# A TEXT BOOK OF

# STRENGTH OF MATERIALS

## FOR
### SEMESTER - I
### SECOND YEAR DEGREE COURSE IN MECHANICAL, MECHANICAL SANDWICH & AUTOMOBILE ENGINEERING

**Strictly According to New Revised Credit System Syllabus of Savitribai Phule Pune University**
**(w.e.f June 2016)**


**Dr. SURESH R. PAREKAR**
M.E. Ph.D. (Structures)
Asso. Prof. & Head,
Civil Engg. Deptt.
AISSM's College of Engineering,
Pune.

**H.M. SOMAYYA**
M.E. (Structures)
Formerly, Asst. Prof.,
Applied Mechanics Deptt.
Maharashtra Institute of Technology
Pune.

**V.N. CHOUGULE**
B.E. (Mech.), M.E. (Mfg. Engg. and Auto.)
Asso. Prof. & Head, Mech., Engg. Deptt.
Modern Eduction Society's College of Engineering
Pune.

N3533

**STRENGTH OF MATERIALS (SE MECH.)**　　　　　ISBN 978-93-86084-07-1

| | | |
|---|---|---|
| Second Edition | : | June 2017 |
| © | : | Authors |




**Published By :**　　　　　　　　　　　　　　　Polyplate

**NIRALI PRAKASHAN**

Abhyudaya Pragati, 1312, Shivaji Nagar,
Off J.M. Road, Pune – 411005
Tel - (020) 25512336/37/39, Fax - (020) 25511379
Email : niralipune@pragationline.com

☞ **DISTRIBUTION CENTRES**

**PUNE**

| | | |
|---|---|---|
| **Nirali Prakashan** | : | 119, Budhwar Peth, Jogeshwari Mandir Lane, Pune 411002, Maharashtra<br>Tel : (020) 2445 2044, 66022708, Fax : (020) 2445 1538<br>Email : bookorder@pragationline.com, niralilocal@pragationline.com |
| **Nirali Prakashan** | : | S. No. 28/27, Dhyari, Near Pari Company, Pune 411041<br>Tel : (020) 24690204 Fax : (020) 24690316<br>Email : dhyari@pragationline.com, bookorder@pragationline.com |

**MUMBAI**

| | | |
|---|---|---|
| **Nirali Prakashan** | : | 385, S.V.P. Road, Rasdhara Co-op. Hsg. Society Ltd.,<br>Girgaum, Mumbai 400004, Maharashtra<br>Tel : (022) 2385 6339 / 2386 9976, Fax : (022) 2386 9976<br>Email : niralimumbai@pragationline.com |

☞ **DISTRIBUTION BRANCHES**

**JALGAON**

| | | |
|---|---|---|
| **Nirali Prakashan** | : | 34, V. V. Golani Market, Navi Peth, Jalgaon 425001,<br>Maharashtra, Tel : (0257) 222 0395, Mob : 94234 91860 |

**KOLHAPUR**

| | | |
|---|---|---|
| **Nirali Prakashan** | : | New Mahadvar Road, Kedar Plaza, 1st Floor Opp. IDBI Bank<br>Kolhapur 416 012, Maharashtra. Mob : 9850046155 |

**NAGPUR**

| | | |
|---|---|---|
| **Pratibha Book Distributors** | : | Above Maratha Mandir, Shop No. 3, First Floor,<br>Rani Jhanshi Square, Sitabuldi, Nagpur 440012, Maharashtra<br>Tel : (0712) 254 7129 |

**DELHI**

| | | |
|---|---|---|
| **Nirali Prakashan** | : | 4593/21, Basement, Aggarwal Lane 15, Ansari Road, Daryaganj<br>Near Times of India Building, New Delhi  110002<br>Mob :  08505972553 |

**BENGALURU**

| | | |
|---|---|---|
| **Pragati Book House** | : | House No. 1, Sanjeevappa Lane, Avenue Road Cross,<br>Opp. Rice Church, Bengaluru – 560002.<br>Tel : (080) 64513344, 64513355,Mob : 9880582331, 9845021552<br>Email:bharatsavla@yahoo.com |

**CHENNAI**

| | | |
|---|---|---|
| **Pragati Books** | : | 9/1, Montieth Road, Behind Taas Mahal, Egmore,<br>Chennai 600008 Tamil Nadu, Tel : (044) 6518 3535,<br>Mob : 94440 01782 / 98450 21552 / 98805 82331,<br>Email : bharatsavla@yahoo.com |

niralipune@pragationline.com  |  www.pragationline.com

Also find us on 🇫 www.facebook.com/niralibooks

# PREFACE TO THE SECOND EDITION

We are glad and excited to announce that the First Edition of this book received an overwhelming response from the engineering student community, compelling us to release its **Second Edition** within a very short period of time.

This thoroughly revised **Second Edition** has been updated with additional matter, many solved problems, including solutions to all University Examination Problems and Numerous Exercises for practice.

Special care has been taken to maintain high degree of accuracy in the theory and numericals throughout the book.

We take this opportunity to express our sincere thanks to Dineshbhai Furia of Nirali Prakashan, a reputed pioneer in the publication field. Our special thanks to Jignesh Furia for their effective cooperation and great care in bringing out this revised edition. We also appreciate the efforts of M. P. Munde and the entire staff of Engineering Books Deptt. of Nirali Prakashan namely Mrs. Deepali Lachake  (Co-ordinator) for bringing this book to the students in a timely manner.

We sincerely hope that this "**Second Edition**" will also be warmly received by all concerned as in the past.

Valuable suggestions from our esteemed readers to improve the book are most welcome and highly appreciated.


**Pune**                                                                                            **Authors**

# PREFACE TO THE FIRST EDITION

It gives us great pleasure in publishing this text book on **"Strength of Materials"** for the students of Second Year Degree Course in Mechanical, Mechanical Sandwich and Automobile Engineering. This book is strictly written according to **New Revised Credit System Syllabus** of Savitribai Phule Pune University (2015 Pattern).

As per the policy of the University, Engineering Syllabi is revised every five years. Last revision was in the year 2012. New revision is coming little earlier, as university has introduced **Online System of Examination** from year 2012.

As per the **New Credit System**, the **In Sem (Online) Examinations** (Combined Phase-I and Phase-II) will be conducted based on first, second, third and fourth units. The **Online** examinations will have objective types of questions with multiple choices. End Semester Examination will be based on all the six units and that will be conducted in traditional way and the Theory Course will have 4 credits.

The subject '**Strength of Materials**' is a foundation stone for any Engineering Course. Today, Engineering applications are mostly interdisciplinary, involving basics of various fundamental subjects. One of such subject of vital importance is '**Strength of Materials**'. The present text is aimed at catering the needs of students appearing for Second Year Degree Course in Mechanical Engineering and Other Competitive Examinations.

The text gives fundamental and simple treatment to the subject with a clear and distinct presentation of theoretical concepts and well graded numerous examples from different universities. The exercise problems at the end of each chapter will help the students to get more refined in application of fundamental principles.

Main feature of this book is, **Complete Coverage** of the new credit system with large number of **Worked (Solved) Examples and Exercises.** Practically, all the questions of previous years' university examination papers have been covered.

**We have given Free Separate book of Multiple Choice Questions (MCQ's), which will be very useful to the students, especially for Online (50 Marks) Examinations.**

We take this opportunity to express our sincere thanks to Shri. Dineshbhai Furia, Shri. Jignesh Furia, Mrs. Nirali Verma and Shri. M. P. Munde and entire team of Nirali Prakashan namely Mrs. Deepali Lachake (Co-ordinator), who really have taken keen interest and untiring efforts in publishing this text.

The advice and suggestions of our esteemed readers to improve the text are most welcomed, and will be highly appreciated.


**27th June 2016**                                                    **Authors**

**Pune**

# SYLLABUS

## Unit I : Simple Stresses and Strains [8 Hrs]

Stress, strain, Hooke's law, Poisson's ratio, Modulus of Elasticity, Modulus of Rigidity, Bulk Modulus. Interrelation between elastic constants,

Stress-strain diagram for ductile and brittle materials, factor of safety.

Stresses and strains in determinate and indeterminate, homogeneous and composite bars under concentrated loads and self weight.

Temperature stresses in simple members.

## Unit II : Shear Force and Bending Moment Diagrams [8 Hrs]

Shear force and bending moment diagrams for statically determinate beam due to concentrated load, uniformly distributed load, uniformly varying load and couple, Relationship between rate of loading, shear force and bending moment.

Maximum bending moment and position of points of contra flexure.

## Unit III Stresses in Machine Elements [8 Hrs]

**Bending Stresses :** Theory of simple bending, assumptions, derivation of flexural formula, second moment of area of common cross sections (rectangular, I,T,C ) with respect to centroidal and parallel axes, bending stress distribution diagrams, moment of resistance and section modulus.

**Shear Stresses:** Concept, derivation of shear stress distribution formula, shear stress distribution diagrams for common symmetrical sections, maximum and average shears stresses, shear connection between flange and web.

## Unit IV [8 Hrs]

**Slope and Deflection of Beams:** Relation between bending moment and slope, slope and deflection of determinate beams, double integration method (Macaulay's method), derivation of formula for slope and deflection for standard cases.

**Strain Energy:** Strain energy due to axial load (gradual, sudden and impact), strain energy due to bending and torsion.

## Unit V [8 Hrs]

**Torsion:** Stresses, strain and deformations in determinate shafts of solid and hollow, homogeneous and composite circular cross section subjected to twisting moment, derivation of torsion equation, stresses due to combined torsion, bending and axial force on shafts.

**Buckling of Columns:** Concept of buckling of columns, derivation of Euler's formula for buckling load for column with hinged ends, concept of equivalent length for various end conditions, limitations of Euler's formula, Rankine's formula, safe load on columns

## Unit VI [8 Hrs]

**Principal Stresses and Strains:** Normal and shear stresses on any oblique plane. Concept of principal planes, derivation of expression for principal stresses and maximum shear stress, position of principal planes and planes of maximum shear.

Graphical solution using Mohr's circle of stresses. Principal stresses in shaft subjected to torsion, bending moment and axial thrust (solid as well as hollow),

Concept of equivalent torsional and bending moments.

**Theories of Elastic Failure:** Maximum principal stress theory, maximum shear stress theory, maximum distortion energy theory – their applications and limitations.

# CONTENTS

◈ ◈ ◈

# Chapter 1

# SIMPLE STRESSES AND STRAINS (PART-I)

## 1.1 INTRODUCTION

The group of studies known as mechanics may be divided and classified in many ways, one of which is indicated below :

$$\text{Mechanics} \begin{cases} \text{Particle and Rigid bodies} \\ \text{(Applied Mechanics)} \\ \text{Deformable bodies} \end{cases} - \begin{cases} \text{Elastic (Strength of materials)} \\ \text{Plastic (Advanced course in plasticity)} \\ \text{Fluid (Hydraulics, Fluid Mechanics, Aerodynamics)} \end{cases}$$

In the usual Applied or Engineering mechanics, all the bodies studied are considered to be particles or rigid bodies - particles when the dimensions of the body are neglected, rigid bodies when the dimensions are considered but the deformations are neglected.

There are many cases in which the distortions of different dimensions of the body must be considered. Structural members, machine parts and springs are usually made of solid materials that deform considerably under the action of external loads but regain their original shape after the load is removed. Such materials are said to be *elastic*.

In all the studies to follow, the free body concept as used in earlier studies in mechanics, will be found indispensable, as will of equations of equilibrium, because the subject "Strength of Materials" is built upon previous knowledge of mechanics with the addition of only a few new concepts.

To illustrate the distinction between the problems of Applied Mechanics and those of Strength of Materials, consider the beam of Fig. 1.1.

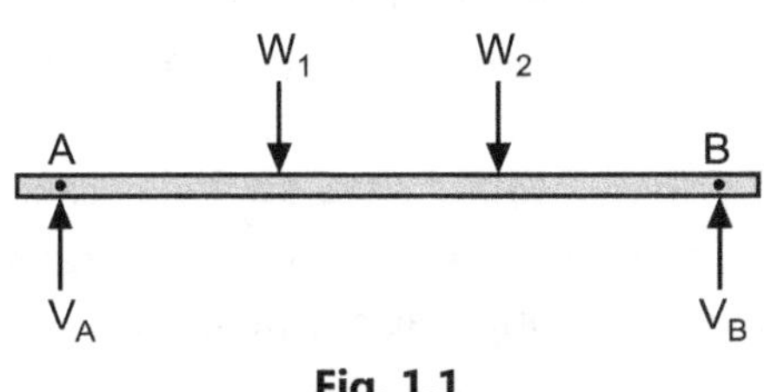


**Fig. 1.1**

In Applied Mechanics, we learned how to apply the equations of equilibrium to the free body in order to determine the unknown reactions $V_A$ and $V_B$, having given the magnitude and spacing of loads. Although the beam does deform due to applied loads, the changes in the dimensions are so small that it has no appreciable effect on the reactions. That is, we consider the beam to be a rigid body.

In Strength of Materials, we shall continue to neglect these deformations while determining the reactions, but we shall be concerned with these deformations while doing other calculations like we may wish to determine how much the beam will deflect or we may be interested in the deformations as a step in determining the internal stresses. Magnitude of these internal stresses must be known in order to proportion a member for a given length and loading.

Throughout this text, we study the principles that govern two fundamental concepts, strength and rigidity. In this first chapter, we start with the simple axial loading, later we consider bending loads, twisting loads and finally we discuss simultaneous combinations of these three basic types of loadings.

## 1.2 LOADS AND THEIR CLASSIFICATION

Loads may be classified in two ways :

**(a) According to manner to their application :** As per this classification, loads may be classified as (i) Dead loads, (ii) Live loads, (iii) Wind loads, (iv) Seismic loads, (v) Temperature loads, (vi) Impact loads, (vii) Erection loads etc.

**(b) According to effect they produce :** Variety of loads acting on structural member produce different types of effect. For convenience, these forces are resolved into components that are normal and tangential to the cross-section as shown in Fig. 1.2. The origin of the reference axis is always taken at the centroid of the cross-section. Each of these components have different structural effects and produces different structural deformation.

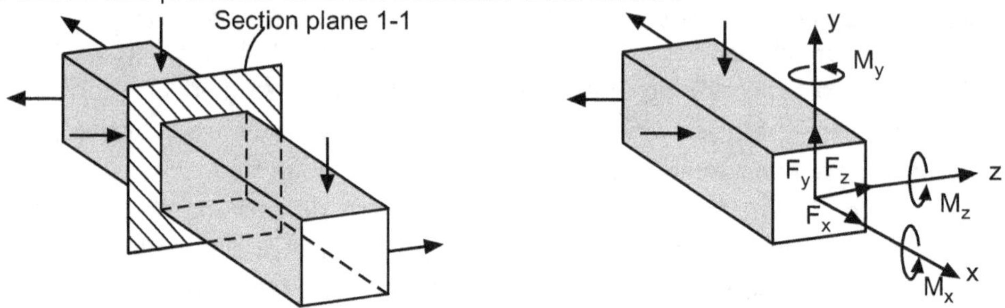


**(a) General loading on member**          **(b) Internal forces at cross-section 1-1**

**Fig. 1.2**

Various components and their structural names are as follows :

**(i)   $F_x$ : Axial force :** The force acting *normal to the cross-section and passing through CG* is called as axial force. The primary effect of axial force is to change the length of member. Axial force may be tensile in nature (pull) which causes increase in the length of a member or compressive in nature (push) which causes decrease in the length of a member.

**(ii)   $F_y$ ; $F_z$ : Shear forces :** The force acting *tangential to the cross-section* is called as shear force. The primary effect of these forces is to cause sliding of one cross-section with respect to other.

**(iii) $M_x$ : Torsional moment :** Net moment vector acting *normal to the cross-section* is called as torsional moment or torque or torsion. The primary effect of torsional moment is to cause rotation of different cross-sections of member with respect to each other about polar axis. This rotation is called as twist.

**(iv) $M_y$ ; $M_z$ : Bending moment :** Net moment vector acting *tangential to the cross-section* is called as bending moment. These moments cause bending of the member @ an axis parallel to the cross-section and ultimately produce slopes and deflection.

The subject 'Strength of Materials' is the study of all above structural actions, corresponding deformations and stresses produced by an individual action or combination thereof.

## 1.3 STRESS

When as elastic body is subjected to loads, it undergoes deformation. While undergoing deformations, the particles of the material offer a resisting force. When this resisting force equals the applied loads, equilibrium is attained and further deformation stops. This internal resistance is called as *stress*. The resistance per unit area is called as intensity of stress. Generally, the word stress refers to *intensity of stress*. Thus, stress is *resistance per unit area*.

## 1.3.1 Types of Stresses

Stresses are of two types : (i) Normal stresses and (ii) Shear stresses.

Stresses which act normal to the section are called as normal stresses while that acting tangential to the section are called shear stresses. It should be noted that *axial force* produces *uniform normal stresses* over the section while *bending moment* produces *linearly varying stresses* over the section within elastic limit, as discussed later in the text. Shear force and torsional moment produces shear stresses over the section. Thus, type of stress produced depends on the type of action the cross-section is subjected to.

Normal stresses can further be classified as tensile or compressive in nature, depending on kind of deformation the member undergoes.

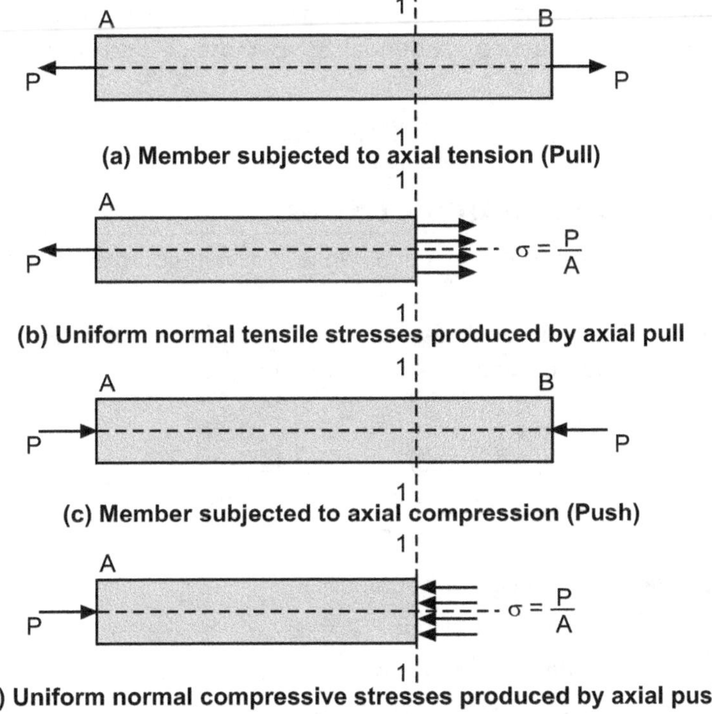



**Fig. 1.3**

Fig. 1.3 (a) shows member subjected to axial tensile force. Consider section 1-1 and FBD of part of the member as shown in Fig. 1.3 (b). For equilibrium, cross-section must offer a resistive force = applied force = P. This resistive force per unit area is called as normal stress.

Thus, for axial force, normal stress = $\sigma_n = \dfrac{P}{A}$        ... (1.1)

where, A = cross-sectional area of member.

Fig. 1.3 (c) and 1.3 (d) respectively show compressive force and corresponding normal stresses.

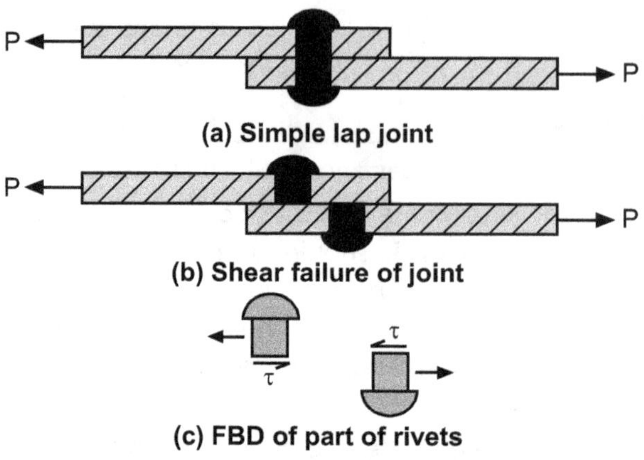

**(a) Simple lap joint**

**(b) Shear failure of joint**

**(c) FBD of part of rivets**

**Fig. 1.4**

Fig. 1.4 shows a simple riveted lap joint and its shear failure. It should be noted that, the force which causes failure of rivet is acting tangential to its cross-section and hence produces shear stress ($\tau$).

$$\text{Shear stress} = \tau = \frac{\text{Shear force}}{\text{Cross-sectional area}} \qquad \ldots (1.2)$$

## 1.3.2 Sign Convention and Unit of Stress

Normal tensile stress is considered positive while normal compressive stress is considered negative.

Shear stress '$\tau$' which produces clockwise couple is considered positive and that producing anticlockwise couple is considered negative as shown in Fig. 1.5.

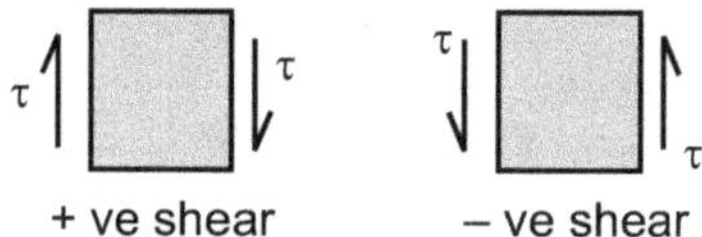

+ ve shear         – ve shear

**Fig. 1.5**

Unit of stress is MPa or GPa (mega or gega Pascal).

**Note :**

$$1 \text{ MPa} = 1 \text{ N/mm}^2$$
$$1 \text{ GPa} = 1 \text{ kN/mm}^2$$
$$\therefore \quad 1 \text{ GPa} = 10^3 \text{ MPa}$$

# 1.4 STRAIN

When an elastic body is subjected to loads, it undergoes deformation. Strain is a *measure of deformation produced by application of external forces.*

## 1.4.1 Types of Strains

Strains are of two types : (i) Linear strain and (ii) Shear strain.

**1.    Linear strain :** It is the ratio of alternation in any dimension of the body to the respective original dimension.

Thus,　　　Linear strain $= \in = \dfrac{\text{Change in dimension}}{\text{Original dimension}}$　　　... (1.3)

In case of an axial force, linear strain produced along the length is called as *longitudinal strain* while that produced along cross-section is called as *lateral strain*.

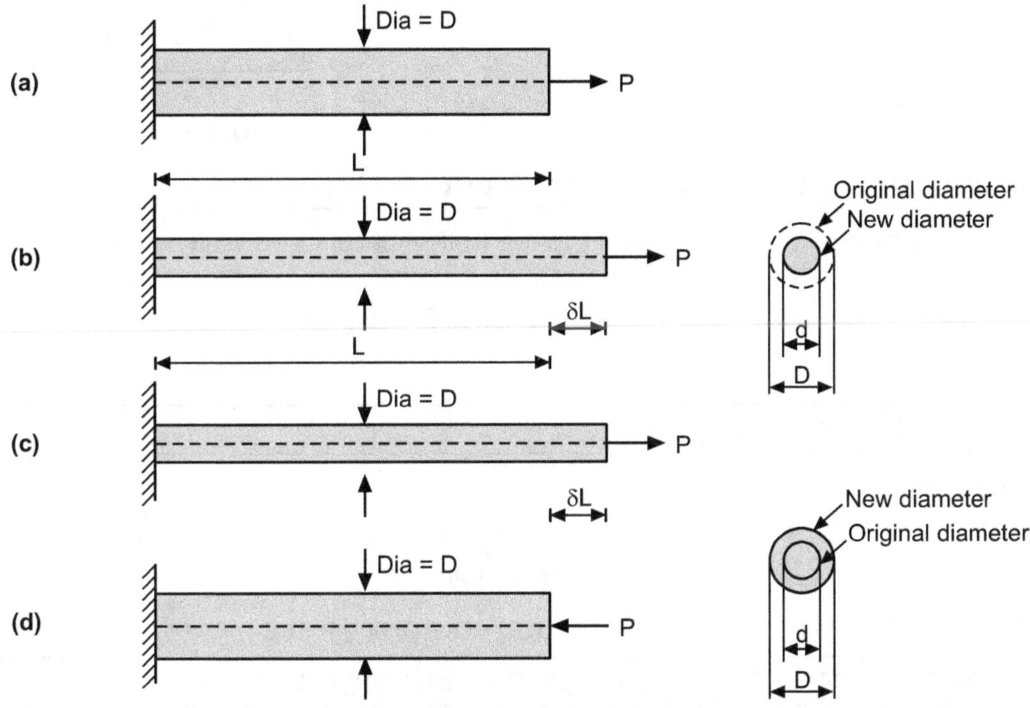


**Fig. 1.6 : Longitudinal and Lateral strains**

Linear strain may be tensile or compressive in nature. Axial pull causes increase in length while decrease in cross-sectional dimensions and axial push causes decrease in length while increase in cross-sectional dimension as shown in Fig. 1.6.

Thus,

$$\text{Longitudinal strain} = \in_L = \frac{\text{Change in length}}{\text{Original length}}$$

$\therefore$　　　　　　　　$\in_L = \dfrac{\delta L}{L}$　　　... (1.4)

$$\text{Lateral strain} = \in_{Lt} = \frac{\text{Change in cross-sectional dimensions}}{\text{Original cross-sectional dimensions}} \quad ... (1.5)$$

For the example of circular bar considered in Fig. 1.6,

$$\text{Lateral strain} = \in_{Lt} = \frac{\text{Change in diameter}}{\text{Original diameter}}$$

**(ii)　Shear strain :** If an element ABCD shown in Fig. 1.7 is subjected to shear stresses $\tau$ on faces AB and CD, then it undergoes angular deformation $\phi$ as shown.

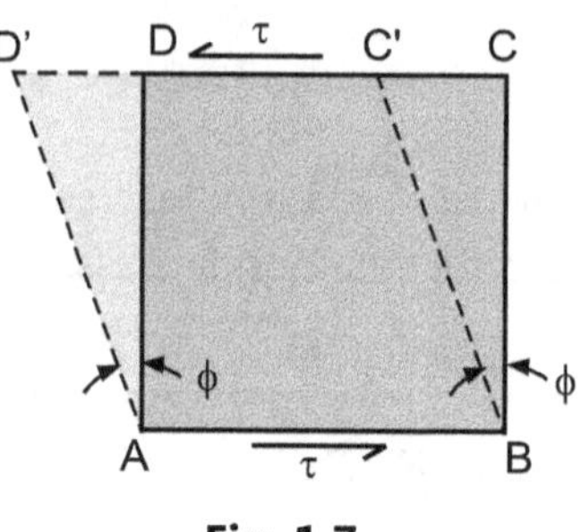


$$\text{Shear strain} = \gamma = \tan\phi = \frac{DD'}{AD} \qquad \text{... (1.6)}$$

Shear strain being very small,

$$\tan\phi \approx \phi$$

## 1.4.2 Sign Convention and Unit of Strain

Linear strain tensile in nature is considered positive while that compressive in nature is considered negative.

Shear strain sign convention is same as explained in article 1.3.2.

Strain does not have any unit.

## 1.5 POISSON'S RATIO ($\mu$)                                        (Dec. 2011)

It is the ratio of lateral strain to linear strain.

Thus,
$$\mu = \frac{\text{Lateral strain}}{\text{Linear strain}} = \frac{\epsilon_{Lt}}{\epsilon_L} \qquad \text{... (1.7)}$$

The value of Poisson's ratio depends on type of material and for most metals it is 0.25 to 0.35.

## 1.6 HOOKE'S LAW AND MODULUS OF ELASTICITY (E)

By experiment it has been established for many structural materials that, within elastic limit, the elongation of the bar is proportional to tensile force. This linear relationship between the force and the elongation produced by it was formulated by Robert Hooke and hence known as *Hooke's law.*

If bars of same material but different lengths and different cross-sectional areas are experimented, it is observed that its elongation is proportional to tensile force, length and inversely proportional to the cross-sectional area.

Thus,
$$\delta L \propto \frac{PL}{A}$$

OR
$$\delta L = \frac{PL}{AE} \qquad \text{... (1.8)}$$

where, E = constant for any given material and is called as **Modulus of elasticity or Young's modulus.**

From equation (1.8), we can further write,

$$E = \frac{\sigma_n}{\epsilon_L} \qquad \text{... (1.9)}$$

as
$$\sigma = \frac{P}{A} \text{ and } \epsilon_L = \frac{\delta L}{L}$$

Thus, Hooke's law states that **stress is proportional to strain.** It should be noted that unit of Modulus of elasticity is same as that of stress.

## 1.7 MODULUS OF RIGIDITY OR SHEAR MODULUS (G)                    (Dec. 2011)

The shear stress $(\tau)$ is proportional to shear strain $(\gamma)$ as long as proportional limit in shear is not exceeded.

Thus,
$$\tau \propto \gamma$$

i.e.
$$\tau = G\gamma$$

or
$$G = \frac{\tau}{\gamma} \qquad \qquad \dots (1.10)$$

where,
$$G = \text{Modulus of rigidity or Shear modulus}$$

It should be noted that the unit of modulus of rigidity is same as that of stress.

## 1.8 VOLUMETRIC STRESS AND VOLUMETRIC STRAIN                    (May 2011)

When an elastic body is subjected to three mutually perpendicular equal direct stresses as shown in Fig. 1.8, it undergoes change in volume without distortion of shape. Such a stress is called as *volumetric stress ($\sigma_v$).* Such a state of stress occurs when a cube is at a large depth in a liquid. The intensity of compressive pressure will have the same magnitude on all the faces. Such a state of stress is also called as *hydrostatic* state of stress.

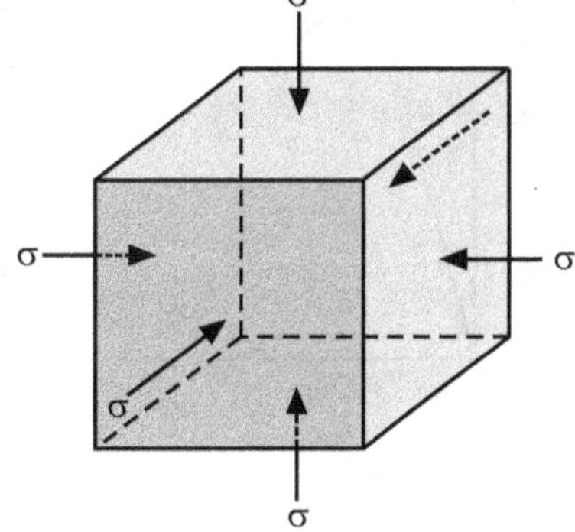


**Fig. 1.8**

The ratio of change in volume to original volume of a body is called as *volumetric strain.*

$$\epsilon_V = \frac{\delta V}{V} \qquad \qquad \dots (1.11)$$

where,
$$\delta V = \text{Change in volume}$$
$$V = \text{Original volume}$$

Let L, b and d be the length, width and depth of an elastic member subjected to external force respectively.

$$\text{Original volume} = V = L \cdot b \cdot d$$
$$\text{Change in volume} = \delta V = \delta L \cdot bd + \delta b \cdot L \cdot d + \delta d \cdot L \cdot b$$
$$\therefore \quad \text{Volumetric strain} = \epsilon_V = \frac{\delta V}{V}$$
$$= \frac{\delta L \cdot bd + \delta b \cdot L \cdot d + \delta d \cdot L \cdot b}{L \cdot b \cdot d}$$

---

$$\frac{\delta V}{V} \ = \ \frac{\delta L}{L} + \frac{\delta b}{b} + \frac{\delta d}{d} \qquad \dots (1.12)$$

*Volumetric strain is thus equal to algebraic sum of linear strains of the three sides.*

Thus, for axial loading,

$$\epsilon_V \ = \ \epsilon_L + \epsilon_{Lt} + \epsilon_{Lt}$$
$$= \ \epsilon_L - \mu\,\epsilon_L - \mu\,\epsilon_L$$
$$= \ \epsilon_L\,(1 - 2\mu) \qquad \dots (1.13)$$

It should be noted that, lateral strain is of opposite sense to that of longitudinal strain.

## 1.9 BULK MODULUS (K)

It is defined as the ratio of volumetric stress ($\sigma_V$) to volumetric strain ($\epsilon_V$).

Thus,            Bulk modulus    $= K = \dfrac{\sigma_V}{\epsilon_V}$                    ... (1.14)

It should be noted that, the unit of Bulk modulus is same as that of stress.

## 1.10 STRESS-STRAIN CURVE                    (May 2011)

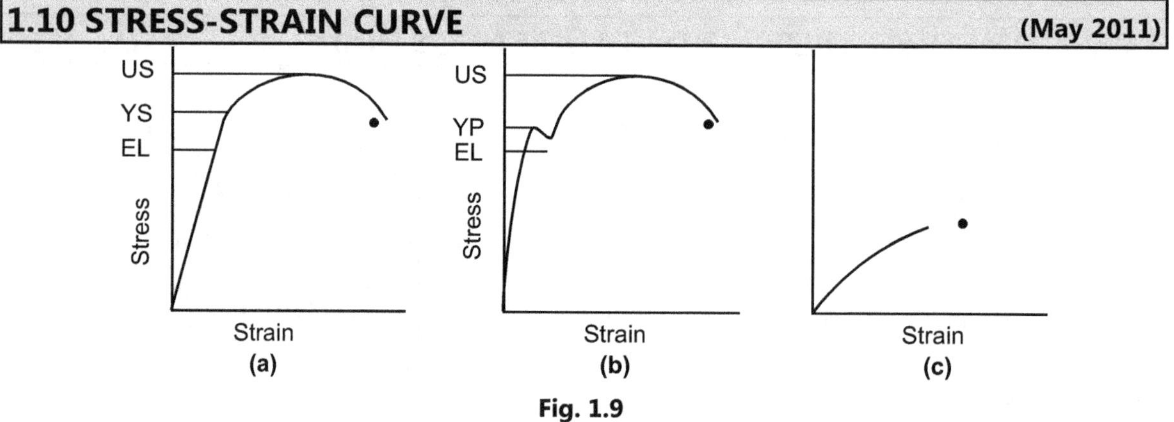


**Fig. 1.9**

In Fig. 1.9, typical stress-strain curves are shown for several common materials. Such curves are obtained by loading a specimen of the material in tension and recording simultaneous observations of both load and elongation. From these readings, stresses and strains are computed and curves are plotted.

**The elastic limit (EL)** is that stress below which the ratio of stress to strain is constant. See Fig. 1.9 (a) and 1.9 (b). More precisely we have defined the proportional limit or proportional elastic limit but the words are often used interchangeably.

**The yield point (YP)** is that stress at which elongation continues without increase in the load. See Fig. 1.9 (b). Low carbon steel is one of the few materials which exhibits a true yield point. For the majority of ductile materials, those which do not exhibit this characteristic, a corresponding value called yield strength is determined.

**Yield strength (YS)** is that stress at which a predetermined permanent set is produced. See Fig. 1.9 (a). The yield point or yield strength each indicates the stress below which a given increment of stress will produce a small strain and above which the same increment of stress will produce a very much larger increment of strain.

The **ultimate strength (US)** is the ratio of maximum load sustained during a tensile test divided by the original cross-sectional area.

One or the other of the curves of Fig. 1.9 (a) and 1.9 (b) is representative of most structural materials. However, the brittle materials, such as concrete and ordinary cast iron, usually exhibit tensile curves similar to Fig. 1.9 (c), breaking with negligible elongation.

The values of yield point, elastic limit and modulus of elasticity are generally determined from tension tests, the results may be applied to problems of compression as well.

## 1.11 ALLOWABLE STRESS AND FACTOR OF SAFETY

The factor of safety allows for errors in estimating design loads, some variations in material quality and perhaps most important of all, errors in the assumptions used in the design calculations.

There are two ways of defining factor of safety :

(i)　**Based on ultimate stress :** It is the ratio of ultimate stress to working stress.

(ii)　**Based on yield stress :** It is the ratio of yield stress to working stress.

It is obvious that the factor of safety based on ultimate stress has larger value than that based on yield stress.

The factor of safety may vary depending upon the judgement of designers and depending upon their experience.

## 1.12 RELATION BETWEEN MODULUS OF ELASTICITY (E)
##　　　AND MODULUS OF RIGIDITY (G)

Consider an elementary rectangular block ABCD of unit thickness, having shear stresses 'τ' acting on faces AD and BC as shown in Fig. 1.10. Assuming AD to be fixed, block ABCD will deform to AB'C'D. Let ϕ be the shear strain.

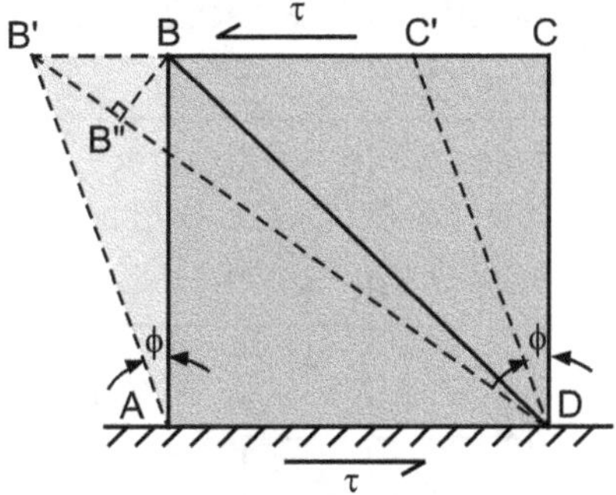


**Fig. 1.10**

$$\text{Linear strain of diagonal BD} \;=\; \frac{DB' - DB}{DB}$$

$$=\; \frac{B'B''}{DB}$$

$$=\; \frac{(BB')\cos 45}{\sqrt{2}\,AB}$$

$$\in_{BD} \ = \ \frac{1}{2}\left(\frac{BB'}{AB}\right) = \frac{1}{2}(\phi) \ \text{(Tensile)} \qquad \qquad \dots (1.15)$$

Similarly, the linear strain of the diagonal AC is also $\frac{1}{2}(\phi)$ but it is compressive in nature.

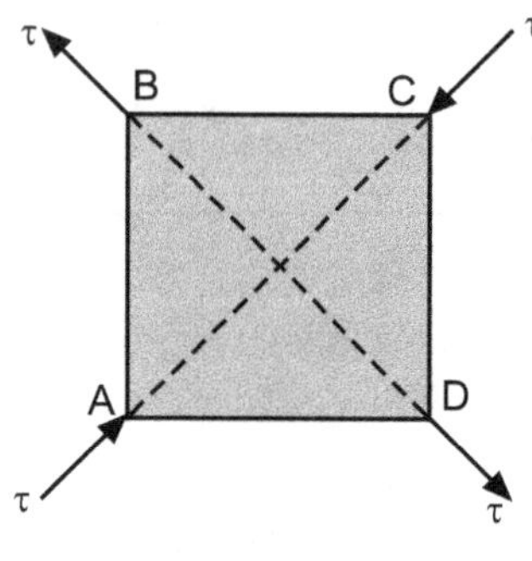

**Fig. 1.11**

Linear strain of diagonal BD can also be derived by considering direct tensile stress $\tau$ across the plane AC, accompanied by the direct compressive stress across the plane BD as shown in Fig. 1.11. This is an equivalent of stress system considered in Fig. 1.10. The combined effect of the two direct stresses on diagonal BD will therefore be tensile strain of magnitude.

$$\in_{BD} \ = \ \frac{\tau}{E}(1 + \mu) \qquad \qquad \dots (1.16)$$

This linear strain is already found to be $\frac{1}{2}(\phi)$ .

∴    Equating equations (1.15) and (1.16), we get

$$\frac{\tau}{E}(1 + \mu) \ = \ \frac{1}{2}(\phi)$$

$$\frac{\tau}{E}(1 + \mu) \ = \ \frac{1}{2}\left(\frac{\tau}{G}\right)$$

∴                    **E = 2 G (1 + μ)** $\qquad \qquad \dots (1.17)$

## 1.13 RELATION BETWEEN MODULUS OF ELASTICITY (E) AND BULK MODULUS (K)

Consider a cube of side 'L' with its faces subjected to direct stresses of intensity ($\sigma$) as shown in Fig. 1.12.

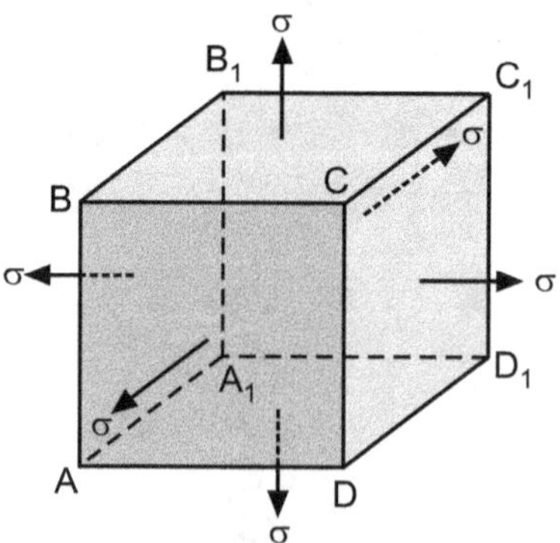

**Fig. 1.12**

The linear strain in any one direction is given by generalised Hooke's law,

Thus,

$$\frac{\delta L}{L} = \frac{1}{E}(\sigma - \mu\sigma - \mu\sigma)$$

$$= \frac{\sigma}{E}(1 - 2\mu) \qquad\qquad \dots (1.18)$$

where,         $\mu$ = Poisson's ratio

Original volume of cube,    $V = L^3$

$\therefore$         $\delta V = 3L^2\,\delta L$

$\therefore$    Volumetric strain $= \epsilon_V = \dfrac{\delta V}{V} = \dfrac{3L^2\,\delta L}{L^3} = 3\cdot\dfrac{\delta L}{L} \qquad\qquad \dots (1.19)$

Substituting for $\dfrac{\delta L}{L}$ from equation (1.18), we get

$$\epsilon_V = 3\cdot\left[\frac{\sigma}{E}(1 - 2\mu)\right] \qquad\qquad \dots (1.20)$$

Bulk modulus,    $K = \dfrac{\sigma}{\epsilon_V} = \dfrac{\sigma}{\dfrac{3\sigma}{E}(1 - 2\mu)}$

$\therefore$         $\mathbf{E = 3K(1 - 2\mu)} \qquad\qquad \dots (1.21)$

From equations (1.17) and (1.21), the relation between four elastic constants is given by

$$\mathbf{E = 2G(1 + \mu) = 3K(1 - 2\mu)} \qquad\qquad \dots (1.22)$$

## SOLVED EXAMPLES

**Example 1.1 :** *A 2.8 m long member is 60 mm deep and 40 mm wide in cross-section. It is subjected to axial tensile force of 210 kN as shown in Fig. 1.13. Determine (i) change in length, (ii) change in cross-sectional dimensions, (iii) change in volume. Assume E = 200 GPa, $\mu$ = 0.3.*

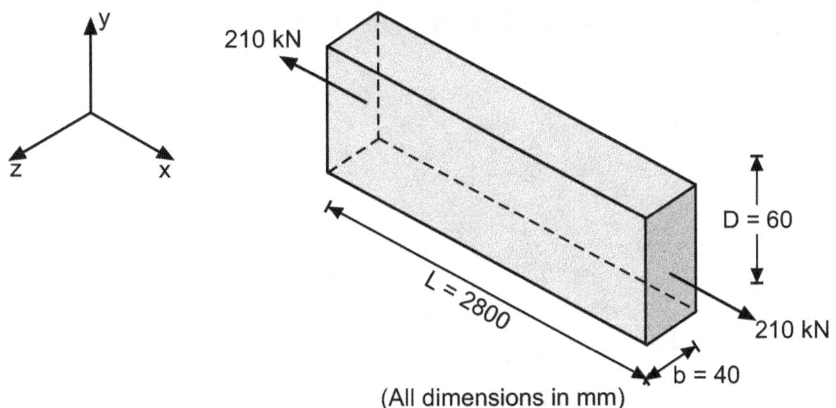


**Fig. 1.13 : Given member**

**Data :** As shown in Fig. 1.13, E = 200 GPa, $\mu$ = 0.3.

**Required :** $\delta L$, $\delta b$, $\delta D$, $\delta V$.

**Concept :** Standard formulae.

**Solution :** (i) Geometric properties : Cross-sectional area = A = $60 \times 40$ = 2400 mm$^2$.

(ii)  Stresses and strains :

$$\text{Normal stress} \ = \ \sigma = \frac{P}{A} = \frac{210 \times 10^3}{2400} = 87.5 \ \text{MPa (Tensile)}$$

$$\text{Longitudinal strain} \ = \ \epsilon_L = \frac{\sigma}{E} = \frac{87.5}{200 \times 10^3} = 4.375 \times 10^{-4} \ \text{(Tensile)}$$

$$\text{Lateral strain} \ = \ \epsilon_{Lt} = \mu \cdot \epsilon_L = 0.3 \times 4.375 \times 10^{-4}$$

$$= \ 1.3125 \times 10^{-4} \ \text{(Compressive)}$$

(iii) Change in dimensions :

$$\text{Change in length,} \quad \delta L \ = \ \epsilon_L \cdot L$$

$$= \ 4.375 \times 10^{-4} \times 2800$$

$$= \ \textbf{1.225 mm (increase)}$$

$$\text{Change in depth,} \quad \delta D \ = \ \epsilon_{Lt} \cdot D$$

$$= \ 1.3125 \times 10^{-4} \times 60$$

$$= \ \textbf{0.0078 mm (decrease)}$$

$$\text{Change in width,} \quad \delta b \ = \ \epsilon_{Lt} \cdot b$$

$$= \ 1.3125 \times 10^{-4} \times 40$$

$$= \ \textbf{0.0052 mm (decrease)}$$

(iv) Change in volume :

$$\text{Volumetric strain,} \ \epsilon_V \ = \ \epsilon_x + \epsilon_y + \epsilon_z$$

$$= \ \epsilon_L + \epsilon_{Lt} + \epsilon_{Lt}$$

$$= \ \epsilon \, (1 - 2\mu)$$

$$= \ 4.375 \times 10^{-4} \, (1 - 2 \times 0.3)$$

$$= \ 1.75 \times 10^{-4}$$

$$\delta V = \epsilon_V \cdot V \ = \ (1.75 \times 10^{-4}) \, (2800 \times 60 \times 40)$$

$$= \ \textbf{1176 mm}^3 \ \textbf{(increase)}$$

---

**Example 1.2 :** *Determine the change in volume of 25 mm cube of aluminium (E = 70 GPa) and* $\mu = \dfrac{1}{3}$ *when dropped at a distance of 8 km in the ocean. Assume density of water = 10 kN/m$^3$.*

---

**Data :** Cube size : 25 mm, E = 70 GPa, $\mu = \dfrac{1}{3}$, $\gamma_{water}$ = 10 kN/m$^3$, h = 8 km

---

**Required :** Change in volume.

**Concept :**　　Water pressure　= Volumetric stress = $\sigma_v = \gamma_h$

$$\text{Bulk modulus}\ =\ K = \frac{E}{3\,(1 - 2\mu)}$$

$$\text{Volumetric strain}\ =\ \epsilon_v = \frac{\sigma_v}{K}$$

**Solution :** (i) Volumetric stress :

$$\sigma_v\ =\ \gamma_h = 10 \times 8000 = 8 \times 10^4 \text{ kN/m}^2 = 80 \text{ MPa}$$

(ii)　Bulk modulus (K) :

$$K\ =\ \frac{E}{3\,(1 - 2\mu)} = \frac{70 \times 10^3}{3\left(1 - 2 \times \dfrac{1}{3}\right)} = 70 \times 10^3 \text{ MPa}$$

(iii) Change in volume ($\delta V$) :

$$\text{Volumetric strain}\ =\ \epsilon_v = \frac{\delta V}{V} = \frac{\sigma_v}{K}$$

$$\therefore \qquad \delta V\ =\ \frac{\sigma_v}{K} \cdot V$$

$$=\ \frac{80}{70 \times 10^3} \times (25)^3$$

$$=\ \textbf{17.85 mm}^3 \textbf{ (decrease)}$$

**Example 1.3 :** *A bar of certain material is 60 mm × 60 mm in cross-section is subjected to an axial pull of 230 kN. The extension over a length of 120 mm is 0.07 mm and decrease in each side is 0.007 mm. Calculate all the elastic constants for material.*

**Data :** Cross-section of member = 60 mm × 60 mm, P = 230 kN (Tensile)

$\delta L$ = 0.07 mm increase, L = 120 mm, $\delta b$ = 0.007 mm (decrease)

**Required :** Elastic constants.

**Concept :** Standard formulae.

**Solution :** (i) Geometric properties :

Cross-sectional area,　　A　= $60 \times 60 = 3600$ mm$^2$

(ii)　Stresses and strains :

$$\text{Normal stress}\ =\ \sigma = \frac{P}{A} = \frac{230 \times 10^3}{3600} = 63.89 \text{ MPa}$$

$$\text{Longitudinal strain}\ =\ \epsilon_L = \frac{\delta L}{L} = \frac{0.07}{120} = 5.83 \times 10^{-4}$$

$$\text{Lateral strain}\ =\ \epsilon_{Lt} = \frac{\delta b}{b} = \frac{0.007}{60} = 1.167 \times 10^{-4}$$

(iii) Elastic constants :

$$\text{Young's modulus,} \quad E = \frac{\sigma}{\in_L} = \frac{63.89}{5.83 \times 10^{-4}} = 109.58 \times 10^3 \text{ MPa} = \mathbf{109.58 \text{ GPa}}$$

$$\text{Poisson's ratio,} \quad \mu = \frac{\in_{Lt}}{\in_L} = \frac{1.167 \times 10^{-4}}{5.83 \times 10^{-4}} = \mathbf{0.2}$$

$$\text{Shear modulus,} \quad G = \frac{E}{2(1+\mu)} = \frac{109.58}{2(1+0.2)} = \mathbf{45.66 \text{ GPa}}$$

$$\text{Bulk modulus,} \quad K = \frac{E}{3(1-2\mu)} = \frac{109.58}{3(1-2\times0.2)} = \mathbf{60.87 \text{ GPa}}$$

**Example 1.4 :** *When a metal tube of external diameter 20 mm and internal diameter 15 mm was subjected to an axial load of 23 kN, the extension on gauge length of 60 mm was 0.05 mm and decrease in outer diameter was 0.005 mm. Find Young's modulus of elasticity (E), Poisson's ratio ($\mu$) and change in volume ($\delta V$) assuming length of tube = 700 mm.*

**Data :** D = 20 mm, d = 15 mm, P = 23 kN, $\delta L$ = 0.05 mm for gauge length of 60 mm, $\delta D$ = 0.005 mm (decrease), Length of tube = L = 700 mm.

**Required :** E, $\mu$, and change in volume ($\delta V$).

**Concept :** Standard formulae.

**Solution :** (i) Geometric properties :

$$\text{Cross-sectional area,} \quad A = \frac{\pi}{4}(D^2 - d^2)$$

$$= \frac{\pi}{4}(20^2 - 15^2)$$

$$= 137.44 \text{ mm}^2$$

(ii)  Stress and strain :

$$\text{Normal stress,} \quad \sigma = \frac{P}{A} = \frac{23 \times 10^3}{137.44} = 167.34 \text{ MPa}$$

$$\text{Longitudinal strain,} \quad \in_L = \frac{\delta L}{L} = \frac{0.05}{60} = 8.33 \times 10^{-4}$$

$$\text{Lateral strain,} \quad \in_{Lt} = \frac{\delta D}{D} = \frac{0.005}{20} = 2.5 \times 10^{-4}$$

(iii) Young's modulus (E) and Poisson's ratio ($\mu$) :

$$E = \frac{\text{Normal stress}}{\text{Longitudinal strain}} = \frac{167.34}{8.33 \times 10^{-4}}$$

$$= 200.89 \times 10^3 \text{ MPa} = 200.89 \text{ GPa}$$

$$\mu = \frac{\text{Lateral strain}}{\text{Longitudinal strain}} = \frac{2.5 \times 10^{-4}}{8.33 \times 10^{-4}} = 0.3$$

(iv) Change in volume ($\delta V$) :

$$\text{Volumetric strain,} \quad \in_v = \in_L (1 - 2\mu)$$

$$= 8.33 \times 10^{-4} (1 - 2 \times 0.3)$$

$$= 3.332 \times 10^{-4}$$

Change in volume,      $\delta V = \epsilon_v \cdot V$

$$= 3.332 \times 10^{-4} (137.44 \times 700)$$

$$= \mathbf{32.05 \ mm^3 \ (increase)}$$

**Example 1.5 :** *A bar of cross-section 8 mm × 8 mm is subjected to axial pull of 7 kN. The lateral dimensions of the bar are found to have reduced by 1.5 × 10⁻³ mm. Find Poisson's ratio and Modulus of elasticity, assuming G = 80 GPa.*

**Data :** Cross-section of member = 8 mm × 8 mm, axial force = 7 kN, change in cross-sectional dimension = $1.5 \times 10^{-3}$ mm, G = 80 GPa.

**Required :** Modulus of elasticity (E) and Poisson's ratio (μ).

**Concept :** Standard formulae.

**Solution :** (i) Stresses and strains :

Normal stress,      $\sigma = \dfrac{P}{A} = \dfrac{7 \times 10^3}{8 \times 8} = 109.375$ MPa

Longitudinal strain,    $\epsilon_L = \dfrac{\sigma}{E} = \dfrac{109.375}{E}$

Lateral strain,    $\epsilon_{Lt}$ = Change in c/s dimension / Original dimension

$$= \dfrac{1.5 \times 10^{-3}}{8}$$

$$= 1.875 \times 10^{-4}$$

(ii)  Modulus of elasticity and Poisson's ratio :

We have,      $\epsilon_{Lt} = \mu \, \epsilon_L$

$$1.875 \times 10^{-4} = \mu \times \dfrac{109.375}{E}$$

$$E = 583.33 \times 10^3 \, \mu \qquad \qquad ...\ (i)$$

Also,      $E = 2G (1 + \mu)$

∴      $E = 2 \times 80 \times 10^3 (1 + \mu)$

$$= 160 \times 10^3 (1 + \mu) \qquad \qquad ...\ (ii)$$

Equating equations (i) and (ii),

$$583.33 \times 10^3 \, \mu = 160 \times 10^3 (1 + \mu)$$

∴      $\mu = \mathbf{0.377}$ , put in (i)

$$E = 220.47 \times 10^3 \text{ MPa}$$

$$= \mathbf{220.47 \ GPa}$$

**Example 1.6 :** *A steel punch can be stressed to a maximum compressive stress of 800 MPa. Find the least diameter of hole which can be punched through a plate of 16 mm thickness if its ultimate shear strength is 300 MPa.*

**Data :** Ultimate compressive and shear stress = 800 MPa and 300 MPa respectively, thickness of plate = 16 mm

**Required :** Diameter of hole which can be punched.

**Concept :** Normal and shear stress.

**Solution :** Let $\phi$ be the diameter of hole in mm.

$$\text{Maximum force on punch} \;=\; \frac{\pi}{4}\phi^2 \cdot \sigma$$

$$=\; \frac{\pi}{4}(\phi)^2 \times 800 \qquad\qquad \ldots \text{(i)}$$

$$\text{Punching shear strength} \;=\; (\pi\,\phi\,t)\,\tau$$

$$=\; \pi\,\phi \times 16 \times 300 \qquad\qquad \ldots \text{(ii)}$$

Equating (i) and (ii),

$$\frac{\pi}{4}(\phi)^2 \times 800 \;=\; \pi\,\phi \times 16 \times 300$$

$$\therefore \qquad\qquad \phi \;=\; \textbf{24 mm}$$

**Example 1.7 :** *A flat plate is connected to gusset plate by four rivets as shown in Fig. 1.14. The normal stress for the flat plate is 120 MPa due to the force P. Find suitable diameter of rivets if permissible shear stress for rivets is 90 MPa. Neglect weakening of plate due to rivet holes.*

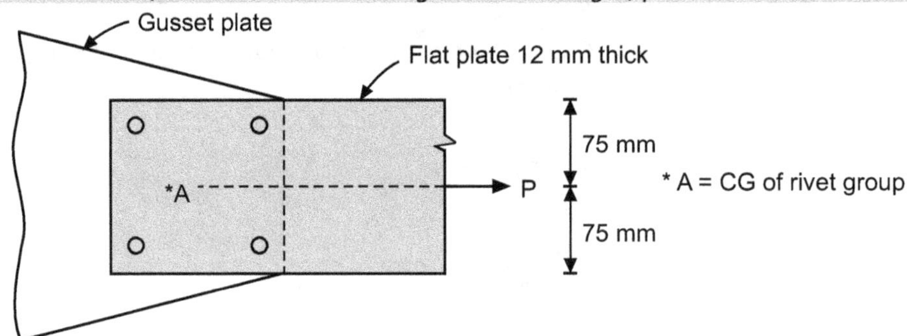


**Fig. 1.14**

**Data :** $\sigma_{flat}$ = 120 MPa, $\tau_{rivets}$ = 90 MPa

**Required :** Diameter of rivets.

**Concept :** Normal and shear stress.

**Solution :** (i) Axial force for flat plate,

$$P \;=\; (\sigma)_{flat} \times \text{cross-sectional area}$$

$$=\; 120 \times (150 \times 12)$$

$$=\; 216000 \text{ N}$$

(ii)   Shear stress for rivets :

$$\text{Force on each rivet} \;=\; \frac{216000}{4} = 54000 \text{ N}$$

Let $\phi$ be the diameter of rivets in mm.

$$\text{Shear stress for each rivet} \; = \; \frac{\text{Force on rivet}}{\text{cross-sectional area}}$$

$$90 \; = \; \frac{54000}{\frac{\pi}{4}\,(\phi)^2}$$

$$\therefore \qquad \phi \; = \; \textbf{27.63 mm}$$

**Example 1.8 :** *Two wooden pieces are joined as shown in Fig. 1.15. Find the safe value of axial load P if the normal stress for wood is limited to 20 MPa and shear stress for joint is limited to 5 MPa.*

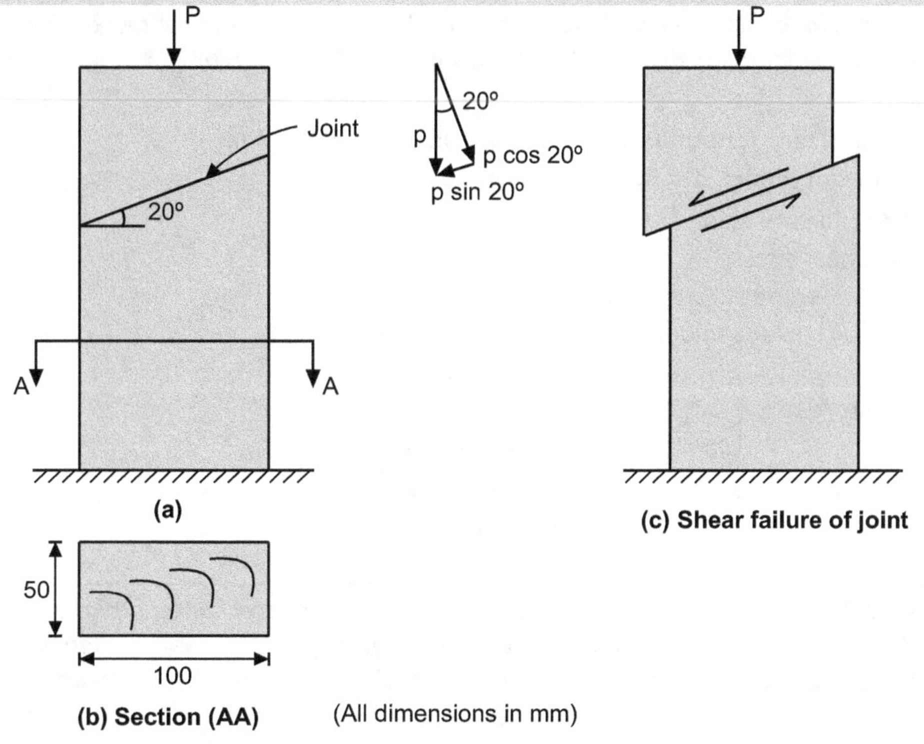


**Fig. 1.15**

**Data :** Normal stress $\sigma > 20$ MPa, shear stress of joint $\tau > 5$ MPa.

**Required :** Safe value of load P.

**Concept :** Normal stress and shear stress.

**Solution :** (i) Magnitude of 'P' from normal stress criterion.

Let P be the value of load in kN.

$$\sigma \; = \; \frac{P}{A}$$

$$20 \; = \; \frac{P \times 10^3}{50 \times 100}$$

$\therefore$ $\qquad\qquad\qquad\qquad\qquad\qquad$ P = 100 kN $\qquad\qquad\qquad\qquad\qquad$ ... (i)

(ii)  Magnitude of 'P' from shear stress criterion :

$$\tau = \frac{\text{Shear force for joint}}{\text{Cross-sectional area of joint}}$$

$$5 = \frac{P \sin 20° \times 10^3}{100 \sec 20° \times 50}$$

P = **77.78 kN** $\qquad\qquad\qquad\qquad\qquad$ ... (ii)

Safe value of P = **77.78 kN** (least of (i) and (ii)).

**Example 1.9 :** *A solid cylinder 100 mm high and 50 mm in diameter is inserted in another cylinder of 50 mm inner diameter and the surfaces of the two cylinders in contact are glued together. If the ultimate shear stress of the glue is 2.6 N/mm², calculate the ultimate load under which the joint will fail.*

**Data :** h = 100 mm, for outer cylinder inner diameter d = 50 mm,

$\qquad\qquad$ for inner cylinder, d = 50 mm, $\tau_{max}$ = 2.6 N/mm²

**Required :** Ultimate load.

**Concept :** Shear stress.

**Solution :** (i) Geometric properties :

$\qquad\qquad$ Area under shear = $100 \times \pi \times 50$

$\qquad\qquad\qquad\qquad\qquad$ = $5000\,\pi$ mm²

(ii)   Ultimate load :

$\qquad\qquad$ Ultimate load = Area under shear $\times \tau_{max}$

$\qquad\qquad\qquad\qquad\qquad$ = $5000\,\pi \times 2.6$

$\qquad\qquad\qquad\qquad\qquad$ = 40840.7 N

$\qquad\qquad\qquad\qquad\qquad$ = **40.84 kN**

**Example 1.10 :** *Two parts of a tie bar of diameter D are connected by a pin joint. The end of one part is formed into a fork, into which the end of the other part fits, a pin of diameter 'd' passing through the two being in double shear. If 'σ' and 'τ' are the tensile and shear stresses in the rod and pin respectively, show that for uniform resistance,*

$$\frac{d}{D} = \sqrt{\frac{\sigma}{2\tau}}$$

**Data :** As shown in Fig. 1.16.

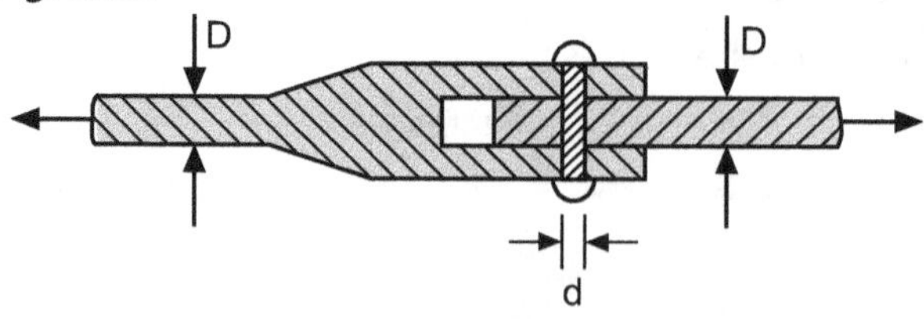


**Fig. 1.16**

**Required :** $\dfrac{d}{D} = \sqrt{\dfrac{\sigma}{2\tau}}$

**Concept :** Normal and shear stress.

**Solution :** (i) Geometric properties :

$$\text{Cross-sectional area of the tie bar} \; = \; A_b = \frac{\pi}{4} D^2$$

$$\text{Cross-sectional area of the pin} \; = \; A_p$$

$$= \; \frac{\pi}{4} d^2$$

$$\text{Area under shear} \; = \; 2 \cdot A_p$$

$$= \; \frac{\pi \, d^2}{4} \times 2 = \frac{\pi}{2} d^2$$

(ii)  Ratio of diameters :

$$\text{Tensile force carried by the tie bar} \; = \; \frac{\pi}{4} D^2 \cdot \sigma$$

$$\text{Shear strength of the pin} \; = \; \frac{\pi}{2} d^2 \cdot \tau$$

$$\text{If tensile strength of the tie bar} \; = \; \text{Shear strength of the pin}$$

$$\frac{\pi}{4} D^2 \, \sigma \; = \; \frac{\pi}{2} d^2 \, \tau$$

$$\frac{d^2}{D^2} \; = \; \frac{\pi \, \sigma}{4} \times \frac{2}{\pi \, \tau}$$

$$\mathbf{\frac{d}{D}} \; = \; \sqrt{\frac{\sigma}{2\tau}}$$

**Example 1.11 :** *A forked end carries an axial pin 25 mm diameter which is in double shear. Calculate the ultimate and safe loads for this pin if the ultimate shear stress of the material is 200 MPa and the ratio between the ultimate and safe stress is to be 5 : 1.*

**Data :** $\phi_{pin}$ = 25 mm, $\tau_{max}$ = 200 MPa, $\dfrac{\tau_{max}}{\tau_{safe}} = \dfrac{5}{1}$

**Required :** Ultimate and safe loads for the pin.

**Concept :** Normal and shear stress.

**Solution :** (i) Geometric properties :

$$\text{Cross-sectional area of the pin, } A_p \; = \; \frac{\pi}{4} (25)^2$$

$$= \; 490 \text{ mm}^2$$

(ii) $\qquad\qquad$ Area under shear $\; = \; 2 \cdot A_p$

$$= \; 2 \times 490$$

$$= \; 980 \text{ mm}^2$$

(iii) $\qquad\qquad$ Ultimate load $\; = \; 980 \times 200$

$$= \; 196 \times 10^3 \text{ N}$$

$$= \; \mathbf{196 \text{ kN}}$$

(iv) $\qquad\qquad$ Safe load $\; = \; \dfrac{196}{5} = \mathbf{39.2 \text{ kN}}$

## 1.14 GENERALISED HOOKE'S LAW

When an elastic body is subjected to normal stresses in x, y and z directions as shown in Fig. 1.17, the corresponding strains in these directions are given by

$$\epsilon_x = \frac{1}{E}(\sigma_x - \mu\,\sigma_y - \mu\,\sigma_z)$$

$$\epsilon_y = \frac{1}{E}(\sigma_y - \mu\,\sigma_x - \mu\,\sigma_z) \qquad \cdots (1.23)$$

$$\epsilon_z = \frac{1}{E}(\sigma_z - \mu\,\sigma_x - \mu\,\sigma_y)$$

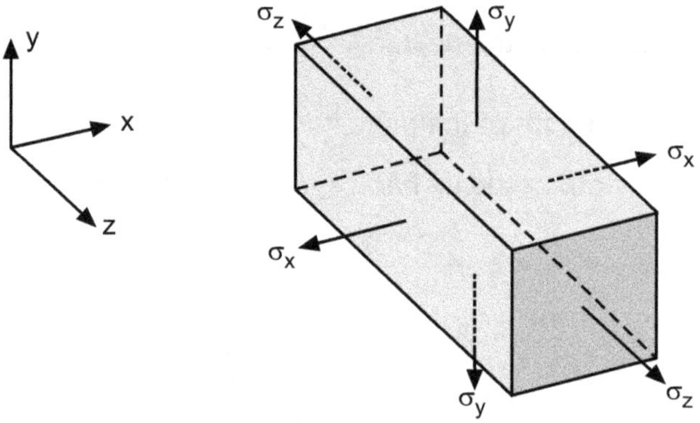

**Fig. 1.17**

**Example 1.12 :** *A rectangular bar 200 mm long, 70 mm wide and 20 mm thick is loaded with an axial tensile load of 150 kN; together with a normal compressive force of 1500 kN on 70 mm × 200 mm face and tensile force of 250 kN on 20 mm × 200 mm face. Calculate change in length, width, thickness and volume. Assume E = 200 GPa and μ = 0.3.*

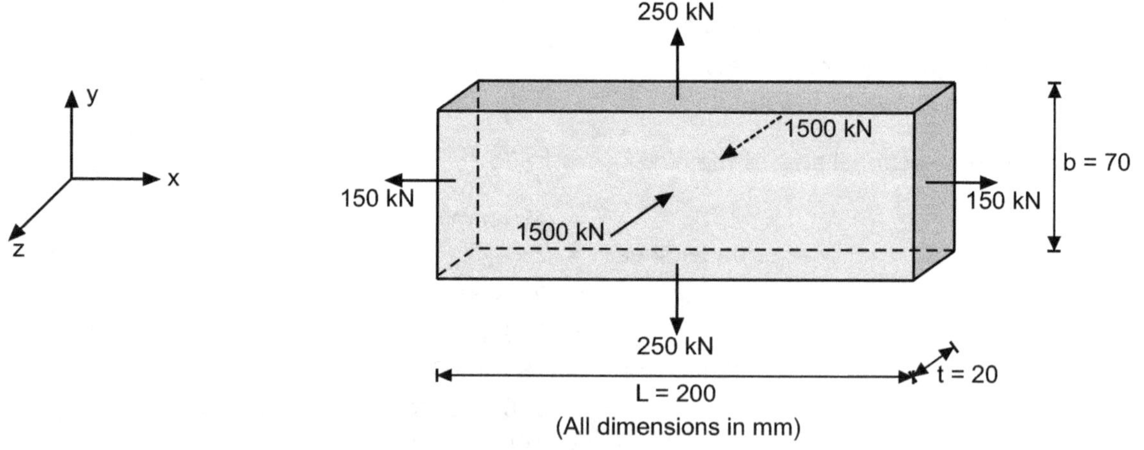


**Fig. 1.18**

**Data :** As shown in Fig. 1.18, E = 200 GPa, μ = 0.3.

**Required :** Change in length, width, thickness and volume.

**Concept :** Generalised Hooke's law.

**Solution :** (i) Normal stresses :

$$\sigma_x = \frac{150 \times 10^3}{20 \times 70} = 107.14 \text{ MPa}$$

$$\sigma_y = \frac{250 \times 10^3}{200 \times 20} = 62.5 \text{ MPa}$$

$$\sigma_z = -\frac{1500 \times 10^3}{200 \times 70} = -107.14 \text{ MPa}$$

**Note :** – ve sign for $\sigma_z$ is due to its compressive nature.

(ii)  Strains :

$$\epsilon_x = \frac{1}{E} (\sigma_x - \mu \sigma_y - \mu \sigma_z)$$

$$= \frac{1}{E} (107.14 - 0.3 \times 62.5 - 0.3 (-107.14))$$

$$= \frac{120.532}{E}$$

$$\epsilon_y = \frac{1}{E} (\sigma_y - \mu \sigma_x - \mu \sigma_z)$$

$$= \frac{1}{E} (62.5 - 0.3 \times 107.14 - 0.3 (-107.14))$$

$$= \frac{62.5}{E}$$

$$\epsilon_z = \frac{1}{E} (\sigma_z - \mu \sigma_x - \mu \sigma_y)$$

$$= \frac{1}{E} (-107.14 - 0.3 \times 107.14 - 0.3 \times 62.5)$$

$$= -\frac{158.03}{E}$$

(iii) Change in dimensions :

$$\delta L = \epsilon_x \cdot L = \frac{120.532}{E} \times 200$$

$$= \frac{120.532}{200 \times 10^3} \times 200 = \mathbf{0.12 \text{ mm (increase)}}$$

$$\delta b = \epsilon_y \cdot b = \frac{62.5}{E} \times 70$$

$$= \frac{62.5}{200 \times 10^3} \times 70 = \mathbf{0.0218 \text{ mm (increase)}}$$

$$\delta t = \epsilon_z \cdot t = \frac{-158.03}{E} \times 20 = \frac{-158.03}{200 \times 10^3} \times 20$$

$$= -0.0158 \text{ mm} = \mathbf{0.0158 \text{ mm (decrease)}}$$

**(iv) Change in volume :**

$$\text{Volumetric strain, } \epsilon_v = \epsilon_x + \epsilon_y + \epsilon_z$$

$$= \frac{1}{E}(120.532 + 62.5 - 158.03)$$

$$= \frac{25.002}{E}$$

$$\text{Change in volume} = \epsilon_v \cdot V$$

$$= \frac{25.002}{200 \times 10^3} \times (200 \times 70 \times 20)$$

$$= \textbf{35 mm}^3 \textbf{ (increase)}$$

**Example 1.13 :** *A mild steel bar 250 mm long and 100 mm × 100 mm in cross-section is subjected to longitudinal axial compressive force of 1000 kN. Determine the values of lateral forces necessary to prevent any transverse strain. Also find change in length and volume.*

*Assume E = 200 GPa and μ = 0.3.*

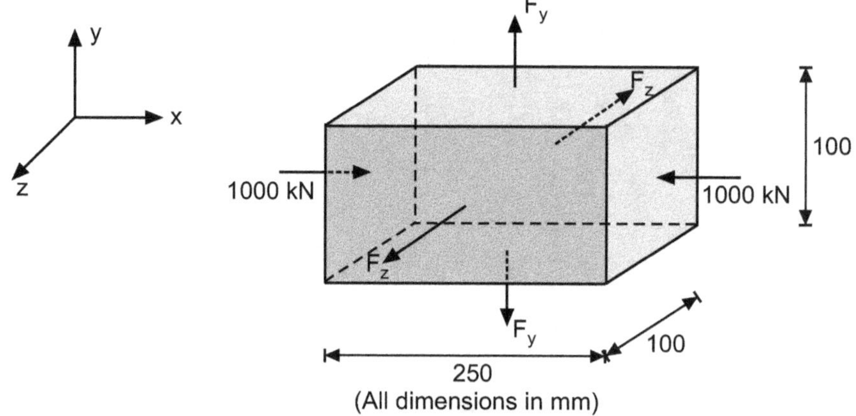


**Fig. 1.19**

**Data :** As shown in Fig. 1.19, E = 200 GPa, μ = 0.3.

**Required :** Forces $F_y$ and $F_z$ in y and z directions respectively such that there is no transverse strain. Let these forces be tensile in nature as shown.

**Concept :** Generalised Hooke's law.

**Solution :** (i) Normal stresses :

$$\sigma_x = \frac{-1000 \times 10^3}{100 \times 100} = -100 \text{ MPa}$$

$$\sigma_y = \frac{F_y \times 10^3}{250 \times 100} = \frac{F_y}{25} \text{ MPa}$$

$$\sigma_z = \frac{F_z \times 10^3}{250 \times 100} = \frac{F_z}{25} \text{ MPa}$$

where, $F_y$ and $F_z$ are forces assumed in kN.

(ii)    Strains :

$$\epsilon_x \;=\; \frac{1}{E}(\sigma_x - \mu\,\sigma_y - \mu\,\sigma_z) \;=\; \frac{1}{E}\left(-100 - 0.3 \times \frac{F_y}{25} - 0.3 \times \frac{F_z}{25}\right)$$

$$=\; -\frac{1}{E}(100 + 0.012\,F_y + 0.012\,F_z)$$

$$\epsilon_y \;=\; \frac{1}{E}(\sigma_y - \mu\,\sigma_x - \mu\,\sigma_z)$$

$$=\; \frac{1}{E}\left(\frac{F_y}{25} - 0.3 \times (-100) - 0.3 \times \frac{F_z}{25}\right)$$

$$=\; \frac{1}{E}(0.04\,F_y + 30 - 0.012\,F_z)$$

$$\epsilon_z \;=\; \frac{1}{E}(\sigma_z - \mu\,\sigma_x - \mu\,\sigma_y)$$

$$=\; \frac{1}{E}\left(\frac{F_z}{25} - 0.3 \times (-100) - 0.3 \times \frac{F_y}{25}\right)$$

$$=\; \frac{1}{E}(0.04\,F_z + 30 - 0.012\,F_y)$$

(iii)    Magnitudes of $F_y$ and $F_z$ for no transverse strains :

It is given that transverse strains $\epsilon_y$ and $\epsilon_z$ are zero.

$$\therefore \qquad \frac{1}{E}(0.04\,F_y + 30 - 0.012\,F_z) \;=\; 0 \qquad\qquad \ldots (i)$$

$$\frac{1}{E}(0.04\,F_z + 30 - 0.012\,F_y) \;=\; 0 \qquad\qquad \ldots (ii)$$

Solving equations (i) and (ii), we get

$$F_y \;=\; -1071.42 \text{ kN}$$
$$F_z \;=\; -1071.42 \text{ kN}$$

**Note :** –ve sign indicates compression.

(iv) Change in length :

$$\epsilon_x \;=\; -\frac{1}{E}(100 + 0.012 \times (-1071.42) + 0.012 \times (-1071.42))$$

$$=\; \frac{-74.28}{E}$$

$$\delta L \;=\; \epsilon_x \cdot L$$

$$\delta L \;=\; \frac{-74.28}{200 \times 10^3} \times 250$$

$$=\; -0.093 \text{ mm} = \mathbf{0.093\ mm\ (decrease)}$$

(v)    Change in volume :

$$\text{Volumetric strain} \;=\; \epsilon_v = \epsilon_x + \epsilon_y + \epsilon_z$$

$$= \frac{-74.28}{E} + 0 + 0$$

$$= \frac{-74.28}{E}$$

$$\text{Change in volume} = \delta V = \epsilon_v \cdot V$$

$$= \frac{-74.28}{200 \times 10^3} (250 \times 100 \times 100)$$

$$= -928.5 \text{ mm}^3$$

$$= \mathbf{928.5 \text{ mm}^3 \textbf{ (decrease)}}$$

**Example 1.14 :** *A plate of uniform thickness is subjected to stresses $\sigma_x$ and $\sigma_y$ as shown in Fig. 1.20. Due to these stresses length of the plate increases by 0.6 mm while width increases by 0.09 mm. Assuming E = 200 GPa and $\mu$ = 0.25, find (i) stresses $\sigma_x$ and $\sigma_y$, (ii) change in thickness, (iii) change in volume.*

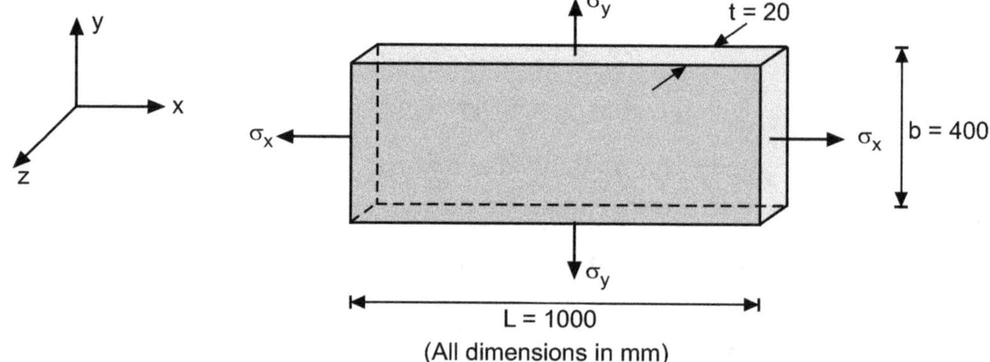


**Fig. 1.20**

**Data :** As shown in Fig. 1.20, E = 200 GPa, $\mu$ = 0.25, $\delta L$ = 0.6 mm, $\delta b$ = 0.09 mm

**Required :** (i) $\sigma_x$ , $\sigma_y$, (ii) $\delta t$, (iii) $\delta V$.

**Concept :** Generalised Hooke's law.

**Solution :** (i) Stresses $\sigma_x$ and $\sigma_y$.

From generalised Hooke's law,

$$\epsilon_x = \frac{1}{E}(\sigma_x - \mu\,\sigma_y)$$

$$\frac{0.6}{1000} = \frac{1}{E}(\sigma_x - 0.25\,\sigma_y) \qquad \text{... (i)}$$

$$\epsilon_y = \frac{1}{E}(\sigma_y - \mu\,\sigma_x)$$

$$\frac{0.09}{400} = \frac{1}{E}(\sigma_y - 0.25\,\sigma_x) \qquad \text{... (ii)}$$

Substituting the value of E, we get

$$\sigma_x - 0.25\,\sigma_y \;=\; 120 \qquad\qquad \dots\text{(i)}$$

$$\sigma_y - 0.25\,\sigma_x \;=\; 45 \qquad\qquad \dots\text{(ii)}$$

Solving equations (i) and (ii),

$$\boldsymbol{\sigma_x \;=\; 140\ MPa \ \ and\ \ \sigma_y = 80\ MPa}$$

(ii)　Change in thickness :

$$\epsilon_z \;=\; \frac{\delta t}{t} = \frac{1}{E}(\sigma_z - \mu\,\sigma_x - \mu\,\sigma_y)$$

$$=\; \frac{1}{200 \times 10^3}\,(0 - 0.25 \times 140 - 0.25 \times 80)$$

$$=\; -\,2.75 \times 10^{-4}$$

$$\therefore \qquad \delta t \;=\; -\,2.75 \times 10^{-4} \times 20$$

$$=\; \mathbf{0.0055\ mm\ (decrease)}$$

(iii) Change in volume :

Volumetric strain

$$=\; \epsilon_v = \epsilon_{xx} + \epsilon_{yy} + \epsilon_{zz}$$

$$=\; \frac{0.6}{1000} + \frac{0.09}{400} - \frac{0.0055}{20}$$

$$=\; 5.5 \times 10^{-4}$$

Change in volume, $\delta V$

$$=\; \epsilon_v \cdot V$$

$$=\; 5.5 \times 10^{-4}\,(1000 \times 400 \times 20)$$

$$=\; \mathbf{4400\ mm^3\ (increase)}$$

---

**Example 1.15 :** *A bar 30 mm diameter was subjected to tensile load of 54 kN. Measured extension on 300 mm gauge length was 0.112 mm and change in diameter was 0.00366 mm. Calculate Poisson's ratio and values of three elastic moduli.* **(Dec. 2002)**

**Data :** $d = 30$ mm, $P = 54$ kN, $l = 300$ mm, $\delta l = 0.112$ mm, $\delta d = 0.00366$ mm

**Required :** $\mu$, E, K and G.

**Concept :** Generalised Hooke's law.

**Solution :**

(i)　　　　Poisson's ratio $=\; \dfrac{\text{Lateral strain}}{\text{Linear strain}}$

$$\mu \;=\; \frac{(\delta d / d)}{\dfrac{\delta l}{l}} \;=\; \frac{(0.0036/30)}{(0.112/300)} = \mathbf{0.32}$$

(ii)　　　　　$\delta l \;=\; \dfrac{PL}{AE}$

$$0.112 \;=\; \frac{54 \times 10^3 \times 300}{\dfrac{\pi}{4} \times (30)^2 \times E}$$

$\therefore$       **E = 204627.78 N/mm²**

(iii)       $E = 3K (1 - 2\mu)$

$204627.78 = 3K (1 - 2 \times 0.32)$

$\therefore$       **K = 189470.17 N/mm²**

(iv)       $E = 2G (1 + \mu)$

$204627.78 = 2G (1 + 0.32)$

$\therefore$       **G = 77510.52 N/mm²**

**Example 1.16 :** *A metallic piece is subjected to forces as shown in Fig. 1.21. Determine the change in volume if E = 200 kN/mm² and Poisson's ratio $\mu$ = 0.25.*       **(Dec. 1997)**

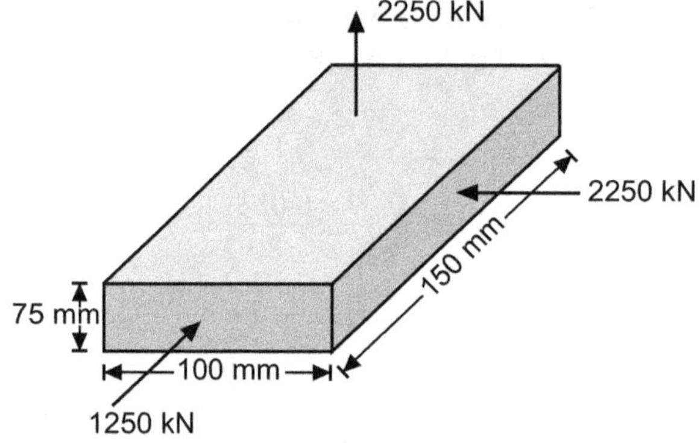


**Fig. 1.21**

**Data :** As shown in Fig. 1.21.

**Required :** Change in volume.

**Concept :** Generalised Hooke's law.

**Solution :**

(i)    Normal stresses :    $\sigma_x = \dfrac{-2250 \times 10^3}{75 \times 150} = -200$ MPa

$\sigma_y = \dfrac{2250 \times 10^3}{150 \times 100} = 150$ MPa

$\sigma_z = \dfrac{-1250 \times 10^3}{75 \times 100} = -166.67$ MPa

**Note :** – ve sign is due to its compressive stress.

(ii)    Strains :    $\epsilon_x = \dfrac{1}{E} \left( \sigma_x - \mu\, \sigma_y - \mu\, \sigma_z \right)$

$= \dfrac{1}{E} [- 200 - 0.25 \times 150 - 0.25 \times (- 166.67)]$

$= -\dfrac{195.83}{200 \times 10^3} = 9.79 \times 10^{-4}$

$$\epsilon_y \;=\; \frac{1}{E}\left(\sigma_y - \mu\sigma_x - \mu\sigma_z\right)$$

$$=\; \frac{1}{E}\left[150 - 0.25 \times (-200) - 0.25\,(-166.67)\right]$$

$$=\; \frac{241.67}{E} \;=\; \frac{241.67}{200 \times 10^3} \;=\; 1.208 \times 10^{-3}$$

$$\epsilon_z \;=\; \frac{1}{E}\left(\sigma_z - \mu\sigma_x - \mu\sigma_y\right)$$

$$=\; \frac{1}{E}\left[-166.67 - 0.25 \times 150 - 0.25 \times (-200)\right]$$

$$=\; -\frac{154.17}{200 \times 10^3} \;=\; -7.71 \times 10^{-4}$$

(iii) Change in volume :

$$\text{Volumetric strain} \;=\; \epsilon_v = \epsilon_x + \epsilon_y + \epsilon_z$$

$$=\; \frac{1}{E}\left(-195.83 + 241.67 - 154.17\right)$$

$$=\; -\frac{108.33}{200 \times 10^3} \;=\; -5.42 \times 10^{-4}$$

$$\therefore \qquad \delta V \;=\; -5.42 \times 10^{-4} \times 75 \times 100 \times 150$$

$$=\; -609.75 \text{ mm}^3$$

Change in volume, $\delta V$ = **609.75 mm³ (decrease)**

**Example 1.17 :** *The following observations were made while testing a mild steel specimen, during tension test, of original diameter 20 mm and gauge length 50 mm.*

| | | |
|---|---|---|
| *(a)* | *Load at limit of proportionality* | *= 80 kN* |
| *(b)* | *Corresponding extension* | *= 0.06 mm* |
| *(c)* | *Yield point load* | *= 85 kN* |
| *(d)* | *Ultimate load* | *= 150 kN* |
| *(e)* | *Diameter at the neck* | *= 15.80 mm* |
| *(f)* | *After fitting the two broken parts neatly together, length between gauge points* | *= 69.50 mm* |

**Calculate :**

*(i)     Young's modulus*

*(ii)    Stress at the limit of proportionality*

*(iii)   Yield stress*

*(iv)    Ultimate tensile stress*

*(v)     Percentage elongation*

*(vi)    Percentage contraction*

**Data :** Load at limit of proportionality     = 80 kN
    Corresponding extension     = 0.06 mm
    Yield point load     = 85 kN
    Ultimate load     = 150 kN
    Diameter at the neck     = 15.80 mm
    Total length     = 69.50 mm
    Gauge length ($l$)     = 50 mm

Cross-sectional area $= \dfrac{\pi}{4} \times (20)^2$     = 314.16 mm²

**Required :** Stress at different conditions, elongation and contraction.
**Concept :** Standard formulae.

**Solution :** (i)
$$\delta l = \frac{PL}{AE}$$

$$0.06 = \frac{80 \times 10^3 \times 50}{314.16\,E}$$

∴     **E = 212206.06 N/mm²**

(ii)   Stress at limit of proportionality,

$$\sigma = \frac{P}{A} = \frac{80 \times 10^3}{314.16} = \mathbf{254.65\ N/mm^2}$$

(iii) Stress at yield point,

$$\sigma = \frac{P}{A} = \frac{85 \times 10^3}{314.16} = \mathbf{270.56\ N/mm^2}$$

(iv) Ultimate tensile stress,

$$\sigma = \frac{P}{A} = \frac{150 \times 10^3}{314.16} = \mathbf{477.46\ N/mm^2}$$

(v)   Percentage elongation :

Elongation, $\delta l = 69.50 - 50 = 19.50$ mm

∴     % elongation $= \dfrac{\delta l}{l} \times 100$

$$= \frac{19.50}{50} \times 100 = \mathbf{39\%}$$

(vi) Percentage contraction :

Contraction, $\delta d = 20 - 15.80 = 4.20$ mm

∴     % contraction $= \dfrac{\delta d}{d} \times 100$

$$= \frac{4.20}{20} \times 100$$

Percentage contraction = **21%**

**Example 1.18 :** *A surveyor's steel tape 30 m long has a cross-section of 6 mm × 0.75 mm. Determine the elongation when the full length is held taut by applying a force of 100 N. The modulus of elasticity is 200 GPa.*

**Data :** $l$ = 30 m, cross-sectional area = 6 × 0.75 mm$^2$, P = 100 N, E = 200 × 10$^3$ MPa

**Required :** $\delta l$

**Concept :** Standard formula.

**Solution :**

$$\delta l = \frac{PL}{AE}$$

$$\therefore \quad \delta l = \frac{100 \times 30.000}{6 \times 0.75 \times 200 \times 10^3}$$

$$\therefore \quad \text{Elongation} = \delta l = \mathbf{3.33\ mm}$$

**Example 1.19 :** *For a certain material, E = 210 MPa. The Poisson's ratio is 0.3. State the relationship to calculate the values of other two elastic constants and find their values.*

**Data :** E = 210 × 10$^3$ MPa, $\mu$ = 0.3.

**Required :** K and G.

**Concept :** Standard formulae.

**Solution :**

(i)    Bulk Modulus (K) :

$$E = 3K\ (1 - 2\mu)$$

$$\therefore \quad K = \frac{210 \times 10^3}{3\ (1 - 2 \times 0.3)}$$

$$\therefore \quad K = \mathbf{175 \times 10^3\ MPa}$$

(ii)    Modulus of rigidity :

$$E = 2G\ (1 + \mu)$$

$$\therefore \quad G = \frac{210 \times 10^3}{2\ (1 + 0.3)}$$

$$\therefore \quad G = \mathbf{80.77 \times 10^3\ MPa}$$

**Example 1.20 :** *A cylinder 150 mm in diameter, 300 mm in length is subjected to axial compressive load of 180 kN which causes increase in diameter 0.0952 mm and a decrease in length by 0.64 mm. Calculate Poisson's ratio and modulus of elasticity.*

**Data :** d = 150 mm, $l$ = 300 mm, P = 180 kN, $\delta d$ = 0.0952 mm, $\delta l$ = 0.64 mm (decrease)

**Required :** $\mu$, E.

**Concept :** Generalised Hooke's law.

**Solution :**

(i)    Poisson's ratio ($\mu$) :

$$\mu = \frac{\text{Lateral strain}}{\text{Linear strain}}$$

$$\text{Lateral strain} \quad = \quad \frac{\delta l}{l} = \frac{0.64}{300} = 0.0021$$

$$\text{Lateral strain} \quad = \quad \frac{\delta d}{d} = \frac{0.0952}{150} = 0.00063$$

$$\therefore \qquad \mu \quad = \quad \frac{0.00063}{0.0021} = \mathbf{0.3}$$

(ii)   Modulus of elasticity :

$$\delta l \quad = \quad \frac{PL}{AE}$$

$$0.64 \quad = \quad \frac{180 \times 10^3 \times 300}{\frac{\pi}{4} \times (150)^2 \times E}$$

$$\therefore \qquad E \quad = \quad 4774.65 \text{ MPa}$$

$$\therefore \qquad E \quad = \quad \mathbf{4.77 \ GPa}$$

**Example 1.21 :** *The cottered joint shown in Fig. 1.22 carries a load of 100 kN. The socket is on square section of sides x mm and the cotter is rectangular b mm × t mm. Find the dimensions d, x, b and t for the following allowable stresses :*

*Tensile stress = 110 N/mm², shear stress = 80 N/mm² and bearing stress = 140 N/mm².*

*Assume double shear 1.875 times as strong as single shear.*

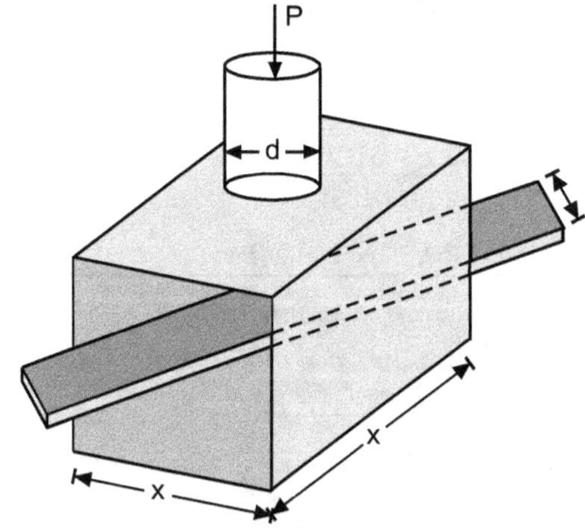


**Fig. 1.22**

**Data :** Tensile stress = 110 N/mm², Shear stress = 80 N/mm²,

Bearing stress = 140 N/mm², P = 100 kN.

**Required :** d, x, b and t.

**Concept :** Stress = $\dfrac{\text{Load}}{\text{Area}}$

**Solution :**

(i)　Diameter (d) :

$$\text{Tensile stress} = \frac{\text{Load}}{\text{Cross-sectional area}}$$

$$110 = \frac{100 \times 10^3}{\frac{\pi}{4} \times d^2}$$

∴　　　**d = 34.02 mm**

(ii)　Dimension (x) :

$$\text{Bearing stress} = \frac{\text{Load}}{\text{Bearing area}}$$

$$140 = \frac{100 \times 10^3}{x \times x}$$

∴　　　**x = 26.73 mm**

(iii) Dimensions b and t : Cotter joint has bearing stress and double shear.

$$\text{Bearing stress} = \frac{\text{Load}}{b \times x}$$

$$140 = \frac{100 \times 10^3}{b \times 26.73}$$

∴　　　**b = 26.73 mm**

$$\text{Shear stress} = \frac{\text{Load}}{\text{Area}}$$

$$\text{Double shear} = 1.875 \times 80 = 150 \text{ MPa}$$

∴　　　$$150 = \frac{100 \times 10^3}{2b \times t}$$

∴　　　**t = 12.47 mm**

**Example 1.22 :** *In a tensile test on a steel tube of external diameter 18 mm and internal diameter 12 mm, an axial pull of 2 kN produced a stretch of $6.72 \times 10^{-3}$ mm in a length of 100 mm and a lateral contraction of $3.62 \times 10^{-4}$ mm in the outer diameter. Calculate the three moduli and Poisson's ratio for the material of the tube.*

**Data :** $D_O = 18$ mm, $D_i = 12$ mm, P = 2 kN, $l = 100$ mm,

　　　$\delta l = 6.72 \times 10^{-3}$ mm, $\delta d = 3.62 \times 10^{-4}$ mm

**Required :** E, μ, K and G.

**Concept :** (i) $\delta l = \dfrac{PL}{AE}$, (ii) Standard formulae.

**Solution :**

(i)　Geometric properties :

$$A = \frac{\pi}{4} \times \left[ D_o^2 - D_i^2 \right]$$

$$= \frac{\pi}{4} \left[ (18)^2 - (12)^2 \right] = 141.37 \text{ mm}^2$$

(ii)　Calculation for E :

$$\delta l = \frac{PL}{AE}$$

$$6.72 \times 10^{-3} = \frac{2 \times 10^3 \times 100}{141.37 \times E}$$

∴　　$E = 210.52 \times 10^3$ MPa = **210.52 GPa**

(iii)　Calculation for μ :

$$\mu = \frac{\text{Lateral strain}}{\text{Linear strain}} = \frac{(\delta d / d)}{(\delta l / l)}$$

∴　　$$\mu = \frac{(3.62 \times 10^{-4} / 18)}{(6.72 \times 10^{-3} / 100)}$$

∴　　$\mu = $ **0.299**

(iv)　Calculation for K :　　$$K = \frac{E}{3(1 - 2\mu)}$$

$$= \frac{210.52 \times 10^3}{3(1 - 2 \times 0.299)}$$

$$K = 117.35 \times 10^3 \text{ MPa}$$

∴　　$K = $ **117.35 GPa**

(v)　Calculation for G :

$$G = \frac{E}{2(1 + \mu)}$$

$$= \frac{210.52 \times 10^3}{2(1 + 0.299)}$$

∴　　$G = 81.03 \times 10^3$ MPa = **81.03 GPa**

**Example 1.23 :** *A rectangular steel plate 1 m long, 0.4 m wide and 20 mm thick is subjected to biaxial stresses $\sigma_x$ and $\sigma_y$ acting along length and width respectively. If the increase in length is 0.6 mm and the increase in width is 0.09 mm, find :*

*(i)　$\sigma_x$ and $\sigma_y$,*

*(ii)　Change in thickness of the plate,*

*(iii)　Change in volume of the plate.*

*E = 200 GPa, Poisson's ratio = 0.25*

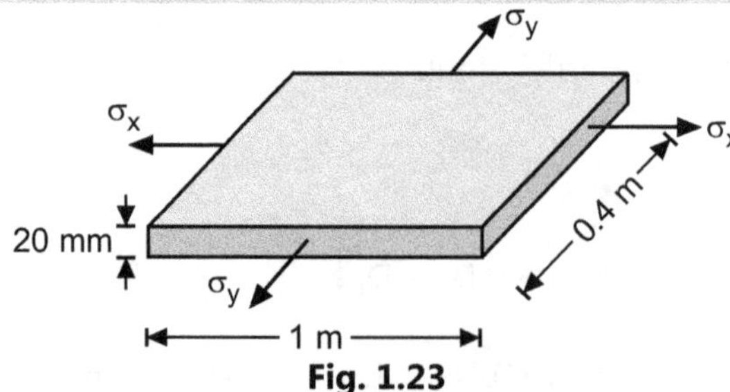


**Fig. 1.23**

**Data :** As shown in Fig. 1.23, E = 200 GPa, μ = 0.25, δ*l* = 0.6 mm, δb = 0.09 mm

**Required :** $\sigma_x$, $\sigma_y$, $\delta t$ and $\delta V$.

**Concept :** Generalised Hooke's law.

**Solution :**

(i)    Calculation for $\sigma_x$ and $\sigma_y$ :

$$\epsilon_x = \frac{\sigma_x}{E} - \frac{\mu\sigma_y}{E} - \frac{\mu\sigma_z}{E}$$

$$\sigma_z = 0$$

$$\epsilon_x = \frac{\delta l}{l}$$

$$\therefore \quad \frac{0.6}{1000} = \frac{\sigma_x - 0.25\,\sigma_y}{200 \times 10^3}$$

$$\therefore \quad \sigma_x - 0.25\,\sigma_y = 120 \qquad \text{... (i)}$$

$$\epsilon_y = \frac{\sigma_y}{E} - \mu\frac{\sigma_x}{E} \qquad (\text{as } \sigma_z = 0)$$

$$\epsilon_y = \frac{\delta b}{b} = \frac{0.09}{400}$$

$$\therefore \quad \frac{0.09}{400} = \frac{\sigma_y - \mu\sigma_x}{200 \times 10^3}$$

$$\therefore \quad \sigma_y - 0.25\,\sigma_x = 45 \qquad \text{... (ii)}$$

Solving equations (i) and (ii),

$$\sigma_x = \textbf{140 MPa}$$

$$\sigma_y = \textbf{80 MPa}$$

(ii)   Change in thickness ($\delta t$) :

$$\frac{\delta t}{t} = \frac{\sigma_z}{E} - \frac{\mu\sigma_x}{E} - \frac{\mu\sigma_y}{E}$$

$$\frac{\delta t}{20} = -\frac{0.25}{200 \times 10^3}\,(140 + 80)$$

$$\therefore \quad \delta t = -5.5 \times 10^{-3} \text{ mm}$$

$$\delta t = \textbf{5.5} \times \textbf{10}^{-3} \textbf{ mm (decrease)}$$

(iii) Change in volume ($\delta V$) :

$$\frac{\delta V}{V} = \epsilon_x + \epsilon_y + \epsilon_z$$

$$\frac{\delta V}{V} = \left(\frac{0.6}{1000}\right) + \left(\frac{0.09}{400}\right) - \left(\frac{5.5 \times 10^{-3}}{20}\right)$$

$$\therefore \quad \delta V = \textbf{4400 mm}^3 \textbf{ (increase)}$$

**Example 1.24 :** *Two rectangular pieces of wood, 100 mm × 50 mm are glued together along the joint, as shown in Fig. 1.24. Determine the maximum safe axial force P, that can be applied to the block if :*

*(i)    The compressive stress in wood is limited to 20 MPa.*

*(ii)   Shear stress of the joint is limited to 5 MPa.*

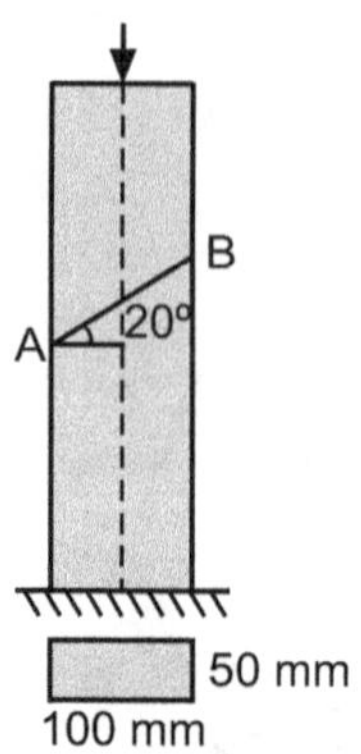

**Fig. 1.24**

**Data :** As shown in Fig. 1.24, compressive stress = 20 MPa, shear stress = 5 MPa

**Required :** Value of P.

**Concept :** Minimum from two.

**Solution :**

(i)   P from compression :

$$\text{Cross-sectional area} = 100 \times 50 = 5000 \text{ mm}^2$$

$$P = \text{Compressive stress} \times \text{Area}$$

$$= 20 \times 5000 = 100 \times 10^3 \text{ N} = 100 \text{ kN}$$

(ii)  P from shear on plane AB :

∴   Shear force along AB is P sin 20.

$$\text{Cross-sectional area} = 50 \times \frac{100}{\cos 20} = 5320.89 \text{ mm}^2$$

∴        $$P \sin 20 = \text{Shear stress} \times \text{Area along force}$$

∴        $$P = \frac{5 \times 5320.89}{\sin 20}$$

$$P = 77786.21 \text{ N}$$

∴        $$P = 77.79 \text{ kN}$$

∴   Maximum axial force is **77.79 kN**

**Example 1.25 :** *A plate 2 m × 2 m × 20 mm is subjected to stresses $\sigma_x$ = 100 MPa tensile and $\sigma_y$ = 50 MPa compressive in the plane of the plate. Modulus of elasticity of the plate is 200 GPa and Poisson's ratio is 0.25. Calculate the volume of the plate.*     **(Dec. 2001)**

**Solution :**

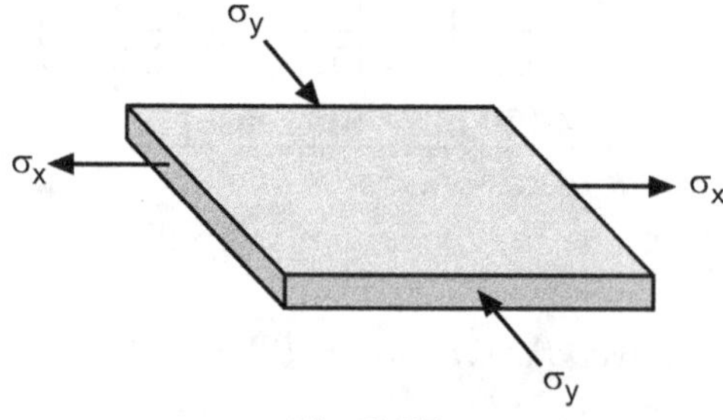


**Fig. 1.25**

(i)　Strains :

$$\epsilon_x = \frac{1}{E}(\sigma_x - \mu\sigma_y - \mu\sigma_z)$$

$$= \frac{1}{E}(100 + 0.25 \times 50) = \frac{112.5}{E}$$

$$\epsilon_y = \frac{1}{E}(\sigma_y - \mu\sigma_x - \mu\sigma_z) = \frac{-75}{E}$$

$$\epsilon_z = \frac{1}{E}(\sigma_z - \mu\,\sigma_x - \mu\,\sigma_y) = \frac{-12.5}{E}$$

$$\epsilon_v = \epsilon_x + \epsilon_y + \epsilon_z = \frac{25}{E}$$

(ii)　Change in volume, $\delta V = \epsilon_v \cdot V = \mathbf{10^4\ mm^3\ (increase)}$

**Example 1.26 :** *A bar of 30 mm diameter was subjected to tensile force of 53 kN and measured extension on 300 mm gauge length was 0.112 mm and change in the diameter was 0.00366 mm. Calculate Poisson's ratio and the values of three moduli.*　　　　　　　**(Dec. 2001)**

**Solution :** (i)　　　　　$A = \frac{\pi}{4}(30)^2 = 706.86\ mm^2$

$$\delta L = \frac{PL}{AE}$$

∴　　　　　$0.112 = \dfrac{53 \times 300}{706.86\ E}$

$$E = 200.838 \times 10^3\ MPa$$

∴　　　　　$\mathbf{E = 200.838\ GPa}$　　　　　　　　　　... (i)

(ii)　　Poisson's radio,　　$\mu = \dfrac{\left(\dfrac{\delta D}{D}\right)}{\left(\dfrac{\delta L}{L}\right)}$

$$= \frac{0.00366}{30} \times \frac{300}{0.112}$$

$$= \mathbf{0.326}$$　　　　　　　　... (ii)

(iii)　　　　　$E = 2G(1 + \mu)$

Substituting from (i) and (ii) and solving, we get

∴　　　　　$G = \mathbf{75.73\ GPa}$

$$E = 3K(1 - 2\mu)$$

Substituting from (i) and (ii) and solving, we get

$$K = \mathbf{192.37\ GPa}$$

**Example 1.27 :** *A bar of steel 40 mm × 40 mm in section and is 120 mm long. It is subjected to loads as shown in Fig. 1.26. Find the change in dimensions of bar and change in volume. Also find what axial longitudinal load alone can produce the same longitudinal strain as in first part ?*

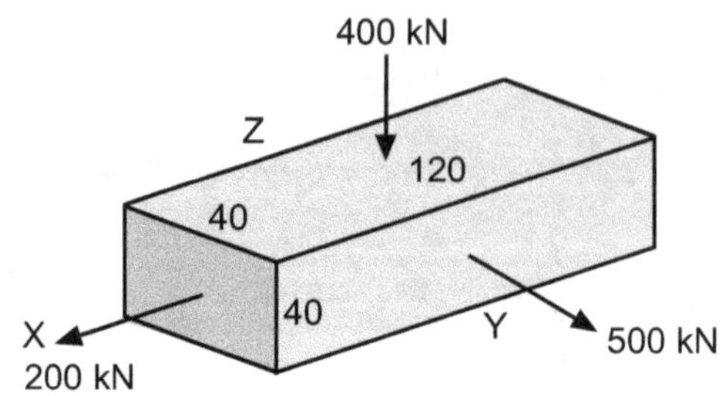



**Fig. 1.26**

$$\sigma_x = \frac{P}{A} = \frac{200 \times 10^3}{40 \times 40} = \mathbf{125 \ N/mm^2}$$

$$\sigma_y = \frac{P}{A} = \frac{500 \times 10^3}{120 \times 40} = \mathbf{104.17 \ N/mm^2}$$

$$\sigma_z = \frac{P}{A} = \frac{400 \times 10^3}{120 \times 40} = \mathbf{-83.33 \ N/mm^2}$$

$$\epsilon_x = \frac{\sigma_x}{E} - \frac{\mu\sigma_y}{E} - \frac{\mu\sigma_z}{E}$$

$$= \frac{125}{2 \times 10^5} - \frac{0.3 \times 104.17}{2 \times 10^5} + \frac{0.3 \times 83.33}{2 \times 10^5}$$

$$\epsilon_x = 5.94 \times 10^{-4}$$

$$\therefore \quad \delta l = 0.0712$$

$$\epsilon_y = \frac{104.17}{2 \times 10^5} - \frac{0.3 \times 125}{2 \times 10^5} + \frac{0.3 \times 83.33}{2 \times 10^5}$$

$$= 4.58 \times 10^{-4}$$

$$\epsilon_z = -\frac{83.33}{2 \times 10^5} - \frac{0.3 \times 125}{2 \times 10^5} - \frac{0.3 \times 104.17}{2 \times 10^5}$$

$$= -7.6 \times 10^{-4}$$

$$\frac{\delta V}{V} = (\epsilon_x + \epsilon_y + \epsilon_z)$$

$$\therefore \quad \delta V = (5.94 + 4.58 - 7.6) \times 10^{-4} \times 40 \times 40 \times 120$$

$$= 56.06 \ mm^3$$

$$\epsilon_x = 5.94 \times 10^{-4}$$

$$\epsilon_x = \frac{\sigma_x}{E}$$

$$\therefore \quad \sigma_x = 5.94 \times 10^{-4} \times E = 5.94 \times 10^{-4} \times 2 \times 10^5 = 118.8$$

$$\therefore \quad P_x = \sigma_x \times c/s \ area = 118.8 \times 40 \times 40$$

$$= \mathbf{190.08 \ kN}$$

190.08 kN force can produce same longitudinal strain as in first part.

**Example 1.28 :** *The shock mount shown in Fig. 1.27 (consisting of a steel tube of inner diameter b and a, central steel bar of diameter d) is used to support an instrument load P and a hollow rubber cylinder of height h bonded to the steel tube and bar.*

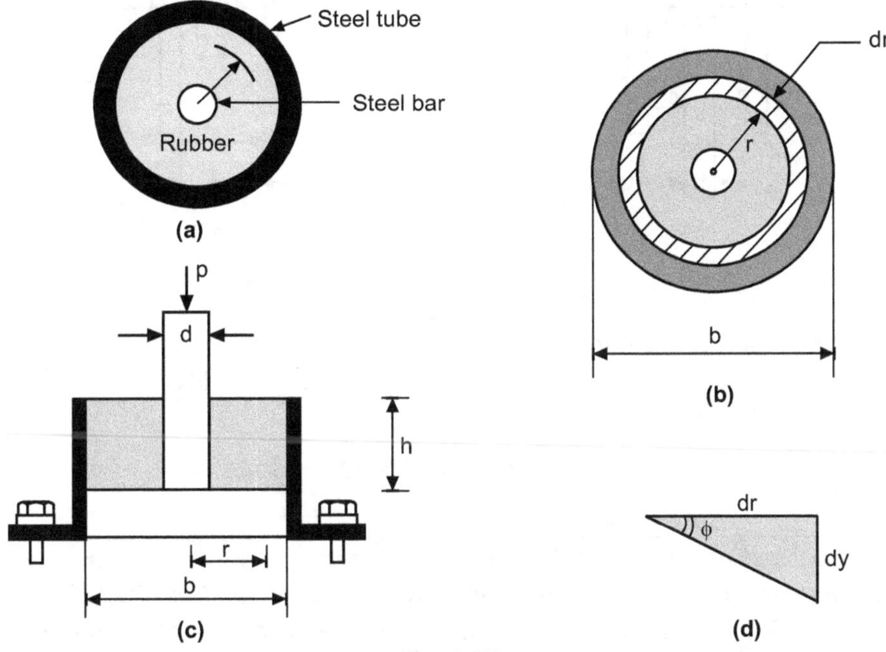


**Fig. 1.27**

*Assuming that G is the shear modulus of elasticity of rubber and that the steel tube is rigid, obtain a formula for the downward displacement of the end of the steel bar in terms of b, d, P, h and G.*

**Solution :** For an elementary ring,

$$A = 2\pi r \cdot dr$$

Downward displacement $= dy$

$$\text{Shear strain} = \tan\phi = \frac{dy}{dr}$$

where,

$$\tan\phi = \frac{\tau}{G} = \frac{P}{2\pi rhG}$$

$$\frac{P}{2\pi rhG} = \frac{dy}{dr}$$

$$\therefore \quad dy = \frac{P}{2\pi hG} = \frac{dr}{r}$$

∴ Total downward displacement,

$$y = \frac{P}{2\pi hG} \int_{d/2}^{b/2} \frac{dr}{r}$$

$$\therefore \quad \mathbf{y = \frac{P}{2\pi hG} \log_e (b/d)}$$

**Example 1.29 :** *An aluminium bar AB is attached to its support by a 16 mm diameter pin at A as shown Fig. 1.28 (a). The thickness of the bar is 15 mm, and its width b is 40 mm. If the allowable tensile stress in the bar is 150 MPa and the allowable shear stress in the pin is 85 MPa, find the allowable load P.*

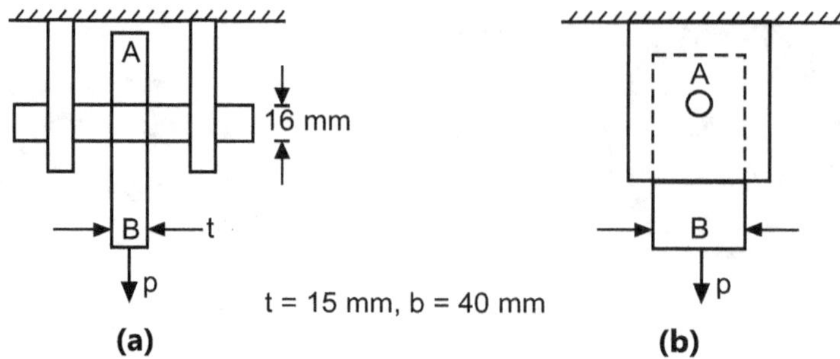



**Fig. 1.28**

**Solution :** (i) Normal stress criteria :

$$P = \sigma A = 150 \times 40 \times 15 \times 10^{-3} = 90 \text{ kN} \qquad \text{... (i)}$$

(ii)   Shear stress criteria :

$$P = 2\left(\frac{\pi}{4}\right) \times 16^2 \times 85 \times 10^{-3} = 34.18 \text{ kN} \qquad \text{... (ii)}$$

**Safe P = 34.18 kN**

**Example 1.30 :** *A steel plate 150 × 100 mm in cross-section is 300 mm long. It carries a tensile load of 500 kN in direction of its length. A compressive load of 5000 kN on its 150 × 300 mm faces and tensile load of 2500 kN on its 100 × 300 mm faces. If E = 2 × 10⁵ MPa and Poisson's ratio is 0.25, find the change in volume of bar. What change must be made in the 5000 kN load in order that there shall be no change in volume of the bar ?* **(Dec. 2006)**

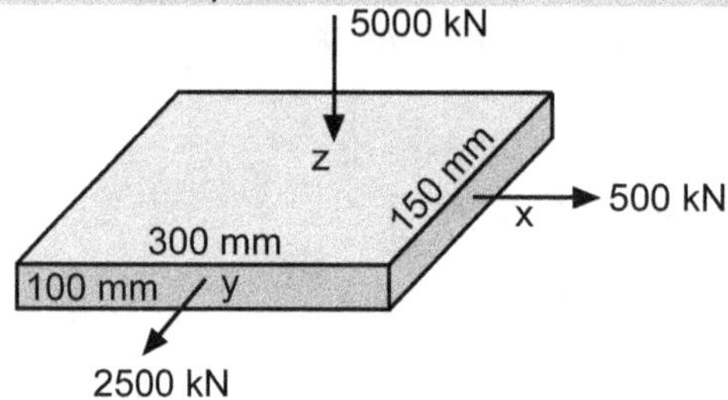



**Fig. 1.29**

**Data :** As shown in Fig. 1.29.

**Required :** Change in volume.

**Concept :** Normliased Hooke's law.

**Solution : (i) Normal stresses :**

$$\sigma_x = \frac{500 \times 10^3}{150 \times 100} = 33.33 \text{ MPa (Tensile)}$$

$$\sigma_y = \frac{2500 \times 10^3}{100 \times 300} = 83.33 \text{ MPa (Tensile)}$$

$$\sigma_z = \frac{5000 \times 10^3}{150 \times 300} = 111.11 \text{ MPa (Comp.)}$$

**(ii) Strains :**

$$\epsilon_x = \frac{1}{E}(\sigma_x - \mu\sigma_y - \mu\sigma_z)$$

$$= \frac{1}{E}(33.33 - 0.25 \times 83.33 + 0.25 \times 111.11)$$

$$= \frac{40.28}{E}$$

$$\epsilon_y = \frac{1}{E}(83.33 - 0.25 \times 33.33 + 0.25 \times 111.11)$$

$$= \frac{102.78}{E}$$

$$\epsilon_z = \frac{1}{E}(-111.11 - 0.25 \times 33.33 - 0.25 \times 83.33)$$

$$= -\frac{140.28}{EI}$$

**(iii) Change in Volume :**

$$\text{Volumetric Strain} = \epsilon_v = \epsilon_x + \epsilon_y + \epsilon_z$$

$$= \frac{40.28}{E} + \frac{102.78}{E} - \frac{140.28}{E} = \frac{2.78}{E}$$

$$\epsilon_v = \frac{\delta v}{v}$$

$$\therefore \quad \delta v = \epsilon_v \times v = \frac{2.78}{2 \times 10^5} \times 150 \times 100 \times 300 = 62.55 \text{ mm}^3$$

$$\text{Increase in volume} = \mathbf{62.55 \ mm^2}$$

**Example 1.31 :** *A specimen of 16 mm diameter was subjected to a tensile test and the following observations were recorded :*                    **(Dec. 2007)**

*Gauge length = 200 mm, Diameter at neck = 10 mm*

| Load (kN) | Extension (mm) | Remarks |
|---|---|---|
| 40 | 0.25 | Elasticity |
| 42 | 37.00 | Yield Point |
| 61 | 50.00 | Maximum Load |
| 59 | 50.00 | Fracture |

**Determine :**

  (i)   Yield stress.        (ii)   Ultimate stress.

  (iii)  Young's modulus.     (iv)  % reduction in cross-section area.

  (v)  % elongation.

**Data :** As given above.

**Required :** Yield stress, ultimate stress, Young's modulus, percentage reduction in cross-section, percentage elongation.

**Concept :** Standard formulae.

**Solution :** (i) Geometric property : $A = \frac{\pi}{4} \times 16^2 = 201.06 \text{ mm}^2$

$$(ii) \qquad \text{Yield stress} = \frac{\text{Yield load}}{\text{Area}} = \frac{42 \times 10^3}{201.06} = \mathbf{208.89 \ N/mm^2}$$

$$(iii) \qquad \text{Ultimate stress} = \frac{\text{Maximum load}}{\text{Area}} = \frac{61 \times 10^3}{201.06} = \mathbf{303.39 \ N/mm^2}$$

(iv) Young's modulus :

$$\delta l = \frac{Pl}{AE}$$

$$0.25 = \frac{40 \times 10^3 \times 200}{201.06 \times E} = \mathbf{159.16 \times 10^3 \ N/mm^2}$$

(v) % Reduction in area :

$$\% \text{ reduction in area} = \left( \frac{\frac{\pi}{4} \times 16^2 - \frac{\pi}{4} \times 10^2}{\frac{\pi}{4} \times 16^2} \right) \times 100 = \mathbf{60.94\%}$$

(vi) Percentage elongation :

$$\% = \frac{50}{200} \times 100 = \mathbf{25\%}$$

**Example 1.32 :** *A square bar 25 mm × 25 mm is subjected to axial forces at different locations as shown in Fig. 1.30. Find total elongation of the bar if E = 200 GPa.*

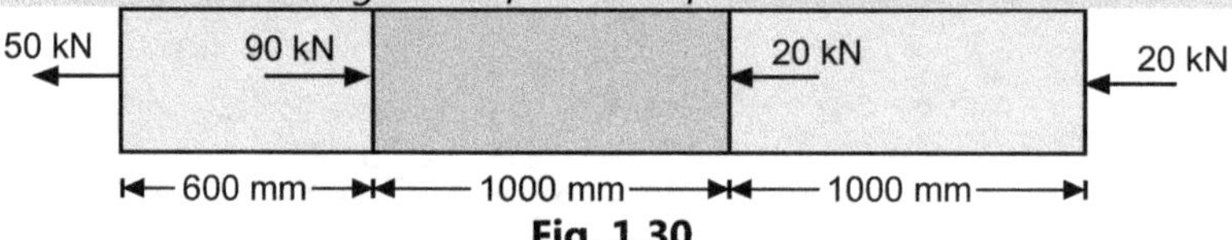


**Fig. 1.30**

**Data :** As shown in Fig. 1.30, square bar : 25 mm × 25 mm, E = 200 GPa.

**Required :** Total elongation.

**Concept :** Standard formulae.

**Solution :** (i) Geometric property :

$$A = 25 \times 25 = 625 \ mm^2$$

(ii) Total deformation :

$$\delta l = \left( \frac{Pl}{AE} \right)_1 + \left( \frac{Pl}{AE} \right)_2 + \left( \frac{Pl}{AE} \right)_3$$

$$= \frac{1}{AE} (P_1 l_1 + P_2 l_2 + P_3 l_3)$$

$$= \frac{1}{AE} (50 \times 10^3 \times 600 - 40 \times 10^3 \times 1000 - 20 \times 10^3 \times 1000)$$

$$= \frac{1}{625 \times 2 \times 10^5} [-30 \times 10^6]$$

$$= -0.24 \ mm = \mathbf{0.24 \ mm \ (contraction)}$$

∴    Total contraction of bar is **0.24 mm**

## EXERCISE

1.  A member 1 m long, 20 mm × 20 mm in cross-section is subjected to axial pull of 20 kN. If modulus of elasticity of material is 200 GPa, find the elongation of member.
    
    ($\delta L$ = 0.25 mm)

2.  Two steel rods AB and BC each 5 m long are connected at B as shown in Fig. 1.31. A load of 200 kN is supported at B as shown.

    (a)    Determine the diameter of each member if allowable stress is 100 MPa.

(b) Determine the vertical displacement of joint B assuming E = 200 GPa.

$(d = 50.46$ mm, $\delta B = 5$ mm $(\downarrow))$

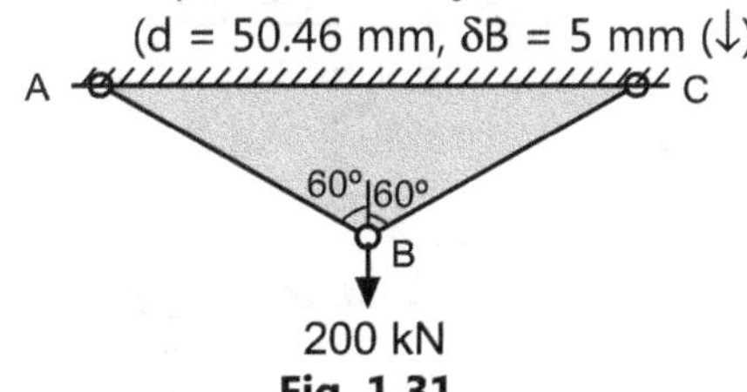


**Fig. 1.31**

3. A hollow circular member is 3 m long, 300 mm outside diameter and thickness of metal 50 mm is subjected to axial load such that stress produced is 75 MPa. If E = 150 GPa, find (i) magnitude of load, (ii) change in length. $(P = 2945.2$ kN, $\delta L = 1.5$ mm$)$

4. The following observations were made during a tensile test on a mild steel specimen 30 mm diameter and 200 mm long.

Elongation with 40 kN load = 0.054 mm

Yield load = 90 kN

Maximum load = 140 kN

Length of specimen at fracture = 241 mm.

Determine (i) Young's modulus of elasticity, (ii) Yield stress, (iii) Ultimate stress, (iv) Percentage elongation. $(E = 209.56$ GPa, Yield stress = 127.32 MPa, Ultimate stress = 198 MPa, Percentage elongation = 20.5%$)$

5. A prismatic steel bar 800 mm long is stretched by 0.7 mm by axial tensile force 'P'. Find the magnitude of force P if the volume of the bar is $450 \times 10^3$ mm$^3$ and E = 210 GPa.

$(P = 103.35$ kN$)$

6. A steel rod 30 mm in diameter, 300 mm long is subjected to axial forces alternating between 18 kN compression and 8 kN tension. Find the difference between the greatest and the least lengths of the rod. Take E = 210 GPa. $(0.0524$ mm$)$

7. Two steel plates are joined together by 16 mm diameter rivets. If plates are pulled apart by a force of 25 kN, as shown in Fig. 1.32, find shear stress in the rivets.

(Shear stress = 62.18 MPa)

**Fig. 1.32**

8. A short cast iron block of rectangular section 50 mm × 20 mm is subjected to an axial compressive load of 49 kN. Calculate the shear and the normal stresses on a section inclined at 30° to the line of action of load. $(\sigma = 12.25$ MPa, $\tau = 21.21$ MPa$)$

## UNIVERSITY QUESTION PAPERS

### MAY 2014

1. A bar of metal 100 mm × 50 mm in cross-section is 250 mm long. It carries a tensile load of 400 kN in the direction of its length, a compressive load of 4000 kN on its 100 mm × 250 mm faces and a tensile load of 2000 kN on its 50 mm × 250 mm faces. If $E = 2 \times 10^5$ N/mm$^2$ and Poisson's ratio is 0.25, find the change in volume of the bar. **[6]**

## DECEMBER 2014

1. A homogeneous 800 kg bar AB is supported at either end by a cable as shown in Fig. 1. Calculate the smallest area of each cable if the stress is not to exceed 90 MPa in bronze and 120 MPa in steel. **[6]**

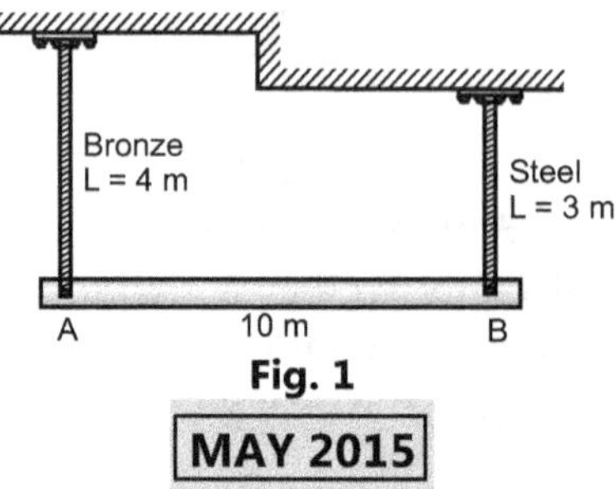


**Fig. 1**

## MAY 2015

1. A steel bar 25 mm diameter and length 250 mm is pulled by 0.001 mm by application of tensile load. Find the diameter of the bar if the linear strain is to be reduced by 10% without changing the load. **[6]**

## NOVEMBER 2015

1. The following data were recorded during the tensile test of a 14 mm diameter mild steel rod. The gauge length was 50 mm. **[6]**

| Load, (N) | Elongation (mm) | Load (N) | Elongation (mm) | Load (N) | Elongation, (mm) |
|---|---|---|---|---|---|
| 0 | 0 | 38090 | 0.061 | 68190 | 7.501 |
| 6500 | 0.011 | 40290 | 0.164 | 59190 | 12.501 |
| 12790 | 0.021 | 41790 | 0.434 | 67990 | 15.501 |
| 18990 | 0.031 | 46390 | 1.251 | 65190 | 20.001 |
| 25290 | 0.041 | 52590 | 2.501 | 61690 | 20.001 |
| 31490 | 0.051 | 58690 | 4.501 | | |

Plot the stress-strain diagram on GRAPH paper and determine the following mechanical properties :

(i)  Proportional limit        (ii) Modulus of elasticity

(iii) Yield point and          (iv) Ultimate strength.

## May 2016

1. A reinforced concrete column is 300 mm × 300 mm in section. The column is provided with 8 bars of 20 mm diameter. The column carries a load of 360 kN. Find the tresses in concrete and the steel bars. Take $E = 2.1 \times 10^5$ N/mm$^2$ and $E = 0.14 \times 10^5$ N/mm$^2$. **[6]**

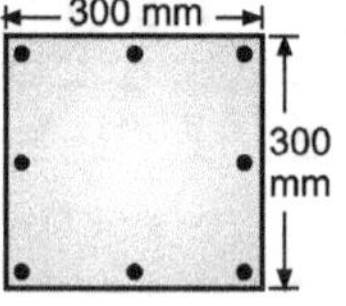


**Fig.2**

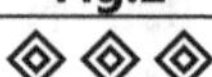

# Chapter 2

# SIMPLE STRESSES AND STRAINS (PART-II)

## 2.1 AXIAL FLEXIBILITY (f)

Axial flexibility (f) is defined as 'the change in length produced by unit axial force'.

We have,
$$\delta L = \frac{PL}{AE}$$

$\therefore$
$$f = \frac{L}{AE} \qquad \text{... (2.1)}$$

*Axial flexibility is directly proportional to length (L) of a member and inversely proportional to product of cross-sectional area and Young's modulus of elasticity* called as **axial rigidity (EA).**

Unit of axial flexibility is mm/N or m/N etc.

## 2.2 AXIAL STIFFNESS (S)

Axial stiffness (S) is defined as 'the axial force required to cause unit change in length'.

We have,
$$\delta L = \frac{PL}{AE}$$

$\therefore$
$$S = \frac{AE}{L} \qquad \text{... (2.2)}$$

*Axial stiffness is directly proportional to axial rigidity (EA) and inversely proportional to length (L).*

Unit of axial stiffness is N/mm or N/m, etc.

It should be noted that axial flexibility and stiffness are reciprocal of each other.

## SOLVED EXAMPLES

**Example 2.1 :** *Find the position of load 'W' for the arrangement shown such that member AB remains horizontal.*

**Data :** As shown in Fig. 2.1 (a).

**Required :** Position of load 'W' for the arrangement shown such that member AB remains horizontal.

**Concept :** Elongation of both, copper and steel wires must be same for member AB to remain horizontal.

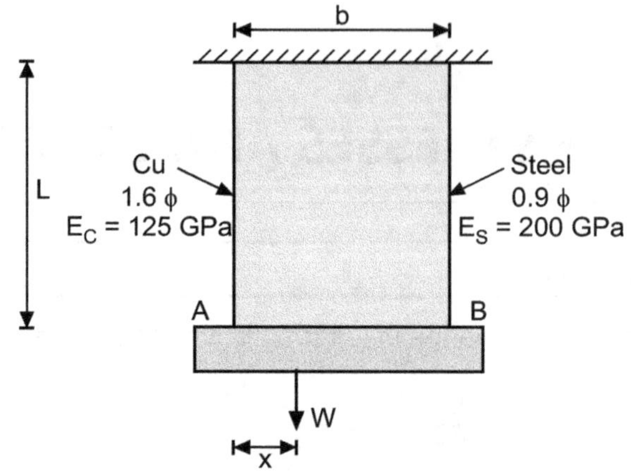



**(a) Given arrangement**

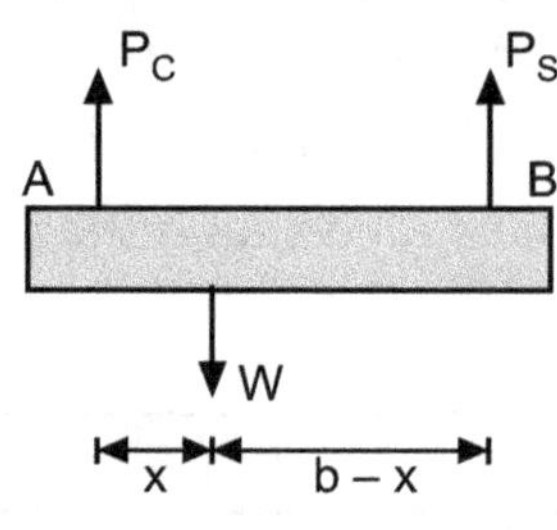



**(b) FBD**

**Fig. 2.1**

**Solution :** (i) Equation of statics :

$$P_C = \frac{W(b-x)}{b} \qquad \text{... (i)}$$

$$P_S = \frac{Wx}{b} \qquad \text{... (ii)}$$

(ii)  For AB to remain horizontal,

$$(\delta L)_{cu} = (\delta L)_{st}$$

$$\left(\frac{PL}{AE}\right)_{cu} = \left(\frac{PL}{AE}\right)_{st}$$

$$\frac{P_C}{\frac{\pi}{4} \times 1.6^2 \times 125 \times 10^3} = \frac{P_S}{\frac{\pi}{4} \times 0.9^2 \times 200 \times 10^3} \qquad \text{... (iii)}$$

$$P_C = 1.97\, P_S$$

Put equations (i) and (ii) in (iii),

$$\frac{W(b-x)}{b} = 1.97 \times \frac{W \cdot x}{b}$$

$$\therefore \qquad b - x = 1.97\, x$$

$$\therefore \qquad x = \frac{\mathbf{b}}{\mathbf{2.97}}$$

**Example 2.2 :** *Two wires AB and AC are supporting weight 'W' as shown in Fig. 2.2. Determine the maximum safe value of 'W' if the axial deformation of members AB and AC is limited to 4 mm and 6 mm respectively, neglect self weight of wires.*

**Data :** As shown in Fig. 2.2.

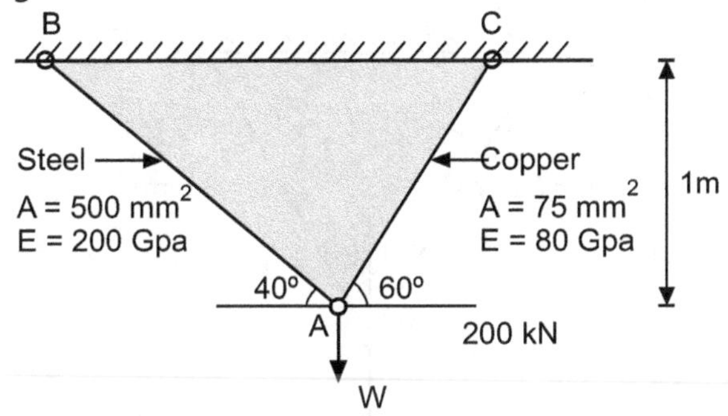


**Fig. 2.2**

**Required :** Maximum safe value of 'W'.

**Concept :** Safe value of W will be the least of that obtained from elongation of two wires.

**Solution :** (i) Equations of equilibrium.

$$\Sigma F_x = 0$$

$$- T_{AB} \cos 40 + T_{AC} \cos 60 = 0$$

$$T_{AB} = (0.65) T_{AC} \qquad \text{... (i)}$$

$$\Sigma F_y = 0$$

$$T_{AB} \sin 40 + T_{AC} \sin 60 - W = 0 \text{ ... (ii)}$$

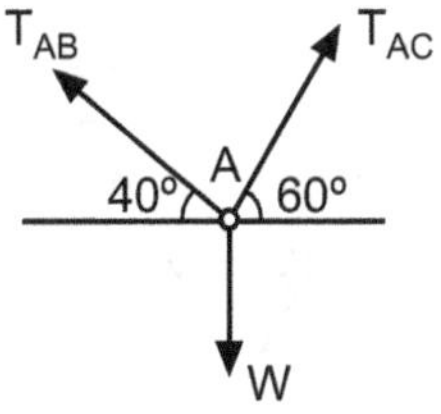

Substitute (i) in (ii),

$$0.65 \, T_{AC} \sin 40 + T_{AC} \sin 60 - W = 0$$

$$T_{AC} = (0.78) \, W$$

$$T_{AB} = (0.5) \, W$$



**Fig. 2.3**

(ii)   Safe value of W :

$$(\delta L)_{AB} = 4 = \left(\frac{PL}{AE}\right)_{AB} = \frac{0.5 \, W \times 1000 / \sin 40}{50 \times 200 \times 10^3}$$

$$4 = 7.77 \times 10^{-5} \, W$$

$$W = 51.4 \times 10^3 \, W$$

$$= 51.4 \text{ kN} \qquad \qquad \text{... (iii)}$$

$$(\delta L)_{AC} = 6 \text{ mm} = \left(\frac{PL}{AE}\right)_{AC}$$

∴

$$6 = \frac{0.78 \, W \times 1000 / \sin 60}{75 \times 80 \times 10^3}$$

$$W = 39.97 \text{ kN} \qquad \qquad \text{... (iv)}$$

$$W_{safe} = \mathbf{39.97 \text{ kN}} \qquad (\because \text{ least of (iii) and (iv)})$$

**Example 2.3 :** *Fig. 2.4 shows two identical bars AB and BC each 3.5 m long and they are connected together at B. A load of 30 kN is supported at B. Assuming all connections to be hinged and ultimate stress for material = 280 MPa with factor of safety of four; calculate (i) diameter of bars, (ii) vertical displacement of B. Take E = 210 GPa.*

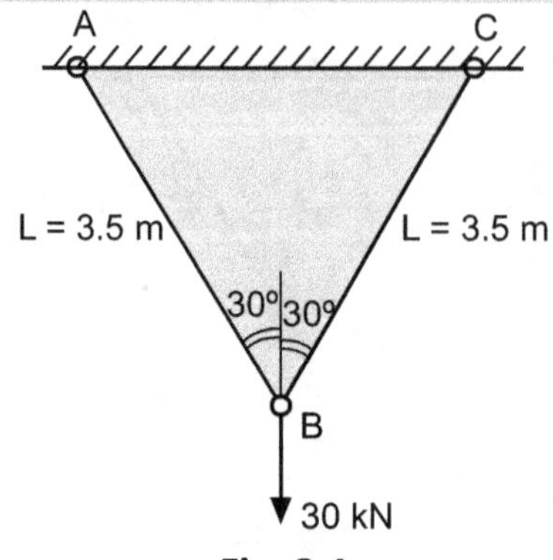



**Fig. 2.4**

**Data :** As shown in Fig. 2.4, Ultimate stress = 280 MPa, factor of safety = 4.

**Required :** (i) Diameter of bars, (ii) Vertical displacement of B.

**Concept :** Statically determinate, Basic formulae.

**Solution :** (i) Analysis of joint B.

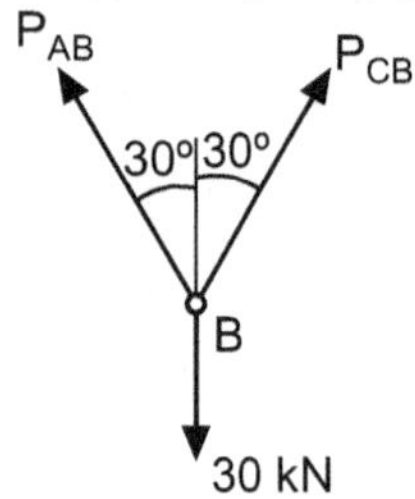



**Fig. 2.5 : FBD of joint B**

$$\Sigma F_x = 0$$

$$- P_{AB} \sin 30 + P_{CB} \sin 30 = 0$$

$$P_{AB} = P_{CB} \qquad \text{... (i)}$$

$$\Sigma F_y = 0$$

$$P_{AB} \cos 30 + P_{CB} \cos 30 - 30 = 0 \qquad \text{... (ii)}$$

Solving equations (i) and (ii),

$$P_{AB} = P_{CB} = 17.32 \text{ kN (Tensile)}$$

(ii)   Diameter of bars :

Let $\phi$ be the diameter of each bar.

$$\text{Safe working stress} = \frac{\text{Ultimate stress}}{\text{Factor of safety}}$$

$$\sigma = \frac{280}{4} = 70 \text{ MPa}$$

$$\therefore \quad \frac{\pi}{4} (\phi)^2 \, \sigma = 17.32 \times 10^3$$

$$\phi^2 = \frac{17.32 \times 10^3 \times 4}{\pi \times 70} = 315.03$$

$$\therefore \quad \phi = \textbf{17.75 mm}$$

(iii) Vertical displacement of joint B :

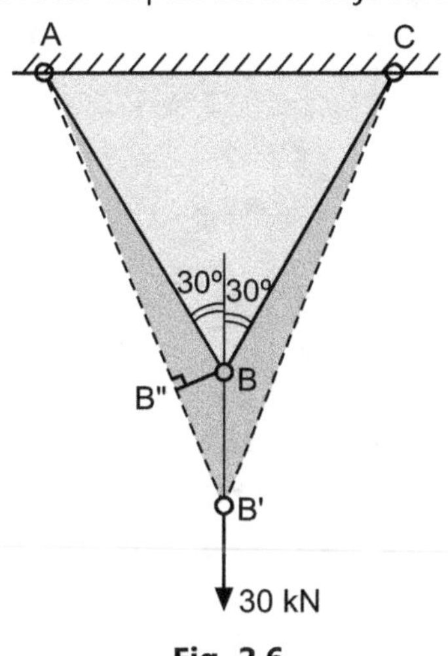



**Fig. 2.6**

Refer Fig. 2.6.

Elongation of each wire

$$= \text{B' B"}$$

$$= \frac{\sigma L}{E} = \frac{70 \times 3500}{210 \times 10^3}$$

$$= 1.167 \text{ mm}$$

Vertical displacement of joint B

$$= BB'$$

$$= \frac{1.167}{\cos 30}$$

$$= \textbf{1.347 mm } (\downarrow)$$

---

**Example 2.4 :** *Length of 2 mm diameter steel wire 'CE' is adjusted such that with no load applied, gap of 1.5 mm exists between the end B and contact point. Assuming E = 200 GPa, determine the position of 25 kg weight so that end B just touches to support.*

**Data :** As shown in Fig. 2.7 (a), E = 200 GPa.

**Required :** Position of 25 kg weight.

**Concept :** From geometry of deformation find elongation of wire, then use equilibrium concepts.

**Solution :** (i) From similar triangles,

$$\frac{1.5}{390} = \frac{(\delta L)_{wire}}{90}$$

$$(\delta L)_{wire} = 0.34 \text{ mm}$$

Force in wire,

$$(\delta L) = \frac{PL}{AE}$$

∴

$$P = \frac{\delta L \cdot AE}{L}$$

$$P = \frac{(0.34) \times \frac{\pi}{4} \times 2^2 \times 200 \times 10^3}{300}$$

$$= 724.9 \text{ N}$$

---

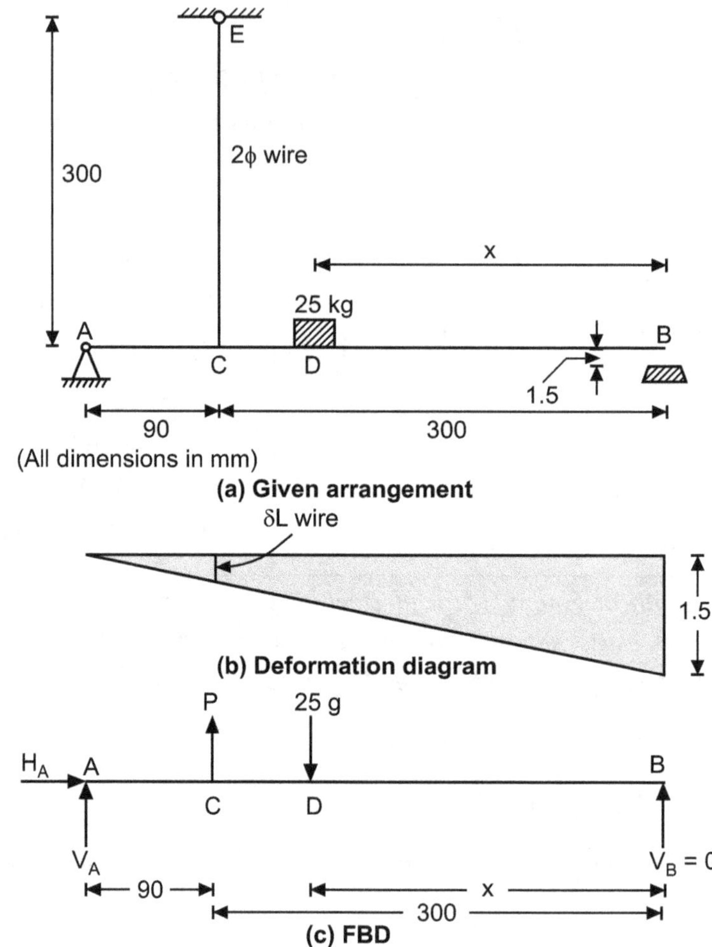



**Fig. 2.7**

(ii)   Position of 25 kg weight (x) :

Refer FBD of member AB as shown in Fig. 2.7 (c),

$$\Sigma M_A = 0$$

$$P \times 90 - 25 \times 9.81 \times (390 - x) = 0$$

$$724.9 \times 90 - 25 \times 9.81 (390 - x) = 0$$

$$\therefore \qquad x = \textbf{124 mm}$$

## 2.3   STRESS AND ELONGATION PRODUCED IN A BAR DUE TO ITS OWN WEIGHT

Let a bar of length L and diameter 'D' be rigidly fixed at the upper end and hanging vertically as shown in Fig. 2.8. Let w be the weight per unit volume of the bar.

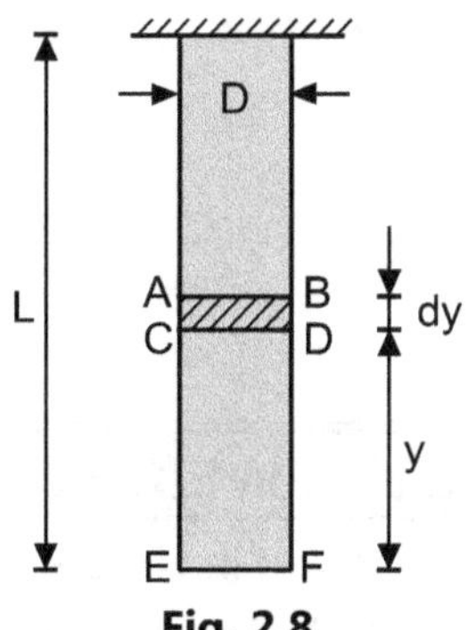

**Fig. 2.8**

Consider a small strip of the bar between the sections AB and CD at a distance 'y' of thickness 'dy' as shown in Fig. 2.8.

Downward force acting at CD is equal to the weight of the bar CDEF $= \frac{\pi}{4} D^2 yw$

$$\text{Stress at section CD} = \sigma = \frac{\text{Force at CD}}{\text{c/s area}} = \frac{\left(\frac{\pi}{4}\right) D^2 yw}{\left(\frac{\pi}{4}\right) D^2}$$

$$\sigma = \mathbf{yw} \qquad \qquad \text{... (2.3)}$$

Thus, stress at any section due to self weight of the bar is directly proportional to y i.e. the distance of the section from the lower end. Stress at the lower end of the bar is zero and at the top it is maximum = wL.

Stresses at the sections AB and CD can be assumed same, since dy is very small. The elongation of length 'dy' $= \frac{\sigma}{E} \cdot dy = \frac{yw}{E} \cdot dy$.

Elongation of entire length of the bar,

$$\delta L = \int_0^L \frac{yw}{E} \cdot dy = \frac{w}{E}\left(\frac{y^2}{2}\right)_0^L$$

$$\delta L = \frac{\mathbf{wL^2}}{\mathbf{2\,E}} \qquad \qquad \text{... (2.4)}$$

**Note :** Elongation produced by the self weight of the bar is equal to that produced by a load of half its weight applied at the end.

**Example 2.5 :** A vertical tie bar of 20 mm ⋅, 2 m long is fixed at the top and supports a downward load of 20 kN at bottom. Calculate the maximum stress and elongation of the bar assuming density = 78 kN/m3 and E = 200 GPa.

**Data :** $\phi$ = 20 mm, L = 2 m, P = 20 kN, w = 78 kN/m³, E = 200 GPa.

**Required :** Maximum stress and elongation due to applied load and self weight.

**Concept :** Standard formulae.

**Solution :** (i) Maximum stress :

$$\sigma = \frac{P}{A} + wL = \frac{20 \times 10^3}{\frac{\pi}{4}(20)^2} + 7.8 \times 10^{-5} \times 2000$$

$$(\geq 78 \text{ kN/m}^3 = 7.8 \times 10^{-5} \text{ N/mm}^3)$$

$$= 63.67 + 0.156 = \mathbf{63.826 \text{ MPa (Tensile)}}$$

(ii)    Maximum elongation :

$$\delta L \;=\; \frac{\sigma L}{E} + \frac{wL^2}{2E}$$

$$=\; \frac{63.67 \times 2000}{200 \times 10^3} + \frac{7.8 \times 10^{-5} \times 2000^2}{2 \times 200 \times 10^3}$$

$$=\; \textbf{0.637 mm (increase)}$$

## 2.4 ELONGATION OF CONICAL BAR DUE TO ITS OWN WEIGHT

A conical rod of length L and base diameter D is rigidly fixed at BC as shown in Fig. 2.9.

Let w be the weight per unit volume of the bar. Consider a small length 'dy' at distance 'y' from A

as shown in Fig. 2.9. Weight of portion AFG $= \left(\dfrac{\pi}{4}d^2 \cdot \dfrac{y}{3}\right)w$

where,                              $d$ = diameter of cross-section FG

$$\text{Stress at section FG} = \sigma \;=\; \frac{\text{Force at FG}}{\text{Area at FG}} \;=\; \frac{\left(\dfrac{\pi}{4}d^2 \cdot \dfrac{y}{3}\right)w}{\dfrac{\pi}{4}d^2}$$

$$\sigma \;=\; \frac{wy}{3} \qquad\qquad \dots (2.5)$$

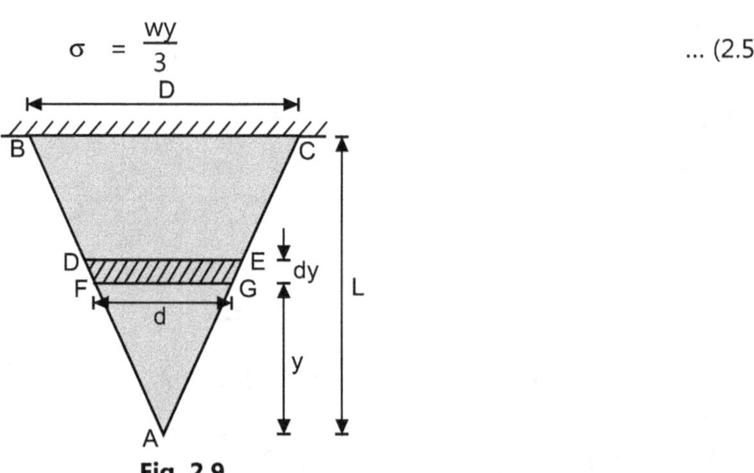


**Fig. 2.9**

$$\text{Elongation of length 'dy'} \;=\; \frac{\sigma}{E}\cdot dy \;=\; \frac{wy}{3E}\cdot dy$$

∴    Elongation of the bar due to self weight

$$=\; \int_0^L \frac{wy}{3E}\cdot dy$$

$$=\; \frac{w}{3E}\left(\frac{y^2}{2}\right)_0^L$$

$$=\; \frac{\mathbf{wL^2}}{\mathbf{6\,E}} \qquad\qquad \dots (2.6)$$

## 2.5 LINEARLY VARYING SECTIONS

For these members, cross-sectional area changes linearly as a function of length of member. Change in length of these members can be computed with the help of integration.

**Example 2.6 :** *A plate of uniform thickness is 60 mm wide at one end and 120 mm wide at other end and 500 mm long. Assuming uniform thickness of 8 mm, find the elongation of plate when subjected to axial tensile force of 50 kN. Take E = 200 GPa.*

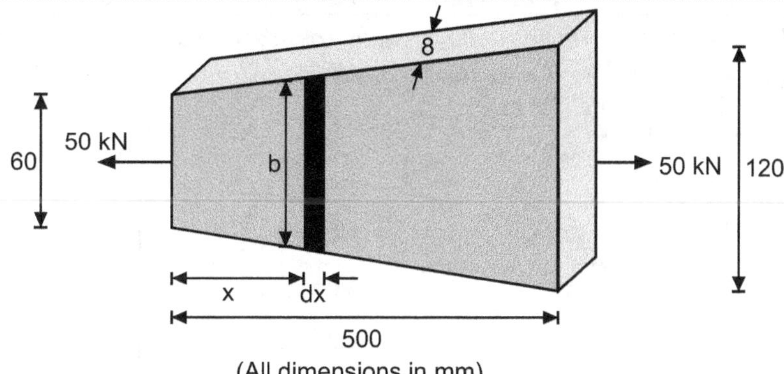


**Fig. 2.10**

**Data :** As shown in Fig. 2.10, E = 200 GPa.

**Required :** Change in length '$\delta L$'.

**Concept :** Member of varying cross-section.

**Solution :** (i) Consider an elementary strip of length 'dx' at a distance 'x' from left end. Let 'b' be the width of the section at x from left end.

Since, width of plate varies linearly,

$$\frac{120 - 60}{500} = \frac{b - 60}{x}$$

$\therefore \qquad\qquad\qquad\qquad b = 60 + 0.12\,x$

$\therefore \qquad$ Cross-sectional area for strip $= A = bt$

$$= (60 + 0.12\,x)\,8$$

$$\text{Change in length of strip} = \frac{PL}{AE}$$

$$= \frac{P\,dx}{(60 + 0.12\,x)\,8E}$$

(ii)   Change in length of member :

$$\delta L = \int_{0}^{500} \frac{P\,dx}{(60 + 0.12 \times 8E)}$$

$$= \frac{P}{8E} \int_{0}^{500} \frac{dx}{(60 + 0.12\,x)}$$

$$= \frac{P}{8E}\left[\log_e (60 + 0.12\,x) \times \frac{1}{0.12}\right]_0^{500}$$

$$= \frac{P}{0.12 \times 8E}\left[\log_e (60 + 0.12 \times 500) - \log_e (60)\right]$$

$$= \frac{0.693\,P}{0.12 \times 8E} = \frac{0.693 \times 50 \times 10^3}{0.12 \times 8 \times 200 \times 10^3}$$

$$= \textbf{0.18 mm (increase)}$$

**Example 2.7 :** *For a member having solid circular cross-section, diameter is 'd' at one end and it linearly increases to 'D' at other end over the length 'L'. Show that its change in length under the action of axial force is given by* $\delta L = \dfrac{4\,PL}{\pi\,D\,dE}$.

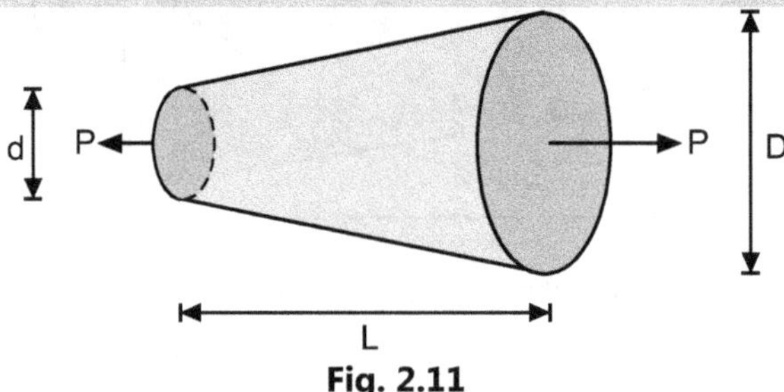

**Fig. 2.11**

**Data :** As shown in Fig. 2.11.

**Required :** Change in length δL.

**Concept :** Member of varying cross-section.

**Solution :** (i) Consider an elementary strip of length 'dx' at a distance x from left end. Let φ be the diameter of section at a distance x from left end as shown in Fig. 2.12.

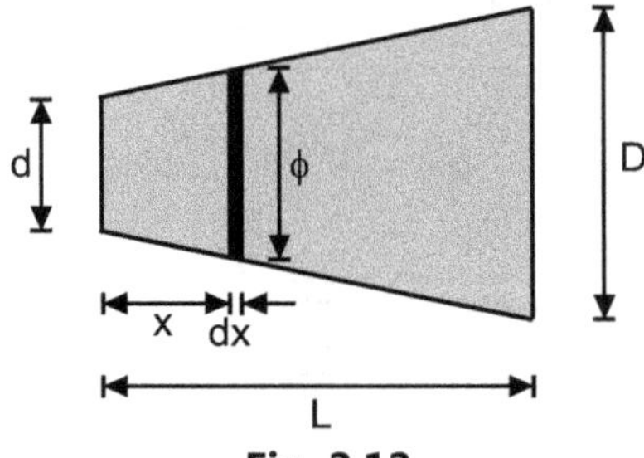

**Fig. 2.12**

Since diameter of bar varies linearly,

$$\frac{D - d}{L} = \frac{\phi - d}{x}$$

∴
$$\phi = d + \frac{(D - d)\,x}{L}$$

Cross-sectional area of strip $= A = \dfrac{\pi}{4}\,\phi^2$

$$= \frac{\pi}{4}\left[d + \left(\frac{D - d}{L}\right)x\right]^2$$

$$\text{Change in length of strip} \;=\; \frac{PL}{AE} = \frac{P\,dx}{\dfrac{\pi}{4}\left[d + \left(\dfrac{D-d}{L}\right)x\right]^2 E}$$

(ii)   Change in length of member :

$$\delta L \;=\; \int_{0}^{L} \frac{P\,dx}{\dfrac{\pi}{4}\left[d + \left(\dfrac{D-d}{L}\right)x\right]^2 E}$$

$$=\; \frac{4P}{\pi E}\left[\frac{-1}{d + \left(\dfrac{D-d}{L}\right)x} \div \frac{D-d}{L}\right]_{0}^{L}$$

$$=\; \frac{-4\,PL}{\pi\,E\,(D-d)}\left[\frac{1}{d + (D-d)} - \frac{1}{d}\right]$$

$$=\; \frac{-4\,PL}{\pi\,E\,(D-d)}\left[\frac{1}{D} - \frac{1}{d}\right] = \frac{-4\,PL}{\pi\,E\,(D-d)}\left[\frac{d-D}{Dd}\right]$$

$$\boldsymbol{\delta L} \;=\; \boldsymbol{\frac{4\,PL}{\pi\,D\,dE}} \qquad\qquad \text{... Hence proved.}$$

**Example 2.8 :** *A circular bar 2.5 m long tapers uniformly from 2.5 cm diameter to 1.2 cm diameter. Determine extension of a rod under a pull of 30 kN. Take E = 200 GPa.*   **(Dec. 2001)**

**Solution :**

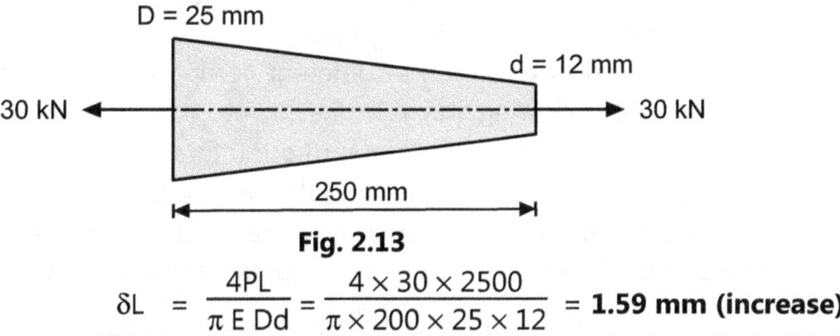


**Fig. 2.13**

$$\delta L \;=\; \frac{4PL}{\pi\,E\,Dd} = \frac{4 \times 30 \times 2500}{\pi \times 200 \times 25 \times 12} = \textbf{1.59 mm (increase)}$$

# 2.6 COMPOUND SECTIONS

When a member consists of *segments or components of different cross-sectional area but of same material,* it is called as compound section. Fig. 2.14 shows a compound section subjected to axial tensile force P.

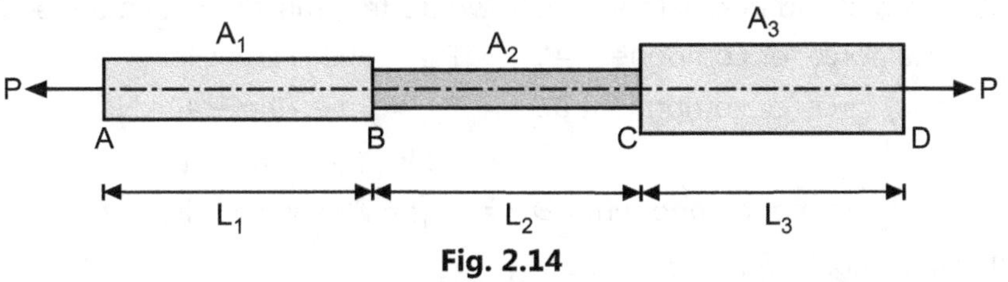


**Fig. 2.14**

Axial force 'P' is constant throughout the length of member but normal stresses are different because of different cross-sectional areas of components. For these sections, change in normal stresses from one component to other is sudden because of sudden change in cross-sectional areas.

Thus, for the compound section considered,

$$(\sigma)_{AB} = \frac{P}{A_1}$$

$$(\sigma)_{BC} = \frac{P}{A_2} \qquad \text{... (2.7)}$$

$$(\sigma)_{CD} = \frac{P}{A_3}$$

Change in length of complete member can be obtained by,

$$\delta L = (\delta L)_{AB} + (\delta L)_{BC} + (\delta L)_{CD} = \left(\frac{PL}{AE}\right)_{AB} + \left(\frac{PL}{AE}\right)_{BC} + \left(\frac{PL}{AE}\right)_{CD}$$

Since, axial force P is constant throughout the length of member,

$$\delta L = P\left[\left(\frac{L}{AE}\right)_{AB} + \left(\frac{L}{AE}\right)_{BC} + \left(\frac{L}{AE}\right)_{CD}\right]$$

$$= P \text{ [Sum of flexibility coefficients of components]} \qquad \text{... (2.8)}$$

However, material being same throughout,

$$\delta L = \frac{P}{E}\left[\left(\frac{L}{A}\right)_{AB} + \left(\frac{L}{A}\right)_{BC} + \left(\frac{L}{A}\right)_{CD}\right] \qquad \text{... (2.9)}$$

**Axial Force Diagram (AFD) :** It is the *diagram which shows variation of axial force along the length of member.* For knowing axial force in different components, method of section is used. Method of section consists of following steps :

- Take a section which cuts the component of our interest.
- Take algebraic addition of all the forces either to the left or to the right of section with due care of sign. Sign convention to be followed is axial tension positive and axial compression negative. The force going away from the section represents tension while towards the section represents compression.

The above procedure is explained further with a numerical example as under :

Let, a compound section be subjected to axial forces as shown in Fig. 2.15 (a).

To find axial forces in components AB, BC and CD, consider sections 1-1, 2-2 and 3-3 respectively. It should be remembered that, member as a whole with given external forces and FBD of components with external and internal forces (shown dotted) must maintain the equilibrium.

Thus,        axial force for component AB   $= P_{AB} = 30$ kN (Tensile)

axial force for component BC   $= P_{BC} = 30 - 70 = -40$ kN

$= 40$ kN (Compressive)

axial force for component CD   $= P_{CD} = 20$ kN (Tensile)

AFD is as shown in Fig. 2.15 (e).

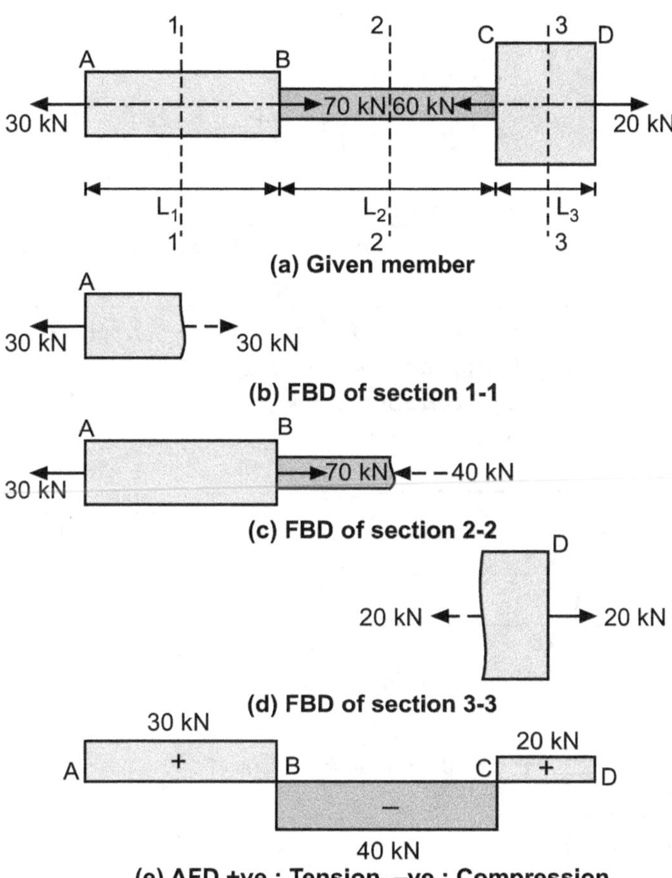



**Fig. 2.15**

**Example 2.9 :** *A compound bar shown in Fig. 2.16 elongates by 0.45 mm when subjected to an axial pull of 150 kN. Calculate Young's modulus of elasticity.*

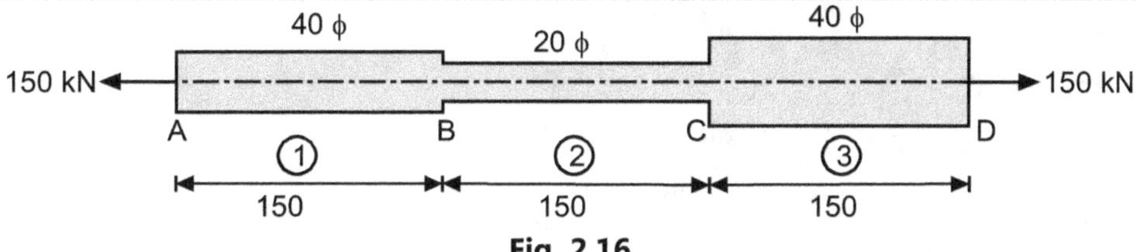



**Fig. 2.16**

**Data :** $\delta L = 0.45$ mm, Refer Fig. 2.16.

**Required :** Young's modulus of elasticity (E).

**Concept :** $\delta L = \delta L_1 + \delta L_2 + \delta L_3$

**Solution :** (i) Geometric properties :

$$A_1 = A_3 = \frac{\pi}{4}(40)^2 = 1256.63 \text{ mm}^2$$

$$A_2 = \frac{\pi}{4}(20)^2 = 314.16 \text{ mm}^2$$

(ii)   Modulus of elasticity (E) :

$$\delta L = \delta L_1 + \delta L_2 + \delta L_3$$

$$= \left(\frac{PL}{AE}\right)_1 + \left(\frac{PL}{AE}\right)_2 + \left(\frac{PL}{AE}\right)_3 = \frac{PL}{E}\left(\frac{1}{A_1} + \frac{1}{A_2} + \frac{1}{A_3}\right)$$

$$0.45 = \frac{150 \times 10^3 \times 150}{E}\left(\frac{1}{1256.63} + \frac{1}{314.16} + \frac{1}{1256.63}\right)$$

$$\therefore \quad E = 238.732 \times 10^3 \text{ MPa} = \textbf{238.732 GPa}$$

**Example 2.10 :** *A 1.75 m long steel bar is having uniform diameter of 30 mm for a length of 750 mm; for next 500 mm length its diameter gradually reduces to 'd' mm; and for remaining 500 mm length, diameter 'd' remains constant. When a load of 100 kN is applied, the extension observed is 2 mm. Assuming E = 200 GPa, find 'd'.*

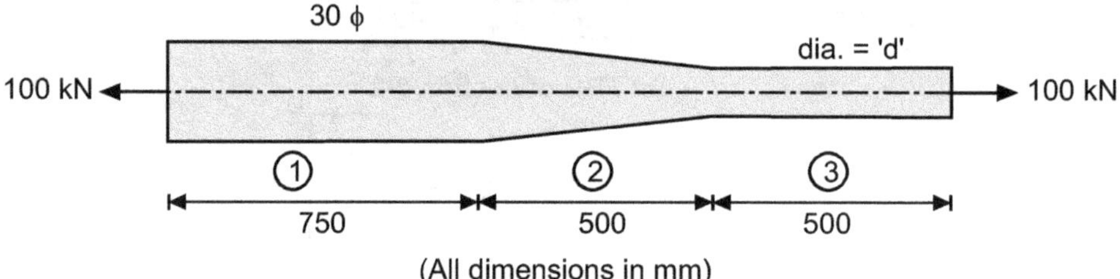


(All dimensions in mm)

**Fig. 2.17**

**Data :** As shown in Fig. 2.17, E = 200 GPa, $\delta L$ = 2 mm

**Required :** Diameter 'd'.

**Concept :** $\delta L = \delta L_1 + \delta L_2 + \delta L_3$

**Solution :** (i) Geometric properties :

$$A_1 = \frac{\pi}{4}(30)^2 = 706.85 \text{ mm}^2$$

$$A_3 = \frac{\pi}{4}(d)^2$$

(ii)   Diameter 'd' :

We have,  $\qquad \delta L = \delta L_1 + \delta L_2 + \delta L_3 \qquad\qquad$ ... (i)

where,  $\qquad \delta L = 2$ mm

$$\delta L_1 = \left(\frac{PL}{AE}\right)_1 = \frac{P \times 750}{706.85\ E} = 1.061\frac{P}{E}$$

$$\delta L_2 = \frac{4\ PL}{\pi\ D\ dE} = \frac{4P \times 500}{\pi \times 30\ dE} = \frac{21.22\ P}{dE}$$

$$\delta L_3 = \left(\frac{PL}{AE}\right)_3 = \frac{P \times 500}{\frac{\pi}{4}(d)^2\ E} = \frac{636.62\ P}{d^2\ E}$$

Substituting in (i),  $\qquad 2 = \frac{P}{E}\left(1.061 + \frac{21.22}{d} + \frac{636.62}{d^2}\right)$

$$= \frac{100 \times 10^3}{200 \times 10^3}\left(1.061 + \frac{21.22}{d} + \frac{636.62}{d^2}\right)$$

$\therefore \quad 2.939\, d^2 - 21.22\, d - 636.62 = 0$

Solving, $\quad\quad\quad\quad\quad\quad\quad d = $ **18.76 mm**

**Example 2.11** : *A mild steel bar 40 mm in diameter and 3m long is subjected to an axial pull of 50 kN. To what length, bar should be centrally bored so that the total extension will increase by 25 % under same axial pull ? Assume diameter of bore as 20 mm and E = 200 GPa.*

**Data** : As shown in Fig. 2.18, E = 200 GPa, $(\delta L)_{\text{case (ii)}} = 1.25\,(\delta L)_{\text{case (i)}}$

**Required** : Length of bore 'x'.

**Concept** : $\delta L = (\delta L)_1 + (\delta L)_2$ for case (ii).

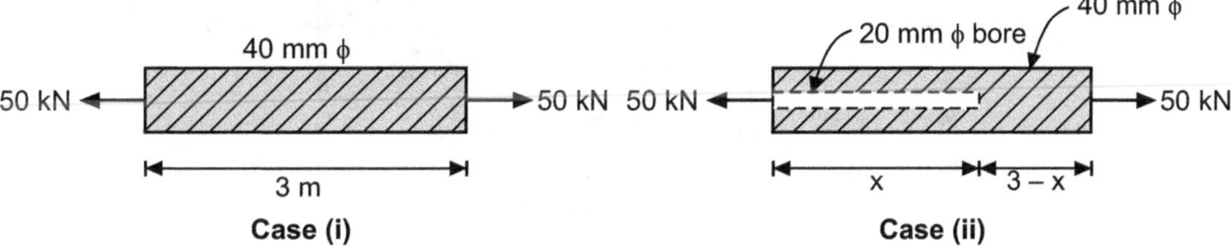


**Fig. 2.18**

**Solution** : (i) Analysis of case (i) :

$$\delta L = \frac{PL}{AE}$$

where, $\quad\quad\quad\quad\quad\quad\quad P = 50 \times 10^3\ \text{N}$

$L = 3000\ \text{mm}$

$A = \frac{\pi}{4}(40)^2 = 1256.63\ \text{mm}^2$

$E = 200 \times 10^3\ \text{MPa}$

Substituting, $\quad\quad\quad \delta L = \dfrac{50 \times 10^3 \times 3000}{1256.63 \times 200 \times 10^3}$

$= 0.5968\ \text{mm}$

(ii) Analysis of case (ii) :

$$\delta L = (\delta L)_1 + (\delta L)_2$$

$$= \left(\frac{PL}{AE}\right)_1 + \left(\frac{PL}{AE}\right)_2 = \frac{P}{E}\left(\frac{L_1}{A_1} + \frac{L_2}{A_2}\right)$$

where, $\quad\quad\quad\quad\quad\quad L_1 = x\ \text{metres}$

$L_2 = (3 - x)\ \text{metres}$

$A_1 = \frac{\pi}{4}(40^2 - 20^2) = 942.47\ \text{mm}^2$

$A_2 = \frac{\pi}{4}(40)^2 = 1256.63\ \text{mm}^2$

Substituting, $\quad\quad\quad \delta L = \dfrac{50 \times 10^3}{200 \times 10^3}\left(\dfrac{x \times 10^3}{942.47} + \dfrac{(3 - x)\,10^3}{1256.63}\right)$

$= (0.2652)\,x + 0.5968 - (0.1989)\,x$

$$= (0.0663)\, x + 0.5968$$

(iii) Length of bore (x) :

We have,     $(\delta L)_{case\ (ii)} = 1.25\,(\delta L)_{case\ (i)}$

$$(0.0663)\, x + 0.5968 = 1.25 \times 0.5968$$

$$\therefore \qquad x = \textbf{2.25 mm}$$

**Example 2.12 :** *For the compound bar ABC shown in Fig. 2.19, (i) Determine the magnitude of P for equilibrium, (ii) Draw axial force diagram, (iii) Find total change in length, (iv) Find displacement of B with respect to A. Assume E = 200 GPa.*

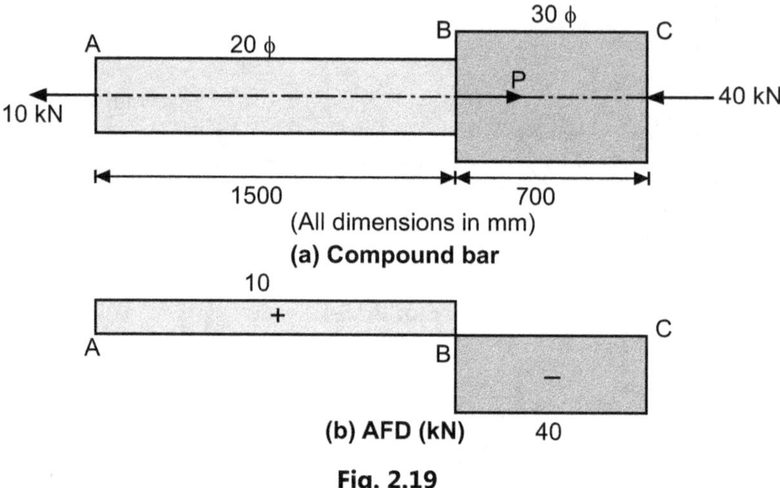


**Fig. 2.19**

**Data :** As shown in Fig. 2.19 (a), E = 200 GPa.

**Required :** (i) P,  (ii) $\delta L$,  (iii) $\delta B/A$.

**Concept :**  (i) $\Sigma\, F_X = 0$ gives magnitude of P.

(ii) $\delta L = (\delta L)_{AB} + (\delta L)_{BC}$

(iii) Displacement of B with respect to A = $(\delta L)_{AB}$

**Solution :** (i) Magnitude of 'P' :

$$\Sigma\, F_X = 0, \quad -10 + P - 40 = 0$$

$$\therefore \qquad\qquad P = 50\ kN$$

(ii)   Axial force diagram :

Taking vertical sections for members AB and BC, we get

Axial force for member AB = $P_{AB}$ = 10 kN (Tensile)

Axial force for member BC = $P_{BC}$ = 40 kN (Compressive)

Axial force diagram is as shown in Fig. 2.19 (b).

(iii) Total change in length :

$$\delta L \;=\; (\delta L)_{AB} + (\delta L)_{BC} \;=\; \left(\frac{PL}{AE}\right)_{AB} + \left(\frac{PL}{AE}\right)_{BC}$$

$$=\; \frac{1}{200 \times 10^3}\left[\frac{10 \times 10^3 \times 1500}{\frac{\pi}{4}(20)^2} + \frac{(-40)\times 10^3 \times 700}{\frac{\pi}{4}(30)^2}\right]$$

$$=\; 0.238 - 0.198$$

$$=\; \textbf{0.04 mm (increase)}$$

(iv) Displacement of B with respect to A :

$$\delta B/A \;=\; (\delta L)_{AB} = \left(\frac{PL}{AE}\right)_{AB}$$

$$=\; \textbf{0.238 mm } (\rightarrow)$$

**Example 2.13 :** *For member ABC shown in Fig. 2.20, find the diameter of portion BC if displacement of C with respect to A is 2 mm. Assume E = 200 GPa.*

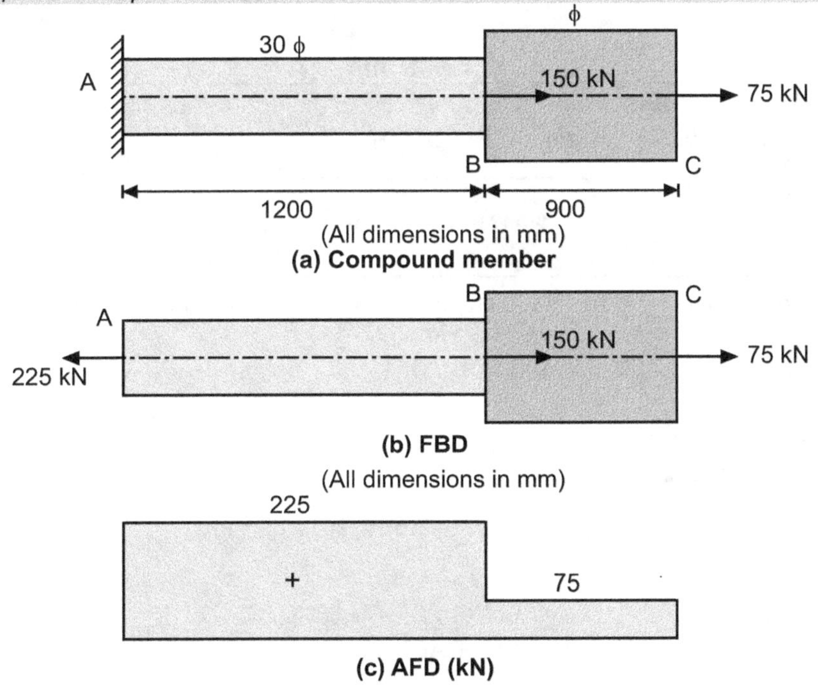


**Fig. 2.20**

**Data :** As shown in Fig. 2.20 (a), E = 200 GPa, $\delta L$ = 2 mm

**Required :** Diameter of portion BC ($\phi$) mm

**Concept :** $\delta L = (\delta L)_{AB} + (\delta L)_{BC}$

**Solution :** (i) Geometric properties :

$$\text{Cross-sectional area of AB} \;=\; A_{AB} = \frac{\pi}{4}(30)^2 = 706.85 \text{ mm}^2$$

$$\text{Cross-sectional area of BC} \;=\; A_{BC} = \frac{\pi}{4}(\phi)^2 \text{ mm}^2$$

(ii)  Analysis :

Let $H_A$ ($\rightarrow$) be the reaction at A.

$\Sigma F_X = 0$,

$$H_A + 150 + 75 = 0$$

$\therefore$  $$H_A = -225 \text{ kN} = 225 \text{ kN} (\leftarrow)$$

FBD of member is as shown in Fig. 2.20 (b).

Axial force diagram is as shown in Fig. 2.20 (c).

**Note :** Axial forces are obtained by taking sections in portions AB and BC.

(iii) Diameter of portion BC :

$$\delta L = (\delta L)_{AB} + (\delta L)_{BC}$$

$$2 = \left(\frac{PL}{AE}\right)_{AB} + \left(\frac{PL}{AE}\right)_{BC}$$

$$= \frac{1}{200 \times 10^3}\left[\frac{225 \times 10^3 \times 1200}{706.85} + \frac{75 \times 10^3 \times 900}{\frac{\pi}{4}(\phi)^2}\right]$$

$$\phi = \mathbf{69.05 \ mm}$$

**Example 2.14 :** *A member 36 mm $\phi$ is subjected to axial forces as shown in Fig. 2.21. Find the total change in length of the bar assuming E = 200 GPa.*

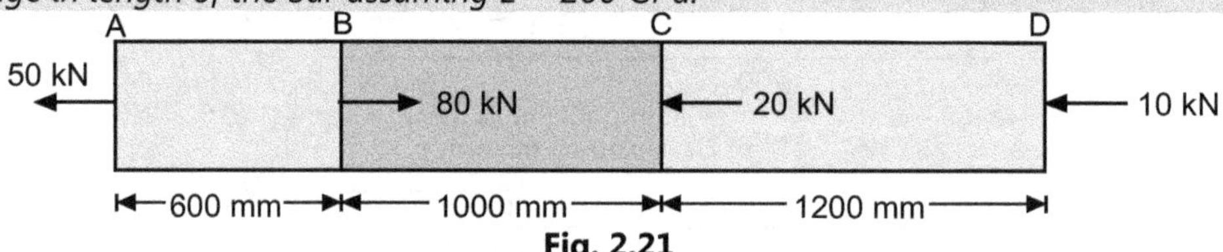


**Fig. 2.21**

**Data :** As shown in Fig. 2.21, $E = 200 \times 10^3$ MPa.

**Required :** $\delta l$

**Concept :** Standard formulae.

**Solution :** (i) Geometric properties :

$$A = \frac{\pi}{4} \times d^2 = \frac{\pi}{4} \times 36^2 = 1017.88 \text{ mm}^2$$

(ii)  Change in length :

$$\delta l = \left(\frac{Pl}{AE}\right)_{AB} + \left(\frac{Pl}{AE}\right)_{BC} + \left(\frac{Pl}{AE}\right)_{CD} = \frac{1}{AE}\left[(Pl)_{AB} + (Pl)_{BC} + (Pl)_{CD}\right]$$

$$= \frac{[(50 \times 10^3 \times 600) - (30 \times 10^3 \times 1000) - (10 \times 10^3 \times 1200)]}{1017.88 \times 200 \times 10^3}$$

$$= -0.118 \text{ mm}$$

$\therefore$  $$\delta l = -0.118 \text{ mm} = \mathbf{0.118 \ mm \ (decrease)}$$

**Example 2.15 :** *A member framed by connecting a steel bar to aluminium bar is shown in Fig. 2.22. Assuming that bars are prevented from buckling sidewise, calculate the magnitude of force P that will cause the total length of member to decrease by 0.33 mm.*

$E_{st} = 210$ GPa, $E_{Al} = 70$ GPa.

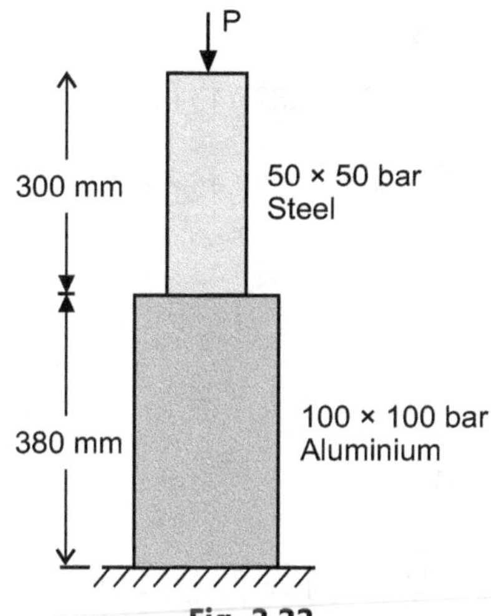


**Fig. 2.22**

**Data :** As shown in Fig. 2.22, $E_{st}$ = 210 × 10³ MPa, $E_{Al}$ = 70 × 10³ MPa, $\delta l$ = 0.33 mm

**Required :** P.

**Concept :** Standard formulae, $\delta l = \dfrac{Pl}{AE}$

**Solution :** (i) Geometric properties :

$$A_{st} = 50 \times 50 = 2500 \text{ mm}^2$$
$$A_{Al} = 100 \times 100 = 10000 \text{ mm}^2$$

(ii)   Calculation for P :

$$\delta l = \left(\frac{Pl}{AE}\right)_{st} + \left(\frac{Pl}{AE}\right)_{Al}$$

As both bars are in compression, so there is decrease in total length.

$\therefore \qquad\qquad \delta l = -0.33$

$$-0.33 = -\left(\frac{P \times 300 \times 10^3}{2500 \times 210 \times 10^3}\right) - \left(\frac{P \times 380 \times 10^3}{10000 \times 70 \times 10^3}\right)$$

$\therefore \qquad\qquad$ P = **296.15 kN (Compression)**

**Example 2.16 :** *A member ABCD is loaded as shown in Fig. 2.23. Determine (a) total deformation of rod, (b) displacement of 'C'. Assume E = 70 GPa.*

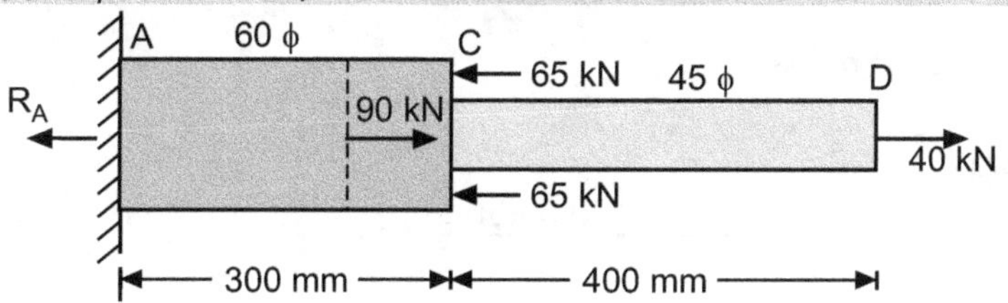


**Fig. 2.23**

**Data :** As shown in Fig. 2.23, E = 70 × 10³ MPa

**Required :** $\delta l$, displacement of C.

**Concept :** Equilibrium equation, $\delta l = \dfrac{Pl}{AE}$

**Solution :** (i) Geometric properties :

$$A_{AB} = \frac{\pi}{4} \times 60^2 = 2827.43 \text{ mm}^2$$

$$A_{BC} = \frac{\pi}{4} \times 60^2 = 2827.43 \text{ mm}^2$$

$$A_{CD} = \frac{\pi}{4} \times 45^2 = 1590.43 \text{ mm}^2$$

(ii)    Equilibrium equation :

$$\Sigma F_X = 0$$
$$- R_A + 90 - 130 + 40 = 0$$
$$\therefore \qquad R_A = 0$$

(iii) Total deformation :

$$\delta l = \left(\frac{Pl}{AE}\right)_{AB} + \left(\frac{Pl}{AE}\right)_{BC} + \left(\frac{Pl}{AE}\right)_{CD}$$

$$= 0 - \left(\frac{90 \times 10^3 \times 200}{2827.43 \times 70 \times 10^3}\right) + \left(\frac{40 \times 10^3 \times 400}{1590.43 \times 70 \times 10^3}\right)$$

$$= -0.091 + 0.1437$$

$$\therefore \qquad \delta l = \mathbf{0.0527 \text{ mm}}$$

(iv) Displacement of point C :

As there is no force on AB, so point B remains on the same point and so C will be displaced by 0.091 mm towards left.

**Example 2.17 :** *A stepped rod is as shown in Fig. 2.24. Find the value of P that will not exceed a maximum overall deformation of 2 mm or a stress in steel of 140 MPa, that in Aluminium 80 MPa and in Brass 120 MPa.* **(Dec. 1998)**

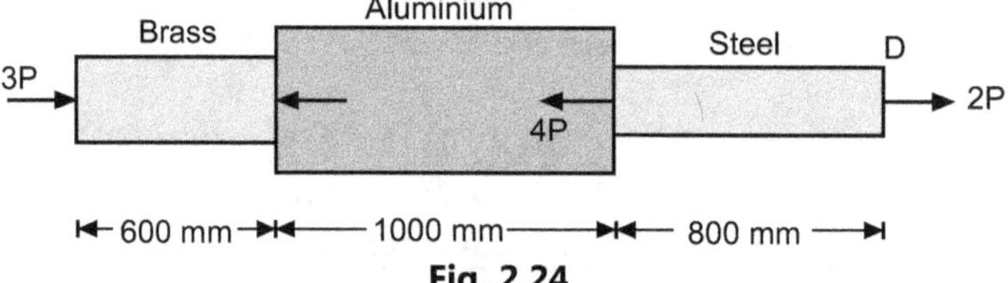


**Fig. 2.24**

**Data :** As shown in Fig. 2.24.

**Required :** P

**Concept :** Standard formulae.

**Solution :**

(i)    P due to Brass :

$$\left(\sigma = \frac{3P}{A}\right)_{Br} \therefore \qquad P = \frac{\sigma A}{3} = \frac{120 \times 450}{3}$$

$$P = 18000 \text{ N} \qquad \qquad \dots \text{(i)}$$

(ii)    P due to Aluminium :

$$\left(\sigma = \frac{2P}{A}\right)_{Al} \therefore \qquad P = \frac{\sigma A}{2} = \frac{80 \times 600}{2}$$

$$P = 24000 \text{ N} \qquad \qquad \text{... (ii)}$$

(iii) P due to Steel :

$$\left(\sigma = \frac{2P}{A}\right)_{Steel} \quad \therefore \quad P = \frac{\sigma A}{2} = \frac{140 \times 300}{2}$$

$$P = 21000 \text{ N} \qquad \qquad \text{... (iii)}$$

(iv) P due to overall deformation :

$$\delta l = \left(\frac{Pl}{AE}\right)_{Br} + \left(\frac{Pl}{AE}\right)_{Al} + \left(\frac{Pl}{AE}\right)_{St}$$

$$2 = \frac{3P \times 600 \times 10^3}{450 \times 83 \times 10^3} + \frac{2P \times 1000 \times 10^3}{600 \times 70 \times 10^3} - \frac{2P \times 800 \times 10^3}{300 \times 200 \times 10^3}$$

$$2 = 0.048\,P + 4.76 \times 10^{-3}\,P - 0.0267\,P$$

$$P = 76.745 \text{ kN}$$

$$P = 76745 \text{ N} \qquad \qquad \text{... (iv)}$$

$$\therefore \quad \text{Value of P} = \mathbf{18000 \text{ N}} = \mathbf{18 \text{ kN}} \qquad \text{[Least of (i), (ii), (iii) and (iv)]}$$

**Example 2.18 :** *A member ABCD is subjected to point loads $P_1$, $P_2$, $P_3$ and $P_4$ as shown in Fig. 2.25. Calculate the force $P_3$ necessary for equilibrium if $P_1$ = 120 kN, $P_2$ = 220 kN and $P_4$ = 160 kN. Determine also the net change in length of the member. Take E = 200 GN/m$^2$.*

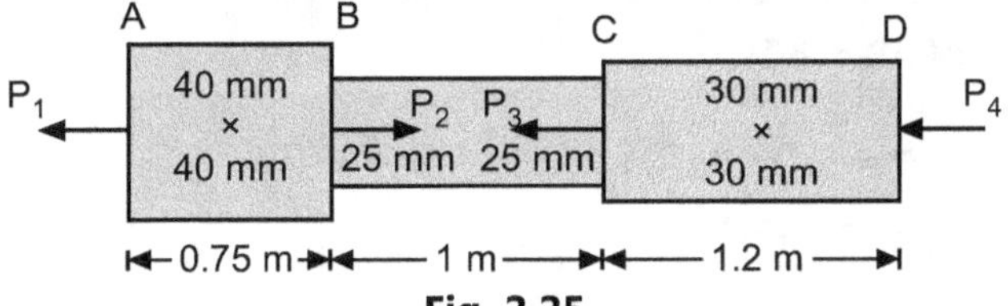


**Fig. 2.25**

**Data :** As shown in Fig. 2.25, $P_1$ = 120 kN, $P_2$ = 220 kN, $P_4$ = 160 kN,

$\quad$ E = 200 GN/m$^2$ = 200 × 10$^3$ N/mm$^2$

**Required :** $P_3$ , $\delta l$.

**Concept :** $\Sigma\, F_x = 0$, standard formulae

**Solution :**

(i) $\qquad \qquad \Sigma\, F_x = 0$

$\therefore \qquad -P_1 + P_2 - P_3 + P_4 = 0$

$\qquad \qquad P_1 + P_3 = P_2 + P_4$

$\therefore \qquad 120 + P_3 = 220 + 160$

$\therefore \qquad \mathbf{P_3 = 260 \text{ kN}}$

(ii) $\qquad \qquad \delta l = \left(\frac{Pl}{AE}\right)_{AB} + \left(\frac{Pl}{AE}\right)_{BC} + \left(\frac{Pl}{AE}\right)_{CD}$

$$\delta l = \left(\frac{120 \times 10^3 \times 750}{40 \times 40 \times 200 \times 10^3}\right) - \left(\frac{100 \times 10^3 \times 1000}{25 \times 25 \times 200 \times 10^3}\right)$$

$$+ \left(\frac{160 \times 10^3 \times 1200}{30 \times 30 \times 200 \times 10^3}\right)$$

$$= 0.28 - 0.8 + 1.067$$

$$\therefore \quad \delta l = \mathbf{0.547\ mm}$$

**Example 2.19 :** *Rod AB has diameter 25 mm, length 800 mm and modulus of elasticity $E_1$, while rod BC has diameter 25 mm and length 550 mm and modulus of elasticity $E_2$. $P_1$, $P_2$ and $P_3$ are axial forces acting on the rod ABC as shown in Fig. 2.26. When $P_1 = 0$, $P_2 = 20$ kN, $P_3 = 20$ kN, elongation of the rod is 1 mm and when $P_1 = 20$ kN, $P_2 = 0$, $P_3 = 20$ kN, elongation of rod ABC is 1.8 mm. Determine the values of $E_1$ and $E_2$.*

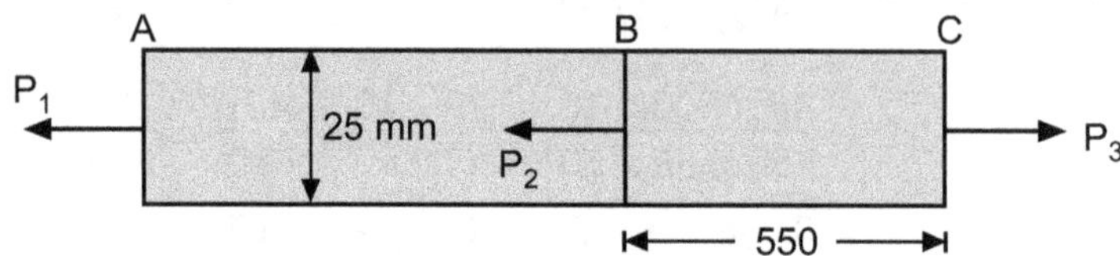


**Fig. 2.26**

**Data :** (i) As shown in Fig. 2.26, $P_1 = 0$, $P_2 = 20$ kN, $P_3 = 20$ kN, $\delta l_1 = 1$ mm

(ii) $P_1 = 20$ kN, $P_2 = 0$, $P_3 = 20$ kN, $\delta l_2 = 1.8$ mm

**Required :** (i) $E_1$ , (ii) $E_2$.

**Concept :** $\delta l = \delta l_{AB} + \delta l_{AC}$

**Solution :** (i) Geometric properties :

Cross-sectional area of AB = BC

$$A_{AB} = A_{BC} = \frac{\pi}{4} \times (25)^2 = 490.87\ mm^2$$

(ii)  Modulus of elasticity $E_1$ and $E_2$ :

$$\delta l_1 = \left(\frac{Pl}{AE}\right)_{AB} + \left(\frac{Pl}{AE}\right)_{BC}$$

$$1 = 0 + \frac{20 \times 10^3 \times 550}{490.87 \times E_2}$$

$$\therefore \quad E_2 = \mathbf{22409.19\ N/mm^2}$$

$$\delta l_2 = \left(\frac{Pl}{AE}\right)_{AB} + \left(\frac{Pl}{AE}\right)_{BC}$$

$$1.8 = \frac{20 \times 10^3 \times 800}{490.87 \times E_1} + \frac{20 \times 10^3 \times 550}{490.87 \times 22409.19}$$

$$1.8 = \frac{32595.19}{E_1} + 1$$

$$\therefore \quad \frac{32595.19}{E_1} = 0.8$$

$$\therefore \quad E_1 = \mathbf{40743.99\ N/mm^2}$$

**Example 2.20 :** *For a member ABC as shown in Fig. 2.27, find the diameter of the portion BC, if the total deformation of the member is 3 mm. Diameter of portion AB is 30 mm. Use E = 200 GPa.*

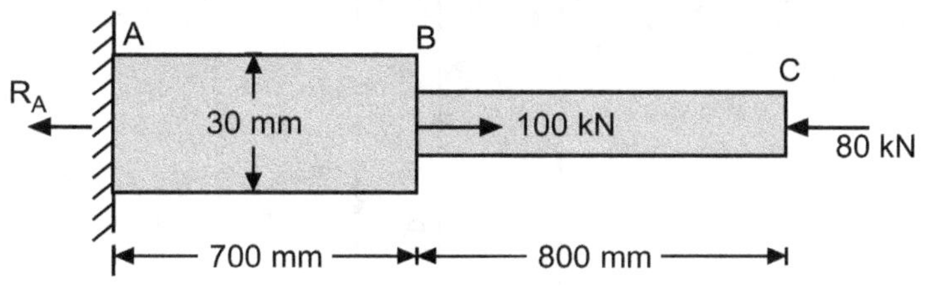


**Fig. 2.27**

**Data :** As shown in Fig. 2.27, E = $200 \times 10^3$ MPa, $\delta l$ = 3 mm

**Required :** Diameter of BC.

**Concept :** $\delta l = \dfrac{Pl}{AE}$

**Solution :** (i) Geometric properties :

$$A_{AB} = \frac{\pi}{4} \times 30^2$$

$$= 706.86 \text{ mm}^2$$

$$A_{BC} = \frac{\pi}{4} \times d^2$$

(ii)   Analysis :        $\Sigma F_X = 0$

$$- H_A + 100 - 80 = 0$$

∴                    $H_A = 20 \text{ kN} (\leftarrow)$

**Note :** As member BC has force larger than AB, so there is decrease in total length of the member.

(iii) Diameter of portion BC :

$$\delta l = \left(\frac{Pl}{AE}\right)_{AB} + \left(\frac{Pl}{AE}\right)_{BC}$$

$$- 3 = \frac{20 \times 10^3 \times 700}{706.86 \times 200 \times 10^3} - \frac{80 \times 10^3 \times 800}{A \times 200 \times 10^3}$$

∴                $A = 103.25 \text{ mm}^2$

∴         $\dfrac{\pi}{4} D^2 = 103.25$

∴                $D = \textbf{11.466 mm}$

**Example 2.21 :** *A steel bar (E = 200 GPa) is supported and loaded as shown in Fig. 2.28. The cross-sectional area of the bar is 250 mm². Determine the force P so that the lower end D of the bar does not move vertically when the loads are applied.*

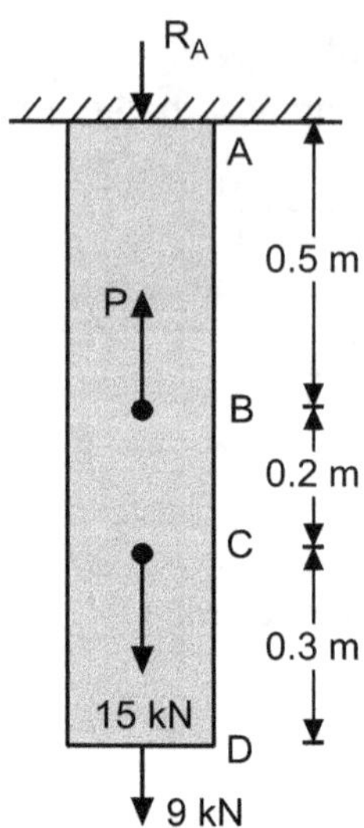


**Fig. 2.28**

**Data :** As shown in Fig. 2.27, A = 250 mm$^2$ , E = 200 GPa, $\delta l$ = 0.

**Required :** P.

**Concept :** (i) $\Sigma$ F$_X$ = 0 gives R$_A$, (ii) $\delta l = \dfrac{Pl}{AE}$

**Solution :**

(i)　Magnitude of reaction :

$$\Sigma F_X = 0$$
$$- R_A + P - 24 = 0$$
$$\therefore \qquad R_A = (P - 24)$$

(ii)　Total change in length :

$$\delta l = 0 = \delta l_{AB} + \delta l_{BC} + \delta l_{CD}$$

$$= \left(\frac{Pl}{AE}\right)_{AB} + \left(\frac{Pl}{AE}\right)_{BC} + \left(\frac{Pl}{AE}\right)_{CD}$$

$$\therefore \qquad 0 = \frac{[- (P - 24) \times 10^3 \times 500] + (24 \times 10^3 \times 200) + (9 \times 10^3 \times 300)}{AE}$$

$$(P - 24) \times 10^3 \times 500 = (24 \times 10^3 \times 200) + (9 \times 10^3 \times 300)$$

$$\therefore \qquad P = \textbf{39 kN}$$

**Example 2.22 :** *A 30 kN weight is supported by means of a pulley as shown in Fig. 2.29. The pulley is supported by a frame ABC. Find the cross-sectional areas for members AC and BC. If the allowable stress in tension is 140 MPa and in compression 96 MPa.*　　　　**(May 2002)**

**Solution :**

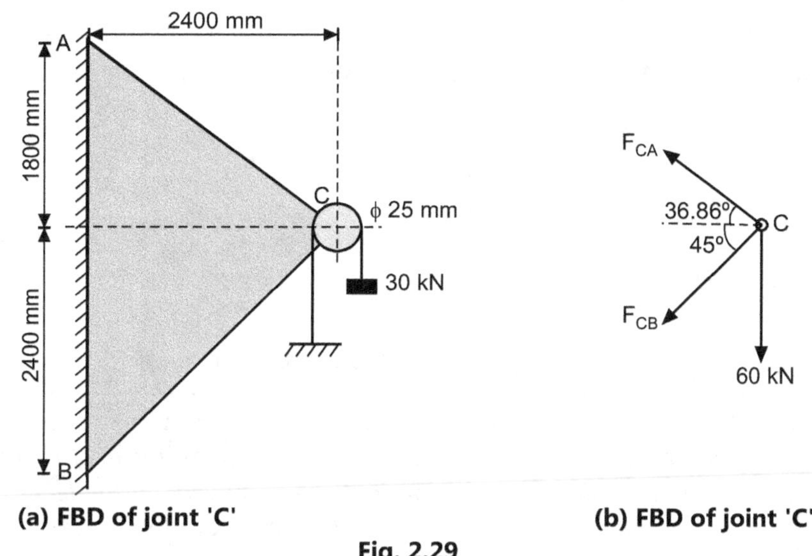

**(a) FBD of joint 'C'**　　　　**(b) FBD of joint 'C'**

**Fig. 2.29**

(i)　　　　$F_{CA}$ = 42.85 kN (Tension)

　　　　$F_{CB}$ = 48.48 kN (Compression)

(ii)　For AC,　　$\sigma = \dfrac{P}{A}$ , $140 = \dfrac{42.85 \times 10^3}{A_{AC}}$

∴　　　　$A_{AC}$ = **306.07 mm²**

　　For BC,　　$\sigma = \dfrac{P}{A}$

　　　　$96 = \dfrac{48.48 \times 10^3}{A_{BC}}$

∴　　　　$A_{BC}$ = 505 mm²

**Example 2.23 :** *A wall bracket is constructed as shown in Fig. 2.30 (a). All joints may be considered pin connected. Steel rod AB has a cross-sectional area of 5 mm². Member BC is a rigid beam. If a 1 m diameter frictionless drum weighing 5 kN is placed in the position shown, what will be the elongation of rod AB ? E = 200 GPa.*　　　　**(May 2003)**

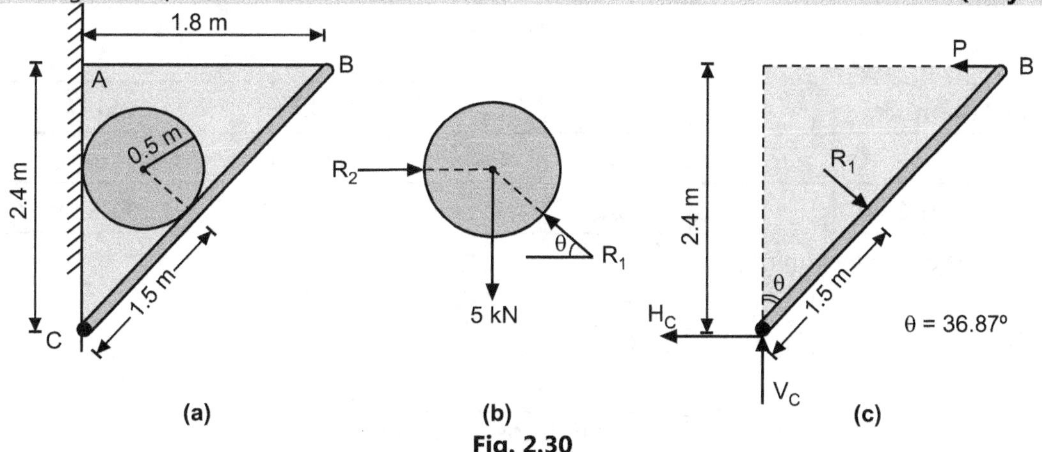

**(a)**　　　　**(b)**　　　　**(c)**

**Fig. 2.30**

**Solution :** (i) FBD as shown in Fig. 2.30 (b) and (c).

(ii)　For drum :　　　　　$\Sigma F_y = -5 + R_1 \sin(36.86) = 0$

　　　　　　　　　　　$R_1 = 8.33$ kN

For beam CB,　　　　$\Sigma M_C = -R_1(1.5) + P(2.4) = 0$

$\therefore$　　　　　　　　　$P = 5.2$ kN

(iii) For AB,　　　　　$\delta L = \dfrac{PL}{AE}$

　　　　　　　　　　　$= \dfrac{5.2 \times 1800}{5 \times 200} = $ **9.36 mm (increase)**

---

**Example 2.24 :** *In the truss ABC shown in Fig. 2.31 (a), cross-sectional area of BC is 8 times that of AB (8A and A). Obtain an expression for the vertical deflection $\delta$ for the joint B in terms of P, L, A, E and $\theta$. If the angle $\theta$ can be adjusted to any desired value, by varying the length of AB and the vertical position of support A without changing L, state the procedure to obtain the angle $\theta$ in order that $\delta$ will be minimum.*　　　　　　　**(May 2003)**

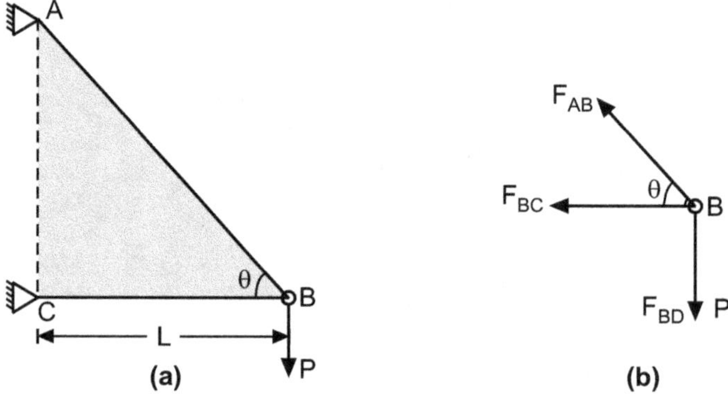


**Fig. 2.31**

**Solution :** (i) Joint A :　　$P_{AB} = \dfrac{P}{\sin \theta}$

and $P_{BC}$　　　　　$= -\dfrac{P}{\tan \theta}$

(ii)

| Member | L | A | P | k | PkL/AE |
|---|---|---|---|---|---|
| AB | $L/\cos \theta$ | A | $P/\sin \theta$ | $1/\sin \theta$ | $(PL/\sin^2 \theta/AE \cos \theta)$ |
| BC | L | 8A | $-P/\tan \theta$ | $-1/\tan \theta$ | $PL/8AE \tan^2 \theta$ |

$\therefore$　　Vertical deflection of joint B :

$$\delta = \frac{\Sigma PkL}{AE}$$

$$\delta = \frac{PL}{AE}\left[\frac{1}{\sin^2 \theta \cos \theta} + \frac{1}{8 \tan^2 \theta}\right]$$

---

For minimum deflection,

$\dfrac{d(\delta)}{d\theta}$ shall be equated to zero and value of $\theta$ shall be obtained. Substituting this value of $\theta$ in above equation, $\delta_{min}$ can be obtained.

**Example 2.25 :** *All bars in the truss shown in Fig. 2.32 have same axial rigidity EA. Find the strain energy of the truss when :*
- *(i) $P_2 = 0$ and only $P_1$ is acting,*
- *(ii) $P_1 = 0$ and only $P_2$ is acting.*
- *(iii) both $P_1$ and $P_2$ act simultaneously.*     **(May 2003)**

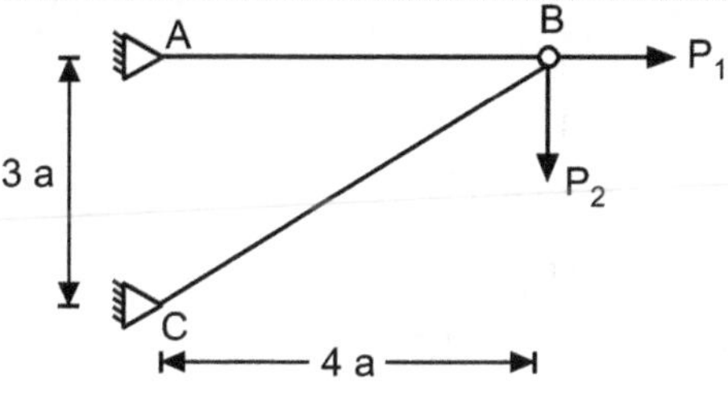


**Fig. 2.32**

**Solution : Case (i) :**  $P_{AB} = P_1$ and $P_{BC} = 0$

$$U = \left[\frac{\sigma^2}{2E} \cdot vol\right]_{AB + BC}$$

$$= \left(\frac{P_1}{A}\right)^2 \times \frac{(A \times 2a)}{2E} = \frac{2P_1^2\,a}{AE}$$

**Case (ii) :**  $P_{AB} = 1.33\,P_2$

$P_{BC} = -1.67\,P_2$

$$U = \left[\frac{\sigma^2}{2E} \cdot vol\right]_{AB + BC}$$

$$= \left(\frac{1.33\,P_2}{A}\right)^2 \times \frac{(A \times 4a)}{2E} + \left(\frac{1.67\,P_2}{A}\right)^2 \times \frac{(A \times 5a)}{2E} = \frac{10.51\,P_2^2}{AE}$$

**Case (iii) :**  $P_{AB} = P_1 + 1.33\,P_2$

and  $P_{BC} = -1.67\,P_2$

$$U = \left[\frac{\sigma^2}{2E} \cdot vol\right]_{AB + BC}$$

$$= \left(\frac{P_1 + 1.33\,P_2}{A}\right)^2 \times \frac{(A \times 4a)}{2E} + \left(\frac{1.67\,P_2}{A}\right)^2 \times \frac{(A \times 5a)}{2E}$$

$$= \frac{2P_1^2\,a + 10.5\,P_2^2\,a + 5.33\,P_1\,P_2\,a}{AE}$$

**Example 2.26 :** *The bar in Fig. 2.33 has E = 200 GPa and area of 225 mm². Find deflection at point D. Does the bar elongate or shorten ?*

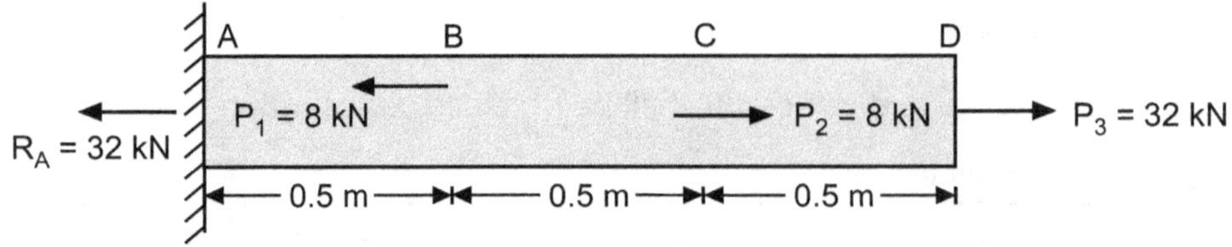


**Fig. 2.33**

**Data :** A = 225 mm², E = 200 GPa, $P_1 = P_2 = 8$ kN, $P_3 = 32$ kN, as shown in Fig. 2.33.

**Required :** Deformation.

**Concept :** Standard formulae.

**Solution :** (i)                     $\sum f_x = 0$

$$- R_A - 8 + 32 + 8 = 0$$

$\therefore$                     $R_A = 32$ kN

$$\delta l = \delta l_{AB} + \delta l_{BC} + \delta l_{CD}$$

$$P_{AB} = 32 \text{ kN (T)}$$

$$P_{BC} = 24 \text{ kN (C)}$$

$$P_{CD} = 32 \text{ kN (T)}$$

$\therefore$     $$\delta l = \frac{32 \times 10^3 \times 500}{225 \times 200 \times 10^3} - \frac{40 \times 10^3 \times 500}{225 \times 200 \times 10^3} + \frac{32 \times 10^3 \times 500}{225 \times 200 \times 10^3}$$

$$= \frac{500 \times 10^3}{225 \times 200 \times 10^3} [32 - 40 + 32] = 0.267 \text{ mm}$$

$\therefore$     Deflection at D is 0.267 mm (increase). Point D will be elongated for the given loading system.

## 2.7 STATICALLY INDETERMINATE PROBLEMS

When laws of static equilibrium, $\sum F_x = 0$, $\sum F_y = 0$ and $\sum M_z = 0$ (3 equations for 2D analysis) are not sufficient enough to evaluate the unknown forces, it is called as statically indeterminate problem. For solution of such problems, additional equations are required to be employed called as equations of **compatibility.**

## 2.8 COMPATIBILITY

In addition to the static equilibrium conditions, it is necessary in any structural analysis, that all conditions of compatibility be satisfied. These conditions refer to continuity of displacements throughout the structure, and are sometimes referred as conditions of geometry. As an example, compatibility conditions must be satisfied at all points of support, where it is necessary that the displacements of the structure be consistent with the support conditions. For instance, at a fixed support, there can be no rotation as well as translation of member.

Compatibility conditions must also be satisfied at all points throughout the interior of structure / structural member. Usually it is compatibility conditions at the joints that are of interest. For example, at a rigid joint between two members, the displacements (translation and rotation) of both members must be the same.

The condition of compatibility required to be employed for the analysis of indeterminate problem must be corresponding to the unknown force selected for analysis i.e. condition of translation must be considered if force is considered as unknown and condition of rotation must be considered if moment is considered as unknown.

## 2.9 PRINCIPLE OF SUPERPOSITION

*The principle states that, the effects produced by several causes can be obtained by combining the effect due to individual causes (forces /actions).*

The principle of superposition is valid whenever linear relations exist between actions and displacements. This occurs whenever following three requirements are satisfied :

(i) the material of structure follows Hooke's law; (ii) the displacements of the structure are small; and (iii) there is no interaction between axial and flexural effects in the member. The first of these requirements means that the material is perfectly elastic and has a linear relationship between stress and strain. The second requirement means that, all calculations involving overall dimensions of the structure can be based upon the original dimension of the structure. The third requirement implies that, the effect of axial force on bending of the member is neglected. This requirement refers to the fact that, axial forces in a member, in combination with even small deflections of the member, will have an effect on the bending moments. The effect is non-linear and can be omitted from the analysis when the axial forces are not large. When all three of these requirements are satisfied, the structure is said to be *linearly elastic.*

**Example 2.27 :** *A steel bar 20 mm diameter is enclosed in a brass tube of 25 mm external diameter and 2 mm thickness. Assuming $\dfrac{E_s}{E_b} = 2$ and initial length of both components = 400 mm, determine the stresses in the steel and brass if the composite section is subjected to an axial compressive force of 50 kN. Assuming $E_s$ = 200 GPa, find change in length of composite section.*

**Data :** As shown in Fig. 2.34, $\dfrac{E_s}{E_b}$ = 2, $E_s$ = 200 GPa.

**Required :** Stresses in steel and brass, change in length.

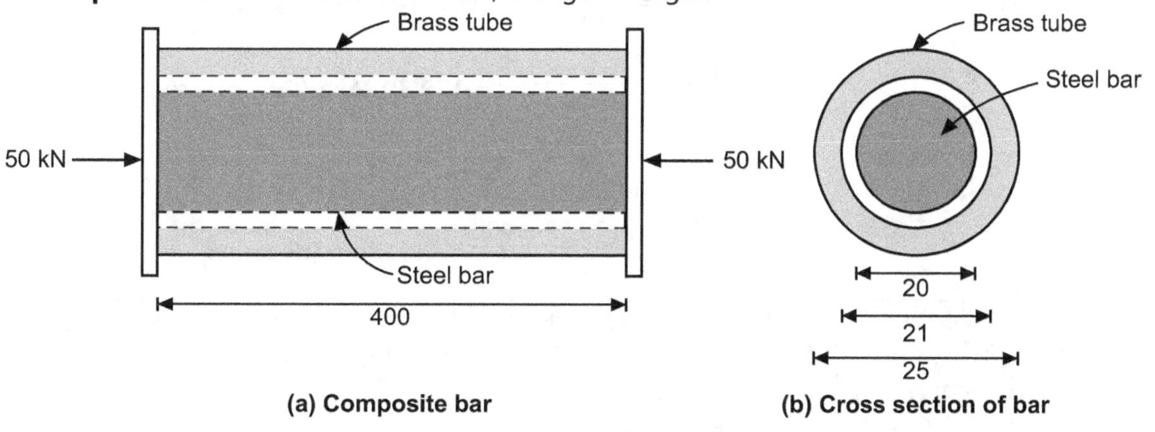


**(a) Composite bar**                    **(b) Cross section of bar**

**Fig. 2.34**

**Concept :** Statically indeterminate.

(i) Equation of statics : $P_b + P_s = P$

i.e. Force in brass tube + Force in steel bar = Total force applied

(ii) Equation of compatibility.

$(\delta L)_b = (\delta L)_s$ i.e. change in length for brass and steel is equal.

**Solution :** (i) Geometric properties :

$$\text{Cross-sectional area of brass tube, } A_b = \frac{\pi}{4}(25^2 - 21^2)$$

$$= 144.51 \text{ mm}^2$$

$$\text{Cross-sectional area of steel bar, } A_s = \frac{\pi}{4}(20)^2 = 314.15 \text{ mm}^2$$

(ii)　Equation of statics :

$$P_b + P_s = P$$

$$\therefore \qquad P_b + P_s = 50 \qquad\qquad \text{... (i)}$$

(iii) Equation of compatibility :

$$(\delta L)_b = (\delta L)_s$$

$$\therefore \qquad \left(\frac{PL}{AE}\right)_b = \left(\frac{PL}{AE}\right)_s$$

$$\frac{P_b}{A_b} = \left(\frac{E_b}{E_s}\right)\left(\frac{P_s}{A_s}\right)$$

$$P_b = 144.51 \times \frac{1}{2} \times \frac{P_s}{314.15}$$

$$P_b = 0.23\, P_s \qquad\qquad \text{... (ii)}$$

(iv) Solution of equations :

Solving equations (i) and (ii),

$$P_s = 40.65 \text{ kN}$$

$$P_b = 9.35 \text{ kN}$$

(v)　Stresses :

$$\sigma_b = \left(\frac{P}{A}\right)_b = \frac{9.35 \times 10^3}{144.51} = \textbf{64.7 MPa (Compressive)}$$

$$\sigma_s = \left(\frac{P}{A}\right)_s = \frac{40.65 \times 10^3}{314.15} = \textbf{129.39 MPa (Compressive)}$$

(vi) Change in length :

$$\delta L = (\delta L)_b \text{ OR } (\delta L)_s$$

$$= \left(\frac{\delta L}{E}\right)_s = \frac{129.39 \times 400}{200 \times 10^3} = \textbf{0.25 mm (decrease)}$$

---

**Example 2.28 :** *A mild steel bar of cross-sectional area 380 mm² is surrounded by copper tube of area 175 mm² as shown in Fig. 2.35. This composite section is carrying a load of 50 kN. It is found that steel bar is longer by 0.2 mm. Find the stresses in each bar.*

*Assume $E_s$ = 200 GPa, $E_c$ = 100 GPa.*

---

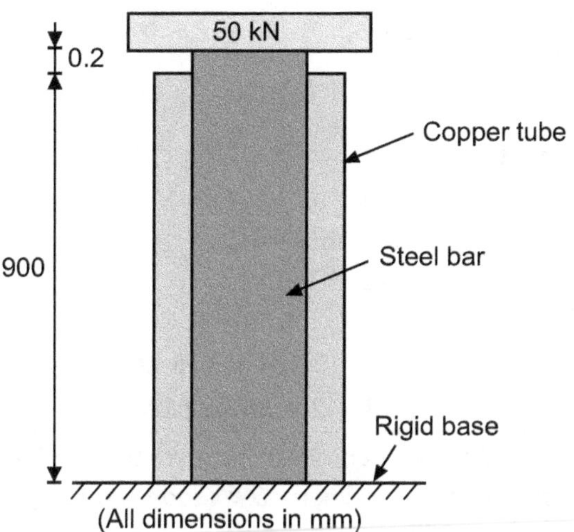


**Fig. 2.35**

**Data :** $A_S = 380$ mm$^2$, $A_C = 175$ mm$^2$, $P = 50$ kN, $E_S = 200$ GPa, $E_C = 100$ GPa

**Required :** Stresses in each bar.

**Concept :**   Load applied = load required to produce 0.2 mm shortening of steel bar (stage I) + load resisted by composite action (stage II)

Let,   $P_I$ = load corresponding to stage I

and   $P_{II}$ = load corresponding to stage II

**Solution :** (i) Stage I :

$$(\delta L)_S = 0.2 = \left(\frac{PL}{AE}\right)_S$$

$$0.2 = \frac{P_I \times 900.2}{380 \times 200 \times 10^3}$$

$$P_I = 16885.13 \text{ N} = 16.88 \text{ kN}$$

Stresses at the end of stage I :

$$\sigma_S = \frac{16.88 \times 10^3}{380} = 44.42 \text{ MPa and } \sigma_C = 0$$

(ii)   Stage II : Equation of statics :

$$P_{II} = P_C + P_S$$

$$(50 - 16.88)\, 10^3 = \sigma_C A_C + \sigma_S A_S$$

$$\therefore \qquad 33.12 \times 10^3 = \sigma_C A_C + \sigma_S A_S \qquad \qquad \text{... (i)}$$

Equation of compatibility :

$$(\delta L)_C = (\delta L)_S$$

$$\left(\frac{\sigma L}{E}\right)_C = \left(\frac{\delta L}{E}\right)_S$$

$$\sigma_C = \frac{E_C}{E_S} \cdot \sigma_S$$

$$= \frac{100}{200} \times \sigma_S$$

$$\sigma_C = 0.5\,\sigma_S \qquad \text{... (ii)}$$

Putting equation (ii) in equation (i),

$$33.12 \times 10^3 = 0.5\,\sigma_S \times 175 + \sigma_S \times 380$$

$$\sigma_S = 70.84 \text{ MPa}$$

$$\therefore \qquad \sigma_C = 35.42 \text{ MPa}$$

(iii) Final stresses :

$$\sigma_S = 44.42 + 70.84 = \mathbf{115.26 \text{ MPa}}$$

$$\sigma_C = 0 + 35.42 = \mathbf{35.42 \text{ MPa}}$$

**Example 2.29 :** *Two bars having geometric properties as shown in Fig. 2.36 are rigidly connected at ends. Find stresses in each bar when 40 kN load is applied axially on composite section. Assume $E_1 = 200$ GPa and $E_2 = 100$ GPa.*

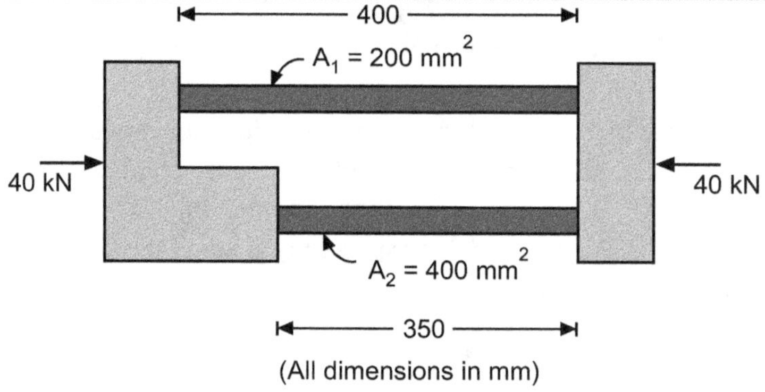


**Fig. 2.36**

**Data :** As shown in Fig. 2.36.

**Required :** Stresses in each bar.

**Concept :** Composite section, statically indeterminate, statics and compatibility.

**Solution :** (i) Equation of statics :

$$P = P_1 + P_2$$

$$40 \times 10^3 = \sigma_1 A_1 + \sigma_2 A_2 \qquad \text{... (i)}$$

(ii)   Equation of compatibility :

$$(\delta L)_1 = (\delta L)_2$$

**Note :** Shortening of the bars is same but not the strain.

$$\left(\frac{\sigma L}{E}\right)_1 = \left(\frac{\sigma L}{E}\right)_2$$

$$\frac{\sigma_1 \times 400}{200 \times 10^3} = \frac{\sigma_2 \times 350}{100 \times 10^3}$$

$$\sigma_1 = 1.75\,\sigma_2 \qquad \text{... (ii)}$$

(iii) Solution of equations :

Put equation (ii) in equation (i),

$$40 \times 10^3 = (1.75\ \sigma_2)(200) + \sigma_2 \times 400$$

$$\therefore \qquad \sigma_2 = \textbf{53.33 MPa}$$

$$\therefore \qquad \sigma_1 = 1.75 \times 53.33$$

$$= \textbf{93.33 MPa}$$

**Example 2.30 :** *A steel bolt of 25 mm diameter passes centrally through a copper tube of internal diameter 40 mm and thickness 8 mm. If length of composite section is 0.5 m, what stresses will be introduced by 60° turn of nut if the pitch of thread is 4 mm ?*

*Assume $E_S$ = 200 GPa, $E_C$ = 100 GPa.*

**Data :** As shown in Fig. 2.37, pitch = 4 mm, $E_S$ = 200 GPa, $E_C$ = 100 GPa

**Required :** Stresses in copper and steel due to 60° turn of nut.

**Concept :** Statically indeterminate.

    (i)    Equation of statics :

Compressive force in copper = Tensile force in steel bolt

    (ii)    Equation of compatibility :

Contraction of copper tube + Extension of steel bolt = Displacement of nut.

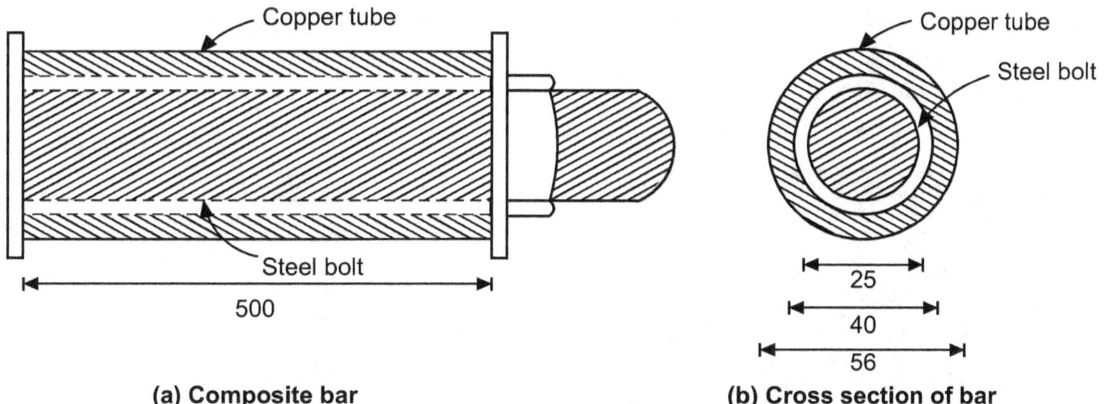


**Fig. 2.37**

**Solution :** (i) Geometric properties :

$$A_c = \text{cross-sectional area of copper tube} = \frac{\pi}{4}(56^2 - 40^2) = 1206.37 \text{ mm}^2$$

$$A_s = \text{cross-sectional area of steel bolt} = \frac{\pi}{4}(25)^2 = 490.87 \text{ mm}^2$$

    (ii)    Equation of statics :

$$P_C = P_S$$

$$\sigma_C\, A_C = \sigma_S\, A_S$$

$$\sigma_c \times 1206.37 = \sigma_s \times 490.87$$
$$\sigma_c = 0.406\,\sigma_s \qquad \text{... (i)}$$

(iii) Equation of compatibility :

$$(\delta L)_c + (\delta L)_s = \text{Displacement of nut}$$

$$\left(\frac{\sigma L}{E}\right)_c + \left(\frac{\sigma L}{E}\right)_s = \frac{60}{360} \times 4$$

$$\left(\frac{\sigma_c}{100 \times 10^3} + \frac{\sigma_s}{200 \times 10^3}\right) 500 = 0.67$$

$$\therefore \qquad 2\sigma_c + \sigma_s = 266.67 \qquad \text{... (ii)}$$

(iv) Solution of equations :

Put equation (i) in equation (ii),

$$2 \times 0.406\,\sigma_s + \sigma_s = 266.67$$
$$\therefore \qquad \sigma_s = \textbf{147.16 MPa (Tensile)}$$
$$\sigma_c = \textbf{59.75 MPa (Compressive)}$$

**Example 2.31 :** *A compound bar is having copper tube of external diameter 70 mm and internal diameter 60 mm inside which there is a steel tube of external diameter 60 mm and internal diameter 50 mm. A steel bolt of 25 mm diameter is inserted through steel tube. Assuming length of composite section as 1 m and system to be stress free initially, find stresses in each material when nut is moved through a distance of 2 mm.*
*Assume $E_s$ = 200 GPa, $E_c$ = 100 GPa.*

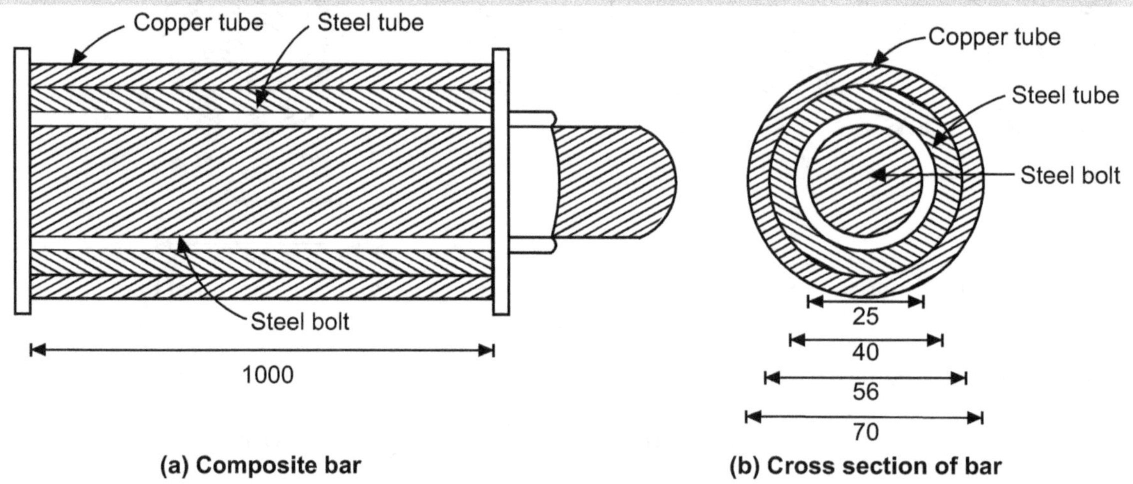


**(a) Composite bar**　　　　　　　　**(b) Cross section of bar**

**Fig. 2.38**

**Data :** As shown in Fig. 2.38, $E_s$ = 200 GPa, $E_c$ = 100 GPa.

**Required :** Stresses in all the materials due to 2 mm displacement of nut.

**Concept :** Statically indeterminate.

(i)　　Equation of statics :

Compressive force in copper tube + Compressive force in steel tube

$$= \text{Tensile force in steel bolt.}$$

(ii)   Equations of compatibility :

(a) Contraction of copper tube = Contraction of steel tube

(b) Contraction of copper or steel tube + Elongation of steel bolt = Displacement of nut

Let $\sigma_c$, $\sigma_s$, $\sigma_b$ = stresses in copper tube, steel tube and steel bolt respectively

**Solution :** (i) Geometric properties :

$$A_c = \text{Area of copper tube} = \frac{\pi}{4}(70^2 - 60^2) = 1021 \text{ mm}^2$$

$$A_s = \text{Area of steel tube} = \frac{\pi}{4}(60^2 - 50^2) = 863.94 \text{ mm}^2$$

$$A_b = \text{Area of steel bolt} = \frac{\pi}{4}(25)^2 = 490.87 \text{ mm}^2$$

(ii)   Equation of statics :

$$P_c + P_s = P_b$$

$$\sigma_c A_c + \sigma_s A_s = \sigma_b A_b$$

$$\sigma_c \times 1021 + \sigma_s \times 863.94 = \sigma_b \times 490.87$$

$$2.08\,\sigma_c + 1.76\,\sigma_s = \sigma_b \qquad \text{... (i)}$$

(iii) Equations of compatibility :

(a)

$$(\delta L)_c = (\delta L)_s$$

$$\left(\frac{\sigma L}{E}\right)_c = \left(\frac{\sigma L}{E}\right)_s$$

$$\sigma_c = \frac{E_c}{E_s} \cdot \sigma_s$$

$$= \frac{100 \times 10^3}{200 \times 10^3}\,\sigma_s$$

$$\sigma_c = 0.5\,\sigma_s \qquad \text{... (ii)}$$

OR

$$\sigma_s = 2\sigma_c$$

(b)

$$(\delta L)_c + (\delta L)_b = \text{Displacement of nut}$$

$$(\delta L)_s + (\delta L)_b = \text{Displacement of nut}$$

$$\therefore \quad (\delta L)_c + (\delta L)_b = 2 \text{ mm}$$

$$\left(\frac{\sigma L}{E}\right)_c + \left(\frac{\sigma L}{E}\right)_b = 2$$

$$\left(\frac{\sigma_c}{100 \times 10^3} + \frac{\sigma_b}{200 \times 10^3}\right) 1000 = 2$$

$$2\sigma_c + \delta_b = 400 \qquad \text{... (iii)}$$

(iv) Solution of equations :

Put equation (ii) in equation (i),

$$2.08\,\sigma_C + 1.76\,(2\,\sigma_C) = \sigma_b$$
$$5.6\,\sigma_C = \sigma_b \qquad \qquad \text{... (iv)}$$

Put equation (iv) in equation (iii),

$$2\sigma_C + 5.6\,\sigma_C = 400$$
$$\sigma_C = \textbf{52.63 MPa (Compressive)}$$
$$\sigma_b = \textbf{294.74 MPa (Tensile)}$$
$$\sigma_S = \textbf{105.26 MPa (Compressive)}$$

**Example 2.32 :** *For the compound section fixed at both ends as shown in Fig. 2.39 (a), find (i) Reactions at both the ends, (ii) Stresses in individual components.*

| | Component | | |
|---|---|---|---|
| | AB | BC | CD |
| Material | Copper | Aluminium | Brass |
| Length (mm) | 500 | 400 | 600 |
| c/s area (mm²) | 400 | 300 | 550 |
| E (GPa) | 120 | 70 | 100 |

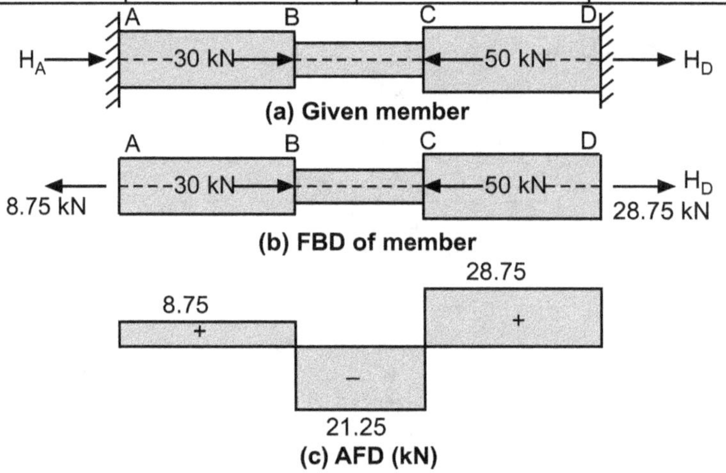

$H_A$ · A · ---30 kN · B · C · 50 kN · D · $H_D$

**(a) Given member**

A · ---30 kN · B · C · 50 kN · D · $H_D$

8.75 kN · 28.75 kN

**(b) FBD of member**

8.75 + · 28.75 + · 21.25 −

**(c) AFD (kN)**

**Fig. 2.39**

**Data :** As shown in Fig. 2.39 (a).

**Required :** (i) Reactions at both fixed ends and (ii) Stresses in individual components.

**Concept :** Statically indeterminate.

(i) Equation of statics : $\Sigma F_X = 0$

(ii) Equation of compatibility : $\delta L = (\delta L)_{AB} + (\delta L)_{BC} + (\delta L)_{CD} = 0$

**Solution :** (i) Equation of statics :

Assuming $H_A$ and $H_D$ both towards right,

$$\Sigma F_X = 0, \qquad H_A + 30 - 50 + H_D = 0$$
$$H_A + H_D = 20 \qquad \qquad \text{... (i)}$$

(ii)   Equation of compatibility :

$$\delta L = (\delta L)_{AB} + (\delta L)_{BC} + (\delta L)_{CD} = 0$$

$$\therefore \quad \left(\frac{PL}{AE}\right)_{AB} + \left(\frac{PL}{AE}\right)_{BC} + \left(\frac{PL}{AE}\right)_{CD} = 0$$

$$\frac{H_A \times 500}{400 \times 120} + \frac{(H_A + 30)\,400}{300 \times 70} + \frac{(H_A + 30 - 50)\,600}{550 \times 100} = 0$$

$$0.0403\,H_A + 0.353 = 0 \qquad\qquad\qquad\qquad \text{... (ii)}$$

(iii) Solution of equations :

Solving equations (i) and (ii),

$$H_A = -8.75 \text{ kN} = 8.75 \text{ kN } (\leftarrow)$$

$$H_D = 28.75 \text{ kN} = 28.75 \text{ kN } (\rightarrow)$$

FBD of member is as shown in Fig. 2.39 (b).

(iv) Axial force diagram :

Considering sections in portions AB, BC and CD,

$$P_{AB} = 8.75 \text{ kN (Tensile)}$$

$$P_{BC} = 8.75 - 30 = -21.25 \text{ kN} = 21.25 \text{ kN (Compressive)}$$

$$P_{CD} = 28.75 \text{ kN (Tensile)}$$

Axial force diagram is as shown in Fig. 2.39 (c).

(v)    Stresses :

$$(\sigma)_{AB} = \left(\frac{P}{A}\right)_{AB} = \frac{8.75 \times 10^3}{400} = \textbf{21.87 MPa (Tensile)}$$

$$(\sigma)_{BC} = \left(\frac{P}{A}\right)_{BC} = \frac{21.25 \times 10^3}{300} = \textbf{70.83 MPa (Compressive)}$$

$$(\sigma)_{CD} = \left(\frac{P}{A}\right)_{CD} = \frac{28.75 \times 10^3}{550} = \textbf{52.27 MPa (Tensile)}$$

---

**Example 2.33 :** *A 20 mm diameter bar is fixed at ends A and B. Two collars weighing 12 kN and 20 kN are placed at C and D respectively as shown in Fig. 2.40. Find*

*(i)    Reactions at ends A and B,*

*(ii)   Stresses in each portion and*

*(iii) Distance through which each collar moves.*

*Assume E = 200 GPa.*

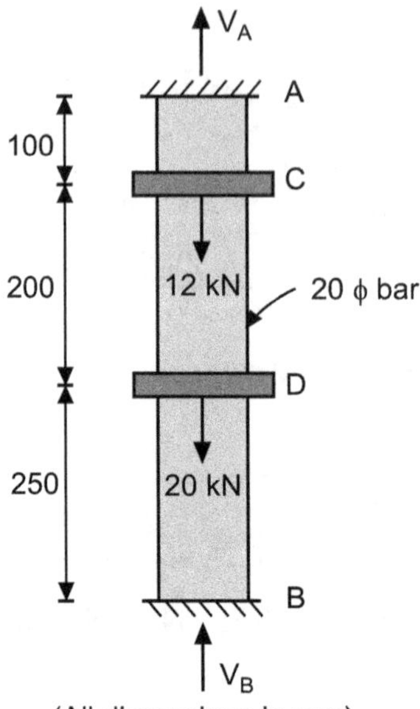


**Fig. 2.40**

**Data :** As shown in Fig. 2.40, E = 200 GPa.

**Required :**　　(i)　Reactions at A and B,

　　　　　(ii)　Stresses in each portion and

　　　　　(iii)　Displacement of each collar.

**Concept :** Statically indeterminate problem. Equations of statics and compatibility.

**Solution :** (i) Geometric properties of bar :

$$A = \frac{\pi}{4}(20)^2 = 314.16 \text{ mm}^2$$

(ii)　Equation of statics :

Assuming $V_A$ and $V_B$ both upwards.

$$\Sigma F_y = 0, \qquad V_A + V_B - 12 - 20 = 0$$

$$\therefore \qquad\qquad V_A + V_B = 32 \qquad\qquad\qquad \text{... (i)}$$

(iii) Equation of compatibility :

$$\delta L = (\delta L)_{AC} + (\delta L)_{CD} + (\delta L)_{DB} = 0$$

$$\therefore \quad \left(\frac{PL}{AE}\right)_{AC} + \left(\frac{PL}{AE}\right)_{CD} + \left(\frac{PL}{AE}\right)_{DB} = 0$$

$$\therefore \quad \frac{1}{AE}[V_A \times 100 + (V_A - 12)\,200 + (V_A - 12 - 20)\,250] = 0$$

$$\therefore \quad \frac{1}{AE}[550\,V_A - 10400] = 0 \qquad\qquad \text{... (ii)}$$

(iv) Solution of equations :

From equation (ii),

$$550\,V_A - 10400 = 0$$

$\therefore$ $\qquad\qquad\qquad\qquad\qquad V_A = 18.9$ kN ($\uparrow$)

Put in (i), $\qquad\qquad\qquad\qquad V_B = 13.1$ kN ($\uparrow$)

(v)  FBD of member and axial force diagram (AFD) :

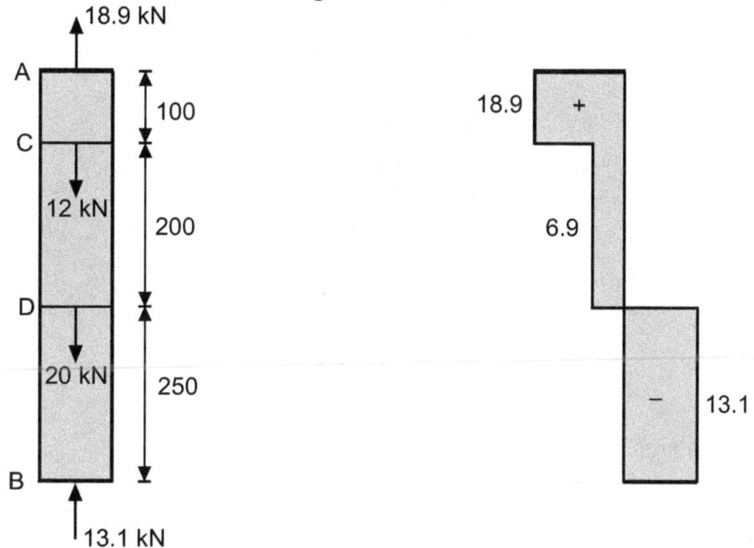


**(a) FBD of member**     (All dimensions in mm)     **(b) AFD (kN)**

**Fig. 2.41**

(vi) Stresses in components :

$$\sigma_{AC} = \left(\frac{P}{A}\right)_{AC} = \frac{18.9 \times 10^3}{314.16} = 60.16 \text{ MPa (Tensile)}$$

$$\sigma_{CD} = \left(\frac{P}{A}\right)_{CD} = \frac{6.9 \times 10^3}{314.16} = 21.96 \text{ MPa (Tensile)}$$

$$\sigma_{DB} = \left(\frac{P}{A}\right)_{DB} = \frac{13.1 \times 10^3}{314.16} = 41.69 \text{ MPa (Compressive)}$$

(vii) Displacements of collars :

$$\text{Displacement of collar C} = (\delta L)_{AC} = \left(\frac{\sigma L}{E}\right)_{AC} = \frac{60.16 \times 100}{200 \times 10^3} = 0.03 \text{ mm } (\neg)$$

$$\text{Displacement of collar D} = (\delta L)_{AD}$$

$$= (\delta L)_{AC} + (\delta L)_{CD} = \left(\frac{\sigma L}{E}\right)_{AC} + \left(\frac{\sigma L}{E}\right)_{CD}$$

$$= \frac{1}{E}(60.16 \times 100 + 21.96 \times 200) = \frac{10408}{200 \times 10^3}$$

$$= \mathbf{0.052 \text{ mm } (\downarrow)}$$

**Example 2.34 :** *A composite bar ABC is rigidly fixed at A and 1 mm above the lower support is loaded as shown in Fig. 2.42. Determine the reactions at the end and the stresses in the two components. Assume E = 200 GPa.*

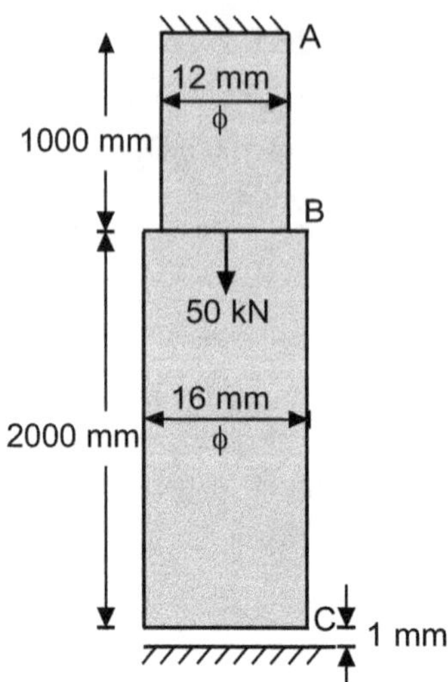



**Fig. 2.42**

**Data :** As shown in Fig. 2.42, $E = 200 \times 10^3$ MPa.

**Required :** Stresses in the bar.

**Concept :** $\delta l = \dfrac{Pl}{AE}$

**Solution :** (i) Geometric properties :

$$A_{AB} = \frac{\pi}{4} \times 12^2 = 113.10 \text{ mm}^2$$

$$A_{BC} = \frac{\pi}{4} \times 16^2 = 201.06 \text{ mm}^2$$

(ii)   Force required to touch the support 'C'.

**Note :** Bar AB is in tension and bar BC is in compression, so stresses are developed in AB due to increase in length.

$$\therefore \qquad \delta l = \left(\frac{Pl}{AE}\right)_{AB}$$

$$1 = \frac{P \times 10^3 \times 1000}{113.10 \times 200 \times 10^3}$$

$$\therefore \qquad P = 22.62 \text{ kN}$$

$$\therefore \qquad \text{Force balanced} = 50 - 22.62$$

$$= 27.380 \text{ kN}$$

(iii) Calculation of stresses :

$$P_{AB1} + P_{BC} = 27.381 \text{ kN} \qquad \qquad \text{... (i)}$$

$$\delta l_{AB} = \delta l_{BC}$$

$$\left(\frac{Pl}{AE}\right)_{AB} = \left(\frac{Pl}{AE}\right)_{BC}$$

$$\frac{P_{AB1} \times 1000}{113.10 \times E} = \frac{P_{BC} \times 2000}{201.06 \times E}$$

$$P_{AB1} = 1.125\ P_{BC} \qquad \qquad ... \text{(ii)}$$

Solving (i) and (ii),
$$P_{BC} = 12.89\ \text{kN}$$
$$P_{AB1} = 14.50\ \text{kN}$$

$\therefore$
$$P_{AB} = P + P_{AB1}$$
$$= 22.62 + 14.50 = 37.12\ \text{kN}$$
$$P_{BC} = 12.89\ \text{kN}$$

$\therefore$
$$\text{Stress in AB} = \frac{P_{AB}}{A_{AB}}$$

$$\sigma_{AB} = \frac{37.12 \times 10^3}{113.10} = \mathbf{328.21\ MPa}$$

$$\text{Stress in BC} = \frac{P_{BC}}{A_{BC}}$$

$$\sigma_{BC} = \frac{12.89 \times 10^3}{201.06} = \mathbf{64.11\ MPa}$$

**Example 2.35 :** *Two steel rods and one copper rod each of 20 mm diameter, together support a load of 20 kN as shown in Fig. 2.43. Find the stresses in rods. Take $E_{st}$ and $E_{Cu}$ as 205 GN/m² and 110 GN/m² respectively.*

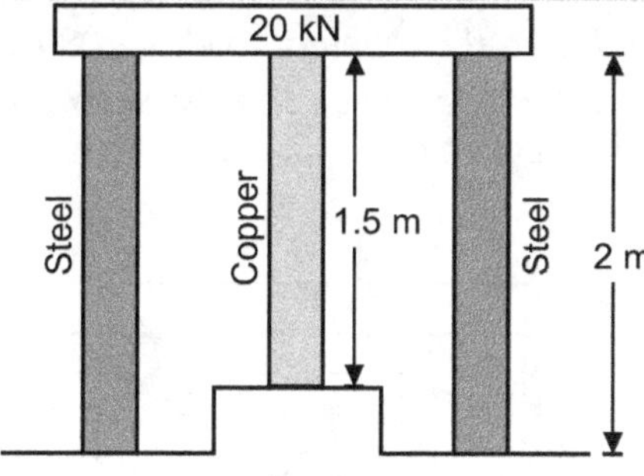


**Fig. 2.43**

**Data :** As shown in Fig. 2.43, $D_{st}$ = 20 mm, $D_{Cu}$ = 20 mm,
$$E_{st} = 205 \times 10^3\ \text{N/mm}^2,\ E_{Cu} = 110 \times 10^3\ \text{N/mm}^2$$

**Required :** Stresses in rods.

**Concept :** Statically indeterminate.

(a)    Forces in rods = Total load

(b)    $\delta_{st} = \delta_{Cu}$

**Solution :** (i) Geometric properties : $A_{st} = A_{Cu} = \dfrac{\pi}{4} \times 20^2 = 314.16\ \text{mm}^2$

(ii)    Equation of equilibrium :
$$P_{st} + P_{Cu} + P_{st} = 20\ \text{kN}$$

$\therefore$
$$2\,P_{st} + P_{Cu} = 20 \qquad \qquad ... \text{(i)}$$

(iii)
$$\delta l_{st} = \delta l_{Cu}$$
$$\left(\frac{Pl}{AE}\right)_{st} = \left(\frac{Pl}{AE}\right)_{Cu}$$

$$\frac{P_{st} \times 10^3 \times 2000}{\frac{\pi}{4} \times 20^2 \times 205 \times 10^3} = \frac{P_{Cu} \times 10^3 \times 1500}{\frac{\pi}{4} \times 20^2 \times 110 \times 10^3}$$

$$P_{st} = 1.4\, P_{Cu} \qquad \qquad \text{... (ii)}$$

Solving equations (i) and (ii),

$$P_{Cu} = 5.26 \text{ kN}$$
$$P_{st} = 7.36 \text{ kN}$$

$\therefore \qquad$ Stress in steel $\quad = \dfrac{P_{st}}{A_{st}} = \dfrac{7.36 \times 10^3}{314.16}$

$\therefore \qquad \sigma_{st} = \textbf{23.43 MPa}$

$\qquad$ Stress in copper $\quad = \dfrac{P_{Cu}}{A_{Cu}} = \dfrac{5.26 \times 10^3}{314.16}$

$\therefore \qquad \sigma_{Cu} = \textbf{16.74 MPa}$

**Example 2.36 :** *Fig. 2.44 shows a round steel rod supported and surrounded by co-axial brass tube. The upper end of the rod is 0.1 mm below that of the tube and axial load is applied to a rigid plate resting on the top of the tube.*

*(i)   Determine the magnitude of the maximum permissible load if the compressive stress in the rod is not to exceed 110 MPa and that in the tube not to exceed 80 MPa.*

*(ii)   Find the amount by which the tube will be shortened by the load if the compressive stress in the tube is same as that in the rod. $E_s$ = 210 GPa, $E_b$ = 90 GPa.*

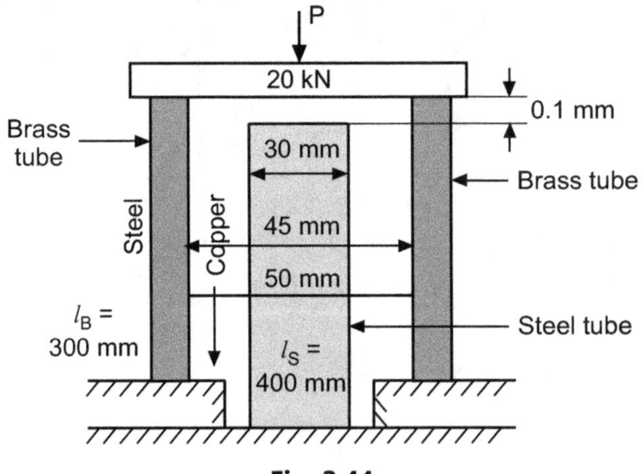


**Fig. 2.44**

**Data :** As shown in Fig. 2.44, $\sigma_{br\ max}$ = 110 MPa,

$\qquad \sigma_{st\ max}$ = 80 MPa, $E_{st}$ = 210 × 10³ MPa, $E_b$ = 90 × 10³ MPa.

**Required :** (i) Maximum value of P.

$\qquad$ (ii) Amount of tube to be shorten.

**Concept :** (a) Force in rods + Force in tube = Total force

$\qquad$ (b) $\qquad \qquad \delta_{br} + 0.1 = \delta_{st}$

**Solution :** (i) Geometric properties :

$$A_{br} = \frac{\pi}{4}(50^2 - 45^2) = 373.06 \text{ mm}^2$$

$$A_{st} = \frac{\pi}{4} \times 30^2 = 706.86 \text{ mm}^2$$

(ii)   Stress developed in brass to shorten by 0.1 mm

$$\delta l = \left(\frac{Pl}{AE}\right)_{Br}$$

$$0.1 = \frac{\sigma_{Br1} \times 300}{90 \times 10^3}$$

$$\therefore \quad \sigma_{Br1} = 30 \text{ MPa}$$

(iii)   $\delta l_{Br} = \delta l_{st}$

$$\left(\frac{Pl}{AE}\right)_{Br} = \left(\frac{Pl}{AE}\right)_{st}$$

$$\frac{\sigma_{Br} \times 300}{90 \times 10^3} = \frac{\sigma_{st} \times 400}{210 \times 10^3}$$

$$\sigma_{Br} = 0.57 \, \sigma_S$$

$$\therefore \quad \sigma_{st} = \frac{50}{0.57}$$

$$= 87.22 \text{ MPa} < 110 \text{ MPa}$$

$$\therefore \quad \text{Force taken by brass} = \sigma_{Br} \times A_{Br}$$

$$= 80 \times 373.06$$

$$P_{Br} = 29.84 \text{ kN}$$

$$\text{Force taken by steel} = \sigma_{st} \times A_{st}$$

$$P_{st} = 87.22 \times 706.85 = 62 \text{ kN}$$

$$P = P_{Br} + P_{st}$$

$$= 29.84 + 62$$

$$= \mathbf{91.84 \text{ kN}}$$

(iv) Amount of tube shorten :   $\delta l = \left(\dfrac{Pl}{AE}\right)_{Br} = \dfrac{\sigma_{Br} \times l}{E}$

$$= \frac{80 \times 300}{90 \times 10^3}$$

$$= 0.267 \text{ mm}$$

---

**Example 2.37 :** *A rigid member ABCD is supported as shown in Fig. 2.45. Find stresses in steel wires at 'B' and 'C'.*

**Data :** As shown in Fig. 2.45 (a).

---

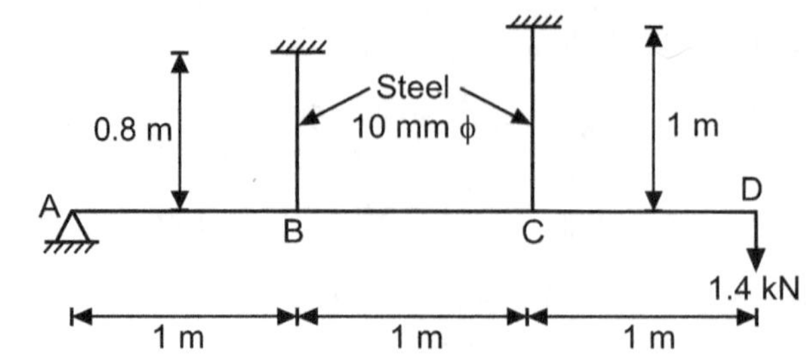



**(a) Given arrangement**

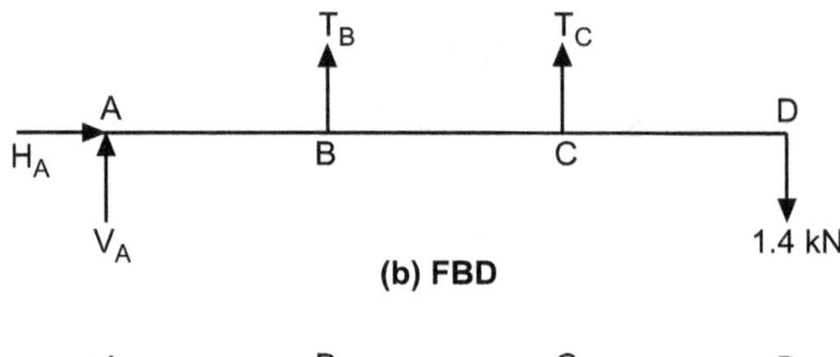



**(b) FBD**

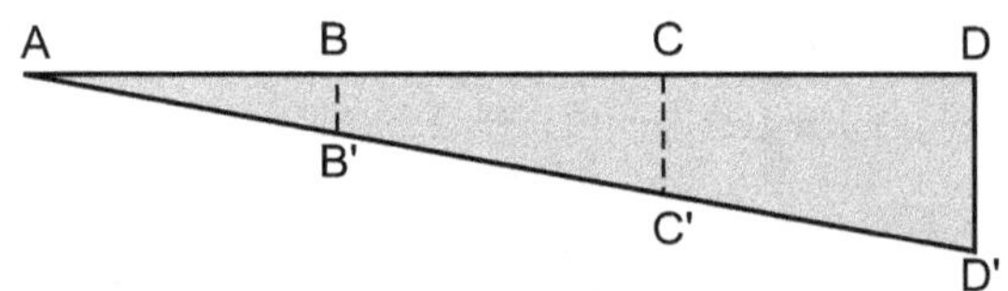



**(c) Deformation diagram**

**Fig. 2.45**

**Required :** Stresses in steel wires at 'B' and 'C'.

**Concept :** Statically indeterminate, statics and compatibility.

**Solution :** (i) Equation of statics :

$$\Sigma M_A = 0$$

$$T_B \times 1 + T_C \times 2 - 1.4 \times 3 = 0$$

$$\therefore \quad T_B + 2T_C = 4.2 \qquad \text{... (i)}$$

(ii)   From compatibility,

$$\frac{CC'}{2} = \frac{BB'}{1}$$

$$\therefore \quad CC' = 2\,BB'$$

$$\therefore \quad \left(\frac{PL}{AE}\right)_C = \left(\frac{2PL}{AE}\right)_B$$

$$\frac{T_C \times 1000}{(AE)} = \frac{2\,T_B \times 800}{(AE)}$$

$$\therefore \quad T_C = 1.6\,T_B \qquad \text{... (ii)}$$

(iii) Solving (i) and (ii),

$$T_B = 1 \text{ kN}$$

$$T_C = 1.6 \text{ kN}$$

(iv) Stresses :

$$\sigma_B \;=\; \frac{1 \times 10^3}{\dfrac{\pi}{4} \times 10^2} = \textbf{12.7 MPa (Tensile)}$$

$$\sigma_C \;=\; \frac{1.6 \times 10^3}{\dfrac{\pi}{4} \times 10^2} = \textbf{20.37 MPa (Tensile)}$$

**Example 2.38 :** *A rigid bar ABC is hinged at 'A' and supported by two wires each 10 mm$\phi$ (E = 200 GPa). Determine the vertical displacement of point C when load of 10 kN is applied.*

**Data :** As shown in Fig. 2.46 (a).

**Required :** Vertical displacement of point C.

**Concept :** Statically indeterminate, statics and compatibility.

**Solution :**

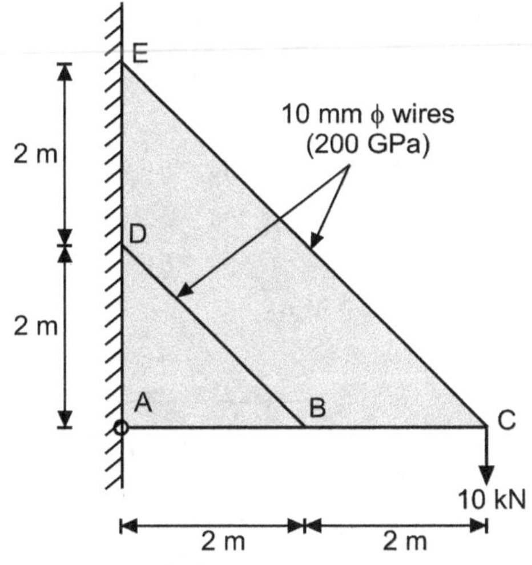


(a) Given arrangement

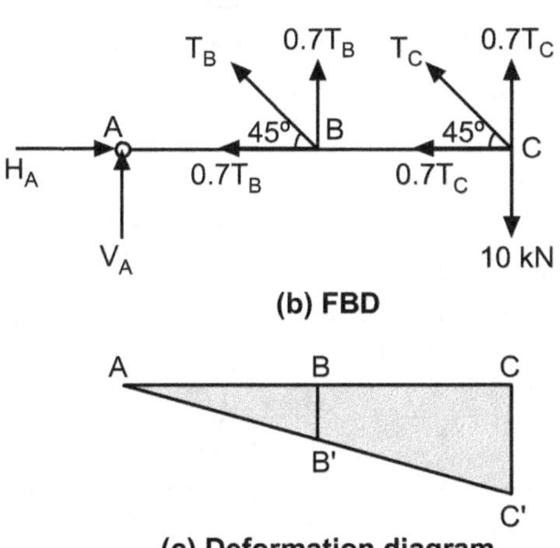


(b) FBD



(c) Deformation diagram

**Fig. 2.46**

(i) Equation of statics :          $\Sigma M_A \;=\; 0$

$$0.7\,T_B \times 2 + 0.7\,T_C \times 4 - 10 \times 4 \;=\; 0$$

$$2T_B + 4T_C \;=\; 57.1 \qquad \text{... (i)}$$

(ii)　Compatibility :
$$\frac{BB'}{2} = \frac{CC'}{4}$$

$\therefore$
$$BB' = \frac{1}{2} \cdot CC'$$

$$(\delta L)_B \times \cos 45 = 0.5\,(\delta L)_C \times \cos 45$$

$\therefore$
$$(\delta L)_B = 0.5\,(\delta L)_C$$

$$\left(\frac{PL}{AE}\right)_B = 0.5 \left(\frac{PL}{AE}\right)_C$$

$$\frac{T_B \times \sqrt{8}}{AE} = 0.5\,\frac{T_C \times \sqrt{32}}{AE}$$

$$T_B = T_C \qquad \text{... (ii)}$$

(iii) Solving (i) and (ii),
$$T_B = 9.51 \text{ kN}$$

$$T_C = 9.51 \text{ kN}$$

$$(\delta L)_C = \left(\frac{PL}{AE}\right)_C$$

$$= \frac{9.51 \times (\sqrt{32}) \times 1000 \times 10^3}{\dfrac{\pi}{4} \times 10^2 \times 200 \times 10^3} = 3.42 \text{ mm}$$

$$(\delta C)_y = 3.42 \cos 45$$

$$= \mathbf{2.4 \text{ mm} (\downarrow)}$$

**Example 2.39 :** *A rigid bar ABC carries a load of 100 kN and supported as shown in Fig. 2.47 (a). Calculate the stresses in steel and brass rod. Assume $E_s$ = 205 GPa, $E_b$ = 82 GPa.*

**Data :** As shown in Fig. 2.47 (a).

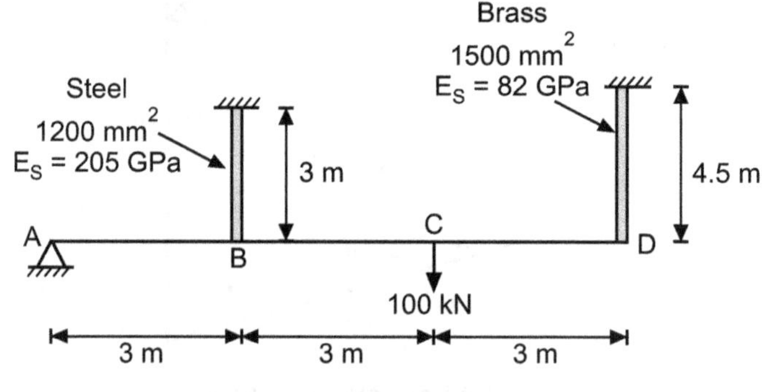


**(a) Given arrangement**

**Fig. 2.47**

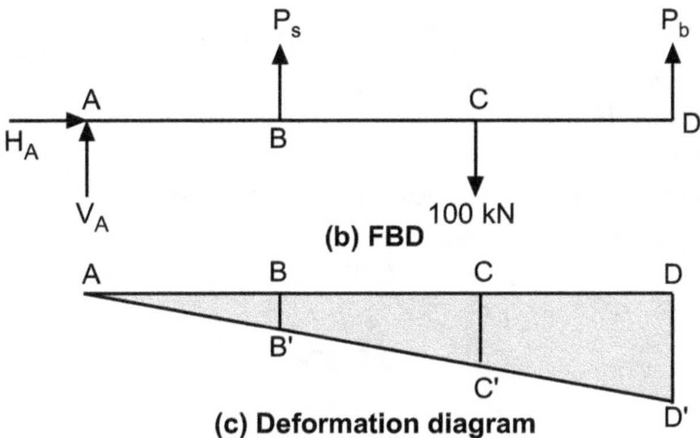



**(c) Deformation diagram**

**Required :** Stresses in steel and brass rod.

**Concept :** Statically indeterminate, statics and compatibility.

**Solution :** (i) Equation of statics :

$$\Sigma M_A = 0$$

$$3\, P_S + 9\, P_B = 100 \times 6 = 600 \qquad \text{... (i)}$$

(ii)   Compatibility :

$$\frac{BB'}{3} = \frac{DD'}{9}$$

$$BB' = \frac{3}{9}(DD')$$

$$\therefore \qquad \left(\frac{PL}{AE}\right)_S = \frac{3}{9}\left(\frac{PL}{AE}\right)_B$$

$$\frac{P_S \times 3000}{1200 \times 205 \times 10^3} = \frac{3}{9}\left(\frac{P_B \times 4500}{1500 \times 82 \times 10^3}\right)$$

$$P_S = P_B \qquad \text{... (ii)}$$

(iii) Solving (i) and (ii),

$$P_S = P_B = 50 \text{ kN}$$

(iv) Stresses :

$$\sigma_S = \frac{P_S}{A_S} = \frac{50 \times 10^3}{1200} = \textbf{41.66 MPa (Tensile)}$$

$$\sigma_B = \frac{P_B}{A_B} = \frac{50 \times 10^3}{1500} = \textbf{33.33 MPa (Tensile)}$$

(v)   **Note :** If deflection under load is required,

$$\frac{BB'}{3} = \frac{CC'}{6}$$

$$BB' = \frac{1}{2}CC'$$

$$CC' = 2\, BB' = 2\left(\frac{PL}{AE}\right)_S = 2\left(\frac{50 \times 10^3 \times 3000}{1200 \times 205 \times 10^3}\right)$$

$$= \textbf{1.2 mm } (\downarrow)$$

**Example 2.40 :** *Find the safe value of 'P' if stresses in steel and brass are restricted to 150 MPa and 70 MPa respectively.*

**Data :** As shown in Fig. 2.48 (a).

**Required :** Safe value of P.

**Concept :** Governing stresses shall be obtained from geometry of deformation.

**Solution :** (i) Geometry of deformation :

$$\frac{CC'}{1.5} = \frac{DD'}{3}$$

$$CC' = 0.5\ DD'$$

$$\left(\frac{\sigma L}{E}\right)_S = 0.5 \left(\frac{\sigma L}{E}\right)_D$$

$$\frac{\sigma_s \times 1500}{200 \times 10^3} = 0.5 \left(\frac{\sigma_b \times 2000}{83 \times 10^3}\right)$$

$$\sigma_s = 1.606\ \sigma_b \qquad \qquad \text{... (i)}$$

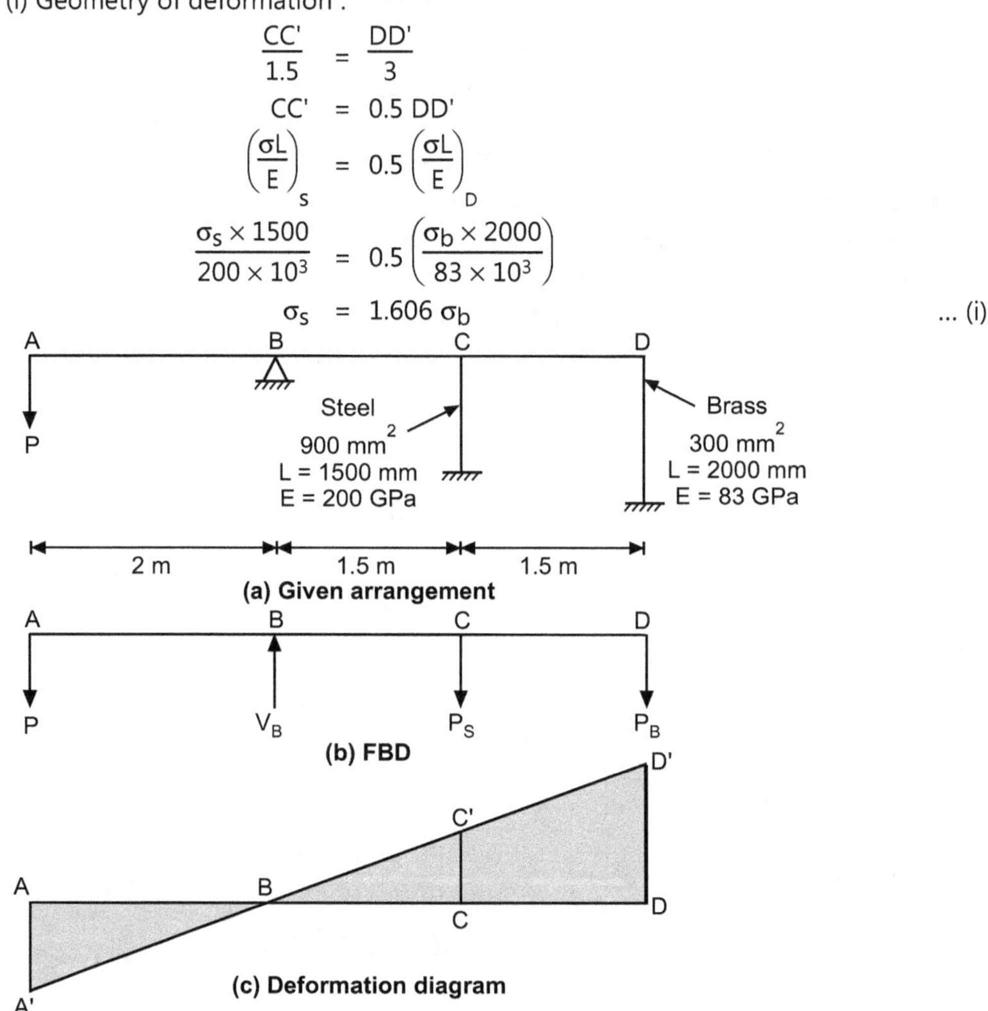


**Fig. 2.48**

(ii)    Stresses :

Let,                                $\sigma_S$ = 150 MPa                    put in (i)

∴                                   $\sigma_b$ = 93.4 MPa > 70 MPa                        ∴ Not allowed

Let,                                $\sigma_b$ = 70 MPa            put in (i)

∴                                   $\sigma_S$ = 112.42 MPa < 150 MPa  ∴ OK

(iii) Forces :                      $P_S$ = $\sigma_S\ A_S$ = $112.42 \times 900 \times 10^{-3}$ = 101.78 kN            ... (ii)

$P_b$ = $\sigma_b\ A_b$ = $70 \times 300 \times 10^{-3}$ = 21 kN

(iv) Safe value of (P),

From FBD,  $\Sigma\,M_B = 0$

$$2\,P - 1.5\,P_s - 3\,P_b = 0 \qquad \text{... (iii)}$$

Put $P_s$ and $P_b$ from (ii) in (iii),

$$2\,P - 1.5 \times 101.78 - 3 \times 21 = 0$$

$\therefore \qquad P = \textbf{107.835 kN}$

**Example 2.41 :** *A uniform bar AB of length L is suspended in a horizontal position under its own weight by two vertical wires attached to it's ends. Both wires are made of same material and have the same cross-sectional area, but the lengths are $L_1$ and $L_2$. Derive a formula for the distance x (from A) to the point on the bar where a vertical load P should be applied if the bar is to remain horizontal.*

**Solution : Data :** $A_{AC} = A_{BD}$, $E_{AC} = E_{BD}$.

**Required :** Expression for distance 'x'.

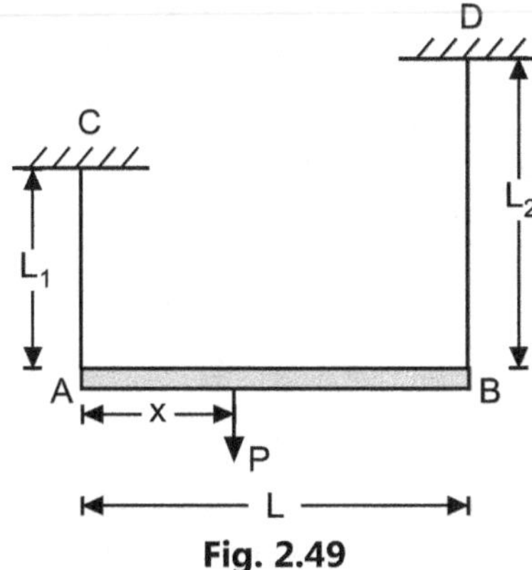


**Fig. 2.49**

Let $P_1$ and $P_2$ be the forces in wires CA and DB.

$\therefore$  Moment @ CA = 0.

$\therefore$
$$P \times x = P_2 \times L$$
$$P_1 + P_2 = P$$

As bar remains horizontal,
$$\delta l_{AC} = \delta l_{BD}$$

$$\frac{P_1 L_1}{AE} = \frac{P_2 L_2}{AE}$$

$$P_1 L_1 = P_2 L_2$$

$\therefore$
$$\frac{P_1}{P_2} = \frac{L_2}{L_1}$$

$$P_1 = P - P_2 = P - \frac{P_1 L_1}{L_2}$$

$$P_1 = \frac{P L_2 - P_1 L_1}{L_2}$$

$$P\,(L_2 + L_1) = P L_2$$

$$\frac{P_1\,(L_2 + L_1)}{L_2}\,x = P_2 \times L$$

$$\frac{P_1}{P_2}\, x = \frac{L_2 \times L}{(L_2 + L_1)}$$

$$\frac{L_2}{L_1}\, x = \frac{L_2 \times L}{(L_2 + L_1)}$$

$$x = \left(\frac{L L_1}{L_2 + L_1}\right)$$

**Example 2.42 :** *Three wires of same material and same cross-sectional area supports load 'P' as shown. Wire no. 1 is 1 m long while wires 2 and 3 are longer by 0.5 mm and 1 mm respectively. Determine the load P which will induce the tensile stress of 250 MPa in wire no. 1. Take c/s area = 10 mm$^2$, E = 200 GPa.*

**Data :** A = 10 mm$^2$ , $\sigma_1$ = 250 MPa,

L$_1$ = 1m, E = 200 GPa.

**Required :** Load P.

**Concept :** Find elongation of each wire and hence forces in them. P = P$_1$ + P$_2$ + P$_3$

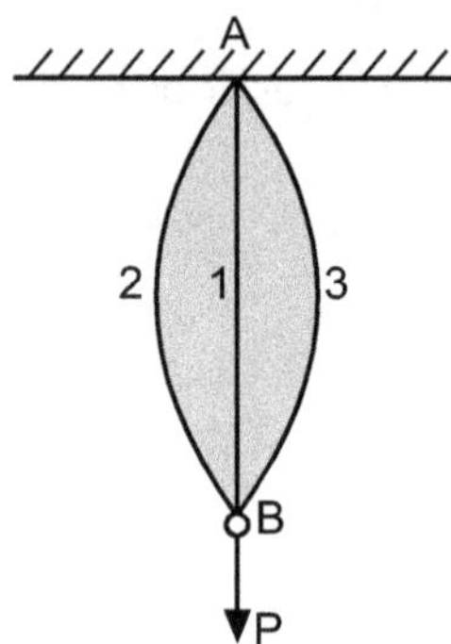


**Fig. 2.50 : Given arrangement**

**Solution :** (i)     $P_1 = \sigma_1 A_1 = 250 \times 10 = 2500$ N

∴     $(\delta L)_1 = \left(\frac{\sigma L}{E}\right)_1 = \left(\frac{250 \times 1000}{200 \times 10^3}\right) = 1.25$ mm

∴     $(\delta L)_2 = 1.25 - 0.5$ mm $= 0.75$ mm

$(\delta L)_3 = 1.25 - 1 = 0.25$ mm

(ii)     $(\delta L)_2 = \left(\frac{\sigma L}{E}\right)_2$

$0.75 = \dfrac{\sigma_2 \times 1000}{200 \times 10^3}$

∴     $\sigma_2 = 150$ MPa

∴     $P_2 = \sigma_2 A_2 = 150 \times 10 = 1500$ N

$(\delta L)_3 = \left(\frac{\sigma L}{E}\right)_3$

$0.25 = \dfrac{\sigma_3 \times 1000}{200 \times 10^3}$

∴     $\sigma_3 = 50$ MPa

∴     $P_3 = \sigma_3 A_3 = 50 \times 10 = 500$ N

∴     Total P $= P_1 + P_2 + P_3$

$$= 2500 + 1500 + 500 = 4500 \text{ N}$$
$$= \mathbf{4.5 \text{ kN}}$$

**Example 2.43 :** *Three wires made of same material and having same c/s area supports load P as shown in Fig. 2.51 (a). Determine stress in each wire in terms of 'P' and 'α'.*

**Data :** As shown in Fig. 2.51 (a).

**Required :** Stress in each wire in terms of 'P' and 'α'.

**Concept :** Statically indeterminate, statics and compatibility.

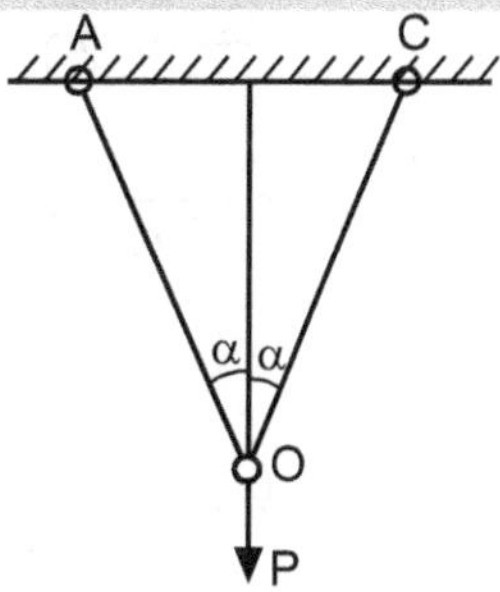

**(a) Given arrangement**

**Solution :** (i) Equation of statics :

Let,
$$T_{OB} = T_1$$
$$T_{OA} = T_{OC} = T_2$$
$$\Sigma F_y = 0$$
$$T_1 + 2T_2 \cos \alpha = P \qquad \ldots (i)$$

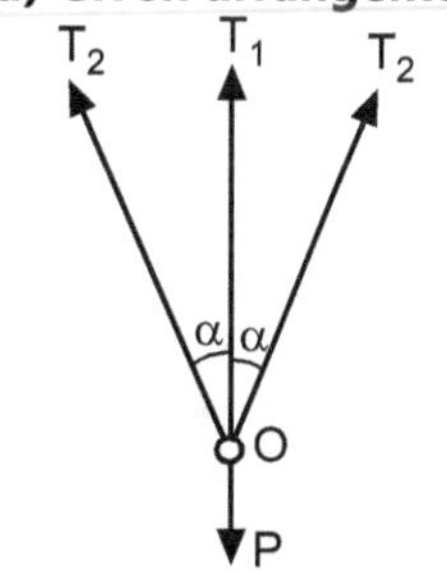

**(b) FBD of joint 'O'**

**Fig. 2.51**

(ii)　Compatibility :

Let elongation of OB = $\delta L$

∴　　Elongation of OA = $\delta L \cos \alpha$

∴
$$\delta L = \left(\frac{PL}{AE}\right)_{OB}$$
$$= \frac{T_1 \times L_{OB}}{AE}$$
$$\delta L \cos \alpha = \left(\frac{PL}{AE}\right)_{OA \text{ or } OC}$$
$$= \frac{T_2 \times L_{OA}}{AE}$$

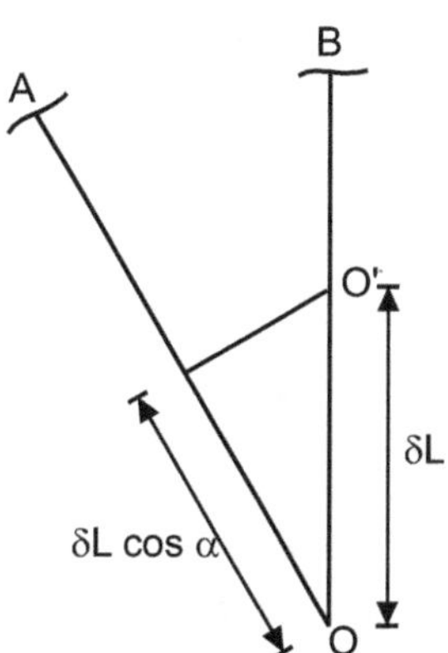

**Fig. 2.51 : (c) Displacement of joint 'O'**

∴
$$\delta L = \frac{T_1 \times L_{OB}}{AE} = \frac{T_2 \times L_{OA}}{AE \cos \alpha}$$

Also, $L_{OA}$
$$= \frac{L_{OB}}{\cos \alpha}$$

$$T_1 \times L_{OB} = \frac{T_2 \cdot L_{OB} / \cos \alpha}{\cos \alpha}$$

$$T_1 = \frac{T_2}{\cos^2 \alpha} \qquad \text{... (ii)}$$

(iii) Put equation (ii) in (i),

$$\frac{T_2}{\cos^2 \alpha} + 2\,T_2 \cos \alpha = P$$

$$T_2 \left( \frac{1}{\cos^2 \alpha} + 2 \cos \alpha \right) = P$$

$$\therefore \quad T_2 = \frac{P \cos^2 \alpha}{1 + 2 \cos^3 \alpha}$$

$$\sigma_{OA} = \sigma_{OC} = \frac{T_2}{A} = \left( \frac{P \cos^2 \alpha}{1 + 2 \cos^3 \alpha} \right) \frac{1}{A}$$

$$T_1 = \frac{T_2}{\cos^2 \alpha}$$

$$= \frac{P \cos^2 \alpha}{1 + 2 \cos^3 \alpha} \cdot \frac{1}{\cos^2 \alpha} = \frac{P}{1 + 2 \cos^3 \alpha}$$

$$\sigma_{OB} = \frac{T_1}{A}$$

$$= \left( \frac{P}{1 + 2 \cos^3 \alpha} \right) \frac{1}{A}$$

---

**Example 2.44 :** *Find the safe load 'W' that can be supported at 'B' if allowable stress for steel and aluminium is 120 MPa and 100 MPa respectively. Take $E_s$ = 200 GPa, $E_a$ = 80 GPa.*

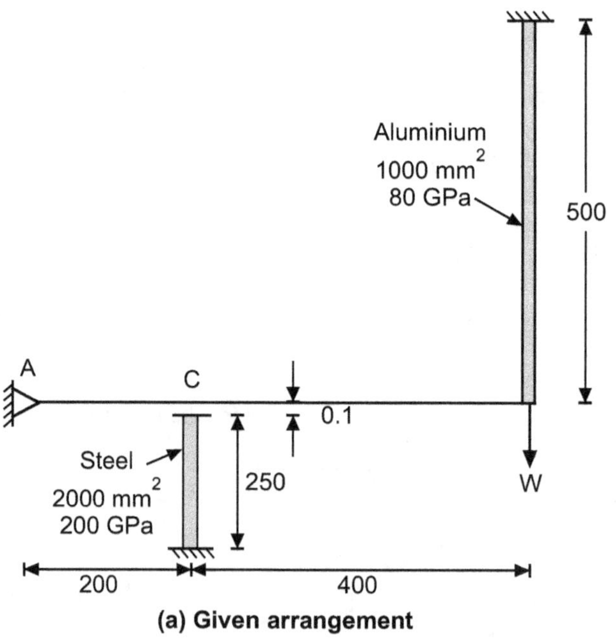


**(a) Given arrangement**

---

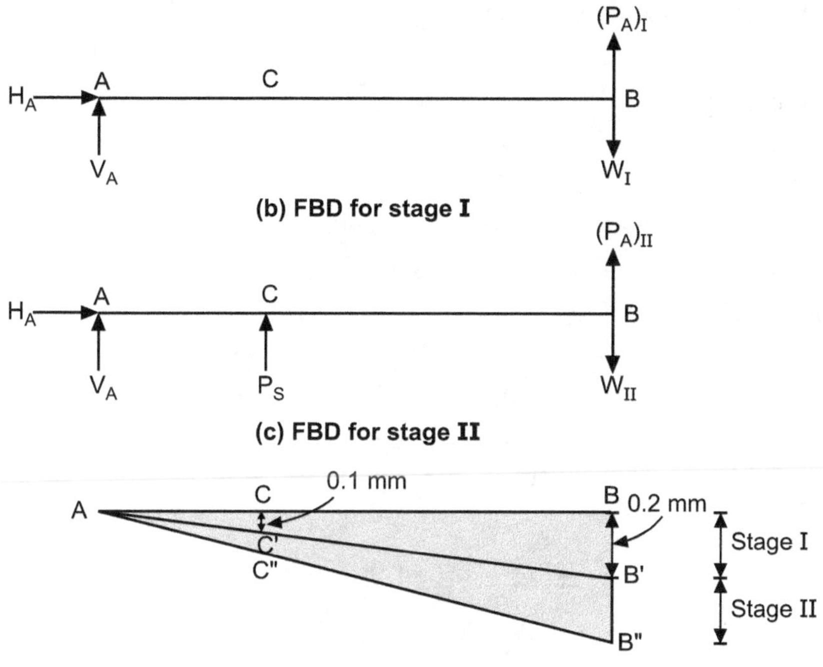



**Fig. 2.52**

**Data :** $\sigma_S > 120$ MPa, $\sigma_A > 100$ MPa, $E_s = 200$ GPa, $E_a = 80$ GPa.

**Required :** Safe load W.

**Concept :** Stage I : Gap at C present : only aluminium bar effective.

∴    No stress in steel.

Stage II : Gap at C closes : aluminium and steel bars both are effective.

**Solution :** (i) Analysis for stage I :

CC' = 0.1 mm

∴ $$BB' = \frac{0.1}{200} \times 600 = 0.3 \text{ mm}$$

Elongation of aluminium bar = BB' = 0.3 mm

∴ Stress in aluminium bar $$= \frac{BB' \times E}{L}$$

$$= \frac{0.3 \times 80 \times 10^3}{500}$$

$$= 48 \text{ MPa}$$

∴ Force in aluminium bar for stage I

$$= (P_A)_I = 48 \times 1000$$

$$= 48000 \text{ N} = 48 \text{ kN}$$

From FBD of stage I,

$\Sigma M_A = 0$ gives,

$$(P_A)_I \times 600 - (W)_I \times 600 = 0$$

$$(P_A)_I = W_I = 48 \text{ kN}$$

(ii)  Analysis of stage II :

Equation of statics :

$\Sigma M_A = 0$ gives

$$P_S \times 200 + (P_A)_{II} \times 600 = W_{II} \times 600$$

$$P_S + 3 (P_A)_{II} = 3 W_{II} \qquad \dots \text{(i)}$$

Equation of compatibility :

$$\frac{C'C''}{200} = \frac{B'B''}{600}$$

$$B'B'' = 3 C'C''$$

$$\therefore \qquad \left(\frac{\sigma L}{E}\right)_A = 3 \left(\frac{\sigma L}{E}\right)_S$$

$$\frac{\sigma_A \times 500}{80 \times 10^3} = 3 \left(\frac{\sigma_S \times 250}{200 \times 10^3}\right)$$

$$\sigma_A = 0.6 \, \sigma_S \qquad \dots \text{(ii)}$$

Reserved stress in aluminium bar  = Allowable stress – stress consumed in stage I

= 100 – 48 = 52 MPa

If stress in aluminium is allowed to reach to its allowable value, then corresponding stress in

steel = $\sigma_S$

$$= \frac{\sigma_A}{0.6} = \frac{52}{0.6}$$

$$= 86.67 \text{ MPa}$$

$$< 120 \text{ MPa (allowable stress in steel)} \qquad \dots \text{OK}$$

$\therefore$  For stage II,  $\sigma_A = 52 \text{ MPa and } \sigma_S = 86.67 \text{ MPa}$

$\therefore$  $(P_A)_{II} = 52 \times 1000 = 52000 \text{ N} = 52 \text{ kN}$

$P_S = 86.67 \times 2000 = 173.34 \times 10^3 \text{ N} = 173.34 \text{ kN}$

Put these values in equation (i),

$$173.34 + 3 \times 52 = 3 W_{II}$$

$\therefore$  $W_{II} = 109.78 \text{ MPa}$

$\therefore$  $W = W_I + W_{II} = 48 + 109.78 = \textbf{157.78 kN}$

**Note :** We have assumed that stress in aluminium reaches to its allowable value and corresponding stress in steel was observed to be less than its allowable stress. In case if this was not satisfied, stress in steel shall be allowed to reach to its allowable value and corresponding stress in aluminium shall be observed to be less than its allowable stress. One of the above two conditions will govern the safe value of load W for stage II.

---

**Example 2.45 :** *Four G.I. wires of 4 mm diameter spaced at an interval of 500 mm as shown in Fig. 2.53 (a) are jointly supporting a rigid bar. Assuming negligible weight of the bar, find stresses in each rod due to load of 3 kN supported at C.*

---

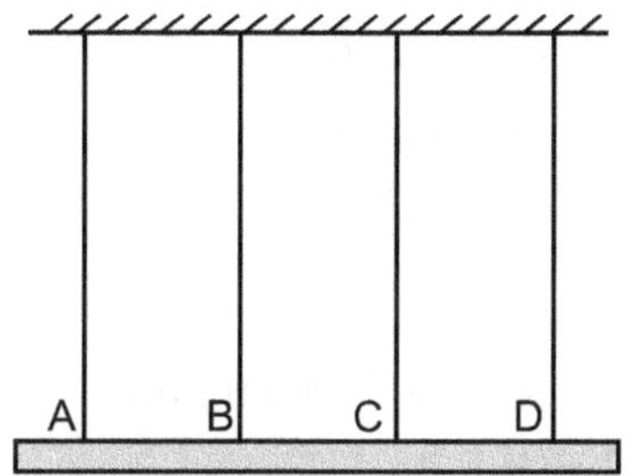

**(a) Right bar supported by wires**

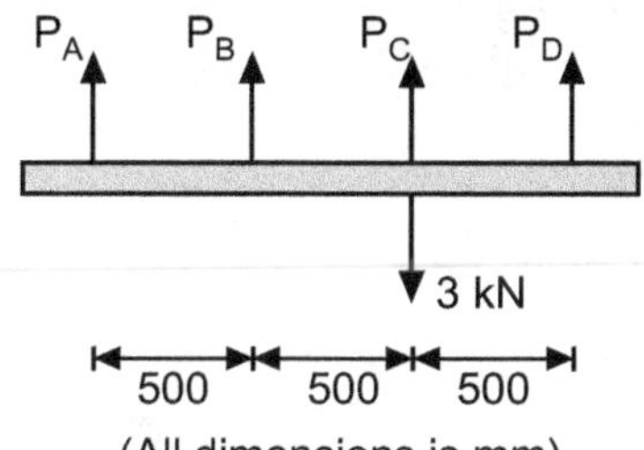

**(b) FBD of rigid bar**

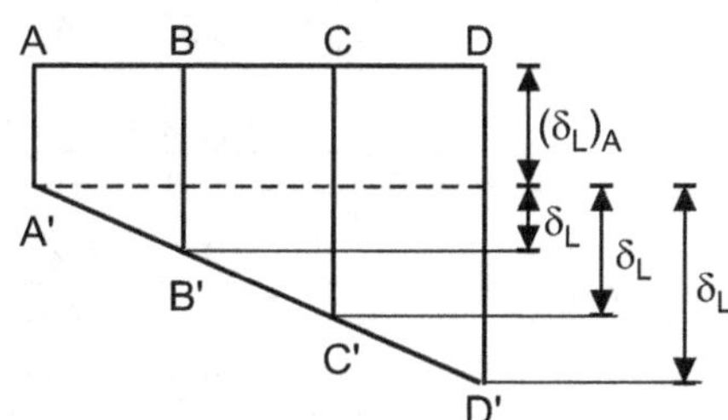

**(c) Deformation of wires**

**Fig. 2.53**

**Data :** As shown in Fig. 2.53 (a).

**Required :** Stresses in each wire.

**Concept :** Statically indeterminate. Equations of statics and compatibility.

**Solution :** (i) Equations of statics :

Let $P_A$, $P_B$, $P_C$ and $P_D$ be the forces in wires A, B, C and D respectively.

Taking moments @ $P_A$,

$$P_B \times 500 + P_C \times 1000 - 3 \times 1000 + P_D \times 1500 = 0$$

$\therefore \qquad\qquad P_B + 2\,P_C + 3\,P_D = 6 \qquad\qquad\qquad \text{... (i)}$

And $\Sigma F_y = 0, \qquad P_A + P_B + P_C + P_D = 3 \qquad\qquad\qquad \text{... (ii)}$

(ii)   Equation of compatibility :

Let,

$$\begin{aligned}
(\delta L)_A &= \text{Elongation of wire A from geometry of Fig. 2.53 (b)} \\
\delta L_A + \delta L &= \text{Elongation of wire B} \\
\delta L_A + 2\delta L &= \text{Elongation of wire C} \\
\delta L_A + 3\delta L &= \text{Elongation of wire D}
\end{aligned}$$

Also, $P_A$ is the force which causes elongation = $\delta L_A$

Let, $P'$ be the force which causes elongation = $\delta L$

$$\therefore \qquad P_B = P_A + P'$$
$$P_C = P_A + 2P' \qquad \qquad \text{... (iii)}$$
$$P_D = P_A + 3P'$$

(iii) Solution of equations : Putting equation (iii) in equation (i), we get

$$P_A + P' + 2\,(P_A + 2P') + 3\,(P_A + 3P') = 6$$
$$6P_A + 14\,P' = 6 \qquad \qquad \text{... (iv)}$$

Putting equation (iii) in equation (ii), we get

$$P_A + (P_A + P') + (P_A + 2P') + (P_A + 3P') = 3$$
$$\therefore \qquad 4P_A + 6P' = 3 \qquad \qquad \text{... (v)}$$

Solving equations (iv) and (v),

$$P_A = 0.3 \text{ kN}$$
$$P' = 0.3 \text{ kN}$$

(iv) Stresses in each wire :

$$\text{Area of each wire} = A = \frac{\pi}{4}\,(4)^2 = 12.56 \text{ mm}^2$$

$$\sigma_A = \frac{P_A}{A} = \frac{0.3 \times 10^3}{12.56} = \mathbf{23.89 \ MPa}$$

$$\sigma_B = \frac{P_B}{A} = \frac{P_A + P'}{A} = \frac{(0.3 + 0.3)\,10^3}{12.56} = \mathbf{47.77 \ MPa}$$

$$\sigma_C = \frac{P_C}{A} = \frac{P_A + 2P'}{A} = \frac{(0.3 + 2 \times 0.3)\,10^3}{12.56} = \mathbf{71.65 \ MPa}$$

$$\sigma_D = \frac{P_D}{A} = \frac{P_A + 3P'}{A} = \frac{(0.3 + 3 \times 0.3)\,10^3}{12.56} = \mathbf{95.54 \ MPa}$$

**Example 2.46 :** *A load of 5 kN is suspended from (i) a frictionless pulley and placed on a continuous rope as shown in Fig. 2.54 (a) and (ii) a rigid platform supported by two ropes as shown in Fig. 2.54 (b). The platform remaining horizontal before and after being loaded. If the area of cross section of each rope is 50 mm², find the stresses in the ropes and the vertical displacement of the load in each case. Assume E = 200 GPa.*

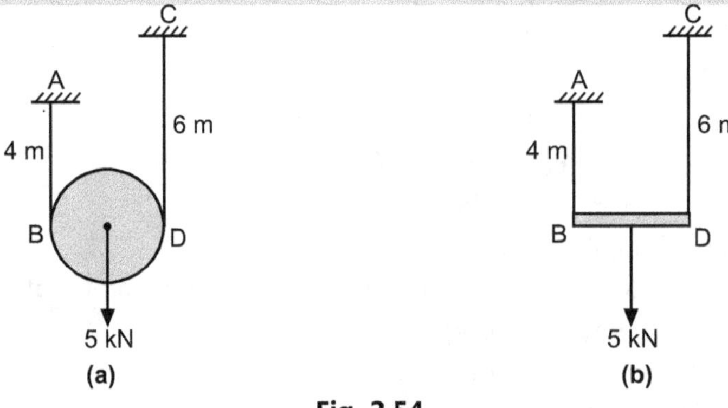


**Fig. 2.54**

**Data :** As shown in Fig. 2.54 (a) and (b), cross-sectional area = 50 mm$^2$,

E = 200 × 10$^3$ MPa and vertical displacement of the platform.

**Concept :** $\delta l_{AB} = \delta l_{CD}$ , $P_{AB} + P_{CD} = 50$ kN

**Solution : Case (i) :** $\qquad \delta l_{AB} = \left(\dfrac{Pl}{AE}\right)_{AB}$ , $\delta l_{CD} = \left(\dfrac{Pl}{AE}\right)_{CD}$

$\therefore \qquad \left(\dfrac{Pl}{AE}\right)_{AB} = \left(\dfrac{Pl}{AE}\right)_{CD}$

$$\dfrac{P_{AB} \times 4000}{50 \times 200} = \dfrac{P_{CD} \times 6000}{50 \times 200}$$

$\therefore \qquad P_{AB} = 1.5\, P_{CD}$

$\therefore \qquad P_{AB} = 30$ kN

$\qquad\quad P_{CD} = 20$ kN

$\therefore \qquad \sigma_{AB} = \dfrac{P_{AB}}{A_{AB}} = \dfrac{30 \times 10^3}{50} = \textbf{600 mm}^2$

$\qquad\quad \sigma_{CD} = \dfrac{P_{CD}}{A_{CD}} = \dfrac{20 \times 10^3}{50} = \textbf{400 mm}^2$

Vertical displacement of pulley,

$$\delta = \left(\dfrac{Pl}{AE}\right)_{AB} = \dfrac{30 \times 10^3 \times 4000}{50 \times 200 \times 10^3}$$

$\therefore \qquad \delta = \textbf{12 mm}$

**Case (ii) :** Same as case (i).

---

**Example 2.47 :** *The bar AB held between rigid supports, has cross-sectional area $A_1$ from A to C and $2A_1$ from C to B. Find the displacement at point D where the load P acts. What are the reactions at supports A and B ? Refer Fig. 2.55.*

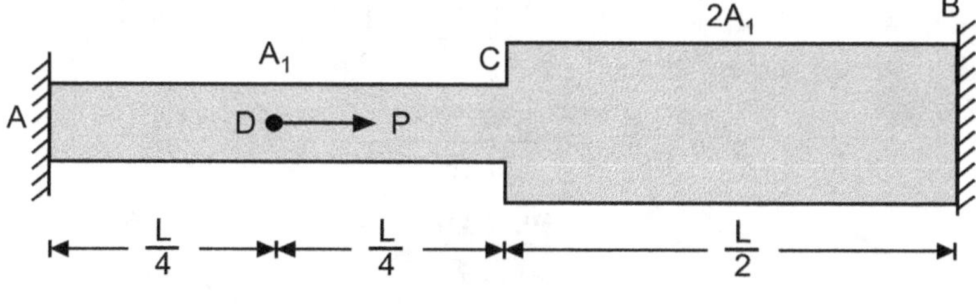


**Fig. 2.55**

**Data :** As shown in Fig. 2.55.

**Required :** Displacement at point D.

**Concept :** Standard formulae.

**Solution :**

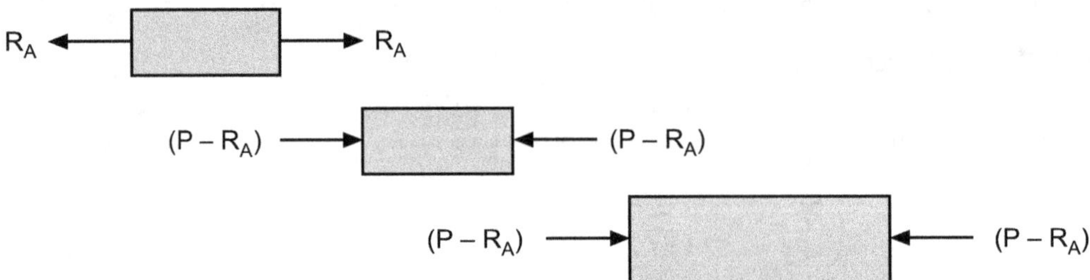

**Fig. 2.56**

Bar AB is in tension, and DC and CB are in compression.

$$\therefore \qquad \delta l_{AB} = \delta l_{DC} + \delta l_{CB}$$

$$\therefore \qquad \frac{R_A \times 10^3}{A_1 \times E} \times \frac{L}{4} = \frac{(P - R_A) \times 10^3}{A_1 \times E} \times \frac{L}{4} + \frac{(P - R_A) \times 10^3}{2A_1 \times E} \times \frac{L}{2}$$

$$R_A = P - R_A + P - R_A$$

$$\therefore \qquad 3R_A = 2P$$

$$\therefore \qquad R_A = \frac{2P}{3}$$

$$\therefore \qquad R_A = \frac{2P}{3} \; (\leftarrow)$$

$$R_B = \frac{P}{3} \; (\leftarrow)$$

$$\text{Displacement at point D} = \frac{Pl}{AE}$$

$$= \frac{R_A \times 10^3}{A_1 \times E} \times \frac{L}{4}$$

$$= \frac{2P \times 10^3}{3A_1 E} \times \frac{L}{4}$$

$$= \frac{PL \times 10^3}{6A_1 E}$$

where P is in kN.

**Example 2.48 :** *The assembly in Fig. 2.57 (a) is made of same material. Find the load ratio $P_2/P_1$ such that the vertical deflection of point C is zero. Your answer should be in terms of areas $A_1$, $A_2$ and lengths $L_1$, $L_2$, $L_3$ and $L_4$.*

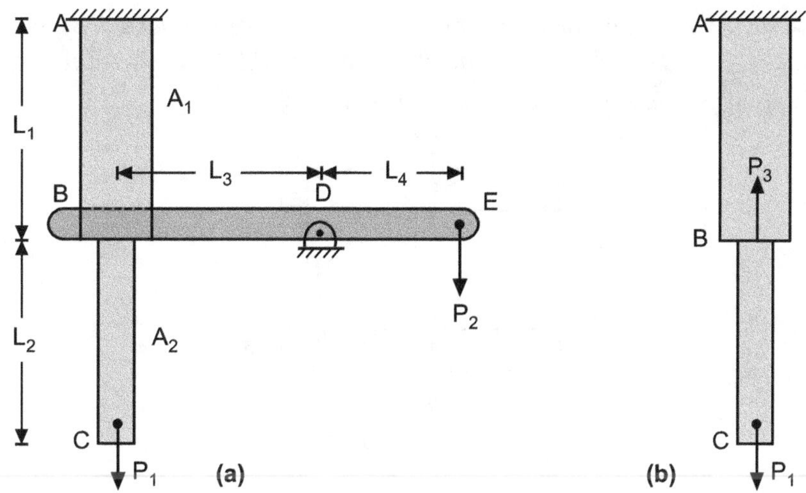

**Fig. 2.57**

**Data :** As shown in Fig. 2.57 (a).

**Required :** $P_2/P_1$.

**Solution :** Bar AB is in compression and bar BC is in tension. If deformation of both is same then deflection at point C is zero. Let $P_3$ be the force acting at point B.

$$\therefore \quad \delta l_{AB} = \delta l_{CB}$$

$$\frac{P_1 L_2}{A_2 E} = \frac{(P_3 - P_1)\, L_1}{A_1 E}$$

$$\therefore \quad \frac{P_1 L_2}{A_2} = \frac{(P_3 - P_1)\, L_1}{A_1}$$

$$\therefore \quad P_1\left(\frac{L_2}{A_2} + \frac{L_1}{A_1}\right) = \frac{P_3 L_1}{A_1}$$

$$\therefore \quad P_3 = P_1 \cdot \frac{A_1}{L_1}\left(\frac{L_2}{A_2} + \frac{L_1}{A_1}\right)$$

$$\frac{\delta l_B}{L_3} = \frac{\delta l_E}{L_4}$$

$$\frac{P_3 L_3}{AE} = \frac{P_2 L_4}{AE}$$

$$\therefore \quad P_3 = P_2 \cdot \frac{L_4}{L_3}$$

$$P_1 \cdot \frac{A_1}{L_1}\left(\frac{L_2}{A_2} + \frac{L_1}{A_1}\right) = \frac{P_2 L_4}{L_3}$$

$$\frac{P_2}{P_1} = \frac{L_3}{L_4}\left(1 + \frac{L_2 A_1}{A_2 L_1}\right)$$

**Example 2.49 :** *Two horizontal rigid bars AB and CD are connected by wires, of length L, modulus of elasticity E, and diameters $d_1$ and $d_2$. Refer Fig. 2.58. What is the increase ($\delta$) in the distance between points E and F where vertical loads P act ?*

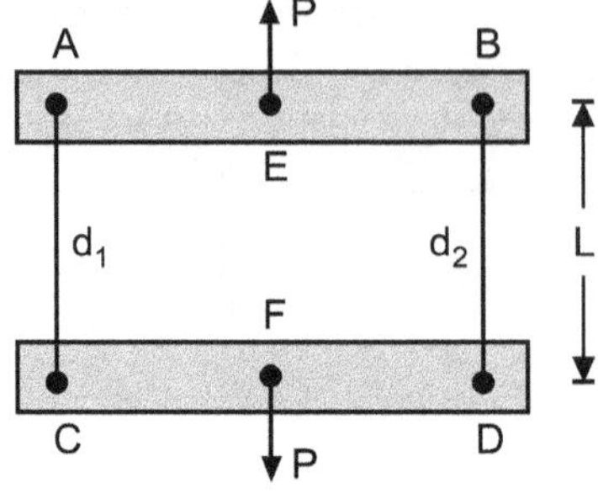


**Fig. 2.58**

**Data :** As shown in Fig. 2.58.

**Required :** Increase ($\delta$) in distance between E and F.

**Solution :** Let $P_A$ and $P_B$ be the forces in wires AC and BD respectively.

$\therefore$    Moment @ AC = 0

$\therefore$
$$P \times \frac{L}{2} = P_B \times L$$

$\therefore$
$$P_B = \frac{P}{2}$$

$\therefore$
$$P_A = \frac{P}{2}$$

Let $\delta l_{AB}$ and $\delta l_{BD}$ be the displacements in members AC and BD.

$\therefore$
$$\delta l_{AB} = \frac{P_A L}{\frac{\pi}{4} d_1^2 \times E} = \frac{2PL}{\pi d_1^2 E}$$

$$\delta l_{BD} = \frac{P_B \times L}{\frac{\pi}{4} \times d_2^2 E} = \frac{2PL}{\pi d_2^2 E}$$

As point E is between AB, so deflection at E is half that of at A and at B.

$\therefore$
$$\delta l_{EF} = \frac{1}{2} [\delta l_{AB} + \delta l_{BD}] = \frac{1}{2} \left[ \frac{2PL}{\pi d_1^2 E} + \frac{2PL}{\pi d_2^2 E} \right]$$

$$= \frac{PL}{\pi E} \left[ \frac{1}{d_1^2} + \frac{1}{d_2^2} \right]$$

**Example 2.50 :** *A 10 m long copper bar of cross-sectional area 8100 mm² and modulus of elasticity 103 GPa under a tensile load of P = 500 kN hangs from a pin supported by two steel pillars. Refer Fig. 2.59. Each pillar has height 1 m, cross-sectional area 7500 mm² and modulus of elasticity 200 GPa. Determine the displacement $\delta$ at point A.*

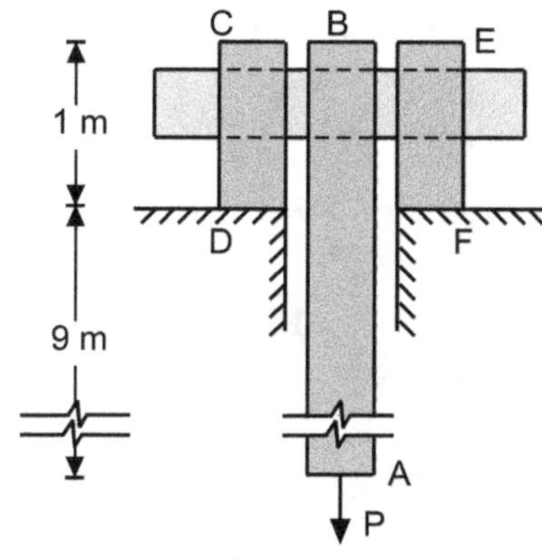

**Fig. 2.59**

**Data :** P = 500 kN, $E_C$ = 103 GPa, $A_C$ = 8100 mm², $E_S$ = 200 GPa, $A_S$ = 7500 mm².

**Required :** Displacement at point A.

**Solution :** Both ends of bar AB are free.

$$\therefore \qquad \delta_A - \delta_B = \left(\frac{PL}{AE}\right)_C$$

In this mechanism, rods CD and EF are in compression. Both are same.

$$\therefore \qquad P_S = \frac{P_C}{2} = \frac{500}{2} = 250 \text{ kN}$$

$$\therefore \qquad \delta_A = \left(\frac{PL}{AE}\right)_C + \delta_B = \left(\frac{PL}{AE}\right)_C + \left(\frac{PL}{AE}\right)_S$$

$$= \frac{500 \times 10^3 \times 10 \times 10^3}{8100 \times 103 \times 10^3} + \frac{250 \times 10^3 \times 1 \times 10^3}{7500 \times 200 \times 10^3}$$

$$= \textbf{6.16 mm}$$

**Example 2.51 :** *A rigid bar is suspended by two vertical rods and hangs in a horizontal position by its own weight (Refer Fig. 2.60 (a)). The rod at 'A' is of brass, length 3 m, cross-sectional area 1000 mm² and modulus of elasticity $1 \times 10^5$ N/mm². The rod at B is of steel, length 5 m, cross-sectional area 445 mm², modulus of elasticity $2 \times 10^5$ N/mm². At what distance from A may a vertical load P be applied if the bar is to remain horizontal after the load is applied ?* **(Dec. 2001)**

**Solution :**

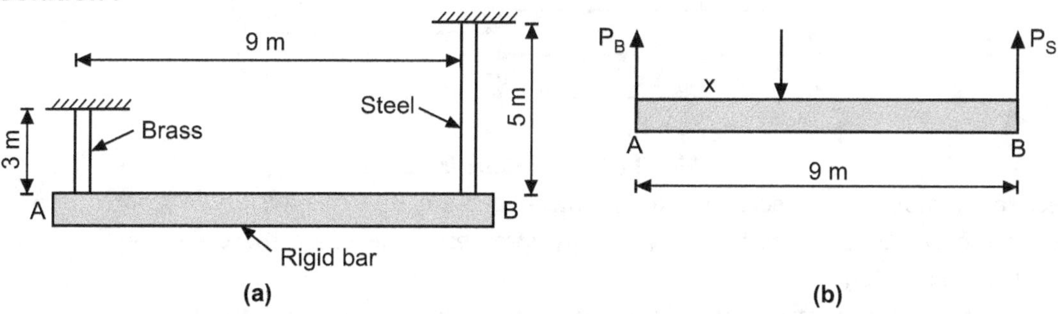

**Fig. 2.60**

(i)    Statics :        $\Sigma F_y = P_B + P_S - P = 0$                    ... (i)

$$\Sigma M_A = -P(x) + P_S(9) = 0 \qquad \text{... (ii)}$$

(ii)  Compatibility :  $(\delta L)_B = (\delta L)_S$

$$\left(\frac{PL}{AE}\right)_B = \left(\frac{PL}{AE}\right)_S$$

$$\frac{P_B \times 3}{1000 \times 1 \times 10^5} = \frac{P_S \times 5}{445 \times 2 \times 10^5}$$

$$\therefore \qquad P_B = \mathbf{1.87\ P_S} \qquad \text{... (iii)}$$

From (i) and (ii),  $P_S = 0.348\ P$

$$P_B = 0.652\ P$$

Put  $P_S = 0.348\ P$ in (ii),

$$\therefore \qquad x = \mathbf{3.132\ m}$$

## 2.10 TEMPERATURE STRESSES

When a member is subjected to temperature change, it is likely to expand or contract. This free expansion or contraction ($\delta L$) is given by

$$\delta L = \alpha t \cdot L \qquad \text{... (2.10)}$$

where,  $\alpha$ = coefficient of thermal expansion

$t$ = change in temperature

$L$ = length of member

$\alpha$ is usually expressed in units of per °C.

When this free expansion or contraction is prevented then only member will be subjected to temperature stresses. In other words, only *statically indeterminate systems* will be subjected to temperature stresses. This temperature stress is given by

$$\sigma = \frac{\delta L \cdot E}{L}$$

$$\sigma = \alpha t E \qquad \text{... (2.11)}$$

It should be noted that, when number is subjected to temperature **rise**, it is likely to expand, and if this expansion is prevented, it is subjected to temperature stress which is **compressive** in nature. Similarly, temperature **fall** will cause **tensile** stresses in a member.

Following are the two situations that we generally come across.

(i)  Members of different cross-sectional areas arranged in series and fixed at both ends.

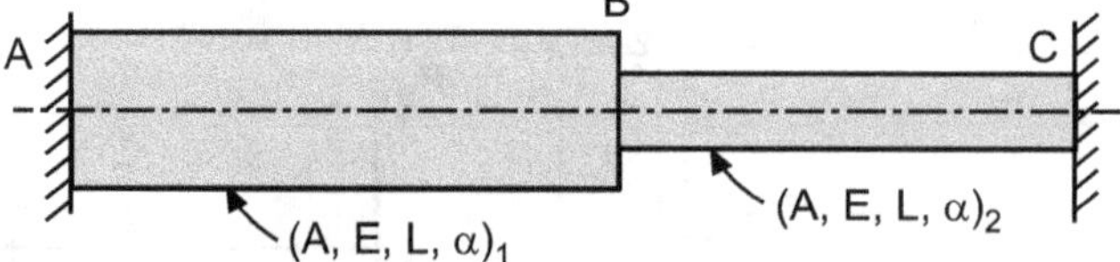


**Fig. 2.61 : Members in series**

If such a member is subjected to temperature change, free expansion or contraction being prevented, it will be subjected to temperature stresses. To evaluate these stresses is a statically indeterminate problem.

The force of internal resistance developed, to prevent the change in length of member as a whole, must be same for both components.

Thus, equation of statics can be written as :

$$P_1 \;=\; P_2$$

i.e.
$$\sigma_1 A_1 \;=\; \sigma_2 A_2 \qquad \ldots (2.12)$$

Equation of compatibility can be written as,

(free change in length possible) – (change in length prevented) = 0

$$[(\alpha\, t\, L)_1 + (\alpha\, t\, L)_2] - \left[\left(\frac{\sigma L}{E}\right)_1 + \left(\frac{\sigma L}{E}\right)_2\right] = 0 \qquad \ldots (2.13)$$

($\because$ change in length of a member as a whole is zero)

Solving equations (2.12) and (2.13), required temperature stresses can be obtained.

In case if any of the support yields, equation (2.13) of compatibility is to be modified as,

$$[(\alpha\, t\, L)_1 - (\alpha\, t\, L)_2] - \left[\left(\frac{\sigma L}{E}\right)_1 + \left(\frac{\sigma L}{E}\right)_2\right] = \text{Amount of yielding of support} \qquad \ldots (2.14)$$

(ii)   Members of two or more materials joined in parallel.

**(a)   Members in parallel**

**(b)   Free expansion of individual members**

**(c)   Actual expansion of composite member**

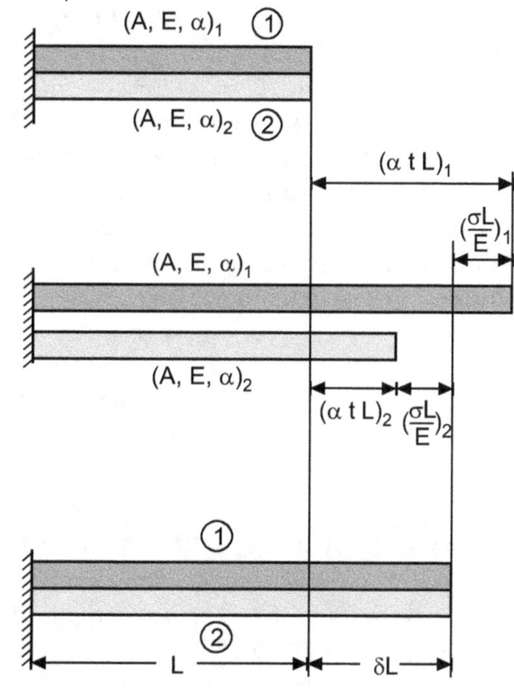


Fig. 2.62

When such a member is subjected to temperature change, actual expansion or contraction of each of the member must be the same.

This actual change in length is different from free change in length as shown in Fig. 2.62.

Hence, members will be subjected to temperature stresses. This is also a statically indeterminate problem.

Equation of statics is same as that of equation (2.12). Since both the components must undergo equal amount of change in length, equation of compatibility can be written as,

$$(\delta L)_1 \;=\; (\delta L)_2$$

$$\left(\alpha t L - \frac{\sigma L}{E}\right)_1 = \left(\alpha t L + \frac{\sigma L}{E}\right)_2$$

The above equation assumes $\alpha_1 > \alpha_2$ as indicated by larger free expansion of member 1 in Fig. 2.62.

Thus, in general, equation of compatibility will be written as,

$$\left(\alpha t L \pm \frac{\sigma L}{E}\right)_1 = \left(\alpha t L \pm \frac{\sigma L}{E}\right)_2 \qquad \qquad ... (2.15)$$

It should be noted that, material having relatively higher value of $\alpha$ will be subjected to compressive stresses, hence the term $\sigma L/E$ for the corresponding material must be assigned –ve sign.

Solving equations (2.12) and (2.15), required temperature stresses can be obtained.

**Example 2.52 :** *A steel rod 1 m long of uniform cross-section is fixed at ends. It is subjected to initial tensile stress of 48 MPa. Find,*

*(a)   Rise in temperature required to make the rod stress free.*

*(b)   Stress in rod if temperature is increased further by 16ºC.*

  *$\alpha = 12 \times 10^{-6}/ºC$ , E = 200 GPa.*

**Data :** L = 1 m, $\sigma$ = 48 MPa , $\alpha = 12 \times 10^{-6}$ /ºC, E = 200 GPa.

**Required :**    (a)   Rise in temperature required to make the rod stress free.

               (b)   Stress in rod if temperature is increased further by 16ºC.

**Concept :** (i) To make the rod stress free, temperature stress = 48 MPa, compressive stress should be developed. (ii) Temperature stress = $\sigma = \alpha t E$.

**Solution :** (i) Rise in temperature :

$$\sigma = \alpha t E$$
$$48 = 12 \times 10^{-6} \times t \times 2 \times 10^5$$

$\therefore$ $\qquad\qquad\qquad\qquad$ t = **20ºC ... (Rise)**

(ii)   Stress in rod : $\qquad \sigma = \alpha t E$
$$= 12 \times 10^{-6} \times 16 \times 2 \times 10^5$$

$\therefore$ $\qquad\qquad\qquad$ $\sigma$ = **38.4 MPa (Compressive)**

**Example 2.53 :** *A steel rod 10 mm $\phi$ and 1 mm long is fixed at ends. If temperature of rod is increased by 50ºC, what will be reaction at supports ? If the rod remains unchanged in length, and if the temperature stress in the rod is to be reduced by 40 %, what should be the yielding of support ? Take E = 100 GPa, $\alpha = 10^{-5}$ /ºC.*

**Data :** d = 10 mm, L = 1 m, t = 50ºC, E = 100 GPa, $\alpha = 10^{-5}$ /ºC.

**Required :** Reaction at supports; yielding of supports.

**Concept :** (i) Reaction at supports = Temperature stress in the member $\times$ cross- sectional area of member.

(ii)   Yielding of support causes decrease in temperature stress.

**Solution :** (i) Geometric properties :

$$\text{Area of steel rod} = A = \frac{\pi}{4}(10)^2 = 78.54 \text{ mm}^2$$

(ii)   Reaction at supports :

$$\sigma = \alpha t E$$

$$= 10^{-5} \times 50 \times 100 \times 10^3$$
$$= 50 \text{ MPa (Compressive)}$$
$$\text{Reaction} = R = \sigma \cdot A$$
$$= 50 \times 78.54 = \textbf{3.9 kN}$$

(iii) Yielding of support :

Stress consumed in yielding of support = 40 % of 50 MPa
$$= 20 \text{ MPa}$$

∴           Yielding of support $= \Delta L = \dfrac{\sigma L}{E} = \dfrac{20 \times 1000}{100 \times 10^3} = \textbf{0.2 mm}$

**Example 2.54 :** *Rails of 10 m length are laid on the track in the morning. The atmospheric temperature then was 12°C. A gap of 1.5 mm was kept between two consecutive rails. At what maximum temperature the rails will remain stress free ? If the temperature is raised further by 10°C, what will be the magnitude and nature of the stresses induced in the rails ?*
*Take α = 12 ×10⁻⁶ /°C, E = 200 GPa.*

**Data :** L = 10 m, ΔL = 1.5 mm, $\alpha = 12 \times 10^{-6}$ /°C, E = 200 GPa.

**Required :** Maximum temperature the rails will remain stress free, magnitude and nature of the stresses induced in the rails when temperature is further raised by 10°C.

**Concept :** Till the time there is a gap between consecutive rails, no temperature stresses are induced.

**Solution :** (i) Let t be the temperature at stress free condition.

Extension for individual rail = 1.5 mm

$$\Delta L = \alpha t L$$
∴           $1.5 = 12 \times 10^{-6} \times (t - 12) \times 10 \times 10^3$
∴           $t = \textbf{24.5 °C}$

(ii)          $\sigma = \alpha t E$
$$= 12 \times 10^{-6} \times 10 \times 200 \times 10^3$$
$$= \textbf{24 MPa (Compressive)}$$

**Example 2.55 :** *Data as shown in Fig. 2.63 below. Find the thermal stresses if the temperature rises by 10 °K. Assume $L_1 = L_2 = L$, $A_1 = 2A_2$. Take α = 11.7 ×10⁻⁶ /°K,    E = 200 GPa.*

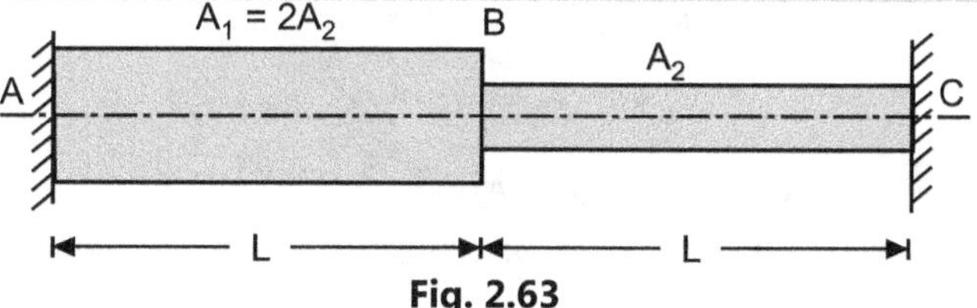


**Fig. 2.63**

**Data :** As shown in Fig. 2.63.

**Required :** Thermal stresses.

**Concept :** Statically indeterminate : Statics and Compatibility.

**Solution :** (i) Equation of statics :

$$\sigma_1 A_1 = \sigma_2 A_2$$
$$\sigma_1 (2A_2) = \sigma_2 A_2$$

∴                          $\sigma_1 = \dfrac{\sigma_2}{2}$                          ... (i) (ii)　Compatibility :

$$(\alpha\, t\, L)_1 + (\alpha\, t\, L)_2 - \left[\left(\frac{\sigma L}{E}\right)_1 + \left(\frac{\sigma L}{E}\right)_2\right] = 0$$

$$2\,\alpha\, t \;=\; \frac{\sigma_1}{E_1} + \frac{\sigma_2}{E_2}$$

∴　　　$(2 \times 11.7 \times 10^{-6} \times 10)\, E \;=\; \sigma_1 + \sigma_2$

∴　　　　　　$\sigma_1 + \sigma_2 \;=\; 46.8\ \text{MPa}$　　　　　　... (ii)

(iii) Thermal stresses :

Solving equations (i) and (ii),　　$\sigma_1 \;=\; \dfrac{\sigma_2}{2}$ from (i) and (ii)

$$\sigma_1 \;=\; \textbf{15.6 MPa (Compressive)}$$
$$\sigma_2 \;=\; \textbf{31.2 MPa (Compressive)}$$

**Example 2.56 :** *Data as shown in Fig. 2.64 below. If the temperature of the bar is raised through 14 °K, find force exerted on supports.*
*$\alpha_S = 11 \times 10^{-6}$ /°K , $E_S = 210$ GPa; $\alpha_B = 20 \times 10^{-6}$ /°K , $E_B = 85$ MPa.*

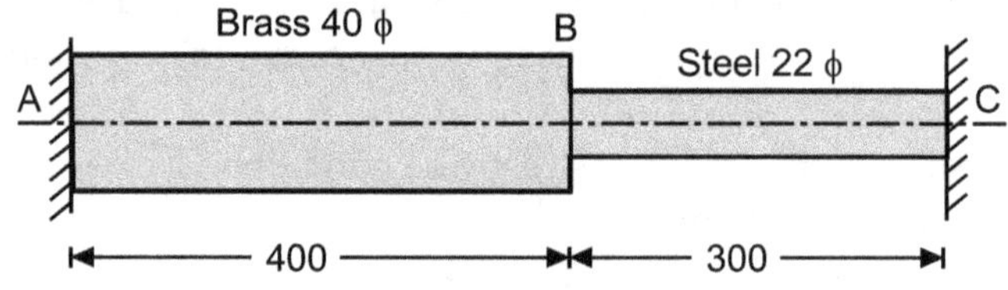


(All dimensions in mm)

**Fig. 2.64 : Given member**

**Data :** As shown in Fig. 2.64.
**Required :** Force exerted on supports.
**Concept :** Statically indeterminate : Statics and Compatibility.
**Solution :** (i) Geometric properties :

Area of steel,　　　　$A_S \;=\; \dfrac{\pi}{4}(22)^2 = 380.12\ \text{mm}^2$

Area of brass,　　　　$A_B \;=\; \dfrac{\pi}{4}(40)^2 = 1256.63\ \text{mm}^2$

(ii)　　　　　　$(\sigma \cdot A)_S \;=\; (\sigma \cdot A)_B$

　　　　$\sigma_S \times 380.12 \;=\; \sigma_B \times 1256.63$

∴　　　　　　$\sigma_S \;=\; 3.30\,\sigma_B$　　　　　　... (i)

(iii) Compatibility :

$$(\alpha\, t\, L)_S + (\alpha\, t\, L)_B - \left[\left(\frac{\sigma L}{E}\right)_S + \left(\frac{\sigma L}{E}\right)_B\right] \;=\; 0$$

$$(11 \times 10^{-6} \times 14 \times 300) + (20 \times 10^{-6} \times 14 \times 400) \;=\; \frac{\sigma_S \times 300}{210 \times 10^3} + \frac{\sigma_B \times 400}{85 \times 10^3}$$

$$0.1582 \;=\; \frac{\sigma_S}{700} + \frac{\sigma_B}{212.5}$$　　　　... (ii)

(iv) Thermal stresses : Solving equations (i) and (ii),

$$\sigma_B = 16.79 \text{ MPa (Compressive)}$$
$$\sigma_S = 55.42 \text{ MPa (Compressive)}$$

(v)    Force at supports :

$$F = \sigma_S A_S = \sigma_B A_B$$
$$= 55.42 \times 380 \times 10^{-3} \text{ kN}$$
$$= \mathbf{21.059 \text{ kN}}$$

**Example 2.57 :** *Data as shown in Fig. 2.65 below. Find the stress in each rod when temperature of aluminium rod only is increased by 50°C.*

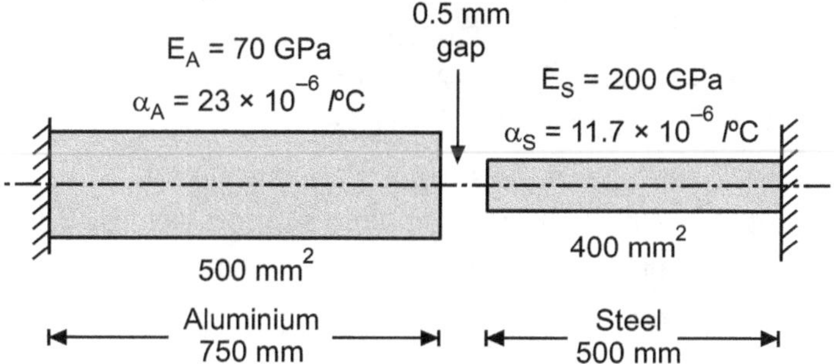


**Fig. 2.65 : Given members**

**Data :** $A_A = 500 \text{ mm}^2$, $A_S = 400 \text{ mm}^2$, $\alpha_A = 23 \times 10^{-6} \text{ /°C}$

$E_A = 70 \text{ GPa}$, $E_S = 200 \text{ GPa}$, $\alpha_S = 11.7 \times 10^{-6} \text{ /°C}$

**Required :** Stress in each rod.

**Concept :** Till the time gap is present, no stresses are developed.

**Solution :** (i) Equation of statics :

$$\sigma_A \cdot A_A = \sigma_S \cdot A_S$$
$$\sigma_A (500) = \sigma_S (400)$$
$$\sigma_A = 0.8 (\sigma_S) \qquad \text{... (i)}$$

(ii)   Equation of compatibility :

$$(\alpha t L)_A + (\alpha t L)_S - \left[\left(\frac{\sigma L}{E}\right)_A + \left(\frac{\sigma L}{E}\right)_S\right] = 0.5$$

$$23 \times 10^{-6} \times 50 \times 750 - \left[\frac{\sigma_A \times 750}{70 \times 10^3} + \frac{\sigma_S \times 500}{200 \times 10^3}\right] = 0.5 \qquad (\geq (\alpha t L)_S = 0)$$

$$\therefore \qquad 0.3625 = \frac{\sigma_A}{93.34} + \frac{\sigma_S}{400} \qquad \text{... (ii)}$$

(iii) Thermal stresses :

Solving equations (i) and (ii),

$$\sigma_S = \mathbf{32.74 \text{ MPa (Compressive)}}$$
$$\sigma_A = \mathbf{26.2 \text{ MPa (Compressive)}}$$

**Example 2.58 :** *A compound member is supported as shown in Fig. 2.66 below. Initially the system is stress free. If the temperature is then dropped by 20°K find (i) stress in each bar if the supports are unyielding, (ii) stress in each bar, if the right hand support yield by 0.1 mm. Assume $\alpha_B = 20 \times 10^{-6}$ /°C, $\alpha_A = 25 \times 10^{-6}$ /°C, $E_B = 90$ GPa and $E_A = 70$ GPa.*

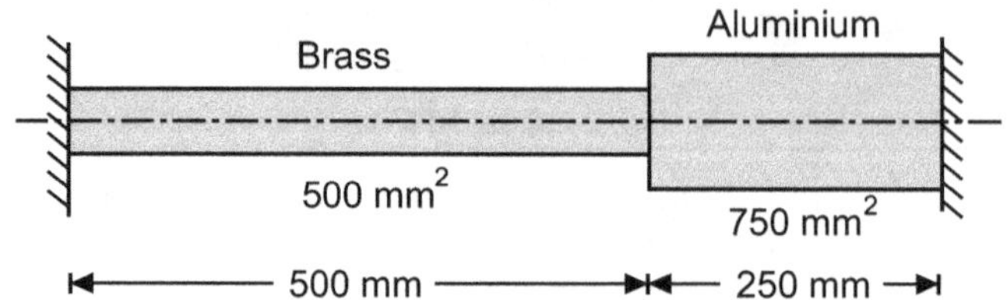


**Fig. 2.66**

**Data :** $A_B = 500$ mm², $A_A = 750$ mm², $\alpha_B = 20 \times 10^{-6}$ /°C.

$\quad \alpha_A = 25 \times 10^{-6}$ /°C, $E_B = 90$ MPa, $E_A = 70$ GPa.

**Required :**  (i) Stress in each bar if the supports are unyielding.

$\qquad\qquad$ (ii) Stress in each bar if the right hand support yield by 0.1 mm.

**Concept :** Statically indeterminate : Statics and Compatibility.

**Solution :** (i) Equation of statics :

$$(\sigma A)_B = (\sigma A)_A$$

$$\sigma_B \times 500 = \sigma_A \times 750$$

$$\sigma_B = 1.5\,\sigma_A \qquad\qquad \text{... (i)}$$

(ii)  Equation of compatibility :

$$(\alpha\,t\,L)_B + (\alpha\,t\,L)_A - \left[\left(\frac{\sigma L}{E}\right)_B + \left(\frac{\sigma L}{E}\right)_A\right] = 0$$

$$(20 \times 10^{-6} \times 20 \times 500) + (25 \times 10^{-6} \times 20 \times 250) = \frac{\sigma_B \times 500}{90 \times 10^3} + \frac{\sigma_A \times 250}{70 \times 10^3}$$

$$0.325 = \frac{\sigma_B}{180} + \frac{\sigma_A}{280} \qquad\qquad \text{... (ii)}$$

(iii) Thermal stresses :

Solving equations (i) and (ii),

$$\sigma_B = \textbf{40.95 MPa (Tensile)}$$

$$\sigma_A = \textbf{27.3 MPa (Tensile)}$$

(iv) When support yields by 0.1 mm, equation of statics remains the same.

$$\sigma_B = 1.5\,\sigma_A \qquad\qquad \text{... (iii)}$$

(v)  Compatibility :

$$(\alpha\,t\,L)_B + (\alpha\,t\,L)_A - \left[\left(\frac{\sigma L}{E}\right)_B + \left(\frac{\sigma L}{E}\right)_A\right] = 0.1$$

$$0.325 = \frac{\sigma_B}{180} + \frac{\sigma_A}{280} + 0.1$$

$$0.225 = \frac{\sigma_B}{180} + \frac{\sigma_A}{280} \qquad\qquad \text{... (iv)}$$

(vi) Thermal stresses :

Solving equations (i) and (iii),

$$\sigma_B \ = \ \textbf{28.55 MPa (Tensile)}$$
$$\sigma_A \ = \ \textbf{19.03 MPa (Tensile)}$$

**Example 2.59 :** *Data as shown in Fig. 2.67. The temperature of the combination is increased by 30ºC. Calculate the stresses induced in the rod and in the tube. Also find actual expansion of composite member.*

Take $\alpha_S = 12 \times 10^{-6}$ /°C, $E_S = 200$ GPa, $\alpha_{Cu} = 16 \times 10^{-6}$ /°C, $E_C = 100$ GPa.

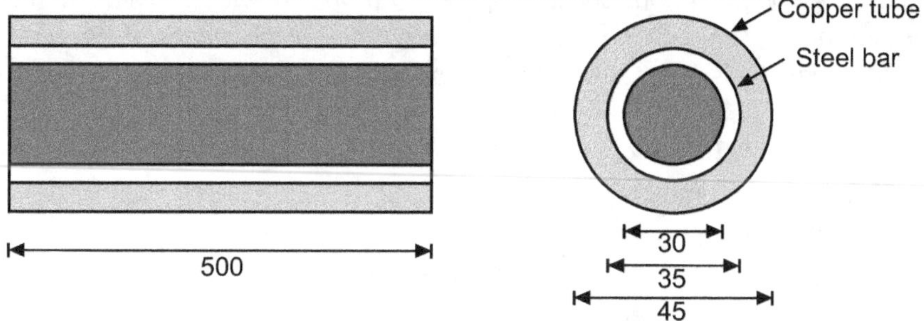


**(a) Given member**          **(b) Cross section of member**

**Fig. 2.67**

**Data :** As shown in Fig. 2.67.

**Required :** Stresses induced in the rod and in the tube; actual expansion of composite member.

**Concept :** Statically indeterminate : Statics and Compatibility.

**Solution :** (i) Geometric properties :

$$\text{Area of steel} \ = \ A_S = \frac{\pi}{4} (30)^2 = 706.8 \text{ mm}^2$$

$$\text{Area of copper} \ = \ A_C = \frac{\pi}{4} (45^2 - 35^2) = 628.3 \text{ mm}^2$$

(ii)   Equation of statics :

$$P_C \ = \ P_S$$
$$\sigma_C \, A_C \ = \ \sigma_S \, A_S$$
$$\sigma_C \ = \ 1.124 \, \sigma_S \qquad \qquad \text{... (i)}$$

(iii) Equation of compatibility :

$$\left( \alpha \, t \, L - \frac{\sigma L}{E} \right)_{Cu} \ = \ \left( \frac{\sigma L}{E} + \alpha \, t \, L \right)_{st}$$

As $\alpha_C > \alpha_{st}$ ; Cu will be subjected to compression.

$$\left( 16 \times 10^{-6} \times 30 - \frac{\sigma_C}{100 \times 10^3} \right) \ = \ \left( 12 \times 10^{-6} \times 30 + \frac{\sigma_S}{200 \times 10^3} \right)$$
$$\sigma_S + 2\sigma_C \ = \ 24 \qquad \qquad \text{... (ii)}$$

(iv) Thermal stresses :

Solving equations (i) and (ii),

$$\sigma_S = \textbf{7.38 MPa (Tensile)}$$
$$\sigma_C = \textbf{8.31 MPa (Compressive)}$$

(v)    Actual expansion :

$$(\delta L)_C = (\delta L)_{st}$$
$$\left(\alpha\, t\, L - \frac{\sigma L}{E}\right)_C = \left(16 \times 10^{-6} \times 30 \times 500 - \frac{8.31 \times 500}{100 \times 10^3}\right)$$
$$\therefore \qquad (\delta L)_C = \textbf{0.198 mm}$$

**Example 2.60 :** *A composite bar consists of steel rod 30 mm diameter enclosed in copper tube 60 mm external diameter. The rod and tube are joined together by means of 24 mm $\phi$ pins, one on each end. Find the shear stress induced in pins if composite section is subjected to temperature rise of 50°C.*

*Take $E_S$ = 210 GPa, $E_C$ = 105 GPa, $\alpha_S$ = 11 $\times 10^{-6}$ /°C, $\alpha_C$ = 17 $\times 10^{-6}$ /°C*

**Data :** For copper, D = 60 mm, d = 30 mm

For steel, d = 30 mm, $\phi_{pins}$ = 24 mm, temperature rise = 50°C.

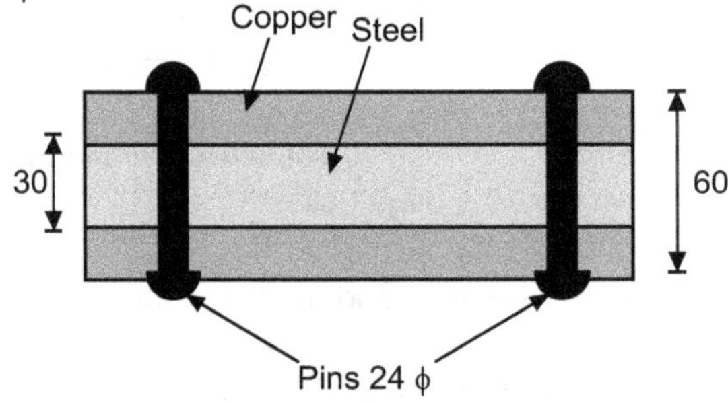


(All dimensions in mm)

**Fig. 2.68 : Given member**

**Required :** Shear stress induced for pins.

**Concept :** (i) Statically indeterminate, (ii) Pins are in double shear.

**Solution :** (i) Geometric properties :

Area of steel rod, $\qquad A_S = \dfrac{\pi}{4}(30)^2 = 706.85 \text{ mm}^2$

Area of copper tube, $\qquad A_C = \dfrac{\pi}{4}(60^2 - 30^2) = 2120.5 \text{ mm}^2$

(ii)    Equation of statics :

$$P_C = P_S$$
$$\sigma_C A_C = \sigma_S A_S$$
$$\sigma_C = \frac{706.85}{2120.5} \cdot \sigma_S$$
$$\therefore \qquad \sigma_C = 0.33\, \sigma_S \qquad\qquad\qquad \text{... (i)}$$

(iii) Equation for compatibility :

As $\alpha_C > \alpha_S$ , Cu is subjected to compression.

$$\left(\alpha\, t\, L - \frac{\sigma L}{E}\right)_C = \left(\alpha\, t\, L + \frac{\sigma L}{E}\right)_S$$

$$\left(17 \times 10^{-6} \times 50 - \frac{\sigma_C}{105 \times 10^3}\right) = \left(11 \times 10^{-6} \times 50 + \frac{\sigma_S}{210 \times 10^3}\right)$$

$$63 = \sigma_S + 2\,\sigma_C \qquad \qquad \ldots \text{(ii)}$$

(iv) Thermal stresses :

Solving equations (i) and (ii),

$$63 = \sigma_S + 2\,(0.33\,\sigma_S)$$
$$63 = 1.67\,\sigma_S$$

$\therefore \qquad \sigma_S = 37.72$ MPa (Tensile)

$\therefore \qquad \sigma_C = 12.45$ MPa (Compressive)

(v)  Axial force :

$$P = \sigma_C\,A_C = \sigma_S\,A_S$$
$$= (706.85)\,(37.72) = 26662.38 \text{ N}$$
$$= 26.66 \text{ kN}$$

(vi) Shear stress for pin :

$$\tau = \frac{P}{2A} \ldots \text{ since pin is subjected to double shear.}$$

$$= \frac{26662.38}{2 \times \dfrac{\pi}{4}\,(24)^2} = \mathbf{29.46 \text{ MPa}}$$

**Example 2.61 :** *Three wires as shown in Fig. 2.69 are supporting a load of 18 kN. The cross-sectional area of each wire is 150 mm². If the lengths of wires are adjusted so as to share the load equally at 20°C, find the stresses in wires at 50°C temperature.*
*Take $E_S = 2 \times 10^5$ MPa, $\alpha_S = 12 \times 10^{-6}$ /°C, $E_C = 1 \times 10^5$ MPa, $\alpha_C = 18 \times 10^{-6}$ /°C.*

**Data :** P = 18 kN, $A_S = A_C = 150$ mm².

**Required :** Stresses in wires at 50°C.

**Concept :** (i) Statically indeterminate

       (ii) Superposition of stresses.

**Solution :** (i) Geometric properties :

Area of steel ($A_S$) = Area of copper ($A_C$) = 150 mm²

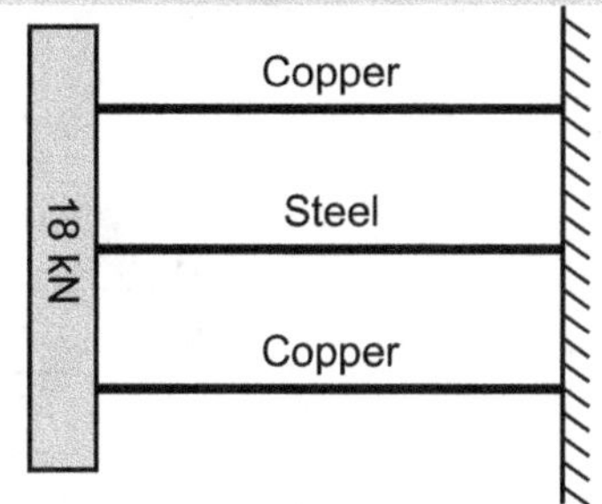


**Fig. 2.69**

(ii)   Equation of statics :

Due to temperature change,

Compressive force in copper wires $=$ Tensile force in steel wire

$$2\,(\sigma_C \times A_C) = (\sigma_S \times A_S)$$
$$2\,\sigma_C = \sigma_S$$
$$\sigma_C = 0.5\,\sigma_S \qquad \qquad \ldots \text{(i)}$$

(iii) Equation of compatibility :

$$\left(\alpha\,t\,L - \frac{\sigma L}{E}\right)_C = \left(\alpha\,t\,L + \frac{\sigma L}{E}\right)_S$$

$$18 \times 10^{-6} \times (50 - 20) - \frac{\sigma_C}{1 \times 10^5} = 12 \times 10^{-6} \times (50 - 20) + \frac{\sigma_S}{2 \times 10^5}$$

$$1.8 \times 10^{-4} = \frac{\sigma_S}{2 \times 10^5} + \frac{\sigma_C}{1 \times 10^5}$$

$$36 = \sigma_S + 2\,\sigma_C \qquad \qquad \ldots \text{(ii)}$$

(iv) Solution of equations : Solving equations (i) and (ii),

$$\sigma_S = 18 \text{ MPa (Tensile)}$$

$$\sigma_C = 9 \text{ MPa (Compressive)}$$

(v)　Stresses due to load :

　　At 20°C, the load is shared equally by three wires.

∴　　　　Load taken by each wire $= \dfrac{18 \times 10^3}{3} = 6 \times 10^3$

∴　　　　Tensile stress in each wire $= \dfrac{6 \times 10^3}{150} = 40$ MPa (Tensile)

(vi) Final stresses :

Stress in steel $= \sigma_S = 18 + 40 =$ **58 MPa (Tensile)**

Stress in copper $= \sigma_C = -9 + 40 =$ **31 MPa (Tensile)**

**Example 2.62 :** *A rigid bar AB is hinged at A and is supported by copper and steel wires as shown in Fig. 2.70 (a). If temperature of the system is raised by 40°C, find the stresses in wires. Assume $E_C = 100$ GPa, $E_S = 200$ GPa, $\alpha_C = 18 \times 10^{-6}$ /°C, $\alpha_S = 12 \times 10^{-6}$ /°C.*

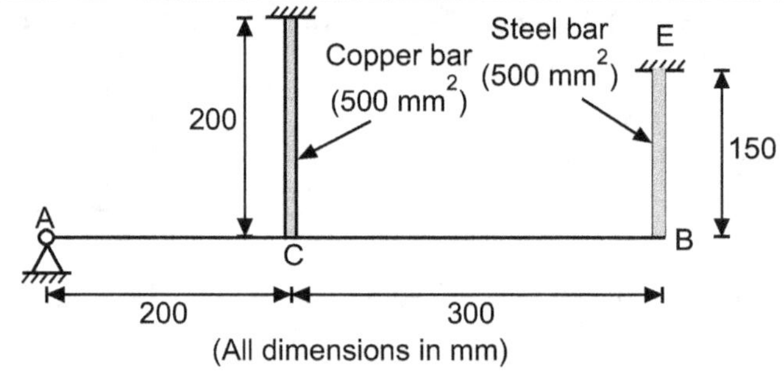


**(a) Given arrangement**

**Fig. 2.70**



**(b) FBD**



**(c) Deformation diagram**

**Data :** As shown in Fig. 2.70 (a).

**Required :** Stresses in copper and steel wires.

**Concept :** Statically indeterminate : Equations of statics and compatibility.

As $(\alpha L)_C > (\alpha L)_S$ , copper will be subjected to compressive stress and steel will be subjected to tensile stress. See Fig. 2.70 (b).

**Solution :** (i) Equation of statics :

Taking moments @ A,

$$\Sigma\, M_A = 0; \qquad\qquad - P_C \times 200 + P_S \times 500 \;=\; 0$$

$$P_C \;=\; 2.5\, P_S$$

$$\sigma_C\, A_C \;=\; 2.5\, \sigma_S\, A_S \qquad\qquad (\because A_C = A_S)$$

$$\therefore\qquad\qquad \sigma_C \;=\; 2.5\, \sigma_S \qquad\qquad\qquad \ldots (i)$$

(ii)　Equation of compatibility :

$$\frac{(\delta L)_C}{200} \;=\; \frac{(\delta L)_S}{500}$$

$$(\delta L)_C \;=\; 0.4\,(\delta L)_S$$

$$\left(\alpha\, t\, L - \frac{\sigma L}{E}\right)_C \;=\; 0.4 \left(\alpha\, t\, L + \frac{\sigma L}{E}\right)_S$$

$$18 \times 10^{-6} \times 40 \times 200 - \frac{\sigma_C \times 200}{100 \times 10^3} \;=\; 0.4 \left[12 \times 10^{-6} \times 40 \times 150 + \frac{\sigma_S \times 150}{200 \times 10^3}\right]$$

$$\therefore\qquad\qquad 0.144 - \frac{\sigma_C}{500} \;=\; 0.0288 + \frac{\sigma_S}{3333.33}$$

$$\therefore\qquad\qquad \sigma_S + 6.67\, \sigma_C \;=\; 384 \qquad\qquad \ldots (ii)$$

(iii) Solution of equations :

Solving equations (i) and (ii),

$$\sigma_S \;=\; \textbf{21.72 MPa (Tensile)}$$

$$\sigma_C \;=\; \textbf{54.31 MPa (Compressive)}$$

---

**Example 2.63 :** *A copper flat 60 mm × 30 mm is joined to another 60 mm × 60 mm steel flat as shown in Fig. 2.71. If the combination is heated through 100°C, determine :*

*(i)　stress produced in each bar,*

*(ii)　the shear force between the flats,*

*(iii)　shear stress.*

---

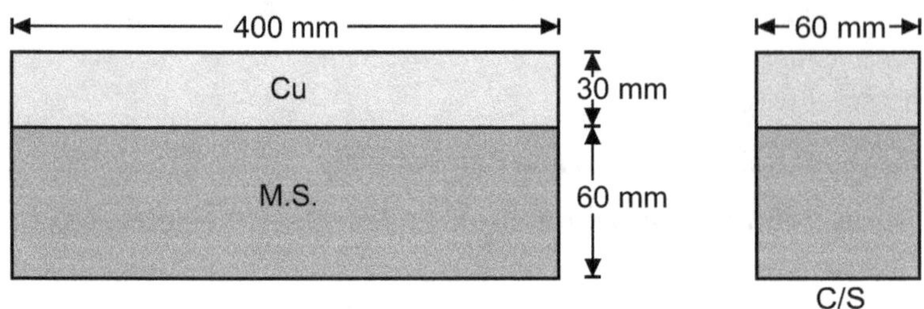

**Fig. 2.71**

**Given :** $\alpha_C = 18.5 \times 10^{-6}$ /°C, $\alpha_S = 12 \times 10^{-6}$ /°C, $E_C = 101$ GPa, $E_S = 220$ GPa.

**Data :** As shown in Fig. 2.71.

**Required :** Stresses induced in the bar, shear force and shear stress.

**Concept :** Statically indeterminate : Statics and compatibility.

**Solution :** (i) Geometric properties :

$$A_{Cu} = 60 \times 30 = 1800 \text{ mm}^2$$
$$A_{St} = 60 \times 60 = 3600 \text{ mm}^2$$

(ii)  Equation of statics :

$$P_{Cu} = P_{St}$$
$$\sigma_{Cu} A_{Cu} = \sigma_{St} A_{St}$$
$$\sigma_{Cu} \times 1800 = \sigma_{St} \times 3600$$
$$\sigma_{Cu} = 2 \times \sigma_{St} \qquad \ldots \text{(i)}$$

(iii) Equation of compatibility :

$$\left(\alpha\, t\, L - \frac{\sigma L}{E}\right)_{Cu} = \left(\frac{\sigma L}{E} + \alpha\, t\, L\right)_{St}$$

As $\alpha_{Cu} > \alpha_{St}$ ; Cu will be subjected to compression.

$$\left(18.5 \times 10^{-6} \times 100 \times 400 - \frac{\sigma_{Cu} \times 400}{101 \times 10^3}\right) = \left(\frac{\sigma_{St} \times 400}{220 \times 10^3} + 12 \times 10^{-6} \times 100 \times 400\right)$$

$$0.74 - 3.96 \times 10^{-3}\, \sigma_{Cu} = \sigma_{St} \times 1.82 \times 10^{-3} + 0.48$$

$$1.82 \times 10^{-3}\, \sigma_{St} + 3.96 \times 10^{-3}\, \sigma_{Cu} = 0.26$$

$$1.82 \times 10^{-3}\, \sigma_{St} + 2 \times 3.96 \times 10^{-3}\, \sigma_{St} = 0.26 \qquad \ldots \text{(ii)}$$

Putting equation (i) in (ii),

$$\sigma_{St} = 26.69 \text{ N/mm}^2$$
$$\therefore \qquad \sigma_{Cu} = 53.39 \text{ N/mm}^2$$

(iv) Shear force between flats :

$$S = \sigma_{Cu} \times A_{Cu} = 53.39 \times 1800$$
$$\therefore \qquad S = \mathbf{96102\ N}$$

---

**Example 2.64 :** *Rails of 15 m length were laid on the track in the morning when the temperature was 16°C. A gap of 1.8 mm was kept between the two rails. At what maximum temperature the rails will remain stress free ? If temperature is further increased by 15°C, what will be the magnitude and nature of stresses induced in the rails ?*

*Assume $\alpha = 12 \times 10^{-6}$ /°C and E = 200 GPa. Assume that rails can expand in one direction.*

---

**Data :** $l$ = 15 m, $\delta l = \dfrac{1.8}{2}$ = 0.9 mm (for each)

t = 16°C, t = (16 + 15) = 31°C, $\alpha$ = 12 × 10⁻⁶ /°C, E = 200 GPa = 200 × 10³ MPa.

**Required :** Maximum temperature for which rails are stress free and stress at 31°C.

**Concept :** $\delta l = l\,\alpha\,t$ and $\sigma = \alpha\,t\,E$

**Solution : Case (i) :**

$$\delta l = l\,\alpha\,t$$
$$0.9 = 15000 \times 12 \times 10^{-6} \times t$$

∴
$$t = \text{change in temperature} = 5°C$$

∴ Maximum temperature at which rails are stress free = (16 + 5) = **21°**

**Case (ii) :** Change in temperature = 31 – 21 = 10°C

∴
$$\sigma = \alpha\,t\,E$$
$$= 12 \times 10^{-6} \times 10 \times 200 \times 10^{3}$$

∴
$$\sigma = \textbf{24 N/mm}^2 \ \textbf{(Compressive)}$$

**Example 2.65 :** *A compound strut consists of a brass portion AB of diameter 75 mm and a steel portion BC 40 mm diameter as shown in Fig. 2.72. Supports at A and C are rigid. If temperature is raised through 140°C, find*

*(i)    Nature and magnitude of stresses developed in brass and steel.*

*(ii)   Force exerted on the supports and*

*(iii) The relative movement at the junction B.*

**Given :** $\alpha_{Br}$ = 20 × 10⁻⁶ /°C, $\alpha_{st}$ = 11 × 10⁻⁶ /°C, $E_{Br}$ = 85 GPa, $E_{st}$ = 210 GPa

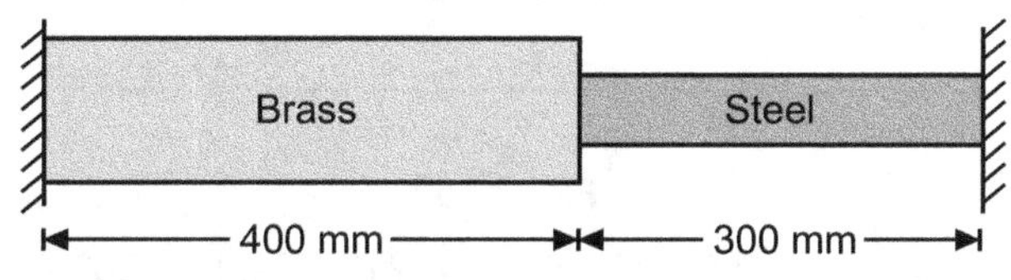


**Fig. 2.72**

**Data :** Brass : d = 75 mm, $l$ = 400 mm, $\alpha$ = 20 × 10⁻⁶ /°C, E = 85 GPa,

Steel : d = 40 mm, $l$ = 300 mm, $\alpha$ = 11 × 10⁻⁶ /°C, E = 210 GPa, t = 140°C

**Required :** Stresses, reaction and relative movement of junction B.

**Concept :** Statically indeterminate, statics and compatibility.

**Solution :**

(i) Geometric properties :

$$A_{Br} = \frac{\pi}{4} \times 75^2 = 4417.86 \ \text{mm}^2$$

$$A_{st} = \frac{\pi}{4} \times 40^2 = 1256.64 \ \text{mm}^2$$

(ii)
$$(\sigma \cdot A)_{Br} = (\sigma \cdot A)_{st}$$
$$\sigma_{Br} \times 4417.86 = \sigma_{st} \times 1256.64$$
∴
$$\sigma_{st} = 3.52\,\sigma_{Br}$$

(iii) Compatibility :

$$(\alpha\,T\,l)_{st} + (\alpha\,t\,l)_{Br} - \left[\left(\frac{\sigma l}{E}\right)_{st} + \left(\frac{\sigma l}{E}\right)_{Br}\right] = 0$$

$$11 \times 10^{-6} \times 140 \times 400 + 20 \times 10^{-6} \times 140 \times 300 - \left[\frac{\sigma_{st} \times 300}{210 \times 10^3} + \frac{\sigma_{Br} \times 400}{85 \times 10^3}\right] = 0$$

$$0.616 + 0.84 - \left[1.43 \times 10^{-3}\,\sigma_{st} + 4.706 \times 10^{-3} \times \sigma_{Br}\right] = 0$$

$$9.7396 \times 10^{-3}\,\sigma_{Br} = 1.456$$
$$\sigma_{Br} = 149.49 \text{ N/mm}^2$$
$$\sigma_{st} = \mathbf{526.21 \text{ N/mm}^2}$$

(iv)
$$\sigma_{st} = \frac{P_{st}}{A}$$
∴
$$P_{st} = \sigma_{st}\,A = 526.21 \times 1256.64$$
∴
$$P_{st} = \mathbf{661.25 \text{ kN}}$$

---

**Example 2.66 :** *The steel wire in Fig. 2.73 is stretched between two rigid supports. The initial stress in the wire is 30 MPa, when the temperature is 20°C. What is the stress in the wire when temperature drops to 0°C ? At what temperature will the stress be zero ? α = 14 × 10⁻⁶/°C and E = 210 GPa.*

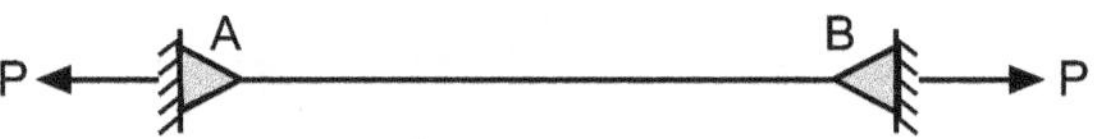


**Fig. 2.73**

**Data :** As shown in Fig. 2.73, $\alpha = 14 \times 10^{-6}/°C$, E = 210 GPa, $t_1 = 20°$, $\sigma$ = 30 MPa.

**Required :** Stress at zero temperature, temperature at zero stress.

**Concept :** Compressive force will be developed due to decrease in temperature and tensile force will be developed due to increase in temperature.

**Solution :** (i) Temperature drops from 20°C to 0°C.

∴
$$\sigma = \alpha t E$$
$$= 14 \times 10^{-6} \times 20 \times 210 \times 10^3$$
$$= 58.8 \text{ MPa}$$

∴ Stress in wire $= -30 + 58.8 = 28.8$ MPa (Compressive)

(ii)  $\sigma = 30$ MPa tensile should be developed to neutralize compressive force.

---

$$\sigma = \alpha t E$$
$$30 = 14 \times 10^{-6} \times t \times 210 \times 10^3$$
$$\therefore \quad t = 10.2°C$$

When temperature is 9.8°C, stress in bar will be zero.

**Example 2.67 :** *A thermometer device, shown in Fig. 2.74, is made of a tungsten bar AC and a magnesium bar BD that are attached to a pointer CDP by pins at C and D. Derive a formula for the upward displacement δ at point P in terms of uniform temperature increase ΔT, coefficients of thermal expansion $\alpha_t$, $\alpha_m$ and the dimensions a, b and L. Suffixes t and m correspond to tungsten and magnesium.*

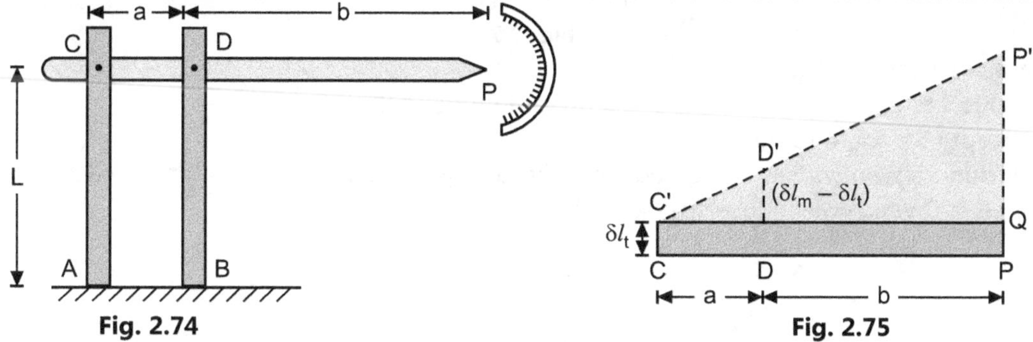

**Fig. 2.74**                                                        **Fig. 2.75**

**Data :** As shown in Fig. 2.74.

**Required :** Formula for displacement.

**Solution :**

$$\delta l = l\alpha t$$
$$CC' = \delta l_t = L\alpha_t \, \Delta T$$
$$DD' = \delta l_m = L\alpha_m \, \Delta T$$

$$P'P = \delta l_p = \delta l_t + P'Q$$

$$= L\alpha_t \, \Delta T + \frac{(\delta l_m - \delta l_t)}{a} \times (a + b)$$

$$= \frac{aL\alpha_t \, \Delta T + (L\alpha_m \, \Delta T - L\alpha_t \, \Delta T)(a + b)}{a}$$

$$= \frac{aL\alpha_t \, \Delta T + aL\alpha_m \, \Delta T + bL\alpha_m \Delta T - aL\alpha_t \, \Delta T - bL\alpha_t \, \Delta T}{a}$$

$$= \frac{aL\alpha_m \Delta T + b(L\alpha_m \Delta T - L\alpha_t \, \Delta T)}{a}$$

$$\delta l_p = L \, \Delta T \left[ \alpha_m + \frac{b}{a}(\alpha_m - \alpha_t) \right]$$

**Example 2.68 :** *For a bar shown in Fig. 2.76, find the reactions produced by upper and lower support on the bar due to applications of load 'P' at 'B', which is utilised to bridge gap of 'X'. The AB part of the far is having cross-sectional area of '3A' and 'L/2' length, whereas 'BC' part is having cross-sectional area 'A' and the length 'L/3'. Assume the modulus of elasticity of bar is 'E'. Also find stresses in the bar AB and BC. Assume relevant units for each parameter.* **(Dec. 2004)**

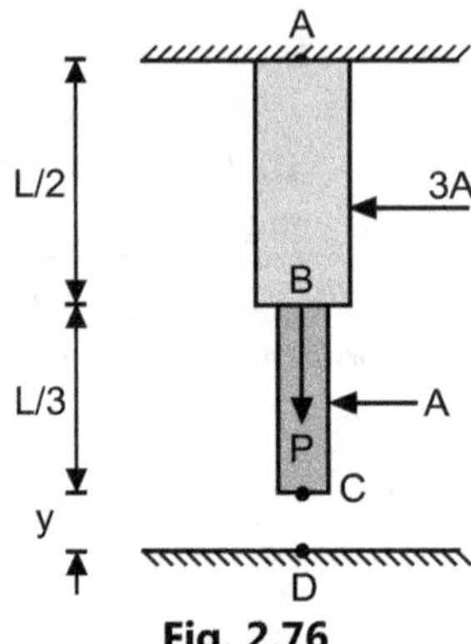


**Fig. 2.76**

**Data :** As shown in Fig. 2.76.

**Required :** Reactions at A and D and stresses in AB and BC.

**Concept :** Standard formulae.

**Solution : (i)** Only AB is elongated for deflection y. Once bar touch point D, reaction will be developed at D which will induce stresses in it.

$$y \;=\; \frac{P_1 l}{AE} = \frac{P_1}{3A} \times \frac{L}{2E} = \frac{P_1 L}{\sigma AE}$$

$\therefore \qquad P_1 \;=\; \dfrac{6\,AEy}{L}$

**(ii)** Remaining force $(P - P_1)$ will develop stresses in bars. The deformations by both should be same (i.e. one tensile and other compressive).

$\therefore \qquad \dfrac{R_A \cdot L}{(3A)^2\,E} \;=\; \dfrac{R_D\,L}{A \times E \times 3}$

$\therefore \qquad R_A \;=\; 2R_D$

$\qquad R_A + R_D \;=\; P - P_1$

$\therefore \qquad 3R_D \;=\; (P - P_1)$

$\therefore \qquad R_D \;=\; \left(\dfrac{P - P_1}{3}\right)$

If, $\qquad P \;=\; P_1,\; R_D = 0$

so that stresses will not develop in the bar AB and BC.

If $\quad P < P_1,\; R_D = 0$ and point C will not touch point D. Stresses will not develop in both bars.

If, $\quad P > P_1,$ stresses will be developed in both bar.

If, $P > P_1$

$\therefore \qquad \text{Stress in AB} \;=\; \dfrac{R_A}{\text{Area}} = \dfrac{2R_D}{3A}$

$$=\; \frac{2\,(P - P_1)}{3 \times 3A} = \frac{2\,(P - P_1)}{9A}$$

$\qquad \text{Stress in BC} \;=\; \dfrac{R_D}{\text{Area}} = \left(\dfrac{P - P_1}{3A}\right)$

**Example 2.69 :** *A copper bar has AB of length 600 mm of a "Tripper circuit box" is placed in position, as shown in Fig. at room temperature with a gap of 0.3 mm between the end B and right wall. Calculate the axial compressive stress in the bar, if the temperature rises to 60° C. For copper bar, take E = 120 GPa and d = 17 × 10⁻⁶ per°C.* **(Dec. 2004)**

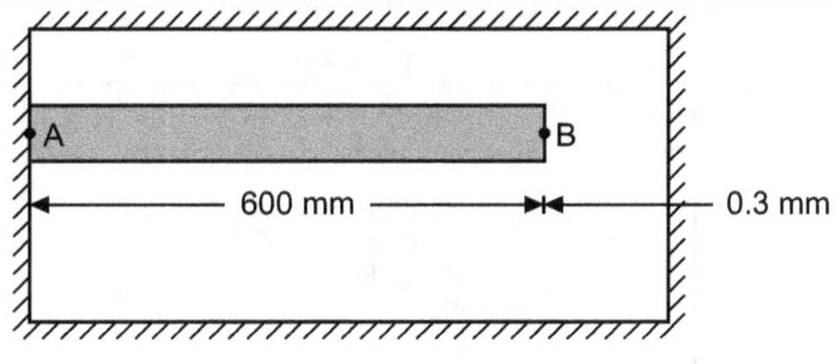


**Fig. 2.77**

**Data :** As shown in figure 2.77.

**Required :** Stress in AB.

**Concept :** Standard formulae.

**Solution :** First calculate temperature increase to get $\delta l$ = 0.3 mm.

Assume,          room temperature  =  25°

$$\delta l \; = \; \alpha \, \delta t. \, l$$

$$0.3 \; = \; 17 \times 10^{-6} \times (t - 25) \times 600$$

$$(t - 25) \; = \; 29.41$$

$\therefore$          $t \; = \; 54.41°C$

Till 54.41°C, no stresses will developed. For remaining temperature (60 – 54.41), sresses will be developed.

$\therefore$

$$\sigma \; = \; \alpha \, \delta t \cdot E.$$

$$= \; 17 \times 10^{-6} (60 - 54.41) \times 120 \times 10^3$$

$$= \; \mathbf{11.40 \ N/mm^2}$$

$\therefore$     The axial compressive stress at 60°C is **11.40 N/mm²**

**Example 2.70 :** *A rigid bar ABC, supported by two links AD and BE [Refer Fig. 2.78] is of uniform cross-sectional area 'A' and of lengths '3h' and 'h' respectively and are made of same material. A force 'F' is applied at point 'B'. Determine the stresses in each link and maximum deflection of point 'B'.* **(Dec. 2004)**

**Data :** As shown in Fig. 2.78

**Required :** Stresses in each link and maximum deflection at B.

**Concept :**   From geometry of deformation, find elongation.

          For stresses are equilibrium concept.

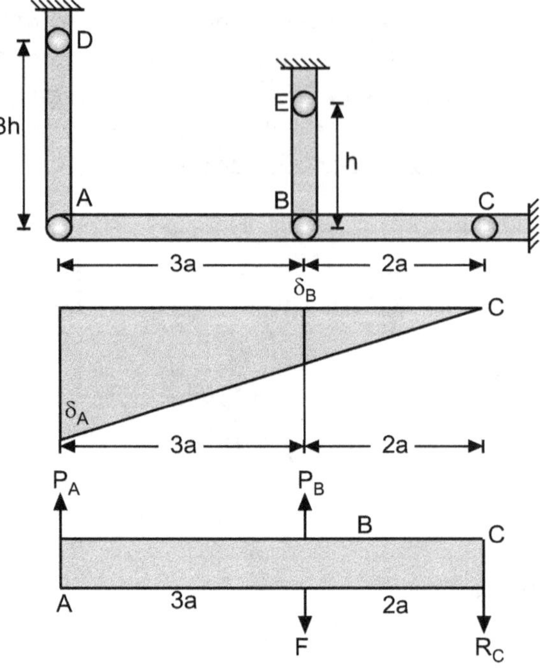



**Fig. 2.78**

**Solution :** (i) From similar triangles,

$$\frac{\delta_B}{2a} = \frac{\delta_A}{5a}$$

$\therefore$
$$\frac{P_B \, l \, (AD)}{2a \, (A) \, (E)} = \frac{P_A \, l \, (BE)}{5a \, (A) \, (E)}$$

$\therefore$
$$\frac{P_B \times 3h}{2} = \frac{P_A \times h}{5}$$

$\therefore$
$$P_A = \left(\frac{15}{2}\right) P_B = 7.5 \, P_B \qquad \qquad …(i)$$

(ii) Apply equilibrium equation to figure (2.78).

take moment @ C.

$\therefore$
$$M @ C = 0$$

$\therefore$
$$2a \times P_B + 5a \times P_A - F \times 2a = 0$$

$$2a \times P_B + 5a \times 7.5 \, P_B - F \times 2a = 0$$

$\therefore$
$$P_B + 18.75 \, P_B = F$$

$$19.75 \, P_B = F$$

$\therefore$
$$P_B = 0.051 \, F$$

$$P_A = 0.38 \, F$$

$\therefore$
$$\text{Stress in bar A} = \frac{P_A}{A} = \left(\frac{\mathbf{0.38 \ F}}{\mathbf{A}}\right) \textbf{tensile}$$

$$\text{Stress in bar B} \;=\; \frac{P_B}{A} = \left(\frac{\textbf{0.051F}}{\textbf{A}}\right) \textbf{tensile}$$

$$\text{Deflection at B} \;=\; \frac{\text{Stress} \times l}{E} = \frac{0.051\ F}{AE} \times h$$

$$=\; \frac{\textbf{0.051 Fh}}{\textbf{AE}}$$

**Example 2.71 :** *A bronze bar is fastened between a steel bar and an aluminium bar as shown in figure. Axial loads are applied at the position shown. Find the largest value of 'P', that will not exceed an overall deformation of 4 mm or the following stresses.*　　　　**(Dec. 2005)**

$\sigma_{st}$ = 140 MPa, $\sigma_b$ = 120 MPa, $\sigma_{al}$ = 80 MPa,

$E_{st}$ = 200 GPa, $E_b$ = 83 GPa, $E_{al}$ = 70 Gpa

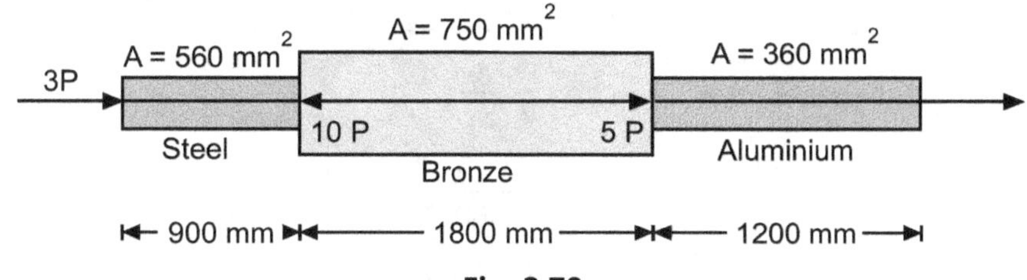


**Fig. 2.79**

**Data :** As shown in figure 2.79.

**Required :** Force P.

**Concept :** Standard formulae.

**Solution :** (i) Geometric properties :

$$\text{Area of Steel} \;=\; 560\ mm^2,$$
$$\text{Area of Bronze} \;=\; 750\ mm^2$$
$$\text{Area of Aluminium} \;=\; 360\ mm^2$$

Consider P is in kN.

$$\delta l \;=\; \delta l_s + \delta l_{Br} + \delta l_{Al}$$

$$\delta l \;=\; 4\ mm$$

$$\delta l_s \;=\; \left(\frac{Pl}{AE}\right)_s = \frac{3P \times 10^3 \times 900}{560 \times 200 \times 10^3} = 0.024\ P \text{ (comp.)}$$

$$\delta l_{Br} \;=\; \left(\frac{Pl}{AE}\right)_{Br} = \frac{7P \times 10^3 \times 1800}{750 \times 83 \times 10^3} = 0.202\ P \text{ (Tensile)}$$

$$(\delta l)_{Al} \;=\; \left(\frac{Pl}{AE}\right)_{Al} = \frac{2P \times 10^3 \times 200}{360 \times 70 \times 10^3} = 0.0952\ P \text{ (Tensile)}$$

$$\therefore \qquad 4 = -\,0.024\,P + 0.202\,P + 0.0952\,P$$

$$\therefore \qquad P = 14.53 \text{ kN} \qquad \qquad \text{...(i)}$$

$$\text{Stress in Steel} = \frac{\text{Force}}{\text{Area}}$$

$$140 = \frac{3P \times 10^3}{560}$$

$$\therefore \qquad P = \textbf{26.13 kN} \qquad \qquad \text{...(ii)}$$

$$\text{Stress in Bronze} = \frac{\text{Force}}{\text{Area}}$$

$$120 = \frac{7P \times 10^3}{750}$$

$$\therefore \qquad P = \textbf{12.85 kN} \qquad \qquad \text{...(iii)}$$

$$\text{Force in Aluminium} = \frac{\text{Force}}{\text{Area}}$$

$$80 = \frac{2P \times 10^3}{360}$$

$$\therefore \qquad P = \textbf{14.4 kN} \qquad \qquad \text{...(iv)}$$

Hence, largest allowable P is minimum of (i), (ii), (iii) and (iv).

$\therefore \qquad$ Largest allowable value of P $= \textbf{12.85 kN}$

**Example 2.72 :** *A steel circular bar PQRS fixed rigidly at P and S. Bar is subjected to axial loads of 60 kN and 120 kN at Q and R as shown in figure. Find the loads shared by each part of the bar and the displacement of the points Q and R. Take E for steel 207 kN/mm².* **(May 2006)**

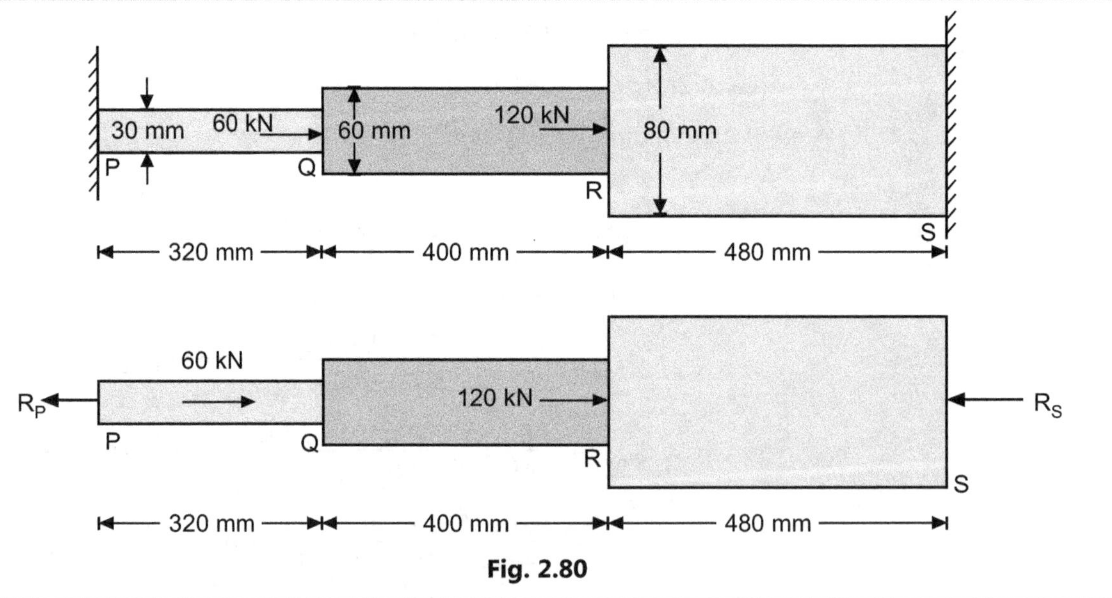


**Fig. 2.80**

**Data :** As shown in Fig. 2.80.

**Required :** Load shared by each part, displacement of Q and R.

**Concept :** Standard formulae.

**Solution :** Let $R_P$ and $R_S$ be the reactions at P and S.

(i) Geometric properties :

$$A_{PQ} = \frac{\pi}{4} \times 30^2$$

$$= 706.86 \text{ mm}^2$$

$$A_{QR} = 2827.43 \text{ mm}^2$$

and $\quad A_{RS} = 5026.55 \text{ mm}^2$

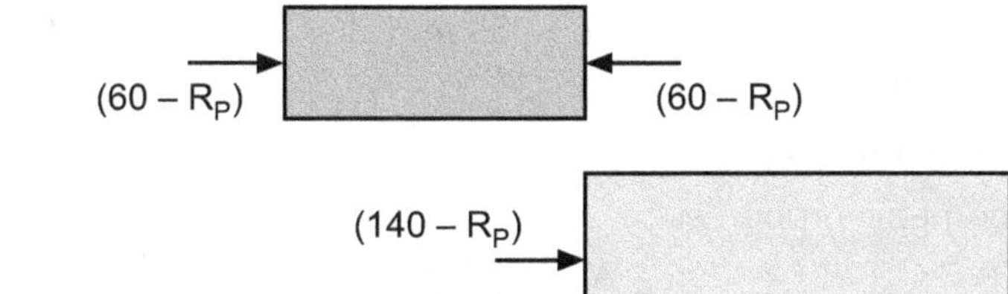


**Fig. 2.81**

Now, $\qquad \delta l = \delta l_{PQ} + \delta l_{QR} + \delta l_{RS}$

$$\delta l_{PQ} = \frac{R_P \times 10^3 \times 320}{706.86 \times 207 \times 10^3}$$

$$= 2.187 \times 10^{-3} \, R_P \text{ (Tensile)}$$

$$\delta l_{QR} = \frac{(60 - R_P) \times 10^3 \times 400}{2827.43 \times 207 \times 10^3}$$

$$= 6.83 \times 10^{-4} \, (60 - R_P) \text{ (Compressive)}$$

$$\delta l_{RS} = \frac{(140 - R_P) \times 10^3 \times 480}{5026.55 \times 207 \times 10^3}$$

$$= 4.61 \times 10^{-4} \, (140 - R_P) \text{ (Compressive)}$$

$\therefore \qquad 0 = 2.18 \times 10^{-3} \, R_P - 6.83 \times 10^{-4} \, (60 - R_P)$

$$- 4.61 \times 10^{-4} \, (140 - R_P)$$

$\therefore \qquad (1055.2) \times 10^{-4} = 3.324 \times 10^{-3} \, R_P$

$\therefore \qquad R_P = 31.74 \text{ kN}$

$$R_S = (140 - R_P)$$

$$= 68.26 \text{ kN}$$

**Displacement of Q :**

$$\delta_Q \;=\; \delta l_{PQ} + \delta l_{QR}$$
$$= 2.18 \times 10^{-3} \times 31.74 + 6.83 \times 10^{-4} (60 - 31.74)$$
$$= 0.069 + 0.019$$
$$= \mathbf{0.088\ mm}$$

**Displacement of R :**

$$\delta l_R \;=\; \delta l_{RS}$$
$$= 4.61 \times 10^{-4} (140 - 31.74)$$
$$= \mathbf{0.05\ mm}$$

---

**Example 2.73 :** *A square bar 50 mm × 50 mm is subjected to a compressive load of 500 kN. The contraction over 200 mm length is 0.5 mm and increase in thickness is 0.04 mm.*

**Calculate :** (i) Poisson's ratio, (ii) Modulus of elasticity, (iii) Bulk modulus, (iv) Volumetric strain.

**Data :** Square bar 50 mm, P = 500 kN, $l$ = 200 mm, $\delta l$ = 0.5 mm, $\delta t$ = 0.04 mm.

**Required :** E, μ, k and $\varepsilon_v$.

**Concept :** Standard formulae.

**Solution :** (i) Geometric properties :

$$A \;=\; 50 \times 50 = 2500\ mm^2$$

(ii) Modulus of elasticity (E) :

$$\delta l \;=\; \frac{Pl}{AE}$$
$$0.5 \;=\; \frac{500 \times 10^3 \times 200}{2500 \times E}$$
$$\therefore \quad E \;=\; 80 \times 10^3\ MPa = \mathbf{80\ GPa}$$

(iii) Poisson's ratio (μ) :

$$\mu \;=\; \frac{\text{Lateral strain}}{\text{Longitudinal strain}}$$
$$= \frac{0.04150}{0.51200} = \mathbf{0.32}$$

(iv) Bulk modulus :

$$k \;=\; \frac{E}{3\,(1 - 2\,\mu)} = \frac{80 \times 10^3}{3\,(1 - 2 \times 0.32)}$$
$$= 74.07 \times 10^3\ MPa$$
$$k \;=\; \mathbf{74.07\ GPa}$$

(v) Volumetric strain ($\varepsilon_v$) :

$$\varepsilon_x \;=\; \frac{\sigma_x}{E}$$
$$= \frac{500 \times 10^3}{2500 \times 80 \times 10^3} = 2.5 \times 10^{-3}$$
$$\varepsilon_v \;=\; \varepsilon_x$$
$$= \mathbf{2.5 \times 10^{-3}}$$

---

**Example 2.74 :** *Two vertical rods one of steel and one of bronze suspended at a distance of 600 mm apart. Each rod is 3 m long, 12 mm in diameter. A horizontal cross bar in connects the lower ends of the rod and on it placed a load of 4500 N so that cross bar remains horizontal. Find the position of the load on the cross bar and stresses in each rod.*

$$E_{steel} = 1.96 \times 10^5 \text{ MPa}$$

$$E_{bronze} = 0.63 \times 10^5 \text{ MPa}$$

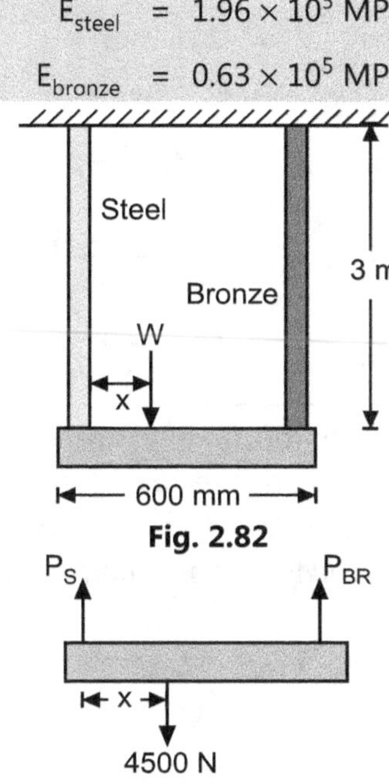


**Fig. 2.82**

**Fig. 2.83**

**Data :** As shown in Fig. 2.82 and 2.83.

**Required :** Distance 'x'.

**Concept :** Elongation of both steel and bronze rod must be same for bar remains horizontal.

**Solution :** (i) Equation of statics :

$$P_{Br} = \frac{4500\, x}{600} = 7.5\, x \qquad \qquad ...(i)$$

$$P_S = \frac{4500\,(600 - x)}{600} = 7.5\,(600 - x) \qquad \qquad ...(ii)$$

(ii) For bar to be horizontal :

$$\delta l_S = \delta l_{Br}$$

$$\frac{P_S l_S}{A_S\, E_S} = \frac{P_{Br} \cdot l_{Br}}{A_{Br}\, E_{Br}}$$

$$\frac{P_S}{1.96 \times 10^5} = \frac{P_{Br}}{0.63 \times 10^5}$$

$$\therefore \qquad P_S = 3.11\, P_{Br}$$

$$\therefore \qquad P_S + P_{Br} = 4500$$

$$\therefore \qquad 3.11\, P_{Br} + P_{Br} = 4500$$

$$\therefore \qquad\qquad P_{Br} \; = \; 1094.89 \text{ N}$$

and $\qquad\qquad\qquad\qquad P_S \; = \; 3405.11 \text{ N}$

Put, $P_{Br}$ in equation (i)

$$\therefore \qquad\qquad 1094.89 \; = \; 7.5 \, x$$

$$\therefore \qquad\qquad x \; = \; \textbf{146 mm}$$

$\therefore \quad$ Bar to be remain horizontal keep load at distance 146 mm from steel rod.

$$\text{Area of rod} \; = \; \frac{\pi}{4} \times 12^2 = 113.1 \text{ mm}^2$$

$$\text{Stress in Bronze rod} \; = \; \frac{P_{Br}}{A} = \frac{1094.89}{113.1} = \textbf{9.68 N/mm}^2$$

$$\text{Stress in Steel rod} \; = \; \frac{P_S}{A} = \frac{3405.11}{113.1} = \textbf{30.11 N/mm}^2$$

---

**Example 2.75 :** *A hollow steel tube of 50 mm in diameter and 3 mm thickness encloses centrally a solid copper bar of 35 mm diameter. The bar and the tube are rigidly connected together at the ends at a temperature of 20°C. Find the stresses in each metal when heated to 170°C. Also find the increase in length, if the original length of assembly is 350 mm.*

*$d_S = 1.08 \times 10^{-5}$ per °C.*

*$E_S = 2 \times 10^5$ MPa*

*$d_C = 1.7 \times 10^{-5}$ per °C*

*$E_C = 1 \times 10^5$ MPa* **(May 2006)**

**Data :** $D_o = 50$ mm, $D_i = 44$ mm, $D_S = 35$ mm, $t_1 = 20°$ C, $t_2 = 170°$ C, $\alpha_S = 1.08 \times 10^{-5}$ per °C, $E_S = 2 \times 10^5$ N/mm$^2$, $\alpha_C = 1.7 \times 10^{-5}$ per °C, $E_C = 1 \times 10^5$ N/mm$^2$

**Required :** Stresses in steel tube and copper rod.

**Concept :** Standard formulae.

**Solution :** (i) Geometric properties :

$$A_S \; = \; \frac{\pi}{4} \, (50^2 - 40^2) = 442.96 \text{ mm}^2$$

$$A_C \; = \; \frac{\pi}{4} \times 35^2 = 962.11 \text{ mm}^2$$

(ii) As it is temporary change, so force in each bar should be same.

$$\therefore \qquad\qquad \sigma_S \cdot A_S \; = \; \sigma_C \, A_C$$

$$\sigma_S \times 442.96 \; = \; \sigma_C \times 962.11$$

$$\therefore \qquad\qquad \sigma_S \; = \; 2.17 \, \sigma_C$$

$$\frac{\sigma_S}{E_S} + \alpha_S \, (t_2 - t_1) \; = \; \alpha_C \, (t_2 - t_1) - \frac{\sigma_C}{E_S}$$

---

$$\frac{2.176_C}{2 \times 10^5} + 1.08 \times 10^{-5}\,(170 - 20) \;=\; 1.7 \times 10^{-5} \times (170 - 20)$$

$$\therefore \qquad 4.17\,\sigma_C \;=\; 93 \times 10^{-4} \times 2 \times 10^{-5} - \frac{\sigma_C}{1 \times 10^{-5}}$$

$$\sigma_C \;=\; \textbf{44.60 N/mm}^2$$

and

$$\sigma_S \;=\; \textbf{96.79 N/mm}^2$$

Stress in copper is 44.60 N/mm$^2$ and steel is 96.79 N/mm$^2$

$$\text{Change in length} \;=\; \frac{\sigma_S l_S}{E_S} + \alpha_S\,l_S\,(t_2 - t_1)$$

$$=\; \frac{96.79 \times 350}{2 \times 10^5} + 1.08 \times 10^{-5} \times 350 \times (170 - 20)$$

$$=\; 0.17\ \text{mm} + 0.57$$

$$=\; \textbf{0.74 mm}$$

$\therefore$    Length of bar will increase by **0.74 mm**.

**Example 2.76 :** *A steel bar shown in Fig. 2.84 of cross-section area of 300 mm$^2$ is held between two end supports and loaded by an axial forces of 30 kN. Determine, (i) Reaction at A and B, (ii) Extension of left portion.* **(Dec. 2006)**

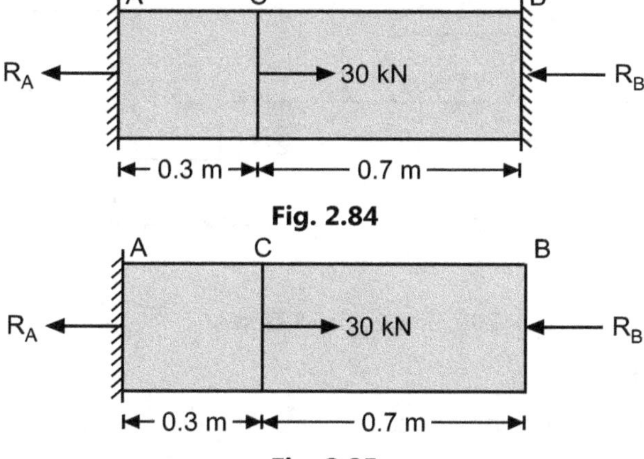


**Fig. 2.84**

**Fig. 2.85**

**Data :** As shown in Fig. 2.84, A = 300 mm$^2$

**Required :** Reactions at A and B and displacement at 'C'.

**Concept :** Total displacement of composite section is zero.

**Solution :** (i) Reactions : Let, $R_A$ and $R_B$ be the reactions at A and B respectively.

$$\delta l \;=\; \delta l_{AC} + \delta l_{BC}$$

$$\therefore \qquad 0 \;=\; \left(\frac{Pl}{AE}\right)_{AC} + \left(\frac{Pl}{AE}\right)_{CB}$$

$$AE = \text{Constant}$$

$$\therefore \quad 0 = \frac{R_A \times 300}{AE} - \frac{(30 - R_A) \times 700}{AE}$$

$$\therefore \quad 0 = 1000\, R_A - 21000$$

$$\therefore \quad R_A = \mathbf{21\ kN}$$

$$\therefore \quad R_B = \mathbf{9\ kN}$$

**(ii) Displacement of C :** Assume $E = 200 \times 10^3$ N/mm$^2$

$$\delta l_{AC} = \left(\frac{Pl}{AE}\right)_{AC} = \frac{21 \times 10^3 \times 300}{300 \times 200 \times 10^3}$$

$$= \mathbf{0.105\ mm}$$

Point 'C' is displaced to left by 0.105 mm.

**Example 2.77 :** *A composite rod, as shown in Fig. 2.86, is loaded by various axial forces. Determine the largest value of 'P' such that the stress in steel does not exceed 150 MPa and that in brass does not exceed 75 MPa. Hence, determine the deformation of the bar.*

*Take $E_{steel} = 200$ GPa and $E_{brass} = 75$ GPa.*

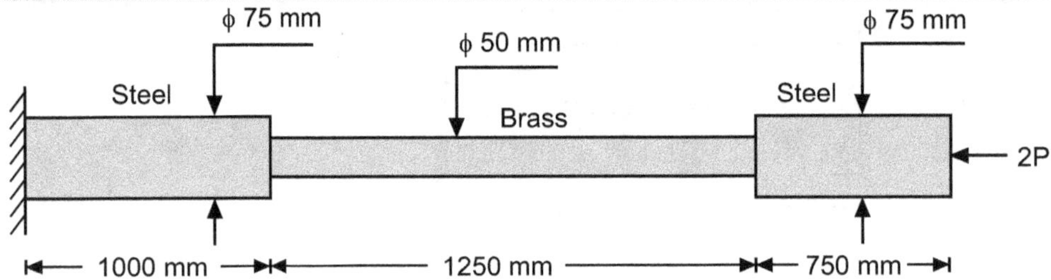


**Fig. 2.86**

**Data :** As shown in figure $E_{St} = 200$ GPa, $E_{Br} = 75$ GPa

**Required :** Deformation of bar.

**Concept :** Find value of P and then calculate deformation.

**Solution :** (i) Geometric properties :

$$A_{St} = \frac{\pi}{4} \times 75^2 = 4417.86\ \text{mm}^2$$

$$A_{Br} = \frac{\pi}{4} \times 50^2 = 1963.50\ \text{mm}^2$$

(ii) Value of 'P' :

$$\sigma_{St} = 150 = \frac{2P}{A}$$

$$\therefore \quad P = \frac{150 \times 4417.86}{2} = 331.34 \times 10^3\ \text{N} \qquad \text{...(i)}$$

$$\sigma_{Br} = \frac{2P}{A}$$

$\therefore \qquad P = \dfrac{75 \times 1963.50}{2} = 73.63 \times 10^3 \text{ N} \qquad \qquad ...(ii)$

Minimum of (i) and (ii)

$\therefore \qquad P = 73.63 \times 10^3 \text{ N}$

(iii) Deformation of bar :

$$\delta l = \left(\frac{Pl}{AE}\right)_{St \to} + \left(\frac{Pl}{AE}\right)_{Br} + \left(\frac{Pl}{AE}\right)_{St}$$

$$= \frac{2 \times 73.63 \times 10^3 \times 1000}{4417.86 \times 200 \times 10^3} + \frac{2 \times 73.63 \times 10^3 \times 1250}{1963.50 \times 75 \times 10^3}$$

$$+ \frac{2 \times 73.63 \times 10^3 \times 750}{4417.86 \times 200 \times 10^3}$$

$\therefore \qquad \delta l = \textbf{1.54 mm (elongation)}$

$\therefore$  Total deformation of bar is **1.54 mm.**

**Example 2.78 :** *A steel rod 30 mm is diameter, 1 m long is heated through 100° K and at the same time subjected to a pull of 'P'. If total extension of the rod is 2 mm, what should be the magnitude of 'P' ?* **(Dec. 2007)**

*Take $\alpha_{steel} = 12 \times 10^{-6}/°K$, $E_{steel} = 200$ GPa.*

**Data :** $D = 30$ mm, $l = 1$m, $\delta t = 100°$ k, $\delta l = 2$ mm, $\alpha_s = 12 \times 10^{-6}/°K$, $E_S = 200$ GPa.

**Required :** Pull 'P'.

**Concept :** Determine elongation due to temperature. Subtract it from total elongation. From remaining elongation find, 'P'.

**Solution :** (i) Elongation due to change in temperature

$$\delta l_T = l \, \alpha \, \delta t$$

$$= 1000 \times 12 \times 10^{-6} \times 100$$

$$= 1.2 \text{ mm}$$

$\therefore \qquad$ Elongation due to pull $= 2 - 1.2 = 0.8$ mm

(ii) Pull 'P' : Let, P is in kN

$\therefore \qquad \qquad \delta l_p = \dfrac{Pl}{AE}$

$$0.8 = \frac{P \times 10^3 \times 1000}{\dfrac{\pi}{4} \times 30^2 \times 200 \times 10^3}$$

$\therefore \qquad \qquad P = \textbf{113.10 kN}$

## EXERCISE

1. A compound bar ABCD is subjected to an axial compressive load of 30 kN as shown in Fig. 2.87. Find stresses in individual components and total change in length of bar. Assume E = 200 GPa.

($\sigma_{AB}$ = 23.87 MPa, $\sigma_{BC}$ = 95.49 MPa, $\sigma_{CD}$ = 42.44 MPa, $\delta L$ = 0.364 mm)

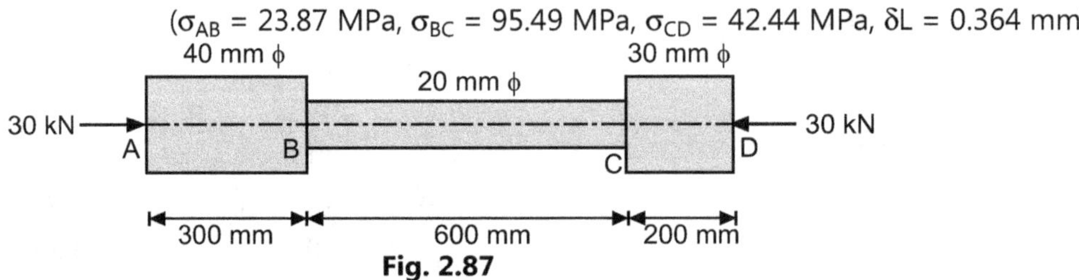


**Fig. 2.87**

2. A compound bar ABCD shown in Fig. 2.88 is subjected to axial compressive load which causes maximum stress of 100 MPa. Find total contraction of member if E = 150 GPa.

($\delta L$ = 0.28 mm)

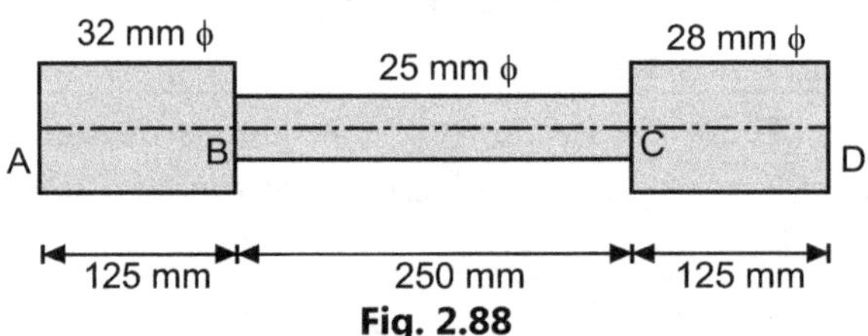


**Fig. 2.88**

3. A member 36 mm φ is subjected to axial forces as shown in Fig. 2.89. Find the total change in length of the bar assuming E = 100 GPa.                    (0.1178 mm contraction)

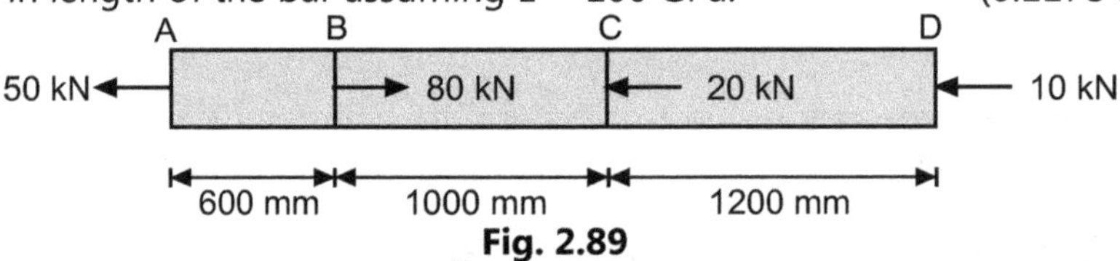


**Fig. 2.89**

4. A straight bar of steel 3 m long has rectangular cross section which varies uniformly from 100 mm × 12 mm at one end to 25 mm × 12 mm at other end. Find change in length of member when subjected to axial load of 35 kN. Assume E = 200 GPa.                    (0.807 mm)

5. A rod tapers uniformly from 40 mm to 22 mm in diameter in a length of 400 mm. If the rod is subjected to an axial load of 40 kN, find the extension of the rod assuming E = 200 GPa.                    (0.115 mm)

6. A member ABCD is subjected to forces as shown in Fig. 2.90. Find force 'P' necessary for equilibrium. Also find total elongation of the bar. Assume E = 210 GPa.

(P = 280 kN, $\delta L$ = 0.476 mm)

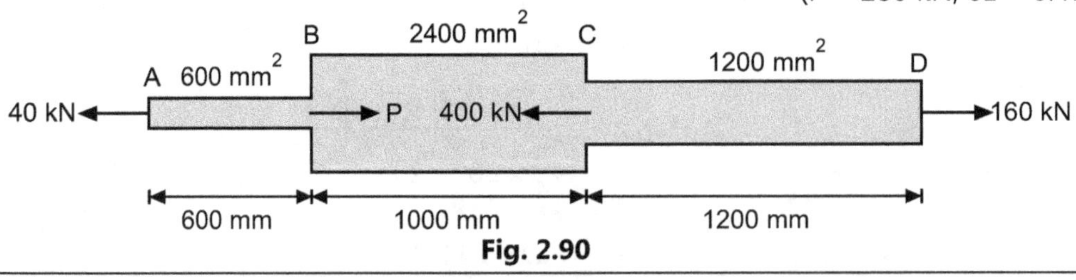


**Fig. 2.90**

7. A cylinder 150 mm in diameter, 300 mm in length is subjected to axial compressive load of 180 kN which causes increase in diameter by 0.0952 mm and a decrease in length by 0.64 mm. Compute the values of Poisson's ratio and modulus of elasticity.

$$(\mu = 0.295, E = 4.78 \text{ GPa})$$

8. A square bar of 20 mm side is held between two rigid supports and loaded as shown in Fig. 2.91. Find the reactions at the supports A and C and the extension of portion AB. Assume E = 200 GPa.

$$(H_A = 60 \text{ kN}, H_C = 90 \text{ kN}, \delta L_{AB} = 0.225 \text{ mm})$$

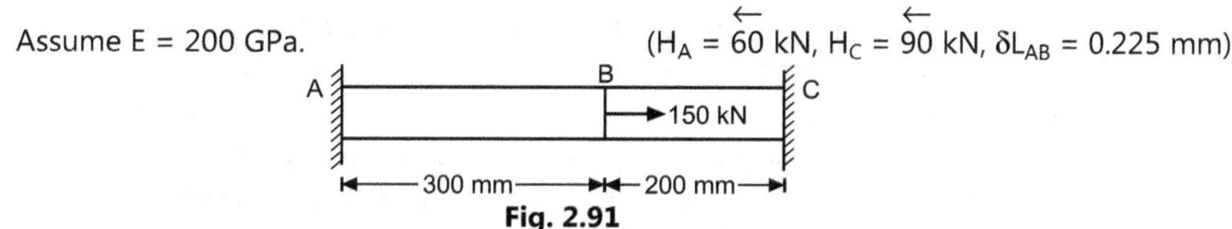


**Fig. 2.91**

9. A member ABCD is loaded as shown in Fig. 2.92. Determine (i) total deformation of rod, (ii) displacement of 'C'. Assume E = 70 GPa.

$$(\delta L = 0.0528 \text{ mm}, \delta C = 0.09 \text{ mm} (\leftarrow))$$

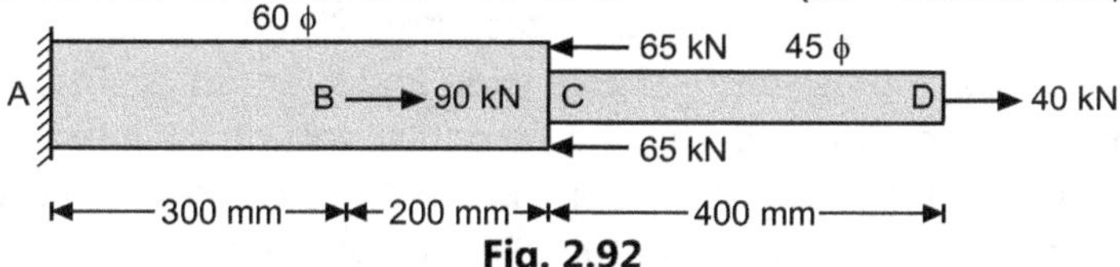


**Fig. 2.92**

10. A square bar is subjected to axial compressive stress $\sigma_x$ in the longitudinal direction. The lateral strains in the direction at right angles are completely prevented by suitable external pressure. Evaluate this external pressure.

$$\left( p = \left( \frac{\mu}{1 - \mu} \right) \sigma_x \, , \, \frac{\sigma_x}{\epsilon_x} = \frac{E}{\mu^2 - 1} \right)$$

11. A short piece of steel pipe is to carry an axial compressive force of 1200 kN with a factor of safety of 1.8 against yielding. If thickness t of the pipe is $\frac{1}{8}$ th of its outside diameter, find minimum required outside diameter. Assume yield stress = 270 MPa.  (153 mm)

12. A metal rod 10 mm diameter when tested under axial pull of 10 kN was found to reduce its diameter by 0.003 mm. Modulus of rigidity for the material is G = 51 GPa. Find other elastic constants.  $(\mu = 0.317, E = 134.3 \text{ GPa}, K = 122.3 \text{ GPa})$

13. A steel bar ABC transmits an axial tensile force such that, total change in length is 0.6 mm. Determine for parts AB and BC the changes in length and diameter. Assume $\mu = 0.3$ and E = 200 GPa.

(For AB, $\delta L = 0.232$ mm, $\delta d = 0.00185$ mm, for BC; $\delta L = 0.368$ mm, $\delta d = 0.00286$ mm)

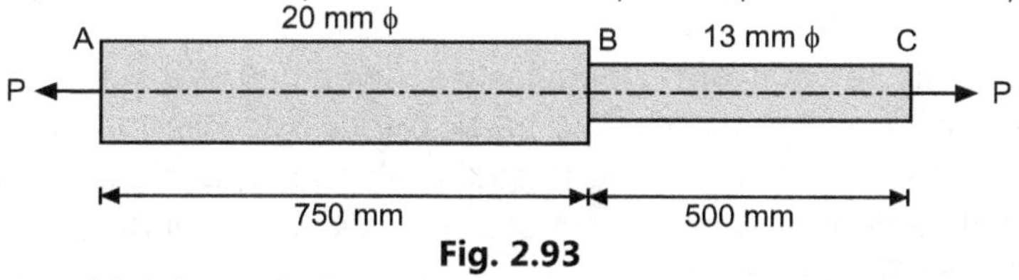

**Fig. 2.93**

14. A column 3 m high has a hollow circular cross-section of external diameter 300 mm and carries an axial compressive load of 500 kN. If stress in the column is limited to 150 MPa and shortening of column is restricted to 2 mm, find the internal diameter required. Also calculate maximum shortening of column, E = 200 GPa.  (205.5 mm, 2 mm)

15. A composite section consists of two bars of equal lengths connected together by sides. If $A_1$ and $A_2$ are their cross-sectional areas and $E_1$ and $E_2$ are their respective modulii of elasticity, show that the equivalent or apparent modulus of elasticity of composite bar is given by $E = \dfrac{E_1\,A_1 + E_2\,A_2}{A_1 + A_2}$ , when loaded axially.

16. A copper bar 36 mm$\phi$ is enclosed in a steel tube having 50 mm external diameter and 5 mm metal thickness. The composite section is subjected to an axial pull of 120 kN. Find stresses induced in both materials and extension of member assuming L = 1.5 m, $E_C$ = 110 GPa and $E_S$ = 200 GPa.                    ($\sigma_C$ = 52 MPa, $\sigma_S$ = 94.7 MPa, $\delta L$ = 0.7 mm)

17. Three vertical rods, equal in lengths, each 12 mm$\phi$ are equispaced in a vertical plane and jointly support the load of 12 kN; the rods being so adjusted to share the load equally. If a further load of 13 kN is added, find the stresses in each rod. Assume      $E_C$ = 110 GPa, $E_S$ = 200 GPa.($\sigma_C$ = 60.18 MPa, $\sigma_S$ = 80.47 MPa)

18. A compound bar consists of a central steel strip 25 mm wide and 6 mm thick placed between two strips of brass each 25 mm wide and t mm thick. The strips are firmly fixed together, to form a compound bar of rectangular section 25 mm wide and (6 + 2t) mm thick. Determine (a) the thickness t of the brass strips which will make apparent modulus of elasticity of the compound bar 140 GPa and (b) the maximum axial pull the bar can then carry if the stress is not to exceed 140 MPa in either the brass or the steel. Assume $E_S$ = 200 GPa, $E_b$ = 110 GPa (t = 5.92 mm, P = 43.7 kN)

19. A solid steel cylinder 500 mm long and 70 mm diameter is placed inside an aluminium cylinder having 75 mm inside diameter and 100 mm outside diameter. The aluminium cylinder is 0.15 mm longer than the steel cylinder. An axial load of 400 kN is applied to the composite section through rigid cover plates. Find stresses developed in each material assuming $E_S$ = 220 GPa, $E_A$ = 70 GPa.          ($\sigma_S$ = 66.34 MPa, $\sigma_A$ = 42.1 MPa)

20. A copper sleeve having 21 mm internal and 27 mm external diameter, surrounds a 20 mm steel bolt, one end of the sleeve being in contact with the shoulder of the bolt. The sleeve is 70 mm long. After putting a rigid washer on the other end of the sleeve, a nut is screwed on the bolt through 10 degrees. If the pitch of the threads is 2.5 mm, find the stresses induced in the copper sleeve and steel bolt.
Take $E_S$ = 210 GPa and $E_C$ = 80 GPa.                    ($\sigma_S$ = 44.78 MPa, $\sigma_C$ = 62.25 MPa)

21. A bar of 2 m length and 20 mm × 15 mm in cross section is subjected to an axial tensile load of 35 kN. Find the final volume of the bar if $\mu$ = 0.25 and E = 200 GPa.
$$(700.175 \times 10^3 \text{ mm}^3)$$

22. A steel block in the form of rectangular parallelopiped has sides 100 mm along x-axis and 50 mm along y and z axes. The block carries a tensile load of 25 kN along x-axis passing through C.G. of block. Find (i) strains along x, y, and z axes (ii) what load should be applied along z-axis so that strain along y-axis is zero under the action of combined loading ? Take E = 200 GPa, $\mu$ = 0.3.
($\epsilon_x$ = 5 × 10$^{-5}$ tensile, $\epsilon_y$ = $\epsilon_z$ = 1.5 × 10$^{-5}$ compressive, $P_z$ = 50 kN compressive)

23. A steel rod 20 mm diameter passes centrally through a steel tube 25 mm internal diameter and 40 mm external diameter. The tube is 800 mm long and is closed by rigid

washers of negligible thickness which are fastened by nuts threaded on the rod. The nuts are tightened until the compressive load on the tube is 20 kN. Calculate the stresses in the tube and the rod. Also find the increase in these stresses when one nut is tightened by one quarter of a turn relative to other. There are 0.4 threads per mm length. Assume E = 210 GPa.

(For 20 kN load on tube, $\sigma_{st}$ = 26.1 MPa compressive, $\sigma_{sr}$ = 63.6 MPa tensile,

When nut is tightened by one quarter, $\sigma_{st}$ = 47.72 MPa compressive,

$\sigma_{sr}$ = 116.34 MPa tensile)

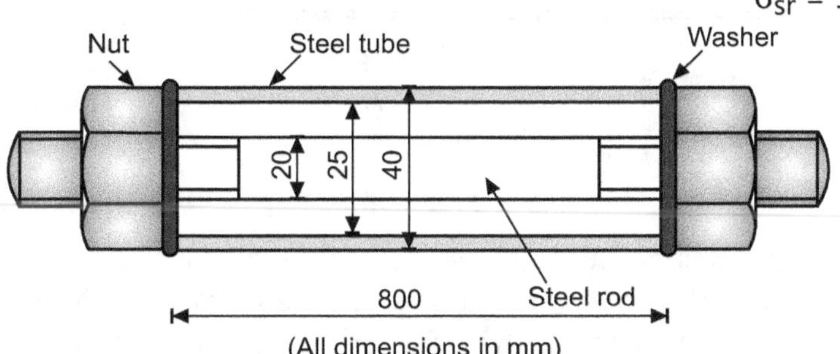


**Fig. 2.94**

24. A mild steel flat 150 mm wide and 20 mm thick is 6 m long. It carries an axial pull of 325 kN. If E = 200 GPa and μ = 0.26, calculate the change in length, width, thickness and volume of the flat.

($\delta L$ = 3.25 mm, $\delta b$ = 0.021 mm, $\delta t$ = 0.0028 mm, $\delta V$ = 4680 mm³)

25. A rigid member ABCD is supported and loaded as shown in Fig. 2.95. Find stresses developed in steel and brass. ($\sigma_C$ = 107.7 MPa, $\sigma_S$ = 107.7 MPa)

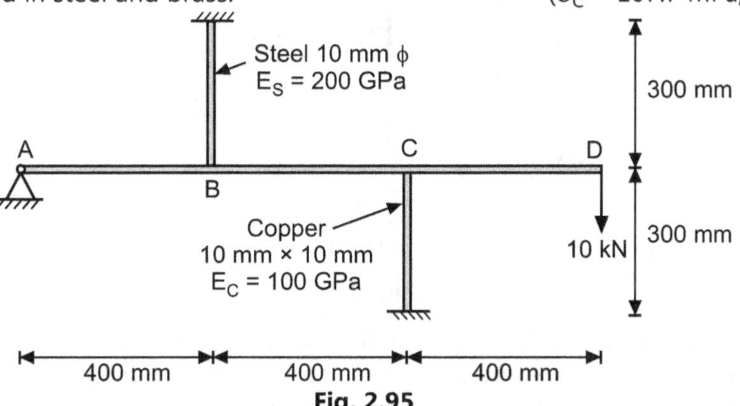


**Fig. 2.95**

26. A steel rod 15 m long is subjected to temperature change of 50°C. Find the temperature stress produced (i) when the expansion of the rod is prevented, (ii) the rod is permitted to expand by 5 mm. Assume $\alpha_s$ = 1.2 × 10⁻⁶ /°C and E = 200 GPa. (120 MPa, 53.33 MPa)

27. A cartwheel of 1.2 m diameter is to be provided with a thin steel tyre. Assuming the wheel to be rigid if the stress in steel is not to exceed 150 MPa, calculate the minimum diameter of the tyre and the minimum temperature to which it should be heated before slipping on to wheel. Assume E = 200 GPa, $\alpha_s$ = 12 × 10⁻⁶ /°C. (1199.1 mm, 62.5°C)

28. A rigid bar 3.5 m in length is hinged at A and supported by wires as shown in Fig. 2.96. Determine (i) stresses in each rod, (ii) elongation of the steel rod. Assume $E_C$ = 120 GPa, $E_S$ = 200 GPa. ($\sigma_S$ = 140.7 MPa, $\sigma_C$ = 64.32 MPa, $\delta L_S$ = 0.7 mm)

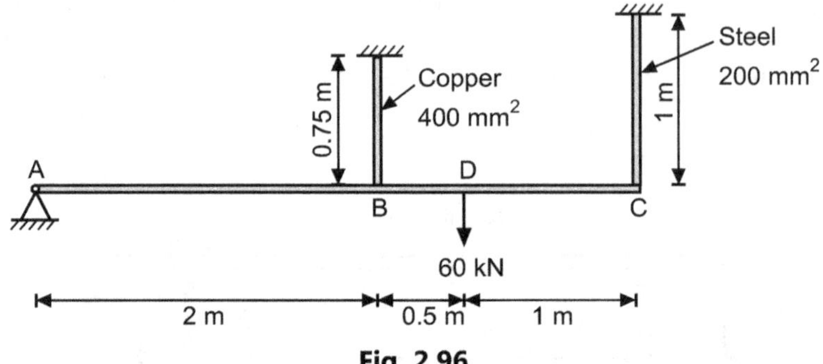


**Fig. 2.96**

29. A rigid beam weighing 200 N is held in horizontal position by three vertical wires as shown in Fig. 2.97. The outer wires of brass are 1.25 mm in diameter and the central steel wire is 0.6 mm in diameter. If the wires are stress free before the beam is attached, estimate the stresses induced in each wire. Assume $E_S$ = 210 GPa, $E_b$ = 86 GPa.

($\sigma_b$ = 63.59 MPa, $\sigma_S$ = 154.48 MPa)

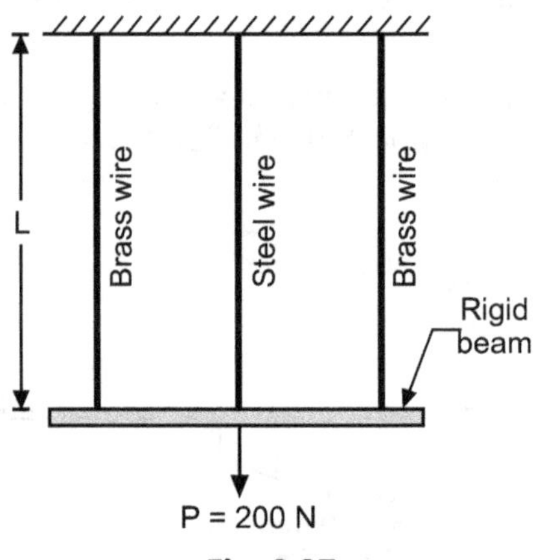


**Fig. 2.97**

30. A surveyor steel tape, nominally 30 metres is 12 mm wide and 1 mm thick. Its length is correct when used at a temperature of 16°C and under a pull of 100 N. By how much it will be in error when used at a temperature of 50°C and under a pull of 50 N ? E = 200 GPa and $\alpha$ = 11 × 10⁻⁶ /°C.    (10.595 mm longer)

31. A bar of steel and two bars of copper, each of the same area and length, have their ends rigidly connected together when a temperature of 25°C so that the steel bar lies between the two copper bars. When the temperature is raised to 275°C, the length of the bar increases by 2 mm. Determine the original length and final stresses in the bar. Take $E_S$ = 200 GPa, $E_C$ = 110 GPa, $\alpha_C$ = 17.5 × 10⁻⁶/°C, $\alpha_S$ = 12 × 10⁻⁶ /°C.

$$(\sigma_C = 71.98 \text{ MPa}, \sigma_S = 143.97 \text{ MPa}, l = 537.55 \text{ mm})$$

32.  A mild steel bar 20 mm in diameter and 300 mm long is encased in a brass tube whose external diameter is 30 mm and internal diameter is 25 mm. The composite bar is heated through 40°C. Calculate the stresses induced in each material.

$\alpha_s = 11.2 \times 10^{-6}$ /°C, $\alpha_b = 16.5 \times 10^{-6}$ /°C, $E_s = 200$ GPa, $E_c = 100$ GPa.

$$(\sigma_b = 15.77 \text{ MPa}, \sigma_s = 10.84 \text{ MPa})$$

33.  A steel rod, 20 mm diameter, 200 mm long is heated through 120°K and at the same time subjected to a pull P. If the total extension of the rod is 0.3 mm, what should be the magnitude of P ? $\alpha_s = 12 \times 10^{-6}$ /°K, E = 215 GPa.            (P = 3.769 kN)

34.  A steel rod 25 mm diameter passes through a brass tube of 25 mm internal diameter and 35 mm external diameter. The nut on the rod is tightened until a stress of 15 MPa is developed in the rod. The temperature of the tube is then raised by 60° K. What are the final stresses in the rod and the tube ?

$E_s = 200$ GPa, $E_b = 80$ GPa, $\alpha_s = 11.7 \times 10^{-6}$ /°K, $\alpha_b = 19 \times 10^{-6}$ /°K.

$$(\sigma_s = 39.16 \text{ MPa tensile}; \sigma_b = 40.79 \text{ MPa compressive})$$

35.  A copper flat 60 mm × 30 mm is joined to another 60 mm × 60 mm steel flat as shown in Fig. 2.98. If the combination is heated through 100°C, determine

(i)      stress produced in each of the bar,

(ii)     shear force between the flats, and

(iii)    shear stress.

$$\alpha_c = 18.5 \times 10^{-6} \text{ /°C}; \alpha_s = 12 \times 10^{-6} \text{ /°C}; E_c = 110 \text{ GPa}; E_s = 220 \text{ GPa}.$$

$$(\sigma_c = 57.2 \text{ MPa}; \sigma_s = 28.6 \text{ MPa, Shear force} = 102.96 \text{ kN; Shear stress} = 4.29 \text{ MPa})$$

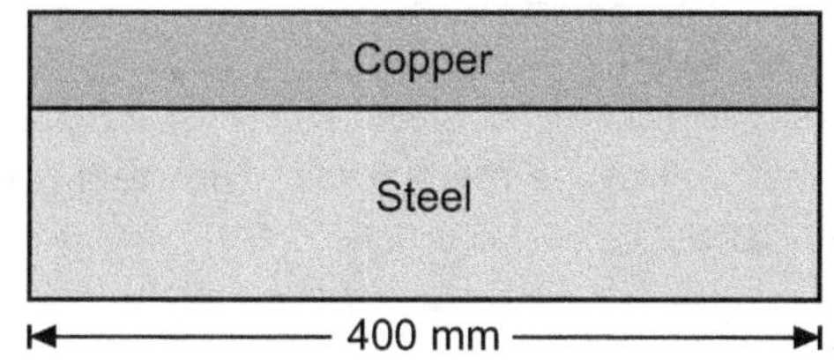


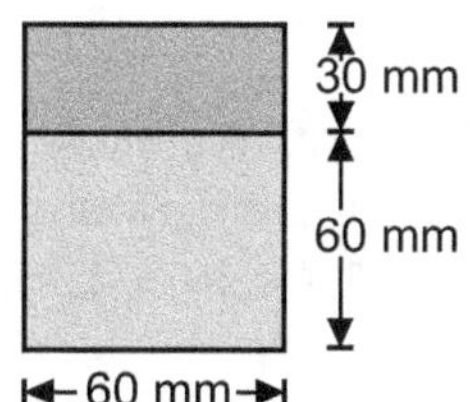


**Fig. 2.98**

36.  A composite bar made up of aluminium and steel is held between two supports as shown in Fig. 2.99. What will be the stresses in the two bars when the temperature is dropped by 30°C if (i) supports are non-yielding, (ii) one of the support yields by 0.1 mm.

$E_s = 210$ GPa; $E_a = 74$ GPa, $\sigma_s = 11.7 \times 10^{-6}$ /°C; $\alpha_a = 23.4 \times 10^{-6}$ /°C

$$(\text{For non-yielding supports}; \sigma_s = 22.09 \text{ MPa}; \sigma_a = 88.38 \text{ MPa};$$
$$\text{For yielding supports}; \sigma_s = 16.85 \text{ MPa}, \sigma_a = 67.41 \text{ MPa})$$

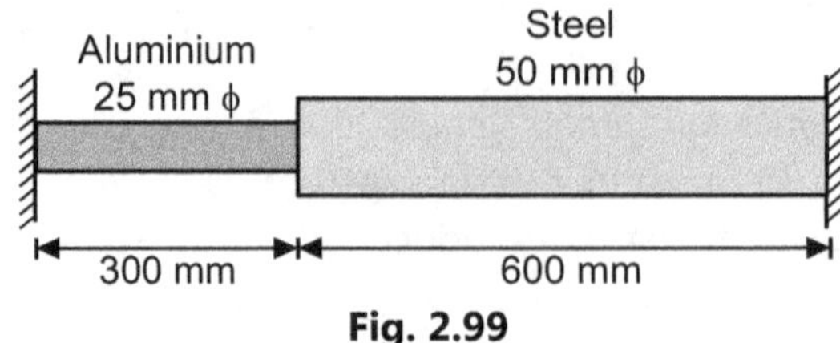

**Fig. 2.99**

37. A compound bar is made up by connecting a steel member and a copper member as shown in Fig. 2.100.

    Take $\alpha_s = 12 \times 10^{-6}$ /°C; $\alpha_c = 15.6 \times 10^{-6}$ /°C; $E_s = 200$ GPa; $E_c = 100$ GPa.

    Estimate the stress induced in the members due to temperature rise of 100°C.

    ($\sigma_c = 26.16$ MPa; $\sigma_s = 26.16$ MPa and 13.08 MPa)

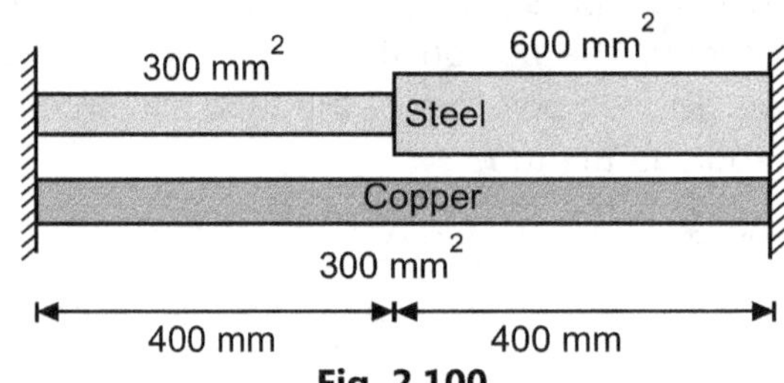

**Fig. 2.100**

38. A circular section tapered bar is rigidly fixed at both ends as shown in Fig. 2.101. If the temperature is raised by 30°C, calculate the maximum stress in the bar.

    $E = 200$ GPa, $\alpha = 12 \times 10^{-6}$/°C.                                         (126 MPa)

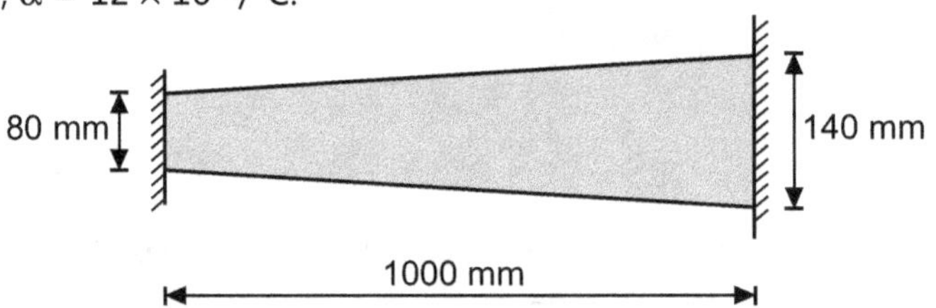

**Fig. 2.101**

39. A rigid bar of negligible weight is supported as shown in Fig. 2.102. If W = 80 kN, compute the temperature change that will cause the stress in the steel rod to be 55 MPa.

    Take $\alpha_s = 11.7 \times 10^{-6}$/°C, $\alpha_b = 18.9 \times 10^{-6}$/°C.               (28.3°C)

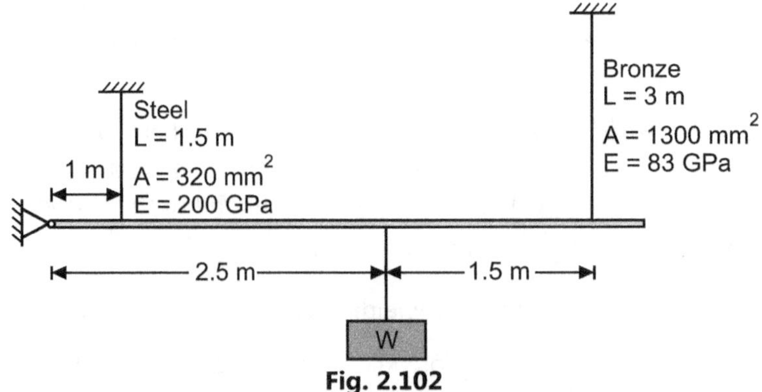

**Fig. 2.102**

## UNIVERSITY QUESTION PAPERS

### MAY 2014

1. A steel rod of 30 mm diameter is enclosed in a brass tube of 42 mm external diameter and 32 mm internal diameter. Each is 360 mm long and the assembly is rigidly held between two stops 360 mm apart. The temperature of the assembly is then raised by 50°C. Determine:

   (i) Stresses in the tube and the rod

   (ii) Stresses in the tube and the rod, if the stops yields by 0.15 mm.

   $E_s$ = 205 GPa,          $E_b$ = 90 GPa

   $\alpha_s = 11 \times 10^{-6}$ per°C,   $\alpha_b = 19 \times 10^{-6}$ per°C          **[6]**

### DECEMBER 2014

1. An aluminum rod is rigidity attached between a steel rod and a bronze rod as shown in the Fig. 1. Axial loads are applied at the positions indicated. Find the maximum value of P that will not exceed a stress in steel of 140 MPa, in aluminum of 90 MPa, or in bronze of 100 MPa.          **[6]**

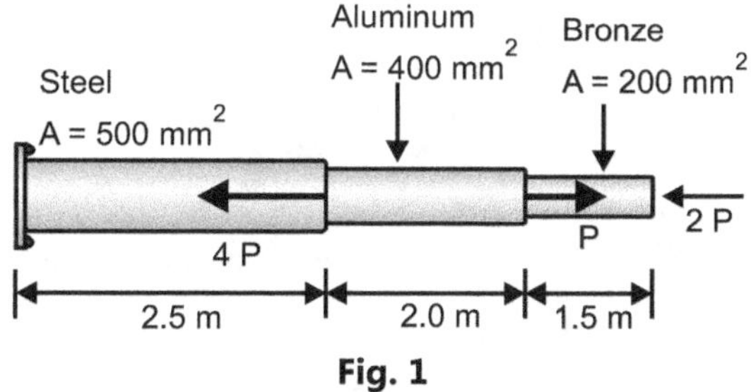


**Fig. 1**

### MAY 2015

1. A steel bar of 35 mm diameter and length 350 mm is pulled by 0.002 mm by application of tensile load. If the diameter of the bar is changed to 30 mm find the change in length for the same load.          **[6]**

## November 2015

1. A hollow steel tube with an inside diameter of 100 mm must carry a tensile load of 400 kN. Determine the outside diameter of the tube if the stress is limited to 120 MN/m$^2$.  **[6]**

## May 2016

1. A steel rod of 32 mm diameter is enclosed in a brass tube of 48 mm external diameter and 34 mm internal diameter. Each is 400 mm long and the assembly is rigidly held between two stops 400 mm apart. The temperature of the assembly is then raised by 60°C. Determine:

    (i)   Stresses in the tube and the rod if the distance between the stops remains constant.

    (ii)  Stresses in the tube and the rod, if the stops yields by 0.25 mm.

    $E_S$ = 200 GPa; $E_b$ = 90 GPa

    $\alpha_s = 12 \times 10^{-6}$ per °C; $\alpha_b = 21 \times 10^{-6}$ per °C.

# Chapter 3

# SHEAR FORCE AND BENDING MOMENT (PART A)

## 3.1 INTRODUCTION

We have so far studied stresses set up in a member due to axial force. As discussed in chapter 1, the axial force may or may not be constant along the length of member. When axial force is not constant along the length of member, we had used method of section to evaluate the axial force at a section of our interest and axial force diagrams were drawn to study the variation of axial force along the length of member. In this chapter, our interest is to study the effect of transverse loading on the member.

*Beam is a structural member which carries lateral or transverse forces i.e. forces at right angles to the axis of the member.* The study of these transverse, loads, however, is complicated by the fact that the loading effects vary from section to section of the beam. As a preliminary to study the stresses in beams, we shall study the variation of shear and bending moment at various cross-sections of the beam. Beams may be straight or curved, but we shall study only straight beams in this chapter. Also the forces applied to the beam will be assumed to lie in the same plane. All the beams discussed will be *statically determinate* i.e. unknown reactions can be determined by applying equations of static equilibrium.

## 3.2 TYPES OF SUPPORTS

In making sketches of structures or structural members it will be convenient to make use of symbols to show the manner in which it is supported. The various types of supports commonly employed in structural arrangements and their description are given in Table 3.1.

**Table 3.1**

| Sr. No. | Support type | Symbol | Description |
|---------|--------------|--------|-------------|
| 1. | Hinged or pinned | | Horizontal or vertical movement of the point of support, A, is prevented but free rotation about the point of support is possible. |
| 2. | Roller/Link | | Movement normal to the plane on which rollers are supported is prevented but movement parallel to the surface of support and rotation about the point of support is possible. |
| 3. | Fixed | | Movement or rotation in any direction is absolutely prevented. |

From the above discussion of various types of supports, it must be clear that, a hinged or a pinned support is capable of resisting a force acting in any direction of the plane. Hence, in general, the reaction at such a support may have two components, one in the horizontal and one in the vertical direction. The roller or link support is capable of resisting a force only in the direction normal to the plane on which it is supported. The fixed support is capable of resisting a force in any direction and is also capable of resisting a couple or a moment.

Thus, two reaction components are possible at hinged end, one reaction component is possible at roller end and three reaction components are possible at the fixed end as shown in  Fig. 3.1.

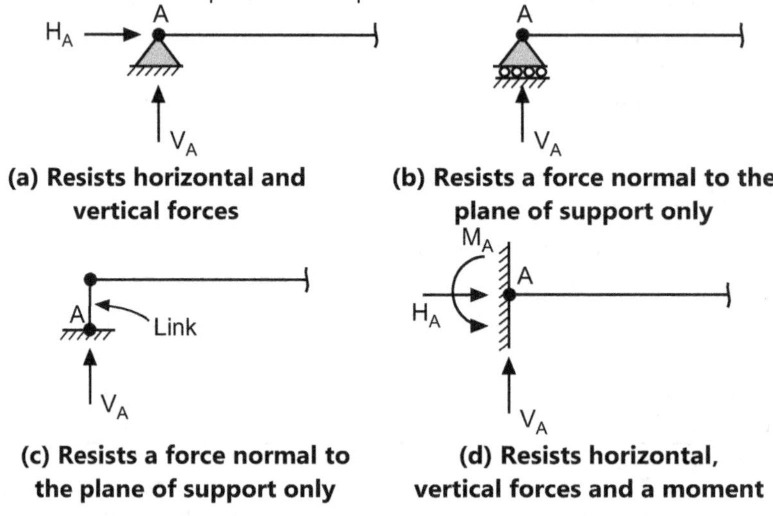


**Fig. 3.1**

## 3.3 TYPES OF LOADS

A beam may be subjected to the following types of loads :

    **(i)**     **Concentrated or point loads :** These loads act on a very small area and hence it can be assumed to act at a point as shown in Fig. 3.2 (a). Magnitude of the point load is expressed in **N** or **kN.**

    **(ii)**     **Uniformly distributed load (UDL) :** A load which is spread over a length of beam such that, each unit length is loaded to the same extent is known as uniformly distributed load (UDL), as shown in Fig. 3.2 (b). The intensity of UDL is expressed in **N/m** or **kN/m.**

    **(iii)**     **Uniformly varying load (UVL) :** A load which is spread over a length of beam such that, its extent varies uniformly on each unit length is known as uniformly varying load (UVL); as shown in Fig. 3.2 (c), (d). The intensity of UVL is expressed in **N/m** or **kN/m.**

    **(iv)**     **Couple or Moment :** A beam may be subjected to couple or moment at a point as shown in Fig. 3.2 (d). The magnitude of couple or moment is expressed in **Nm** or **kNm.**

    **(v)**     **Bracket loads :** A beam may be subjected to a bracket load as shown in Fig. 3.2 (g) which ultimately result in **point load** and **couple** at the point of attachment of bracket with the beam.

The reactions from secondary beams, columns, brackets etc. are generally idealized as concentrated or point loads. The self weight of beam, live load etc. are generally uniformly distributed over the length of beam. Loading on side walls of water tanks, lintels, retaining walls etc. is uniformly varying load. Point loads on brackets or point loads eccentric to the axis of the member result in couples.

There may also be various combinations of these loadings. All these loads are assumed to act in one plane, called as plane of loading. To get the reactions set up by various *distributed loads*, one needs only to consider the load replaced by an *equivalent concentrated load acting at its centre of gravity.*

## 3.4 REACTIONS

If a body, subjected to forces acting in a plane, is at rest, there are three conditions of equilibrium which must be satisfied.

$$\sum F_x = 0; \; \sum F_y = 0 \text{ and } \sum M_z = 0$$

It follows that, in determining the reactions acting on the body, the loads being known, not more than three unknown quantities can be found. There are three things which must be known about each force in order to have it fully determined : *its magnitude, its direction, and its point of application or line of action.* If knowledge of all these concerning one reaction is lacking, then the magnitude, direction and point of application or line of action of all other forces acting on the structure must be known. This reaction would then hold the body at equilibrium.

It must be remembered that, the number of unknowns which can be determined is fixed by the number of equations available, and it makes no difference whether they pertain to one reaction or to several reactions as long as the unknown quantities do not exceed in number of independent equations.

To find the reactions of given beam or structure, first of all we remove the supports and show the respective reaction components in their places and draw complete free body diagram (FBD). Then apply laws of statics to get the required unknown reactions. *Sign convention* used for applying laws of *statics* is as under :

    (i)     All horizontal forces to the right are considered positive.

    (ii)    All vertical forces acting upwards are considered positive.

    (iii)   All anticlockwise moments are considered positive.

Forces, moments, opposite of above are considered negative.

## 3.5 TYPES OF BEAMS

Beams are basically classified as statically determinate and statically indeterminate beams. When unknown reactions can be obtained by use of equations of static equilibrium alone, it is called as statically determinate. The various types of statically determinate beams are (i) Simply supported beam, (ii) Simple beam, (iii) Cantilever beam (iv) Overhanging beam etc. While the various types of statically indeterminate beams are (i) Fixed beams (ii) Continuous beams, (iii) Propped cantilevers etc. These various types of beams are shown in Fig. 3.2.

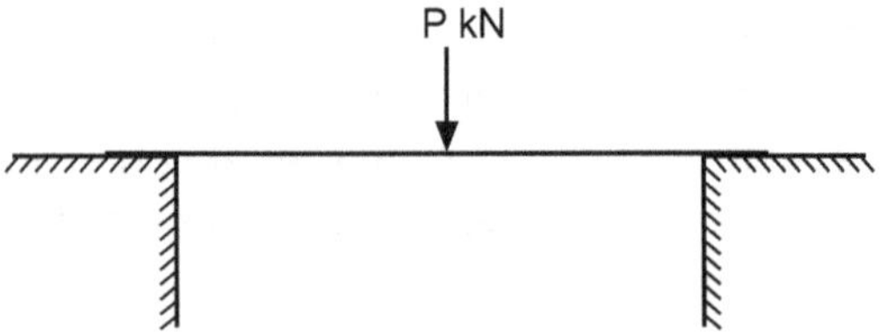

**(a) Simply supported beam**

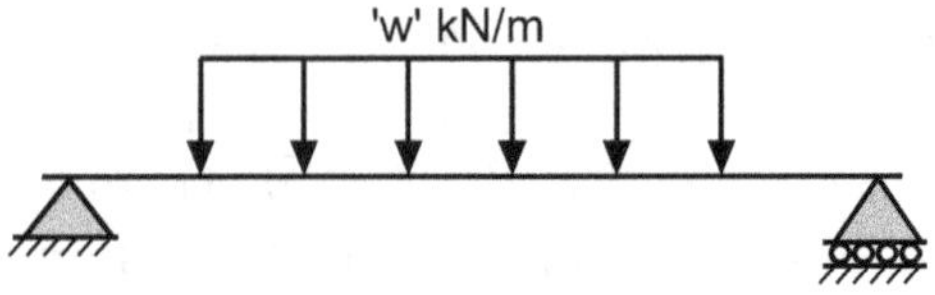

**(b) Simple beam**

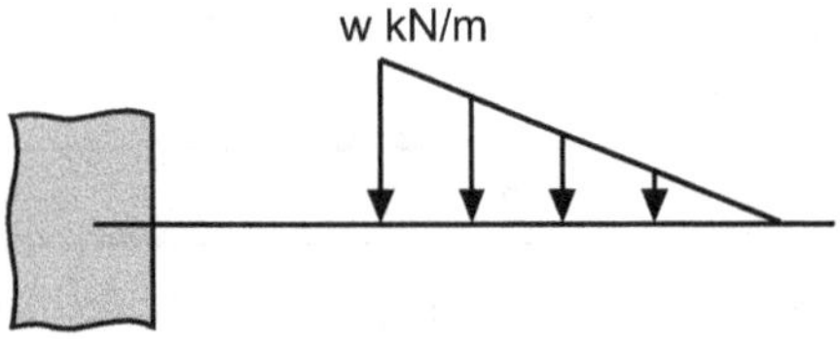

**(c) Cantilever beam**

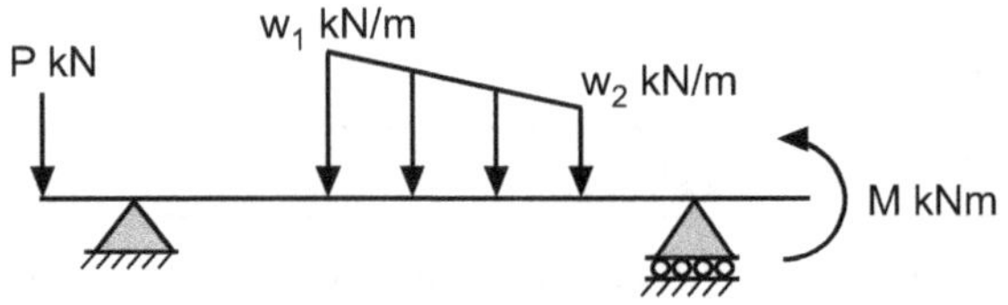

**(d) Overhanging beam**

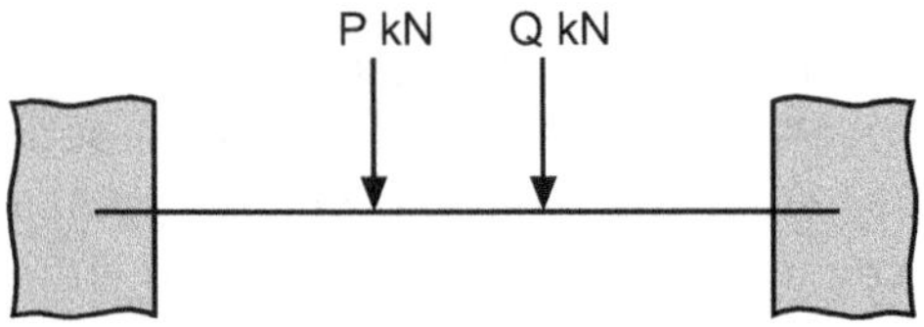

**(e) Fixed beam**

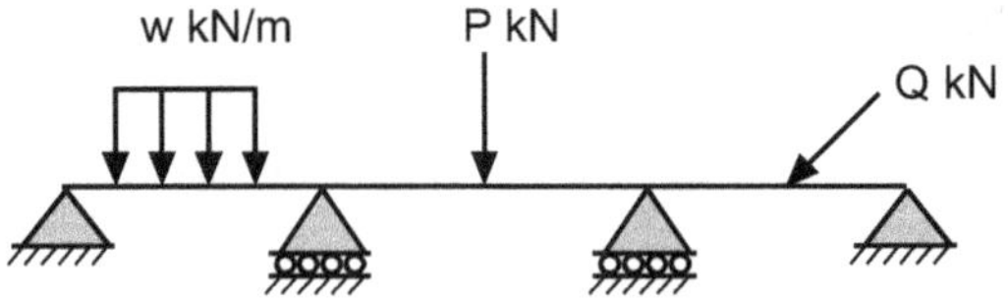

**(f) Continuous beam**

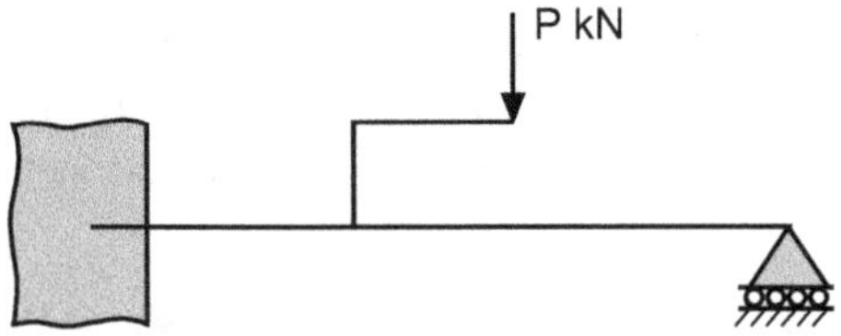

**(g) Propped cantilever**

**Fig. 3.2 : Various types of beams**

## 3.6 SHEAR FORCE AND BENDING MOMENT

Consider a FBD of beam as shown in Fig. 3.3 (a). The unknown reactions are determined by equations of laws of statics and having obtained the unknown reactions, *method of section* is used to find shear force and bending moment at a cross-section.

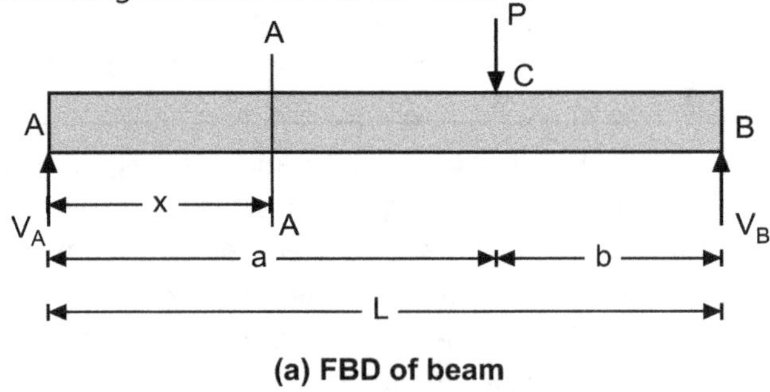

**(a) FBD of beam**

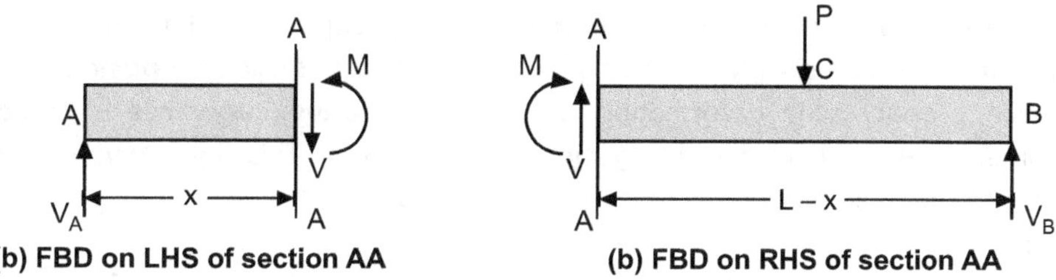

**(b) FBD on LHS of section AA**          **(b) FBD on RHS of section AA**

**Fig. 3.3**

Fig. 3.3 (b) shows the FBD of part of the beam on left hand side of the section considered at a distance x from A. Since, the beam and all its parts are in equilibrium, this section of the beam must be in equilibrium. First consider the equilibrium of the vertical forces i.e. $\sum F_y = 0$. This equation shows that, there must be a downward vertical force equal in magnitude to the reaction at left support. The only surface on which such a force can act is that on the right end of the free body. This downward force is called as the shear force and is designated as V or SF. Since, there are no horizontal forces, a moment equation is all that remains to be satisfied for equilibrium of the element shown. We can, ofcourse, write a moment equation about any point in the plane of the diagram, but it is convenient to write it with respect to the right hand end of the section. Assuming unknown couple at this section of magnitude M, we have

$$M - V_A\,(x) \;=\; 0$$

$$\therefore \qquad\qquad M \;=\; V_A\,(x)$$

This quantity is known as the bending moment and is designated as M or BM.

Fig. 3.3 (c) shows FBD of part of the beam on right hand side of the section considered. *It should be noted that magnitude and nature of the shear force and bending moment at a section whether computed from left or right hand side of the section remains the same.* The side to be chosen for calculation is that side on which fewer external forces are acting and the *section is to be considered normal to the axis of the beam.*

Thus, shear force and bending moment at a section can be defined as follows :

**Shear Force :** It is the algebraic sum of all the external forces acting parallel to the section, on any one side of the section.

**Bending Moment :** It is the algebraic sum of the moments of all the external forces acting on any one side of the section taken about the centre of gravity of section.

## 3.6.1 Sign Conventions for Shear Force and Bending Moment

**(a) Shear force :** An upward shear force to the left of the section or downward shear force to the right of the section is considered as positive; otherwise it will be negative. See Fig. 3.4 (a).

This sign convention of shear force leads to the shear effect as shown in Fig. 3.4 (b).

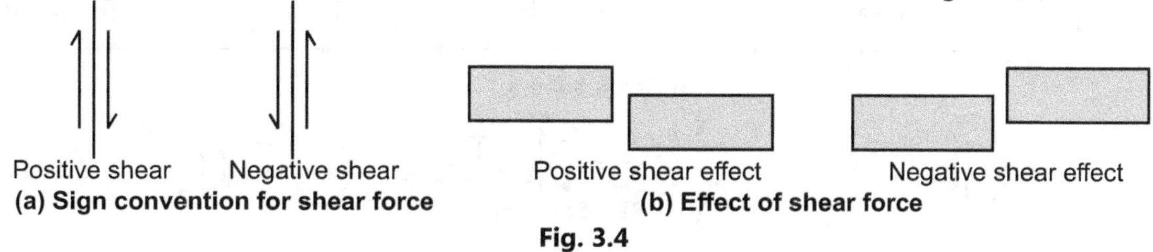



**(a) Sign convention for shear force**          **(b) Effect of shear force**

**Fig. 3.4**

**(b) Bending moment :** The bending moment which produces the deformation of the beam **concave upwards** is called **sagging** bending moment and it is considered **positive**. The bending moment which produces the deformation of the beam **convex upwards** is called **hogging** bending moment and it is considered **negative**. See Fig. 3.5 (a). This sign convention of bending moment leads to the bending effect as shown in Fig. 3.5 (b).

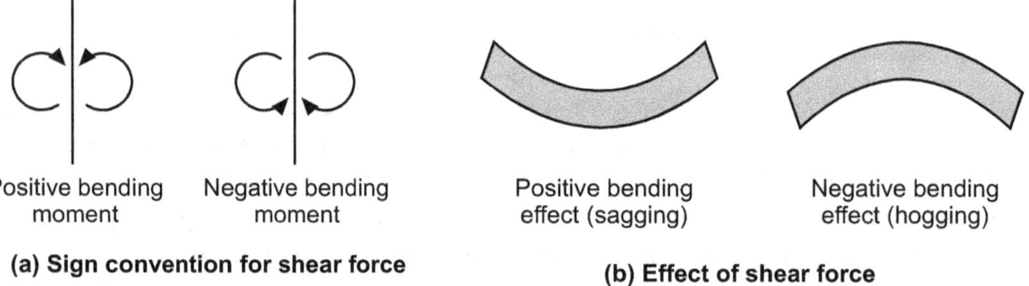



**(a) Sign convention for shear force**          **(b) Effect of shear force**

**Fig. 3.5**

It should be noted that, for a horizontal beam, upward external forces cause positive bending moments with respect to any section while the downward external forces cause negative bending moments.

## 3.7  SHEAR FORCE AND BENDING MOMENT DIAGRAMS (SFD AND BMD)

The shear force and bending moment can be calculated numerically at any particular section. But from the design point of view, we are interested in knowing the manner in which these values vary, along the length of beam. This can be done by plotting the shear force or the bending moment as ordinate and the position of the cross-section as abscissa to give shear force diagram (SFD) and bending moment diagram (BMD) respectively. While plotting these diagrams, positive values are plotted above the reference line and negative values below it. The shear force and bending moment diagrams can be plotted from shear force and bending moment equations written for respective zones. The nature of these curves depend on the type of loading the beam is subjected to. This is illustrated in following simple examples.

## SOLVED EXAMPLES

**Example 3.1 :** *Draw SFD and BMD for the following cantilever beams.*

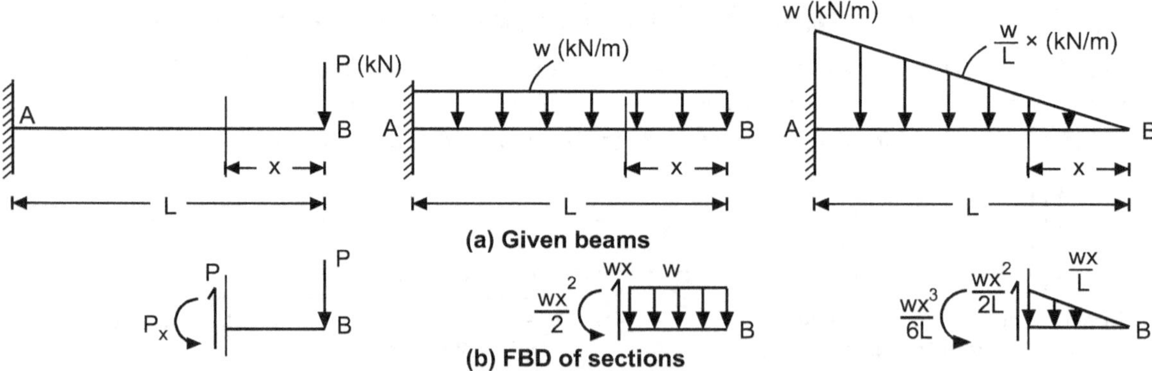

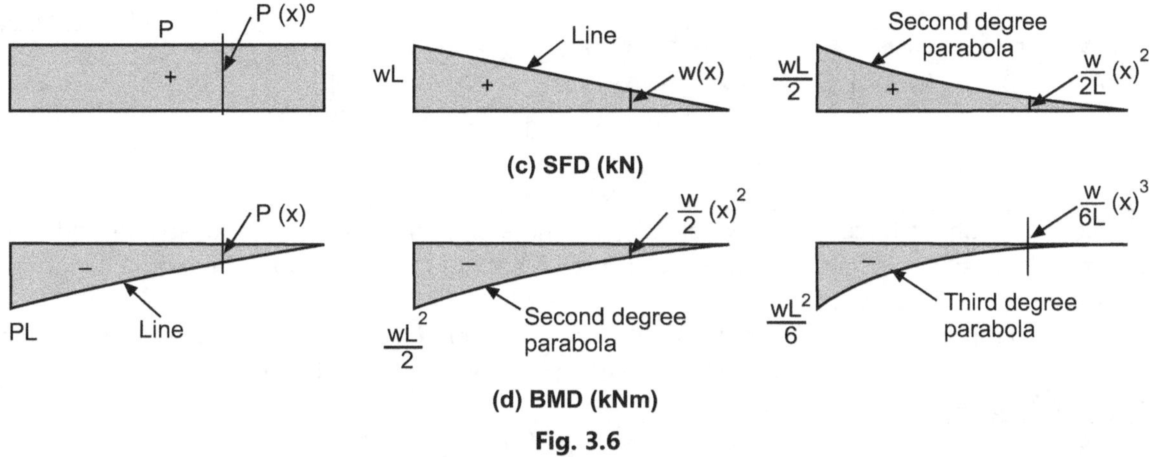

**(c) SFD (kN)**

**(d) BMD (kNm)**

**Fig. 3.6**

**Data**        :  Given beams as shown in Fig. 3.6 (a).

**Required**    :  SFD and BMD.

**Concept**     :  Consider a section at a distance 'x' from free end B as shown in Fig. 3.6 (a) and write the equations of SF and BM for the respective beams.

**Solution**    :  **(i) Case I :** Cantilever beam with point load at free end.

| Zone | Origin | Limits | $SF_{(x)}$ | $BM_{(x)}$ | SF at | | BM at | |
|------|--------|--------|------------|------------|-------|-------|-------|-------|
|      |        |        |            |            | x = 0 | x = L | x = 0 | x = L |
| BA   | B      | $0-L$  | P          | $-Px$      | P     | P     | 0     | $-PL$ |

**Note :** (i) Shear force is independent of position of section defined by distance 'x'. Therefore, shear force is constant throughout the beam; and SFD is as shown in Fig. 3.6 (c).

(ii) Bending moment is linear function of 'x'. Therefore, bending moment is zero at free end and maximum at fixed end. The variation of BM is linear along the length of beam as shown in Fig. 3.6 (d).

**(ii) Case II :** Cantilever beam with UDL throughout the span.

| Zone | Origin | Limits | $SF_{(x)}$ | $BM_{(x)}$ | SF at | | BM at | |
|------|--------|--------|------------|------------|-------|-------|-------|-------|
|      |        |        |            |            | x = 0 | x = L | x = 0 | x = L |
| BA   | B      | $0-L$  | wx         | $-\dfrac{wx^2}{2}$ | 0 | wL | 0 | $-\dfrac{wL^2}{2}$ |

**Note :** (i) Shear force is linear function of 'x'. Therefore, shear force is zero at free end and maximum at fixed end. The variation of shear is linear along the length of beam as shown in Fig. 3.6 (c).

(ii) Bending moment is function of $(x)^2$. Therefore, bending moment is zero at free end and maximum at fixed end. The variation of bending moment is second degree parabolic along the length of beam as shown in Fig. 3.6 (d).

**(iii) Case III :** Cantilever beam carrying triangular load (UVL) as shown in Fig. 3.6 (a). Intensity of triangular load at a distance 'x' from free end is given by $\dfrac{wx}{L}$ from similar triangles.

| Zone | Origin | Limits | $SF_{(x)}$ | $BM_{(x)}$ | SF at | | BM at | |
|------|--------|--------|-----------|-----------|-------|-------|-------|-------|
| | | | | | $x = 0$ | $x = L$ | $x = 0$ | $x = L$ |
| BA | B | $0 - L$ | $\dfrac{1}{2} x \left(\dfrac{wx}{L}\right)$ $= \dfrac{wx^2}{2L}$ | $-\dfrac{wx^2}{2L}\left(\dfrac{x}{3}\right) =$ $-\dfrac{wx^3}{6L}$ | 0 | $\dfrac{wL}{2}$ | 0 | $-\dfrac{wL^2}{6}$ |

**Note :** (i) Shear force is a function of $(x)^2$. Therefore, shear force is zero at free end and maximum at fixed end. The variation of shear force is second degree parabolic along the length of beam as shown in Fig. 3.6 (c).

(ii) Bending moment is a function of $(x)^3$. Therefore, bending moment is zero at free end and maximum at fixed end. The variation of bending moment is third degree parabolic along the length of beam as shown in Fig. 3.6 (d).

**Example 3.2 :** *Draw SF and BM diagrams for the following simple beams.*

**Data**     :  As shown in Fig. 3.7 (a).

**Required**  :  SFD and BMD.

**Solution**  :  **(i) Case I :** Simple beam with single point load.

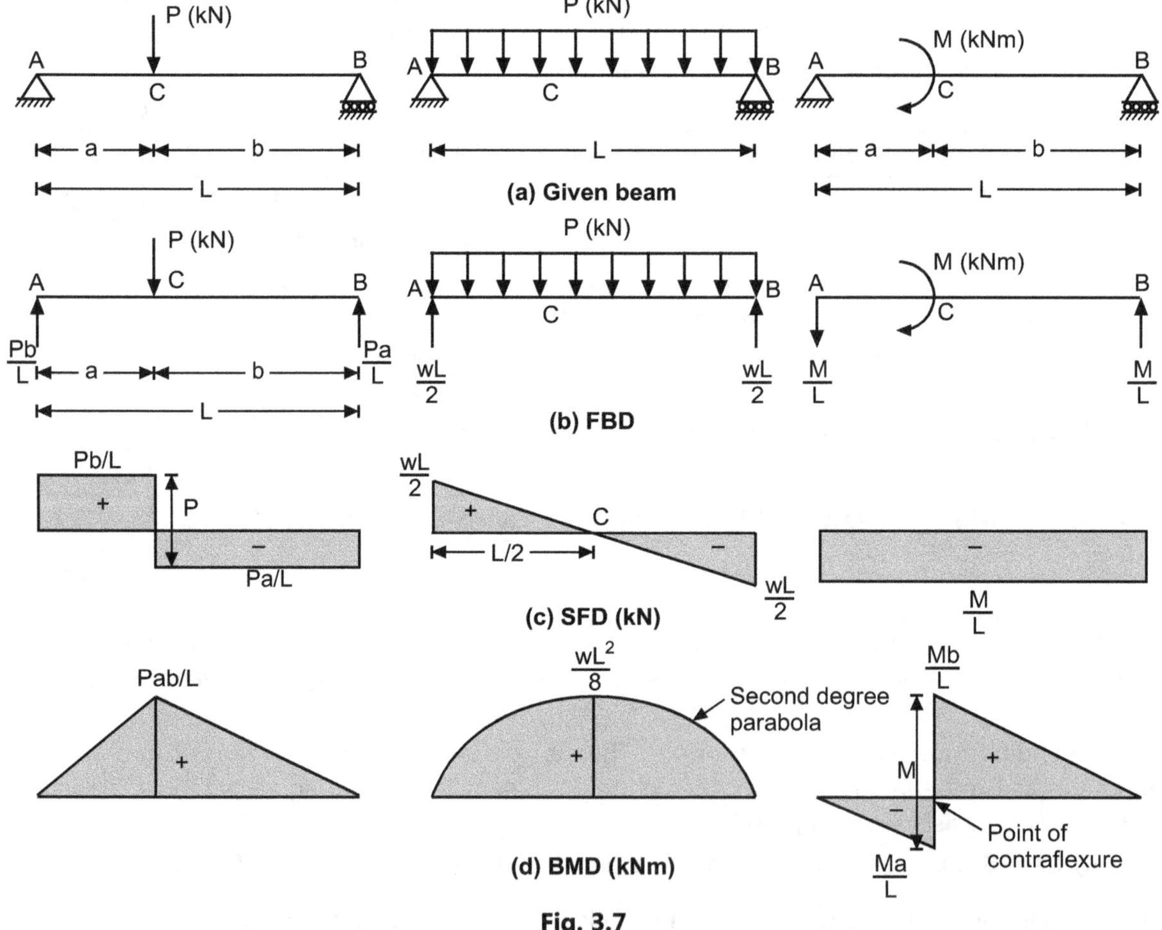

(a) Given beam

(b) FBD

(c) SFD (kN)

(d) BMD (kNm)

**Fig. 3.7**

**Reactions** :  $\sum M_A = 0$;          $V_B \times L - Pa = 0$          $\therefore$   $V_B = \dfrac{Pa}{L}$ ($\uparrow$)

$\sum F_y = 0$;      $\therefore$  $V_A + V_B - P = 0$

$\therefore$  $V_A = P - \dfrac{Pa}{L} = \dfrac{P\,b}{L}$ ($\uparrow$)

FBD of beam is as shown in Fig. 3.6 (b).

**SF calculations :**          $SF_A$  $= \dfrac{Pb}{L}$

SF (just to the left of C) $= \dfrac{Pb}{L}$

SF (just to the right of C) $= \dfrac{Pb}{L} - P = -\dfrac{Pa}{L}$

$SF_B$  $= -\dfrac{Pa}{L}$

**Note :** It is important to find shear force on either side of the concentrated force. SFD is as shown in Fig. 3.7 (c).

**BM calculations :**          $BM_A$  $= BM_B = 0$

$BM_C$  $= \left(\dfrac{Pb}{L}\right) a = \dfrac{Pab}{L}$

BMD is as shown in Fig. 3.7 (d).

**Note :** (i) SFD is parallel to the reference line.

(ii)     Bending moment variation is linear along the length of beam.

(iii)    Vertical drop in SFD indicates sudden change in the value of shear force at a section. The magnitude of drop in SF diagram is equal to the magnitude of point load acting at a section.

(iv)    Bending moment is maximum at 'C' where, shear force changes the sign.

**(ii)    Case II :** Simple beam with UDL.

**Reactions** :   By symmetry ; $V_A = V_B = \dfrac{wL}{2}$ ($\uparrow$)

FBD of beam is as shown in Fig. 3.6 (b).

**SF calculations :** Consider a section at a distance 'x' from A; FBD of part of the beam is as shown in Fig. 3.8.

Shear force at a distance 'x' $= SF_x = V = \dfrac{wL}{2} - wx$          ... (i)

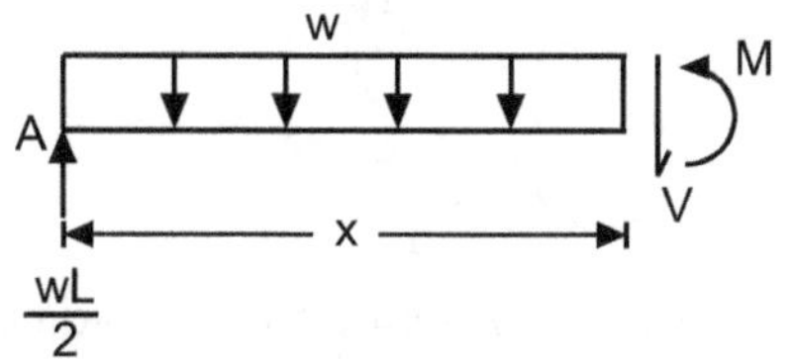

**Fig. 3.8**

Put x = 0 for shear force at A, $SF_A = \dfrac{wL}{2}$

Put x = L for shear force at B, $SF_B = \dfrac{wL}{2} - wL = \dfrac{-wL}{2}$

Equating equation (i) to zero, we can locate the section of zero shear force as,

$$\dfrac{wL}{2} - wx = 0 \quad \therefore x = \dfrac{L}{2}$$

SFD is as shown in Fig. 3.7 (c).

**BM calculations :** From Fig. 3.8, BM at a distance x

$$= BM_x = M = \dfrac{wL}{2}(x) - \dfrac{wx^2}{2} \qquad \qquad \text{... (ii)}$$

Put x = 0 for bending moment at A, $BM_A = 0$

Put x = L for bending moment at B, $BM_B = \dfrac{wL^2}{2} - \dfrac{wL^2}{2} = 0$

Put $x = \dfrac{L}{2}$ for BM at point of zero SF i.e. at C, $BM_C = \dfrac{wL}{2}\left(\dfrac{L}{2}\right) - \dfrac{w}{2}\left(\dfrac{L}{2}\right)^2$

$$BM_C = \dfrac{wL^2}{4} - \dfrac{wL^2}{8} = \dfrac{wL^2}{8}$$

BMD is as shown in Fig. 3.7 (d).

**Note :** (i) Shear force variation is linear along the length of beam.

(ii)　Bending moment variation is second degree parabolic along the length of beam.

(iii)　Bending moment is maximum at C where shear force changes the sign. *For locating the section of zero shear force, shear force equation for the respective zone shall be equated to zero.*

**(iii)　Case III :** Simple beam carrying a couple.

**Reaction** ：$\sum M_A = 0$ ;　　　$V_B \times L - M = 0$　　　　$\therefore$　　$V_B = \dfrac{M}{L}$ $(\uparrow)$

　　　　　　　$\sum F_y = 0$ ;　　　$V_A + V_B = 0$　　　　$\therefore$　　$V_A = -\dfrac{M}{L} = \dfrac{M}{L}$ $(\downarrow)$

FBD of beam is as shown in Fig. 3.7 (b).

**SF calculations :** Since there is no vertical loading on the beam, shear force is constant throughout and SF $= -\dfrac{M}{L}$ .

SFD is as shown in Fig. 3.7 (c).

**BM calculations :**　　　　　$BM_A = BM_B = 0$

$$\text{BM (just to the left of C)} = -\dfrac{M}{L}a$$

$$\text{BM (just to the right of C)} = \dfrac{M}{L}b.$$

**Note :** It is important to find bending moment on either side of a couple.

BMD is as shown in Fig. 3.7 (d).

**Note :** (i) SFD is parallel to the reference line.

(ii)　　Bending moment variation is linear along the length of beam.

(iii)　　At a section where couple is acting, shear force does not change.

(iv)　　Section where bending moment changes its sign is called as *point of contraflexure*. Since change of sign is possible only when bending moment at point of contraflexure is zero, it is also called as point of zero bending moment or *point of inflection*. It should be understood that a point of contraflexure is necessarily a point of inflection but point of inflection need not be a point of contraflexure. *For locating point of contraflexure, bending moment equation in the respective zone shall be equated to zero.*

(v)　　Vertical drop in the BMD indicates sudden change in the value of bending moment at a section. The magnitude of drop in the BM diagram is equal to the magnitude of couple acting at a section.

## 3.8　RELATIONSHIP BETWEEN LOAD, SHEAR AND BENDING MOMENT

The relationship between load, shear and bending moment can be derived as under. Consider a beam supported and loaded as shown in Fig. 3.9 (a).

Let, $V_x$ and $M_x$ be the shear and bending moment on a section at a distance 'x' from A. Likewise $V_x + dV_x$ and $M_x + dM_x$ are the shear and bending moment on a section at a distance x + dx from A. The free body diagram of the segment of the beam which is dx in length is shown in Fig. 3.9 (b).

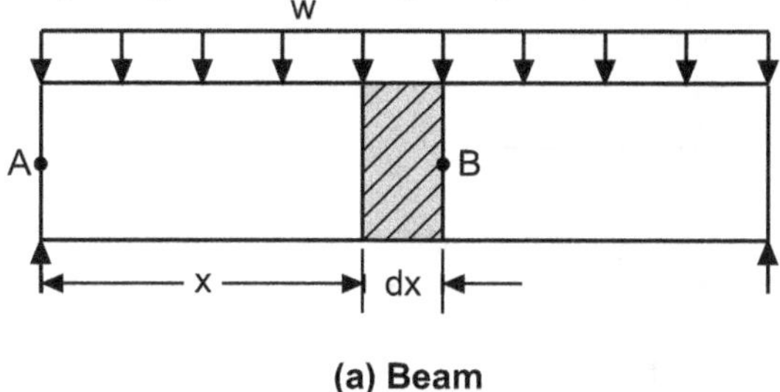


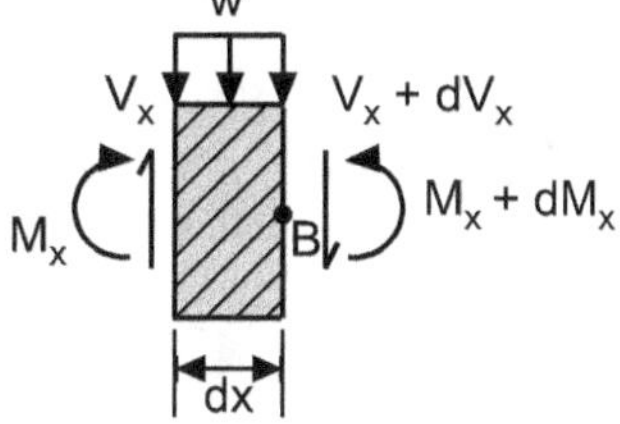


(a) Beam　　　　　　　　　(b) FBD of beam segement

**Fig. 3.9**

Applying equations of equilibrium to FBD of segment as under :

$$\Sigma F_y = 0 \quad \Rightarrow \quad V_x - (V_x + dV_x) - w \cdot dx = 0$$

$$dV_x = - w \cdot dx$$

$$\therefore \qquad \frac{dV_x}{dx} = - w \qquad \qquad \dots (3.1)$$

Thus, *the rate of decrease of shear force with respect to x, on any section at a distance 'x' from left end of the beam is equal to the intensity of load at the section.*

$$\Sigma M_B = 0 \Rightarrow \quad V_x \cdot dx + M_x = M_x + dM_x + w \frac{dx^2}{2}$$

The term $w \dfrac{dx^2}{2}$ being very small; can be neglected.

$$dM_x = V_x \cdot dx$$

$$\frac{dM_x}{dx} = V_x \qquad\qquad \text{... (3.2)}$$

Thus, *the rate of increase of bending moment with respect to 'x', on any section at a distance 'x' from left end of the beam, is equal to shear at the section.*

**Example 3.3 :** *The beam is supported and loaded as shown in Fig. 3.10 (a). Draw SFD, BMD indicating all the important values.*

**Data**        :   As shown in Fig. 3.10 (a).

**Required**   :   SFD, BMD.

**Solution**    :   (i) Reactions :

$\sum F_y = 0;$ $\qquad\qquad$ $V_A - 20 - 30 = 0$ $\qquad\qquad$ $\therefore\quad V_A = 50\ kN\ (\uparrow)$

$\sum M_A = 0;$ $\qquad\qquad$ $M_A - 20 \times 1 - 30 \times 2.5 = 0$ $\qquad \therefore\quad M_A = 95\ kNm\ (\circlearrowleft)$

$\sum F_x = 0;$ $\qquad\qquad$ $H_A = 0$

FBD of beam is as shown in Fig. 3.10 (b).

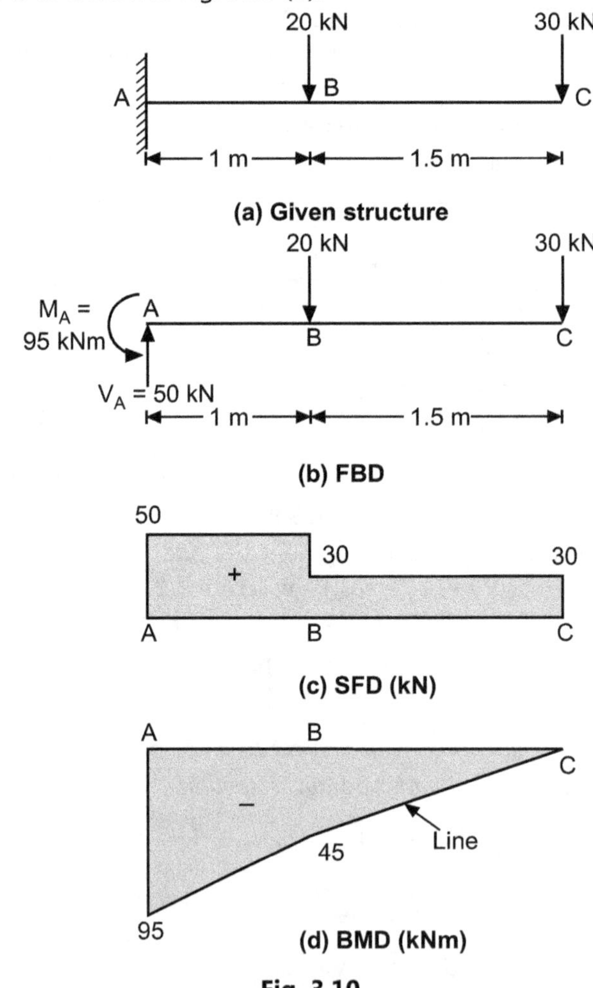


**Fig. 3.10**

(ii)   SF calculations :       $SF_A$  =  50 kN

$SF_B$  (just to the left) = 50 kN

$SF_B$  (just to the right) = 50 – 20 = 30 kN

$SF_C$  = 30 kN

SFD is as shown in Fig. 3.10 (c).

(iii)   BM calculations :

$$BM_A = -95 \text{ kN.m}$$

$$BM_B = -30 \times 1.5 = -45 \text{ kN.m}$$

$$BM_C = 0$$

BMD is as shown in Fig. 3.10 (d).

**Example 3.4 :** *The beam is supported and loaded as shown in Fig. 3.11 (a). Draw SFD, BMD indicating all important values.*

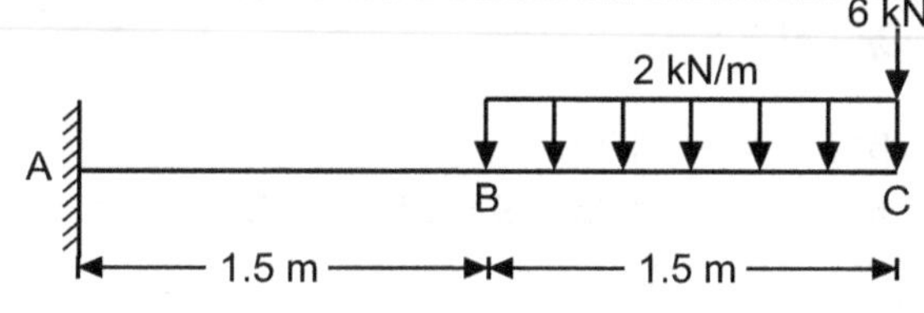


**(a) Given structure**

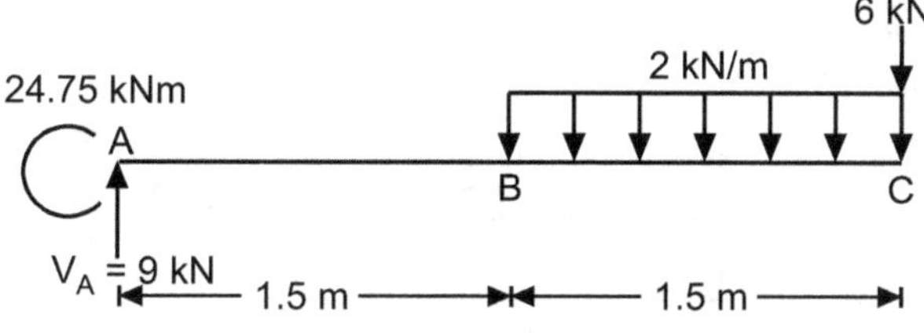


**(b) FBD**

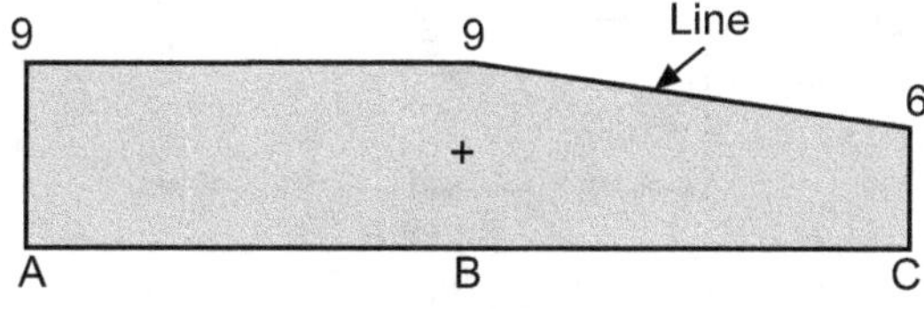


**(c) SFD (kN)**

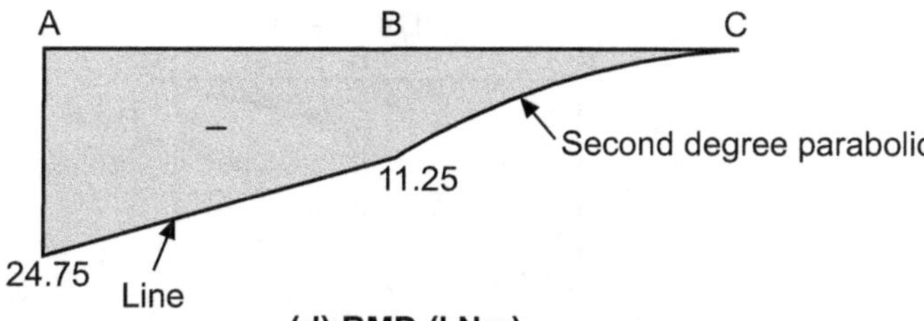


**(d) BMD (kNm)**

**Fig. 3.11**

**Data**　　　　: As shown in Fig. 3.11 (a).

**Required**　: SFD, BMD.

**Solution**　: (i) Reactions :

$$\sum F_y = 0; \qquad 'V_A - 2 \times 1.5 - 6 = 0$$

$$\therefore \qquad\qquad V_A = 9 \text{ kN } (\uparrow)$$

$$\sum M_A = 0; \qquad M_A - 2 \times 1.5 \times 2.25 - 6 \times 3 = 0$$

$$M_A = 24.75 \text{ kN.m } (\circlearrowleft)$$

$$\sum F_x = 0; \qquad H_A = 0$$

FBD of beam is as shown in Fig. 3.11 (b).

(ii)　　SF calculations :

$$SF_A = SF_B = 9 \text{ kN}$$

$$SF_C = 6 \text{ kN}$$

SFD is as shown in Fig. 3.11 (c).

(iii)　　BM calculations :

$$BM_A = -24.75 \text{ kN.m}$$

$$BM_B = -24.75 + 9 \times 1.5 = -11.25 \text{ kN.m}$$

$$BM_C = 0$$

BMD is as shown in Fig. 3.11 (d).

**Example 3.5 :** *The beam is supported and loaded as shown in Fig. 3.12 (a). Draw SFD and BMD indicating all the important values.*

**Data :**　　　As shown in Fig. 3.12 (a).

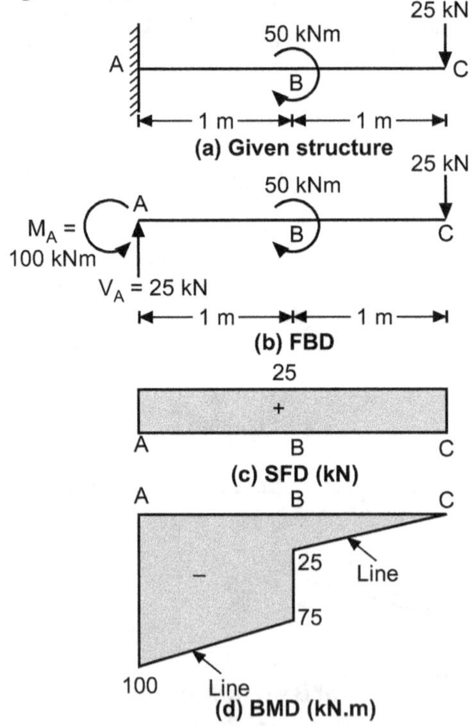


**Fig. 3.12**

**Required** : SFD, BMD.

**Solution** : (i) Reactions :

$$\sum F_y = 0; \qquad V_A - 25 = 0 \quad \therefore V_A = 25 \text{ kN } (\uparrow)$$

$$\sum M_A = 0; \qquad M_A - 50 - 25 \times 2 = 0$$

$$\therefore \qquad M_A = 100 \text{ kN.m } (\circlearrowleft)$$

$$\sum F_x = 0; \qquad H_A = 0$$

FBD of beam is as shown in Fig. 3.12 (b).

(ii) SF calculations :

$$SF_A = SF_B = SF_C = 25 \text{ kN}$$

SFD is as shown in Fig. 3.12 (c).

(iii) BM calculations :

$$BM_A = -100 \text{ kN.m}$$

$$BM_B \text{ (just to the left)} = -100 + 25 \times 1 = -75 \text{ kN.m}$$

$$BM_B \text{ (just to the right)} = -75 + 50 = -25 \text{ kN.m}$$

$$BM_C = 0$$

BMD is as shown in Fig. 3.12 (d).

**Example 3.6 :** *The beam is supported and loaded as shown in Fig. 3.13 (a). Draw SFD, BMD indicating all the important values.*

**Data** : As shown in Fig. 3.13 (a).

**Required** : SFD, BMD.

**Solution** : (i) Reactions :

$$\sum F_y = 0; \qquad V_A - 10 \times 2 = 0 \qquad\qquad \therefore \qquad V_A = 20 \text{ kN } (\uparrow)$$

$$\sum M_A = 0; \qquad M_A - 25 - 10 \times \frac{2^2}{2} = 0 \qquad \therefore \qquad M_A = 45 \text{ kN.m } (\circlearrowleft)$$

$$\sum F_x = 0; \qquad H_A = 0$$

FBD of beam is as shown in Fig. 3.13 (b).

(ii) SF calculations :

$$SF_A = 20 \text{ kN}$$

$$SF_C = 0$$

SFD is as shown in Fig. 3.13 (c).

(iii) BM calculations :

$$BM_A = -45 \text{ kN.m}$$

$$BM_B \text{ (just to the left)} = -45 + 20 \times 1 - 10 \times \frac{1^2}{2} = -30 \text{ kN.m}$$

$$BM_B \text{ (just to the right)} = -30 + 25 = -5 \text{ kN.m}$$

$$BM_C = 0$$

BMD is as shown in Fig. 3.13 (d).

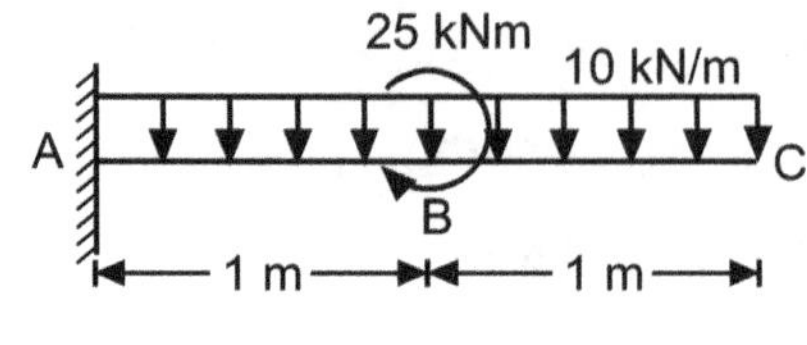

**(a) Given structure**

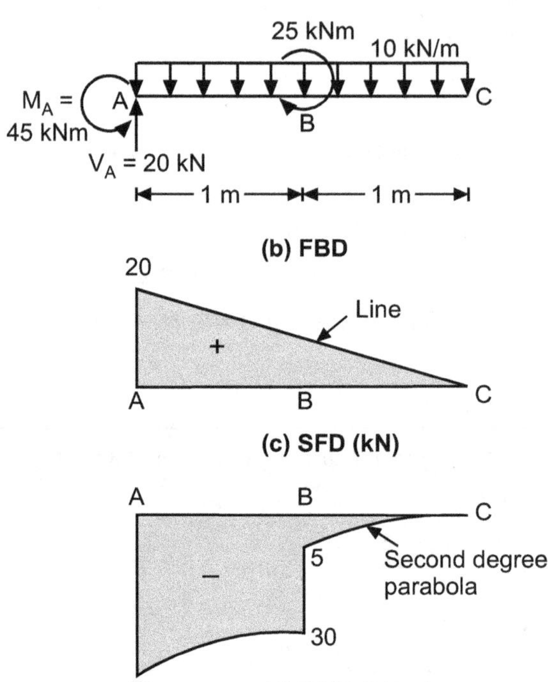

**(b) FBD**

**(c) SFD (kN)**

**(d) BMD (kN.m)**

**Fig. 3.13**

**Example 3.7 :** *The beam is supported and loaded as shown in Fig. 3.14 (a). Draw SFD and BMD indicating all the important values.*

**Data**      :    As shown in Fig. 3.14 (a).

**Required**    :    SFD, BMD.

**Solution**    :    (i) Reactions :

$$\Sigma F_y = 0; \qquad V_A = 0$$

$$\Sigma M_A = 0; \qquad M_A - 75 + 25 - 50 = 0$$

$$\therefore \qquad M_A = 100 \text{ kN.m } (\circlearrowleft)$$

FBD of beam is as shown in Fig. 3.14 (b).

(ii)     SF calculations :

Beam is not subjected to any shear force.

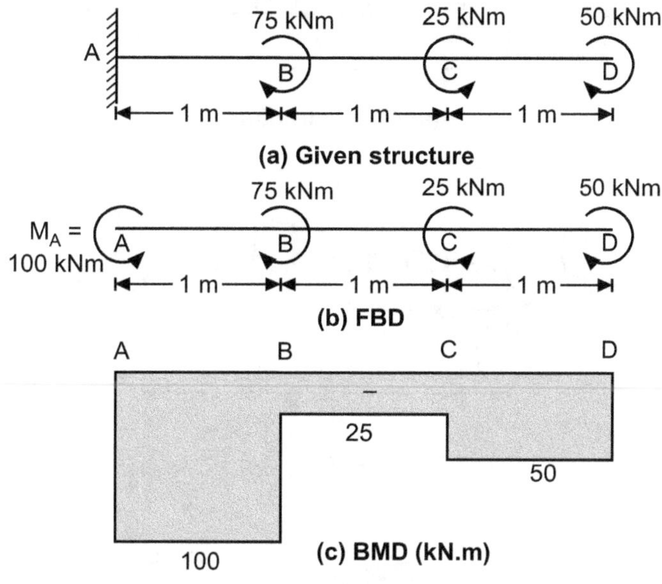



**Fig. 3.14**

(iii)     BM calculations :

$$BM_A = -100 \text{ kN.m}$$

$$BM_B \text{ (just to the left)} = -100 \text{ kN.m}$$

$$BM_B \text{ (just to the right)} = -100 + 75 = -25 \text{ kN.m}$$

$$BM_C \text{ (just to the left)} = -25 \text{ kN.m}$$

$$BM_C \text{ (just to the right)} = -25 - 25 = -50 \text{ kN.m}$$

$$BM_D = -50 \text{ kN.m}$$

BMD is as shown in Fig. 3.14 (c).

**Example 3.8 :** *Draw SFD, BMD for the cantilever beam shown in Fig. 3.15 (a).*

**Data**          :     As shown in Fig. 3.15 (a).

**Required**     :     SFD, BMD.

**Solution**     :     (i) Reactions :

$$\sum F_y = 0 ; \qquad V_A - \frac{1}{2} \times w \times L = 0 \qquad \therefore \quad V_A = \frac{wL}{2} (\uparrow)$$

$$\sum M_A = 0 ; \qquad M_A - \frac{wL}{2} \times \frac{2L}{3} = 0 \qquad \therefore \quad M_A = \frac{wL^2}{3} (\circlearrowleft)$$

FBD of beam is as shown in Fig. 3.15 (b).

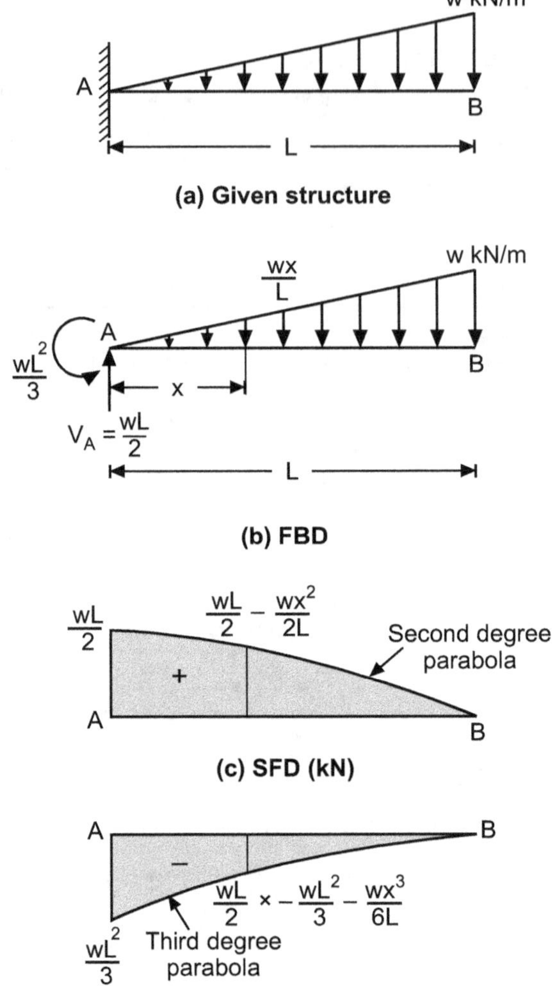



**Fig. 3.15**

(ii)     SF and BM :

| Zone | Origin | Limits | $SF_{(x)}$ | $BM_{(x)}$ | SF at $x = 0$ | SF at $x = L$ | BM at $x = 0$ | BM at $x = L$ |
|------|--------|--------|------------|------------|---------------|---------------|---------------|---------------|
| AB | A | $0 - L$ | $\dfrac{wL}{2} - \dfrac{wx^2}{2L}$ | $\dfrac{wL}{2}x - \dfrac{wL^2}{3} - \dfrac{wx^3}{6L}$ | $\dfrac{wL}{2}$ | $0$ | $\dfrac{wL^2}{3}$ | $0$ |

SFD and BMD are as shown in Fig. 3.15 (c) and Fig. 3.15 (d) respectively.

**Example 3.9 :** *The beam is supported and loaded as shown in Fig. 3.16 (a). Draw SFD, BMD indicating all important values.*

**Data**        :   As shown in Fig. 3.16 (a).

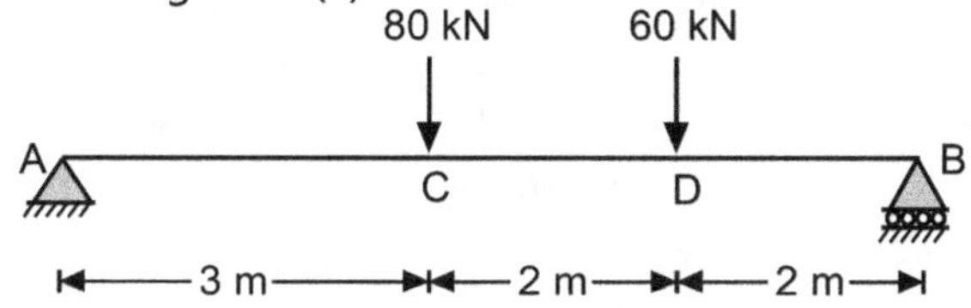


**(a) Given structure**

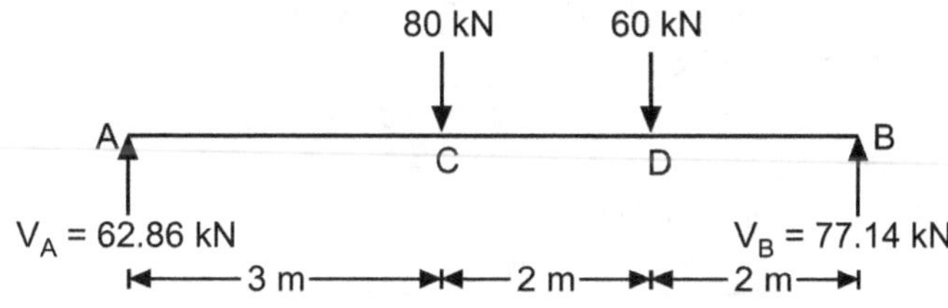


**(b) FBD**

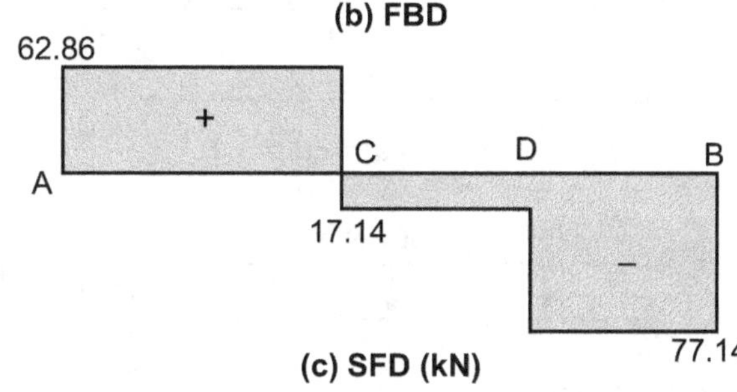


**(c) SFD (kN)**

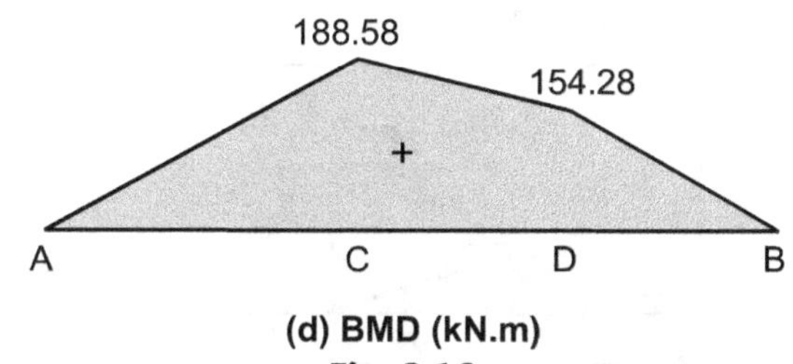


**(d) BMD (kN.m)**
**Fig. 3.16**

**Required**   :   SFD, BMD.

**Solution**   :   (i) Reactions :

$\sum M_A = 0$;          $V_B \times 7 - 60 \times 5 - 80 \times 3 = 0$

$\therefore$          $V_B = 77.14$ kN ($\uparrow$)

$\sum F_y = 0$;          $V_A + V_B - 80 - 60 = 0$

$\therefore$          $V_A = 62.86$ kN ($\uparrow$)

$\sum F_x = 0$; $H_A = 0$

FBD of beam is as shown in Fig. 3.16 (b).

(ii)     SF calculations :

$SF_A$ = 62.86 kN

$SF_C$ (just to the left) = 62.86 kN

$SF_C$ (just to the right) = 62.86 − 80 = − 17.14 kN

$SF_D$ (just to the left) = − 17.14 kN

$SF_D$ (just to the right) = − 17.14 − 60 = − 77.14 kN

$SF_B$ = − 77.14 kN

SFD is as shown in Fig. 3.16 (c).

(iii)    BM calculations :    $BM_A$ = $BM_B$ = 0

$BM_C$ = 62.86 × 3 = 188.58 kN.m

$BM_D$ = 77.14 × 2 = 154.28 kN.m

BMD is as shown in Fig. 3.16 (d).

**Example 3.10 :** *The beam is supported and loaded as shown in Fig. 3.17 (a). Draw SFD, BMD indicating all the important values.*

**Data**        :    As shown in Fig. 3.17 (a).

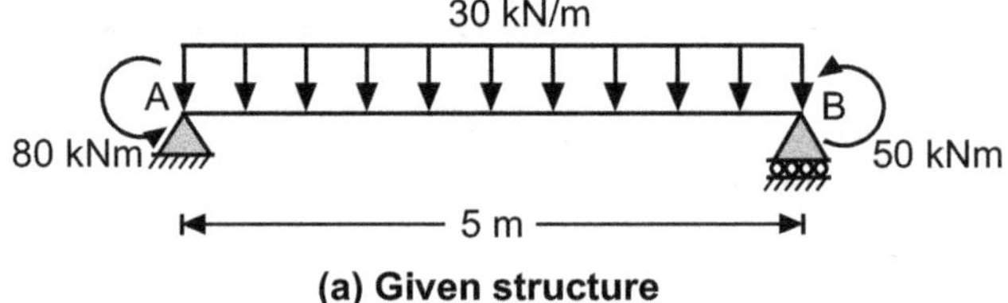


**(a) Given structure**

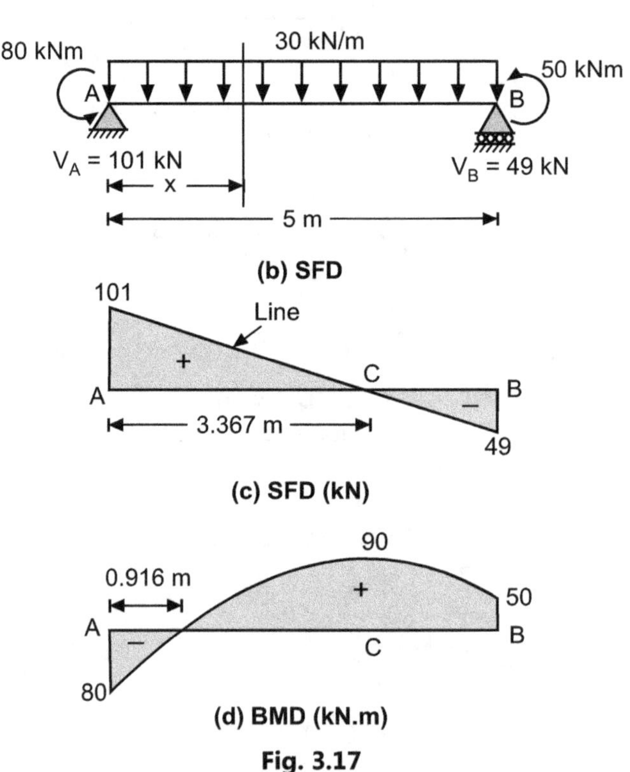


**Fig. 3.17**

**Required** : SFD, BMD.

**Solution** : (i) Reactions :

$$\Sigma M_A = 0; \qquad V_B \times 5 + 50 - 30 \times \frac{5^2}{2} + 80 = 0$$

$$\therefore \qquad V_B = 49 \text{ kN } (\uparrow)$$

$$\Sigma F_y = 0; \qquad V_A + V_B - 30 \times 5 = 0$$

$$\therefore \qquad V_A = 101 \text{ kN } (\uparrow)$$

FBD of beam is as shown in Fig. 3.17 (b).

(ii) SF calculations :

Consider a section at a distance 'x' from 'A'.

$$SF_x = 101 - 30 \, x \qquad\qquad\qquad \dots (i)$$

put x = 0; $\qquad SF_A = 101$ kN

put x = 5 m; $\qquad SF_B = 101 - 30 \times 5 = -49$ kN

To locate point of zero SF, equate equation (i) to zero.

$$101 - 30 \, x = 0$$

$$\therefore \qquad x = 3.367 \text{ m from A}$$

SFD is as shown in Fig. 3.17 (c).

(iii) BM calculations :

$$BM_x = 101 \, x - 80 - \frac{30 \, x^2}{2} = 101 \, x - 80 - 15 \, x^2 \qquad\qquad \dots (ii)$$

put x = 0; $\qquad BM_A = -80$ kN.m

x = 3.367 m; $\qquad BM_C = 101 \times 3.367 - 80 - 15 \, (3.367)^2 = 90$ kN.m

x = 5 m; $\qquad BM_B = 101 \times 5 - 80 - 15 \, (5)^2 = 50$ kN.m

To locate point of contraflexure, equate equation (ii) to zero.

$$BM_x = 101 \, x - 80 - 15 \, x^2 = 0$$

Solving $\qquad x = 0.916$ m from A

BMD is as shown in Fig. 3.17 (d).

**Example 3.11 :** *The beam is supported and loaded as shown in Fig. 3.18 (a). Draw SFD, BMD indicating all important values.*

**Data** : As shown in Fig. 3.18 (a).

**Required** : SFD, BMD.

**Solution** : (i) Reactions :

Couple at D = $5 \times 2 \times 0.375 = 3.75$ kN.m ($\circlearrowleft$)

$$\Sigma M_A = 0; \qquad V_B \times 3 - 5 \times 2.625 - 3.75 - 5 \times 0.375 = 0$$

$$\therefore \qquad V_B = 6.25 \text{ kN } (\uparrow)$$

$$\Sigma F_y = 0; \qquad V_A + V_B - 5 - 5 = 0$$

$$V_A = 3.75 \text{ kN } (\uparrow)$$

$$\Sigma F_x = 0 \quad H_A = 0$$

FBD of beam is as shown in Fig. 3.18 (b).

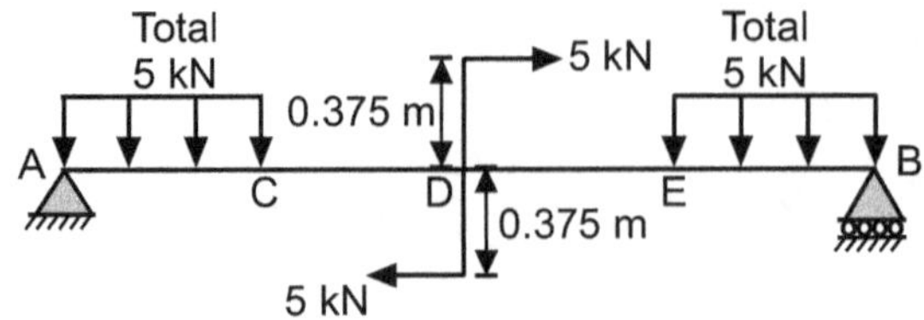

**(a) Given structure**

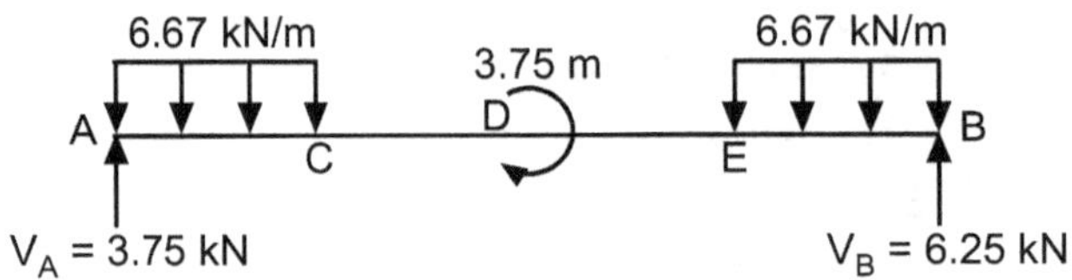

**(b) FBD**

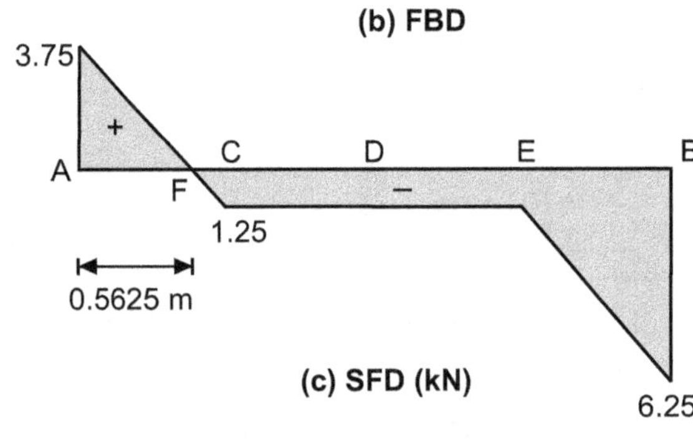

**(c) SFD (kN)**

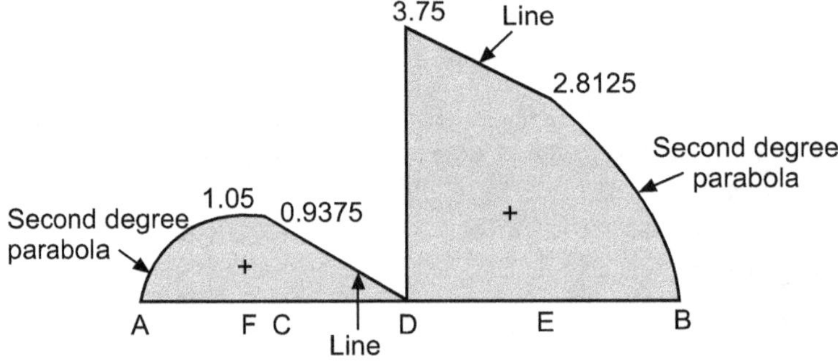

**(d) BMD (kN.m)**

**Fig. 3.18**

(ii)　　SF calculations :

$$SF_A = 3.75 \text{ kN}$$

$$SF_C = 3.75 - 5 = -1.25 \text{ kN}$$

$$SF_B = -6.25 \text{ kN}$$

To locate point of zero SF, consider a section at a distance 'x' from A in zone AC,

$$SF_x = 3.75 - 6.67\,x = 0$$

$\therefore$  $\qquad x = 0.5625$ m from A

SFD is as shown in Fig. 3.18 (c).

(iii)  BM calculations :

$$BM_A = BM_B = 0$$

$$BM_C = 3.75 \times 0.75 - 5 \times \frac{0.75}{2} = 0.9375 \text{ kN.m}$$

BM at point of zero SF $= BM_F = 3.75 \times 0.5625 - 6.67 \times \dfrac{0.5625^2}{2} = 1.05$ kN.m

$BM_D$ (just to the left) $= 3.75 \times 1.5 - 5 \times 1.125 = 0$

$BM_D$ (just to the right) $= 0 + 3.75 = 3.75$ kN.m

$$BM_E = 6.25 \times 0.75 - 5 \times \frac{0.75}{2} = 2.8125 \text{ kN.m}$$

---

**Example 3.12 :** *The beam is supported and loaded as shown in Fig. 3.19 (a). Draw SFD, BMD indicating all important values.*

**Data**      :  As shown in Fig. 3.19 (a).

**Required**  :  SFD, BMD.

**Solution**  :  (i) Reactions :

$\sum M_A = 0;$  $\qquad V_B \times 8 - 100 - 50 - 75 \times 1 = 0$

$\qquad\qquad\qquad V_B = 28.125$ kN ($\uparrow$)

$\sum F_y = 0;$  $\qquad V_A + V_B - 75 = 0$

$\qquad\qquad\qquad V_A = 46.875$ kN ($\uparrow$)

$\sum F_x = 0;\ H_A = 0$

FBD of beam is as shown in Fig. 3.19 (b).

(ii)  SF calculations :  $\qquad SF_A = 46.875$ kN

$\qquad\qquad\qquad SF_C$ (just to the left) $= 46.875$ kN

$\qquad\qquad\qquad SF_C$ (just to the right) $= 46.875 - 75$

$\qquad\qquad\qquad\qquad = -28.125$ kN

$\qquad\qquad\qquad SF_D = SF_E = SF_B = -28.125$ kN

SFD is as shown in Fig. 3.19 (c).

---

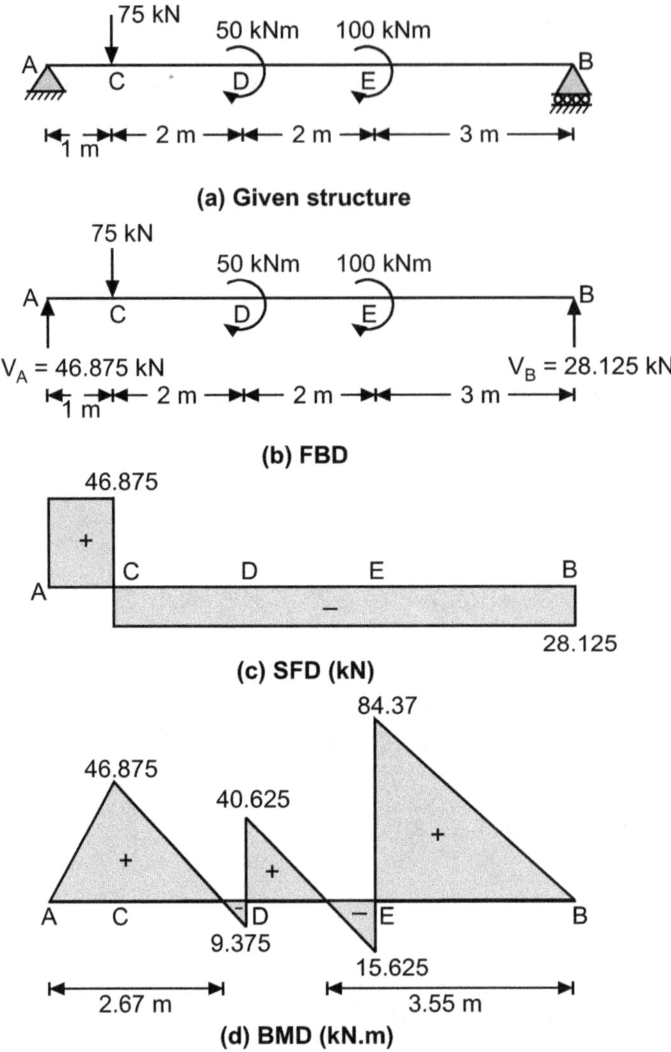



**Fig. 3.19**

(iii)　BM calculations :

$$BM_A = BM_B = 0$$

$$BM_C = 46.875 \times 1 = 46.875 \text{ kN.m}$$

$$BM_D \text{ (just to the left)} = 46.875 \times 3 - 75 \times 2$$

$$= -9.375 \text{ kN.m}$$

$$BM_D \text{ (just to the right)} = -9.375 + 50$$

$$= 40.625 \text{ kN.m}$$

$$BM_E \text{ (just to the right)} = 28.125 \times 3$$

$$= 84.375 \text{ kN.m}$$

$$BM_E \text{ (just to the left)} = 84.375 - 100$$

$$= -15.625 \text{ kN.m}$$

To locate point of contraflexure in zone CD, consider a section at a distance 'x' from 'A' in zone CD.

$$BM_x = 46.875\,x - 75\,(x - 1) = 0$$

$$\therefore \qquad x = 2.67 \text{ m from 'A'}$$

To locate point of contraflexure in zone DE, consider a section at a distance 'x' from B in zone DE.

$$BM_x = 28.125\,x - 100 = 0$$

$$\therefore \qquad x = \textbf{3.55 m from B}$$

BMD is as shown in Fig. 3.19 (d).

**Example 3.13 :** *The beam is supported and loaded as shown in Fig. 3.20 (a). Draw SFD, BMD indicating all important values.*

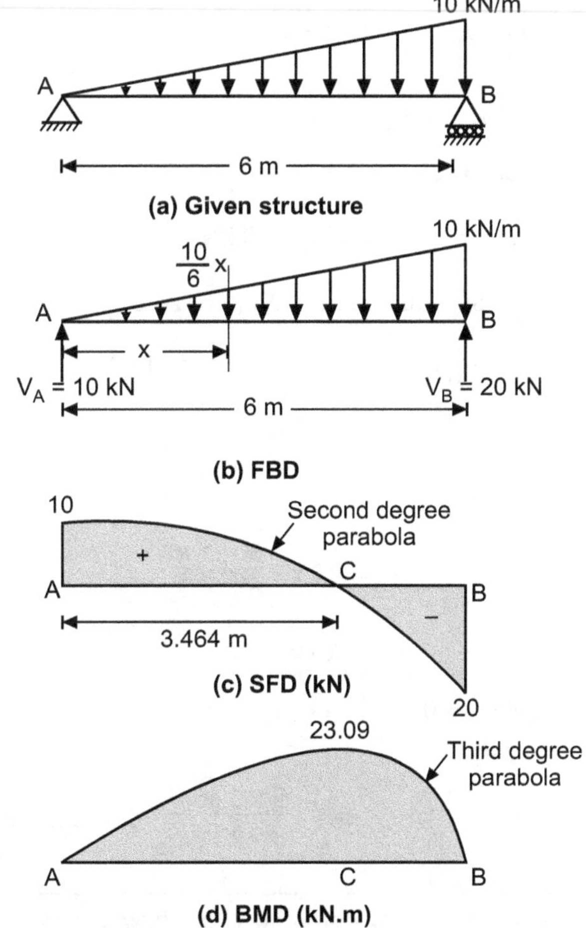


**Fig. 3.20**

**Data** 　　: 　As shown in Fig. 3.20 (a).

**Required** 　: 　SFD, BMD.

**Solution**    :    (i) Reactions :

$$\sum M_A = 0 ; \qquad V_B \times 6 - \frac{1}{2} \times 6 \times 10 \times \frac{2}{3} \times 6 = 0$$

$$\therefore \qquad V_B = 20 \text{ kN } (\uparrow)$$

$$\sum F_y = 0 ; \qquad V_A + V_B - \frac{1}{2} \times 6 \times 10 = 0$$

$$\therefore \qquad V_A = 10 \text{ kN } (\uparrow)$$

$$\sum F_x = 0 ; \qquad H_A = 0$$

FBD of beam is as shown in Fig. 3.20 (b).

(ii)    SF calculations :

$$\text{Intensity of UVL at 'x' from A} = \frac{10}{6} x$$

$$\text{SF at a distance 'x' from A, } SF_x = 10 - \frac{1}{2} \times x \times \frac{10}{6} x$$

$$\therefore \qquad SF_x = 10 - \frac{5}{6} x^2 \qquad \qquad \text{... (i)}$$

$$\text{put } x = 0 ; \qquad SF_A = 10 \text{ kN}$$

$$\text{put } x = 6 \text{ m} ; \qquad SF_B = 10 - \frac{5}{6} (6)^2 = -20 \text{ kN}$$

To locate point of zero SF, equate equation (i) to zero.

$$10 - \frac{5}{6} x^2 = 0 \therefore x = 3.464 \text{ m from A.}$$

SFD is as shown in Fig. 3.20 (c).

(iii)    BM calculations :

$$\text{BM at a distance 'x' from A} \quad = BM_x$$

$$= 10 x - \frac{5}{6} x^2 \times \frac{x}{3}$$

$$= 10 x - \frac{5x^3}{18} \qquad \qquad \text{... (ii)}$$

$$\text{put } x = 0 ; \qquad BM_A = 0$$

$$\text{put } x = 0 ; \qquad BM_B = 0$$

$$\text{put } x = 3.464 \text{ m}; \qquad BM_C = 10 \times 3.464 - \frac{5 \times 3.464^3}{18} = 23.09 \text{ kN.m}$$

BMD is as shown in Fig. 3.20 (d).

**Example 3.14 :** *The beam is supported and loaded as shown in Fig. 3.21 (a). Draw SFD, BMD indicating all the important values.*

**Data :**      As shown in Fig. 3.21 (a).

**Required**   :   SFD, BMD.

**Solution** : (i) Reactions :

$$V_A = V_B = \frac{1}{2}\left[\frac{1}{2} \times L \times w\right] = \frac{wL}{4} \ (\uparrow)$$

FBD of beam is as shown in Fig. 3.21 (b).

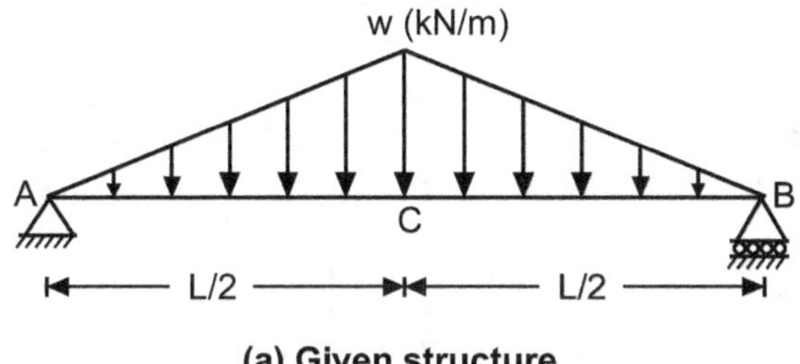


**(a) Given structure**

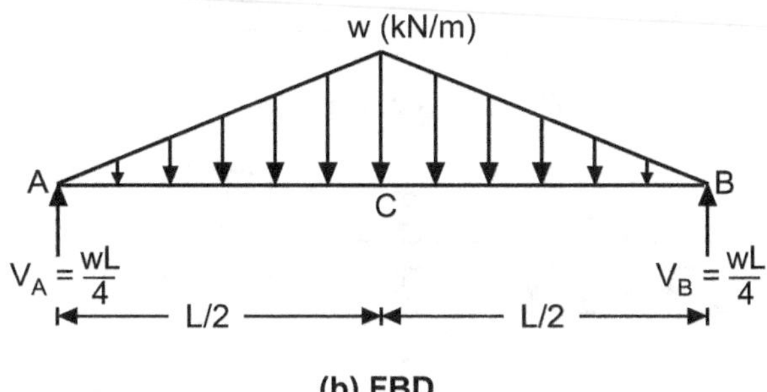


**(b) FBD**

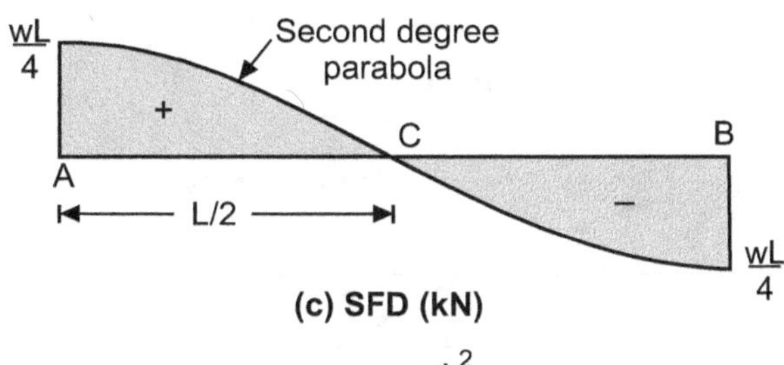


**(c) SFD (kN)**

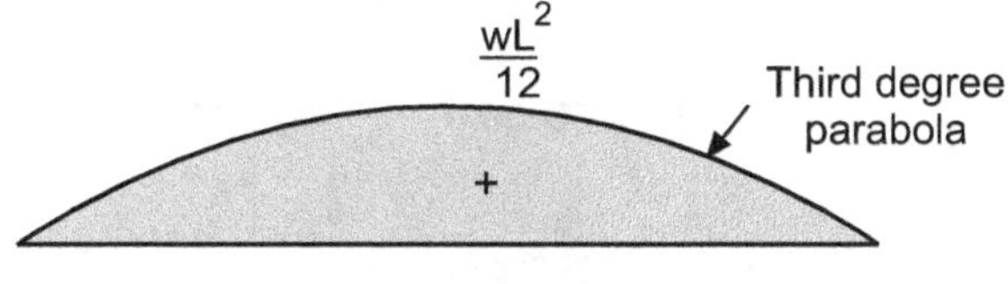


**(c) BMD (kN.m)**

**Fig. 3.21**

(ii)    SF calculations :

$$SF_A = \frac{wL}{4}$$

$$SF_B = -\frac{wL}{4}$$

$$SF_C = 0 \ (\text{By symmetry})$$

SFD is as shown in Fig. 3.21 (c).

(iii)   BM calculations :

$$BM_A = BM_B = 0$$

$$BM_C = \frac{wL}{4} \times \frac{L}{2} - \frac{1}{2} \times \frac{L}{2} \times w \times \frac{1}{3} \times \frac{L}{2} = \frac{wL^2}{8} - \frac{wL^2}{24} = \frac{wL^2}{12}$$

BMD is as shown in Fig. 3.21 (d).

**Example 3.15 :** *The beam is supported and loaded as shown in Fig. 3.22 (a). Draw SFD, BMD indicating all the important values.*

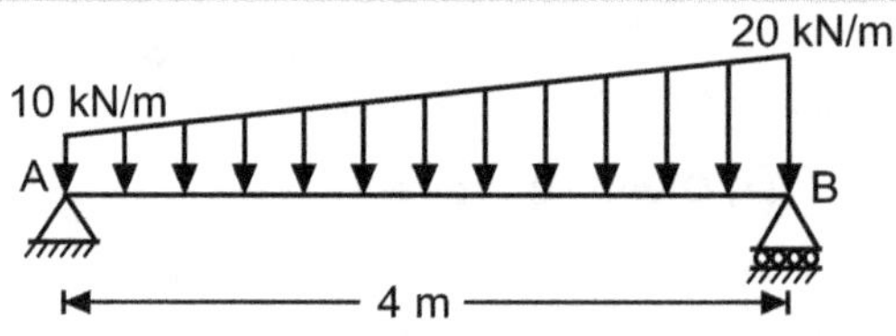


**(a) Given structure**

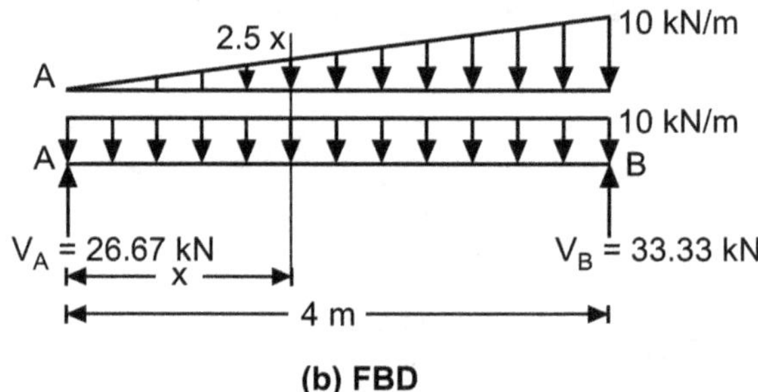


**(b) FBD**

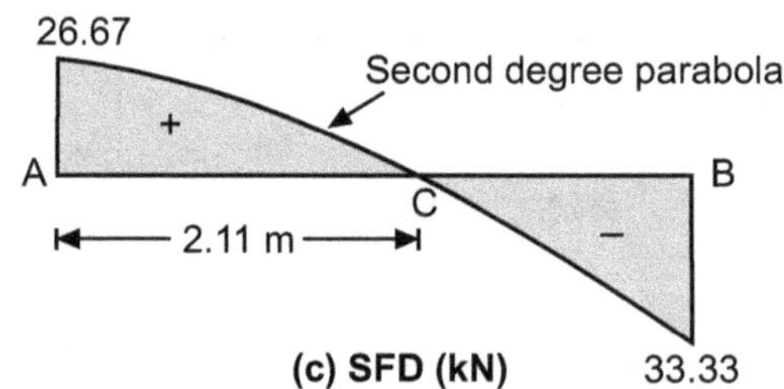


**(c) SFD (kN)**        33.33

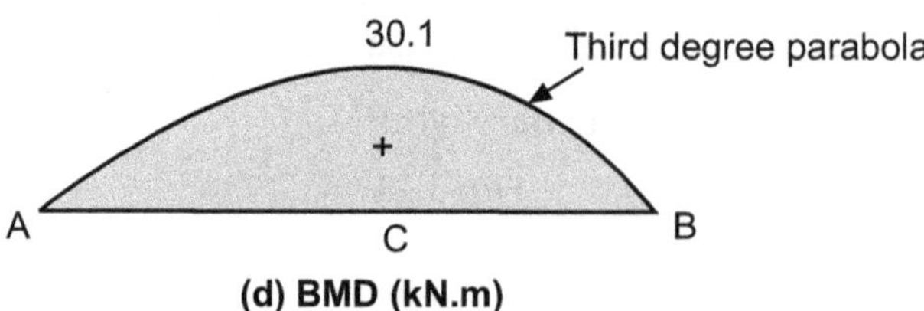


**(d) BMD (kN.m)**

**Fig. 3.22**

**Data**       :   As shown in Fig. 3.22 (a).

**Required**   :   SFD, BMD.

**Solution**   :   (i) Reactions :

$$\sum M_A = 0 \; ; \qquad V_B \times 4 - 10 \times \frac{4^2}{2} - \frac{1}{2} \times 10 \times 4 \times \frac{2}{3} \times 4 = 0$$

$$\therefore \qquad V_B = 33.33 \text{ kN } (\uparrow)$$

$$\sum F_y = 0 \; ; \qquad V_A + V_B = 10 \times 4 + \frac{1}{2} \times 10 \times 4$$

$$V_A = 26.67 \text{ kN } (\uparrow)$$

$$\sum F_x = 0 \; ; \qquad H_A = 0$$

FBD of beam is as shown in Fig. 3.22 (b).

(ii)  SF calculations :

Consider a section at a distance 'x' from 'A'.

$$SF_x = 26.67 - 10 \, x - \frac{1}{2} \times x \times x \times 2.5 \, x$$

$$= 26.67 - 10 \, x - 1.25 \, x^2 \qquad \qquad \text{... (i)}$$

$$\text{put } x = 0 \; ; \qquad SF_A = 26.67 \text{ kN}$$

$$\text{put } x = 4 \text{ m} \; ; \qquad SF_B = 26.67 - 10 \times 4 - 1.25 \times 4^2 = -33.33 \text{ kN}$$

To locate point of zero SF, equate equation (i) to zero.

$$SF_x = 26.67 - 10 \, x - 1.25 \, x^2 = 0$$

$$\text{Solving ; } x = 2.11 \text{ m from A}$$

SFD is as shown in Fig. 3.22 (c).

(iii)  BM calculations :

$$BM_x = 26.67 \, x - 10 \frac{x^2}{2} - 1.25 \, x^2 \times \frac{x}{3}$$

$$= 26.67 \, x - 5 \, x^2 - \frac{x^3}{2.4} \qquad \qquad \text{... (ii)}$$

$$\text{put } x = 0 \; ; \qquad BM_A = 0$$

$$\text{put } x = 4 \text{ m} \; ; \qquad BM_B = 0$$

$$\text{put } x = 2.11 \text{ m} \; ; \qquad BM_C = 26.67 \times 2.11 - 5 \, (2.11)^2 - \frac{(2.11)^3}{2.4} = 30.1 \text{ kN.m}$$

BMD is as shown in Fig. 3.22 (d).

**Example 3.16 :** *The beam is supported and loaded as shown in Fig. 3.23 (a). Draw SFD, BMD indicating all the important values.*

**Data**      :   As shown in Fig. 3.23 (a).

**Required**   :   SFD, BMD.

**Solution**   :   (i) Reactions :

$$\sum M_A = 0 ; \qquad V_B \times 6 - \frac{1}{2} \times 3 \times 10 \times \frac{2}{3} \times 3 + \frac{1}{2} \times 3 \times 10 \times \left(3 + \frac{1}{3} \times 3\right) = 0$$

$$\therefore \qquad V_B = -5 \text{ kN} = 5 \text{ kN} (\downarrow)$$

$$\sum F_y = 0 ; \qquad V_A + V_B - \frac{1}{2} \times 3 \times 10 + \frac{1}{2} \times 3 \times 10 = 0$$

$$\therefore \qquad V_A = 5 \text{ kN} (\uparrow)$$

$$\sum F_x = 0 ; \qquad H_A = 0$$

FBD of beam is as shown in Fig. 3.23 (b).

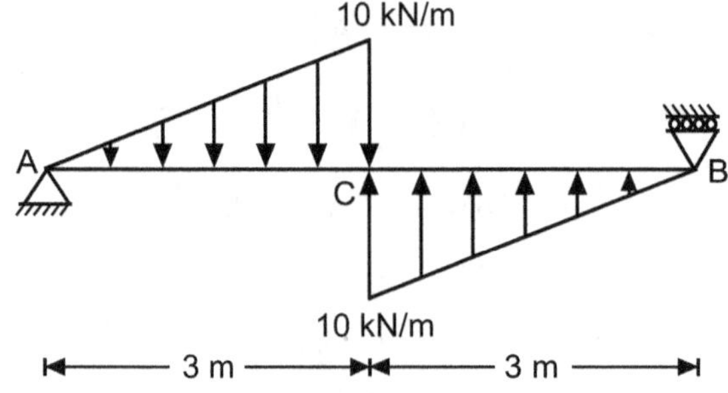


**(a) Given structure**

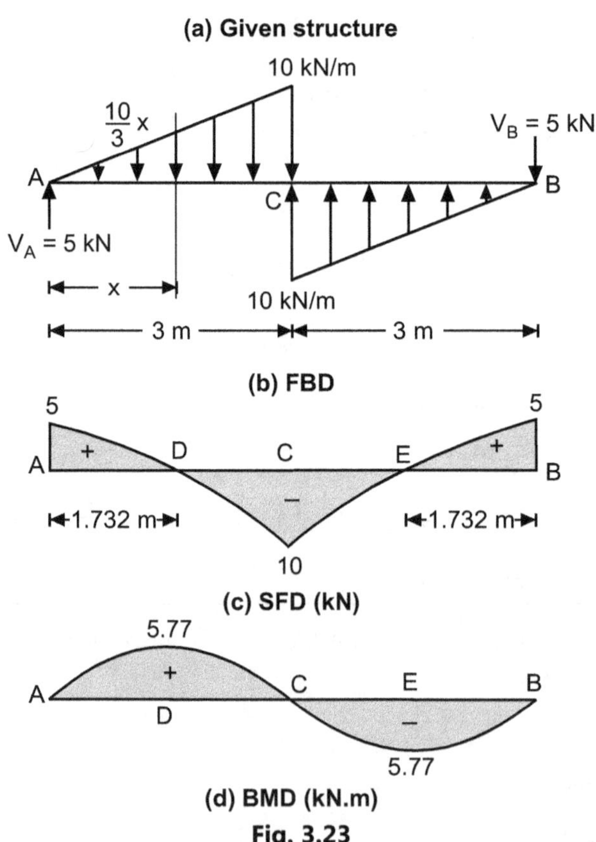


**(b) FBD**



**(c) SFD (kN)**



**(d) BMD (kN.m)**

**Fig. 3.23**

(ii)   SF calculations : Consider a section at a distance 'x' from A in zone AC.

$$SF_x = 5 - \frac{1}{2} \times x \times \frac{10}{3} x = 5 - \frac{5}{3} x^2 \quad ... (i)$$

put x = 0 ;          $SF_A = 5$ kN

put x = 3 m ;        $SF_C = 5 - \frac{5}{3}(3)^2 = -10$ kN

To locate point of zero SF, equate equation (i) to zero.

$$5 - \frac{5}{3} x^2 = 0 \quad \therefore \quad x = 1.732 \text{ m from A}$$

SFD for zone BC will be same as that of zone AC by symmetry.
SFD is as shown in Fig. 3.23 (c).

(iii)  BM calculations :

$$BM_x = 5x - \frac{5}{3} x^2 \times \frac{x}{3} = 5x - \frac{5}{9} x^3 \quad ... (ii)$$

put x = 0 ;          $BM_A = 0$

put x = 3 m ;        $BM_C = 5 \times 3 - \frac{5}{9}(3)^3 = 0$

put x = 1.732 m ;    $BM_D = 5 \times 1.732 - \frac{5}{9}(1.732)^3 = 5.77$ kN.m

BMD for zone BC will be same as that of zone AC by symmetry.
BMD is as shown in Fig. 3.23 (d).

**Example 3.17 :** *The beam PQ is supported and loaded as shown in Fig. 3.24 (a). Determine the magnitude of couple 'M' at C such that reaction at P is zero. Draw SFD and BMD.*

**Data**       :   As shown in Fig. 3.24 (a).

**Required**   :   Magnitude of couple 'M' and SFD, BMD.

**Solution**   :   (i) Reactions and magnitude of couple 'M' :

$$\sum F_y = 0 ; \qquad V_P + V_Q - \frac{1}{2} \times 1.8 \times 2.4 = 0$$

$$\therefore \qquad V_Q = 2.16 \text{ kN } (\uparrow) \qquad (\because V_P = 0)$$

$$\sum M_P = 0 ; \qquad V_Q \times 3 - M - \frac{1}{2} \times 1.8 \times 2.4 \times \frac{1}{3} \times 1.8 = 0$$

$$M = 5.184 \text{ kN.m}$$

FBD of beam is as shown in Fig. 3.24 (b).

(ii)   SF calculations :

$$SF_P = 0$$

$$SF_D = -\frac{1}{2} \times 1.8 \times 2.4 = -2.16 \text{ kN.m}$$

$$SF_Q = -2.16 \text{ kN.m}$$

SFD is as shown in Fig. 3.24 (c).

(iii)  BM calculations :

$$BM_P = BM_Q = 0$$

$$BM_C \text{ (just to the right)} = 2.16 \times 0.6 = 1.296 \text{ kN.m}$$

$$BM_C \text{ (just to the left)} = 1.296 - 5.184 = -3.888 \text{ kN.m}$$

$$BM_D = -\frac{1}{2} \times 1.8 \times 2.4 \times \frac{2}{3} \times 1.8 = -2.592 \text{ kN.m}$$

BMD is as shown in Fig. 3.24 (d).

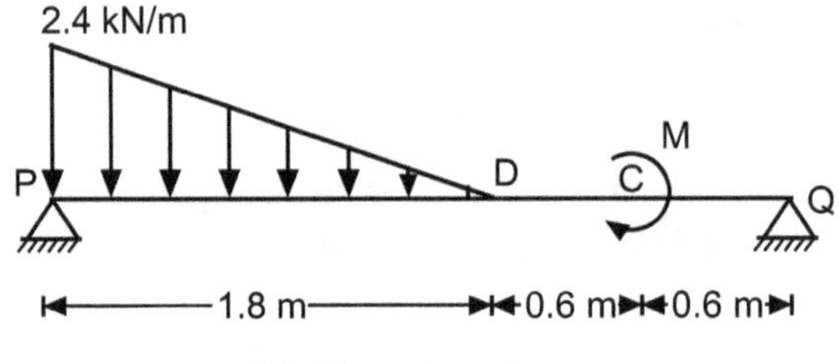


**(a) Given structure**

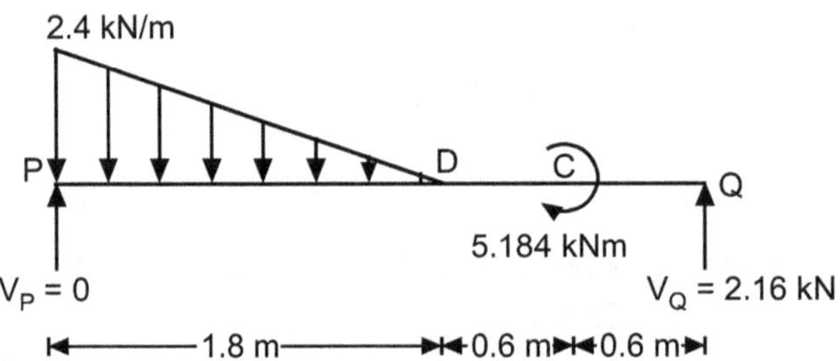


**(b) FBD**

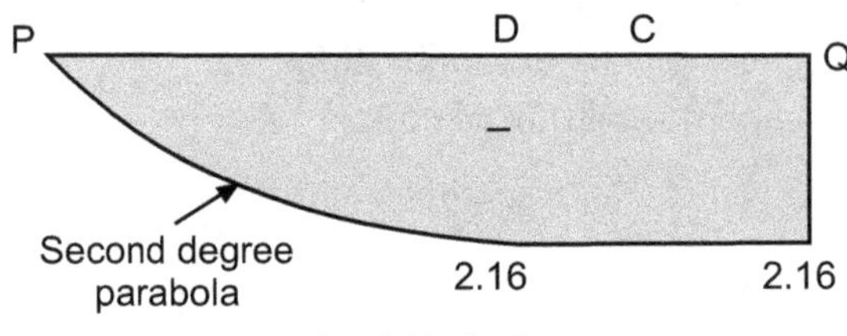


**(c) SFD (kN)**

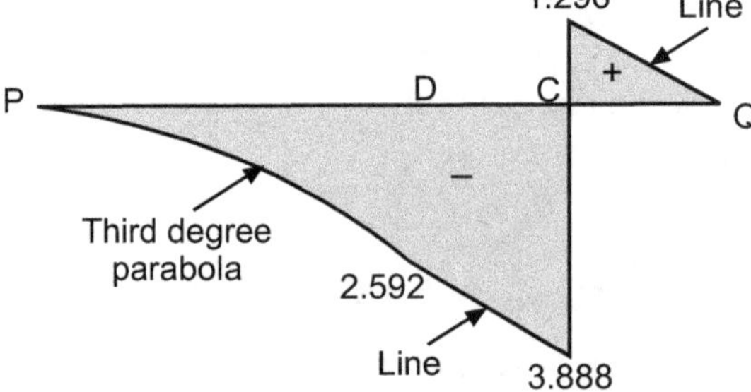


**(d) BMD (kN.m)**

**Fig. 3.24**

**Example 3.18 :** *The beam is supported and loaded as shown in Fig. 3.25 (a). Draw SFD, BMD indicating all important values.*

**Data** : As shown in Fig. 3.25 (a).

**Required** : SFD, BMD.

**Solution** : (i) Reactions :

$$\sum M_A = 0 \; ; \qquad\qquad -10 \times 5.5 \times \frac{5.5}{2} + V_B \times 4 = 0$$

$$\therefore \qquad\qquad V_B = 37.8 \text{ kN } (\uparrow)$$

$$\sum F_y = 0 \; ; \qquad\qquad V_A + V_B - 10 \times 5.5 = 0$$

$$\therefore \qquad\qquad V_A = 17.2 \text{ kN } (\uparrow)$$

FBD of beam is as shown in Fig. 3.25 (b).

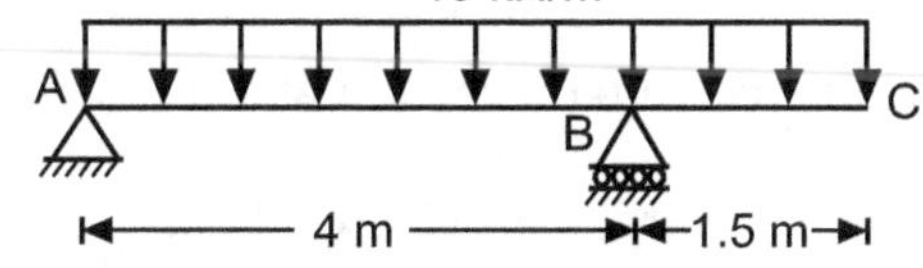


**(a) Given structure**

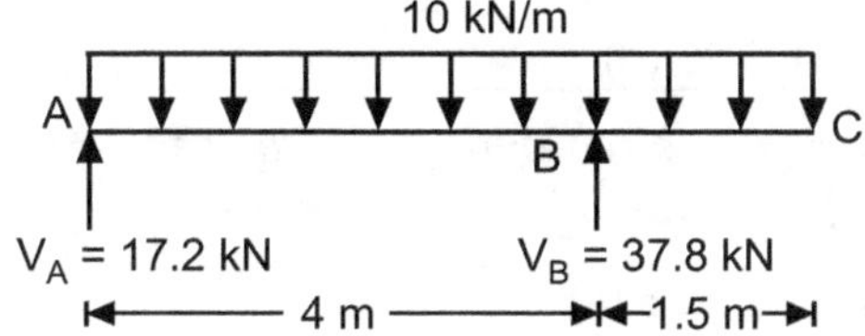


**(b) FBD**

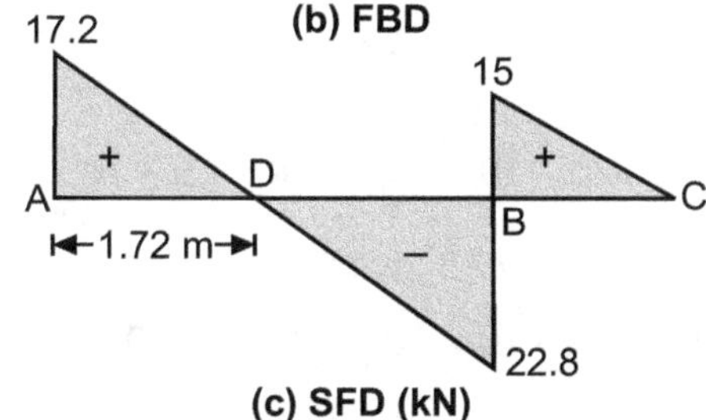


**(c) SFD (kN)**

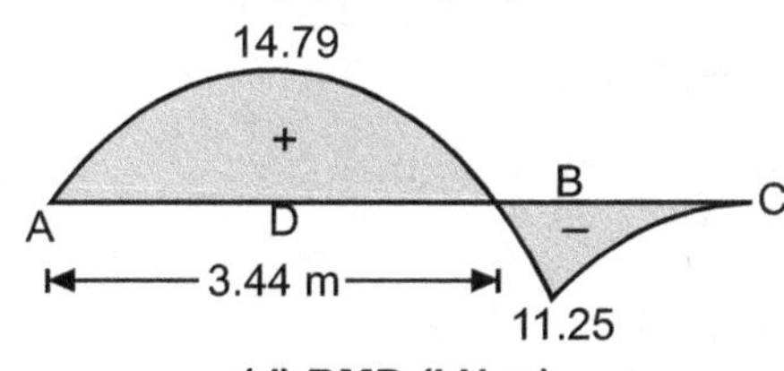


**(d) BMD (kN.m)**

**Fig. 3.25**

(ii)　SF calculations :

$$SF_A = 17.2 \text{ kN}$$

$$SF_B \text{ (just to the left)} = 17.2 - 10 \times 4 = -22.8 \text{ kN}$$

$$SF_B \text{ (just to the right)} = -22.8 + 37.8 = 15 \text{ kN}$$

$$SF_C = 0$$

To locate point of zero SF, consider a section at a distance x from A in zone AB.

$$SF_X = 17.2 - 10\,x = 0$$

$$\therefore \qquad x = 1.72 \text{ m from A}$$

SFD is as shown in Fig. 3.25 (c).

(iii)    BM calculations :    $BM_A = BM_C = 0$

$$BM_B = -10 \times \frac{1.5^2}{2} = -11.25 \text{ kN.m}$$

$$\text{BM at point of zero SF} = BM_D = 17.2 \times 1.72 - 10 \times \frac{1.72^2}{2}$$

$$= 14.79 \text{ kN.m}$$

To locate point of contraflexure, consider a section at a distance x from A in zone AB,

$$BM_X = 17.2\,x - 10\,\frac{x^2}{2} = 0$$

$$x = 3.44 \text{ m from A.}$$

BMD is as shown in Fig. 3.25 (d).

**Example 3.19 :** *The beam is supported and loaded as shown in Fig. 3.26 (a). Draw SFD, BMD indicating all important values.*

**Data**    :    As shown in Fig. 3.26 (a).

**Required**    :    SFD, BMD.

**Solution**    :    (i) Reactions :

$$\sum M_A = 0 ; \qquad V_B \times 20 - 10 \times \frac{10^2}{2} - 20 \times 15 - 30 \times 25 = 0$$

$$\therefore \qquad V_B = 77.5 \text{ kN} (\uparrow)$$

$$\sum F_y = 0 ; \qquad V_A + V_B - 10 \times 10 - 20 - 30 = 0$$

$$\therefore \qquad V_A = 72.5 \text{ kN} (\uparrow)$$

$$\sum F_x = 0 ; \qquad H_A = 0$$

FBD of beam is as shown in Fig. 3.26 (b).

(ii)    SF calculations :

$$SF_A = 72.5 \text{ kN}$$

$$SF_C = 72.5 - 10 \times 10 = -27.5 \text{ kN}$$

$$SF_D \text{ (just to the left)} = -27.5 \text{ kN}$$

$$SF_D \text{ (just to the right)} = -27.5 - 20 = -47.5 \text{ kN}$$

$$SF_B \text{ (just to the right )} = 30 \text{ kN}$$

$$SF_B \text{ (just to the left)} = 30 - 77.5 = -47.5 \text{ kN}$$

$$SF_E = 30 \text{ kN}$$

To locate point of zero SF, consider a section at a distance x from A in zone AC,

$$SF_X = 72.5 - 10\,x = 0$$

$$\therefore \quad x = 7.26 \text{ m from A}$$

SFD is as shown in Fig. 3.26 (c).

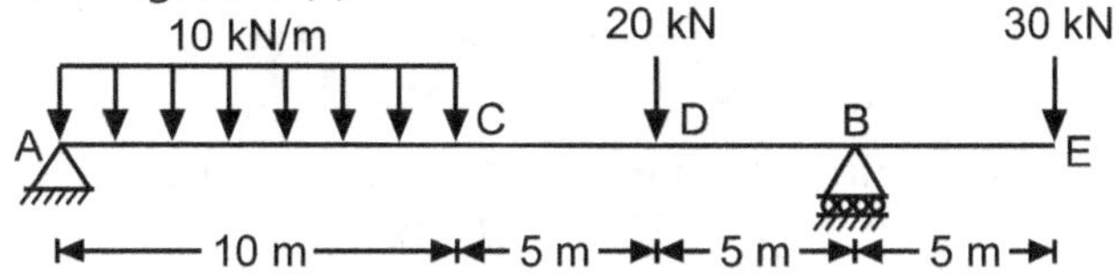

**(a) Given structure**

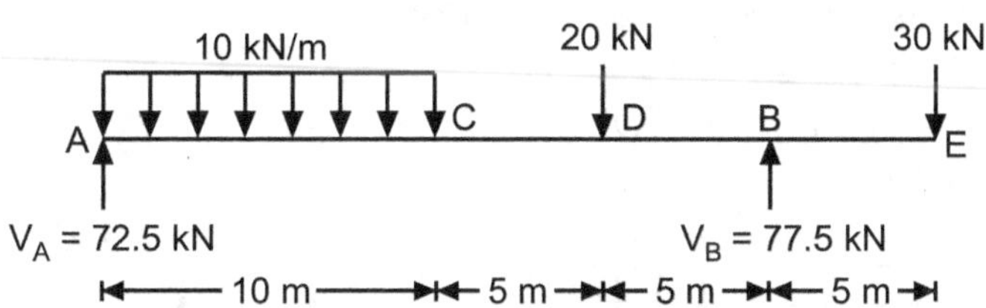

**(b) FBD**

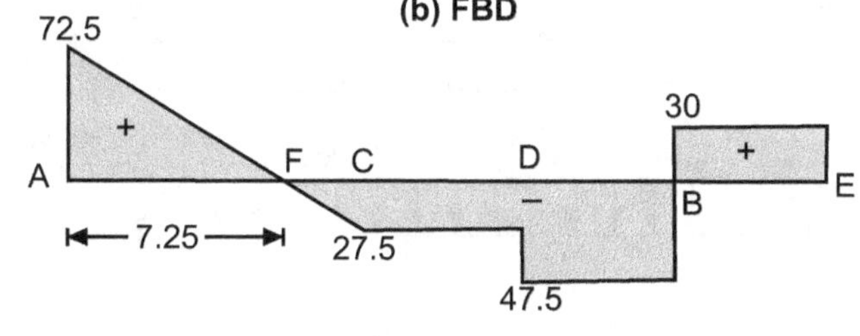

**(c) SFD (kN)**

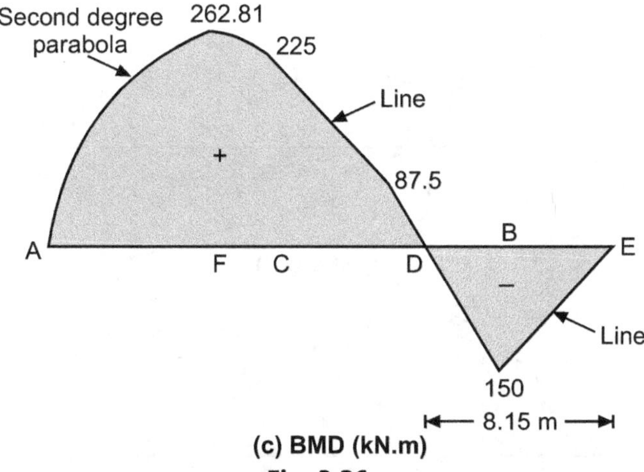

**(c) BMD (kN.m)**

**Fig. 3.26**

(iii)　　BM calculations :

$$BM_A = BM_E = 0$$

$$BM_C \;=\; 72.5 \times 10 - 10 \times \frac{10^2}{2} = 225 \text{ kN.m}$$

$$\text{BM at a point of zero SF} \;=\; BM_F = 72.5 \times 7.25 - 10 \times \frac{7.25^2}{2}$$

$$= 262.81 \text{ kN.m}$$

$$BM_D \;=\; 77.5 \times 5 - 30 \times 10 = 87.5 \text{ kN.m}$$

$$BM_B \;=\; -30 \times 5 = -150 \text{ kN.m}$$

To locate point of contraflexure, consider a section at a distance 'x' from E in zone DB.

$$BM_X \;=\; -30x + 77.5(x-5) = 0$$

$$\therefore \qquad x \;=\; 8.15 \text{ m from E}$$

BMD is as shown in Fig. 3.26 (d).



**Data**        :   As shown in Fig. 3.27 (a).

**Required**   :   SFD, BMD.

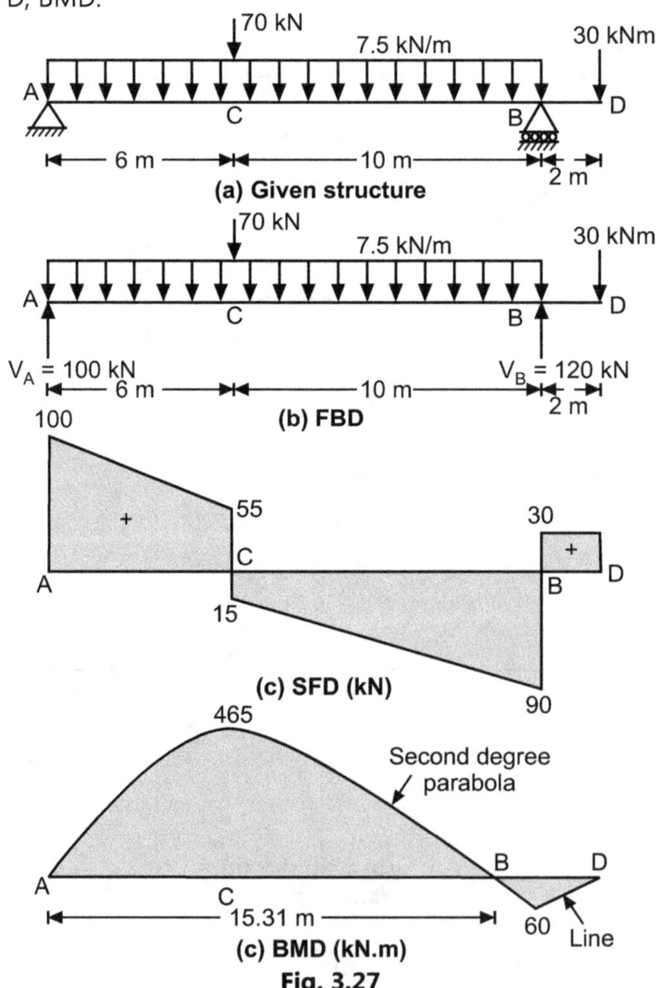


**Fig. 3.27**

**Solution** : (i) Reactions :

$$\Sigma M_A = 0 ; \qquad V_B \times 16 - 30 \times 18 - 7.5 \times \frac{16^2}{2} - 70 \times 6 = 0$$

$$\therefore \qquad V_B = 120 \text{ kN } (\uparrow)$$

$$\Sigma F_y = 0 ; \qquad V_A + V_B - 70 - 30 - 7.5 \times 16 = 0$$

$$\therefore \qquad V_A = 100 \text{ kN } (\uparrow)$$

$$\Sigma F_x = 0 ; \qquad H_A = 0$$

FBD of beam is as shown in Fig. 3.27 (b).

(ii)   SF calculations :

$$SF_A = 100 \text{ kN}$$

$$SF_C \text{ (just to the left)} = 100 - 7.5 \times 6 = 55 \text{ kN}$$

$$SF_C \text{ (just to the right)} = 55 - 70 = -15 \text{ kN}$$

$$SF_B \text{ (just to the left)} = 30 - 120 = -90 \text{ kN}$$

$$SF_B \text{ (just to the right)} = 30 \text{ kN}$$

$$SF_D = 30 \text{ kN}$$

SFD is as shown in Fig. 3.27 (c).

(iii)   BM calculations :

$$BM_A = BM_D = 0$$

$$BM_C = 100 \times 6 - 7.5 \times \frac{6^2}{2} = 465 \text{ kN.m}$$

$$BM_B = -30 \times 2 = -60 \text{ kN.m}$$

To locate point of contraflexure, consider a section at a distance x from A in the zone CB.

$$BM_x = 100 \, x - 7.5 \frac{x^2}{2} - 70 \,(x - 6) = 0$$

$$\therefore \qquad x^2 - 8x - 112 = 0$$

Solving ; $\qquad x = 15.31 \text{ m or} - 7.31 \text{ m}$

Neglecting negative value, x = 15.31 m from A.

**Example 3.21 :** *The beam is supported and loaded as shown in Fig. 3.28 (a). Draw SFD, BMD indicating all important values.*

**Data**       :   As shown in Fig. 3.28 (a).

**Required**   :   SFD, BMD.

**Solution**   :   (i) Reactions :

$$\Sigma M_A = 0 ; \qquad V_D \times 8 - 7.5 \times 10 - 10 \times 6 - 10 \times 2 - 15 \times \frac{10^2}{2} = 0$$

$$\therefore \qquad V_D = 113.125 \text{ kN } (\uparrow)$$

$$\Sigma F_y = 0 ; \qquad V_A + V_D = 10 + 10 + 7.5 + 15 \times 10$$

$$\therefore \qquad V_A = 64.375 \text{ kN } (\uparrow)$$

$$\Sigma F_x = 0 ; \qquad H_A = 0$$

FBD of beam is as shown in Fig. 3.28 (b).

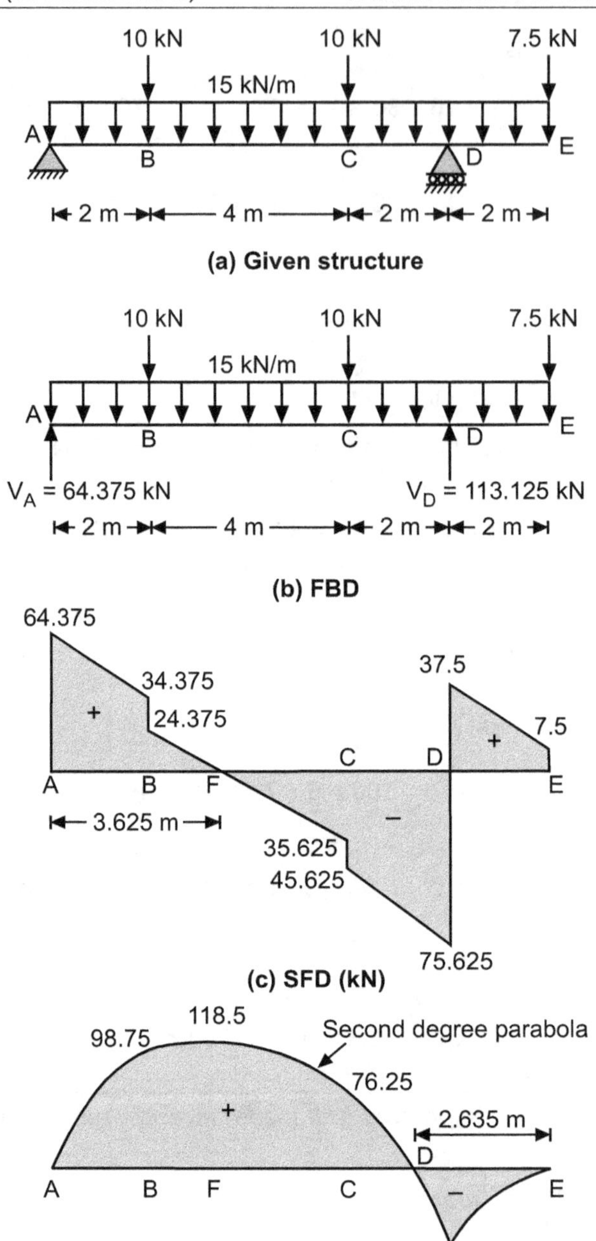



**Fig. 3.28**

(ii)    SF calculations :

$$SF_A = 64.375 \text{ kN}$$

$$SF_B \text{ (just to the left)} = 64.375 - 15 \times 2 = 34.375 \text{ kN}$$

$$SF_B \text{ (just to the right)} = 34.375 - 10 = 24.375 \text{ kN}$$

$SF_C$ (just to the left) $= 64.375 - 10 - 15 \times 6 = -35.625$ kN

$SF_C$ (just to the right) $= -35.625 - 10 = -45.625$ kN

$SF_D$ (just to the right) $= 7.5 + 15 \times 2 = 37.5$ kN

$SF_D$ (just to the left) $= 37.5 - 113.125 = -75.625$ kN

$SF_E = 7.5$ kN

To locate point of zero SF, consider a section at a distance x from A in zone BC.

$$SF_x = 64.375 - 15\,x - 10 = 0$$

$\therefore \qquad x = 3.625$ m from A

(iii)    BM calculations :

$$BM_A = BM_E = 0$$

$$BM_B = 64.375 \times 2 - 15 \times \frac{2^2}{2}$$

$$= 98.75 \text{ kN.m}$$

BM at point of zero SF $= BM_F$

$$= 64.375 \times 3.625 - 15 \times \frac{3.625^2}{2} - 10 \times 1.625$$

$$= 118.55 \text{ kN.m}$$

$$BM_C = -7.5 \times 4 - 15 \times \frac{4^2}{2} + 113.125 \times 2$$

$$= 76.25 \text{ kN.m}$$

$$BM_D = -7.5 \times 2 - 15 \times \frac{2^2}{2}$$

$$= -45 \text{ kN.m}$$

To locate point of contraflexure, consider a section at a distance x from 'E' in zone CD.

$$BM_x = -7.5\,x - 15\,\frac{x^2}{2} + 113.125\,(x - 2) = 0$$

$$-7.5\,x^2 + 105.625\,x - 226.25 = 0$$

Solving; $\qquad x = 2.635$ m from E.

BMD is as shown in Fig. 3.28 (d).

**Example 3.22 :** *The beam is supported and loaded as shown in Fig. 3.29 (a). Locate the position of support 'C' such that mid-point of the beam 'E' is point of contraflexure. Also draw SFD and BMD.*

**Data**        :    As shown in Fig. 3.29 (a).

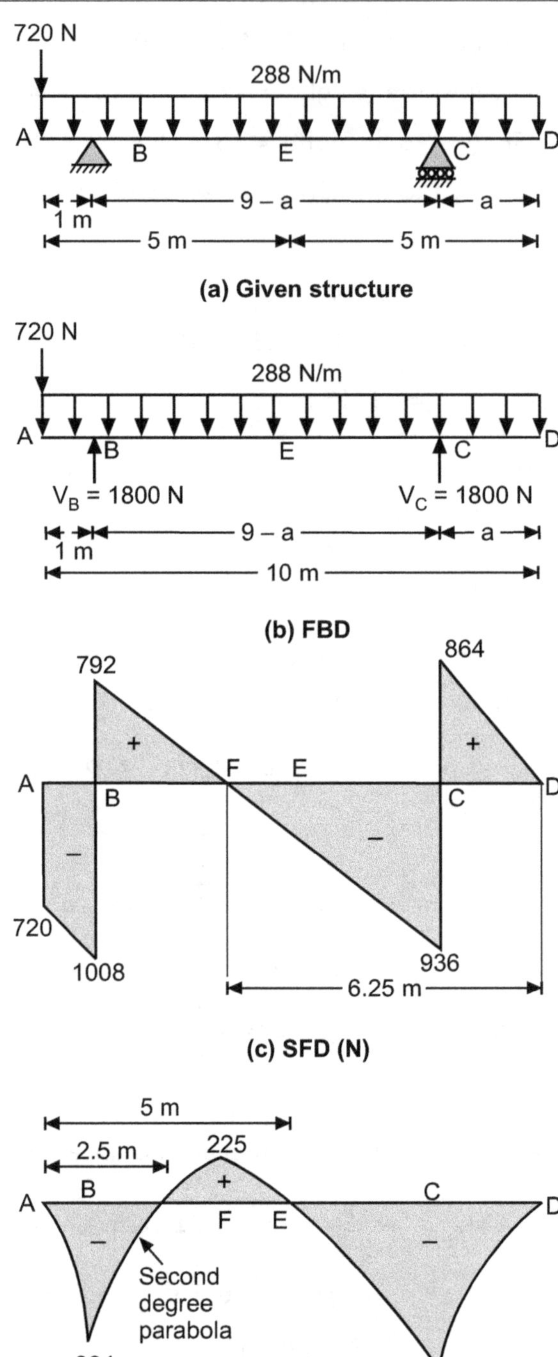



**Fig. 3.29**

**Required** : SFD, BMD.

**Solution** : (i) Reactions and position of support 'C'.

As mid-point of the beam, 'E' is a point of contraflexure

$$\Sigma M_{E\,(LHS)} = \Sigma M_{E\,(RHS)} = 0$$

$$\Sigma M_{E\,(LHS)} = 0 \;;\qquad -V_B \times 4 + 720 \times 5 + 288 \times \frac{5^2}{2} = 0$$

$$\therefore \qquad\qquad V_B \;=\; 1800 \text{ N } (\uparrow)$$

$$\Sigma F_y = 0 \;;\qquad V_B + V_C - 720 - 288 \times 10 = 0$$

$$\therefore \qquad\qquad V_C \;=\; 1800 \text{ N } (\uparrow)$$

$$\Sigma M_{E\,(RHS)} = 0 \;;\qquad V_C\,(5 - a) - 288 \times \frac{5^2}{2} = 0$$

$$\therefore \qquad\qquad 1800\,(5 - a) - 288 \times \frac{5^2}{2} = 0$$

$$\therefore \qquad\qquad a \;=\; 3 \text{ m}$$

$$\Sigma F_x = 0 \;;\qquad H_B \;=\; 0$$

FBD of beam is as shown in Fig. 3.29 (b).

(ii)    SF calculations :

$$SF_A = -720 \text{ N}$$

$$SF_B \text{ (just to the left)} = -720 - 288 \times 1 = -1008 \text{ N}$$

$$SF_B \text{ (just to the right)} = -1008 + 1800 = 792 \text{ N}$$

$$SF_D = 0$$

$$SF_C \text{ (just to the right)} = 288 \times 3 = 864 \text{ N}$$

$$SF_C \text{ (just to the left)} = 864 - 1800 = -936 \text{ N}$$

To locate point of zero SF, consider a section at a distance 'x' from D in zone BC,

$$SF_x \;=\; 288\,x - 1800 = 0$$

$$x \;=\; 6.25 \text{ m from D}$$

SFD is as shown in Fig. 3.29 (c).

(iii)    BM calculations :

$$BM_A \;=\; BM_E = BM_D = 0$$

$$BM_B \;=\; -720 \times 1 - 288 \times \frac{1^2}{2} = -864 \text{ N.m}$$

$$BM_F \;=\; -288 \times \frac{6.25^2}{2} + 1800\,(6.25 - 3) = 225 \text{ N.m}$$

$$BM_C \;=\; -288 \times \frac{3^2}{2} = -1296 \text{ N.m}$$

To locate point of contraflexure, consider a section at a distance x from A in zone BE,

$$BM_x \;=\; -720\,x - 288\,\frac{x^2}{2} + 1800\,(x - 1) = 0$$

$$x^2 - 7.5\,x + 12.5 \;=\; 0$$

Solving,        $x \;=\; 2.5$ m and 5 m.

BMD is as shown in Fig. 3.29 (d).

**Example 3.23 :** *The beam is supported and loaded as shown in Fig. 3.30 (a). Draw SFD, BMD indicating all important values.*

**Data**　　　:　As shown in Fig. 3.30 (a).

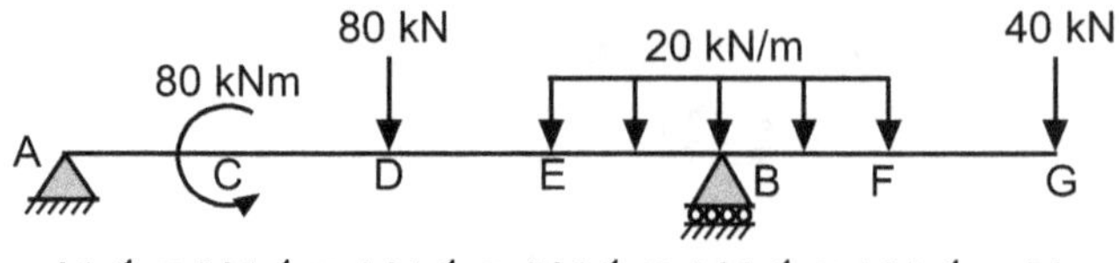


**(a) Given structure**

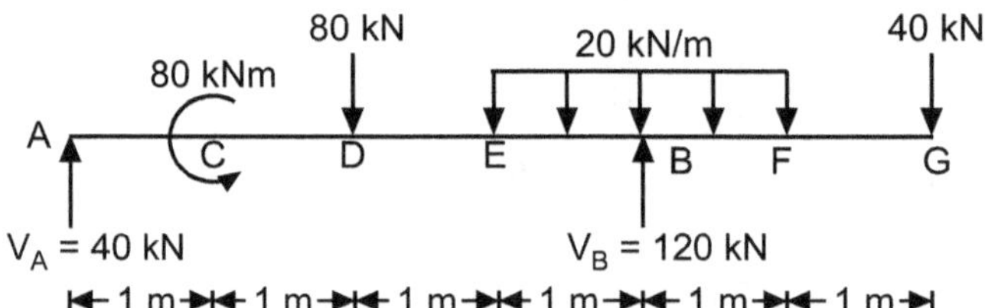


**(b) FBD**

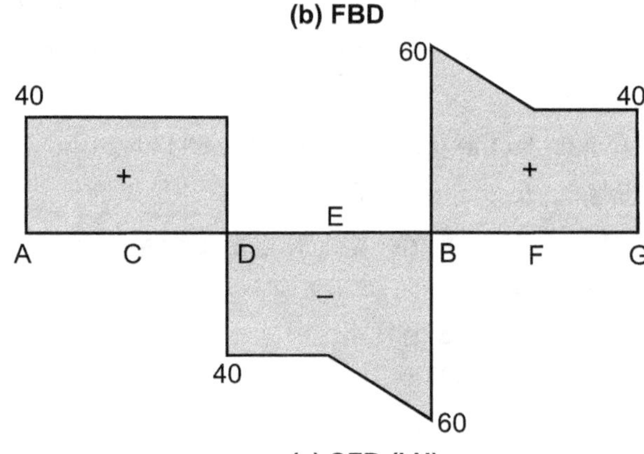


**(c) SFD (kN)**

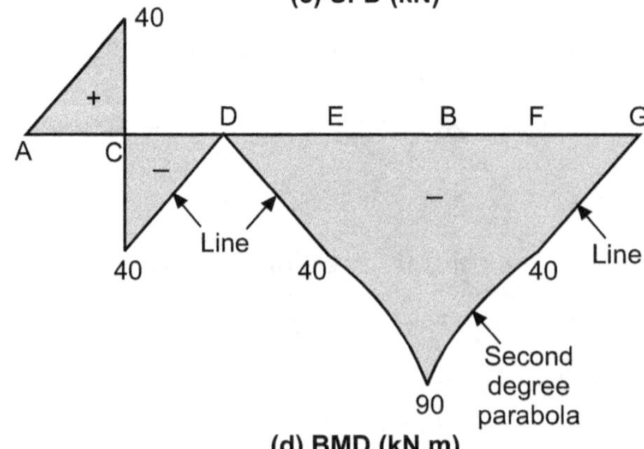


**(d) BMD (kN.m)**

**Fig. 3.30**

**Required** : SFD, BMD.

**Solution** : (i) Reactions :

$$\sum M_A = 0 ; \qquad V_B \times 4 - 40 \times 6 - 20 \times 2 \times 4 - 80 \times 2 + 80 = 0$$

$$V_B = 120 \text{ kN } (\uparrow)$$

$$\sum F_y = 0 ; \qquad V_A + V_B - 80 - 20 \times 2 - 40 = 0$$

$$\therefore \qquad V_A = 40 \text{ kN } (\uparrow)$$

$$\sum F_x = 0 ; \qquad H_A = 0$$

FBD of beam is as shown in Fig. 3.30 (b).

(ii) SF calculations :

$$SF_A = 40 \text{ kN}$$

$$SF_C = 40 \text{ kN}$$

$$SF_D \text{ (just to the left)} = 40 \text{ kN}$$

$$SF_D \text{ (just to the right)} = 40 - 80 = -40 \text{ kN}$$

$$SF_E = 40 - 80 = -40 \text{ kN}$$

$$SF_B \text{ (just to the left)} = 40 - 80 - 20 \times 1 = -60 \text{ kN}$$

$$SF_B \text{ (just to the right)} = -60 + 120 = 60 \text{ kN}$$

$$SF_F = SF_G = 40 \text{ kN}$$

SFD is as shown in Fig. 3.30 (c).

(iii) BM calculations :

$$BM_A = BM_G = 0$$

$$BM_C \text{ (just to the left)} = 40 \times 1 = 40 \text{ kN.m}$$

$$BM_C \text{ (just to the right)} = 40 - 80 = -40 \text{ kN.m}$$

$$BM_D = 40 \times 2 - 80 = 0$$

$$BM_E = 40 \times 3 - 80 - 80 \times 1 = -40 \text{ kN.m}$$

$$BM_B = -40 \times 2 - 20 \times \frac{1^2}{2} = -90 \text{ kN.m}$$

$$BM_F = -40 \times 1 = -40 \text{ kN.m}$$

BMD is as shown in Fig. 3.30 (d).

**Example 3.24 :** *The beam is supported and loaded as shown in Fig. 3.31 (a). Draw SFD, BMD indicating all important values.*

**Data** : As shown in Fig. 3.31 (a).

**Required** : SFD, BMD.

**Solution** : (i) Reactions :

$$\sum M_B = 0 ; \qquad V_E \times 6 - 40 \times 7.8 - 40 - 100 \times 1.8 - 15 \times \frac{1.8^2}{2} + 15 \times \frac{1.2^2}{2} = 0$$

$$\therefore \qquad V_E = 90.92 \text{ kN } (\uparrow)$$

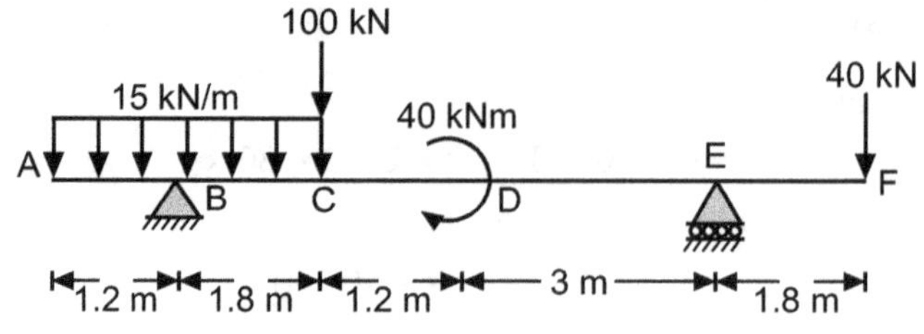

**(a) Given structure**

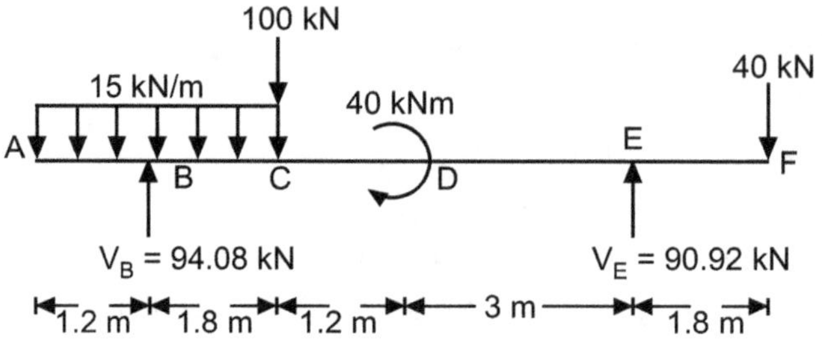

**(b) FBD**

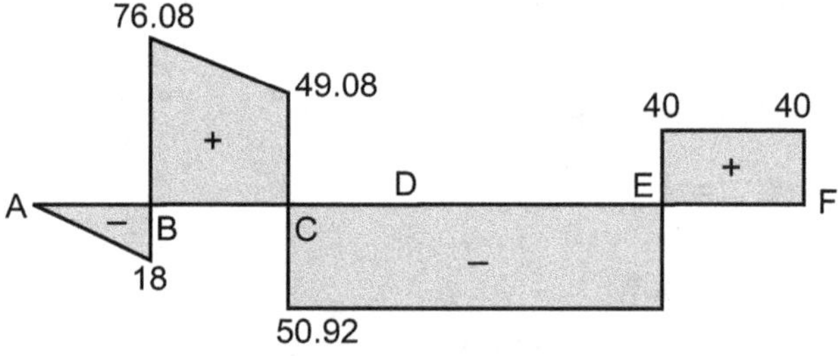

**(c) SFD (kN)**

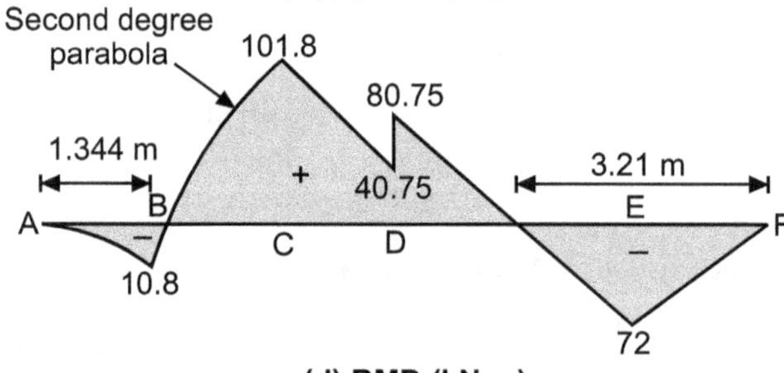

**(d) BMD (kN.m)**

**Fig. 3.31**

$$\sum F_y = 0 ; \qquad V_B + V_E - 15 \times 3 - 100 - 40 = 0$$

$$\therefore \qquad V_B = 94.08 \text{ kN } (\uparrow)$$

$$\sum F_x = 0 ; \qquad H_A = 0$$

FBD of beam is as shown in Fig. 3.31 (b).

(ii)    SF calculations :

$$SF_A = 0$$

$$SF_B \text{ (just to the left)} = -15 \times 1.2 = -18 \text{ kN}$$

$$SF_B \text{ (just to the right)} = -18 + 94.08 = 76.08 \text{ kN}$$

$$SF_C \text{ (just to the left)} = 94.08 - 15 \times 3 = 49.08 \text{ kN}$$

$$SF_C \text{ (just to the right)} = 49.08 - 100 = -50.92 \text{ kN}$$

$$SF_F = 40 \text{ kN}$$

$$SF_E \text{ (just to the right)} = 40 \text{ kN}$$

$$SF_E \text{ (just to the left)} = 40 - 90.92 = -50.92 \text{ kN}$$

SFD is as shown in Fig. 3.31 (c).

(iii)   BM calculations :

$$BM_A = BM_F = 0$$

$$BM_B = -15 \times \frac{(1.2)^2}{2} = -10.8 \text{ kN.m}$$

$$BM_C = -15 \times \frac{3^2}{2} + 94.08 \times 1.8 = 101.8 \text{ kN.m}$$

$$BM_D \text{ (just to the left)} = 94.08 \times 3 - 15 \times 3 \times \left(1.2 + \frac{3}{2}\right) - 100 \times 1.2$$

$$= 40.75 \text{ kN.m}$$

$$BM_D \text{ (just to the right)} = 40.75 + 40$$

$$= 80.75 \text{ kN.m}$$

$$BM_E = -40 \times 1.8 = -72 \text{ kN.m}$$

To locate point of contraflexure, consider a section at a distance x from 'F' in zone ED.

$$BM_x = -40x + 90.92 (x - 1.8) = 0$$

$$\therefore \quad x = 3.21 \text{ m from F}$$

To locate another point of contraflexure, consider a section at a distance 'x' from A in zone BC.

$$BM_x = -15 \frac{x^2}{2} + 94.08 (x - 1.2) = 0$$

$$\therefore \quad x = 1.344 \text{ m from A.}$$

BMD is as shown in Fig. 3.31 (d).

---

**Example 3.25 :** *The beam is supported and loaded as shown in Fig. 3.32 (a). Find the magnitude of load W such that support reactions at A and B are equal. Draw SFD and BMD.*

**Data**       :   As shown in Fig. 3.32 (a).

**Required**   :   Magnitude of load W and SFD, BMD.

---

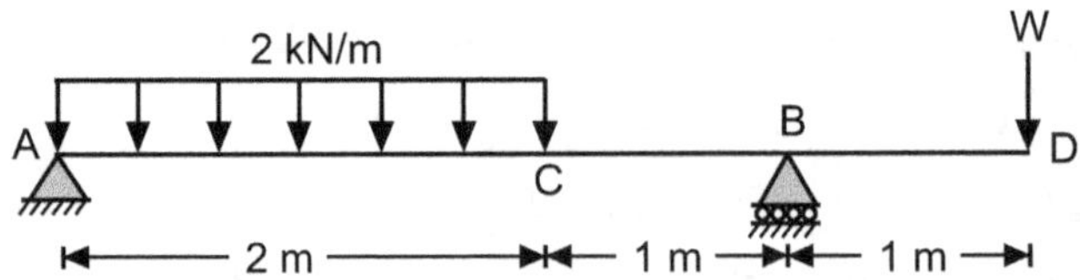

**(a) Given structure**

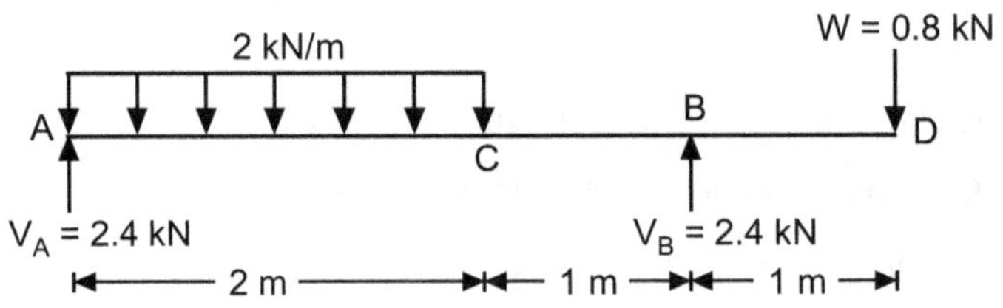

**(b) FBD**

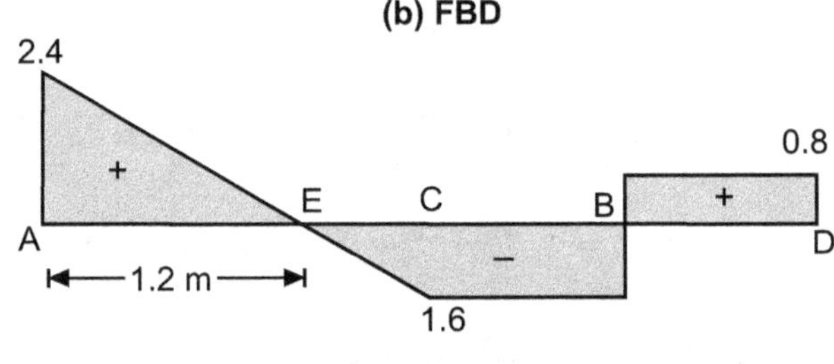

**(c) SFD (kN)**

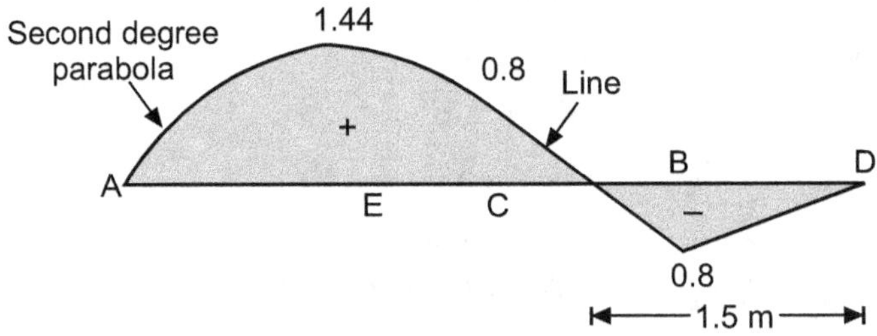

**(d) BMD (kN.m)**

**Fig. 3.32**

**Solution    :**   (i) Reactions and magnitude of load 'W' :

Let,                      $V_A = V_B = V$ (say)

$\sum M_A = 0$ ;          $V \times 3 - W \times 4 - 2 \times \dfrac{2^2}{2} = 0$

$\therefore$                      $V = \dfrac{4}{3}(W + 1)$                      ... (i)

$\sum F_y = 0$ ;          $2V - 2 \times 2 - W = 0$

$\therefore$                      $V = \dfrac{W}{2} + 2$                      ... (ii)

Equating equations (i) and (ii),

$$\frac{4}{3}(W + 1) = \frac{W}{2} + 2$$

$$\therefore \qquad W = 0.8 \text{ kN}$$

$$\text{Reactions} = V_A = V_B = \frac{W}{2} + 2 = 2.4 \text{ kN } (\uparrow)$$

FBD of beam is as shown in Fig. 3.32 (b).

(ii)     SF calculations :

$$SF_A = 2.4 \text{ kN}$$

$$SF_C = 2.4 - 2 \times 2 = -1.6 \text{ kN}$$

$$SF_B \text{ (just to the left)} = -1.6 \text{ kN}$$

$$SF_B \text{ (just to the right)} = -1.6 + 2.4 = 0.8 \text{ kN}$$

$$SF_D = 0.8 \text{ kN}$$

To locate point of zero SF, consider a section at a distance 'x' from A in zone AC,

$$SF_x = 2.4 - 2x = 0$$

$$\therefore \qquad x = 1.2 \text{ m from A.}$$

SFD is as shown in Fig. 3.32 (c).

(iii)    BM calculations :

$$BM_A = BM_D = 0$$

$$BM_C = 2.4 \times 2 - 2 \times \frac{2^2}{2} = 0.8 \text{ kN.m}$$

$$\text{BM at point of zero SF} = BM_E = 2.4 \times 1.2 - 2 \times \frac{1.2^2}{2} = 1.44 \text{ kN.m}$$

$$BM_B = -0.8 \times 1 = -0.8 \text{ kN.m}$$

To locate point of contraflexure, consider a section at a distance x from D in zone CB,

$$BM_x = -0.8 x + 2.4 (x - 1) = 0$$

$$\therefore \qquad x = 1.5 \text{ m from D.}$$

BMD is as shown in Fig. 3.32 (d).

**Example 3.26 :** *For the beam ABCD shown in Fig. 3.33 (a), find the position of supports at B and C such that, the maximum BM is minimum possible. Also draw SFD and BMD.*

**Data**        :   As shown in Fig. 3.33 (a).

**Required**   :   Position of supports SFD, BMD.

**Solution**   :   (i) Position of supports :

Hogging moments at supports B and C $= \dfrac{wa^2}{2}$        ... (i)

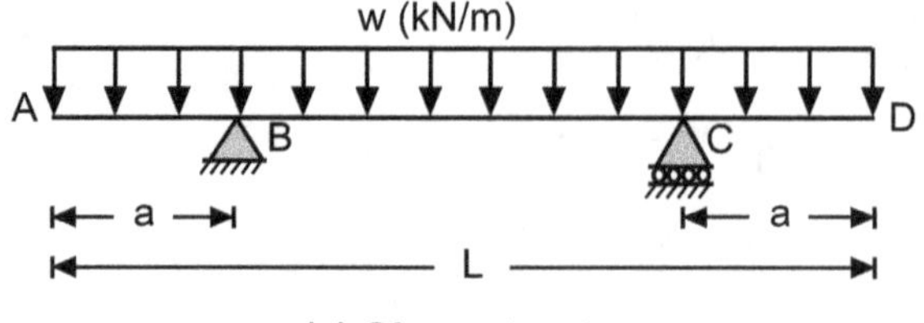

**(a) Given structure**

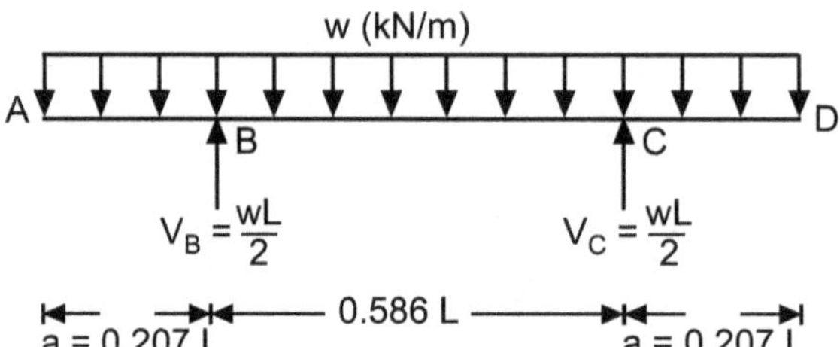

**(b) FBD**

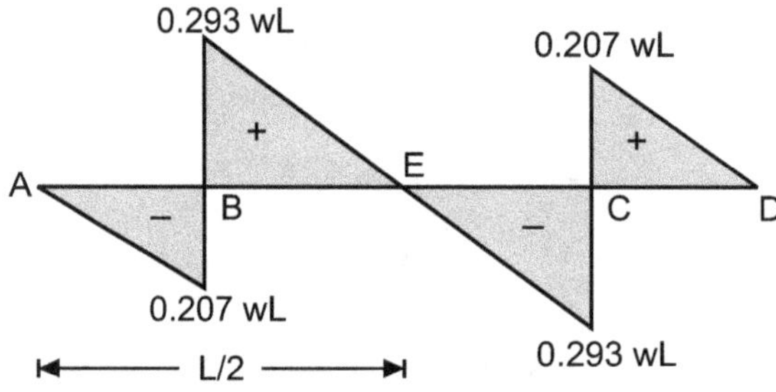

**(c) SFD (kN)**

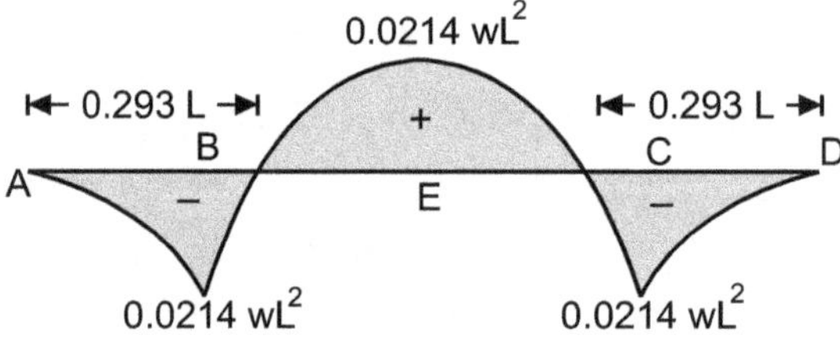

**(d) BMD (kN.m)**

**Fig. 3.33**

Maximum sagging moment at midspan

$$= \frac{w}{8}(L - 2a)^2 - \frac{wa^2}{2} \qquad \ldots \text{(ii)}$$

For maximum bending moment to be minimum, equating equations (i) and (ii),

$$\therefore \qquad \frac{wa^2}{2} = \frac{w}{8}(L - 2a)^2 - \frac{wa^2}{2}$$

$$\therefore \qquad a^2 = \frac{(L-2a)^2}{4} - a^2$$

$$\therefore \qquad a^2 + La - \frac{L^2}{4} = 0$$

Solving ; $\qquad a = 0.207\,L$

$$\text{Reactions} = V_A = V_B = \frac{wL}{2}\,(\uparrow)\ \text{by symmetry.}$$

FBD of beam is as shown in Fig. 3.33 (b).

(ii)   SF calculations :

$$SF_A = SF_D = 0$$

$$SF_B\ (\text{just to the left}) = -0.207\,wL$$

$$SF_B\ (\text{just to the right}) = -0.207\,wL + 0.5\,wL = 0.293\,wL$$

By symmetry, SF is zero at midspan.

SFD is drawn using symmetry as shown in Fig. 3.33 (c).

(iii)   BM calculations :

$$BM_A = BM_D = 0$$

Hogging moment at supports B and C

$$= \text{Sagging moment at midspan.}$$

$$= \frac{wa^2}{2}\ \text{where a} = 0.207\,L = \frac{w\,(0.207\,L)^2}{2}$$

$$= 0.0214\,wL^2$$

To locate point of contraflexure, consider a section at a distance 'x' from A in zone BC,

$$BM_x = -\frac{wx^2}{2} + \frac{wL}{2}\,(x - 0.207\,L) = 0$$

$$\therefore \qquad x^2 - Lx + 0.207\,L^2 = 0$$

Solving ; $\qquad x = 0.293\,L$

BMD is as shown in Fig. 3.33 (d).

**Example 3.27 :** *The beam is supported and loaded as shown in Fig. 3.34 (a). Draw AFD, SFD, BMD for beam ABC indicating all the important values.*

**Data**        :   As shown in Fig. 3.34 (a).

**Required**   :   AFD, SFD, BMD.

**Solution**   :   (i) Reactions :

Vertical component of 50 kN force at D

$$= 50 \times \frac{3}{5} = 30\ \text{kN}\ (\uparrow)$$

Horizontal component of 50 kN force at D

$$= 50 \times \frac{4}{5} = 40\ \text{kN}\ (\rightarrow)$$

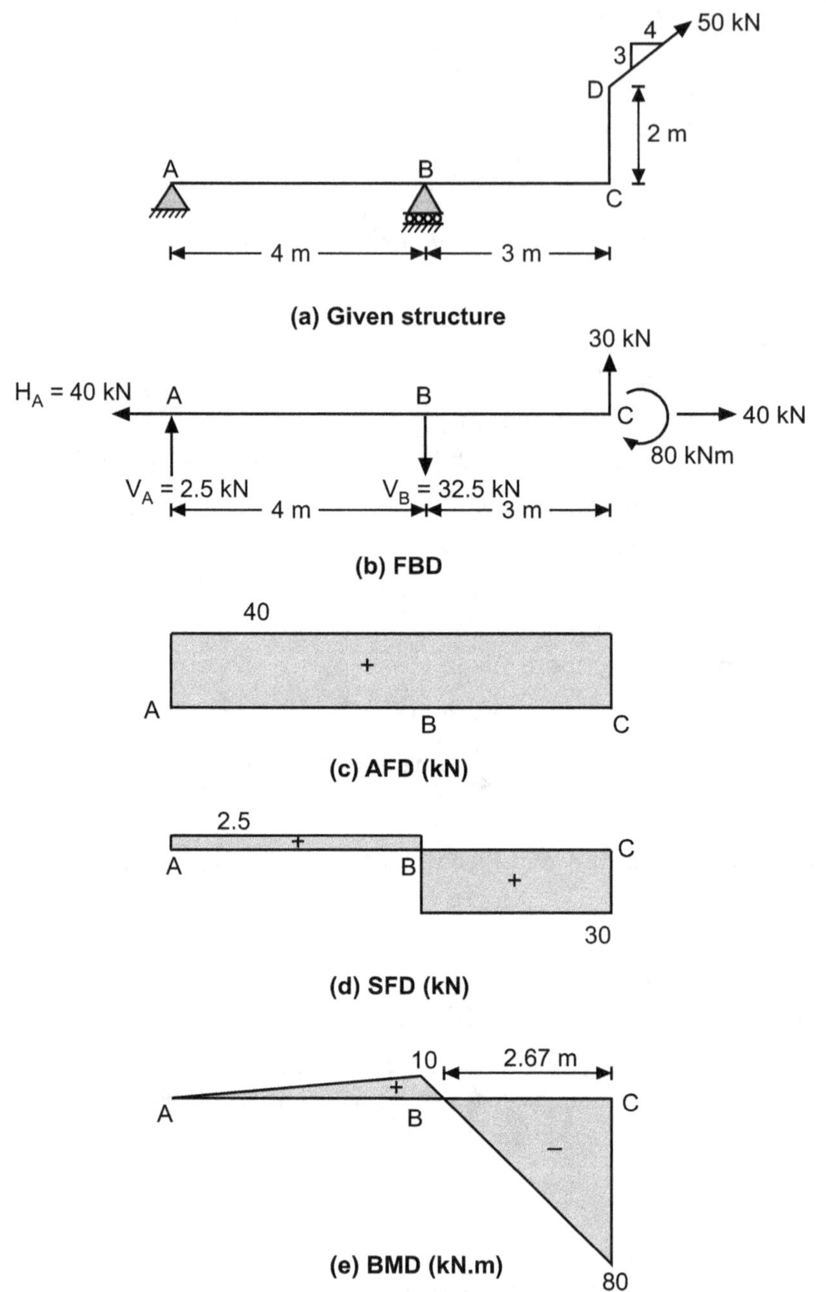



**Fig. 3.34**

Force components at D are transferred at C as shown in Fig. 3.34 (b).

$$\sum M_A = 0 ; \qquad V_B \times 4 - 80 + 30 \times 7 = 0$$

$$\therefore \qquad V_B = -32.5 \text{ kN} = 32.5 \text{ kN} (\downarrow)$$

$$\sum F_y = 0 ; \qquad V_A + V_B + 30 = 0$$

$$\therefore \qquad V_A = 2.5 \text{ kN} (\uparrow)$$

$$\Sigma F_x = 0 ; \qquad H_A = 40 \text{ kN} (\leftarrow)$$

FBD of beam is as shown in Fig. 3.34 (b).

(ii)  Axial force :

Member ABC is subjected to axial tension of 40 kN. AFD is as shown in Fig. 3.34 (c).

(iii)  SF calculations :

$$SF_A = 2.5 \text{ kN}$$
$$SF_B \text{ (just to the left) } = 2.5 \text{ kN}$$
$$SF_B \text{ (just to the right) } = 2.5 - 32.5 = -30 \text{ kN}$$
$$SF_C = -30 \text{ kN}$$

SFD is as shown in Fig. 3.34 (d).

(iv)  BM calculations :

$$BM_A = 0$$
$$BM_B = 2.5 \times 4 = 10 \text{ kN.m}$$
$$BM_C = -80 \text{ kN.m}$$

To locate point of contraflexure, consider a section at a distance 'x' from 'C' in zone BC,

$$BM_x = 30x - 80 = 0$$
$$x = 2.67 \text{ m from C.}$$

BMD is as shown in Fig. 3.34 (e).

**Example 3.28 :** *The beam is supported and loaded as shown in Fig. 3.35 (a). Draw SFD and BMD indicating all the important values.*

**Data**       :  As shown in Fig. 3.35 (a).

**Required**  :  SFD, BMD.

**Solution**  :  (i) Reactions :

$$\Sigma M_A = 0 ; \qquad V_B \times 7 - 10 \times \frac{3^2}{2} + 50 - 30 \times 1 \times 7.5 = 0$$

$$\therefore \qquad V_B = 31.43 \text{ kN} (\uparrow)$$

$$\Sigma F_y = 0 ; \qquad V_A + V_B - 10 \times 3 - 30 \times 1 = 0$$

$$V_A = 28.57 \text{ kN} (\uparrow)$$

$$\Sigma F_x = 0 ; \qquad H_A = 0$$

FBD of beam is as shown in Fig. 3.35 (b).

(ii)  SF calculations :

$$SF_A = 28.57 \text{ kN}$$
$$SF_C = 28.57 - 10 \times 3 = -1.43 \text{ kN}$$
$$SF_B \text{ (just to the right) } = 30 \text{ kN}$$
$$SF_B \text{ (just to the left) } = 30 - 31.43 = -1.43 \text{ kN}$$
$$SF_E = 0$$

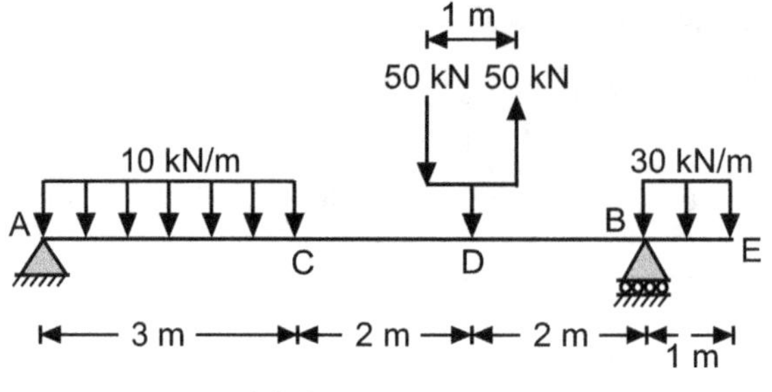

**(a) Given structure**

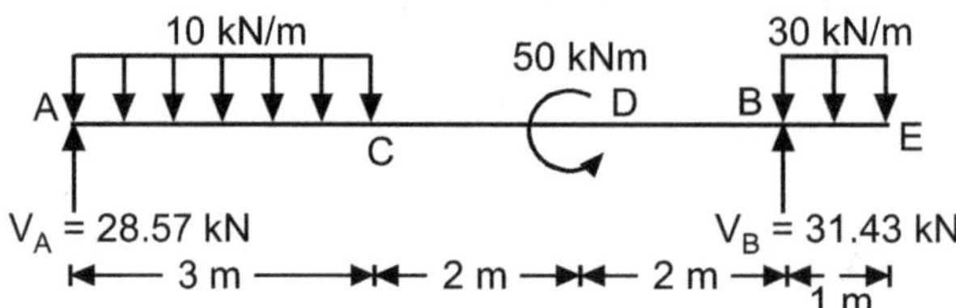

**(b) FBD**

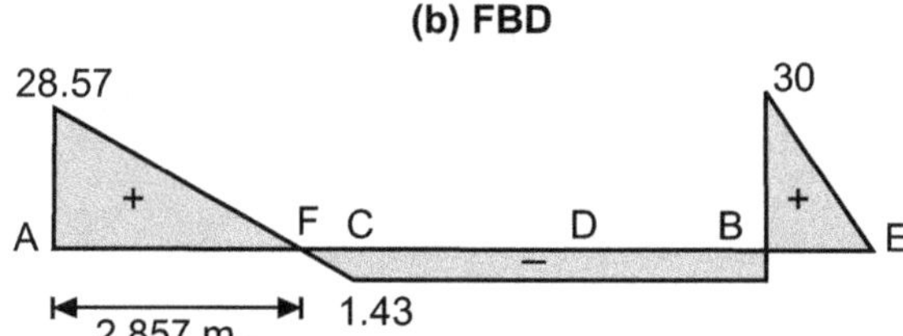

**(c) SFD (kN)**

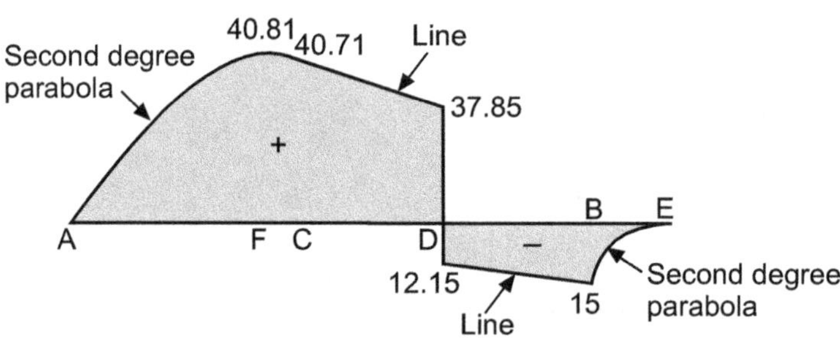

**(d) BMD (kN.m)**

**Fig. 3.35**

To locate point of zero SF, consider a section at a distance 'x' from A in zone AC,

$$SF_x = 28.57 - 10x = 0$$

$$\therefore \qquad x = 2.857 \text{ m from A.}$$

SFD is as shown in Fig. 3.35 (c).

(iii)　BM calculations :

$$BM_A = BM_E = 0$$

BM at point of zero SF $= BM_F$

$$= 28.57 \times 2.857 - 10 \times \frac{2.857^2}{2}$$

$$= 40.81 \text{ kN.m}$$

$$BM_C = 28.57 \times 3 - 10 \times \frac{3^2}{2} \quad = 40.71 \text{ kN.m}$$

$$BM_D \text{ (just to the left)} \quad = 28.57 \times 5 - 10 \times 3 \times 3.5$$

$$= 37.85 \text{ kN.m}$$

$$BM_D \text{ (just to the right)} \quad = 37.85 - 50 = -12.15 \text{ kN.m}$$

$$BM_B = -30 \times \frac{1^2}{2} \quad = -15 \text{ kN.m}$$

BMD is as shown in Fig. 3.35 (d).

**Example 3.29 :** *The beam is supported and loaded as shown in Fig. 3.36 (a). Draw AFD, SFD, BMD indicating all the important values.*

**Data**          :     As shown in Fig. 3.36 (a).

**Required**   :     AFD, SFD, BMD.

**Solution**    :     (i) Reactions :

$$\sum M_A = 0 ; \qquad V_D \times 3.4 - 21.21 \times 1 + 21.21 - 20 \times 2.2 - 15 \times 2.4 \times 3.4 = 0$$

$$\therefore \qquad V_D = 48.94 \text{ kN } (\uparrow)$$

$$\sum F_y = 0 ; \qquad V_A + V_D - 21.21 - 20 - 15 \times 2.4 = 0$$

$$\therefore \qquad V_A = 28.27 \text{ kN } (\uparrow)$$

$$\sum F_x = 0 ; \qquad H_A = 21.21 \text{ kN } (\rightarrow)$$

(ii)     Axial force :

Portion AB has axial compressive force of 21.21 kN.

AFD is as shown in Fig. 3.36 (c).

(iii)     SF calculations :

$$SF_A = 28.27 \text{ kN}$$

$$SF_B \text{ (just to the left)} = 28.27 \text{ kN}$$

$$SF_B \text{ (just to the right)} = 28.27 - 21.21 = 7.06 \text{ kN}$$

$$SF_C \text{ (just to the left)} = 7.06 \text{ kN}$$

$$SF_C \text{ (just to the right)} = 7.06 - 20 = -12.94 \text{ kN}$$

$$SF_D \text{ (just to the right)} = 15 \times 1.2 = 18 \text{ kN}$$

$$SF_D \text{ (just to the left)} = 18 - 48.94 = -30.94 \text{ kN}$$

SFD is as shown in Fig. 3.36 (d).

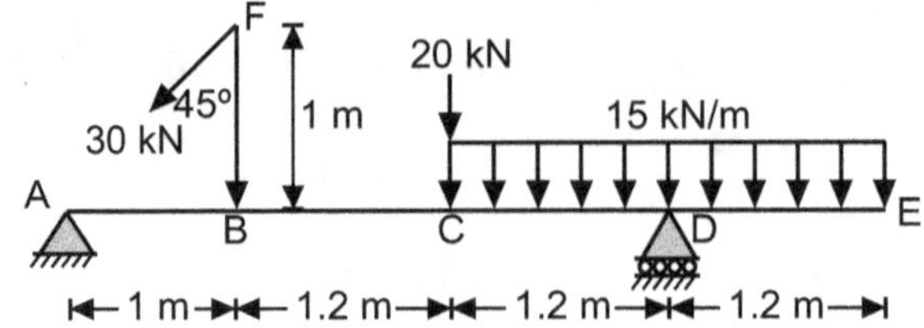

**(a) Given structure**

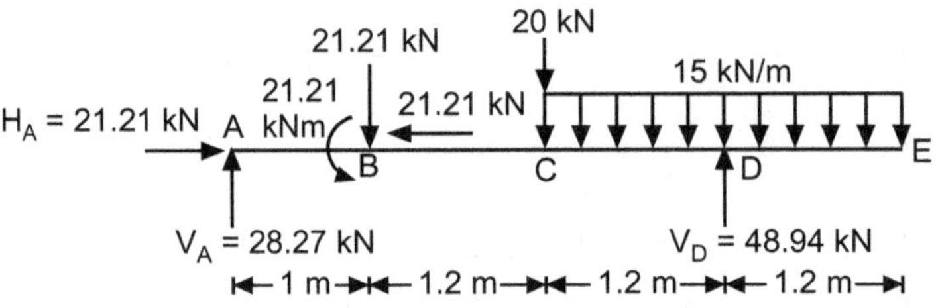

**(b) FBD**

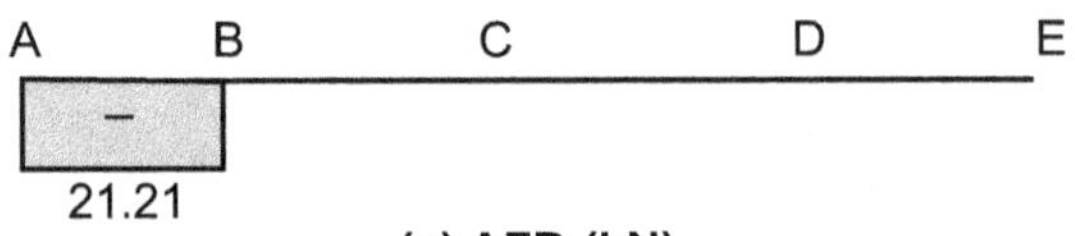

**(c) AFD (kN)**

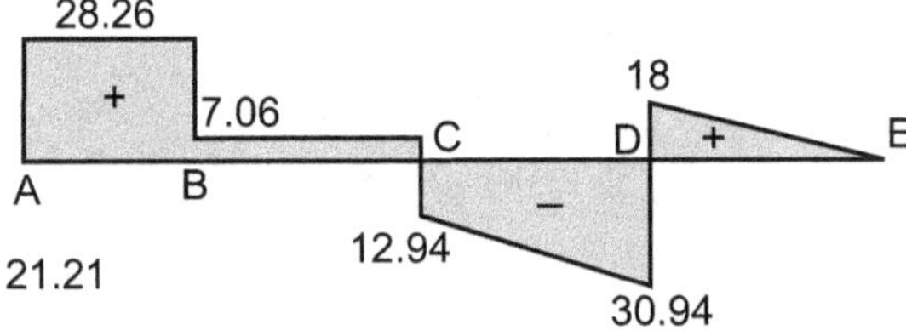

**(d) SFD (kN)**

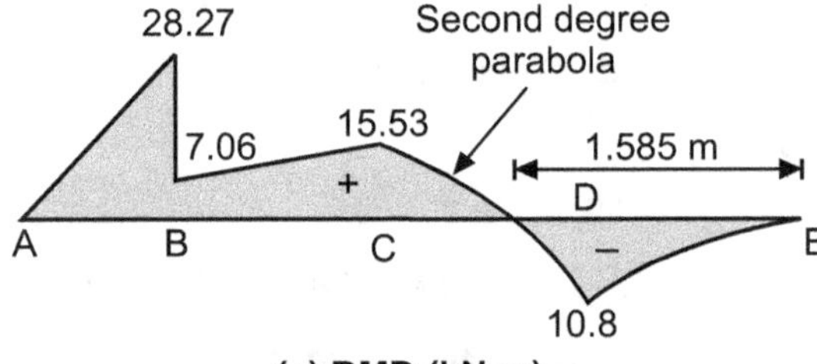

**(e) BMD (kN.m)**

**Fig. 3.36**

(iv)　BM calculations :　　$BM_A = BM_E = 0$

$BM_B$ (just to the left) $= 28.27 \times 1 = 28.27$ kN.m

$BM_B$ (just to the right) $= 28.27 - 21.21 = 7.06$ kN.m

$BM_C = 28.27 \times 2.2 - 21.21 - 21.21 \times 1.2 = 15.53$ kN.m

$$BM_D = -15 \times \frac{(1.2)^2}{2} = -10.8 \text{ kN.m}$$

To locate point of contraflexure, consider a section at a distance 'x' from 'E' in zone CD,

$$BM_x = -15\frac{x^2}{2} + 48.94\,(x - 1.2) = 0$$

Solving ;          x = 1.585 m from E.

BMD is as shown in Fig. 3.36 (e).

**Example 3.30 :** *The beam is supported and loaded as shown in Fig. 3.37 (a). Draw SFD, BMD indicating all the important values.*

**Data**      :   As shown in Fig. 3.37 (a).

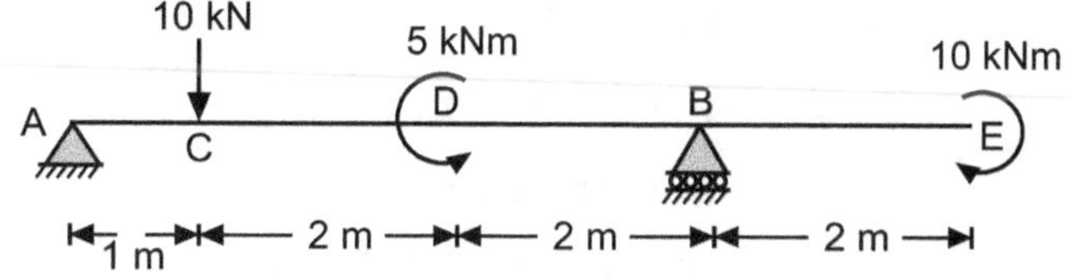

(a) Given structure

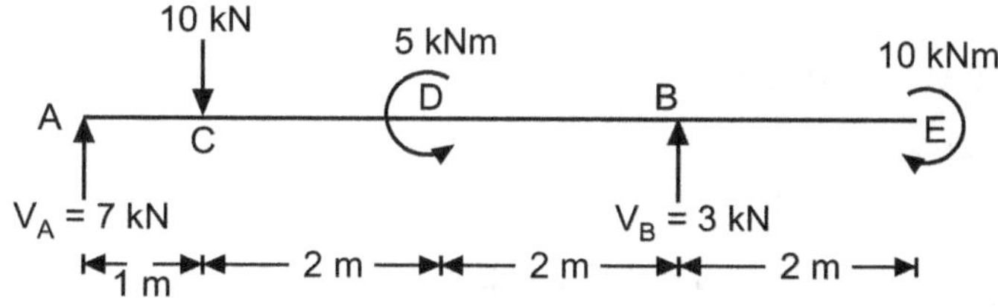

(b) FBD

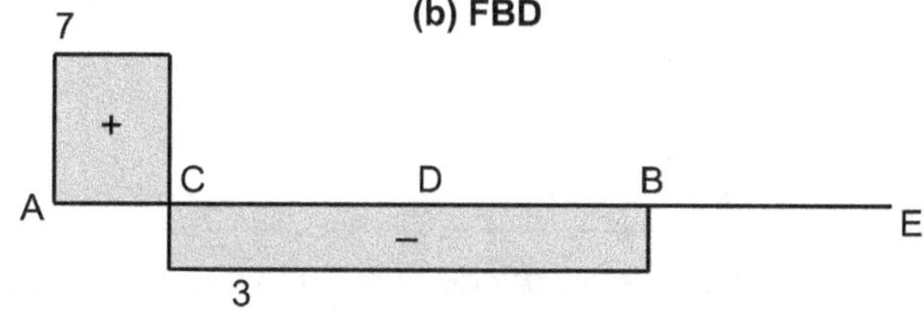

(c) SFD (kN)

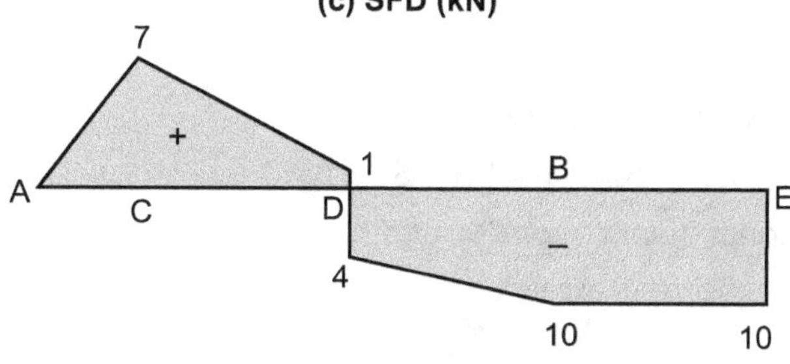

(d) BMD (kN.m)

**Fig. 3.37**

**Required** : SFD, BMD.

**Solution** : (i) Reactions :

$$\Sigma\, M_A = 0\; ; \qquad V_B \times 5 - 10 \times 1 + 5 - 10 = 0$$
$$\therefore \qquad\qquad V_B \;=\; 3 \text{ kN } (\uparrow)$$
$$\Sigma\, F_y = 0\; ; \qquad V_A + V_B - 10 = 0$$
$$\therefore \qquad\qquad V_A \;=\; 7 \text{ kN } (\uparrow)$$
$$\Sigma\, F_x = 0\; ; \qquad H_A \;=\; 0$$

FBD of beam is as shown in Fig. 3.37 (b).

(ii)    SF calculations :

$$SF_A = 7 \text{ kN}$$
$$SF_C \text{ (just to the left) } = 7 \text{ kN}$$
$$SF_C \text{ (just to the right) } = 7 - 10 = -3 \text{ kN}$$
$$SF_B \text{ (just to the left) } = -3 \text{ kN}$$
$$SF_B \text{ (just to the right) } = -3 + 3 = 0$$
$$SF_E = 0$$

SFD is as shown in Fig. 3.37 (c).

(iii)    BM calculations :

$$BM_A = 0$$
$$BM_C = 7 \times 1 = 7 \text{ kN.m}$$
$$BM_D \text{ (just to the left) } = 7 \times 3 - 10 \times 2 = 1 \text{ kN.m}$$
$$BM_D \text{ (just to the right) } = 1 - 5 = -4 \text{ kN.m}$$
$$BM_D = BM_E = -10 \text{ kN.m}$$

BMD is as shown in Fig. 3.37 (d).

**Example 3.31 :** *The beam is supported and loaded as shown in Fig. 3.38 (a). Find the magnitude of couple 'M' such that reaction at A will be $\dfrac{1}{4}$ th of the reaction at B. Draw SFD, BMD indicating all the important values.*

**Data** : As shown in Fig. 3.38 (a).

**Required** : Magnitude of couple 'M' and SFD, BMD.

**Solution** : (i) Magnitude of couple 'M' and reactions :

Let $V_A$ and $V_B$ be the vertical reaction components at A and B respectively.

We have ;

$$V_A \;=\; \frac{1}{4} V_B \qquad\qquad\qquad \text{... (i)}$$

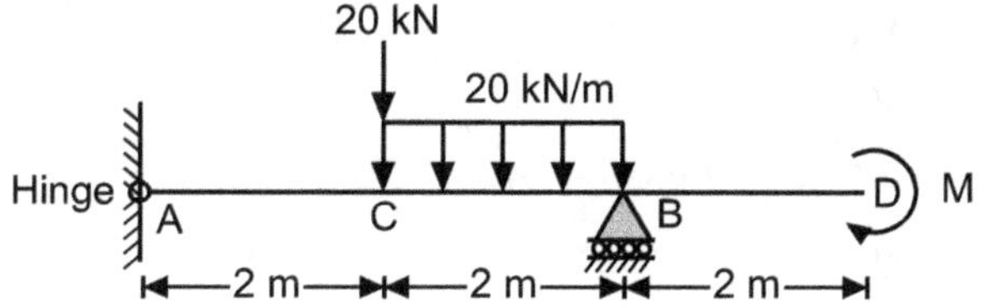

**(a) Given structure**

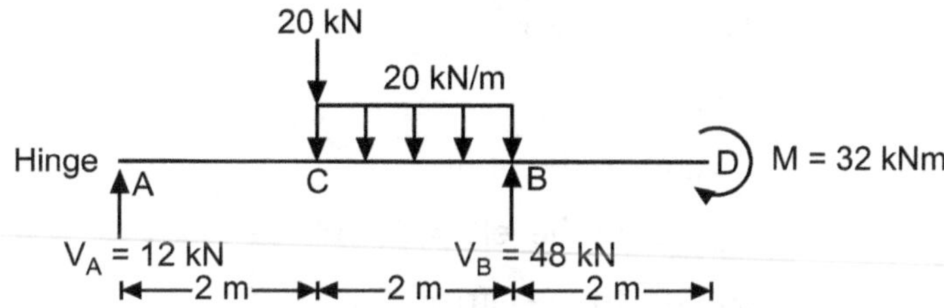

**(a) Given structure**

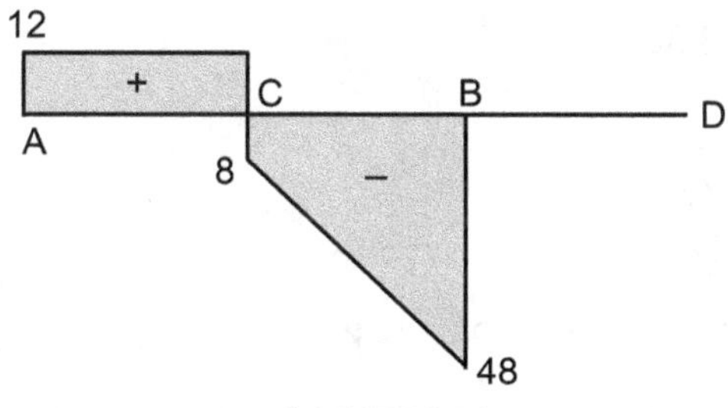

**(c) SFD (kN)**

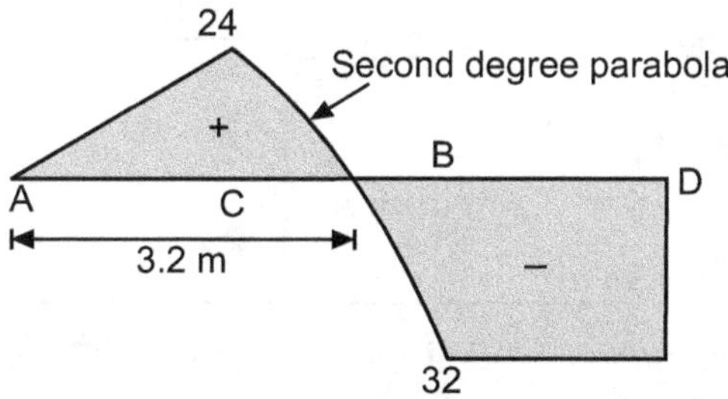

**(d) BMD (kN.m)**

**Fig. 3.38**

$\sum M_A = 0 \; ; \qquad V_B \times 4 - M - 20 \times 2 \times 3 - 20 \times 2 = 0$

$$\therefore \qquad V_B = \frac{M}{4} + 40 \qquad \qquad \text{... (ii)}$$

$\sum F_y = 0 \; ; \qquad V_A + V_B - 20 \times 2 - 20 = 0$

$$\therefore \qquad V_A + V_B = 60 \qquad \qquad \text{... (iii)}$$

Put equation (i) in equation (iii)

$$\frac{1}{4} V_B + V_B = 60$$

$$\therefore \qquad V_B \ = \ 48 \ kN \ (\uparrow)$$

$$\therefore \qquad V_A \ = \ 12 \ kN \ (\uparrow)$$

$$\therefore \qquad M \ = \ 32 \ kN.m \ (\circlearrowleft)$$

$$\sum F_X = 0 ; \qquad H_A \ = \ 0$$

FBD of beam is as shown in Fig. 3.38 (b).

(ii)    SF calculations :

$$SF_A \ = \ 12 \ kN$$

$$SF_D \ = \ 0$$

$$SF_B \ (just \ to \ the \ right) = 0$$

$$SF_B \ (just \ to \ the \ left) = 0 - 48 = -48 \ kN$$

$$SF_C \ (just \ to \ the \ left) = 12 \ kN$$

$$SF_C \ (just \ to \ the \ right) = 12 - 20 = -8 \ kN$$

SFD is as shown in Fig. 3.38 (c).

(iii)   BM calculations :

$$BM_A \ = \ 0$$

$$BM_B \ = \ BM_D = -32 \ kN.m$$

$$BM_C \ = \ 12 \times 2 = 24 \ kN.m$$

To locate point of contraflexure, consider a section at a distance 'x' from A in zone CB,

$$BM_X \ = \ 12\,x - 20\,(x-2) - \frac{20\,(x-2)^2}{2} = 0$$

$$\therefore \qquad x^2 - 3.2\,x \ = \ 0$$

$$\therefore \qquad x \ = \ 3.2 \ m \ from \ A.$$

BMD is as shown in Fig. 3.38 (d).

---

**Example 3.32 :** *The beam is supported and loaded as shown in Fig. 3.39 (a). Draw SFD, BMD indicating all the important values.*

**Data**        :   As shown in Fig. 3.39 (a).

**Required**   :   SFD, BMD.

**Solution**   :   (i) Reactions :

$$\sum M_A = 0 ; \qquad V_B \times 3.5 - 4 \times 2 \times 2.5 - 6 \times 4 - \frac{1}{2} \times 4 \times 1.5 \times \frac{1}{3} \times 1.5 = 0$$

$$\therefore \qquad V_B = 13 \ kN \ (\uparrow)$$

$$\sum F_y = 0 ; \qquad V_A + V_B - \frac{1}{2} \times 4 \times 1.5 - 4 \times 2 - 6 = 0$$

$$\therefore \qquad V_A = 4 \ kN \ (\uparrow)$$

---

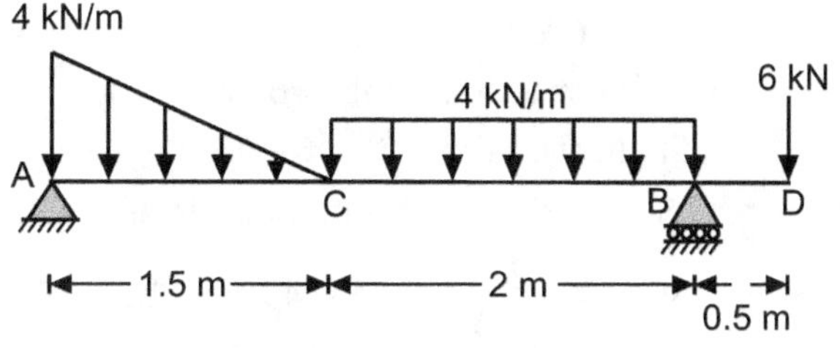

**(a) Given structure**

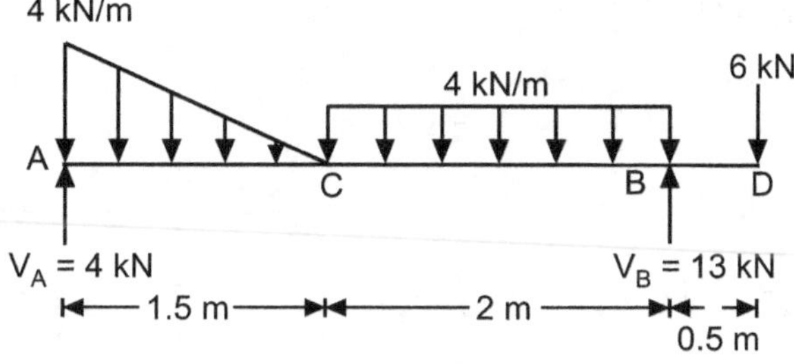

**(b) FBD**

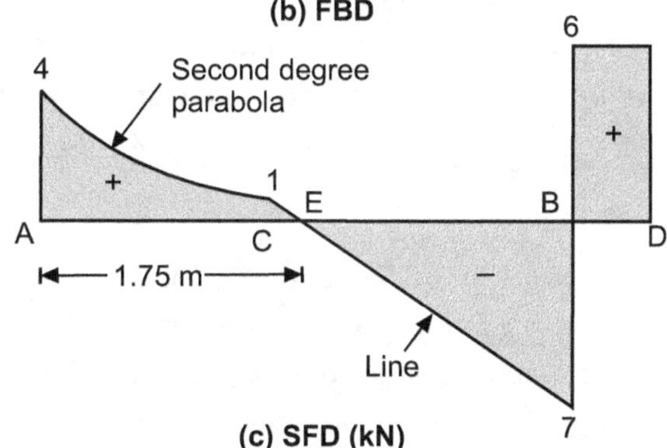

**(c) SFD (kN)**

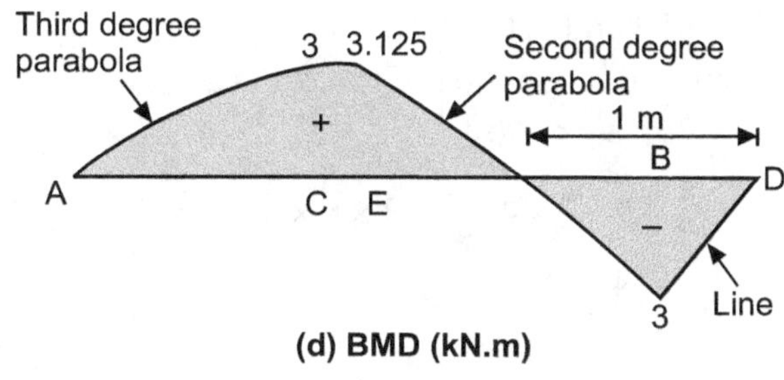

**(d) BMD (kN.m)**

**Fig. 3.39**

$$\Sigma F_X = 0 ; \qquad H_A = 0$$

FBD of beam is as shown in Fig. 3.39 (b).

(ii)    SF calculations :

$$SF_A = 4 \text{ kN}$$

$$SF_C = 4 - \frac{1}{2} \times 4 \times 1.5 = 1 \text{ kN}$$

$$SF_D = 6 \text{ kN}$$

$$SF_B \text{ (just to the right)} = 6 \text{ kN}$$

$$SF_B \text{ (just to the left)} = 6 - 13 = -7 \text{ kN}$$

To locate point of zero SF, consider a section at a distance x from A in zone CB,

$$SF_X = 4 - \frac{1}{2} \times 4 \times 1.5 - 4 \times (x - 1.5) = 0$$

$$\therefore \qquad x = 1.75 \text{ m from A}$$

SFD is as shown in Fig. 3.39 (c).

(iii)   BM calculations :

$$BM_A = BM_D = 0$$

$$BM_C = 4 \times 1.5 - \frac{1}{2} \times 4 \times 1.5 \times \frac{2}{3} \times 1.5 = 3 \text{ kN.m}$$

$$\text{BM at point of zero SF} = BM_E = 4 \times 1.75 - \frac{1}{2} \times 4 \times 1.5 \times \left(\frac{2}{3} \times 1.5 + 0.25\right) - 4 \times \frac{0.25^2}{2}$$

$$= 3.125 \text{ kN.m}$$

$$BM_B = -6 \times 0.5 = -3 \text{ kN.m}$$

To locate point of contraflexure, consider a section at a distance x from D in zone BC,

$$BM_X = -6x + 13 (x - 0.5) - 4 \frac{(x - 0.5)^2}{2} = 0$$

$$\therefore \qquad x^2 - 4.5 \, x + 3.5 = 0$$

Solving,      $x = 1 \text{ m} > 0.5 \text{ m and} < 2.5 \text{ m OK}$

or      $x = 3.5 \text{ m} > 2.5 \text{ m, hence neglected.}$

**Example 3.33 :** *The beam is supported and loaded as shown in Fig. 3.40 (a). Find the magnitude of force P such that reactions at A and B are equal. Also draw SFD and BMD.*

**Data**      :   As shown in Fig. 3.40 (a).

**Required**   :   Magnitude of P and SFD, BMD.

**Solution**   :   (i) Reactions and magnitude of force 'P'.

Let,      $V_A = V_B = V$ (say)

$$\sum M_A = 0 ; \qquad V \times 3 - P \times 4 - \frac{1}{2} \times 3 \times 6 \times \frac{1}{3} \times 3 = 0$$

$$\therefore \qquad V = \frac{4}{3} P + 3 \qquad \qquad \dots \text{(i)}$$

$$\sum F_y = 0 ; \qquad 2V - \frac{1}{2} \times 3 \times 6 - P = 0$$

$$\therefore \qquad V = \frac{P}{2} + 4.5 \qquad \qquad \dots \text{(ii)}$$

Equating equations (i) and (ii),

$$\frac{4}{3} P + 3 = \frac{P}{2} + 4.5$$

$$\therefore \qquad P = 1.8 \text{ kN}$$

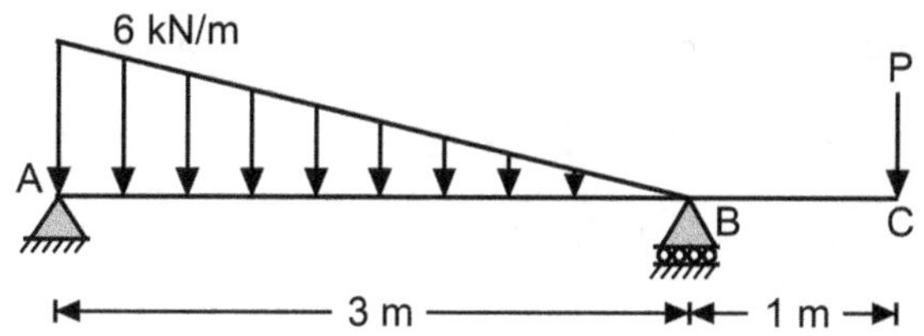

**(a) Given structure**

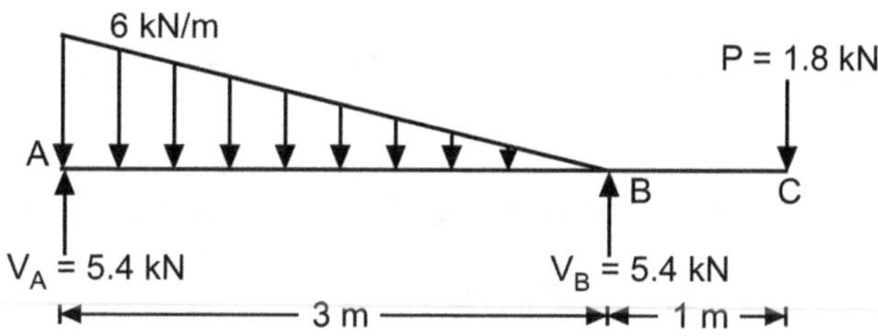

**(b) FBD**

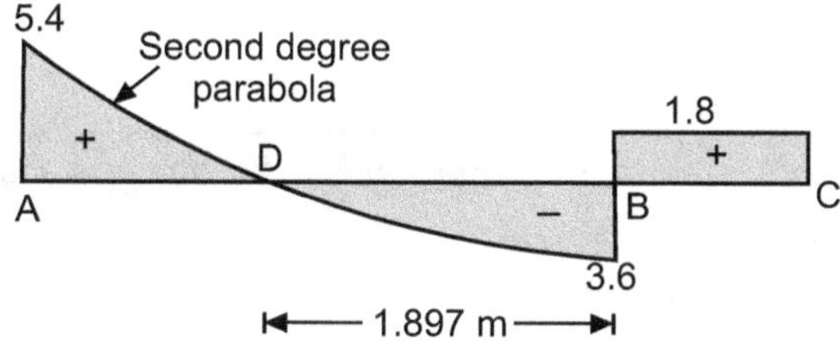

**(c) SFD (kN)**

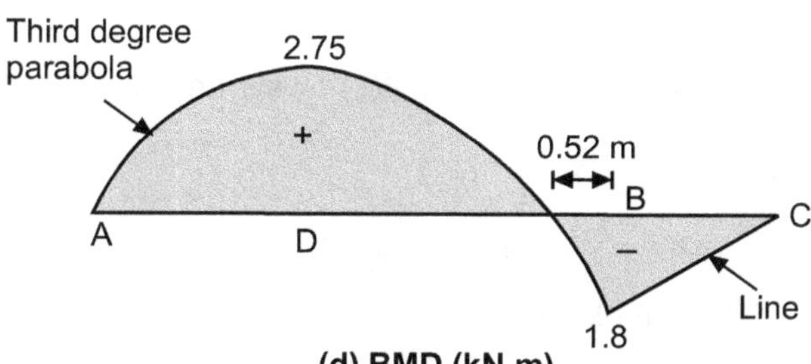

**(d) BMD (kN.m)**

**Fig. 3.40**

$$\therefore \qquad V_A = V_B = \frac{P}{2} + 4.5 = \frac{1.8}{2} + 4.5 = 5.4 \text{ kN } (\uparrow)$$

(ii)　　SF calculations :

$$SF_A = 5.4 \text{ kN}$$

$$SF_B \text{ (just to the left)} = 5.4 - \frac{1}{2} \times 3 \times 6 = -3.6 \text{ kN}$$

$$SF_B \text{ (just to the right)} = -3.6 + 5.4 = 1.8 \text{ kN}$$

$$SF_C = 1.8 \text{ kN}$$

To locate point of zero SF, consider a section at a distance x from B in zone BA,

$$SF_x = -3.6 + \frac{1}{2} \times x \times 2x = 0$$

$$\therefore \quad x = 1.897 \text{ m from B.}$$

(iii)   BM calculations :

$$BM_A = BM_C = 0$$

$$BM_B = -1.8 \times 1 = -1.8 \text{ kN.m}$$

BM at point of zero SF $= BM_D = -1.8 \times 2.897 + 5.4 \times 1.897 - \frac{1}{2} \times 1.897 \times 2 \times 1.897 \times \frac{1.897}{3}$

$$= 2.75 \text{ kN.m}$$

To locate point of contraflexure, consider a section at a distance x from 'B' in zone BA,

$$BM_x = -1.8\,(x + 1) - \frac{1}{2} \times x \times 2x \times \frac{x}{3} + 5.4\,x = 0$$

$$\therefore \quad 3.6\,x - \frac{x^3}{3} - 1.8 = 0$$

Solving by trial and error.

$$x = 0.52 \text{ m from B.}$$


**Example 3.34 :** *The beam is supported and loaded as shown in Fig. 3.41 (a). Draw SFD, BMD indicating all important values.*

**Data**        :   As shown in Fig. 3.41 (a).

**Required**   :   SFD, BMD.

**Solution**    :   (i) Reactions :

For member DE ;

$$V_D = V_E = \frac{40}{2} = 20 \text{ kN } (\uparrow) \text{ by symmetry.}$$

For member ABC ;

$$\sum M_A = 0 ; \qquad V_B \times 4 - 20 \times 5 - 20 \times \frac{4^2}{2} = 0$$

$$\therefore \qquad V_B = 65 \text{ kN } (\uparrow)$$

$$\sum F_y = 0 ; \qquad V_A + V_B - 20 \times 4 - 20 = 0$$

$$\therefore \qquad V_A = 35 \text{ kN } (\uparrow)$$

FBD of members is as shown in Fig. 3.41 (b).

(ii)   SF calculations :

$$SF_A = 35 \text{ kN}$$

$$SF_B \text{ (just to the left)} = 35 - 20 \times 4 = -45 \text{ kN}$$

$$SF_B \text{ (just to the right)} = -45 + 65 = 20 \text{ kN}$$

$$SF_E = -20 \text{ kN}$$

$$SF_F \text{ (just to the right)} = -20 \text{ kN}$$

$$SF_F \text{ (just to the left)} = -20 + 40 = 20 \text{ kN}$$

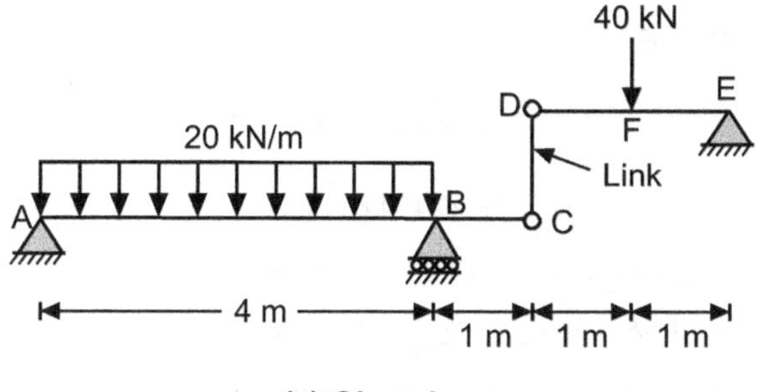

**(a) Given beam**

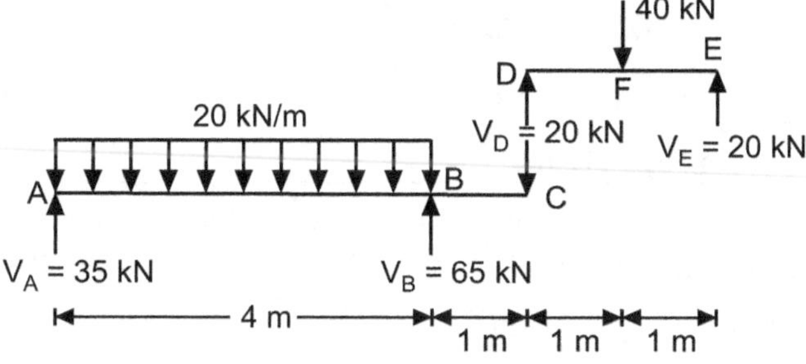

**(b) FBD of members**

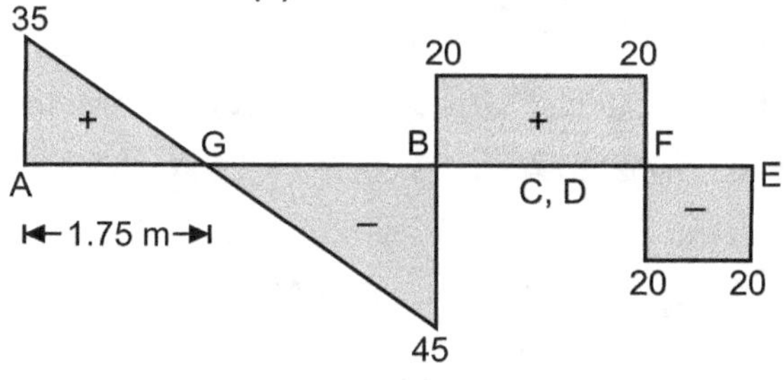

**(c) SFD (kN)**

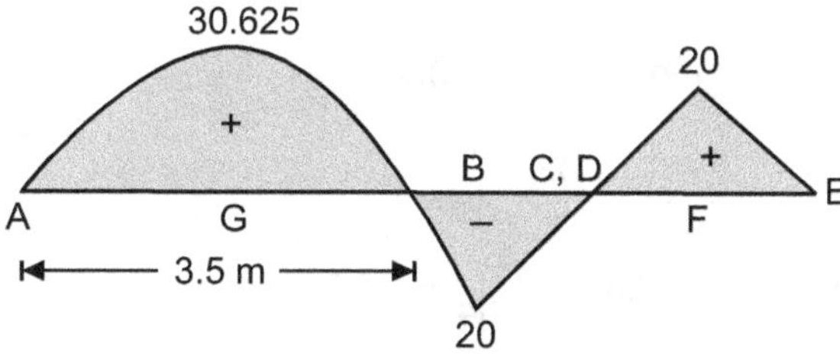

**(d) BMD (kN.m)**

**Fig. 3.41**

To locate point of zero SF, consider a section at a distance 'x' from A in zone AB,

$$SF_x = 35 - 20\,x = 0 \therefore x = 1.75 \text{ m from A}$$

SFD is as shown in Fig. 3.41 (c).

(iii)   BM calculations :

$$BM_A = BM_C = BM_D = BM_E = 0$$

$$\text{BM at point of zero SF} = BM_G$$

$$= 35 \times 1.75 - 20 \times \frac{1.75^2}{2}$$

$$= 30.625 \text{ kN.m}$$

$$BM_B = -20 \times 1 = -20 \text{ kN.m}$$

$$BM_F = 20 \times 1 = 20 \text{ kN.m}$$

To locate point of contraflexure, consider a section at a distance 'x' from A in zone AB,

$$BM_x = 35x - 20\frac{x^2}{2} = 0$$

$$\therefore \qquad x = 3.5 \text{ m from A.}$$

BMD is as shown in Fig. 3.41 (d)



**Data**        :   As shown in Fig. 3.42 (a).

**Required**   :   AFD, SFD, and BMD.

**Solution**   :   (i) Reactions :

Total vertical load due to UDL = $10 \times 3 = 30$ kN ($\downarrow$)

Component of load normal to AB = 30 cos 30 = 26 kN ($\searrow$)

Component of load parallel to AB = 30 sin 30 = 15 kN ($\swarrow$)

By symmetry, reactions at A and B normal to AB

$$= \frac{26}{2} = 13 \text{ kN } (\nwarrow)$$

Reaction at A along AB = 15 kN ($\nearrow$)

FBD of beam is as shown in Fig. 3.42 (b).

$$\text{Length of beam AB} = \frac{3}{\cos 30} = 3.464 \text{ m.}$$

$$\text{Intensity of UDL normal to AB} = \frac{26}{3.464} = 7.5 \text{ kN/m.}$$

$$\text{Intensity of UDL tangential to AB} = \frac{15}{3.464} = 4.33 \text{ kN/m.}$$

(ii)    Axial force, SF and BM equations :

Consider a section at a distance 'x' from 'A' along AB.

| Zone | Origin | Limits (m) | $AF_x$ (kN) | $SF_x$ (kN) | $BM_x$ (kN.m) |
|---|---|---|---|---|---|
| AB | A | 0 – 3.464 | – 15 + 4.33 x | 13 – 7.5 x | $13\,x - 7.5\dfrac{x^2}{2}$ |

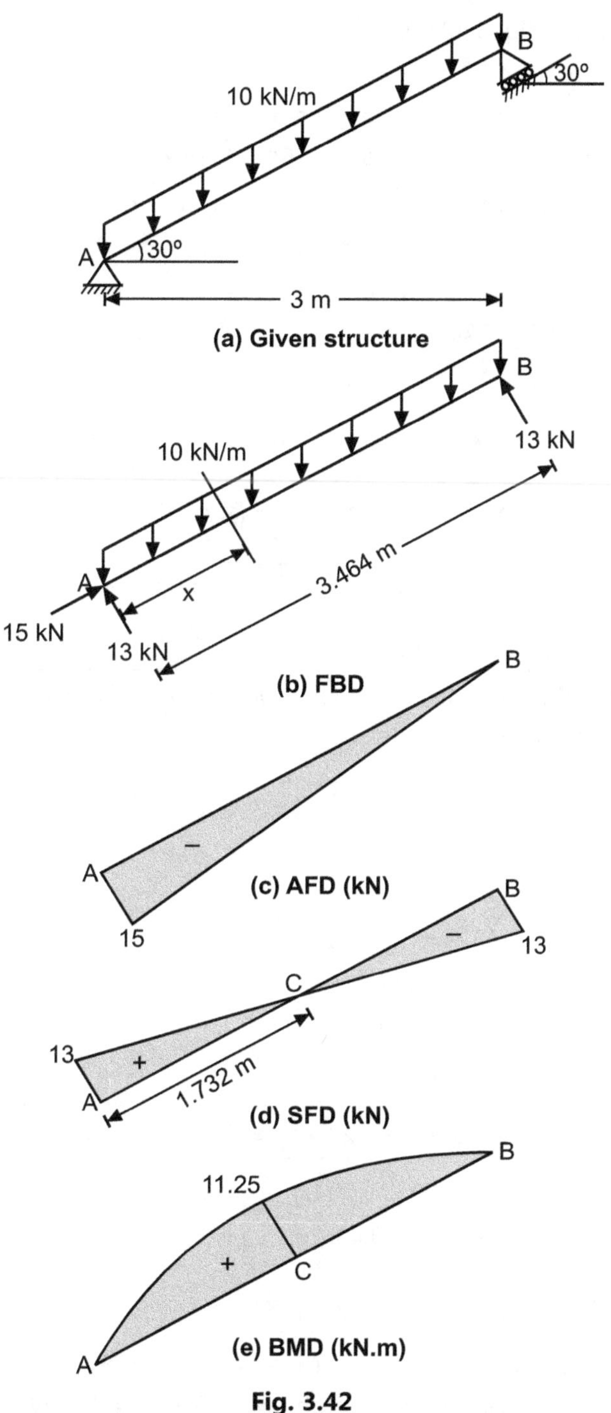



**Fig. 3.42**

(iii)  Axial force :

put x = 0 ;  $AF_A = -15 + 4.33 \times 0 = -15$ kN

put x = 3.464 m ;  $AF_B = -15 + 4.33 \times 3.464 = 0$

AFD is as shown in Fig. 3.42 (c).

(iv)  Shear force :

put $x = 0$ ;          $SF_A = 13 - 7.5 \times 0 = 13$ kN

put $x = 3.464$ m ;     $SF_B = 13 - 7.5 \times 3.464 = -13$ kN

To locate point of zero SF ; equate SF equation to zero.

$$SF_X = 13 - 7.5\, x = 0$$

$\therefore$          $x = 1.733$ m from A.

SFD is as shown in Fig. 3.42 (d).

(v)  Bending moment :

put $x = 0$ ;          $BM_A = 13 \times 0 - \dfrac{7.5}{2}(0) = 0$

put $x = 1.732$ m ;     $BM_C = 13 \times 1.733 - \dfrac{7.5}{2}(1.733)^2 = 11.25$ kN.m

put $x = 3.464$ m ;     $BM_B = 13 \times 3.464 - \dfrac{7.5}{2}(3.464)^2 = 0$

BMD is as shown in Fig. 3.42 (e).

**Example 3.36 :** *The beam is supported and loaded as shown in Fig. 3.43 (a). Draw SFD, BMD, indicating all the important values.*

**Data**          :   As shown in Fig. 3.43 (a).

**Required**    :   SFD, BMD.

**Solution**    :   (i) Reactions :

$\sum M_C = 0$ (LHS) ;     $-V_B \times 4 + 20 \times \dfrac{6^2}{2} = 0$

$\therefore$          $V_B = 90$ kN ($\uparrow$)

$\sum F_y = 0$ ;          $V_B + V_D - 20 \times 8 = 0$

$\therefore$          $V_D = 70$ kN ($\uparrow$)

$\sum M_C = 0$ (RHS) ;     $70 \times 2 - M_D - 20 \times \dfrac{2^2}{2} = 0$

$\therefore$          $M_D = 100$ kN.m ($\circlearrowleft$)

FBD of beam is as shown in Fig. 3.43 (b).

(ii)  SF calculations :

$$SF_A = 0$$

$SF_B$ (just to the left) $= -20 \times 2 = -40$ kN

$SF_B$ (just to the right) $= -40 + 90 = 50$ kN

$$SF_D = -70 \text{ kN}$$

To locate point of zero SF, shear force at a distance x from D in zone DB,

$$= SF_X = -70 + 20\,x = 0$$

$$\therefore \qquad x = 3.5 \text{ m from D.}$$

SFD of beam is as shown in Fig. 3.43 (c).

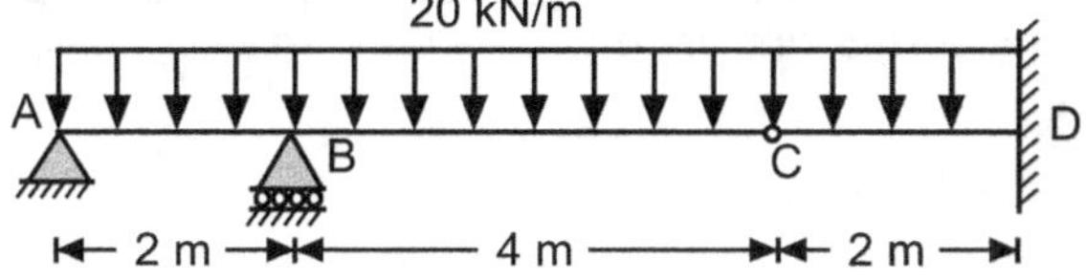



**(a) Given beam**

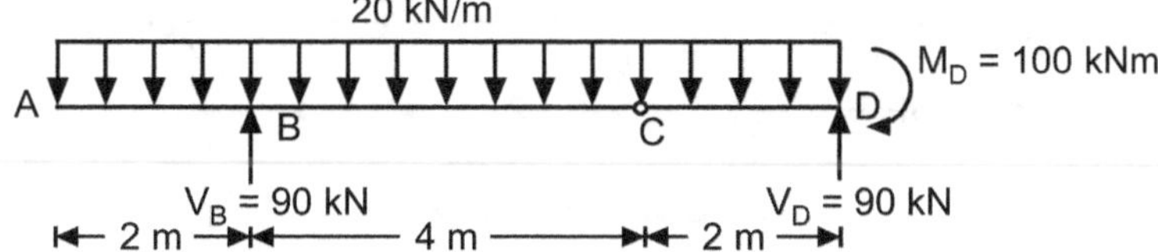



**(b) FBD of beam**

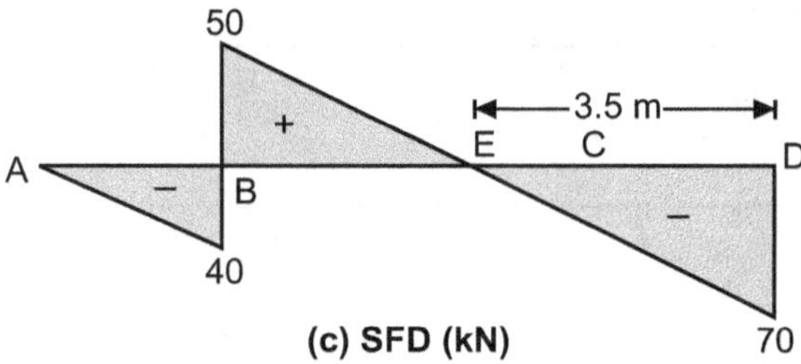



**(c) SFD (kN)**

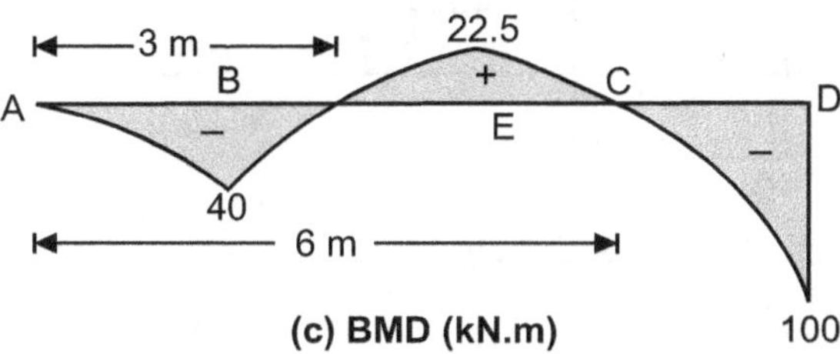



**(c) BMD (kN.m)**

**Fig. 3.43**

(iii)    BM calculations :

$$BM_A = BM_C = 0$$

$$BM_B = \frac{-20 \times 2^2}{2} = -40 \text{ kN.m}$$

BM at point of zero SF $= BM_E = 90 \times 2.5 - 20 \times \dfrac{4.5^2}{2} = 22.5$ kN.m

$$BM_D = -100 \text{ kN.m}$$

To locate point of contraflexure, consider a section at a distance 'x' from A in the zone BC,

$$BM_X = 90\,(x - 2) - 20\,\frac{x^2}{2} = 0$$

$$\therefore \qquad 90x - 180 - 10x^2 = 0$$
$$\therefore \qquad x^2 - 9x + 18 = 0$$

Solving ; $\qquad x = 3$ m and 6 m.

BMD is as shown in Fig. 3.43 (d).

**Example 3.37 :** *The beam is supported and loaded as shown in Fig. 3.44 (a). Draw SFD, BMD indicating all the important values.*

**Data**       :   As shown in Fig. 3.44 (a).

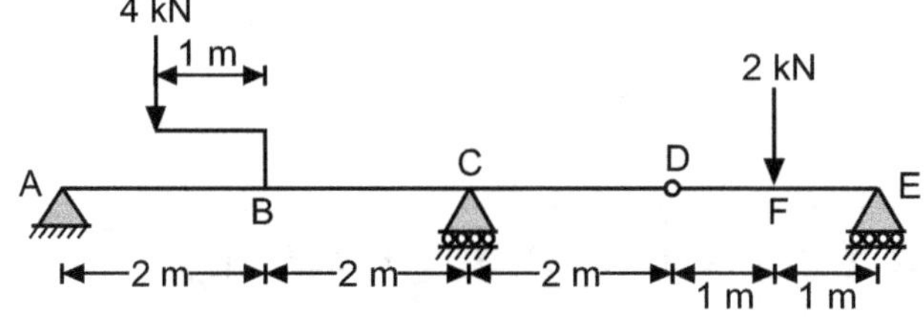

**(a) Given structure**

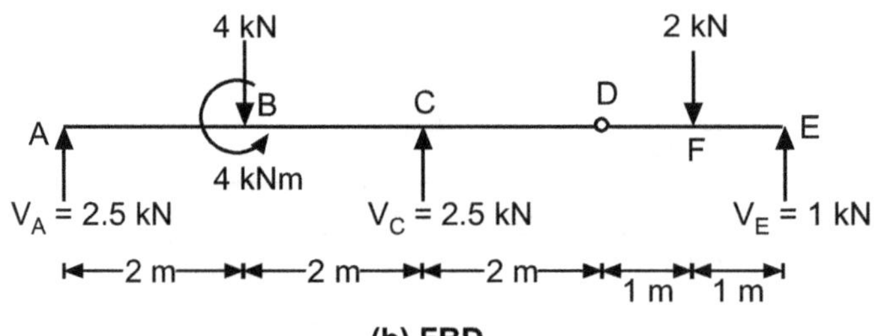

**(b) FBD**

**(c) SFD (kN)**

**(d) BMD (kN.m)**

**Fig. 3.44**

**Required**   :   SFD, BMD.

**Solution**   :   (i) Reactions :

At D, internal hinge is provided hence,

$$\Sigma\, M_{D\,(LHS)} = \Sigma\, M_{D\,(RHS)} = 0$$

$$\Sigma\, M_D = 0\ _{(RHS)}\,;\qquad V_E \times 2 - 2 \times 1 = 0$$

$$\therefore\qquad V_E = 1\ kN\ (\uparrow)$$

$$\Sigma\, M_A = 0\,;\qquad V_C \times 4 + V_E \times 8 - 2 \times 7 - 4 \times 2 + 4 = 0$$

$$\therefore\qquad V_C = 2.5\ kN\ (\uparrow)$$

$$\Sigma\, F_y = 0\,;\qquad V_A + V_C + V_E - 4 - 2 = 0$$

$$\therefore\qquad V_A = 2.5\ kN\ (\uparrow)$$

$$\Sigma\, F_x = 0\,;\qquad H_A = 0$$

FBD of beam is as shown in Fig. 3.44 (b).

(ii)    SF calculations :

$$SF_A = 2.5\ kN$$

$$SF_B\ (just\ to\ the\ left) = 2.5\ kN$$

$$SF_B\ (just\ to\ the\ right) = 2.5 - 4 = -1.5\ kN$$

$$SF_C\ (just\ to\ the\ left) = -1.5\ kN$$

$$SF_C\ (just\ to\ the\ right) = -1.5 + 2.5 = 1\ kN$$

$$SF_E = -1\ kN$$

$$SF_F\ (just\ to\ the\ right) = -1\ kN$$

$$SF_F\ (just\ to\ the\ left) = -1 + 2 = 1\ kN$$

SFD is as shown in Fig. 3.44 (c).

(iii)    BM calculations :

$$BM_A = BM_D = BM_E = 0$$

$$BM_B\ (just\ to\ the\ left) = 2.5 \times 2 = 5\ kN.m$$

$$BM_B\ (just\ to\ the\ right) = 5 - 4 = 1\ kN.m$$

$$BM_C = 1 \times 4 - 2 \times 3 = -2\ kN.m$$

$$BM_F = 1 \times 1 = 1\ kN.m$$

To locate point of contraflexure, consider a section at a distance x from A in zone BC.

$$BM_x = 2.5\,x - 4 - 4\,(x - 2) = 0$$

$$x = 2.67\ m\ from\ A.$$

BMD is as shown in Fig. 3.44 (d).

**Example 3.38 :** *The beam is supported and loaded as shown in Fig. 3.45 (a). Draw SFD, BMD indicating all the important values.*

**Data**       :    As shown in Fig. 3.45 (a).

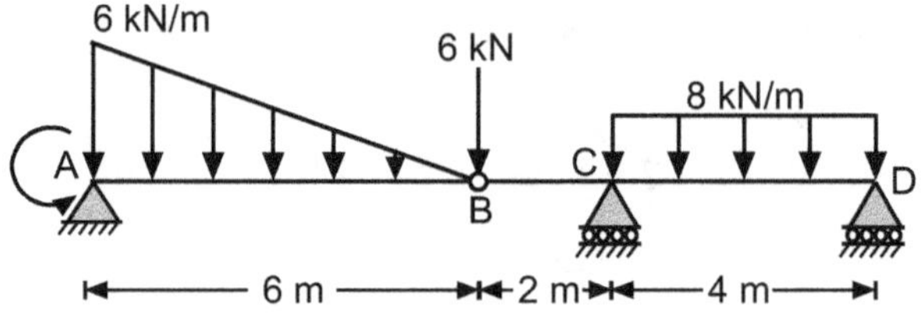

**(a) Given structure**

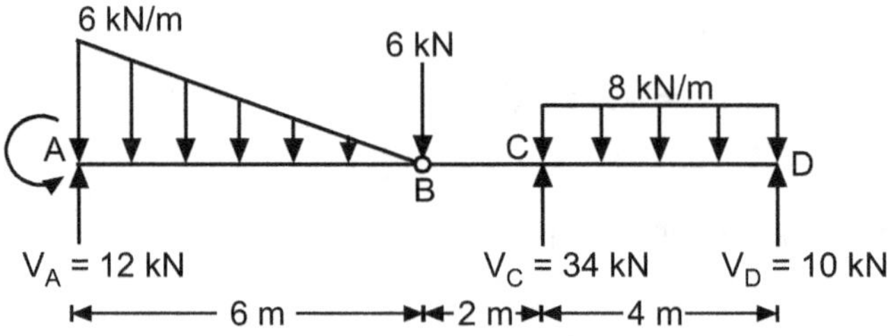

**(b) FBD**

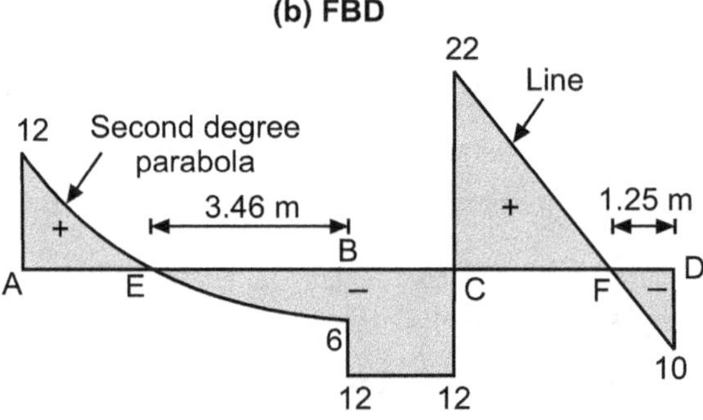

**(c) SFD (kN)**

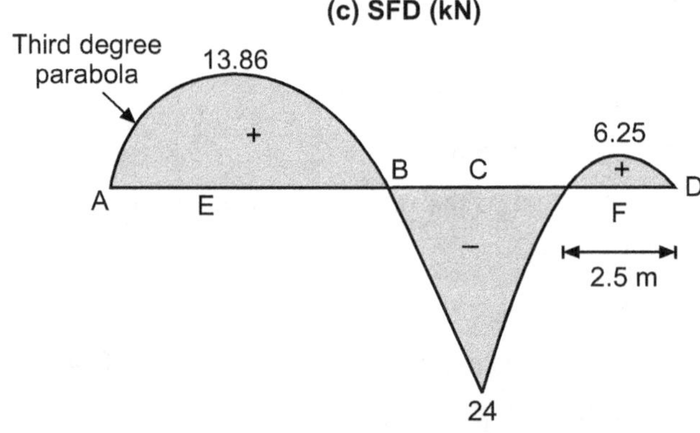

**(d) BMD (kN.m)**

**Fig. 3.45**

**Required** : SFD, BMD.

**Solution** : (i) Reactions :

At B, there is an internal hinge hence ;

$$\Sigma\, M_{B\,(LHS)} = \Sigma\, M_{B\,(RHS)} = 0$$

$$\Sigma\, M_{B\,(LHS)} = 0\,; \qquad -V_A \times 6 + \frac{1}{2} \times 6 \times 6 \times \frac{2}{3} \times 6 = 0$$

$$\therefore \qquad V_A = 12 \text{ kN } (\uparrow)$$

$$\Sigma\, M_D = 0\,; \qquad -V_A \times 12 - V_C \times 4 + \frac{1}{2} \times 6 \times 6 \times (6+4) + 6 \times 6 + 8 \times \frac{4^2}{2} = 0$$

$$\therefore \qquad V_C = 34 \text{ kN } (\uparrow)$$

$$\Sigma\, F_y = 0\,; \qquad V_A + V_C + V_D - \frac{1}{2} \times 6 \times 6 - 6 - 8 \times 4 = 0$$

$$\therefore \qquad V_A = 10 \text{ kN } (\uparrow)$$

FBD of beam is as shown in Fig. 3.45 (b).

(ii)    SF calculations :    $SF_A = 12$ kN

$$SF_B \text{ (just to the left)} = 12 - \frac{1}{2} \times 6 \times 6 = -6 \text{ kN}$$

$$SF_B \text{ (just to the right)} = -6 - 6 = -12 \text{ kN}$$

$$SF_D = -10 \text{ kN}$$

$$SF_C \text{ (just to the right)} = -10 + 8 \times 4 = 22 \text{ kN}$$

$$SF_C \text{ (just to the left)} = 22 - 34 = -12 \text{ kN.}$$

To locate point of zero SF in zone AB, consider a section at a distance x from B,

$$SF_x = -6 + \frac{1}{2} \times x \times \frac{6}{6} x = 0$$

$$\therefore \qquad -6 + \frac{x^2}{2} = 0 \qquad \therefore x = 3.46 \text{ m from B.}$$

To locate point of zero SF in zone DC, consider a section at a distance 'x' from D.

$$SF_x = -10 + 8x = 0 \therefore x = 1.25 \text{ m from D.}$$

SFD is as shown in Fig. 3.45 (c).

(iii)    BM calculations :

$$BM_A = BM_B = BM_D = 0$$

$$BM_E = 6 \times 3.46 - \frac{1}{2} \times 3.46 \times 3.46 \times \frac{1}{3} \times 3.46 = 13.85 \text{ kN.m}$$

$$BM_C = 10 \times 4 - 8 \times \frac{4^2}{2} = -24 \text{ kN.m}$$

$$BM_F = 10 \times 1.25 - \frac{8 \times 1.25^2}{2}$$

$$= 6.25 \text{ kN.m}$$

To locate point of contraflexure, consider a section at a distance x from D in zone DC,

$$BM_x = 10\,x - \frac{8x^2}{2} = 0$$

$$\therefore \qquad x = 2.5 \text{ m from D.}$$

BMD is as shown in Fig. 3.45 (d).

**Example 3.39 :** *The beam is supported and loaded as shown in Fig. 3.46 (a). Draw SFD and BMD indicating all the important values.*

**Data**        :   As shown in Fig. 3.46 (a).

**Required**  :   SFD, BMD.

**Solution**   :   (i) Reactions :

Consider FBD of member as shown in Fig. 3.46 (b).

For member BC ;

$\sum M_B = 0$ ;          $V_C \times 4 - 4 \times 2 \times 3 - 10 \times 2 = 0$

$\therefore$          $V_C = 11$ kN ($\uparrow$)

$\sum F_y = 0$ ;          $V_B + V_C - 10 - 4 \times 2 = 0$

$\therefore$          $V_B = 7$ kN ($\uparrow$)

For member AB ;

$\sum F_y = 0$ ;          $V_A - 7 = 0$          $\therefore$    $V_A = 7$ kN ($\uparrow$)

$\sum M_A = 0$ ;          $M_A - 7 \times 3 = 0$          $\therefore$    $M_A = 21$ kN.m ($\circlearrowleft$)

$\sum F_x = 0$ ;          $H_A = 0$

For member CD :

$\sum F_y = 0$ ;          $V_D - 11 - \dfrac{1}{2} \times 5 \times 4 = 0$          $\therefore$    $V_D = 21$ kN ($\uparrow$)

$\sum M_D = 0$ ;          $- M_D + 11 \times 4 + \dfrac{1}{2} \times 5 \times 4 \times \dfrac{4}{3} = 0$

$\therefore$          $M_D = 57.33$ kN.m ($\circlearrowright$)

$\sum F_x = 0$ ;          $H_D = 0$

FBD of beam is as shown in Fig. 3.46 (c).

(ii)     SF calculations :

$SF_A = 7$ kN

$SF_E$ (just to the left) $= 7$ kN

$SF_E$ (just to the right) $= 7 - 10 = - 3$ kN

$SF_C = 7 - 10 - 4 \times 2 = - 11$ kN

$SF_D = - 21$ kN

SFD is as shown in Fig. 3.46 (d).

(iii)    BM calculations :

$BM_B = BM_C = 0$

$BM_A = - 21$ kN.m

$BM_E = 7 \times 2 = 14$ kN.m

$BM_D = - 57.33$ kN.m

BMD is as shown in Fig. 3.46 (e).

10 kN
4 kN/m
5 kN/m
A
B
E
C
D
3 m
2 m
2 m
4 m
(a) Given structure
10 kN
4 kN/m
B
E
C
V_B = 7 kN
V_C = 11 kN
7 kN
11 kN
5 kN/m
M_A = 21 kNm
A
B
M_D = 57.33 kNm
V_A = 7 kN
C
D
V_D = 21 kN
(b) FBD of members
10 kN
4 kN/m
5 kN/m
M_A = 21 kNm
A
B
E
C
D
M_D = 57.33 kNm
V_A = 7 kN
V_D = 21 kN
3 m
2 m
2 m
4 m
(c) FBD of beam
7
+
A
B
E
C
D
3
11
Second degree parabola
21
(d) SFD (kN)
14
Line
Second degree parabola
+
A
B
E
C
D
21
Third degree parabola
(e) BMD (kN.m)
57.33

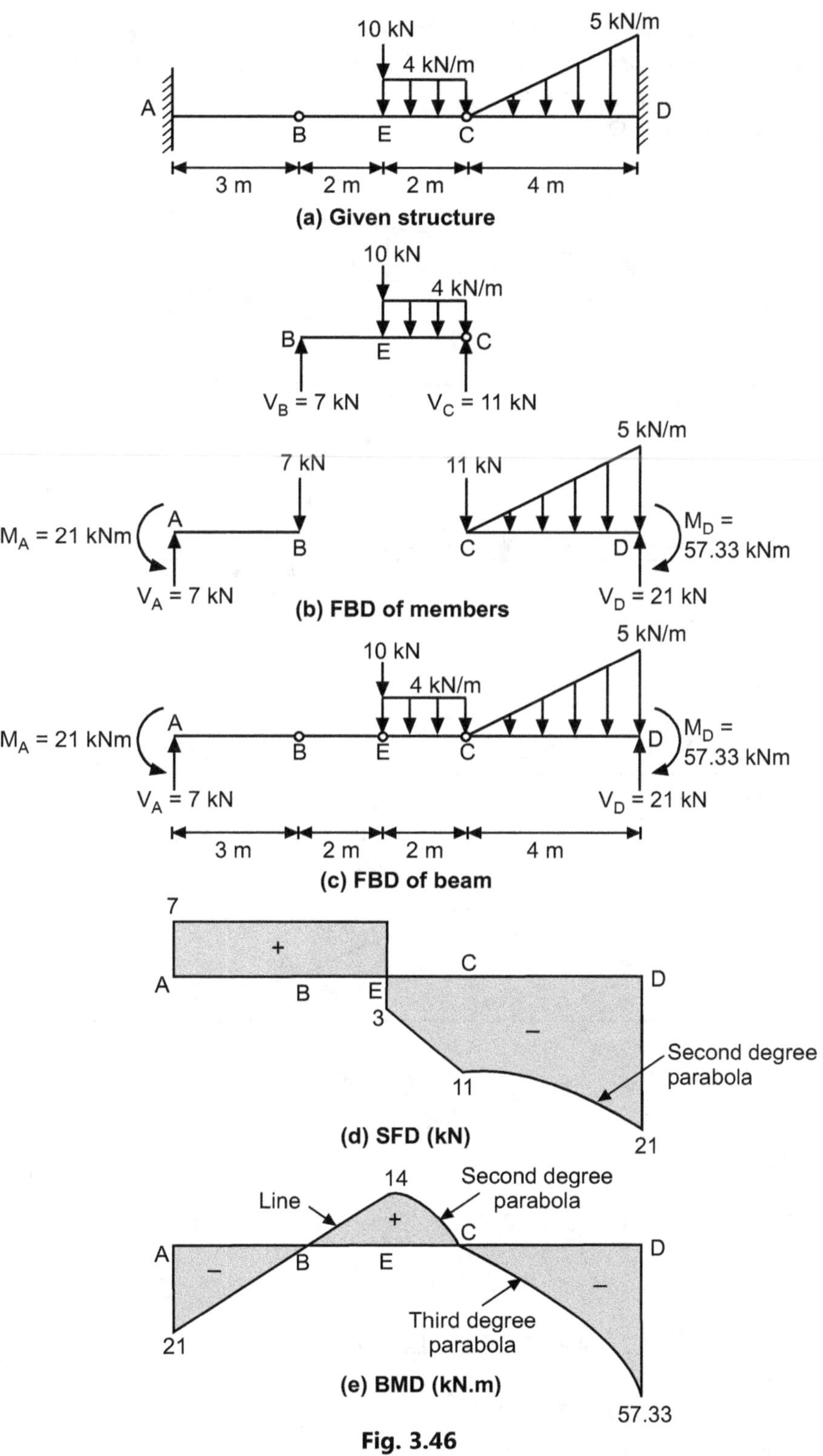

**Fig. 3.46**

**Example 3.40 :** *Draw SFD and BMD for the beam shown in Fig. 3.47. A is a hinged support. Reaction offered by soil is uniformly distributed over length CD of the beam. Locate point of contraflexure and point of maximum B.M.*          **(Dec. 1999)**

**Data :** As shown in Fig. 3.47.

**Required :** BMD.

**Solution :**

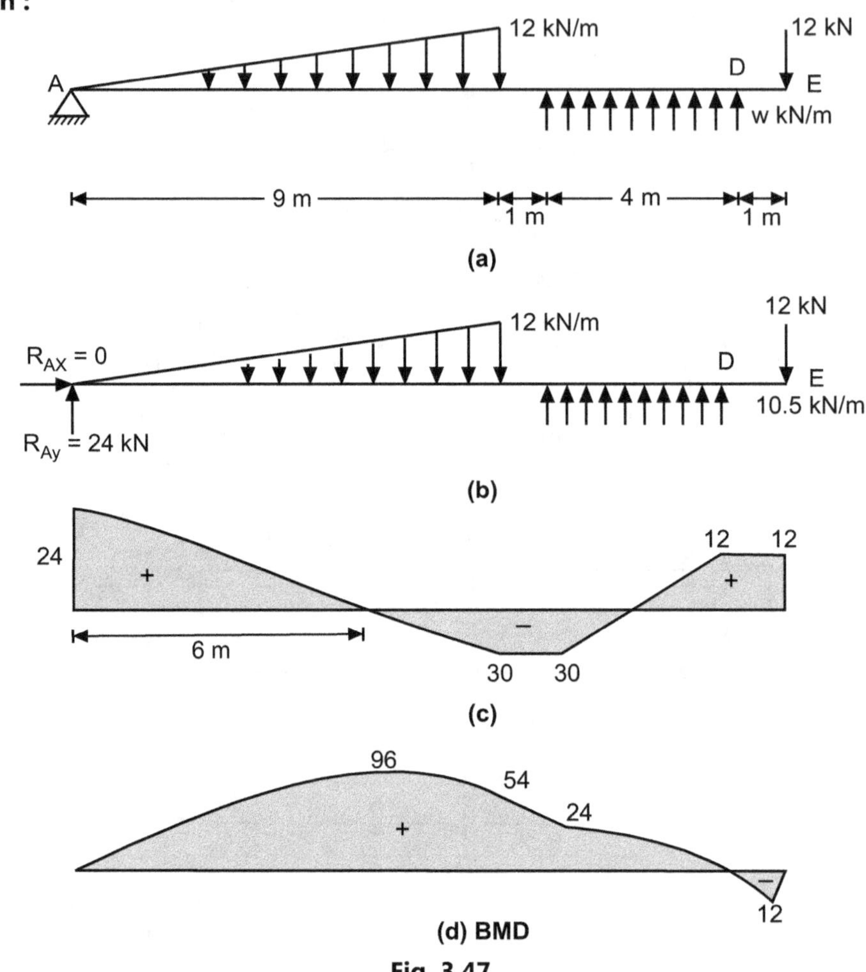


**Fig. 3.47**

(i)   Reactions :

$$\sum M @ A = 0; \quad -\frac{1}{2} \times 12 \times 9 \times 6.0 + w \times 4 \times 12 - 12 \times 15 = 0$$

$$\therefore \qquad\qquad w = 10.5 \text{ kN/m}$$

$$\sum F_y = 0; \quad R_{Ay} - \frac{1}{2} \times 12 \times 9 + 10.5 \times 4 - 12 = 0$$

$$\therefore \qquad\qquad R_{Ay} = 24 \text{ kN } (\uparrow)$$

$$\sum F_x = 0; \qquad\qquad R_{Ax} = 0$$

(ii)  SF calculations :

$$SF_A = 24 \text{ kN}$$

$$SF_B = 24 - \frac{1}{2} \times 12 \times 9 = -30 \text{ kN}$$

$$SF_C = -30 \text{ kN}$$

$$SF_D = -30 + 10.5 \times 4 = 12 \text{ kN}$$

$$SF_E = 12 \text{ kN}$$

To locate point of zero SF, consider a section at a distance x from A in zone AB.

$$\therefore \qquad \frac{12}{9} = \frac{y}{x} \qquad\qquad \therefore \ y = \frac{4}{3}x$$

$$\therefore \qquad SF_x = 24 - \frac{1}{2} \times x \times y = 0$$

$$24 - \frac{1}{2} \times x \times \frac{4}{3}x = 0$$

$$\therefore \qquad x = 6 \text{ m from A.}$$

SFD is as shown in Fig. 3.47 (c).

(iii) BM calculations :

$$BM_A = BM_E = 0$$

$$\text{BM at a point of zero SF} = BM_F$$

$$= 24 \times 6 - \frac{1}{2} \times 6 \times \frac{4}{3} \times 6 \times \frac{6}{3}$$

$$= 96 \text{ kN.m}$$

$$BM_B = 24 \times 9 - \frac{1}{2} \times 12 \times 9 \times 3 = 54 \text{ kN.m}$$

$$BM_C = 24 \times 10 - \frac{1}{2} \times 12 \times 9 \times 4 = 24 \text{ kN.m}$$

$$BM_D = 24 \times 14 - \frac{1}{2} \times 12 \times 9 \times 8 + 10.5 \times 4 \times 2$$

$$= -12 \text{ kN.m}$$

To locate point of contraflexure, consider a section at a distance x from E in zone CD.

$$BM_x = -12 \times (x + 1) + 10.5 \frac{x^2}{2} = 0$$

$$= -2.286\, x - 2.286 + x^2 = 0$$

$$\therefore \qquad x = \frac{2.286 \pm \sqrt{(-2.286)^2 - 4 \times 1 \times (-2.286)}}{2}$$

$$= 3.04 \text{ m from E}$$

BMD is shown in Fig. 3.47 (d).

**Example 3.41 :** *A simply supported beam ABC is loaded as shown in Fig. 3.48. Determine the location at which a concentrated load 5 kN must act from end A to make the reactions at A and B equal. Draw SFD and BMD.*

**Data :** As shown in Fig. 3.48.

**Required :** x, SFD, BMD.

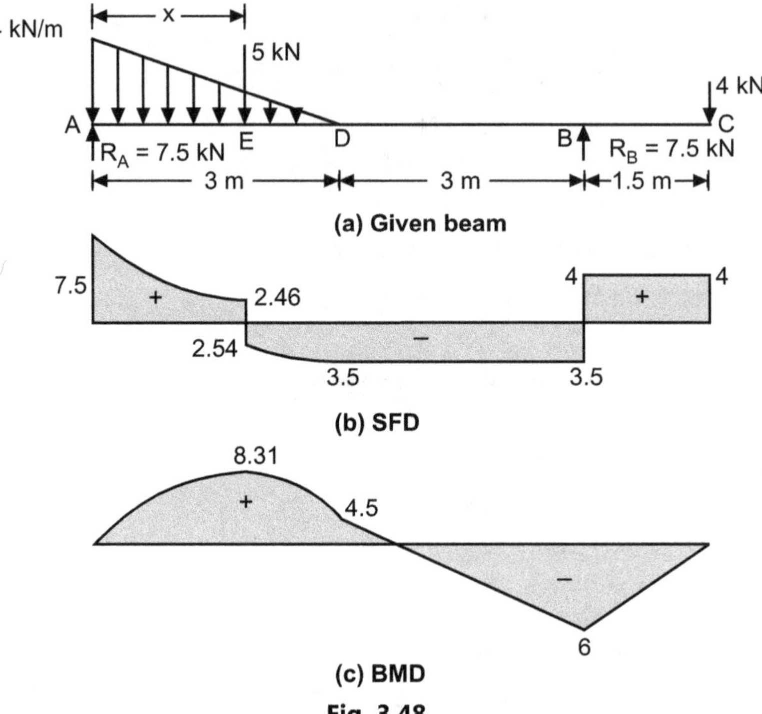


**Fig. 3.48**

**Solution :** (i) Reactions :

$$R_A = R_B$$

$$\therefore \quad R_A = R_B = \frac{\text{Total load}}{2} = \frac{\frac{1}{2} \times 4 \times 3 + 5 + 4}{2} = 7.5 \text{ kN}$$

(ii)  Position of x :

$$\sum M @ A = 0; \ -\frac{1}{2} \times 4 \times 3 \times \frac{3}{3} - 5 \times x + 7.5 \times 6 - 4 \times 7.5 = 0$$

$$\therefore \quad x = \textbf{1.8 m from A}$$

(iii) SF calculations :

$$SF_A = 7.5 \text{ kN}$$

$$SF_E \text{ (just to the left)} = 7.5 - \frac{(4 + 1.6)}{2} \times 1.8 = 2.46 \text{ kN}$$

$$SF_E \text{ (just to the right)} = 2.46 - 5 = -2.54 \text{ kN}$$

$$SF_D = -2.54 - \frac{1}{2} \times 1.6 \times 1.2 = -3.5 \text{ kN}$$

$$SF_B \text{ (just to the left)} = -3.5 \text{ kN}$$

$$SF_B \text{ (just to the right)} = -3.5 + 7.5 = 4.0 \text{ kN}$$

$$SF_C = 4 \text{ kN}$$

SFD is as shown in Fig. 3.48 (b).

(iv) BM calculations :

$$BM_A = 0$$

$$BM_E = 7.5 \times 1.8 - \left[\frac{1}{2} \times (4 + 1.6) \times 1.8 \left(\frac{2 \times 4 + 1.6}{4 + 1.6}\right) \times \frac{1.8}{3}\right]$$

$$= 8.316 \text{ kN.m}$$

$$BM_D = 7.5 \times 3 - \frac{1}{2} \times 4 \times 3 \times 2 - 5 \times 1.2 = 4.5 \text{ kN.m}$$

$$BM_B = 7.5 \times 6 - \frac{1}{2} \times 4 \times 3 \times 5 - 5 \times 4.2 = -6 \text{ kN.m}$$

$$BM_C = 0$$

BMD is as shown in Fig. 3.48 (c).

**Example 3.42 :** *For a beam loaded as shown in Fig. 3.49, draw SFD and BMD, indicating all the important values.*

**Data :** As shown in Fig. 3.49.

**Required :** SFD and BMD.

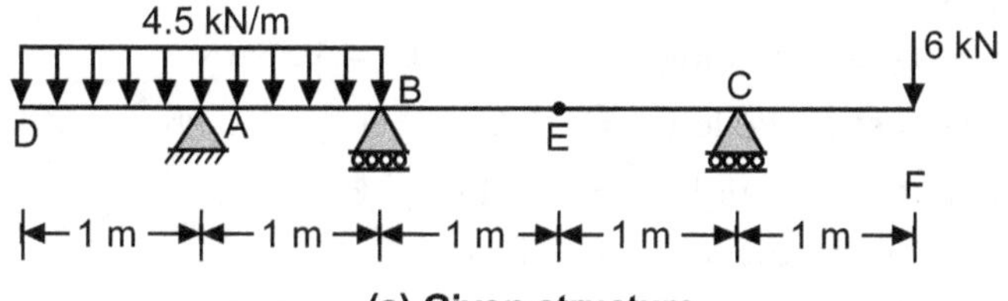


**(a) Given structure**

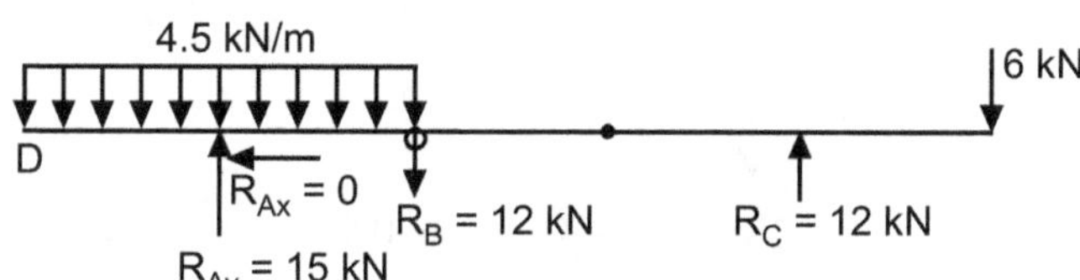


**(b) FBD**

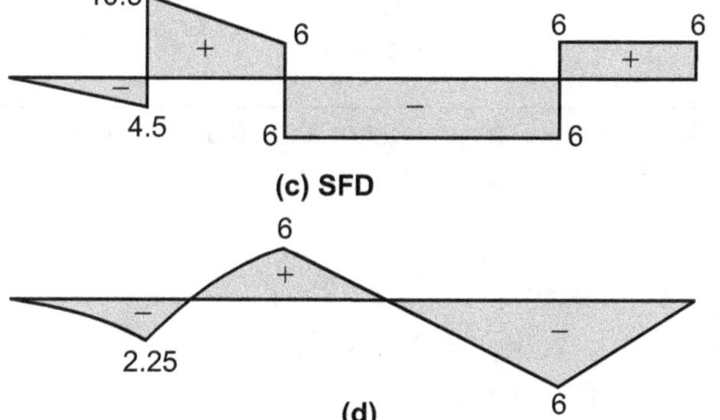


**(c) SFD**



**(d)**

**Fig. 3.49**

**Solution :** (i) Reactions :

$$\sum M @ E = 0 \text{ (Right part of hinge)}$$

$\therefore \qquad R_C \times 1 - 6 \times 2 = 0 \qquad\qquad \therefore R_C = 12$ kN

$\sum M @ E = 0$ (Left part of hinge)

$- R_{Ay} \times 2 - R_B \times 1 + 4.5 \times 2 \times 2 = 0$

$\therefore \qquad 2 R_{Ay} + R_B = 18$

$\sum F_y = 0$

$\therefore \qquad R_{Ay} + R_B + R_C - 4.5 \times 2 - 6 = 0$

$\therefore \qquad R_{Ay} + 18 - 2 R_{Ay} + 12 - 15 = 0$

$\therefore \qquad R_{Ay} = + 15$ kN $(\uparrow)$

$2 R_{Ay} + R_B = 18$

$\therefore \qquad R_B = - 12$ kN

$= 12$ kN $(\downarrow)$

(ii)  SF calculations :

$SF_A$ (just to the left) $= - 4.5 \times 1 = - 4.5$ kN

$SF_A$ (just to the right) $= - 4.5 + 15 = 10.5$ kN

$SF_B$ (just to the left) $= 10.5 - 4.5 \times 1 = 6.0$ kN

$SF_B$ (just to the right) $= 6 - 12 = - 6$ kN

$SF_C$ (just to the left) $= - 6$ kN

$SF_C$ (just to the right) $= - 6 + 12 = 6$ kN

$SF_F = 6$ kN

SFD is as shown in Fig. 3.49 (c).

(iii) BM calculations :

$BM_D = 0$

$BM_A = - 4.5 \times 1 \times 0.5 = - 2.25$ kN.m

$BM_B = - 4.5 \times 2 \times 1 + 15 \times 1 = 6$ kN.m

$BM_E = - 4.5 \times 2 \times 2 + 15 \times 2 - 12 \times 1 = 0$

$BM_C = - 4.5 \times 2 \times 3 + 15 \times 3 - 12 \times 2$

$= - 6$ kN.m

BMD is as shown in Fig. 3.49 (d).

**Example 3.43 :** *Draw SFD and BMD for the beam loaded as shown in Fig. 3.50.*

**Data :** As shown in Fig. 3.50.

**Required :** SFD, BMD.

**Solution :** (i) Reactions :

$\sum M @ A = 0$; $V_B \times 6 - 10 - 10 \times 2 - 3 \times 4 \times 6 = 0$

$\therefore \qquad V_B = 17$ kN $(\uparrow)$

$\sum F_y = 0$; $\qquad V_A + V_B - 10 - 3 \times 4 = 0$

$\therefore \qquad V_A = 5$ kN $(\uparrow)$

(ii)  SF calculations :

$SF_A = 5$ kN

$SF_C = 5 - 10 = - 5$ kN

$SF_D = - 5$ kN

$$\text{SF}_B \text{ (just to the left)} \ = \ -5 - 3 \times 2 = -11 \text{ kN}$$

$$\text{SF}_B \text{ (just to the right)} \ = \ -11 + 17 = 6 \text{ kN}$$

$$\text{SF}_E \ = \ 6 - 6 = 0$$

SFD is as shown in Fig. 3.50 (c).

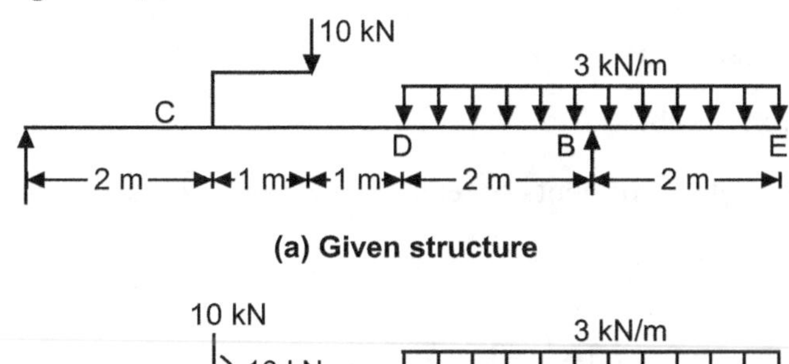


**(a) Given structure**

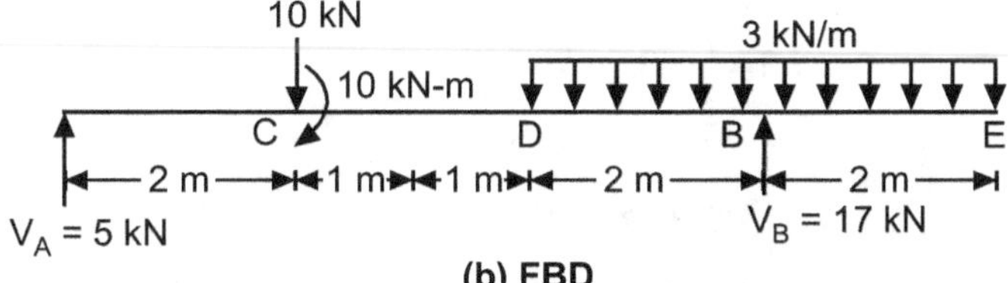


**(b) FBD**

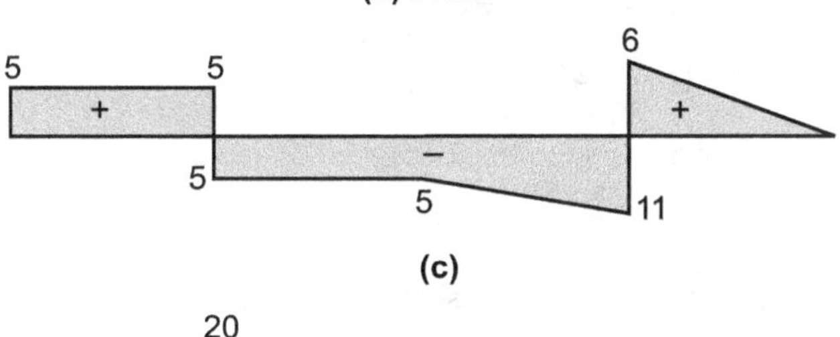


**(c)**

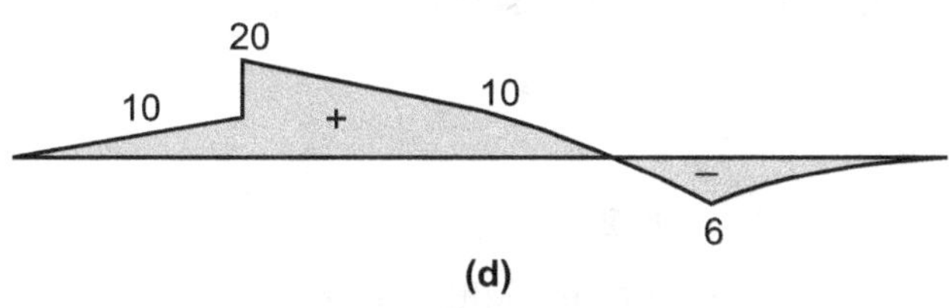


**(d)**

**Fig. 3.50**

(iii) BM calculations :         $\text{BM}_A \ = \ 0$

$$\text{BM}_C \text{ (just to the left)} \ = \ 5 \times 2 = 10 \text{ kN.m}$$

$$\text{BM}_C \text{ (just to the right)} \ = \ 5 \times 2 + 10 = 20 \text{ kN.m}$$

$$\text{BM}_D \ = \ 5 \times 4 + 10 - 10 \times 2 = 10 \text{ kN.m}$$

$$\text{BM}_B \ = \ 5 \times 6 + 10 - 10 \times 4 - 3 \times 2 \times 1 = -6 \text{ kN.m}$$

$$\text{BM}_E \ = \ 5 \times 8 + 10 - 10 \times 6 - 3 \times 4 \times 2 + 17 \times 2$$

$$= \ 0$$

BMD is as shown in Fig. 3.50 (d).

**Example 3.44 :** *The beam ABC is supported and loaded as shown in Fig. 3.51 (a). Draw AFD, SFD and BMD, indicating all the important values.*

**Data**        :   As shown in Fig. 3.51 (a).

**Required**   :   AFD, SFD and BMD.

**Solution**   :   (i) Reactions :

Let, T be the tension in wire.

Horizontal and vertical components of tension in wire = 0.7 T as shown in Fig. 3.51 (b).

$$\sum M_A = 0 ; \qquad 0.7\,T \times 4 - 40 \times 5 - 30 \times \frac{5^2}{2} = 0$$

$$\therefore \qquad 0.7\,T = 143.75 \text{ kN}$$

$$\sum F_y = 0 ; \qquad V_A + 0.7\,T - 30 \times 5 - 40 = 0$$

$$\therefore \qquad V_A = 46.25 \text{ kN } (\uparrow)$$

$$\sum F_x = 0 ; \qquad H_A - 143.75 = 0$$

$$\therefore \qquad H_A = 143.75 \text{ kN } (\rightarrow)$$

FBD of beam is as shown in Fig. 3.51 (b).

(ii)    Axial force :

Beam is subjected to axial compressive force of 143.75 kN from A to B. AFD is as shown in Fig. 3.51 (c).

(iii)   SF calculations :

$$SF_A = 46.25 \text{ kN}$$

$$SF_B \text{ (just to the left)} = 46.25 - 30 \times 4 = -73.75 \text{ kN}$$

$$SF_B \text{ (just to the right)} = -73.75 + 143.75 = 70 \text{ kN}$$

$$SF_C = 40 \text{ kN}.$$

To locate point of zero SF, consider a section at a distance x from A in zone AB.

$$SF_x = 46.25 - 30\,x = 0$$

$$\therefore \qquad x = 1.54 \text{ m from A.}$$

SFD is as shown in Fig. 3.51 (c).

(iv)   BM calculations :

$$BM_A = BM_C = 0$$

$$BM_B = -40 \times 1 - 30 \times \frac{1^2}{2} = -55 \text{ kN.m}$$

D
45°
Wire
40 kN
30 kN/m
Hinge
A
B
C
4 m
1 m
(a) Given structure

07T = 143.75
40 kN
30 kN/m
H_A = 143.75 kN
A
07T = 143.75
B
C
V_A = 46.25 kN
4 m
1 m
(b) FBD

A
B
C
−
143.75
(c) AFD (kN)

70
46.25
40
+
D
+
A
B
C
1.54 m
−
73.75
(d) SFD (kN)

35.65
+
B
A
D
−
C
3.08 m
55
(e) BMD (kN.m)

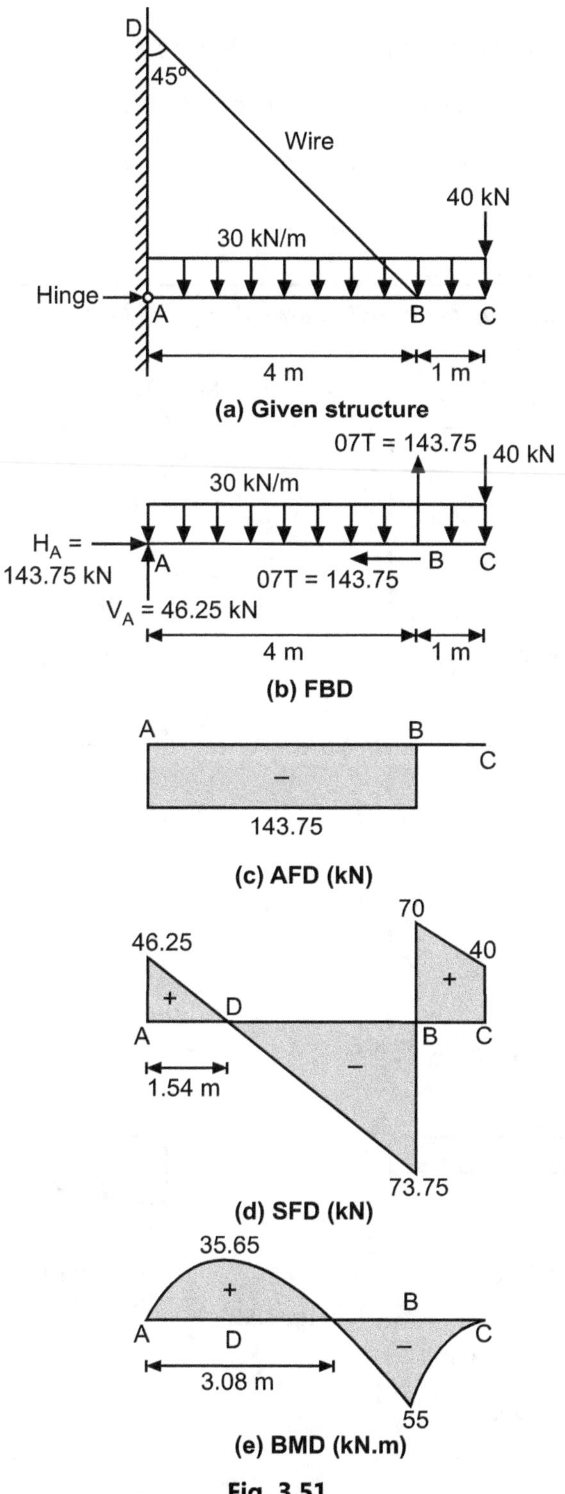

**Fig. 3.51**

BM at point of zero SF = $BM_D = 46.25 \times 1.54 - 30 \times \dfrac{(1.54)^2}{2} = 35.65$ kN.m

To locate point of contraflexure, consider a section at a distance 'x' from A in zone AB,

$$BM_x = 46.25\,x - 30\,\frac{x^2}{2} = 0$$

$\therefore$        x = 3.08 m from 'A'.

BMD is as shown in Fig. 3.51 (d).

**Example 3.45 :** *For a bent up beam ABC shown in Fig. 3.52 (a), draw AFD, SFD, BMD.*

**Data :**      As shown in Fig. 3.52 (a).

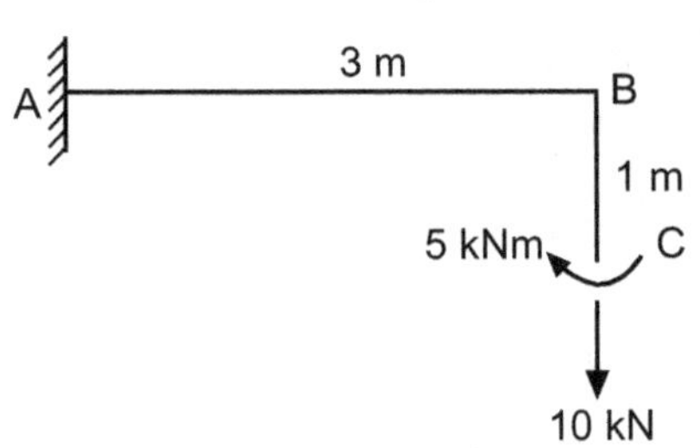


**(a) Given structure**           **(b) FBD of structure**

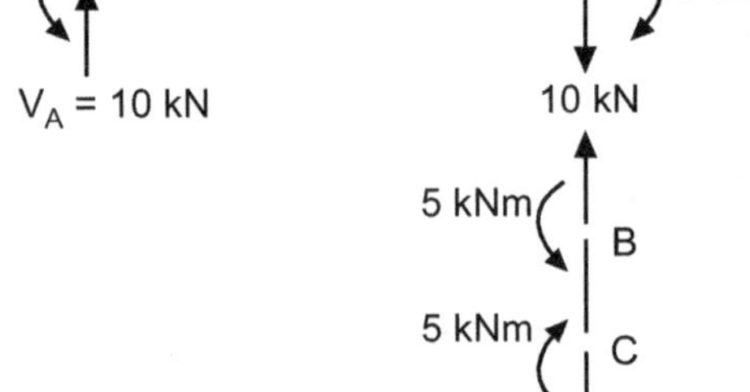


**(c) FBD of members**           **(d) AFD (kN)**

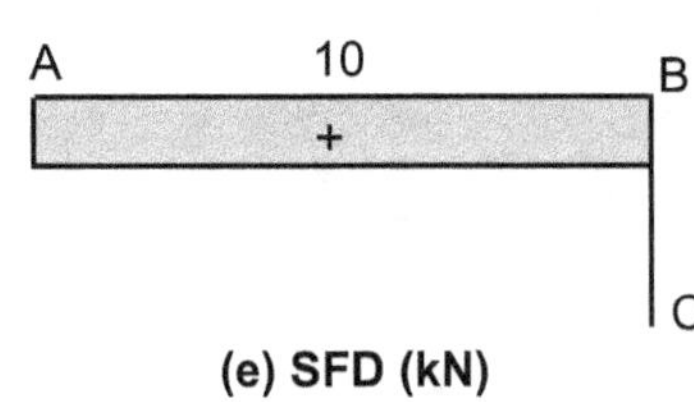


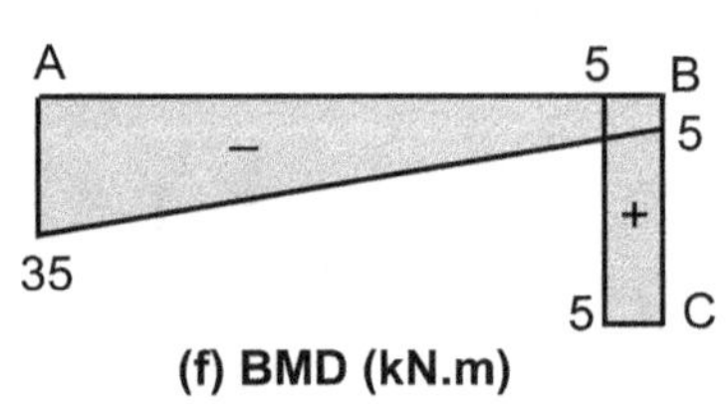


**(e) SFD (kN)**           **(f) BMD (kN.m)**

**Fig. 3.52**

**Required**    :    AFD, SFD, BMD.

**Solution**    :    (i) Reactions :

     $\Sigma\,F_y = 0$ ;          $V_A - 10 = 0$          $\therefore$    $V_A = 10$ kN ($\uparrow$)

     $\Sigma\,F_x = 0$ ;          $H_A = 0$

$$\sum M_A = 0 ; \qquad M_A - 5 - 10 \times 3 = 0 \qquad \therefore \quad M_A = 35 \text{ kN.m } (\circlearrowleft)$$

FBD of structure is as shown in Fig. 3.52 (b).

Also considering equilibrium of individual members,

FBD of members is as shown in Fig. 3.52 (c).

(ii)    Axial force : Member BC is subjected to axial tensile force of 10 kN.

AFD is as shown in Fig. 3.52 (d).

(iii)    SFD is as shown in Fig. 3.52 (e).

(iv)    BM calculations :

For member AB,

$$BM_A \ = \ -35 \text{ kN.m}$$
$$BM_B \ = \ -5 \text{ kN.m}$$

For member BC,

$$BM_B \ = \ 5 \text{ kN.m}$$
$$BM_C \ = \ 5 \text{ kN.m}$$

BMD is as shown in Fig. 3.52 (f).

**Example 3.46 :** *For the cantilever beam ABCD as shown in Fig. 3.53 (a), draw AFD, SFD and BMD.*

**Data**        :   As shown in Fig. 3.53 (a).

**Required**   :   AFD, SFD and BMD.

**Solution**   :   (i) Reactions :

$$\sum F_x = 0 ; \qquad H_A = 0$$
$$\sum F_y = 0 ; \qquad V_A - 4 = 0 \qquad\qquad \therefore \quad V_A = 4 \text{ kN } (\uparrow)$$
$$\sum M_A = 0 ; \qquad M_A - 4 \times 1 = 0 \qquad \therefore \quad M_A = 4 \text{ kN.m } (\circlearrowleft)$$

FBD of structure is as shown in Fig. 3.53 (b).

Also considering equilibrium of individual members,

FBD of members is as shown in Fig. 3.53 (c).

(ii)    Axial force : Member BC is subjected to axial tensile force of 4 kN.

AFD is as shown in Fig. 3.53 (d).

(iii)    SFD is as shown in Fig. 3.53 (e).

(iv)    BM calculations :

for member AB, $BM_A = -4$ kN.m, $BM_B = 8$ kN.m

for member BC, $BM_B = -8$ kN.m, $BM_C = -8$ kN.m

for member CD, $BM_C = -8$ kN.m, $BM_D = 0$

BMD is as shown in Fig. 3.53 (f).

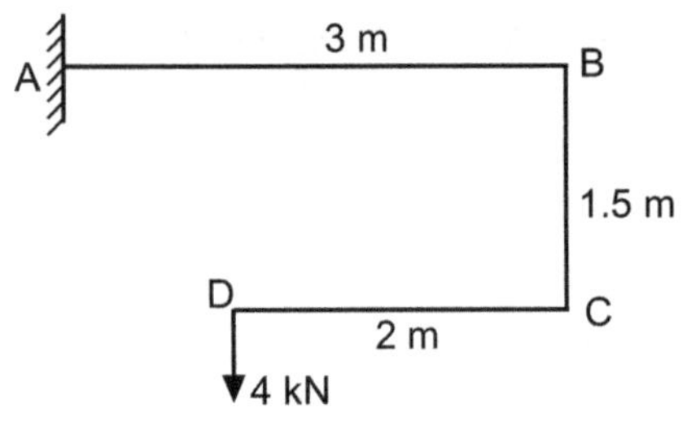

**(a) Given structure**

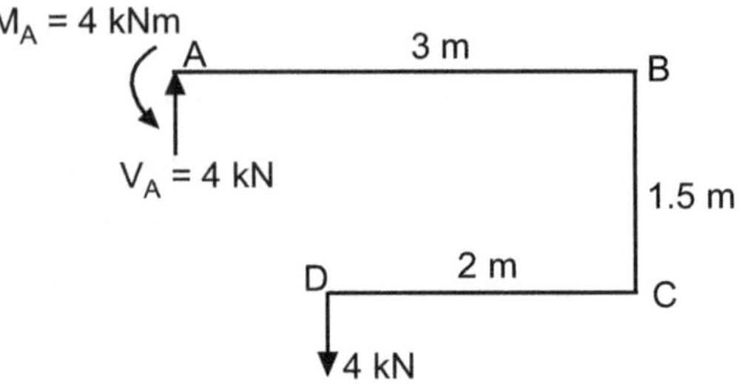

**(b) FBD of structure**

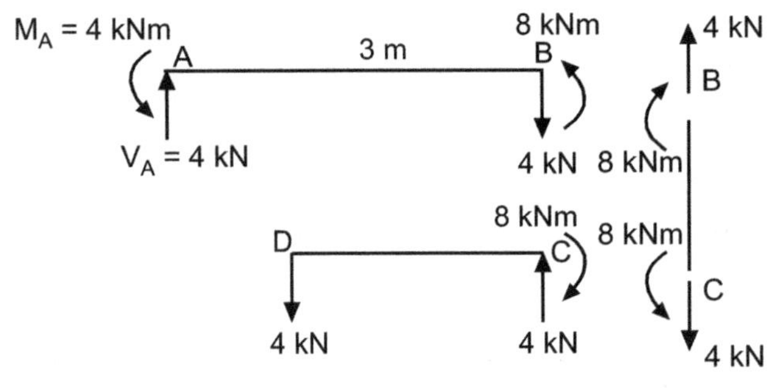

**(c) FBD of members**

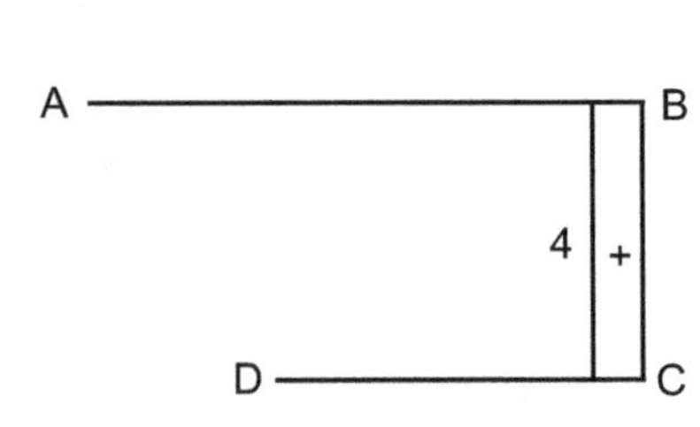

**(b) AFD (kN)**

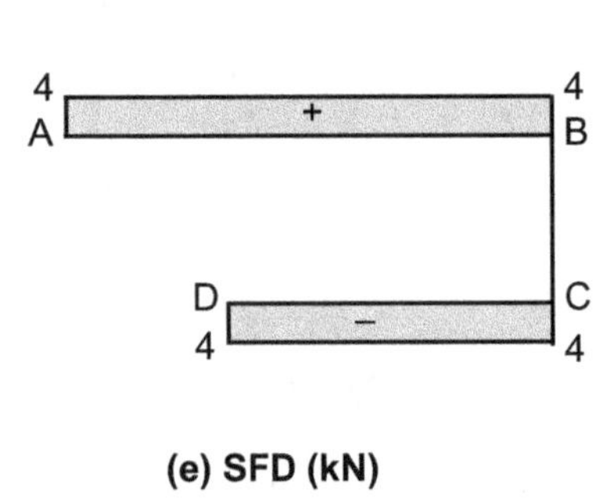

**(e) SFD (kN)**

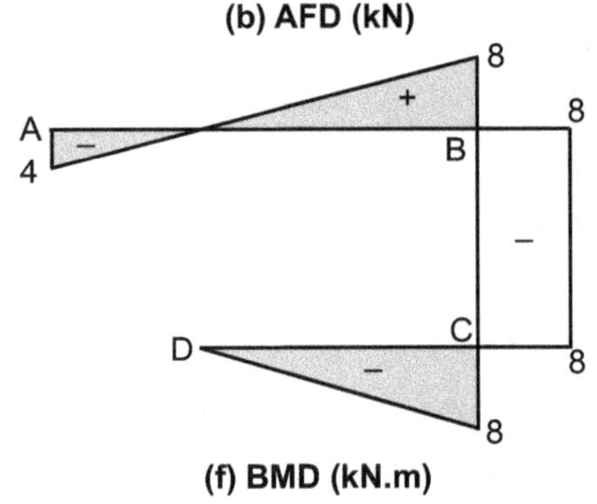

**(f) BMD (kN.m)**

**Fig. 3.53**

**Example 3.47 :** *For a rigid jointed frame ABCD shown in Fig. 3.54 (a), draw AFD, SFD and BMD.*

**Data**　　: As shown in Fig. 3.54 (a).

**Required**　: AFD, SFD and BMD.

**Solution**　: (i) Reactions :

$$\sum M_A = 0 ; \qquad V_D \times 6 + 28.66 \times 1 - 20 \times \frac{6^2}{2} - 30 \times 4 = 0$$

$$\therefore \qquad V_D = 75.22 \text{ kN } (\uparrow)$$

$$\sum F_y = 0 ; \qquad V_A + V_D - 20 \times 6 = 0$$

$$\therefore \qquad V_A = 44.78 \text{ kN } (\uparrow)$$

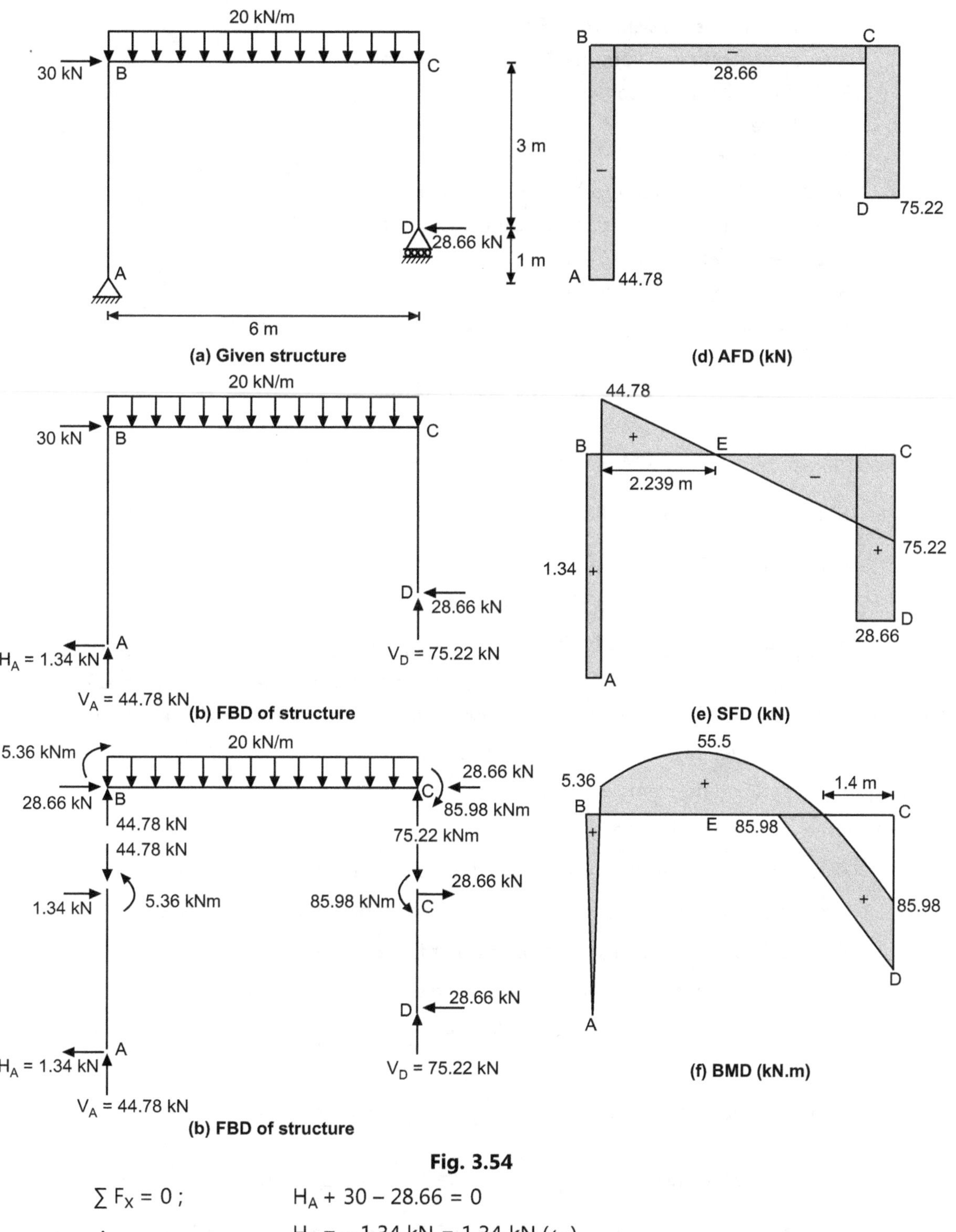


**Fig. 3.54**

$$\sum F_X = 0 \; ; \qquad H_A + 30 - 28.66 = 0$$

$$\therefore \qquad H_A = -1.34 \text{ kN} = 1.34 \text{ kN } (\leftarrow)$$

FBD of structure is as shown in Fig. 3.54 (b).

Also considering equilibrium of individual members,

FBD of members is as shown in Fig. 3.54 (c).

(ii)    Axial force :

Member AB is subjected to axial compression of 44.78 kN.

Member BC is subjected to axial compression of 28.66 kN.

Member CD is subjected to axial compression of 75.22 kN.

AFD is as shown in Fig. 3.54 (d).

(iii)    SFD is as shown in Fig. 3.54 (e).

(iv)    BM calculations :

For member AB,

$$BM_A = 0 \; ; \; BM_B = 5.36 \text{ kN.m}$$

For member BC,

$$BM_B = 5.36 \text{ kN.m} \; ; \; BM_C = -85.98 \text{ kN.m}$$

$$BM \text{ at point of zero SF} = BM_E = 44.78 \times 2.24 + 5.36 - 20 \times \frac{(2.24)^2}{2} = 55.5 \text{ kN.m}$$

For member CD,

$$BM_D = 0 \; ; \quad BM_C = 85.98 \text{ kN.m}$$

BMD is as shown in Fig. 3.54 (f).

**Example 3.48 :** *A beam ABCD is simply supported at A and fixed at D. Shear force diagram for the beam is as shown in Fig. 3.55 (a). Obtain the load diagram and hence construct BMD.*

**Data**    :    Given SFD as shown in Fig. 3.55 (a).

**Required**    :    Load diagram and BMD.

**Solution**    :    (i) Load diagram :

Rise in SFD at A indicates upward point force of magnitude 40 kN at A.

Drop in SFD at B indicates downward point force of magnitude 20 kN at B.

Drop in SFD at C indicates downward point force of magnitude 15 kN at C.

Rise in SFD at D indicates upward point force of magnitude 35 kN at D.

$$\text{Zone AB ; intensity of UDL} = \frac{dV}{dx} = \frac{35 - 40}{2} = -2.5 \text{ kN/m.}$$

$$\text{Zone BC ; intensity of UDL} = \frac{dV}{dx} = \frac{-5 - 15}{8} = -2.5 \text{ kN/m.}$$

$$\text{Zone CD ; intensity of UDL} = \frac{dV}{dx} = \frac{-35 - (-20)}{6} = -2.5 \text{ kN/m.}$$

Thus, there is downward UDL of intensity 2.5 kN/m throughout the length of beam.

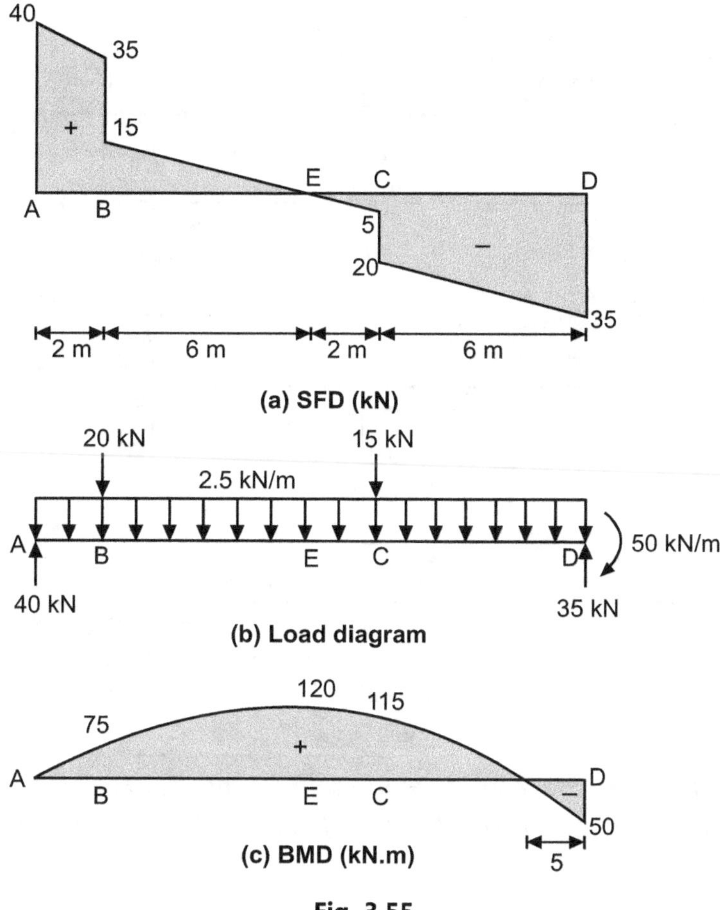



**Fig. 3.55**

(ii)　Equilibrium of beam from load diagram :

$$\Sigma\, F_y = 40 + 35 - 20 - 15 - 2.5 \times 16 = 0$$

$$\Sigma\, M_A = 35 \times 16 - 2.5 \times \frac{16^2}{2} - 15 \times 10 - 20 \times 2 = 50 \text{ kN.m}$$

Moment equilibrium is not satisfied.

Hence, moment at fixed end D = − 50 kN.m = 50 kN.m

Load diagram is as shown in Fig. 3.55 (b).

(iii)　BMD is as shown in Fig. 3.55 (c).

---

**Example 3.49 :** *Draw the S.F.D. and B.M.D. for the beam shown in Fig. 3.56. Indicate the numerical values at all important sections. Find the position of contraflexure, magnitude and position of maximum BM.*　　　　**(Dec. 2001)**

---

**Solution :**

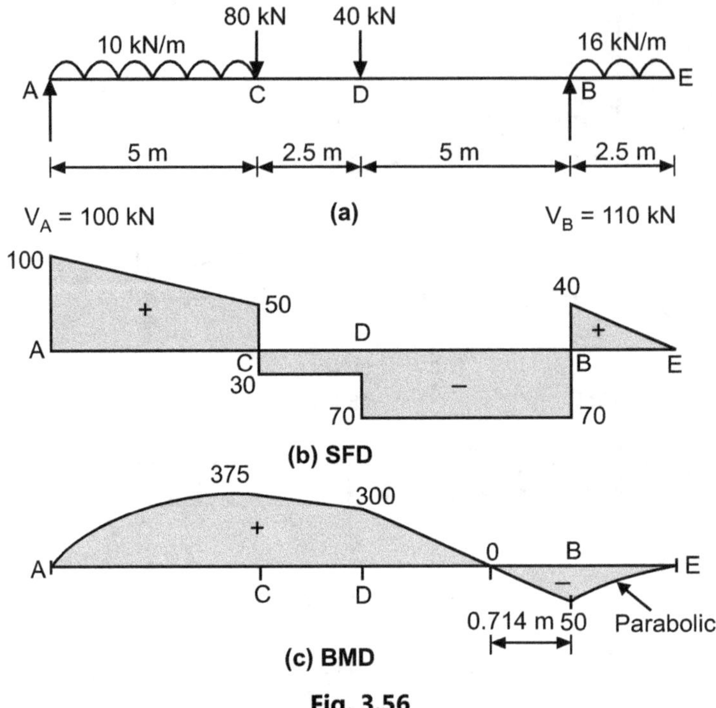

Fig. 3.56

**Example 3.50 :** *Draw the SFD and BMD for a simply supported beam of span 4 m, carrying a uniformly varying load, varying from zero at one end to 10 kN/m at the other end.* **(Dec. 2001)**

**Solution :**

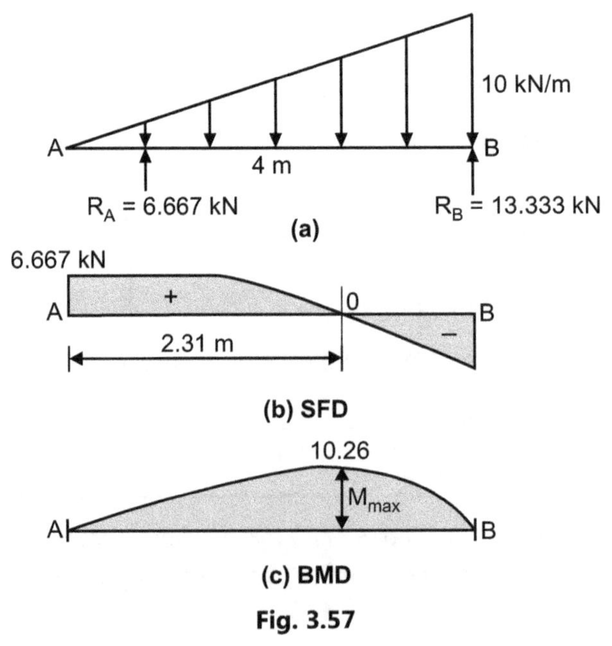

Fig. 3.57

**Example 3.51 :** *A horizontal beam AD 10 m long carries a uniformly distributed load of 20 kN/m along with a concentrated load of 60 kN at the left hand end 'A'. The beam is supported at 'B' 1 m from 'A' and at 'C' 'x' m from D. Determine the value of 'x' if the mid-section of the beam is a point of contraflexure. Locate any other point of inflection and plot SFD and BMD.* **(May 2002)**

**Solution :**

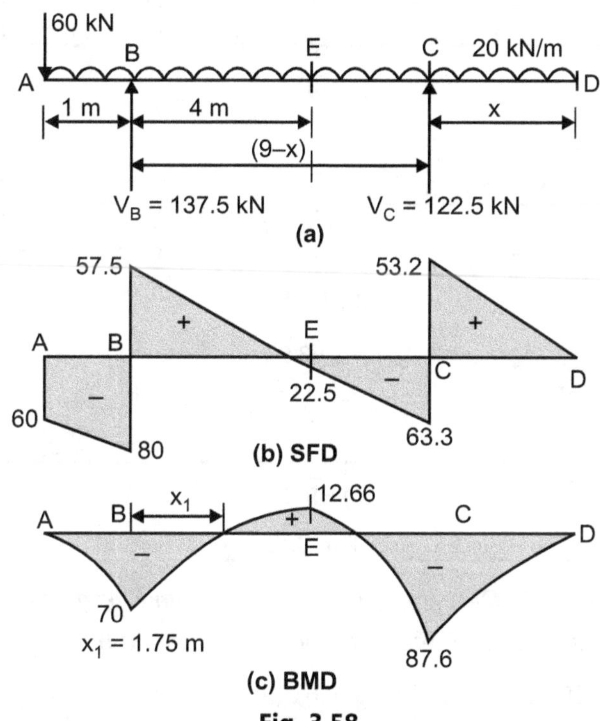


**Fig. 3.58**

**Example 3.52 :** *A simply supported beam with overhanging ends, carries transverse load as shown in Fig. 3.59. If wL = P, what is the ratio a/L for which the bending moment at middle of the beam will be zero ?* **(May 2002)**

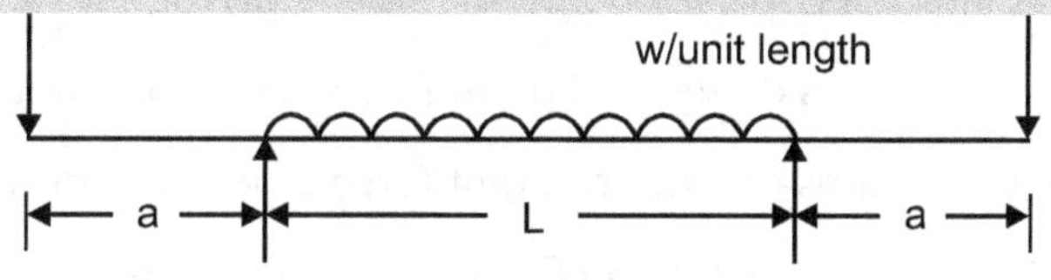


**Fig. 3.59**

**Solution :** Due to symmetry,

$$\text{Reactions} = P + \frac{wL}{2} = 1.5\ wL$$

$$\text{B.M. at centre} = -P(a + 0.5\ L) + 1.5\ wL(0.5\ L) - (w/2)(0.5\ L)^2 = 0$$

$\therefore$    $-wLa - 0.5\ wL^2 + 0.75\ wL^2 - 0.125\ wL^2 = 0$

$\therefore$    $a = 0.125\ L$

$\therefore$    $\dfrac{a}{L} = \dfrac{1}{8}$

**Example 3.53 :** *Draw shear force and bending moment diagrams for the beam loaded as shown in Fig. 3.60. Find maximum bending moment on the beam.* **(Dec. 2002)**

**Solution :**

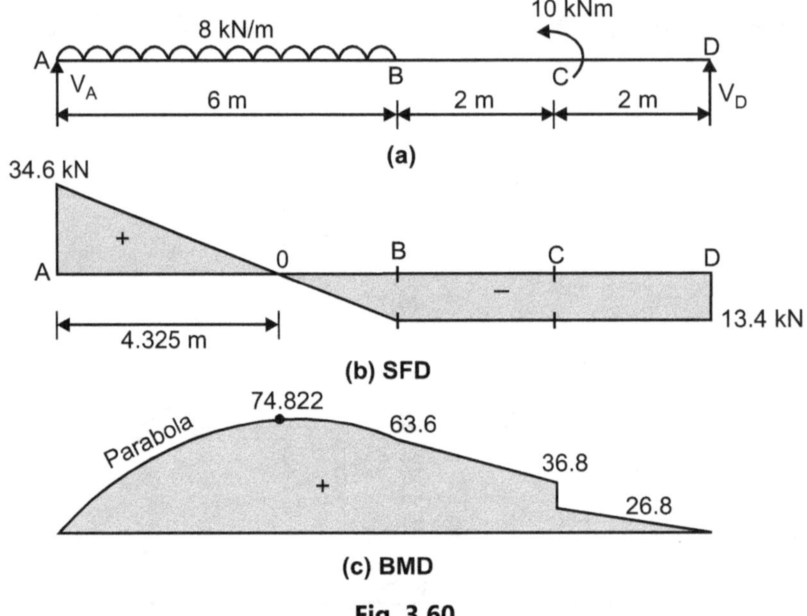


**Fig. 3.60**

---

**Example 3.54 :** *A beam ABCD is simply supported at A and fixed at D. Shear force diagram for the beam is as shown in Fig. 3.61 (a). Obtain the load diagram and hence construct BMD.*

**Data**        :   Given SFD as shown in Fig. 3.61 (a).

**Required**   :   Load diagram and BMD.

**Solution**   :   (i) Load diagram :

Rise in SFD at A indicates upward point force of magnitude 40 kN at A.

Drop in SFD at B indicates downward point force of magnitude 20 kN at B.

Drop in SFD at C indicates downward point force of magnitude 15 kN at C.

Rise in SFD at D indicates upward point force of magnitude 35 kN at D.

Zone AB ; intensity of UDL $= \dfrac{dV}{dx} = \dfrac{35 - 40}{2} = -2.5$ kN/m.

Zone BC ; intensity of UDL $= \dfrac{dV}{dx} = \dfrac{-5 - 15}{8} = -2.5$ kN/m.

Zone CD ; intensity of UDL $= \dfrac{dV}{dx} = \dfrac{-35 - (-20)}{6} = -2.5$ kN/m.

Thus, there is downward UDL of intensity 2.5 kN/m throughout the length of beam.

---

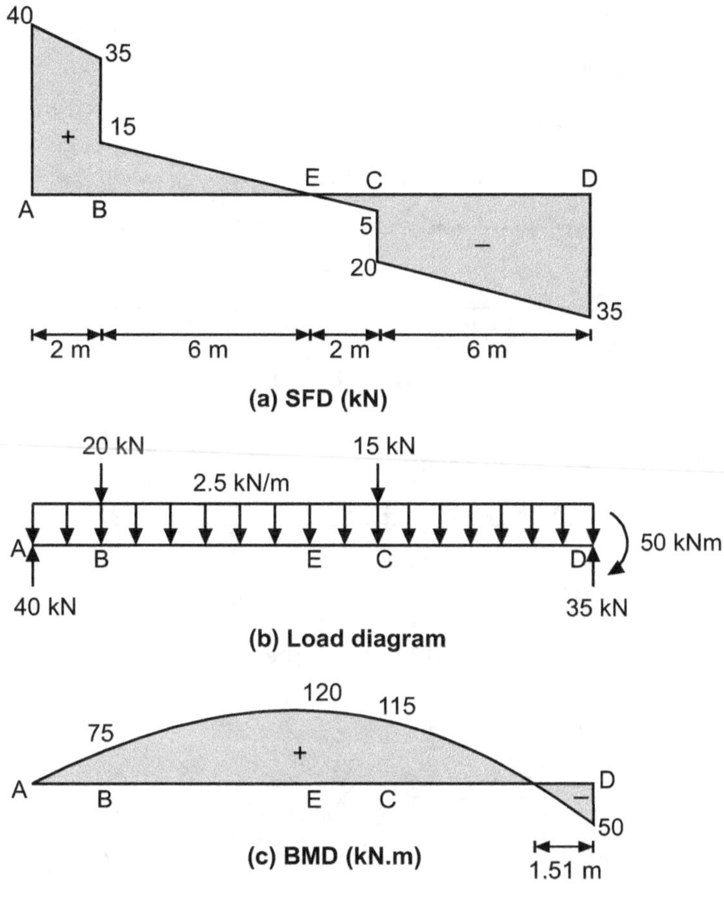



**Fig. 3.61**

(ii)   Equilibrium of beam from load diagram :

$$\Sigma\, F_y = 40 + 35 - 20 - 15 - 2.5 \times 16 = 0$$

$$\Sigma\, M_A = 35 \times 16 - 2.5 \times \frac{16^2}{2} - 15 \times 10 - 20 \times 2 = 50 \text{ kN.m}$$

Moment equilibrium is not satisfied.

Hence, moment at fixed end D = – 50 kN.m = 50 kN.m (↺)

Load diagram is as shown in Fig. 3.61 (b).

(iii)   BMD is as shown in Fig. 3.61 (c).

**Example 3.55 :** *A beam ABC is simply supported at A and B. Supports at A and B are 3 m apart and overhang BC = 1 m. The shear force diagram for the beam is as shown in Fig. 3.63 (a). Obtain the load diagram and hence construct BMD. Assume that there is no couple acting on the beam.*

**Data**   :   Given SFD as shown in Fig. 3.62 (a).

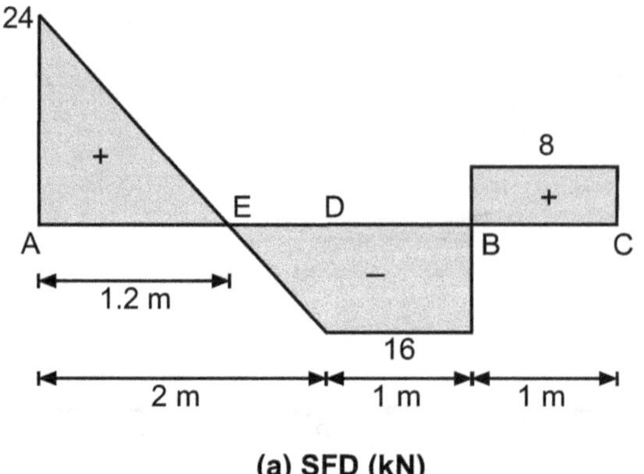

**(a) SFD (kN)**

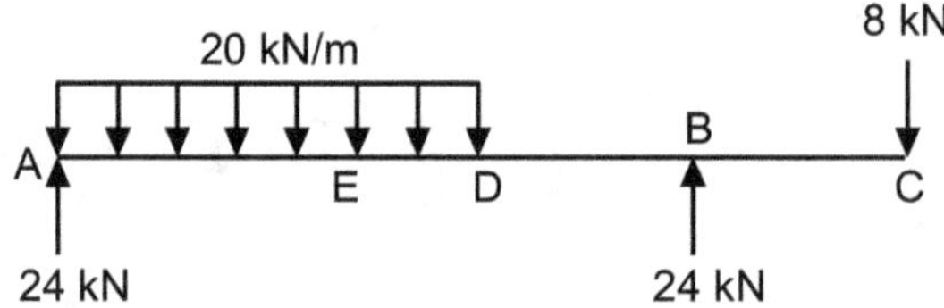

**(b) Load diagram**

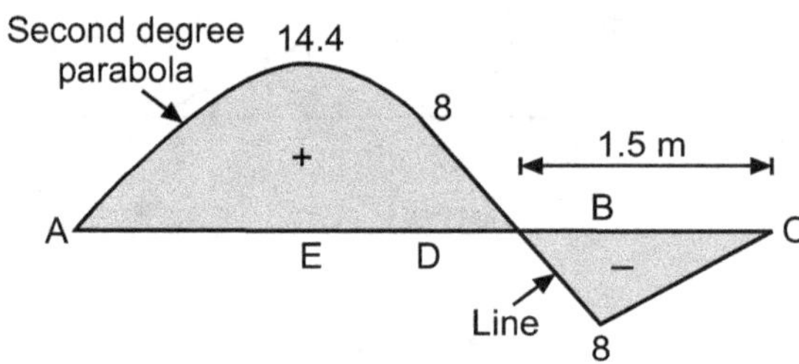

**(c) BMD (kN.m)**

**Fig. 3.62**

**Required**  :  Load diagram and BMD.

**Solution**  :  (i) Load diagram :

Rise in SFD at A indicates upward point force of 24 kN at A.

Zone AD, intensity of UDL $= \dfrac{dV}{dx} = \dfrac{-16 - (24)}{2} = -20$ kN/m

Thus, there is a downward UDL from A to D of intensity 20 kN/m.

Rise in SFD at B indicates upward point force of 24 kN at B.

Drop in SFD at C indicates downward point force of 8 kN at C.

Load diagram is as shown in Fig. 3.62 (b).

(ii)  Equilibrium of beam from load diagram :

$$\Sigma\, F_y \;=\; 24 + 24 - 20 \times 2 - 8 = 0$$

$$\Sigma\, M_A \;=\; -8 \times 4 + 24 \times 3 - 20 \times \dfrac{2^2}{2} = 0$$

Thus, the load diagram obtained is justified.

(iii)　BMD as shown in Fig. 3.62 (c).

**Example 3.56 :** *A beam ABC is simply supported at A and B. Supports at A and B are 6 m apart and overhang BC = 1 m. The bending moment diagram for the beam is as shown in Fig. 3.63 (a). Construct SFD and load diagram.*

**Data :** Given BMD as shown in Fig. 3.63 (a).

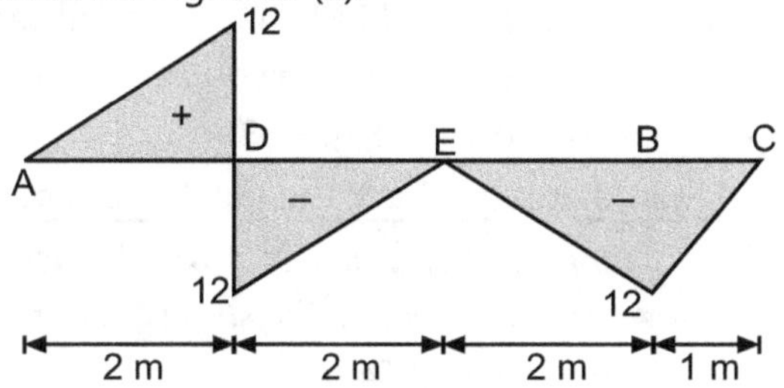

**(a) BMD (kN.m)**

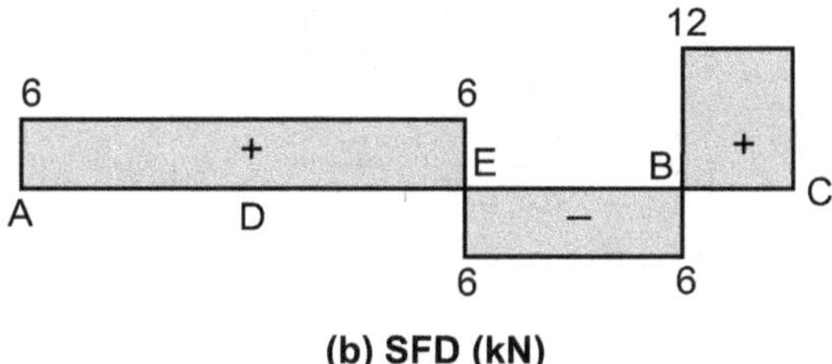

**(b) SFD (kN)**

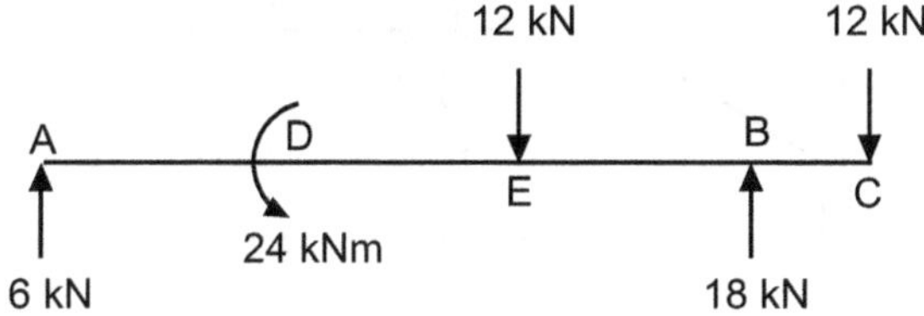

**(c) Load diagram**

**Fig. 3.63**

**Required**　:　SFD and load diagram.

**Solution**　:　(i) SFD :

Zone AD ;　　$SF = \dfrac{dM}{dx} = \dfrac{12 - 0}{2} = 6$ kN

Zone DE ;　　$SF = \dfrac{dM}{dx} = \dfrac{0 - (-12)}{2} = 6$ kN

Zone EB ;　　$SF = \dfrac{dM}{dx} = \dfrac{-12 - 0}{2} = -6$ kN

Zone BC ;　　$SF = \dfrac{dM}{dx} = \dfrac{0 - (-12)}{1} = 12$ kN

SFD is as shown in Fig. 3.63 (b).

(ii)    Load diagram :

Rise in SFD at A indicates upward point force of magnitude 6 kN at A.

Drop in SFD at E indicates downward point force of magnitude 12 kN at E.

Rise in SFD at B indicates upward point force of magnitude 18 kN at B.

Drop in SFD at C indicates downward point force of magnitude 12 kN at C.

Also, at D, drop in BM diagram = 24 kN.m and BM changes from sagging to hogging from left of D to right of D, hence, there must be an anticlockwise couple of magnitude 24 kN.m at D.

The load diagram for the beam is as shown in Fig. 3.63 (c).

**Note :** Having obtained the load diagram, check the equilibrium of beam to justify the results.

**Example 3.57 :** *A beam ABC is supported on roller at A and hinged at C. The bending moment diagram for the beam ABC is as shown in Fig. 3.64 (a). Construct SFD and load diagram.*

**Data**       :    Given BMD as shown in Fig. 3.64 (a).

**Required**   :    SFD and load diagram.

**Solution**   :    (i) SFD :

$$\text{Zone AB} ; \qquad SF = \frac{dM}{dx} = \frac{5 - (-10)}{1} = 15 \text{ kN}$$

$$\text{Zone BC} ; \qquad SF = \frac{dM}{dx} = \frac{10 - (-5)}{1} = 15 \text{ kN}$$

SFD is as shown in Fig. 3.64 (b).

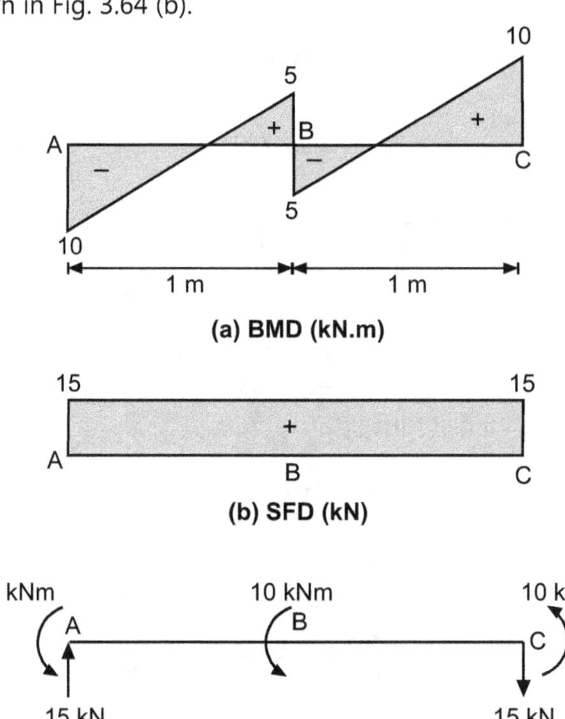


**(a) BMD (kN.m)**



**(b) SFD (kN)**

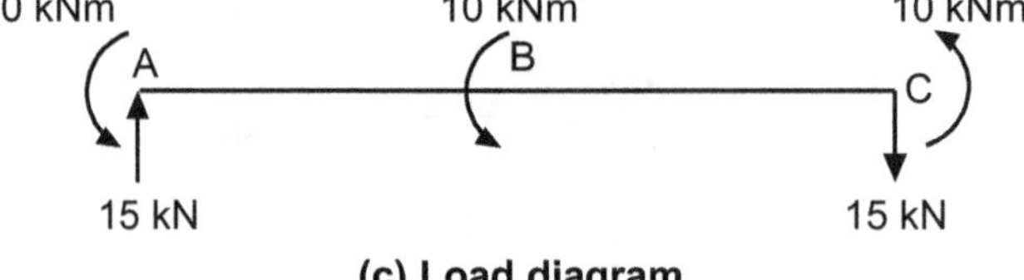


**(c) Load diagram**

**Fig. 3.64**

(ii)    Load diagram :

In zone AC ; constant SF = 15 kN.

∴      Upward reaction at A = 15 kN and downward reaction at C = 15 kN.

At A, BM = – 10 kN.m which indicates anticlockwise couple of magnitude 10 kN.m at A.

At B, drop in BM diagram = 10 kN.m and BM changes from sagging to hogging from left of B to right of B, hence there must be an anticlockwise couple of magnitude 10 kN.m at B.

At C, BM = 10 kN.m which indicates anticlockwise couple of magnitude 10 kN.m at C.

The load diagram for the beam is as shown in Fig. 3.64 (c).

**Note :** Having obtained the load diagram, check the equilibrium of beam to justify the results.

**Example 3.58 :** *Fig. 3.65 shows a SFD for a simply supported beam AB. Draw BMD for the beam.*

**Data :** Given SFD as shown in Fig. 3.65.

**Required :** BMD.

**Solution :** (i) Load diagram : Rise in SFD at A indicates upward point force 12.5 kN at A.

Horizontal line between A to C shows no load between A to C.

Rise in SFD at B indicates upward point force of 7.5 kN at B.

**Zone CD :** Intensity of UDL = $\dfrac{dV}{dx} = \dfrac{-7.5 - 12.5}{4} = -5$ kN.m.

Load diagram is as shown in Fig. 3.65 (b).

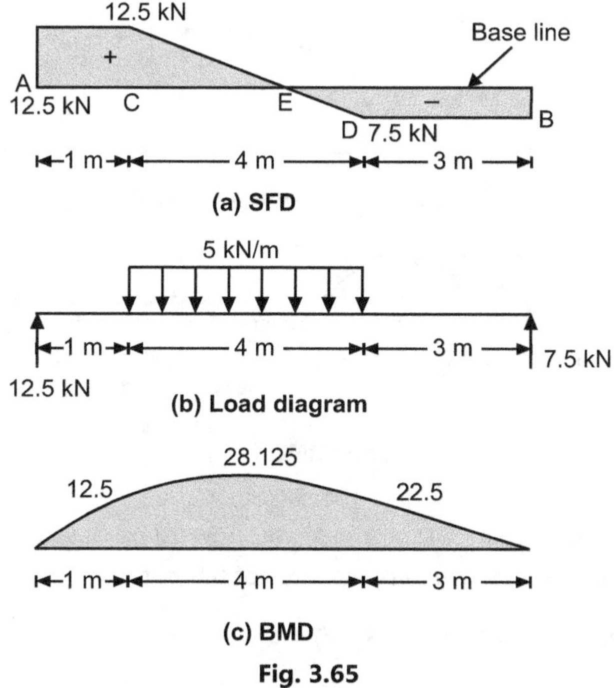


**Fig. 3.65**

(ii)     BMD : Bending moment, maximum at SF is zero.

$$\therefore \qquad x = \frac{12.5}{5} = 2.5 \text{ m (from starting point of UDL)}$$

BMD is as shown in Fig. 3.65 (c).

**Example 3.59 :** *The SFD of a 4 m long beam is a second degree curve as shown in Fig. 3.66 (a), with the maximum negative SF of 3 kN at the beam centre. Assuming that no couples act on the beam, draw the loading and BMD. Locate the position of maximum BM and their magnitudes. Points of contraflexure if any, too, should be located.*                    **(Dec. 2003)**

**Data :** SFD as shown in Fig. 3.66 (a).

**Required :** Loading diagram and BMD.

**Solution :**

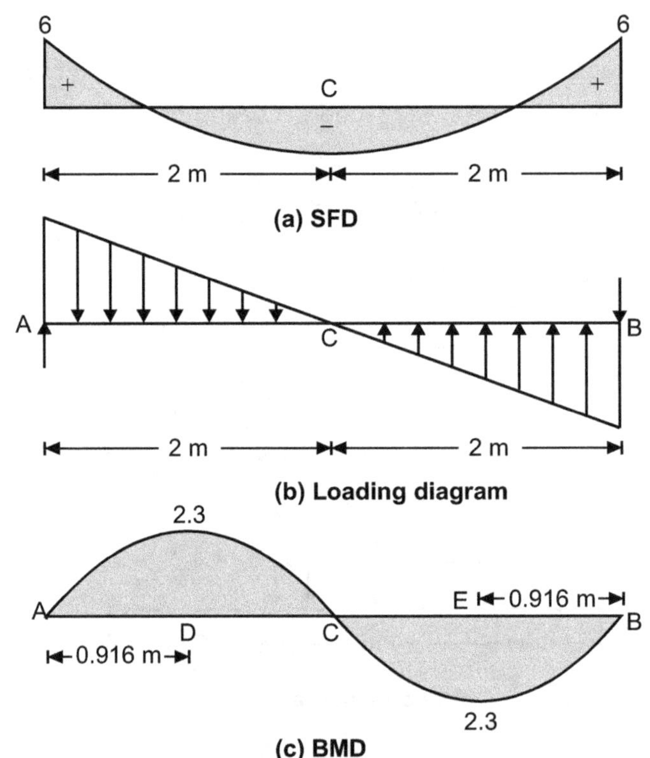


**Fig. 3.66**

(i)     **Loading diagram :** Rise in SFD at A indicates upward point force of 6 kN at A.
Drop in SFD at B indicates downward point force of 6 kN at B.

**Zone A to C :**  Intensity of UVL  $= (-3 - 6) = \frac{1}{2} w \times l$

$$-9 = \frac{1}{2} \times w \times 2$$

$\therefore \qquad w = -9 \text{ kN.m}$

**Zone C to B :** Intensity of UVL $= 6 - (-3) = \frac{1}{2} w \times l$

$\therefore \qquad w = 9 \text{ kN.m}$

To locate point of zero SF, consider a section at a distance x from A in zone AC.

$$SF_x = 6 - (\text{Area of trapezoidal load diagram}) = 0$$

$$\frac{9}{2} = \frac{y}{x} \qquad\qquad \therefore y = 4.5 x$$

$$\therefore \qquad 6 - \frac{(9 + 4.5 x)}{2} \times x = 0$$

$$9x + 4.5x^2 - 12 = 0$$

$$\therefore \qquad x^2 + 2x - 2.67 = 0$$

$$x = -2 \pm \frac{\sqrt{(2)^2 - 4 \times 1 (-2.67)}}{2}$$

$$= 0.916 \text{ m from A and B.}$$

(As beam is symmetrical, so points of zero SF are at same distance from both ends.)

Loading diagram is as shown in Fig. 3.66 (b).

(ii)    BM calculations :

$$BM_A = BM_B = 0$$

BM at zero SF, $\quad BM_D = 6 \times 0.916 - \text{Moment due to trapezoidal loading diagram}$

$$= 6 \times 0.916 - \frac{(9 + 4.5 \times 1.084)}{2} \times 0.916 \times \left(\frac{4.878 + 9 \times 2}{4.878 + 9}\right) \times \frac{0.916}{3}$$

$$= 2.3 \text{ kN.m}$$

$$BM_C = 6 \times 2 - \frac{1}{2} \times 9 \times 2 \times \frac{2}{3} \times 2$$

$$= 0$$

$$BM_E = -2.3 \text{ kN.m}$$

BMD is as shown in Fig. 3.66 (c).

**Example 3.60 :** *The BMD of a simply supported beam is linear in the 1.5 m long portion AC and parabolic in the 3 m long portion CDEB. There is no slope discontinuity anywhere in the BMD. The moments of D and E are 28.125 kN.m and 22.5 kN.m respectively. Draw the SFD and loading diagrams for the beam and highlight all the significant values.*    **(May 2004)**

**Data :** BMD as shown in Fig. 3.67 (a).

**Required :** Loading diagram and SFD.

**Solution :**

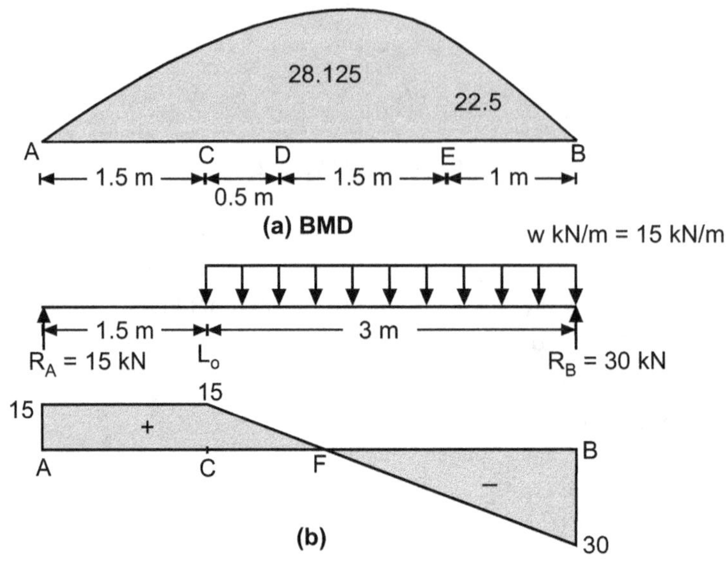



**Fig. 3.67**

(i)　w and reactions :

$$M_E = R_B \times 1 - \frac{w \times 1^2}{2}$$

$$= 22.5$$

$$R_B - 0.5\,w = 22.5 \qquad \qquad \text{... (i)}$$

$$M_D = R_B \times 2.5 - \frac{w \times 2.5^2}{2}$$

$$= 28.125$$

$$\therefore \qquad R_B - 1.25\,w = 11.25 \qquad \qquad \text{... (ii)}$$

Solving equations (i) and (ii),

$$w = 15 \text{ kN/m},\ R_B = 30 \text{ kN } (\uparrow)$$

$$\Sigma F_y = 0; \qquad R_A + R_B - w \times 3 = 0$$

$$R_A = 15 \text{ kN } (\uparrow)$$

(ii)　Loading diagram as shown in Fig. 3.67 (b).

(iii) SF calculations :

$$SF_A = 15 \text{ kN}$$

$$SF_C = 15 \text{ kN}$$

$$SF_B = 15 - 15 \times 3 = -30 \text{ kN}$$

To locate point of SF, consider a section at a distance x from B in portion BC.

$$\therefore \qquad SF_X = 30 - 15 \times x = 0$$

$$\therefore \qquad x = 2 \text{ m from B.}$$

(iv) Maximum BM is at 2 m from B.

$$\therefore \qquad BM_F = 30 \times 2 - 15 \times 2 \times 1 = 30 \text{ kN.m}$$

SFD is as shown in Fig. 3.67 (c).

**Example 3.61 :** *The bending moment diagram for a beam ABCDE is as shown in Fig. 3.68. Portions AB, CD and DE have linear curves whereas portion BC has a second degree curve with a peak located at 1.8 m from B and enjoys slope continuity at C. Draw the shear force and loading diagrams for the beam. Hence or otherwise locate the points of contraflexure.* **(May 2003)**

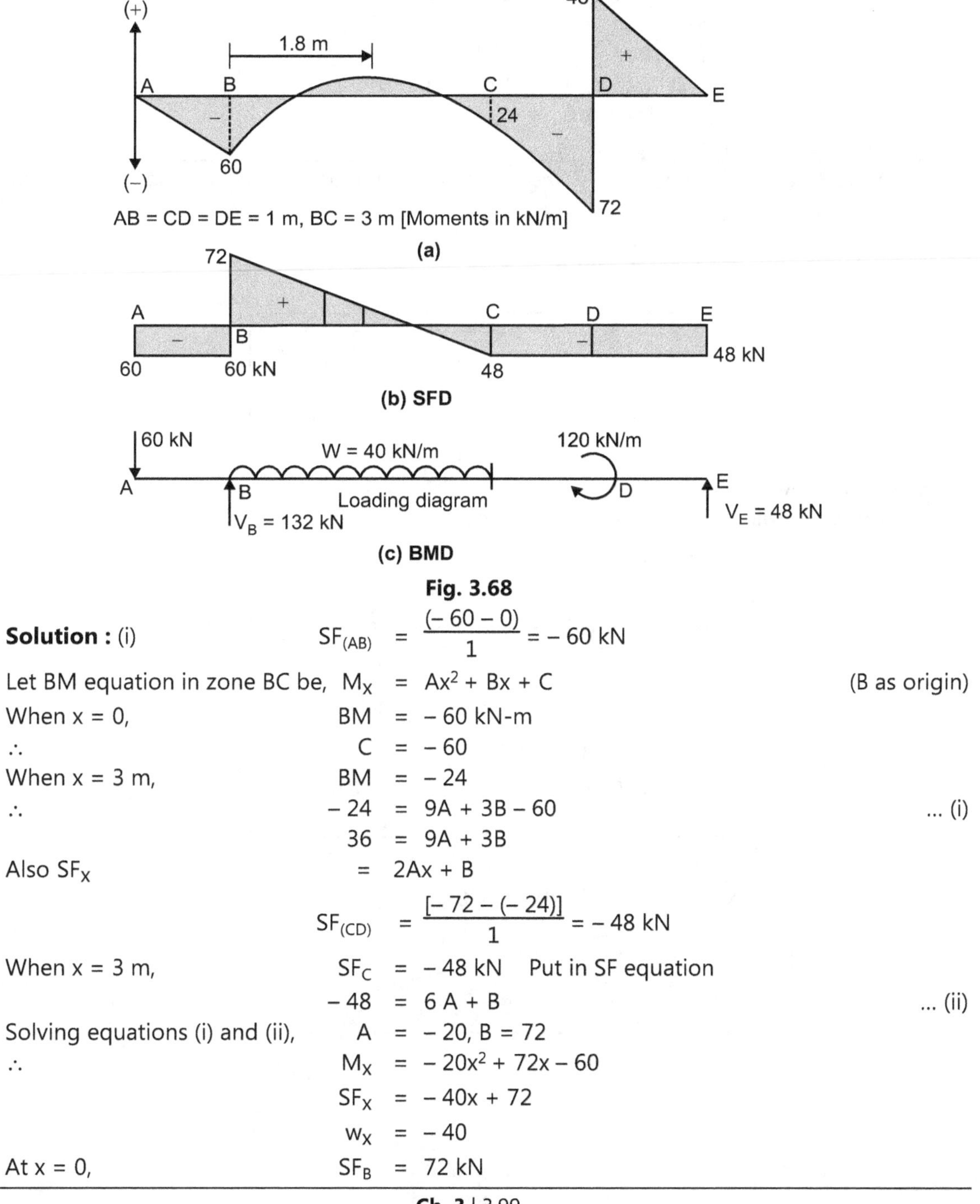



Fig. 3.68

**Solution :** (i)

$$SF_{(AB)} = \frac{(-60 - 0)}{1} = -60 \text{ kN}$$

Let BM equation in zone BC be, $M_X = Ax^2 + Bx + C$  (B as origin)

When $x = 0$, $\quad BM = -60$ kN-m

$\therefore \quad C = -60$

When $x = 3$ m, $\quad BM = -24$

$\therefore \quad -24 = 9A + 3B - 60$  ... (i)

$\quad 36 = 9A + 3B$

Also $SF_X \quad = 2Ax + B$

$$SF_{(CD)} = \frac{[-72 - (-24)]}{1} = -48 \text{ kN}$$

When $x = 3$ m, $\quad SF_C = -48$ kN    Put in SF equation

$\quad -48 = 6A + B$  ... (ii)

Solving equations (i) and (ii), $\quad A = -20, B = 72$

$\therefore \quad M_X = -20x^2 + 72x - 60$

$\quad SF_X = -40x + 72$

$\quad w_X = -40$

At $x = 0$, $\quad SF_B = 72$ kN

At x = 3 m, $\qquad SF_C = -48$ kN

$$SF_{(DE)} = \frac{(0-48)}{1} = -48 \text{ kN}$$

SFD is as shown in Fig. 3.68 (b).

(ii) 　　　　Point load at A $= 60$ kN $(\downarrow)$
　　　　　　Point load at B $= 60 + 72 = 132$ kN $(\uparrow)$
　　　　　　UDL in zone BC $= 40$ kN/m $(\uparrow)$
　　　　　　Couple at D $= 120$ kN/m $(\circlearrowleft)$
　　　　　　Point load at E $= 48$ kN $(\uparrow)$

Load diagram is shown in Fig. 3.68 (c).

**Example 3.62 :** *Fig. 3.69 shows the shear force for beam ABCD. Draw the loading diagram and bending moment diagram.*

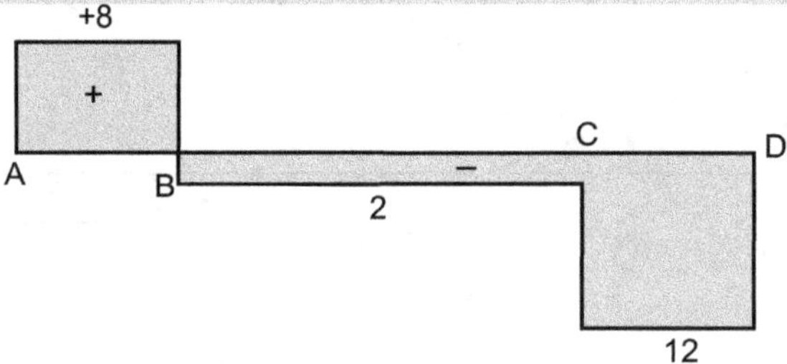


**Fig. 3.69**

**Data :** As shown in Fig. 3.69.

**Required :** Loading diagram and bending moment diagram.

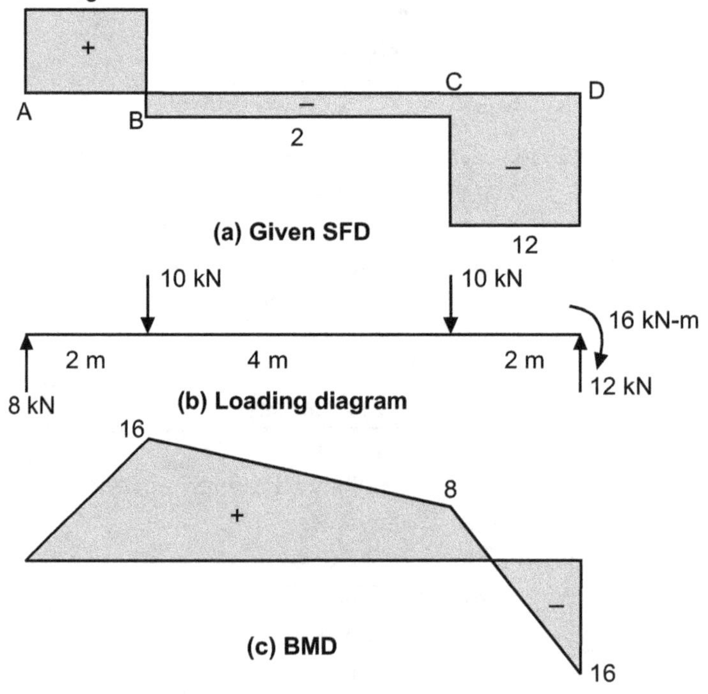


**Fig. 3.70**

**Example 3.63 :** Shown in Fig. 3.71 is the shear force diagram of a beam. The curve in portion AB is a second-degree curve that has zero slope at 'A'. Draw completely the loading diagram of the beam.

**(Dec. 2002)**

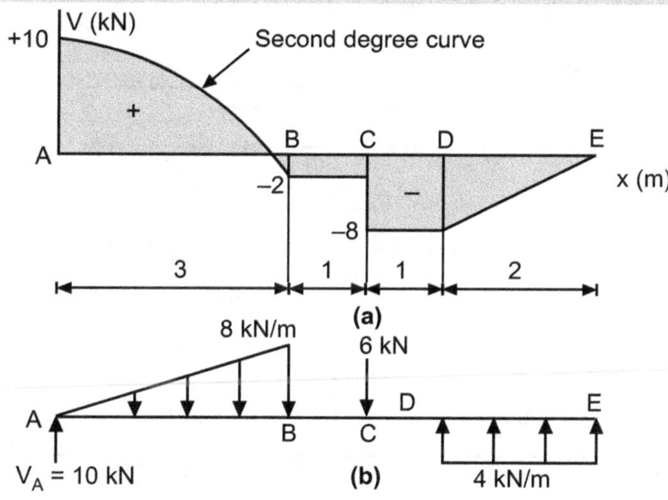


**Fig. 3.71**

**Solution :** At 'A' upward point load of 10 kN.

SF equation in zone AB $= Ax^2 + B$

When $x = 0$,     SF $= 10$ kN,     $\therefore$   B $= 10$

When $x = 3$ m,     SF $= -2$ kN     $\therefore$   A $= -1.33$

$\therefore$     $SF_{(x)} = -1.33\, x^2 + 10$     ... (i)

$\therefore$     $w_{(x)} = -2.67\, x$     ... (ii)

When $x = 0$,     $w = 0$

When $x = 3$ m,     $w = 8$ kN/m

Thus in zone AB, we have triangular load with zero intensity at A and 8 kN/m at B.

At 'C' downward point load of 6 kN is present.

Intensity of UDL from D to E $= \dfrac{0 - (-8)}{2} = 4$ kN/m ($\uparrow$)

Load diagram is as shown in Fig. 3.71.

## EXERCISE

Draw shear force and bending moment diagrams for the following beams indicating all important values :

1.

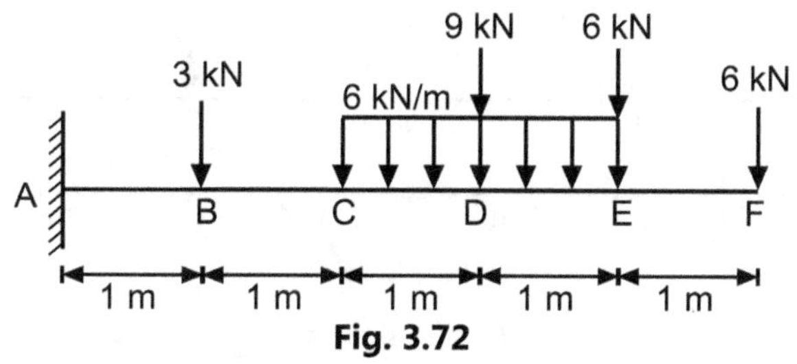


**Fig. 3.72**

$(BM_A = -120$ kN.m, $BM_B = -84$ kN.m, $BM_C = -51$ kN.m,

$BM_D = -21$ kN.m, $BM_E = -6$ kN.m, $BM_F = 0)$

2.

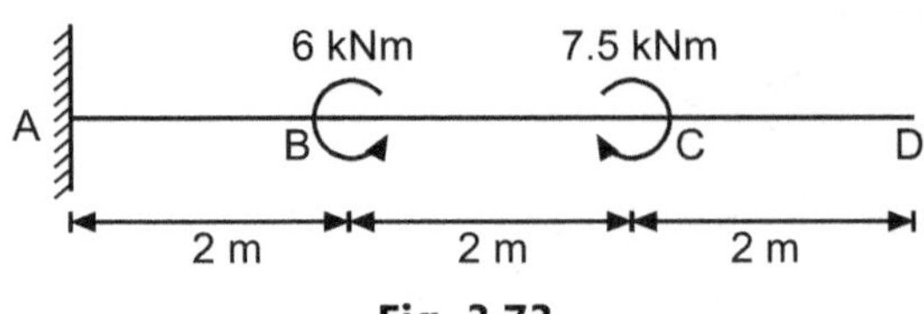

**Fig. 3.73**

$(BM_A = -1.5$ kN.m, $BM_{B\,(L)} = -1.5$ kN.m, $BM_{B\,(R)} = -7.5$ kN.m,

$BM_{C\,(L)} = -7.5$ kN.m, $BM_{C\,(R)} = 0$, $BM_D = 0)$

3.

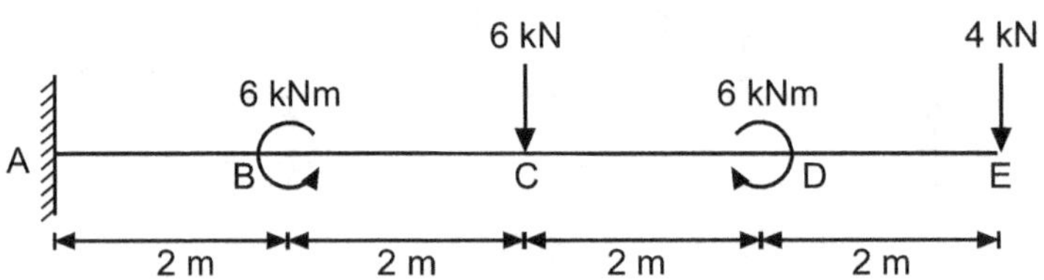

**Fig. 3.74**

$(BM_A = -58$ kN.m, $BM_{B\,(L)} = -38$ kN.m, $BM_{B\,(R)} = -42$ kN.m, $BM_C = -22$ kN.m,

$BM_{D\,(L)} = -14$ kN.m, $BM_{D\,(R)} = -8$ kN.m, $BM_E = 0)$

4.

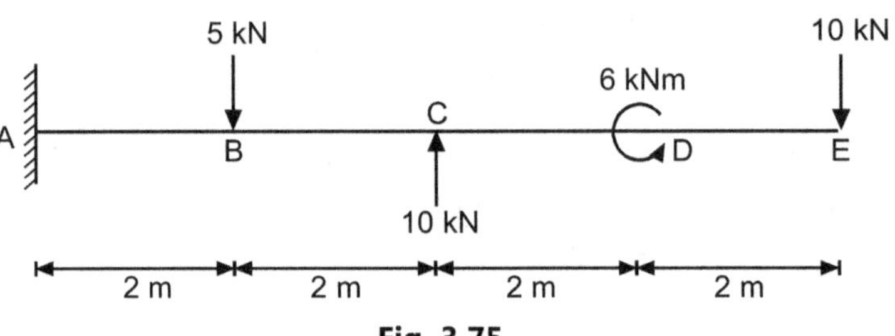

**Fig. 3.75**

$(BM_A = 10$ kN.m, $BM_B = 20$ kN.m, $BM_C = 20$ kN.m, $BM_{D\,(L)} = 40$ kN.m,

$BM_{D\,(R)} = -20$ kN.m, $BM_E = 0)$

5.

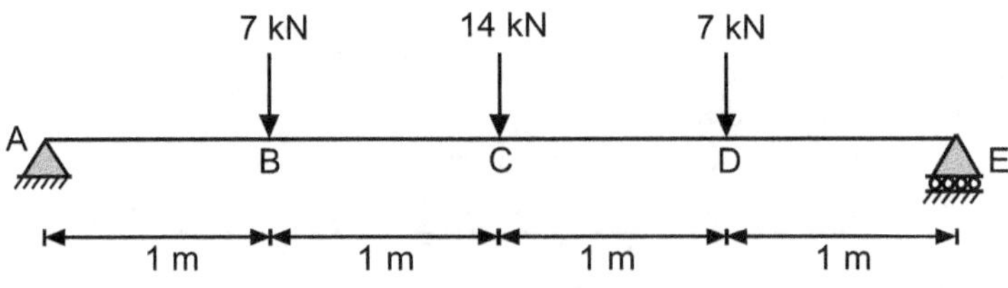

**Fig. 3.76**

$(BM_A = BM_E = 0$, $BM_B = 14$ kN.m, $BM_C = 21$ kN.m, $BM_D = 14$ kN.m$)$

6.

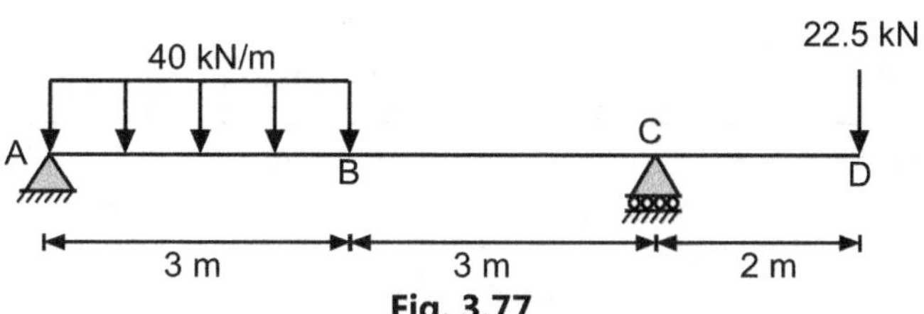

**Fig. 3.77**

(BM$_A$ = BM$_D$ = 0, BM$_B$ = 67.5 kN.m, BM$_C$ = − 45 kN.m, BM$_{max}$ = 84.93 m at 2.06 m from A)

7.

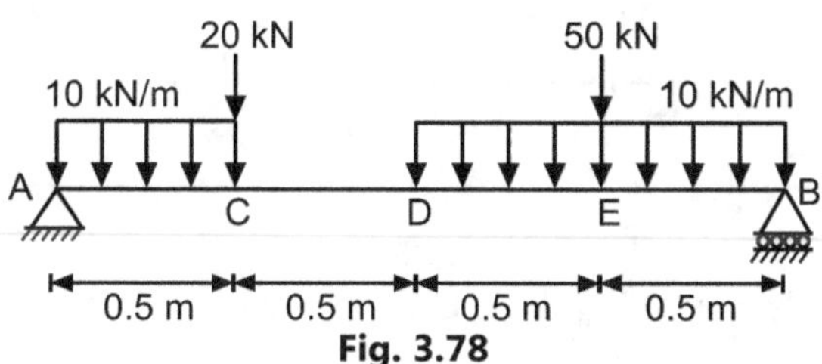

**Fig. 3.78**

(BM$_A$ = BM$_B$ = 0, BM$_C$ = 16.5 kN.m, BM$_D$ = 21 kN.m, BM$_E$ = 24.25 kN.m)

8.

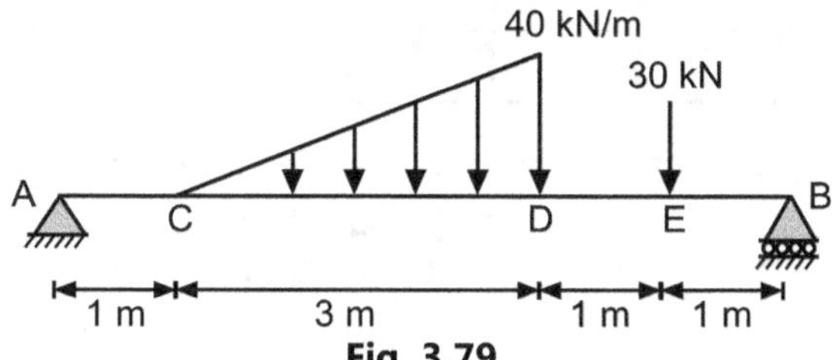

**Fig. 3.79**

(BM$_A$ = BM$_B$ = 0, BM$_C$ = 35 kN.m, BM$_D$ = 80 kN.m, BM$_E$ = 55 kN.m,

BM$_{max}$ = 88.46 kN.m at 3.29 m from A)

9.

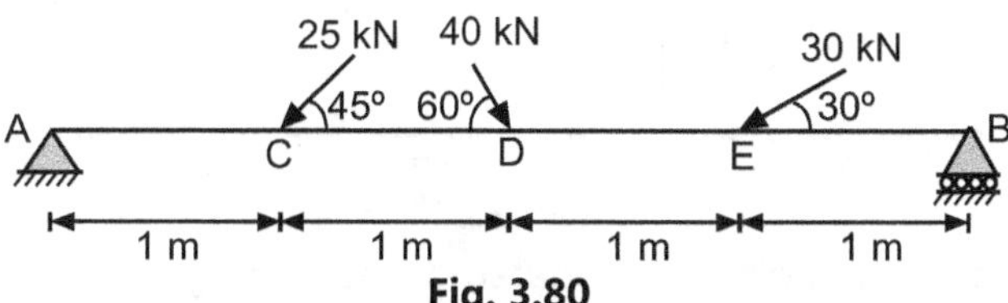

**Fig. 3.80**

(BM$_A$ = BM$_B$ = 0, BM$_C$ = 34.33 kN.m, BM$_D$ = 50.985 kN.m, BM$_E$ = 32.995 kN.m)

10.

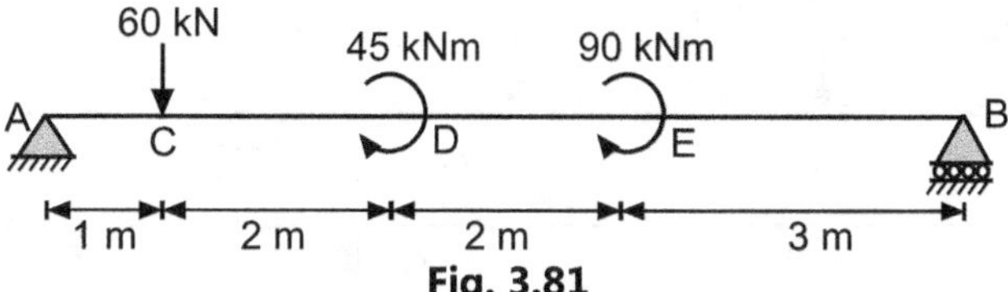

**Fig. 3.81**

(BM$_A$ = BM$_B$ = 0, BM$_C$ = 35.625 kN.m, BM$_{D\ (L)}$ = − 13.125 kN.m,

BM$_{D\ (R)}$ = 31.875 kN.m, BM$_{E\ (L)}$ = − 16.875 kN.m, BM$_{E\ (R)}$ = 73.125 kN.m)

11.

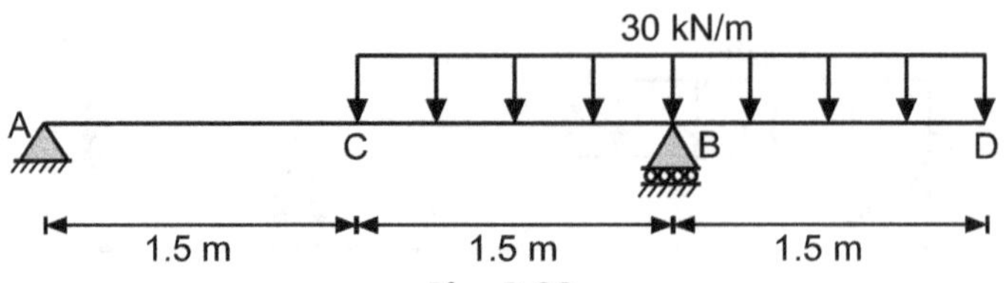

Fig. 3.82

$$(BM_A = BM_D = BM_C = 0, BM_B = -33.75 \text{ kN.m})$$

12.

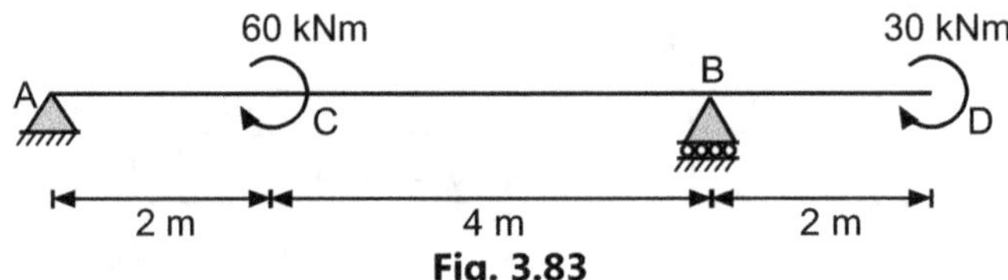

Fig. 3.83

$$(BM_A = 0, BM_{C(L)} = -30 \text{ kN.m}, BM_{C(R)} = 30 \text{ kN.m}, BM_B = BM_D = -30 \text{ kN.m})$$

13.

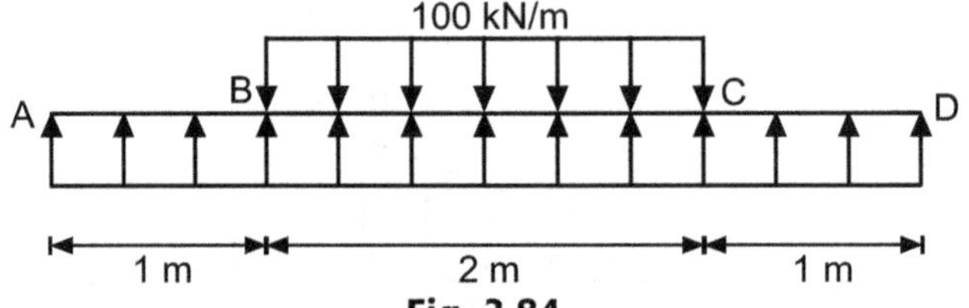

Fig. 3.84

$$(BM_A = BM_D = 0, BM_B = BM_C = 25 \text{ kN.m}, BM_{max} \text{ at centre} = 50 \text{ kN.m})$$

14.

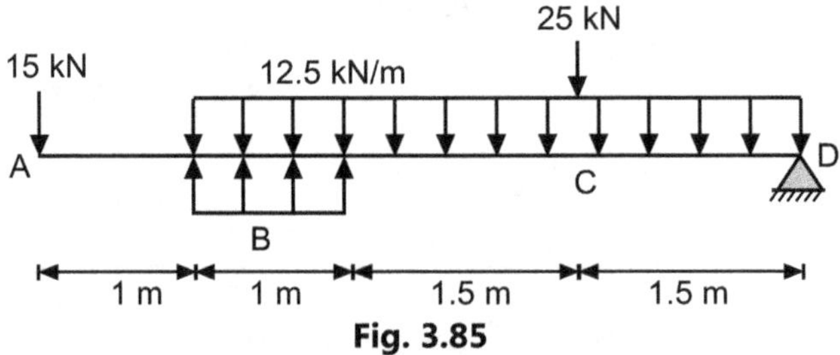

Fig. 3.85

**Hint :** Reaction at B is uniformly distributed over 1 m length.

$$(BM_A = BM_D = 0, BM_B = -15 \text{ kN.m}, BM_C = 29.875 \text{ kN.m})$$

15.

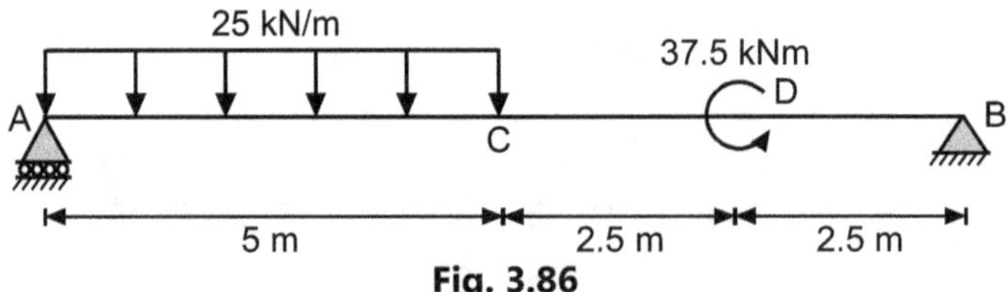

Fig. 3.86

$$(BM_A = BM_B = 0, BM_C = 343.75 \text{ kN.m}, BM_{D(L)} = 359.375 \text{ kN.m},$$
$$BM_{D(R)} = -15.625 \text{ kN.m})$$

16.

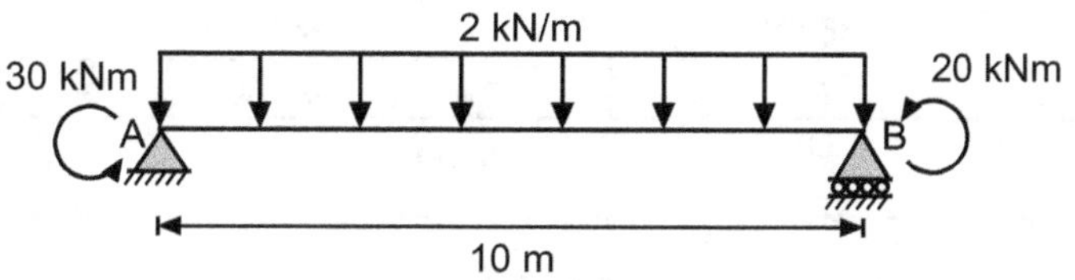

**Fig. 3.87**

$(BM_A = -30 \text{ kN.m}, BM_B = 20 \text{ kN.m}, BM_{max} = 26.25 \text{ kN.m at 7.5 m from A})$

17.

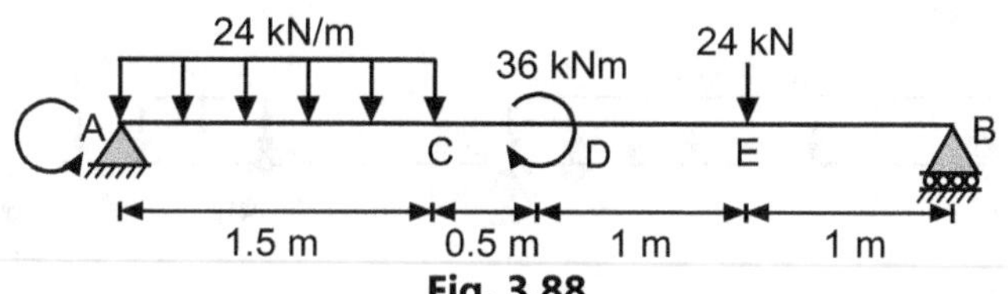

**Fig. 3.88**

$(BM_A = BM_B = 0, BM_C = 12.38 \text{ kN.m, BM at zero SF in zone AC} = 14.34 \text{ kN.m},$

$BM_{D (L)} = 7.48 \text{ kN.m}, BM_{D (R)} = 43.48 \text{ kN.m}, BM_E = 33.74 \text{ kN.m})$

18.

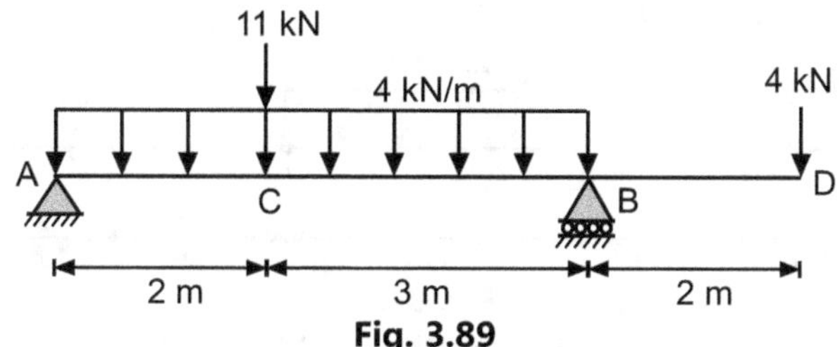

**Fig. 3.89**

$(BM_A = 0, BM_C = 22 \text{ kN.m}, BM_B = -8 \text{ kN.m})$

19.

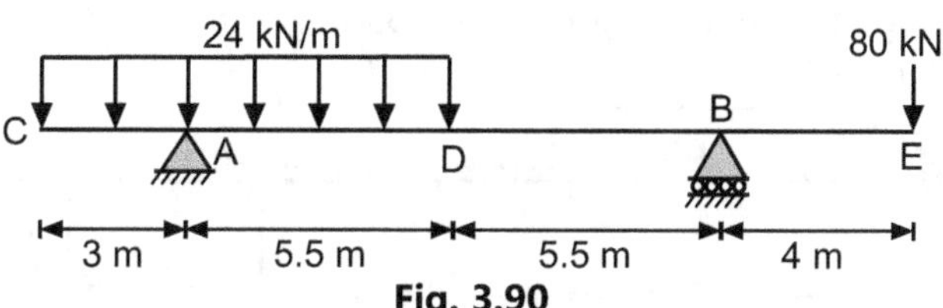

**Fig. 3.90**

$(BM_C = BM_E = 0; BM_A = -108 \text{ kN.m}, BM_B = -32.68 \text{ kN.m}, BM_B = -320 \text{ kN.m};$

$BM \text{ at zero SF in zone AD} = 24.16 \text{ kN.m, at 6.32 m from C})$

20.

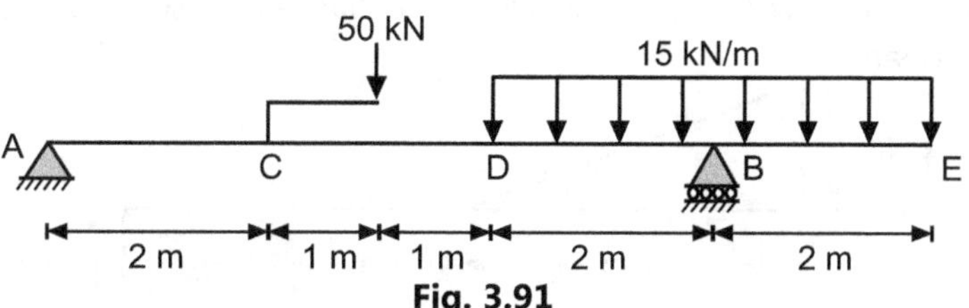

**Fig. 3.91**

$(BM_A = BM_E = 0, BM_{C (L)} = 50 \text{ kN.m}, BM_{C (R)} = 100 \text{ kN.m}, BM_D = 50 \text{ kN.m},$

$BM_B = -30 \text{ kN.m})$

21.

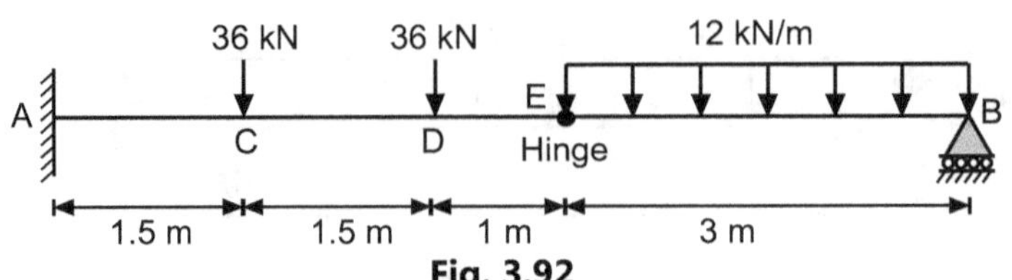

**Fig. 3.92**

($BM_E = BM_B = 0$; $BM_A = -234$ kN.m, $BM_C = -99$ kN.m, $BM_D = -18$ kN.m, BM at zero SF in zone BE = 13.5 kN.m)

22.

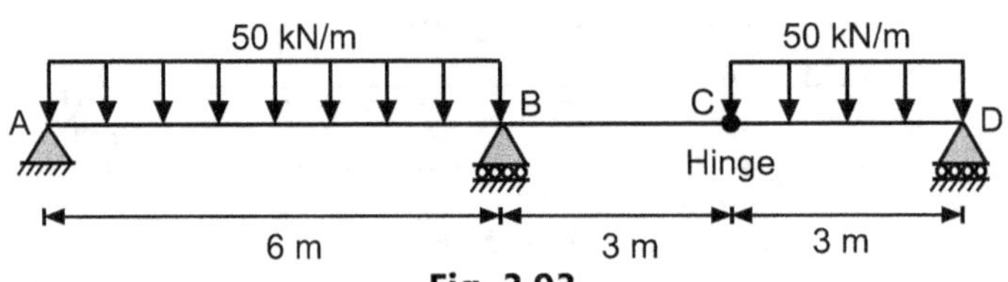

**Fig. 3.93**

($BM_A = BM_C = BM_D = 0$; $BM_B = -225$ kN.m, BM at zero SF in zone AB = 126.56 kN.m at 2.25 m from A; BM at zero SF in zone CD = 56.25 kN.m 1.5 m from D)

23.

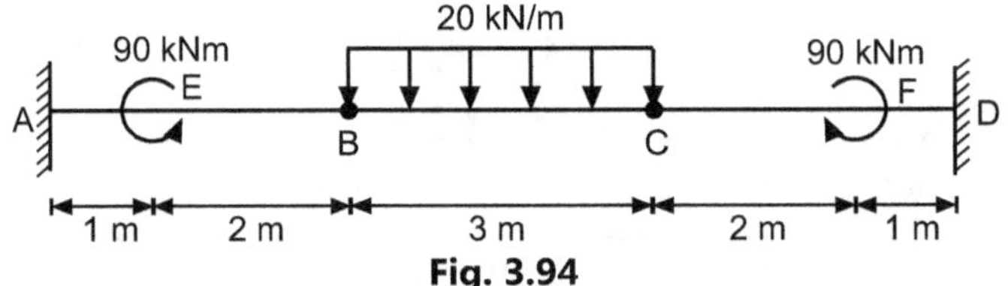

**Fig. 3.94**

($BM_A = BM_B = BM_C = BM_D = 0$; $BM_{E\,(L)} = 30$ kN.m $= BM_{F\,(R)}$; $BM_{E\,(R)} = -60$ kN.m $= BM_{F\,(L)}$; BM at zero SF in zone BC = 22.5 kN.m)

24.  Draw the bending moment diagram and loading diagram from the given shear force diagram. (Refer Fig. 3.95)

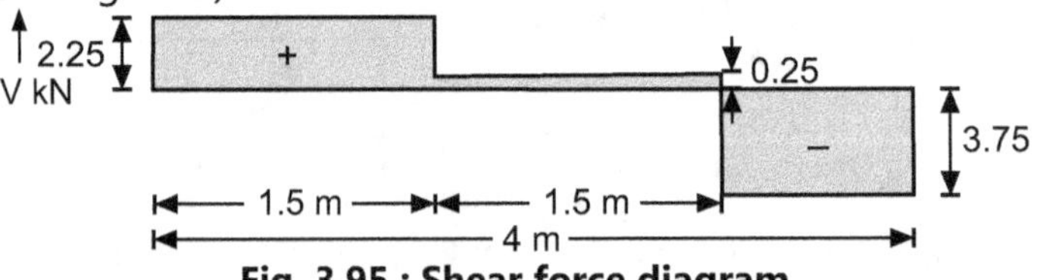

**Fig. 3.95 : Shear force diagram**

25.  The shear force diagram for a simple beam is shown in Fig. 3.96. Determine the loading on the beam and draw the bending moment diagram, assuming that no couples act as loads on the beam.

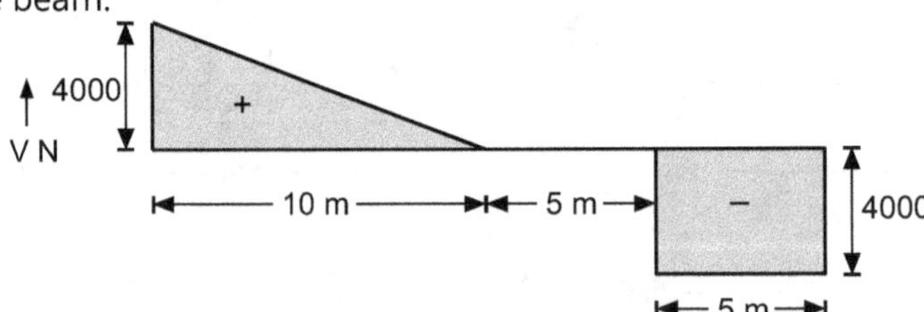

**Fig. 3.96 : Shear force diagram**

26. The shear force diagram for a beam is as shown in Fig. 3.97. Assuming that no couple act as load on the beam, draw the bending moment diagram and also show the loading diagram.

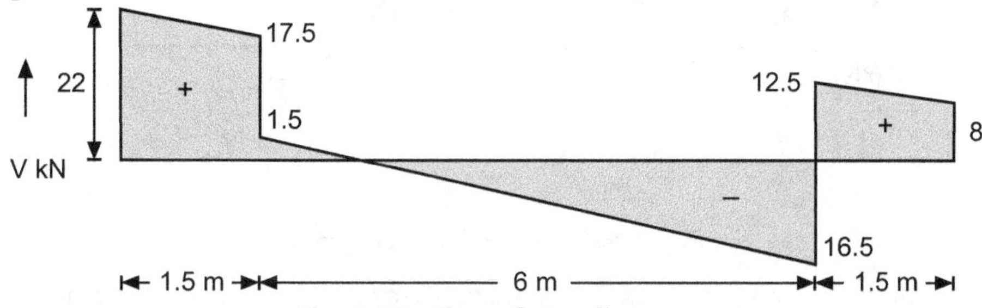

**Fig. 3.97 : Shear force diagram**

27. Construct the loading and shear force diagram for the beam with an overhang as shown in Fig. 3.98.

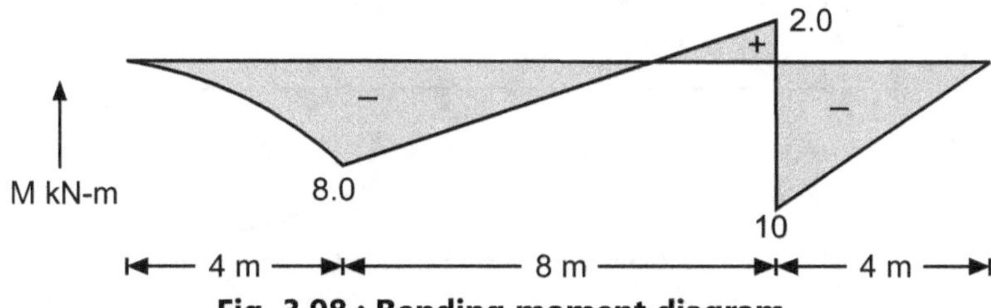

**Fig. 3.98 : Bending moment diagram**

28. Construct the shear force diagram and loading diagram for the cantilever beam shown in Fig. 3.99.

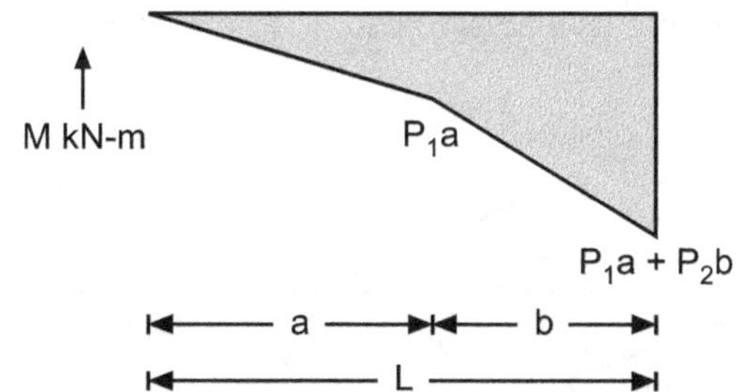

**Fig. 3.99 : Bending moment diagram**

29. Construct the bending moment diagram and loading diagram for the simply supported beam as shown in Fig. 3.100.

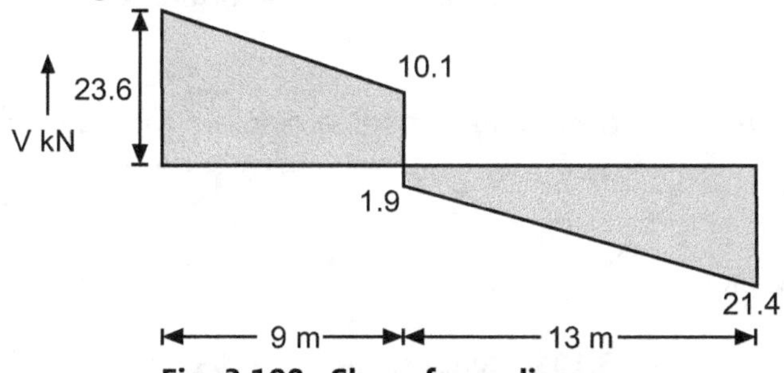

**Fig. 3.100 : Shear force diagram**

30. Draw the bending moment diagram and loading diagram from shear for the simply supported beam as shown in Fig. 3.101.

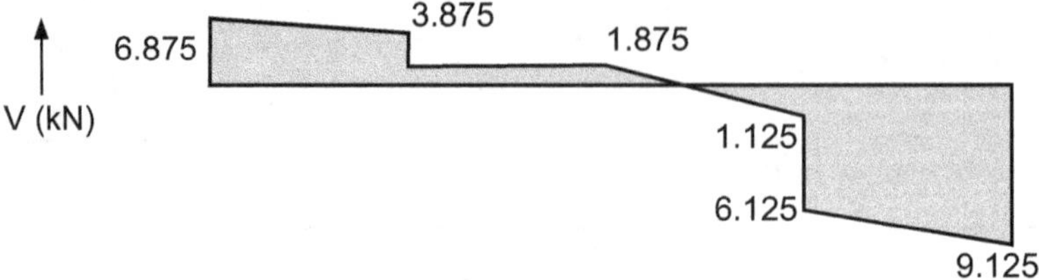


**Fig. 3.101 : Shear force diagram**

31. Draw bending moment diagram and loading diagram from shear force diagram for simply supported beam as shown in Fig. 3.102.

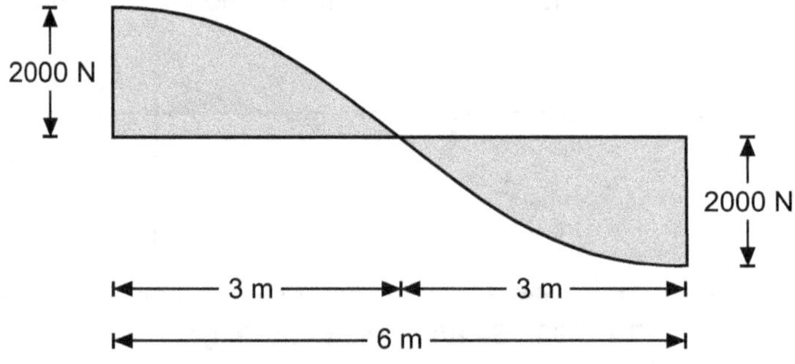


**Fig. 3.102 : Shear force diagram**

32. Construct bending moment diagram and loading diagram for the overhanging beam shown in Fig. 3.103.

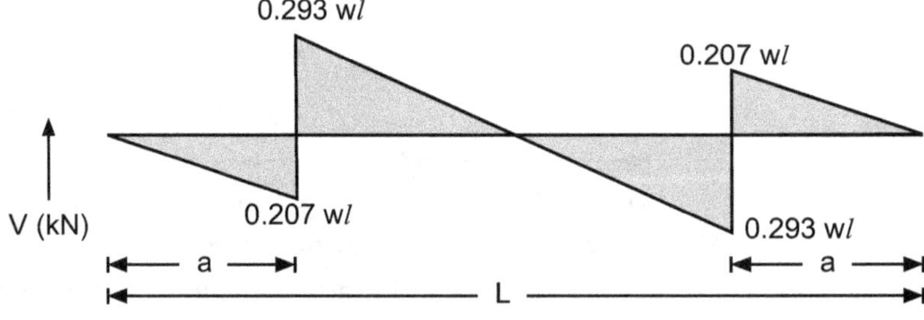


**Fig. 3.103 : Shear force diagram**

33. Construct the shear force diagram and loading diagram for the beam shown in Fig. 3.104.

**Fig. 3.104 : Bending moment diagram**

## UNIVERSITY QUESTION PAPERS

### MAY 2014

1. A beam AB 10 meters long has supports at its ends A and B. It carries a point load of 5 kN at 3 meters from A and a point load of 5 kN at 7 meters from A and a uniformly distributed load of 1 kN per meter between the point loads. Draw SF and BM diagrams for the beam. **[6]**

2. Draw SF and BM diagrams for the beam ABCDE shown in following Fig. 1. **[6]**

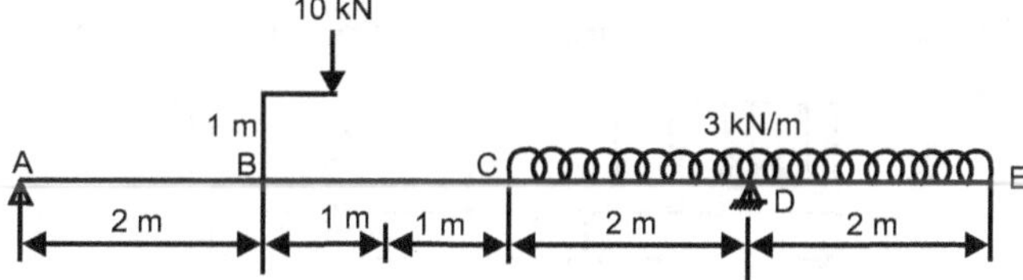


**Fig. 1**

### DECEMBER 2014

1. Draw SFD and BMD for the beam loaded as shown in the Fig. 1 below : **[6]**

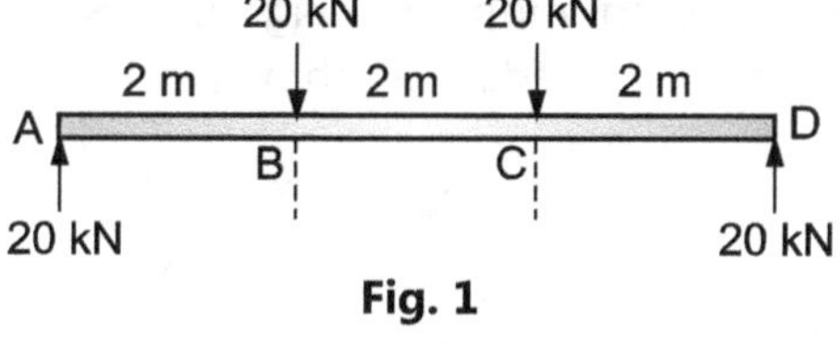


**Fig. 1**

**OR**

2. Draw SFD and BMD for the beam loaded as shown in the Fig. 2. **[6]**

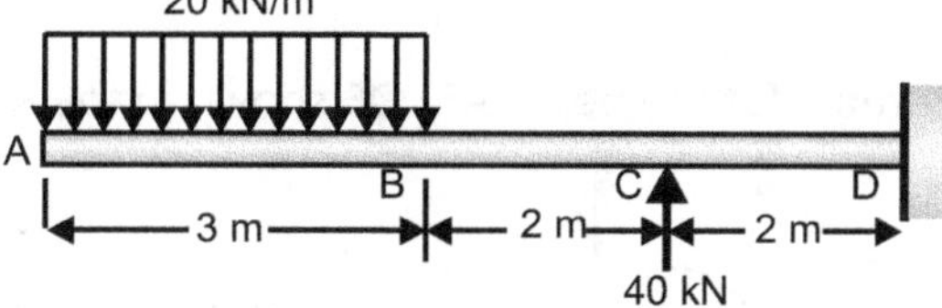


**Fig. 2**

### MAY 2015

1. Draw SFD and BMD for the beam loaded as shown in Fig. 1 below. **[6]**

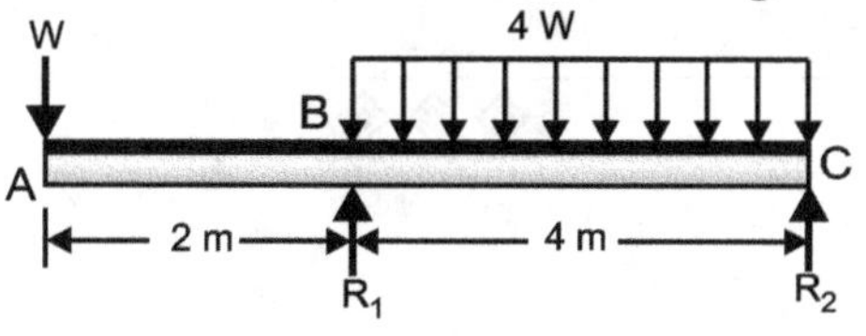


**Fig. 1**

1. Draw SFD and BMD for the beam loaded as shown in Fig. 2 below. **[6]**

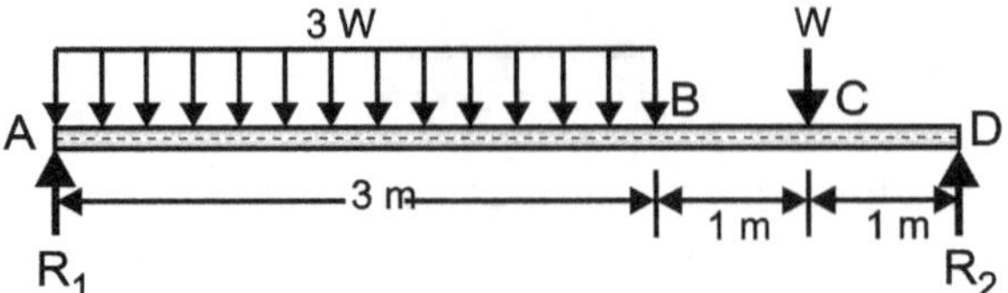

**Fig. 2**

## November 2015

1. Draw SFD and BMD for the beam loaded as shown in Fig. 1 below. **[6]**

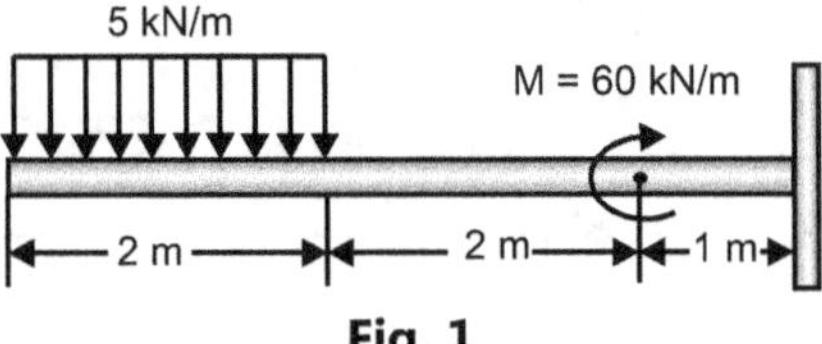

**Fig. 1**

## May 2016

1. Draw shear force and bending moment diagrams [SFD and BMD] for a single side overhanging beam subjected to loading as shown in Fig. 1 given below. Locate points of contra flexure, if any. **[6]**

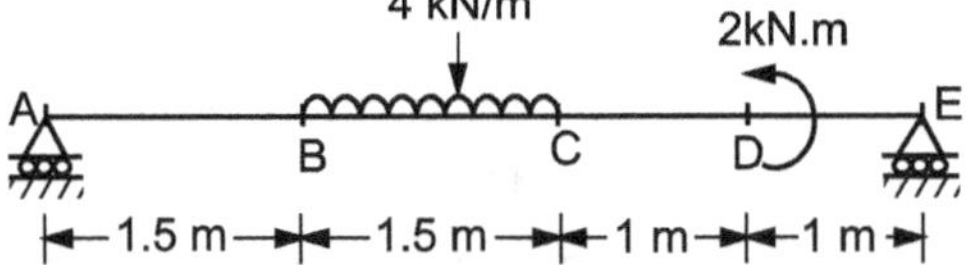

**Fig. 1**

2. Draw SF and BM diagrams for the beam ABCDE shown in the following Fig. 2

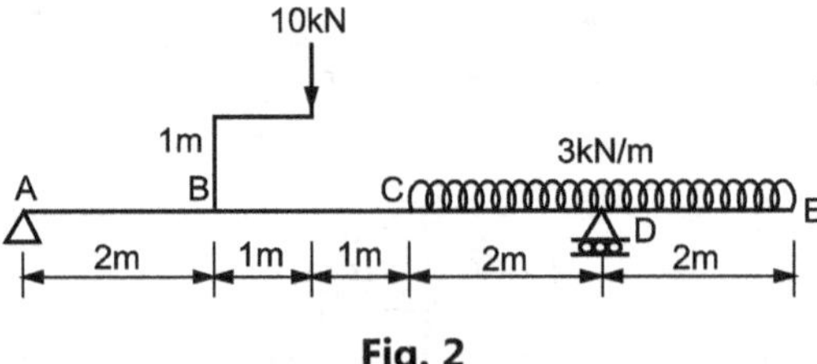

**Fig. 2**

◈ ◈ ◈

# Chapter 4

# SHEAR FORCE AND BENDING MOMENT (PART B)

## 4.1 RELATIONSHIP BETWEEN LOAD, SHEAR AND BENDING MOEMENT

The relationship between load, shear and bending moment can be derived as under. Consider a beam supported and loaded as shown in Fig. 4.1 (a).

Let $V_x$ and $M_x$ be the shear and bending moment on a section at a distance 'x' from A. Likewise $V_x$ + $dV_x$ and $M_x$ and $dM_x$ are the shear and bending moment at a section at a distance $x + dx$ from A. The free body diagram of the segment of the beam which is dx in length is shown in Fig. 4.1 (b).

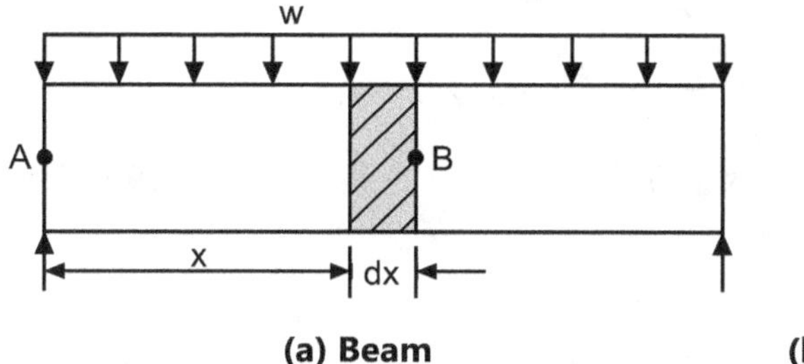


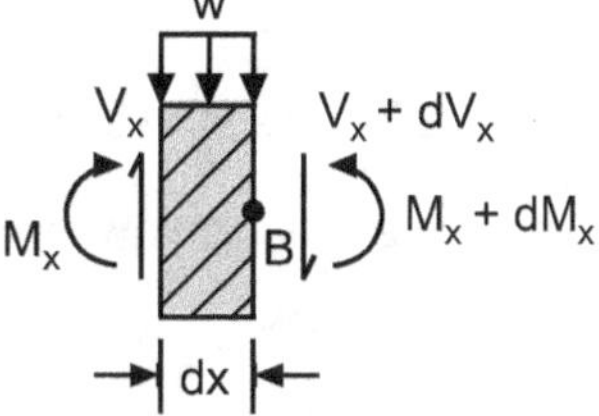


(a) Beam     (b) FBD of beam segment

**Fig. 4.1**

Applying equations of equilibrium to FBD of segment as under :

$$\Sigma F_y = 0 \Rightarrow \qquad V_x - (V_x + dV_x) - w \cdot dx = 0$$

$$dV_x = -w \cdot dx$$

$$\therefore \qquad \frac{dV_x}{dx} = -w \qquad \qquad \dots (4.1)$$

*Thus, the rate of decrease of shear force with respect to x, on any section at a distance 'x' from left end of the beam is equal to the intensity of load at the section.*

$$\Sigma M_B = 0 \Rightarrow \qquad V_x \cdot dx + M_x = M_x + dM_x + w\frac{dx^2}{2}$$

The term $w\dfrac{dx^2}{2}$ being very small, can be neglected.

$$dM_x = V_x \cdot dx$$

$$\frac{dM_x}{dx} = V_x \qquad \qquad \dots (4.2)$$

*Thus, the rate of increase of bending moment with respect to 'x', on any section at a distance 'x' from left end of the beam, is equal to shear at the section.*

# SOLVED EXAMPLES

**Example 4.1 :** A beam ABCD is simply supported at A and fixed at D. Shear force diagram for the beam is as shown in Fig. 4.2 (a). Obtain the load diagram and hence construct BMD.

**Data**        :   Given SFD as shown in Fig. 4.2 (a).

**Required**   :   Load diagram and BMD.

**Solution**   :   (i) Load diagram :

Rise in SFD at A indicates upward point force of magnitude 40 kN at A.

Drop in SFD at B indicates downward point force of magnitude 20 kN at B.

Drop in SFD at C indicates downward point force of magnitude 15 kN at C.

Rise in SFD at D indicates upward point force of magnitude 35 kN at D.

$$\text{Zone AB : Intensity of udl} = \frac{dV}{dx} = \frac{35 - 40}{2} = -2.5 \text{ kN/m.}$$

$$\text{Zone BC : Intensity of udl} = \frac{dV}{dx} = \frac{-5 - 15}{8} = -2.5 \text{ kN/m.}$$

$$\text{Zone CD : Intensity of udl} = \frac{dV}{dx} = \frac{-35 - (-20)}{6} = -2.5 \text{ kN/m.}$$

Thus, there is downward udl of intensity 2.5 kN/m throughout the length of beam.

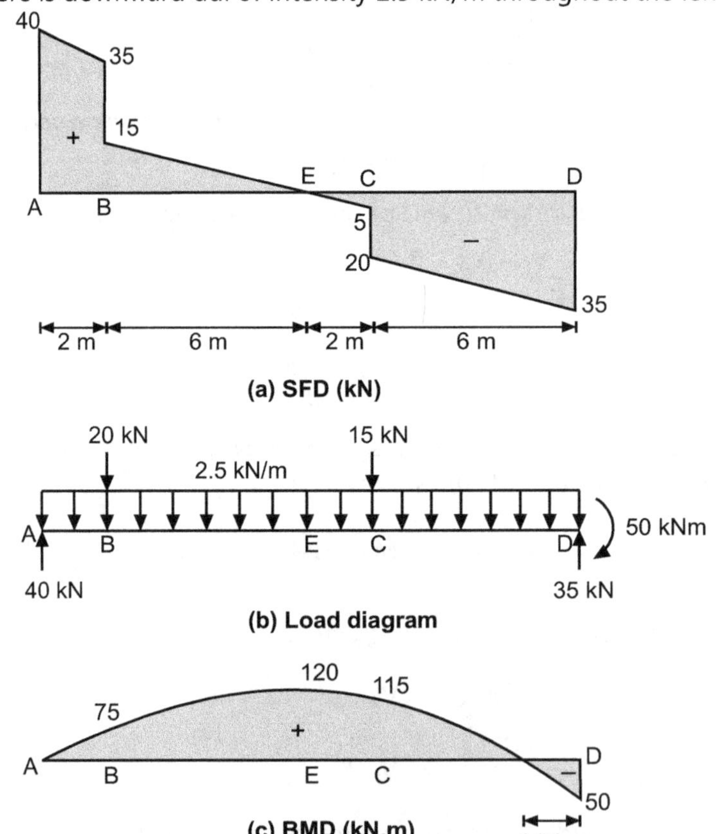


**Fig. 4.2**

(ii)     Equilibrium of beam from load diagram :

$$\sum F_y = 40 + 35 - 20 - 15 - 2.5 \times 16 = 0$$

$$\sum M_A = 35 \times 16 - 2.5 \times \frac{(16)^2}{2} - 15 \times 10 - 20 \times 2 = 50 \text{ kN.m}$$

Moment equilibrium is not satisfied.

Hence, moment at fixed end D = $-$ 50 kN.m = 50 kN.m ($\circlearrowleft$)

Load diagram is as shown in Fig. 4.2 (b).

(iii)    BMD is as shown in Fig. 4.2 (c).

**Example 4.2 :** A beam ABC is simply supported at A and B. Supports at A and B are 3 m apart and overhang BC = 1 m. The shear force diagram for the beam is as shown in Fig. 4.3 (a). Obtain the load diagram and hence construct BMD. Assume that there is no couple acting on the beam.

**Data :**     Given SFD as shown in Fig. 4.3 (a).

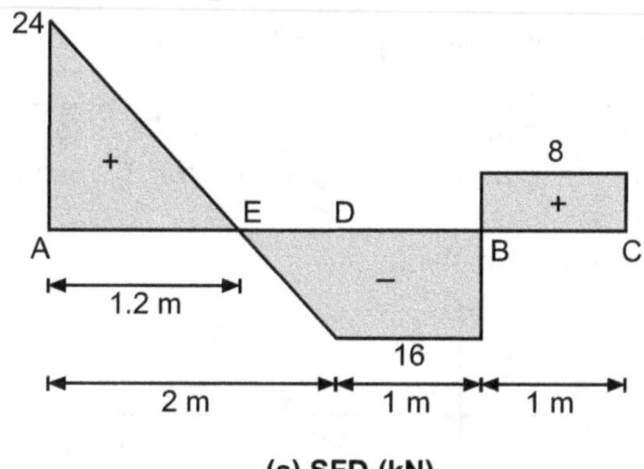


**(a) SFD (kN)**

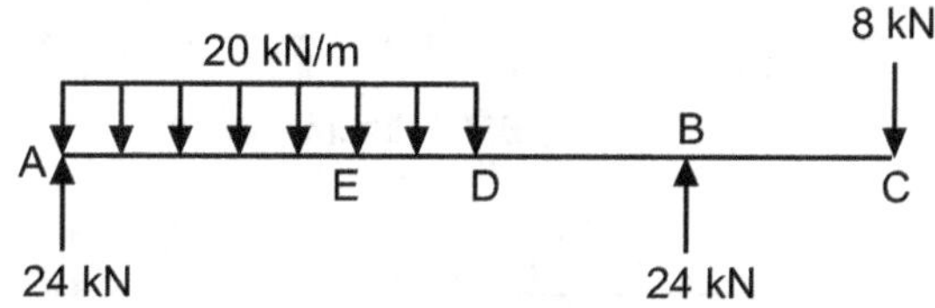


**(b) Load diagram**

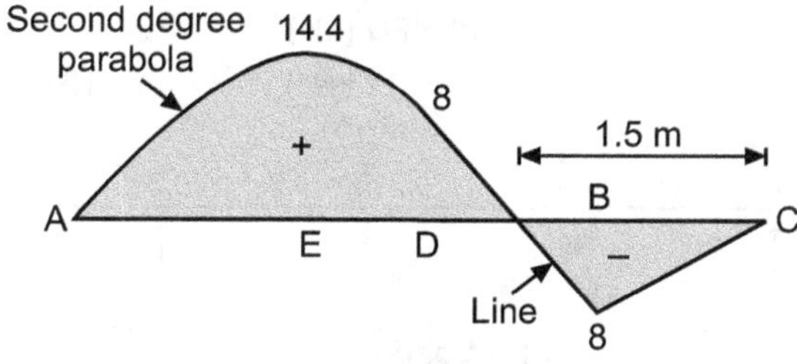


**(c) BMD (kN.m)**

**Fig. 4.3**

**Required** : Load diagram and BMD.

**Solution** : (i) Load diagram :

Rise in SFD at A indicates upward point force of 24 kN at A.

Zone AD, intensity of udl $= \dfrac{dV}{dx} = \dfrac{-16 - (24)}{2} = -20$ kN/m

Thus, there is a downward udl from A to D of intensity 20 kN/m.

Rise in SFD at B indicates upward point force of 24 kN at B.

Drop in SFD at C indicates downward point force of 8 kN at C.

Load diagram is as shown in Fig. 4.3 (b).

(ii) Equilibrium of beam from load diagram :

$$\sum F_y \ = \ 24 + 24 - 20 \times 2 - 8 = 0$$

$$\sum M_A \ = \ -8 \times 4 + 24 \times 3 - 20 \times \dfrac{2^2}{2} = 0$$

Thus the load diagram obtained is justified.

(iii) BMD as shown in Fig. 4.3 (c).

**Example 4.3 :** A beam ABC is simply supported at A and B. Supports at A and B are 6 m apart and overhang BC = 1 m. The bending moment diagram for the beam is as shown in Fig. 4.4 (a). Construct SFD and load diagram.

**Data** : Given BMD as shown in Fig. 4.4 (a).

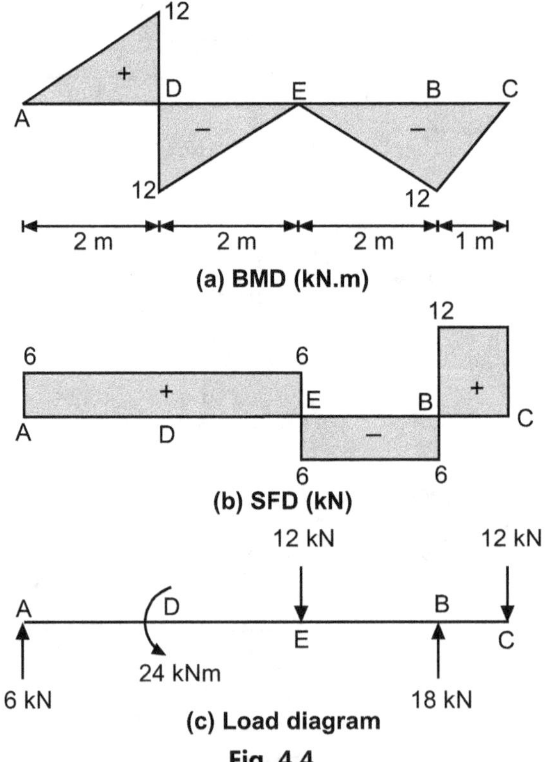


**Fig. 4.4**

**Required** : SFD and load diagram.

**Solution** : (i) SFD :

Zone AD : $\qquad$ SF $= \dfrac{dM}{dx} = \dfrac{12 - 0}{2} = 6$ kN

Zone DE : $\qquad$ SF $= \dfrac{dM}{dx} = \dfrac{0 - (-12)}{2} = 6$ kN

Zone EB : $\qquad$ SF $= \dfrac{dM}{dx} = \dfrac{-12 - 0}{2} = -6$ kN

Zone BC : $\qquad$ SF $= \dfrac{dM}{dx} = \dfrac{0 - (-12)}{1} = 12$ kN

SFD is as shown in Fig. 4.4 (b).

(ii) Load diagram :

Rise in SFD at A indicates upward point force of magnitude 6 kN at A.

Drop in SFD at E indicates downward point force of magnitude 12 kN at E.

Rise in SFD at B indicates upward point force of magnitude 18 kN at B.

Drop in SFD at C indicates downward point force of magnitude 12 kN at C.

Also, at D, drop in BM diagram = 24 kN.m and BM changes from sagging to hogging from left of D to right of D, hence there must be an anticlockwise couple of magnitude 24 kN.m at D.

The load diagram for the beam is as shown in Fig. 4.4 (c).

**Note :** Having obtained the load diagram, check the equilibrium of beam to justify the results.

**Example 4.4 :** A beam ABC is supported on roller at A and hinged at C. The bending moment diagram for the beam ABC is as shown in Fig. 4.5 (a). Construct SFD and load diagram.

**Data** : Given BMD as shown in Fig. 4.5 (a).

**Required** : SFD and load diagram.

**Solution** : (i) SFD :

Zone AB : $\qquad$ SF $= \dfrac{dM}{dx} = \dfrac{5 - (-10)}{1} = 15$ kN

Zone BC : $\qquad$ SF $= \dfrac{dM}{dx} = \dfrac{10 - (-5)}{1} = 15$ kN

SFD is as shown in Fig. 4.5 (b).

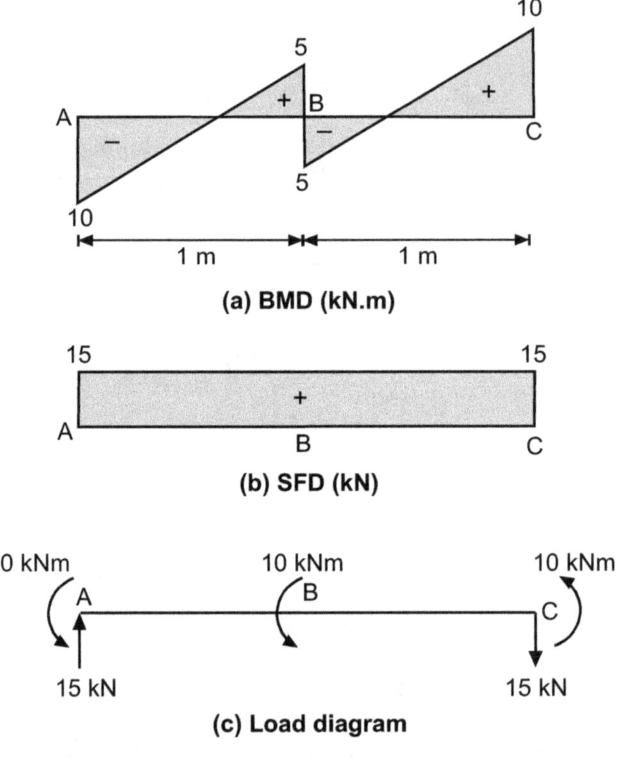



**(a) BMD (kN.m)**



**(b) SFD (kN)**



**(c) Load diagram**

**Fig. 4.5**

(ii)　　Load diagram :

In zone AC, constant SF = 15 kN.

∴　　Upward reaction at A = 15 kN and downward reaction at C = 15 kN.

At A, BM = – 10 kN.m which indicates anticlockwise couple of magnitude 10 kN.m at A.

At B, drop in BM diagram = 10 kN.m and BM changes from sagging to hogging from left　of B to right of B, hence there must be an anticlockwise couple of magnitude 10 kN.m at B.

At C, BM = 10 kN.m which indicates anticlockwise couple of magnitude 10 kN.m at C.

The load diagram for the beam is as shown in Fig. 4.5 (c).

**Note :** Having obtained the load diagram, check the equilibrium of beam to justify the results.

**Example 4.5 :** Fig. 4.6 shows SFD for a simply supported beam AB. Draw BMD for the beam.

**Data :** Given SFD as shown in Fig. 4.6.

**Required :** BMD.

**Solution :** (i) Load diagram : Rise in SFD at A indicates upward point force 12.5 kN at A.

Horizontal line between A to C shows no load between A to C.

Rise in SFD at B indicates upward point force of 7.5 kN at B.

**Zone CD :** Intensity of UDL $= \dfrac{dV}{dx} = \dfrac{-7.5 - 12.5}{4} = -5$ kN.m.

Load diagram is as shown in Fig. 4.6 (b).

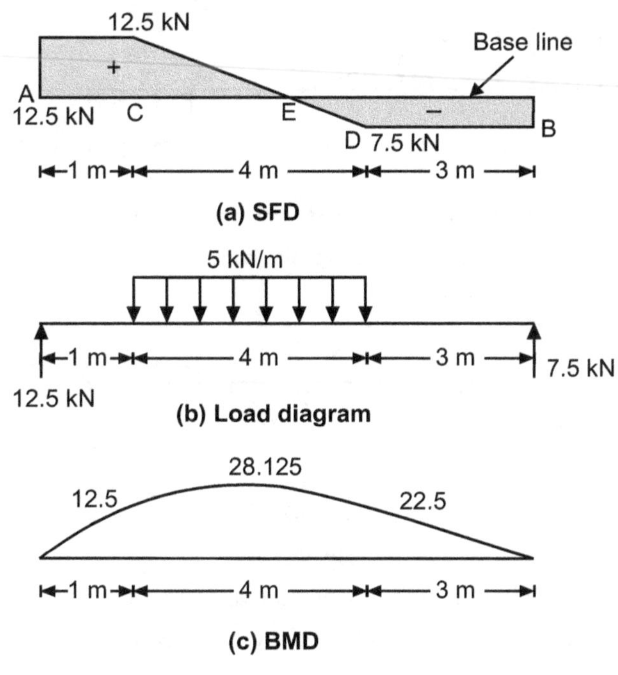


**Fig. 4.6**

(ii)     BMD : Bending moment, maximum at SF is zero.

$\therefore$           $x = \dfrac{12.5}{5} = 2.5$ m (from starting point of UDL)

BMD is as shown in Fig. 4.6 (c).

**Example 4.6 :** The SFD of a 4 m long beam is a second degree curve as shown in Fig. 4.7 (a), with the maximum −ve SF of 3 kN at the beam centre. Assuming that no couples act on the beam, draw the loading and BMD. Locate the position of maximum BM and their magnitudes. Points of contraflexure if any, too, should be located.                    **(Dec. 2003)**

**Data :** SFD as shown in Fig. 4.7 (a).

**Required :** Loading diagram and BMD.

**Solution :**

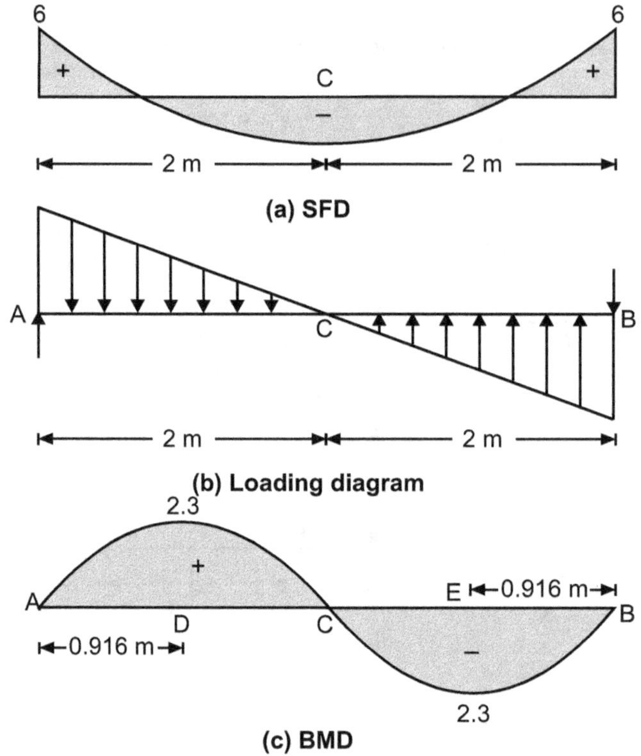



**Fig. 4.7**

(i)     **Loading diagram :** Rise in SFD at A indicates upward point force of 6 kN at A.
Drop in SFD at B indicates downward point force of 6 kN at B.

**Zone A to C :** Intensity of UVL $= (-3 - 6) = \dfrac{1}{2} w \times l$

$$-9 \ = \ \dfrac{1}{2} \times w \times 2$$

$\therefore \qquad\qquad\qquad w \ = \ -9 \text{ kN.m}$

**Zone C to B :** Intensity of UVL $= 6 - (-3) = \dfrac{1}{2} w \times l$

$\therefore \qquad\qquad\qquad w \ = \ 9 \text{ kN.m}$

To locate point of zero SF, consider a section at a distance x from A in zone AC.

$$SF_x \ = \ 6 - (\text{Area of trapezoidal load diagram}) = 0$$

$$\dfrac{9}{2} \ = \ \dfrac{y}{x} \qquad\qquad \therefore \ \ y = 4.5\, x$$

$$\therefore \quad 6 - \frac{(9 + 4.5\,x)}{2} \times x = 0$$

$$9x + 4.5x^2 - 12 = 0$$

$$\therefore \quad x^2 + 2x - 2.67 = 0$$

$$x = -2 \pm \frac{\sqrt{(2)^2 - 4 \times 1\,(-2.67)}}{2}$$

$$= 0.916 \text{ m from A and B.}$$

(As beam is symmetrical, so points of zero SF are at same distance from both ends.)

Loading diagram is as shown in Fig. 4.7 (b).

(ii)   BM calculations :

$$BM_A = BM_B = 0$$

BM at zero SF :   $BM_D = 6 \times 0.916 -$ Moment due to trapezoidal loading diagram

$$= 6 \times 0.916 - \frac{(9 + 4.5 \times 1.084)}{2} \times 0.916 \times \left(\frac{4.878 + 9 \times 2}{4.878 + 9}\right) \times \frac{0.916}{3}$$

$$= 2.3 \text{ kN.m}$$

$$BM_C = 6 \times 2 - \frac{1}{2} \times 9 \times 2 \times \frac{2}{3} \times 2$$

$$= 0$$

$$BM_E = -2.3 \text{ kN.m}$$

BMD is as shown in Fig. 4.7 (c).

---

## EXERCISE

1.   Draw the bending moment diagram and loading diagram from the given shear force diagram. (Refer Fig. 4.8)

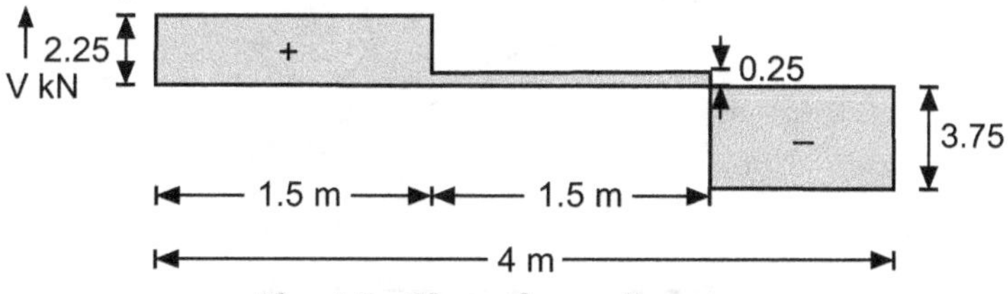


**Fig. 4.8 : Shear force diagram**

2.   The shear force diagram for a simple beam is shown in Fig. 4.9. Determine the loading on the beam and draw the bending moment diagram, assuming that no couples act as loads on the beam.

---

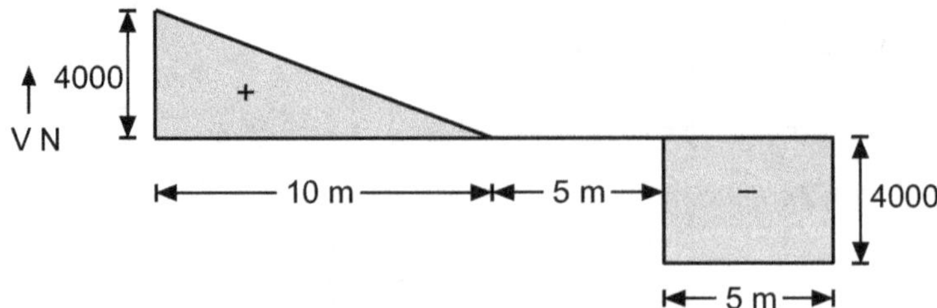

**Fig. 4.9 : Shear force diagram**

3.  The shear force diagram for a beam is as shown in Fig. 4.10. Assuming that no couples act as load on the beam, draw the bending moment diagram and also show the loading diagram.

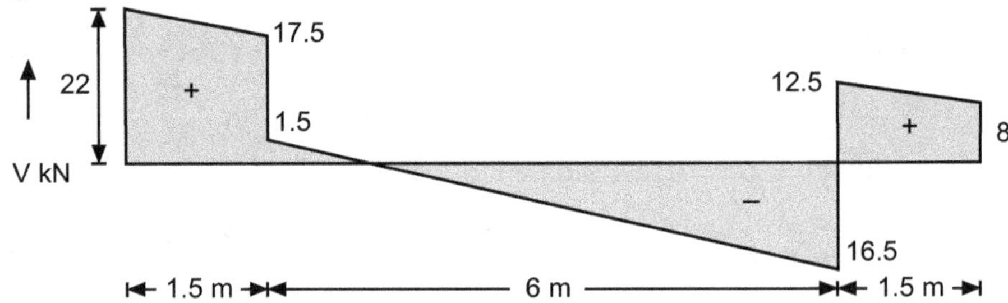

**Fig. 4.10 : Shear force diagram**

4.  Construct the loading and shear force diagram for the beam with an overhang as shown in Fig. 4.11.

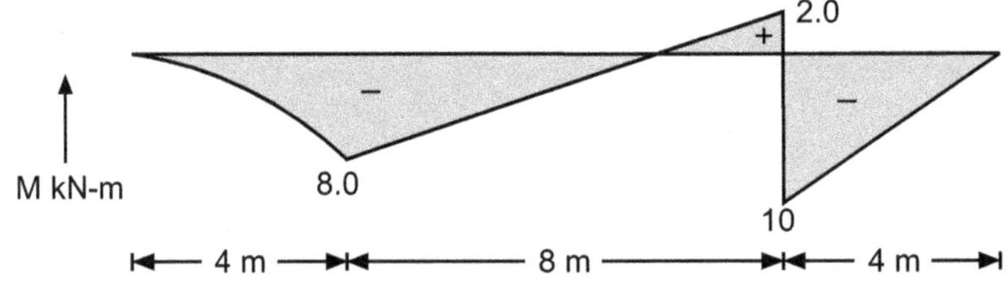

**Fig. 4.11 : Bending moment diagram**

5.  Construct the shear force diagram and loading diagram for the cantilever beam shown in Fig. 4.12.

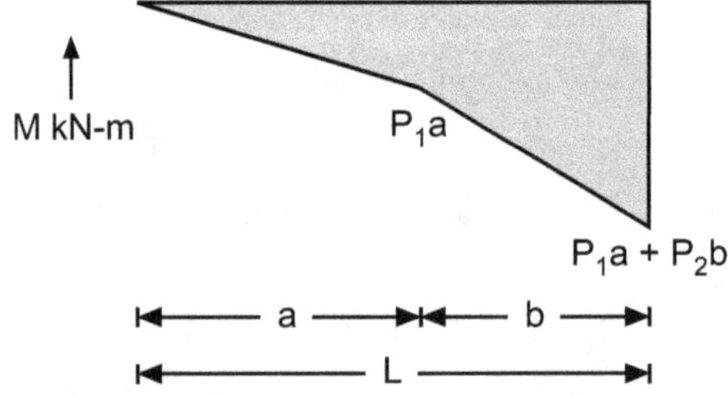

**Fig. 4.12 : Bending moment diagram**

6.  Construct the bending moment diagram and loading diagram for the simply supported beam as shown in Fig. 4.13.

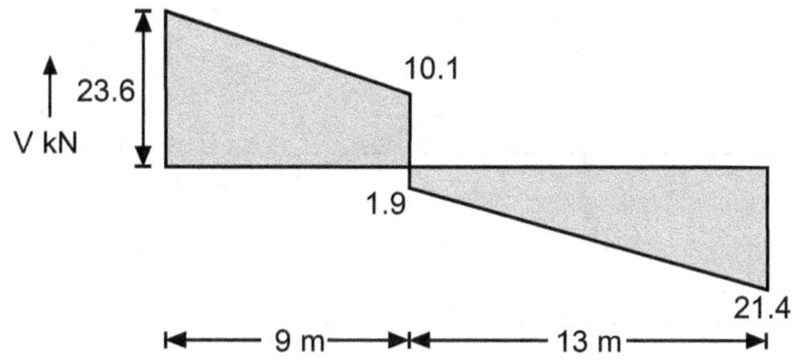

**Fig. 4.13 : Shear force diagram**

7. Draw the bending moment diagram and loading diagram from shear for the simply supported beam as shown in Fig. 4.14.

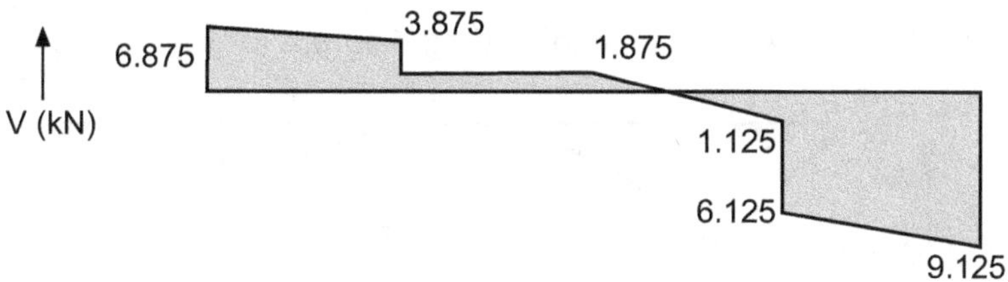

**Fig. 4.14 : Shear force diagram**

8. Draw bending moment diagram and loading diagram from shear force diagram for simply supported beam as shown in Fig. 4.15.

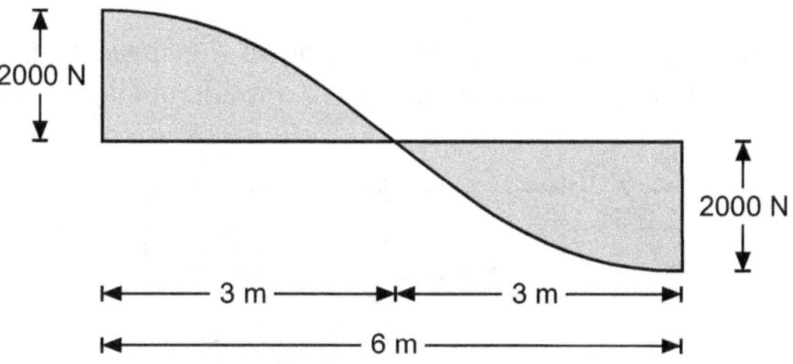

**Fig. 4.15 : Shear force diagram**

9. Construct bending moment diagram and loading diagram for the overhanging beam shown in Fig. 4.16.

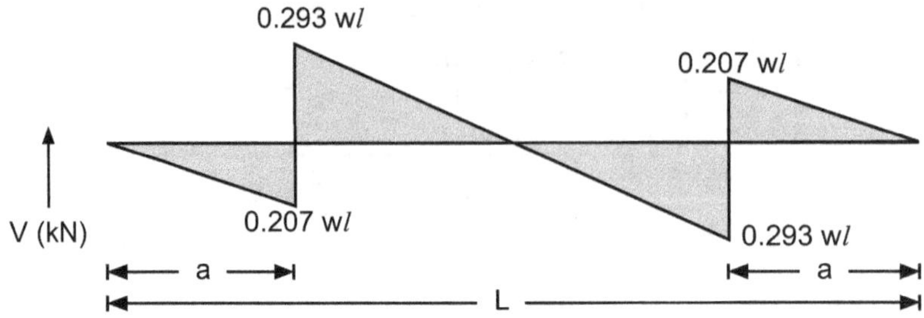


**Fig. 4.16 : Shear force diagram**

10. Construct the shear force diagram and loading diagram for the beam shown in Fig. 4.17.

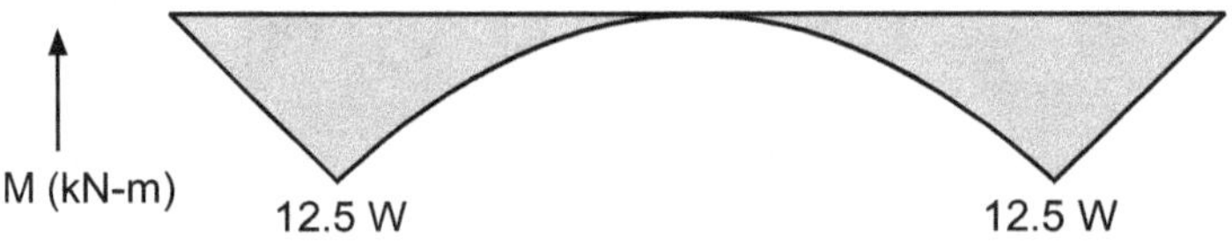


**Fig. 4.17 : Bending moment diagram**

# UNIVERSITY QUESTION PAPERS

## November 2015

**1** Draw moment and load diagrams corresponding to the shear diagram as shown in Fig. 2 below. Specify values at all change of load positions and at all points of zero shear.

**[6]**

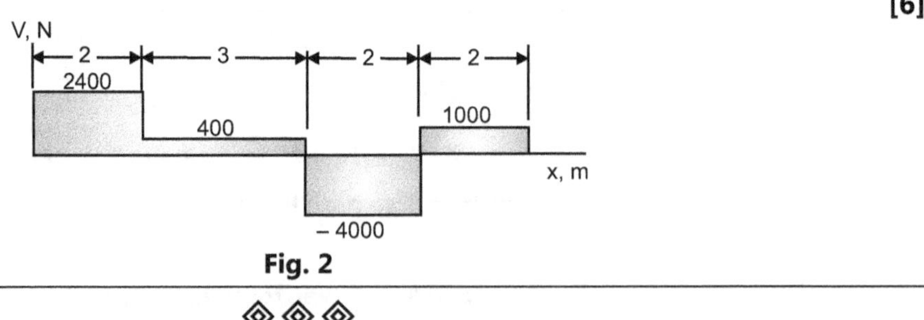


**Fig. 2**

◈ ◈ ◈

# Chapter 5

# BENDING STRESSES IN BEAMS

## 5.1 INTRODUCTION

The stresses caused by bending moment are called as *bending* or *flexural stresses*. In this chapter, we shall study the relation between bending moment and flexural stress.

In deriving these relations, following assumptions are made :

- A transverse section of the beam, which is plane before bending will remain plane after bending.

- The material of the beam is homogeneous, isotropic (same elastic properties in all the directions), and it obeys Hooke's law.

- The value of the Young's modulus is the same for the beam material in tension as well as compression.

- The beam is initially straight and of constant cross-section.

- The plane of loading must contain a principal axis of the beam cross-section and the loads must be perpendicular to the longitudinal axis of the beam.

## 5.2 DERIVATION OF FLEXURE FORMULA

Fig. 5.1 (a) shows a beam AB subjected to couple M at each end. It is easily seen that, between A and B, BM is constant and there is no shear force at all between A and B. This condition of the beam between A and B is called *pure bending or simple bending*.

Consider two adjacent sections ab and cd, separated by small distance dx as shown in Fig. 5.1 (a). Because of the bending, sections ab and cd rotate relative to each other by an amount $d\theta$ as shown in Fig. 5.1 (b) but remains straight and undistorted in accordance with the assumption (i) in article 5.1.

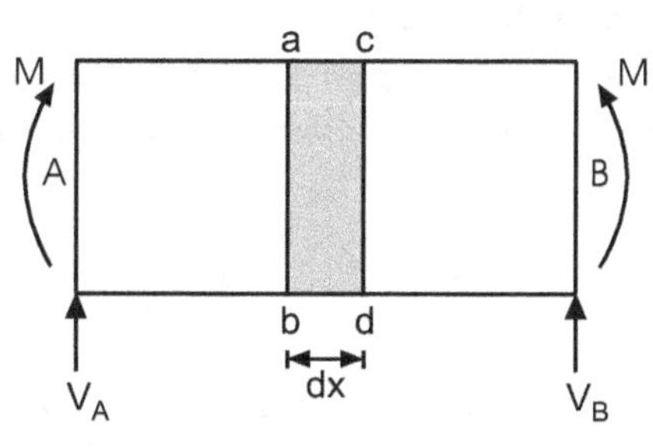


**(a) Beam**

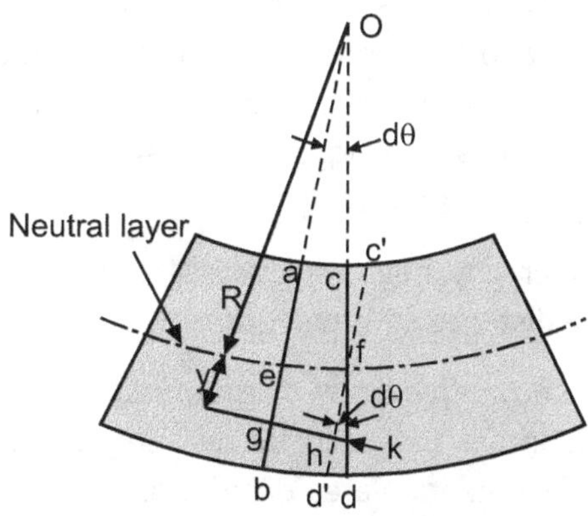


**(b) Bending deformation**

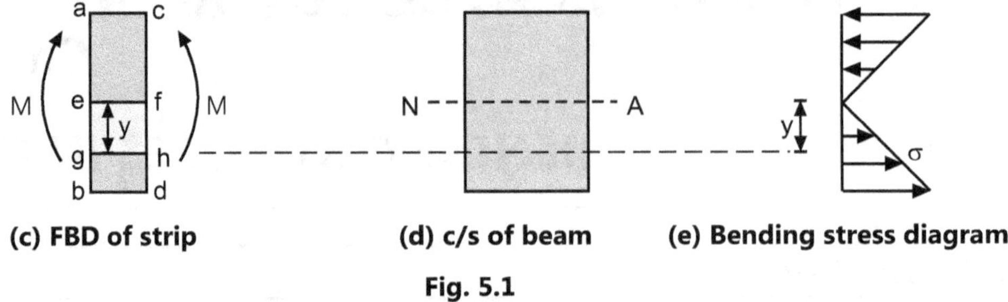

**(c) FBD of strip**          **(d) c/s of beam**          **(e) Bending stress diagram**

**Fig. 5.1**

Fibre ac at the top gets shortened while fibre bd at the bottom gets elongated. Somewhere between them is fibre ef whose length is unchanged. Drawing a line c'd' through f parallel to ab shows that fibre ac gets shortened by an amount cc' and is in compression while fibre bd gets elongated by an amount d'd and is in tension.

The plane containing fibres like ef is called as *neutral layer* because these fibres will remain unchanged in length and hence carry no stress. The line of intersection of neutral layer and cross-section of the beam is called as *neutral axis* abbreviated as NA.

Now consider deformation of typical fibre gh located at a distance 'y' from neutral layer. Its elongation hk is the arc of a circle of radius y subtended by an angle dθ and is given by

$$\delta L = hk = y\,d\theta$$

$$\therefore \quad \text{Longitudinal strain} = \epsilon = \frac{dL}{L} = \frac{y\,d\theta}{ef} = \frac{y\,d\theta}{R\,d\theta} = \frac{y}{R}$$

where, R = Radius of curvature of neutral layer.

Because the material is homogeneous and obeys Hook's law; stress (σ) in the fibre gh is given by

$$\sigma = E \cdot \epsilon = E \cdot \left(\frac{y}{R}\right) \qquad \qquad \dots (5.1)$$

where, E = Young's modulus of elasticity

Equation (5.1) indicates that; stress in any fibre varies directly with respect to its location y from neutral layer and therefore variation of bending stress over the cross-section of member is linear within elastic limit with zero stress at neutral layer and maximum at extreme fibres. Bending stress diagram is as shown in Fig. 5.1 (e). It should be noted that, bending stress diagram is irrespective of shape of cross-section.

Now consider any beam subjected to transverse loading as shown in Fig. 5.2 (a). Consider a section at a distance x from support A.

Fig. 5.2 (b) shows free body diagram of beam element AC. The external loads that act on one side of the section are balanced by resisting shear V and bending moment M. For this equilibrium, consider an elementary area dA of cross-section. The state of forces on this elementry area for the beam element is as shown in Fig. 5.2 (c).

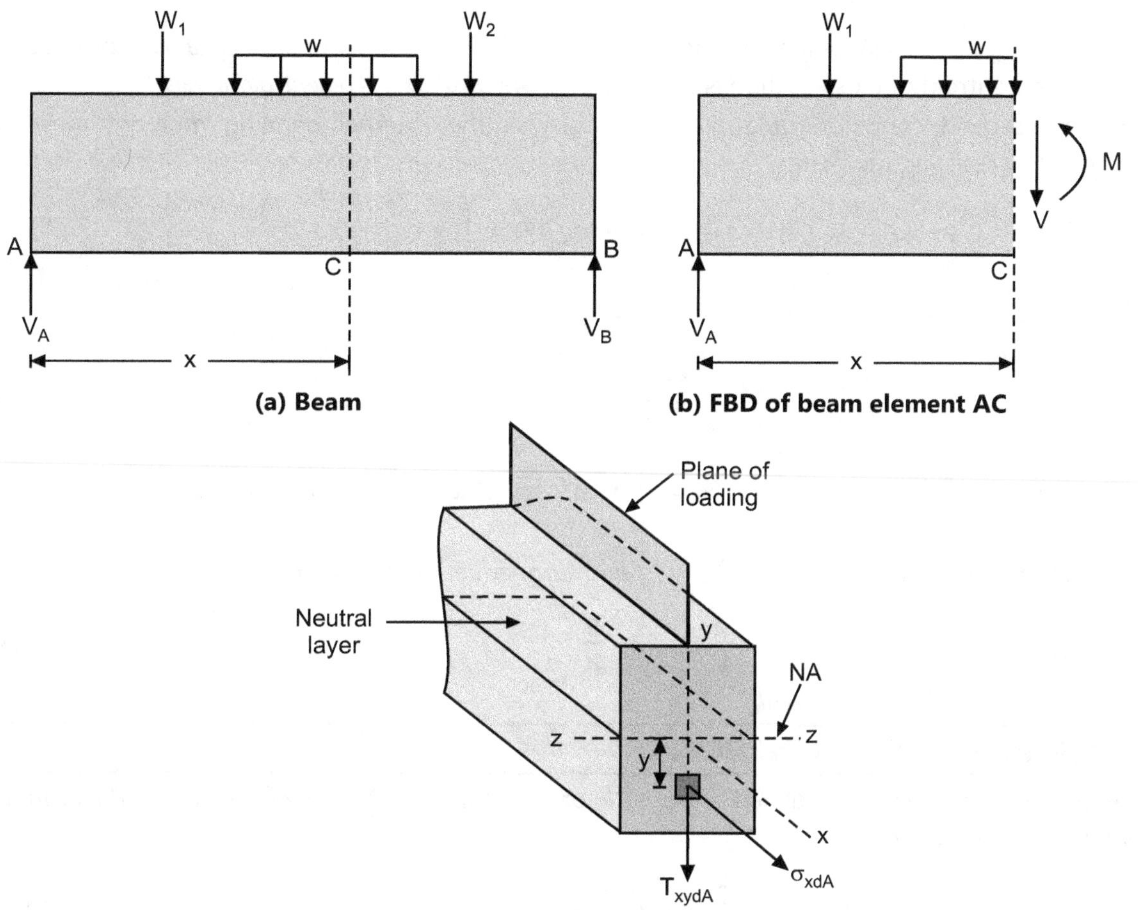



**(c) Forces on typical element of beam cross-section**

**Fig. 5.2**

As per assumption (v) of article (5.1), there is no external force normal to the cross-section, hence

$$\sum F_x = 0 \quad \therefore \qquad \int \sigma_x \cdot dA = 0 \qquad \qquad \ldots (5.2)$$

$$[\because \sigma_x = \sigma \text{ of equation (5.1)}]$$

Put equation (5.1) in equation (5.2)

$$\therefore \qquad \int \frac{E}{R}(y)\, dA = 0$$

$$\therefore \qquad \frac{E}{R} \int y\, dA = 0$$

$$\therefore \qquad \frac{E}{R} A\,\bar{y} = 0 \qquad \qquad \ldots (5.3)$$

where, $\dfrac{E}{R}$ is constant and $A\,\bar{y}$ = total moment of area.

To satisfy equation (5.3), only $\bar{y}$ in that equation can be zero which means distance from neutral axis to the centroid of cross-section is zero. *Thus, the neutral axis is a centroidal axis.*

Applying second condition of equilibrium; because the external bending moment must be balanced by resisting moment;

$$\sum M_z = 0 \text{ we get;} \qquad M = \int y \, (\sigma_x \, dA) = \int y \cdot \left(\frac{E}{R} \cdot y\right) dA$$

$$= \frac{E}{R} \int y^2 \, dA$$

$$M = \frac{E}{R} I \qquad \qquad \dots (5.4)$$

where; $\qquad\qquad\qquad I = \int y^2 \, dA = $ moment of inertia @ neutral axis.

From equation (5.1); $\qquad \dfrac{\sigma}{y} = \dfrac{E}{R}$ and from equation (5.4), $\dfrac{M}{I} = \dfrac{E}{R}$

$$\therefore \qquad\qquad \frac{M}{I} = \frac{\sigma}{y} = \frac{E}{R} \qquad\qquad \dots (5.5)$$

This is called *flexure formula*.

## 5.3 IMPORTANT DEFINITIONS

**Section Modulus (Z) :** It is defined as the *ratio of moment of inertia of cross-section to the distance of farthest fibre from NA.*

$$\text{Thus,} \qquad\qquad Z = \frac{I}{y_{max}} \qquad\qquad \dots (5.6)$$

Unit of section modulus is $mm^3$.

**Moment of Resistance (MR) :** It is defined as *capacity of section to resist bending moment and is given by product of section modulus and allowable bending stress.*

Let, $\sigma_{bc}$ and $\sigma_{bt}$ = Allowable stresses in bending compression and tension respectively.

If $\sigma_{bc} = \sigma_{bt}$ ; we shall indicate allowable stress in bending as '$\sigma_b$'.

Thus, in general, $\qquad MR = Z \cdot \sigma_b \qquad\qquad \dots (5.7)$

Following are the different possibilities, we may come across while finding MR of given section.

(i) Symmetric or unsymmetric section with $\sigma_{bc} = \sigma_{bt} = \sigma_b$ (say)

$$MR = Z \cdot \sigma_b$$

(ii) Symmetric section with $\sigma_{bc} \neq \sigma_{bt}$

$$MR_c = Z \cdot \sigma_{bc} \quad \text{and} \quad MR_t = Z \cdot \sigma_{bt}$$

where, $MR_c$ and $MR_t$ = Moment of resistance with reference to compression and tension side respectively.

Governing safe MR = Least of $MR_c$ and $MR_t$.

(iii) Unsymmetric section with $\sigma_{bc} \neq \sigma_{bt}$

$$MR_c = \frac{I}{y_{c,\,max}}\,\sigma_{bc} = Z_c \cdot \sigma_{bc} \text{ and}$$

$$MR_t = \frac{I}{y_{t,\,max}}\,\sigma_{bt} = Z_t \cdot \sigma_{bt}$$

where, $Z_c$ and $Z_t$ = Section modulus with respect to compression and tension side respectively.

Governing safe MR = Least of $MR_c$ and $MR_t$.

Following points must be noted while calculating geometric properties of cross-section.

- Moment of inertia of section shall be calculated about axis of bending (NA) and distance of extreme fibre is to be measured perpendicular to NA.
- Sagging BM produces compression above NA and tension below NA while hogging BM produces tension above NA and compression below NA, hence depending on the nature of bending moment, position of extreme compressive or tensile fibre shall be decided and accordingly distances $y_{c,\,max}$ or $y_{t,\,max}$ shall be written.

**Note :** In all the examples, x and y axes are considered as the axes of the cross-section since it is convenient for two-dimensional study. But actual reference axes are as shown in Fig. 5.2.

## SOLVED EXAMPLES

**Example 5.1 :** *Find moment of resistance of the beam section shown in Fig. 5.3 in following cases :*

(i)   *Permissible stress in bending, $\sigma_b$ = 100 MPa.*

(ii)  *Permissible stress in bending compression and tension is 80 MPa and 100 MPa respectively.*

**Data :** Cross-section as shown in Fig. 5.3.

Case (i) :    $\sigma_b$ = 100 MPa

Case (ii) :   $\sigma_{bc}$ = 80 MPa; $\sigma_{bt}$ = 100 MPa

**Required :** Moment of resistance.

**Concept :** (i) For symmetric sections with same allowable stress in bending compression and tension,

$$MR = Z_{xx} \times \sigma_b$$

(ii)  For symmetric sections with different allowable stresses in bending compression and tension,

$$MR = (Z_{xx}) \cdot (\text{least of } \sigma_{bc} \text{ and } \sigma_{bt})$$

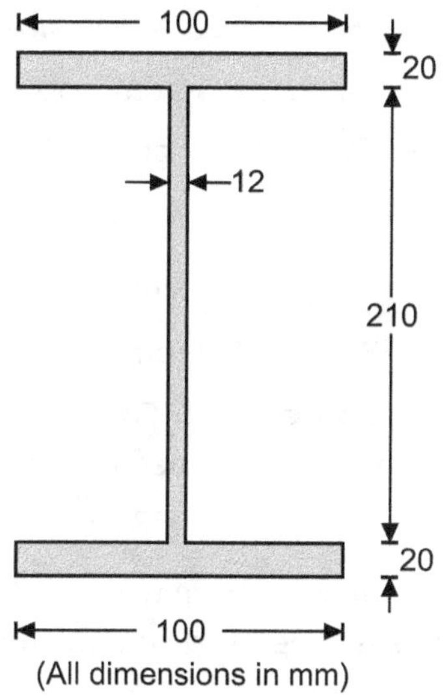


**Fig. 5.3 : C/s of beam**

**Solution :** (i) Geometric properties :

$$I_{xx} = \frac{100 \times 250^3}{12} - \frac{88 \times 210^3}{12} = 62.29 \times 10^6 \text{ mm}^4$$

$$y_{max} \;=\; \frac{250}{2} = 125 \text{ mm}$$

$$Z_{xx} \;=\; \frac{I_{xx}}{y_{max}} = \frac{62.29 \times 10^6}{125} = 498.35 \times 10^3 \text{ mm}^3$$

(ii)    Moment of resistance :

Case (i) : When          $\sigma_b$  =  100 MPa

$$MR \;=\; Z_{xx} \cdot \sigma_b$$

$$=\; 498.35 \times 10^3 \times 100 \times 10^{-6} \text{ kN.m}$$

$$=\; \textbf{49.835 kN.m}$$

Case (ii) : When          $\sigma_{bc}$  =  80 MPa and $\sigma_{bt}$ = 100 MPa

$$MR \;=\; Z_{xx} \times \sigma_{bc} \qquad\qquad (\because \sigma_{bc} < \sigma_{bt})$$

$$=\; 498.35 \times 10^3 \times 80 \times 10^{-6} \text{ kN.m}$$

$$=\; \textbf{39.868 kN.m}$$

**Example 5.2 :** *Find moment of resistance of the beam section shown in Fig. 5.4. @ xx axis in following cases :*

(i)    *Permissible stress in bending is 100 MPa.*

(ii)   *Permissible stress in bending compression and tension is 80 MPa and 100 MPa respectively. Assume sagging BM for cross-section.*

**Data :** Cross-section as shown in Fig. 5.4.

Case (i) :        $\sigma_b$  =  100 MPa

Case (ii) :       $\sigma_{bc}$  =  80 MPa ;

$\sigma_{bt}$  =  100 MPa

**Required :** Moment of resistance.

**Concept :** (i) For unsymmetric sections with same allowable stress in bending compression and tension;

$$MR \;=\; Z_{xx} \cdot \sigma_b$$

(ii) For unsymmetric sections with different allowable stresses in bending compression and tension;

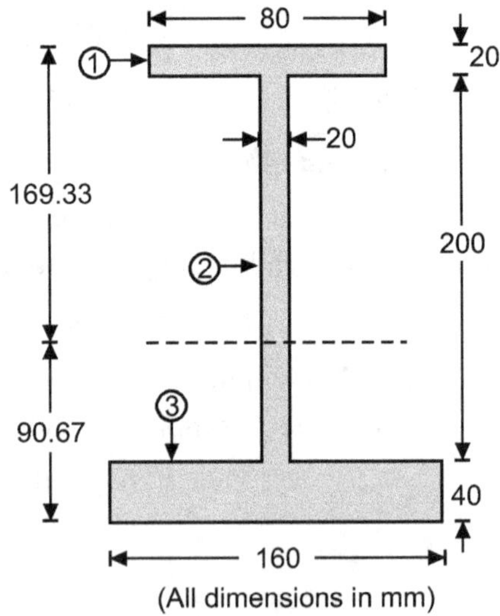


**Fig. 5.4 : C/s of beam**

$$(MR)_c \;=\; (Z_{xx})_c \,(\sigma_{bc})$$

$$(MR)_t \;=\; (Z_{xx})_t \,(\sigma_{bt})$$

Governing MR     =   Least of $(MR)_c$ and $(MR)_t$

**Solution :** (i) Geometric properties.

Considering bottom fibre as reference for CG.

$$a_1 = 80 \times 20 = 1600 \text{ mm}^2 ; \quad y_1 = 250 \text{ mm}$$

$$a_2 = 200 \times 20 = 4000 \text{ mm}^2; \quad y_2 = 140 \text{ mm}$$

$$a_3 = 160 \times 40 = 6400 \text{ mm}^2; \quad y_3 = 20 \text{ mm}$$

$$\bar{y} = \frac{1600 \times 250 + 4000 \times 140 + 6400 \times 20}{1600 + 4000 + 6400}$$

$$= 90.67 \text{ mm from bottom}$$

$$= 169.33 \text{ mm from top}$$

$$I_{xx} = I_{xx_1} + I_{xx_2} + I_{xx_3}$$

$$I_{xx_1} = \frac{80 \times 20^3}{12} + (1600)(250 - 90.67)^2 = 40.67 \times 10^6 \text{ mm}^4$$

$$I_{xx_2} = \frac{20 \times 200^3}{12} + (4000)(140 - 90.67)^2 = 23.06 \times 10^6 \text{ mm}^4$$

$$I_{xx_3} = \frac{160 \times 40^3}{12} + (6400)(90.67 - 20)^2 = 32.82 \times 10^6 \text{ mm}^4$$

$\therefore \qquad I_{xx} = (40.67 + 23.06 + 32.82) \times 10^6$

$$= \mathbf{96.55 \times 10^6 \ mm^4}$$

(ii)     Moment of resistance :

Case (i) : When $\sigma_b$ = 100 MPa

$$MR = Z_{xx} \cdot \sigma_b$$

$$= \frac{I_{xx}}{y_{max}} \cdot \sigma_b$$

$$= \frac{96.55 \times 10^6}{169.33} \times 100 \times 10^{-6} \text{ kN.m}$$

$$= 57.02 \text{ kN.m}$$

Case (ii) : When $\sigma_{bc}$ = 80 MPa and $\sigma_{bt}$ = 100 MPa.

As the cross-section is subjected to sagging bending moment,

$y_c$ = 169.33 mm and $y_t$ = 90.67 mm, as sagging BM causes compression above neutral axis and tension below neutral axis.

$\therefore \qquad (Z_{xx})_c = \dfrac{I_{xx}}{y_c} = \dfrac{96.55 \times 10^6}{169.33} = 570.19 \times 10^3 \text{ mm}^3$

$\qquad (Z_{xx})_t = \dfrac{I_{xx}}{y_t} = \dfrac{96.55 \times 10^6}{90.67} = 1064.85 \times 10^3 \text{ mm}^3$

$\qquad (MR)_c = (Z_{xx})_c \, (\sigma_{bc})$

$$= 570.19 \times 10^3 \times 80 \times 10^{-6} \text{ kN.m}$$

$$= 45.62 \text{ kN.m}$$
$$(MR)_t = (Z_{xx})_t \cdot (\sigma_{bt})$$
$$= 1064.85 \times 10^3 \times 100 \times 10^{-6} \text{ kN.m}$$
$$= 106.485 \text{ kN.m}$$

$\therefore$    Governing    MR  =  Least of $(MR)_c$ and $(MR)_t$

$$= \textbf{45.62 kN.m}$$

**Example 5.3 :** *A beam has the cross-sectional dimensions as shown in Fig. 5.5 (a). If the allowable stress in bending is 50 MPa, find the intensity of UDL the beam can carry over simply supported span of 4 m.*

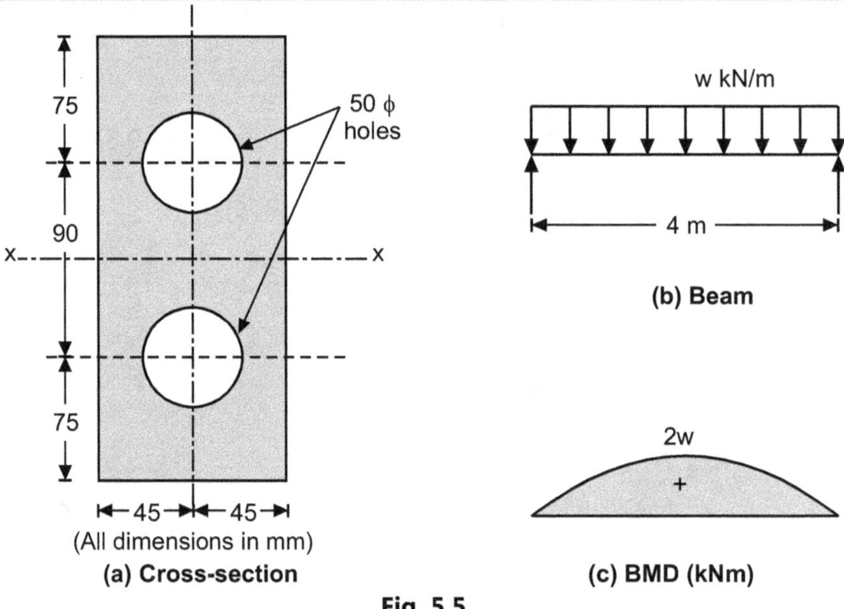


**(a) Cross-section**        **(b) Beam**

**(c) BMD (kNm)**

**Fig. 5.5**

**Data**         :  $\sigma_b$ = 50 MPa
**Required**    :  Safe UDL on beam.
**Concept**     :  Equate max BM and MR.
**Solution**    :  (i) Geometric properties :

$$I_{xx} = \frac{90 \times 240^3}{12} - 2\left[\frac{\pi}{64}(50)^4 + \frac{\pi}{4}(50)^2 \times 45^2\right]$$

$$= 95.11 \times 10^6 \text{ mm}^4$$

$$y_{max} = \frac{240}{2} = 120 \text{ mm}$$

$$Z_{xx} = \frac{I_{xx}}{y_{max}} = \frac{95.11 \times 10^6}{120} = 792.58 \times 10^3 \text{ mm}^3$$

(ii)    Analysis of beam.

Let,                    w  =  Intensity of UDL in kN/m.

$\therefore$    Maximum BM at centre $= \dfrac{wl^2}{8} = \dfrac{w\,(4)^2}{8}$

$$= 2w \text{ kN/m}$$

(iii)    Safe value of 'w'.

Equating maximum BM and MR,

$$2w = Z_{XX} \cdot \sigma_b$$
$$= 792.58 \times 10^3 \times 50 \times 10^{-6}$$
$$\therefore \qquad w = \mathbf{19.8\ kN/m}$$

**Example 5.4 :** *A groove in the form of a triangle is cut symmetrically from a beam section as shown in Fig. 5.6. If the stress in bending is not to exceed 25 MPa, find safe UDL which the beam can carry on a simply supported span of 4 m.*

**Data :** Cross-section of beam as shown in Fig 5.6;

$$\sigma_b = 25 \text{ MPa}$$

**Required :** Safe UDL the beam can carry over a simply supported span of 4 m.

**Concept :** Equate maximum BM to MR.

**Solution :** (i) Geometric properties :

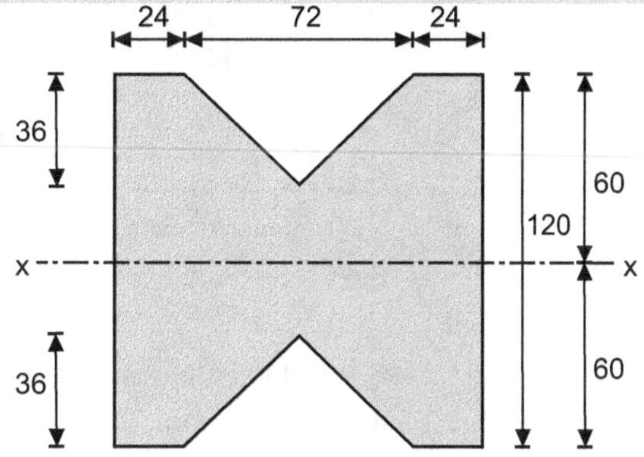


(All dimensions in mm)

**Fig. 5.6 : C/s of beam**

$$I_{XX} = \frac{120 \times 120^3}{12} - 2\left[\frac{72 \times 36^3}{36} + \frac{1}{2} \times 72 \times 36\left(60 - \frac{1}{3} \times 36\right)^2\right]$$
$$= 17.28 \times 10^6 - 6.16 \times 10^6$$
$$= 11.12 \times 10^6 \text{ mm}^4$$
$$y_{max} = 60 \text{ mm}$$
$$Z_{XX} = \frac{I_{XX}}{y_{max}} = \frac{11.12 \times 10^6}{60} = 185.36 \times 10^3 \text{ mm}^3$$

(ii)    Safe UDL for the beam.

$$MR = Z_{XX} \cdot \sigma_b = 185.36 \times 10^3 \times 25 \times 10^{-6} = 4.634 \text{ kN.m}$$
$$\text{Maximum BM} = \frac{wl^2}{8} = \frac{w\,(4)^2}{8} = 2\,w \text{ kN.m}$$

where            $w = $ UDL in kN/m

Equating MR and maximum BM,

$$4.634 = 2\,w$$
$$w = \mathbf{2.317\ kN/m\ (Inclusive\ of\ self\ weight)}$$

**Example 5.5 :** *The cross-section shown in Fig. 5.7 is used as a simply supported beam on a span of 4 m. If allowable stress in bending compression and tension is 100 MPa and 165 MPa respectively, find the safe UDL the beam can carry.*

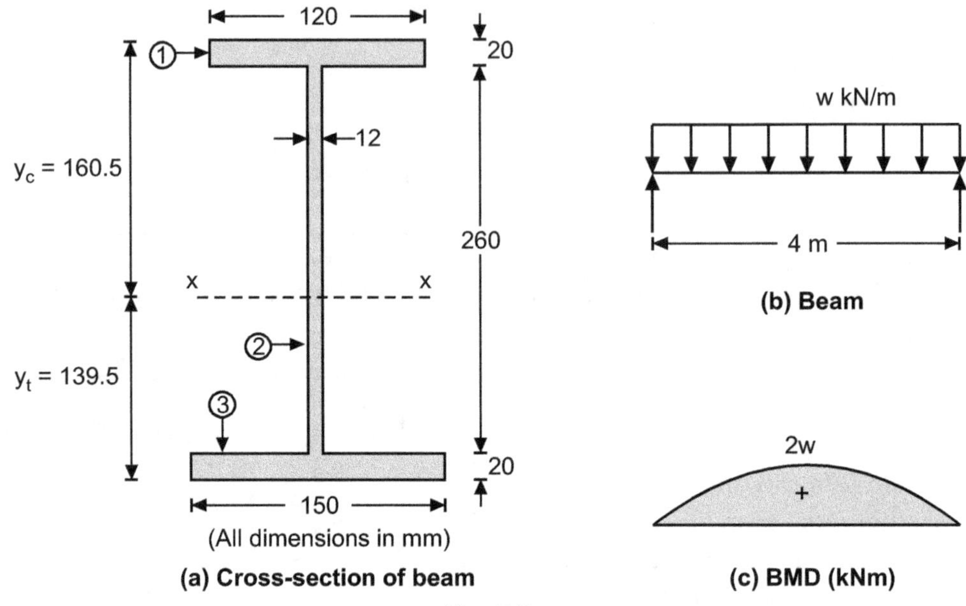



**(a) Cross-section of beam**       **(b) Beam**

                                      **(c) BMD (kNm)**

**Fig. 5.7**

**Data**      :    As shown in Fig. 5.7 (a) ; $\sigma_{bc}$ = 100 MPa ; $\sigma_{bt}$ = 165 MPa

**Required** :    Safe UDL on beam.

**Concept**  :    Find MR w.r.t. tension and compression side.

                   Governing MR = Least of the two; then equate maximum BM = MR.

**Solution**  :    (i) Geometric properties :

Taking bottommost fibre as reference for C.G.

$$a_1 \;=\; 120 \times 20 = 2400 \text{ mm}^2; \quad y_1 = 290 \text{ mm}$$

$$a_2 \;=\; 260 \times 10 = 2600 \text{ mm}^2; \quad y_2 = 150 \text{ mm}$$

$$a_3 \;=\; 150 \times 20 = 3000 \text{ mm}^2; \quad y_3 = 10 \text{ mm}$$

$$\bar{y} \;=\; \frac{2400 \times 290 + 2600 \times 150 + 3000 \times 10}{2400 + 2600 + 3000}$$

$$=\; 139.5 \text{ mm from bottom.}$$

$\therefore$            $y_c$ = 160.5 mm and $y_t$ = 139.5 mm             ($\because$ sagging BM)

$$I_{xx} \;=\; I_{xx_1} + I_{xx_2} + I_{xx_3}$$

$$I_{xx_1} \;=\; \frac{120 \times 20^3}{12} + 2400\,(290 - 139.5)^2 = 54.44 \times 10^6 \text{ mm}^4$$

$$I_{xx_2} \;=\; \frac{10 \times 260^3}{12} + 2600\,(150 - 139.5)^2 = 14.93 \times 10^6 \text{ mm}^4$$

$$I_{xx_3} \;=\; \frac{150 \times 20^3}{12} + 3000\,(139.5 - 10)^2 = 50.41 \times 10^6 \text{ mm}^4$$

$$I_{xx} \;=\; (54.44 + 14.93 + 50.41) \times 10^6 = 119.78 \times 10^6 \text{ mm}^4$$

$$(Z_{xx})_c = \frac{I_{xx}}{y_c} = \frac{119.78 \times 10^6}{160.5} = 746.29 \times 10^3 \text{ mm}^3$$

$$(Z_{xx})_t = \frac{I_{xx}}{y_t} = \frac{119.78 \times 10^6}{139.5} = 858.63 \times 10^3 \text{ mm}^3$$

(ii)    Moment of resistance (MR) :

$$(MR)_c = (Z_{xx})\, \sigma_{bc} = 746.29 \times 10^3 \times 100 \times 10^{-6} \text{ kN.m}$$
$$= 74.629 \text{ kN.m}$$
$$(MR)_t = (Z_{xx})\, \sigma_{bt} = 858.63 \times 10^3 \times 165 \times 10^{-6} \text{ kN.m}$$
$$= 141.67 \text{ kN.m}$$

Governing               MR $=$ least of $(MR)_c$ and $(MR)_t$
$$= 74.629 \text{ kN.m}$$

(iii)    Safe UDL on beam :

$$\text{Maximum BM} = \frac{wL^2}{8} = \frac{w\,(4)^2}{8} = 2\,w \text{ kN.m}$$

where;                $w = $ UDL in kN/m

Equating maximum BM and MR

$$2\,w = 74.629$$

$\therefore$                       $w = $ **37.32 kN/m (Inclusive of self weight)**

---

**Example 5.6 :** *A cast iron test beam 30 mm square in cross-section, 500 mm long is simply supported at ends. It fails at central point load at 4.32 kN. What load at free end will cause the failure of cantilever beam of 1 m span made of same material 30 mm × 60 mm in cross-section ?*

**Data**      :    For simply supported beam : cross-section = 30 mm × 30 mm ;
                   span = L = 0.5 m ; failure load = 4.32 kN applied at centre of span.
                   For cantilever beam : cross-section = 30 mm × 60 mm ; span = 1 m

**Required :**   Failure load for cantilever beam (P) : applied at free end.

**Concept :**   From the case of simply supported beam, obtain permissible stress in bending and then for cantilever beam equating Maximum BM to MR, obtain the failure load (P).

**Solution :**   (i) Case of simply supported beam :

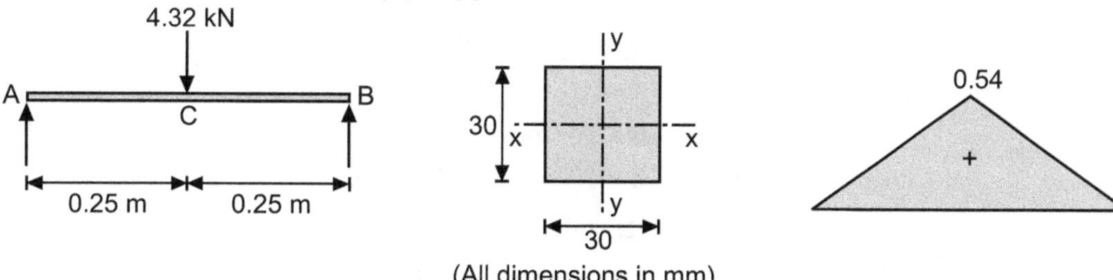


       **(a) Beam**              **(b) C/s of beam**           **(c) BMD (kN.m)**

**Fig. 5.8**

$$I_{xx} = \frac{30 \times 30^3}{12} = 67.5 \times 10^3 \ \text{mm}^4$$

$$y_{max} = \frac{30}{2} = 15 \ \text{mm}$$

$$Z_{xx} = \frac{I_{xx}}{y_{max}} = \frac{67.5 \times 10^3}{15} = 4.5 \times 10^3 \ \text{mm}^3$$

Let; $\quad \sigma_b$ = Permissible stress in bending for cast iron

$\therefore \quad MR = Z_{xx} \cdot \sigma_b$

$$= 4.5 \times 10^3 \times \sigma_b \ \text{Nmm}$$

Maximum $\quad BM = \dfrac{4.32 \times 0.5}{4} = 0.54 \ \text{kN.m}$

Equating maximum BM and MR

$$0.54 = 4.5 \times 10^3 \times \sigma_b \times 10^{-6}$$

$$\sigma_b = \textbf{120 MPa}$$

(ii)　Case of cantilever beam :

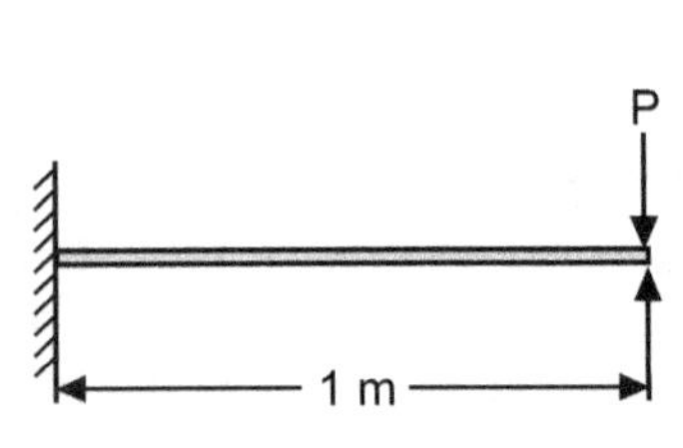

**(a) Beam**

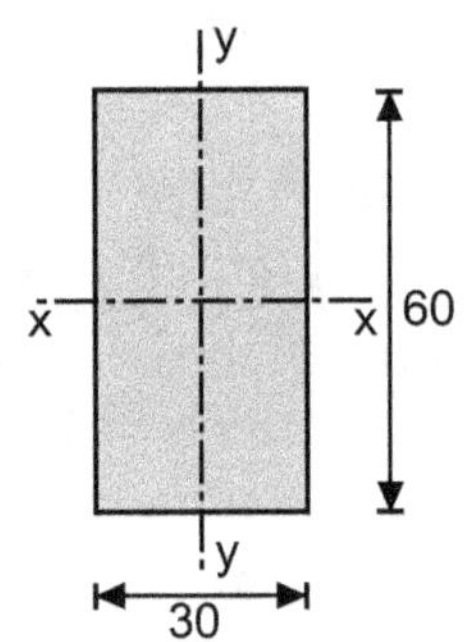

**(b) C/s of beam**

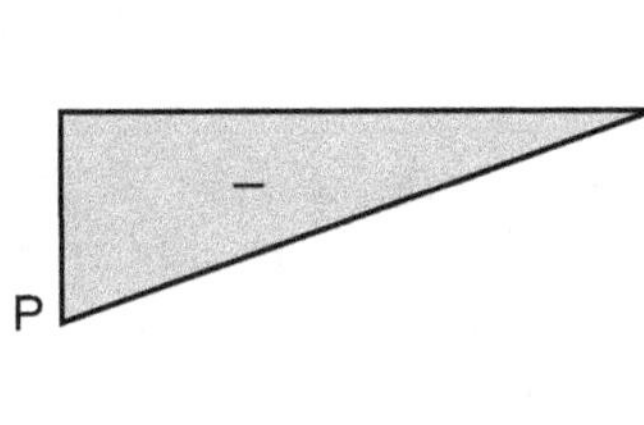

**(c) BMD (kN.m)**

**Fig. 5.9**

$$I_{xx} = \frac{30 \times 60^3}{12} = 540 \times 10^3 \ \text{mm}^4$$

$$y_{max} = \frac{60}{2} = 30 \ \text{mm}$$

$$Z_{xx} = \frac{I_{xx}}{y_{max}} = \frac{540 \times 10^3}{30}$$

$$= 18 \times 10^3 \ \text{mm}^3$$

$$MR = Z_{xx} \cdot \sigma_b = 18 \times 10^3 \times 120 \times 10^{-6} \ \text{kN.m}$$

$$= 2.16 \ \text{kN.m}$$

Maximum BM = 'P' kN.m ; where P = failure load in kN

Equating maximum BM and MR

$$P = \textbf{2.16 kN}$$

**Example 5.7 :** *A water main having 600 mm external diameter and 10 mm thickness is made of mild steel plate and is running full. If the allowable bending stress is 60 MPa, find the maximum span for simply supported condition that the water main can be used. Assume density of steel as 78.5 kN/m³ and that of water as 9.81 kN/m³.*

**Data**        :   $D$ = 600 mm ; $d$ = 580 mm ; $\sigma_b$ = 60 MPa ; Density of steel and water

  = 78.5 kN/m³ and 9.81 kN/m³ respectively.

**Required** :   Simply supported span (L).

**Concept**  :   From cross-section dimensions and permissible stress, find moment of resistance (MR) and obtain maximum BM in terms of span. Equating MR and max. BM, span can be found out.

**Solution**   :   (i) Geometric properties :

$$I_{xx} = \frac{\pi}{64}(D^4 - d^4)$$

$$= \frac{\pi}{64}(600^4 - 580^4)$$

$$= 806.75 \times 10^6 \text{ mm}^4$$

$$y_{max} = \frac{600}{2} = 300 \text{ mm}$$

$$Z_{xx} = \frac{I_{xx}}{y_{max}} = \frac{806.75 \times 10^6}{300}$$

$$= 2.69 \times 10^6 \text{ mm}^3$$

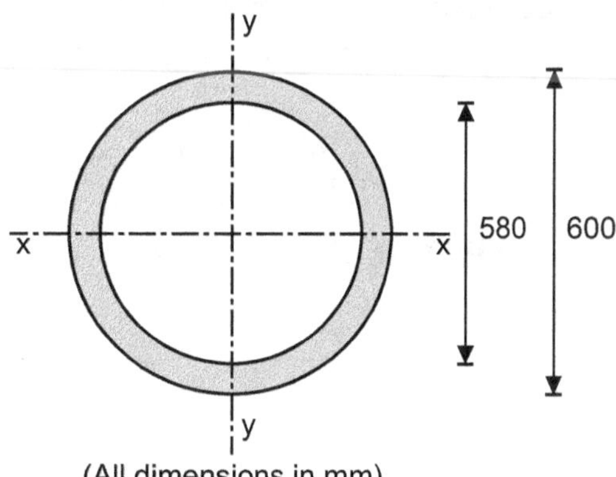


(All dimensions in mm)

**Fig. 5.10 : C/s of water main**

(ii)    Analysis :

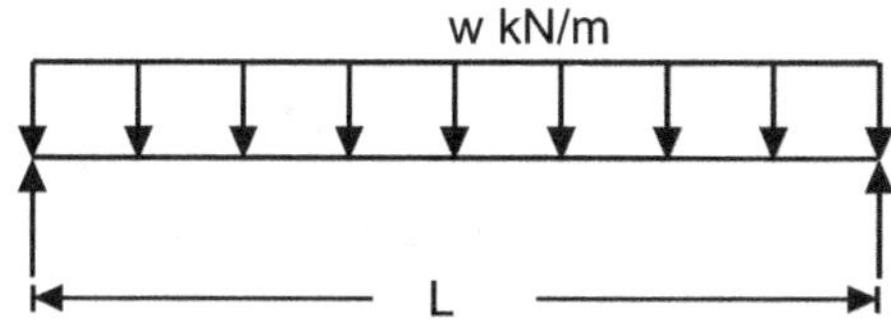


**Fig. 5.11**

Let,                          $L$  =  span in metres

  $w$  =  Total UDL due to self weight of pipe and water.

$$= \left(\frac{\pi}{4}(600^2 - 580^2) \times 78.5 + \frac{\pi}{4}(580)^2 \times 9.81\right) \times 10^{-6}$$

$$= 4.05 \text{ kN/m}$$

∴          Maximum BM  $= \dfrac{wL^2}{8} = 4.05 \times \dfrac{L^2}{8} = (0.50625)\, L^2 \text{ kN.m}$

(iii)    Moment of Resistance (MR) :

$$MR = Z_{xx} \cdot \sigma_b$$

$$= 2.69 \times 10^6 \times 60 \times 10^{-6} \text{ kN.m}$$

$$= 161.4 \text{ kN.m}$$

(iv)    Span of water main (L) :

Equating maximum BM and MR

$$(0.50625)\ L^2\ =\ 161.4$$

$$\therefore \qquad\qquad L\ =\ \mathbf{17.85\ m}$$

**Example 5.8 :** *Fig. 5.12 shows the cross-section of a beam. What is the ratio of moment of resistance about yy-axis to that about xx-axis, if permissible bending stress is same in either directions ?*

**Data**       :   As shown in Fig. 5.12.

**Required**  :   $\dfrac{(MR)_y}{(MR)_x}$

**Concept**  :   Since permissible.
Stress in either direction
is same.

$$\dfrac{(MR)_y}{(MR)_x} = \dfrac{Z_{yy}}{Z_{xx}}$$

**Solution**  :   (i) To find $Z_{yy}$ :

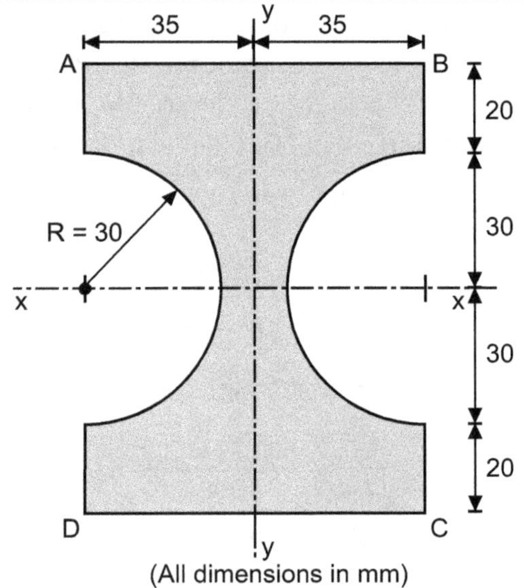


**Fig. 5.12 : C/s of beam**

$I_{yy} = I_{yy}$ of rectangle ABCD $-$ 2 ($I_{yy}$ of semicircle).

$I_{yy}$ of rectangle ABCD $= \dfrac{100 \times 70^3}{12} = 2.86 \times 10^6\ mm^4.$

$I_{yy}$ of semicircle about vertical axis passing through its C.G.

$$
\begin{aligned}
I_{GG} &= \frac{\pi}{8}\, r^4 - \frac{\pi r^2}{2}\left(\frac{4r}{3\pi}\right)^2 \\[2mm]
&= \frac{\pi}{8}\,(30)^{\,4} - \frac{\pi\,(30)^2}{2}\left(\frac{4 \times 30}{3\pi}\right)^2 \\[2mm]
I_{GG} &= 88.9 \times 10^3\ mm^4 \\[2mm]
I_{yy}\ \text{of semicircle} &= I_{GG} + Ak^2 \\[2mm]
&= I_{GG} + \frac{\pi r^2}{2}\left(35 - \frac{4r}{3\pi}\right)^2 \\[2mm]
&= 88.9 \times 10^3 + \frac{\pi \times 30^2}{2}\left(35 - \frac{4 \times 30}{3\pi}\right)^2 \\[2mm]
&= 789.89 \times 10^3\ mm^4
\end{aligned}
$$

$\therefore\ I_{yy}$ of cross-section of beam $=\ 2.86 \times 10^6 - 2\ (789.89 \times 10^3)$

$$
\begin{aligned}
&=\ 1.28 \times 10^6\ mm^4 \\[2mm]
y_{max} &=\ 35\ mm
\end{aligned}
$$

$\therefore$      $Z_{yy} = \dfrac{I_{yy}}{y_{max}} = \dfrac{1.28 \times 10^6}{35} = \mathbf{36.58 \times 10^3\ mm^3}$

(ii)    To find $Z_{xx}$ :     $I_{xx}$ = $I_{xx}$ of rectangle ABCD − $I_{xx}$ of circle with r = 30 mm

$$= 70 \times \dfrac{100^3}{12} - \dfrac{\pi}{4}(30)^4 = 5.197 \times 10^6\ mm^4$$

$$y_{max} = 50\ mm$$

$$Z_{xx} = \dfrac{I_{xx}}{y_{max}} = \dfrac{5.197 \times 10^6}{50} = \mathbf{103.94 \times 10^3\ mm^3}$$

(iii)    $\dfrac{MR\ @\ yy\text{-}axis}{MR\ @\ xx\text{-}axis} = \dfrac{Z_{yy}}{Z_{xx}} = \dfrac{36.58 \times 10^3}{103.94 \times 10^3} = \mathbf{0.35}$

---

**Example 5.9 :** *A simply supported beam has square cross-section throughout its length.*

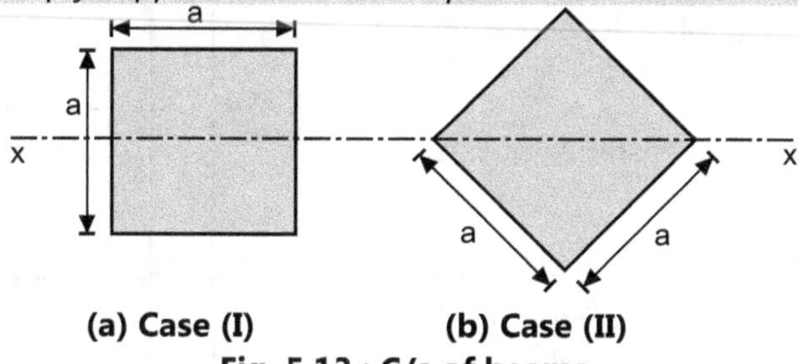

**(a) Case (I)**         **(b) Case (II)**

**Fig. 5.13 : C/s of beams**

The side of square is 'a'. The section carries BM = M. Calculate maximum bending stresses developed in beam when;

(i)    side of square is kept vertical and

(ii)    diagonal of square is kept horizontal; as shown in Fig. 5.13.

**Data**      :    As shown in Fig. 5.13.

**Required** :    Bending stresses.

**Concept** :          $\sigma_b = \dfrac{M}{Z_{xx}}$

**Solution** :    (i) Analysis of case I :

$$I_{xx} = \dfrac{a^4}{12} \ ; \ y_{max} = \dfrac{a}{2}$$

$\therefore$      $Z_{xx} = \dfrac{I_{xx}}{y_{max}} = \dfrac{a^4}{12} \times \dfrac{2}{a} = \dfrac{a^3}{6}$

$\therefore$    Bending stresses, $\sigma_b = \pm \dfrac{M}{Z_{xx}} = \pm \dfrac{M}{a^3/6} = \pm \dfrac{\mathbf{6\ M}}{\mathbf{a^3}}$

(ii) Analysis of case II :    $I_{xx} = 2\left(\dfrac{b\,h^3}{12}\right) = \dfrac{b\,h^3}{6} = \dfrac{(\sqrt{2}\,a)\,(a/\sqrt{2})^3}{6} = \dfrac{a^4}{12}$

$$y_{max} = \dfrac{a}{\sqrt{2}}$$

$\therefore$      $Z_{xx} = \dfrac{I_{xx}}{y_{max}} = \dfrac{a^4}{12} \times \dfrac{\sqrt{2}}{a} = \dfrac{a^3}{6\sqrt{2}}$

---

$$\text{Bending stresses} = \sigma_b = \pm\frac{M}{Z_{xx}} = \pm\frac{M}{a^3/6\sqrt{2}} = \pm\frac{(6\sqrt{2})\,M}{a^3}$$

**Note :** Bending stresses for case II are higher than that of case I.

**Example 5.10 :** *A hollow rectangular beam is formed by joining four wooden pieces together as shown in Fig. 5.14. The Young's modulus of elasticity is same for all pieces. However, the permissible stress in bending is 10 MPa and 6 MPa for horizontal and vertical pieces respectively. Determine the moment of resistance of beam section.*

**Data :** Cross-section of beam as shown in Fig. 5.14.

$\sigma_b$ = 10 MPa and 6 MPa for horizontal and vertical pieces.

**Required :** Moment of resistance of beam section.

**Concept :** Moment of resistance will be governed by allowable stress in bending for horizontal pieces or for vertical pieces, whichever gives the least value.

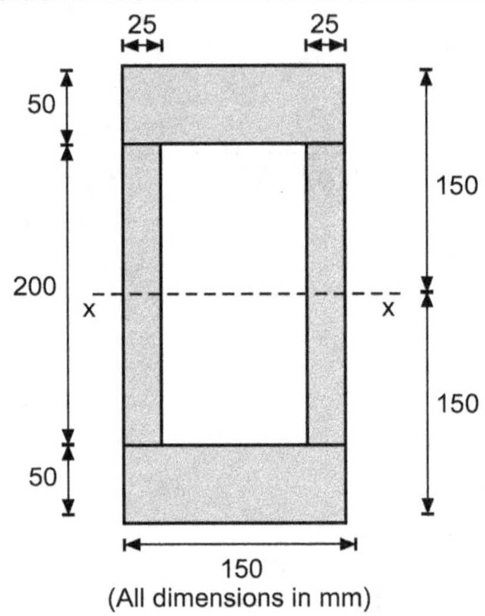


**Fig. 5.14 : C/s of beam**

**Solution :** (i) Geometric properties of cross-section :

$$I_{xx} = \frac{150 \times 300^3}{12} - \frac{100 \times 200^3}{12} = \mathbf{270.83 \times 10^6 \ mm^4}$$

(ii) MR based on allowable stress of horizontal pieces :

$$(MR)_1 = (I_{xx})\left(\frac{\sigma_b}{y_{max}}\right) \text{ for horizontal pieces.}$$

$$= 270.83 \times 10^6 \left(\frac{10}{150}\right) \times 10^{-6} \text{ kN.m}$$

$$= \mathbf{18.05 \ kN.m} \qquad \ldots (i)$$

(iii) MR based on allowable stress of vertical pieces.

$$(MR)_2 = (I_{xx})\left(\frac{\sigma_b}{y_{max}}\right) \text{ for vertical pieces.}$$

$$= 270.83 \times 10^6 \times \left(\frac{6}{100}\right) \times 10^{-6} \text{ kN.m}$$

$$= \mathbf{16.25 \ kN.m} \qquad \ldots (ii)$$

$$\text{Governing MR} = \text{Least of } (MR)_1 \text{ and } (MR)_2$$

$$= 16.25 \text{ kN.m}$$

**Example 5.11 :** *For the beam shown in Fig. 5.15, find bending stresses at cross-sections C and B.*

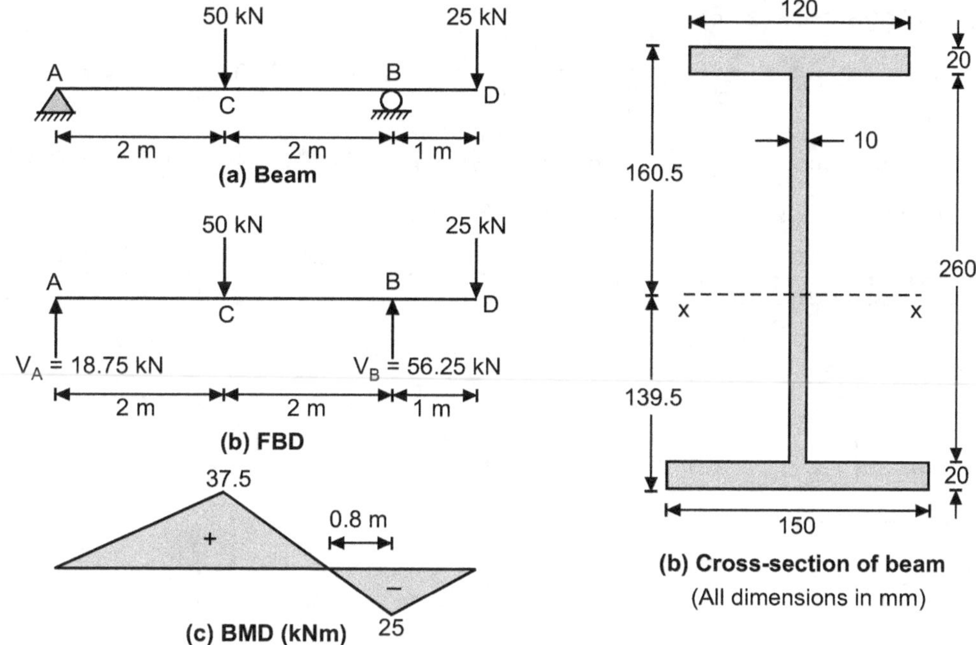


**Fig. 5.15**

**Data**       :   As shown in Fig. 5.15 (a) and 5.15 (b).

**Required**  :   Bending stresses at 'C' and 'B'.

**Concept**   :   $\sigma_b = \dfrac{M}{I} \times y$; Note the nature of BM at cross-sections C and B.

**Solution**  :   (i) Geometric properties :

    Distance of CG   =   139.5 mm from bottom.

$$I_{XX} = \mathbf{119.78 \times 10^6\ mm^4}$$

(ii) Analysis of beam :

For reactions ;

  $\Sigma M_A = 0$ ;  $V_B \times 4 - 50 \times 2 - 25 \times 5 = 0$

  $\therefore$      $V_B = 56.25$ kN $(\uparrow)$

  $\Sigma F_y = 0$ ;  $V_A + V_B - 50 - 25 = 0$

  $\therefore$      $V_A = 18.75$ kN $(\uparrow)$

  $\Sigma F_x = 0$ ;  $H_A = 0$

      $BM_C = 18.75 \times 2 = 37.5$ kN.m (Sagging)

      $BM_B = -25 \times 1 = -25$ kN.m $= 25$ kN.m (Hogging)

  BMD is shown in Fig. 5.15 (d).

(iii) Bending stresses at 'C' :

$$(\sigma_b)_{top} = \frac{BM_C}{I_{XX}}\,(y)\,top = \frac{37.5 \times 10^6}{119.78 \times 10^6} \times 160.5 = 50.24 \text{ MPa (Compressive)}$$

$$(\sigma_b)\text{bottom} = \frac{BM_C}{I_{xx}}(y)\text{ bottom} = \frac{37.5 \times 10^6}{119.78 \times 10^6} \times 139.5 = 43.67 \text{ MPa (Tensile)}$$

(iv) Bending stresses at 'B' :

$$(\sigma_b)\text{top} = \frac{BM_B}{I_{xx}} \cdot (y)\text{top} = \frac{25 \times 10^6}{119.78 \times 10^6} \times 160.5 = 33.49 \text{ MPa (Tensile)}$$

$$(\sigma_b)\text{bottom} = \frac{BM_B}{I_{xx}}(y)\text{ bottom} = \frac{25 \times 10^6}{119.78 \times 10^6} \times 139.5 = 29.11 \text{ MPa (Compressive)}$$

(v)   Bending stress diagram is as shown in Fig. 5.16.

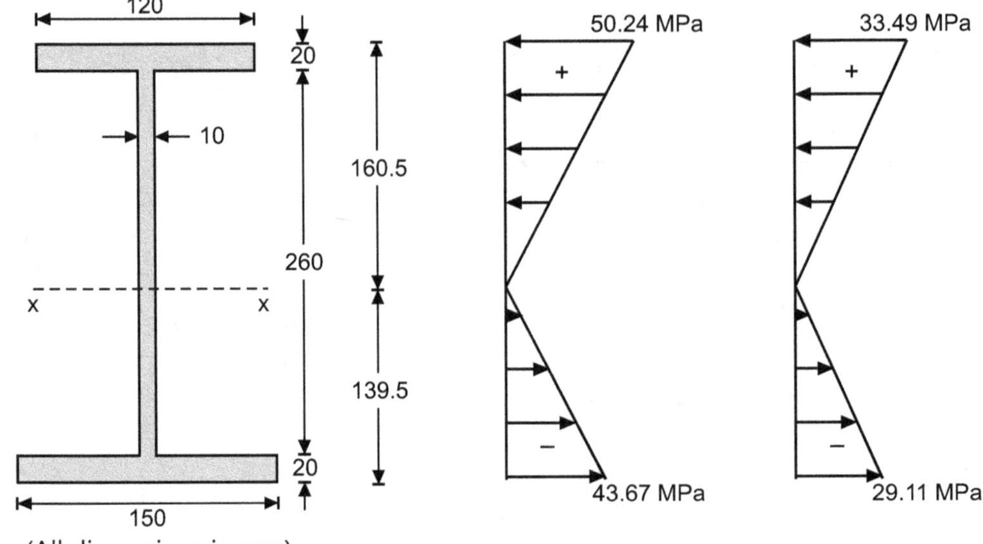

(All dimensions in mm)

**(a) Cross-section of beam  (b) Bending stresses at 'C'  (c) Bending stresses at 'B'**

**Fig. 5.16**

**Example 5.12 :** *A beam of constant section and symmetrical about the neutral axis is simply supported over a span of 8 m. The beam has to carry a concentrated load of 40 kN at midspan and a UDL of 15 kN/m on the entire span. If the central deflection is limited to $\left[\dfrac{1}{480}\right]^{th}$ of span and maximum fibre stress due to bending is not to exceed 118 MPa, determine the required depth of beam and its moment of inertia. Assume E = 200 GPa.*

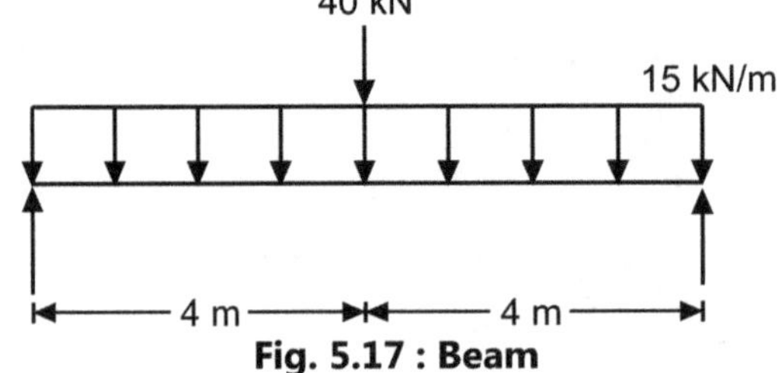

**Fig. 5.17 : Beam**

**Data**      :   $\Delta_{max} = \left(\dfrac{1}{480}\right)^{th}$ span;

$\sigma_b$ = 118 MPa; E = 200 GPa. Loading as shown in Fig. 5.17.

**Required** : Depth of beam and M.I.

**Concept** : Find the value of moment of inertia knowing central deflection and then find depth of beam from bending stress criteria.

**Solution** : (i) M.I. from deflection criteria.

Maximum deflection for given beam will occur at centre. By principle of superposition,

$$\Delta_{max} = \frac{5}{384}\frac{wL^4}{EI} + \frac{PL^3}{48\,EI} = \frac{5}{384}\cdot\frac{15\times 8000^4}{EI} + \frac{40\times 10^3 \times 8000^3}{48\,EI}$$

$$\Delta_{max} = \frac{1.226\times 10^{15}}{EI}\ \text{mm};$$

where EI = flexural rigidity in Nmm$^2$

$$\text{Allowable deflection} = \left(\frac{1}{480}\right)^{th}\text{span}$$

$$= \frac{8000}{480}$$

$$= 16.67\ \text{mm}$$

Equating $\Delta_{max}$ and allowable deflection,

$$\frac{1.226\times 10^{15}}{EI} = 16.67$$

$$EI = 7.356\times 10^{13}\ \text{Nmm}^2$$

We have; $\quad E = 200$ GPa

$$\therefore \quad I = \frac{7.356\times 10^{13}}{200\times 10^3}$$

$$= 367.8\times 10^6\ \text{mm}^4$$

(ii) Depth of beam from bending stress criteria.

$$\text{Maximum BM at mid-span} = M = \frac{wL^2}{8} + \frac{PL}{4}$$

$$= \frac{15\times 8^2}{8} + \frac{40\times 8}{4}$$

$$M = 200\ \text{kN.m}$$

$$\text{Bending stress} = \frac{M}{I}\times y_{max}$$

$$118 = \frac{200\times 10^6}{367.8\times 10^6}\cdot y_{max}$$

$$\therefore \quad y_{max} = 217\ \text{mm}$$

$$\therefore \quad \text{Depth of beam} = 2\,y_{max} = \textbf{434 mm} \qquad (\because \text{symmetry @ N.A.})$$

**Example 5.13 :** *The cross-section of beam shown in Fig. 5.18 (a) is to be used as a cantilever beam to carry a UDL over a span of 2 m. If permissible bending stress is 160 MPa, find the intensity of UDL that the beam can carry. Also find the shear stresses at neutral axis. The section is placed such that web of the channel forms tension flange for the beam.*

**Data**       :   As shown in Fig. 5.18 (a) and 5.18 (b).

**Required**   :   Safe UDL 'w'.

**Concept**    :   Equate maximum BM = MR.

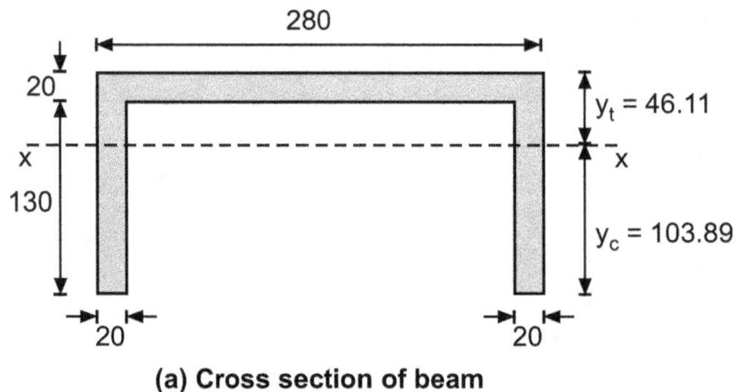

**(a) Cross section of beam**

(All dimensions in mm)

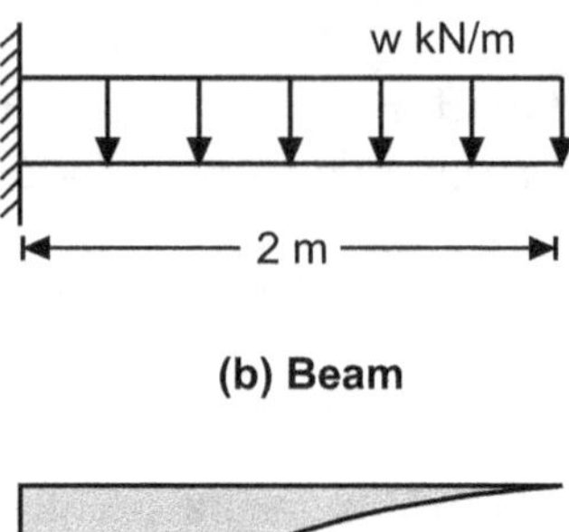

**(b) Beam**

**(c) BMD (kNm)**

**Fig. 5.18**

**Solution :** (i) Geometric properties :

Taking bottommost fibre as reference for CG of cross-section,

$$a_1 = 280 \times 20 = 5600 \text{ mm}^2; \quad y_1 = 140 \text{ mm}$$

$$a_2 = a_3 = 130 \times 20 = 2600 \text{ mm}^2; y_2 = y_3 = 65 \text{ mm}$$

$$\bar{y} = \frac{5600 \times 140 + 2 \times 2600 \times 65}{5600 + 2 \times 2600} = 103.89 \text{ mm from bottom}$$

$$I_{xx} = I_{xx_1} + I_{xx_2} + I_{xx_3}$$

$$I_{xx_1} = \frac{280 \times 20^3}{12} + (5600)(140 - 103.89)^2 = 7.49 \times 10^6 \text{ mm}^4$$

$$I_{xx_2} = I_{xx_3} = \frac{20 \times 130^3}{12} + (2600)(103.89 - 65)^2 = 7.59 \times 10^6 \text{ mm}^4$$

$$I_{xx} = (7.49 + 2 \times 7.59) \times 10^6 = 22.67 \times 10^6 \text{ mm}^4$$

$$y_{max} = 103.89 \text{ mm}$$

$$Z_{xx} = \frac{I_{xx}}{y_{max}} = \frac{22.67 \times 10^6}{103.89} = \mathbf{218.21 \times 10^3 \text{ mm}^3}$$

(ii)   Moment of resistance :

$$MR = Z_{xx} \cdot \sigma_b$$

$$= 218.21 \times 10^3 \times 160 \times 10^{-6} \text{ kN.m}$$

$$= 34.91 \text{ kN.m}$$

(iii)   Safe UDL :

Let,          $w$ = Intensity of UDL in 'kN/m'

$$\text{Max. BM} = \frac{wL^2}{2} = w \times \frac{(2)^2}{2} = 2w \text{ kN.m}$$

Equating maximum BM and MR,

---

$$2\,w = 34.91$$

$$\therefore \qquad w = \textbf{17.4 kN/m}$$

**Example 5.14 :** *A simply supported beam 6 m long carrying UDL throughout has cross-section shown in Fig. 5.19 (b). If permissible stresses in bending compression and tension are 100 MPa and 120 MPa respectively, determine the safe intensity of UDL.*

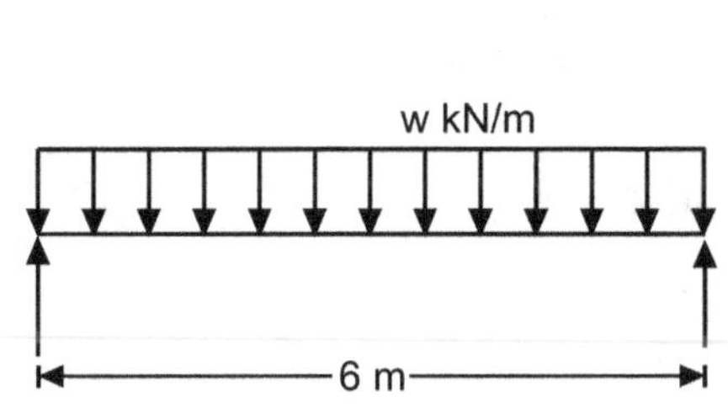


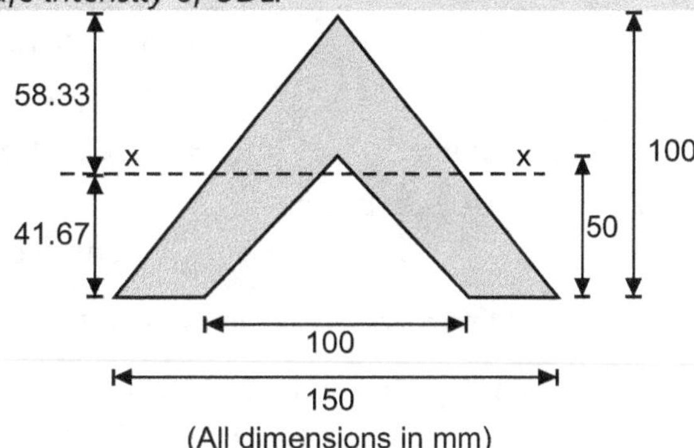


**(a) Beam**                                   **(b) C/s of beam**

**Fig. 5.19**

**Data**       :   $\sigma_{bc}$ = 100 MPa; $\sigma_{bt}$ = 120 MPa.

**Required**  :   Intensity of UDL.

**Concept**   :   Equate maximum BM and MR.

**Solution**  :   (i) Geometric properties :

Consider bottommost fibre as reference for locating C.G.

$$a_1 = \frac{1}{2} \times 150 \times 100 = 7500 \text{ mm}^2 \; ; \quad y_1 = \frac{100}{3} \text{ mm}$$

$$a_2 = \frac{1}{2} \times 100 \times 50 = 2500 \text{ mm}^2 \; ; \quad y_2 = \frac{50}{3} \text{ mm}$$

$$\bar{y} = \frac{a_1 y_1 - a_2 y_2}{a_1 - a_2} = \frac{7500 \times 100/3 - 2500 \times 50/3}{7500 - 2500}$$

$$= 41.67 \text{ mm from bottom}$$

$$\therefore \qquad y_c = 58.33 \text{ mm and } y_t = 41.67 \text{ mm} \quad (\because \text{ sagging BM})$$

$$I_{xx} = I_{xx_1} - I_{xx_2}$$

$$I_{xx_1} = \frac{150 \times 100^3}{36} + 7500 \left(41.67 - \frac{100}{3}\right)^2 = 4.69 \times 10^6 \text{ mm}^4$$

$$I_{xx_2} = \frac{100 \times 50^3}{36} + 2500 \left(41.67 - \frac{50}{3}\right)^2 = 1.91 \times 10^6 \text{ mm}^4$$

$$\therefore \qquad I_{xx} = (4.69 - 1.91) \times 10^6 = 2.78 \times 10^6 \text{ mm}^4$$

$$(Z_{xx})_c = \frac{I_{xx}}{y_c} = \frac{2.78 \times 10^6}{58.33} = \textbf{47.66} \times \textbf{10}^3 \textbf{ mm}^3$$

$$(Z_{xx})_t = \frac{I_{xx}}{y_t} = \frac{2.78 \times 10^6}{41.67} = \textbf{66.71} \times \textbf{10}^3 \textbf{ mm}^3$$

(ii)    Moment of resistance of cross-section :

$$(MR)_c = (Z_{xx})_c \cdot \sigma_{bc} = 47.66 \times 10^3 \times 100 \times 10^{-6} \text{ kN.m}$$

$$= \textbf{4.766 kN.m} \qquad \qquad \text{... (i)}$$

$$(MR)_t = (Z_{xx})_t \cdot \sigma_{bt}$$

$$= 66.71 \times 10^3 \times 120 \times 10^{-6} \text{ kN.m}$$

$$= \textbf{8 kN.m} \qquad \qquad \text{... (ii)}$$

Governing        MR  = **4.766 kN.m**  ($\because$ Least of (i) and (ii))

(iii)   Safe UDL on beam :

Let,                    w  =  intensity of safe UDL in kN/m

$$\therefore \quad \text{Maximum BM at mid-span} = \frac{wl^2}{8} = \frac{w \times 6^2}{8} = 4.5 \ w \text{ kN.m}$$

Equating maximum BM and MR,

$$4.5 \ w = 4.766$$

$$\therefore \qquad w = \textbf{1.059 kN/m}$$

**Example 5.15 :** *An unequal ISA 125 $\times$ 75 $\times$ 8 is used as a simply supported beam over a span of 3 m; with longer leg placed vertical. Find the safe UDL, the beam can carry if allowable bending stress in tension = 120 MPa. Also find the maximum compressive stress induced, assuming bending about xx-axis.*

**Data**          :   ISA 125 $\times$ 75 $\times$ 8 ; L = 3 m simply supported; $\sigma_{bt}$ = 120 MPa.

**Required**   :   Safe UDL and stress in bending compression.

**Concept**    :   Using MR of tension side, find safe UDL and then evaluate stress in bending compression $(\sigma_{bc})_{cal}$.

**Solution**   :

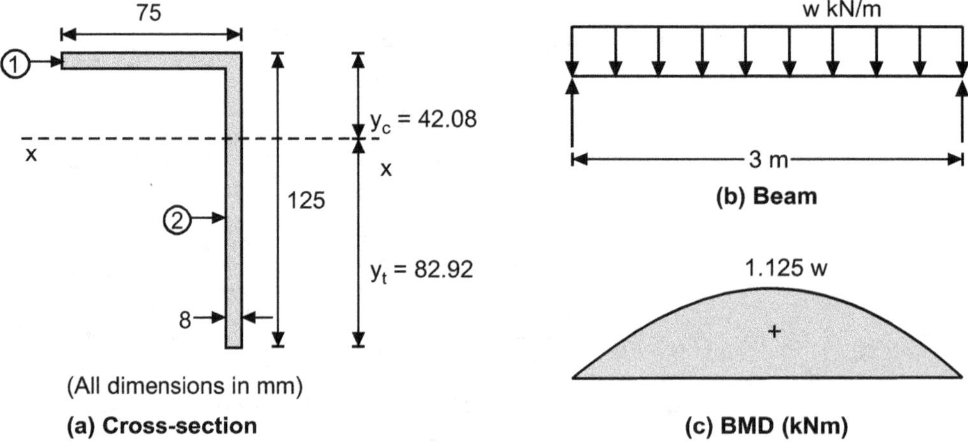



**(a) Cross-section**            **(b) Beam**

**(c) BMD (kNm)**

**Fig. 5.20**

(i)     Geometric properties :
Taking topmost fibre as a reference for CG.

$$a_1 = 75 \times 8 = 600 \text{ mm}^2 \quad ; \quad y_1 = 4 \text{ mm}$$

$$a_2 = (125 - 8)\,8 = 936 \text{ mm}^2; \quad y_2 = 8 + \left(\frac{125 - 8}{2}\right) = 66.5 \text{ mm}$$

$$\bar{y} = \frac{600 \times 4 + 936 \times 66.5}{600 + 936} = 42.08 \text{ mm from AB}$$

$$I_{xx} = 75 \times \frac{8^3}{12} + (600)\,(42.08 - 4)^2 + \frac{8 \times (125 - 8)^3}{12} + 936\,(66.5 - 42.08)^2$$

$$= 2.5 \times 10^6 \text{ mm}^4$$

$$y_c = 42.08 \text{ mm} \quad \text{and} \quad y_t = 82.92 \text{ mm}$$

$$(Z_{xx})_c = \frac{I_{xx}}{y_c} = \frac{2.5 \times 10^6}{42.08} = \mathbf{59.41 \times 10^3 \text{ mm}^3}$$

$$(Z_{xx})_t = \frac{I_{xx}}{y_t} = \frac{2.5 \times 10^6}{82.92} = \mathbf{30.15 \times 10^3 \text{ mm}^3}$$

(ii)    Safe UDL (w) :

$$(MR)_t = (Z_{xx})_t \times \sigma_{bt} = 30.15 \times 10^3 \times 120 \times 10^{-6} \text{ kN.m}$$

$$= 3.618 \text{ kN.m}$$

$$\text{Maximum} \quad BM = \frac{wL^2}{8} = \frac{w\,(3)^2}{8} = (1.125\ w) \text{ kN.m}$$

where;         $w$ = UDL in kN/m

Equating maximum BM and MR,

$$(1.125)\ w = 3.618$$

$$\therefore \qquad w = \mathbf{3.216 \text{ kN/m (inclusive of self weight)}}$$

(iii)    Stress in bending compression.

$$(\sigma_{bc})_{cal} = \frac{BM}{(Z_{xx})_c} = \frac{(1.125)\ w \times 10^6}{59.41 \times 10^3} = \mathbf{60.9 \text{ MPa}}$$

**Example 5.16 :** *A uniform beam in pure bending has trapezoidal cross-section as shown in Fig. 5.21 (a). If allowable working stress in tension and compression is 40 MPa and 60 MPa respectively, calculate the ratio of $b_1$ to $b_2$ for maximum economy. Assume the cross-section to carry sagging bending moment.*

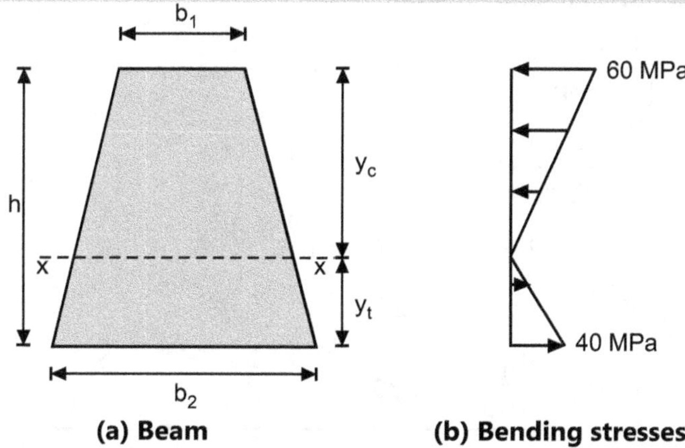


(a) Beam                    (b) Bending stresses

**Fig. 5.21**

**Data**       :   $\sigma_{bt} = 40$ MPa ; $\sigma_{bc} = 60$ MPa

**Required**   :   Ratio $\dfrac{b_1}{b_2}$

**Concept**    :   For maximum economy, stresses in tension and compression should reach to the permissible limits simultaneously.

**Solution**   :   (i) Geometric properties :

C.G. of cross-section from bottom $= \left[\dfrac{b_2 + 2\,b_1}{b_2 + b_1}\right]\dfrac{h}{3}$.

Due to sagging BM ;

$$y_t = \left[\dfrac{b_2 + 2\,b_1}{b_2 + b_1}\right]\dfrac{h}{3} \qquad \ldots \text{(i)}$$

(ii)   Relation between $y_c$ and $y_t$.

From bending stress diagram ; $\dfrac{60}{y_c} = \dfrac{40}{y_t}$

$$\therefore \qquad y_t = \dfrac{2}{3}\,y_c \qquad \ldots \text{(ii)}$$

Also;          $y_t + y_c = h \qquad \ldots \text{(iii)}$

Put equation (ii) in equation (iii)

$$\left(\dfrac{2}{3}\right) y_c + y_c = h$$

$$\therefore \qquad y_c = \mathbf{0.6\ h} \qquad\qquad \therefore \quad y_t = \mathbf{0.4\ h} \qquad \ldots \text{(iv)}$$

(iii)   Ratio of $b_1$ and $b_2$.

Equating equation (i) and equation (iv),

$$\left[\dfrac{b_2 + 2\,b_1}{b_2 + b_1}\right]\dfrac{h}{3} = 0.4\ h$$

$$\dfrac{b_2 + 2\,b_1}{b_2 + b_1} = 1.2$$

$$\therefore \qquad b_2 + 2\,b_1 = 1.2\,(b_2 + b_1)$$

$$0.8\,b_1 = 0.2\,b_2$$

$$\therefore \qquad \dfrac{b_1}{b_2} = \mathbf{0.25}$$

**Example 5.17 :** *A simply supported timber beam 5 m span carries UDL of 12 kN/m and a point load of 12 kN at 2 m from left support. If the permissible bending stress in timber is 10 MPa, design suitable cross-section of beam if b = 0.4 D.*

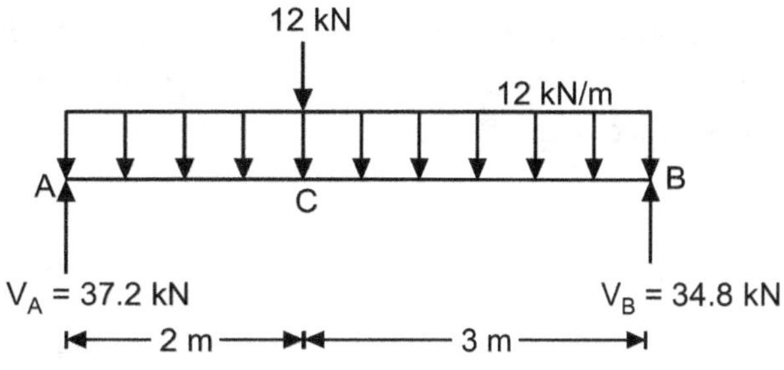



**(a) FBD**

**Data :** Loading on beam as shown in Fig. 3.22 (a).

**Required :** Design of cross section of beam.

**Concept :** Maximum bending moment shall be obtained from analysis and equate maximum BM to MR.

**Solution :** (i) Analysis of beam :

$$\sum M_A = 0; \; V_B \times 5 - 12 \times \frac{5^2}{2} - 12 \times 2 = 0$$

$$\therefore \quad V_B = 34.8 \text{ kN } (\uparrow)$$

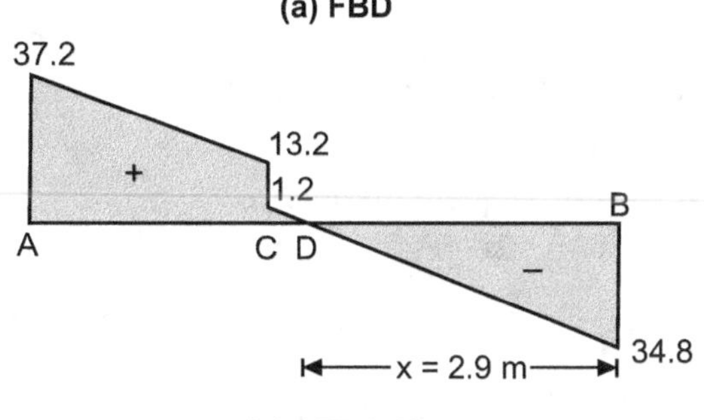



**(b) SFD (kN)**

**Fig. 5.22**

$$\sum F_y = 0; \quad V_A + V_B - 12 - 12 \times 5 = 0$$

$$\therefore \quad V_A = 37.2 \text{ kN } (\uparrow)$$

SFD is as shown in Fig. 3.22 (b).

$$x = \left[\frac{34.8}{34.8 + 1.2}\right] 3 = 2.9 \text{ m}$$

$$BM_{max} = BM_D = 34.8 \times 2.9 - 12 \times \frac{(2.9)^2}{2} = \textbf{50.46 kNm}$$

(ii)    Design of cross section :

$$MR = Z_{xx} \cdot \sigma_b$$

$$= \frac{1}{6} bD^2 \times \sigma_b$$

$$= \frac{1}{6} (0.4 \, D) \, D^2 \times 10$$

$$= \frac{2}{3} D^3$$



**Fig. 3.23 : c/s of beam**

Equating $BM_{max}$ to MR,

$$50.46 \times 10^6 = \frac{2}{3} D^3$$

$$\therefore \qquad D = 423 \text{ mm; say } 425 \text{ mm, } b = 0.4, D = 170 \text{ mm}$$

$$\therefore \quad \text{Use} \qquad b = \textbf{170 mm} \quad \text{and} \quad D = \textbf{425 mm}$$

**Example 5.18 :** *A hollow circular beam having outside diameter twice the inside diameter is subjected to a BM of 50 kN-m. If the permissible bending stress in the beam is 105 MN/m², find the diameters of the beam.*

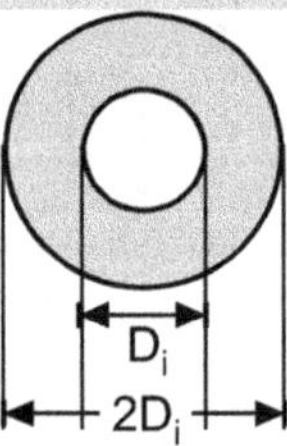


**Fig. 5.24**

**Data :** As shown in Fig. 5.24, M = 50 kN-m, $\sigma_b$ = 105 MN/m².

**Required :** $D_i$, $D_o$.

**Concept :** Equate maximum BM to MR.

**Solution :** Geometric properties :

$$I_{xx} = \frac{\pi}{64} \times (D_o^4 - D_i^4) = \frac{\pi}{64} \times ((2D_i)^4 - D_i^4) = \frac{\pi}{64} \times 15\, D_i^4$$

$$y_{max} = \frac{D_o}{2} = \frac{2D_i}{2} = D_i$$

$$\therefore \quad Z_{xx} = \frac{I_{xx}}{Y_{xx}} = \frac{\frac{15\pi}{64} D_i^4}{D_i} = \frac{15\pi}{64} D_i^3$$

$$\therefore \quad BM = MR = \sigma_b \times Z_{xx}$$

$$\therefore \quad 50 \times 10^6 = 105 \times \frac{15\pi}{64} D_i^3$$

$$\therefore \quad D_i = \textbf{86.48 mm}$$

$$D_o = \textbf{172.96 mm}$$

**Example 5.19 :** *A square beam 20 mm × 20 mm in section and 2m long is supported at the ends. The beam fails when a point load of 400 N is applied at the centre of the beam. What UDL will break a cantilever of the same material 40 mm wide, 60 mm deep and 3 m long ?*

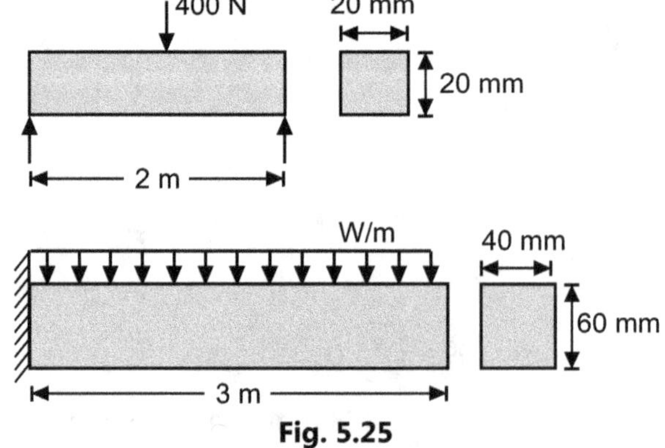


**Fig. 5.25**

**Data :** As shown in Fig. 5.25.

**Required :** w/m run.

**Concept :** (i) BM = MR

$$\therefore \qquad BM \;=\; \frac{Wl}{4} \;=\; \frac{400 \times 2}{4} \;=\; 200 \text{ N-m}$$

$$I_{xx} \;=\; \frac{bd^3}{12} \;=\; \frac{20 \times 20^3}{12} \text{ mm}^4, \; y_{max} = \frac{20}{2} = 10 \text{ mm}$$

$$Z_{xx} \;=\; \frac{I_{xx}}{y_{max}} \;=\; \frac{20^4 \times 10}{12} \;=\; 13333.33 \text{ mm}^3$$

$$\therefore \qquad 200 \times 10^3 \;=\; \sigma_b \times 13333.33$$

$$\therefore \qquad \sigma_b \;=\; 15 \text{ MPa}$$

(ii)   Calculations for UDL :

$$MR \;=\; BM$$

$$MR \;=\; \sigma_b \times Z_{xx}$$

$$I_{xx} \;=\; \frac{bd^3}{12} \;=\; \frac{40 \times 60^3}{12} \;=\; 720 \times 10^3$$

$$Z_{xx} \;=\; \frac{I_{xx}}{y_{max}} \;=\; 24 \times 10^3 \text{ mm}^3$$

$$\therefore \qquad BM \;=\; MR$$

$$\frac{wl^2}{2} \;=\; 15 \times 24 \times 10^3$$

$$w \;=\; \textbf{80 N/m}$$

**Example 5.20 :** *The cross-section of the steel girder is as shown in Fig. 5.26. If the allowable bending compressive and bending tensile stress is 125 N/mm² and 165 N/mm² respectively, then determine the moment carrying capacity of the section under gravity loads.*

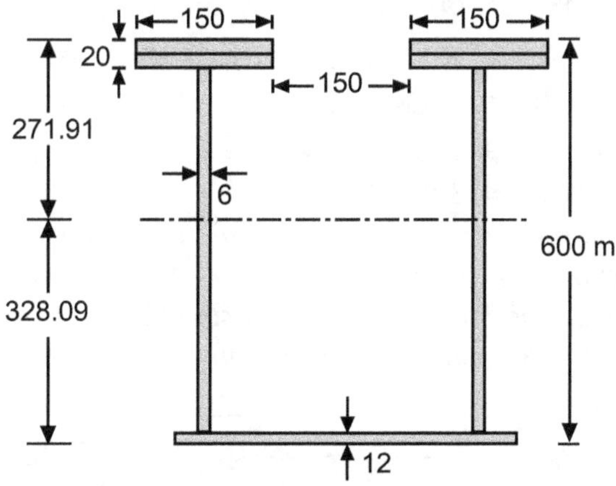


**Fig. 5.26**

**Data :** As shown in Fig. 5.26.

**Required :** MR

**Concept :** Standard formulae.

**Solution :** Geometric properties. Consider bottommost fibre as reference for locating C.G.

$$a_1 = 20 \times 150 = 3000 \text{ mm}^2, \; y_1 = 590 \text{ mm}$$
$$a_2 = 6 \times 568 = 3408 \text{ mm}^2, \; y_2 = 296 \text{ mm}$$
$$a_3 = 12 \times 350 = 4200 \text{ mm}^2, \; y_3 = 6 \text{ mm}$$

$\therefore$
$$\bar{y} = \frac{2(a_1 y_1) + (2a_2 y_2) + a_3 y_3}{2a_1 + 2a_2 + a_3}$$

$$\bar{y} = \frac{2(3000 \times 590) + 2(3408 \times 296) + (4200 \times 6)}{(2 \times 3000) + (2 \times 3408) + 4200}$$

$$\bar{y} = 328.09 \text{ mm}$$

$$I_{xx} = 2 I_{xx_1} + 2 I_{xx_2} + I_{xx_3}$$

$$= 2 \times \left(\frac{150 \times 20^3}{12}\right) + 2 (150 \times 20)(261.91)^2$$

$$+ 2 \left(\frac{6 \times 568^3}{12}\right) + 2 (6 \times 568)(32.09)^2$$

$$+ \left(\frac{350 \times 12^3}{12}\right) + (350 \times 12)(322.09)^2$$

$$= 200 \times 10^3 + 205.79 \times 10^6 + 183.25 \times 10^6$$
$$+ 7.02 \times 10^6 + 50.4 \times 10^3 + 435.72 \times 10^6$$

$$= 832.03 \times 10^6 \text{ mm}^4$$

$$Z_{xx_t} = \frac{I}{y_t} = \frac{832.03 \times 10^6}{271.91} = 3.06 \times 10^6 \text{ mm}^3$$

$$Z_{xx_b} = \frac{I}{y_b} = \frac{832.03 \times 10^6}{328.09} = 2.54 \times 10^6 \text{ mm}^3$$

$\therefore$
$$MR_c = \sigma_{bc} \times Z_{xx_t}$$
$$= 125 \times 3.06 \times 10^6 = 382.5 \times 10^6 \text{ N-mm}$$
$$MR_t = \sigma_{bt} \times Z_{xx_b}$$
$$= 165 \times 2.54 \times 10^6 = 419.1 \times 10^6 \text{ N-mm}$$

$\therefore$ MR of section $= \mathbf{382.5 \text{ kN-m}}$

**Example 5.21 :** *A rail road sleeper is subjected to two concentrated loads P acting as shown in Fig. 5.27. The reaction q of the ballast may be assumed to be uniformly distributed over the length of the sleeper. Calculate the maximum bending stress in the sleeper assuming P = 200 kN, L = 1676 mm, a = 500 mm, b = 300 mm and h = 250 mm.*                    **(Dec. 2003)**

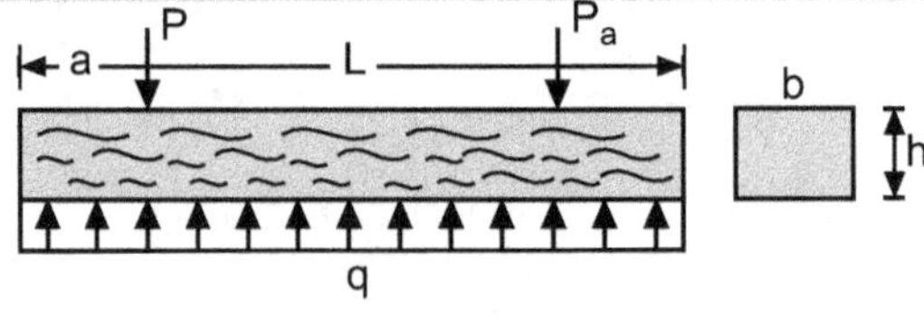

**Fig. 5.27**

**Data :** As shown in Fig. 5.27.

**Required :** Maximum bending stress and q.

**Concept :** Equilibrium and BM = MR

**Solution :** (i) Calculation for q :

$$\sum F_y = 0; \quad 2P - q \times (L + 2a) = 0$$

$$\therefore \quad q = \frac{2 \times 200}{(1.676 + 0.5 \times 2)} = 149.48 \text{ kN/m}$$

(ii)  Bending stress : Maximum BM will be at the centre, as beam is symmetrical with centre.

$$\therefore \quad BM = 200 \times \frac{L}{2} - \frac{149.48 \times \left(\frac{L}{2} + a\right)^2}{2}$$

$$= 200 \times \frac{1.676}{2} - \frac{149.48 \left(\frac{1.676}{2} + 0.5\right)^2}{2}$$

$$= 33.79 \text{ kN-m}$$

$$MR = \sigma \times Z_{XX}$$

$$I_{XX} = \frac{bd^3}{12} = \frac{300 \times 250^3}{12} = 3.91 \times 10^8 \text{ mm}^4$$

$$Z_{XX} = \frac{I_{XX}}{\frac{b}{2}} = 3.128 \times 10^6 \text{ mm}^3$$

$$BM = MR$$

$$33.79 \times 10^6 = \sigma_b \times 3.128 \times 10^6$$

$$\therefore \quad \sigma_b = 10.8 \text{ MPa}$$

∴    Maximum bending stress is 10.8 MPa.

## 5.4 FITCHED BEAMS

Fitched beam section may be defined as 'a section, made up of two or more different materials, joined together, in such a manner that they behave like a single piece and each material bends to the same radius of curvature'.

Such beams are used when a beam of one material, if used alone, requires quite a large cross-sectional area, which does not suit the space available. A material is reinforced with some other materials with higher strength in order to reduce the cross-sectional area of the beam and suit the space available.

Total moment of resistance = Moment of resistance of two sections.

Consider a section of two materials as shown in Fig. 5.28.

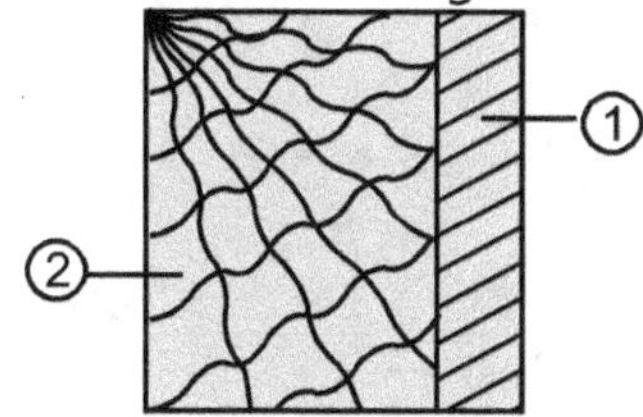


**Fig. 5.28**

Let,                    $E_1$ and $E_2$  —  Moduli of elasticity of part I and part II.

$I_1$ and $I_2$  –  M.I. of part I and part II

$Z_1$ and $Z_2$  –  Section modulus of part I and part II

$\sigma_1$ and $\sigma_2$  –  Bending stresses of part I and part II

R  –  Radius of curvature of beam.

$\therefore$  $M_1 = \sigma_1 \times Z_1$

$M_2 = \sigma_2 \times Z_2$

$\therefore$  $M = M_1 + M_2 = \sigma_1 \times Z_1 + \sigma_2 \times Z_2$

We also know that at any distance, from the neutral axis, the strain in both the materials is same.

Strain of part I  =  Strain of part II

$$\frac{\sigma_1}{E_1} = \frac{\sigma_2}{E_2}$$

$$\sigma_1 = \frac{E_1}{E_2}\sigma_2$$

$$\sigma_1 = m \cdot \sigma_2$$

where m :  modular ratio  $= E_1/E_2$

Thus from the above, the MR of composite section can be determined.

---

**Example 5.22 :** *A flitched timber beam made up of steel and timber has a section as shown in Fig. 5.29. Determine the moment of resistance of the beam. Stress in steel = 100 MPa and stress in timber = 5 MPa.*

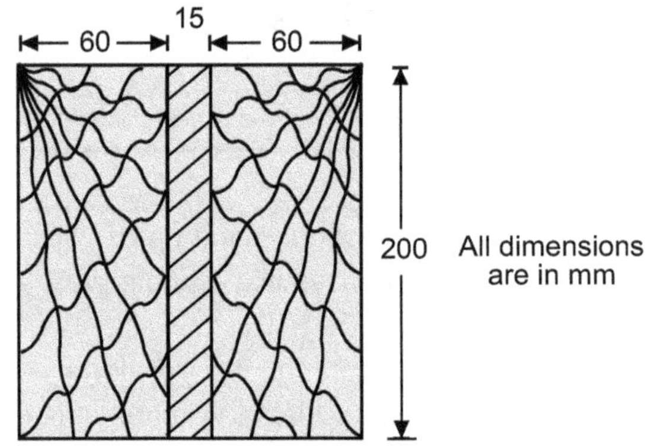


**Fig. 5.29**

**Data :** As shown in Fig. 5.29, $\sigma_{st}$ = 100 MPa, $\sigma_t$ = 5 MPa.

**Required :** Moment of resistance.

**Concept :** MR = $MR_{st}$ = $MR_t$.

**Solution :** (i) Geometric properties :

$$Z_{st} = \frac{bd^2}{6} = \frac{15 \times 200^2}{6} = 100 \times 10^3 \, mm^3$$

$$Z_t = 2 \times \frac{bd^2}{6} = \frac{2 \times 60 \times 200^2}{6} = 800 \times 10^3 \, mm^3$$

(ii)  MR of steel :  $MR_{st} = \sigma_{st} \times Z_{st} = 100 \times 100 \times 10^3$

---

$$MR_{st} = 100 \times 10^5 \text{ N-mm}$$

(iii) MR of timber : $\quad MR_t = \sigma_t \times Z_t = 5 \times 800 \times 10^3$

$\therefore \qquad MR_t = 40 \times 10^5 \text{ N-mm}$

(iv) MR of section :

$\therefore \qquad MR = MR_{st} + MR_t$

$\qquad\qquad MR = 100 \times 10^5 + 40 \times 10^5$

$\qquad\qquad MR = 140 \times 10^5 \text{ N-mm} = 14 \text{ kN-m}$

**Example 5.23 :** *A timber beam 120 mm wide and 300 mm deep is strengthened by a steel plate 120 mm wide and 10 mm deep screwed at the bottom surface of the timber as shown in Fig. 5.30. Calculate the moment of resistance of the beam, if the safe stresses in timber and steel are 10 N/mm² and 140 N/mm² respectively. Take $E_s = 20\, E_t$.*

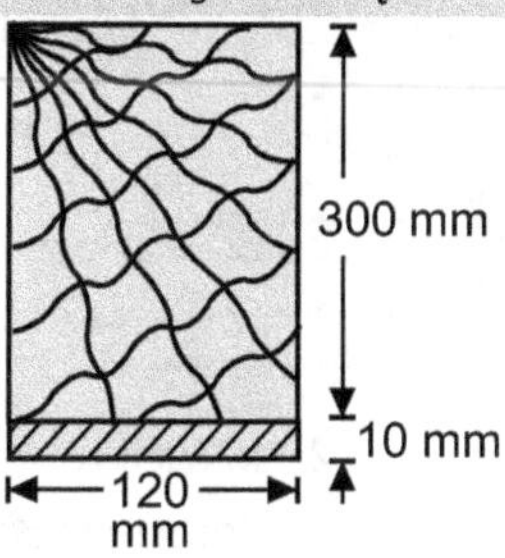


**Fig. 5.30**

**Data :** As shown in Fig. 5.30, stress in timber = 10 N/mm², stress in steel = 140 N/mm², $E_s = 20\, E_t$.

**Required :** Moment of resistance.

**Concept :** $MR = MR_{st} + MR_t$.

**Solution :** (i) N.A. calculation :

$$\therefore \qquad \bar{y} = \frac{300 \times 120 \times 160 + 20 \times 120 \times 10 \times 5}{(300 \times 120) + (20 \times 120 \times 10)}$$

$$\bar{y} = 98 \text{ mm}$$

(ii)  Moment of inertia :

$$I = \frac{120 \times 300^3}{12} + 120 \times 300 \times (160 - 98)^2$$

$$+ \frac{20 \times 120 \times 10^3}{12} + 20 \times 120 \times 10\,(98 - 5)^2$$

$$= 6.16 \times 10^8 \text{ mm}^4$$

(iii) Calculation for M.R.

$$y_c = 310 - 98 = 212 \text{ mm}$$

$$y_t = 98 \text{ mm}$$

$\therefore$   Stress in uppermost fibre is 10 MPa.

$\therefore$   Stress in lowermost fibre $= \dfrac{10}{212} \times 98 = 4.62$ MPa.

$\therefore$     Actual stress in steel $= 20 \times 4.62 = 92.4$ MPa $< 150$ MPa $\therefore$ O.K.

$$\therefore \qquad MR = \frac{I}{y_{max}} \cdot \sigma_t = \frac{6.16 \times 10^8}{212} \times 10$$

$$MR = 29.06 \times 10^6 \text{ N-mm}$$

$$MR = 29.06 \text{ kN-m}$$

**Example 5.24 :** *A simply supported beam of 4 m span has the cross-section, as shown in Fig. 5.31. It carries uniformly distributed load of intensity 20 kN/m over the middle half of the span. If m = 15, calculate the maximum stresses in timber and steel.*

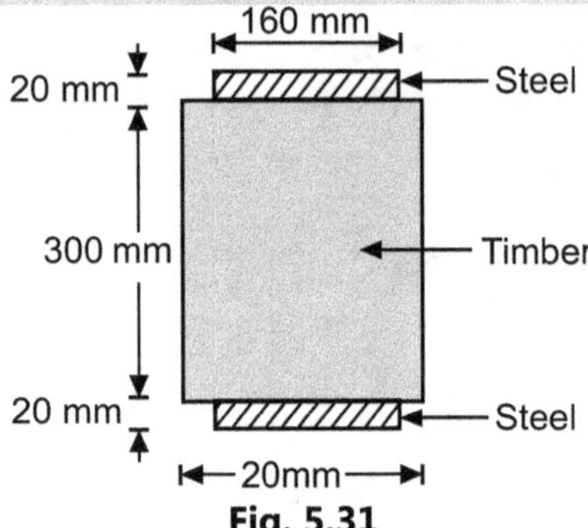


**Fig. 5.31**

**Data :** As shown in Fig. 5.31, $l$ = 4 m, w = 20 kN/m, m = 15.

**Required :** Maximum stress in steel and maximum stress in timber.

**Concept :** $\dfrac{M}{I} = \dfrac{\sigma}{y}$.

**Solution :** (i) M.I. (I)

$$\bar{y} = y_c = y_t = 170 \text{ mm}$$

$$\therefore \qquad I = 2\left[\left(\frac{15 \times 160 \times 10^3}{12}\right) + 15 \times 160 \times 10\,(170-10)^2\right] + \frac{200 \times 300^3}{12}$$

$$= 1.68 \times 10^9 \text{ mm}^4$$

(ii)　BM calculation :

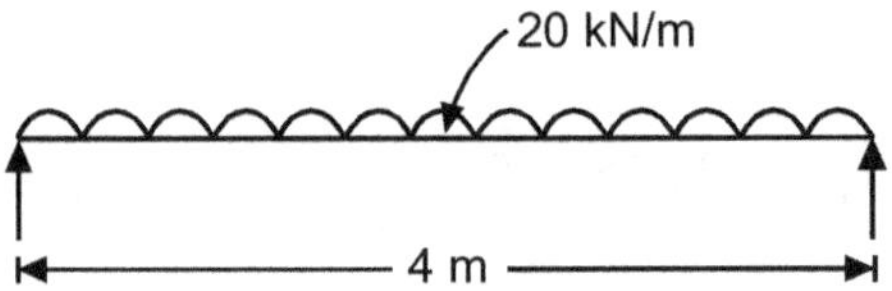

**Fig. 5.32**

$$M = \frac{20 \times 4^2}{8} = 40 \text{ kN-m}$$

(iii) Stress calculation :

$$\sigma = \frac{M}{I} \cdot y = \frac{40 \times 10^6}{1.68 \times 10^9} \times 170$$

$$\sigma = 4.05 \text{ MPa}$$

$$\therefore \qquad \sigma_{st} = 15 \times 4.05 = 60.75 \text{ MPa}$$

$$\sigma_t = \frac{M}{I} \cdot y = \frac{40 \times 10^6}{1.68 \times 10^9} \times 150$$

$$\sigma_{t\,max} = 3.57 \text{ MPa.}$$

**Example 5.25 :** *State the expression for bending stress for curved bar subjected to pure bending in the plane of the curve. Explain the terms in the expression with sign convention.* **(Dec. 2001)**

**Solution :** $\sigma_o$ = bending stress at outer face of curved bar = $\dfrac{M}{AR}\left[1 + \left(\dfrac{R^2}{h^2}\right)\left(\dfrac{y_2}{R + y_2}\right)\right]$

$\sigma_i$ = bending stress at inner face = $\dfrac{M}{AR}\left[1 - \left(\dfrac{R^2}{h^2}\right)\left(\dfrac{y_1}{R + y_1}\right)\right]$

where,

$M$ = Couple (B.M.) applied at the ends of curved bar, positive if B.M. tends to increase curvature.

$A$ = Cross-sectional area of bar.

$R$ = Initial radius of bar upto centroidal axis of section.

$h^2$ = Factor according to cross-section of bar as per Winkler Batch theory.

$y$ = Distance of a fibre from centroidal axis of cross-section, positive towards convex side of bar.

($y_2$ for outer fibre and $y_1$ for inner fibre)

Bending stress distribution is hyperbolic.

**Example 5.26 :** *Fig. 5.33 shows a cast iron beam section, which is subjected to sagging bending moment causing maximum tensile stress of 30 MPa. Determine a magnitude of bending moment and maximum compressive stress.* **(May 2002)**

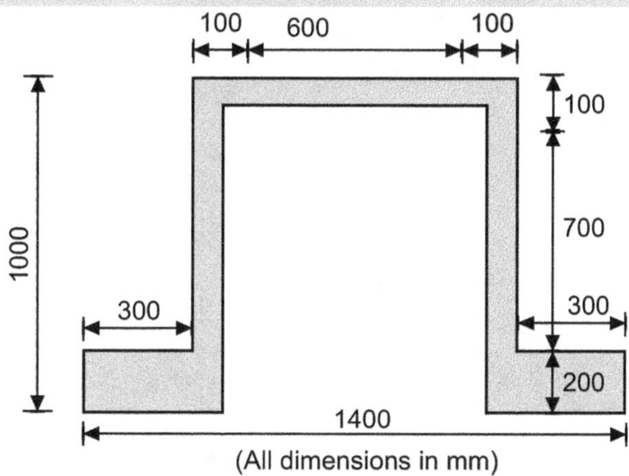


**Fig. 5.33**

**Solution :** (i) CG and MI

$a_1$ = $800 \times 100 = 8 \times 10^4$ mm², $\qquad$ $y_1$ = 950 mm

$a_2$ = $2 \times 100 \times 700 = 14 \times 10^4$ mm², $\qquad$ $y_2$ = 550 mm

$a_3$ = $2 \times 400 \times 200 = 16 \times 10^4$ mm², $\qquad$ $y_3$ = 100 mm

∴ $\bar{y}$ = $y_t$ = 447.73 mm ∴ $y_c$ = 555.27 mm

$I_x$ = $\dfrac{800 \times 100^3}{12} + 8 \times 10^4 (950 - 447.73)^2 +$

$$\frac{200 \times 700^3}{12} + 14 \times 10^4 (550 - 447.73)^2 +$$

$$\frac{800 \times 200^3}{12} + 16 \times 10^4 (447.73 - 100)^2$$

$$= 47.3 \times 10^9 \text{ mm}^4$$

(ii)
$$\frac{M}{I} = \frac{\sigma_c}{y_c} = \frac{\sigma_t}{y_t}$$

$$\frac{M \times 10^6}{47.3 \times 10^9} = \frac{\sigma_x}{555.27} = \frac{30}{447.73}$$

$$M = \textbf{3169.96 kN.m}$$

$$\sigma_c = \textbf{37.2 MPa}$$

**Example 5.27 :** *A beam with the cross-section shown in Fig. 5.34 is to be subjected to a constant bending moment. Due to practical limitations, it is decided to keep the beam width B and angle $\alpha$ as constant. Determine the optimum value of h in order to minimize the stresses in the outer fibres.*

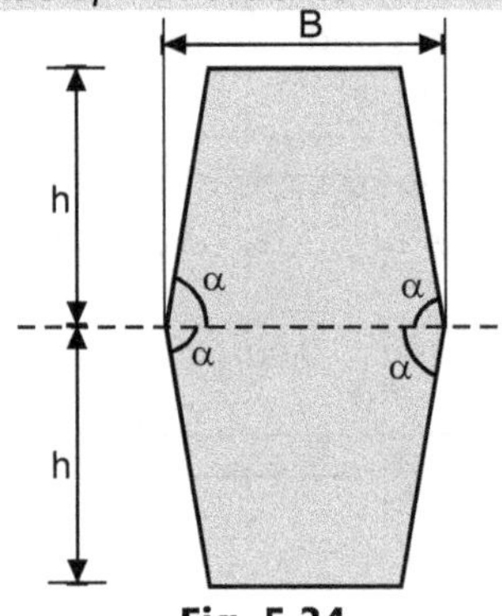


**Fig. 5.34**

**Solution :**

$$I = I_{rectangle} + 4 \, (I)_{triangle} \, @ \, base$$

$$= \frac{(B - 2h \cot (\alpha)) \, (2h)^3}{12} + 4 \left\{ \frac{h \cdot \cot (\alpha) \, h^3}{12} \right\}$$

$$= \frac{h^3}{12} \{8B - 16 \, h \cdot \cot (\alpha) + 4h \cdot \cot (\alpha)\} = \frac{2}{3} Bh^3 - h^4 \cot (\alpha)$$

$$z = \frac{I}{y_{max}} = \frac{2}{3} Bh^2 - h^3 \cot (\alpha)$$

For optimum value of h (i.e. $z_{max}$)

$$\frac{d}{dh} (z) = \frac{4}{3} Bh - 3h^2 \cot (\alpha) = 0$$

$$\therefore \qquad h = \frac{4}{9} B \cdot \tan (\alpha)$$

**Example 5.28 :** *A beam in pure bending has a trapezoidal cross-section as shown in  Fig. 5.35 with the top of the beam in compression. The allowable stresses in tension and compression are in the ratio $\sigma_t/\sigma_c = \alpha$ Determine the ratio $b_1/b_2$ of the base dimensions   (in terms of $\alpha$) in order that the stresses at both the top and bottom of the beam have the maximum allowable values. What is the permissible range of values of $\alpha$ for the trapezoidal cross-section ?*

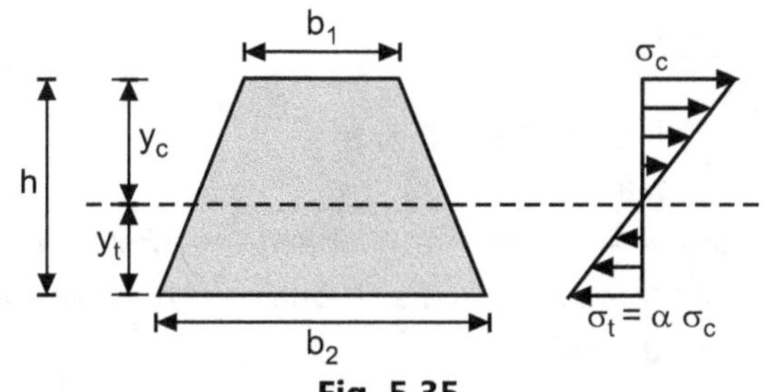

**Fig. 5.35**

**Solution :**

$$\sigma_t/y_t = \sigma_c/y_c$$

$\therefore \qquad y_t/y_c = \sigma_t/\sigma_c = \alpha \qquad \qquad \text{... (i)}$

$$y_t = \{(b_2 + 2b_1)/(b_2 + b_1)\}\, h/3 \qquad \qquad \text{... (ii)}$$

Also $\qquad y_c + y_t = h \qquad \qquad \text{... (iii)}$

From (i) and (iii),

$$y_c = h/(1 + \alpha) \text{ and } y_t = (\alpha/1 + \alpha)\, h \qquad \qquad \text{... (iv)}$$

Equating $y_t$ from (ii) and (iv)

$$\alpha/(1 + \alpha) = [(b_2 + 2b_1)/(b_2 + b_1)]\, 1/3$$

$$3\,\alpha\,(b_2 + b_1) = (b_2 + 2b_1)\,(1 + \alpha)$$

$$2\alpha\, b_2 + \alpha\, b_1 = b_2 + 2b_1$$

$$b_1/b_2 = \frac{(2\alpha - 1)}{(2 - \alpha)}$$

For trapezoidal section, value of $b_1/b_2$ can vary from 0 to 1.

For $b_1/b_2 = 0$, $\alpha = \dfrac{1}{2}$ (Triangular section)

For $b_1/b_2 = 1$, $\alpha = 1$ (Rectangular section).

**Example 5.29 :** *A wooden beam ABC of square cross-section is supported at A and B and carries a uniform load on BC as shown in Fig. 5.36. Calculate the required dimensions of the cross-section if the allowable stress in bending is 12 MPa. Include the weight of the beam assuming the specific weight of wood to be 5.5 kN/m³.* **(May 2003)**

**Solution :**

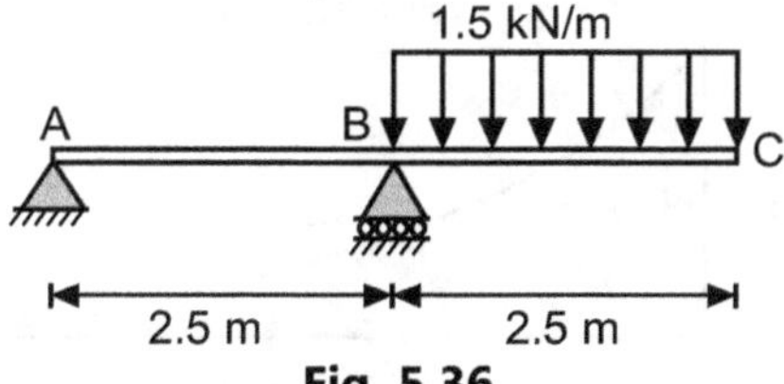


**Fig. 5.36**

**(i) Analysis of beam :** Line of action of self weight of beam passes through support B, hence does not affect BM.

$$\text{Max. BM at B} = \frac{-1.5 \times 2.5^2}{2} = -4.6875 \text{ kN-m}$$

$$= 4.6875 \text{ kN-m (hogging)}$$

**(ii) Design of beam :** $\qquad M/I = \sigma/y \; \therefore \; M/\sigma = I/y$

$$\therefore \qquad \frac{4.6875 \times 10^6}{12} = \frac{b^3}{6}$$

$$\therefore \qquad b = 132.82 \text{ mm}$$

Use 133 mm × 133 mm sq. beam.

**Example 5.30 :** *The cantilever beam AB, loaded as shown in Fig. 5.37, is constructed of a channel section. Find the maximum tensile and compressive stresses due to bending if I = 1.2 ×10⁶ mm⁴ about the neutral axis.*

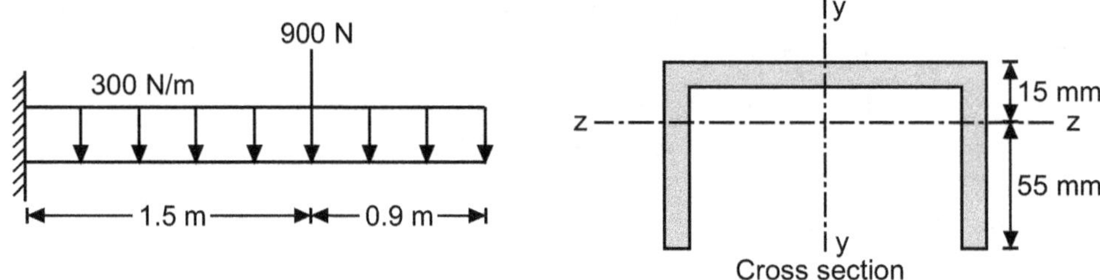


**Fig. 5.37 (a) : Given beam**

**Data :** As shown in Fig. 5.37 (a).

**Required :** Bending stresses.

**Solution :** (i) Reactions :

$$\sum f_y = 0, \qquad \therefore R_A = 300 \times 2.7 + 900$$

$$= 1710 \text{ N}$$

$$\sum M @ A = 0, \qquad \therefore M_A = 300 \times 2.7 \times \frac{2.7}{2} + 900 \times 1.5$$

$$= 2443.5 \text{ N-m}$$

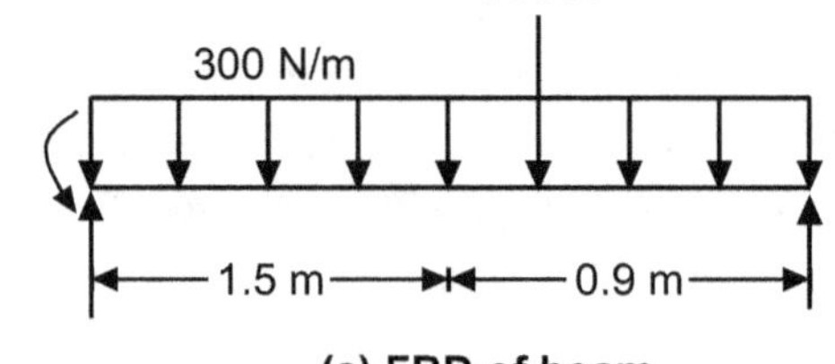


**(a) FBD of beam**

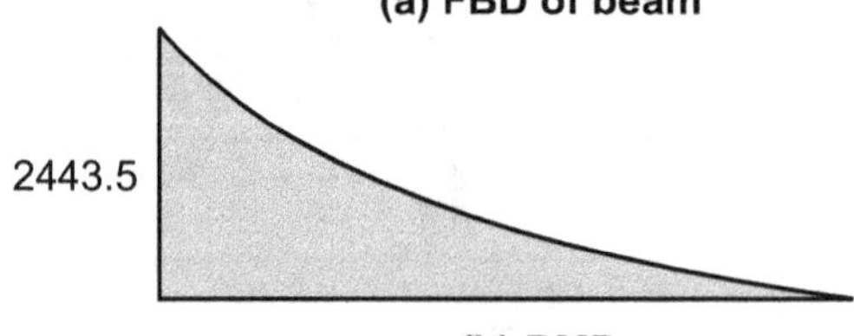


**(b) BMD**

**Fig. 5.37 (b)**

(ii)   Bending stresses :

Maximum compressive (bottom) stresses :

$$\therefore \qquad \sigma_{bc} = \frac{M}{I} \times y_b = \frac{2443.5 \times 10^3}{1.2 \times 10^6} \times 55$$

$$= 111.99 \text{ N/mm}^2$$

Maximum tensile stresses (top) :

$$\sigma_{bt} \;=\; \frac{M}{I} \times y_t = \frac{2443.5 \times 10^3}{1.2 \times 10^6} \times 15 = 30.54 \ \text{N/mm}^2$$

**Example 5.31 :** *The 100 mm $\times$ 150 mm portion of beam cross-section shown in Fig. 5.38 (a) and (b) is made up of wood ($E_W$ = 10 GPa) whereas 100 mm $\times$ 8 mm portion of steel ($E_S$ = 210 GPa). Find the maximum bending stress in wood and steel if the 3 m long beam is subjected to a central load of 5 kN.*

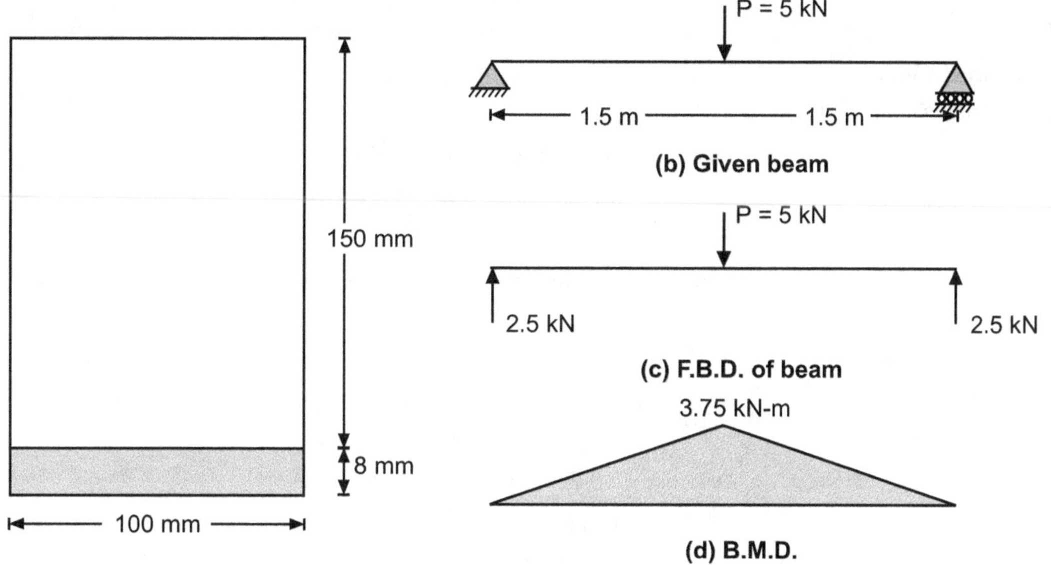


**Fig. 5.38**

**Data :** As shown in Fig. 5.38 (a) and (b).

**Required :** Maximum bending stress.

**Solution :** $M = \dfrac{E_s}{E_c} = \dfrac{210}{10} = 21$

$$\bar{y} \;=\; \frac{A_1 y_1 + A_2 y_2}{A_1 + A_2} = \frac{150 \times 100 \times 75 + 21 \times 100 \times 8 \times 154}{150 \times 100 + 21 \times 100 \times 8}$$

$$= 116.73 \ \text{m from top.}$$

$$I \;=\; \frac{100 \times 150^3}{12} + 100 \times 150 \times (116.73 - 75)^2$$

$$+ \frac{21 \times 100 \times 8^3}{12} + 21 \times 100 \times 8 \, (154 - 116.73)^2$$

$$= 77.67 \times 10^6 \ \text{mm}^4$$

$\therefore$　Bending stress in timber,

$$\sigma \;=\; \frac{M}{I} \times y_{max} = \frac{3.75 \times 10^6}{77.67 \times 10^6} \times 116.73 = 5.64 \ \text{MPa}$$

$\therefore$　　　　　　Stress in steel $= 21 \times \dfrac{5.64}{116.73} \times 43.27 = 43.90 \ \text{MPa}$

**Example 5.32 :** *A wood beam 100 mm × 250 mm is supported as shown in Fig. 5.39. Determine the maximum permissible P if the allowable bending stress is 10 MPa. Consider the self weight of the beam which has a specific weight 5.5 kN/m³, a = 0.6 m and L = 2.5 m.*

**Fig. 5.39**

**Data :** a = 0.6 m, L = 2.5 m, w = 5.5 kN/m³, $\sigma_{bc}$ = 10 MPa, beam 100 mm × 250 mm.

**Required :** Value of P.

**Solution :** Geometric properties :

$$A = 100 \times 250 = 25 \times 10^3 \text{ mm}^2$$

$$I = \frac{bd^3}{12} = \frac{100 \times 250^3}{12} = 130.21 \times 10^6 \text{ mm}^4$$

$$\text{S.W.} = \text{specific weight} \times \text{area} = 5.5 \times 0.1 \times 0.25 = 0.14 \text{ kN/m}$$

$$\sigma = \frac{M}{I} \times y$$

$$10 = \frac{(0.6\,P + 0.084) \times 10^6}{130.21 \times 10^6} \times 125$$

$$10.42 = 0.6\,P + 0.084$$

$$\therefore \quad P = 17.22 \text{ kN}$$

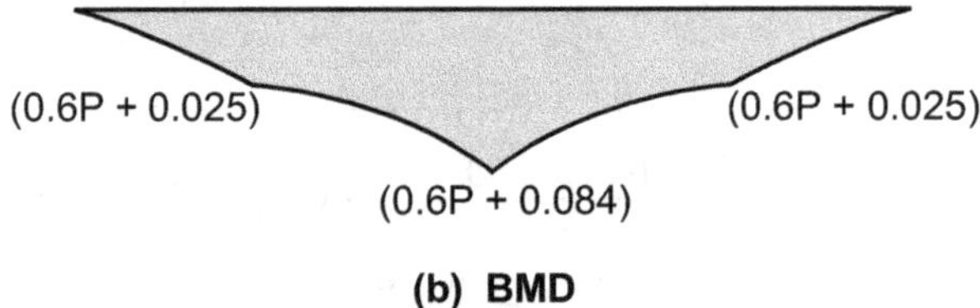

(a)  Given beam

(b)  BMD

**Fig. 5.40**

**Example 5.33 :** *The cross-section of the beam is as shown in Fig. 5.41 which is simply supported at ends and has a span of 5 m. The beam carries UDL of 25 kN/m. Determine thickness 't' if maximum bending compressive stress is not to exceed 150 MPa. Also check whether the section will remain safe in sharing if the maximum allowable shear stress is   100 MPa.*

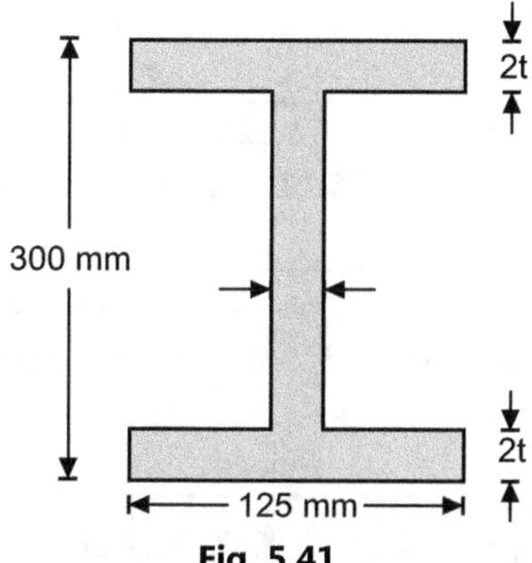



**Fig. 5.41**

**Data :** As shown in Fig. 5.41, w = 25 kN/m, $l$ = 5m.

$\sigma_c$ = 150 MPa, $\tau_{max}$ = 100 MPa

**Required :** Thickness 't'.

**Concept :** Determine t for bending stress and check for shear stress.

**Solution :** (i) Thickness 't' :

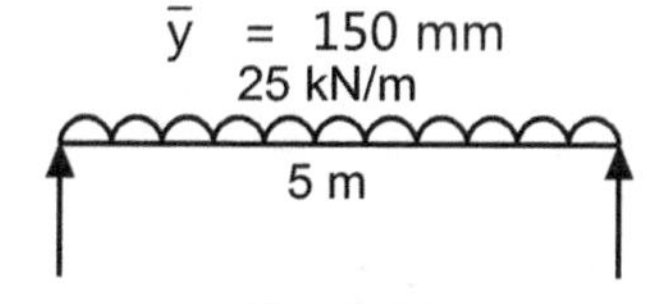



**Fig. 5.42**

$$\text{B.M.} = M = \frac{wl^2}{8} = \frac{25 \times 5^2}{8} = 78.13 \text{ kN-m}$$

$$\therefore \quad \frac{M}{I} = \frac{\sigma}{y}$$

$$\frac{78.13 \times 10^6}{I} = \frac{150}{150}$$

$$\therefore \quad I = 78.13 \times 10^6 \text{mm}^4$$

$$I = \left[ 125 \times \frac{300^3}{12} - \frac{(125 - t)(300 - 4t)^3}{12} \right]$$

$$\therefore \quad 78.125 \times 10^6 = 281.25 \times 10^6 - \frac{(125 - t)(300 - 4t)^3}{12}$$

Solving above equation **t = 6.49 mm**

(ii) Check for shear stress :

$$S = \frac{wl}{2} = \frac{25 \times 5}{2} = 62.5 \text{ kN}$$

$$\tau = \frac{SA\bar{y}}{Ib}$$

$$A\bar{y} = 125 \times 12.98 \times (150 - 6.49) + 137.02 \times 6.49 \times \frac{137.02}{2}$$

$$= 293.77 \times 10^3 \text{ mm}^3$$

$$\tau_{max} = \frac{62.5 \times 10^3 \times 293.77 \times 10^3}{78.125 \times 10^6 \times 6.49}$$

$$\tau_{max} = \mathbf{36.21 \text{ N/mm}^2} < 100 \text{ N/mm}^2$$

∴    Section will remain safe.

**Example 5.34 :** *A rectangular beam 300 mm deep is simply supported over a span of 4m. What UDL the beam may carry if the bending stress is not to exceed 120 MPa ?*

*Take I = 8 × 10⁶ mm⁴.*                                                      **(Dec. 2007)**

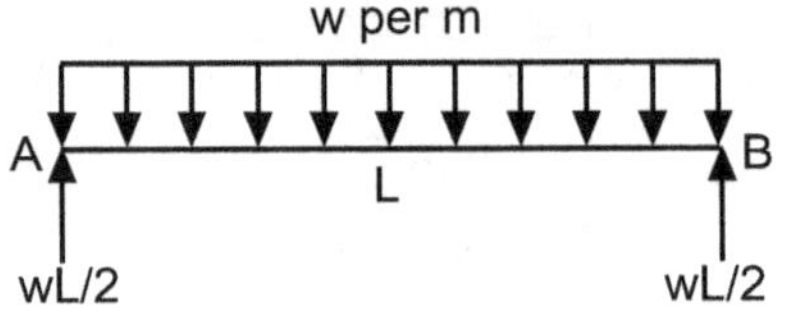


**Fig. 5.43**

**Data :** $D = 300$ mm, $l = 4$m, $\sigma_b = 120$ MPa, $I = 8 \times 10^6$ mm⁴

**Required :** UDL on beam.

**Concept :** Standard formulae.

**Solution :**

$$\frac{M}{I} = \frac{\sigma}{y}$$

$$M = \frac{120 \times 8 \times 10^6}{150} = 6.4 \times 10^6 \text{ N-mm.}$$

$$= 6.4 \text{ kN.m}$$

Let 'w' be the UDL on beam.

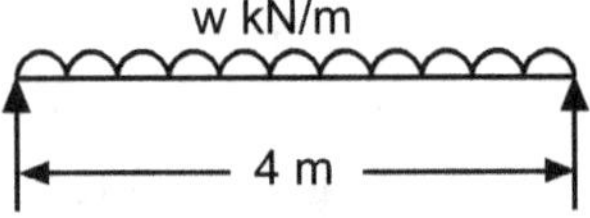


**Fig. 5.44**

$$\text{B.M.} = \frac{wl^2}{8} = \frac{w \times 4^2}{8} = 2w$$

$$\text{M.R.} = \text{B.M.}$$

$$6.4 = 2w$$

∴                                           $$w = \mathbf{3.2 \text{ kN/m}}$$

**Example 5.35 :** *A beam having a cross-section in the form of a channel as shown in Fig. 5.45 is subjected to a bending moment about X-X axis. Calculate the thickness 't' of the channel in order that the bending stresses at the top and at the bottom of the beam will be in the ratio 7 : 3.*

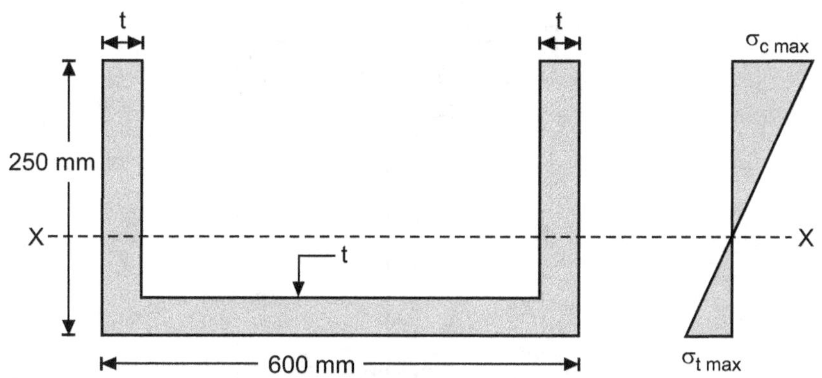


**Fig. 5.45**

**Data :** As shown in figure $\sigma_{top} : \sigma_{bottom} = 7 : 3$

**Required :** Thickness 't'.

**Concept :** Standard Formulae.

**Solution :**

$$\frac{\sigma_{top}}{\sigma_{bottom}} = \frac{7}{3}$$

$$\frac{250 - y_b}{y_b} = \frac{7}{3}$$

$$750 - 3y_b = 7y_b$$

$\therefore$      $y_b = 75$ mm

and      $y_t = 175$ mm

$$y_b = \frac{250 \times t \times 125 \times 2 + (600 - 2t)\, t \times \dfrac{t}{2}}{[(250 \times t) \times 2 + (600 - 2t) \times t]}$$

$\therefore$      $$75 = \frac{62500\, t + 300\, t^2 - t^3}{500\, t + 600\, t - 2t^2}$$

$\therefore$      $62500t + 300\, t^2 - t^3 = 82500\, t - 150\, t^2$

$\therefore$      $t^3 - 450\, t^2 + 2000t = 0$

Solving quadratic equation,

$$t = \mathbf{50\ mm}$$

$\therefore$   Thickness of channel is **50 mm**

---

**Example 5.36 :** *A symmetric I-section has flanges of size 180 mm × 10 mm and its overall depth is 500 mm. The thickness of the web is 8 mm. It is strengthened with a plate of size 240 mm × 12 mm on compressive side. Find the moment of resistance of the section, A = 10320 mm² if permissible stress is 150 N/mm². How much uniformly distributed load it can carry, if it is used as a cantilever of span 3 m ?*                    **(Dec. 2005)**

---

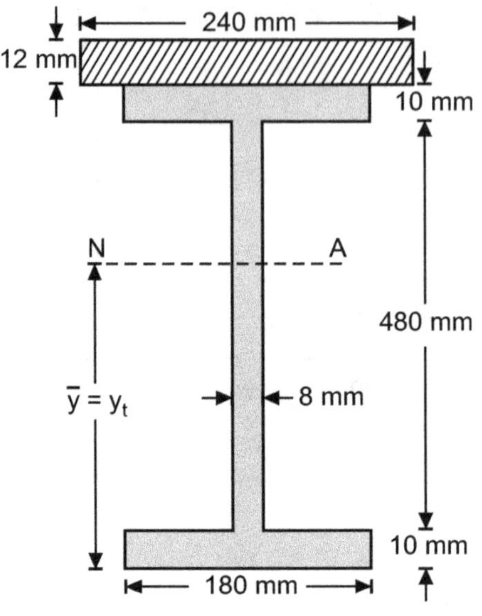


**Fig. 5.46**

**Data :** As shown in Fig. 5.46 $\sigma$ = 150 N/mm$^2$, $l$ = 3m.

**Required :** Moment of resistance.

**Concept :** Standard formulae.

**Solution :** (i) N.A. :

$$\bar{y}_{top} = \frac{240 \times 12 \times 6 + 180 \times 10 \times 17 + 480 \times 8 \times 262 + 180 \times 10 \times 507}{240 \times 12 + 180 \times 10 + 480 \times 8 + 180 \times 10}$$

$$= 190.56 \text{ mm}$$

$$I_{xx} = \frac{240 \times 12^3}{12} + 240 \times 12 \times (190.56 - 6)^2 + \frac{180 \times 10^3}{12}$$

$$+ 180 \times 10 (190.56 - 17)^2 + 480 \times 8 \times (262 - 190.56)^2$$

$$+ \frac{480^3 \times 8}{12} + \frac{180 \times 10^3}{12} + 180 \times 10 \times (507 - 190.56)^2$$

$$= 425.95 \times 10^6 \text{ mm}^4$$

Now,    $$\frac{M}{I} = \frac{\sigma}{y}$$

$\therefore$    $$M.R. = \frac{\sigma \times I}{y}$$

$$= \frac{150 \times 425.95 \times 10^6}{321.44}$$

$$= 198.77 \times 10^6 \text{ N.mm}$$

$\therefore$    M.R. = 198.77 kN.m

$\therefore$    M.R. = B.M. = **198.77 kN.m.**

**Example 5.37 :** *The cross-section of beam is a shown in Fig. 5.47. Determine maximum tensile and compressive stresses when the beam is subjected to uniformly distributed load of 2 kN/m and length of span is 3 m for : (i) Cantilever, (ii) Simply supported.*

*The beam resist bending moment about neutral axis.*                    **(May 2006)**

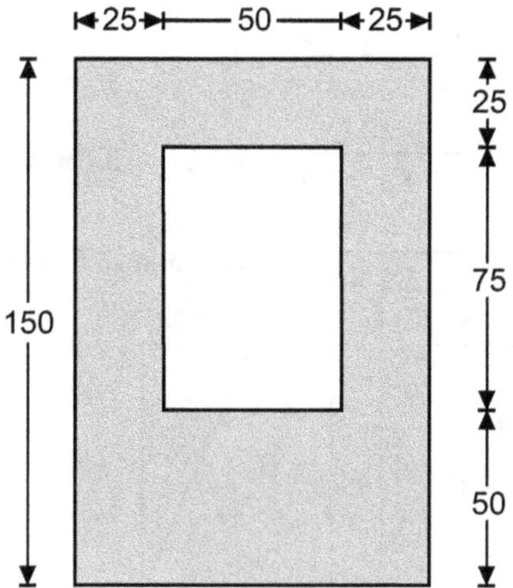

**Fig. 5.47**

**Data :** w = 2 kN/m, $l$ = 3m, as shown in Fig. 5.47.

**Required :** Tensile and compressive stresses.

**Concept :** $\sigma_b = \dfrac{M}{I} \cdot y$

**Solution :** (i) Geometric properties :

$$\bar{y}_{top} = \frac{150 \times 100 \times 75 - 50 \times 75 \times 62.5}{(150 \times 100 - 50 \times 75)} = 79.17 \text{ mm}$$

$$I = \frac{100 \times 150^3}{12} + 100 \times 150 \times (79.17 - 75)^2$$

$$- \frac{50 \times 75^3}{12} - 50 \times 75 \times (79.17 - 62.5)$$

$$= \mathbf{25.59 \times 10^6 \ mm^4}$$

(ii) Cantilever :

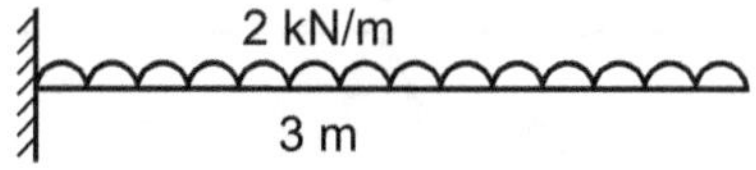

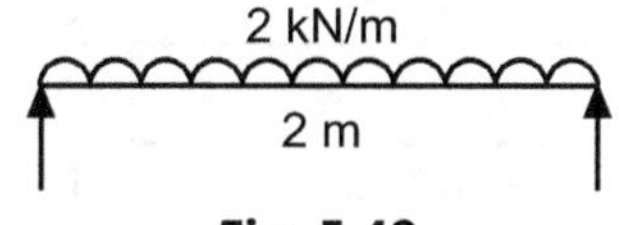


**Fig. 5.48**

$$\text{Maximum B.M.} = \frac{wl^2}{2} = \frac{2 \times 3^2}{2} = 9 \text{ kN.m}$$

$\therefore$

$$\sigma_{top} = \frac{M}{I} y_{top} = \frac{9 \times 10^6}{25.59 \times 10^6} \times 79.170 \text{ (Tension)}$$

$$= \mathbf{27.84 \ N/mm^2}$$

$$\sigma_{bottom} = \frac{9 \times 10^6}{25.59 \times 10^6} \times 70.83 = 24.91 \text{ N/mm}^2 \text{ (Comp.)}$$

(iii) Simply Supported :



**Fig. 5.49**

$$\text{Maximum B.M.} = \frac{wl^2}{8} = \frac{2 \times 2^2}{8} = 1 \text{ kN.m}$$

$$\therefore \quad \sigma_{top} = \frac{1 \times 10^6}{25.59 \times 10^6} \times 79.17 = \textbf{3.09 N/mm}^2$$

$$\sigma_{bottom} = \frac{1 \times 10^6}{25.59 \times 10^6} \times 70.83 = \textbf{2.77 N/mm}^2$$

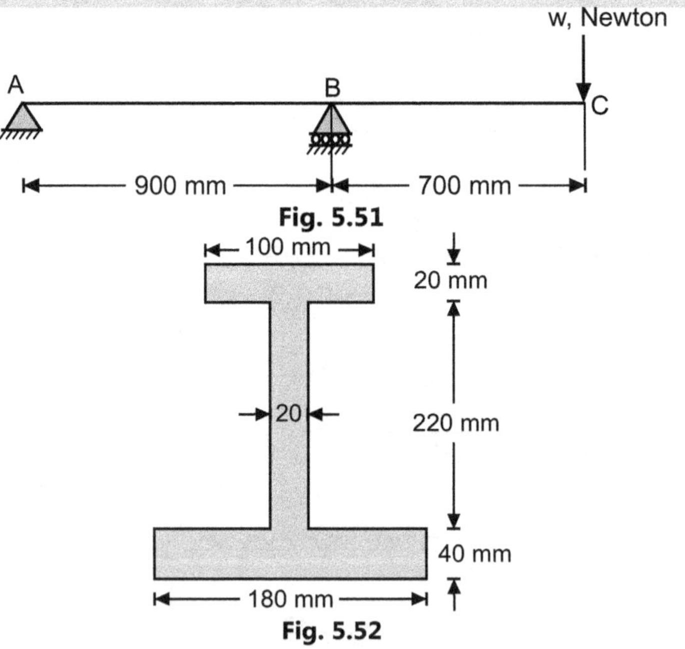


**Fig. 5.50**

**Example 5.48 :** *A simply supported beam with overhang is loaded with point load as shown in Fig. 5.51 and 5.52. The cross-section of beam is I-section. The allowable bending stresses in tension and compression are $\sigma_t$ = 150 MPa and $\sigma_c$ = 100 MPa. Find the safe value of load 'W' on the overhang.* **(Dec. 2006)**



**Fig. 5.51**



**Fig. 5.52**

**Data :** As shown in Fig. 5.51 and 5.52.

**Required :** Value of W.

**Concept :** M.R. = B.M.

**Solution :** (i) Geometric Properties :

$$\bar{y}_{top} = \frac{100 \times 20 \times 10 + 220 \times 20 \times 130 + 180 \times 40 \times 260}{100 \times 20 + 220 \times 20 + 180 \times 40}$$

$$= 181.18 \text{ mm}$$

$$I = \frac{100 \times 20^3}{12} + 100 \times 20 \times (181.18 - 10)^2$$

$$+ \frac{20 \times 220^3}{12} + 20 \times 220 \, (181.18 - 130)^2$$

$$+ \frac{180 \times 40^3}{12} + 180 \times 40 \, (260 - 181.18)^2$$

$$= 133.63 \times 10^6 \text{ mm}^4$$

(ii) Maximum B.M. :

$$\sum M @ A = 0$$

$$\therefore \quad W \times 1.6 - R_B \times 0.9 = 0$$

$$\therefore \quad R_B = 1.78 \, W \, (\uparrow) \text{ and } R_A = \textbf{(0.78 W)} \downarrow$$

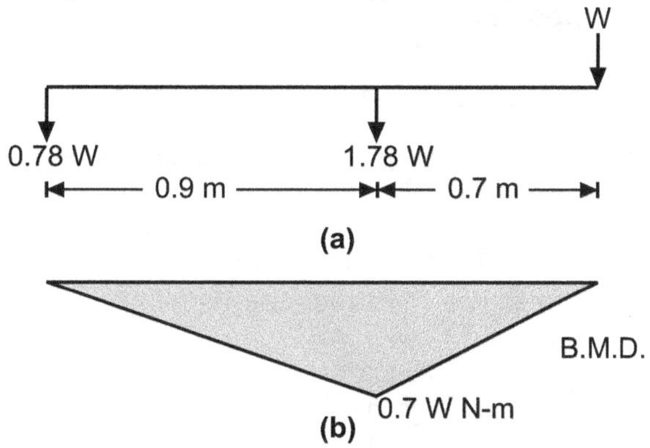

**Fig. 5.53**

$$M.R._1 = \frac{\sigma \times I}{y_{top}} = \frac{150 \times 133.63 \times 10^6}{181.87} = 110.21 \times 10^6 \text{ N.mm}$$

$$\therefore \quad 700 \, W = 110.21 \times 10^6$$

$$\therefore \quad W = 158.06 \times 10^3 \text{ N}$$

$$\therefore \quad W = \textbf{158 kN}$$

## EXERCISE

1. A steel rod of 16 mm diameter is to be bent to a circular arc. Find the minimum radius of curvature to which it should be bent, so that stress in steel may not exceed 120 MPa. Assume E = 200 GPa.     (13.33 m)

2. A rectangular beam 300 mm deep is simply supported over a span of 5 m. Find the intensity of safe UDL the beam can carry if bending stress is not to exceed 120 MPa. Assume $I = 8 \times 10^7$ mm$^4$. (20.48 kN/m)

3. A 4m long simply supported beam is loaded as shown in Fig. 5.54. The beam is rectangular in cross-section, 100 mm wide and 200 mm deep. Determine the maximum bending stress in the beam . (210.93 MPa)

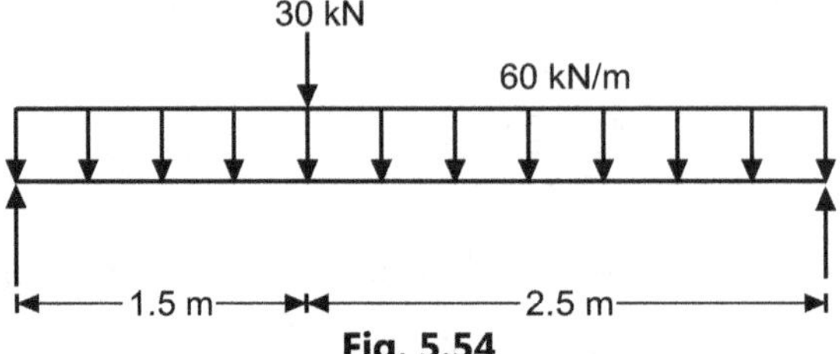


**Fig. 5.54**

4. An unequal angle bar 150 mm × 75 mm, thickness of metal 8 mm is used as a joist, simply supported over a span of 4 m with its longer leg placed vertically. Find the safe UDL the beam can carry if the maximum permissible bending stress is 130 MPa in tension. Also calculate maximum bending compressive stress induced.

(W = 23.91 kN/m; $\sigma_{bc;\ cal}$ = 71.23 MPa)

5. A rectangular section of beam 40 mm × 200 mm is simply supported and carries UDL of 8 kN/m. If the bending stress is not to exceed 125 MPa, determine the longest span over which beam can be supported. (5.77 m)

6. Determine the dimensions of timber beam rectangular in section, simply supported over 8 m span to carry a brick masonry wall 230 mm thick, 4 m high. Assume density of brick masonry as 20 kN/m$^3$, allowable bending stress = 8 MPa and b = $\dfrac{d}{2}$ for the cross-section.

(b = 302.2 mm, d = 604.4 mm)

9. Find the width of flange 'b' for the cross-section of beam shown in Fig. 5.55 such that, bending compressive stress is three times the bending tensile stress, when subjected to sagging bending moment. (b = 200 mm)

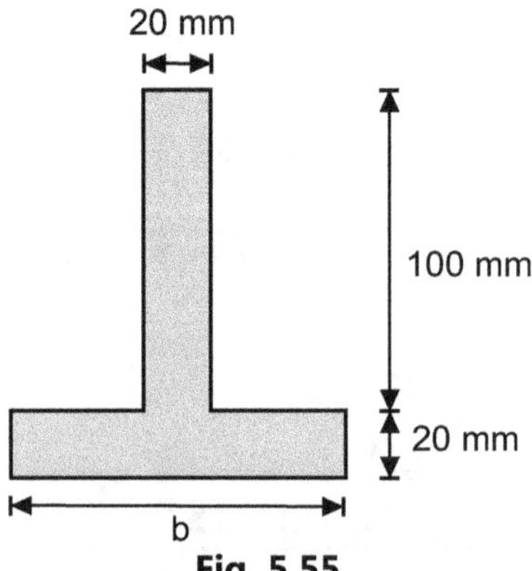


**Fig. 5.55**

7. The floor is supported on rectangular timber beams 100 mm × 300 mm, 4 m long. If the total floor load is 10 kN/m$^2$, calculate the spacing of beams such that the bending stress in beams does not exceed 10 MPa. (0.75 m)

8. A hollow circular bar having outside diameter twice the inside diameter is subjected to bending moment of 50 kN.m. If allowable bending stress is 120 MPa, find outside and inside diameters of bar.                    (D = 165.42 mm; d = 82.71 mm)

10. The cross-section of a simply supported beam of 5 m span is as shown in Fig. 5.56. If permissible stresses are 100 MPa in compression and 40 MPa in tension, find the safe UDL the beam can carry.(42.26 kN/m)

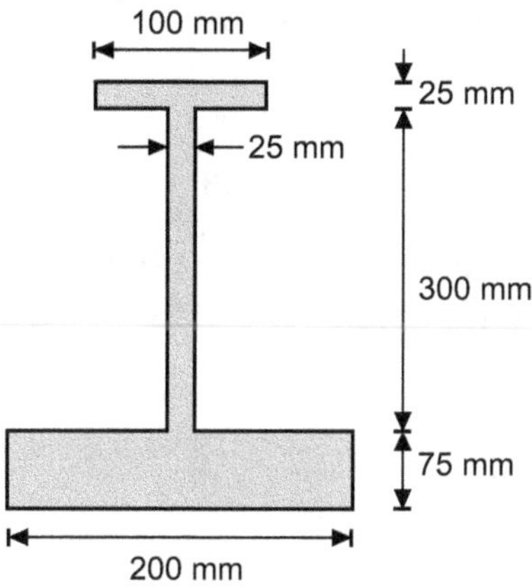


**Fig. 5.56**

11. The cross-section of cantilever bracket is as shown in Fig. 5.57. If allowable bending stresses are 90 MPa and 140 MPa in tension and compression respectively, find the maximum value of vertical point load it can support at free end. Assume span of bracket as 1.2 m.                    (127 kN)

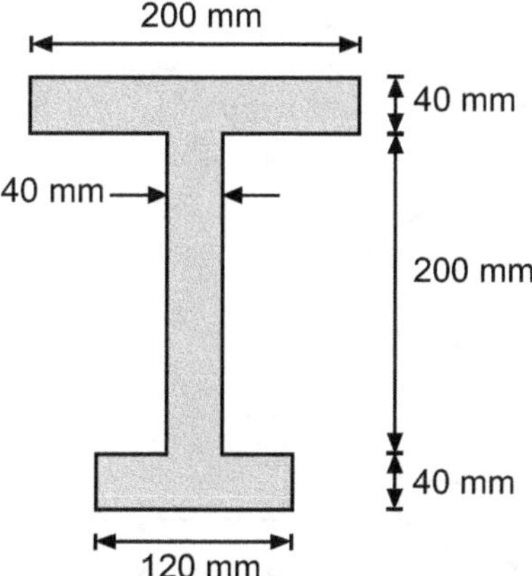


**Fig. 5.57**

12. A simply supported beam with an overhang is loaded as shown in Fig. 5.45. The cross-section of the beam is also shown in Fig. 5.58. Determine the bending stresses induced in the section at C and B.

(At C; BM = 9.18 kN.m; $\sigma_{bc,\ cal}$ = 70.59 MPa, $\sigma_{bt,\ (a)}$ = 187.12 MPa.

At B; BM = − 8.64 kN.m, $\sigma_{bc,\ cal}$ = 176.11 MPa; $\sigma_{bt,\ cal}$ = 66.43 MPa)

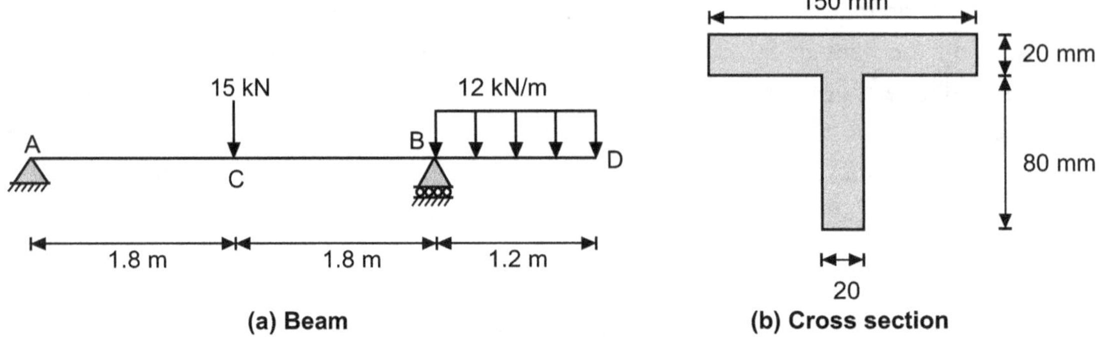

**(a) Beam**                              **(b) Cross section**

**Fig. 5.58**

13.  A beam having cross-section in the form of a channel is as shown in Fig. 5.59. It is subjected to bending moment about x-x-axis. Calculate the thickness 't' of the channel in order that the bending stresses at the top and at the bottom of the section will be in the ratio 7 : 3.                                                                              (50 mm)

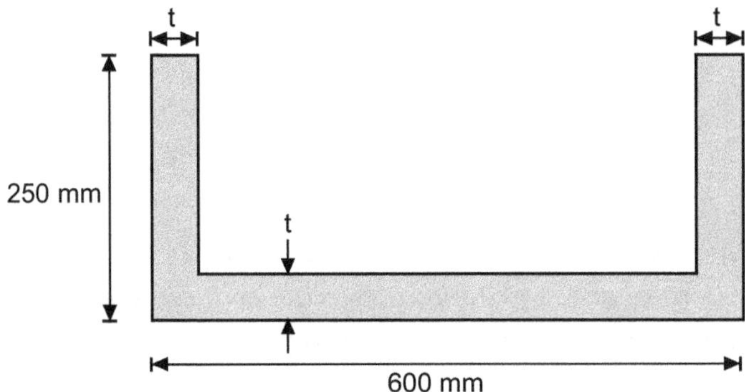

**Fig. 5.59**

14.  A simply supported beam, 4 m span of cross-section shown in Fig. 5.60 is to carry UDL throughout the span. Calculate the intensity of UDL if the tensile and compressive stresses must not exceed 25 MPa and 45 MPa respectively.                          (3.07 kN/m)

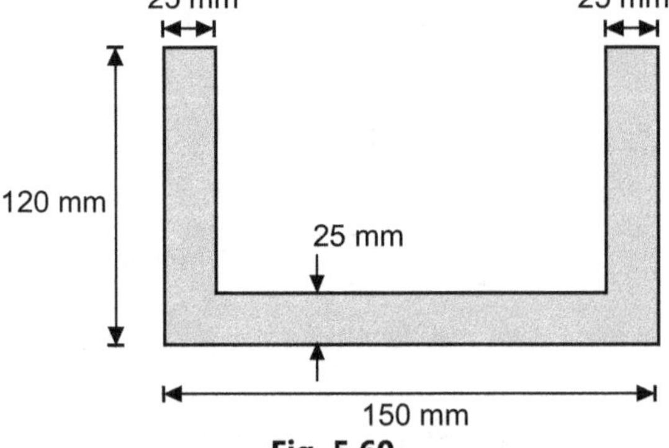

**Fig. 5.60**

15.  Fig. 5.61 shows the cross-section of beam when this section is subjected to bending moment, the tensile stress at the bottom is 40 MPa. Calculate : (i) the value of bending moment, (ii) stress induced at the top edge.

(BM = 40 kN.m; $\sigma_{b, top}$ = 53.32 MPa compressive)

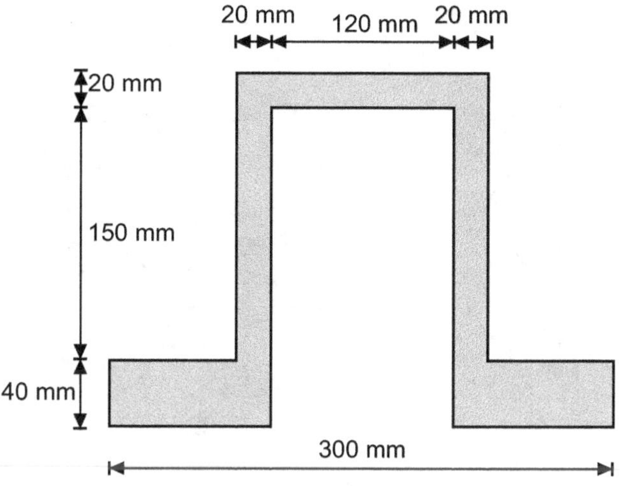

**Fig. 5.61**

16. A horizontal cantilever 2.5 m long is of rectangular cross-section 50 mm wide throughout its length and depth varying uniformly from 50 mm at the free end to 150 mm at the fixed end. A load of 5 kN acts at free end. Find the position of highest stressed section and the value of maximum bending stress induced. Neglect the self weight of cantilever.

$$(x = 1.25 \text{ m}; \sigma_{b, max} = 75 \text{ MPa})$$

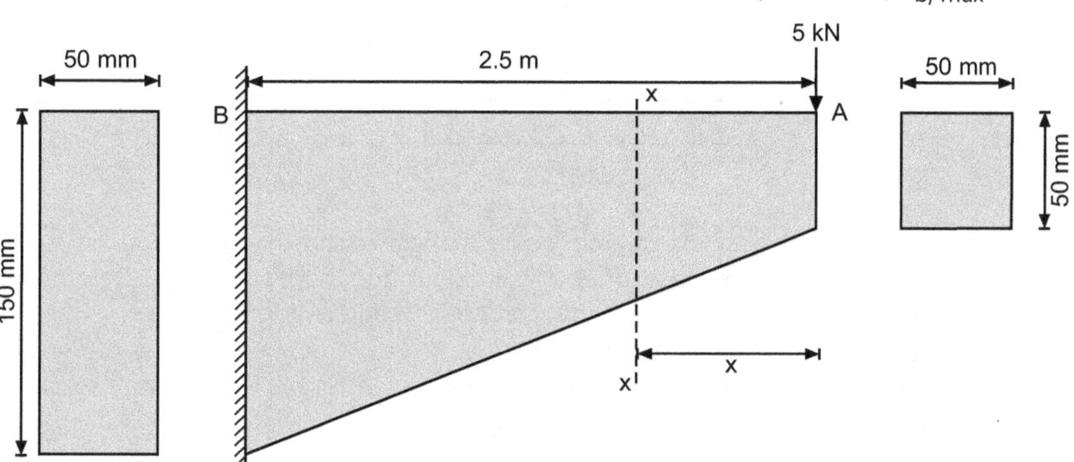

**Fig. 5.62**

17. A metallic tube of internal diameter 25 mm and 5 mm thickness is simply supported on a span of 1 m and the load at mid-span just sufficient to bring the stress to elastic limit is found to be 1 kN. Four such tubes are firmly clamped to each other to form a single beam, the centres of the tubes forming a square of 35 mm side with two sides of this square horizontal. Calculate the maximum UDL this beam can carry over a span of 1 m without exceeding the elastic limit. (14.59 kN/m)

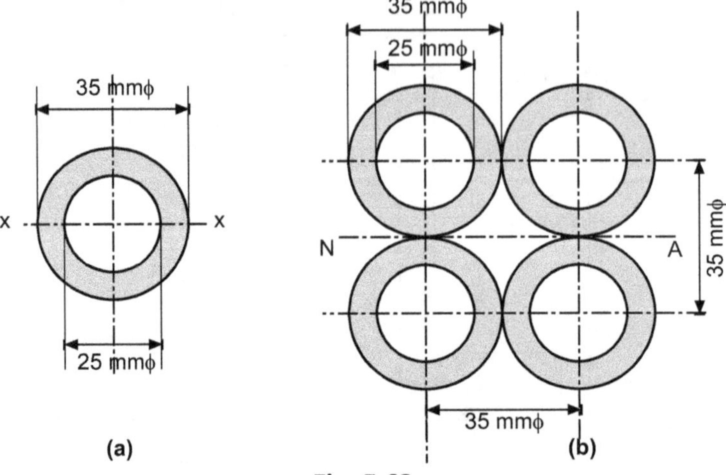


**Fig. 5.63**

18.  Fig. 5.64 shows the cross-section of a simply supported beam. The permissible stresses in bending compression and tension are 90 MPa and 30 MPa respectively. It is desired to achieve a balanced design so that the largest possible bending stresses are reached simultaneously. Find (i) the width of the flange, (ii) the magnitude of concentrated load that can be applied to the beam at its centre if the span is 6 m.(b = 270 mm, P = 7.776 kN)

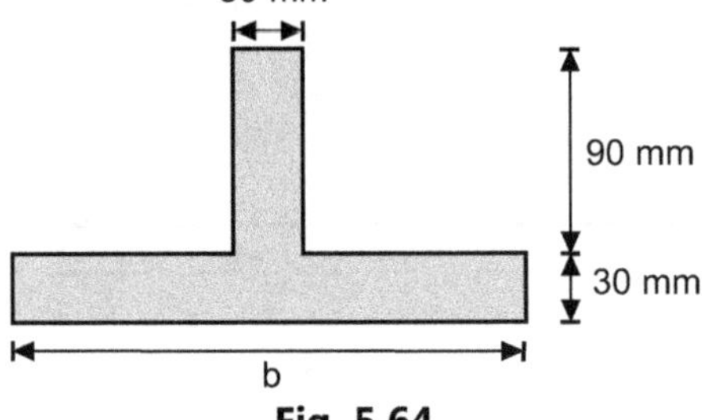


**Fig. 5.64**

19.  A beam has the cross-section of an isosceles triangle as shown in Fig. 5.65. It is subjected to sagging bending moment of 5 kN.m about the horizontal axis. Determine the magnitude and position of the resultant compressive and tensile forces.

(Tensile and compressive forces = 59.25 kN.

Position of compressive force from top = 50 mm.

Position of tensile force from bottom = 15.61 mm)

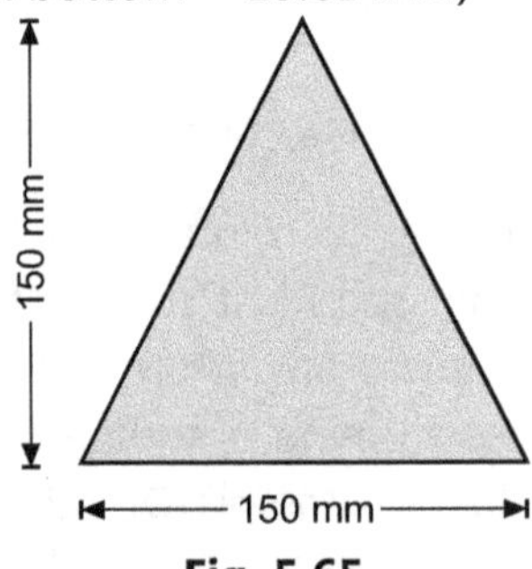


**Fig. 5.65**

## UNIVERSITY QUESTION PAPERS

### MAY 2014

1. A cast iron pipe of internal diameter 450 mm is 15 mm thick and is supported on a span of 8 m. Find the maximum bending stress in the pipe when it is full of water. Take specific weight of cast iron = 71600 N/m$^3$ and that of water = 9810 N/m$^3$. **[6]**

2. A horizontal beam of the section shown in following Fig. 1 is 3 m long and is simply supported at the ends. Find the maximum uniformly distributed load it can carry, if the compressive and tensile stresses must not exceed 55 N/mm$^2$ and 30 N/mm$^2$ respectively.

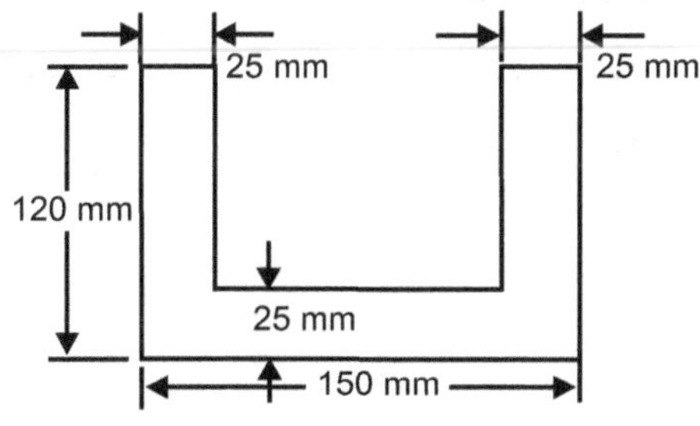


**Fig. 1**

### DECEMBER 2014

1. A cantilever beam, 30 mm wide by 100 mm high and 3 m long, carries a load that varies uniformly from zero at the free end to 2000 N/m at the wall. Compute the magnitude and location of the maximum flexural stress. **[6]**

### MAY 2015

1. A rectangular steel bar, 15 mm wide by 30 mm high and 6 m long, is simply supported at its ends. If the density of steel is 7850 kg/m$^3$, determine the maximum bending stress caused by the self-weight of the bar. **[6]**

2. Determine the minimum height h of the beam shown in Fig. 1 below if the flexural stress is not to exceed 20 MPa. **[6]**

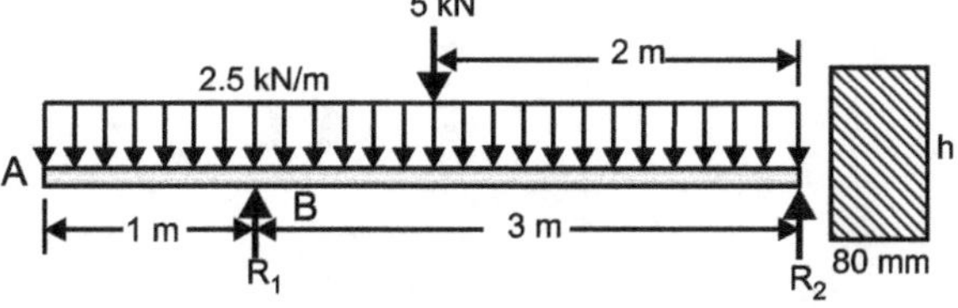


**Fig. 1**

## November 2015

1.  A cantilever beam, 60 mm wide by 100 mm high and 2 m long, carries UDL of 3000 N/m over entire span. Compute the magnitude and location of the maximum flexural stress. **[6]**

## May 2016

1.  A square beam 20 mm $\times$ 20 mm in section and 2 m long is supported at the ends. The beam fails when a point load of 400 N is applied at the centre of the beam. What uniformly distributed load per meter length will break a cantilever of the same material 40 mm wide, 60 mm. Deep and 3 m long? **[6]**

# Chapter 6

# SHEAR STRESSES DISTRIBUTION IN BEAMS

## 6.1 INTRODUCTION

The shearing force at any cross-section of a beam will set up a shear stress on transverse sections which in general will vary across the section. Following two assumptions are made in the analysis of shearing stress :

(i)   The shearing stress is uniform along the width i.e. parallel to neutral axis of the beam.

(ii)   The shearing stress does not affect the distribution of bending stress.

Second assumption cannot be strictly true because of distortion of the transverse plane due to shearing stress.

## 6.2 DERIVATION OF FORMULA FOR HORIZONTAL SHEARING STRESS

Consider two adjacent sections in a beam seperated by a small distance 'dx' as shown in Fig. 6.1 (a). Fig. 6.1 (b) shows bending stresses on two cross-sections. Assuming bending moment at cross-section 'cd' to be greater than that at cross-section 'ab', therefore the resulting horizontal force at cross-section 'cd', $F_{cd}$ will be greater than that at 'ab', $F_{ab}$.

Let it be required to find the shear stress intensity at '$y_1$' from NA. Consider free body diagram of elementary length 'dx' as shown in Fig. 6.1 (c) and Fig. 6.1 (e). Above this layer, difference in horizontal forces at two cross-sections will be resisted by shear force 'dF' acting on the bottom face of the free body since no external force acts on the section in this direction.

Thus, for equilibrium,

$$\sum F_x = 0; \qquad dF = F_{cd} - F_{ab}$$

$$= \int_{y_1}^{y_{max}} \sigma_{cd} \cdot dA - \int_{y_1}^{y_{max}} \sigma_{ab} \cdot dA$$

$$= \frac{M_{cd}}{I} \int_{y_1}^{y_{max}} y \cdot dA - \frac{M_{ab}}{I} \int_{y_1}^{y_{max}} y \cdot dA$$

$$= \frac{M_{cd} - M_{ab}}{I} \int_{y_1}^{y_{max}} y \cdot dA \qquad \qquad \ldots (6.1)$$

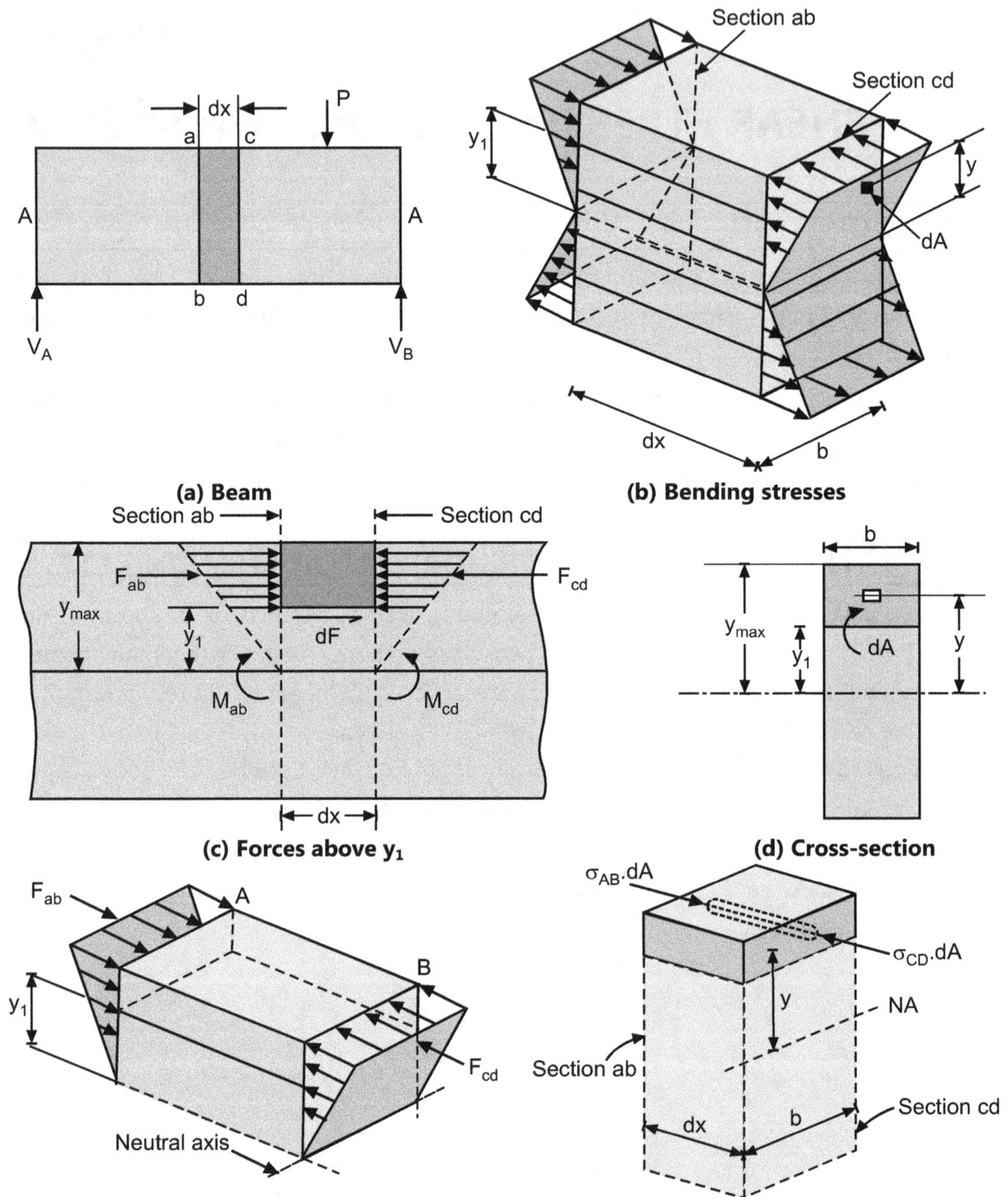



**Fig. 6.1 : Derivation of horizontal shearing stress**

where; $M_{ab}$ and $M_{cd}$ = Bending moments at cross-sections 'ab' and 'cd' respectively.

From Fig. 6.1 (c),

$$dF = \tau \cdot b \cdot dx \qquad \qquad \text{... (6.2)}$$

where; $\quad \tau$ = average shear stress on area of length 'dx' and width 'b'.

Equating equations (6.1) and (6.2),

$$\tau \cdot b \cdot dx = \frac{M_{cd} - M_{ab}}{I} \int_{y_1}^{y_{max}} y \cdot dA$$

$$\therefore \quad \tau = \frac{M_{cd} - M_{ab}}{dx} \cdot \frac{1}{bI} \int_{y_1}^{y_{max}} y \cdot dA = \frac{S}{bI} \int_{y_1}^{y_{max}} y \cdot dA$$

where;  $\quad S$ = vertical shear force at a section

$$= \frac{M_{cd} - M_{ab}}{dx} = \text{rate of change of bending moment}$$

$$\therefore \quad \tau = \frac{SA\,\bar{y}}{b\,I} \qquad \qquad \text{... (6.3)}$$

where;  $\quad A\,\bar{y} = \int_{y_1}^{y_{max}} y \cdot dA$

= Moment of area above or below the level at which shear stress is required about the neutral axis.

**Note :** It is the vertical shear force which comes in the equation (6.3) of calculating horizontal shear stress. However, horizontal shear stress is always accompanied by equal vertical shear stress as shown in Fig. 6.2.

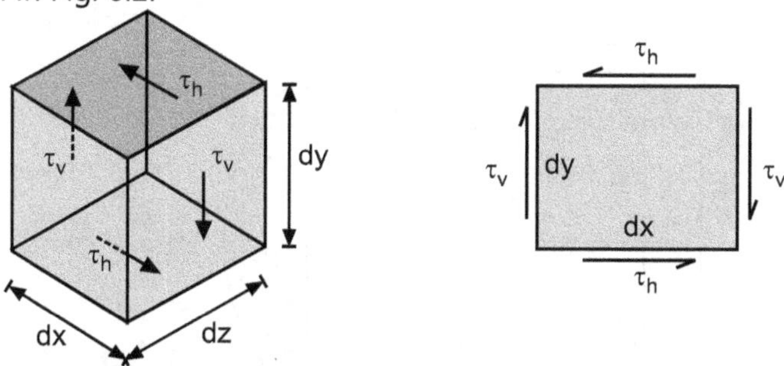

**Fig. 6.2 : State of shear stress on typical beam element**

# 6.3 DESIGN OF SHEAR CONNECTORS

Consider a wooden plank placed on top of another as shown in Fig. 6.3. If these planks act as a beam and are not interconnected, they will slide over each other at their contact surface. The interconnection of these components is necessary so that, they act as one unit.

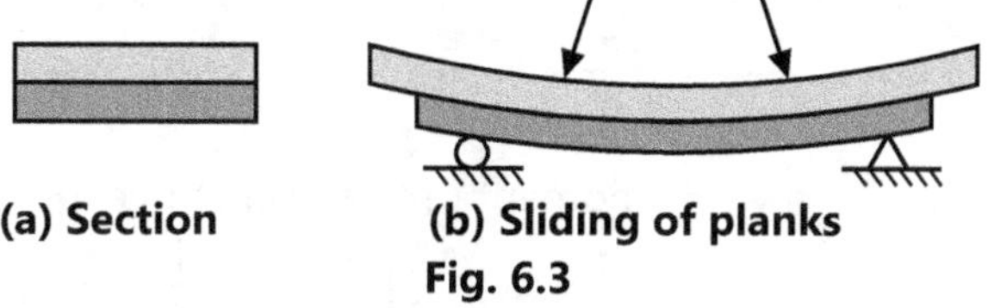

**(a) Section**  **(b) Sliding of planks**

**Fig. 6.3**

If the shear stress is multiplied by the width of cross-section, we get longitudinal force per unit length transmitted across the section (q) at the respective level. This quantity (q) is called as *shear flow.*

Thus, horizontal shear per unit length

$$= q \;=\; \tau \cdot b \;=\; \frac{SA\,\bar{y}}{I} \qquad\qquad \text{... (6.4)}$$

Let,　p  = pitch of rivets or nails along the length of member.

Then, to avoid shear failure and to make components behave as one unit,

$$q \cdot p \;=\; \text{Strength of rivet or nail} \qquad\qquad \text{... (6.5)}$$

From equation (6.5), pitch of the shear connectors can be obtained.

# SOLVED EXAMPLES

**Example 6.1 :** *Derive the relation between* $\tau_{max}$ *and* $\tau_{avg}$ *for*

*(i)　Rectangular section.*

*(ii)　Circular section.*

**Data**　　　:　Shear stresses for rectangular section and circular section as shown in Fig. 6.4 (a) and Fig. 6.5 (a).

**Required**　:　Relation between $\tau_{max}$ and $\tau_{avg}$ for rectangular and circular section.

**Concept**　:　Actual shear stress $= \tau = \dfrac{SA\,\bar{y}}{b\,I}$ and $\tau_{avg} = \dfrac{\text{Shear force}}{\text{Cross-sectional area}}$.

**Solution**　:　(I) Rectangular section :

(i)　　Geometric properties of cross-section : $I_{xx} = \dfrac{bd^3}{12}$

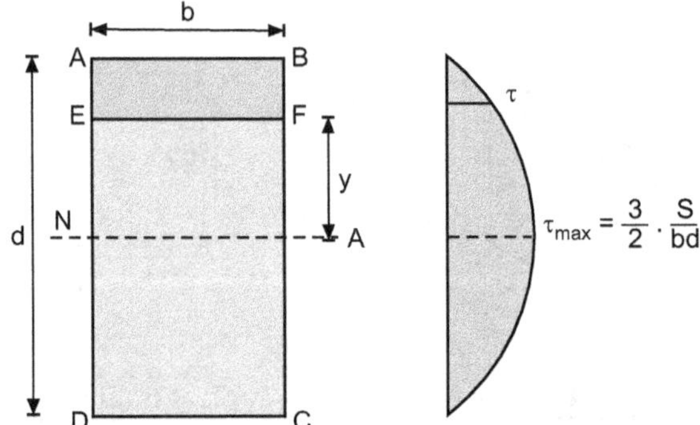



**(a) C/s of beam**　　　**(b) Shear stress distribution diagram**

**Fig. 6.4**

(ii)　　Stress Analysis :

Intensity of shear stress at level EF

$$\tau \;=\; \frac{Sa\,\bar{y}}{bI}$$

where;　　　　　　　　　　　$a\,\bar{y}$　= moment of the area above EF

$$\therefore \qquad a\,\bar{y} \;=\; b\left(\frac{d}{2} - y\right) \cdot \frac{1}{2}\left(\frac{d}{2} + y\right) = \frac{b}{2}\left(\frac{d^2}{4} - y^2\right)$$

$\therefore \qquad \tau = \dfrac{S}{b\,I} \cdot \dfrac{b}{2}\left(\dfrac{d^2}{4} - y^2\right) = \dfrac{12}{bd^3} \cdot \dfrac{S}{b} \cdot \dfrac{b}{2}\left(\dfrac{d^2}{4} - y^2\right) = \dfrac{6\,S}{bd^3}\left(\dfrac{d^2}{4} - y^2\right)$

At the top edge i.e. at $\qquad y = \dfrac{d}{2}; \ \tau = 0$

At the neutral axis, i.e. at $\qquad y = 0$

$$\tau = \dfrac{6\,S}{bd^3} \cdot \dfrac{d^2}{4} = \dfrac{3}{2} \cdot \dfrac{S}{bd}$$

Average shear stress $\qquad \tau_{avg} = \dfrac{S}{bd}$

$$\tau_{max} = \dfrac{3}{2}\,\tau_{avg}.$$

Hence, the maximum shear stress intensity for a rectangular section is 1.5 times the average shear stress.

(II)    Circular section :

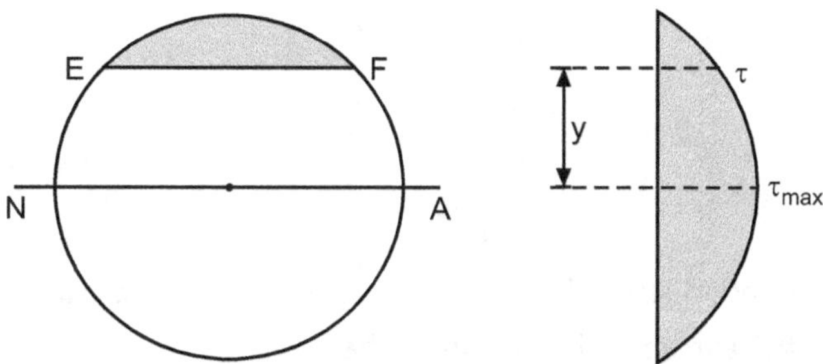


**(a) C/s of beam**    **(b) Shear stress distribution diagram**

**Fig. 6.5**

(i)    Geometric properties of cross-section.

$$I_{XX} = \dfrac{\pi\,r^4}{4}$$

(ii)    Stress Analysis.

Consider any level EF at a distance "y" from the neutral axis.

Width of the section at the level EF.

$$= 2\sqrt{r^2 - y^2}$$

Moment of the area above EF @ the NA.

$$a\,\bar{y} = \int\limits_{y}^{r} 2y\sqrt{r^2 - y^2}\ dy$$

Let, $\qquad 2\sqrt{r^2 - y^2} = u$

$$4(r^2 - y^2) = u^2$$

$$-8y \cdot dy = 2u \cdot du$$

$$y \cdot dy = -\dfrac{1}{4}u \cdot du$$

$$a\,\bar{y} \;=\; \int_{u}^{0} -\frac{1}{4}\,u \cdot du = \frac{1}{4}\int_{0}^{u} u^2 \cdot du = \frac{u^3}{12}$$

Shear stress at level EF, $\quad \tau \;=\; \dfrac{Sa\,\bar{y}}{b\,I}$

where; $\qquad\qquad\qquad\qquad$ b $\;=\;$ width of the section at level EF

$\qquad\qquad\qquad\qquad\qquad$ $=\;$ EF $= 2\sqrt{r^2 - y^2} = u$

$\therefore \qquad\qquad\qquad \tau \;=\; \dfrac{S}{I}\cdot\dfrac{u^3}{12u} = \dfrac{S}{12\,I}\,u^2$

$$\tau \;=\; \frac{S}{12\,I}\cdot 4\,(r^2 - y^2)$$

$$=\; \frac{S}{3\,I}\cdot (r^2 - y^2)$$

$$=\; \frac{S\times 4}{3\pi\,r^4}\cdot (r^2 - y^2)$$

$$=\; \frac{4}{3}\,\frac{S}{\pi r^4}\cdot (r^2 - y^2)$$

Hence, the shear stress distribution is according to a parabolic law.

At $\quad$ y = r; i.e. at the extreme distance from the neutral axis.

$$\tau \;=\; 0$$

At $\quad$ y = 0; i.e. at the neutral axis, the shear stress

$$\tau_{max} \;=\; \frac{4}{3}\cdot\frac{S}{\pi r^2}$$

But the average shear stress $=\;\; \tau_{avg} = \dfrac{S}{\pi r^2}$

$\therefore \qquad\qquad\qquad \tau_{max} \;=\; \dfrac{4}{3}\,\tau_{avg}$

---

**Example 6.2 :** *Two cross-sections of timber beam; square and solid circular, are subjected to shear force of 53 kN. If maximum allowable shear stress for timber is 8 MPa, design the cross-sectional dimensions.*

**Data** $\qquad$ : $\quad$ SF = 53 kN ; $\tau_{max}$ = 8 MPa

**Required** $\quad$ : $\quad$ Cross-sectional dimensions.

**Concept** $\qquad$ : $\quad$ $\tau_{max}$ = 1.5 $\tau_{avg}$ for rectangular or square cross-section and $\tau_{max} = \dfrac{4}{3}\,\tau_{avg}$ for solid circular cross-section.

**Solution** $\quad$ : $\quad$ (i) Design of square cross-section.

$\qquad$ Let, $\qquad\qquad\qquad\qquad$ a $\;=\;$ side of square in mm

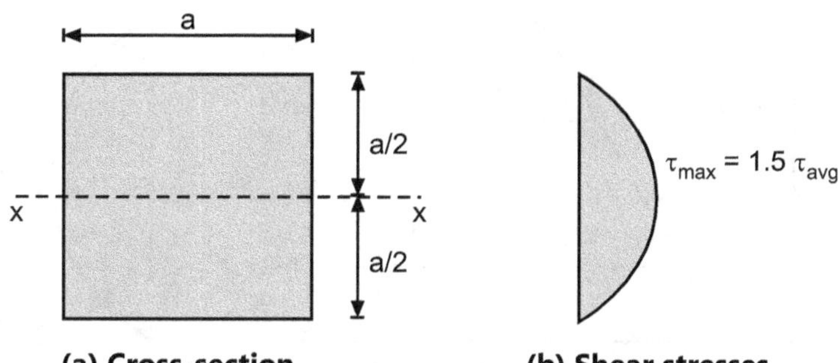



**(a) Cross-section**　　　　**(b) Shear stresses**

**Fig. 6.6**

$$\therefore \quad \tau_{avg} = \frac{SF}{c/s\ area} = \frac{53 \times 10^3}{a^2}$$

$$\therefore \quad \tau_{max} = \frac{1.5 \times 53 \times 10^3}{a^2} = 8\ MPa \quad (\because Given)$$

$$\therefore \quad a = 99.68\ mm$$

$$\cong \mathbf{100\ mm\ (say).}$$

∴　　Use **100 mm × 100 mm beam**

(ii)　　Design of solid circular cross-section.

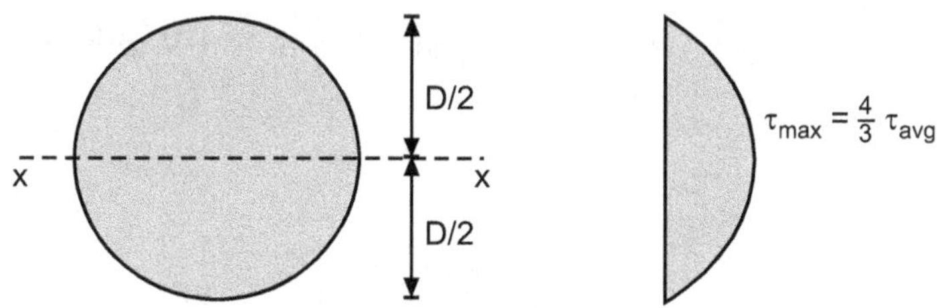



**(a) Cross-section**　　**(b) Shear stresses**

**Fig. 6.7**

Let,　　　　　　　$D$ = Diameter of section in mm

$$\therefore \quad \tau_{avg} = \frac{SF}{c/s\ area} = \frac{53 \times 10^3}{\frac{\pi}{4} \cdot D^2}$$

$$\tau_{max} = \frac{4}{3} \times \frac{53 \times 10^3}{\left(\frac{\pi}{4}\right) D^2} = 8\ MPa \quad (\because given)$$

$$\therefore \quad D = 106.05\ mm$$

∴　　Use　　　　　$D$ = **107 mm**

**Example 6.3 :** *A beam is triangular in section having a base "b" and an altitude "h". It is placed with its base horizontal. If at a certain section of the beam, the shear force is "S", find the maximum shear stress and the shear stress at the neutral axis.*

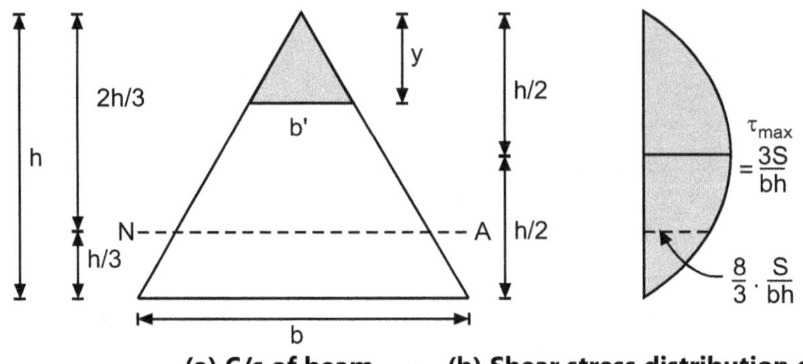

**(a) C/s of beam        (b) Shear stress distribution diagram**

**Fig. 6.8**

**Data**        :   As shown in Fig. 6.8.

**Required**    :   Maximum shear stress and shear stress at the neutral axis.

**Concept**     :   $\tau = \dfrac{SA\,\bar{y}}{b\,I}$

**Solution**    :   (i) Geometric properties of cross-section :

$$I_{xx} = \frac{bh^3}{36}$$

(ii)    Stress Analysis :

Let the shear stress intensity be "$\tau$" at a depth "$y$" from top. Width of the beam at a depth "$y$" from the top is say $b'$.

$$b' = \frac{b}{h}\cdot y$$

$$\tau = \frac{Sa\,\bar{y}}{I\,b'} = \frac{S\left(\dfrac{y}{2}\cdot\dfrac{by}{h}\right)\left(\dfrac{2}{3}h-\dfrac{2}{3}y\right)}{\left(\dfrac{bh^3}{36}\right)\left(\dfrac{by}{h}\right)}$$

$$\tau = \frac{12\,S}{bh^3}\,y\,(h-y)$$

For $\tau$ to be maximum;

$$\frac{d\tau}{dy} = \frac{12\,S}{bh^3}\,(h-2y) = 0$$

$\therefore$

$$y = \frac{h}{2}$$

$$\tau_{max} = \frac{12\,S}{bh^3}\cdot\frac{h}{2}\cdot\frac{h}{2} = \frac{3\,S}{b\,h}$$

To find shear stress at the neutral axis; put $y = \dfrac{2}{3}h$

$$\tau = \frac{12\,S}{bh^3}\cdot\frac{2}{3}h\cdot\frac{h}{3} = \frac{8}{3}\cdot\frac{S}{b\,h}$$

**Example 6.4 :** *A beam of square section is placed with one diagonal horizontal. If the shear force at a section of the beam is S, draw the shear stress distribution diagram for the section.*

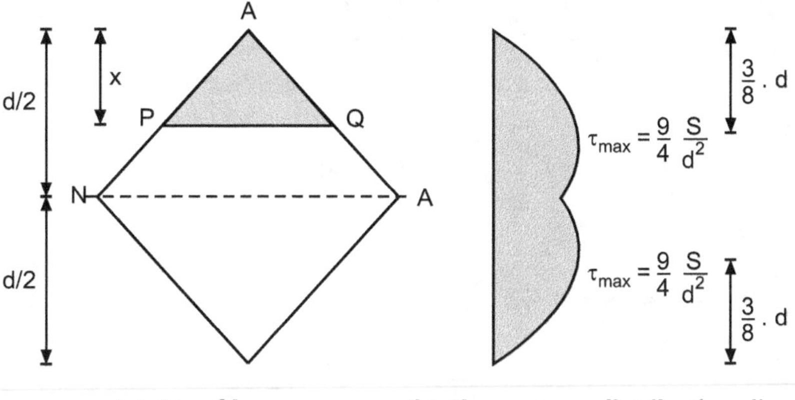

(a) C/s of beam                   (b) Shear stress distribution diagram

**Fig. 6.9**

**Data**          :   As shown in Fig. 6.9 (a).

**Required**   :   Shear stress distribution diagram for the section.

**Concept**   :   $\tau = \dfrac{SA\,\bar{y}}{b\,I}$

**Solution**   :   (i) Geometric properties of cross-section :

$$I_{xx} = 2\,\frac{d\left(\dfrac{d}{2}\right)^3}{12} = \frac{d^4}{48}$$

(ii)    Stress Analysis :

Consider a point in the section at a depth x from A. Shear stress at this point is given by

$$\tau = \frac{Sa\,\bar{y}}{b\,I}$$

where;                              a  = area above the level PQ

$\bar{y}$  = centroidal distance of the shaded area from the neutral axis.

b  = width of the beam at a depth x from A

∴                              $a = x^2$ and $\bar{y} = \left(\dfrac{d}{2} - \dfrac{2}{3}x\right) = \dfrac{1}{6}(3d - 4x)$

$$b = 2x$$

$$\tau = Sx^2 \dfrac{\frac{1}{6}(3d - 4x)}{\left(\dfrac{d^4}{48}\right) \times 2x}$$

$$\therefore \quad \tau = \frac{4S}{d^4} x (3d - 4x)$$

At  $x = 0$; i.e. at A, $\tau = 0$

At  $x = \dfrac{d}{2}$; i.e. at the neutral axis,

$$\tau_{na} = \frac{4S}{d^4} \cdot \frac{d}{2}\left(3d - \frac{4d}{2}\right) = \frac{2S}{d^2}$$

Average shear stress  $= \tau_{avg} = \dfrac{S}{\text{area of beam section}}$

$$\frac{S}{\left(\dfrac{d^2}{2}\right)} = \frac{2S}{d^2}$$

$$\tau_{avg} = \tau_{na}$$

For shear stress to be a maximum,

$$\frac{d\tau}{dx} = \frac{4S}{d^4}(3d - 8x) = 0$$

i.e.  $$x = \frac{3}{8} \cdot d$$

Hence, at a distance of $\dfrac{3}{8} \cdot d$ from 'A', maximum shear stress occurs.

Putting $x = \dfrac{3}{8}d$ in the general expression for the shear stress, the maximum shear stress is

given by

$$\tau_{max} = \frac{4S}{d^4} \cdot \frac{3}{8} \cdot d \left(3d - 4 \times \frac{3}{8} \cdot d\right)$$

$$= \frac{9}{4} \cdot \frac{S}{d^2} = \frac{9}{8} \cdot \left(\frac{2S}{d^2}\right)$$

$$\tau_{max} = \frac{9}{8}\,\tau_{avg}$$

---

**Example 6.5 :** *Draw shear stress distribution diagram for the cross-section of beam shown in Fig. 6.10 (a) if SF = 100 kN.*

---

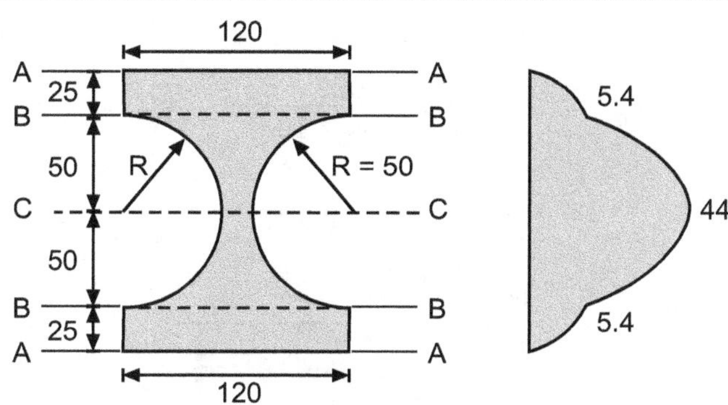



**(a) C/s of beam　(b) Shear stress distribution diagram (MPa)**

**Fig. 6.10**

**Data**　　　:　SF = 100 kN ; c/s as shown in Fig. 6.10 (a).

**Required**　:　Shear stress distribution diagram.

**Concept**　　:　Shear stress = $\tau = \dfrac{SA\,\bar{y}}{b\,I}$.

**Solution**　:　(i) Geometric properties of cross-section :

$$I_{XX} = \frac{120 \times 150^3}{12} - \frac{\pi}{4}(50)^4 = 28.84 \times 10^6 \text{ mm}^4$$

(ii)　　Shear stress analysis :

$$\tau_{AA} = 0$$

$$\tau_{BB} = \frac{SA\,\bar{y}}{b\,I}$$

Refer Fig. 6.11.

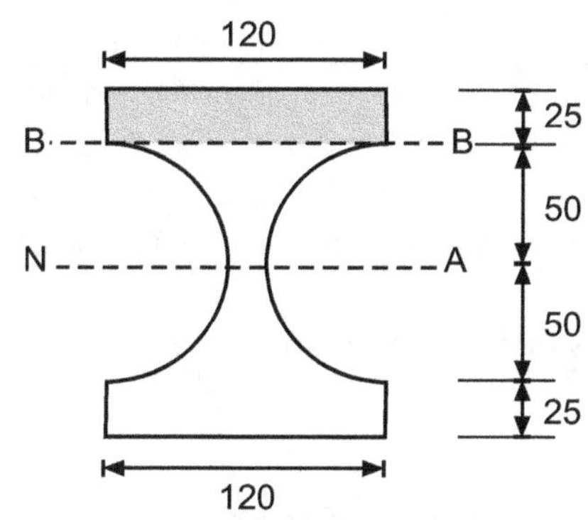



(All dimensions in mm)

**Fig. 6.11**

where;

$$S = 100 \text{ kN}$$

$$A = 120 \times 25 = 3000 \text{ mm}^2$$

$$\bar{y} = 50 + \frac{25}{2} = 62.5 \text{ mm}$$

$$b = 120 \text{ mm}$$

$$I = 28.84 \times 10^6 \text{ mm}^4$$

$$\therefore \quad \tau_{BB} = \frac{100 \times 10^3 \times 3000 \times 62.5}{120 \times 28.84 \times 10^6} = 5.4 \text{ MPa.}$$

$$\tau_{CC} = \frac{SA\,\bar{y}}{bI}, \text{ Refer Fig. 6.12}$$

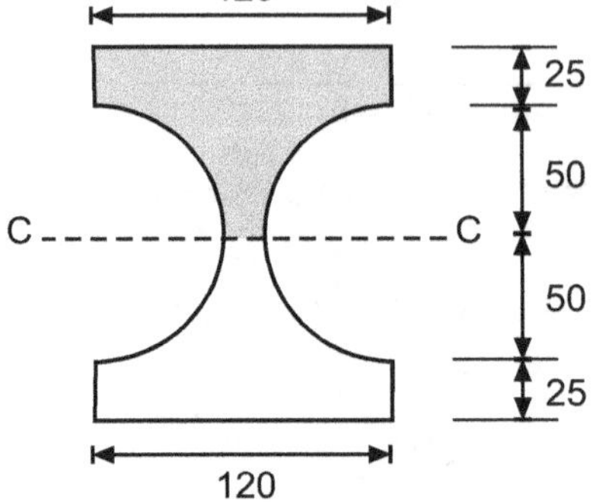

(All dimensions in mm)

**Fig. 6.12**

where;

$$A\,\bar{y} = 120 \times 75 \times \frac{75}{2} - \frac{\pi}{2}(50)^2 \times \frac{4 \times 50}{3\pi}$$

$$= 254.16 \times 10^3 \text{ mm}^3$$

$$\therefore \quad b = 120 - 2 \times 50 = 20 \text{ mm}$$

$$\therefore \quad \tau_{CC} = \frac{100 \times 10^3 \times 254.16 \times 10^3}{20 \times 28.84 \times 10^6} = \textbf{44 MPa}$$

$\therefore$ Shear stress distribution diagram is as shown in Fig. 6.10 (b).

**Example 6.6 :** *A simply supported beam of span 4 m carries UDL of 6 kN/m throughout the span. The cross-section of the beam is as shown in Fig. 6.13 (c). Draw shear stress distribution diagram for cross-section at 1 m from support. Also find average shear stress.*

**Data** : Span = 4 m ; simply supported ; UDL = 6 kN/m ; cross-section as shown in Fig. 6.13 (c).

**Required** : Shear stress distribution diagram for c/s at 1 m from left support.

**Concept** : $\tau = \dfrac{SA\,\bar{y}}{b\,I}$

**Solution** : (i) Geometric properties of cross-section :
Consider bottom most fibre as a reference for locating CG.

$$a_1 = 100 \times 10 = 1000 \text{ mm}^2; \quad y_1 = 105 \text{ mm}$$

$$a_2 = 100 \times 10 = 1000 \text{ mm}^2; \quad y_2 = 50 \text{ mm}$$

$$\bar{y} = \frac{a_1 y_1 + a_2 y_2}{a_1 + a_2} = \frac{1000 \times 105 + 1000 \times 50}{1000 + 1000}$$

$$= 77.5 \text{ mm from bottom}$$

$$I_{xx} = I_{xx_1} + I_{xx_2}$$

$$I_{xx_1} = \frac{100 \times 10^3}{12} + (1000)(105 - 77.5)^2 = 764.58 \times 10^3 \text{ mm}^4$$

$$I_{xx_2} = \frac{10 \times 100^3}{12} + (1000)(77.5 - 50)^2$$

$$= 1.589 \times 10^6 \text{ mm}^4$$

$$\therefore \quad I_{xx} = (764.58 + 1.589) \times 10^3 = \mathbf{2.354 \times 10^6 \text{ mm}^4}$$

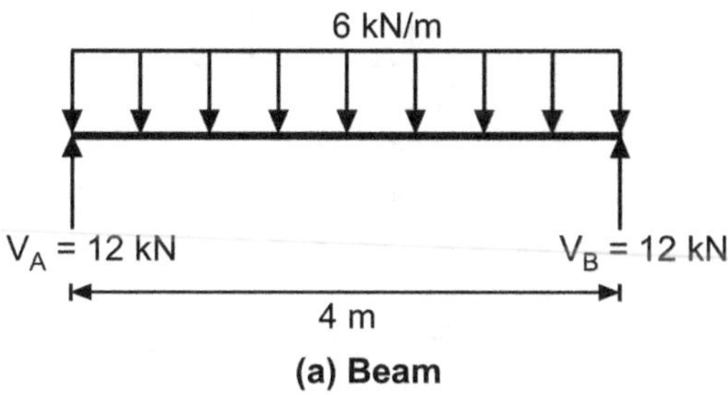


**(a) Beam**

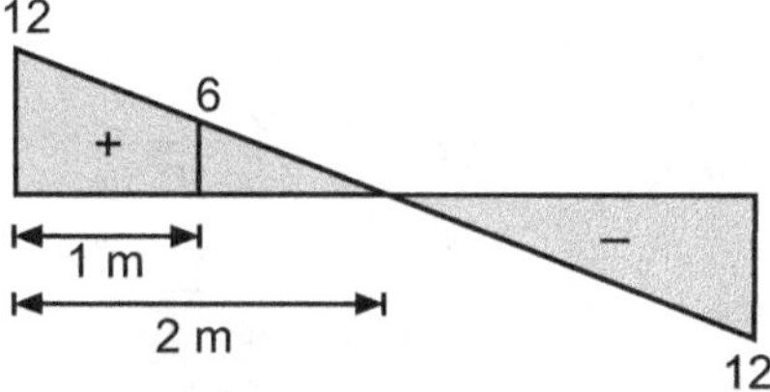


**(b) SFD (kN)**

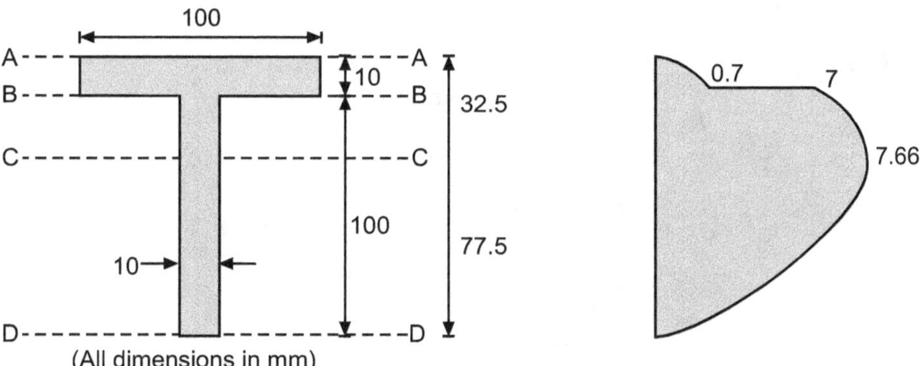


**(c) C/s**          **(d) Shear stresses (MPa) at c/s 1m from LHS**

**Fig. 6.13**

(ii)     Analysis of beam :

Reactions :     $V_A = V_B = \dfrac{6 \times 4}{2} = 12$ kN (↑)

SF at 1m from LHS = **6 kN**

(iii)    Shear stress analysis :

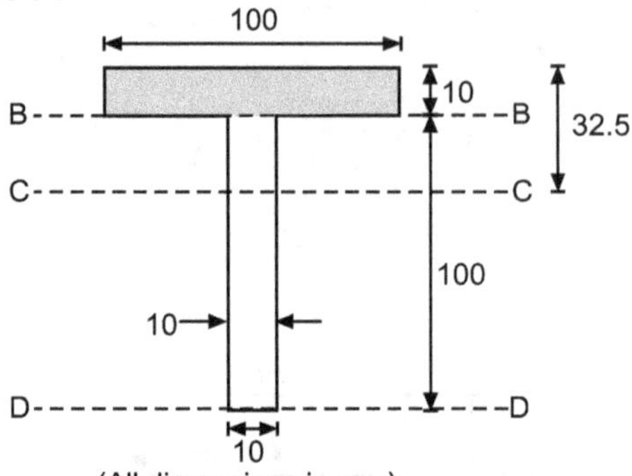


**Fig. 6.14**

$$\tau_{AA} = \tau_{DD} = 0$$

$$\tau_{BB} = \frac{SA\,\bar{y}}{b\,I} \text{, Refer Fig. 6.14.}$$

where;                      $A = 100 \times 10 = 1000 \text{ mm}^2$,  $\bar{y} = 32.5 - 5 = 27.5 \text{ mm}$

Substituting;            $\tau_{BB} = \dfrac{6 \times 10^3 \times 1000 \times 27.5}{100 \times 2.354 \times 10^6} = 0.7 \text{ MPa}$

$$\tau_{BB}' = \frac{\tau_{BB} \times b, \text{ just below "BB"}}{b, \text{ just above "BB"}} = \frac{0.7}{10} \times 100 = 7 \text{ MPa}$$

**Note :** Sudden change in width of cross-section at BB.

$$\tau_{CC} = \frac{SA\,\bar{y}}{b\,I}$$

Refer Fig. 6.15.

where;                  $A = 77.5 \times 10 = 775 \text{ mm}^2$

$$\bar{y} = \frac{77.5}{2} = 38.75 \text{ mm}$$

$$\tau_{CC} = \frac{6 \times 10^3 \times 775 \times 38.75}{10 \times 2.354 \times 10^6} = \textbf{7.66 MPa}$$

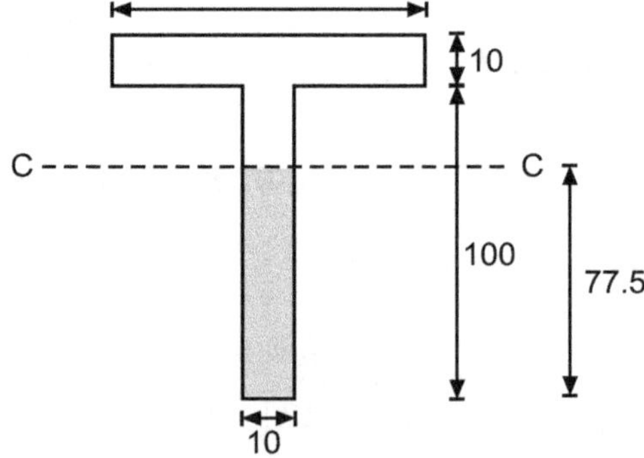


**Fig. 6.15**

Shear stress distribution diagram is as shown in Fig. 6.13 (d).

(iv)　Average shear stress :

$$\tau_{avg} \;=\; \frac{SF}{c/s\ area} = \frac{6 \times 10^3}{2000} = \textbf{3 MPa}$$

---

**Example 6.7 :** *A wooden beam consists of three horizontal pieces each 50 mm × 100 mm giving on overall size of beam as 100 mm wide and 150 mm deep. The joints are glued together. The maximum permissible shear stress for the glued joint is 0.8 MPa. If the beam is 2 m long simply supported at ends, find what safe load can be applied at mid-span.*

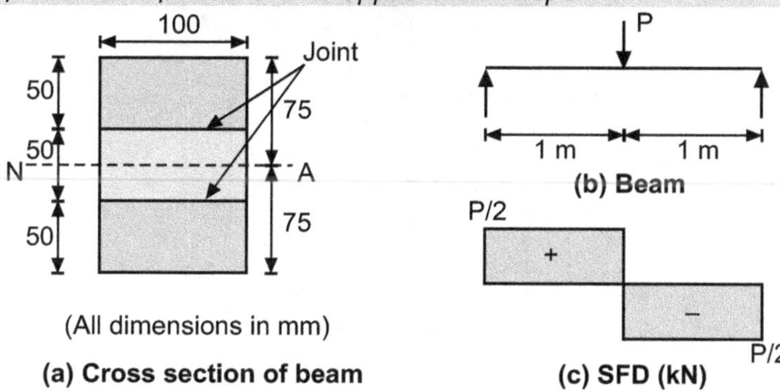


**Fig. 6.16**

**Data**　　　:　$\tau_{joint}$ = 0.8 MPa, as shown in Fig. 6.16 (a) and (b).

**Required**　:　Safe value of 'P'.

**Concept**　:　Shear stress at joint in terms of 'P' shall be equated to allowable shear stress.

**Solution**　:　(i) Geometric properties :

$$I_{XX} \;=\; \frac{100 \times 150^3}{12} = \textbf{28.125} \times \textbf{10}^6\,\textbf{mm}^4$$

(ii)　Shear stress at the level of joint and magnitude of (P)

$$\tau \;=\; \frac{SA\,\bar{y}}{b\,I}$$

where　　　　　$S$ = SF at support = $\dfrac{P}{2}$ (kN)

$A\,\bar{y}$ = Moment of area above or below the joint @ NA

　　　= $100 \times 50 \times 50 = 250 \times 10^3\ mm^3$

$b$ = width of cross-section at joint = 100 mm

$I$ = $28.125 \times 10^6\ mm^4$

Substituting　　$\tau = \dfrac{\left(\dfrac{P}{2}\right) \times 10^3 \times 250 \times 10^3}{100 \times 28.125 \times 10^6} = 0.044\ P\ MPa = 0.8\ MPa$

(∵ Allowable shear stress)

∴　　　　　　　$P$ = **18 kN**

---

**Example 6.8 :** *A wooden beam is prepared by connecting three pieces; as shown in Fig. 6.17. If the cross-section of the beam is subjected to maximum shear force of 25 kN, determine the spacing of the connectors assuming their shear strength to be 7.5 kN.*

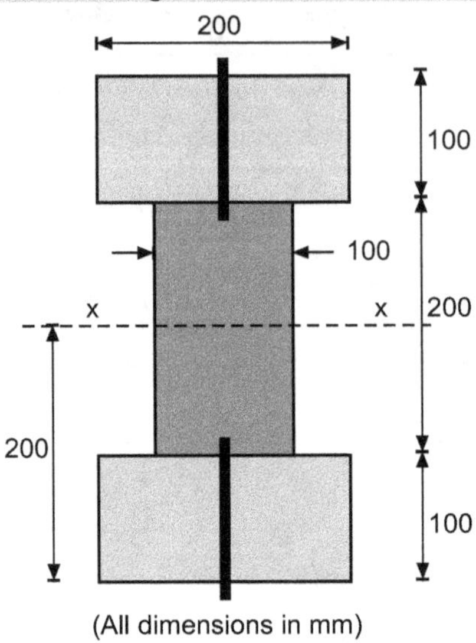


**Fig. 6.17 : C/s of beam**

**Data**     :    SF = 25 kN ;  shear strength of connectors = 7.5 kN ; c/s of beam as shown in Fig. 6.17.

**Required**   :    Spacing of shear connectors.

**Concept**   :    This connection is to be designed for horizontal shear between flange and web.

**Solution**  :    (i) Horizontal shear / mm run between flange and web.

$$q = \tau b = \frac{SA\,\bar{y}}{I}$$

where;

$S$ = Shear force = 25 kN

$A$ = Area above or below the level considered

$\quad$ = $200 \times 100 = 2 \times 10^4$ mm$^2$

$\bar{y}$ = Distance of CG of area 'A' from NA

$\quad$ = $100 + 50 = 150$ mm

$I$ = MI of section @ NA = $I_{xx}$

$$= \frac{200 \times 400^3}{12} - \frac{100 \times 200^3}{12} = 1 \times 10^9 \text{ mm}^4$$

Substituting,

$$q = \frac{25 \times 2 \times 10^4 \times 150}{1 \times 10^9} = \textbf{0.075 kN/mm}$$

(ii)    Spacing of shear connectors.

Let    $p$ = pitch of shear connectors in 'mm'

$\therefore$    $0.075\,p$ = 7.5

$\therefore$    $p$ = **100 mm c/c.**

**Example 6.9 :** *The cross-section shown in Fig. 6.18 (a) is used as a simply supported beam over an effective span of 3 m. If the permissible stress in bending compression and tension is 100 MPa and 150 MPa respectively, find the safe value of 'P'. Neglect weakening of tension flange due to rivet holes. Also find pitch of rivets at supports assuming diameter of rivets as 16 mm and allowable shear stress for rivets is 100 MPa. Also comment on curtailment of flange plates.*

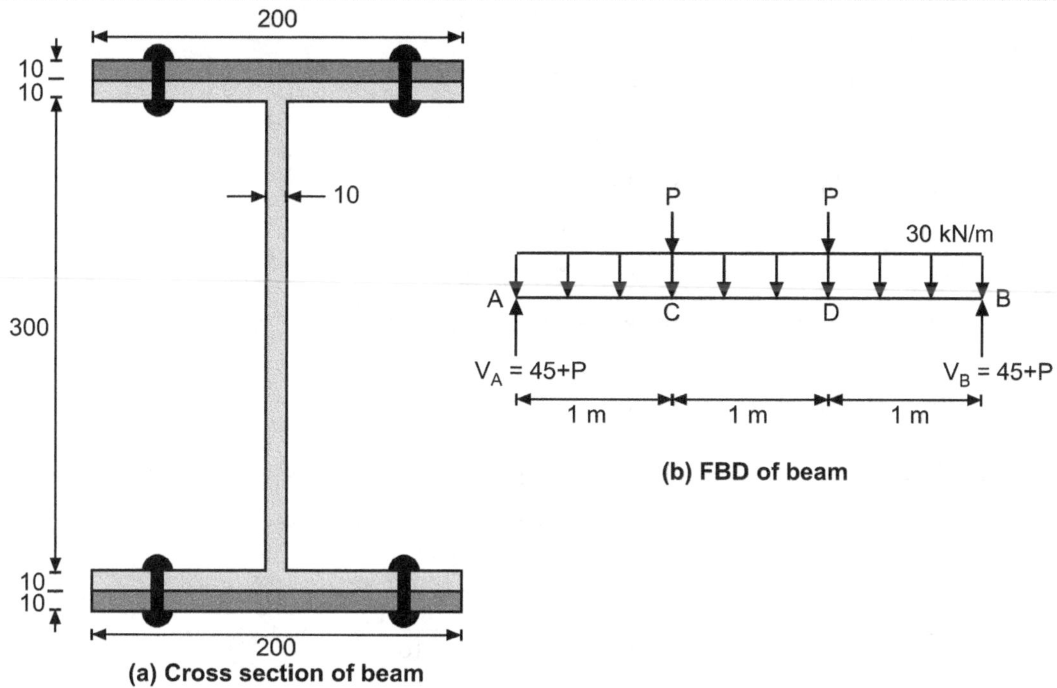



**Fig. 6.18**

**Data**          :   $\sigma_{bc}$ = 100 MPa ; $\sigma_{bt}$ = 150 MPa ; $\phi$ for rivets = 16 mm ;

$\tau$ for rivets = 100 MPa.

**Required**   :   Magnitude of 'P' and pitch of rivets.

**Concept**   :   Magnitude of 'P' will be governed by flexure criteria while pitch of rivets is to be designed for horizontal shear between flange plate and flange of 'I' section.

**Solution**   :   (i) Geometric properties :

$$I_{xx} = \frac{200 \times 340^3}{12} - \frac{190 \times 300^3}{12} = 227.57 \times 10^6 \, mm^4$$

$$y_{max} = 170 \, mm$$

$$Z_{xx} = \frac{I_{xx}}{y_{max}} = \frac{227.57 \times 10^6}{170} = \mathbf{1.34 \times 10^6 \, mm^3}$$

(ii)   Moment of resistance.

MR will be governed by allowable stress in bending compression.

$$MR = Z_{xx} \cdot \sigma_{bc} = 1.34 \times 10^6 \times 100 \times 10^{-6}$$

$$= \mathbf{133.86\ kN\text{-}m}$$

(iii)   Magnitude of 'P'

Let  'P' be the magnitude in kN.

Due to symmetry ;   $V_A = V_B = \dfrac{30 \times 3}{2} + P = 45 + P\ (\uparrow)$

Maximum BM at centre   $= (45 + P)\,1.5 - 30 \times \dfrac{1.5^2}{2} - P \times 0.5$

$$= 33.75 + P$$

Equating maximum BM and MR,

$$33.75 + P = 133.86$$

$$P = \mathbf{100.11\ kN}$$

(iv)   Design of connection between flange plate and flange of 'I' section.

Horizontal shear/mm run $= \tau = \dfrac{SA\,\bar y}{I}$

where          $A\bar y = (200 \times 10)(150 + 10 + 5) = 330 \times 10^3\ mm^3$

$S$  $=$ shear force $= 45 + P = 45 + 100.11 = 145.11$ kN

$I$  $= I_{xx} = 227.57 \times 10^6\ mm^4$

Substituting          $q = \dfrac{145.11 \times 330 \times 10^3}{227.57 \times 10^6} = 0.21$ kN/mm

Let          $p =$ pitch of rivets in mm

$q \times p = 2$ (strength of rivet)          ($\because$ 2 rivets for each flange)

$0.21 \times p = 2 \times \dfrac{\pi}{4} \times 16^2 \times 100 \times 10^{-3}$

$$p = \mathbf{191.4\ mm\ say\ 190\ mm\ c/c}$$

(v)   Curtailment of flange plates :

When maximum BM > MR of 'I' section alone, flange plates are connected to it to enhance the M.I. and hence MR. Design of cross-section for flexure is always governed by maximum BM. However, BM is not constant over the length of beam. (As for simply supported beam it reduces to zero at supports and for cantilevers it reduces to zero at free end etc.) Hence, the section designed for flexure is not fully utilized throughout the length of beam and thus results in uneconomical design.

At a section where BM to be resisted equals the moment of resistance of 'I' section alone (without flange plates), flange plates can theoretically be curtailed as illustrated below :

$I_{xx}$ of I section alone   $= \dfrac{200 \times 320^3}{12} - \dfrac{190 \times 300^3}{12}$

$$= 118.63 \times 10^6\ mm^4$$

$$y_{max} = 160 \text{ mm}$$

$$Z_{XX} \text{ of I section alone} = \frac{118.63 \times 10^6}{160}$$

$$= 741.46 \times 10^3 \text{ mm}^3$$

$$\text{MR of I section alone} = (Z_{XX}) \text{ I section} \times \sigma_{bc}$$

$$= 741.46 \times 10^3 \times 100 \times 10^{-6}$$

$$= 74.146 \text{ kN-m} \qquad \text{... (i)}$$

Let the section of curtailment for flange plates occur in zones 'AC' and 'DB'.

BM at a distance 'x' from support in these zones

$$M_x = V_A(x) - 30\left(\frac{x^2}{2}\right)$$

$$= (45 + 100.11)x - 15x^2$$

$$M_x = 145.11x - 15x^2 \qquad \text{... (ii)}$$

Equating (i) and (ii),  $74.146 = 145.11x - 15x^2$

Solving;  $x = 0.54 \text{ m}$

Thus; flange plates can theoretically be curtailed at 0.54 m from either supports.

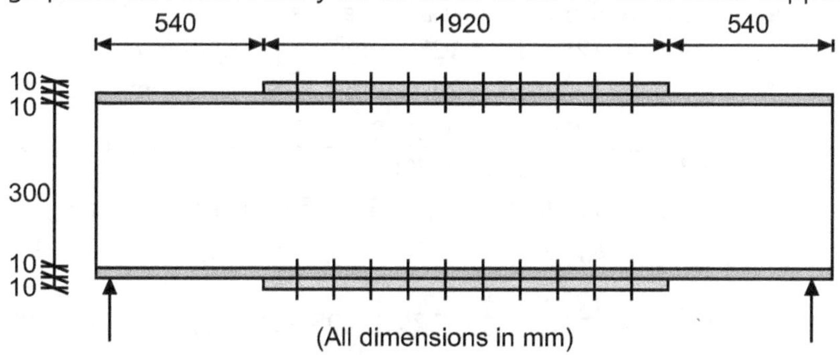

**Fig. 6.19 : Curtailment of flange plates**

**Note :** If the curtailment of flange plate is done, connection shall be designed in similar way by taking shear force at point of cut-off as design shear force.

**Example 6.10 :** *A simply supported beam of span 4 m is loaded with concentrated load 'P' acting at centre. Determine the magnitude of load 'P' if the maximum bending stress allowed is 165 MPa and the section used for the beam is as shown in Fig. 6.20 (a). Also determine the maximum shear stress in the section.*

**Data**  :  As shown in Fig. 6.20 (a); $\sigma_b = 165$ MPa.

**Required**  :  Safe value of 'P' and maximum shear stress induced.

**Concept**  :  Equating MR and maximum BM, find magnitude of 'P'. Maximum shear stress occurs at neutral axis of support section.

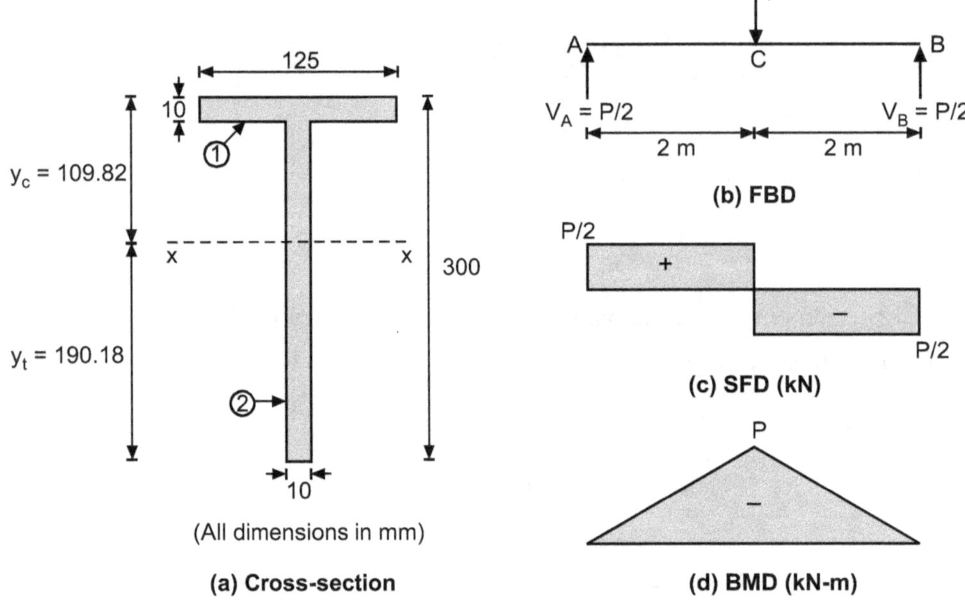



**(a) Cross-section**

**Fig. 6.20**

**Solution** : (i) Geometric properties :

To locate CG, consider bottommost fibre as a reference.

$$a_1 = 125 \times 10 = 1250 \text{ mm}^2; \quad y_1 = 295 \text{ mm}$$

$$a_2 = 290 \times 10 = 2900 \text{ mm}^2; \quad y_2 = 145 \text{ mm}$$

$$\bar{y} = \frac{1250 \times 295 + 2900 \times 145}{1250 + 2900} = 190.18 \text{ mm from bottom}$$

$$\therefore \quad y_c = 109.82 \text{ mm} ; \quad y_t = 190.18 \text{ mm as shown in Fig. 6.20 (a)}$$

$$I_{xx} = I_{xx_1} + I_{xx_2}$$

$$I_{xx_1} = \frac{125 \times 10^3}{12} + (1250)(295 - 190.18)^2 = 13.74 \times 10^6 \text{ mm}^4$$

$$I_{xx_2} = \frac{10 \times 290^3}{12} + (2900)(190.18 - 145)^2 = 26.24 \times 10^6 \text{ mm}^4$$

$$I_{xx} = (13.74 + 26.24) \times 10^6 = \mathbf{39.98 \times 10^6 \text{ mm}^4}$$

$$y_{max} = 190.18 \text{ mm}$$

$$Z_{xx} = \frac{I_{xx}}{y_{max}} = \frac{39.98 \times 10^6}{190.18} = \mathbf{210.22 \times 10^3 \text{ mm}^3}$$

(ii) Analysis of beam :

$$\text{Maximum} \quad BM = \frac{PL}{4} = \frac{P(4)}{4} = P \text{ kN-m}$$

where; $P$ = magnitude of point load in kN

SF and BM diagram are drawn as shown in Fig. 6.20 (c) and (d).

(iii) Magnitude of (P) :

$$\text{Moment of resistance} = MR = Z_{xx} \cdot \sigma_b = 210.22 \times 10^3 \times 165 \times 10^{-6} \text{ kN/m}$$

$$= 34.68 \text{ kN-m}$$

Equating maximum BM and MR

$$P = 34.68 \text{ kN}$$

(iv)   Maximum shear stresses ($\tau_{max}$) :

Maximum shear stress will occur at neutral axis of support section.

$$\tau_{max} = \tau_{NA} = \frac{SA\,\bar{y}}{b\,I}$$

where;

$$S = \text{Shear force} = \frac{P}{2} = \frac{34.68}{2} = 17.34 \text{ kN}$$

$$A = \text{Area above or below the NA} = 10 \times 190.18 = 1901.8 \text{ mm}^2$$

$$\bar{y} = \text{Distance of CG of area 'A' from NA} = \frac{190.18}{2}$$

$$= 95.09 \text{ mm}$$

$$b = \text{Width of cross-section at NA} = 10 \text{ mm}$$

$$I = I_{XX} = 39.98 \times 10^6 \text{ mm}^4$$

Substituting;

$$\tau_{NA} = \frac{17.34 \times 10^3 \times 1901.8 \times 95.09}{10 \times 39.98 \times 10^6}$$

$$= \mathbf{7.84 \text{ MPa}}$$



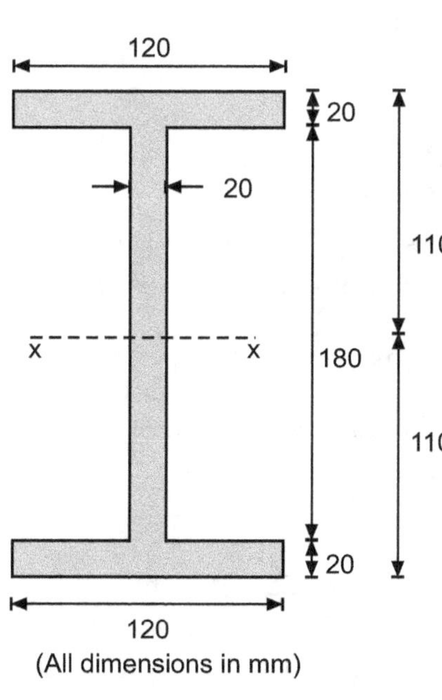

**(a) Cross-section of beam**

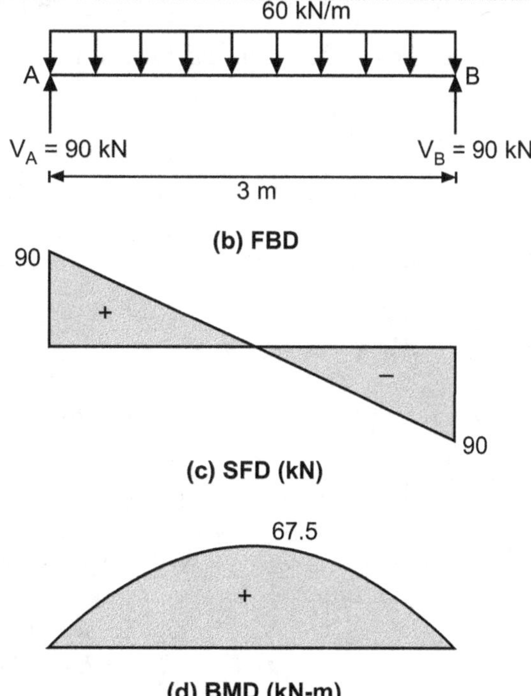

**(b) FBD**

**(c) SFD (kN)**

**(d) BMD (kN-m)**

**Fig. 6.21**

**Data**        :   As shown in Fig. 6.21 (a) and (b).

**Required**    :   Bending and shear stresses.

**Concept**     :   Bending stress $\sigma_b = \dfrac{M}{I_{xx}} \cdot y$. Shear stresses $= \tau = \dfrac{SA\,\bar{y}}{b\,I}$.

**Solution**    :   (i) Geometric properties :

C.G. : by symmetry.

$$I_{xx} = \frac{120 \times 220^3}{12} - \frac{100 \times 180^3}{12} = 57.88 \times 10^6 \text{ mm}^4$$

$$y_{max} = 110 \text{ mm}$$

$$Z_{xx} = \frac{I_{xx}}{y_{max}} = \frac{57.88 \times 10^6}{110} = \mathbf{526.18 \times 10^3\ mm^3}$$

(ii)    Analysis of beam

$$\text{Reactions} = 90 \text{ kN ( ) by symmetry.}$$

$$\text{Central BM} = \frac{wL^2}{8} = \frac{60 \times 3^2}{8} = \mathbf{67.5\ kN\text{-}m\ \ (sagging)}$$

SF and BM diagrams are as shown in Fig. 6.21 (c) and (d).

(iii)   Bending stresses at mid-span.

$$\sigma_b = \pm \frac{BM}{Z_{xx}} = \pm \frac{67.5 \times 10^6}{526.18 \times 10^3} = \pm\ \mathbf{128.28\ MPa}$$

(iv)    Shear stresses at support section.

$$\tau_{AA} = 0$$

$$\tau_{BB} = \frac{SA\,\bar{y}}{b\,I} = \frac{90 \times 10^3 \times (120 \times 20)\,(90 + 10)}{120 \times 57.88 \times 10^6}$$

$$= 3.1 \text{ MPa } (\because \text{ shear stress at a section within the flange,}$$

very close to junction of flange and web)

$$\tau_{BB'} = \frac{SA\,\bar{y}}{b\,I} = \frac{3.1 \times 120}{20} = 18.6 \text{ MPa}$$

($\because$ shear stress at a section within the web, very close to junction of flange and web)

$$\tau_{NA} = \frac{SA\,\bar{y}}{b\,I}$$

where,      $A\,\bar{y} = 120 \times 20 \times 100 + 90 \times 20 \times 45 = 321 \times 10^3 \text{ mm}^3$

Substituting;

$$\tau_{NA} = \frac{90 \times 10^3 \times 321 \times 10^3}{20 \times 57.88 \times 10^6} = 24.96 \text{ MPa}$$

Bending and shear stress diagrams are as shown in Fig. 6.22 (b) and (c).

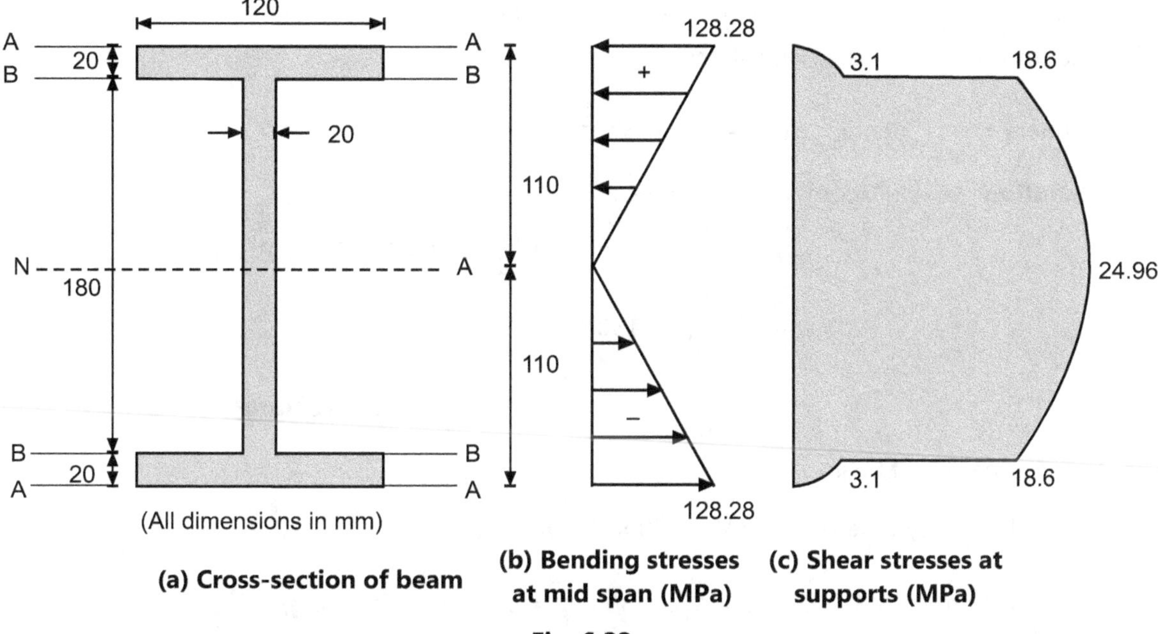



**(a) Cross-section of beam**  **(b) Bending stresses at mid span (MPa)**  **(c) Shear stresses at supports (MPa)**

**Fig. 6.22**

**Example 6.12 :** *A simply supported beam of cross-section in Fig. 6.23 (a) having 6 m span carries UDL of 30 kN/m throughout the span. Draw bending stress distribution diagram at mid-span and shear stress distribution diagram at support section.*

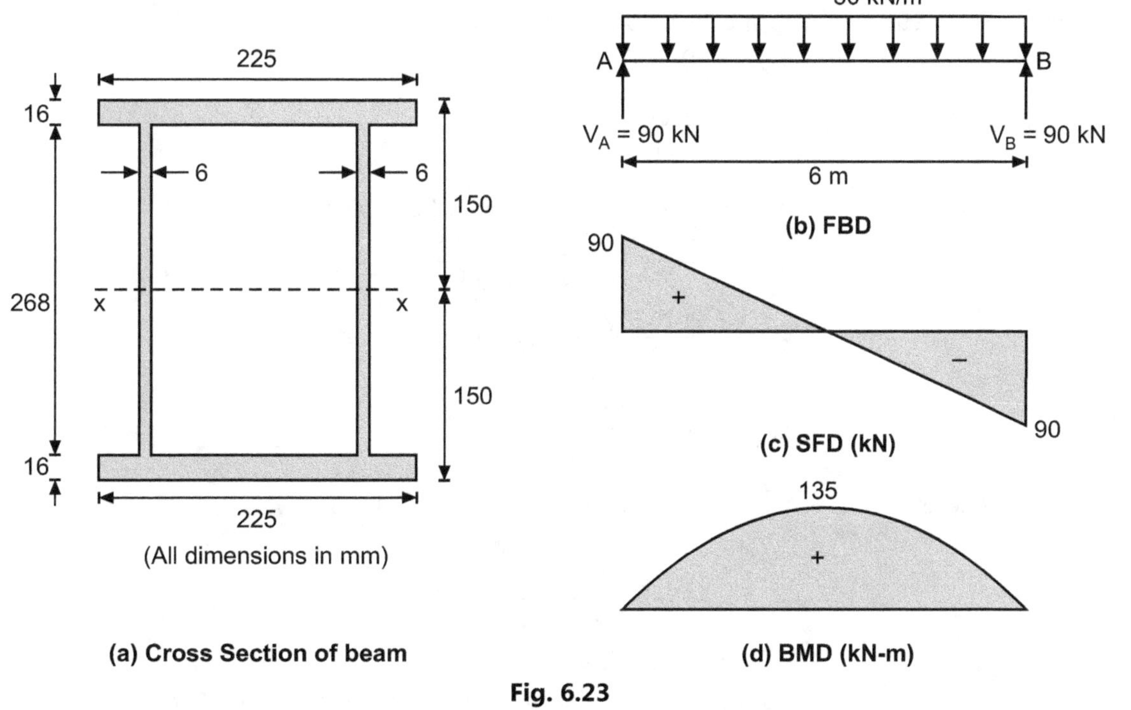



**(a) Cross Section of beam**  **(b) FBD**  **(c) SFD (kN)**  **(d) BMD (kN-m)**

**Fig. 6.23**

**Data** : As shown in Fig. 6.23 (a) and 6.23 (b).

**Required** : Bending and shear stresses.

**Concept** : Bending stresses $= \sigma_b = \dfrac{M}{Z_{xx}}$ ; Shear stresses $= \tau = \dfrac{SA\,\bar{y}}{b\,I}$ .

**Solution** : (i) Geometric properties :

$$I_{xx} = \frac{225 \times 300^3}{12} + \frac{213 \times 268^3}{12} = 164.58 \times 10^6 \text{ mm}^4$$

$$y_{max} = \frac{300}{2} = 150 \text{ mm}$$

$$Z_{xx} = \frac{I_{xx}}{y_{max}} = \frac{164.58 \times 10^6}{150} = \textbf{1.097} \times \textbf{10}^6 \textbf{ mm}^3$$

(ii)　Analysis of beam :

Due to symmetry; $V_A = V_B = 30 \times \dfrac{6}{2} = 90$ kN ($\uparrow$)

Maximum BM at centre $= \dfrac{wL^2}{8} = 30 \times \dfrac{6^2}{8} = 135$ kN-m (sagging)

SF and BM diagrams are as shown in Fig. 6.23 (c) and 6.23 (d).

(iii)　Bending stresses at mid-span section.

$$\sigma_{bc};\, cal = \sigma_{bt,\, cal} = \frac{M}{Z_{xx}} = \frac{135 \times 10^6}{1.097 \times 10^6} = 123.04 \text{ MPa}$$

(iv)　Shear stresses at support section.

$$\tau_{AA} = 0$$

$$\tau_{BB} = \frac{SA\,\bar{y}}{b\,I}$$

where　　$A\bar{y} = (225 \times 16) \times 142 = 511.2 \times 10^3 \text{ mm}^3$

$\therefore$　　$\tau_{BB} = \dfrac{90 \times 10^3 \times 511.2 \times 10^3}{225 \times 164.58 \times 10^6} = 1.24$ MPa

$$\tau_{BB'} = \frac{1.24 \times 225}{2 \times 6} = 23.29 \text{ MPa}$$

$$\tau_{max} = \tau_{NA} = \frac{SA\,\bar{y}}{b\,I}$$

where;　　$A\,\bar{y} = (225 \times 16 \times 142) + 2 \times (134 \times 6 \times 67)$

$\phantom{A\bar y} = 618.936 \times 10^3 \text{ mm}^3$

$\therefore$　　$\tau_{NA} = \dfrac{90 \times 10^3 \times 618.936 \times 10^3}{2 \times 6 \times 164.58 \times 10^6}$

$$= \textbf{28.2 MPa}$$

(v)　Bending and shear stress distribution diagrams are as shown in Fig. 6.24 (b) and 6.24 (c).

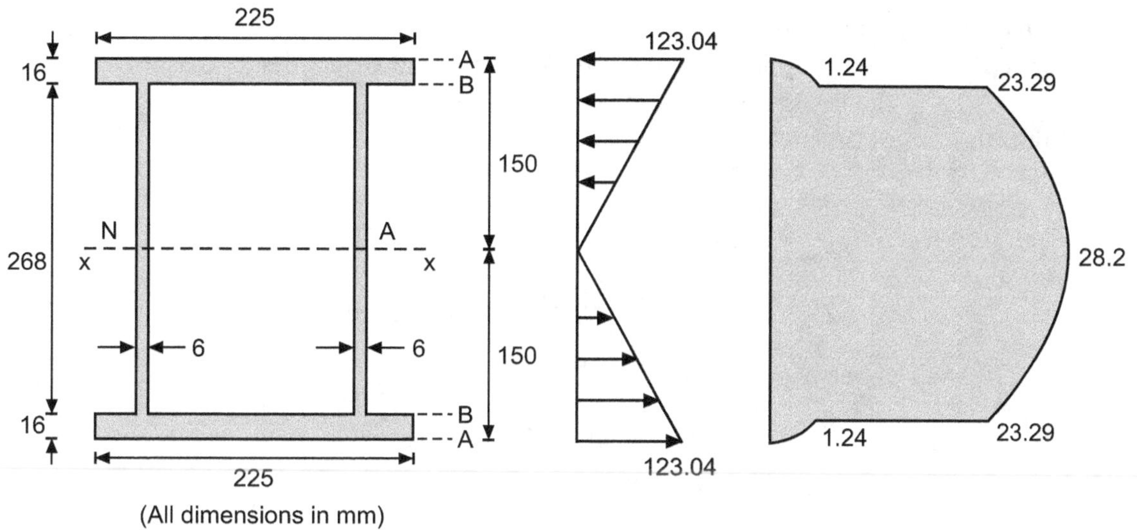

**(a) Cross-section of beam**     **(b) Bending stresses at mid-span (MPa)**     **(c) Shear stresses at supports (MPa)**

**Fig. 6.24**

**Example 6.13 :** *Fig. 6.25 (a) and 6.25 (b) show a simply supported beam and its cross-section. The maximum permissible stress in bending is 125 MPa and the shear stress is 84 MPa. Find the maximum allowable value of 'P' neglecting self weight of the beam.*

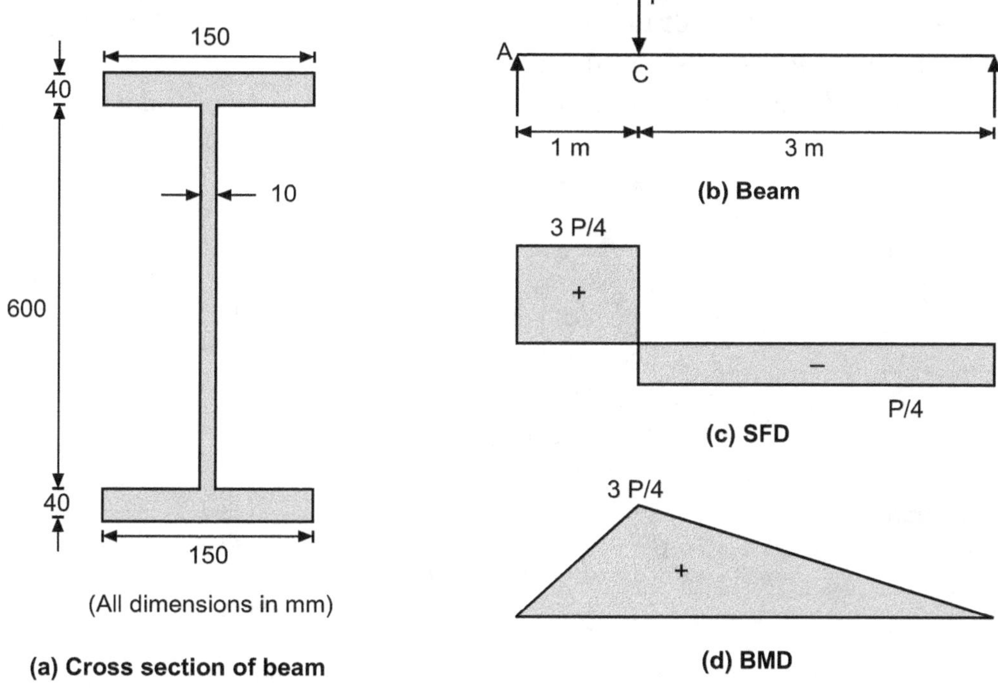

**Fig. 6.25**

**Data**       :   $\sigma_b$ = 125 MPa ; $\tau_{max}$ = 84 MPa; as shown in Fig. 6.25 (a) and 6.25 (b).

**Required** : Safe value of 'P'.

**Concept** : Find magnitude of 'P' from BM criteria and shear criteria. Least of the two is safe value of 'P'.

**Solution** : (i) Geometric properties :

$$I_{XX} = \frac{150 \times 680^3}{12} - \frac{140 \times 600^3}{12} = 1.41 \times 10^9 \text{ mm}^4$$

$$y_{max} = 340 \text{ mm}$$

$$Z_{XX} = \frac{I_{XX}}{y_{max}} = \frac{1.41 \times 10^9}{340} = 4.15 \times 10^6 \text{ mm}^3$$

(ii)　Analysis of beam :

$$V_A = \frac{Pb}{L} = \frac{3\,P}{4}\ (\downarrow) \text{ and } V_B = \frac{Pa}{L} = \frac{P}{4}\ (\uparrow)$$

$$\text{BM at 'C'} = \frac{Pab}{L} = \frac{3\,P}{4}$$

SF and BM diagrams are drawn as shown in Fig. 6.25 (c) and 6.25 (d).

(iii)　Magnitude of 'P' from BM criteria.

Let 'P' be the force in kN.

Maximum　　BM　=　MR

$$\frac{3P}{4} = 4.15 \times 10^6 \times 125 \times 10^{-6}$$

∴　　　　　P　=　**691.67 kN**　　　　　　　　　　　... (i)

(iv)　Magnitude of 'P' from shear criteria.

Maximum shear stress will occur at neutral axis of cross-section at support 'A'.

$$\tau_{NA} = \tau_{max} = \frac{SA\,\bar{y}}{b\,I}$$

where;　　　　$S$ = shear force at support A = $\dfrac{3P}{4}$ kN

$A\,\bar{y}$ = Moment of area above or below the NA @ NA

= $150 \times 40 \times 320 + 300 \times 10 \times 150$

= $2.37 \times 10^6 \text{ mm}^3$

$b$ = width of cross-section at NA = 10 mm

$I$ = $I_{XX}$ of section = $1.41 \times 10^9 \text{ mm}^4$

Substituting;

$$\tau_{max} = \frac{\left(\dfrac{3P}{4}\right) \times 10^3 \times 2.37 \times 10^6}{10 \times 1.41 \times 10^9} = 0.126\ (P)\ \text{MPa}$$

= 84 MPa　　　　　　　　(∵ Allowable stress)

∴　　　　　P　=　666.67 kN　　　　　　　　　　　... (ii)

∴　　Safe value of P　=　**666.67 kN**　　　　　(∵ Least of (i) and (ii))

**Example 6.14 :** *For a cantilever beam shown in Fig. 6.26 (a), calculate principal stresses, locate principal planes, maximum shear stresses and locate planes of maximum shear for elements "A" and "B" as shown.*

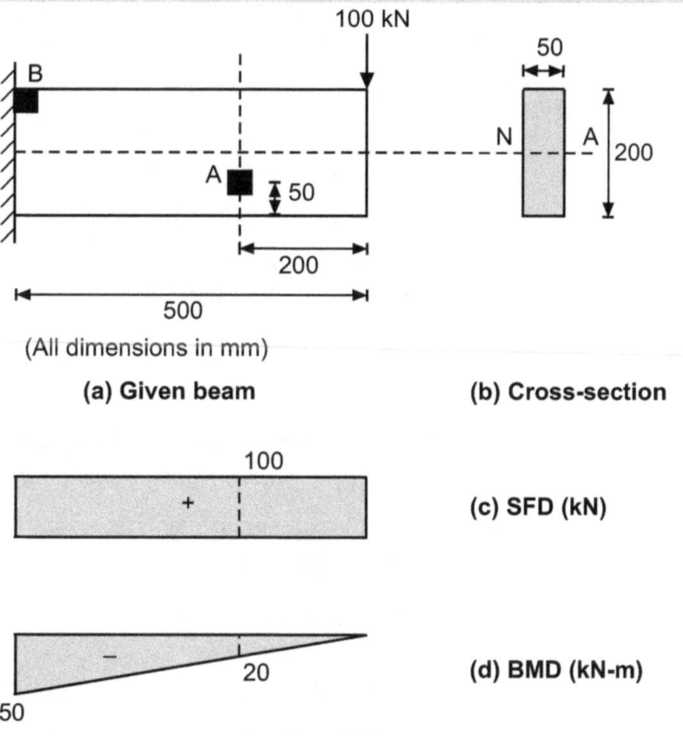


**(a) Given beam**　　　　　　**(b) Cross-section**

**(c) SFD (kN)**

**(d) BMD (kN-m)**

**Fig. 6.26**

**Data**　　　:　As shown in Fig. 6.26 (a) and 6.26 (b).

**Required**　:　Principal planes, Principal stresses, Maximum shear stresses and planes of maximum shear for elements "A" and "B".

**Concept**　:　Bending moment will cause normal stresses while shear force will cause shear stresses.

**Solution**　:　(i) Geometric properties of cross-section :

$$I_{xx} = \frac{50 \times 200^3}{12} = \mathbf{33.33 \times 10^6 \ mm^4}$$

(ii)　Analysis of beam.

$$BM_A = -100 \times 0.2 = -20 \ kN.m = \mathbf{20 \ kN\text{-}m \ (Hogging)}$$

$$BM_B = -100 \times 0.5 = -50 \ kN.m = \mathbf{50 \ kN\text{-}m \ (Hogging)}$$

SF and BM diagrams are drawn as shown in Fig. 6.26 (c) and 6.26 (d).

(iii)　Stress analysis at element "A" :

$$\text{Bending stresses} = \sigma_b = \frac{M}{I} \times y_A$$

$$= \frac{20 \times 10^6}{33.33 \times 10^6} \times 50$$

$$= 30 \text{ MPa (Compressive)}$$

**Note :** Hogging BM produces compression below NA.

$$\text{Shear stresses} \ = \ \tau = \frac{SA\,\bar{y}}{b\,I}$$

where;  $S$ = SF at A = 100 kN

$A$ = Area above or below the level of element "A" of cross section

$\quad = 50 \times 50 = 2500 \text{ mm}^2$

$\bar{y}$ = Distance of CG of area "A" from NA

$\quad = 50 + 25 = 75 \text{ mm}$

$b$ = Width of cross-section at the level of element "A"

$\quad = 50 \text{ mm}$

$I$ = M.I. of cross-section @ NA

$\quad = 33.33 \times 10^6 \text{ mm}^4$

Substituting,  $\tau = \dfrac{100 \times 10^3 \times 2500 \times 75}{50 \times 33.33 \times 10^6}$

$$\tau = \mathbf{11.25 \ MPa}$$

State of stress for element "A" is as shown in Fig. 6.27.

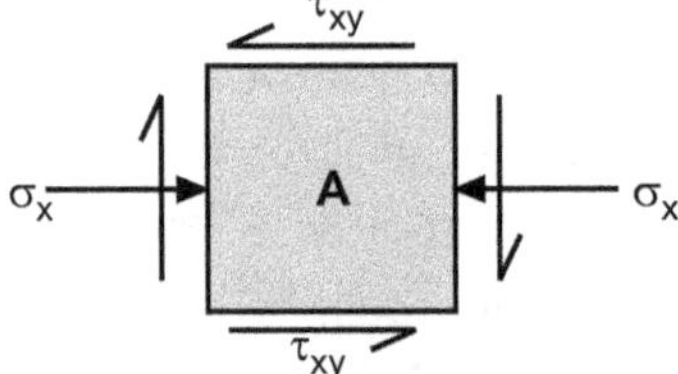


**Fig. 6.27**

$$\sigma_x \ = \ -30 \text{ MPa} \ (\because \text{Compressive})$$

$$\tau_{xy} \ = \ 11.25 \text{ MPa}$$

$\therefore$  Principal stresses $= \sigma_1 ; \sigma_2 = \dfrac{\sigma_x}{2} \pm \sqrt{\left(\dfrac{\sigma_x}{2}\right)^2 + \tau_{xy}^2}$

$$= -\frac{30}{2} \pm \sqrt{\left(\frac{-30}{2}\right)^2 + 11.25^2}$$

$$= -15 \pm 18.75$$

$$\sigma_1 \ = \ \mathbf{-33.75 \ MPa}$$

$$= 33.75 \text{ MPa (Compressive)}$$

$$\sigma_2 = \textbf{3.75 MPa (Tensile)}$$

Principal planes : $\tan(2\theta_1) = -\dfrac{2\,\tau_{xy}}{\sigma_x}$

$$= \dfrac{2 \times 11.25}{30} = 0.75 \qquad (\because \sigma_x \text{ is } - ve)$$

$\therefore \qquad \theta_1 = 18.43^o$

$\therefore \qquad \theta_2 = \theta_1 + 90^o = 108.43^o$

Maximum shear stress :

$$\tau_{max} = \dfrac{\sigma_1 - \sigma_2}{2} = \dfrac{3.75 - (-33.75)}{2} = \textbf{18.75 MPa}$$

Planes of maximum shear :

$$\theta_3 = \theta_1 + 45^o = 18.43^o + 45^o = \textbf{63.43}^\mathbf{o}$$

$$\theta_4 = \theta_3 + 90^o = 63.43^o + 90^o = \textbf{153.43}^\mathbf{o}$$

(iv)    Stress analysis at element "B".

$$\text{Bending stress} = \sigma_b = \dfrac{M}{I} \times y_\mathbf{B}$$

$$= \dfrac{50 \times 10^6}{33.33 \times 10^6} \times 100$$

$$= \textbf{150 MPa (Tensile)}$$

**Note :** Hogging BM produces tension above NA.

Shear stress for element B = $\tau$ = 0.

$\therefore$    State of stress for element B is as shown in Fig. 6.28.

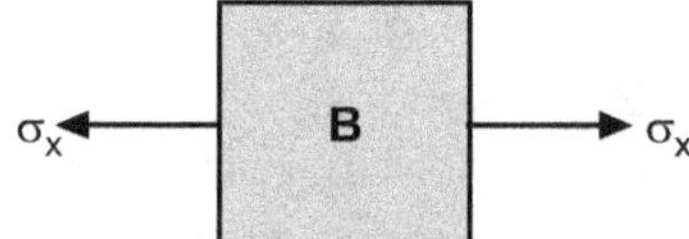


**Fig. 6.28**

$$\sigma_x = 150 \text{ MPa (Tensile)}$$

$\therefore$    Principal stresses : $\sigma_1 = 150$ MPa (Tensile)

$$\sigma_2 = 0.$$

Principal planes : $\theta_1 = 0^o \quad \therefore \theta_2 = 90^o$

Maximum shear stress $= \tau_{max} = \dfrac{\sigma_1 - \sigma_2}{2} = \dfrac{150 - 0}{2}$

$$= 75 \text{ MPa}$$

Planes of maximum shear :    $\theta_3 = \theta_1 + 45^o = \textbf{45}^\mathbf{o}$

$$\theta_4 = \theta_3 + 90^o = \textbf{135}^\mathbf{o}$$

**Example 6.15 :** *A rectangular beam spans 1 m and is loaded with a vertical downward load of 100 kN at mid-span as shown in Fig. 6.29 (a). Find the principal stresses and locate principal planes at points A, B, C and D. Self weight of beam may be neglected.*

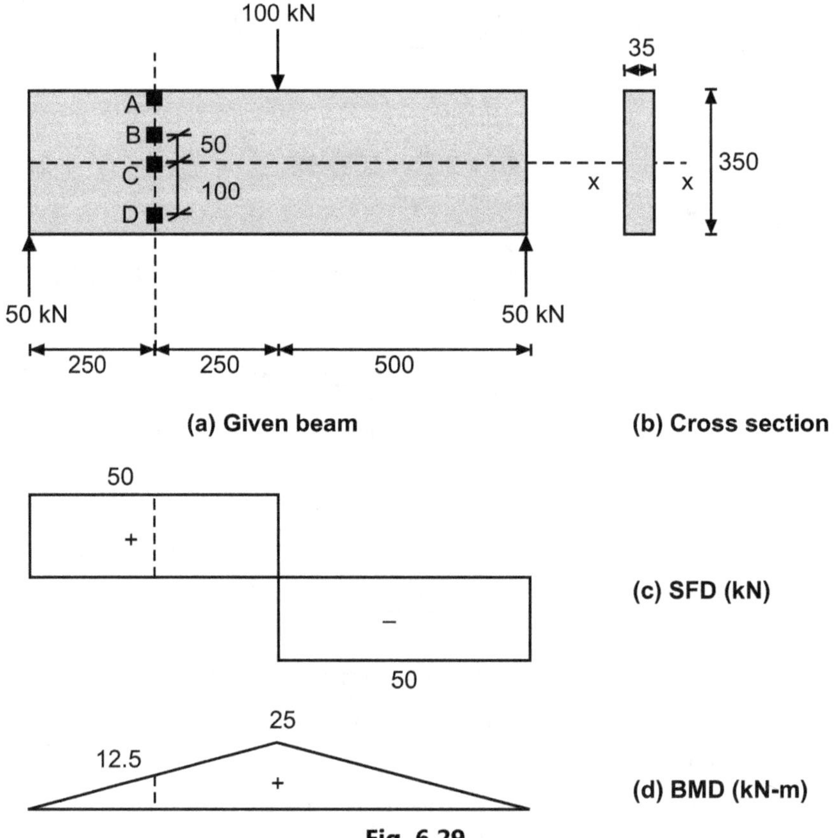



**Fig. 6.29**

**Data** :　　As shown in Fig. 6.29 (a) and 6.29 (b).

**Required** :　Principal stresses and principal planes for elements A, B, C and D.

**Concept** :　Bending moment will cause normal stresses while shear force will cause shear stresses.

**Solution** :　(i) Geometric properties of cross-section :

$$I_{XX} = \frac{35 \times 350^3}{12}$$

$$= 125.05 \times 10^6 \text{ mm}^4$$

(ii)　Analysis of beam :

$$\text{Reactions} : \frac{100}{2} = 50 \text{ kN (By symmetry)}$$

$$\text{BM at centre} = \frac{PL}{4} = \frac{100 \times 1}{4} = 25 \text{ kN-m}$$

BM at 250 mm from left support = $50 \times 0.25$ = **12.5 kN-m.**

SF and BM diagrams are drawn as shown in Fig. 6.29 (c) and 6.29 (d).

(iii)    Stress analysis at element "A",

$$\text{Bending stress, } \sigma_b = \frac{M}{I_{xx}} \times y_A = \frac{12.5 \times 10^6}{125.05 \times 10^6} \times 175$$

$$= 17.49 \text{ MPa (Compressive)}$$

(Sagging BM produces compression above NA.)

Shear stress for element "A" = 0.

$\therefore$    State of stress for element "A" is as shown in Fig. 6.30.

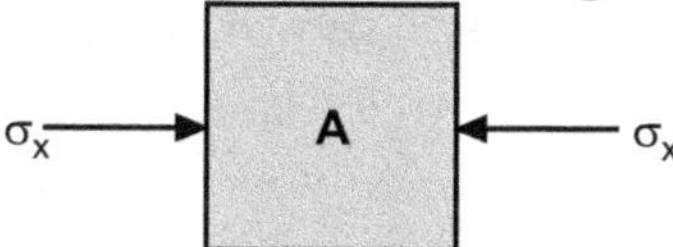


**Fig. 6.30**

$$\sigma_x = 17.49 \text{ MPa}$$

$\therefore$    Principal stresses :    $\sigma_1 = 17.49 \text{ MPa (Compressive)}$

$$\sigma_2 = 0$$

$$\text{Principal planes} : \theta_1 = 0^\circ$$

$\therefore$    $\theta_2 = \theta_1 + 90^\circ = 90^\circ$

(iv)    Stress analysis for element "B"

$$\text{Bending stress} = \sigma_b = \frac{M}{I_{xx}} \times y_B$$

$$= \frac{12.5 \times 10^6}{125.05 \times 10^6} \times 50 = 5 \text{ MPa (Compressive)}$$

(Sagging BM produces compression above NA.)

$$\text{Shear stress} = \tau = \frac{S A \bar{y}}{b I} . \text{ Refer Fig. 6.31}$$

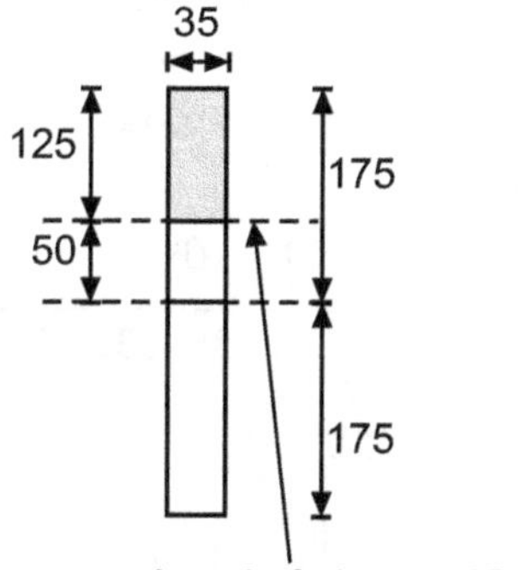

**Fig. 6.31**

where;        $S = 50$ kN

$A$ = Area of cross-section above or below the level of element "B"

$= 125 \times 35 = 4375 \text{ mm}^2$

$\bar{y}$ = Distance of CG of area A from NA

$$= 50 + \frac{125}{2} = 112.5 \text{ mm}$$

$b$ = Width of cross-section at the level of element "B"

$= 35$ mm

$I = I_{xx} = 125.05 \times 10^6 \text{ mm}^4$

Substituting; $\tau = \dfrac{50 \times 10^3 \times 4375 \times 112.5}{35 \times 125.05 \times 10^6} = 5.62$ MPa

∴ State of stress for element "B" is as shown in Fig. 6.32.

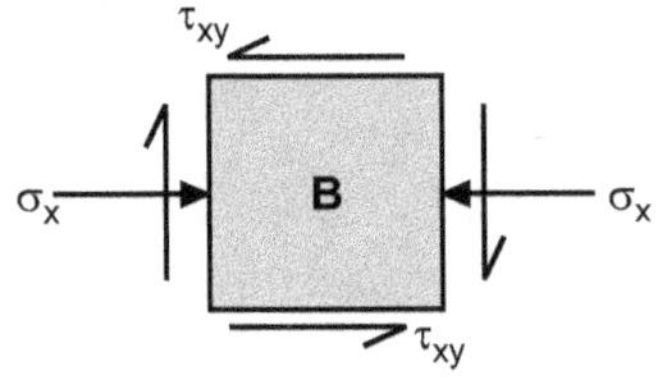

$\sigma_x = 5$ MPa (Compressive)

$= -5$ MPa

$\tau_{xy} = 5.62$ MPa

**Fig. 6.32**

Principal stresses : $\sigma_1 ; \sigma_2 = \dfrac{\sigma_x}{2} \pm \sqrt{\left(\dfrac{\sigma_x}{2}\right)^2 + \tau_{xy}^2} = \dfrac{-5}{2} \pm \sqrt{\left(\dfrac{-5}{2}\right)^2 + (5.62)^2}$

$= -2.5 \pm 6.15$

∴ $\sigma_1 = 3.65$ MPa (Tensile)

$\sigma_2 = -8.65$ MPa $= 8.65$ MPa (Compressive)

Principal planes : $\tan(2\theta_1) = -\dfrac{2\,\tau_{xy}}{\sigma_x} = \dfrac{2 \times 5.62}{5}$ $\quad (\because \sigma_x \text{ is } - ve)$

∴ $\theta_1 = \mathbf{33^o}$

∴ $\theta_2 = \theta_1 + 90^o = \mathbf{123^o}$

(v) Stress analysis at element "C" :

Bending stresses for element "C" = 0 $(\because$ "C" is at NA)

Shear stresses = $\tau = \dfrac{SA\,\bar{y}}{b\,I}$ . Refer Fig. 6.33.

$$= \dfrac{50 \times 10^3 \times (175 \times 35)\left(\dfrac{175}{2}\right)}{35 \times 125.05 \times 10^6} = \mathbf{6.12 \ MPa}$$

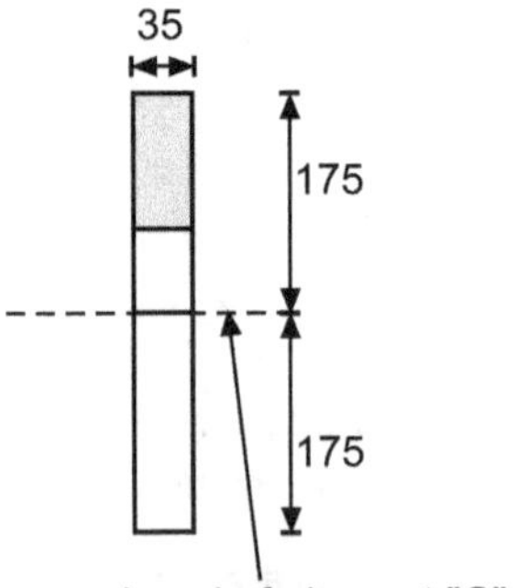

Level of element "C"

**Fig. 6.33**

State of stress for element "C" is as shown in Fig. 6.34.

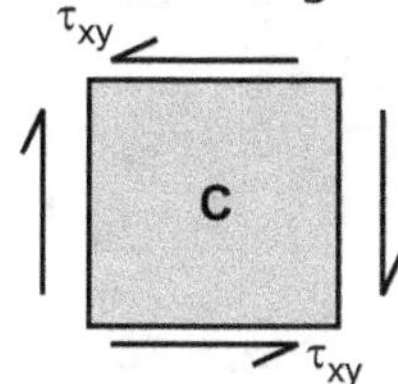

**Fig. 6.34**

$$\tau_{xy} \;=\; 6.12 \text{ MPa}$$

$$\therefore \quad \text{Principal stresses} : \sigma_1 ; \sigma_2 \;=\; \frac{\sigma_x}{2} \pm \sqrt{\left(\frac{\sigma_x}{2}\right)^2 + \tau_{xy}^2}$$

$$\therefore \quad \sigma_1 = -\sigma_2 = \tau_{xy} \;=\; 6.12 \text{ MPa}$$

$$\text{Principal planes} = \tan(2\theta_1) = \frac{\sin(2\theta_1)}{\cos(2\theta_1)} = -\frac{2\,\tau_{xy}}{\sigma_x}$$

$$\sigma_x = 0 \quad \therefore \quad \cos(2\theta_1) \;=\; 0$$

$$\therefore \quad \theta_1 \;=\; \mathbf{45^o}$$

$$\therefore \quad \theta_2 \;=\; \theta_1 + 90^o = \mathbf{135^o}$$

(vi)   Stress analysis at element "D".

$$\text{Bending stress} \;=\; \sigma_b = \frac{M}{I_{xx}} \times y_D$$

$$=\; \frac{12.5 \times 10^6}{125.05 \times 10^6} \times 100$$

$$=\; 10 \text{ MPa (Tensile)}$$

(Sagging BM produces tension below NA.)

$$\text{Shear stresses} = \tau \;=\; \frac{SA\,\bar{y}}{b\,I} \quad \text{Refer Fig. 6.35.}$$

$$=\; \frac{50 \times 10^3 \times (75 \times 35)\,(137.5)}{35 \times 125.05 \times 10^6}$$

$$=\; \mathbf{4.12 \text{ MPa}}$$

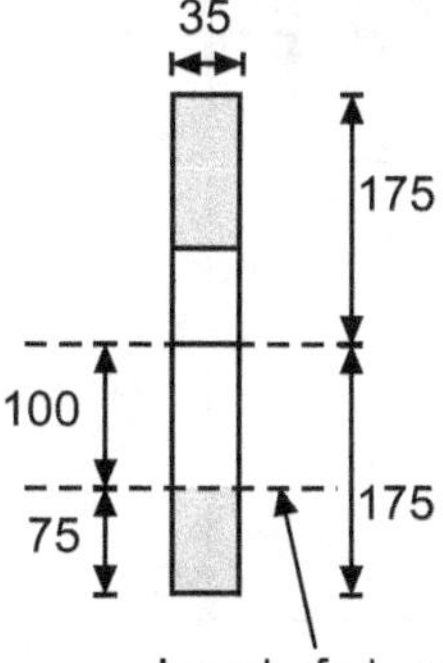



**Fig. 6.35**

$\therefore$   State of stress for element "D" is as shown in Fig. 6.36.

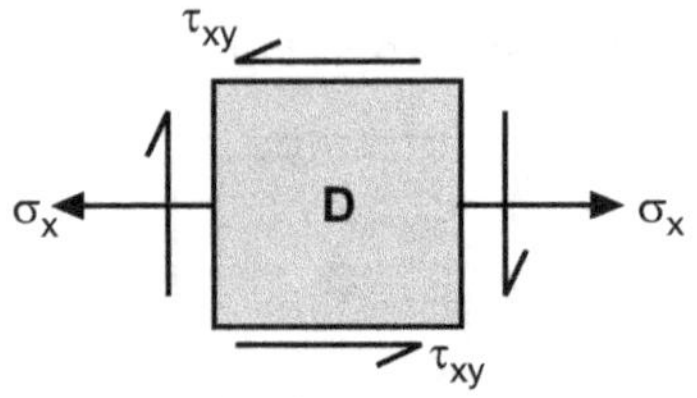

**Fig. 6.36**

$$\sigma_x = 10 \text{ MPa (Tensile)}$$

$$\tau_{xy} = 4.12 \text{ MPa}$$

$$\text{Principal stresses : } \sigma_1 ; \sigma_2 = \frac{\sigma_x}{2} \pm \sqrt{\left(\frac{\sigma_x}{2}\right)^2 + \tau_{xy}^2} = \frac{10}{2} \pm \sqrt{\left(\frac{10}{2}\right)^2 + (4.12)^2}$$

$$= 5 \pm 6.47$$

$$\therefore \quad \sigma_1 = 11.47 \text{ MPa}$$

$$\sigma_2 = -1.47 \text{ MPa}$$

$$\text{Principal planes; } \tan(2\theta_1) = -\frac{2\,\tau_{xy}}{\sigma_x} = -\frac{2 \times 4.12}{10}$$

$$\therefore \quad \theta_1 = -19.74^\circ$$

$$\theta_2 = -(\theta_1 + 90^\circ) = -109.24^\circ$$

**Note :** (i) Element "A" is subjected to normal stress in x direction only, hence this normal stress itself is a principal stress.

(ii) Elements "B" and "D" are subjected to combined normal and shear stresses, hence principal stresses are evaluated as above.

(iii) Element "C" is in the state of pure shear for which principal stresses $\sigma_1 ; \sigma_2 = \pm \tau_{xy}$ at $45^\circ$ and $135^\circ$ respectively called as *diagonal tension* and *compression*.

**Example 6.16 :** *A simply supported beam, 'L' m carries a UDL of 16 kN/m over the entire span. The cross-section of the beam is as shown in Fig. 6.37. If the maximum flexural stress is 40 MPa, find the span of the beam. Find the maximum shear stress developed. Draw the shear stress distribution diagram.*

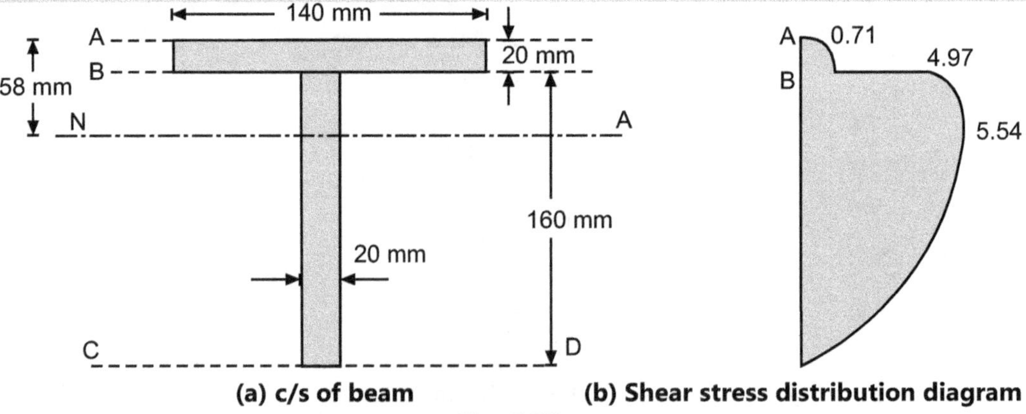

(a) c/s of beam    (b) Shear stress distribution diagram

**Fig. 6.37**

**Data :** As shown in Fig. 6.37 (a).

**Required :** Span, shear stress diagram.

**Concept :** B.M. = M.R.,  standard formulae.

**Solution :** (i) Geometric properties :

$$a_1 = 140 \times 20 = 2800 \text{ mm}^2, \quad y_1 = 160 + 10 = 170 \text{ mm}$$

$$a_2 = 160 \times 20 = 3200 \text{ mm}^2, \quad y_2 = \frac{160}{2} = 80 \text{ mm}$$

$$\bar{y} = \frac{a_1 y_1 + a_2 y_2}{a_1 + a_2} = \frac{2800 \times 170 + 3200 \times 80}{2800 + 3200}$$

$$= 122 \text{ mm}$$

$$y_c = 58 \text{ mm}, \quad y_t = 122 \text{ mm}$$

$$I_{XX_1} = \frac{140 \times 20^3}{12} + 140 \times 20 \times (58 - 10)^2 = 6.45 \times 10^6 \text{ mm}^4$$

$$I_{XX_2} = \frac{20 \times 160^3}{12} + 160 \times 20 (122 - 80)^2 = 12.47 \times 10^6 \text{ mm}^4$$

$$I_{XX} = I_{XX_1} + I_{XX_2} = 6.45 \times 10^6 + 12.47 \times 10^6 = 18.92 \times 10^6 \text{ mm}^4$$

(ii)   Span calculation :   B.M. = M.R.

$$Z_{XX} = \frac{I}{y_{max}} = \frac{18.92 \times 10^6}{122} = 155.08 \times 10^3 \text{ mm}^3$$

$$\therefore \quad \frac{wl^2}{8} = \sigma_b \times Z_{XX}$$

$$\frac{16 \times l^2}{8} = 40 \times 155.08 \times 10^3 \times 10^{-6}$$

$$\therefore \quad l = 1.76 \text{ m}$$

(iii) Shear stress calculations :

$$\tau = \frac{SA\bar{y}}{Ib}$$

$$S = \frac{wl}{2} = \frac{16 \times 1.76}{2} = 14.08 \text{ kN}$$

$$S = 14.08 \text{ kN}$$

$$I = I_{XX} = 18.92 \times 10^6 \text{ mm}^4$$

$$\tau_{AA} = \frac{SA\bar{y}}{Ib}$$

$$A - \text{Area above AA} = 0$$

$$\tau_{AA} = \tau_{CC} = 0$$

$$\tau_{BB} = \frac{SA\bar{y}}{Ib}$$

$$A - \text{Area above BB} = 140 \times 20 = 2800 \text{ mm}^2$$

$$\bar{y} - \text{C.G. of area from N.A.} = (58 - 10) = 48 \text{ mm}$$

$$b = 140 \text{ mm}$$

$$\therefore \qquad \tau_{BB} = \frac{14.08 \times 10^3 \times 2800 \times 48}{18.92 \times 10^6 \times 140} = 0.71 \text{ MPa}$$

$$\tau_{B'B'} = \tau_{BB} \times \frac{140}{20} = 4.97 \text{ MPa}$$

$$\tau_{NA} = \frac{SA\,\bar{y}}{Ib}$$

$$A\bar{y} = (140 \times 20 \times 48) + (20 \times 38 \times 19)$$
$$= 148840 \text{ mm}^3$$

$$\therefore \qquad \tau_{NA} = \frac{14.08 \times 10^3 \times 148840}{18.92 \times 10^6 \times 20} = 5.54 \text{ MPa}$$

Shear stress distribution diagram is as shown in Fig. 6.37 (b).

**Example 6.17 :** *A steel section shown in Fig. 6.38 is subjected to a shear force 200 kN. Draw shear stress distribution diagram. Also find the ratio of maximum shear stress to average shear stress.*

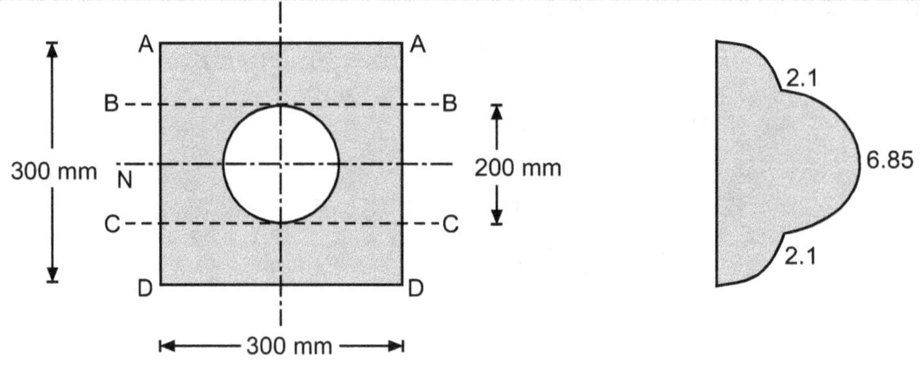


**(a) c/s of beam**          **(b) Shear stress distribution diagram**

**Fig. 6.38**

**Data :** As shown in Fig. 6.38 (a); S = 200 kN.

**Required :** $\dfrac{\text{Maximum shear stress}}{\text{Average shear stress}}$

**Concept :** $\tau = \dfrac{SA\,\bar{y}}{Ib}$

**Solution :** (i) Geometric properties :

$$\text{M.I.} = \frac{bd^3}{12} - \frac{\pi}{64} D^4$$

$$= \frac{300 \times 300^3}{12} - \frac{\pi}{64} \times 200^4 = 5.96 \times 10^8 \text{ mm}^4$$

(ii)   Shear stress calculation :

Shear stress at A-A and D-D = 0.

Shear stress at B-B :

$$\tau_{BB} \;=\; \frac{SA\,\bar{y}}{Ib}$$

$$S \;=\; 200 \text{ kN} = 200 \times 10^3 \text{ N}$$

$$I \;=\; 5.96 \times 10^8 \text{ mm}^4$$

$$A \;=\; \text{Area above B-B} = 300 \times 50 = 15000 \text{ mm}^2$$

$$\bar{y} \;=\; 125 \text{ mm}, \quad b = 300 \text{ mm}$$

$$\tau_{BB} \;=\; \frac{200 \times 10^3 \times 15000 \times 125}{5.96 \times 10^8 \times 300}$$

$$\tau_{BB} = \tau_{CC} \;=\; 2.10 \text{ N/mm}^2$$

$$\tau_{NA} \;=\; \frac{SA\,\bar{y}}{Ib}$$

$$A\bar{y} \;=\; 300 \times 150 \times 75 - \frac{1}{2} \times \frac{\pi}{4} \times 200^2 \times \frac{4 \times 200}{3 \times \pi}$$

$$=\; 2041666.7 \text{ mm}^3$$

$$\therefore \qquad \tau_{NA} \;=\; \frac{200 \times 10^3 \times 2041666.7}{5.96 \times 10^8 \times 100}$$

$$=\; 6.85 \text{ N/mm}^2$$

**Example 6.18 :** *A timber section as shown in Fig. 6.39 is subjected to a shearing force of 15 kN.*

*If the permissible shear stress for the material of section is 2 N/mm$^2$, determine the safety of section.*

*Further, the top flange is connected to vertical web by means of nails spaced at 200 K. Determine the minimum shear strength of the nail required to be provided for safety of joint.*

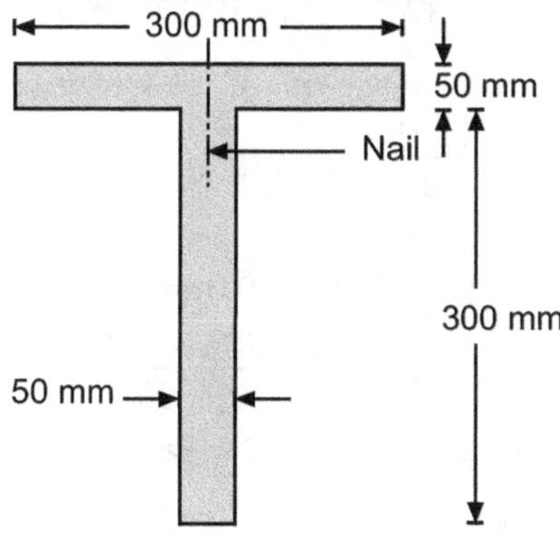


**Fig. 6.39 : C/s of beam**

**Data :** As shown in Fig. 6.39, $\tau_{max}$ = 2 N/mm$^2$, S.F. = 15 kN.

**Required :** Check for safety, minimum shear strength of web.

**Concept :** Standard formulae.

**Solution :**                       $q \;=\; \dfrac{SA\,\bar{y}}{Ib}$

$S = S.F. \;=\; 15 \text{ kN}$

(i)    Geometric properties :

To locate CG, consider bottommost fibre as a reference.

$$a_1 \;=\; 300 \times 50 = 15000 \text{ mm}^2, \; y_1 = \; 325 \text{ mm}$$

$$a_2 \;=\; 50 \times 300 = 15000 \text{ mm}^2, \; y_2 = 150 \text{ mm}$$

$$\bar{y} \;=\; \frac{a_1 y_1 + a_2 y_2}{a_1 + a_2} = \frac{15000 \times 325 + 15000 \times 150}{15000 + 15000}$$

$$\bar{y} \;=\; 237.5 \text{ mm (from bottom)}$$

$$y_c \;=\; 112.5 \text{ mm}, \; y_t = 237.5 \text{ mm}$$

$$I_{xx_1} \;=\; \frac{300 \times 50^3}{12} + 300 \times 50 \left(112.5 - \frac{50}{2}\right)^2$$

$$\;=\; 117.97 \times 10^6 \text{ mm}^4$$

$$I_{xx_2} \;=\; \frac{50 \times 300^3}{12} + 50 \times 300 \,(237.5 - 150)^2$$

$$\;=\; 2.27 \times 10^8 \text{ mm}^4$$

$$I_{xx} \;=\; 117.97 \times 10^6 + 2.27 \times 10^8 = 3.45 \times 10^8 \text{ mm}^4$$

$$Z_{xx} \;=\; \frac{I_{xx}}{y_{max}} = \frac{3.45 \times 10^8}{237.5} = 1.45 \times 10^6 \text{ mm}^3$$

(ii)   Shear stress :                $q \;=\; \dfrac{SA\,\bar{y}}{Ib}$

$$S \;=\; 15 \times 10^3 \text{ N}$$

$$A \;=\; \text{Area above or below N.A.}$$

$$\;=\; (237.5 \times 50) = 11875 \text{ mm}^2$$

$$\bar{y} \;=\; \text{Distance of C.G. of area from N.A.}$$

$$\;=\; \frac{237.5}{2} = 118.75 \text{ mm}$$

$$b \;=\; 50 \text{ mm}$$

$$I \;=\; I_{xx} = 3.45 \times 10^8 \text{ mm}^4$$

$$\tau_{NA} \;=\; \frac{15 \times 10^3 \times 11875 \times 118.75}{3.45 \times 10^8 \times 50}$$

$$\tau_{NA} \;=\; 1.23 \text{ MPa} < 2 \text{ MPa}$$

$\therefore$    Section is safe.

(iii) Shear stress at the connection of flange and web :

$$\tau_j \;=\; \frac{SA\,\bar{y}}{Ib}$$

$$S \;=\; 15 \text{ kN} = 15 \times 10^3 \text{ N}$$

$$A = \text{Area above junction} = 300 \times 50 = 15000 \text{ mm}^2$$

$$\bar{y} = \text{C.G. of area from N.A.} = (112.5 - 25) = 87.5 \text{ mm}$$

$$I = I_{xx} = 3.45 \times 10^8 \text{ mm}^4$$

$$b = 300 \text{ mm}$$

$$\therefore \quad \tau_j = \frac{15 \times 10^3 \times 15000 \times 87.5}{3.45 \times 10^8 \times 300} = 0.19 \text{ MPa}$$

Shear force developed due to S.F.

$$= \text{Required strength of nail}$$
$$= \tau_j \times b \times l = 0.19 \times 300 \times 200 = 11400 \text{ N}$$
$$= 11.4 \text{ kN}$$

Minimum shear strength of nail required = 11.4 kN.

**Example 6.19 :** *A timber box beam having cross-section shown in Fig 6.40 carries a vertical load W at mid-span over a simply supported span of 2 m. If allowable working stress in bending is 8 MPa, find the spacing of the screws. Each screw can transmit a shear force of 3000 N.*

**Solution :**

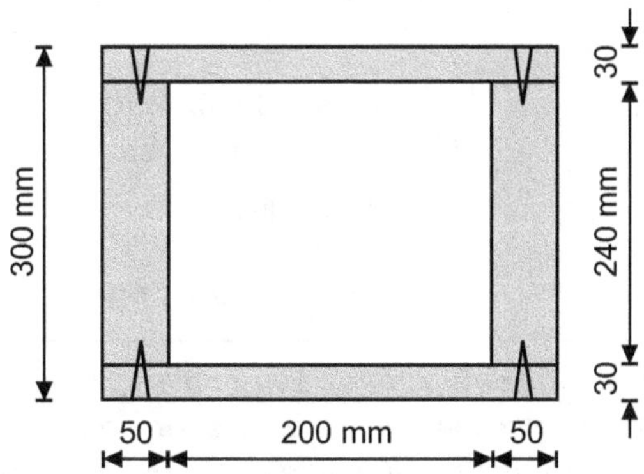


**Fig. 6.40**

(i)      CG and MI $= (1/12)\,(300^4 - 200 \times 240^3)$

$$= 444.6 \times 10^6 \text{ mm}^4$$

(ii)      $\dfrac{M}{I} = \dfrac{\sigma}{y}$,   where $M = \dfrac{WL}{4} = 0.5$ kN-m

$$\frac{0.5\,W \times 10^6}{444.6 \times 10^6} = \frac{8}{150} \quad \therefore W = 47.42 \text{ kN}$$

(iii)      Shear per mm run $= SA\bar{y}\,/I$

i.e.      $q = \dfrac{(47.42) \times 300 \times 30 \times 135}{444.6 \times 10^6} = 0.0648$ kN/mm

$$0.0648 \times \text{pitch} = 2 \times \text{shear strength of each screw}$$
$$0.0648\,p = 2 \times 3$$
$$p = 92.59 \text{ mm}$$

**Example 6.20 :** *A circular hole is to be punched through a 5 mm thick aluminium plate. If the ultimate shear strength of aluminium is 120 MPa and safe compressive strength for the punch is 80 MPa, determine the maximum diameter of the hole that can be punched.* **(May 2002)**

**Solution :**     Normal force on punch   =  Shear force on portion removed

$$\left(\frac{\pi}{4}\,\phi^2\right)\sigma \;=\; (\pi\,\phi\,t)\,\tau$$

$$\frac{\pi}{4}\,(\phi^2)\,80 \;=\; \pi\,\phi \times 5 \times 120$$

$$\therefore \qquad \phi \;=\; 30 \text{ mm}$$

**Example 6.21 :** *A section of beam is an isosceles triangle with base 260 mm and base angles 45°. It is used with base horizontal and carries a shear force of 62 kN at a particular section. Find the maximum intensity of shear stress and shear stress at neutral axis.*          **(May 2002)**

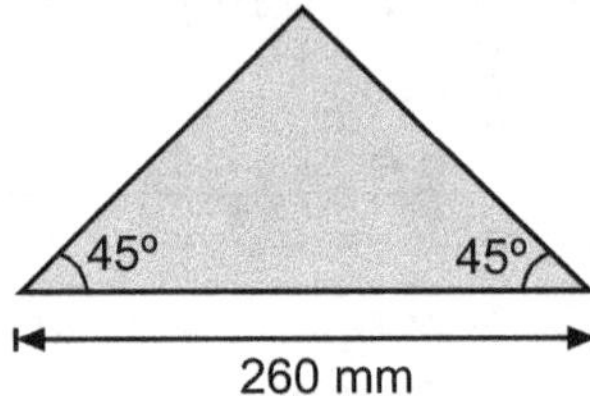


**Fig. 6.41**

**Solution :**

$$\tau_{max} \;=\; \frac{3\,S}{bh} = \frac{3 \times 62 \times 10^3}{260 \times 130}$$

$$= \textbf{5.502 MPa}$$

$$\tau_{NA} \;=\; \frac{2.67\,S}{bh} = \textbf{4.89 MPa}$$

**Example 6.22 :** *A cylindrical tube of diameter 100 mm is to be anchored in a concrete block as shown in Fig. 6.42. if the maximum allowable shear stress in concrete is 0.5 MPa, find minimum length of cylindrical anchor tube, so that it will not be pulled out from concrete block under a force of 200 kN.*          **(Dec. 2002)**

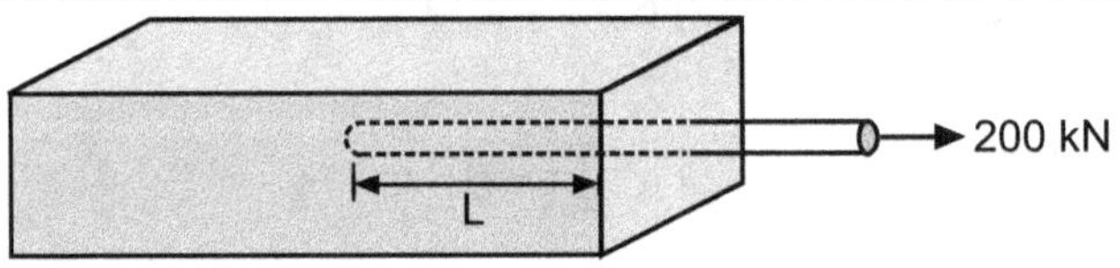


**Fig. 6.42**

**Solution :**     Axial force on tube   =  Shear force on contact area

$$200 \;=\; (\pi dL)\,\tau$$

$$= (\pi \times 100 \times L) \times 0.5 \times 10^{-3}$$

$$\therefore \qquad L \;=\; \textbf{1273.24 mm}$$

**Example 6.23 :** *The cross-section of a beam is a tee-section as shown in Fig. 6.43. Find the maximum intensity of shear stress and sketch the distribution of stress across the section, if it has a resist to shear force of 100 kN.*          **(Dec. 2002)**

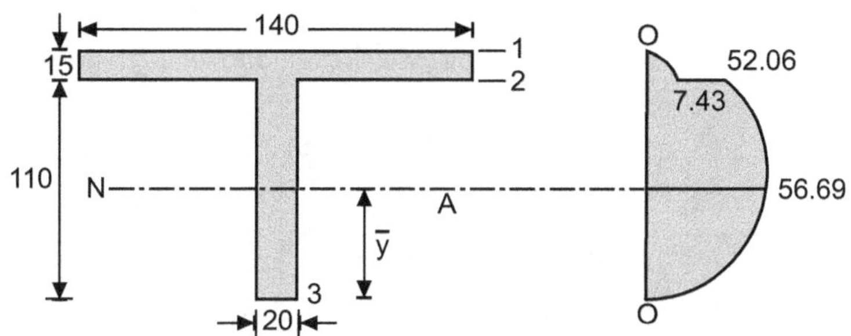


**Fig. 6.43**

**Solution :** (i) CG and MI :     $\bar{y}$ = 85.52 mm from bottom

$I_x$ = $6.45 \times 10^6$ mm$^4$

(ii)   $\tau_1 = \tau_3 = 0,$

$$\tau_2 \text{ (just above)} = \frac{SA\,\bar{y}}{bI}$$

$$= \frac{100 \times 10^3 \times (140 \times 15)\,(31.98)}{140 \times 6.45 \times 10^6}$$

$$= \textbf{7.43 MPa}$$

$$\tau_2 \text{ (just below)} = \frac{7.43 \times 140}{20} = \textbf{52.06 MPa}$$

$$\tau_{NA} = \frac{SA\,\bar{y}}{bI} = \frac{100 \times 10^3 \times (85.52 \times 20)\,42.76}{20 \times 6.45 \times 10^6}$$

$$= \textbf{56.69 MPa}$$

---

**Example 6.24 :** *The cross-section and loading of a timber beam is as shown in Fig. 6.44. If the allowable stresses in bending and shear are respectively 12 MPa and 0.9 MPa, find the required dimensions of the beam (breadth and depth).*     **(May 2003)**

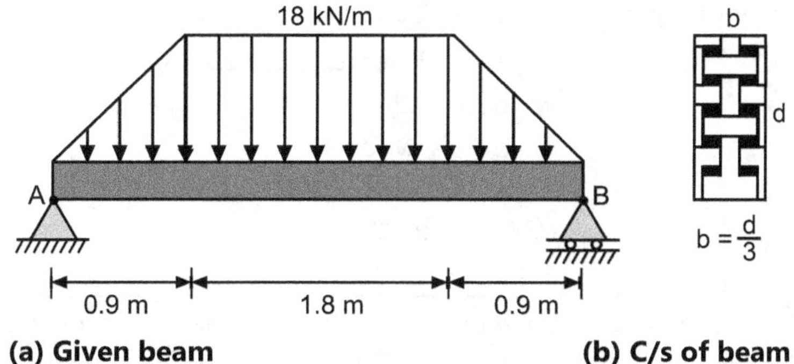


**(a) Given beam**                    **(b) C/s of beam**

**Fig. 6.44**

**Solution :** (i) Analysis of beam :

$$V_A = V_B = \frac{1}{2} \text{ (Total load)}$$

$$= \frac{1}{2} \{(3.6 + 1.8)/2 \times 18\}$$

$$= 24.3 \text{ kN}$$

$$\therefore \quad SF_{max} = 24.3 \text{ kN}$$

$$BM_{max \text{ (at centre)}} = 24.3 \times 1.8 - (1/2 \times 0.9 \times 18)(0.9 + 0.9/3)$$

$$- (0.9 \times 18)(0.45)$$

$$= \textbf{26.73 kN-m}$$

(ii)   For c/s of beam :

$$I = bd^3/12 = d^4/36$$

$$y_{max} = d/2$$

(iii) Design for bending :

$$\frac{M}{I} = \frac{\sigma}{y}$$

$$\frac{26.73 \times 10^6}{d^4/36} = \frac{12}{d/2}$$

$$\therefore \quad d = 342.26 \text{ mm}$$

(iv) Design for shear :

$$\tau_{max} = 1.5 \{S/bd\}$$

$$0.9 = 1.5 \{(24.3 \times 10^3)/(d^2/3)\}$$

$$\therefore \quad d = \textbf{348.57 mm}$$

use,     $$d = \textbf{349 mm and } b = \textbf{117 mm}$$

**Example 6.25 :** *A wooden beam of rectangular cross-section is simply supported and uniformly loaded. The height of the beam is 200 mm, and the allowable stresses in bending and shear are 8.2 MPa and 1.0 MPa respectively, determine the span length L below which the shear stress governs the permissible load and above which the bending stress governs.*     **(May 2003)**

**Solution :** (i) Shear design :     $$\tau_{max} = 1.5 \{S/bd\}$$

$$1 = 1.5 \{(wL/2) 10^3/200 \, b\}$$

$$\therefore \quad wL/b = 0.267 \quad \text{...(i)}$$

(ii)   Flexure design :     $$\sigma = 6M/bd^2$$

$$8.2 = (6 \times wL^2/8) 10^6/b \times 200^2$$

$$wL^2/b = 0.437 \quad \text{... (ii)}$$

Dividing equation (ii) by (i),     $$L = \textbf{1.636 m}$$

**Example 6.26 :** *A beam is constructed of two boards, 50 mm × 250 mm in cross-section that are attached by two 25 × 250 mm boards as shown in Fig. 6.45. The boards are nailed to the beams at a longitudinal spacing of 100 mm. If each nail has an allowable shear force of 1300 N, what is the maximum permissible shear force V ?*     **(May 2003)**

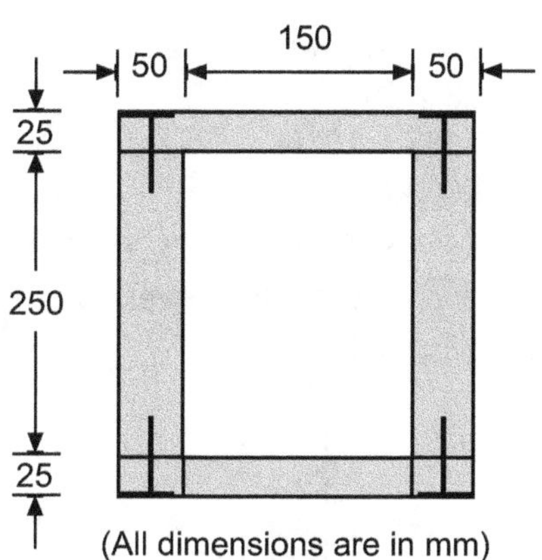


**Fig. 6.45**

**Solution :** (i)          $I = 250 \times 300^3/12 - 150 \times 250^3/12$
$$= 367.18 \times 10^6 \text{ mm}^4$$

(ii)          $(SA\,\bar{y}\,/I)\,p = 2$ (shear strength of nail)

$S \times (250 \times 25)\,(137.5) \times 100/367.18 \times 10^6 = 2 \times 1.3$

∴          $S = \textbf{11.1 kN}$

**Example 6.27 :** *A wooden box beam is built up of four 50 mm $\times$ 200 mm members. If the longitudinal spacing of the nails is 125 mm and allowable load per nail is 1.8 kN, find the allowable shear force that the section can carry.*

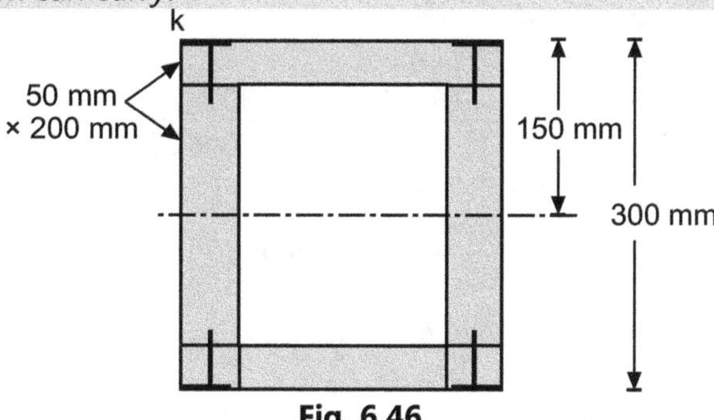


**Fig. 6.46**

**Data :** As shown in Fig. 6.46.
**Required :** Shear force.
**Solution :** Let S be the shear force.
Maximum shear stress is at centre.

∴          $A\bar{y} = 50 \times 200 \times 125 + 50 \times 100 \times 50$
$$= 1.5 \times 10^6 \text{ mm}^3$$

$$I = 2\left[\frac{200 \times 50^3}{12} + 50 \times 200 \times 125^2\right] + 2\left[\frac{50 \times 200^3}{12}\right]$$
$$= 383.33 \times 10^6 \text{ mm}^4$$

∴          $q = \dfrac{SA\bar{y}}{I} = \dfrac{S \times 1.5 \times 10^6}{383.33 \times 10^6} = 3.91 \times 10^{-3}\,S$

$\therefore$ $\quad$ q × spacing of nails $\quad=$ Shear strength of nail

$\quad$ $3.91 \times 10^{-3}\, S \times 125 \;=\; 1.8 \times 10^3$

$\therefore$ $\qquad\qquad\qquad\qquad S \;=\; 3.683 \times 10^3\, N$

$\qquad\qquad\qquad\qquad\qquad =\; 3.68\ kN$

$\therefore$ $\quad$ Allowable shear force that the section can carry is 3.68 kN.

**Example 6.28 :** *Determine the maximum shear stress in the web of the T-section shown in Fig. 6.47 when subjected to shear force of 68 kN.*

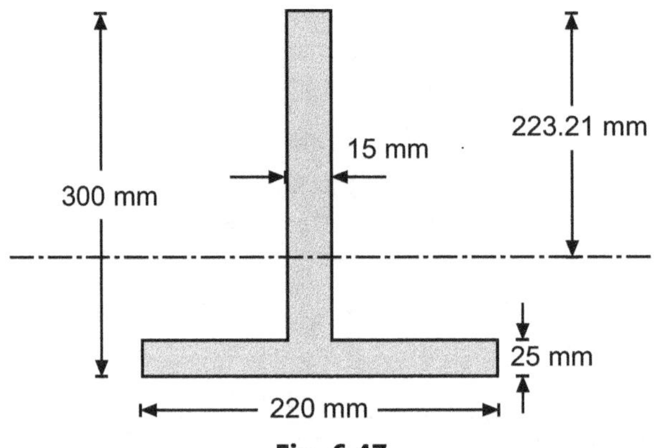


**Fig. 6.47**

**Data :** As shown in Fig. 6.47, S.F. = 68 kN.

**Required :** Maximum shear stress.

**Solution :** Maximum shear stress is at N.A.

$$\bar{x} \text{ from top} \;=\; \frac{275 \times 15 \times 137.5 + 220 \times 25 \times 287.5}{275 \times 15 + 220 \times 25}$$

$$=\; 223.21\ mm$$

$$\text{Moment of inertia} \;=\; \frac{15 \times 275^3}{12} + 15 \times 275 \times (223.21 - 137.5)^2$$

$$+\; \frac{220 \times 25^3}{12} + 220 \times 25\,(287.5 - 223.21)^2$$

$$=\; 79.32 \times 10^6\ mm^4$$

$\therefore$ 
$$q \;=\; \frac{S A \bar{y}}{I b}$$

$$S \;=\; 68\ kN = 68 \times 10^3\ N$$

$$A\bar{y} \;=\; 223.21 \times 15 \times \frac{223.21}{2} = 373.67 \times 10^3\ mm^3$$

$$b \;=\; 15\ mm$$

$\therefore$ 
$$q_{\text{N.A.}} \;=\; \frac{68 \times 10^3 \times 373.67 \times 10^3}{79.32 \times 10^6 \times 15} = 21.36\ N/mm^2$$

$\therefore$ $\quad$ Maximum shear stress is 21.36 N/mm².

**Example 6.29 :** *Fig. 6.48 shows the cross-section of a beam which is subjected to a shear force of 20 kN. Draw shear stress distribution across the depth marking values at salient points.*

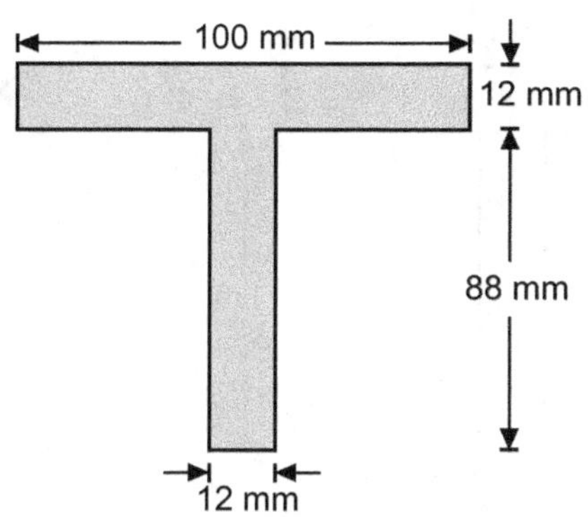


**Fig. 6.48**

**Data :** As shown in figure  6.48, shear force = 20 kN.

**Required :** Shear stress diagram.

**Concept :** Standard formulae.

**Solution :** (i) Geometric properties :

$$\bar{y} = \frac{100 \times 12 \times 6 + 88 \times 12 \times 56}{100 \times 12 + 88 \times 12}$$

$$= 29.4 \text{ mm from top}$$

$$I = \frac{100 \times 12^3}{12} + 100 \times 12 \, (29.4 - 6)^2$$

$$+ \frac{12 \times 88^3}{12} + 12 \times 88 \, (56 - 29.4)^2$$

$$= 2.1 \times 10^6 \text{ mm}^4$$

**(ii) Shear stress :**
$$q = \frac{SA\bar{y}}{Ib}$$

(a)
$$q_{1-1} = q_{4-4} = 0$$

(b)
$$q_{2-2} : A\bar{y} = 100 \times 12 \times (23.4) = 28080 \text{ mm}^3$$

$$q_{2-2} = \frac{20 \times 10^3 \times 28080}{2.1 \times 10^6 \times b} = \frac{267.42}{b}$$

$$q_{2-2 \text{ just above}} = \frac{267.42}{100} = 2.67 \text{ N/mm}^2$$

$$q_{2-2 \text{ just below}} = \frac{267.42}{12} = 22.29 \text{ N/mm}^2$$

$$q_{3-3} \, A\bar{y} = 100 \times 12 \times 23.4 + 12 \times 23.4 \times \frac{23.4}{2}$$

$$= 31365.36 \text{ mm}^3$$

$$q_{3-3} = \frac{20 \times 10^3 \times 31365.36}{2.1 \times 10^6 \times 12}$$

$$= \mathbf{24.89 \text{ N/mm}^2}$$

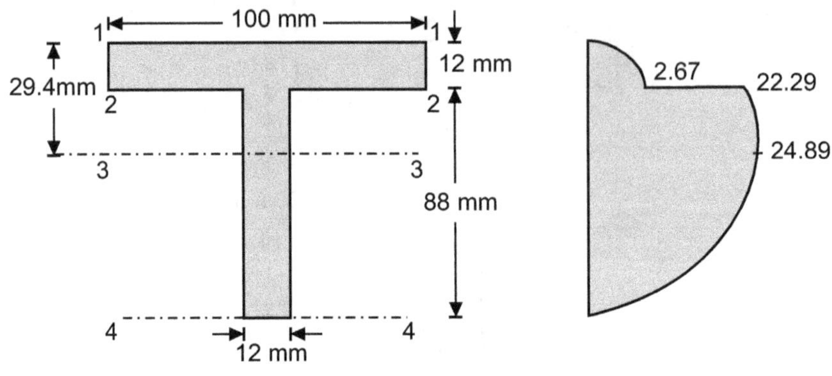


**Fig. 6.49**

**Example 6.30 :** *A beam of extruded magnesium has the cruciform cross-section shown in Fig. 6.50. Calculate the shear stress at the junction AB, if the total force on the cross-section is 225 kN.*
**(Dec. 2005)**

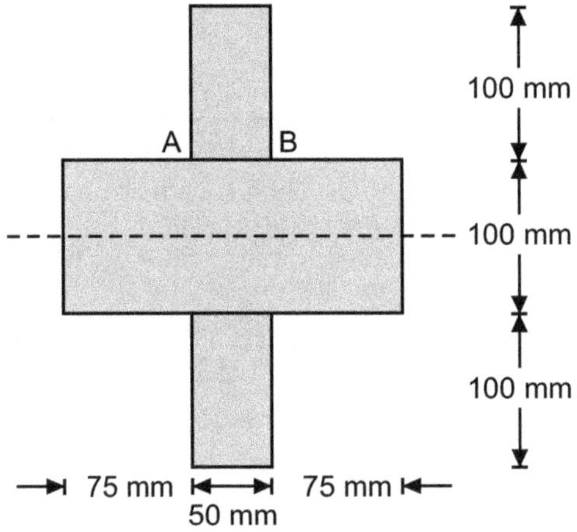


**Fig. 6.50**

**Data :** S = 225 kN, as shown in Fig. 6.50.

**Required :** Stress at AB.

**Concept :** Standard formulae.

**Solution :** (i) Geometric properties :

$$\bar{y} = 150 \text{ mm at centre}$$

$$\therefore \quad I = \frac{50 \times 300^3}{12} + \frac{150 \times 100^3}{12} = 125 \times 10^6 \text{ mm}^4$$

(ii) Shear Stress :

$$q = \frac{S A \bar{y}}{I b} = \frac{225 \times 10^3 \times 50 \times 100 \times 150}{125 \times 10^6 \times b} = \frac{900}{b}$$

$$q_{\text{just above AB}} = \frac{900}{50} = \textbf{18 Mpa}$$

$$q_{\text{just below AB}} = \frac{900}{200} = \textbf{4.5 Mpa}$$

**Example 6.31 :** *Figure 6.31 shows cross-section of beam is subjected to shear of 200 kN. Draw shear stress diagram and find the value of maximum shear stress.*

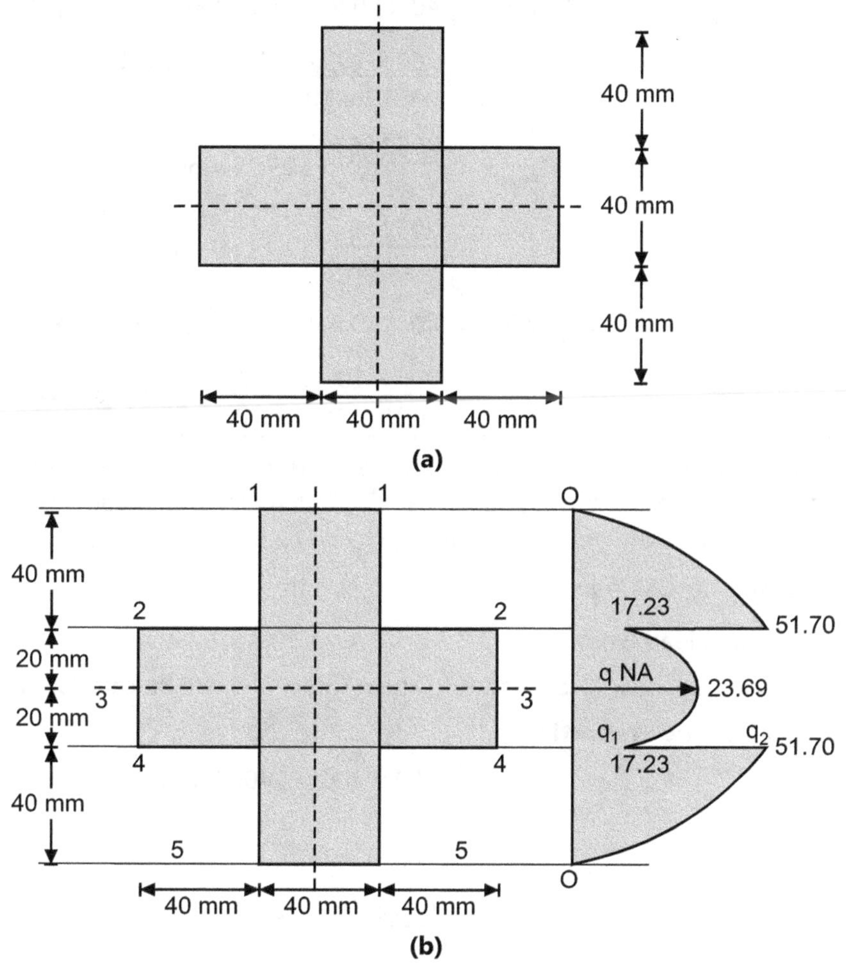


**Fig. 6.51**

**Data :** As shown in Fig. 6.51.

**Required :** Shear stress diagram.

**Concept :** Standard formuale.

**Solution :** (i) Geometric properties :

$$\bar{y}_{top} \;=\; 60 \text{ mm}$$

$$I \;=\; \frac{40 \times 120^3}{12} + \frac{80 \times 40^3}{12} = 6.19 \times 10^6 \text{ mm}^4$$

(ii) Shear stress :

$$\tau \;=\; \frac{SA\bar{y}}{Ib}$$

$$q_{1-1} = q_{5-5} = 0$$

$$q_{2-2} : A\bar{y} = 40 \times 40 \times 40 = 64000 \text{ mm}^3$$

$$q_{2-2} = \frac{200 \times 10^3 \times 64000}{6.19 \times 10^6 \times b} = \frac{2067.85}{b}$$

$$q_{2-2 \text{ just above}} = \frac{2067.85}{40} = 51.70 \text{ N/mm}^2$$

$$q_{2-2 \text{ just below}} = \frac{2067.85}{120} = 17.23 \text{ N/mm}^2$$

$$q_{3-3} : A\bar{y} = 40 \times 40 \times 40 + 20 \times 120 \times 10 = 88000 \text{ mm}^2$$

$$q_{3-3} = \frac{200 \times 10^3 \times 88000}{6.19 \times 10^6 \times 120} = \textbf{23.69 N/mm}^2$$



**Data :** $b = 120$ mm, $D = 200$ mm, $l = 4$m, $Z_{max} = 5$ N/mm².

**Required :** Maximum load (w).

**Concept :** First find out shear force. Knowing shear force load can be calculated.

**Solution : (i) Geometric Properties :**

$$A = 120 \times 200 = 24000 \text{ mm}^2$$

For a rectangular section,
$$q_{max} = \frac{3S}{2bd}$$

$$S = \frac{(5)\,(2)\,(120)\,(200)}{3} = 80 \times 10^3 \text{ N}$$

$$S = 80 \text{ kN}$$

Beam is simply supported at end with UDL$_w$ in / kN/m

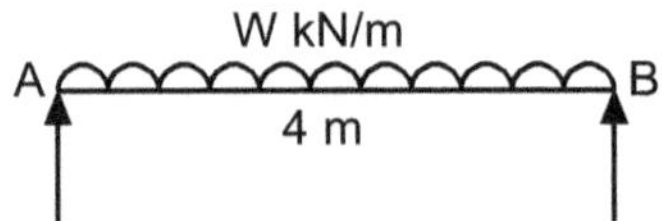


**Fig. 6.52**

Now,
$$\frac{w\,(l)}{2} = S$$

$$\therefore \quad \frac{w\,(4)}{2} = 80$$

$$\therefore \quad \textbf{w = 40 kN/m}$$

## EXERCISE

1. Fig. 6.53 shows the cross-section of beam. Draw shear stress distribution diagram if this cross-section is subjected to a shear force of 150 kN.

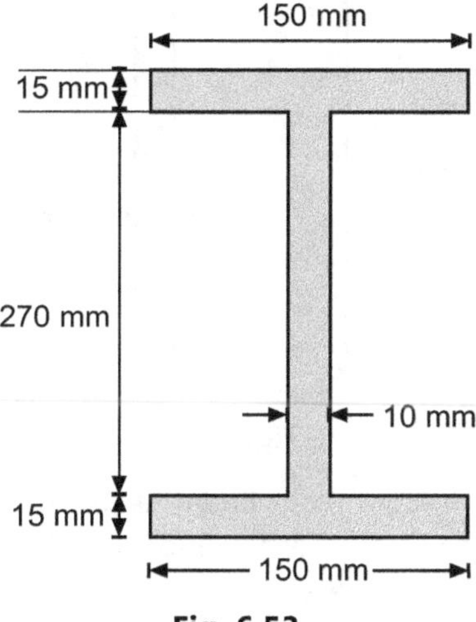


**Fig. 6.53**

(Shear stress at the junction of web and flange = 2.97 MPa, 44.58 MPa and $\tau_{max}$ = 57.25 MPa)

2. For the cross-section of beam shown in Fig. 6.48, find the percentage of bending moment resisted by flanges and percentage of shear force resisted by web. (Bending moment resisted by flanges = 84.77%, shear force resisted by web = 95.48%)

3. Find the ratio of maximum shear stress to average shear stress for the cross-section of beam shown in Fig. 6.54.

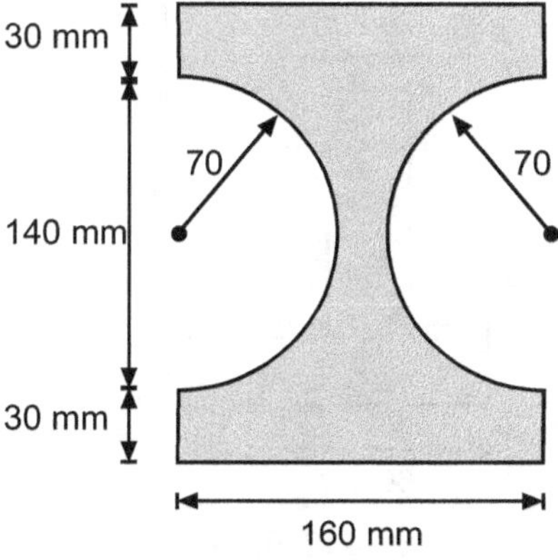


**Fig. 6.54**

4. Fig. 6.55 shows the cross-section of a beam. If this section is subjected to a shear force of 70 kN, draw the shear stress distribution diagram.

(Shear stress at the junction of web and flange = 6.67 MPa; 62.44 MPa; $\tau_{max}$ = 79.56 MPa)

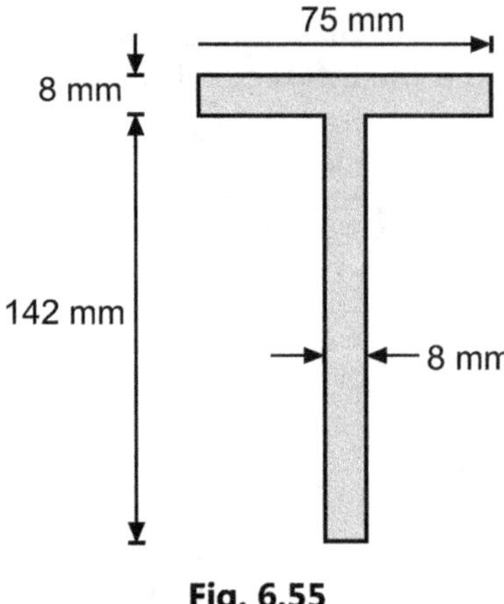

**Fig. 6.55**

5. Fig. 6.56 shows the cross-section of a beam. If this cross-section is subjected to a shear force of 15 kN, draw shear stress distribution diagram and find the ratio of maximum shear stress to minimum shear stress.

(Shear stress at the junction of web and flange = 2.75 MPa; 13.23 MPa;

$$\tau_{max} = 13.78 \text{ MPa, } \frac{\tau_{max}}{\tau_{avg}} = 2.206)$$

6. A compound beam of cross-section 100 mm wide and 300 mm deep is made up from three uniform wooden sections 100 mm × 100 mm each glued together. Calculate the maximum intensity of UDL that a simply supported beam of 4m span of above cross-section can carry if permissible horizontal shear per unit length of glued joint is 7 N/mm.

(0.7876 kN/m)

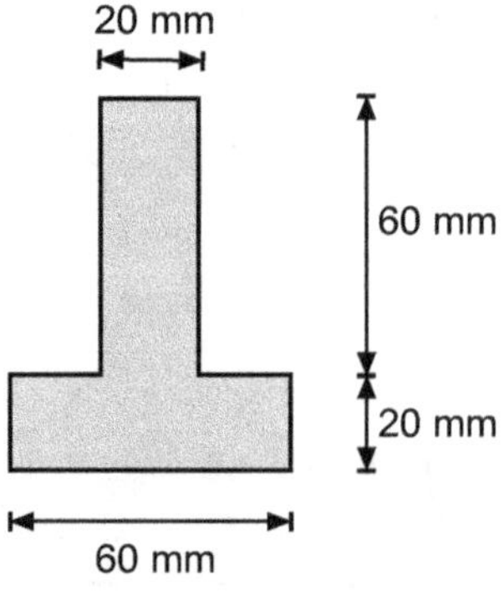

**Fig. 6.56**

7. Determine the shear stress distribution for the cross-section of a beam shown in Fig. 6.57 when subjected to shear force of 400 kN.

(Shear stress at the junction of flange and web = 4 MPa; 47.94 MPa; $\tau_{NA}$ = 4.168 MPa)

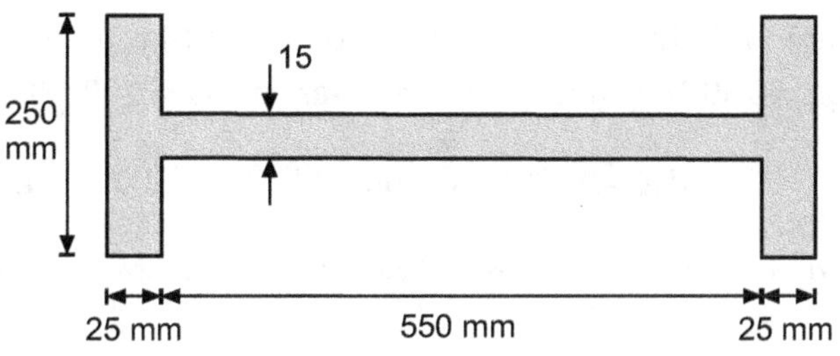


**Fig. 6.57**

8.   Fig. 6.58 shows the cross-section of beam made out of five wooden planks glued

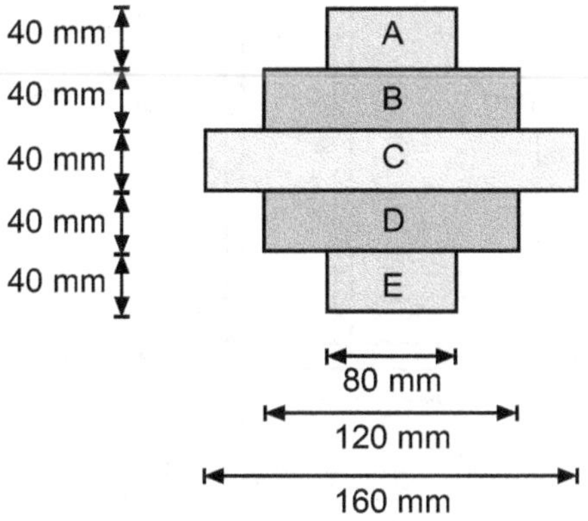


**Fig. 6.58**

together. A simply supported beam of the given cross-section is carrying UDL of 5 kN/m over 2m span. Find : (i) the maximum bending stress (ii) what should be the strength of the glued joint ? (iii) what is the percentage contribution of the plank B towards the moment of resistance at 0.5 m from the support. (iv) what is their contribution in resisting shear at the same section ? (Maximum bending stress = 4.34 MPa; strength of glued joint = 38.88 N/mm; percentage contribution of B = 28.96% towards moment and 19.1% towards shear)

9.   A circular pipe having 80 mm external diameter and 60 mm internal diameter is subjected to a shear force of 30 kN at a certain section. Calculate the intensity of maximum shear stress.                                                                          (26.92 MPa)

10.   For a hollow circular section whose external diameter is twice the internal diameter, find the ratio of maximum shear stress to average shear stress.                                (1.866)

11.   A simply supported beam AB of span 8 m carries UDL of 25 kN/m over the entire span. The beam is also subjected to clockwise couple of 75 kN.m at centre. Check the safety of

section for flexure and shear with following data : (i) Maximum flexural stress in tension and compression = 150 MPa (ii) Maximum shear  stress = 100 MPa.

$$(I_{XX} = 8.71 \times 10^8 \text{ mm}^4, \text{SF}_{max} = 109.375 \text{ kN}, \text{BM}_{max} = 237.5 \text{ kN.m}$$

$\sigma_{b,\ max} = 93$ MPa $< 150$ MPa, $\tau_{max} = 17.81$ MPa $< 100$ MPa. $\therefore$ Safe in flexure andshear).

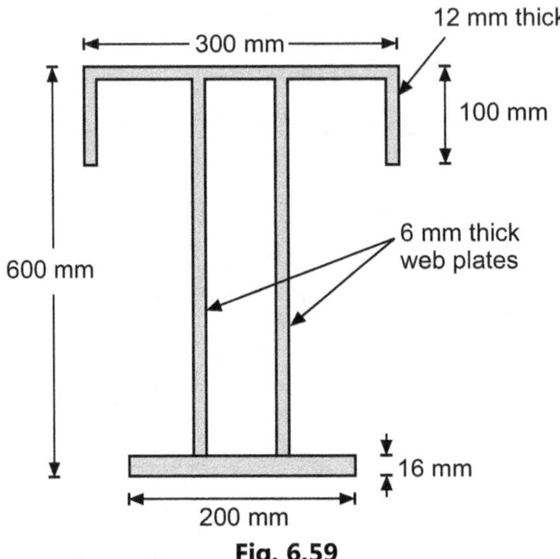


**Fig. 6.59**

## UNIVERSITY QUESTION PAPERS

### May 2016

1. A simply supported beam carriers a uniformly distributed load of intensity  30 N/mm over the entire span of 1 m. The cross-section of the beam is a T-section having the dimension as shown in Fig. 1. Calculate the maximum shear for the section of the beam.  **[6]**

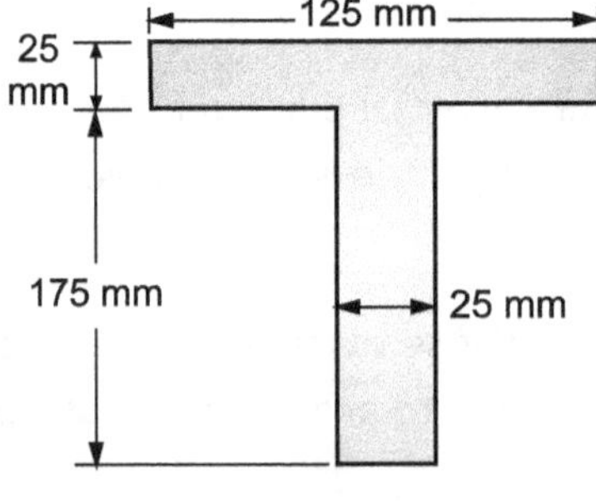


**Fig. 1**

# Chapter 7

# SLOPE AND DEFLECTION OF BEAMS (MACAULAY'S METHOD)

## 7.1 INTRODUCTION

Under the action of external loads the beam deflects from its initial position. Exact values of deflections are required in many designs. For example, in buildings, floor beams shall not deflect beyond the specified limit to maintain the sense of security of the occupants. Also study of deflection is necessary to check the dimensional accuracy of various machine elements, under the action of variety of loads.

Basically beam is subjected to flexure and shear. Both of these actions are responsible for causing deflection. However, deflections due to shear are generally neglected, being smaller in magnitude as compared to that due to bending.

When the cross section of beam is designed to resist bending stresses safely, it is called as design for *strength criterion*. And when the cross section of beam is designed such that deflection is within specified limit, it is called as *stiffness criterion* of design. Practically, design of flexure member is required for strength as well as stiffness criteria.

## 7.2 ASSUMPTIONS

When line members are subjected to bending without twisting (i.e. the plane of the external forces acting on member must pass through the shear centre of the cross section) their axis does not elongate and their cross sections do not twist. Moreover, because the dimensions of the cross sections of line members are small compared to their length, the following assumptions as to the geometry of their deformed configuration can be made.

   (i)   Plane sections normal to the axis of a line member prior to the deformation can be considered plane subsequent to deformation, that is the warping of cross section of a line member is assumed negligible.

   (ii)  Plane sections normal to the axis of a line member before deformation can be considered normal to its deformed axis subsequent to deformation. This implies that, the effect of shearing components of strain on transverse components of translation of cross sections is negligible.

## 7.3 SLOPE, DEFLECTION AND RADIUS OF CURVATURE

A segment of initially straight beam is shown in a deformed state in Fig. 7.1. The deflected axis of the beam is called *elastic curve*, which bends into an arc of a circle with radius of curvature R as shown in Fig. 7.1. The elastic curve is very flat and its slope at any point is very small.

$$\tan \theta \ = \ \frac{dy}{dx}$$

$$\therefore \qquad \theta = \frac{dy}{dx} \qquad \qquad \dots (7.1)$$

$$\therefore \qquad \frac{d\theta}{dx} = \frac{d^2y}{dx^2} \qquad \qquad \dots (7.2)$$

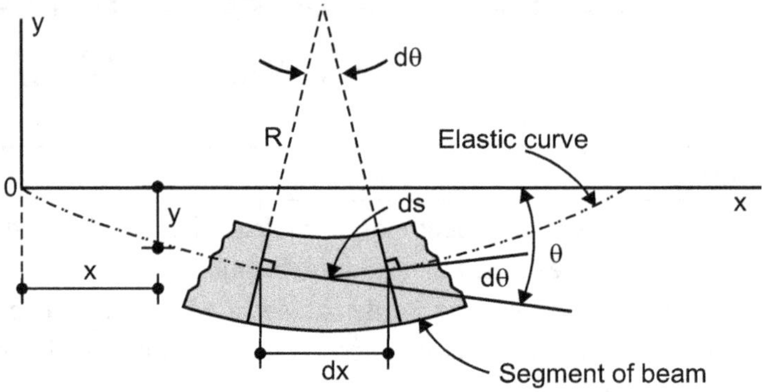

**Fig. 7.1**

From Fig. 7.1,

$$ds = R\, d\theta \qquad \qquad \dots (7.3)$$

where,
$$R = \text{radius of curvature for arc of length ds}$$

$$\therefore \qquad \frac{1}{R} = \frac{d\theta}{ds} \approx \frac{d\theta}{dx} = \frac{d^2y}{dx^2} \qquad \qquad \dots (7.4)$$

In deriving the flexure formula, we have obtained

$$\frac{1}{R} = \frac{M}{EI} \qquad \qquad \dots (7.5)$$

Equating values of $\frac{1}{R}$ from equations (7.4) and (7.5), we get

$$EI\frac{d^2y}{dx^2} = M \qquad \qquad \dots (7.6)$$

Equation (7.6) is known as differential equation of the elastic curve of a beam. The product EI is called *flexural rigidity* of the beam.

The exact value of $\frac{1}{R}$ is given by

$$\frac{1}{R} = \frac{\dfrac{d^2y}{dx^2}}{\left[1 + \left(\dfrac{dy}{dx}\right)^2\right]^{3/2}} \qquad \qquad \dots (7.7)$$

However, $\frac{dy}{dx}$ being very small its square is still smaller compared to unity and hence neglected.

Assuming EI = constant along the length of beam and integrating equation (7.6), we get

$$EI\frac{dy}{dx} = \int M\, dx + C_1 \qquad \qquad \dots (7.8)$$

Equation (7.8) is a slope equation, where M represents the bending moment equation in terms of x and $C_1$ is the constant of integration to be evaluated knowing the boundary conditions.

Integrating equation (7.8), we get

$$EIy = \int \int M\,dx + C_1 x + C_2 \qquad \text{... (7.9)}$$

Equation (7.9) is a deflection equation, where $C_2$ is another constant of integration to be evaluated knowing the boundary conditions.

## 7.4 METHODS OF DISPLACEMENT ANALYSIS

Several methods are available for determining slopes and deflections of beams. Although based on the same principles, they differ in technique and their immediate objective. The three methods that are discussed in detail are ;

(i)   Macaulay's method

(ii)  Moment area method and

(iii) Conjugate beam method.

## 7.5 MACAULAY'S METHOD

This is a convenient method of displacement analysis particularly when the beam is subjected to different loading conditions. In this method, single bending moment equation is written such that it becomes continuous for the entire length of beam inspite of the discontinuity of loading.

For example, consider a beam AB supported and loaded as shown in Fig. 7.2.

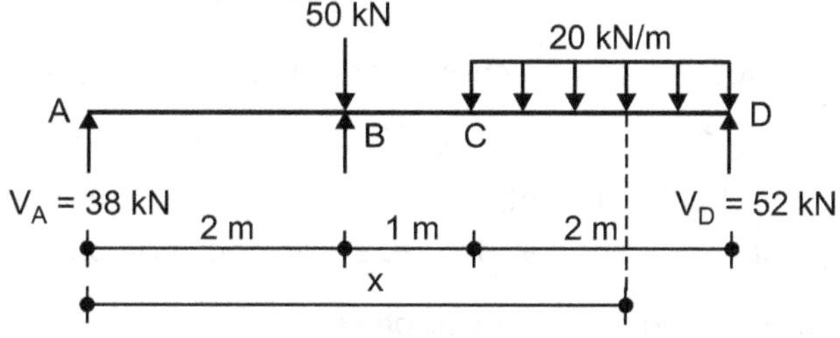


**Fig. 7.2**

Reactions $V_A$ and $V_D$ are obtained from statics as shown in Fig. 7.2.

Bending moment equations for different zones can be written as under;

$$M_{AB} = 38\,x$$

$$M_{BC} = 38\,x - 50\,(x - 2)$$

$$M_{CD} = 38\,x - 50\,(x - 2) - \frac{20\,(x - 3)^2}{2}$$

It should be noted that bending moment equation of zone CD is valid for zones AB and BC also provided that the terms $(x - 2)$ and $(x - 3)^2$ are neglected for values of x less than 2 m and 3 m respectively. For the ease of working, the section shall be considered in the last zone and bending moment equation for it shall be written with vertical lines of division as shown

$$EI\,\frac{d^2y}{dx^2} \;=\; M_x \;=\; 38\,x\;\bigg|\;-50\,(x-2)\;\bigg|\;-\;\frac{20\,(x-3)^2}{2} \qquad \text{... (a)}$$

The above equation is valid for the complete length of beam if we neglect the negative values of terms in brackets.

Thus, equation (a) is the general equation of bending moment for the beam considered.

Integrating equation (a) with respect to x, we get

$$EI\cdot\frac{dy}{dx} \;=\; 38\,\frac{x^2}{2} + C_1\;\bigg|\;-\frac{50\,(x-2)^2}{2}\;\bigg|\;-\frac{20\,(x-3)^3}{6}$$

$$=\; 19x^2 + C_1\;\bigg|\;-25\,(x-2)^2\;\bigg|\;-3.33\,(x-3)^3 \qquad \text{... (b)}$$

Equation (b) is general equation of slope for the beam considered. Integrating this equation further with respect to x, we get

$$EI\cdot y \;=\; \frac{19x^3}{3} + C_1x + C_2\;\bigg|\;\frac{-25\,(x-2)^3}{3}\;\bigg|\;-\frac{3.33\,(x-3)^4}{4}$$

$$=\; 6.33\,x^3 + C_1x + C_2\;\bigg|\;-8.33\,(x-2)^3\;\bigg|\;-0.83\,(x-3)^4 \qquad \text{... (c)}$$

Equation (c) is general equation of deflection for the beam considered.

In equations (b) and (c) $C_1$, $C_2$ are constants of integrations which can be evaluated using boundary conditions. Then substituting different values of x and considering proper terms from equations (b) and (c) slope and deflection at desired sections can be obtained.

Following points must be noted regarding slope and deflection equations :

(i)　Constants of integration $C_1$ and $C_2$ must be written before the first vertical line of division.

(ii)　Terms in the bracket shall be integrated as a whole. For example,

$$\int (x-a)\,dx \;=\; \frac{(x-a)^2}{2}$$

## 7.6  BOUNDARY CONDITIONS

For the solution of beam deflection Examples, in addition to the differential equations, boundary conditions must be prescribed. Several types of homogeneous boundary conditions are as shown in Table 7.1.

**Table 7.1 : Boundary conditions**

| Support type | Displacements restrained | Displacements allowed |
|---|---|---|
| Fixed | $\Delta_x$ , $\Delta_y$ , $\theta_z$ | NIL |
| Hinged | $\Delta_x$, $\Delta_y$ | $\theta_z$ |
| Horizontal Roller | $\Delta_y$ | $\Delta_x$, $\theta_z$ |
| Horizontal Guide | $\Delta_y$, $\theta_z$ | $\Delta_x$ |

**Note 1 :** $\Delta_x$ ; $\Delta_y$ indicate translations in x and y directions respectively while $\theta_z$ represents rotation @ z-axis.

**Note 2 :** All the supports are assumed in x-y plane.

## 7.7 SIGN CONVENTIONS

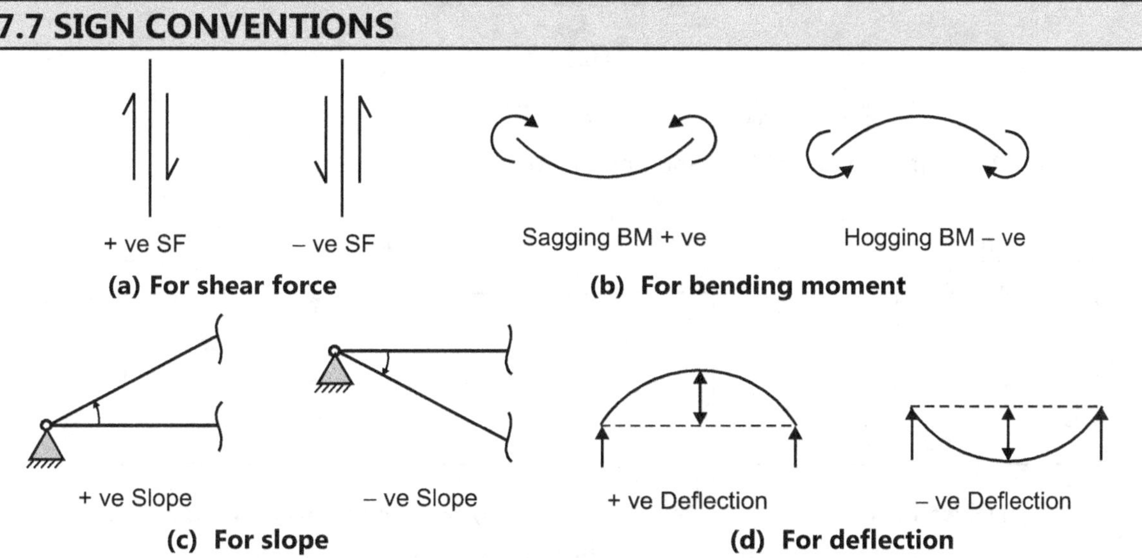


**Fig. 7.3 : Sign conventions**

## 7.8 BENDING MOMENT EQUATIONS FOR MACAULAY'S METHOD

Following are some of the variety of loadings that we generally come across for displacement analysis. Bending moment equations are written after each type of loading considering extreme left end of the beam as origin. Few cases of simply supported beams are discussed, while cantilever beams and beams with overhangs can be analysed based on same principles.

**Case (i) :** Beam with point loads :

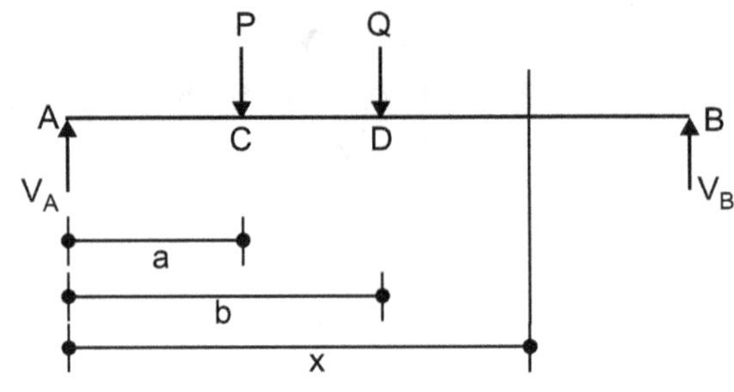

**Fig. 7.4**

$$EI \frac{d^2y}{dx^2} = V_A(x) \bigg| - P(x-a) \bigg| - Q(x-b)$$

**Case (ii) :** Beam with partial UDL and point load :

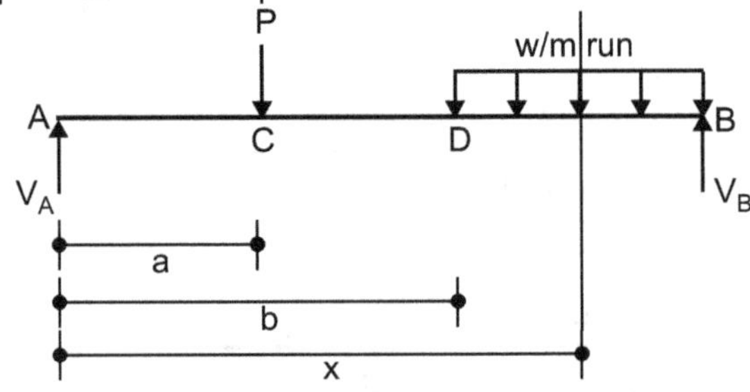

**Fig. 7.5**

$$EI \cdot \frac{d^2y}{dx^2} = V_A(x) \bigg| - P(x-a) \bigg| - \frac{w}{2}(x-b)^2$$

**Case (iii) :** Beam with partial UDL and point load :

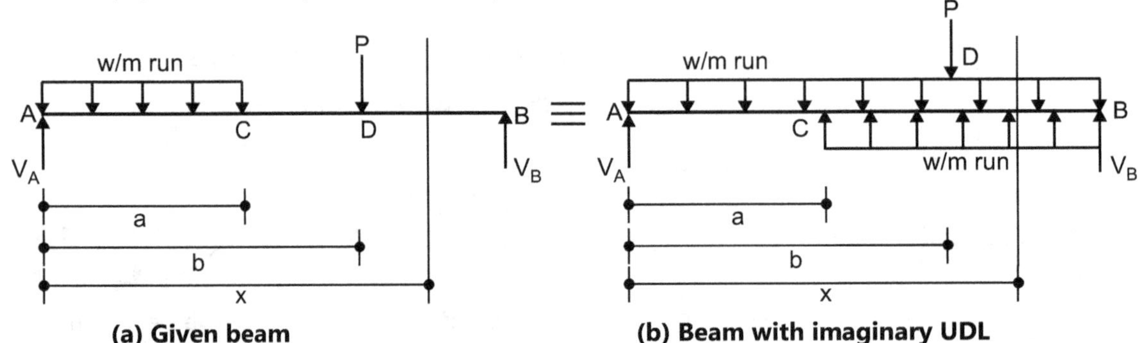

**(a) Given beam**　　　　　**(b) Beam with imaginary UDL**

**Fig. 7.6**

In case if partial UDL does not continue upto last zone i.e. DB as shown in Fig. 7.6 (a); an imaginary UDL is required to be considered to maintain the continuity of bending moment equation as shown in Fig. 7.6 (b). Bending moment equation for the above case now can be

written as,　　　　$$EI \cdot \frac{d^2y}{dx^2} = V_A(x) - \frac{w}{2}(x)^2 \bigg| + \frac{w}{2}(x-a)^2 \bigg| - P(x-b)$$

**Case (iv) :** Beam with point load and couple :

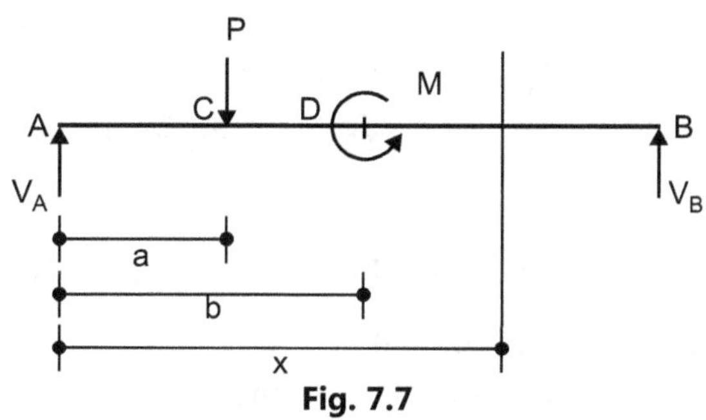

**Fig. 7.7**

$$EI \cdot \frac{d^2y}{dx^2} = V_A(x) \Big| -P(x-a) \Big| -M(x-b)^0$$

## SOLVED EXAMPLES

**Example 7.1 :** *Derive expressions for slope and deflection at free end of cantilever beam carrying point load 'P' at free end.*

**Solution :**

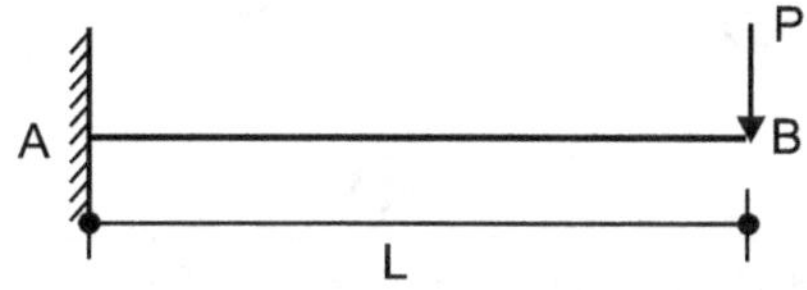

**(a) Given beam**

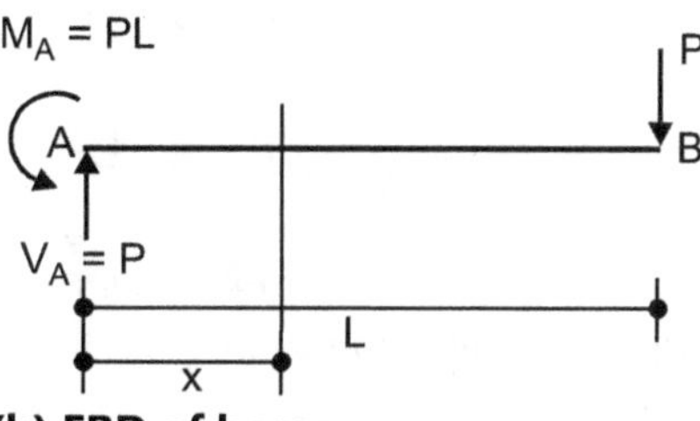

**(b) FBD of beam**

**Fig. 7.8**

(i)　　Reactions for equilibrium :

$\sum M_A = 0$;　　$M_A - PL = 0$　　　　　　　$\therefore$　　　$M_A = PL$ (↺)

$\sum F_y = 0$;　　$V_A - P = 0$　　　　　　　$\therefore$　　　$V_A = P$ (↑)

$\sum F_x = 0$;　　　$H_A = 0$

(ii) Equations of BM; slope and deflection.

　　Consider section at a distance 'x' from 'A'.

$$EI\left(\frac{d^2y}{dx^2}\right) = P(x) - PL(x)^0 \qquad \text{... (I)}$$

$$EI\left(\frac{dy}{dx}\right) = \frac{P}{2}(x)^2 - PL(x) + C_1 \qquad \text{... (II)}$$

$$EI(y) = \frac{P}{6}(x)^3 - \frac{PL}{2}(x)^2 + C_1(x) + C_2 \qquad \text{... (III)}$$

**Note :** For simplicity of equations; BM at a distance 'x' from 'A' can be written from RHS as

$$EI\frac{d^2y}{dx^2} = -P(L-x)$$

$$EI\left(\frac{dy}{dx}\right) = \frac{-P}{2}(L-x)^2 + C_1$$

$$EI\,(y) = \frac{-P}{6}(L-x)^3 + C_1\,(x) + C_2$$

However, now values of $C_1$ and $C_2$ will not be zero as obtained in the present analysis.

(iii) Boundary conditions

At A i.e. $x = 0$; $\dfrac{dy}{dx} = 0$ put in equation (II)  $\qquad\qquad \therefore \qquad C_1 = 0$

At A i.e. $x = 0$; $y = 0$  put in equation (III)  $\qquad\qquad \therefore \qquad C_2 = 0$

Substituting $C_1$ and $C_2$, equations (II) and (III) are written as

$$EI\left(\frac{dy}{dx}\right) = \frac{P}{2}(x)^2 - PL\,(x) \qquad\qquad\qquad \text{... (II)}$$

$$EI\,(y) = \frac{P}{6}(x)^3 - \frac{PL}{2}(x)^2 \qquad\qquad\qquad \text{... (III)}$$

(iv) Slope and deflections :

For slope and deflection at free end put $x = L$ in equations (II) and (III) respectively.

$$EI\left(\frac{dy}{dx}\right)_B = \frac{P}{2}(L)^2 - PL\,(L) \qquad \therefore \left(\frac{dy}{dx}\right)_B = \frac{-PL^2}{2\,EI} = \frac{PL^2}{2\,EI}\ (\circlearrowleft)$$

$$EI\,(y)_B = \frac{P}{6}(L)^3 - \frac{PL}{2}(L)^2 \qquad \therefore\ (y)_B = \frac{-PL^3}{3\,EI} = \frac{PL^3}{3\,EI}\ (\downarrow)$$

**Example 7.2 :** *Derive the expressions for slope and deflection at free end of cantilever beam carrying UDL throughout the span.*

**Solution :**

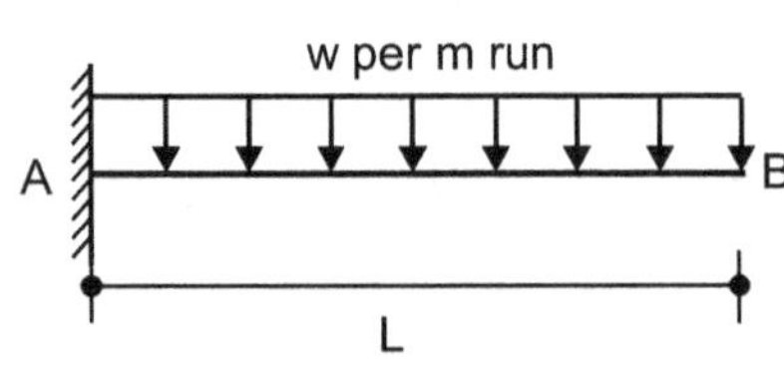



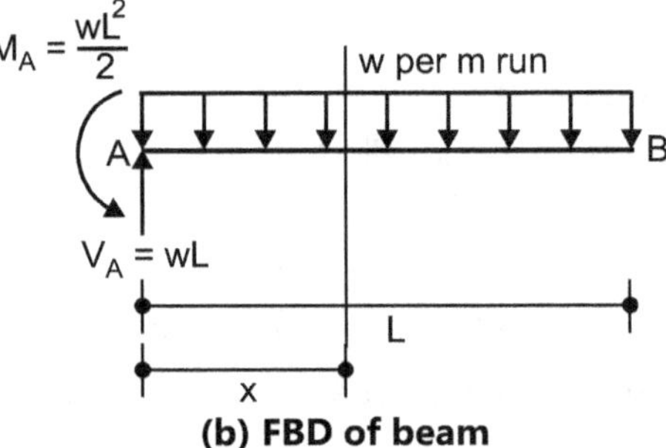



**Fig. 7.9**

(i)  Reactions for equilibrium.

$\sum M_A = 0;$  $\qquad M_A - \dfrac{wL^2}{2} = 0$  $\qquad\qquad \therefore\ M_A = \dfrac{wL^2}{2}\ (\circlearrowleft)$

$\sum F_y = 0;$  $\qquad V_A - wL = 0$  $\qquad\qquad \therefore\ V_A = wL\ (\uparrow)$

$\sum F_x = 0;$  $\qquad H_A = 0$

(ii)  Equations of BM; slope and deflection.

Consider a section at a distance 'x' from 'A'.

$$EI\left(\frac{d^2y}{dx^2}\right) = wL\,(x) - \frac{wL^2}{2}(x)^{\circ} - \frac{wx^2}{2} \qquad\qquad \text{... (I)}$$

$$EI\left(\frac{dy}{dx}\right) = \frac{wL}{2}(x)^2 - \frac{wL^2}{2}(x) - \frac{w(x)^3}{6} + C_1 \qquad \ldots \text{(II)}$$

$$EI(y) = \frac{wL}{6}(x)^3 - \frac{wL^2}{4}(x)^2 - \frac{w(x)^4}{24} + C_1(x) + C_2 \qquad \ldots \text{(III)}$$

**Note :** For simplicity of equations ; BM at a distance 'x' from 'A' can be written from R.H.S. as

$$EI\left(\frac{d^2y}{dx^2}\right) = -\frac{w}{2}(L-x)^2$$

$$EI\left(\frac{dy}{dx}\right) = -\frac{w}{6}(L-x)^3 + C_1$$

$$EI(y) = -\frac{w}{24}(L-x)^4 + C_1(x) + C_2$$

However, now values of $C_1$ and $C_2$ will not be zero as obtained in present analysis.

(iii)    Boundary conditions.

At A i.e. $x = 0$; $\dfrac{dy}{dx} = 0$; put in equation (II)         $\therefore$     $C_1 = 0$

At A i.e. $x = 0$; $y = 0$; put in equation (III)         $\therefore$     $C_2 = 0$

Substituting values of $C_1$ and $C_2$ ; equations (II) and (III) are written as

$$EI\left(\frac{dy}{dx}\right) = \frac{wL}{2}(x)^2 - \frac{wL^2}{2}(x) - \frac{w}{6}(x)^3 \qquad \ldots \text{(II)}$$

$$EI(y) = \frac{wL}{6}(x)^3 - \frac{wL^2}{4}(x)^2 - \frac{w}{24}(x)^4 \qquad \ldots \text{(III)}$$

(iv) Slope and deflection.

For slope and deflection at free end; put $x = L$ in equations (II) and (III) respectively.

$$EI\left(\frac{dy}{dx}\right)_B = \frac{wL}{2}(L)^2 - \frac{wL^2}{2}(L) - \frac{w}{6}(L)^3$$

$$\therefore \qquad \left(\frac{dy}{dx}\right)_B = -\frac{wL^3}{6\,EI} = \mathbf{\frac{wL^3}{6\,E\,I}}\,(\circlearrowleft)$$

$$EI(y)_B = \frac{wL}{6}(L)^3 - \frac{wL^2}{4}(L)^2 - \frac{w}{24}(L)^4$$

$$(y)_B = \frac{-wL^4}{8\,EI} = \mathbf{\frac{wL^4}{8\,EI}}\,(\downarrow)$$



**Solution :**

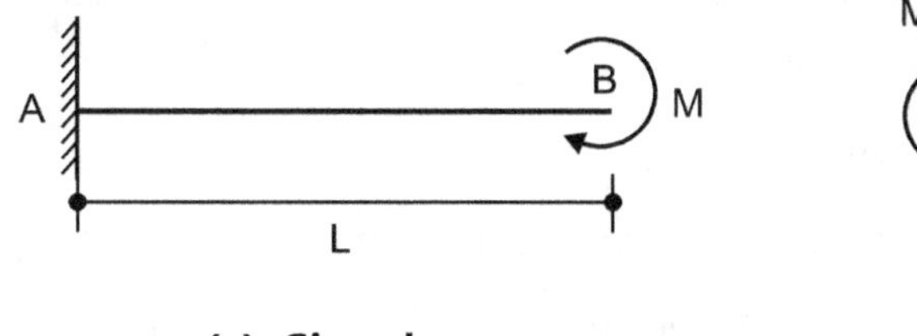


**(a) Given beam**

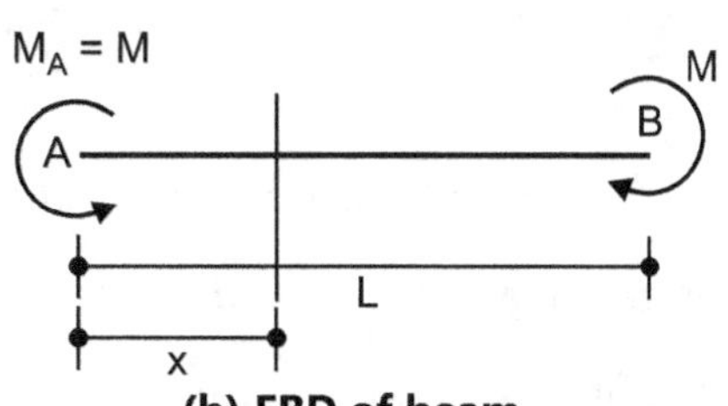


**(b) FBD of beam**

**Fig. 7.10**

(i)   Reactions for equilibrium.  $M_A = M$ (↺)

(ii)  Equations of BM ; slope and deflection.

$$EI\left(\frac{d^2y}{dx^2}\right) = -M(x)^0 \qquad \text{... (I)}$$

$$EI\left(\frac{dy}{dx}\right) = -M(x) + C_1 \qquad \text{... (II)}$$

$$EI(y) = \frac{-M(x)^2}{2} + C_1(x) + C_2 \qquad \text{... (III)}$$

(iii) Boundary conditions.

At $x = 0$ ; $\frac{dy}{dx}$ and $y = 0$   $\therefore$  $C_1 = C_2 = 0$

(iv) Slope and deflections.

Substituting $x = L$ in equations (II) and (III)

$$\left(\frac{dy}{dx}\right)_B = \frac{\mathbf{ML}}{\mathbf{EI}}\text{(↺)}$$

$$(y)_B = \frac{\mathbf{ML^2}}{\mathbf{2\ EI}}\text{(↓)}$$

**Example 7.4 :** *Derive expression for slope and deflection at free end of cantilever shown in Fig. 7.11 (a).*

**Solution :**

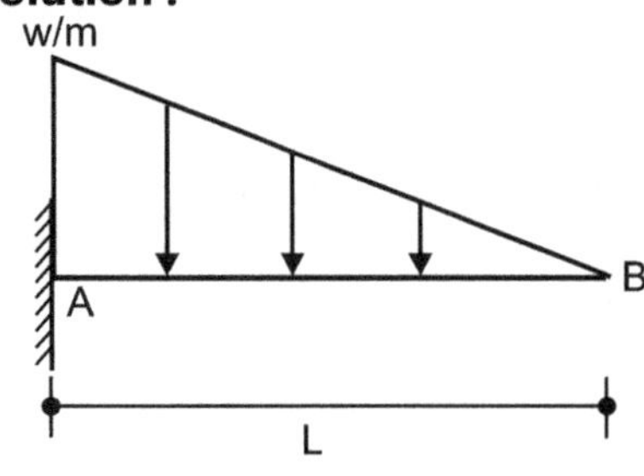


**(a) Given beam**

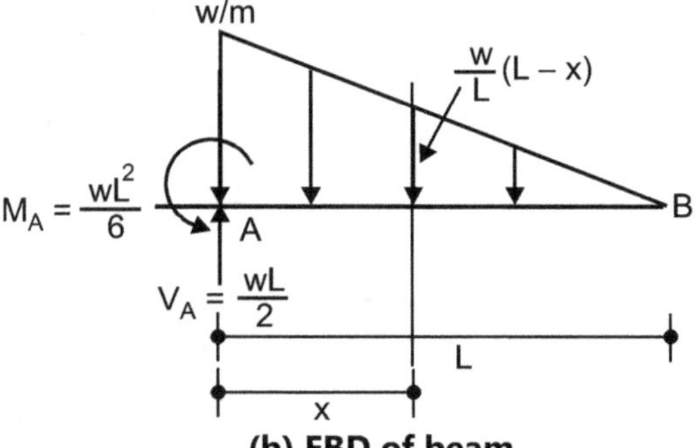


**(b) FBD of beam**

**Fig. 7.11**

(i)   Reactions for equilibrium.

$$\sum M_A = 0; \qquad M_A - \frac{1}{2}(w \times L) \times \frac{1}{3}(L) = 0 \qquad \therefore \quad M_A = \frac{wL^2}{6}\text{(↺)}$$

$$\sum F_y = 0; \qquad V_A - \frac{1}{2}(w \times L) = 0 \qquad \therefore \quad V_A = \frac{wL}{2}\text{(↑)}$$

$$\sum F_x = 0; \qquad H_A = 0$$

(ii)  Equations of BM; slope and deflection.

Considering a section at a distance 'x' from 'A', intensity of load at this section $= \frac{w}{L}(L-x)$ .

**Note :** BM equation is written from RHS for simplicity.

$$EI\left(\frac{d^2y}{dx^2}\right) = -\frac{1}{2}(L-x)\left[\frac{w}{L}(L-x)\right]\frac{(L-x)}{3}$$

$$= -\frac{w}{6L}[L-x]^3 \qquad \ldots (I)$$

$$EI\left(\frac{dy}{dx}\right) = \frac{-w}{24L}(L-x)^4 + C_1 \qquad \ldots (II)$$

$$EI(y) = \frac{-w}{120L}(L-x)^5 + C_1(x) + C_2 \qquad \ldots (III)$$

(iii) Boundary conditions.

At A i.e. $x = 0$ ; $\dfrac{dy}{dx} = 0$ ; put in equation (II)

$$\therefore \qquad C_1 = -\frac{wL^3}{24}$$

At A i.e. $x = L$ ; $y = 0$ put in equation (III)

$$\therefore \qquad C_2 = \frac{wL^4}{120}$$

Substituting values of $C_1$ and $C_2$, equations (II) and (III) are written as

$$EI\left(\frac{dy}{dx}\right) = -\frac{w}{24L}(L-x)^4 - \frac{wL^3}{24} \qquad \ldots (II)$$

$$EI(y) = -\frac{w}{120L}(L-x)^5 - \frac{wL^3}{24}(x) + \frac{wL^4}{120} \qquad \ldots (III)$$

(iv) Slope and deflections.

For slope and deflection at free end, put $x = L$ in equations (II) and (III) respectively.

$$EI\left(\frac{dy}{dx}\right)_B = \frac{-wL^3}{24}$$

$$\therefore \qquad \left(\frac{dy}{dx}\right)_B = \mathbf{\frac{wL^3}{24\,EI}}\,(\circlearrowleft)$$

$$EI(y)_B = \frac{-wL^3}{24}(L) + \frac{wL^4}{120}$$

$$\therefore \qquad (y)_B = \frac{-wL^4}{30\,EI} = \mathbf{\frac{wL^4}{30\,EI}}\,(\downarrow)$$

**Special case :** Find slope and deflection at free end of cantilever shown in Fig. 7.12.

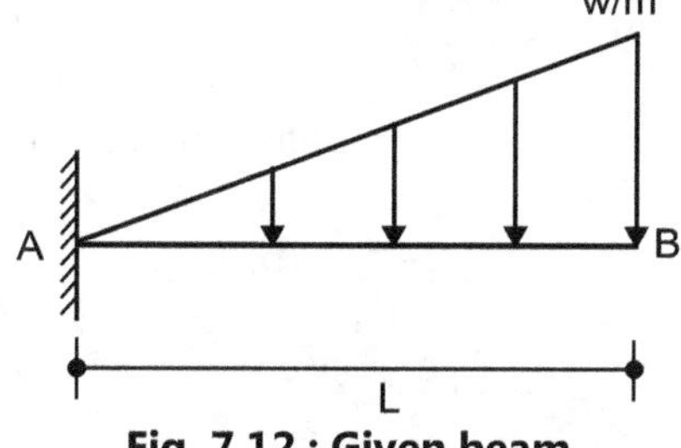


**Fig. 7.12 : Given beam**

Using principle of superposition.

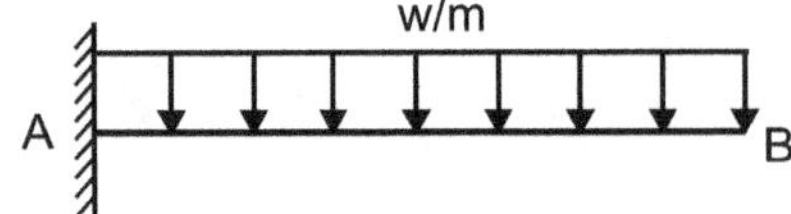

**Fig. 7.13 : Beam with UDL**

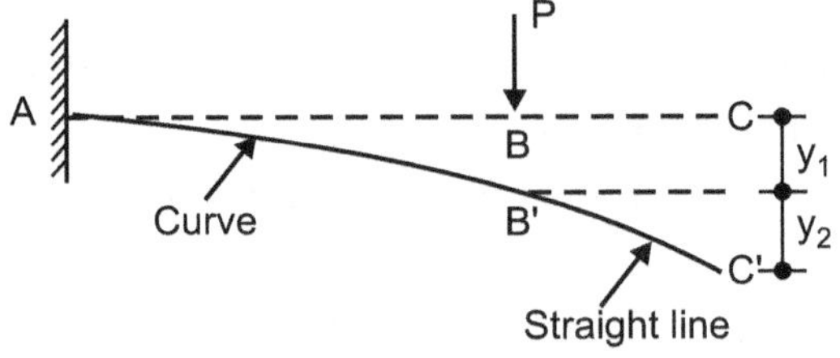

**Fig. 7.14 : Beam with UVL**

$$\left(\frac{dy}{dx}\right)_B = -\frac{wL^3}{6\,EI}$$

$$\left(\frac{dy}{dx}\right)_B = \frac{wL^3}{24\,EI}$$

$$(y)_B = -\frac{wL^4}{8\,EI}$$

$$(y)_B = \frac{wL^4}{30\,EI}$$

$\therefore$ For the given beam ; $\left(\dfrac{dy}{dx}\right)_B = \dfrac{-wL^3}{6\,EI} + \dfrac{wL^3}{24\,EI}$

$$= \frac{-wL^3}{8\,EI} = \frac{wL^3}{8\,EI}\ (\circlearrowleft)$$

$$(y)_B = \frac{-wL^4}{8\,EI} + \frac{wL^4}{30\,EI} = -\frac{11}{120}\frac{wL^4}{EI} = \frac{11}{120}\frac{wL^4}{EI}\ (\downarrow)$$

**Special tricks for cantilever beam :**

(i)

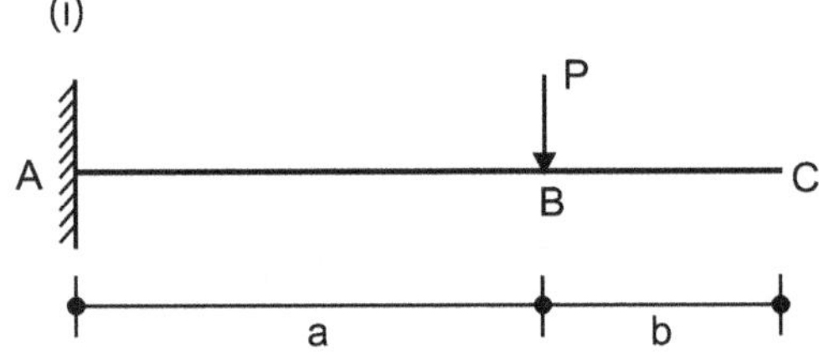

**(a) Beam**



**(b) Elastic curve**

**Fig. 7.15**

$$\text{Slope at B} = \frac{-P\,a^2}{2\,E\,I}$$

$$\text{Deflection at B} = \frac{-P\,a^3}{3\,E\,I}$$

$$\text{Slope at C} = \text{Slope at B} = \frac{-P\,a^2}{2\,E\,I}$$

$$\text{Deflection at C} = y_1 + y_2 = \text{deflection at B} + \text{slope at B} \times L\ (BC)$$

$$= \frac{-Pa^3}{3\,EI} - \frac{Pa^2}{2\,EI}\ (b)$$

$$= \frac{-P}{EI}\left(\frac{a^3}{3} + \frac{a^2 b}{2}\right)$$

$$= \frac{-Pa^2}{EI}\left(\frac{a}{3} + \frac{b}{2}\right)$$

(ii)

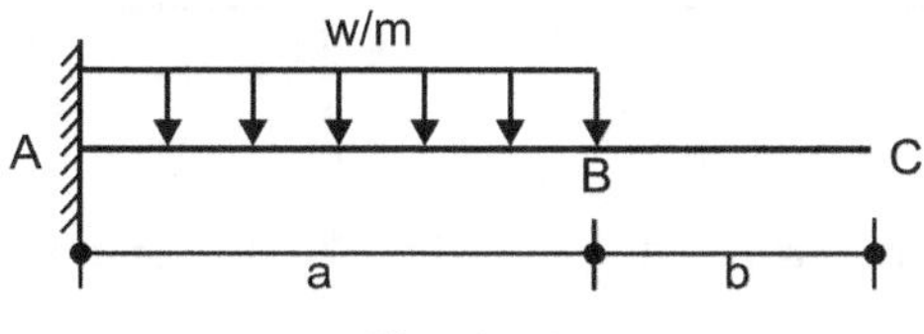

**Fig. 7.16**

$\therefore$     Slope at B $=$ Slope at C $= -\dfrac{w\,a^3}{6\,E\,I}$

Deflection at B $= -\dfrac{w\,a^4}{8\,E\,I}$

Deflection at C $= -\dfrac{wa^4}{8\,EI} - \dfrac{wa^3}{6\,EI}$ (b)

$$= -\frac{w\,a^3}{E\,I}\left(\frac{a}{8} + \frac{b}{6}\right)$$

(iii)

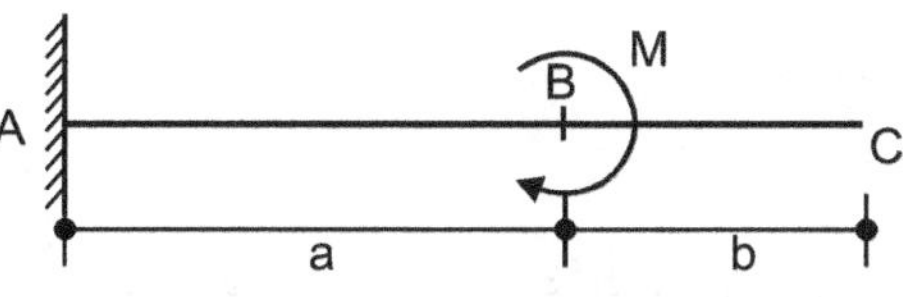

**Fig. 7.17**

Slope at B $=$ Slope at C $= -\dfrac{M\,a}{E\,I}$

Deflection at B $= -\dfrac{M\,a^2}{2\,E\,I}$

Deflection at C $= -\dfrac{Ma^2}{2\,EI} - \dfrac{Ma}{EI}$ (b)

$$= -\frac{Ma}{EI}\left(\frac{a}{2} + b\right)$$

**Example 7.5 :** *Find slope and deflection at 'C' for cantilever beam shown in Fig. 7.18.*

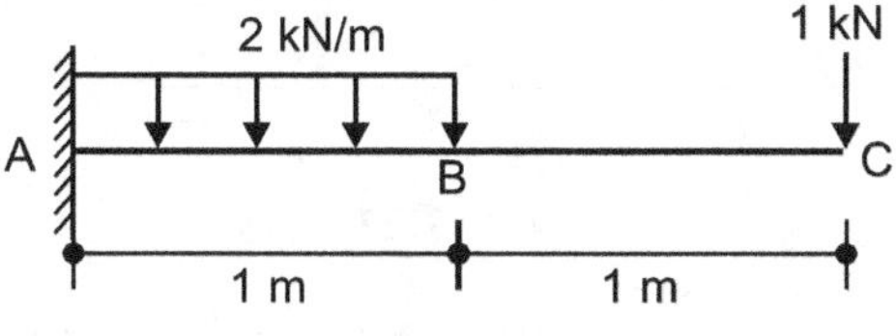

**Fig. 7.18**

**Solution :** Using principle of superposition and standard results.

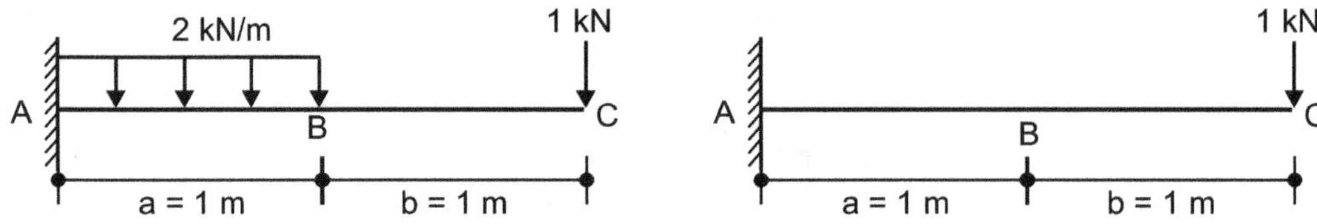

**Fig. 7.19 : Beam with UDL**          **Fig. 7.20 : Beam with point load**

$$\left(\frac{dy}{dx}\right)_C = \frac{-wa^3}{6\,EI} = \frac{-2\,(1)^3}{6\,EI} \qquad \left(\frac{dy}{dx}\right)_C = \frac{-PL^2}{2\,EI} = \frac{-1\,(2)^2}{2\,EI}$$

$$= \frac{-1}{3\,EI} \qquad\qquad\qquad = \frac{-2}{EI}$$

$$(\because a + b = L = 2m)$$

$$(y)_C = \frac{-wa^3}{EI}\left(\frac{a}{8} + \frac{b}{6}\right) \qquad (y)_C = \frac{-PL^3}{3\,EI} = \frac{-1\times 2^3}{3\,EI}$$

$$= \frac{-2\times 1^3}{EI}\left(\frac{1}{8} + \frac{1}{6}\right) \qquad\qquad = \frac{-2.67}{EI}$$

$$= \frac{-0.583}{EI}$$

$$\therefore \qquad \text{Slope at C} \;=\; \frac{-1}{EI}\left(\frac{1}{3} + 2\right) = \frac{-2.33}{EI} = \frac{2.33}{EI}\;(\circlearrowleft)$$

$$\text{Deflection at C} \;=\; \frac{-1}{EI}(0.583 + 2.67)$$

$$= \frac{-3.25}{EI} = \frac{\mathbf{3.25}}{\mathbf{E\,I}}\;(\circlearrowleft)$$

---

**Example 7.6 :** *For the cantilever beam shown in Fig. 7.21, find the magnitude of couple 'M', so that deflection at free end is zero.*

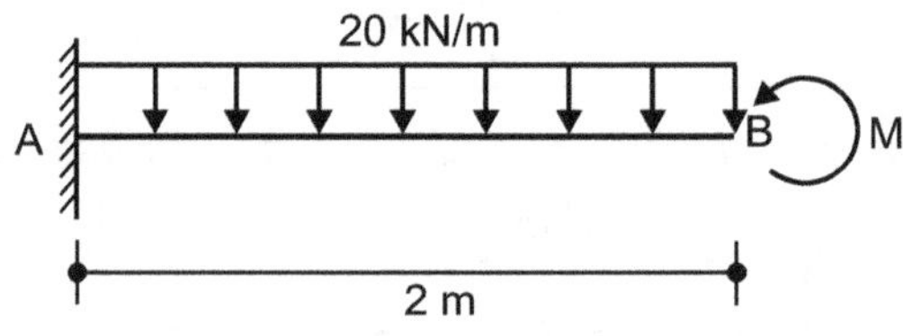

**Fig. 7.21**

**Solution :** Using principle of superposition and standard results,

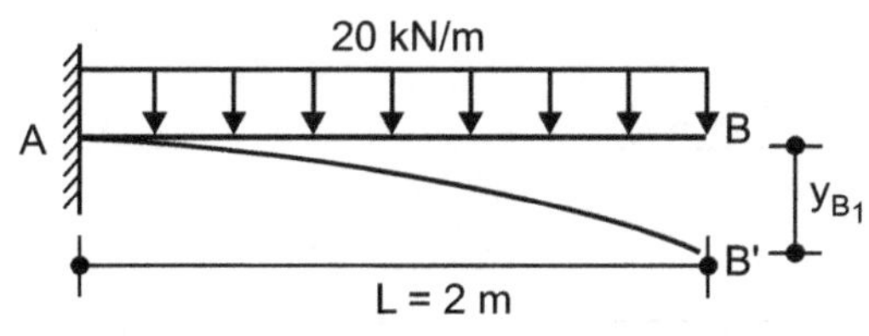

**Fig. 7.22 : Beam with UDL**

$$y_{B_1} = \frac{-wL^4}{8\,EI} = \frac{-20\,(2)^4}{8\,EI}$$

$$= \frac{-40}{EI}$$

**Fig. 7.23 : Beam with couple**

$$y_{B_2} = \frac{ML^2}{2\,EI} = \frac{M\,(2)^2}{2\,EI} = \frac{2\,M}{EI}$$

For deflection at free end, $y_B = 0$

$$y_{B_1} + y_{B_2} = \frac{-40}{EI} + \frac{2\,M}{EI} = 0$$

$$\therefore \qquad M = \textbf{20 kN.m}$$

---

**Example 7.7 :** *Find slope and deflection at free end of cantilever beam shown in Fig. 7.24 (a). If cross section of beam is 100 mm wide and 200 mm deep. Assume E = 11 GPa.*

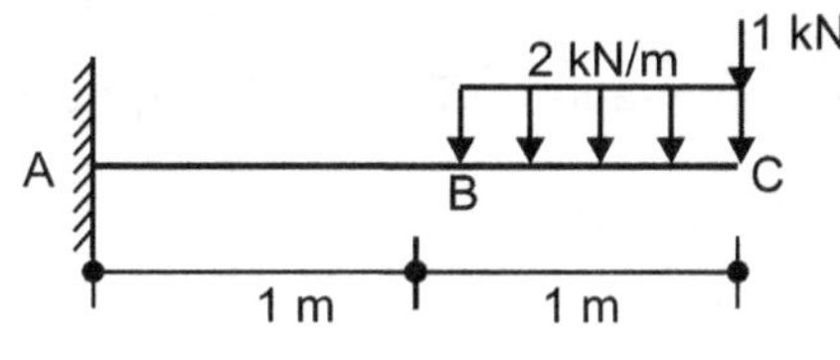

**(a) Given beam**

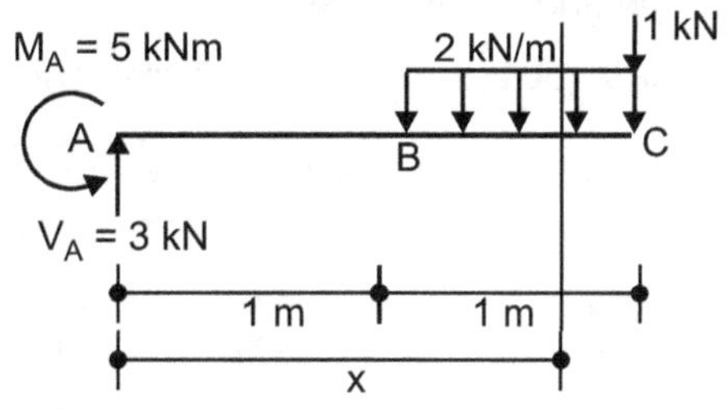

**(b) FBD of beam**

**Fig. 7.24**

**Data** : As shown in Fig. 7.24.

**Required** : Slope and deflection at C.

**Concept** : Consider 'A' as origin and section at a distance 'x' from A for BM equation.

**Solution** : (i) Reactions for equilibrium.

$$\sum M_A = 0 \; ; \qquad M_A - 2 \times 1 \times 1.5 - 1 \times 2 = 0 \qquad \therefore \quad M_A = 5 \text{ kNm } (\circlearrowleft)$$

$$\sum F_y = 0; \qquad V_A - 2 \times 1 - 1 = 0 \qquad \therefore \quad V_A = 3 \text{ kN } (\uparrow)$$

$$\sum F_x = 0; \qquad H_A = 0$$

(ii)  Equations of BM ; slope and deflection.

$$EI\left(\frac{d^2y}{dx^2}\right) = 3x - 5\,(x)^0 \left|\; \frac{-\,2\,(x-1)^2}{2}\right. \qquad \ldots \text{(I)}$$

$$EI\left(\frac{dy}{dx}\right) = 1.5\,x^2 - 5\,(x) + C_1 \left|-\,0.33\,(x-1)^3\right. \qquad \ldots \text{(II)}$$

$$EI\,(y) = 0.5\,x^3 - 2.5\,(x)^2 + C_1\,(x) + C_2 \left|-\,0.0825\,(x-1)^4\right. \qquad \ldots \text{(III)}$$

(iii) Boundary conditions.

At A i.e. $x = 0$ ; $\dfrac{dy}{dx} = 0$  and  $y = 0$

Substituting in equations (II) and (III)

$\therefore \qquad\qquad C_1 = C_2 = 0$

$\therefore$  Equations (II) and (III) are written as ;

$$EI\left(\frac{dy}{dx}\right) = 1.5\,(x)^2 - 5\,(x) \left|-\,0.33\,(x-1)^3\right. \qquad \ldots \text{(II)}$$

$$EI\,(y) = 0.5\,(x)^3 - 2.5\,(x)^2 \left|-\,0.0825\,(x-1)^4\right. \qquad \ldots \text{(III)}$$

(iv) Slope and deflections.

For slope and deflection at free end, put $x = 2$ m in equations (II) and (III) respectively.

$$EI\left(\frac{dy}{dx}\right)_C = 1.5\,(2)^2 - 5\,(2) - 0.33\,(2-1)^3$$

$$\left(\frac{dy}{dx}\right)_C = \frac{-\,4.33}{EI}$$

$$EI\,(y)_C = 0.5\,(2)^3 - 2.5\,(2)^2 - 0.0825\,(2-1)^4$$

$$(y)_C = \frac{-\,6.0825}{EI}$$

$$I = \frac{bD^3}{12} = \frac{100 \times 200^3}{12} = 66.67 \times 10^6 \text{ mm}^4$$

$$E = 11 \text{ GPa}$$

$$\therefore \qquad EI = 11 \times 66.67 \times 10^6 \text{ kNmm}^2$$

$$= 733.33 \text{ kNm}^2$$

$$\therefore \qquad \left(\frac{dy}{dx}\right)_C = \frac{-\,4.33}{733.33} = \mathbf{2.9 \times 10^{-3}\ rad\ (\circlearrowright)}$$

$$(y)_C = \frac{-\,6.0825}{733.33} \times 10^3 = \mathbf{8.29\ mm\ (\downarrow)}$$

**Example 7.8 :** *Find slope and deflections at 'C' and 'D' of cantilever beam shown in Fig. 7.25 (a) in terms of EI.*

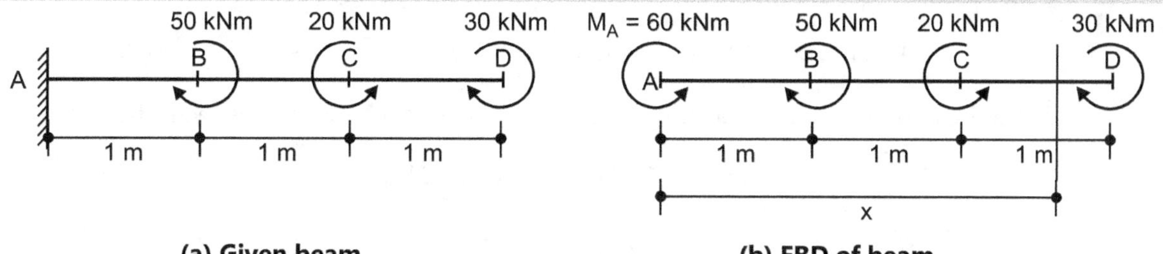


**(a) Given beam**                    **(b) FBD of beam**

**Fig. 7.25**

**Data**        :   As shown in Fig. 7.25

**Required**    :   Slope and deflection at free end ds and C.

**Concept**     :   Consider 'A' as origin and section at a distance 'x' from 'A' in zone CD for BM equation.

**Solution**    :   (i) Reactions for equilibrium.

$\sum M_A = 0$  ;                $M_A - 50 + 20 - 30 = 0$        $\therefore$    $M_A = 60$ kNm ($\uparrow$)

$\sum F_y = 0$;                              $V_A = 0$

$\sum F_x = 0$;                              $H_A = 0$

(ii)   Equations of BM; slope and deflection.

$$EI \left(\frac{d^2y}{dx^2}\right) = -60\,(x)^0 \,\Big|\, + 50\,(x-1)^0 \,\Big|\, - 20\,(x-2)^0 \qquad \ldots \text{(I)}$$

$$AB$$
$$BC$$
$$CD$$

$$EI \left(\frac{dy}{dx}\right) = -60\,(x) + C_1 \,\Big|\, + 50\,(x-1)\,\Big|\, - 20\,(x-2) \qquad \ldots \text{(II)}$$

$$EI\,(y) = -30\,(x)^2 + C_1\,(x) + C_2 \,\Big|\, + 15\,(x-1)^2 \,\Big|\, - 10\,(x-2)^2 \qquad \ldots \text{(III)}$$

(iii) Boundary conditions.

At A i.e. $x = 0$ ; $\frac{dy}{dx} = 0$ and $y = 0$, put in equations (II) and (III).

We get ; $C_1 = C_2 = 0$ $\therefore$  equations (II) and (III) are written as

$$EI \left(\frac{dy}{dx}\right) = -60\,(x) \,\Big|\, + 50\,(x-1)\,\Big|\, - 20\,(x-2) \qquad \ldots \text{(II)}$$

$$EI\,(y) = -30\,(x)^2 \,\Big|\, + 25\,(x-1)^2 \,\Big|\, - 10\,(x-2)^2 \qquad \ldots \text{(III)}$$

(iv) Slope and deflections.

For slope and deflection at C; put $x = 2$ m in equations (II) and (III) respectively.

$$EI \left(\frac{dy}{dx}\right)_C = -60(2) + 50(2-1) \qquad \therefore \qquad \left(\frac{dy}{dx}\right)_C = \frac{-70}{EI} = \frac{70}{EI} \, (\circlearrowleft)$$

$$EI\,(y)_C = -30(2)^2 + 25(2-1)^2 \qquad \therefore \qquad (y)_C = \frac{-95}{EI} = \frac{95}{EI} \, (\downarrow)$$

For slope and deflection at D ; put x = 3 m in equations (II) and (III) respectively.

$$EI \left(\frac{dy}{dx}\right)_D = -60(3) + 50(3-1) - 20(3-2)$$

$$\therefore \qquad \left(\frac{dy}{dx}\right)_D = \frac{-100}{EI} = \mathbf{\frac{100}{EI}} \, (\circlearrowleft)$$

$$EI\,(y)_D = -30(3)^2 + 15(3-1)^2 - 10(3-2)^2$$

$$\therefore \qquad (y)_D = \frac{-180}{EI}$$

$$= \mathbf{\frac{180}{EI}} \, (\downarrow)$$

---

**Example 7.9 :** *Derive the expression for slope at supports, deflection under the load and maximum deflection for the beam shown in Fig. 7.26.*

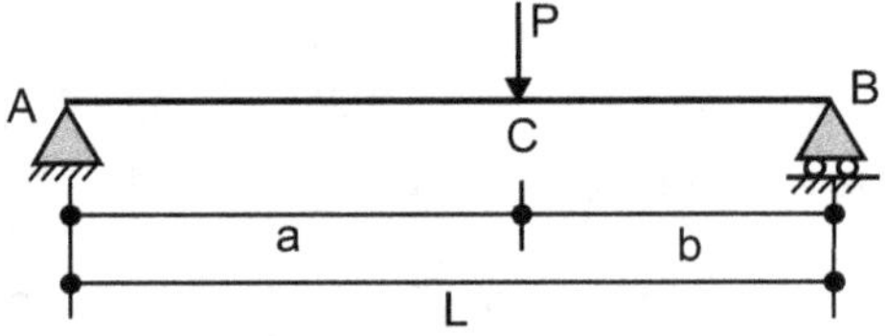


**Fig. 7.26 : Given beam**

**Data**         :   As shown in Fig. 7.26.

**Required**     :   Slopes at supports ; deflection under load and maximum deflection.

**Concept**      :   (i) Consider 'A' as origin and section at a distance 'x' from 'A' in zone CB for BM equation.

(ii) At a section of maximum deflection, slope is zero hence to locate the section of maximum deflection; slope equation for the assumed zone is equated to zero. The zone of maximum deflection shall be decided by inspection. As in the present case assuming a > b; maximum deflection will occur in zone AC.

**Solution**     :   (i) Reactions for equilibrium.

$$\Sigma M_A = 0 \; ; \qquad\qquad V_B \times L - P \times a = 0 \qquad \therefore \qquad V_B = \frac{Pa}{L} \, (\uparrow)$$

$$\Sigma F_y = 0; \qquad\qquad V_A + V_B - P = 0 \qquad \therefore \qquad V_A = P - \frac{Pa}{L} = \frac{Pb}{L} \, (\uparrow)$$

$$\Sigma F_x = 0; \qquad\qquad\qquad H_A = 0$$

FBD of beam is as shown in Fig. 7.27.

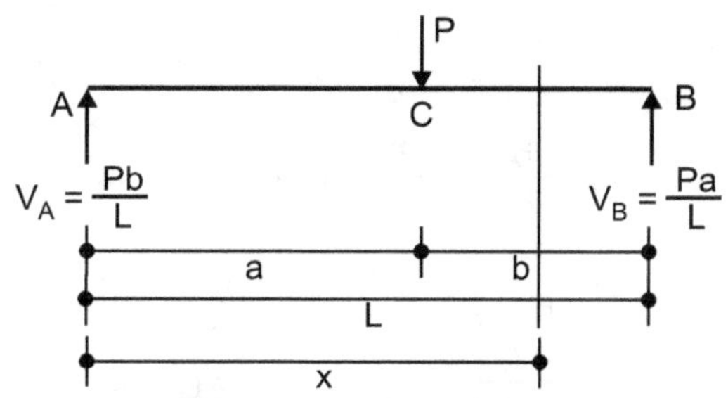

**Fig. 7.27 : FBD of beam**

(ii)    Equations for BM; slope and deflection.

$$EI\left(\frac{d^2y}{dx^2}\right) = \frac{Pb}{L}(x) \Big| - P(x-a) \qquad \text{... (I)}$$

$$EI\left(\frac{dy}{dx}\right) = \frac{Pb}{2L}(x)^2 + C_1 \left|\frac{-P(x-a)^2}{2}\right. \qquad \text{... (II)}$$

$$EI(y) = \frac{Pb}{6L}(x)^3 + C_1(x) + C_2 \left|\frac{-P(x-a)^3}{6}\right. \qquad \text{... (III)}$$

(iii) Boundary conditions.

At 'A' i.e. $x = 0$; $y = 0$ put in equation (III)          $\therefore$          $C_2 = 0$

At 'B' i.e. $x = L$; $y = 0$ put in equation (III)

$$0 = \frac{Pb}{6L}(L)^3 + C_1(L) + C_2 - \frac{P}{6}(L-a)^3$$

$$\therefore \quad 0 = \frac{Pb}{6}(L)^2 - L\,C_1 - \frac{Pb^3}{6}$$

$$\therefore \quad C_1 = \frac{-Pb}{6L}(L^2 - b^2)$$

Substituting values of $C_1$ and $C_2$, equations, (II) and (III) are written as ;

$$EI\left(\frac{dy}{dx}\right) = \frac{Pb}{2L}(x)^2 - \frac{Pb}{6L}(L^2 - b^2) \left| - \frac{P}{2}(x-a)^2 \right. \qquad \text{... (II)}$$

$$EI(y) = \frac{Pb}{6L}(x)^3 - \frac{Pb}{6L}(L^2 - b^2)(x) \left| - \frac{P}{6}(x-a)^3 \right. \qquad \text{... (III)}$$

(iv) Slope and deflections.

For slopes at A and B; put $x = 0$ and $x = L$ in equation (II) respectively.

$$EI\left(\frac{dy}{dx}\right)_A = -\frac{Pb(L^2 - b^2)}{6L}$$

$$\therefore \quad \left(\frac{dy}{dx}\right)_A = \frac{\mathbf{Pb}}{\mathbf{6EIL}}\mathbf{(L^2 - b^2)}\,(\circlearrowleft) \qquad \text{... (E}_1\text{)}$$

$$\therefore \quad EI \left(\frac{dy}{dx}\right)_B = \frac{Pb}{2L}(L)^2 - \frac{Pb}{6L}(L^2 - b^2) - \frac{P}{2}(L-a)^2$$

$$= \frac{Pb}{2}(L) - \frac{Pb}{6L}(L^2 - b^2) - \frac{P}{2}(b)^2$$

$$= \frac{Pb}{6L}[2L^2 + b^2 - 3Lb]$$

$$= \frac{P(L-a)}{6L}[2L^2 - L^2 - 2La + a^2 - 3L^2 + 3La]$$

$$(\because b = L - a)$$

$$= \frac{P(L-a)}{6L}[La + a^2]$$

$$= \frac{Pa}{6L}[L^2 - a^2]$$

$$\therefore \quad \left(\frac{dy}{dx}\right)_B = \frac{P \cdot a}{6EIL}(L^2 - a^2) \; (\circlearrowleft) \qquad \ldots (E_2)$$

For deflection under load; put $x = a$ in equation (III)

$$EI(y)_C = \frac{Pb}{6L}(a)^3 - \frac{Pb}{6L}(L^2 - b^2)a$$

$$= -\frac{Pab}{6L}(L^2 - b^2 - a^2)$$

$$= -\frac{Pab}{6L}[a^2 + b^2 + 2ab - b^2 - a^2) \; (\because a + b = L)$$

$$= -\frac{Pa^2 b^2}{3L}$$

$$\therefore \quad y_C = \frac{Pa^2 b^2}{3EIL} (\downarrow) \qquad \ldots (E_3)$$

For maximum deflection; equating slope equation for zone 'AC' to zero.

$$0 = \frac{Pb}{2L}(x)^2 - \frac{Pb}{6L}(L^2 - b^2)$$

$$\therefore \quad x^2 = \frac{L^2 - b^2}{3}$$

$$\therefore \quad x = \sqrt{\frac{L^2 - b^2}{3}} \qquad \ldots (E_4)$$

Put in equation (III)

$$EI(y)_{max} = \frac{Pb}{6L}\left[\sqrt{\frac{L^2 - b^2}{3}}\right]^2 - \frac{Pb}{6L}(L^2 - b^2)\left[\sqrt{\frac{L^2 - b^2}{3}}\right]$$

$$= \frac{-Pb}{6L}(L^2 - b^2)^{3/2}\left[\frac{1}{\sqrt{3}} - \frac{1}{3^{3/2}}\right]$$

$$= \frac{-Pb}{6L}(L^2 - b^2)^{3/2}\left(\frac{2\sqrt{3}}{9}\right)$$

$$= \frac{- Pb (L^2 - b^2)^{3/2}}{9\sqrt{3} \cdot L}$$

$$\therefore \qquad y_{max} = \frac{Pb (L^2 - b^2)^{3/2}}{9\sqrt{3}\,EIL}\,(\downarrow) \qquad \qquad ...\,(E_5)$$

**Special case 1 :** For simply supported beam carrying point load 'P' at centre, find slope at supports and maximum deflection.

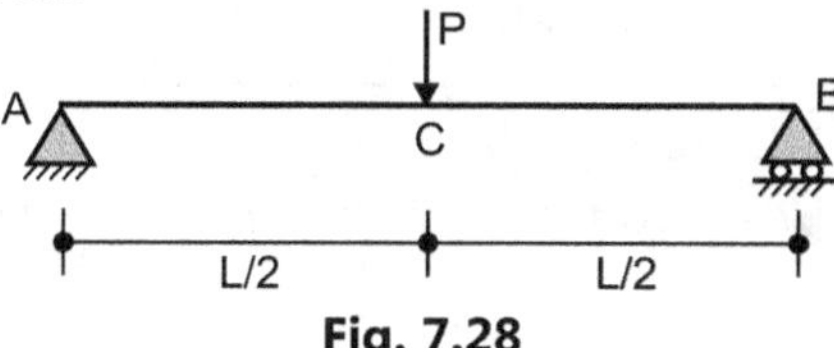

**Fig. 7.28**

For slope at supports using equations $(E_1)$ and $(E_2)$ and substituting $a = b = \dfrac{L}{2}$

By symmetry,

$$-\left(\frac{dy}{dx}\right)_A = \left(\frac{dy}{dx}\right)_B = \frac{P L^2}{16\,EI} \qquad \qquad ...\,(E_6)$$

Also, maximum deflection occurs at centre i.e.; under point load. Using equation $(E_3)$ and substituting $a = b = \dfrac{L}{2}$

$$y_{max} = \frac{P L^3}{48\,EI}\,(\downarrow) \qquad \qquad ...\,(E_7)$$

**Special case 2 :** For the beam shown in Fig. 7.29 (a), find 'a' in terms of 'L' such that central deflection is same as that of deflection at free ends.

$$\text{Deflection at centre} = \frac{P L^3}{48\,EI} \qquad \qquad ...\,(I)$$

$$\text{Deflection at ends A/E} = \text{Slope at support} \times \text{Length of overhang}$$

$$= \frac{P L^2}{16\,EI}\,(a) \qquad \qquad ...\,(II)$$

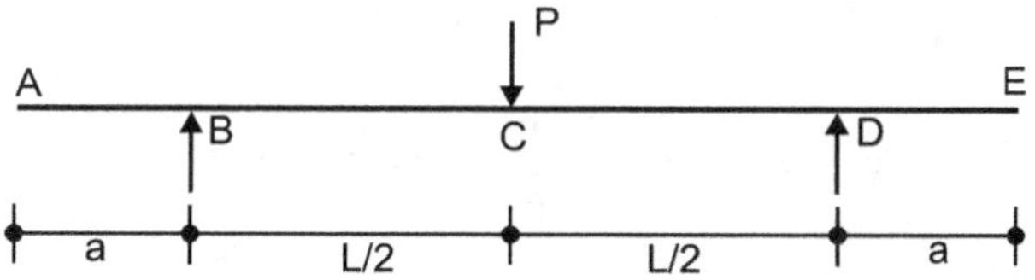

**(a) Given beam**

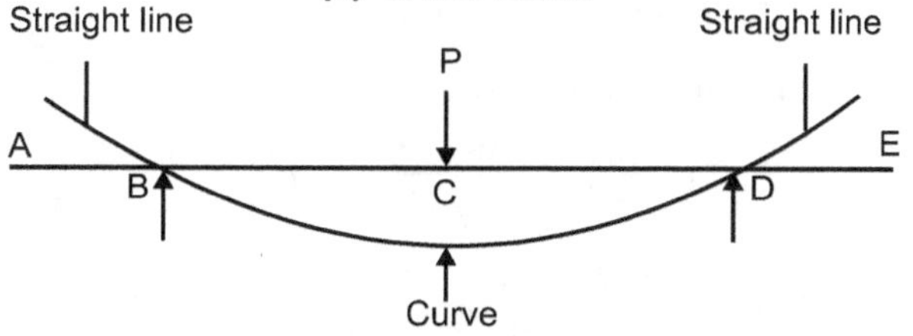

**(b) Elastic curve**

**Fig. 7.29**

Equating (I) and (II),

$$\frac{PL^3}{48\,EI} = \frac{PL^2}{16\,EI} \quad (a)$$

$$a = \frac{L}{3}$$

Thus ; for $a = \frac{L}{3}$, deflection at ends = midspan deflection.

**Example 7.10 :** *Derive the expressions for slope at supports and maximum deflection for the simply supported beam carrying UDL throughout the span.*

**Solution :**

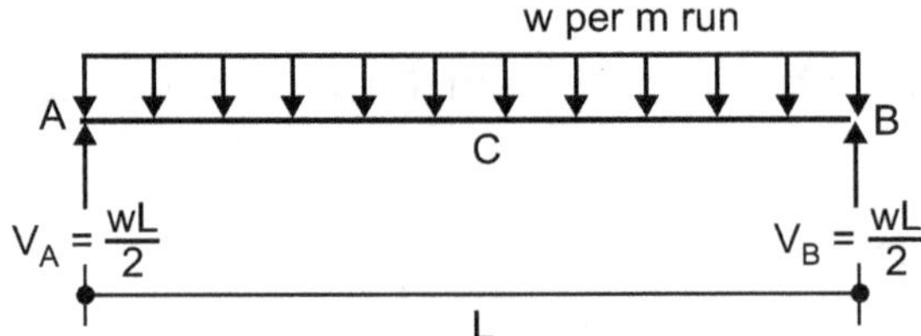


**Fig. 7.30 : FBD of beam**

Let; 

$w$ = Intensity of UDL

$L$ = Span of the beam.

(i) Reactions for equilibrium.

$$V_A = V_B = \frac{wL}{2}\ (\uparrow) \qquad\qquad (\because \text{symmetry})$$

(ii) Equations of BM; slope and deflection.

$$EI\left(\frac{d^2y}{dx^2}\right) = \frac{wL}{2}(x) - \frac{w(x)^2}{2} \qquad\qquad \dots (I)$$

$$EI\left(\frac{dy}{dx}\right) = \frac{wL}{4}(x)^2 - \frac{w}{6}(x)^3 + C_1 \qquad\qquad \dots (II)$$

$$EI(y) = \frac{wL}{12}(x)^3 - \frac{w}{24}(x)^4 + C_1(x) + C_2 \qquad\qquad \dots (III)$$

(iii) Boundary conditions.

At A i.e. $x = 0$ ; $y = 0$ put in equation (III) $\therefore C_2 = 0$

At B i.e. $x = L$ ; $y = 0$ put in equation (III)

$$0 = \frac{wL}{12}(L)^3 - \frac{w(L)^4}{24} + C_1(L)$$

$$\therefore \qquad C_1 = -\frac{wL^3}{24}$$

Substituting values of $C_1$ and $C_2$, equations (II) and (III) are written as

$$EI \left(\frac{dy}{dx}\right) = \frac{wL}{4}(x)^2 - \frac{w}{6}(x)^3 - \frac{wL^3}{24} \qquad \text{... (II)}$$

$$EI(y) = \frac{wL}{12}(x)^3 - \frac{w}{24}(x)^4 - \frac{wL^3}{24}(x) \qquad \text{... (II)}$$

(iv) Slope and deflections.

For slope at support A put x = 0 in equation (II).

$$EI \left(\frac{dy}{dx}\right)_A = -\frac{wL^3}{24} \qquad \therefore \quad \left(\frac{dy}{dx}\right)_A = \frac{wL^3}{24\,EI} \ (\circlearrowleft)$$

$$\left(\frac{dy}{dx}\right)_B = \frac{wL^3}{24\,EI} \ (\circlearrowright)$$

Maximum deflection will occur at midspan due to symmetry ; put $x = \frac{L}{2}$ in equation (III).

$$EI(y)_{max} = \frac{wL}{12}\left(\frac{L}{2}\right)^3 - \frac{w}{24}\left(\frac{L}{2}\right)^4 - \frac{wL^3}{24}\left(\frac{L}{2}\right)$$

$$\therefore \qquad y_{max} = -\frac{5}{384} \cdot \frac{wL^4}{EI}$$

**Example 7.11** : *Derive the expressions for slope at supports and deflection at point of application of couple for the beam shown in Fig. 7.31.*

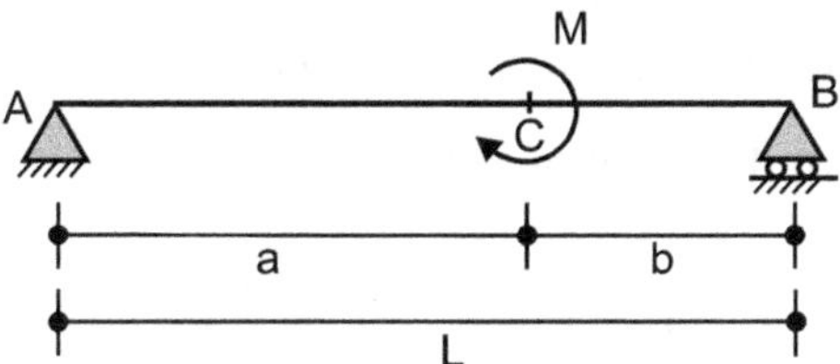


**Fig. 7.31 : Given beam**

**Data**      :   As shown in Fig. 7.31.

**Required**  :   Slope at supports and deflection at 'C'.

**Concept**   :   Consider 'A' as origin and section at a distance 'x' from 'A' in zone CB for BM equation.

**Solution:**   (i) Reactions for equilibrium.

$$\sum M_A = 0; \ V_B \times L - M \qquad = 0 \ \therefore \qquad V_B \quad = \frac{M}{L} \ (\uparrow)$$

$$\sum F_y = 0; \ V_A + V_B \qquad = 0 \ \therefore \qquad V_A \quad = \frac{M}{L} \ (\downarrow)$$

FBD of beam is as shown in Fig. 7.32.

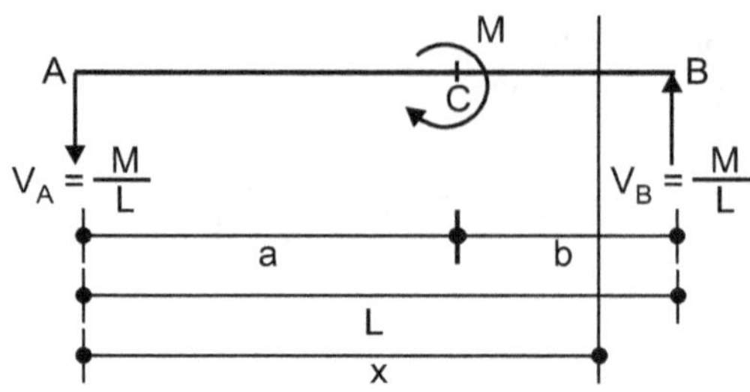

**Fig. 7.32 : FBD of beam**

(ii)    Equation of BM ; slope and deflection.

$$EI\left(\frac{d^2y}{dx^2}\right) = -\frac{M}{L}(x) + M(x-a)^0 \qquad \text{... (I)}$$

AC

CB

$$EI\left(\frac{dy}{dx}\right) = -\frac{M}{2L}(x)^2 + C_1 \bigg| + M(x-a) \qquad \text{... (II)}$$

$$EI(y) = -\frac{M}{6L}(x)^3 + C_1(x) + C_2 \bigg| + \frac{M}{2}(x-a)^2 \qquad \text{... (III)}$$

(iii) Boundary conditions.

At A i.e. x = 0; y = 0 put in equation (III) $\therefore$  $C_2 = 0$

At B i.e. x = L ; y = 0 put in equation (III)

$$0 = -\frac{M}{6L}(L)^3 + L\cdot C_1 + \frac{M}{2}(L-a)^2$$

$$\therefore \qquad C_1 = -\frac{M}{6L}(2L^2 - 6La + 3a^2)$$

Substituting values of $C_1$ and $C_2$, equations (II) and (III) can be written as

$$EI\left(\frac{dy}{dx}\right) = -\frac{M}{2L}(x)^2 - \frac{M}{6L}(2L^2 - 6La + 3a^2) \bigg| + M(x-a) \qquad \text{... (II)}$$

$$EI(y) = -\frac{M}{6L}(x)^3 - \frac{M}{6L}(2L^2 - 6La + 3a^2)x \bigg| + \frac{M}{2}(x-a)^2 \qquad \text{... (III)}$$

(iv) Slope and deflections.

For slope at 'A' put x = 0 in equation (II).

$$EI\left(\frac{dy}{dx}\right)_A = -\frac{M}{2L}(0) - \frac{M}{6L}(2L^2 - 6La + 3a^2)$$

$$\therefore \qquad \left(\frac{dy}{dx}\right)_A = -\frac{M}{6\ EIL}\ (2\ L^2 - 6\ La + 3a^2) \qquad \qquad \dots (E_1)$$

For slope at 'B' put $x = L$ in equation (II).

$$EI\left(\frac{dy}{dx}\right)_B = -\frac{M}{2\ L}\ (L)^2 - \frac{M}{6\ L}\ (2\ L^2 - 6\ La + 3a^2)\ + M\ (L - a)$$

$$= -\frac{M}{6\ L}\ (3\ L^2 + 2\ L^2 - 6\ La + 3a^2 - 6\ L^2 + 6\ La)$$

$$= -\frac{M}{6\ L}\ (3a^2 - L^2)$$

$$\therefore \qquad \left(\frac{dy}{dx}\right)_B = -\frac{M}{6\ EIL}\ (3a^2 - L^2) \qquad \qquad \dots (E_2)$$

For deflection at C; put $x = a$ in equation (III).

$$EI\ (y_C) = -\frac{M}{6\ L}\ (a)^3 - \frac{M}{6\ L}\ (2\ L^2 - 6\ La + 3a^2)\ a$$

$$= -\frac{Ma}{6\ L}\ [a^2 + 2\ L^2 - 6\ La + 3a^2]$$

$$= -\frac{Ma}{3\ L}\ (L - a)\ (L - 2a)$$

$$\therefore \qquad y_C = -\frac{Ma}{3\ EIL}\ (L - a)\ (L - 2a) \qquad \qquad \dots (E_3)$$

**Special case :** Find slope at supports and deflection at point of application of couple for simply supported beam carrying couple 'M' at centre.

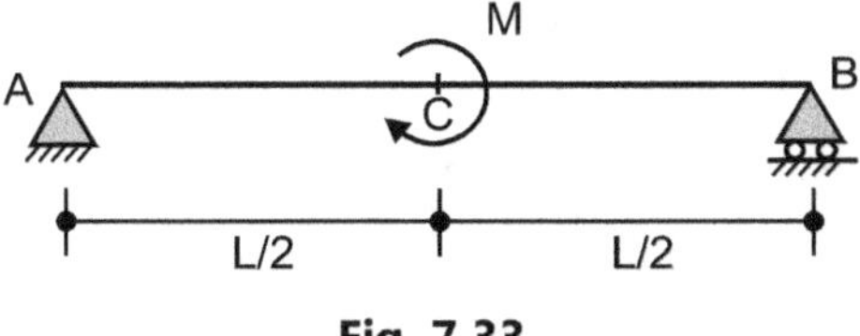


**Fig. 7.33**

For slope ; put $a = \dfrac{L}{2}$ in equation $(E_1)$ or $(E_2)$.

$$\left(\frac{dy}{dx}\right)_A = \left(\frac{dy}{dx}\right)_B = \frac{ML}{24\ EI}\ (\circlearrowleft)$$

For deflection, put $a = \dfrac{L}{2}$ in equation $(E_3)$

$$(y)_C = 0$$

**Example 7.12 :** *Find slope at supports, central and maximum deflection for the beam shown in Fig. 7.34 (a).*

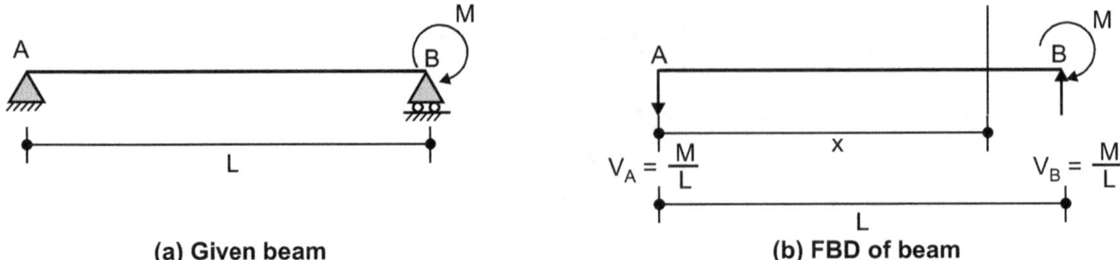

(a) Given beam                         (b) FBD of beam

**Fig. 7.34**

**Data**        :   As shown in Fig. 7.34 (a).

**Required**   :   Slope at supports and maximum deflection.

**Concept**    :   Consider 'A' as origin and a section at a distance 'x' from 'A' for BM
equation.

**Solution:**    (i) Reactions for equilibrium.

$$\sum M_A = 0; \quad V_B \times L - M = 0 \quad \therefore \quad V_B = \frac{M}{L} (\uparrow)$$

$$\sum F_y = 0; \quad V_A + V_B = 0 \quad \therefore \quad V_A = \frac{M}{L} (\downarrow)$$

$$\sum F_x = 0; \quad H_A = 0$$

FBD of beam is as shown in Fig. 7.34 (b).

(ii)   Equations of BM; slope and deflection.

$$EI\left(\frac{d^2y}{dx^2}\right) = -\frac{M}{L}(x) \qquad \qquad \text{... (I)}$$

$$EI\left(\frac{dy}{dx}\right) = -\frac{M}{2L}(x)^2 + C_1 \qquad \qquad \text{... (II)}$$

$$EI(y) = -\frac{M}{6L}(x)^3 + C_1 x + C_2 \qquad \qquad \text{... (III)}$$

(iii) Boundary conditions.

At A ; x = 0 ; y = 0 put in equation (III) $\therefore C_2 = 0$

At B ; x = L ; y = 0 put in equation (III)

$$0 = -\frac{M}{6L}(L)^3 + L \cdot C_1$$

$$\therefore \qquad C_1 = \frac{ML}{6}$$

Substituting values of $C_1$ and $C_2$, equations (II) and (III) can be written as

$$EI\left(\frac{dy}{dx}\right) = -\frac{M}{2L}(x)^2 + \frac{ML}{6} \qquad \qquad \text{... (II)}$$

$$EI(y) = -\frac{M}{6L}(x)^3 + \frac{ML}{6}(x) \qquad \qquad \text{... (III)}$$

(iv) Slope and deflections.

For slope at A; put x = 0 in equation (II).

$$EI\left(\frac{dy}{dx}\right)_A = \frac{ML}{6} \quad \therefore \quad \left(\frac{dy}{dx}\right)_A = \frac{ML}{6\ EI} \ (\circlearrowleft)$$

For slope at B ; put x = L in equation (II).

$$EI\left(\frac{dy}{dx}\right)_B = -\frac{M}{2L}(L)^2 + \frac{ML}{6}$$

$$\therefore \quad \left(\frac{dy}{dx}\right)_B = -\frac{ML}{3\ EI} = \frac{ML}{3\ EI} \ (\circlearrowright)$$

For deflection at centre, put $x = \frac{L}{2}$ in equation (III).

$$EI\ (y)\ \text{centre} = -\frac{M}{6L}\left(\frac{L}{2}\right)^3 + \frac{ML}{6}\left(\frac{L}{2}\right)$$

$$= -\frac{ML^2}{48} + \frac{ML^2}{12}$$

$$\therefore \quad y_{\text{centre}} = \frac{ML^2}{16\ EI} \ (\uparrow)$$

For maximum deflection equating slope equation to zero.

$$0 = -\frac{M}{2L}(x)^2 + \frac{ML}{6}$$

$$\therefore \quad x = \left(\sqrt{\frac{1}{3}}\right) L$$

Put in equation (III).

$$EI\ (y)_{\text{max}} = -\frac{M}{6L}\left(\sqrt{\frac{1}{3}}\ L\right)^3 + \frac{ML}{6}\left(\sqrt{\frac{1}{3}} \cdot L\right)$$

$$= (-\ 0.032 + 0.0962)\ ML^2$$

$$= 0.0642\ ML^2$$

$$\therefore \quad y_{\text{max}} = 0.0642\ \frac{ML^2}{EI} \ (\uparrow)$$

**Special case :** Find slope at supports for the beam loaded as shown in Fig. 7.35.

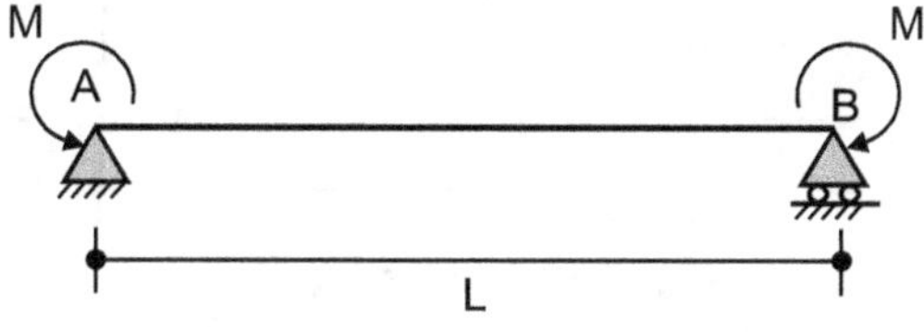


**Fig. 7.35**

Using principle of superposition.

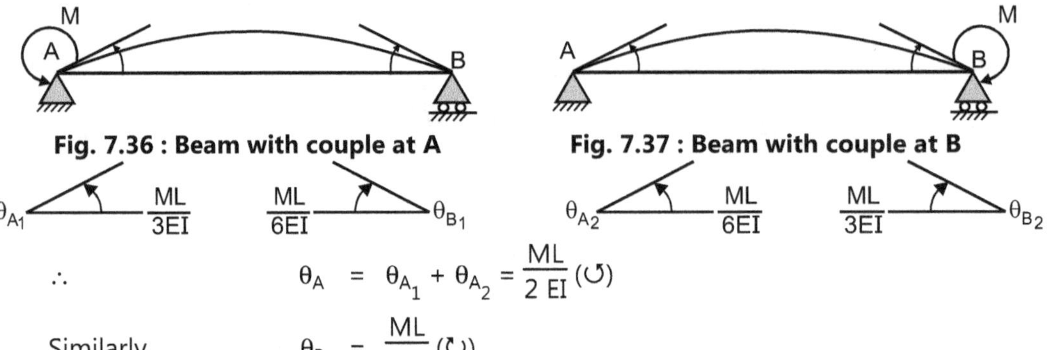

**Fig. 7.36 : Beam with couple at A**　　　　**Fig. 7.37 : Beam with couple at B**

$$\theta_{A_1} \quad \frac{ML}{3EI} \qquad \frac{ML}{6EI} \quad \theta_{B_1} \qquad\qquad \theta_{A_2} \quad \frac{ML}{6EI} \qquad \frac{ML}{3EI} \quad \theta_{B_2}$$

$$\therefore \qquad \theta_A = \theta_{A_1} + \theta_{A_2} = \frac{ML}{2\,EI}\ (\circlearrowleft)$$

Similarly

$$\theta_B = \frac{ML}{2\,EI}\ (\circlearrowright)$$

**Note :** Maximum deflection for this case occurs at centre and is given by $\dfrac{ML^2}{8\,EI}\ (\uparrow)$ .

**Example 7.13 :** *Find slope at supports and deflection at centre for the beam shown in Fig. 7.38.*

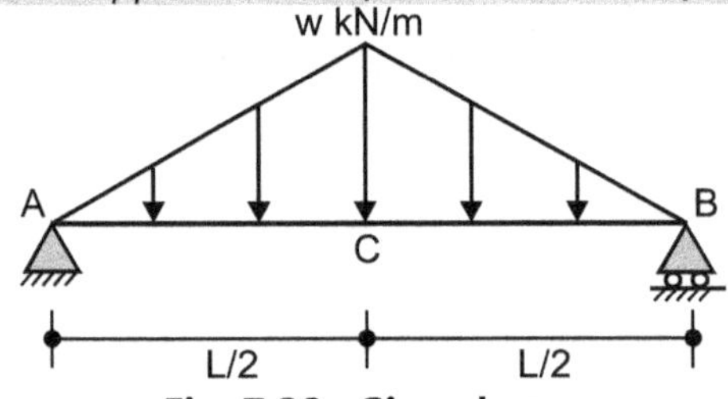

**Fig. 7.38 : Given beam**

**Data** ：As shown in Fig. 7.38.

**Required** ：Slope at supports and deflection at centre.

**Concept** ：By considering section at a distance 'x' from 'A' in zone 'CB', BM equation will be complicated. Hence consider section in zone AC and make use of symmetry.

**Solution:** (i) Reactions for equilibrium.

$$V_A = V_B = \frac{wL}{4}\ (\uparrow)$$

FBD of beam is as shown in Fig. 7.39.

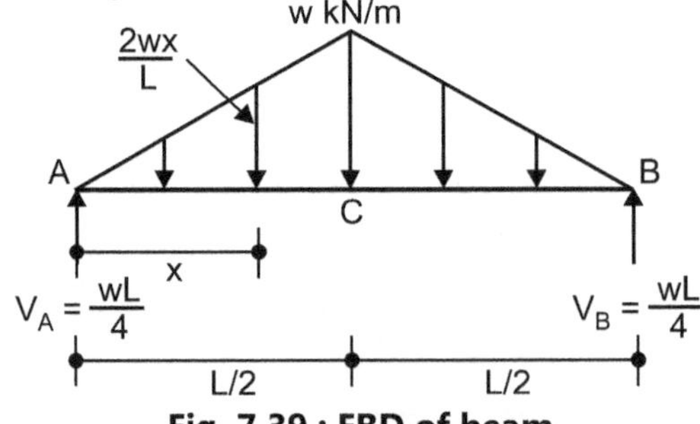

**Fig. 7.39 : FBD of beam**

(ii) Equation of BM; slope and deflection.

Intensity of load at a distance 'x' from 'A' $= \dfrac{2\,wx}{L}$

$$\therefore \qquad EI\left(\frac{d^2y}{dx^2}\right) = \frac{wL}{4}(x) - \frac{1}{2}(x)\frac{2wx}{L}\left(\frac{x}{3}\right) \qquad \left(\because 0 \le x \le \frac{L}{2}\right)$$

$$= \frac{wL}{4}(x) - \frac{wx^3}{3L} \qquad \qquad \text{... (I)}$$

$$AC$$

$$EI\left(\frac{dy}{dx}\right) = \frac{wL}{8}(x)^2 - \frac{w}{12L}(x)^4 + C_1 \qquad \text{... (II)}$$

$$EI(y) = \frac{wL}{24}(x)^3 - \frac{w}{60L}(x)^5 + C_1(x) + C_2 \qquad \text{... (III)}$$

(iii)   Boundary conditions.

At A i.e. $x = 0$ ; $y = 0$ put in equation (II) $\therefore C_2 = 0$

Due to symmetry, maximum deflection occurs at centre.

$$\therefore \quad \text{At C i.e. } x = \frac{L}{2} ; \frac{dy}{dx} = 0 \text{ put in equation (II)}$$

$$0 = \frac{wL}{8}\left(\frac{L}{2}\right)^2 - \frac{w}{12L}\left(\frac{L}{2}\right)^4 + C_1$$

$$C_1 = \frac{-5}{192}wL^3$$

**Note :** Condition of $x = L$ ; $y = 0$ cannot be employed because BM equation is applicable only for zone AC.

Substituting values of $C_1$ and $C_2$, equations (II) and (III) are written as

$$EI\left(\frac{dy}{dx}\right) = \frac{wL}{8}(x)^2 - \frac{w}{12L}(x)^4 - \frac{5}{192}wL^3 \qquad \text{... (II)}$$

$$EI(y) = \frac{wL}{24}(x)^3 - \frac{w}{60L}(x)^5 - \frac{5}{192}wL^3(x) \qquad \text{... (III)}$$

(iv)   Slope and deflections.

For slope at A ; put $x = 0$ in equation (II).

$$EI\left(\frac{dy}{dx}\right)_A = -\frac{5}{192}wL^3 \quad \therefore \quad \left(\frac{dy}{dx}\right)_A = \frac{5}{192}\frac{wL^3}{EI}\ (\circlearrowleft)$$

By symmetry, $\qquad \left(\dfrac{dy}{dx}\right)_B = \dfrac{5\,wL^3}{192\,EI}\ (\circlearrowright)$

For deflection at 'C' ; put $x = \dfrac{L}{2}$ in equation (III).

$$EI(y)_C = \frac{wL}{24}\left(\frac{L}{2}\right)^3 - \frac{w}{60L}\left(\frac{L}{2}\right)^5 - \frac{5}{192}wL^3\left(\frac{L}{2}\right)$$

$$\therefore \qquad y_C = -\frac{wL^4}{120\,EI}$$

$$y_C = \frac{wL^4}{120\,EI}\ (\downarrow)$$

$$= y_{max}$$

**Example 7.14 :** *For the beam shown in Fig. 7.40, find slope at A, B, and C. Also find deflection at C; at centre of A, B and maximum deflection between A and B.*

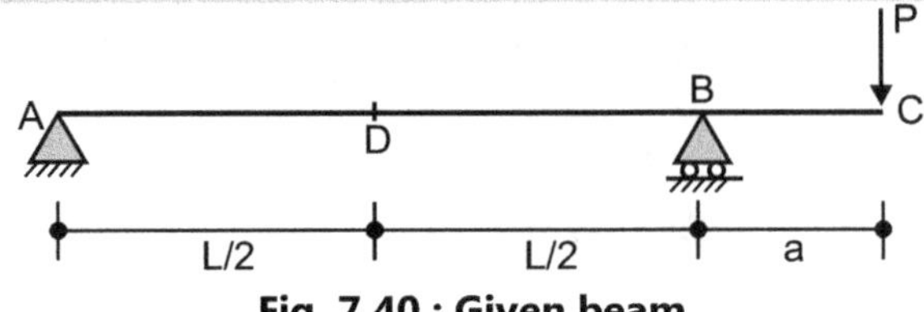

**Fig. 7.40 : Given beam**

**Data**         :   As shown in Fig. 7.40.

**Required**     :   Slope at A, B, C and deflection at D, C and maximum deflection between AB.

**Concept**      :   For slope and deflection at C ; we shall work from first principles. Slope at A, B; maximum deflection between AB and deflection at 'D' can be obtained by using standard results as illustrated.

**Solution:**      (i) Reactions for equilibrium.

$$\sum M_A = 0; \qquad V_B \times L - P(L + a) = 0 \qquad \therefore \qquad V_B = \frac{P}{L}(L + a) \ (\uparrow)$$

$$\sum F_y = 0; \qquad V_A + V_B - P = 0 \qquad \therefore \qquad V_A = \frac{Pa}{L} \ (\downarrow)$$

$$\sum F_x = 0; \quad H_A \qquad\qquad\qquad = 0$$

FBD of beam is as shown in Fig. 7.41.

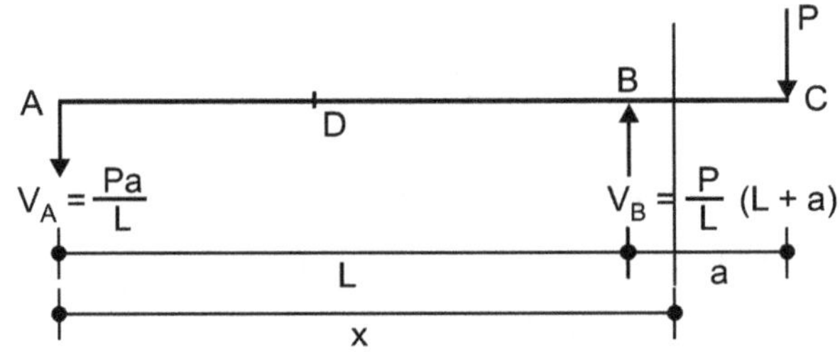

**Fig. 7.41 : FBD of beam**

(ii)   Equation of BM; slope and deflection.

$$EI\left(\frac{d^2y}{dx^2}\right) = \left. -\frac{Pa}{L}(x) \right|_{AB} + \frac{P}{L}(L + a)(x - L) \qquad\qquad \ldots (I)$$

$$\underbrace{\phantom{-\frac{Pa}{L}(x)}}_{AB}$$

$$\underbrace{\phantom{-\frac{Pa}{L}(x) + \frac{P}{L}(L+a)(x-L)}}_{BC}$$

$$EI\left(\frac{dy}{dx}\right) = \left. -\frac{Pa}{2L}(x)^2 + C_1 \right| + \frac{P(L + a)}{2L}(x - L)^2 \qquad\qquad \ldots (II)$$

$$EI\,(y) \;=\; -\frac{Pa}{6\,L}\,(x)^3 + C_1\,(x) + C_2 \;\Big|\; + \frac{P\,(L + a)}{6\,L}\,(x - L)^3 \qquad\qquad \ldots \text{(III)}$$

(iii) Boundary conditions.

At A i.e. $x = 0$; $y = 0$ put in equation (III) $\therefore$ $C_2 = 0$

At B i.e. $x = L$; $y = 0$ put in equation (III)

$$0 \;=\; -\frac{Pa}{6\,L}\,(L)^3 + C_1\,(L) + \frac{P\,(L + a)}{6\,L}\,(L - L)^3$$

$$\therefore \qquad C_1 \;=\; \frac{PaL}{6}$$

Substituting values of $C_1$ and $C_2$; equations (II) and (III) are written as

$$EI\left(\frac{dy}{dx}\right) \;=\; -\frac{Pa}{2\,L}\,(x)^2 + \frac{PaL}{6} \;\Big|\; + \frac{P}{2\,L}\,(L + a)\,(x - L)^2 \qquad\qquad \ldots \text{(II)}$$

$$EI\,(y) \;=\; -\frac{Pa}{6\,L}\,(x)^3 + \frac{PaL}{6}\,(x) \;\Big|\; + \frac{P}{6\,L}\,(L + a)\,(x - L)^3 \qquad\qquad \ldots \text{(III)}$$

(iv) Slope and deflection at 'C'.

Put $x = (L + a)$ in equations (II) and (III) respectively.

$$EI\left(\frac{dy}{dx}\right)_C \;=\; -\frac{Pa}{2\,L}\,(L + a)^2 + \frac{PaL}{6} + \frac{P}{2\,L}\,(L + a)\,(L + a - L)^2$$

$$\therefore \qquad \left(\frac{dy}{dx}\right)_C \;=\; -\frac{Pa}{6\,EI}\,(2\,L + 3a) = \frac{Pa}{6\,EI}\,(2\,L + 3a)\;(\circlearrowleft)$$

$$EI\,(y)_C \;=\; -\frac{Pa}{6\,L}\,(L + a)^3 + \frac{PaL}{6}\,(L + a) + \frac{P}{6\,L}\,(L + a)\,(L + a - L)^3$$

$$y_C \;=\; -\frac{Pa^2}{3\,EI}\,(L + a) = \frac{Pa^2}{3\,EI}\,(L + a)\;(\downarrow)$$

(v)  Use of standard results.

Load at C is transferred to B as force couple system as shown in Fig. 7.42.

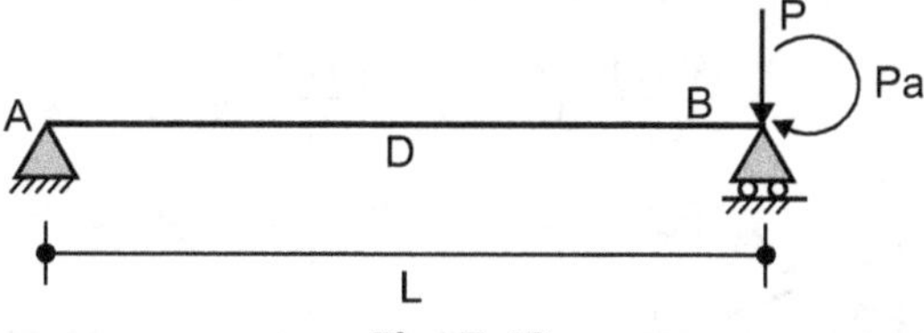


**Fig. 7.42**

Load P acting at B does not produce any slope or deflection for the beam. Hence beam can be considered to have only couple at 'B' of magnitude M = Pa.

$\therefore$    Using equations derived for simply supported beam with couple acting at end of the beam,

$$\left(\frac{dy}{dx}\right)_A \;=\; \frac{ML}{6\,EI} = \frac{PaL}{6\,EI}\;(\circlearrowleft)$$

$$\left(\frac{dy}{dx}\right)_B = \frac{ML}{3\,EI} = \frac{PaL}{3\,EI}\;(\circlearrowleft)$$

$$y_D = \frac{ML^2}{16\,EI} = \frac{PaL^2}{16\,EI}\;(\uparrow)$$

Maximum deflection between AB occurs at $\left(\sqrt{\dfrac{1}{3}}\right)L$ from A and its magnitude is $y_{max}$.

$$= 0.0642\,\frac{ML^2}{EI}$$

$$= \mathbf{0.0642\,\frac{PaL^2}{EI}\;(\uparrow)}$$

**Example 7.15 :** *Find the magnitude of 'W' for the beam shown in Fig. 7.43 such that deflection at free end A of the beam is zero.*

**Data**        :   As shown in Fig. 7.43.

**Required**   :   Magnitude of W for deflection at 'A' to be zero.

**Concept**    :   Principle of superposition.

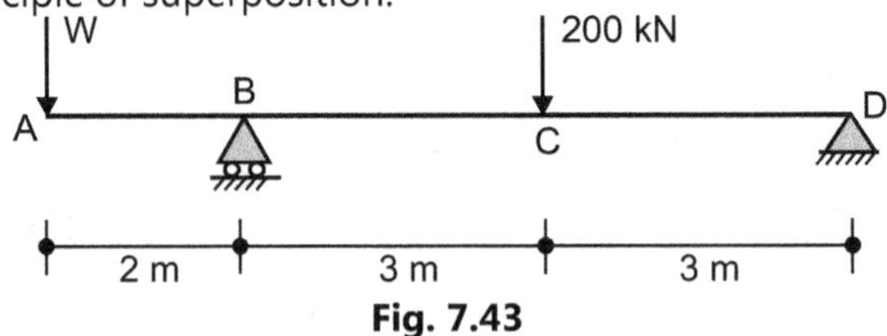


**Fig. 7.43**

**Solution :**

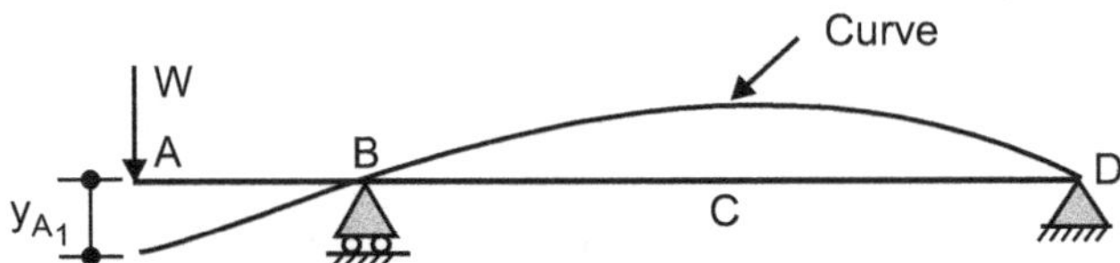


**Fig. 7.44 : Elastic curve due to W**

$$y_{A_1} = \frac{Wa^2}{3\,EI}(L + a)$$

$$= \frac{W\,(2)^2}{3\,EI}(6 + 2) = \frac{10.67}{EI}\,W\;(\downarrow)$$

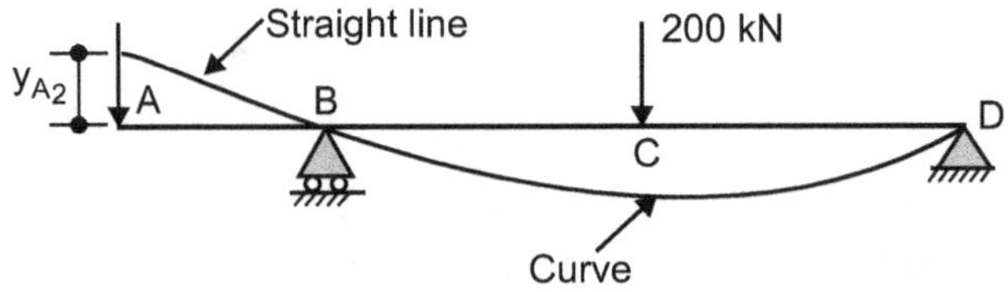

**Fig. 7.45 : Elastic curve due to 200 kN load**

$$y_{A_2} = \text{slope at B} \times l\,(AB)$$

$$= \frac{PL^2}{16\ EI} \times l\ (AB)$$

$$= \frac{200 \times 6^2}{16\ EI} \times 2$$

$$= \frac{900}{EI}\ (\uparrow)$$

For $y_A = 0$;  $\qquad\qquad y_{A_1} = y_{A_2}$

$$\frac{10.67\ W}{EI} = \frac{900}{EI}$$

$\therefore \qquad\qquad W = \mathbf{84.375\ kN}$

**Example 7.16** : *For the beam shown in Fig. 7.46, find slope at each support, deflection at centre and free end of the beam.*

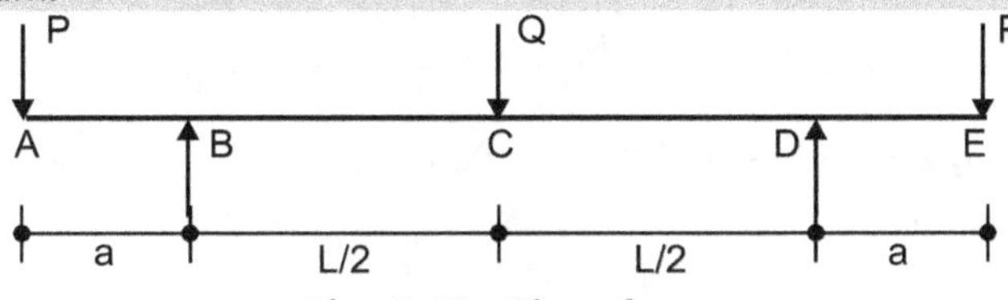


**Fig. 7.46 : Given beam**

**Data**         :   As shown in Fig. 7.46.

**Required**   :   Slope at B, C and deflections at A, C.

**Concept:**     Use of standard results and principle of superposition.

**Solution:**    (i) Analysis for load 'Q'.

Slope at B/D $\qquad = \dfrac{QL^2}{16\ EI}$

Deflection at centre $= \dfrac{QL^3}{48\ EI}\ (\downarrow)$

Deflection at A/E $\quad =$

$\dfrac{QL^2}{16\ EI}\ (a)\ (\uparrow)$

$(\because\ \text{Slope at supports} \times \text{length a})$

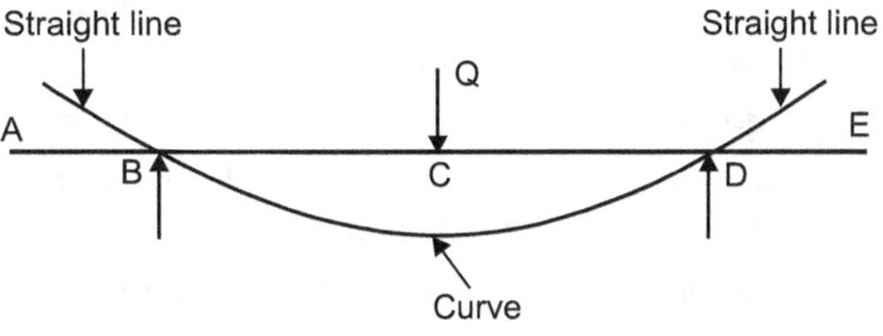


**Fig. 7.47 : Elastic curve due to load 'Q'**

(ii) Analysis for load 'P'.

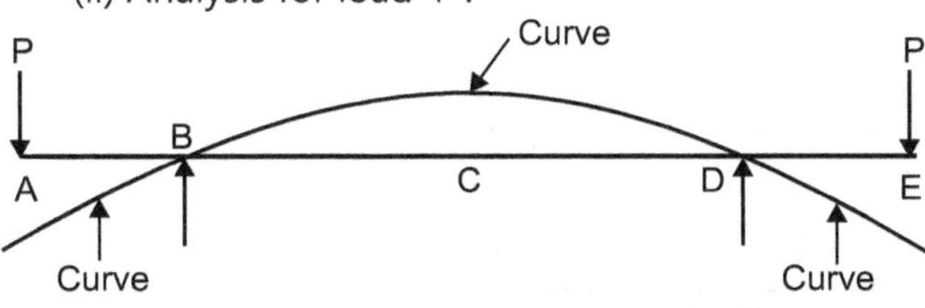


**Fig. 7.48 : Elastic curve due to load 'P'**

By considering two couples each at B and D, Couple = M = Pa.

Slope at B/D $= \dfrac{PaL}{2\ EI}$

$$\left( \because\ \frac{ML}{2\ EI} \right)$$

Deflection at centre $= \dfrac{PaL^2}{8\ EI}\ (\uparrow)$

$$\left( \because \text{ Central deflection } = \frac{ML^2}{8\ EI}\ ; M = Pa \right)$$

Deflection at A/E = deflection due to slope at B/D

+ deflection due to cantilever action.

$$= \frac{PaL}{2\ EI} \times (a) + \frac{Pa^3}{3\ EI} = \frac{Pa^2}{6\ EI}(2a + 3\ L)\ (\downarrow)$$

(iii) Superposition.

$$\text{Net slope at B/D } = \frac{QL^2}{16\ EI} - \frac{PaL}{2\ EI} = \frac{L}{16\ EI}(QL - 8\ Pa)$$

$$\text{Net deflection at centre } = -\frac{QL^3}{48\ EI} + \frac{PaL^2}{8\ EI} = \frac{L^2}{48\ EI}(6\ Pa - QL)$$

$$\text{Net deflection at free ends } = \frac{QL^2}{16\ EI}(a) - \frac{Pa^2}{6\ EI}(2a + 3\ L)$$

---

**Example 7.17 :** *For the beam shown in Fig. 7.49, find slope at supports; deflection under the load and maximum deflection.*

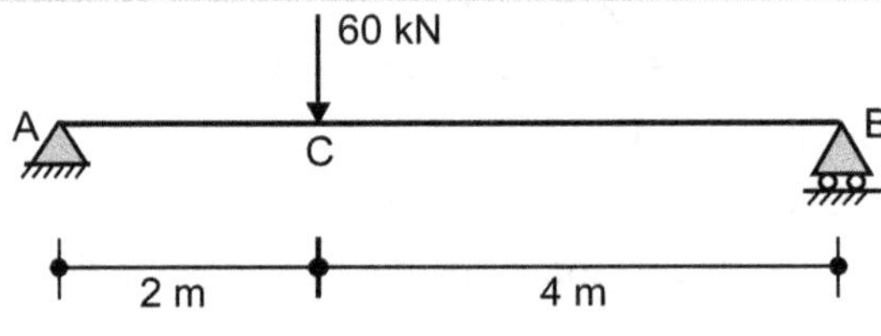


**Fig. 7.49 : Given beam**

**Data**         :   As shown in Fig. 7.49.

**Required**   :   Slope at A; B; deflection at C and maximum deflection.

**Concept**    :   Consider 'A' as origin and section at a distance 'x' from A in zone CB
for BM equation.

**Solution**   :   (i) Reactions for equilibrium.

$\sum M_A = 0;\ V_B \times 6 - 60 \times 2 \qquad = 0\quad \therefore \qquad V_B \quad = 20\text{ kN }(\uparrow)$

$\sum F_y = 0; \qquad\qquad V_A + V_B - 60\ =\ 0 \qquad \therefore \qquad V_A\ =\ 40\text{ kN }(\uparrow)$

$\sum F_x = 0;\ \ H_A \qquad\qquad\qquad = 0$

FBD of beam is as shown in Fig. 7.50.

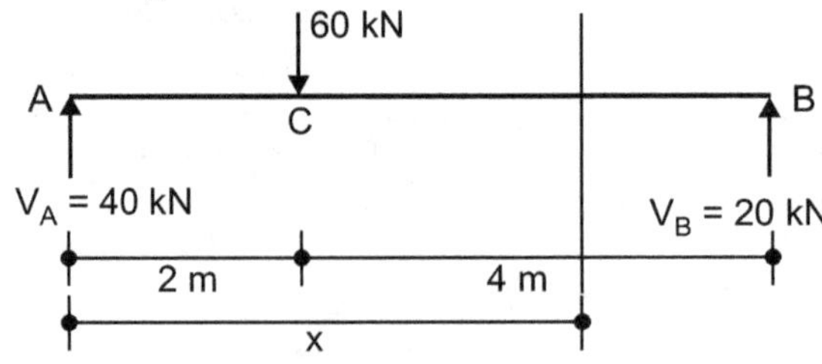


**Fig. 7.50 : FBD of beam**

---

(ii)    Equations of BM, slope and deflection.

$$EI\left(\frac{d^2y}{dx^2}\right) = 40\,(x)\ \Big|\ -60\,(x-2) \qquad \text{... (I)}$$

$$EI\left(\frac{dy}{dx}\right) = 20\,(x)^2 + C_1\ \Big|\ -30\,(x-2)^2 \qquad \text{... (II)}$$

$$EI\,(y) = \frac{20}{3}\,(x)^3 + C_1\,(x) + C_2\ \Big|\ -10\,(x-2)^3 \qquad \text{... (III)}$$

(iii) Boundary conditions.

At A i.e. $x = 0$ ; $y = 0$ put in equation (III).

$$0 = 0 + 0 + C_2 \qquad \therefore\ C_2 = 0$$

At B i.e. $x = 6$ m ; $y = 0$ put in equation (III).

$$0 = \frac{20}{3}\,(6)^3 + C_1\,(6) + C_2 - 10\,(6-2)^3 \quad (\because C_2 = 0)$$

$$0 = 1440 + 6\,C_1 - 640$$

$$\therefore \qquad C_1 = -133.33$$

Substituting values of $C_1$ and $C_2$, equations (II) and (III) are written as

$$EI\left(\frac{dy}{dx}\right) = 20\,(x)^2 - 133.33\ \Big|\ -30\,(x-2)^2 \qquad \text{... (II)}$$

$$EI\,(y) = \frac{20}{3}\,(x)^3 - 133.33\,(x)\ \Big|\ -10\,(x-2)^3 \qquad \text{... (III)}$$

(iv) Slopes and deflections.

For slope at 'A' put $x = 0$ in equation (II).

$$EI\left(\frac{dy}{dx}\right)_A = 0 - 133.33 \qquad \therefore\ \left(\frac{dy}{dx}\right)_A = \frac{-133.33}{EI} = \mathbf{\frac{133.33}{EI}}\ (\circlearrowleft)$$

For slope at 'B' put $x = 6$ m in equation (II).

$$EI\left(\frac{dy}{dx}\right)_B = 20\,(6)^2 - 133.33 - 30\,(6-2)^2$$

$$\therefore \qquad \left(\frac{dy}{dx}\right)_B = \frac{106.67}{EI} = \mathbf{\frac{106.67}{EI}}\ (\circlearrowright)$$

For deflection at 'C' put $x = 2$ m in equation (III).

$$EI\,(y)_C = \frac{20}{3}\,(2)^3 - 133.33\,(2)$$

$$\therefore \qquad y_C = \frac{-213.33}{EI} = \mathbf{\frac{213.33}{EI}}\ (\downarrow)$$

For maximum deflection;

let  maximum deflection occurs in zone CB i.e. (2 < x < 6)

Equating slope equation (II) for zone CB to zero.

$$0 = 20\,(x)^2 - 133.33 - 30\,(x - 2)^2$$

$$0 = 10x^2 - 120x + 253.33$$

Solving                $x = 2.73$ m  Assumption is OK.

Put x = 2.73 m in equation (III) to get maximum deflection.

$$EI\,(y)_{max} = \frac{20}{3}\,(2.73)^3 - 133.33\,(2.73) - 10\,(2.73 - 2)^3$$

$$(y)_{max} = \frac{-232.24}{EI} = \frac{\mathbf{232.24}}{\mathbf{EI}}\,(\downarrow)$$

---

**Example 7.18** : *Find slope at supports ; deflection under loads and maximum deflection for the beam shown in Fig. 7.51. Assume E = 200 GPa ; I = 3 ×10⁸ mm⁴.*

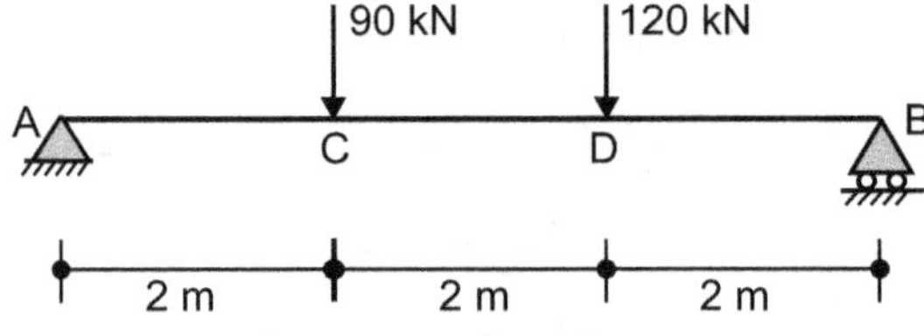


**Fig. 7.51 : Given beam**

**Data**          :   As shown in Fig. 7.51 ;

$$EI = 200 \times 3 \times 10^8 = 6 \times 10^{10}\ kN.mm^2 = 6 \times 10^4\ kN.m^2$$

**Required**  :   Slopes at A, B; and deflection at C, D and maximum deflection.

**Concept**   :   Consider 'A' as origin and section at a distance 'x' from A in zone DB for BM equation.

**Solution**   :   (i) Reactions for equilibrium.

$$\sum M_A = 0;\ V_B \times 6 - 120 \times 4 - 90 \times 2 \qquad = 0 \ \therefore \qquad V_B \quad = \ 110\ kN\ (\uparrow)$$

$$\sum F_y = 0;\ V_A + V_B - 90 - 120 \qquad = 0 \ \therefore \qquad V_A \quad = \ 100\ kN\ (\uparrow)$$

$$\sum F_x = 0;\ H_A \qquad = 0$$

FBD of beam is as shown in Fig. 7.52.

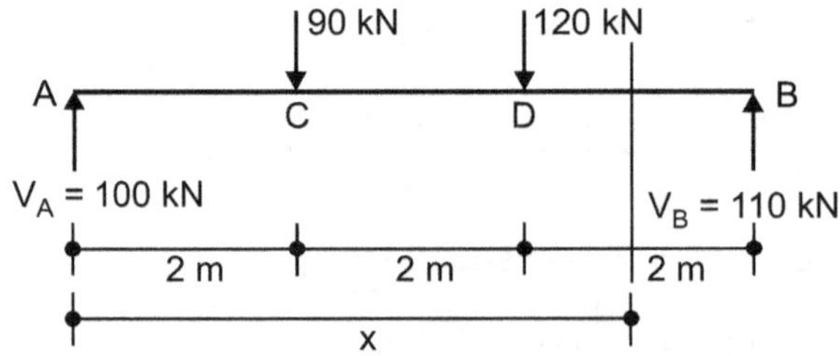


**Fig. 7.52 : FBD of beam**

(ii)   Equations of BM, slope and deflection.

$$EI\left(\frac{d^2y}{dx^2}\right) = 100\,(x)\Big| - 90\,(x-2)\Big| - 120\,(x-4) \qquad \text{... (I)}$$

$$EI\left(\frac{dy}{dx}\right) = 50\,(x)^2 + C_1 \Big| - 45\,(x-2)^2 \Big| - 60\,(x-4)^2 \qquad \text{... (II)}$$

$$EI\,(y) = 16.67\,(x)^3 + C_1\,(x) + C_2 \Big| - 15\,(x-2)^3 \Big| - 20\,(x-4)^3 \qquad \text{... (III)}$$

(iii) Boundary conditions.

At 'A' i.e. $x = 0$ ; $y = 0$; put in equation (III).

$$C_2 = 0$$

At 'B' i.e. $x = 6$ m ; $y = 0$;  put in equation (III).

$$0 = 16.67\,(6)^3 + C_1\,(6) + C_2 - 15\,(6-2)^3 - 20\,(6-4)^3$$

$$\therefore \qquad C_1 = -413.45$$

Substituting values of $C_1$ and $C_2$, equations (II) and (III) are written as

$$EI\left(\frac{dy}{dx}\right) = 50\,(x)^2 - 413.45 \Big| - 45\,(x-2)^2 \Big| - 60\,(x-4)^2 \qquad \text{... (II)}$$

$$EI\,(y) = 16.67\,(x)^3 - 413.45\,(x) \Big| - 15\,(x-2)^3 \Big| - 20\,(x-4)^3 \qquad \text{... (III)}$$

(iv) Slopes and deflections.

For slope at 'A' put $x = 0$ in equation (II).

$$EI\left(\frac{dy}{dx}\right)_A = -413.45 \quad \therefore \quad \left(\frac{dy}{dx}\right)_A = \frac{413.45}{EI}\;(\circlearrowleft)$$

$$\therefore \qquad \left(\frac{dy}{dx}\right)_A = \frac{413.45}{6 \times 10^4} = \mathbf{6.89 \times 10^{-3}\ rad}\;\mathbf{(\circlearrowleft)}$$

For slope at B ; put $x = 6$ m in equation (II).

$$EI\left(\frac{dy}{dx}\right)_B = 50\,(6)^2 - 413.45 - 45\,(6-2)^2 - 60\,(6-4)^2$$

$$\therefore \qquad \left(\frac{dy}{dx}\right)_B = \frac{426.55}{EI}$$

$$\therefore \qquad \left(\frac{dy}{dx}\right)_B = \frac{426.55}{6 \times 10^4} = \mathbf{7.11 \times 10^{-3}\ rad}\;\mathbf{(\circlearrowleft)}$$

For deflection at 'C' put $x = 2$ m in equation (III).

$$EI\,(y)_C = 16.67\,(2)^3 - 413.45\,(2)$$

$$\therefore \qquad (y)_C \;=\; \frac{-693.54}{EI} \;=\; \frac{-693.54}{6 \times 10^4} \;=\; -0.01155 \text{ m} = 11.55 \text{ mm} (\downarrow)$$

For deflection at 'D' put x = 4 m in equation (III).

$$EI\,(y)_D \;=\; 16.67\,(4)^3 - 413.45\,(4) - 15\,(4-2)^3$$

$$y_D \;=\; \frac{-706.92}{EI} \;=\; \textbf{11.78 mm } (\downarrow)$$

For maximum deflection ;

let maximum deflection occurs in zone CD i.e. 2 < x < 4.

∴  Equating slope equation (II) for zone CD to zero.

$$0 \;=\; 50\,(x)^2 - 413.45 - 45\,(x-2)^2$$

$$0 \;=\; 5\,x^2 + 180\,x - 593.45$$

$$\therefore \qquad x \;=\; 3.04 \text{ m Assumption is OK.}$$

Put $\qquad\qquad x \;=\; 3.04$ m in equation (III)

$$EI\,(y_{max}) \;=\; 16.67\,(3.04)^3 - 413.45\,(3.04) - 15\,(3.04-2)^3$$

$$\therefore \qquad y_{max} \;=\; \frac{-805.43}{EI}$$

$$=\; \textbf{13.42 mm } (\downarrow)$$

---

**Example 7.19 :** *Find slope at 'B', 'C' and deflection at 'C' and 'D' for the beam shown in Fig. 7.53. Assume E = 200 GPa ; I = $2 \times 10^8$ mm$^4$.*

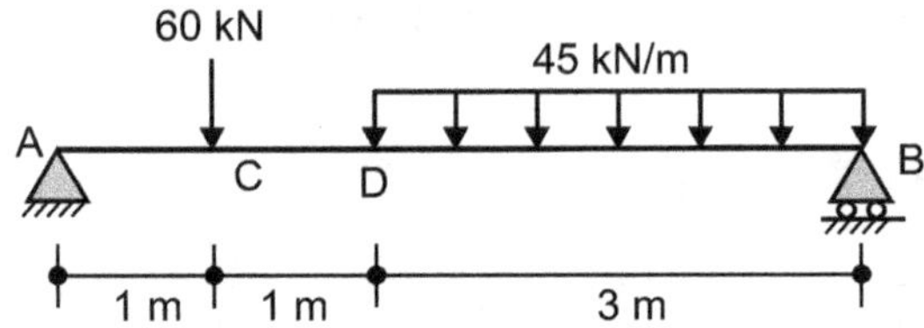


**Fig. 7.53 : Given beam**

**Data**        :  As shown in Fig. 7.53 ; EI = $4 \times 10^4$ kN.m$^2$.

**Required**  :  Slope at 'B', 'C' and deflection at 'C' and 'D'.

**Concept**   :  Consider 'A' as origin and section at a distance 'x' from 'A' in zone DB for BM equation.

**Solution**  :  (i) Reactions for equilibrium.

$\Sigma M_A = 0;$ $\qquad V_B \times 5 - 45 \times 3 \times 3.5 - 60 \times 1 \;=\; 0 \qquad \therefore \qquad V_B \;=\; 106.5$ kN (↑)

$\Sigma F_y = 0;$ $\qquad\qquad V_A + V_B - 60 - 45 \times 3 \;=\; 0 \qquad \therefore \qquad V_A \;=\; 88.5$ kN (↑)

$\Sigma F_x = 0;$ $\qquad H_A \qquad\qquad\qquad\qquad\qquad = \; 0$

FBD of beam is as shown in Fig. 7.54.

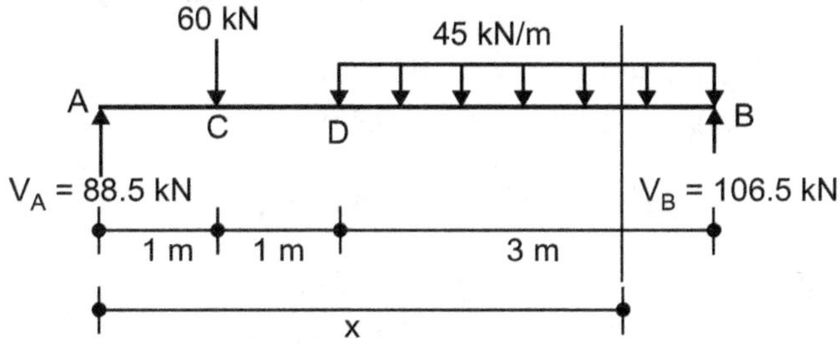

**Fig. 7.54 : F.B.D. of beam**

(ii) Equations of BM ; slope and deflection.

$$EI \left(\frac{d^2y}{dx^2}\right) = 88.5\,(x) \Big| - 60\,(x-1) \Big| - 45\,\frac{(x-2)^2}{2} \qquad \text{... (I)}$$

$$EI \left(\frac{dy}{dx}\right) = 44.25\,(x)^2 + C_1 \Big| - 30\,(x-1)^2 \Big| - 7.5\,(x-2)^3 \qquad \text{... (II)}$$

$$EI\,(y) = 14.75\,(x)^3 + C_1\,(x) + C_2 \Big| - 10\,(x-1)^3 \Big| - 1.875\,(x-2)^4 \qquad \text{... (III)}$$

(iii) Boundary conditions.

At A i.e. $x = 0$ ; $y = 0$ put in equation (III).

$$C_2 = 0$$

At B i.e. $x = 5$ m ; $y = 0$ put in equation (III).

$$0 = 14.75\,(5)^3 + C_1\,(5) - 10\,(5-1)^3 - 1.875\,(5-2)^4$$

$$\therefore \qquad C_1 = -210.375$$

Substituting values of $C_1$ and $C_2$, equations (II) and (III) are written as

$$EI \left(\frac{dy}{dx}\right) = 44.25\,(x)^2 - 210.375 \Big| - 30\,(x-1)^2 \Big| - 7.5\,(x-2)^3 \qquad \text{... (II)}$$

$$EI\,(y) = 14.75\,(x)^3 - 210.375\,(x) \Big| - 10\,(x-1)^3 \Big| - 1.875\,(x-2)^4 \qquad \text{... (III)}$$

(iv) Slopes and deflections.

For slope at 'B' put $x = 5$ m in equation (II).

$$EI \left(\frac{dy}{dx}\right)_B = 44.25\,(5)^2 - 210.375 - 30\,(5-1)^2 - 7.5\,(5-2)^3$$

$$\therefore \qquad \left(\frac{dy}{dx}\right)_B = \frac{213.375}{EI} = \mathbf{5.33 \times 10^{-3}\ rad\ (\circlearrowleft)}$$

For slope at 'C' put $x = 1$ m in equation (II)

$$EI \left(\frac{dy}{dx}\right)_C = 44.25\,(1)^2 - 210.375$$

$$\left(\frac{dy}{dx}\right)_C = \frac{-166.125}{EI} = 4.153 \times 10^{-3} \text{ rad } (\circlearrowleft)$$

For deflection at 'C' put x = 1 m in equation (III).

$$EI\,(y)_C = 14.75\,(1)^3 - 210.375\,(1)$$

$$\therefore \qquad y_C = \frac{-195.625}{EI} = 4.89 \text{ mm } (\downarrow)$$

For deflection at 'D' put x = 2 m in equation (III).

$$EI\,(y)_D = 14.75\,(2)^3 - 210.375\,(2) - 10\,(2-1)^3$$

$$\therefore \qquad y_D = \frac{-312.75}{EI} = 7.82 \text{ mm } (\downarrow)$$

**Example 7.20 :** *Find slope at 'C' and deflection at 'C' and 'D' for the beam shown in Fig. 7.55. Assume EI = 4 × 10⁴ kN.m².*

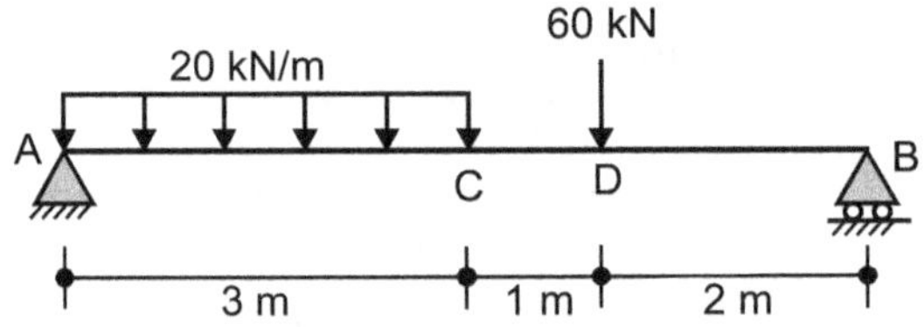


**Fig. 7.55 : Given beam**

**Data**      : As shown in Fig. 7.55 ; EI = 4 × 10⁴ kN.m².

**Required**  : Slope at 'C' ; deflection at 'C' and 'D'.

**Concept**   : Consider 'A' as origin and section at a distance 'x' from 'A' in zone DB
               for BM equation.

**Solution**  : (i) Reactions for equilibrium.

$$\sum M_A = 0; \qquad V_B \times 6 - 60 \times 4 - 20 \times \frac{3^2}{2} = 0 \qquad \therefore \quad V_B = 55 \text{ kN } (\uparrow)$$

$$\sum F_y = 0; \qquad V_A + V_B - 20 \times 3 - 60 = 0 \qquad \therefore \quad V_A = 65 \text{ kN } (\uparrow)$$

$$\sum F_x = 0; \qquad H_A = 0$$

FBD of beam is as shown in Fig. 7.56.

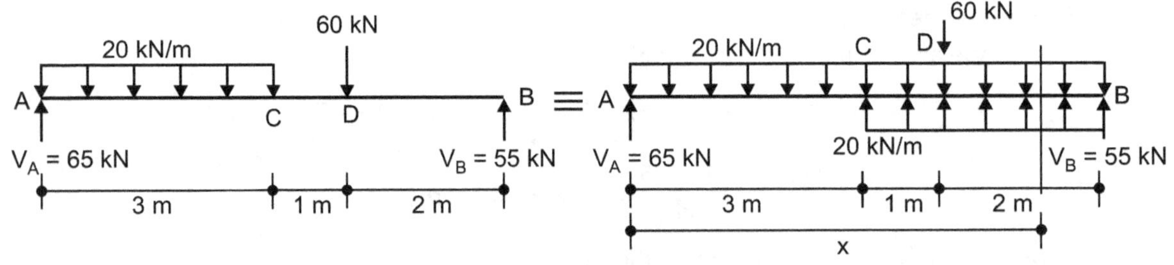


**(a) FBD of beam**                    **(b) Beam with imaginary UDL**

**Fig. 7.56**

(ii) Equations of BM ; slope and deflection.

$$EI\left(\frac{d^2y}{dx^2}\right) = 65\,(x) - 20\left(\frac{x^2}{2}\right)\Bigg| + 20\,\frac{(x-3)^2}{2}\Bigg| - 60\,(x-4)$$

$$= 65\,(x) - 10\,(x)^2\Big| + 10\,(x-3)^2\Big| - 60\,(x-4) \qquad \dots \text{(I)}$$

AC

CD

DB

$$EI\left(\frac{dy}{dx}\right) = 32.5\,(x)^2 - 3.33\,(x)^3 + C_1\Big| + 3.33\,(x-3)^3\Big| - 30\,(x-4)^2 \qquad \dots \text{(II)}$$

$$EI\,(y) = 10.83\,(x)^3 - 0.83\,(x)^4 + C_1\,(x) + C_2\Big| + 0.83\,(x-3)^4\Big| - 10\,(x-4)^3 \qquad \dots \text{(III)}$$

(iii) Boundary conditions.

At A i.e. $x = 0$; $y = 0$ put in equation (III).
$$C_2 = 0$$

At B i.e. $x = 6$ m; $y = 0$ put in equation (III).
$$0 = 10.83\,(6)^3 - 0.83\,(6)^4 + 6\,C_1 + 0.83\,(6-3)^4 - 10\,(6-4)^3$$
$$\therefore \qquad C_1 = -208.47$$

Substituting values of $C_1$ and $C_2$, equations (II) and (III) are written as ;

$$EI\left(\frac{dy}{dx}\right) = 32.5\,(x)^2 - 3.33\,(x)^3 - 208.47\Big| + 3.33\,(x-3)^3\Big| - 30\,(x-4)^2 \qquad \dots \text{(II)}$$

$$EI\,(y) = 10.83\,(x)^3 - 0.83\,(x)^4 - 208.47\,(x)\Big| + 0.83\,(x-3)^4\Big| - 10\,(x-4)^3 \qquad \dots \text{(III)}$$

(iv) Slopes and deflections.

For slope at 'C' put $x = 3$ m in equation (II).

$$EI\left(\frac{dy}{dx}\right)_C = 32.5\,(3)^2 - 3.33\,(3)^3 - 208.47$$

$$\therefore \qquad \left(\frac{dy}{dx}\right)_C = \frac{-5.88}{EI} = \frac{5.88}{4 \times 10^4} = \mathbf{1.47 \times 10^{-4}\ rad\ (\circlearrowleft)}$$

For deflection at 'C' put $x = 3$ m in equation (III).

$$EI\,(y)_C = 10.83\,(3)^3 - 0.83\,(3)^4 - 208.47\,(3)$$

$$\therefore \qquad y_C = \frac{-400.23}{EI} = \mathbf{10\ mm\ (\downarrow)}$$

For deflection at 'D' put $x = 4$ m in equation (III).

$$EI\,(y)_D = 10.83\,(4)^3 - 0.83\,(4)^4 - 208.47\,(4) + 0.83\,(4-3)^4$$

$$\therefore \qquad y_D = -\frac{352.41}{EI} = \mathbf{-8.81\ mm\ (\downarrow)}$$

---

**Example 7.21 :** *For the beam shown in Fig. 7.57, find slope and deflection at 'C' and 'D'. Assume E = 210 GPa and I = 3.6 ×10$^7$ mm$^4$.*

---

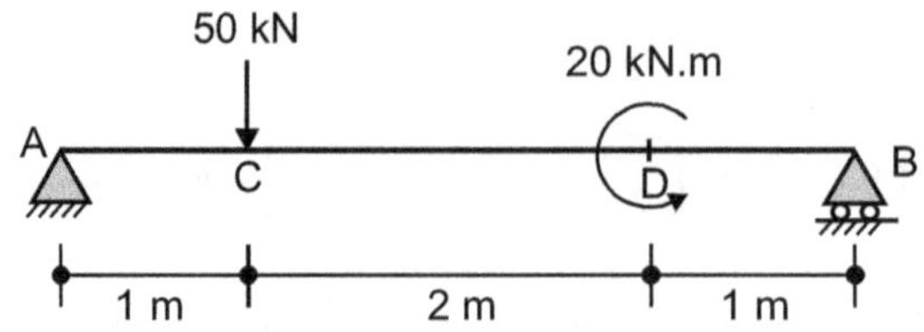

**Fig. 7.57 : Given beam**

**Data**　　　:　As shown in Fig. 7.57 ; EI = 7560 kN.m$^2$.

**Required**　:　Slope and deflection at C and D.

**Concept**　:　Consider 'A' as origin and section at a distance 'x' from 'A' in zone DB
　　　　　　　for BM equation.

**Solution**　:　(i) Reactions for equilibrium.

$\sum M_A = 0$;　　　　　　$V_B \times 4 + 20 - 50 \times 1 = 0$　　　　$\therefore$　　$V_B = 7.5$ kN ($\uparrow$)

$\sum F_y = 0$;　　　　　　　　$V_A + V_B = 50$　　　　$\therefore$　　$V_A = 42.5$ kN ($\uparrow$)

$\sum F_x = 0$;　　　　　　　　　$H_A = 0$

FBD of beam is as shown in Fig. 7.58.

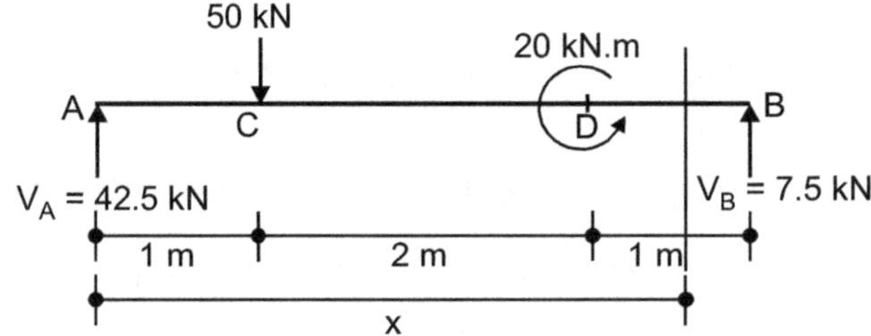

**Fig. 7.58 : FBD of beam**

(ii) Equations for BM ; slope and deflection.

$$EI \left(\frac{d^2y}{dx^2}\right) = 42.5\,(x) \Big| - 50\,(x-1) \Big| - 20\,(x-3)^0 \qquad \text{... (I)}$$

$$EI \left(\frac{dy}{dx}\right) = 21.25\,(x)^2 + C_1 \Big| - 25\,(x-1)^2 \Big| - 20\,(x-3) \qquad \text{... (II)}$$

$$EI\,(y) = 7.08\,(x)^3 + C_1 x + C_2 \Big| - 8.33\,(x-1)^3 \Big| - 10\,(x-3)^2 \qquad \text{... (III)}$$

(iii) Boundary conditions.

　　At 'A' i.e. x = 0; y = 0 put in equation (III) $\therefore$　$C_2 = 0$

　　At 'B' i.e. x = 4 m; y = 0 put in equation (III).

$$0 = 7.08\,(4)^3 + 4\,C_1 - 8.33\,(4-1)^3 - 10\,(4-3)^2$$

$$\therefore \qquad C_1 = -54.55$$

Substituting values of $C_1$ and $C_2$, equations (II) and (III) are written as

$$EI\left(\frac{dy}{dx}\right) = 21.25\,(x)^2 - 54.55 \Big| -25\,(x-1)^2 \Big| -20\,(x-3) \qquad \text{... (II)}$$

$$EI\,(y) = 7.08\,(x)^3 - 54.55\,x \Big| -8.33\,(x-1)^3 \Big| -10\,(x-3)^2 \qquad \text{... (III)}$$

(iv) Slopes and deflections.

For slope and deflection at 'C' put $x = 1$ m in equations (II) and (III) respectively.

$$EI\left(\frac{dy}{dx}\right)_C = 21.25\,(1)^2 - 54.55$$

$$\therefore \qquad \left(\frac{dy}{dx}\right)_C = \frac{-33.3}{EI} = \mathbf{4.4 \times 10^{-3}\ rad\ (\circlearrowleft)}$$

$$EI\,(y)_C = 7.08\,(1)^3 - 54.55\ (\uparrow)$$

$$y_C = \frac{-47.47}{EI} = \mathbf{6.28\ mm\ (\downarrow)}$$

For slope and deflection at D ; put $x = 3$ m in equations (II) and (III) respectively.

$$EI\left(\frac{dy}{dx}\right)_D = 21.25\,(3)^2 - 54.55 - 25\,(3-1)^2$$

$$\left(\frac{dy}{dx}\right)_D = \frac{36.7}{EI} = \mathbf{4.85 \times 10^{-3}\ rad\ (\circlearrowleft)}$$

$$EI\,(y)_D = 7.08\,(3)^3 - 54.55\,(3) - 8.33\,(3-1)^3$$

$$y_D = \frac{-39.13}{EI} = \mathbf{5.18\ mm\ (\downarrow)}$$

---

**Example 7.22 :** *Find slope at C and deflection at 'C' and 'D' for the beam shown in Fig. 7.59. Assume EI = 32.5 × 10³ kN.m².*

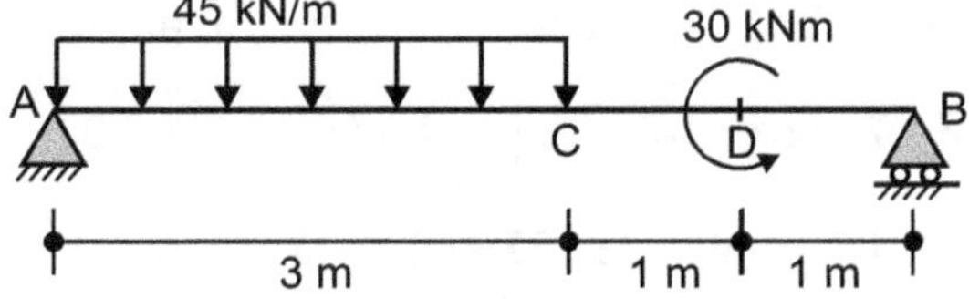


**Fig. 7.59 : Given beam**

**Data**          :   As shown in Fig. 7.59 ; EI = 32.5 × 10³ kN.m².

**Required**   :   Slope at 'C' and deflection at 'C' and 'D'.

---

**Concept**    :  Consider 'A' as origin and section at a distance 'x' from 'A' in zone
'DB' for BM equation.

**Solution**    :  (i) Reactions for equilibrium.

$$\sum M_A = 0; \qquad V_B \times 5 + 30 - 45 \times \frac{3^2}{2} = 0 \qquad \therefore \quad V_B = 34.5 \text{ kN } (\uparrow)$$

$$\sum F_y = 0; \qquad V_A + V_B - 45 \times 3 = 0 \qquad \therefore \quad V_A = 100.5 \text{ kN } (\uparrow)$$

$$\sum F_x = 0; \qquad H_A = 0$$

FBD of beam is as shown in Fig. 7.60.

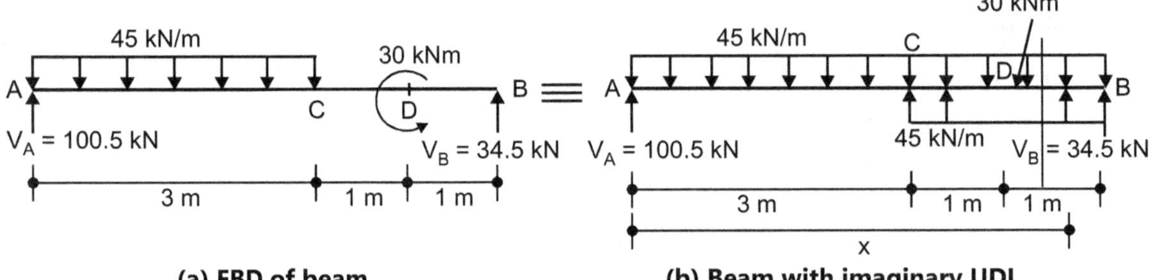


**(a) FBD of beam**              **(b) Beam with imaginary UDL**

**Fig. 7.60**

(ii) Equations of BM ; slope and deflection.

$$EI\left(\frac{d^2y}{dx^2}\right) = 100.5\,(x) - 45\,\frac{(x)^2}{2}\bigg| + 45\,\frac{(x-3)^2}{2}\bigg| - 30\,(x-4)^0 \qquad \dots (I)$$

$$\underbrace{\qquad}_{AC}$$
$$\underbrace{\qquad\qquad}_{CD}$$
$$\underbrace{\qquad\qquad\qquad}_{DB}$$

$$EI\left(\frac{dy}{dx}\right) = 50.25\,(x)^2 - 7.5\,(x)^3 + C_1\bigg| + 7.5\,(x-3)^3\bigg| - 30\,(x-4) \qquad \dots (II)$$

$$EI\,(y) = 16.75\,(x)^3 - 1.875\,(x)^4 + C_1\,(x) + C_2\bigg| + 1.875\,(x-3)^4\bigg| - 15\,(x-4)^2 \qquad \dots (III)$$

(iii) Boundary conditions.

At 'A' i.e. x = 0 ; y = 0 put in equation (III) $\therefore$ $C_2 = 0$

At 'B' i.e. x = 5 m ; y = 0 put in equation (III).

$$0 = 16.75\,(5)^3 - 1.875\,(5)^4 + 5\,C_1 + 1.875\,(5-3)^4 - 15\,(5-4)^2$$

$$\therefore \qquad C_1 = -187.375$$

Substituting values of $C_1$ and $C_2$, equations (II) and (III) are written as

$$EI\left(\frac{dy}{dx}\right) = 50.25\,(x)^2 - 75\,(x)^3 - 187.375\bigg| + 7.5\,(x-3)^3\bigg| - 30\,(x-4) \qquad \dots (II)$$

$$EI\,(y) = 16.75\,(x)^3 - 1.875\,(x)^4 - 187.375\,(x)\bigg| + 1.875\,(x-3)^4\bigg| - 15\,(x-4)^2 \qquad \dots (III)$$

(iv) Slopes and deflections.

For slope and deflection at 'C' put x = 3 m i.e. equations (II) and (III) respectively.

$$EI\left(\frac{dy}{dx}\right)_C = 50.25\,(3)^2 - 7.5\,(3)^3 - 187.375$$

$$\therefore \quad \left(\frac{dy}{dx}\right)_C = \frac{62.375}{EI} = \mathbf{1.91 \times 10^{-3} \ rad \ (\circlearrowleft)}$$

$$EI \ (y)_C = 16.75 \ (3)^3 - 1.875 \ (3)^4 - 187.375 \ (3)$$

$$\therefore \quad y_C = \frac{-261.75}{EI} = \mathbf{8.05 \ mm \ (\downarrow)}$$

For deflection at 'D' put x = 4 m in equation (III).

$$EI \ (y)_D = 16.75 \ (4)^3 - 1.875 \ (4)^4 - 187.375 \ (4) + 1.875 \ (4-3)^4$$

$$\therefore \quad y_D = \frac{-155.625}{EI} = \mathbf{4.79 \ mm \ (\downarrow)}$$

**Example 7.23 :** *Find slope and deflections at 'C' and 'D' for the beam shown in Fig. 7.61 (a) in terms of EI.*

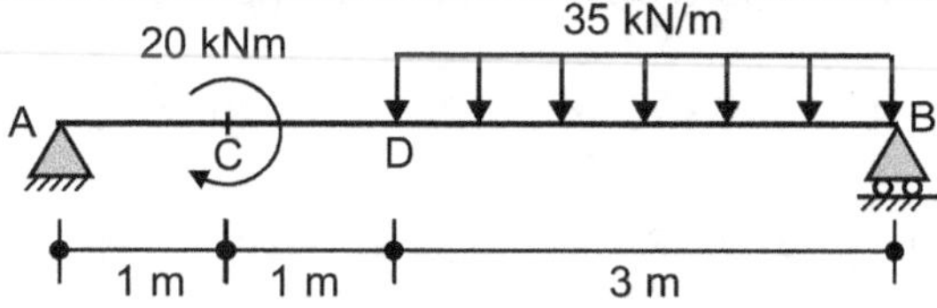


**Fig. 7.61 (a) : Given beam**

**Data**        :   As shown in Fig. 7.61 (a).

**Required**    :   Slope and deflections at 'C' and 'D'.

**Concept**     :   Consider 'A' as origin and section at a distance 'x' from 'A' in zone 'DB' for BM equation.

**Solution:**   (i) Reactions for equilibrium.

$\Sigma M_A = 0;$ $\qquad V_B \times 5 - 35 \times 3 \times 3.5 - 20 = 0 \qquad \therefore \quad V_B = 77.5 \ kN \ (\uparrow)$

$\Sigma F_y = 0;$ $\qquad V_A + V_B - 35 \times 3 = 0 \qquad \therefore \quad V_A = 27.5 \ kN \ (\uparrow)$

$\Sigma F_x = 0;$ $\qquad H_A = 0$

FBD of beam is as shown in Fig. 7.61 (b).

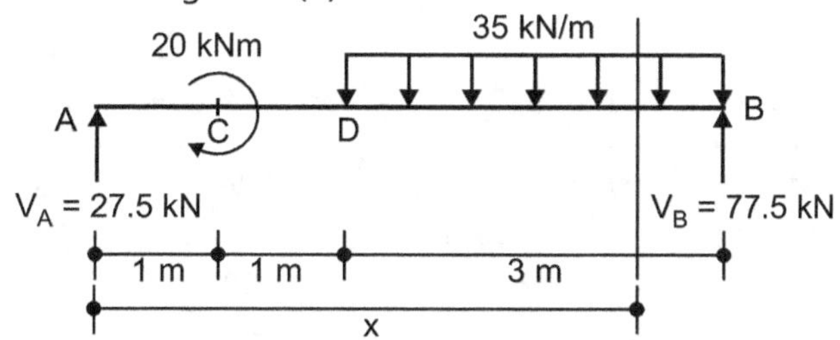


**Fig. 7.61 (b) : FBD of beam**

(ii) Equations for BM ; slope and deflection.

$$EI \left(\frac{d^2y}{dx^2}\right) = 27.5 \ (x) \ \bigg| \ + 20 \ (x-1)^0 \ \bigg| \ \frac{-35 \ (x-2)^2}{2} \qquad \qquad \dots (I)$$

AC

CD

DB

$$EI\left(\frac{dy}{dx}\right) = 13.75\,(x)^2 + C_1 \Big| + 20\,(x-1) \Big| - 5.83\,(x-2)^3 \qquad \text{... (II)}$$

$$EI\,(y) = 4.58\,(x)^3 + C_1\,(x) + C_2 \Big| + 10\,(x-1)^2 \Big| - 1.46\,(x-2)^4 \qquad \text{... (III)}$$

(iii) Boundary conditions.

At 'A' i.e. $x = 0$; $y = 0$ put in equation (III) $\therefore$ $C_2 = 0$

At 'B' i.e. $x = 5$ m; $y = 0$ put in equation (III).

$$0 = 4.58\,(5)^3 + 5\,C_1 + 10\,(5-1)^2 - 1.46\,(5-2)^4$$

$$\therefore \qquad C_1 = -122.85$$

Substituting values of $C_1$ and $C_2$ in equations (II) and (III),

$$EI\left(\frac{dy}{dx}\right) = 13.75\,(x)^2 - 122.85 \Big| + 20\,(x-1) \Big| - 5.83\,(x-2)^3 \qquad \text{... (II)}$$

$$EI\,(y) = 4.58\,(x)^3 - 122.85 \Big| + 10\,(x-1)^2 \Big| - 1.46\,(x-2)^4 \qquad \text{... (III)}$$

(iv) Slopes and deflections.

For slope and deflection at 'C' put $x = 1$ m in equations (II) and (III) respectively.

$$EI\left(\frac{dy}{dx}\right)_C = 13.75\,(1)^2 - 122.85 \quad \therefore \quad \left(\frac{dy}{dx}\right)_C = \frac{\mathbf{109.1}}{\mathbf{EI}}\,(\circlearrowleft)$$

$$EI\,(y_C) = 4.58\,(1)^3 - 122.85\,(1) \therefore \quad y_C = \frac{\mathbf{118.27}}{\mathbf{EI}}\,(\downarrow)$$

For slope and deflection at 'D' put $x = 2$ m in equations (II) and (III) respectively.

$$EI\left(\frac{dy}{dx}\right)_D = 13.75\,(2)^2 - 122.85 + 20\,(2-1) \therefore \left(\frac{dy}{dx}\right)_D = \frac{\mathbf{47.85}}{\mathbf{EI}}\,(\circlearrowleft)$$

$$EI\,(y_D) = 4.58\,(2)^3 - 122.85\,(2) + 10\,(2-1)^2 \therefore y_D = \frac{\mathbf{199.06}}{\mathbf{EI}}\,(\downarrow)$$

**Example 7.24 :** *For the beam shown in Fig. 7.62, derive equation of elastic curve and find deflection at centre in terms of EI.*

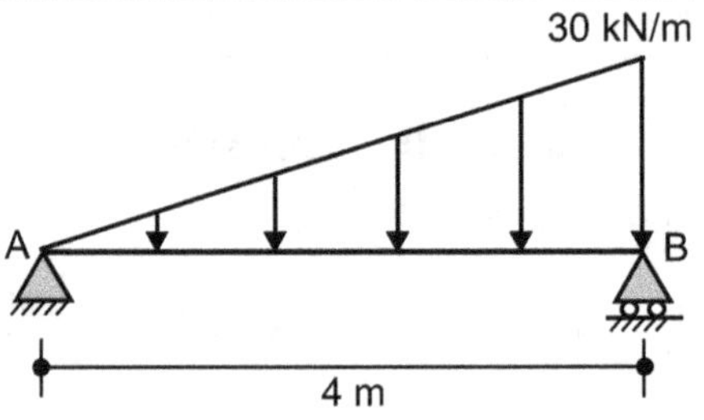


**Fig. 7.62 : Given beam**

**Data**        :   As shown in Fig. 7.62.

**Required**   :   Equation of elastic curve ; deflection at centre.

**Concept**     :  Equation of elastic curve is nothing but the deflection equation.

**Solution:**     (i) Reactions for equilibrium.

$\sum M_A = 0;$     $V_B \times 4 - \left(\dfrac{1}{2} \times 30 \times 4\right)\dfrac{2}{3} \times 4 = 0$     $\therefore$     $V_B = 40$ kN ($\uparrow$)

$\sum F_y = 0;$     $V_A + V_B - \dfrac{1}{2} \times 30 \times 4 = 0$     $\therefore$     $V_A = 20$ kN ($\uparrow$)

$\sum F_x = 0;$     $H_A = 0$

FBD of beam is as shown in Fig. 7.63.

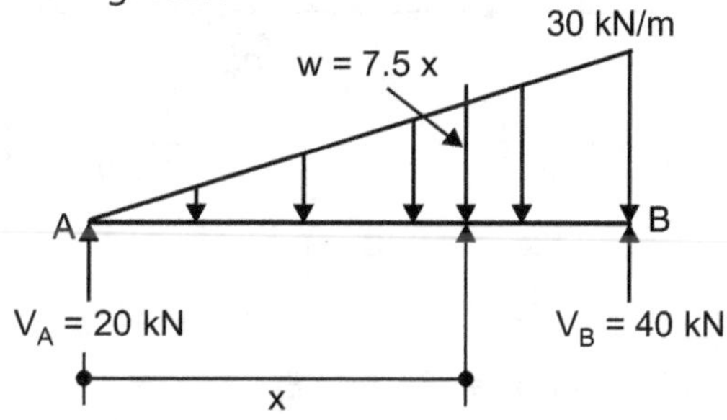


**Fig. 7.63 : FBD of beam**

(ii)    Equations of BM ; slope and deflection.

Considering section at a distance 'x' from 'A'.

Intensity of load at 'x' from 'A' $= W = \dfrac{30}{4}x = 7.5\,x$

$\therefore$     $EI\left(\dfrac{d^2y}{dx^2}\right) = 20\,x - \dfrac{1}{2}(x \times 7.5\,x)\dfrac{x}{3}$

$EI\left(\dfrac{d^2y}{dx^2}\right) = 20\,x - 1.25\,x^3$     ... (I)

$$\underset{AB}{\vdash\!\!\!-\!\!\!-\!\!\!-\dashv}$$

$EI\left(\dfrac{dy}{dx}\right) = 10\,(x)^2 - 0.3125\,(x)^4 + C_1$     ... (II)

$EI\,(y) = 3.33\,(x)^3 - 0.0625\,(x)^5 + C_1\,x + C_2$     ... (III)

(iii) Boundary conditions.

At A i.e. x = 0 ; y = 0 put in equation (III) $\therefore$ $C_2 = 0$

At B i.e. x = 4 m ; y = 0 put in equation (III).

$0 = 3.33\,(4)^3 - 0.0625\,(4)^5 + 4\,C_1$

$\therefore$     $C_1 = -37.28$

Substituting values of $C_1$ and $C_2$, equations (II) and (III) are written as ;

$EI\left(\dfrac{dy}{dx}\right) = 10\,(x)^2 - 0.3125\,(x)^4 - 37.28$     ... (II)

$EI\,(y) = 3.33\,(x)^3 - 0.0625\,(x)^5 - 37.28\,x$     ... (III)

Equation (III) is the required equation of elastic curve.

(iv) Deflection at centre ($y_C$).

Put  x = 2 m in equation (III).

$$EI\,(y_C) = 3.33\,(2)^3 - 0.0625\,(2)^5 - 37.28 \times 2$$

$$\therefore \qquad y_C = \frac{50}{EI}\,(\downarrow)$$

**Example 7.25 :** *Find slope and deflections at 'D' and 'E' for the beam shown in Fig. 7.64. Assume E = 200 GPa and I = 6.2 × 10⁷ mm⁴·*

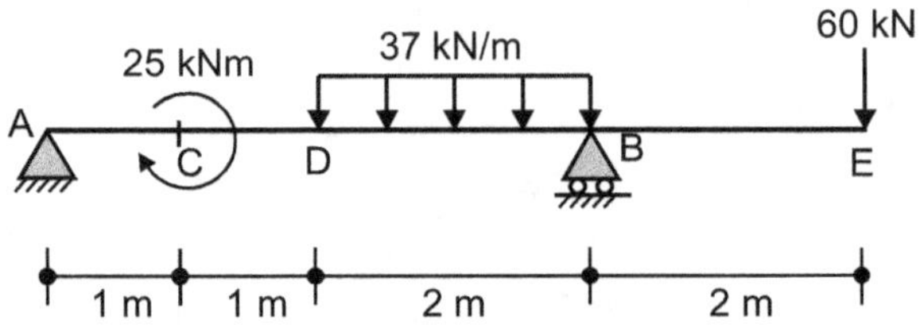


**Fig. 7.64 : Given beam**

**Data**       :  As shown in Fig. 7.64 ; $EI = 12.4 \times 10^3$ kN.m².

**Required**   :  Slope and deflections at 'D' and 'E'.

**Concept**    :  Consider 'A' as origin and section at a distance 'x' from 'A' in zone BE from BM equation. Imaginary UDL is required to be considered in zone BE.

**Solution:**   (i) Reactions for equilibrium.

$\sum M_A = 0;$ $\qquad V_B \times 4 - 37 \times 2 \times 3 - 60 \times 6 - 25 = 0$ $\qquad \therefore \qquad V_B = 151.75$ kN $(\uparrow)$

$\sum F_y = 0;$ $\qquad V_A + V_B - 37 \times 2 - 60 = 0$ $\qquad \therefore \qquad V_A = -17.75$ kN

$\sum F_x = 0;$ $\qquad\qquad\qquad H_A = 0$ $\qquad\qquad = 17.75$ kN $(\downarrow)$

FBD of beam is as shown in Fig. 7.65.

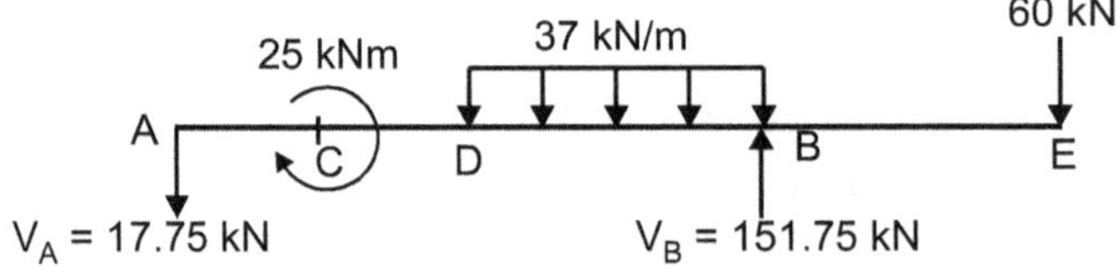


**(a) FBD of beam**

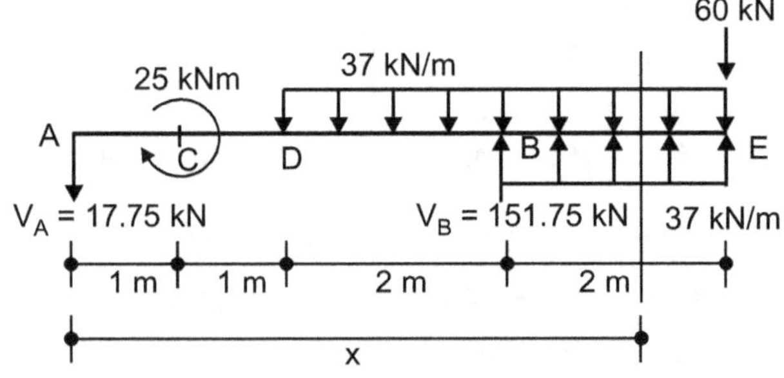


**(b) Beam with imaginary UDL**

**Fig. 7.65**

(ii) Equations of BM; slope and deflection.

$$EI\frac{d^2y}{dx^2} = -17.75\,(x)\,\Big| + 25\,(x-1)^0\,\Big| - 37\,\frac{(x-2)^2}{2}\,\Big| + 151.75\,(x-4) + \frac{37\,(x-4)^2}{2} \qquad \dots \text{(I)}$$

AC

CD

DB

BE

$$EI\frac{dy}{dx} = -8.87\,(x)^2 + C_1\,\Big| + 25\,(x-1)\,\Big| - 6.17\,(x-2)^3\,\Big| + 75.875\,(x-4)^2 + 6.17\,(x-4)^3$$

$$\dots \text{(II)}$$

$$EI\,(y) = -2.96\,(x)^3 + C_1\,(x) + C_2\,\Big| + 12.5\,(x-1)^2\,\Big| - 1.54\,(x-2)^4\,\Big| + 25.29\,(x-4)^3$$

$$+\,1.54\,(x-4)^4 \quad \dots \text{(III)}$$

(iii) Boundary conditions.

At A i.e. $x = 0$; $y = 0$  put in equation (III)  $\therefore\ C_2 = 0$

At B i.e. $x = 4$ m; $y = 0$ put in equation (III).

$$0 = -2.96\,(4)^3 + 4\,C_1 + 12.5\,(4-1)^2 - 1.54\,(4-2)^4$$

$$\therefore \qquad C_1 = 25.4$$

Substituting values of $C_1$ and $C_2$, equations (II) and (III) can be written as

$$EI\left(\frac{dy}{dx}\right) = -8.875\,(x)^2 + 25.4\,\Big| + 25\,(x-1)\,\Big| - 6.17\,(x-2)\,\Big| +$$

$$75.875\,(x-4)^2 + 6.17\,(x-4)^3 \ \dots \text{(II)}$$

$$EI\,(y) = 2.96\,(x)^3 + 25.4\,(x)\,\Big| + 12.5\,(x-1)^2\,\Big| - 1.54\,(x-2)^4\,\Big| +$$

$$25.29\,(x-4)^3 + 1.54\,(x-4)^4 \ \dots \text{(III)}$$

(iv) Slopes and deflections.

For slope and deflection at 'D' put $x = 2$ m in equations (II) and (III) respectively.

$$EI\left(\frac{dy}{dx}\right)_D = -8.875\,(2)^2 + 25.4 + 25\,(2-1)$$

$$\therefore \qquad \left(\frac{dy}{dx}\right)_D = \frac{14.9}{EI} = \mathbf{1.2 \times 10^{-3}\,rad} \quad (\circlearrowleft)$$

$$EI\,(y_D) = -2.96\,(2)^3 + 25.4\,(2) + 12.5\,(2-1)^2$$

$$\therefore \qquad y_D = \frac{39.62}{EI} = \mathbf{3.19\,mm\ (\uparrow)}$$

For slope and deflection at 'E' put $x = 6$ m in equations (II) and (III) respectively.

$$EI\left(\frac{dy}{dx}\right)_E = -8.875\,(6)^2 + 25.4 + 25\,(6-1) - 6.17\,(6-2)^3$$

$$+\,75.875\,(6-4)^2 + 6.17\,(6-4)^3$$

$$\left(\frac{dy}{dx}\right)_E = \frac{-211.12}{EI} = 17.03 \times 10^3 \text{ rad } (\circlearrowleft)$$

$$EI\,(y)_E = -2.96\,(6)^3 + 25.4\,(6) + 12.5\,(6-1)^2 - 1.54\,(6-2)^4 + $$
$$25.29\,(6-4)^3 + 1.54\,(6-4)^4$$

$$\therefore \qquad y_E = \frac{-341.74}{EI} = 27.56 \text{ mm } (\downarrow)$$

**Example 7.26 :** *Find deflections at 'C' and 'D' for the beam, shown in Fig. 7.66. Assume EI = 8.4 × 10³ kN.m².*

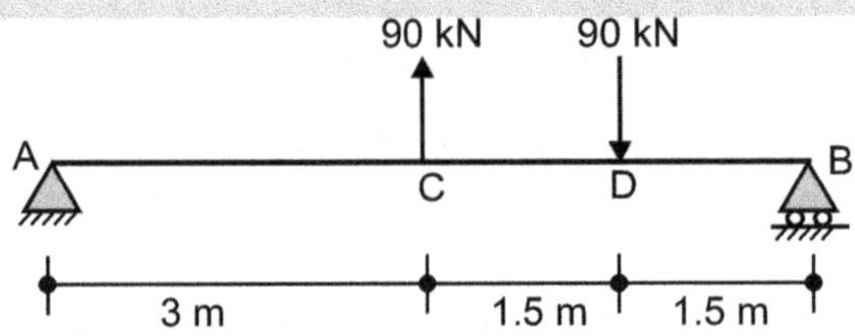


**Fig. 7.66 : Given beam**

**Data**         :   As shown in Fig. 7.66 ; EI = 8.4 × 10³ kN.m².

**Required**   :   Deflections at 'C' and 'D'.

**Concept**    :   Consider 'A' as origin and section at a distance 'x' from 'A' in zone DB for BM equation.

**Solution:**   (i) Reactions for equilibrium.

$\sum M_A = 0;$ $\qquad V_B \times 6 - 90 \times 4.5 + 90 \times 3 = 0$ $\qquad \therefore \qquad V_B = 22.5$ kN $(\uparrow)$

$\sum F_y = 0;$ $\qquad\qquad\qquad V_A + V_B = 0$ $\qquad \therefore \qquad V_A = 22.5$ kN $(\downarrow)$

$\sum F_x = 0;$ $\qquad\qquad\qquad\qquad H_A = 0$

FBD of beam is as shown in Fig. 7.67.

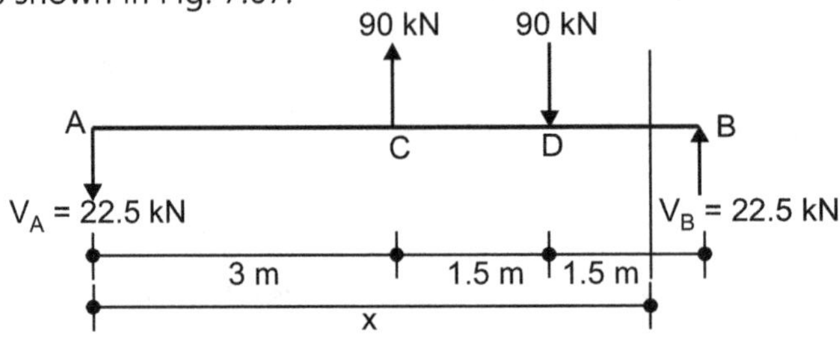


**Fig. 7.67 : FBD of beam**

(ii) Equations of BM; slope and deflection.

$$EI\left(\frac{d^2y}{dx^2}\right) = -22.5\,(x)\,\Big| + 90\,(x-3)\,\Big| - 90\,(x-4.5) \qquad\qquad \dots \text{(I)}$$

AC

CD

DB

$$EI\left(\frac{dy}{dx}\right) = -11.25\,(x)^2 + C_1\,\Big| + 45\,(x-3)^2\,\Big| - 45\,(x-4.5)^2 \qquad\qquad \dots \text{(II)}$$

$$EI\,(y) = -3.75\,(x)^3 + C_1\,(x) + C_2\,\big|\, + 15\,(x-3)^3\,\big| - 15\,(x-4.5)^3 \qquad \text{... (III)}$$

(iii) Boundary conditions.

At A i.e. $x = 0$ ; $y = 0$ put in equation (III) $\therefore$ $C_2 = 0$

At B i.e. $x = 6$ m ; $y = 0$ put in equation (III).

$$0 = -3.75\,(6)^3 + C_1\,(6) + 15\,(6-3)^3 - 15\,(6-4.5)^3$$

$$\therefore \quad C_1 = 75.94$$

Substituting values of $C_1$ and $C_2$, equation (III) is written as

$$EI\,(y) = -3.75\,(x)^3 + 75.94\,(x)\,\big| + 15\,(x-3)^3\,\big| - 15\,(x-4.5)^3 \qquad \text{... (III)}$$

(iv) Deflections at 'C' and 'D'.

For deflection at 'C' put $x = 3$ m in equation (III).

$$EI\,(y)_C = -3.75\,(3)^3 + 75.94\,(3)$$

$$\therefore \quad y_C = \frac{126.57}{EI} = \textbf{15.07 mm (}\uparrow\textbf{)}$$

For deflection at 'D' put $x = 4.5$ m in equation (III).

$$EI\,(y)_D = -3.75\,(4.5)^3 + 75.94\,(4.5) + 15\,(4.5-3)^3$$

$$\therefore \quad y_D = \frac{50.64}{EI} = \textbf{6.03 mm (}\uparrow\textbf{)}$$

**Example 7.27** : *For the beam shown in Fig. 7.68, find position and magnitude of maximum deflection. Assume E = 210 GPa ; I = 8 ×10⁷ mm⁴.*

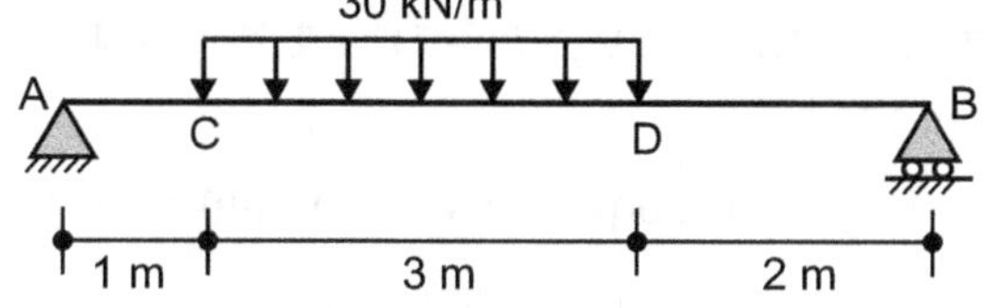


**Fig. 7.68 : Given beam**

**Data**        :   As shown in Fig. 7.68 ; $EI = 16.8 \times 10^3$ kN.m².

**Required**   :   Position and magnitude of maximum deflection.

**Concept:**   (i)   Consider 'A' as origin and section at a distance 'x' from 'A' in zone DB for BM equation.

(ii)   Imaginary UDL is required in zone DB.

**Solution:**   (i) Reactions for equilibrium.

$\sum M_A = 0$ ;          $V_B \times 6 - 30 \times 3 \times 2.5 = 0$          $\therefore$          $V_B = 37.5$ kN $(\uparrow)$

$\sum F_y = 0$ ;          $V_A + V_B - 30 \times 3 = 0$          $\therefore$          $V_A = 52.5$ kN $(\uparrow)$

$\sum F_x = 0$ ;                    $H_A = 0$

FBD of beam is as shown in Fig. 7.69.

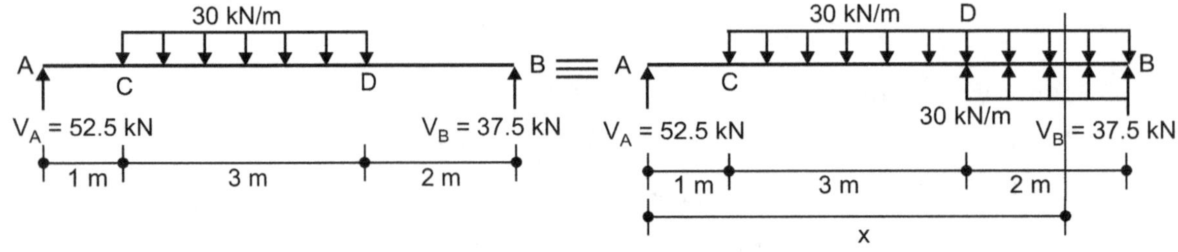

**(a) FBD of beam**          **(b) Beam with imaginary UDL**

**Fig. 7.69**

(ii) Equations of BM ; slope and deflection.

$$EI\left(\frac{d^2y}{dx^2}\right) = 52.5\,(x) \left|\frac{-30\,(x-1)^2}{2}\right| + \frac{30\,(x-4)^2}{2} \qquad \dots \text{(I)}$$

$$\underbrace{\phantom{AC}}_{AC} \quad \underbrace{\phantom{CD}}_{CD} \quad \underbrace{\phantom{DB}}_{DB}$$

$$EI\left(\frac{dy}{dx}\right) = 26.25\,(x)^2 + C_1 \left|-5\,(x-1)^3\right| + 5\,(x-4)^3 \qquad \dots \text{(II)}$$

$$EI\,(y) = 8.75\,(x)^3 + C_1\,(x) + C_2 \left|-1.25\,(x-1)^4\right| + 1.25\,(x-4)^4 \qquad \dots \text{(III)}$$

(iii) Boundary conditions.

At A i.e. $x = 0$; $y = 0$ put in equation (III) $\therefore$ $C_2 = 0$

At B i.e. $x = 6$ m; $y = 0$ put in equation (III).

$$0 = 8.75\,(6)^3 + C_1\,(6) - 1.25\,(6-1)^4 + 1.25\,(6-4)^4$$

$$\therefore \qquad C_1 = -188.12$$

Substituting values of $C_1$ and $C_2$, equations (II) and (III) are written as

$$EI\left(\frac{dy}{dx}\right) = 26.25\,(x)^2 - 188.12 \left|-5\,(x-1)^3\right| + 5\,(x-4)^3 \qquad \dots \text{(II)}$$

$$EI\,(y) = 8.75\,(x)^3 - 188.12\,(x) \left|-1.25\,(x-1)^4\right| + 1.25\,(x-4)^4 \qquad \dots \text{(III)}$$

(iv) Maximum deflection.

Assuming maximum deflection to occur in zone CD. Hence equating slope equation for CD to zero,

$$0 = 26.25\,(x)^2 - 188.12 - 5\,(x-1)^3$$

Solving by trial and error, $x = 2.916$ m. $\therefore$ Assumption is OK.

For maximum deflection; put $x = 2.916$ m in equation (III).

$$EI\,(y)_{max} = 8.75\,(2.916)^3 - 188.12\,(2.916) - 1.25\,(2.916-1)^4$$

$$\therefore \qquad y_{max} = \frac{-348.49}{EI} = \textbf{20.74 mm } (\downarrow)$$

**Example 7.28 :** *For the beam shown in Fig. 7.70, find the magnitude of 'P' such that deflection at 'C' is 10 mm ($\downarrow$). Assume EI = 19.2 $\times$ 10³ kN.m².*

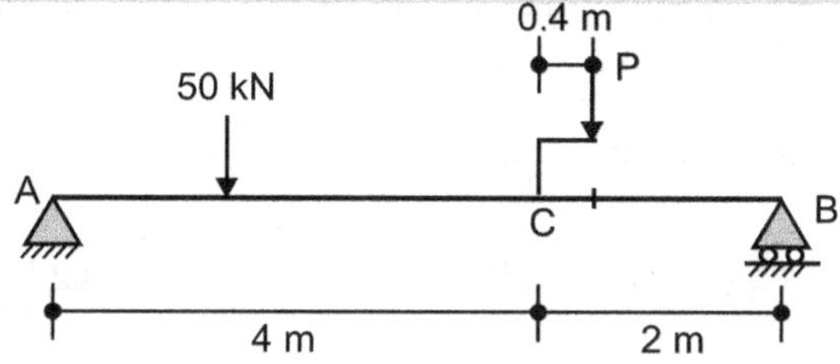

**Fig. 7.70 : Given beam**

**Data**        :   Deflection at 'C' = 10 mm ($\downarrow$) ; EI = 19.2 $\times$ 10³ kN.m².

**Required**    :   Magnitude of 'P'.

**Concept**     :   Force on bracket will be transferred at 'C' as force couple system as shown in Fig. 7.71.

**Solution:**   (i) Reactions for equilibrium.

$\Sigma M_A = 0$;              $V_B \times 6 - 4P - 0.4P = 0$          $\therefore$    $V_B = \dfrac{22}{30} P \;(\uparrow)$

$\Sigma F_y = 0$;                    $V_A + V_B - P = 0$              $\therefore$    $V_A = \dfrac{8}{30} P \;(\uparrow)$

$\Sigma F_x = 0$;                          $H_A = 0$

FBD of beam is as shown in Fig. 7.71.

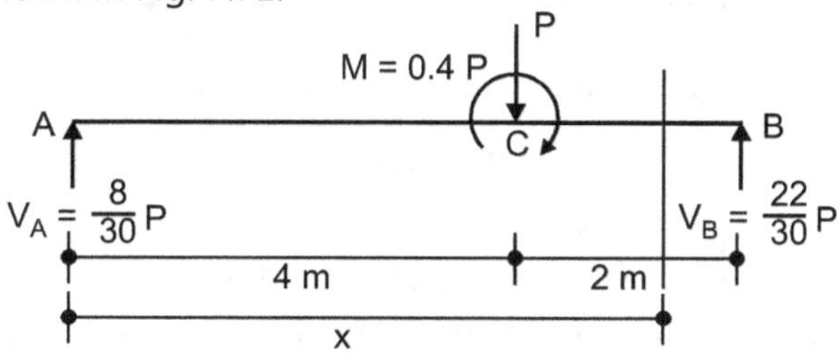

**Fig. 7.71 : FBD of beam**

(ii) Equations of BM ; slope and deflection.

$$EI \left(\dfrac{d^2y}{dx^2}\right) = \dfrac{8}{30} \cdot P\,(x) \left|\; - P(x-4) + 0.4\,P\,(x-4)^0 \right. \qquad \text{... (I)}$$

$$EI \left(\dfrac{dy}{dx}\right) = \dfrac{4}{30}(P)(x)^2 + C_1 \left|\; \dfrac{-P}{2}(x-4)^2 + 0.4\,P\,(x-4) \right. \qquad \text{... (II)}$$

$$EI\,(y) = \dfrac{4}{90}(P)(x)^3 + C_1(x) + C_2 \left|\; \dfrac{-P}{6}(x-4)^3 + 0.2\,P\,(x-4)^2 \right. \qquad \text{... (III)}$$

(iii) Boundary conditions.

At A i.e. x = 0; y = 0 put in equation (III) $\therefore$ $C_2 = 0$

At B i.e. $x = 6$ m; $y = 0$ put in equation (III).

$$0 = \frac{4}{90}(P)(6)^3 + 6\,C_1 - \frac{P}{6}(6-4)^3 + 0.2\,P\,(6-4)^2$$

$$\therefore \qquad C_1 = -1.51\,P$$

Substituting values of $C_1$ and $C_2$, equation (III) can be written as

$$EI\,(y) = \frac{4}{90}(P)(x)^3 - 1.51\,P\,(x)\ \left|\ \frac{-P}{6}(x-4)^3 + 0.2\,P\,(x-4)^2 \right. \qquad \dots \text{(III)}$$

(iv) Magnitude of "P".

At 'C' i.e. $x = 4$ m; $y_C = 10$ mm ($\lnot$) given;

$$\therefore \qquad y_C = \frac{-10}{10^3}\ \text{m} = -0.01\ \text{m substituting;}$$

$$-19.2 \times 10^3 \times 0.01 = \frac{4}{90}(P)(4)^3 - 1.51\,(P)(4)$$

$$\therefore \qquad\qquad P = \mathbf{60\ kN}$$

**Example 7.29 :** *Determine central deflection and slope at supports for the beam shown in Fig. 7.72.*

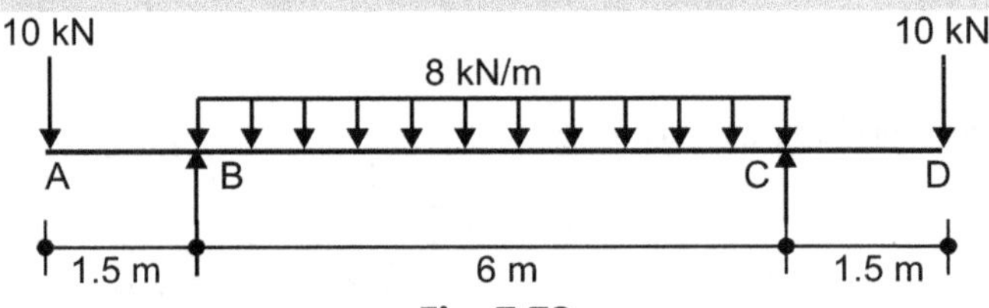


**Fig. 7.72**

**Data**　　　　:　As shown in Fig. 7.72.

**Required**　　:　Slope at supports and deflection at centre.

**Concept**　　:　Due to symmetry, maximum deflection in zone BC will occur at centre, hence this condition will be used to evaluate constant of integration and only half the part of beam will be considered for analysis.

**Solution:**　　(i) Reactions for equilibrium.

$$V_B = V_C = \frac{1}{2}\,(\text{Total load}) = \frac{1}{2}\,[2 \times 10 + 8 \times 6] = 34\ \text{kN}\ (\uparrow)$$

FBD of beam is as shown in Fig. 7.73.

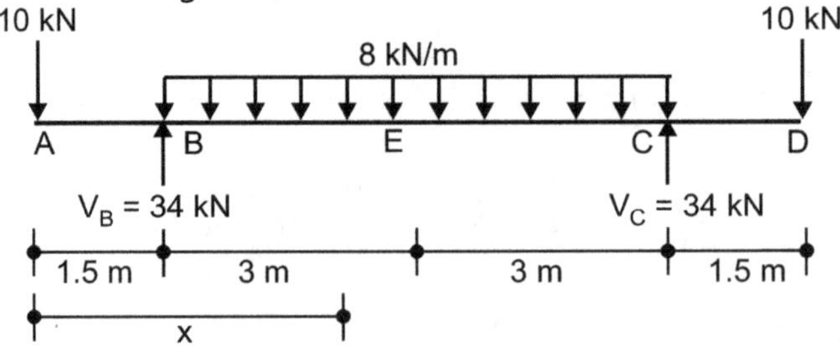


**Fig. 7.73 : FBD of beam**

(ii) Equations of BM ; slope and deflection.

For section in zone BE $(0 \leq x \leq 4.5\ m)$

$$EI \left(\frac{d^2y}{dx^2}\right) = -10\ x \ \Big| + 34\ (x - 1.5) - \frac{8\ (x - 1.5)^2}{2} \qquad \text{... (I)}$$

$$EI \left(\frac{dy}{dx}\right) = -5x^2 + C_1 \Big| + 17\ (x - 1.5)^2 - 1.33\ (x - 1.5)^3 \qquad \text{... (II)}$$

$$EI\ (y) = -1.67\ x^3 + C_1\ (x) + C_2 \Big| + 5.67\ (x - 1.5)^3 - 0.33\ (x - 1.5)^4 \qquad \text{... (III)}$$

(iii) Boundary conditions.

At E i.e. $x = 4.5\ m;\ \dfrac{dy}{dx} = 0$ ; put in equation (II).

$$0 = -5\ (4.5)^2 + C_1 + 17\ (4.5 - 1.5)^2 - 1.33\ (4.5 - 1.5)^3$$

$$\therefore \qquad C_1 = -15.84$$

At B i.e. $x = 1.5\ m$ ; $y = 0$ put in equation (III).

$$0 = -1.67\ (1.5)^3 + (-15.84)\ (1.5) + C_2$$

$$\therefore \qquad C_2 = +29.4$$

Substituting values of $C_1$ and $C_2$, equations (II) and (III) are written as ;

$$EI \left(\frac{dy}{dx}\right) = -5\ (x)^2 - 15.84 \ \Big| + 17\ (x - 1.5)^2 - 1.33\ (x - 1.5)^3 \qquad \text{... (II)}$$

$$EI\ (y) = -1.67\ (x)^3 - 15.84\ (x) + 29.4 \ \Big| + 5.67\ (x - 1.5)^3 - 0.33\ (x - 1.5)^4 \qquad \text{... (III)}$$

(iv) Slope and deflections.

For slope at supports, put $x = 1.5\ m$ in equation (II).

$$EI \left(\frac{dy}{dx}\right)_B = -5\ (1.5)^2 - 15.84$$

$$\therefore \qquad \left(\frac{dy}{dx}\right)_B = \frac{-27.09}{EI} = \left(\frac{dy}{dx}\right)_C$$

For deflection at centre, put $x = 4.5\ m$ in equation (III).

$$EI\ (y)_E = -1.67\ (4.5)^3 - 15.84\ (4.5) + 29.4 + 5.67\ (4.5 - 1.5)^3 - 0.33\ (4.5 - 1.5)^4$$

$$\therefore \qquad (y)_E = \frac{-67.69}{EI}$$

**Note :** Above example can be solved by using principle of superposition and standard results as under.

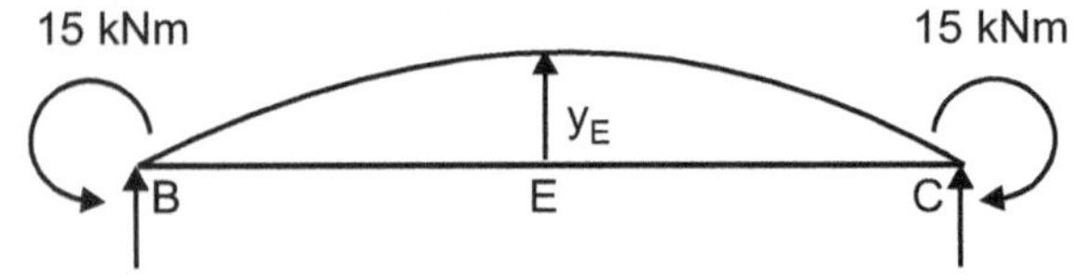


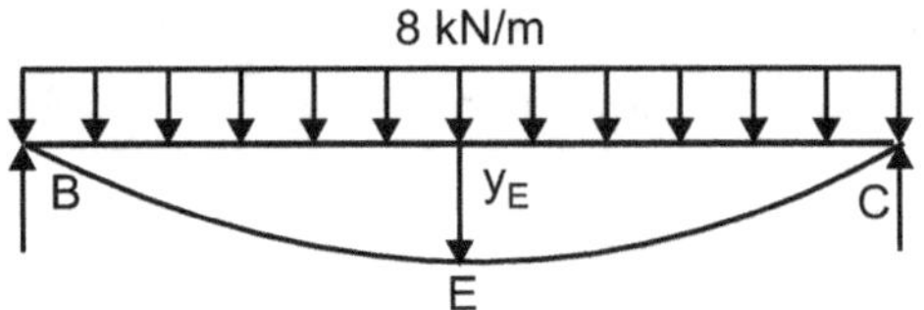


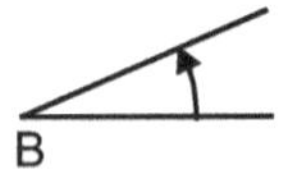


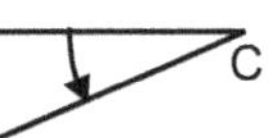


**Fig. 7.74 : Beam with end couples**       **Fig. 7.75 : Beam with UDL**

$$\left(\frac{dy}{dx}\right)_B = -\left(\frac{dy}{dx}\right)_C = \frac{ML}{2\,EI} = \frac{15 \times 6}{2\,EI}$$

$$-\left(\frac{dy}{dx}\right)_B = \left(\frac{dy}{dx}\right)_C = \frac{wL^3}{24\,EI} = \frac{8 \times 6^3}{24\,EI}$$

$$= \frac{45}{EI}$$

$$= \frac{72}{EI}$$

$$y_E = \frac{ML^2}{8\,EI} = \frac{15 \times 6^2}{8\,EI} = \frac{67.5}{EI}$$

$$y_E = \frac{5}{384}\left(\frac{wL^4}{EI}\right) = \frac{5}{384}\left(\frac{8 \times 6^4}{EI}\right)$$

$$= \frac{135}{EI}$$

$$\therefore \quad \text{Slope at supports} = \frac{45 - 72}{EI} = \frac{27}{EI} \; (\text{At B } (\neq) \text{ and At C } (\circlearrowleft))$$

$$\text{Deflection at centre} = \frac{67.5 - 135}{EI} = \frac{-67.5}{EI} \; \text{i.e. downward.}$$

**Example 7.30 :** *Calculate the uniform bending moment which must be applied to a steel rod 12 mm $\phi$ in order to bend it into a circular arc of 12 m radius. If the bar is 2 m long, find the central deflection. Assume E = 200 GPa.*

**Data**　　　 : 　L = 2 m ; $\phi$ = 12 mm ; R = 12 m ; E = 200 GPa.

**Required**　 : 　Uniform bending moment M and central deflection y.

**Concept**　　 : 　Flexure formula.

**Solution**　　 : 　(i) Geometric properties.

$$I = \frac{\pi}{64}(\phi)^4 = \frac{\pi}{64}(12)^4 = 1017.88 \text{ mm}^4$$

(ii) Bending moment (M).

$$\frac{M}{I} = \frac{\sigma}{y} = \frac{E}{R}$$

$$\therefore \qquad M = \frac{E}{R}(I) = \frac{200 \times 10^3}{12 \times 10^3} \times 1017.88$$

$$\therefore \qquad M = 16.96 \times 10^3 \text{ N.mm}$$

$$= 16.96 \times 10^{-3} \text{ kN.m}$$

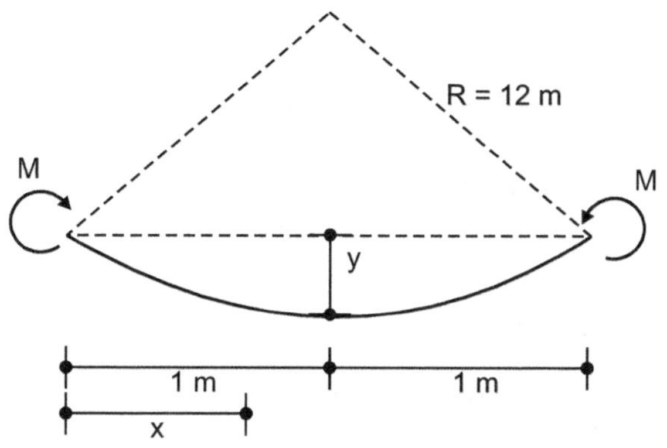


**Fig. 7.76**

(ii) Central deflection $(y)_C$.

$$EI \left(\frac{d^2y}{dx^2}\right) = M (x)^0 \qquad \qquad \text{... (I)}$$

$$EI \left(\frac{dy}{dx}\right) = M (x) + C_1 \qquad \qquad \text{... (II)}$$

$$EI (y) = \frac{M}{2} (x)^2 + C_1 (x) + C_2 \qquad \qquad \text{... (III)}$$

For $x = 0$ ; $y = 0$ put in equation (III) $\qquad \qquad \therefore \ C_2 = 0$

For $x = 2$ m ; $y = 0$ put in equation (III) $\qquad \qquad \therefore \ C_1 = -M$

For central deflection put $x = 1$ m in equation (III).

$$EI (y)_C = \frac{M}{2} (1)^2 - M (1)$$

$$\therefore \qquad (y)_C = \frac{-M}{2 \, EI} ; \qquad \text{where,} \qquad E = 200 \text{ kN.m}^2$$

$$I = 1017.88 \text{ mm}^4$$

$$\therefore \qquad EI = 0.204 \text{ kN.m}^2 \text{ and } M = 16.96 \times 10^{-3} \text{ kN.m}$$

$$\therefore \qquad y_C = \frac{-16.96 \times 10^{-3}}{2 \times 0.204}$$

$$= -0.0415 \text{ m} = 41.5 \text{ mm} (\downarrow)$$

**Example 7.31 :** *A beam of length 6 is simply supported at its ends and carries a point load of 50 kN at 4 m from the support. Find the deflection under the load and the maximum deflection. Also find the point at which the maximum deflection occurs. Given I for beam = $7.33 \times 10^7$ mm⁴ and E = 200 GPa. Use Macaulay's method.*

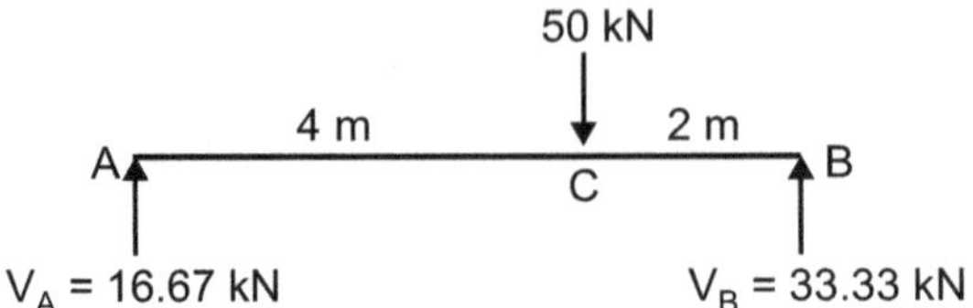



**Fig. 7.77**

**Solution :** (i) Reactions :

$$V_A = 16.67 \text{ kN}, \ V_B = 33.33 \text{ kN}$$

(ii)  Equations :  $$EI \frac{d^2y}{dx^2} = 16.67 \, (x) - 50 \, (x - 4) \qquad \text{... (i)}$$

$$EI \frac{dy}{dx} = 8.33 \, (x)^2 + C_1 - 25 \, (x - 4)^2 \qquad \text{... (ii)}$$

$$EI \cdot y = 2.78 \, (x)^3 + C_1 x + C_2 - 8.33 \, (x - 4)^3 \qquad \text{... (iii)}$$

(iii) Boundary conditions :

At $x = 0$, $y = 0$ $\quad \therefore C_2 = 0$

At $x = 6$ m, $y = 0$ $\quad \therefore C_1 = -89$

(iv) Slope and deflection :

Put $x = 4$ m in equation (iii),

$$y_C = \frac{-178.08}{EI} = 12.12 \text{ mm } (\neg)$$

Let, $y_{max}$ occur in zone AC.

$$EI \frac{dy}{dx} = 0 = 8.33 \, x^2 - 89$$

$$x = 3.268 \text{ m} < 4 \text{ m} \quad \text{... Assumption is O.K.}$$

For $y_{max}$, put $x = 3.268$ m in equation (iii).

$$y_{max} = -\frac{193.82}{EI} = \textbf{13.22 mm } (\downarrow)$$

---

**Example 7.32 :** *A beam 'AB' of span 4 m is hinged at 'B' and simply supported at 'A' is subjected to an end moment of 20 kN-m at 'B'. Locate the point and amount of maximum deflection.*

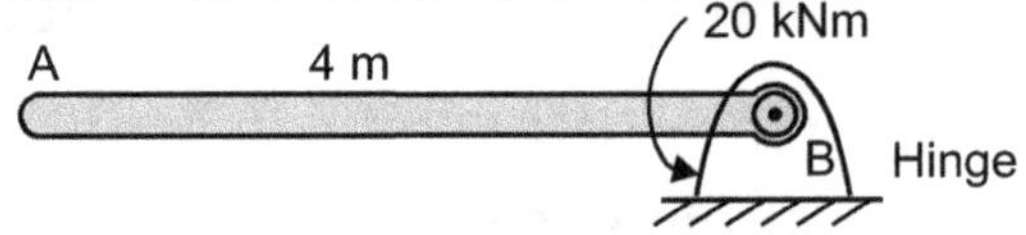



**Fig. 7.78 (Given beam)**

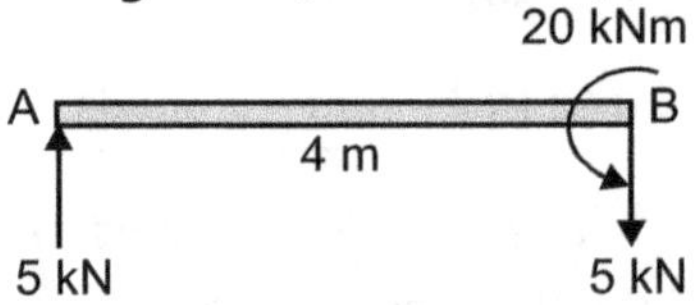

**Fig. 7.79 : F.B.D.**

**Solution :** (i) Reactions :   $V_A = \dfrac{20}{4} = 5$ kN (≠), $V_B = 5$ kN (¬)

---

(ii)    Equations :

$$EI \cdot \frac{d^2y}{dx^2} = 5\,(x) \qquad \ldots (i)$$

$$EI\frac{dy}{dx} = 2.5\,x^2 + C_1 \qquad \ldots (ii)$$

$$EI \cdot y = 0.833\,x^3 + C_1\,(x) + C_2 \qquad \ldots (iii)$$

(iii)    Boundary conditions :

At $x = 0$, $y = 0$,      $C_2 = 0$

At $x = 4$ m, $y = 0$,      $C_1 = -13.33$

(iv)    For maximum deflection :

$$EI\frac{dy}{dx} = 0 = 2.5\,x^2 - 13.33$$

$$x = 2.31 \text{ m  Put in equation (iii).}$$

$$y_{max} = \frac{\mathbf{20.52}}{\mathbf{EI}} (\downarrow)$$

**Example 7.33 :** *Calculate the maximum deflection $\delta_{max}$ of the beam shown in Fig. 7.80. Take E = 200 GPa, I = 1.20 $\times 10^9$ mm$^4$ and use Macaulay's method.*

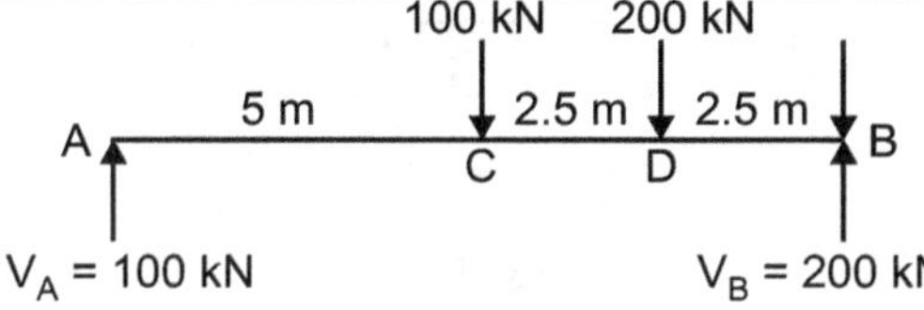



**Fig. 7.80**

**Solution :** (i) Reactions : $V_A = 100$ kN, $V_B = 200$ kN

(ii)    Equations :

$$\frac{EI \cdot d^2y}{dx^2} = 100\,(x) - 100\,(x-5) - 200\,(x-7.5) \qquad \ldots (i)$$

$$\frac{EI \cdot dy}{dx} = 50\,(x)^2 + C_1 - 50\,(x-5)^2 - 100\,(x-7.5)^2 \qquad \ldots (ii)$$

$$EI \cdot y = 16.67\,(x)^3 + C_1\,(x) + C_2 - 16.67\,(x-5)^3 - 33.33\,(x-7.5)^3 \qquad \ldots (iii)$$

(iii)    Boundary conditions :

At $x = 0$, $y = 0$      $\therefore$    $C_1 = 0$

At $x = 10$ m, $y = 0$   $\therefore$    $C_1 = -1406.54$

(iv)    Maximum deflection : Let 5m $< x <$ 7.5 m

$\therefore$
$$\frac{EI \cdot dy}{dx} = 50\,(x)^2 - 1406.54 - 50\,(x-5)^2 = 0$$

$\therefore$
$$x = 5.31 \text{ m Put in equation (iii)}$$

$\therefore$
$$y_{max} = -\frac{4973.37}{EI}$$

$$= \mathbf{20.72 \text{ mm}} (\downarrow) \qquad (EI = 240 \times 10^3 \text{ kNm}^2)$$

## EXERCISE

Solve following examples by Macaulay's method.

1.  A 2 m long cantilever made of steel tube 150 mm external diameter and 10 mm thickness is loaded as shown in Fig. 7.81. Determine the maximum deflection. Assume E = 200 GPa.

$$(13.98 \text{ mm } (\downarrow))$$

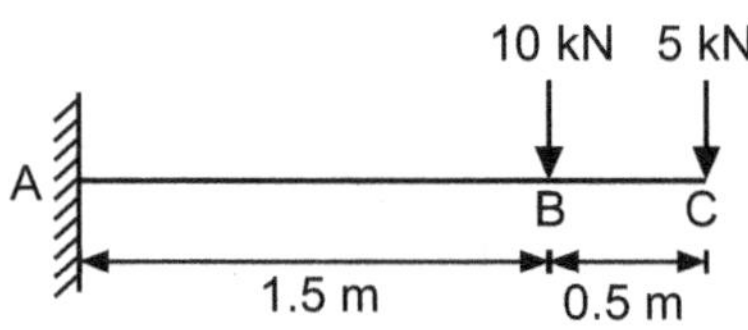


**Fig. 7.81**

2.  A 2 m long cantilever is of rectangular section 100 mm wide and 200 mm deep. It is loaded as shown in Fig. 7.82. Find deflection at free end assuming E = 10 GPa.

$$(19.39 \text{ mm } (\downarrow))$$

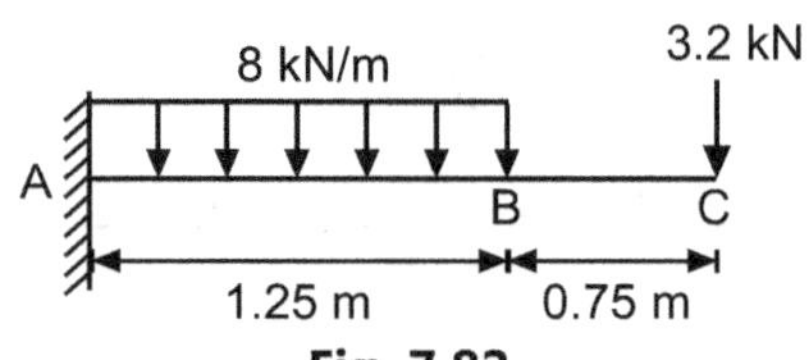


**Fig. 7.82**

3.  A horizontal cantilever of uniform section and span 'L' is loaded as shown in Fig. 7.83. Find the deflection at free end.

$$\left(\frac{26.76}{EI} \, (\downarrow)\right)$$

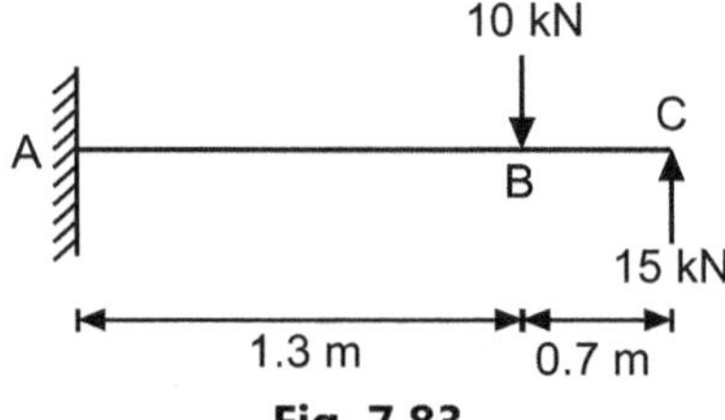


**Fig. 7.83**

4.  A cantilever of uniform section is loaded as shown in Fig. 7.84. Find the deflection at B. If the cantilever is propped at B, find the reaction at prop assuming there is no deflection at B.

$$\left(y_B = \frac{33.75}{EI} \, (\downarrow) \, ; \, V_B = 30 \text{ kN } (\uparrow)\right)$$

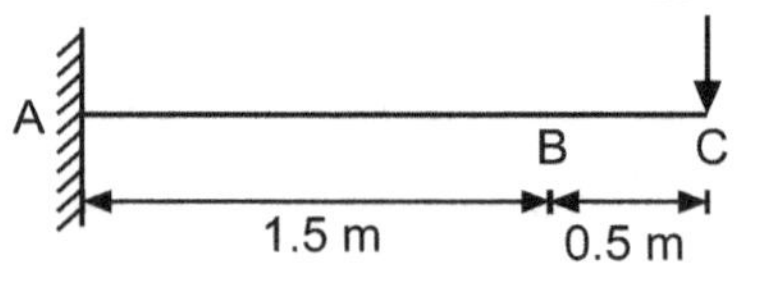

**Fig. 7.84**

5.    A vertical post AB of constant flexural rigidity 4000 kNm$^2$ is fixed at the base A and subjected to a horizontal load of 20 kN at C as shown in Fig. 7.85. Determine the necessary force in horizontal tie at B such that the deflection at B is limited to 20 mm to the left.

(5.13 kN)

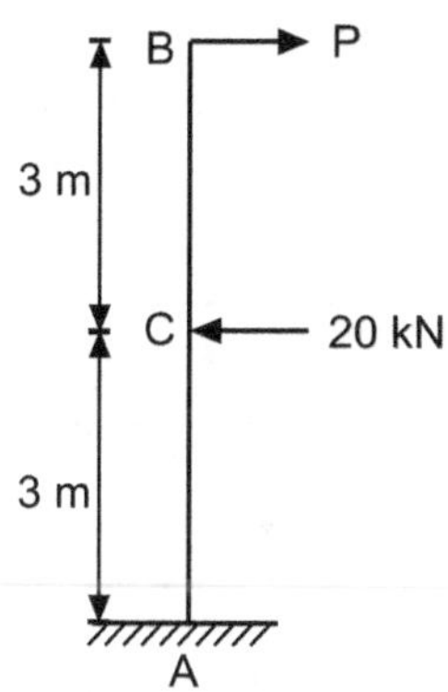


**Fig. 7.85**

6.    Two equal steel beams are built in at one end and connected by a steel rod as shown in Fig. 7.86. Show that the pull in the rod is

$$P = \frac{5\,wL^3}{32\left(\dfrac{6\,aI}{\pi d^2} + L^3\right)}$$

where        d  =  diameter of the rod

and          I  =  M.I. of each beam

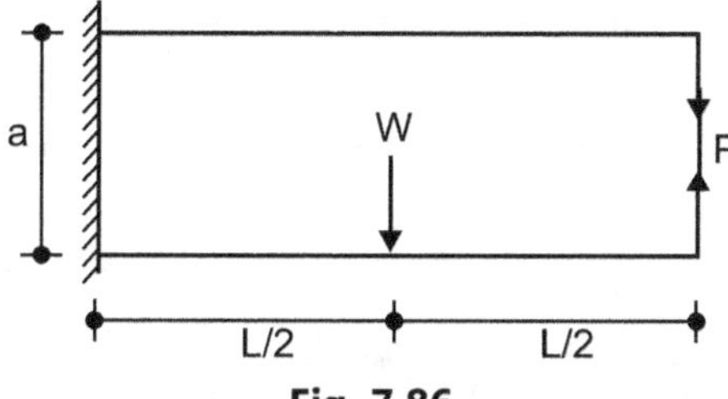


**Fig. 7.86**

7.    For the beam shown in Fig. 7.87, show that the deflection under load is $\dfrac{W}{3.2\ EI}$.

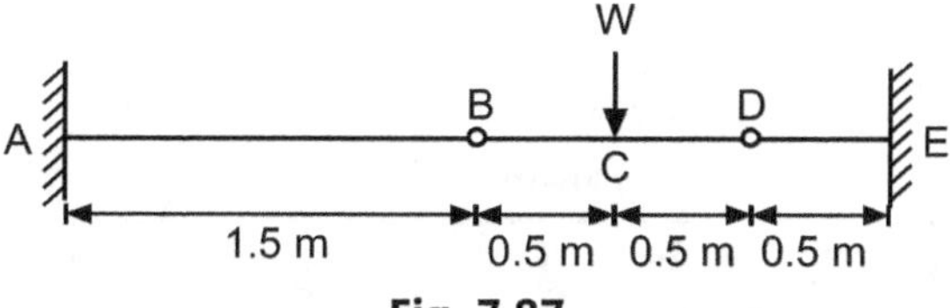


**Fig. 7.87**

8.    A timber beam carries a UDL of 10 kN/m over a span of 6 m. The ends of the beam are simply supported. Determine the section of the beam if the central deflection is limited to 15 mm and the maximum bending stress to 10 MPa. Take E = 12 GPa.

$$(b = 154 \text{ mm}, d = 417 \text{ mm})$$

9.  The beam is supported and loaded as shown in Fig. 7.88. Find (i) the deflection under the load, (ii) the position and the amount of maximum deflection.

    Assume $E = 200$ GPa and $I = 50 \times 10^6$ mm$^4$

    $$(y_C = 6 \text{ mm } (\downarrow); \ y_{max} = 6.53 \text{ mm } (\downarrow) \text{ at } 2.45 \text{ m from A})$$

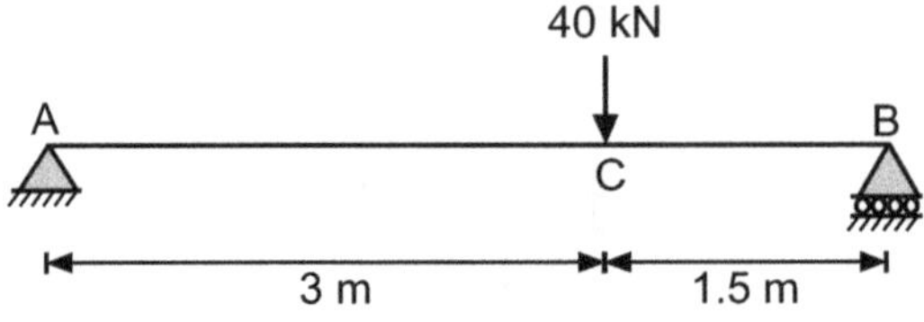


**Fig. 7.88**

10. The beam is supported and loaded as shown in Fig. 7.89. Find (i) the deflection under loads, (ii) the maximum deflection. Assume $E = 200$ GPa, $I = 70 \times 10^8$ mm$^4$.

    $$(y_C = 2.34 \text{ mm } (\downarrow) \ ; \ y_D = 2.98 \text{ mm } (\downarrow) \ ; \ y_{max} = 3.54 \text{ mm } (\downarrow) \text{ at } 6.87 \text{ m from A})$$

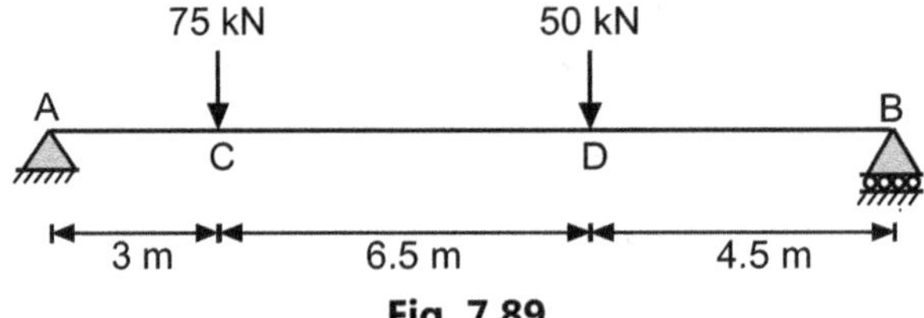


**Fig. 7.89**

11. The beam is supported and loaded as shown in Fig. 7.90. Determine the position and amount of maximum deflection. $EI = 1.39 \times 10^{11}$ kNmm$^2$.

    $$(y_{max} = 6.82 \text{ mm } (\downarrow) \text{ at } 4.97 \text{ m from A})$$

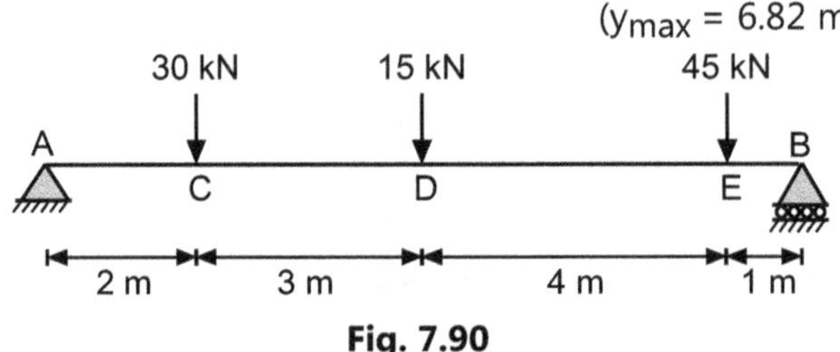


**Fig. 7.90**

12. The beam is supported and loaded as shown in Fig. 7.91. Find deflection at C.

    $$\left(y_C = \frac{3.75}{EI} \ (\downarrow)\right)$$

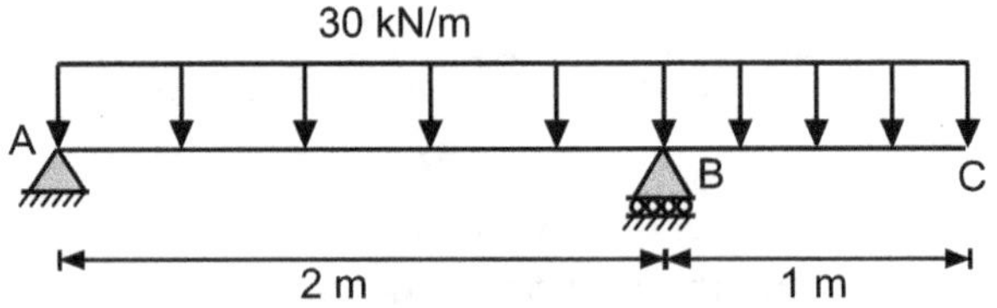

**Fig. 7.91**

13. The beam is supported and loaded as shown in Fig. 7.92. Assuming E = 200 GPa, I = $40 \times 10^6$ mm$^4$, find (i) the deflection at C; (ii) the maximum deflection, and (iii) slope at end A.

$(y_C = 8.74$ mm $(\downarrow)$; $y_{max} = 8.75$ mm $(\downarrow)$ at 1.958 m from A; $\theta_A = 0.417°$ $(\circlearrowleft))$

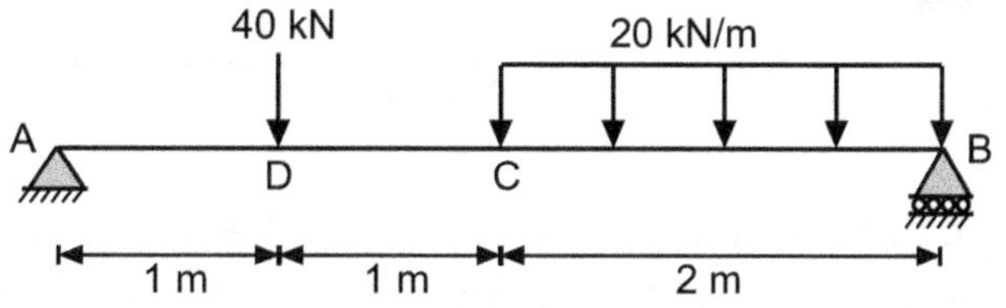

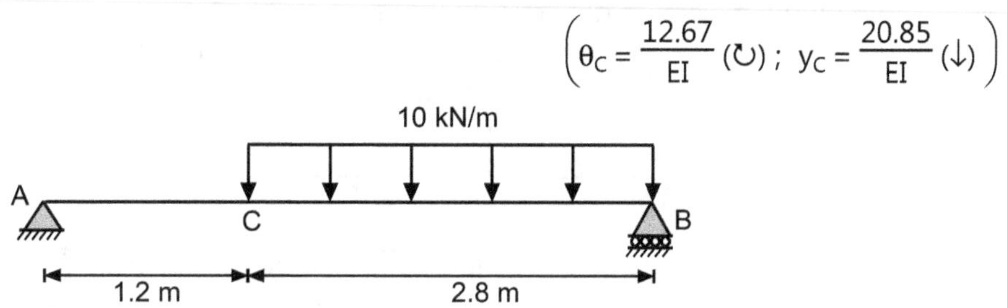


**Fig. 7.92**

14. The beam is supported and loaded as shown in Fig. 7.93. Calculate slope and deflection at point C.

$$\left( \theta_C = \frac{12.67}{EI} \; (\circlearrowleft) \; ; \; y_C = \frac{20.85}{EI} \; (\downarrow) \right)$$

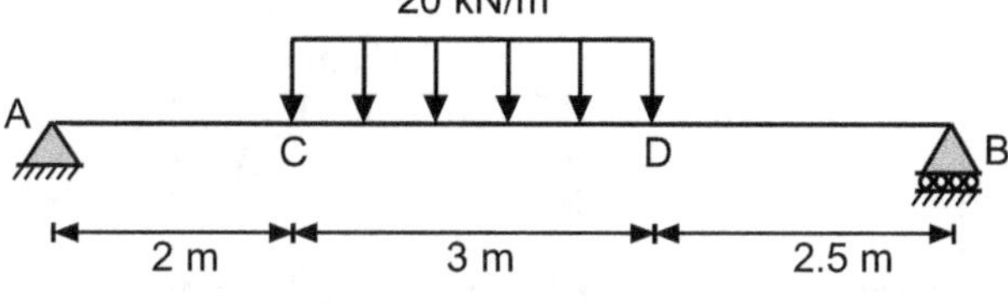


**Fig. 7.93**

15. A beam of constant section, symmetric about neutral axis is simply supported over a span of 8 m. The beam has to carry a concentrated load of 40 kN at the midspan and a UDL of 15 kN/m over the entire span. If the central deflection is limited to $\frac{1}{480}$th of the span and the maximum fibre stresses due to bending are not to exceed 118 MPa, determine the required depth of the beam and moment of inertia.

$(d = 435$ mm ; $I_{xx} = 3.686 \times 10^8$ mm$^4)$

16. The beam is supported and loaded as shown in Fig. 7.94. Determine the deflections at C and D and maximum deflection, assuming EI = $3 \times 10^{10}$ kNmm$^2$.

$(y_C = 12.09$ mm $(\downarrow)$; $y_D = 13.81$ mm $(\downarrow)$; $y_{max} = 16.22$ mm $(\downarrow)$ at 3.7 m from A)



**Fig. 7.94**

17. Find slope and deflections at C and E for the beam supported and loaded as shown in Fig. 7.95. Assume E = 200 GPa, I = $2 \times 10^7$ mm$^4$.

$(\theta_C = 0.0047^\circ \;(\circlearrowleft); \; y_C = 12.5 \text{ mm} \;(\downarrow); \; \theta_E = 0.568^\circ \;(\varnothing); \; y_E = 9.916 \text{ mm} \;(\uparrow))$

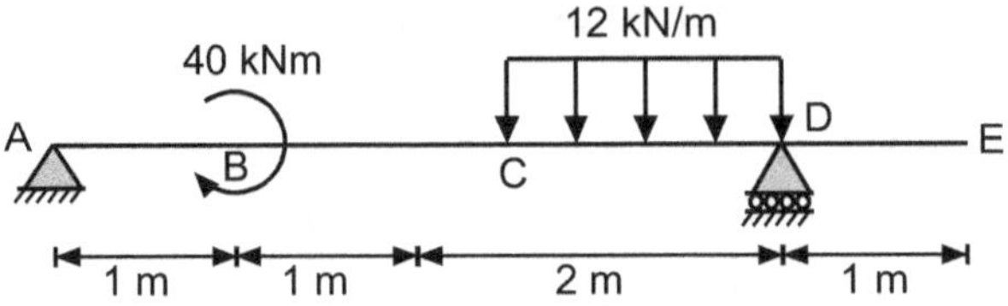

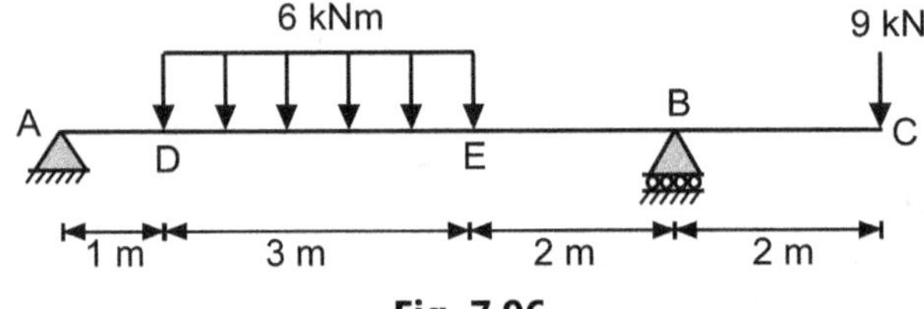

**Fig. 7.95**

18. A simply supported beam AB of length 'L' just touches a spring of midspan in unloaded condition. Find the stiffness k of the spring that will make the forces on the supports and on the spring equal for a uniformly distributed load. Assume EI = constant.    $(54.857 \; EI/L^3)$

19. The beam is supported and loaded as shown in Fig. 7.96. Determine (i) the deflection at C and (ii) the maximum deflection between A and B. Assume EI = 2700 kNm$^2$.      $(y_C = 10.08 \text{ mm} \;(\downarrow); \; y_{max} \text{ in zone AB} = 11.4 \text{ mm} \;(\downarrow) \text{ at 2.46 m from A})$

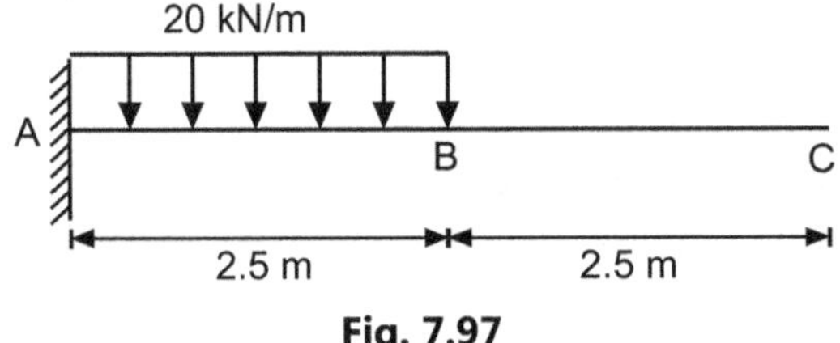

**Fig. 7.96**

20. Determine slope and deflection at free end of a cantilever shown in Fig. 7.97. Assume uniform flexural rigidity. Take $E = 2 \times 10^5$ MPa; $I = 8.5 \times 10^7$ mm$^4$.

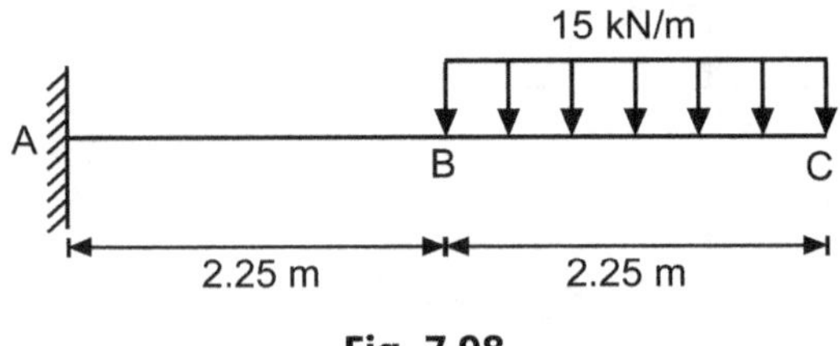

**Fig. 7.97**

$[\theta_C = 0.175^\circ \;(\circlearrowleft), \; y_C = 13.40 \text{ mm} \;(\downarrow)]$

21. Find slope and deflection at free end of a cantilever shown in Fig. 7.98. Assume uniform flexural rigidity. Take $E = 2 \times 10^5$ MPa; $I = 2.5 \times 10^8$ mm$^4$.

**Fig. 7.98**

$\left[\theta_C = 0.228^\circ \;(\circlearrowleft), \; y_C = 13.13 \text{ mm} \;(\downarrow)\right]$

22. Find midspan and maximum deflection for cantilever beam of uniform section shown in Fig. 7.99. Take EI = 7560 kNm$^2$.

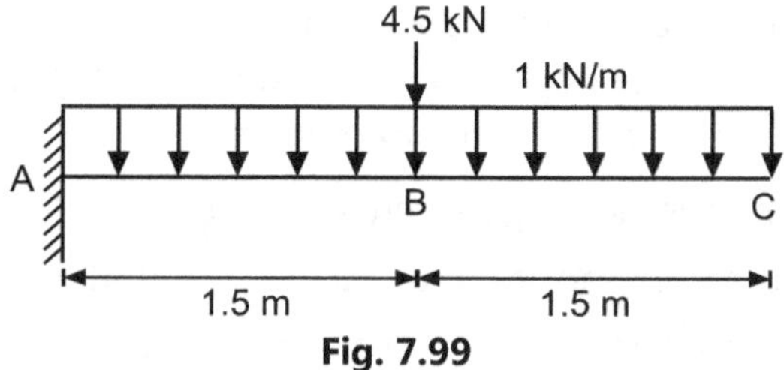

**Fig. 7.99**

$$\left[ y_B = 11.44 \text{ mm } (\downarrow),\ y_{max} = 30.1 \text{ mm } (\downarrow) \right]$$

23. A cantilever beam shown in Fig. 7.100 has a uniform rectangular cross section having d = 2b. Find the values of b, d if maximum deflection is not to exceed 15 mm.

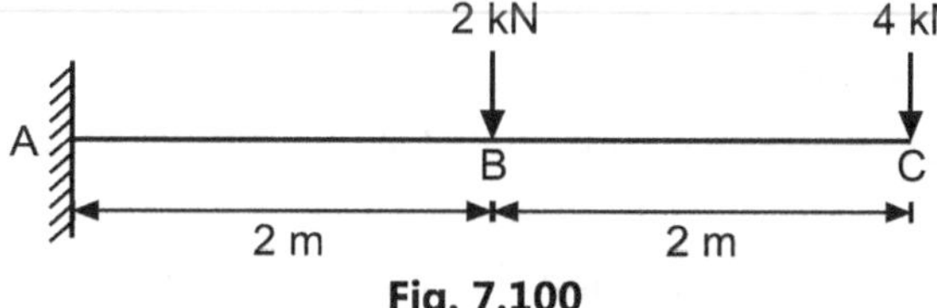

**Fig. 7.100**

$$[b = 217.5 \text{ mm};\ d = 435 \text{ mm}]$$

24. Find the deflection at free end of a cantilever shown in Fig. 7.101.
Take E = $2 \times 10^5$ MPa, I = $4 \times 10^6$ mm$^4$. $\qquad \left[ y_C = 8.33 \text{ mm } (\uparrow) \right]$

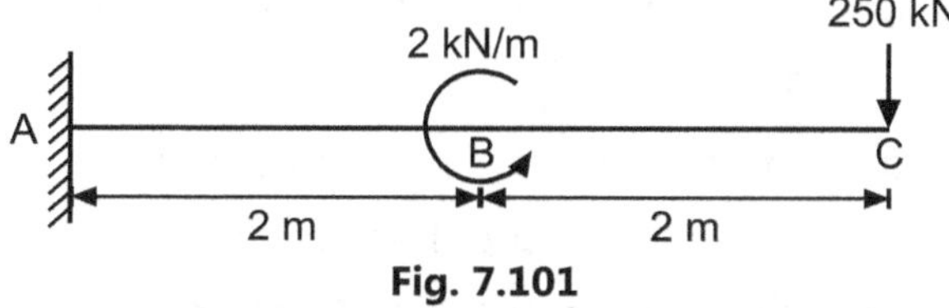

**Fig. 7.101**

## UNIVERSITY QUESTION PAPERS

## MAY 2014

1. Following Fig. 1 shows a simply supported beam of uniform section whose moment of inertia is $4.3 \times 10^8$ mm$^4$. For the loading shown, find the position and magnitude of the maximum deflection. Take E = 200 kN/mm$^2$. **[6]**

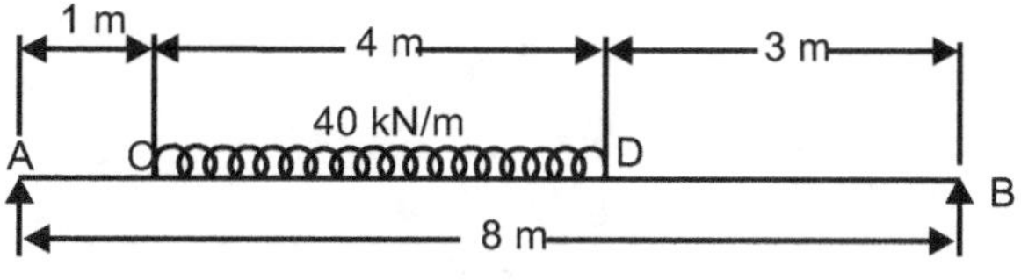

**Fig. 1**

## DECEMBER 2014

1. The cantilever beam has rectangular cross-section of 50 mm (W) × 150 mm (H) is 3 m long and loaded by an end force of 10 kN. The material is steel with E = 210 GPa. Find the maximum deflection of the beam and maximum stress. Take E = 200 GPa. **[6]**

2. The cantilever beam has rectangular cross-section of 50 mm (W) × 150 mm (H) is 3 m long and loaded by an end force of 10 kN. The material is steel with E = 210 GPa determine the slope of free end of the cantilever beam. **[6]**

## MAY 2015

1. Determine the deflection at the free end of a cantilever of length 4 m carrying a uniformly distributed load of 12 kN/m over a length of 3 m from fixed end.

   Take EI = $2 \times 10^{13}$ N/mm$^2$. **[6]**

2. a cantilever of length 4 m carrying a uniformly distributed load of 12 kN/m over a length of 3 m from fixed end.

   Take EI = $2 \times 10^{13}$ N/mm$^2$.determine the slope at the free end of the cantilever. **[6]**

## November 2015

1. A cantilever beam, 60 mm wide by 100 mm high and 2 m long, carries UDL of 3000 N/m over entire span. find the maximum deflection and slope (in radians) of the beam. Take E = 210 GPa. **[6]**

2. A simply supported beam length 3 m is loaded centrally by a point load of 5 kN, find the location and values of maximum deflection and slope (in radians) of the beam. Take flexural rigidity of the beam section as 400 kN-m$^2$. **[6]**

## May 2016

1. A cantilever of length 'L' carrier a uniformly distributed load of 'w' N/m for a length of 'a' from the fixed end, find the deflection at the free end. **[6]**

2. A horizontal cantilever of uniform section of length L carries two point loads W at the free end and 2 W at a distance of 'a' from the free end. Find the

# Chapter 8

# STRAIN ENERGY

## 8.1 INTRODUCTION

When a load is applied on any elastic member, there is deformation. The kind of deformation, that the member undergoes, depends on the type of load applied. For example, axial load causes elongation or contraction of the member depending on whether the axial load is tensile or compressive in nature. Similarly, torsional moment causes angular deformation called as twist. Bending moment also causes angular deformation. Thus, the applied load does some work on a member. When the external loads are removed, member has a capacity to regain its original shape, provided the loads were applied within elastic limit. Thus, the work done on a member is stored in the body as energy and that is why body has capacity to regain its original size and shape. This stored energy, which is by virtue of strain, is called as *strain energy*. Our main interest in this chapter is to study strain energy due to axial force.

## 8.2 STRAIN ENERGY DUE TO AXIAL FORCE

When a member is subjected to axial load, it undergoes axial deformation i.e. change in length. Also, resistance is set up in the member gradually. Within the limit of proportionality, the relation between resistance set up and deformation is always linear as shown in Fig. 8.1.

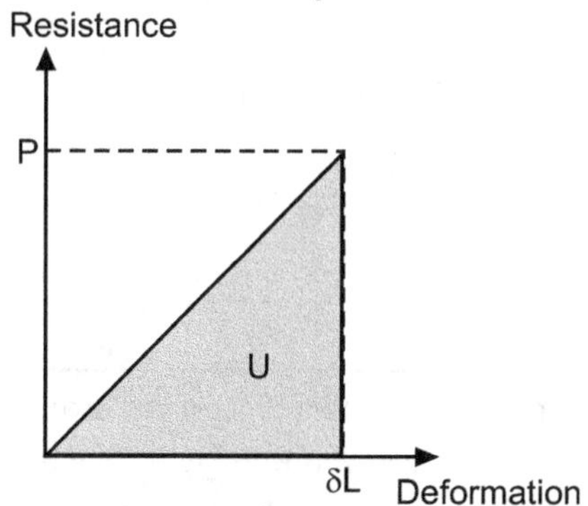


**Fig. 8.1 : Relation between resistance and deformation within elastic limit**

Symbols :

$R$ = Resistance

$\sigma$ = Normal stress

$A$ = Cross-sectional area

$\delta L$ = Axial deformation

$L$ = Length of member

$E$ = Young's modulus of elasticity

$P$ = Applied load

$$U = \text{Strain energy}$$

From Fig. 8.1, area under resistance deformation diagram indicates strain energy U.

$$\therefore \quad U = \frac{1}{2} R \cdot \delta L$$

$$= \frac{1}{2} (\sigma A)\, \delta L \qquad\qquad (\because R = \sigma A)$$

$$= \frac{1}{2} (\sigma A) \left( \frac{\sigma L}{E} \right) \qquad\qquad \left( \because \delta L = \frac{\sigma L}{E} \right)$$

$$= \frac{\sigma^2}{2E} \cdot (AL)$$

$$= \frac{\sigma^2}{2E} \cdot \text{Volume} \qquad\qquad (\because \text{Volume} = AL)$$

OR

$$U = \frac{1}{2} \sigma A \cdot \delta L \times \frac{L}{L} \qquad\qquad \text{(multiply and divide by L)}$$

$$= \frac{1}{2} \cdot \sigma \cdot \varepsilon \cdot AL \qquad\qquad \left( \because \text{linear strain} = \varepsilon = \frac{\delta L}{L} \right)$$

$$= \frac{1}{2} \sigma \cdot \varepsilon \cdot \text{Volume}$$

Thus, various forms of expression of strain energy are,

$$U = \frac{1}{2} \sigma A \cdot \delta L \qquad\qquad \text{... (8.1 a)}$$

OR

$$U = \frac{\sigma^2}{2E} \cdot \text{Volume} \qquad\qquad \text{... (8.1 b)}$$

OR

$$U = \frac{1}{2} \sigma \cdot \varepsilon \cdot \text{Volume} \qquad\qquad \text{... (8.1 c)}$$

Unit of strain energy is Nm.

## 8.3 PROOF RESILIENCE

It is defined as the *maximum strain energy which can be stored by a body without undergoing permanent deformation*. Obviously, it is the strain energy at elastic limit.

Let

$$F_y = \text{Stress at elastic limit}$$

$$\therefore \quad \text{Proof resilience} = \frac{F_y^2}{2E} \cdot \text{Volume} \qquad\qquad \text{... (8.2)}$$

Unit of proof resilience is same as that of strain energy i.e. Nm.

## 8.4 MODULUS OF RESILIENCE

It is defined as *proof resilience per unit volume*.

$$\therefore \quad \text{Modulus of Resilience} = \frac{F_y^2}{2E} \qquad\qquad \text{... (8.3)}$$

Unit of Modulus of Resilience is MPa.

## 8.5 STRESS DUE TO VARIOUS TYPES OF AXIAL LOADS

### 8.5.1 Gradually Applied Load

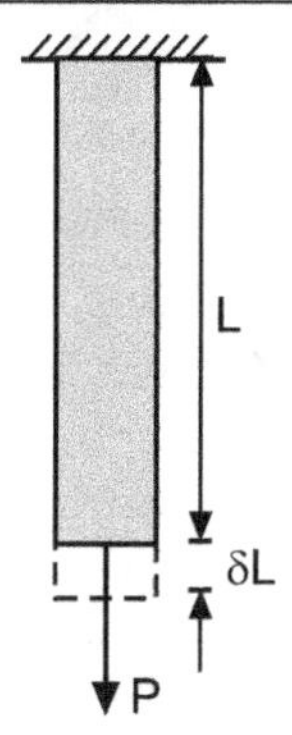

(a) Gradually applied axial load

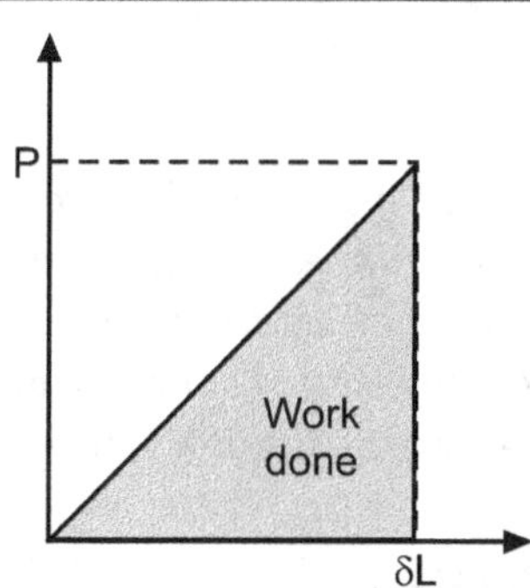


(b) Relation between gradual load and deformation within elastic limit

Fig. 8.2

Let the load P be gradually applied to a member of uniform cross-sectional area A and length L which means magnitude of P increases from zero to final value P. Initially, when load P is zero, the corresponding deformation is also zero. When the magnitude of load is equal to P, the corresponding deformation is δL. Fig. 8.2 (b) shows this relation of gradually applied load and corresponding deformation.

Equating work done to strain energy,

$$\frac{1}{2}P \cdot \delta L = \frac{1}{2}\sigma A \cdot \delta L$$

$$\therefore \qquad \sigma = \frac{P}{A} \qquad \qquad \dots (8.4)$$

### 8.5.2 Suddenly Applied Load

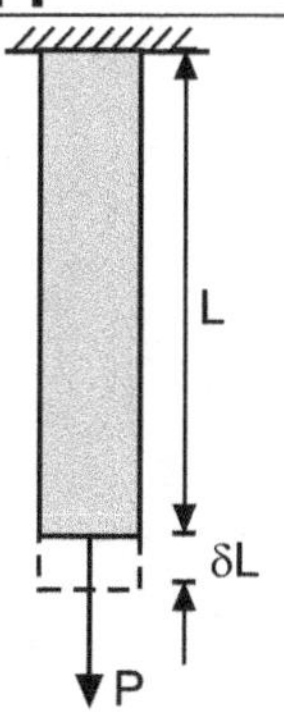

(a) Suddenly applied axial load

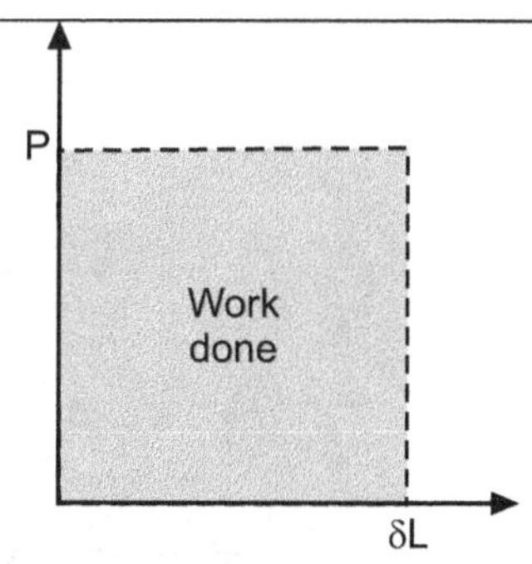


(b) Relation between suddenly applied load and deformation within elastic limit

Fig. 8.3

Let, the load P be suddenly applied to a member of uniform cross-sectional area A and length L. In this case, magnitude of load P is constant throughout the process of extension. Fig. 8.3 (b) shows this relation of gradually applied load and corresponding deformation.

Equating work done to strain energy,

$$\therefore \quad P \cdot \delta L = \frac{1}{2} \sigma \cdot A \cdot \delta L$$

$$\therefore \quad \sigma = \frac{2P}{A} \qquad \qquad \dots (8.5)$$

*It is important here to note that stress produced by suddenly applied load is twice that of gradually applied load. After the instantaneous extension due to suddenly applied load, the state of equilibrium is not reached. As the force of resistance is double the applied load, it sets the motion of vibration into a member like suddenly loaded spring. The equation (8.5) gives maximum instantaneous stress developed in a member due to suddenly applied load.*

### 8.5.3 Impact Load

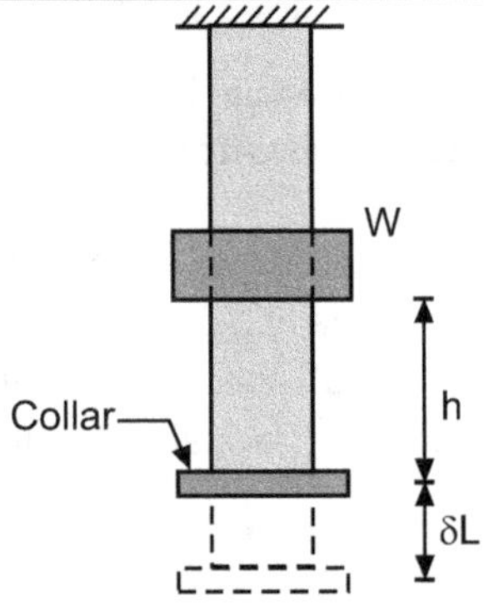


**Fig. 8.4**

Let, the load W fall freely through a distance h before it strikes the rigid collar attached at the bottom of the bar as shown in Fig. 8.4. This is the case of impact loading.

$$\text{Work done} = W(h + \delta L)$$

$$\text{Strain energy} = \frac{1}{2}\sigma A \cdot \delta L$$

Equation of instantaneous stress produced by impact load can be derived by equating work done to strain energy and substituting $\delta L = \dfrac{\sigma L}{E}$.

$$W\left(h + \frac{\sigma L}{E}\right) = \frac{1}{2}\sigma A \cdot \frac{\sigma L}{E}$$

$$\therefore \quad \frac{\sigma^2}{2E} \cdot AL - \left(\frac{WL}{E}\right)\sigma = Wh$$

$$\sigma^2 - \left(\frac{2W}{A}\right)\sigma = \frac{2WhE}{AL}$$

$$\therefore \quad \left(\sigma - \frac{W}{A}\right)^2 = \frac{2WhE}{AL} + \frac{W^2}{A^2}$$

$$\therefore \quad \sigma - \frac{W}{A} = \pm\sqrt{\frac{2WhE}{AL} + \frac{W^2}{A^2}}$$

$$\therefore \quad \sigma = \frac{W}{A} \pm \sqrt{\frac{2WhE}{AL} + \frac{W^2}{A^2}} \qquad \dots (8.6)$$

Other form of equation (8.6) can be derived as,

$$\sigma = \frac{W}{A} \pm \sqrt{\frac{2WhE}{AL} \cdot \frac{WA}{WA} + \frac{W^2}{A^2}}$$

$$= \frac{W}{A} \pm \sqrt{\frac{2h}{WL/AE} \cdot \frac{W^2}{A^2} + \frac{W^2}{A^2}}$$

$$= \frac{W}{A}\left[1 \pm \sqrt{\frac{2h}{\delta_{st}} + 1}\right] \qquad \dots (8.7)$$

where, $\qquad \delta_{st}$ = axial deformation produced by gradually applied load called

$$\text{as axial deformation produced by static load} = \frac{WL}{AE}$$

It should be noted that, in equation (8.7) if h = 0,

$$\sigma = \frac{2W}{A} = \text{instantaneous stress produced by suddenly applied load.}$$

## SOLVED EXAMPLES

**Example 8.1 :** *A vertical steel bar 1.5 m long is fixed at top. A weight can slide freely along the rod and its fall is arrested at the bottom by collar. When weight falls through 40 mm, the maximum instantaneous stress developed in the bar is 200 MPa. Determine the stress in the same bar when same weight is (i) gradually applied; (ii) suddenly applied; (iii) with free fall of 50 mm.*

**Data** : L = 1.5 m = 1500 mm; h = 40 mm which produces $\sigma_{max}$ = 200 MPa;

E = 200 GPa.

**Required** : Maximum stress for gradually applied; suddenly applied load and maximum stress with the same weight falling through height of 50 mm.

**Concept** : Knowing instantaneous stress $\sigma_{max}$ = 200 MPa for h = 40 mm, find $\dfrac{W}{A}$ and

then evaluate stresses for different types of loads applied.

**Solution** : (i) For $\qquad$ h = 40 mm ; $\sigma_{max}$ = 200 MPa

$$\sigma_{max} = \frac{W}{A} \pm \sqrt{\frac{2\,WhE}{AL} + \frac{W^2}{A^2}}$$

$$200 = \frac{W}{A} \pm \sqrt{\frac{2 \times W \times 40 \times 200 \times 10^3}{A \times 1500} + \frac{W^2}{A^2}}$$

Let, $\qquad \dfrac{W}{A} = x$

$\therefore \qquad 200 = x \pm \sqrt{10.67 \times 10^3\,(x) + x^2}$

$(200 - x)^2 = 10.67 \times 10^3\,(x) + x^2$

$40 \times 10^3 - 400\,x + x^2 = 10.67 \times 10^3\,(x) + x^2$

$40 \times 10^3 - 400\,x = 10.67 \times 10^3\,(x)$

$\therefore \qquad x = 3.62$ MPa

$$\frac{W}{A} = 3.62 \text{ MPa}$$

(ii) $\sigma_{max}$ when load is gradually applied :

$$\sigma_{max} = \frac{W}{A} = \textbf{3.62 MPa}$$

(iii) $\sigma_{max}$ when load is suddenly applied :

$$\sigma_{max} = \frac{2W}{A} = 2 \times 3.62 = \textbf{7.24 MPa}$$

(iv) $\sigma_{max}$ when load falls through height of 50 mm :

$$\sigma_{max} = \frac{W}{A} \pm \sqrt{\frac{2\,WhE}{AL} + \frac{W^2}{A^2}}$$

$$= 3.62 \pm \sqrt{\frac{2 \times 3.62 \times 50 \times 200 \times 10^3}{(1500)} + (3.62)^2}$$

$$= \mathbf{223.35\ MPa}$$

**Example 8.2 :** *Water under pressure of 10 MPa is suddenly admitted on to a plunger of 100 mm diameter, attached to a rod 28 mm diameter, 3 m long. Find the maximum instantaneous stress and deformation of the rod if E = 210 GPa.*

**Data**   : Water pressure p = 10 MPa ; Diameter of plunger = 100 mm; Diameter of rod = 28 mm ; Length of rod = L = 3000 mm ; E = 210 GPa.

**Required** : Maximum instantaneous stress and elongation for rod.

**Concept** : Knowing pressure intensity and area of plunger, find force on the rod.

Stress due to suddenly applied load = $\sigma = \dfrac{2\,P}{A}$ .

**Solution** : (i) Geometric properties :

Cross-sectional area of plunger = $\dfrac{\pi}{4}\,(100)^2 = 7853.98\ mm^2$

Cross-sectional area of rod = $\dfrac{\pi}{4}\,(28)^2 = 615.75\ mm^2$

(ii) Force on rod,    P = Water pressure × C/s area of plunger

            = 10 × 7853.98 = 78539.8 N

(iii) Maximum instantaneous stress for rod,

$$\sigma_{max} = \frac{2\,P}{A} \qquad \text{... (\textbf{Note :} Sudden application of force)}$$

$$= \frac{2 \times 78539.8}{615.75} = \mathbf{255.1\ MPa}$$

(iv) Maximum instantaneous elongation,

$$\delta L = \frac{\sigma \cdot L}{E} = \frac{255.1 \times 3000}{210 \times 10^3} = \mathbf{3.64\ mm}$$

**Example 8.3 :** *A bar 50 mm in diameter, 2 m long has to transmit shock energy of 100 joules. Calculate maximum instantaneous stress developed and maximum elongation if E = 200 GPa.*

**Data**   : d = 50 mm ; L = 2000 mm ; U = 100 joules

     ∴ U = 100 Nm = 100 × 10³ Nmm; E = 200 GPa

**Required** : $\sigma_{max}$ and $\delta L_{max}$.

**Concept** : Equate shock energy to strain energy and find maximum instantaneous stress and hence elongation.

**Solution**  :  (i) Maximum instantaneous stress :

$$\text{Strain energy} = \frac{\sigma_{max}^2}{2\,E} \times \text{Volume}$$

$$100 \times 10^3 = \frac{\sigma_{max}^2}{2 \times 200 \times 10^3} \times \frac{\pi}{4}(50)^2 \times 2000$$

$$\therefore \qquad \sigma_{max} = 100.9 \text{ MPa}$$

(ii)  Maximum elongation :

$$\delta L_{max} = \frac{\sigma_{max} \cdot L}{E} = \frac{100.9 \times 2000}{200 \times 10^3} = \mathbf{1\ mm}$$

**Example 8.4 :** *A vertically suspended steel bar, circular in cross-section, is subjected to load of 5 kN which falls by 20 mm on rigid collar provided at lower end of bar. If maximum allowable strain for bar is $\dfrac{1}{1250}$, find suitable diameter of rod.*

*Assume E = 200 GPa and length of bar = 2 m.*

**Data**       :  W = 5 kN ;  h = 20 mm ;  Strain $= \dfrac{1}{1250}$ ;

E = 200 GPa ;  L = 2000 mm as shown in Fig. 8.5

**Required**   :  Diameter of bar.

**Concept**    :  Knowing strain, elongation and stress for
the bar can be obtained, then use basic work equation.

**Solution**   :  (i) Work equation.

$$W(h + \delta L) = \frac{\sigma^2}{2\,E} \times \text{Volume}$$

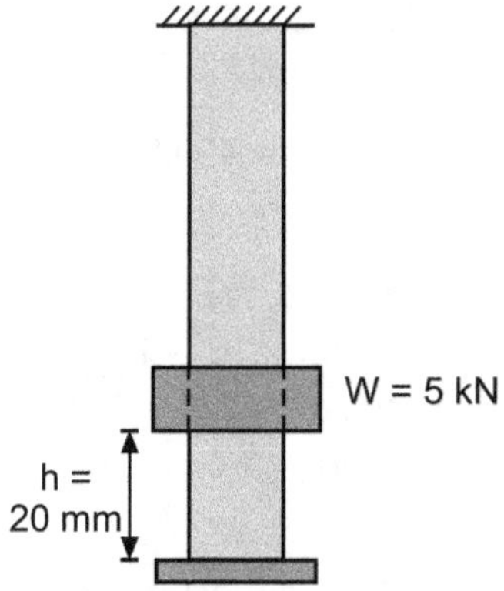

W = 5 kN

h =
20 mm

**Fig. 8.5**

where       $\delta L$ = Strain $\times$ L $= \dfrac{1}{1250} \times 2000$

$\qquad\qquad\quad$ = 1.6 mm

$\qquad\quad \sigma$ = Strain $\times$ E $= \dfrac{1}{1250} \times 200 \times 10^3 = 160$ MPa

Substituting,

$$5 \times 10^3 (20 + 1.6) = \frac{160^2}{2 \times 200 \times 10^3} \times \frac{\pi}{4} (\phi)^2 \times 2000$$

$$\phi = \mathbf{32.78 \ mm}$$

**Example 8.5 :** *A bar of 25 mm diameter stretches 2 mm under gradually applied load of 65 kN. If a weight of 2 kN is dropped on to a collar at the lower end of this bar, through a height of 40 mm, calculate maximum instantaneous stress and elongation of bar. Assume E = 200 GPa.*

**Data**      :  $\phi$ = 25 mm ; $\delta L$ = 2 mm for gradually applied
load of 65 kN; W = 2 kN ; h = 40 mm ;
E = 200 GPa  as shown in Fig. 8.6.

**Required**  :  Maximum instantaneous stress and elongation.

**Concept**  :  Length of bar can be obtained by knowing
elongation due to gradually applied load ;
then use standard formulae for impact loading.

**Solution**  :  (i) Geometric properties :

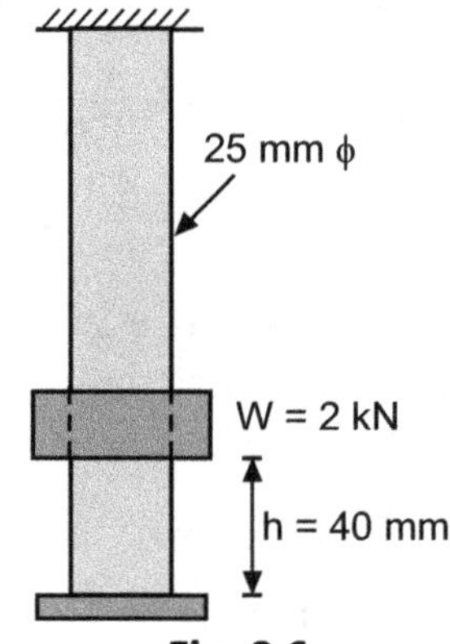


**Fig. 8.6**

$$A = \frac{\pi}{4} (25)^2 = 490.87 \ mm^2$$

(ii) Gradually applied load :

$$\delta L = \frac{PL}{AE}$$

$$2 = \frac{65 \times 10^3 \times L}{490.87 \times 200 \times 10^3}$$

$$\therefore \quad L = 3020.76 \ mm$$

(iii) Stress for impact loading,

$$\sigma = \frac{W}{A} \pm \sqrt{\frac{2 \ WhE}{AL} + \frac{W^2}{A^2}}$$

$$= \frac{2 \times 10^3}{490.87} \pm \sqrt{\frac{2 \times 2 \times 10^3 \times 40 \times 200 \times 10^3}{490.87 \times 3020.76} + \left(\frac{2000}{490.87}\right)^2}$$

$$= \mathbf{151.03 \ MPa}$$

(iv) Elongation for impact loading,

$$\delta L = \frac{\sigma L}{E} = \frac{151.03 \times 3020.76}{200 \times 10^3}$$

$$\delta L = \mathbf{2.281 \ mm}$$

**Example 8.6 :** *A vertical steel bar having 16 mm diameter ; 1.5 m long is provided with a collar at lower end. Find the maximum weight that can be dropped through a height of 100 mm over the collar if maximum permissible tensile stress is 150 MPa. Assume E = 200 GPa.*

**Data**       :   $\phi$ = 16 mm ;  L = 1500 mm ; h = 100 mm ; $\sigma_{max}$ = 150 MPa ;  E = 200 GPa

                   as shown in Fig. 8.7.

**Required**  :  Weight W.

**Concept**   :  Standard formulae.

**Solution**   :  (i) Geometric properties :

$$A = \frac{\pi}{4}(16)^2 = 201.06 \ mm^2$$

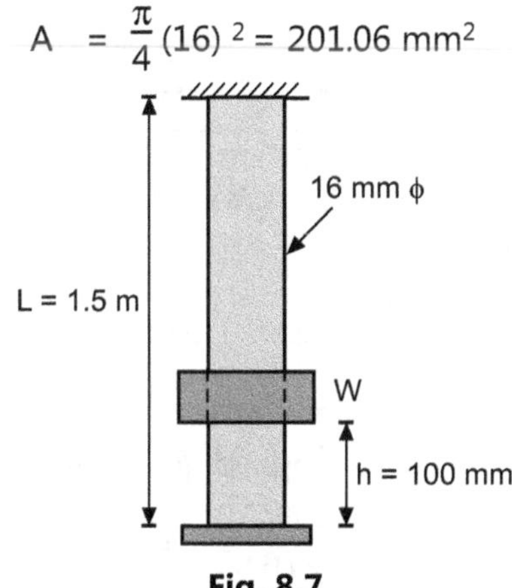


**Fig. 8.7**

(ii)   Maximum weight :

$$\sigma_{max} = \frac{W}{A} \pm \sqrt{\frac{2\,WhE}{AL} + \frac{W^2}{A^2}}$$

Let           $\dfrac{W}{A} = x$

$$150 = x \pm \sqrt{\frac{2x \times 100 \times 200 \times 10^3}{1500} + x^2}$$

$$150 = x \pm \sqrt{26.67 \times 10^3\,x + x^2}$$

$$(150 - x)^2 = 26.67 \times 10^3\,x + x^2$$

$$22500 - 300\,x + x^2 = 26.67 \times 10^3\,x + x^2$$

$$x = 0.834 = \frac{W}{A}$$

$\therefore$              $W = 0.834 \times 201.06$

                 $W = \mathbf{167.75 \ N}$

**Example 8.7 :** *A solid vertical prismatic steel bar of equilateral triangular section of side 25 mm is firmly fixed at top. A rigid collar is attached at the lower end at a distance of 600 mm from top. Compute the strain energy in each of the following cases :*

*(i)   When a pull of 10 kN is applied gradually.*
*(ii)  When a force of 8 kN is suddenly applied.*
*(iii) When a weight of 4 kN falls through 120 mm. Assume E = 210 GPa.*

**Data**      :  c/s of bar;  equilateral triangular section with
                 25 mm side ; L = 600 mm ; E = 210 GPa.

**Required**  :  Strain energy for different given cases.

**Concept**   :  Standard formulae.

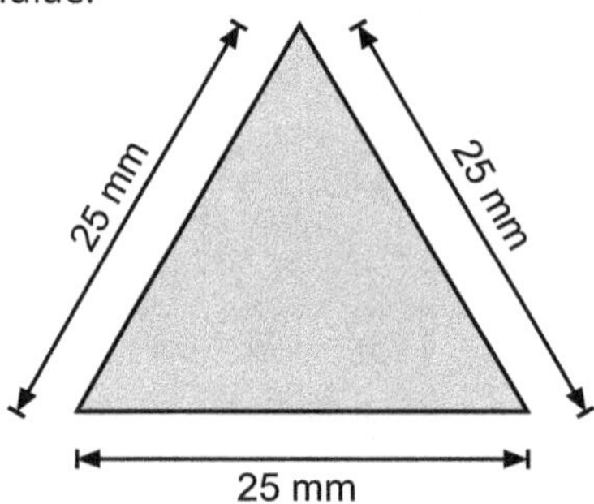


**Fig. 8.8 : c/s of bar**

**Solution**   :  (i) Geometric properties :

$$A = \frac{1}{2} \times \text{Base} \times \text{Height} = \frac{1}{2} \times 25 \times \left(\frac{25}{2} \times \tan 60\right)$$

$$= 270.63 \text{ mm}^2$$

(ii)   Strain energy, when pull of 10 kN is applied gradually :

$$\sigma_{max} = \frac{P}{A} = \frac{10 \times 10^3}{270.63} = 36.95 \text{ MPa}$$

$$U = \frac{\sigma_{max}^2}{2E} \times \text{Volume} = \frac{(36.95)^2}{2 \times 210 \times 10^3} \times 270.63 \times 600$$

$$= 527.85 \text{ N.mm}$$

(ii)   Strain energy, when a force of 8 kN is suddenly applied :

$$\sigma_{max} = \frac{2P}{A} = \frac{2 \times 8 \times 10^3}{270.63} = 59.12 \text{ MPa}$$

$$U = \frac{\sigma_{max}^2}{2E} \times \text{Volume} = \frac{(59.12)^2}{2 \times 210 \times 10^3} \times 270.63 \times 600$$

$$= \mathbf{1351.28 \text{ N.mm}}$$

(iii) When a weight of 4 kN falls through 120 mm,

$$\sigma_{max} = \frac{W}{A} \pm \sqrt{\frac{2\,WhE}{AL} + \frac{W^2}{A^2}}$$

$$= \frac{4 \times 10^3}{270.63} \pm \sqrt{\frac{2 \times 4 \times 10^3 \times 120 \times 210 \times 10^3}{270.63 \times 600} + \left[\frac{4 \times 10^3}{270.63}\right]^2}$$

$$= 14.78 \pm 1114.3 = \mathbf{1129.125 \text{ MPa}}$$

$$\text{Strain energy, } U = \frac{\sigma_{max}^2}{2E} \times \text{Volume}$$

$$= \frac{(1129.125)^2}{2 \times 210 \times 10^3} \times 270.63 \times 600$$

$$= \mathbf{492.90 \times 10^3 \ N.mm}$$

**Example 8.8 :** *A mass of 20 kg is dropped from a height of 1 m on to the centre of small rigid platform as shown in Fig. 8.9. The two steel rods supporting the platform are 25 mm × 50 mm in cross-section and 3 m long. If one half of the energy is effective in producing stress in the two rods, determine (i) the equivalent static load and (ii) the deflection of platform. Assume E = 200 GPa.*

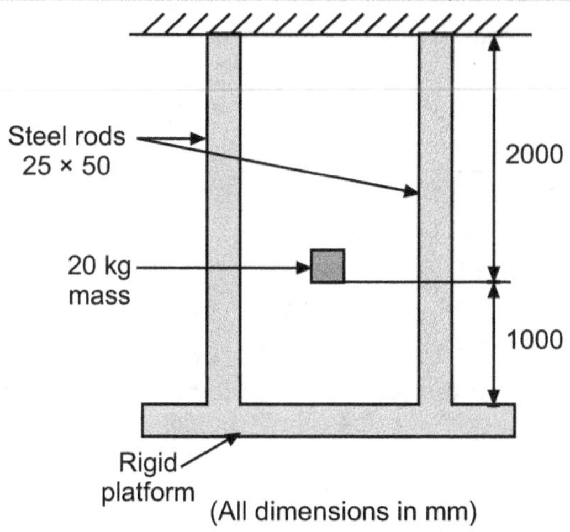


**Fig. 8.9**

| | | |
|---|---|---|
| **Data** | : | As shown in Fig. 8.9. |
| **Required** | : | Equivalent static load and deflection of platform. |
| **Concept** | : | Considering only half the energy effective in producing stress, write work equation. |
| **Solution** | : | (i) Geometric properties : Cross-sectional area = A = 25 × 50 = 1250 mm² |

Volume = A × L = 1250 × 3000 = 3.75 × 10⁶ mm³

(ii)   Work equation :

$$\frac{1}{2} \times W(h + \delta L) = 2\left(\frac{\sigma^2}{2E} \cdot \text{Volume}\right)$$

**Note :** Only half the energy is effective in producing stress.

Substituting
$$\delta L = \frac{\sigma L}{E}$$

$$\frac{1}{2} \times W\left(h + \frac{\sigma L}{E}\right) = 2\left(\frac{\sigma^2}{2E} \cdot \text{Volume}\right)$$

$$\frac{20 \times 9.81}{2}\left(1000 + \frac{\sigma \times 3000}{200 \times 10^3}\right) = 2\left(\frac{\sigma^2}{2 \times 200 \times 10^3} \times 3.75 \times 10^6\right)$$

$$98.1 (1000 + 0.015\ \sigma) = 18.75\ \sigma^2$$
$$5232 + 0.07848\ \sigma = \sigma^2$$

Solving, $\sigma = 72.37$ MPa.

(ii)  Deflection of platform :

Deflection of platform = Instantaneous elongation of rod

$$= \frac{\sigma L}{E}$$

$$= \frac{72.37 \times 3000}{200 \times 10^3}$$

$$= \textbf{1.085 mm}$$

(iii) Equivalent static load.

Let P = effective static load in kN

$$\frac{PL}{AE} = 1.085$$

$$\frac{P \times 10^3 \times 3000}{2 \times 1250 \times 200 \times 10^3} = 1.085$$

$$P = 180.83 \text{ kN}$$

$\therefore$ Actual static load $= 2 \times 180.83$

$$= \textbf{361.66 kN}$$

**Example 8.9 :** *A steel specimen 16 mm $\phi$ stretches by 0.12 mm over 150 mm length under an axial load of 35 kN. Calculate the strain energy stored in the specimen at this stage. If the load at the elastic limit for the specimen is 50 kN, calculate the elongation at elastic limit and the proof resilience.*

**Data**       :   $\phi = 16$ mm ;  for W = 35 kN; $\delta L = 0.12$ mm;
L = 150 mm ; for elastic limit W = 50 kN.

**Required**  :   Strain energy of bar for W = 35 kN; elongation at elastic limit; proof resilience.

**Concept**   :   Standard formula.

**Solution**  :   (i) Geometric properties :

$$A = \frac{\pi}{4}(16)^2 = 201.06 \text{ mm}^2$$

(ii)  Strain energy of bar for W = 35 kN

$$U = \frac{1}{2}W \cdot \delta L$$

$$= \frac{1}{2} \times 35 \times 10^3 \times 0.12$$

$$= 2100 \text{ N.mm}$$

$$= 2.1 \text{ N.m}$$

$$= \textbf{2.1 J}$$

(iii) Elongation at elastic limit.

Elongation due to 35 kN load = 0.12 mm

$\therefore$ Elongation due to 50 kN load $= 0.12 \times \dfrac{50}{35}$

$$= \textbf{0.171 mm}$$

(iv)        Proof resilience  = Maximum strain energy stored in the member at elastic limit

$$= \frac{1}{2} \cdot W \cdot \delta L$$

$$= \frac{1}{2} \times 50 \times 10^3 \times 0.171$$

$$= 4275 \text{ N.mm}$$

$$= \mathbf{4.275 \ N.m = 4.275 \ J}$$

**Example 8.10 :** *A uniform bar of cross-sectional area 500 mm$^2$ is 2.5 m long. Find the proof resilience and modulus of resilience, if the elastic limit for the bar material is 250 MPa. Also find maximum value of suddenly applied load that the member can carry.*

*Assume = E = 200 GPa.*

**Data**       :  A = 500 mm$^2$ ; L = 2.5 m = 2500 mm ; $F_y$ = 250 MPa ; E = 200 GPa.

**Required**  :  Proof resilience; Modulus of resilience and suddenly applied load.

**Concept**  :  Standard formulae.

**Solution**  :  (i) Proof resilience,

$$U_{max} = \frac{\sigma_{max}^2}{2E} \times \text{Volume}$$

$$= \frac{(250)^2}{2 \times 200 \times 10^3} (500 \times 2500)$$

$$= 195312.5 \text{ N.mm}$$

$$= 195.312 \text{ N.m}$$

$$= 195.312 \text{ J}$$

(ii)        Modulus of resilience  = Maximum strain energy per unit volume

$$= \frac{\sigma_{max}^2}{2E}$$

$$= \frac{250^2}{2 \times 200 \times 10^3}$$

$$= 0.156 \text{ MPa}$$

(iii) Maximum suddenly applied load,

$$\sigma_{max} = \frac{2P}{A}$$

$$250 = \frac{2P}{500}$$

$$\therefore \qquad P = 62500 \text{ N}$$

$$= 62.5 \text{ kN}$$

**Example 8.11 :** *A uniform rod AB is made of brass for which yield stress $F_y$ = 125 MPa and E = 105 GPa. Collar 'D' moves along the rod and has a speed of 3 m/s as it strikes a small plate attached to end B of the rod. Using factor of safety of 4, determine the largest allowable mass of collar if the* *rod is not to be permanently deformed. Will the answer be different, if rod is held vertical and mass is moving downward ? Why ?*

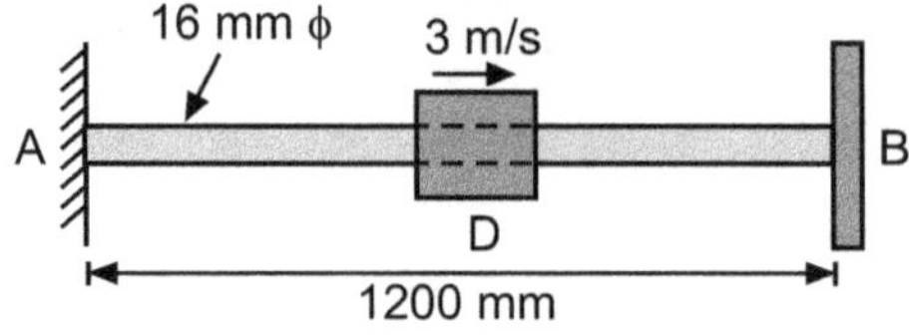


**Fig. 8.10**

**Data**        :   $F_y$ = 125 MPa;  E = 105 GPa;  V = 3 m/s;  Factor of safety = 4.

**Required**   :   Mass of collar.

**Concept**    :   Kinetic energy of collar will get converted to strain energy of rod. If the rod is held vertically, the answer will be different because then the motion of collar is with uniform acceleration due to gravity.

**Solution**   :   (i) K.E. of collar :

Let mass of collar be 'm' kg.

$$\text{K.E.} = \frac{1}{2}mV^2$$

$$= \frac{1}{2}m \times 3^2$$

$$= 4.5 \text{ m N.m}$$

(ii)    Strain energy of rod,    $U = \dfrac{\sigma_{max}^2}{2E} \times \text{Volume}$

with factor of safety   =   4 ;

$$\sigma_{max} = \frac{F_y}{4} = \frac{125}{4} = 31.25 \text{ MPa}$$

∴                    $U = \dfrac{(31.25)^2}{2 \times 105 \times 10^3} \times \dfrac{\pi}{4}(16)^2 \times 1200$

$$U = 1121.986 \text{ N.mm}$$

(iii) Mass of collar :

Equating kinetic energy to strain energy, we get

$$4.5 \text{ m} = 1121.98 \times 10^{-3}$$

$$m = \mathbf{0.249 \text{ kg}}$$

---

**Example 8.12 :** *A wagon weighing 20 kN is attached to a wire rope and is moving at the speed of 5.4 kmph. The rope suddenly jams and wagon is brought to rest. If length of rope is 50 m and diameter is 36 mm, find maximum instantaneous stress and elongation of rope assuming E = 200 GPa.*

**Data**        :   W = 20 kN; V = 5.4 kmph = 1.5 m/s; L = 50 m ; φ = 36 mm; E = 200 GPa.

---

**Required** : Maximum instantaneous stress and elongation of rope.

**Concept** : Kinetic energy of wagon will be converted to strain energy of rope.

**Solution** : (i) Kinetic energy of wagon,

$$K.E. = \frac{1}{2}mV^2$$

$$= \frac{1}{2}\left(\frac{20 \times 10^3}{9.81}\right) \times (1.5)^2$$

$$= 2293.58 \text{ Nm}$$

$$= 2293.58 \times 10^3 \text{ N.mm}$$

(ii)  Strain energy of rope,  $U = \dfrac{\sigma_{max}^2}{2\,E} \times \text{Volume}$

$$= \frac{\sigma_{max}^2}{2 \times 200 \times 10^3}\left(\frac{\pi}{4}(36)^2 \times 50 \times 10^3\right)$$

$$= 127.23\,\sigma_{max}^2$$

(iii) Maximum instantaneous stress :

Equating kinetic energy and strain energy, we get

$$2293.58 \times 10^3 = 127.23\,\sigma_{max}^2$$

$$\sigma_{max} = \textbf{134.26 MPa}$$

(iv) Maximum instantaneous elongation,

$$\delta L_{max} = \frac{\sigma_{max} \cdot L}{E} = \frac{134.26 \times 50 \times 10^3}{200 \times 10^3}$$

$$= \textbf{33.56 mm}$$

---

**Example 8.13 :** *A lift weighing 20 kN is to function at a speed of 1 m/s. Length of rope connecting lift is 40 m. If yield stress for rope material is 300 MPa, find suitable diameter of rope assuming factor of safety of 2. Assume E = 200 GPa.*

**Data** : W = 20 kN; V = 1 m/s; L = 40 m ; $F_y$ = 300 MPa;

Factor of safety = 2;  E = 200 GPa.

**Required** : Diameter of rope.

**Concept** : Same as Example 8.12. In the following analysis, static stress due to self weight of lift is neglected. However, for the exact analysis, see Example   No. 8.14.

**Solution** : (i) Kinetic energy of lift

$$K.E. = \frac{1}{2}mV^2$$

$$= \frac{1}{2}\left(\frac{20 \times 10^3}{9.81}\right) \times (1)^2$$

$$= 1019.36 \text{ N.m}$$

$$= 1019.36 \times 10^3 \text{ N.mm}$$

(ii)  Strain energy of rope,    $U = \dfrac{\sigma_{max}^2}{2E} \cdot \text{Volume}$

Maximum safe stress  $= \sigma_{max} = \dfrac{\text{Yield stress}}{\text{Factor of safety}}$

$\therefore \qquad \sigma_{max} = \dfrac{300}{2} = 150 \text{ MPa}$

$\therefore \qquad U = \dfrac{(150)^2}{2 \times 200 \times 10^3}\left(\dfrac{\pi}{4}\,(\phi)^2 \times 40 \times 10^3\right)$

$$= 1767.14\ \phi^2$$

(iii) Diameter of rope :

Equating kinetic energy and strain energy, we get

$$1019.36 \times 10^3 = 1761.14\ \phi^2$$

$\therefore \qquad\qquad \phi = \mathbf{24\ mm}$

---

**Example 8.14 :** *A crane chain lowers a load of 8 kN at uniform rate of 0.6 m/s. When length of chain unwound is 10 m, it suddenly gets jammed. Estimate the instantaneous stress induced in it due to the sudden stoppage and the maximum elongation, if each link is 'O' shaped and made of 10 mm $\phi$ steel rod. Also find impulsive force on each link. Assume E = 200 GPa.*

**Data**      :  W = 8 kN;  V = 0.6 m/s;  L = 10 m;  $\phi$ = 10 mm for O shaped link.

**Required**  :  Maximum instantaneous stress ; elongation and impulsive force.

**Concept**   :  Maximum instantaneous stress = Stress due to impulsive force + Stress due to static load.

**Solution**  :  (i) Geometric properties :

Cross-sectional area of each O-shaped link

$$= 2 \times \dfrac{\pi}{4} \times (10)^2$$

$$= 157.08 \text{ mm}^2$$

(ii) Kinetic energy,    $\text{K.E.} = \dfrac{1}{2}\,m \cdot V^2$

$$\text{K.E.} = \dfrac{1}{2}\left(\dfrac{8 \times 10^3}{9.81}\right) \times (0.6)^2$$

$$= 146.79 \text{ N.m}$$

$$= 146.79 \times 10^3 \text{ N.mm}$$

(iii) Strain energy,

$$U = \frac{\sigma^2}{2E} \cdot \text{Volume}$$

$$= \frac{\sigma^2}{2 \times 200 \times 10^3} \times (157.08 \times 10 \times 10^3)$$

$$U = 3.927 \, \sigma^2$$

(iv) Instantaneous stress :

Equating kinetic energy to strain energy, we get

$$146.79 \times 10^3 = 3.927 \, \sigma^2$$

$$\sigma = 193.34 \text{ MPa} \qquad\qquad \text{(Stress due to impulse)}$$

In addition to above impulsive stress, static stress due to load of 8 kN

$$= \frac{8 \times 10^3}{157.08} = 50.93 \text{ MPa}$$

Maximum instantaneous stress,

$$\sigma_{max} = \text{Stress due to impulse} + \text{Static stress}$$

$$= 193.34 + 50.93$$

$$= \mathbf{244.27 \text{ MPa}}$$

(v)  Maximum instantaneous elongation,

$$\delta L = \sigma_{max} \cdot \frac{L}{E}$$

$$= \frac{244.27 \times 10 \times 10^3}{200 \times 10^3}$$

$$= \mathbf{12.21 \text{ mm}}$$

(vi) Impulsive force :

$$\text{Impulsive force} = F = \sigma_{max} \times A$$

$$= 244.27 \times 157.08$$

$$= 38.37 \times 10^3 \text{ N}$$

$$= \mathbf{38.37 \text{ kN}}$$

**Example 8.15 :** *A load P is supported at B by two rods of same material and the same cross-sectional area A as shown in Fig. 8.11. Determine the strain energy of system. Let 'E' be the modulus of elasticity.*

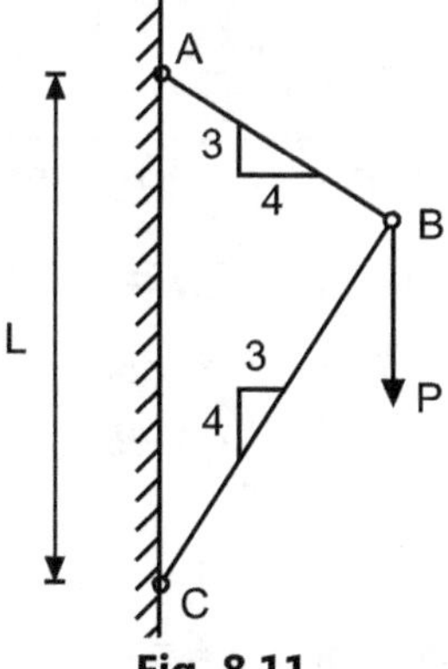


**Fig. 8.11**

**Data** : As shown in Fig. 8.11.

**Required** : Strain energy of system.

**Concept** : Analyse joint P and get forces in members AB and BC and then find total strain energy of system.

**Solution** : (i) Force in members :

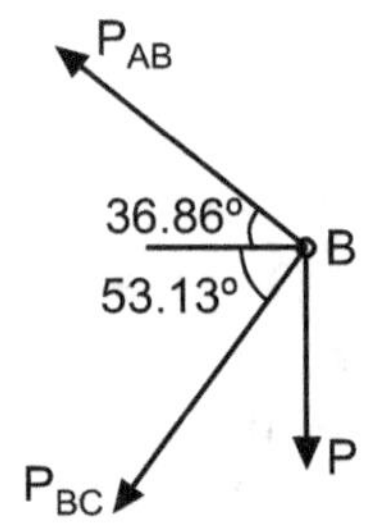


**Fig. 8.12 : FBD of joint B**

$$\frac{P}{\sin (90)} = \frac{P_{AB}}{\sin (36.86)} = \frac{P_{BC}}{\sin (233.14)}$$

$$P_{AB} = 0.6\,P$$

$$P_{BC} = -0.8\,P = 0.8\,P \ \ ... \text{(Compressive)}$$

(ii) Strain energy of system :

$$U = \left(\frac{\sigma^2}{2E} \times \text{Volume}\right)_{AB} + \left(\frac{\sigma^2}{2E} \times \text{Volume}\right)_{BC}$$

where    $\sigma_{AB} = \dfrac{0.6\,P}{A}$ and $\sigma_{BC} = \dfrac{0.8\,P}{A}$

By geometry,

$$\frac{L}{\sin (90)} = \frac{L_{AB}}{\sin (36.86)} = \frac{L_{BC}}{\sin (53.13)}$$

$\therefore$    $L_{AB} = 0.6\,L$ and $L_{BC} = 0.8\,L$

$\therefore$  Volume of AB $= A \times (0.6\,L) = 0.6\,AL$

and  Volume of BC $= A \times (0.8\,L) = 0.8\,AL$

Substituting,  $U = \left(\dfrac{0.6\,P}{A}\right)^2 \times \dfrac{0.6\,AL}{2E} + \left(\dfrac{0.8\,P}{A}\right)^2 \times \dfrac{0.8\,AL}{2E}$

$$U = 0.364\,\frac{P^2 L}{AE}$$

**Example 8.16 :** *Show that for a member subjected to principal stresses $\sigma_1$ and $\sigma_2$, the strain energy per unit volume is given by $\dfrac{1}{2E}\left(\sigma_1^2 + \sigma_2^2 - 2\,\mu\,\sigma_1\,\sigma_2\right)$*

*where    $E$ = Young's modulus and*

*      $\mu$ = Poisson's ratio*

**Data** : Principal stresses are $\sigma_1$ and $\sigma_2$.

**Required** : Strain energy per unit volume.

**Concept** : Generalised Hook's law and $U = \dfrac{1}{2}\sigma \cdot E$

**Solution** : (i) Principal strains :

$$\in_1 = \frac{1}{E}(\sigma_1 - \mu\,\sigma_2)$$

$$\in_2 = \frac{1}{E}(\sigma_2 - \mu\,\sigma_1)$$

(ii) Strain energy per unit volume,

$$U = \frac{1}{2}\sigma_1\in_1 + \frac{1}{2}\sigma_2\in_2$$

$$= \frac{1}{2}\sigma_1\left[\frac{1}{E}(\sigma_1 - \mu\,\sigma_2)\right] + \frac{1}{2}\sigma_2\left[\frac{1}{E}(\sigma_2 - \mu\,\sigma_1)\right]$$

$$U = \frac{1}{2E}\left[\sigma_1^2 + \sigma_2^2 - 2\,\mu\,\sigma_1\,\sigma_2\right]$$

**Example 8.17 :** *Determine the diameter of aluminium shaft designed to store same amount of strain energy per unit volume as that of 50 mm $\phi$ steel bar of same length, when both shafts are subjected to same axial load. Take $E_S$ = 200 GPa and $E_A$ = 67 GPa.*

*Also find the ratio of stresses developed in two bars.*

**Data** : Diameter of steel shaft = 50 mm ; $E_S$ = 200 GPa ; $E_A$ = 67 GPa ; $U_A = U_S$

**Required** : Diameter of aluminium shaft and ratio of stresses developed.

**Concept** : Equate strain energy of aluminium and steel shaft and get relation between stresses and then find diameter of aluminium shaft.

**Solution** : (i) Ratio of stresses :

$$U_A = U_S \text{ for unit volume}$$

$$\therefore \quad \left(\frac{\sigma_{max}^2}{2E}\right)_A = \left(\frac{\sigma_{max}^2}{2E}\right)_S$$

$$\frac{\left(\sigma_{max}^2\right)_A}{2\times 67\times 10^3} = \frac{\left(\sigma_{max}^2\right)_S}{2\times 200\times 10^3}$$

$$(\sigma_{max})_A = (0.578)\,(\sigma_{max})_S$$

$$\therefore \quad \frac{(\sigma_{max})_A}{(\sigma_{max})_S} = 0.578$$

OR

$$\frac{(\sigma_{max})_S}{(\sigma_{max})_A} = 1.727$$

(ii) Diameter of aluminium shaft :

$$\left(\frac{P}{A}\right)_A = 0.578\left(\frac{P}{A}\right)_S \qquad\qquad (\because P_A = P_S)$$

$$\therefore \quad \frac{1}{\frac{\pi}{4}(\phi)_A^2} = 0.578\left(\frac{1}{\frac{\pi}{4}(50)^2}\right)$$

$$\therefore \quad \phi_A = \textbf{65.76 mm}$$

**Example 8.18 :** *A copper rod of 30 mm diameter is enclosed in a steel tube having 45 mm internal diameter and 5 mm thickness. The length of composite member is 2 m. It is fixed at top and provided with a rigid collar at bottom. A body of mass 50 kg is allowed to slide down freely through a height (h). If maximum instantaneous stress developed in copper is not to exceed 75 MPa, find height and elongation of composite bar. Take $E_s$ = 200 GPa and $E_c$ = 120 GPa.*

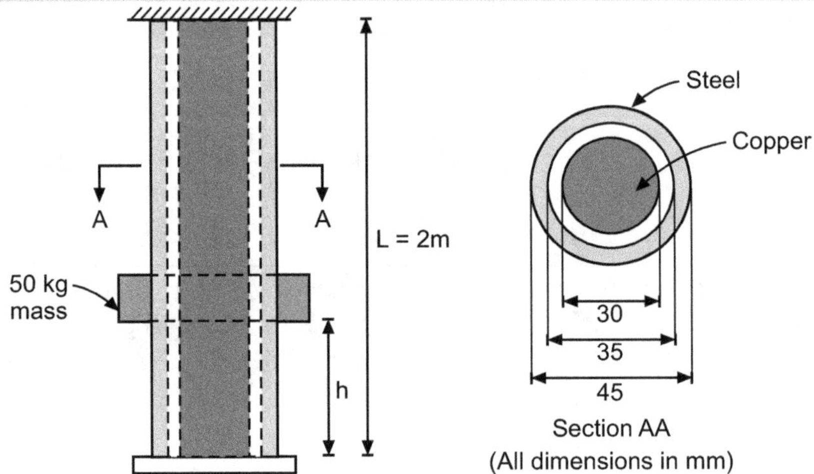


**Fig. 8.13**

**Data**        :   As shown in Fig. 8.13.

**Required**    :   h and $\delta L$.

**Concept**     :   Use basic work equation along with compatibility as $(\delta L)_s = (\delta L)_c$.

**Solution**    :   (i) Geometric properties :

$$A_c = \frac{\pi}{4}(30)^2 = 706.85 \text{ mm}^2$$

$$A_s = \frac{\pi}{4}(45^2 - 35^2) = 628.32 \text{ mm}^2$$

(ii)   Work equation :

$$W(h + \delta L) = \left(\frac{\sigma_{max}^2}{2E} \times \text{Volume}\right)_c + \left(\frac{\sigma_{max}^2}{2E} \times \text{Volume}\right)_s$$

We have,        $(\delta L)_c = (\delta L)_s$

$\therefore$        $\sigma_s = \dfrac{E_s}{E_c} \times \sigma_c$

$$= \frac{200}{120} \times 75$$

$$= 125 \text{ MPa}$$

Also,        $W = 50 \text{ kg} = 50 \times 9.81 = 490.5 \text{ N}$

Instantaneous elongation $\quad = \delta L \;=\; \left(\dfrac{\sigma L}{E}\right)_c = \left(\dfrac{\sigma L}{E}\right)_s$

$$= \dfrac{75 \times 2000}{120 \times 10^3}$$

$$= \mathbf{1.25\ mm}$$

Substituting,

$$490.5\,(h + 1.25) = \dfrac{(75)^2}{2 \times 120 \times 10^3} \times 706.85 \times 2000 + \dfrac{(125)^2}{2 \times 200 \times 10^3} \times 628.32 \times 2000$$

$$490.5\,(h + 1.25) = 82.22 \times 10^3$$

$$\therefore \qquad\qquad h = \mathbf{166.37\ mm}$$

**Example 8.19 :** *A copper bar is enclosed in a steel tube 36 mm external diameter and 4 mm thickness. A composite bar is held vertically fixed at top and provided with a collar at bottom. A weight of 2.5 kN falls freely through height of 20 mm. Length of composite section is 1.5 m. Find diameter of copper bar if maximum instantaneous stress developed in steel is 150 MPa. Assume $E_c = 100$ GPa ; $E_s = 200$ GPa.*

**Data**          :   As shown in Fig. 8.14.

**Required**   :   Diameter of copper bar and maximum elongation of composite section.

**Concept**    :   Same as Example 8.18.

**Solution**   :

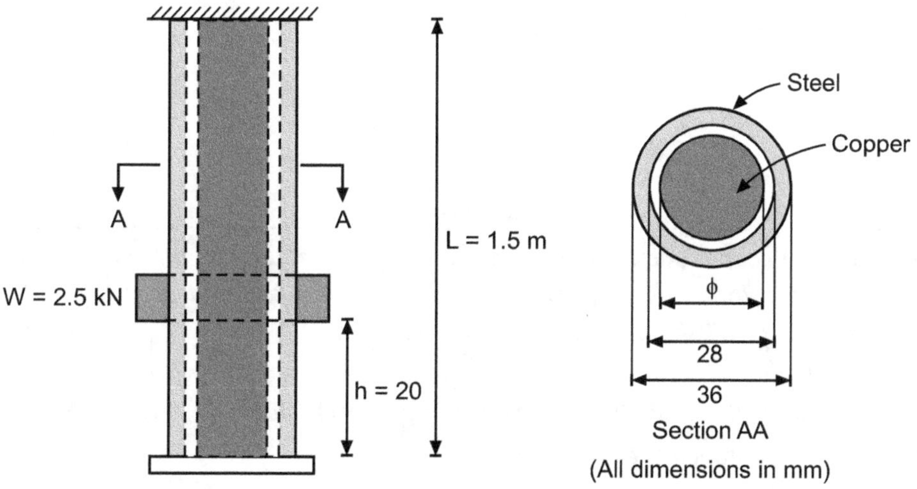


**Fig. 8.14**

(i)    Geometric properties :

$$A_s = \dfrac{\pi}{4}\,[(36)^2 - (28)^2] = 402.12\ mm^2$$

$$A_c = \text{Unknown}$$

(ii)   Work equation :

$$W (h + \delta L) \;=\; \left(\frac{\sigma^2}{2\,E} \cdot \text{Volume}\right)_c + \left(\frac{\sigma^2}{2\,E} \cdot \text{Volume}\right)_s$$

We have,

$$(\delta L)_c \;=\; (\delta L)_s$$

$$\left(\frac{\sigma L}{E}\right)_c \;=\; \left(\frac{\sigma L}{E}\right)_s$$

$$\sigma_c \;=\; \frac{E_c}{E_s} \cdot \sigma_s = \frac{100}{200} \cdot \sigma_s$$

$$\sigma_c \;=\; 0.5\,\sigma_s$$

$$=\; 0.5 \times 150$$

$$=\; 75 \text{ MPa}$$

$$W (h + \delta L) \;=\; \frac{(75)^2}{2 \times 100 \times 10^3} \times A_c \times 1500 + \frac{(150)^2}{2 \times 200 \times 10^3}(402.12 \times 1500)$$

$$W (h + \delta L) \;=\; 42.18\, A_c + 33928.875$$

Substituting,

$$W \;=\; 2.5 \text{ kN} = 2500 \text{ N}$$

$$h \;=\; 20 \text{ mm}$$

$$\delta L \;=\; \left(\frac{\sigma L}{E}\right)_s = \frac{150 \times 1500}{200 \times 10^3}$$

$$=\; 1.125 \text{ mm}$$

$\therefore \qquad 2500\,(20 + 1.125) \;=\; 42.18\, A_c + 33928.875$

$$A_c \;=\; 447.69 \text{ mm}^2$$

$$\frac{\pi}{4}(\phi)^2 \;=\; 447.69$$

$\therefore \qquad\qquad\qquad\qquad \phi \;=\; \textbf{23.87 mm}$

---

**Example 8.20 :** *A copper bar 20 mm $\phi$ is enclosed in a steel tube 30 mm external diameter and 3 mm thickness. The composite bar is held vertically, fixed at top and provided with a collar at bottom. A weight of 2 kN falls freely through height of 20 mm.*
*If length of bar is 2 m, find :*

*(i)   Maximum instantaneous stress developed in each material.*

*(ii)   Maximum instantaneous elongation.*

*Assume $E_s$ = 200 GPa ; $E_c$ = 110 GPa.*

**Data**        :   As shown in Fig. 8.15.

**Required**   :   $\sigma_{max}$ for copper and steel, $\delta L$.

**Concept**   :   Same as Example 8.18.

**Solution**   :

---

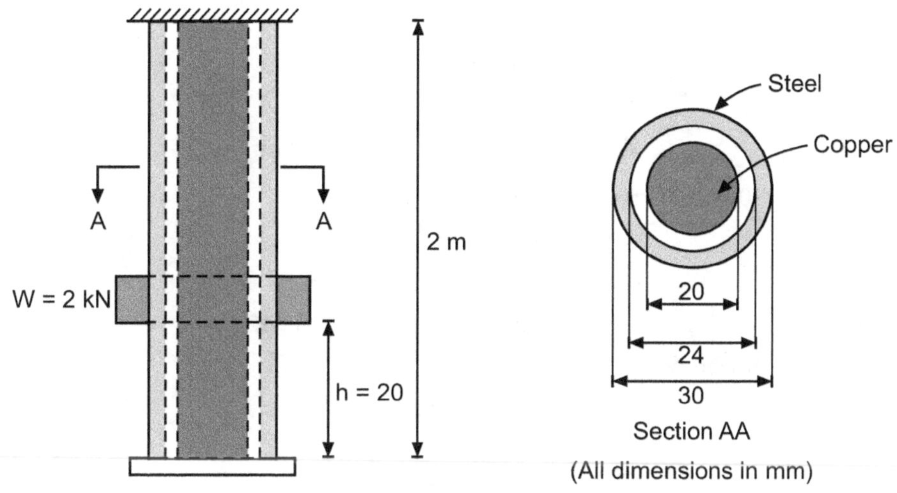



**Fig. 8.15**

(i)　Geometric properties :　$A_C = \dfrac{\pi}{4}(20)^2 = 314.16 \text{ mm}^2$

$$A_S = \frac{\pi}{4}[(30)^2 - (24)^2] = 254.47 \text{ mm}^2$$

(ii)　Work equation :

$$W(h + \delta L) = U_C + U_S$$

$$= \left[\frac{\sigma_{max}^2}{2E} \times \text{Volume}\right]_C + \left[\frac{\sigma_{max}^2}{2E} \times \text{Volume}\right]_S$$

We have,　　　　　$(\delta L)_C = (\delta L)_S$

$$\left(\frac{\sigma L}{E}\right)_C = \left(\frac{\sigma L}{E}\right)_S$$

$$\frac{\sigma_C}{E_C} = \frac{\sigma_S}{E_S}$$

$$\therefore \qquad \sigma_C = \frac{E_C}{E_S} \cdot \sigma_S$$

$$= \frac{110}{200} \cdot \sigma_S$$

$$\sigma_C = 0.55\,\sigma_S$$

$$\therefore \quad W(h + \delta L) = \frac{(0.55\,\sigma_S)^2}{2 \times 110 \times 10^3} \times 314.16 \times 2000 + \frac{\sigma_S^2}{2 \times 200 \times 10^3} \times 254.47 \times 2000$$

$$\therefore \quad W(h + \delta L) = 2.136\,\sigma_S^2$$

Substituting for　　　　　$\delta L = \dfrac{\sigma_S L_S}{E_S}$

$$= \frac{\sigma_S \times 2000}{200 \times 10^3}$$

$$= 0.01\,\sigma_S$$

and $\qquad W = 2\text{ kN} = 2000\text{ N}\,;\ h = 20\text{ mm}$

$$2000\,(20 + 0.01\,\sigma_S) = 2.136\,\sigma_S^2$$

Solving, $\qquad \sigma_S = \mathbf{141.6\ MPa}$

$$\sigma_C = 0.55 \times \sigma_S$$

$$= 0.55 \times 141.6 = \mathbf{77.88\ MPa}$$

(iii) Maximum elongation δL :

$$\delta L = \left(\frac{\sigma L}{E}\right)_C = \left(\frac{\sigma L}{E}\right)_S$$

$$= \frac{77.88 \times 2000}{110 \times 10^3}$$

$$= \mathbf{1.416\ mm}$$

**Example 8.21 :** *A vertical steel rod 1.5 m long is fixed at top and provided with collar at bottom. The upper 900 mm length of bar is 28 mm $\phi$, while the lower 600 mm bar is 16 mm $\phi$. A weight of magnitude 150 N falls freely through a height of 60 mm. Find*

*(i)    Maximum instantaneous stress,*

*(ii)   Maximum elongation,*

*(iii)  Total strain energy stored.*

*Assume E = 200 GPa*

**Data**          :    As shown in Fig. 8.16.

**Required**   :    $\sigma_{max}$ , $\delta L_{max}$ and U

**Concept**    :    Use of equation (8.7) where,

$$\delta_{st} = \left(\frac{PL}{AE}\right)_1 + \left(\frac{PL}{AE}\right)_2$$

**Solution**   :    (i) Geometric properties :

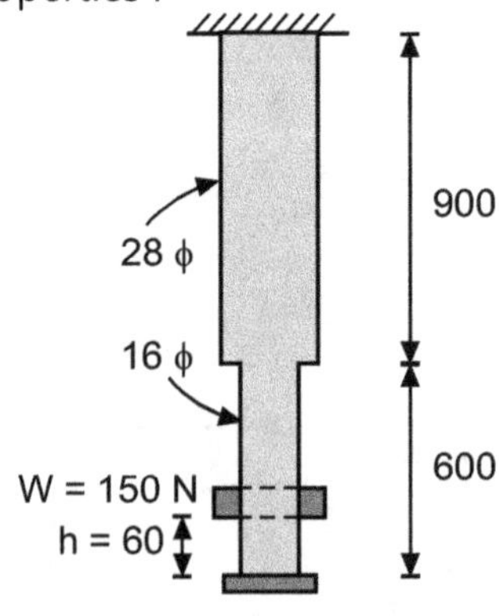


(All dimensions in mm)

**Fig. 8.16**

Let,
$$A_1 = \frac{\pi}{4}(28)^2 = 615.75 \text{ mm}^2$$

$$A_2 = \frac{\pi}{4}(16)^2 = 201.06 \text{ mm}^2$$

(ii)  Maximum instantaneous stress,

$$\sigma_{max} = \frac{W}{A}\left[1 \pm \sqrt{1 + \frac{2h}{\delta_{st}}}\right]$$

where
$$\delta_{st} = \left(\frac{PL}{AE}\right)_1 + \left(\frac{PL}{AE}\right)_2 = \left[\frac{150 \times 900}{615.75} + \frac{150 \times 600}{201.06}\right] \times \frac{1}{200 \times 10^3}$$

$$= 3.33 \times 10^{-3} \text{ mm}$$

$$\therefore \quad \sigma_{max} = \frac{150}{201.06}\left[1 \pm \sqrt{1 + \frac{2 \times 60}{3.33 \times 10^{-3}}}\right] = \mathbf{142.28 \text{ MPa}}$$

**Note :** Maximum stress occurs in the portion of relatively smaller area.

(iii)  Maximum instantaneous elongation :

We have,
$$\sigma_1 A_1 = \sigma_2 A_2$$

$$\sigma_1 \times 615.75 = 142.28 \times 201.06$$

$$\sigma_1 = 46.46 \text{ MPa}$$

$$\delta L_{max} = \frac{1}{E}(\sigma_1 L_1 + \sigma_2 L_2)$$

$$= \frac{1}{200 \times 10^3}(46.46 \times 900 + 142.28 \times 600)$$

$$= \mathbf{0.6359 \text{ mm}}$$

(iv) Total strain energy U :
$$U = W(h + \delta L_{max})$$

$$= 150(60 + 0.6359)$$

$$= 9095.3 \text{ N.mm}$$

$$= \mathbf{9.09 \text{ J}}$$

**Example 8.22 :** *A hammer of weight 75 N falls freely through a distance of 100 mm on a bar as shown in Fig. 8.17. Assuming E = 200 GPa, find instantaneous stress developed in bar at top and bottom.*

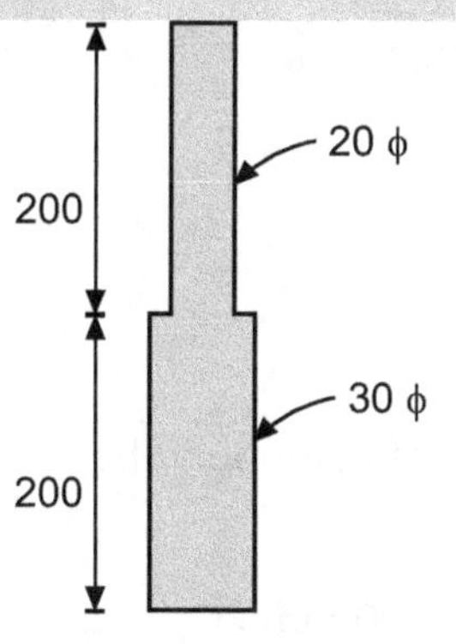


(All dimensions in mm)

**Fig. 8.17**

**Data :** W = 75 N ; h = 100 mm ;
E = 200 GPa

**Required :** Instantaneous stress at top and bottom.

**Concept :** Same as Example 8.21.

**Solution :** (i) Geometric properties :

$$A_1 \;=\; \frac{\pi}{4}(20)^2 = 314.16 \text{ mm}^2;$$

$$A_2 \;=\; \frac{\pi}{4}(30)^2 = 706.86 \text{ mm}^2$$

(ii)  Stresses :

$$\sigma_{max} \;=\; \sigma_1 = \frac{W}{A}\left[1 + \sqrt{1 + \frac{2\,h}{\delta_{st}}}\right] \quad \{\textbf{Note : } \sigma_1 > \sigma_2\}$$

where

$$\delta_{st} \;=\; \left(\frac{WL}{AE}\right)_1 + \left(\frac{WL}{AE}\right)_2$$

$$=\; \frac{75}{200 \times 10^3}\left[\frac{200}{314.16} + \frac{200}{706.86}\right]$$

$$=\; 3.448 \times 10^{-4}$$

$$\therefore \qquad \sigma_{max} = \sigma_1 \;=\; \frac{75}{314.16}\left[1 + \sqrt{1 + \frac{2 \times 100}{3.448 \times 10^{-4}}}\right]$$

$$\sigma_1 \;=\; \textbf{182 MPa}$$

Also $\sigma_1 A_1$

$$=\; \sigma_2 A_2$$

$$182 \times 314.16 \;=\; \sigma_2 \times 706.86$$

$$\therefore \qquad \sigma_2 \;=\; \textbf{80.91 MPa}$$

---

**Example 8.23 :** *A steel bar 4 m long has details as shown in Fig. 8.18. This bar is given an axial blow transmitting a shock energy of 100 Nm. Calculate the maximum instantaneous stress induced and maximum instantaneous elongation of the bar. E = 210 GPa.*

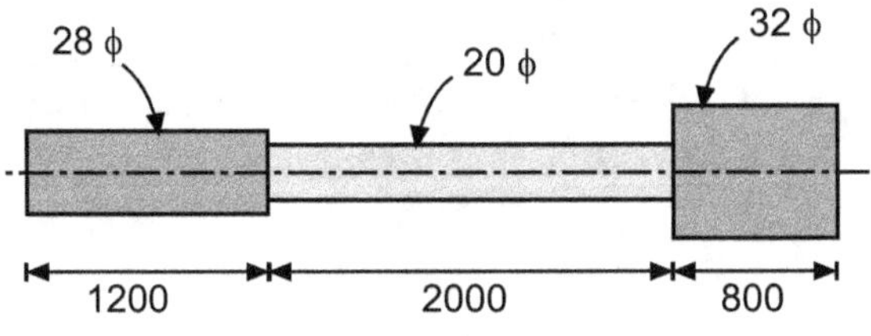


(All dimensions in mm)

**Fig. 8.18**

**Data**       :  Shock energy = 100 N.m ;  E = 210 GPa.

**Required**   :  Maximum instantaneous stress and elongation.

**Concept**    :  Shock energy shall be equated to strain energy of compound bar.

**Solution**   :  (i) Geometric properties :

$$A_1 \;=\; \frac{\pi}{4}(28)^2 = 615.75 \text{ mm}^2; \quad L_1 = 1200 \text{ mm}$$

$$\therefore \qquad \text{Volume}_1 \;=\; A_1 \times L_1 = 615.75 \times 1200 = 738.9 \times 10^3 \text{ mm}^3$$

---

$$A_2 = \frac{\pi}{4}(20)^2 = 314.16 \text{ mm}^2 \,; L_2 = 2000 \text{ mm}$$

$$\text{Volume}_2 = A_2 \times L_2 = 314.16 \times 2000 = 628.32 \times 10^3 \text{ mm}^3$$

$$A_3 = \frac{\pi}{4}(32)^2 = 804.25 \text{ mm}^2 \,; L_3 = 800 \text{ mm}$$

$$\text{Volume}_3 = A_3 \times L_3 = 804.25 \times 800 = 643.39 \times 10^3 \text{ mm}^3$$

(ii)   Instantaneous stress :

$$U = \left(\frac{\sigma^2}{2E} \cdot \text{Volume}\right)_1 + \left(\frac{\sigma^2}{2E} \cdot \text{Volume}\right)_2 + \left(\frac{\sigma^2}{2E} \cdot \text{Volume}\right)_3$$

We have $\qquad \sigma_1 A_1 = \sigma_2 A_2 = \sigma_3 A_3$

$$\sigma_1 \times 615.75 = \sigma_2 \times 314.16 = \sigma_3 \times 804.25$$

$\therefore \qquad \sigma_1 = 0.51\,\sigma_2$ and $\sigma_3 = 0.39\,\sigma_2$ $\qquad\qquad$ ($\because \sigma_2$ = Maximum stress)

Substituting,

$$100 \times 10^3 = \frac{1}{2E}[(0.51\,\sigma_2)^2 \times 738.9 \times 10^3 + \sigma_2^2 \times 628.32 \times 10^3$$

$$+ (0.39\,\sigma_2)^2 \times 643.39 \times 10^3]$$

$$100 \times 10^3 = 459.18 \times 10^3 \cdot \frac{\sigma_2^2}{E} = \frac{459.18 \times 10^3}{210 \times 10^3} \cdot \sigma_2^2$$

$\therefore \qquad\qquad \sigma_2 = $ **213.85 MPa**

$\therefore \qquad\qquad \sigma_1 = $ 109.06 MPa and $\sigma_3 = 83.4$ MPa

(iii) Instantaneous elongation,

$$\delta L = \delta L_1 + \delta L_2 + \delta L_3$$

$$= \left(\frac{\sigma L}{E}\right)_1 + \left(\frac{\sigma L}{E}\right)_2 + \left(\frac{\sigma L}{E}\right)_3$$

$$= \frac{1}{E}[\sigma_1 L_1 + \sigma_2 L_2 + \sigma_3 L_3]$$

$$= \frac{1}{210 \times 10^3}[109.06 \times 1200 + 213.85 \times 2000 + 83.4 \times 800]$$

$$= \textbf{2.977 mm}$$

**Example 8.24 :** *Two bars A and B of circular cross-section and of the same material have dimensions as shown in Fig. 8.19. An axial blow is given to 'A', which produces maximum instantaneous stress of 100 MPa in it.*

   *(i)    Calculate the maximum instantaneous stress produced by same axial blow given to 'B' assuming $U_A = U_B$.*

   *(ii)   If each bar is stressed to elastic limit, calculate the ratio of resilience of 'A' to that of 'B'.*

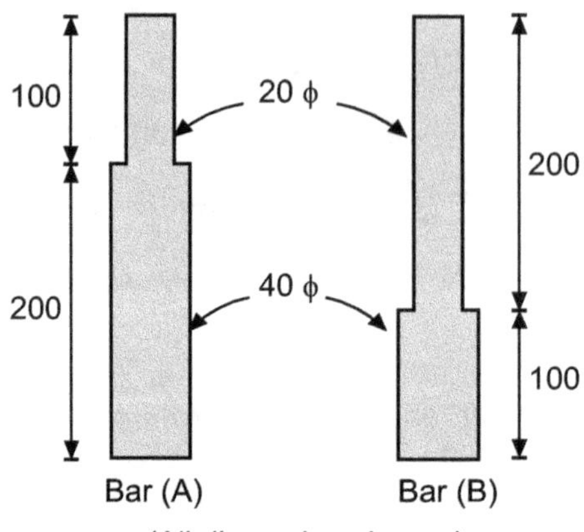


(All dimensions in mm)

**Fig. 8.19**

**Data**        :   As shown in Fig. 8.19.

**Required**    :   $\sigma_{max}$ for bar B and ratio of resilience of A to B.

**Concept**     :   Standard formulae.

**Solution**    :   (i) Geometric properties :

Let $A_1$ and $A_2$ be the cross-sectional areas of bar 'A' for 20 mm ϕ and 40 mm ϕ components respectively. $A_3$ and $A_4$ be the cross-sectional areas of bar 'B' for 20 mm ϕ and 40 mm ϕ components respectively.

$$\therefore \qquad A_1 = \frac{\pi}{4}(20)^2 = 314.16 \text{ mm}^2 = A_3$$

$$A_2 = \frac{\pi}{4}(40)^2 = 1256.64 \text{ mm}^2 = A_4$$

$V_1$ and $V_2$ = Volumes of bar 'A' for components of 20 mm ϕ and 40 mm ϕ respectively.

$$V_1 = 314.16 \times 100 = 31.416 \times 10^3 \text{ mm}^3$$

$$V_2 = 1256.64 \times 200 = 251.328 \times 10^3 \text{ mm}^3$$

$V_3$ and $V_4$ = Volumes of bar 'B' for components of 20 mm ϕ and 40 mm ϕ respectively.

$$V_3 = 314.16 \times 200 = 62.832 \times 10^3 \text{ mm}^3$$

$$V_4 = 1256.64 \times 100 = 125.664 \times 10^3 \text{ mm}^3$$

$\sigma_1, \sigma_2$ = Stresses developed in bar 'A' for components of 20 mm ϕ and 40 mm ϕ respectively and

$\sigma_3, \sigma_4$ = Stresses developed in bar 'B' for components of 20 mm ϕ and 40 mm ϕ respectively.

(ii)   Strain energy of bar 'A',

$$U_A = \left(\frac{\sigma^2}{2E} \cdot \text{Volume}\right)_1 + \left(\frac{\sigma^2}{2E} \cdot \text{Volume}\right)_2$$

We have, $\qquad \sigma_1 A_1 = \sigma_2 A_2$

$\qquad 100 \times 314.16 = \sigma_2 \times 1256.64$

$\therefore \qquad \sigma_2 = 25$ MPa

$\therefore \qquad U_A = \dfrac{(100)^2}{2E} \times 31.416 \times 10^3 + \dfrac{(25)^2}{2E} \times 251.328 \times 10^3$

$\qquad\qquad = \dfrac{235.62 \times 10^6}{E}$

(iii) Strain energy of bar 'B',

$$U_B = \left(\dfrac{\sigma^2}{2E} \cdot \text{Volume}\right)_3 + \left(\dfrac{\sigma^2}{2E} \cdot \text{Volume}\right)_4$$

We have, $\qquad \sigma_3 A_3 = \sigma_4 A_4$

$\qquad \sigma_3 \times 314.16 = \sigma_4 \times 1256.64$

$\qquad\qquad \sigma_3 = 4 \cdot \sigma_4$

OR $\qquad\qquad \sigma_4 = 0.25\,\sigma_3$

$$U_B = \dfrac{\sigma_3^2}{2E} \times 62.832 \times 10^3 + \dfrac{(0.25\,\sigma_3)^2}{2E} \times 125.664 \times 10^3$$

$$U_B = 35343 \cdot \dfrac{\sigma_3^2}{E} \qquad\qquad\qquad \textbf{(Note :}\ \sigma_3 > \sigma_4)$$

(iv)  Maximum instantaneous stress for bar 'B' : Equating strain energy of 'A' to that of 'B',

$$\dfrac{235.62 \times 10^6}{E} = 35343\,\dfrac{\sigma_3^2}{E}$$

$\therefore \qquad\qquad \sigma_3 = 81.65$ MPa

(v)  Ratio of resilience when each bar is stressed to elastic limit :

Let, $\qquad\qquad F_y = $ yield stress

**Note :** Material for bar 'A' and bar 'B' being same, yield stress is same for both the bars. Also for bar 'A', $\sigma_1 > \sigma_2$, hence $\sigma_1 = F_y$ and for bar B , $\sigma_3 > \sigma_4$, hence $\sigma_3 = F_y$.

$$\text{Resilience of 'A'} = \left(\dfrac{\sigma^2}{2E} \cdot \text{Volume}\right)_1 + \left(\dfrac{\sigma^2}{2E} \cdot \text{Volume}\right)_2$$

where $\qquad\qquad \sigma_1 = F_y$ and $\sigma_2 = 0.25\,F_y$

Substituting,

$$\text{Resilience of 'A'} = \dfrac{1}{2E}\left(F_y^2 \times 31.416 \times 10^3 + (0.25\,F_y)^2 \times 251.328 \times 10^3\right)$$

$$= 23562\,\dfrac{F_y^2}{E}$$

$$\text{Resilience of 'B'} = \left(\dfrac{\sigma^2}{2E} \cdot \text{Volume}\right)_3 + \left(\dfrac{\sigma^2}{2E} \cdot \text{Volume}\right)_4$$

where $\qquad\qquad \sigma_3 = F_y$ and $\sigma_4 = 0.25\,F_y$

Substituting,

$$\text{Resilience of B} = \frac{1}{2E}[F_y^2 \times 62.832 \times 10^3 + (0.25\,F_y)^2 \times 125.664 \times 10^3]$$

$$= 35343\,\frac{F_y^2}{E}$$

$$\frac{\text{Resilience of A}}{\text{Resilience of B}} = 23562\,\frac{F_y^2}{E} \times \frac{E}{35343\,F_y^2}$$

$$= \frac{1}{1.5}$$

**Example 8.25 :** *A 300 mm long stepped bar 'A' has a diameter of 20 mm for a length of 100 mm and a diameter of 40 mm for the remaining length. Another bar 'B' made of same material has a diameter of 30 mm throughout the entire length of 300 mm. Compare the values of maximum strain energy stored in them, if permissible stresses for the material are same.*

**Data**        :   As shown in Fig. 8.20.

**Required**   :   $\dfrac{U_A}{U_B}$ .

**Concept**    :   Standard formulae.

**Solution**   :

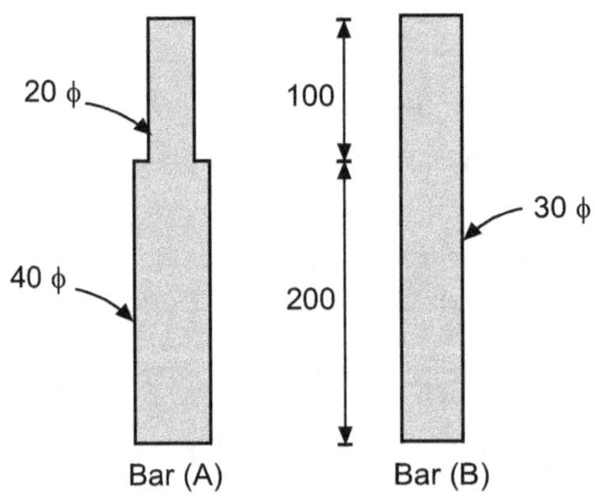


**Fig. 8.20**

**Solution**    :   (i) Strain energy of bar A :

Let $\sigma_1$ and $\sigma_2$ be the stresses developed in portions 20 mm φ and 40 mm φ of bar A respectively.

$$U_A = \left(\frac{\sigma^2}{2E}\cdot\text{Volume}\right)_1 + \left(\frac{\sigma^2}{2E}\cdot\text{Volume}\right)_2$$

where        $\text{Volume}_1 = \dfrac{\pi}{4}(20)^2 \times 100 = 31.42 \times 10^3 \text{ mm}^3$

$$\text{Volume}_2 \;=\; \frac{\pi}{4}(40)^2 \times 200 = 251.33 \times 10^3 \text{ mm}^3$$

$$\sigma_1 A_1 \;=\; \sigma_2 A_2$$

$$\sigma_1 \times \frac{\pi}{4}(20)^2 \;=\; \sigma_2 \times \frac{\pi}{4}(40)^2$$

$$\therefore \qquad \sigma_1 \;=\; 4\,\sigma_2 \quad \text{OR} \quad \sigma_2 = 0.25\,\sigma_1$$

Substituting,
$$U_A \;=\; \frac{\sigma_1^2}{2\,E} \times 31.42 \times 10^3 + \frac{(0.25\,\sigma_1)^2}{2\,E} \times 251.33 \times 10^3$$

$$=\; \left(\frac{23.56 \times 10^3}{E}\right)\sigma_1^2$$

Note that $\sigma_1 > \sigma_2$, hence $U_A$ is obtained in terms of $\sigma_1$.

(ii)   Strain energy of bar B :

Let $\sigma_3$ be the stress developed in bar B.

$$U_B \;=\; \frac{\sigma_3^2}{2\,E} \times \text{Volume}$$

$$=\; \frac{\sigma_3^2}{2\,E} \times \frac{\pi}{4}(30)^2 \times 300$$

$$=\; \left(\frac{106.02 \times 10^3}{E}\right)\sigma_3^2$$

(iii) Comparison of $U_A$ and $U_B$ :

$$\frac{U_A}{U_B} \;=\; \left(\frac{23.56 \times 10^3}{E}\right)\sigma_1^2 \times \frac{E}{106.02 \times 10^3\,\sigma_3^2}$$

$$=\; \frac{1}{4.5}$$

**Note :** Material for bars A and B being same, E = constant and $\sigma_1 = \sigma_3$.

**Example 8.26 :** *A uniform rod of cross-sectional area = A ; length = L is held vertically as shown in Fig. 8.21. Derive the expression for strain energy due to self weight. Assume Young's modulus of elasticity 'E' and mass density '$\rho$'.*

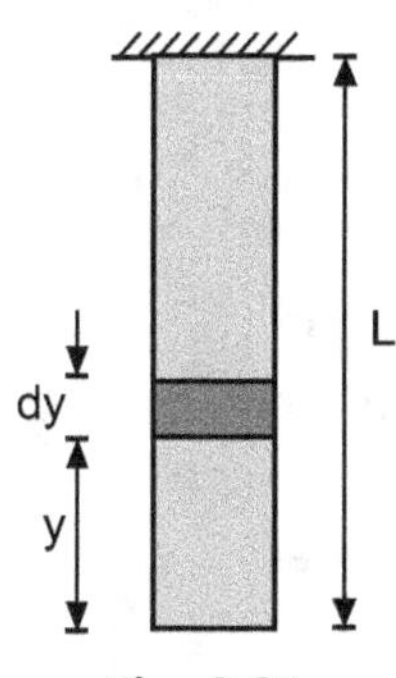


**Fig. 8.21**

**Data :** A, L, E, $\rho$.

**Required :** Expression for strain energy due to self weight.

**Concept :** Strain energy due to self weight by integration.

**Solution :** Consider an elementary strip of thickness 'dy' at a distance 'y' from bottom as shown in Fig. 8.21.

$$\text{Axial force on elementary strip} = F = \text{Volume below the strip} \times \text{Weight density}$$

$$= A \cdot y \cdot \rho \cdot g$$

$$\text{Normal stress on elementary strip} = \sigma = \frac{F}{\text{Cross-sectional area of strip}} = \frac{A \cdot y \cdot \rho \cdot g}{A}$$

$$\sigma = y \cdot \rho \cdot g$$

$$\text{Strain energy of strip} = dU = \frac{\sigma^2}{2\,E} \times \text{Volume of strip}$$

$$= \frac{(y\,\rho \cdot g)^2}{2\,E} \times (A \cdot dy)$$

$$\text{Strain energy of member} = U = \int_0^L dU = \int_0^L \frac{y^2\,\rho^2\,g^2 \cdot A}{2\,E} \cdot dy$$

$$= \frac{\rho^2 \cdot g^2 \cdot A \cdot L^3}{6\,E}$$

**Example 8.27 :** *A solid right circular cone is held vertically as shown in Fig. 8.22. Derive the expression for strain energy stored in it due to self weight using standard notation.*

**Data**       :   As shown in Fig. 8.22.

**Required**   :   Expression for strain energy due to self weight.

**Concept**    :   Same as Example 8.26.

**Solution**   :   Consider an elementary strip of thickness 'dy' at a distance 'y' from bottom as shown in Fig. 8.22.

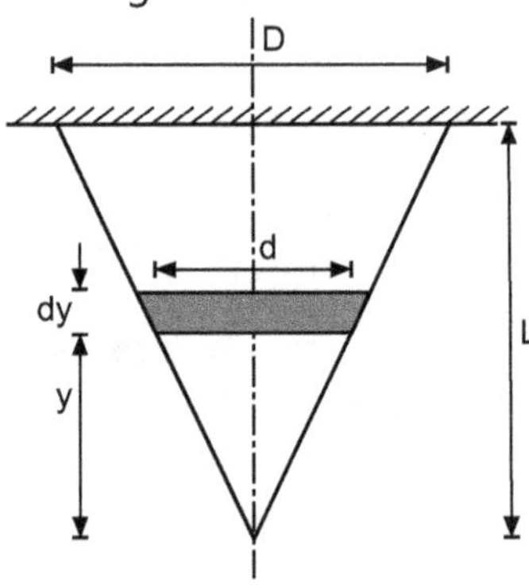


**Fig. 8.22**

Let,                               D = Diameter of cone at fixed end

d = Diameter of cone at 'y' from bottom

L = Height of cone

$\rho$ = Mass density of cone material

g = Gravitational acceleration

E = Modulus of elasticity

Axial force on elementary strip $\;=\;$ Volume below the strip $\times$ Weight density

$$= \left(\frac{1}{3} A_y \cdot y\right) \cdot \rho \cdot g$$

where $A_y$ = area of cross section at 'y' from bottom.

$\therefore\qquad$ Normal stress on elementary strip $= \sigma \;=\; \dfrac{F}{A_y}$

$$= \frac{y \cdot \rho \cdot g}{3}$$

$\therefore\qquad$ Strain energy of elementary strip $\;=\; dU$

$$= \frac{\sigma^2}{2\,E} \times \text{Volume of strip}$$

$\therefore\qquad dU \;=\; \left(\dfrac{y \cdot \rho \cdot g}{3}\right)^2 \cdot \dfrac{1}{2\,E} \cdot (A_y \cdot dy)$

$\therefore\qquad dU \;=\; \dfrac{y^2 \cdot \rho^2 \cdot g^2}{18\,E} \cdot (A_y \cdot dy)$

where,$\qquad A_y \;=\; \dfrac{\pi}{4} d^2 = \dfrac{\pi}{4}\left[\dfrac{D}{L} \cdot y\right]^2$

Total strain energy for cone $= U = \displaystyle\int_0^L dU$

$\therefore\qquad U \;=\; \displaystyle\int_0^L \frac{y^2 \rho^2 g^2}{18\,E}\left[\frac{\pi}{4}\left(\frac{D}{L} \cdot y\right)^2\right] dy$

$$= \frac{\rho^2 g^2 \pi D^2}{72\,E\,L^2} \cdot \left[\frac{L^5}{5}\right]$$

$$= \frac{\rho^2 g^2 \cdot \pi D^2}{360\,E} \cdot L^3$$

**Example 8.28 :** *A vertical round steel rod 1.82 metre long is securely held at its upper end. A weight can slide freely on the rod and its fall is arrested by a slop provided at the lower end of the rod. When the weight falls from a height of 30 mm above the stop the maximum stress reached in the rod is estimated to be 157 N/mm². Determine the stress in the rod if the load had been applied gradually and also the minimum stress if the load had fallen from a height of 47.5 mm.*

*Take E = 2.1 $\times 10^5$ GPa.*

**Data :** L = 1820 mm, h = 30 mm, $\sigma_i$ = 157 N/mm², E = 2.1 GPa.

**Required :** Stress in rod and minimum stress for h = 47.5 mm

**Concept :** Standard formulae.

**Solution :** (i) Stress in rod :

$$\sigma_i = \frac{W}{A}\left[1 + \sqrt{1 + \frac{2hEA}{WL}}\right]$$

$$= \sigma\left[1 + \sqrt{1 + \left(\frac{2 \times 30 \times 2.1 \times 10^5}{1820\sigma}\right)}\right]$$

$$157 = \sigma + \sigma\sqrt{1 + \frac{6923.08\sigma}{\sigma}}$$

$$(157 - \sigma)^2 = \sigma^2\left(1 + \frac{6923.08}{\sigma}\right)$$

$$24649 - 3146 + \sigma^2 = \sigma^2 + 6923.08\,\sigma$$

$$\therefore \qquad \sigma = \textbf{3.41 N/mm}^2 \textbf{ (Tensile)}$$

(ii) $\sigma_i$ due to h = 47.5 mm

$$\sigma_i = 3.41\left[1 + \sqrt{1 + \frac{2 \times 47.5 \times 2.1 \times 10^5}{1820\,\sigma}}\right]$$

$$\sigma_i = \textbf{196.7 MPa}$$

---

**Example 8.29 :** *A 10 mm diameter mild steel bar of 1.5 m is stressed by a weight of 120 N dropping freely through a distance of 20 mm before commencing to stretch the bar. Find maximum instantaneous stress and the elongation produced in the bar. Take E = 2 $\times$ 10$^5$ N/mm$^2$.* **(Dec. 2007)**

**Solution :** Formula for maximum instantaneous stress due to impact load is :

$$\sigma_{max} = \frac{W}{A}\left[1 + \sqrt{1 + \frac{2hEA}{LW}}\right]$$

Now, 
$$A = \frac{\pi}{4}(10)^2 = 78.54 \text{ mm}^2$$

$$\therefore \qquad \sigma_{max} = \left[\frac{120}{78.54}\right]\left[1 + \sqrt{1 + \frac{2\,(20)\,(2 \times 10^5)\,(78.54)}{(1500)\,(120)}}\right]$$

$$\therefore \qquad \sigma_{max} = 91.81 \text{ MPa}$$

Using, 
$$\delta L = \frac{\sigma L}{E} \text{ we get } (\delta L)_{max}$$

$$= \textbf{0.69 mm [elongation]}$$

---

## EXERCISE

1. A bar 75 mm in diameter, 3.2 m long has to transmit shock energy of 175 joules. Calculate maximum instantaneous stress developed and maximum elongation if E = 200 GPa.

$$(\sigma_{max} = 70.36 \text{ MPa} ; \delta L_{max} = 1.125 \text{ mm})$$

2. A vertical steel bar 1.75 m long is fixed at top. A weight can slide freely along the rod and its fall is arrested at the bottom by collar. When weight falls through 50 mm, the maximum instantaneous stress developed in the bar is 200 MPa. Determine the stress in the same bar when weight is (i) gradually applied, (ii) suddenly applied, (iii) with free fall of 60 mm.          ((i) $\sigma_{max}$ = 3.38 MPa, (ii) $\sigma_{max}$ = 6.76 MPa, (iii) $\sigma_{max}$ = 218.706 MPa)

3. A uniform bar of cross-sectional area 485 mm² is 8.85 m long. Find the proof resilience and modulus of resilience if the elastic limit for the bar material is 250 MPa. Also find the maximum value of suddenly applied load, the member can carry. Assume  E = 200 GPa.

(Proof resilience = 215.976 joules, Modulus of resilience = 0.156 MPa,

Suddenly applied load = 60.625 kN)

4. A vertical steel rod 1.7 m long is fixed at top and provided with collar at bottom. The upper 1000 mm length of bar is 30 mm $\phi$, while the lower 700 mm is of 15 mm $\phi$. A weight of magnitude 175 N falls freely through a height of 75 mm. Find (i) maximum instantaneous stress, (ii) maximum elongation, (iii) total strain energy stored. Assume E = 200 GPa.          ((i) $\sigma_{max}$ = 177.84 MPa, (ii) $\delta L$ = 0.848 mm (iii) U = 13.273 joules)

5. A vertical steel bar 15 mm diameter, 1.4 m long is provided with a collar at lower end. Find the maximum weight that can be dropped through a height of 95 mm over the collar if maximum permissible tensile stress is 150 MPa. Assume E = 200 GPa.      (W = 144.88 N)

6. A bar of 20 mm diameter stretches 1 mm under gradually applied load of 50 kN. If a weight of 1.5 kN is dropped on to a collar at the lower end of this bar through a height of 35 mm, calculate the maximum instantaneous stress and elongation of the bar. Take E = 200 GPa.          ($\sigma_{max}$ = 235.46 MPa ; $\delta L$ = 1.479 mm)

7. Water under pressure of 10 MPa is suddenly admitted on to a plunger of 125 mm diameter attached to a rod 30 mm diameter, 4 m long. Find the maximum instantaneous stress and deformation of the rod if E = 210 GPa.          ($\sigma_{max}$ = 347.22 MPa ; $\delta L$ = 6.9 mm)

8. A steel specimen 15 mm $\phi$ stretches by 0.1 mm over 175 mm length under an axial load of 40 kN. Calculate the strain energy stored in the specimen at this stage. If the load at the elastic limit for the specimen is 50 kN, calculate the elongation at elastic limit and proof resilience.          (U = 2 joules ; $\delta L$ = 0.125 mm, Proof resilience = 3.125 joules)

9. A vertically suspended steel bar, circular in cross-section, is subjected to load of 7.5 kN, which falls by 15 mm on rigid collar provided at lower end of the bar. If maximum allowable strain for the bar is $\dfrac{1}{1300}$, find suitable diameter of bar. Assume E = 200 GPa and length of bar = 3 m.(30.512 mm)

10. A wagon weighing 25 kN is attached to a wire rope and is moving at the speed of 5.5 kmph. The rope suddenly jams and the wagon is brought to rest. If length of the rope is 45 m and diameter 40 mm, find maximum instantaneous stress and elongation of rope, assuming E = 200 GPa. ($\sigma_{max}$ = 145.04 MPa ; $\delta L_{max}$ = 32.63 mm)

11. A lift weighing 22 kN is connected by 24 mm diameter and 42 m long rope. If yield stress for the rope material is 300 MPa and factor of safety = 2.1, E = 200 GPa, find the safe working speed for the lift.   (0.9 m/s)

12. A copper rod 25 mm diameter is enclosed in a steel tube 30 mm internal diameter and 3 mm thickness. The length of composite member is 2.4 m. It is fixed at top and provided with a rigid collar at bottom. A body of mass 44 kg is allowed to slide down freely through a height 'h'. If maximum instantaneous stress developed in copper is not to exceed 70 MPa, find height and elongation of composite bar, $E_s$ = 200 GPa; $E_c$ = 120 GPa.

(h = 113.17 mm;  $\delta L$ = 1.4 mm)

13. A copper bar 18 mm $\phi$ is enclosed in a steel tube 28 mm external diameter and 3.2 mm thickness. The composite bar is held vertically and provided with a rigid collar at bottom. A weight of 1.75 kN falls freely through a height of 22 mm. If length of the bar is 2.5 m, find (i) Maximum instantaneous stress developed in each material and (ii) Maximum instantaneous elongation. $E_s$ = 200 GPa, $E_c$ = 110 GPa.

($\sigma_s$ = 130.36 MPa, $\sigma_c$ = 71.7 MPa,  $\delta L$ = 1.629 mm)

14. A copper tube is enclosed in a steel tube 35 mm external diameter and 5 mm thickness. This composite bar is held vertically fixed at top and provided with a rigid collar at bottom. A weight of 2 kN falls freely through a height of 25 mm. Length of composite member is 3m. Find diameter of copper bar if maximum instantaneous stress developed in steel is 150 MPa. Assume $E_c$ = 100 GPa, $E_s$ = 200 GPa.                    (21.1 mm)

15. A 500 mm long stepped bar 'A' has a diameter of 25 mm for a length of 200 mm and a diameter of 45 mm for the remaining length. Another bar 'B' made of same material has a

diameter of 30 mm throughout the entire length of 500 mm. Compare the values of maximum strain energy stored in them if permissible stress for the material is same.

(1 : 2.46)

16. A vertical steel bar is fixed at top and provided with rigid collar at bottom as shown in Fig. 3.23. Compute maximum stress induced in a member if 30 N weight falls through a height of 200 mm.
$(\sigma_{max} = 107.4$ MPa)

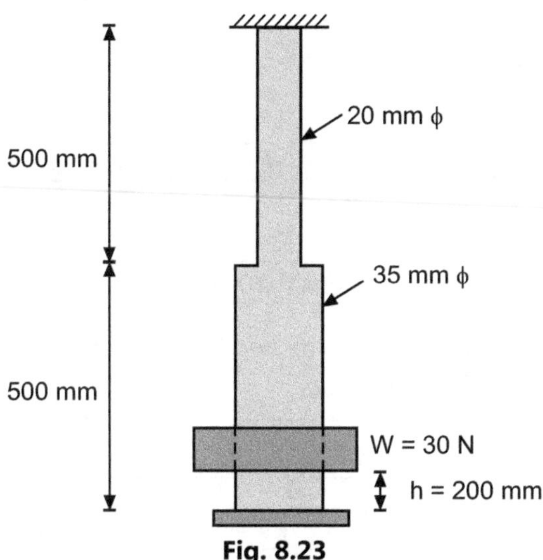


**Fig. 8.23**

17. An unknown weight 'W' falls through a height of 10 mm on a collar rigidly attached to the lower end of a vertical bar 5 m long and 600 mm² in section. If the maximum extension of the rod is to be 3 mm, what is the corresponding stress and magnitude of unknown weight ? E = 200 GPa.
(W = 8.3 kN)

18. A vertical steel rod of 25 mm diameter checks the fall on its end of weight 2.5 kN which drops through a distance of 4 mm before it strikes the rod. Find the shortest length of rod which will bear the impact if the stress is not to exceed 150 MPa. E = 210 GPa.  (407.9 mm)

19. A bar 1 m long as shown in Fig. 8.24 is subjected to an axial pull such that the maximum stress is equal to 160 MPa. If E = 200 GPa, calculate the strain energy stored in the bar.

(3.359 N.m)

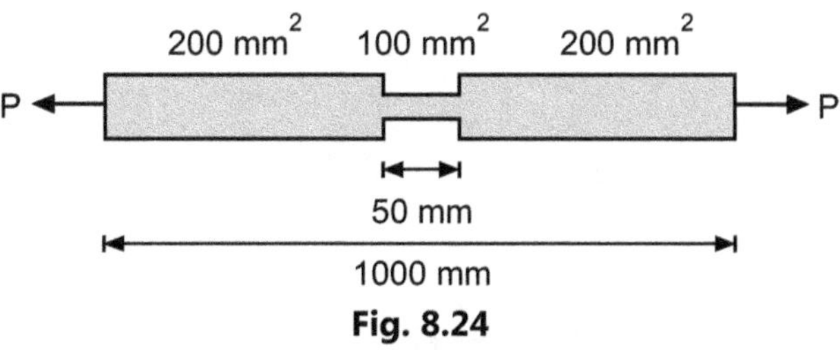


**Fig. 8.24**

20. Two circular bars of some material have the same length L. One bar has diameter 'd' for a length $\frac{L}{3}$ and diameter '2d' for the remaining length. The order bar has a diameter '2d' for a length $\frac{2L}{3}$ and the diameter '3d' for the remaining length. The bars are subjected to same axial loads. Compare the amount of strain energy in the bar. Compare also the amount of strain energy in them when the maximum stress induced in both the bars is same, the stress being within elastic limit. $\left(\dfrac{27}{11}, \dfrac{27}{176}\right)$

## UNIVERSITY QUESTION PAPERS

### MAY 2014

1. Compare the strain energy stored in the two bars of the same material shown in following Fig. 1, if gradually applied load is same. **[6]**

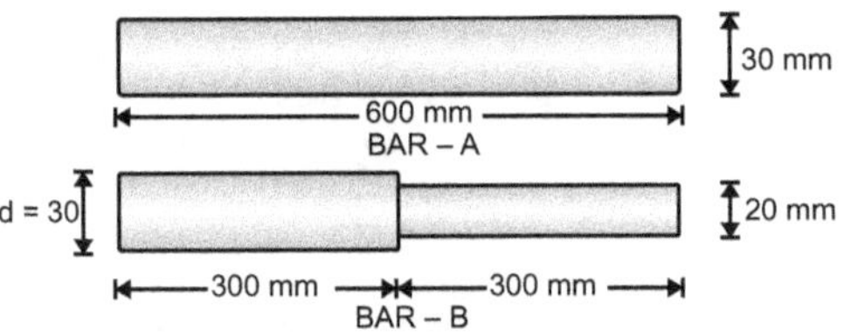

**Fig. 1**

◈ ◈ ◈

# Chapter 9

# TORSION

## 9.1 INTRODUCTION

In this chapter, study is aimed at evaluation of stresses and deformation within elastic range due to torque applied on solid and hollow circular shafts. In practice, members that transmit torque, such as shafts of motors or power equipments etc. are predominantly circular or tubular in cross-section. Hence, the scope is restricted to circular sections only. Various situations for statically determinate and indeterminate shafts subjected to pure torque are illustrated. But in practice, members are generally subjected to bending and torsion or bending, torsion and axial force which involve evaluation of stresses and strains due to each of these actions and then by using principle of superposition, resultant stresses are obtained. Evaluation of principal stresses and strains for such combined actions is of prime importance from practical design point of view.

## 9.2 BASICS OF TORSION

Torsion is defined as the *resultant moment on any one side of the section about longitudinal or polar axis of the member*. It is also called as torque or torsional moment or twisting moment.

Deformation corresponding to torque is rotation about polar axis called as *twist*. Thus, various cross-sections of shaft subjected to torque tend to rotate relatively with respect to each other; about polar axis which developes shear stresses normal to shaft within elastic limit, magnitude of angle of twist and shear stresses are proportional to the magnitude of torque section is subjected to.

## 9.3 METHOD OF SECTION

For analysis of members subjected to torques, the basic approach of method of section is used. First the system as a whole is examined for equilibrium. Section is considered perpendicular to the axis of the member and then equilibrium of any one side of the section is examined. Internal torque necessary for equilibrium of isolated part on any one side of the section is then evaluated by using equation of statics viz. $\sum$ M @ polar axis = 0. This is illustrated in following example :

**Note :** Sign convention

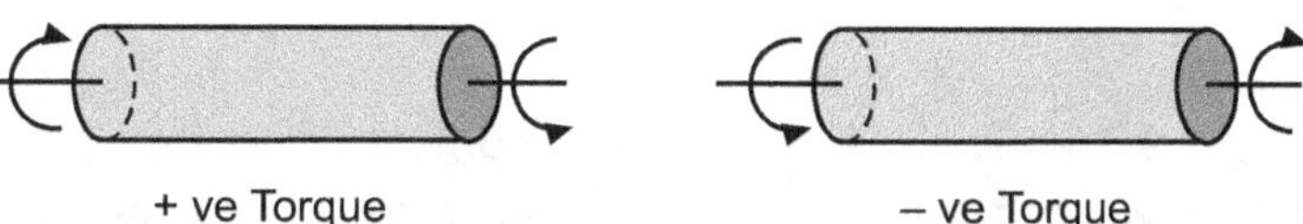



**Fig. 9.1 : Sign convention**

Consider a shaft ABC subjected to torques $T_A$ = 30 kN.m, $T_B$ = 80 kN.m and $T_C$ = 50 kN.m as shown in Fig. 9.2 (a). Let, it be required to find torque for portions AB and BC. Consider sections 1-1 and 2-2 in segments AB and BC respectively as shown.

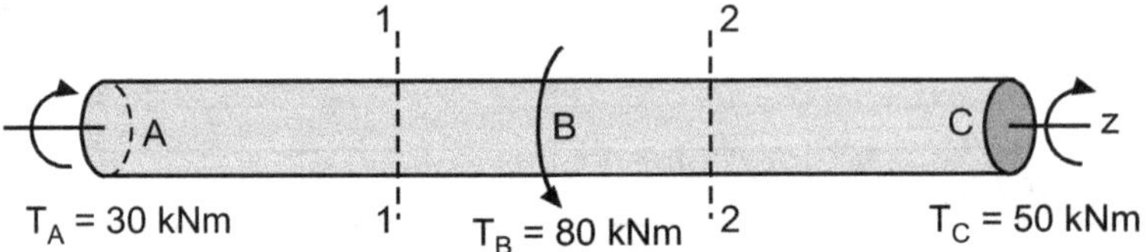


**(a) Shaft ABC**

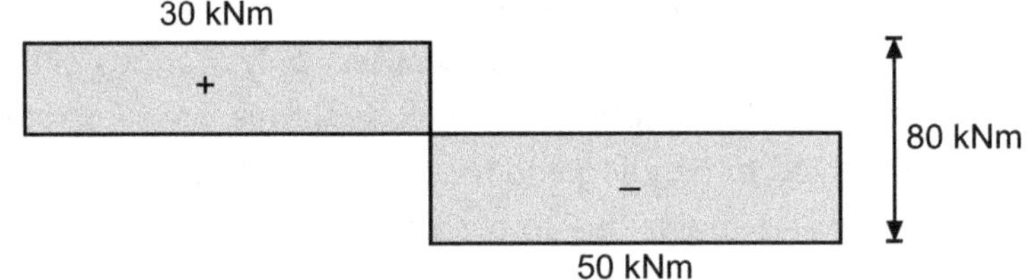


**(b) Torsional moment diagram**

**Fig. 9.2**

$\sum M_z$ on LHS of section 1-1 = 30 kN.m, OR

$\sum M_z$ on RHS of section 1-1 = − 50 + 80 = 30 kN.m

$\sum M_z$ on LHS of section 2-2 = 30 − 80 = − 50 kN.m OR

$\sum M_z$ on RHS of section 2-2 = − 50 kN.m

Thus, the torque of 30 kN.m is constant in portion AB and torque of − 50 kN.m is constant in portion BC. It should be noted that, torque just to the left of c/s B is + 30 kN.m and just to the right of c/s B is − 50 kN.m.

## 9.3.1 Torsional Moment Diagram

It is the diagram which shows variation of torsional moment along the length of member. With above discussion, torsional moment diagram for the shaft ABC is drawn as shown in Fig. 9.2 (b).

**Note :** There is a vertical drop or rise in torsional moment diagram at a section of application of torque and magnitude of drop or rise in the diagram is equal to magnitude of torque acting at that section.

Above example illustrates drawing of torsional moment diagram for shaft subjected to concentrated torques. However, torque can be uniformly distributed over the length of a member as shown in Fig. 9.3 (a). Torsional moment diagram for such a shaft will vary linearly as shown in Fig. 9.3 (b).

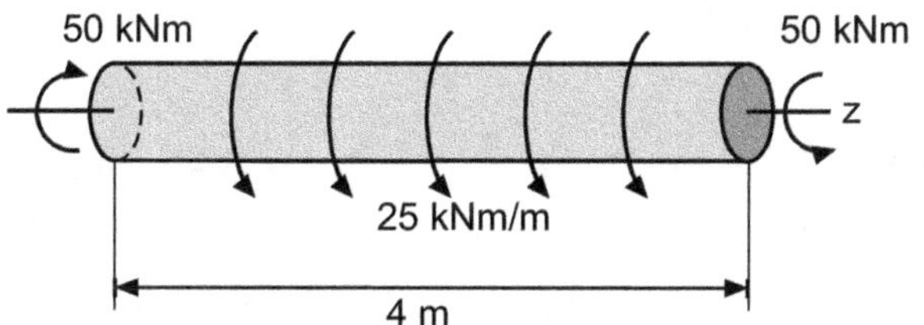

**(a) Uniformly distributed torque on a member**

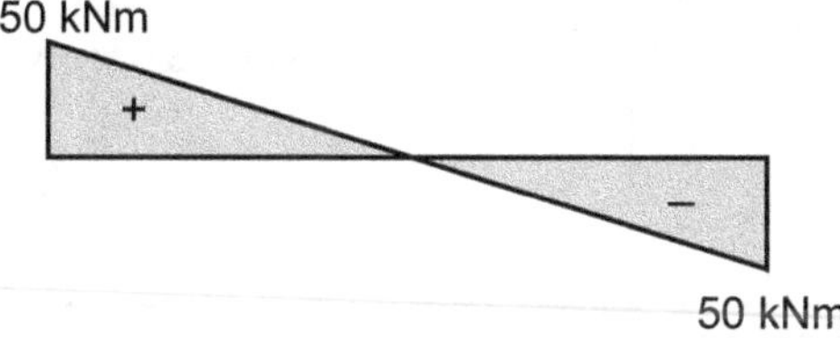

**(b) Torsional moment diagram**

**Fig. 9.3**

However, intensity of torque along the length of member can be varying. Such situations are not discussed in the present text.

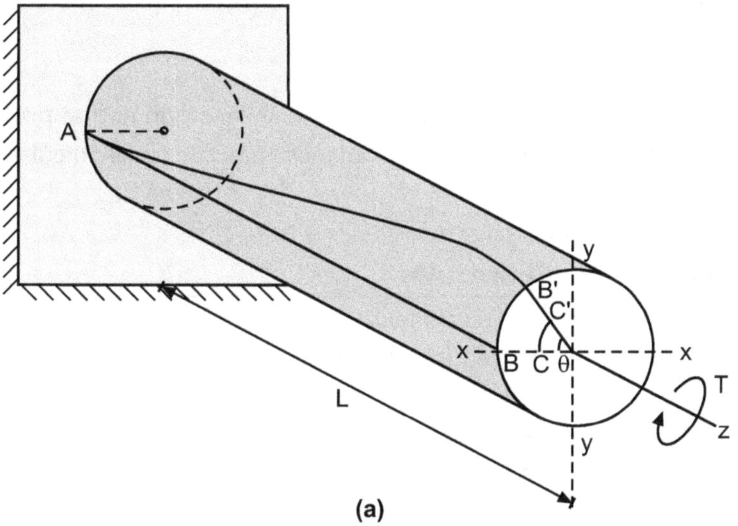

(a)

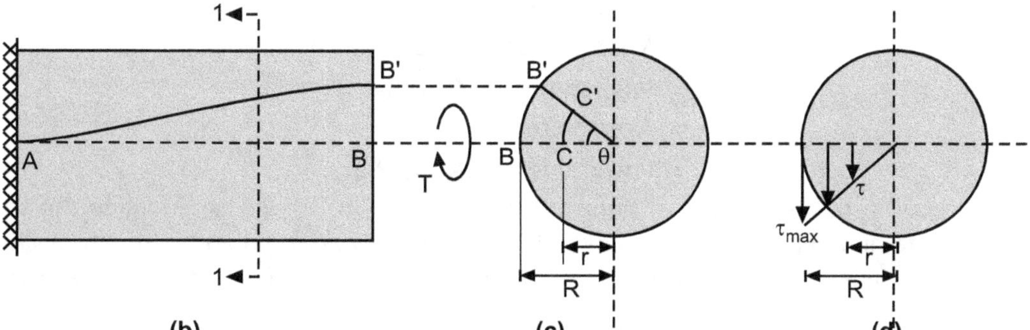

(b)      (c)      (d)

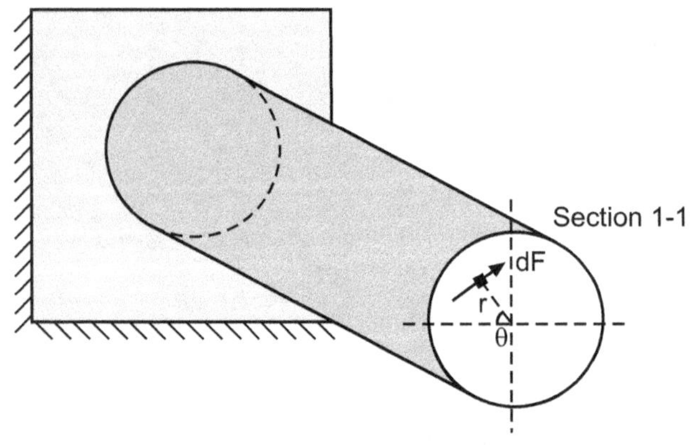


(a)   Shaft subjected to torque
(b)   Side view of shaft
(c)   Angular deformation in cross-section
(d)   Shear stress variation over the cross-section
(e)   Section 1-1

**Fig. 9.4**

# 9.4 THEORY OF TORSION

## 9.4.1 Assumptions

In deriving the torsion formulae, following assumptions are made :

- Plane sections remain plane and do not warp.
- Stresses do not exceed the limit of proportionality.
- Radial lines remain radial after twisting.
- Material is elastic and obeys Hook's law.

  i.e. Shear stress at any point is proportional to shear strain at that point.
- Shaft is loaded by twisting couples in planes that are perpendicular to the axis of the shaft.
- Circular sections remain circular.

## 9.4.2 Derivation of Torsion Formula

Symbols :

$$\begin{aligned}
T &= \text{Torsional moment} \\
L &= \text{Length of shaft} \\
R &= \text{Radius of shaft} \\
r &= \text{Radial distance} \\
\theta &= \text{Angle of twist} \\
G &= \text{Shear modulus} \\
\tau &= \text{Shear stress} \\
\tau_{max} &= \text{Maximum shear stress} \\
J &= \text{Polar moment of inertia} \\
T_a &= \text{Average torque} \\
P &= \text{Power transmitted by shaft}
\end{aligned}$$

Consider a circular shaft subjected to pure torque as shown in Fig. 9.4 (a). Imagine the shaft to consist of infinite number of circular laminas which individually are rigid and joined to each other by elastic fibres. Thus, due to the application of torque each lamina rotates with respect to each other.

Consider now any internal fibre located at radial distance 'r' from origin. The deformation of such a fibre is marked by CC' in the Fig. 9.4 (c). It should be noted that deformation is maximum at outermost periphery marked by BB' and zero at the centre of the shaft. Thus, axis passing through centre of the shaft and normal to the cross-section is neutral axis (Polar axis). It is clearly seen from Fig. 9.4 that deformation of a fibre is directly proportional to its distance from polar axis and hence the stress. The shear stress variation over the cross-section when loaded within elastic limit is also shown in Fig. 9.4 (a).

Thus,  $\qquad BB' = R\theta$  and  $CC' = r\theta$  ... (9.1)

Shear deformation per unit length of fibre at a distance 'r'

$$= \frac{CC'}{L} = \frac{r\theta}{L}$$

$\therefore$  Shear strain $= \gamma = \dfrac{r\theta}{L}$

Shear stress $= \tau = \dfrac{Gr\theta}{L} = \left(\dfrac{G\theta}{L}\right) r$  ... (9.2)

*"Thus, shear stress along any radius varies linearly with the radial distance of the shaft."*

$\therefore$  $\qquad \dfrac{\tau}{r} = \dfrac{\tau_{max}}{R} = \dfrac{G\theta}{L}$  ... (9.3)

## Torsional Resistance

Consider FBD of section 1-1 as shown in Fig. 9.4 (e). An elementary area dA is considered at a distance r from axis of the shaft on which shear stress is equal to $\tau$. By considering area to be infinitesimally shall, we can assume stress to be uniform over area dA. Shear force acting on elementary area $= dF = dA \cdot \tau$. This force dF must be normal to the radius vector as it has to resist the applied torque as efficiently as possible so that energy is conserved.

Small twisting moment produced by dF about polar axis $= dT = dF \cdot r$

$\therefore$  $\qquad T = \displaystyle\int_0^R dF \cdot r = \int_0^R (dA \cdot \tau)\, r$

$\qquad = \displaystyle\int_0^R dA \cdot \frac{G\theta}{L} \cdot r^2 = \frac{G\theta}{L} \int_0^R dA \cdot r^2$

$\therefore$  $\qquad T = \dfrac{G\theta}{L} J$  ... (9.4)

Since  $\qquad J = \displaystyle\int_0^R dA \cdot r^2 = $ polar moment of inertia of cross-section

From equations (9.3) and (9.4),

$$\frac{T}{J} = \frac{\tau_{max}}{R} = \frac{G\theta}{L}$$  ... (9.5)

## 9.5  IMPORTANT TERMS

### 9.5.1 Torsional Stiffness

*It is the torque required to produce unit angle of twist.*

Thus,          torsional stiffness  $= \dfrac{GJ}{L}$

Unit of torsional stiffness is Nm/radian.

### 9.5.2 Torsional Flexibility

*It is the angle of twist produced by unit torque applied.*

Thus,          torsional flexibility  $= \dfrac{L}{GJ}$

Unit of torsional flexibility is radian/N.m.

It should be noted that stiffness and flexibility coefficients are reciprocal of each other.

### 9.5.3 Torsional Rigidity

*Product of shear modulus and polar moment of inertia of cross-section is called as torsional rigidity (GJ).*

Unit of torsional rigidity is N.m$^2$.

### 9.5.4 Torsional Section Modulus

*Ratio of polar moment of inertia of cross-section to its radius is called as torsional section modulus (J/R).*

Unit of torsional section modulus is m$^3$.

**Torsional section modulus for solid circular shaft**

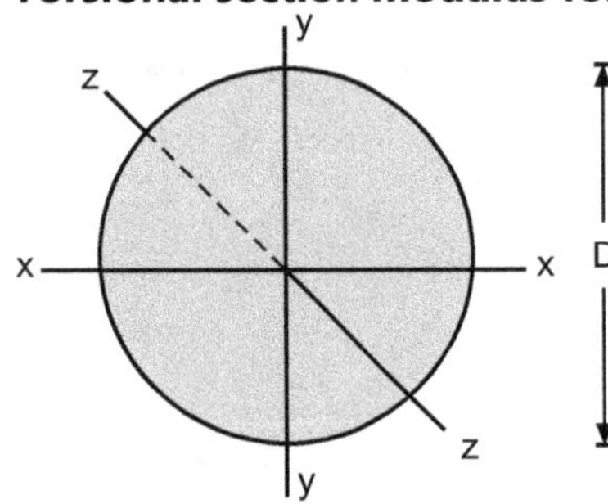

$$I_{xx} = I_{yy} = \frac{\pi}{64} D^4$$

$$J = I_{zz} = I_{xx} + I_{yy} = 2 \times \frac{\pi}{64} D^4 = \frac{\pi}{32} D^4$$

$$R = \frac{D}{2}$$

$$\therefore \quad \frac{J}{R} = \frac{\pi}{32} D^4 \times \frac{2}{D} = \frac{\pi}{16} D^3 \qquad \dots (9.6)$$

**Fig. 9.5**

**Torsional section modulus for hollow circular shaft**

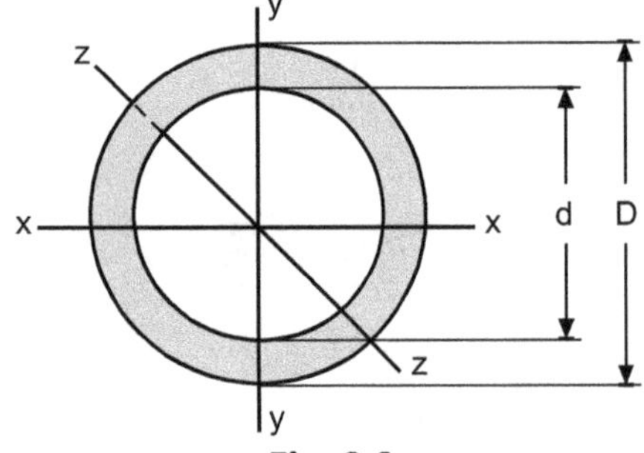

$$I_{xx} = I_{yy} = \frac{\pi}{64} (D^4 - d^4)$$

$$J = I_{zz} = I_{xx} + I_{yy} = 2 \times \frac{\pi}{64} (D^4 - d^4) = \frac{\pi}{32} (D^4 - d^4)$$

$$R = \frac{D}{2}$$

$$\therefore \quad \frac{J}{R} = \frac{\pi}{32} (D^4 - d^4) \times \frac{2}{D}$$

$$= \frac{\pi}{16\,D} (D^4 - d^4) \qquad \dots (9.7)$$

**Fig. 9.6**

## 9.5.5 Power Transmitted by Shaft

*It is the product of average torque and corresponding angle turned per unit duration of time.*

$$\text{Power} = \text{Average torque} \times \text{Angle of rotation/sec.}$$

$$= T_a \times \frac{2\pi N}{60}$$

$$\therefore \quad \mathbf{P = Power} = \frac{2\pi N\, T_a}{60} \qquad \qquad \dots (9.8)$$

where N = No. of revolutions per minute (RPM). Unit of power is Nm/s or watts.

However, power can also be expressed in Horse power (H.P.) unit.

$$1 \text{ H.P.} = \frac{2\pi N\, T_a}{4500} \qquad \qquad \dots (9.9)$$

## SOLVED EXAMPLES

**Example 9.1 :** *Find power transmitted by a shaft having 60 mm diameter rotating at 150 rpm. If maximum permissible shear stress = 80 MPa.*

**Data**         :   D = 60 mm;  N = 150 r.p.m.;  $\tau_{max}$ = 80 MPa

**Required**   :   Power transmitted.

**Concept**    :   Find the value of torque based on shear stress criteria and then use equation of power.

**Solution**   :   (i) Geometric properties :

$$J = \frac{\pi}{32} \cdot D^4 = \frac{\pi}{32} (60)^4 = 1.272 \times 10^6 \text{ mm}^3$$

$$R = \frac{D}{2} = \frac{60}{2} = 30 \text{ mm}$$

(ii)    Torque corresponding to shear stress,

$$T = \frac{J}{R} \cdot \tau_{max}$$

$$= \frac{1.272 \times 10^6}{30} \times 80$$

$$= 3.392 \times 10^6 \text{ N.mm}$$

$$\therefore \quad T = 3.392 \times 10^3 \text{ N.m}$$

(iii)    Power transmitted,    $P = \frac{2\pi N\, T_a}{60}$

$$= \frac{2 \times \pi \times 150 \times 3.392 \times 10^3}{60}$$

$$= 53281.41 \text{ W}$$

$$\therefore \quad P = \mathbf{53.281 \text{ kW}}$$

**Example 9.2 :** *A hollow circular shaft of 150 mm external diameter; thickness of metal 20 mm is rotating at 200 rpm. The angle of twist on 3 m length was found to be 0.7°. Calculate the power transmitted and maximum shear stress induced in the material.*

Assume G = 80 GPa.

**Data** : $D = 150$ mm ; $t = 20$ mm ; $N = 200$ r.p.m. ; $\theta = 0.7° = 0.0122$ rad.;
$G = 80$ GPa ; $L = 3000$ mm.

**Required** : Power transmitted (P) and maximum shear stress ($\tau_{max}$).

**Concept** : Find torque based on angle of twist criteria and then use equation of power.

**Solution** : (i) Geometric properties :

$$d = \text{Internal diameter of shaft}$$
$$= 150 - 2 \times 20$$
$$= 110 \text{ mm}$$

$$J = \frac{\pi}{32}(D^4 - d^4)$$

$$= \frac{\pi}{32}(150^4 - 110^4)$$

$$= 35.32 \times 10^6 \text{ mm}^4$$

$$R = \frac{150}{2} = 75 \text{ mm}$$

$$\therefore \quad \frac{J}{R} = \frac{35.32 \times 10^6}{75} = 471.03 \times 10^3 \text{ mm}^3$$

(ii) Torque corresponding to angle of twist.

$$T = \left(\frac{G \cdot \theta}{L}\right) \cdot J$$

$$= \frac{80 \times 10^3 \times 0.0122}{3000} \times 35.32 \times 10^6$$

$$= 11.49 \times 10^6 \text{ N.mm}$$

$$\therefore \quad T = 11.49 \times 10^3 \text{ N.m}$$

(iii) Power transmitted (P)

$$P = \frac{2\pi N \, T_a}{60} = \frac{2 \times \pi \times 200 \times 11.49 \times 10^3}{60}$$

$$= 240.66 \times 10^3 \text{ W}$$

$$= \mathbf{240.66 \ kW}$$

(iv) Maximum shear stress ($\tau_{max}$)

$$\tau_{max} = \frac{T}{J/R} = \frac{11.49 \times 10^6}{471.03 \times 10^3}$$

$$= \mathbf{24.39 \ MPa}$$

---

**Example 9.3 :** *A hollow circular shaft has external diameter of 100 mm and internal diameter of 80 mm. Find the safe power that can be transmitted if allowable shear stress is 100 MPa and maximum angle of twist is 3° for 2 m length. Take speed of shaft = 2.5 revolutions per second and maximum torque to exceed by mean torque by 20%. Take G = 80 GPa.*

**Data** : $D = 100$ mm ; $d = 80$ mm ; $\tau_{max} = 100$ MPa ; $\theta = 3° = 0.0524$ rad ;

$$L = 2000 \text{ mm} \; ; \; N = 2 \text{ r.p.s.} \; ; \; G = 80 \text{ GPa} \; ; \; T = 1.2 \, T_a$$

**Required**  :  Safe power.

**Concept**  :  Safe torque is the least of that obtained from shear stress and angle of twist criteria.

**Solution**  :  (i) Geometric properties :

$$J = \frac{\pi}{32}(D^4 - d^4)$$

$$= \frac{\pi}{32}(100^4 - 80^4)$$

$$= 5.796 \times 10^6 \text{ mm}^4$$

$$R = \frac{100}{2} = 50 \text{ mm}$$

$$\therefore \quad \frac{J}{R} = \frac{5.796 \times 10^6}{50} = 115.93 \times 10^3 \text{ mm}^3$$

(ii)  Torque based on strength criteria :

$$T = \left(\frac{J}{R}\right) \cdot \tau_{max}$$

$$= 115.93 \times 10^3 \times 100$$

$$= 11.59 \times 10^6 \text{ N.mm} \qquad \qquad \dots \text{(i)}$$

(iii)  Torque based on stiffness criteria.

$$T = \left(\frac{G\theta}{L}\right) J$$

$$= \frac{80 \times 10^3 \times 0.0524}{2000} \times 5.796 \times 10^6$$

$$= 12.15 \times 10^6 \text{ N.mm} \qquad \qquad \dots \text{(ii)}$$

(iv)  Safe maximum torque (T) :

$$T = \text{Least of (i) and (ii)}$$

$$= 11.59 \times 10^6 \text{ N.mm}$$

$$= \mathbf{11.59 \times 10^3 \ N.m}$$

$$\therefore \quad \text{Safe average torque, } T_a = \frac{T}{1.2}$$

$$= \frac{11.59 \times 10^3}{1.2}$$

$$= \mathbf{9.66 \times 10^3 \ N.m}$$

(v)  Safe power (P) :     $P = 2\pi N \, T_a$     ... (**Note :** N = 2.5 revolutions per second)

$$= 2\pi \times 2.5 \times 9.66 \times 10^3$$

$$= 151.74 \times 10^3 \text{ W}$$

$$= \mathbf{151.74 \ kW}$$

**Example 9.4 :** *A steel bar with 38 mm diameter and 450 mm long when tested under an axial tensile load of 100 kN found to stretch by 0.2 mm. The same bar when subjected to a torque of 1.27 kN.m is found to twist by 1.922º. Determine the values of four elastic constants.*

**Data**        :   $D = 38$ mm ;  $L = 450$ mm;  $P = 100$ kN ;   $\delta L = 0.2$ mm;

                    $T = 1.27$ kN.m ;  $\theta = 1.922º$.

**Required**    :   $E$ ;  $G$ ;  $K$ and $\mu$.

**Concept**     :   Standard formulae

**Solution**    :   (i) Geometric properties :

$$A = \frac{\pi}{4}(D)^2 = \frac{\pi}{4}(38)^2 = 1134.12 \text{ mm}^2$$

$$J = \frac{\pi}{32}(D^4) = \frac{\pi}{32}(38)^4 = 204.7 \times 10^3 \text{ mm}^4$$

(ii)    Modulus of elasticity (E) :

$$\delta L = \frac{PL}{AE}$$

$$0.2 = \frac{100 \times 10^3 \times 450}{1134.12 \; E}$$

$\therefore$              $E = 198.39 \times 10^3$

                    $= \mathbf{198.39 \text{ GPa}}$

(iii)   Modulus of rigidity (G) :

$$\theta = \frac{TL}{GJ} \quad \therefore \quad 1.922 \times \frac{\pi}{180} = \frac{1.27 \times 10^6 \times 450}{G \times 204.7 \times 10^3}$$

$\therefore$              $G = 83.23 \times 10^3$ MPa $= \mathbf{83.23 \text{ GPa.}}$

(iv)    Poisson's ratio ($\mu$) :

$$E = 2G(1 + \mu)$$

$$198.39 = 2 \times 83.23(1 + \mu)$$

$$\mu = \mathbf{0.19}$$

(v)     Bulk modulus (K) :

$$E = 3K(1 - 2\mu)$$

$$198.39 = 3K(1 - 2 \times 0.19)$$

$\therefore$              $K = \mathbf{106.66 \text{ GPa}}$

**Example 9.5 :** *A metal bar 16 mm $\phi$ subjected to a pull of 35 kN elongates by 0.40 mm over a gauge length of 500 mm. In a torsion test on the same material, maximum shear stress of 45 MPa was measured on a bar of 40 mm $\phi$ and angle of twist over a length of 400 mm was measured to be 0.6º. Determine Poisson's ratio for the material.*

**Data**          :   For axial pull : P = 35 kN ; $\delta L$ = 0.40 mm; D = 16 mm ;  L = 500 mm

For torsion test : $\tau$ = 45 MPa; D = 40 mm; $\theta$ = 0.6° = 0.01047;  L = 400 mm.

**Required**   :   Poisson's ratio ($\mu$)

**Concept**    :   Standard formulae

**Solution**    :   (i) For axial pull :

$$\delta L = \frac{PL}{AE}$$

$$0.40 = \frac{35 \times 10^3 \times 500}{\frac{\pi}{4}(16)^2 \times E}$$

$$\therefore \quad E = 217.59 \times 10^3 \text{ MPa}$$

$$= \mathbf{217.59 \text{ GPa}}$$

(ii)     For torsion test :

$$\frac{\tau}{R} = \frac{G\theta}{L}$$

$$\therefore \quad G = \frac{\tau L}{R\theta}$$

$$= \frac{45 \times 400}{0.01047 \times 20}$$

$$= 85.96 \times 10^3 \text{ MPa}$$

$$= \mathbf{85.96 \text{ GPa}}$$

(iii)     Poisson's ratio ($\mu$) :

$$E = 2G(1 + \mu)$$

$$217.59 = 2 \times 85.96(1 + \mu)$$

$$\mu = \mathbf{0.266}$$

## 9.6 DESIGN OF SHAFTS

For the design of circular shafts (solid or hollow), following are the two criteria :

   **(i)**     **Strength criteria :** It means, with the designed diameter, shear stress shall not exceed the allowable value.

   **(ii)**     **Stiffness criteria :** It means, with the designed diameter, angle of twist shall not exceed the allowable value.

Diameter of the shaft is obtained using above two conditions and greater of the two is to be used.

## 9.7 SOLID & HOLLOW CIRCULAR SHAFTS FOR THE SAME TORQUE

When solid shaft is replaced by hollow shaft, there is saving in material. This is due to the fact that for solid shaft, material very near to the polar axis contributes very little for resisting the applied torque while the same material placed away from polar axis provides greater polar moment of inertia and section modulus in case of hollow shaft $\left( \because J = \int_{0}^{R} da\, r^2 \right)$.

However, the hollow circular shaft requires more space to accommodate as compared to solid shaft.

**Example 9.6 :** *Design the diameter of solid circular shaft to transmit 50 kW power rotating at 150 r.p.m. Maximum torque is likely to exceed mean torque by 25%. Permissible shear stress = 60 MPa. Also calculate angle of twist for 2 m length. Assume G = 85 GPa.*

**Data :**      $P = 50$ kW ; $N = 150$ r.p.m. ; $T = 1.25\, T_a$ ;

$\tau_{max} = 60$ MPa ; $L = 2000$ mm ; $G = 85$ GPa.

**Required**   :   Diameter of shaft (D) and angle of twist ($\theta$).

**Concept**    :   Design based on strength criteria.

**Solution**   :   (i) Average torque ($T_a$) :

We have;       $P \; = \; \dfrac{2\pi N\, T_a}{60}$

$\therefore$          $50 \times 10^3 \; = \; \dfrac{2\pi \times 150 \times T_a}{60}$

$T_a \; = \; 3183.1$ N.m

$= \; \mathbf{3183.1 \times 10^3}$ **N.mm**

(ii)    Maximum torque (T) :

$T \; = \; 1.25\, T_a = 1.25 \times 3183.1 \times 10^3$

$= \; \mathbf{3978.87 \times 10^3}$ **N.mm**

(iii)   Diameter based on strength criteria :

$$T \; = \; \frac{J}{R} \cdot \tau_{max}$$

$$3978.87 \times 10^3 \; = \; \frac{\pi}{16}\, (D)^3 \times 60$$

$\therefore$          $D \; = \; \mathbf{69.64}$ **mm say 70 mm.**

(iv)    Angle of twist ($\theta$) :       $\dfrac{T}{J} \; = \; \dfrac{G\theta}{L} \qquad \therefore \quad \theta = \dfrac{T\,L}{G\,J}$

where          $J \; = \; \dfrac{\pi}{32}\, (70)^4 = 2.357 \times 10^6$ mm$^4$

$\therefore$          $\theta \; = \; \dfrac{3978.87 \times 10^3 \times 2000}{85 \times 10^3 \times 2.357 \times 10^6}$

$= \; 0.0397$ rad.

$\theta \; = \; \mathbf{2.27^o}$

**Example 9.7 :** *A steel shaft of solid circular cross-section has to transmit 200 kW at 180 r.p.m. The maximum shear stress is not to exceed 50 MPa and the angle of twist must not be more than 1.6$^o$ in a length of 2.6 m. Design suitable diameter of shaft. Take G = 80 GPa.*

**Data**       :   $P = 200$ kW; $N = 180$ r.p.m.; $\tau_{max} = 50$ MPa;

$\theta = 1.6^o = 0.0279$ rad; $L = 2600$ mm; $G = 80$ GPa.

**Required**   :   Design of cross-section of shaft.

**Concept**    :   Design based on strength and stiffness criteria. Diameter to be used is
greater of that obtained from above two conditions.

**Solution**    :    (i) Average torque $(T_a)$ :

We have, $\qquad\qquad\qquad\qquad P = \dfrac{2\pi N\, T_a}{60}$

$$200 \times 10^3 = \dfrac{2\pi \times 180 \times T_a}{60}$$

$$T_a = \mathbf{10.61 \times 10^3\ N.m}$$

Assuming maximum torque, $\qquad T = T_a = 10.61 \times 10^3\ N.m$

$$= \mathbf{10.61 \times 10^6\ N.mm}$$

(**Note** : Relation between maximum torque and average torque is not given.)

(ii)    Diameter based on strength criteria :

$$T = \left(\dfrac{J}{R}\right) \cdot \tau_{max}$$

$$10.61 \times 10^6 = \left(\dfrac{\pi}{16} \cdot D^3\right) \cdot 50$$

$\therefore \qquad\qquad\qquad\qquad D = \mathbf{102.62\ mm} \qquad\qquad\qquad\qquad\qquad\qquad$ ... (i)

(iii)    Diameter based on stiffness criteria :

$$\dfrac{T}{J} = \dfrac{G\theta}{L} \quad \therefore \quad J = \dfrac{T\,L}{G\theta}$$

$$\dfrac{\pi}{32} \cdot D^4 = \dfrac{10.61 \times 10^6 \times 2600}{80 \times 10^3 \times 0.0279}$$

$\therefore \qquad\qquad\qquad\qquad D = 105.92\ mm \qquad\qquad\qquad\qquad\qquad\qquad$ ... (ii)

$\therefore \qquad\qquad\qquad\qquad D = \mathbf{105.92\ mm}$

$\qquad\qquad\qquad\qquad\qquad \mathbf{say\ 106\ mm} \qquad\qquad\qquad$ (Greater of (i) and (ii))

**Example 9.8** : *Design the cross-section of hollow shaft for which internal diameter is $\left(\dfrac{3}{4}\right)^{th}$ of its external diameter to resist a torque of 1600 N.m such that shear stress does not exceed 60 MPa and angle of twist does not exceed $2^0$ for 1.8 m length. Assume G = 80 GPa.*

**Data**    :    $d = \dfrac{3}{4}D$;   $T = 1600$ N.m;   $\tau_{max} = 60$ MPa;

$\qquad\qquad\qquad \theta = 2^0 = 0.0349$ rad;   $L = 1800$ mm;   $G = 80$ GPa.

**Required**    :    Design of cross-section of shaft.

**Concept**    :    Same as Example (9.7).

**Solution**    :    (i) Diameter based on strength criteria :

$$T = \left(\dfrac{J}{R}\right) \tau_{max}$$

$$1600 \times 10^3 = \dfrac{\pi}{16\,D}\,(D^4 - d^4)\,60$$

$$1600 \times 10^3 = \dfrac{\pi}{16\,D}\left[D^4 - \left(\dfrac{3}{4}D\right)^4\right]60$$

$$D = 58.35\ mm$$

(ii)   Diameter based on stiffness criteria :

$$\frac{T}{J} = \frac{G\theta}{L} \quad \therefore \quad J = \frac{TL}{G\theta}$$

$$\frac{\pi}{32}(D^4 - d^4) = \frac{1600 \times 10^3 \times 1800}{80 \times 10^3 \times 0.0349}$$

$$\frac{\pi}{32}\left[D^4 - \left(\frac{3}{4}D\right)^4\right] = 1.031 \times 10^6$$

$$D = 62.61 \text{ mm}$$

$\therefore$   Use        $D = 62.61 \text{ mm} \cong \textbf{63 mm and}$

$$d = \frac{3}{4}(63) = 47.25 \text{ mm} \cong \textbf{47 mm}$$

---

**Example 9.9 :** *A hollow steel shaft 2.5 m long transmits a torque of 15 kN.m. Total angle of twist is not to exceed 2.5⁰ and permissible shear stress = 80 MPa. Determine inside and outside diameter of shaft. G = 82 GPa.*

**Data**        :   L = 2500 mm;  T = 15 kN.m;  $\theta$ = 2.5⁰ = 0.0436 rad

$\tau_{max}$ = 80 MPa;  G = 82 GPa

**Required**   :   Design of cross section of shaft.

**Concept**    :   Generally cross-section of shaft is designed for strength and stiffness criteria and dimensions to be provided are governed by greater of the requirement for above two conditions. For the design of hollow shaft, relation between external and internal diameter must be known to use the conventional procedure. In this example, this relation is not given.

**Solution**   :   (i) External diameter of shaft (D) :

Using;                    $$\frac{\tau_{max}}{R} = \frac{G\theta}{L}$$

$$\frac{80}{D/2} = \frac{82 \times 10^3 \times 0.0436}{2500}$$

$\therefore$              $D = \textbf{111.9 mm  say 112 mm.}$

(ii)   Polar M.I. of shaft :

$$\frac{T}{J} = \frac{G\theta}{L}$$

$\therefore$              $$J = \frac{TL}{G\theta} = \frac{15 \times 10^6 \times 2500}{82 \times 10^3 \times 0.0436}$$

$$J = \textbf{10.49} \times \textbf{10}^\textbf{6}\,\textbf{mm}^\textbf{4}$$

(iii)  Internal diameter of shaft

$$J = \frac{\pi}{32}(D^4 - d^4)$$

$$10.49 \times 10^6 = \frac{\pi}{32}(112^4 - d^4) = \textbf{84.3 mm  say 84 mm}$$

Thus;                 $D = \textbf{112 mm}$ and $d$ = **84 mm**

(**Note :** Internal diameter shall be rounded off on lower side.)

---

**Example 9.10 :** *A hollow shaft has 60 mm external diameter and 50 mm internal diameter. Determine the twisting moment it can resist if permissible shear stress is 100 MPa. Determine the diameter of solid circular shaft made of the same material which can transmit same twisting moment. Hence, compare their weights per metre length. Take G = 80 GPa.*

**Data**        :   D = 60 mm; d = 50 mm for hollow shaft; $\tau_{max}$ = 100 MPa; G = 80 GPa.

**Required**  :   Twisting moment; Diameter of solid shaft; Comparison of weights.

**Concept**   :   Hollow shaft is economical as compared to solid shaft.

**Solution**  :   (i) Geometric properties :

$$\text{For hollow shaft;} \quad J = \frac{\pi}{32}(D^4 - d^4)$$

$$= \frac{\pi}{32}(60^4 - 50^4)$$

$$= 658.75 \times 10^3 \text{ mm}^4$$

$$R = \frac{60}{2} = 30 \text{ mm}$$

$$\therefore \quad \frac{J}{R} = \frac{658.75 \times 10^3}{30} = \mathbf{21.96 \times 10^3 \text{ mm}^3}$$

(ii) Torque based on shear stress (T) :

$$T = \left(\frac{J}{R}\right)\tau_{max}$$

$$= 21.96 \times 10^3 \times 100$$

$$= \mathbf{2.196 \times 10^6 \text{ N.mm}}$$

(iii)    Diameter of solid shaft ($D_1$) :

$$T = \left(\frac{J}{R}\right)\tau_{max}$$

$$2.196 \times 10^6 = \left(\frac{\pi}{16}D_1^3\right)100$$

$$D_1 = 48.18 \text{ mm} \cong \mathbf{49 \text{ mm}}$$

(iv)    Comparison of weights :

$$(A)_{solid} = \frac{\pi}{4}D_1^2 = \frac{\pi}{4}(49)^2 = \mathbf{1885.74 \text{ mm}^2}$$

$$(A)_{hollow} = \frac{\pi}{4}(D^2 - d^2) = \frac{\pi}{4}(60^2 - 50^2) = \mathbf{863.94 \text{ mm}^2}$$

$$\frac{\text{Weight of solid shaft}}{\text{Weight of hollow shaft}} = \frac{(A)_{solid}}{(A)_{hollow}} = \frac{1885.74}{863.94} = \mathbf{2.18}$$

**Example 9.11 :** *Design diameter of solid shaft for resisting torque of 2500 N.m. Also design cross-section of hollow shaft made of same material assuming internal diameter as 0.7 times the external diameter for the same torque. Hence, comment on percentage saving in weight and shear stress for shaft. Assume allowable angle of twist 2° for 1 m length of both shafts. Take G = 80 GPa.*

**Data**        :   T = 2500 N.m; d = 0.7 D for hollow shaft;

$$\theta = 2° = 0.0349 \text{ rad}; \quad L = 1000 \text{ mm}; \quad G = 80 \text{ GPa}.$$

**Required** : Comparison of hollow and solid shaft.

**Concept** : Design of shafts based on stiffness criteria.

**Solution** : (i) Design of solid shaft :

Let,
$$D_1 = \text{Diameter of solid shaft}$$

$$\frac{T}{J} = \frac{G\theta}{L} \quad \therefore \quad J = \frac{TL}{G\theta}$$

$$\therefore \quad \frac{\pi}{32} D_1^4 = \frac{2500 \times 10^3 \times 1000}{80 \times 10^3 \times 0.0349}$$

$$= 895.41 \times 10^3 \text{ mm}^4$$

$$\therefore \quad D_1 = \textbf{54.95 mm}$$

(ii) Design of hollow shaft : $\quad J = \dfrac{TL}{G\theta}$

$$\frac{\pi}{32}(D^4 - d^4) = 895.41 \times 10^3 \text{ mm}^4$$

$$\frac{\pi}{32}[D^4 - (0.7\,D)^4] = 895.41 \times 10^3$$

$$D = \textbf{58.85 mm}$$

$$\therefore \quad d = \textbf{41.19 mm}$$

(iii) Comparison of weights :

$$A_s = \frac{\pi}{4}\left(D_1^2\right) = \frac{\pi}{4} \times 54.95^2 = \textbf{2.37} \times \textbf{10}^3 \text{ mm}^2$$

$$A_h = \frac{\pi}{4}(D^2 - d^2) = \frac{\pi}{4}[(58.85)^2 - (41.19)^2]$$

$$= \textbf{1.387} \times \textbf{10}^3 \text{ mm}^2$$

$$\text{Percentage saving in weight} = \frac{A_s - A_h}{A_s} \times 100$$

$$= \frac{(2.37 - 1.387) \times 10^3}{2.37 \times 10^3} \times 100$$

$$= \textbf{41.47 \%}$$

(iv) Comparison of shear stresses :

For solid shaft,
$$\frac{J}{R} = \frac{895.41 \times 10^3}{\dfrac{54.95}{2}} = \textbf{32.59} \times \textbf{10}^3 \text{ mm}^3$$

$$\tau_s = \frac{T}{J/R} = \frac{2500 \times 10^3}{32.59 \times 10^3} = \textbf{76.71 MPa}$$

For hollow shaft,
$$\frac{J}{R} = \frac{895.41 \times 10^3}{58.85/2}$$

$$= \textbf{30.43} \times \textbf{10}^3 \text{ mm}^3$$

$$\tau_h = \frac{T}{J/R} = \frac{2500 \times 10^3}{30.43 \times 10^3} = \textbf{82.15 MPa}$$

Thus; $\qquad \dfrac{\tau_s}{\tau_h} = \dfrac{76.71}{82.15} = 0.93$

$\therefore \qquad \tau_s = 0.93\,\tau_h$

i.e. $\qquad \tau_h = \mathbf{1.075\,\tau_s}$

**Note :** For the same torque when solid and hollow shafts are designed from stiffness criteria, there is saving in weight when hollow shaft is used. However, shear stress developed for hollow shaft is of higher magnitude than that of solid shaft. If this stress of comparatively higher magnitude for hollow shaft is less than permissible stress, then only replacement of solid shaft by hollow shaft will be possible.

It should also be noted that for stress criteria of design, polar section modulii (J/R) of solid and hollow shafts are same while for stiffness criteria of design, polar moment of inertia (J) of solid and hollow shafts are same.

**Example 9.12 :** *Design diameter of solid shaft for resisting torque of 2500 N.m. Also design cross-section of hollow shaft made of same material assuming internal diameter as 0.7 times the external diameter for the same torque. Hence, comment on percentage saving in weight and angle of twist per unit length of shafts. Assume permissible shear stress = 60 MPa.*

**Data** : $T = 2500$ N.m; $d = 0.7\,D$ for hollow shaft; $\tau_{max} = 60$ MPa.

**Required** : Comparison of hollow and solid shaft.

**Concept** : Design of shafts based on strength criteria.

**Solution** : (i) Design of solid shaft :

Let $\qquad D_1$ = Diameter of solid shaft

$$T = \left(\frac{J}{R}\right)\tau_{max}$$

$\therefore \qquad 2500 \times 10^3 = \left[\frac{\pi}{16}\left(D_1^3\right)\right]60$

$\therefore \qquad D_1 = \mathbf{59.64\ mm}$

(ii) Design of hollow shaft :

$$T = \left(\frac{J}{R}\right)\tau_{max}$$

$$2500 \times 10^3 = \frac{\pi}{16\,D}(D^4 - d^4) \times 60$$

$$= \frac{\pi}{16\,D}(D^4 - (0.7\,D)^4) \times 60$$

$\therefore \qquad D = \mathbf{65.36\ mm}$

$\therefore \qquad d = 0.7\,D$

$\qquad = 0.7 \times 65.36$

$\qquad = \mathbf{45.75\ mm}$

(iii) Comparison of weights :

$$A_{solid} = \frac{\pi}{4}D_1^2 = \frac{\pi}{4}(59.64)^2 = 2.79 \times 10^3\ mm^2$$

$$A_{hollow} = \frac{\pi}{4}(D^2 - d^2) \quad = \frac{\pi}{4}\left((65.36)^2 - (45.75)^2\right)$$

$$= \mathbf{1.71 \times 10^3 \ mm^2}$$

$$\text{Percentage saving in weight} \quad = \frac{A_{solid} - A_{hollow}}{A_{solid}} \times 100$$

$$= \frac{(2.79 - 1.71) \times 10^3}{2.79 \times 10^3} \times 100$$

$$= \mathbf{38.7 \ \%}$$

(iv)  Comparison of angle of twist :

For solid shaft,
$$J = \frac{\pi}{32} \cdot D_1^4 = \frac{\pi}{32}(59.64)^4$$

$$= \mathbf{1.242 \times 10^6 \ mm^4}$$

For hollow shaft,
$$J = \frac{\pi}{32}(D^4 - d^4) = \frac{\pi}{32}\left((65.36)^4 - (45.75)^4\right)$$

$$= \mathbf{1.36 \times 10^6 \ mm^4}$$

Angle of twist for solid shaft

$$\theta_s = \frac{TL}{GJ_s}$$

$$= \frac{TL}{G \times 1.242 \times 10^6}$$

Angle of twist for hollow shaft $= \ \theta_h = \dfrac{TL}{GJ_h}$

$$\theta_h = \frac{TL}{G \times 1.36 \times 10^6}$$

$$\therefore \qquad \frac{\theta_s}{\theta_h} = \frac{TL}{G \times 1.242 \times 10^6} \times \frac{G \times 1.36 \times 10^6}{TL}$$

$$\frac{\theta_s}{\theta_h} = 1.095$$

$$\therefore \qquad \theta_s = \mathbf{1.095 \ \theta_h}$$

i.e. $\qquad \theta_h = \mathbf{0.913 \ \theta_s}$

**Note :** For the same torque when solid and hollow shafts are designed from strength criteria there is saving in weight if hollow shaft is used. Also angle of twist for hollow shaft is smaller than that of solid shaft. Hence, if stress is the criteria of design, hollow shaft has advantage over solid shaft.

**Example 9.13 :** *Compare the weights of equal lengths of hollow and solid shaft to resist same torsional moment for same maximum shear stress. Assume internal diameter 0.8 times the external diameter for hollow shaft.*

**Data**      :    d = 0.8 D for hollow shaft :

**Required**  :    Ratio of weights for hollow and solid shaft.

**Concept**   :    Design based on strength criteria and then comparison of weights.

**Solution** : (i) For solid shaft

Let, $\quad D_1$ = diameter of solid shaft

$$\tau_{max} = \left(\frac{T}{J}\right) \cdot R = \frac{T}{J/R}$$

$$= \frac{T}{\left(\frac{\pi}{16}\right) D_1^3} \qquad \dots (i)$$

(ii) For hollow shaft

Let $\quad D$ = External diameter

$\quad d$ = 0.8 D = Internal diameter

$\therefore \quad \tau_{max} = \left(\frac{T}{J}\right) \cdot R = \frac{T}{(J/R)}$

$$= \frac{T}{\left(\frac{\pi}{16\,D}\right)(D^4 - d^4)}$$

$$= \frac{T}{\left(\frac{\pi}{16\,D}\right)(D^4 - (0.8\,D)^4)}$$

$$= \frac{T}{\left(\frac{\pi}{16}\right) \cdot (0.59\,D^3)} \qquad \dots (ii)$$

(iii) Relation between diameter of solid and hollow shaft :

Equating (i) and (ii)

$$\frac{T}{\left(\frac{\pi}{16}\right) D_1^3} = \frac{T}{\left(\frac{\pi}{16}\right)(0.59\,D^3)}$$

$$D_1 = \mathbf{0.84\,D}$$

(iv) Comparison of weights :

Cross-sectional area of solid shaft = $A_s = \frac{\pi}{4} \cdot D_1^2$

$$= \frac{\pi}{4}(0.84\,D)^2$$

$$= (0.7056) \cdot \frac{\pi}{4}\,D^2$$

Cross-sectional area of hollow shaft = $A_h = \frac{\pi}{4}(D^2 - d^2)$

$$= \frac{\pi}{4}(D^2 - (0.8\,D)^2)$$

$$= (0.36) \cdot \frac{\pi}{4} \cdot D^2$$

$\therefore \quad \dfrac{\text{Weight of hollow shaft}}{\text{Weight of solid shaft}} = \dfrac{A_h}{A_s} = \dfrac{0.36}{0.7056} = \mathbf{0.51}$

**Example 9.14 :** *A solid shaft of 200 mm diameter has the same cross-sectional area as that of hollow shaft of the same materials of inside diameter 150 mm.*

   *(i)      Find the ratio of power transmitted by the two shafts of same angular velocity.*

   *(ii)     Compare angle of twist in equal lengths of these shafts when stressed equally.*

**Data :** $d = 150$ mm for hollow shaft, $D_1 = 20$ mm for solid shaft

**Required :** Comparison of hollow and solid shaft.

**Concept :** Design of shafts based on stiffness criteria.

**Solution :** (i) Outside diameter of hollow shaft :

$$\frac{\pi}{4}(D^2 - d^2) = \frac{\pi}{4}D_1^2$$

$$(D^2 - 150^2) = 200^2$$

$$D = 250 \text{ mm}$$

(ii)    Ratio of power transmitted :

$$\frac{\text{Power transmitted by hollow shaft}}{\text{Power transmitted by solid shaft}} = \frac{\text{Torque transmitted by hollow shaft}}{\text{Torque transmitted by solid shaft}}$$

$$\text{Torque transmitted by hollow shaft} = \left(\frac{J}{R}\right)\tau_{max}.$$

$$\therefore \qquad T = \pi\frac{(250^4 - 150^4)}{16 \times 250} \times \tau_{max}$$

$$= 2.67 \times 10^6\,\tau_{max}$$

$$T_1 = \frac{\pi}{16}D^3\,\tau_{max}$$

$$= \frac{\pi}{16} \times 200^3 \times \tau_{max}$$

$$= 1.57 \times \tau_{max}$$

$$\therefore \qquad \frac{T}{T_1} = \frac{2.67 \times 10^6 \times \tau_{max}}{1.57 \times \tau_{max}}$$

$$\therefore \qquad \frac{P}{P_1} = \frac{T}{T_1} = 1.7$$

(iii) Comparison of angle of twist :

$$\frac{\tau_{max}}{R} = \frac{G\theta}{l}$$

$$\therefore \qquad \theta_{hollow} = \frac{\tau_{max} \times l}{G \times 125}$$

$$\therefore \qquad \theta_{solid} = \frac{\tau_{max} \times l}{G \times 100}$$

$$\therefore \qquad \frac{\theta_{hollow}}{\theta_{solid}} = \frac{100}{125} = 0.8$$

$$\therefore \qquad \boldsymbol{\theta_{hollow} = 0.8\,\theta_{solid}}$$

**Example 9.15 :** *A hollow circular shaft having internal diameter 50 % of its external diameter transmits 600 kW at 150 r.p.m. Determine the external diameter of the shaft if the shear stress is not to exceed 65 N/mm² and a twist in a length of 3 m should not exceed 1.4°.*

*Assume : $T_{max}$ = 1.2 ($T_{mean}$) , G = 100 GPa.*

**Data :** $d = \dfrac{D}{2}$, $\tau_{max}$ = 65 N/mm², $\theta$ = 1.4° = 0.0244 rad, $L$ = 3000 mm, G = 100 GPa,

$$P = 600 \text{ kW, } N = 150 \text{ r.p.m.}$$

**Required :** External diameter.

**Concept :** Design based on strength and stiffness criteria.

**Solution :** (i) Torque calculation :

$$P = \frac{2\pi NT}{60}$$

$$T = \frac{P \times 60}{2\pi N} = \frac{600 \times 10^3 \times 60}{2\pi \times 150}$$

$$= 38.197 \times 10^3 \text{ N-m}$$

$$T_{max} = 1.2 \times T = 1.2 \times 38.197 \times 10^6 = 45.384 \times 10^6 \text{ N.mm}$$

(ii)　Diameter based on strength criteria :

$$T = \frac{J}{R}\,\tau_{max}$$

$$45.384 \times 10^6 = \frac{\pi}{16D}(D^4 - d^4)\,65$$

$$45.384 \times 10^6 = \frac{\pi}{16D}\left(D^4 - \frac{D^4}{16}\right)65$$

$$D = 156.47 \text{ mm}$$

(iii) Diameter based on stiffness criteria :

$$\frac{T}{J} = \frac{G\theta}{L} \qquad\qquad \therefore\, J = \frac{T\,L}{G\theta}$$

$$\frac{\pi}{32}(D^4 - d^4) = \frac{45.384 \times 10^6 \times 3000}{100 \times 10^3 \times 0.0244}$$

$$D = \textbf{156.92 mm say 160 mm}$$

# 9.8 SHAFTS IN SERIES

When two or more shafts are connected length-wise, they are said to be in series. It is also called as *compound shaft*. For the analysis of shafts in series, following points are to be noted :

(i)　　All the component shafts are co-axially connected i.e. polar axis is common for all the shafts.

(ii)　　Joint between the components is rigid i.e. there is no relative rotation between the two adjacent shafts at a joint.

Consider a compound shaft ABC subjected to torque 'T' as shown in Fig. 9.7.

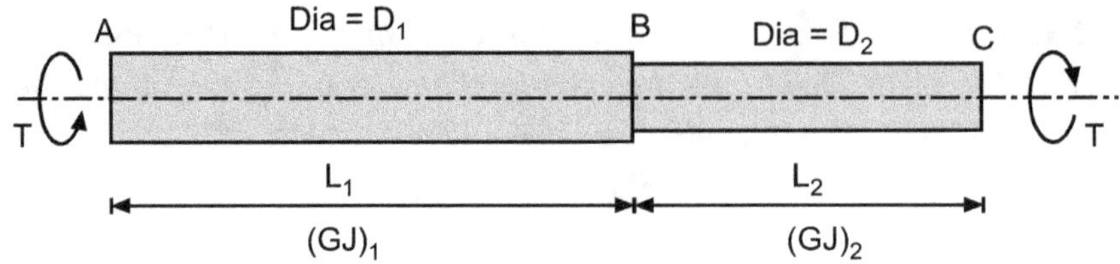

**Fig. 9.7 : Shafts in series**

Shear stress for portion AB = $\tau_1 = \dfrac{T}{J_1}\left(\dfrac{D_1}{2}\right)$

Shear stress for portion BC = $\tau_2 = \dfrac{T}{J_2}\left(\dfrac{D_2}{2}\right)$

Total angle of twist at C relative to A

$$= (\theta)_{AC} = (\theta)_{AB} + (\theta)_{BC}$$

$$= \left(\dfrac{TL}{GJ}\right)_{AB} + \left(\dfrac{TL}{GJ}\right)_{BC}$$

$$= T\left[\dfrac{L_1}{(GJ)_1} + \dfrac{L_2}{(GJ)_2}\right] \qquad \text{... (9.10 a)}$$

$$= T \text{ [Sum of flexibility coefficients for components]}$$

If material for shafts AB and BC is same,

$$(\theta)_{AC} = \dfrac{T}{G}\left[\dfrac{L_1}{J_1} + \dfrac{L_2}{J_2}\right] \qquad \text{... (9.10 b)}$$

**Example 9.16 :** *A compound shaft ABCD has details as shown in Fig. 9.8. Determine inside diameter of portion AB such that shear stresses developed in portions AB and CD are equal. Also find total angle of twist if shaft is subjected to torque of 1.1 kN.m. Assume G = 80 GPa.*

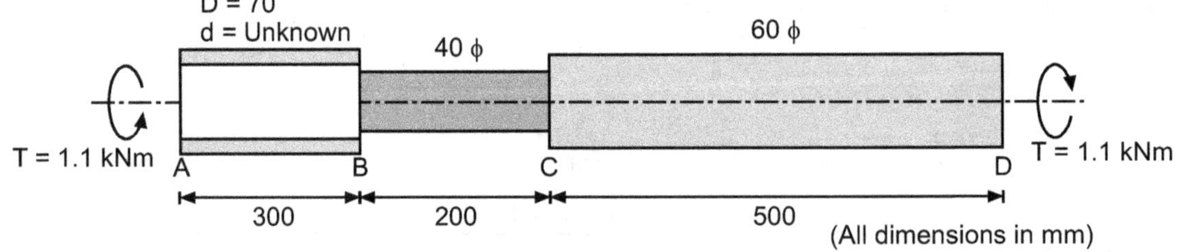


**Fig. 9.8**

**Data**      :   As shown in Fig. 9.8; T = 1.1 kN.m; G = 80 GPa; $\tau_{AB} = \tau_{CD}$.

**Required**  :   Inside diameter (d) for AB and total angle of twist.

**Concept**   :   (i) Equating shear stress for portions AB and CD, get the diameter of portion AB.

(ii) Total angle of twist at D relative to A = $\theta_{AD} = \theta_{AB} + \theta_{BC} + \theta_{CD}$.

**Solution**  :   (i) Geometric properties :

| Component | J (mm$^4$) | R (mm) | (J/R) (mm$^3$) |
|---|---|---|---|
| AB | $\dfrac{\pi}{32}(70^4 - d^4)$ | $\dfrac{70}{2} = 35$ | $\dfrac{\pi}{1120}(70^4 - d^4)$ |
| BC | $\dfrac{\pi}{32}(40)^4 = 251.33 \times 10^3$ | $\dfrac{40}{2} = 20$ | $12.57 \times 10^3$ |
| CD | $\dfrac{\pi}{32}(60)^4 = 1272.35 \times 10^3$ | $\dfrac{60}{2} = 30$ | $42.41 \times 10^3$ |

(ii)      Inside diameter for AB :

$$\tau_{AB} = \tau_{CD}$$

$$\left(\frac{T}{J/R}\right)_{AB} = \left(\frac{T}{J/R}\right)_{CD}$$

$$\therefore \quad \left(\frac{J}{R}\right)_{AB} = \left(\frac{J}{R}\right)_{CD}$$

$$\frac{\pi}{1120}(70^4 - d^4) = 42.41 \times 10^3$$

$$\therefore \quad d = 54.605 \text{ mm}$$

$$\therefore \quad (J)_{AB} = \frac{\pi}{32}(70^4 - 54.605^4)$$

$$\therefore \quad (J)_{AB} = \mathbf{1.484 \times 10^6 \ mm^4}$$

(iii)      Total angle of twist :

$$\theta = \theta_{AB} + \theta_{BC} + \theta_{CD}$$

$$= \left(\frac{T}{G}\right)\left[\left(\frac{L}{J}\right)_{AB} + \left(\frac{L}{J}\right)_{BC} + \left(\frac{L}{J}\right)_{CD}\right]$$

$$= \frac{1.1 \times 10^6}{80 \times 10^3}\left[\frac{300}{1.484 \times 10^6} + \frac{200}{251.33 \times 10^3} + \frac{500}{1272.35 \times 10^3}\right]$$

$$= 0.01912 \text{ rad.}$$

$$\theta = \mathbf{1.095^o}$$

**Example 9.17 :** *A compound shaft consists of brass and steel components coaxially attached; fixed at one end and subjected to torque T at free end as shown in Fig. 9.9. Find the safe value of torque T at free end subjected to following conditions :*

*(i) $\tau_{brass} \leq 40$ MPa  (ii) $\tau_{steel} \leq 60$ MPa  (iii) $\theta \leq 2.5^o$ .*

*Assume $G_S = 80$ GPa and $G_b = 35$ GPa.*

*Also find actual stresses developed in each part.*

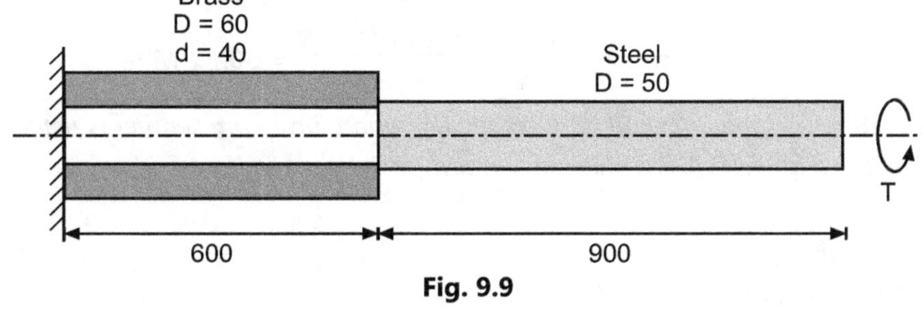


**Fig. 9.9**

**Data**　　　：　As shown in Fig. 9.9; $\tau_B \le 40$ MPa; $\tau_S \le 60$ MPa; $\theta \le 2.5^\circ$; $G_S = 80$ GPa; $G_b = 35$ GPa.

**Required**　：　Safe torque (T) at free end and shear stresses.

**Concept**　：　Safe torque (T) is the least of that obtained from given conditions of strength and stiffness.

**Solution**　：　(i) Geometric properties :

| Component | $J$ (mm$^4$) | $R$ (mm) | $\left(\dfrac{J}{R}\right)$ (mm$^3$) |
|---|---|---|---|
| Brass | $\dfrac{\pi}{32}(60^4 - 40^4) = 1.021 \times 10^6$ | $\dfrac{60}{2} = 30$ | $34.03 \times 10^3$ |
| Steel | $\dfrac{\pi}{32}(50)^4 = 613.59 \times 10^3$ | $\dfrac{50}{2} = 25$ | $24.54 \times 10^3$ |

(ii)　Torque based on strength criteria :

(a)　$\tau_B \le 40$ MPa.

$\therefore$　　　　$T = \left(\dfrac{J}{R}\right)_B \times \tau_B = 34.03 \times 10^3 \times 40$

$\therefore$　　　　$T = \mathbf{1361.2 \times 10^3}$ **N.mm**　　　　　　　　... (i)

(b)　$\tau_S \le 60$ MPa

$\therefore$　　　　$T = \left(\dfrac{J}{R}\right)_S \cdot \tau_S$

　　　　　　$= 24.54 \times 10^3 \times 60 = \mathbf{1472.4 \times 10^3}$ **N.mm**　　　　... (ii)

(iii)　Torque based on stiffness criteria ($\theta \le 2.5^\circ$)

Maximum angle of twist at free end $= \theta_B + \theta_S$

$$2.5 \times \frac{\pi}{180} = T\left[\left(\frac{L}{GJ}\right)_B + \left(\frac{L}{GJ}\right)_S\right]$$

$$= T\left[\frac{600}{35 \times 10^3 \times 1.021 \times 10^6} + \frac{900}{80 \times 10^3 \times 613.59 \times 10^3}\right]$$

$\therefore$　　　　$T = \mathbf{1242.227 \times 10^3}$ **N.mm**　　　　　　... (iii)

$\therefore$ Safe torque　　$T = \mathbf{1242.227 \times 10^3}$ **N.mm**　　(Least of (i), (ii), and (iii))

(iv)　Shear stresses :　　$\tau_B = \dfrac{T}{(J/R)_B} = \dfrac{1242.227 \times 10^3}{34.03 \times 10^3} = \mathbf{36.50}$ **MPa**

　　　　　　　　　　$\tau_S = \dfrac{T}{(J/R)_S} = \dfrac{1242.227 \times 10^3}{24.54 \times 10^3} = \mathbf{50.62}$ **MPa**

---

**Example 9.18 :** *A compound shaft consists of steel and aluminium segments acted upon by two torques as shown in Fig. 9.10. Determine maximum permissible value of 'T' subjected to following conditions.*

*(i) $\tau_S \le 80$ MPa　(ii) $\tau_a \le 55$ MPa　(iii) $\theta \le 6^\circ$*

*Assume $G_S = 83$ GPa and $G_a = 28$ GPa.*

---

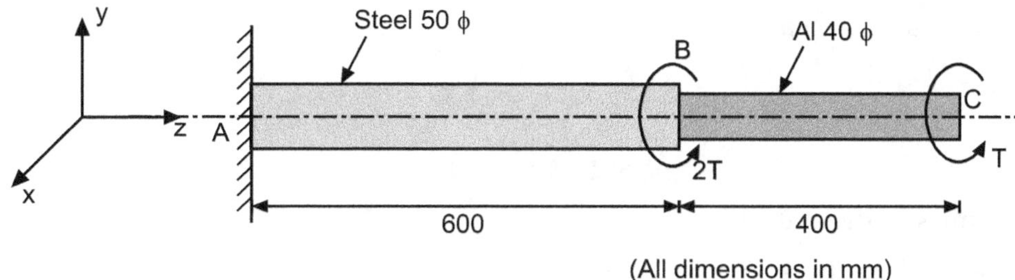



**Fig. 9.10**

**Data**    :  As shown in Fig. 9.10; $\tau_s \le 80$ MPa; $\tau_a \le 55$ MPa;

$\theta \le 6°$; $G_s = 83$ GPa; $G_a = 28$ GPa.

**Required**  :  Safe value of torque 'T'.

**Concept**  :  Reactive torque at fixed end; torsional moment diagram; strength criteria; stiffness criteria.

**Solution**  :  (i) Analysis :

From statistics;

$$\sum M_z = 0 \text{ gives reactive torque at fixed end A} = 3\,T \;(\rightarrow)$$

FBD of shaft and torsional moment diagram is as shown in Fig. 9.11.

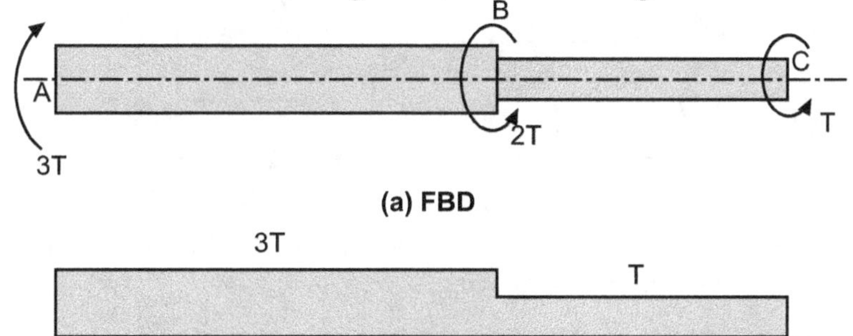



**(a) FBD**



**(b) TMD**

**Fig. 9.11**

(ii)    Geometric properties :

| Component | J (mm⁴) | R (mm) | $\left(\dfrac{J}{R}\right)$ (mm³) |
|---|---|---|---|
| Steel | $\dfrac{\pi}{32}(50)^4 = 613.59 \times 10^3$ | $\dfrac{50}{2} = 25$ | $24.54 \times 10^3$ |
| Aluminium | $\dfrac{\pi}{32}(40)^4 = 251.33 \times 10^3$ | $\dfrac{40}{2} = 20$ | $12.57 \times 10^3$ |

(iii)    Strength criteria :

    (a)    $\tau_s \le 80$ MPa

$$3T = \left(\frac{J}{R}\right)_s \cdot \tau_s = 24.54 \times 10^3 \times 80$$

$$\therefore \quad T = \mathbf{654.4 \times 10^3\ N.mm} \qquad \qquad \dots (i)$$

(b) $\quad \tau_a \leq 55$ MPa

$$T = \left(\frac{J}{R}\right)_a \cdot \tau_a = 12.57 \times 10^3 \times 55$$

$$= \mathbf{691.35 \times 10^3 \ N.mm} \qquad \qquad \dots \text{(ii)}$$

(iv)　Stiffness criteria ($\theta \leq 6^0$) :

$\theta_{max}$ at free end $= 6^0 = \theta_{AB} + \theta_{BC}$

$$6 \times \frac{\pi}{180} = \left(\frac{TL}{GJ}\right)_{AB} + \left(\frac{TL}{GJ}\right)_{BC}$$

$$= \frac{3T \times 600}{83 \times 10^3 \times 613.59 \times 10^3} + \frac{T \times 400}{28 \times 10^3 \times 251.33 \times 10^3}$$

$$T = \mathbf{1135.98 \times 10^3 \ N.mm} \qquad \qquad \dots \text{(iii)}$$

Safe value of T$= \mathbf{654.4 \times 10^3 \ N.mm}$ $\qquad$ (Least of (i), (ii) and (iii))

**Example 9.19 :** *The shaft shown in Fig. 9.12 below rotates at 200 r.p.m. with 40 H.P. and 20 H.P. taken off at A and B respectively and 60 H.P. applied at C. Find the maximum shear stress developed in the shaft and angle of twist of gear 'A' relative to gear 'C'. G = 85 GPa.*

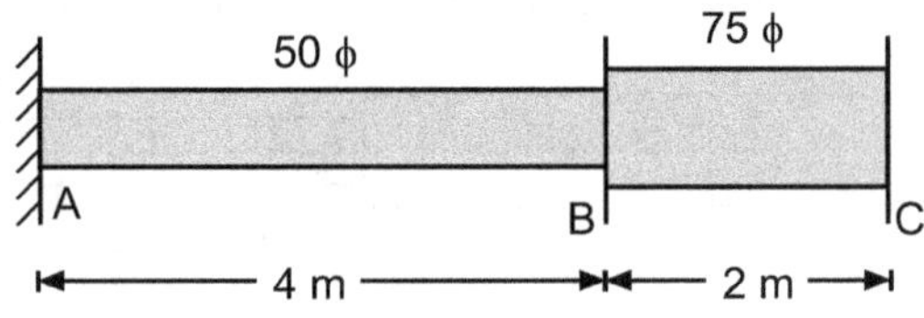


**Fig. 9.12**

**Data** : $\quad$ N = 200 r.p.m.; at A and B 40 H.P. and 20 H.P. taken off, while at C 60 HP applied; G = 85 GPa.

**Required** : $\quad$ Maximum shear stress and angle of twist at A w.r.t. C.

**Concept** : $\quad$ From the given power, find torques at A, B and C, draw torsional moment diagram and then analyse for stresses and angle of twist.

**Solution** : $\quad$ (i) Analysis and T.M.D.

$$P_A = 40 \text{ H.P.} = \frac{2\pi \, NT_A}{4500} = \frac{2\pi \times 200 \times T_A}{4500}$$

$\therefore \qquad T_A = \mathbf{143.24 \ N.m} \ (\circlearrowleft)$

$$P_B = 20 \text{ H.P.} = \frac{2\pi \, NT_B}{4500} = \frac{2\pi \times 200 \times T_B}{4500}$$

$\therefore \qquad T_B = \mathbf{71.62 \ N.m} \ (\circlearrowleft)$

$$P_C = 60 \text{ H.P.} = \frac{2\pi \, NT_C}{4500} = \frac{2\pi \times 200 \times T_C}{4500}$$

$\therefore \qquad T_C = \mathbf{214.86 \ N.m} \ (\circlearrowright)$

Fig. 9.13 (a) below shows FBD and Fig. 9.13 (b) shows torsional moment diagram for the shaft.

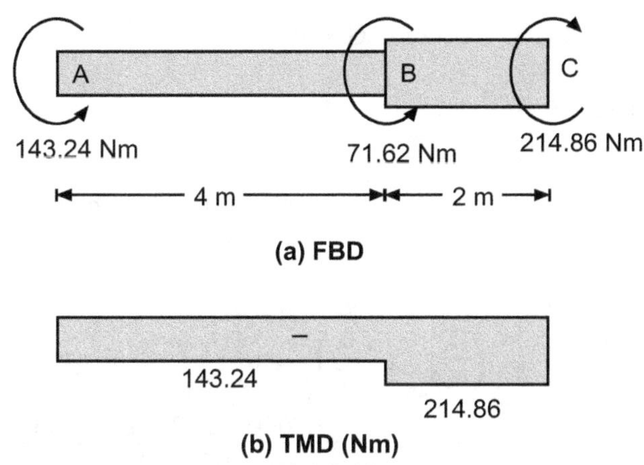



**(a) FBD**



**(b) TMD (Nm)**

**Fig. 9.13**

(ii)    Geometric properties :

| Component | $J$ (mm⁴) | $R$ (mm) | $\left(\dfrac{J}{R}\right)$ (mm³) |
|---|---|---|---|
| AB | $\dfrac{\pi}{32}(50)^4 = 613.59 \times 10^3$ | $\dfrac{50}{2} = 25$ | $24.54 \times 10^3$ |
| BC | $\dfrac{\pi}{32}(75)^4 = 3106.31 \times 10^3$ | $\dfrac{75}{2} = 37.5$ | $82.83 \times 10^3$ |

(iii)   Shear stresses :

$$\tau_{AB} = \frac{T_{AB}}{(J/R)_{AB}} = \frac{143.24 \times 10^3}{24.54 \times 10^3} = \textbf{5.83 MPa}$$

$$\tau_{BC} = \frac{T_{BC}}{(J/R)_{BC}} = \frac{214.86 \times 10^3}{82.83 \times 10^3} = \textbf{2.59 MPa}$$

$$\therefore \qquad \tau_{max} = \textbf{5.83 MPa}$$

(iv)    Angle of twist of gear 'A' w.r.t. gear 'C'

$$\theta_{AC} = \theta_{AB} + \theta_{BC} = \left(\frac{TL}{GJ}\right)_{AB} + \left(\frac{TL}{GJ}\right)_{BC}$$

$$= \frac{1}{85 \times 10^3}\left[\frac{143.24 \times 10^3 \times 4000}{613.59 \times 10^3} + \frac{214.86 \times 10^3 \times 2000}{3106.31 \times 10^3}\right]$$

$$= 0.0126 \text{ rad} = \textbf{0.7219}°$$

**Example 9.20 :** *An aluminium shaft of constant diameter 80 mm is loaded by torques applied to gears attached to it, as shown in Fig. 9.14. Determine the angle of twist of gear A relative to gear D. G = 30 GPa.*

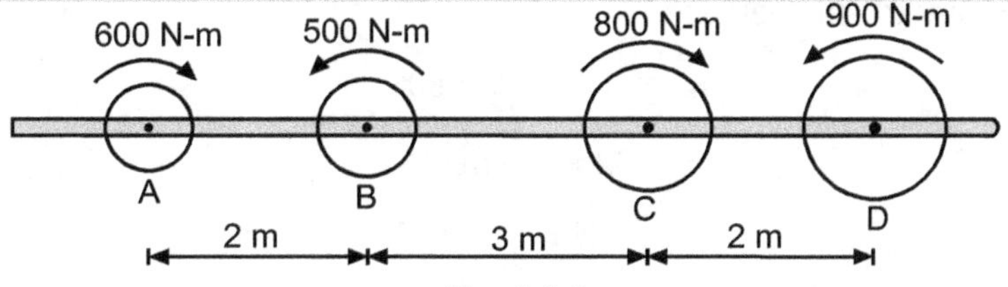



**Fig. 9.14**

**Data :** As shown in Fig. 9.14,  D = 80 mm, G = 30 GPa.

**Required :** Twist at D w.r. to A.

**Concept :** $\theta_{A/D} = \theta_A + \theta_B + \theta_C + \theta_D$.

**Solution :** (i) Geometric properties :

$$J \;=\; \frac{\pi}{32}\,D^4 = \frac{\pi}{32} \times 80^4 \;=\; 4.02 \times 10^6 \text{ mm}^4$$

(ii)      Calculation for $\theta_{A/D}$

$$\theta_{A/D} \;=\; \theta_A + \theta_B + \theta_C + \theta_D$$

$$=\; \left(\frac{TL}{JG}\right)_{AB} + \left(\frac{TL}{JG}\right)_{BC} + \left(\frac{TL}{JG}\right)_{CD} \;=\; \frac{1}{JG}\left[(TL)_{AB} + (TL)_{BC} + (TL)_{CD}\right]$$

$$=\; \frac{[-\,600 \times 10^3 \times 2000 - 100 \times 10^3 \times 3000 - 900 \times 10^3 \times 2000]}{4.02 \times 10^6 \times 30 \times 10^3}$$

$$\theta_{A/D} \;=\; \textbf{0.027 radians = 1.57}$$

**Example 9.21 :** *A stepped shaft is subjected the couples (in the same direction) at change in section at the free end as shown in Fig. 9.15 (a). The length of each section is 0.5 m and diameters are 80 mm, 60 mm and 40 mm. If G = 80 GPa, find the angle of twist $\theta$ in degrees at the free end   .*

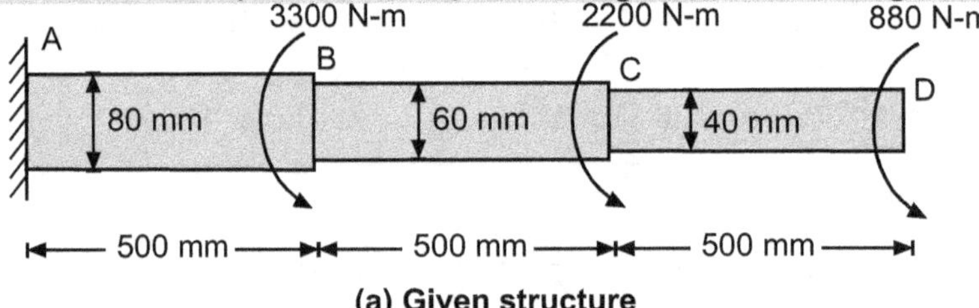



**(a) Given structure**

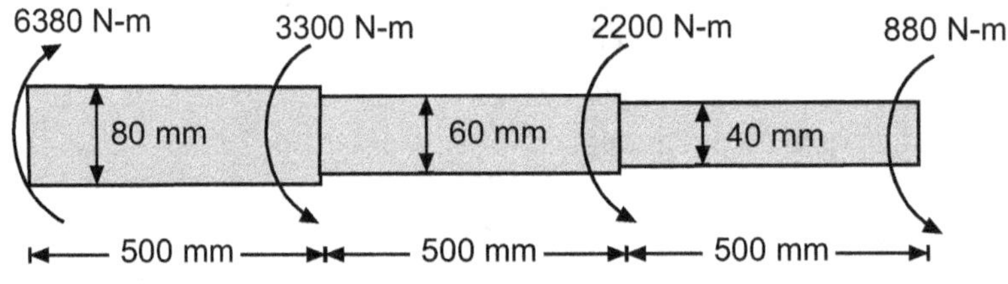



**(b) FBD**

**Fig. 9.15**

**Data :** As shown in Fig. 9.15 (a), G = 80 GPa.

**Required :** Angle of twist '$\theta$' at the free end.

**Concept :** $\theta = \theta_{AB} + \theta_{BC} + \theta_{CD}$.

**Solution :** (i) Geometric properties :

$$J_{AB} \;=\; \frac{\pi}{32}\,D^4 = \frac{\pi}{32} \times 80^4$$

$$=\; 4.02 \times 10^6 \text{ mm}^4$$

$$J_{BC} \;=\; \frac{\pi}{32}\,D^4 = \frac{\pi}{32} \times 60^4$$

$$=\; 1.27 \times 10^6 \text{ mm}^4$$

$$J_{CD} = \frac{\pi}{32} D^4 = \frac{\pi}{32} \times 40^4$$

$$= 251.33 \times 10^3 \text{ mm}^4$$

**(ii)**   Torsion in members :

$$T_{AB} = 3300 + 2200 + 880 = 6380 \text{ N.m}$$

$$= 6.38 \times 10^6 \text{ N.mm}$$

$$T_{BC} = 2200 + 880 = 3080 \text{ N.m}$$

$$= 3.08 \times 10^6 \text{ N.mm}$$

$$T_{CD} = 880 \text{ N-m}$$

$$= 880 \times 10^3 \text{ N.mm}$$

$$\theta = \theta_{AB} + \theta_{BC} + \theta_{CD}$$

$$= \left(\frac{TL}{GJ}\right)_{AB} + \left(\frac{TL}{GJ}\right)_{BC} + \left(\frac{TL}{GJ}\right)_{CD}$$

$$= \frac{L}{G}\left[\left(\frac{T}{J}\right)_{AB} + \left(\frac{T}{J}\right)_{BC} + \left(\frac{T}{J}\right)_{CD}\right]$$

$$= \frac{500}{80 \times 10^3}\left[\frac{6.38 \times 10^6}{4.02 \times 10^6} + \frac{3.08 \times 10^6}{1.27 \times 10^6} + \frac{880 \times 10^3}{251.33 \times 10^3}\right]$$

$$\theta = \mathbf{0.047 \text{ radians} = 2.69°.}$$

# 9.9 STATICALLY INDETERMINATE PROBLEMS

## 9.9.1 Shafts Fixed at Both Ends

*When equations of statics are not sufficient to evaluate the unknown forces, it is called as statically indeterminate problem.* For example, consider a shaft fixed at two ends and subjected to torque T as shown in Fig. 9.16.

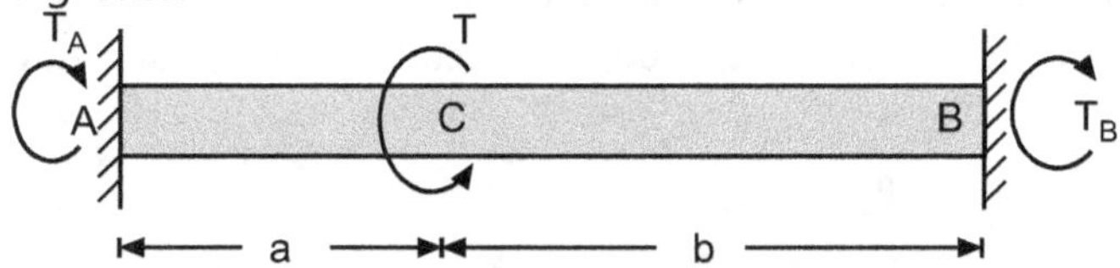

**Fig. 9.16 : Shaft fixed at both ends**

Unknown reactions = $T_A$ and $T_B$ i.e. resistive torques at A and B.

Equation of statics : $\sum M_z = 0$ gives

$$T_A + T_B = T \qquad\qquad\qquad \text{... (9.11)}$$

Second equation can be formulated using the fact that angle of twist of C ($\theta_{CA}$) due to torque '$T_A$' acting over length AC is equal to angle of twist at C ($\theta_{CB}$) due to torque '$T_B$' acting over length CB.

$$\theta_{CA} = \theta_{CB}$$

$$\left(\frac{TL}{GJ}\right)_{CA} = \left(\frac{TL}{GJ}\right)_{CB} \qquad\qquad\qquad \text{... (9.12)}$$

Substituting geometric properties for portions CA and CB in equation (9.12), relation between $T_A$ and $T_B$ can be obtained. Then by using equation (9.11), $T_A$ and $T_B$ can be evaluated.

**Note :** Equation (9.12) is the condition of deformation called as **equation of compatibility** wherein member deformation is assumed continuous.

The above situation will be called as externally indeterminate because equations of statics are not sufficient enough to evaluate external reactive torques $T_A$ and $T_B$. However, member can be internally indeterminate also as discussed below.

### 9.9.2  Shafts in Parallel

*When one shaft is surrounded by other shaft, the two shafts are said to be in parallel.*

Consider two shafts placed in parallel as shown in Fig. 9.17.

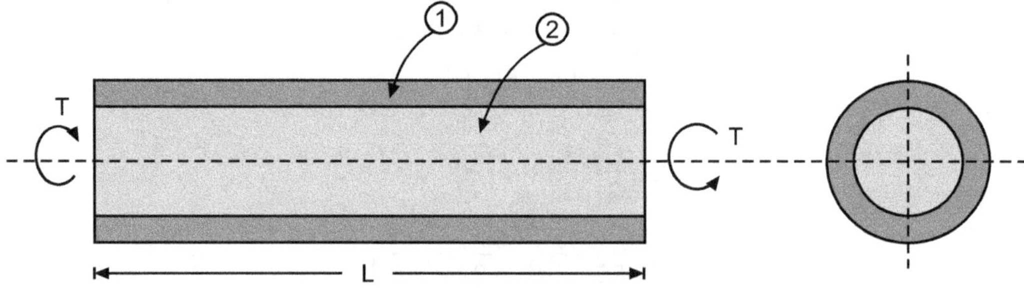

**Fig. 9.17 : Shafts in parallel**

Let,          T  = Total torque acting on the shaft

$T_1 ; T_2$  = Torque resisted by individual components 1 and 2 respectively.

Unknown torques are $T_1$ and $T_2$ while the equation of statics available is only one i.e.

$$\sum M_z = 0 \Rightarrow \quad T = T_1 + T_2 \qquad \text{... (9.13)}$$

Second equation can be formulated using the fact that the angle of twist for both the shafts for a given length under the action of given torque, is constant. This is the equation of **compatibility** here.

Thus,              $\theta_1 = \theta_2$

$$\left(\frac{TL}{GJ}\right)_1 = \left(\frac{TL}{GJ}\right)_2 \qquad \text{... (9.14 a)}$$

Lengths of both components being same for the shaft considered in Fig. 9.17,

$$\left(\frac{T}{GJ}\right)_1 = \left(\frac{T}{GJ}\right)_2 \qquad \text{... (9.14 b)}$$

Solving equations (9.13) and (9.14), values of $T_1$ and $T_2$ can be obtained.

The above situation will be called as internally indeterminate because equations of statics are not sufficient enough to evaluate internal resistive torques $T_1$ and $T_2$.

**Note :** In the above analysis, it is assumed that the shafts are co-axially fitted and there is no relative rotation between the two components.

**Example 9.22 :** *A uniform bar AB of length 'L' is fixed at A and B. It is subjected to torque 'T' at 'C' at a distance 'a' from left end and 'b' from right end. Derive expressions for reactive torques developed at A and B and draw torsional moment diagram.*

**Data**          :    As shown in Fig. 9.18 (a).

**Required**   :    Expressions for reactive torques.

**Concept**    :    Statically indeterminate; equation of statics and compatibility.

**Solution**    :    (i) Equation of statics :

$$\sum M_z = 0 ; \quad T_A + T_B = T \qquad \qquad \text{... (i)}$$

(ii)   Equation of compatibility :

$$\theta_{CA} = \theta_{CB}$$

$$\left(\frac{TL}{GJ}\right)_{CA} = \left(\frac{TL}{GJ}\right)_{CB}$$

$$T_A \cdot a = T_B \cdot b \quad \therefore \quad T_A = \frac{b}{a} T_B \qquad \qquad \text{... (ii)}$$

(iii)   Solution of equations :

Solving (i) and (ii),

$$T_A = \frac{Tb}{L} \, (\circlearrowleft) \quad \text{and} \quad T_B = \frac{Ta}{L} \, (\circlearrowleft)$$

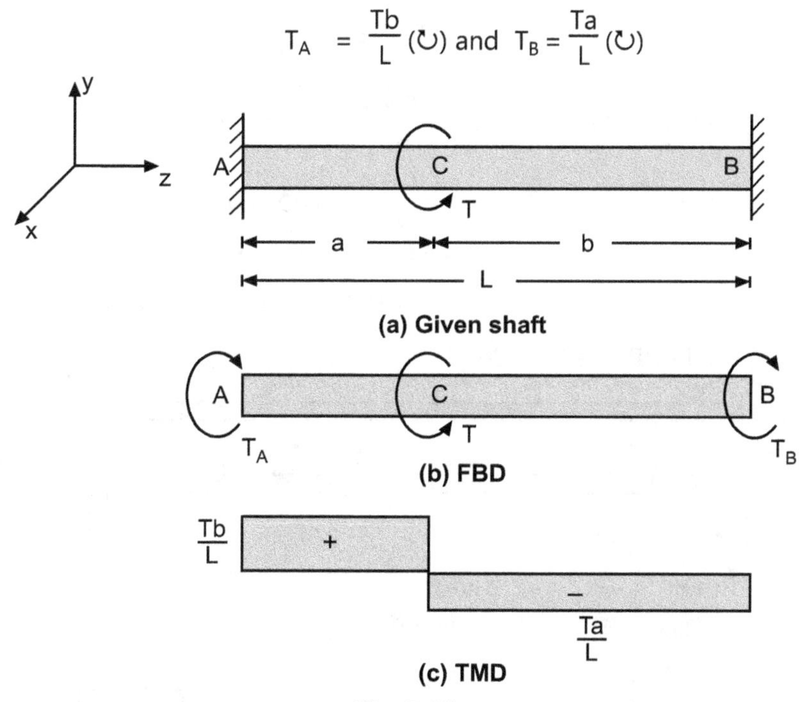


**Fig. 9.18**

**Example 9.23 :** *A steel shaft ABCD is subjected to torques as shown in Fig. 9.19. (i) Determine reactive torques at fixed ends, (ii) Draw torsional moment diagram, (iii) Find maximum shear stress and angle of twist. Assume G = 80 GPa.*

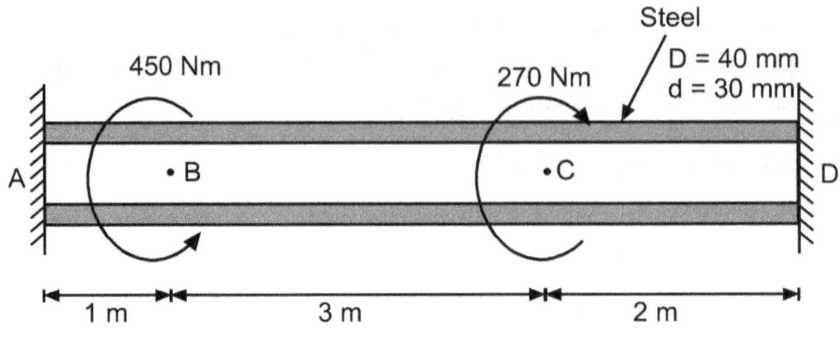


**Fig. 9.19**

**Data**        :   As shown in Fig. 9.19;  G = 80 GPa.

**Required**    :   Reactive torques at A and D; TMD; Maximum shear stress and angle of twist.

**Concept**     :   Statically indeterminate problem, use of standard results and principle of superposition.

**Solution**    :   (i) Reactive torques :

Using standard result and principle of superposition.

Reactions due to 450 N.m ($\circlearrowleft$)       $T_A = \dfrac{450 \times 5}{6} = $ **375 N.m** ($\circlearrowleft$)

$$T_D = \dfrac{450 \times 1}{6} = \textbf{75 N.m} \ (\circlearrowleft)$$

Reactions due to 270 N.m ($\circlearrowright$)       $T_A = \dfrac{270 \times 2}{6} = $ **90 N.m** ($\circlearrowright$)

$$T_D = \dfrac{270 \times 4}{6} = \textbf{180 N.m} \ (\circlearrowright)$$

Final reactions,          $T_A = 375 - 90 = $ **285 N.m** ($\circlearrowleft$)

$$T_B = 75 - 180 = -105 \ \text{N.m} = \textbf{105 N.m} \ (\circlearrowright)$$

(ii)    FBD and torsional moment diagram.

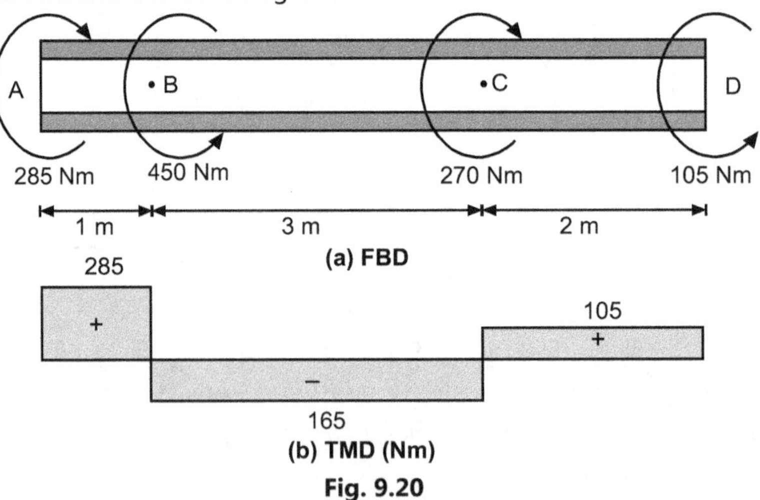


**Fig. 9.20**

(iii)    Geometric properties :

$$J = \frac{\pi}{32}(40^4 - 30^4) = 171.8 \times 10^3 \text{ mm}^4$$

$$R = \frac{40}{2} = 20 \text{ mm}$$

$$\frac{J}{R} = \frac{171.8 \times 10^3}{20} = \textbf{8.59} \times \textbf{10}^3 \textbf{ mm}^3$$

(iv)    Maximum shear stress ($\tau_{max}$)

Maximum shear stress will occur in portion AB.

$$\therefore \qquad \tau_{max} = \frac{T_{AB}}{(J/R)} = \frac{285 \times 10^3}{8.59 \times 10^3} = \textbf{33.18 MPa}$$

(v)    Maximum angle of twist.

$$\theta_{AB} = \left(\frac{TL}{GJ}\right)_{AB} = \frac{285 \times 10^3 \times 1000}{80 \times 10^3 \times 171.8 \times 10^3} = \textbf{0.0207 rad} \ (\circlearrowleft)$$

$$\theta_{BC} = \left(\frac{TL}{GJ}\right)_{BC} = \frac{165 \times 10^3 \times 3000}{80 \times 10^3 \times 171.8 \times 10^3} = \textbf{0.036 rad} \ (\circlearrowright)$$

$$\theta_{CD} = \left(\frac{TL}{GJ}\right)_{CD} = \frac{105 \times 10^3 \times 2000}{80 \times 10^3 \times 171.8 \times 10^3} = \textbf{0.0153 rad} \ (\circlearrowleft)$$

$\therefore$    Maximum angle of twist = 0.036 rad = 2.063° which occurs in portion BC.

**Note :** Total angle of twist from A to D

$$= \theta_{AB} + \theta_{BC} + \theta_{BD}$$

$$= -0.0207 + 0.036 - 0.0153$$

$$= 0 \text{ (Ends A and D are fixed).}$$

**Example 9.24 :** *A compound shaft shown in Fig. 9.21 is attached to rigid supports. Determine the ratio of lengths 'b' to 'a' so that each material is stressed to its permissible limit. What torque T is applied ? Assume $G_b$ = 42 GPa; $G_s$ = 84 GPa; $\tau_b \leq 70$ MPa; $\tau_s \leq 100$ MPa.*

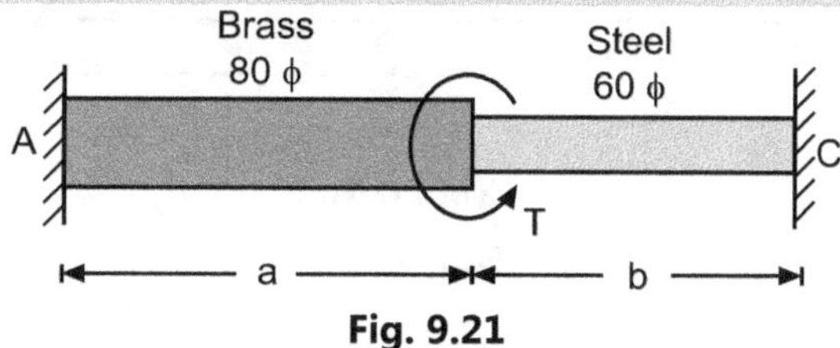


**Fig. 9.21**

**Data**          :    As shown in Fig. 9.21.

**Required**   :    Ratio $\dfrac{b}{a}$ and T.

**Concept**    :    Both materials brass and steel are stressed to their permissible limit, hence torques on portions AB and BC are known. Equation of equilibrium and compatibility.

**Solution**   :    (i) Geometric properties :

| Component | $J$ (mm$^4$) | $R$ (mm) | $\left(\dfrac{J}{R}\right)$ (mm$^3$) |
|---|---|---|---|
| Brass | $\dfrac{\pi}{32}(80)^4 = 4.02 \times 10^6$ | $\dfrac{80}{2} = 40$ | $100.5 \times 10^3$ |
| Steel | $\dfrac{\pi}{32}(60)^4 = 1.27 \times 10^6$ | $\dfrac{60}{2} = 30$ | $42.41 \times 10^3$ |

(ii)  Torque for components :

$$T_{brass} = \text{Reactive torque at A} = T_A$$

$$= \left(\frac{J}{R}\right)_b \cdot \tau_b$$

$$= 100.5 \times 10^3 \times 70$$

$$= \mathbf{7.035 \times 10^6 \ N.mm}$$

$$T_{steel} = \text{Reactive torque at C} = T_C$$

$$= \left(\frac{J}{R}\right)_s \cdot \tau_s$$

$$= 42.41 \times 10^3 \times 100$$

$$= \mathbf{4.241 \times 10^6 \ N.mm}$$

(iii)  FBD and torsional moment diagram :

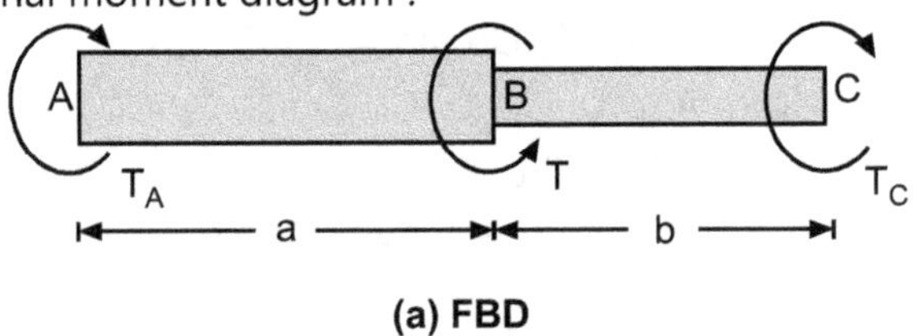


**(a) FBD**

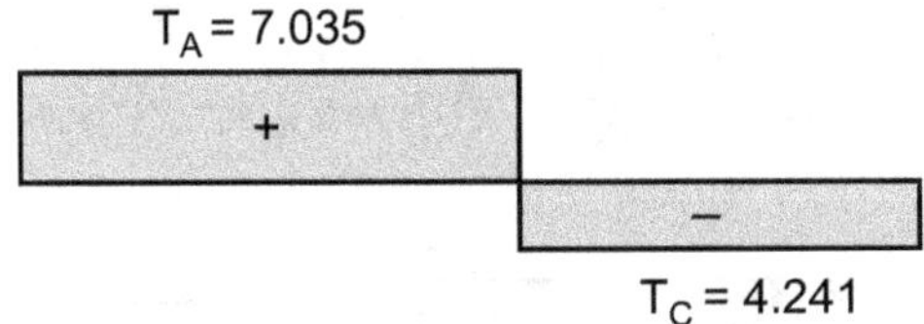


**(b) TMD (kNm)**

**Fig. 9.22**

(iv)  Compatibility :

$$\theta_{BA} = \theta_{BC}$$

$$\left(\frac{TL}{GJ}\right)_{BA} = \left(\frac{TL}{GJ}\right)_{BC}$$

$$\frac{7.035 \times 10^6 \times a}{42 \times 10^3 \times 4.02 \times 10^6} = \frac{4.241 \times 10^6 \times b}{84 \times 10^3 \times 1.27 \times 10^6}$$

$$\therefore \quad \frac{b}{a} = \mathbf{1.048}$$

(v)     Equilibrium :
$$T = T_A + T_C$$
$$= (7.035 + 4.241) \times 10^6$$
$$= \mathbf{11.276 \times 10^6 \ N.mm}$$

**Example 9.25 :** *A shaft ABC fixed at 'A' and 'B' is subjected to torque of 42.5 N.m at 'C' as shown in Fig. 9.23. Calculate the end reactions and shear stresses in both components. Also find angle of twist at junction 'C'.*

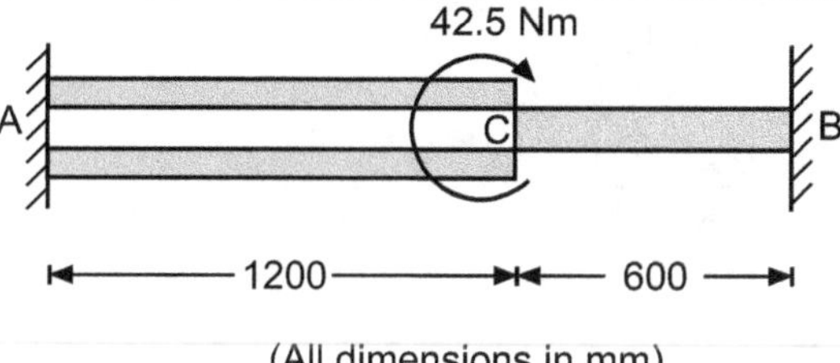


**Fig. 9.23**

**Data :** As shown in Fig. 9.23.

**Required :** End reactions; shear stresses; and angle of twist at 'C'.

**Concept :** Equations of equilibrium and compatibility.

| AC | CB |
|---|---|
| **Brass** | **Steel** |
| D = 30 mm | D = 20 mm |
| d = 20 mm |  |
| $G_b$ = 39 GPa | $G_s$ = 79 GPa |

**Solution   :**   (i) Geometric properties :

| Component | J (mm⁴) | R (mm) | $\left(\dfrac{J}{R}\right)$ (mm³) |
|---|---|---|---|
| Brass | $\dfrac{\pi}{32}(30^4 - 20^4) = 63.81 \times 10^3$ | $\dfrac{30}{2} = 15$ | $4.254 \times 10^3$ |
| Steel | $\dfrac{\pi}{32}(20^4) = 15.71 \times 10^3$ | $\dfrac{20}{2} = 10$ | $1.571 \times 10^3$ |

(ii)    Equation of statics :
$$T = T_A + T_B$$
$$42.5 = T_A + T_B \qquad \text{... (i)}$$

(iii)   Equation of compatibility :
$$\theta_{CA} = \theta_{CB}$$
$$\left(\frac{TL}{GJ}\right)_{CA} = \left(\frac{TL}{GJ}\right)_{CB}$$
$$\frac{T_A \times 1200}{39 \times 10^3 \times 63.81 \times 10^3} = \frac{T_B \times 600}{79 \times 10^3 \times 15.71 \times 10^3}$$
$$T_A = T_B \qquad \text{... (ii)}$$

(iv)    Solution of equations :
Solving equations (i) and (ii),
$$\mathbf{T_A = T_B = 21.25 \ N.m}$$

(v)     Shear stresses :

$$\tau_{brass} = \left(\frac{T}{J/R}\right)_{brass} = \frac{21.25 \times 10^3}{4.254 \times 10^3} = \mathbf{4.99 \ MPa}$$

$$\tau_{steel} = \left(\frac{T}{J/R}\right)_{steel} = \frac{21.25 \times 10^3}{1.571 \times 10^3} = \mathbf{13.52 \ MPa}$$

(vi)    Angle of twist at C :

$$\theta_{CA} = \theta_{CB} = \left(\frac{TL}{GJ}\right)_{brass} \ OR \ \left(\frac{TL}{GJ}\right)_{steel}$$

$$= \frac{21.25 \times 10^3 \times 1200}{39 \times 10^3 \times 63.81 \times 10^3}$$

$$= 0.0102 \ rad.$$

$$= \mathbf{0.587^o}$$

**Example 9.26 :** *For a compound shaft ABC shown in Fig. 9.24 if allowable shear stress is 70 MPa, find the safe value of torque T at C.*

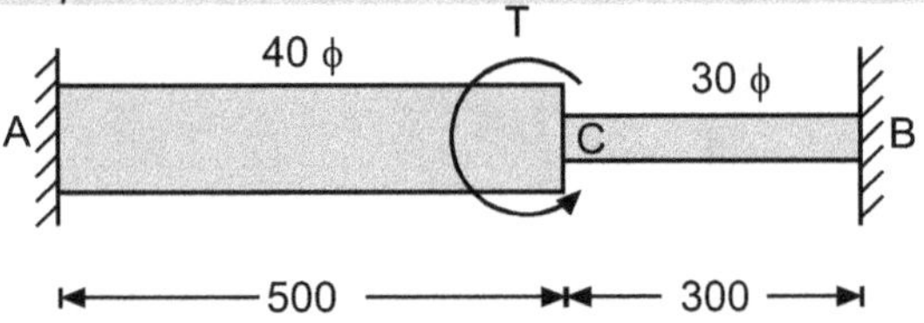


(All dimensions in mm)

**Fig. 9.24**

**Data**         :    As shown in Fig. 9.24; $\tau_{max}$ = 70 MPa

**Required**     :    Safe value of torque T at C.

**Concept**      :    Equations of statics and compatibility.

**Solution**     :    (i) Geometric properties :

| Component | J (mm⁴) | R (mm) | $\left(\dfrac{J}{R}\right)$ (mm³) |
|---|---|---|---|
| AC | $\dfrac{\pi}{32}(40)^4 = 251.33 \times 10^3$ | $\dfrac{40}{2} = 20$ | $12.57 \times 10^3$ |
| CB | $\dfrac{\pi}{32}(30)^4 = 79.52 \times 10^3$ | $\dfrac{30}{2} = 15$ | $5.3 \times 10^3$ |

(ii)    Equation of compatibility :

$$\theta_{CA} = \theta_{CB}$$

$$\left(\frac{TL}{GJ}\right)_{CA} = \left(\frac{TL}{GJ}\right)_{CB}$$

$$\frac{T_A \times 500}{251.33 \times 10^3} = \frac{T_B \times 300}{79.52 \times 10^3} \qquad (\because G = constant)$$

$$\therefore \qquad T_A = \mathbf{1.896 \ T_B} \qquad \qquad ... (i)$$

(iii)    Equation of equilibrium :

$$T = T_A + T_B$$

Let, stress in portion CB reaches to allowable value of 70 MPa.

$\therefore$

$$T_B = \left(\frac{J}{R}\right)_{CB} \tau_{CB} = 5.3 \times 10^3 \times 70$$

$$= \mathbf{371 \times 10^3 \ N.mm}$$

$\therefore$    Put $T_B$ in equation (i)

$$T_A = 1.896 \times 371 \times 10^3$$

$$= \mathbf{703.416 \times 10^3 \ N.mm}$$

$\therefore$

$$\tau_{AC} = \frac{T_A}{(J/R)_{AC}} = \frac{703.416 \times 10^3}{12.57 \times 10^3} = 55.96 \ MPa < 70 \ MPa \ (OK)$$

$\therefore$

$$T = (703.416 + 371) \times 10^3$$

$$= 1074.416 \times 10^3 \ N.mm$$

$$= \mathbf{1074.416 \ N.m}$$

**Note :** If stress calculated for portion AC is greater than 70 MPa, allow portion AC to get stressed to 70 MPa and find corresponding stress in portion CB. Stress calculated for portion CB will then be less than 70 MPa.

---

**Example 9.27 :** *A composite shaft consists of copper rod 40 mm $\phi$ enclosed in a steel tube of 50 mm external diameter and 5 mm thickness. There is no relative motion between the two and shafts are coaxially fixed. Determine shear stresses developed in copper and steel rods if both the shafts have equal lengths. Assume $G_C = 40$ GPa; $G_S = 80$ GPa and torque = 1400 N.m.*

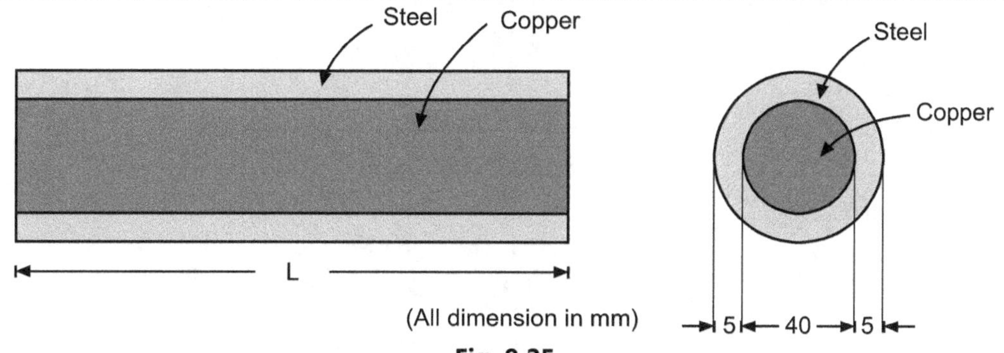


**Fig. 9.25**

**Data**           :   As shown in Fig. 9.25; $G_C = 40$ GPa; $G_S = 80$ GPa; T = 1400 N.m.

**Required**   :   Shear stresses for steel and copper.

**Concept**     :   Statically indeterminate problem; Equation of statics : $T_S + T_C = T$.

Equation of compatibility : $\theta_S = \theta_C$.

**Solution**    :   (i) Geometric properties :

---

For copper;
$$J_c = \frac{\pi}{32}(40)^4 = 251.33 \times 10^3 \text{ mm}^4$$

$$R = \frac{40}{2} = 20 \text{ mm}$$

$\therefore$
$$\left(\frac{J}{R}\right)_c = \frac{251.33 \times 10^3}{20} = \mathbf{12.56 \times 10^3 \text{ mm}^3}$$

For s teel;
$$J_s = \frac{\pi}{32}(50^4 - 40^4) = \mathbf{362.26 \times 10^3 \text{ mm}^4}$$

$$R = \frac{50}{2} = 25$$

$$\left(\frac{J}{R}\right)_s = \frac{362.26 \times 10^3}{25} = \mathbf{14.49 \times 10^3 \text{ mm}^3}$$

(ii)  Equation of statics :

$$T = T_c + T_s$$
$$1400 = T_c + T_s \qquad \qquad \text{... (i)}$$

(iii)  Equation of compatibility :

$$\theta_c = \theta_s$$
$$\left(\frac{TL}{GJ}\right)_c = \left(\frac{TL}{GJ}\right)_s \qquad \qquad \left[\because L_c = L_s\right]$$

$$\frac{T_c}{40 \times 10^3 \times 251.33 \times 10^3} = \frac{T_s}{80 \times 10^3 \times 362.26 \times 10^3}$$

$\therefore$
$$T_c = \mathbf{0.3469\ T_s} \qquad \qquad \text{... (ii)}$$

(iv)  Solution of equations :
Solving (i) and (ii) ;
$$T_c = \mathbf{360.58 \text{ N.m}}$$
$$T_s = \mathbf{1039.42 \text{ N.m}}$$

(v)  Shear stresses :

For copper;
$$\tau_c = \frac{T_c}{(J/R)_c} = \frac{360.58 \times 10^3}{12.56 \times 10^3} = \mathbf{28.7 \text{ MPa}}$$

For steel;
$$\tau_s = \frac{T_s}{(J/R)_s} = \frac{1039.42 \times 10^3}{14.49 \times 10^3} = \mathbf{71.73 \text{ MPa}}$$

**Example 9.28 :** *A composite shaft is made of 40 mm $\phi$ steel core enclosed in alloy tube of 60 mm external diameter and 10 mm thickness. There is no relative motion between the two and shafts are coaxially fitted. Permissible shear stress for steel and alloy are 60 MPa and 40 MPa respectively. Find maximum power transmitted by composite shaft at 500 r.p.m. Assume $G_s = 80$ GPa and $G_a = 44$ GPa.*

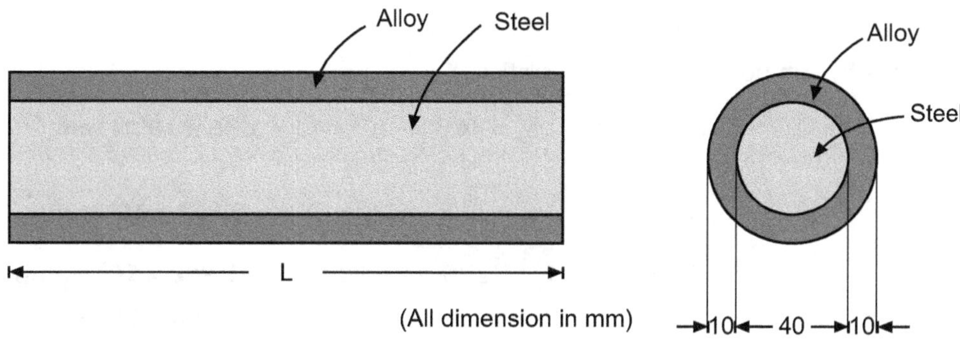


**Fig. 9.26**

**Data**        :   $\tau_s = 60$ MPa; $\tau_a = 40$ MPa; $G_s = 80$ GPa; $G_a = 44$ GPa; $N = 500$ r.p.m.

**Required**    :   Power transmitted by composite shaft.

**Concept**     :   Permissible shear stresses for the two materials are given. It does not mean that both the materials are subjected to given values of stresses. Hence governing stresses shall be found out from angle of twist which is constant for both the shafts.

**Solution**    :   (i) Geometric properties :

$$\text{For steel; } J_s \quad = \quad \frac{\pi}{32}(40)^4 = 251.33 \times 10^3 \text{ mm}^4$$

$$R \quad = \quad \frac{40}{2} = 20 \text{ mm}$$

$$\therefore \quad \left(\frac{J}{R}\right)_s \quad = \quad \frac{251.33 \times 10^3}{20} = \mathbf{12.57 \times 10^3 \ mm^3}$$

$$\text{For alloy; } \quad J_a \quad = \quad \frac{\pi}{32}(60^4 - 40^4) = 1021.01 \times 10^3$$

$$R \quad = \quad \frac{60}{2} = 30 \text{ mm}$$

$$\therefore \quad \left(\frac{J}{R}\right)_a \quad = \quad \frac{1021.01 \times 10^3}{30} = \mathbf{34.03 \times 10^3 \ mm^3}$$

(ii)   Governing stresses using compatibility.

$$\theta_s \quad = \quad \theta_a$$

$$\left(\frac{\tau L}{GR}\right)_s \quad = \quad \left(\frac{\tau L}{GR}\right)_a \qquad \left(\because \text{ using } \frac{\tau}{R} = \frac{G\theta}{L}\right)$$

$$\frac{\tau_s}{80 \times 10^3 \times 20} \quad = \quad \frac{\tau_a}{44 \times 10^3 \times 30}$$

$$\tau_s \quad = \quad \mathbf{1.21 \ \tau_a} \qquad \qquad \dots \text{(i)}$$

Let, stress in alloy is allowed to reach to 40 MPa.

$$\text{Stress in steel} \quad = \quad \tau_s = 1.21 \times 40 = \mathbf{48.4 \ MPa < 60 \ MPa} \qquad \dots \text{(OK)}$$

**Note :** If this condition is not satisfied, give second trial by allowing stress in steel to reach its permissible value and find stress in alloy using equation (i) and compare it with permissible stress.

Thus; in our case, $\tau_a = 40$ MPa and $\tau_s = 48.4$ MPa

(iii)    Torque by composite shafts from statics :

$$T_a = \left(\frac{J}{R}\right)_a \times \tau_a = 34.03 \times 10^3 \times 40 = \mathbf{1.36 \times 10^6 \ N.mm}$$

$$T_s = \left(\frac{J}{R}\right)_s \times \tau_s = 12.57 \times 10^3 \times 48.4 = \mathbf{0.608 \times 10^6 \ N.mm}$$

$$\therefore \quad T = T_a + T_s = (1.36 + 0.608) \times 10^6 = \mathbf{1.968 \times 10^6 \ N.mm}$$

$$= \mathbf{1.968 \times 10^3 \ N.m.}$$

(iv)    Power transmitted (P) :

$$P = \frac{2\pi\ NT}{60} = \frac{2\pi \times 500 \times 1.968 \times 10^3}{60} = 103.04 \times 10^3 \ W$$

$$= \mathbf{103.04 \ kW}$$

**Example 9.29 :** *A shaft of 80 mm diameter transmits 150 kN power at 180 r.p.m. A flanged coupling is keyed to the shaft by means of a key 100 mm long and 30 mm wide. The coupling has 6 bolts of 20 mm diameter symmetrically arranged along a bolt circle of 200 mm diameter. Calculate the shear stress in the shaft, the key and the bolts of the coupling.*

**Solution :** (i) For shaft,

$$J = (\pi/32)\,(80)^4 = 4.02 \times 10^6 \ \text{mm}^4$$

$$P = \frac{(2\pi NT)}{60}$$

$$150 \times 10^3 = \frac{2\pi \times 180 \times T}{60} \qquad \therefore \ T = \mathbf{7957.74 \ N.m}$$

$$\tau = (T/J) \times R = \frac{7957.74 \times 10^3}{4.02 \times 10^6} \times 40 = \mathbf{79.18 \ MPa}$$

(ii)    For key,     Shear force $= \dfrac{T}{R} = \dfrac{7957.74 \times 10^3}{40} = \mathbf{198943.5 \ N}$

Shear stress $= \dfrac{198943.5}{100 \times 30} = \mathbf{66.31 \ MPa}$

(iii) For bolts,

$$\tau = (T/J) \times R'$$

$$= \frac{7957.74 \times 10^3}{6 \times (\pi/4) \times (20)^2 \times 100^2}\,(100) = \mathbf{42.21 \ MPa}$$

**Example 9.30 :** *A bar of steel is 40 mm in diameter and 450 mm long. A tensile load of 100 kN is found to stretch the bar by 0.25 mm. The same bar when subjected to a torque of 1.2 kN-m, is found to twist through 2°. Find the values of four elastic constants.*

**Solution :** (i)

$$A = 1256.63 \ \text{mm}^2$$

$$J = 251.32 \times 10^3 \ \text{mm}^4$$

(ii)

$$\delta_L = \frac{PL}{AE}$$

$$\therefore \quad 0.25 = \frac{100 \times 450}{1256.63 \ E}$$

$$\therefore \quad E = \mathbf{143.24 \ GPa}$$

(iii)
$$\theta = \frac{TL}{GJ}$$

$$\frac{2\pi}{180} = \frac{1.2 \times 10^3 \times 450}{G \times 251.32 \times 10^3} \qquad \therefore G = \mathbf{61.55\ GPa}$$

(iv)
$$E = 2G\,(1 + \mu) = 3K\,(1 - 2\mu)$$

$\therefore$
$$\mu = \mathbf{0.163};\ K = \mathbf{70.96\ GPa}$$

**Example 9.31 :** *A steel shaft (G = 80 GPa) of total length 4 m is encased over half its length by a brass tube (40 GPa) that is securely bonded to the steel as shown in Fig. 9.27. The diameters of the shaft and tube are 70 mm and 90 mm respectively.*

(i)　　*Determine the allowable torque $T_1$ if the angle of twist $\theta$ between ends A and C is limited to $\theta = 12°$.*

(ii)　*Determine the allowable torque $T_2$ if the shear stress in brass is limited to $\tau_b = 100$ MPa.*

(iii)　*Determine the allowable torque $T_3$ if the shear stress in steel is limited to $\tau_s = 80$ MPa.*

(iv)　*What is the allowable torque T, if all three of the preceding conditions must be satisfied ?*

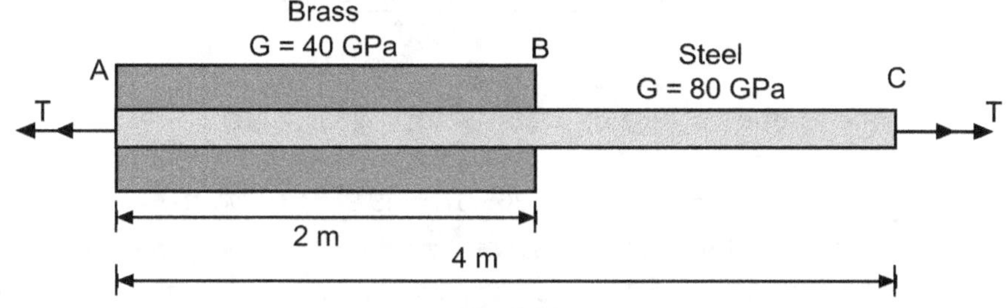


**Fig. 9.27**

**Solution :** (i)
$$J_{AB} = J_{Brass} = 4.084 \times 10^6 \text{ mm}^4$$
$$J_{BC} = J_{steel} = 2.35 \times 10^6 \text{ mm}^4$$

Apparent shear modulus for portion AB
$$G' = \frac{G_S J_S + G_B J_B}{J_S + J_B} = 54.609 \text{ GPa}$$

(ii)　For $\theta \le 12°$,
$$\theta_{A/C} = \{TL/GJ\}_{AB\,+\,BC}$$
$$\frac{12\pi}{180} = (T \times 2000)\,\{(1/54.609 \times 10^3 \times 6.434 \times 10^6) + (1/80 \times 10^3 \times 2.35 \times 10^6)\}$$
$$T = \mathbf{12.82 \times 10^6\ N.mm} \qquad\qquad \text{... (i)}$$

(iii)　For $\tau_B \le 100$ MPa,
$$\theta = \left(\frac{\tau L}{GR}\right)_S = \left(\frac{\tau L}{GR}\right)_B$$

$\therefore$
$$\frac{\tau_S \times 2000}{80 \times 10^3 \times 35} = \frac{\tau_B \times 2000}{40 \times 10^3 \times 45}$$

$\therefore$
$$\tau_S = 155.55 \text{ MPa (equating angle of twist)}$$
$$T = \{(J/R) \cdot \tau\}_B + \{(J/R) \cdot \tau\}_S = 19.51 \times 10^6$$
$$= 19.51 \times 10^6 \text{ N-mm} \qquad\qquad \text{... (ii)}$$

(iv)    For $\tau_s \leq 80$ MPa,

$$T = \{(J/R)\,\tau\}_s = 2.35 \times 10^6 \times 80/35$$

$$= \mathbf{5.37 \times 10^6\ N.mm} \qquad \text{... (iii)}$$

If all above conditions are to be satisfied, safe torque = **5.37 kN/m.**

**Example 9.32 :** *A 2.5 m long solid steel shaft of 30 mm diameter rotates at a frequency of 30 Hz. Determine the maximum power that the shaft may transmit, knowing that the allowable shearing stress is 50 MPa and that the angle of twist must not exceed 7.5°. G = 80 GPa.*

**Solution :** (i)     $\qquad J = 79.52 \times 10^3\ mm^4$

(ii)    Strength criteria :     $\dfrac{T}{J} = \dfrac{\tau_{max}}{R}$

$$T = 79.52 \times 10^3 \times \frac{50}{15} = 265.07 \times 10^3\ N.mm \qquad \text{... (i)}$$

(iii)   Stiffness criteria :     $\dfrac{T}{J} = \dfrac{G\theta}{L}$

$$T = \frac{79.52 \times 10^3 \times 80 \times 10^3 \times 7.5\pi}{180 \times 2500}$$

$$= \mathbf{333.1 \times 10^3\ N.mm} \qquad \text{...(ii)}$$

Safe torque $= 265.07 \times 10^3$ N.mm $= 265.07$ N.m

(iv)    Power $= 2\pi\ NT$

$$= 2\pi \times 30 \times 265.07 = 49.96 \times 10^3\ watts$$

**Example 9.33 :** *A tube of 50 mm outside diameter and 2 mm thickness is attached to a solid shaft of 25 mm diameter as shown in Fig. 9.28. If both the tube and the shaft are of the same material, what percentage of applied torque T is carried by the tube ?*

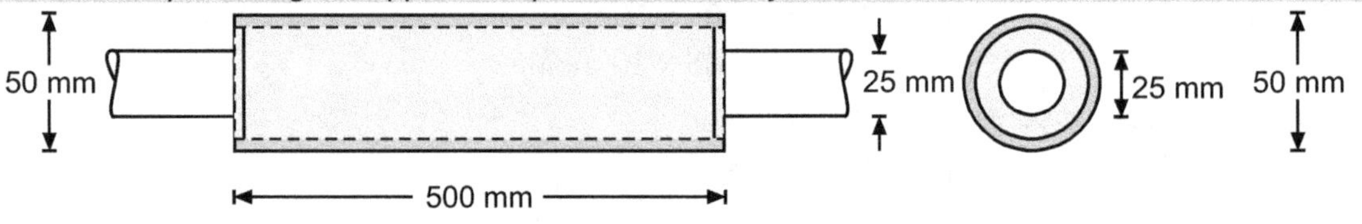


**Fig. 9.28**

**Data :** As shown in Fig. 9.28.

**Required :** Torque carried by the tube.

**Solution :** $\qquad T = T_t + T_s$

$$J_t = \frac{\pi}{32}\,(50^4 - 46^4)$$

$$= 174.02 \times 10^3\ mm^4$$

$$J_s = \frac{\pi}{32}\,D^4 = \frac{\pi}{32} \times 25^4$$

$$= 38.35 \times 10^3\ mm^4$$

$$Q_t = Q_s$$

$$\therefore \qquad \left(\frac{TL}{GJ}\right)_t = \left(\frac{TL}{GJ}\right)_s$$

$$\frac{T_t \times 500}{G \times 174.02 \times 10^3} = \frac{T_s \times 500}{G \times 38.35 \times 10^3}$$

$$T_t = 4.54\, T_s$$

$$\therefore \qquad T = T_t + 0.22\, T_t$$

$$\therefore \qquad T_t = \frac{T}{1.22} = 0.820\, T$$

∴      82% torque is carried by the tube.

**Example 9.34 :** *Modulus of rigidity of steel and brass are respectively $G_s = 80$ GPa and $G_b = 36$ GPa for the shaft shown in Fig. 9.29. If the allowable shear stresses in steel and brass are respectively $\tau_s = 82$ MPa and $\tau_b = 50$ MPa, determine the maximum permissible torque T that may be applied to the shaft.*

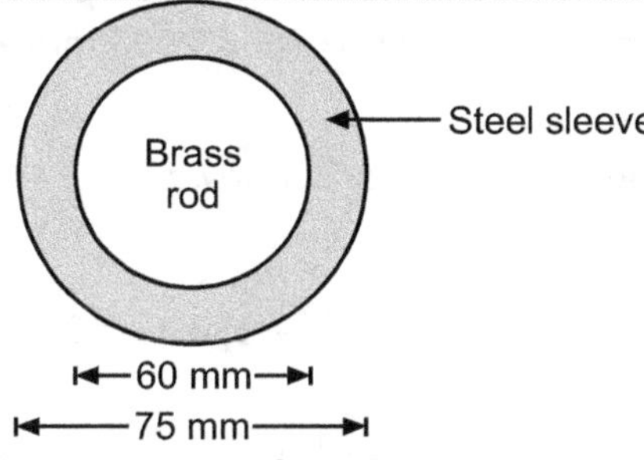


**Fig. 9.29**

**Data :** $G_s = 80$ GPa, $G_b = 36$ GPa, $\tau_s = 82$ MPa, $\tau_b = 50$ MPa.

**Required :** Torque.

**Solution :** (i) Geometric properties :

$$A_b = \frac{\pi}{4} \times 60^2 = 2827.43 \text{ mm}^2$$

$$A_s = \frac{\pi}{4}(75^2 - 60^2) = 1590.43 \text{ mm}^2$$

$$J_b = \frac{\pi}{32} \times 60^4 = 1.27 \times 10^6 \text{ mm}^4$$

$$J_s = \frac{\pi}{32}(75^4 - 60^4) = 18.68 \times 10^6 \text{ mm}^4$$

(ii)    Governing stresses using compatibility :

$$\theta_b = \theta_s$$

$$\left(\frac{\tau L}{GR}\right)_b = \left(\frac{\tau L}{GR}\right)_s$$

$$\frac{\tau_b \times L}{36 \times 10^3 \times 30} = \frac{\tau_s \times L}{80 \times 10^3 \times \left(\dfrac{75}{2}\right)}$$

$$\therefore \qquad \tau_b = 0.36\, \tau_s$$

Let us assume stress in steel is 82 MPa.

$$\therefore \qquad \tau_b = 29.52 \text{ MPa} < 50 \text{ MPa}$$

$$\therefore \qquad \tau_b = 29.52 \text{ MPa and } \tau_s = 82 \text{ MPa}$$

$$T = T_b + T_s$$

$$= \left(\frac{J}{R}\right)_b \times \tau_b + \left(\frac{J}{R}\right)_s \times \tau_s$$

$$= \frac{1.27 \times 10^6}{30} \times 29.52 + \frac{18.68 \times 10^6}{37.5} \times 82 = 42.1 \times 10^6 \text{ N-mm}$$

$$= 42.1 \text{ kN-m}$$

**Example 9.35 :** *A hollow circular shaft 200 mm external diameter and thickness of metal 25 mm is transmitting power at 200 r.p.m. The angle of twist over a length of 2 m was found to be 0.5. Calculate the power transmitted and the maximum shear stress induced in the section. The modulus of rigidity of material is 84 kN/mm².*

**Data :** $D_o$ = 200 mm, $D_i$ = 150 mm, N = 200 r.p.m., l = 2000 mm, $\theta$ = 0.5 , G = $84 \times 10^3$ N/mm²

**Required :** Power transmitted.

**Concept :** Find torque and then use equation of power.

**Solution :** (i) Geometric properties :

$$A = \frac{\pi}{4} \times (200^2 - 150^2) = 13.74 \times 10^3 \text{ mm}^2$$

and

$$J = \frac{\pi}{32}(200^4 - 150^4) = 107.38 \times 10^6 \text{ mm}^4$$

(ii) Torque corresponding to twist :

$$T = \left(\frac{G\theta}{L}\right) J$$

$$\theta = 0.5 \times \frac{\pi}{180} = 8.73 \times 10^{-3} \text{ rad}$$

$$T = \frac{84 \times 10^3 \times 8.73 \times 10^{-3}}{2000} \times 107.38 \times 10^6$$

$$= 39.37 \times 10^6 \text{ N.mm}$$

$$= 39.37 \times 10^3 \text{ N.m}$$

$$\text{Power} = \frac{2\pi NT}{60} = \frac{2\pi \times 200 \times 39.37 \times 10^3}{60}$$

$$= 824.56 \times 10^3 \text{ watt} = 824.56 \text{ kW}$$

$$\therefore \qquad \text{Power transmitted} = \textbf{824.56 kW}$$

(iii) Shear stress :

$$\frac{\tau}{R} = \frac{T}{J}$$

$$\frac{\tau_{max}}{100} = \frac{39.37 \times 10^6}{107.38 \times 10^6}$$

$$\therefore \qquad \tau_{max} = \textbf{36.66 N/mm}^2$$

## EXERCISE

1. Find the power transmitted by a shaft having 50 mm diameter at 150 r.p.m. if maximum permissible shear stress is 80 MPa.                                    (P = 30.834 kW)

2. A hollow circular shaft of 125 mm external diameter thickness of metal 25 mm is rotating at 150 r.p.m. The angle of twist on 5 m length was found to be 0.8°.   Calculate the power transmitted and maximum shear stress induced in the material. Assume G = 80 GPa.

$$(P = 73.19 \text{ kW}, \tau_{max} = 13.96 \text{ MPa})$$

3. A hollow circular shaft has external diameter of 125 mm and internal diameter of 100 mm. Find the safe power that can be transmitted if allowable shear stress is 100 MPa and maximum angle of twist is 4° for 3.5 m length. Take speed of shaft = 3 revolutions per second and maximum torque to exceed by mean torque by 25%. Take G = 80 MPa.

$$(P = 340.498 \text{ kW})$$

4. Design the diameter of solid circular shaft to transmit 40 kW power rotating at 120 r.p.m. Maximum torque is likely to exceed mean torque by 20%. Permissible shear stress = 60 MPa. Also calculate angle of twist for 2.5 m length, assume G = 85 GPa.

$$(D = 68.698 \text{ mm}, \theta = 2.9435°)$$

5. A steel shaft of solid circular cross-section has to transmit 220 kW at 200 r.p.m. The maximum shear stress is not to exceed 50 MPa and angle of twist must not be more than 1.5° in a length of 2.5 m. Design suitable diameter of shaft. Take G = 80 MPa.

$$(D \text{ (based on strength criteria)} = 102.278 \text{ mm},$$
$$D \text{ (based on stiffness criteria)} = 86.798 \text{ mm} \therefore D = 102.278 \text{ mm})$$

6. Design the cross-section of hollow shaft for which internal diameter is 3/4th of its external diameter to resist a torque of 2000 Nm such that shear stress does not exceed 60 MPa and angle of twist does not exceed 2° for 2m length, assume G = 80 GPa.

$$(D \text{ (based on strength criteria)} = 62.85 \text{ mm}, D \text{ (based on stiffness criteria)} = 67.96 \text{ mm}$$
$$\therefore D = 67.96 \text{ mm}, d = 50.977 \text{ mm})$$

7. A hollow steel shaft 3 m long transmits a torque of 2 kN.m. Total angle of twist is not to exceed 3° and permissible shear stress = 80 MPa. Determine inside and outside diameters of shaft, G = 85 MPa.                              (D = 107.85 mm, d = 105.05 mm)

8. A hollow shaft has 75 mm external diameter and 50 mm internal diameter. Determine the twisting moment it can resist if permissible shear stress is 110 MPa. Determine the diameter of solid circular shaft made of same material which can transmit same twisting moment. Hence compare their weights per metre length. Take G = 80 MPa.

$$(T = 7.312 \times 10^6 \text{ N.mm}, D_{(solid\ shaft)} = 69.69 \text{ mm}, \frac{\text{Weight of solid shaft}}{\text{Weight of hollow shaft}} = 1.55)$$

9. Design diameter of solid shaft for resisting torque of 3000 N.m. Also design cross-section of hollow shaft made of same material assuming internal diameter as 0.75 times the external diameter for the same torque. Hence, comment on percentage saving in weight

and shear stress for shaft. Assume allowable angle of twist 2.5° for 2 m length of both shafts. Take G = 80 GPa.

$(D_{solid}$ = 64.686 mm, $(D_{ext})_{hollow}$ = 71.139 mm, $(D_{int})_{hollow}$ = 53.354 mm

% saving in weight = 47.085%

$\tau_{solid}$ = 0.909 $\tau_{hollow}$ or $\tau_{hollow}$ = 1.099 $\tau_{solid})$

10. Design diameter of solid shaft for resisting torque of 3000 N.m. Also design cross-section of hollow shaft made of same material assuming internal diameter 0.75 times the external diameter for the same torque. Hence, comment on percentage saving in weight and angle of twist per unit length of shafts. Assume permissible shear stress as 60 MPa.

$(D_{solid}$ = 63.384 mm, $(D_{ext})_{hollow}$ = 71.952 mm, $(D_{int})_{hollow}$ = 53.965 mm

% saving in wt. = 43.625%, $\theta_s$ = 1.135 $\theta_h$ or $\theta_h$ = 0.88 $\theta_s)$

11. Compare the weights of equal lengths of hollow and solid shaft to resist same torsional moment for same maximum shear stress, assume internal diameter 0.75 times the external diameter for hollow shaft.

$$\left(\frac{\text{wt. of hollow shaft}}{\text{wt. of solid shaft}} = 0.564\right)$$

12. The shaft shown in Fig. 9.30 below rotates at 250 r.p.m. with 40 H.P. and 20 HP taken off at A and B respectively and 60 HP applied at C. Find the maximum shear stress developed in the shaft and angle of twist of gear A relative to gear C. G = 85 GPa.

$(\tau_{max}$ = 11.399 MPa, $\theta$ = 2.034°)

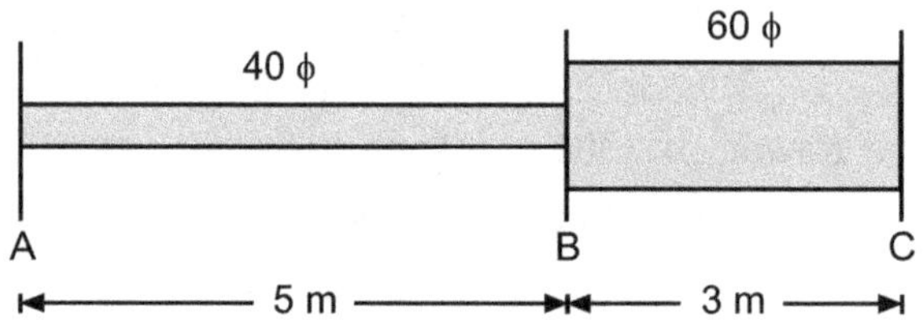

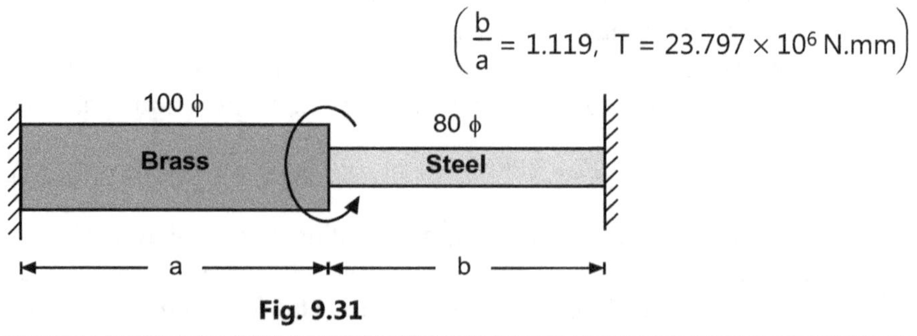


**Fig. 9.30**

13. A compound shaft as shown in Fig. 9.31 is attached to rigid supports. Determine the ratio of lengths 'b' to 'a' so that each material is stressed to its permissible limit. What torque T is applied ? Assume $G_b$ = 42 GPa, $G_s$ = 84 GPa, $\tau_b \leq$ 70 MPa, $\tau_s \leq$ 100 MPa.

$$\left(\frac{b}{a} = 1.119, \; T = 23.797 \times 10^6 \text{ N.mm}\right)$$



**Fig. 9.31**

14.  A shaft ABC fixed at A and B is subjected to torque of 45 N.m at C as shown in Fig. 9.32. Calculate the end reactions and shear stresses in both components. Also find angle of twist at junction C.

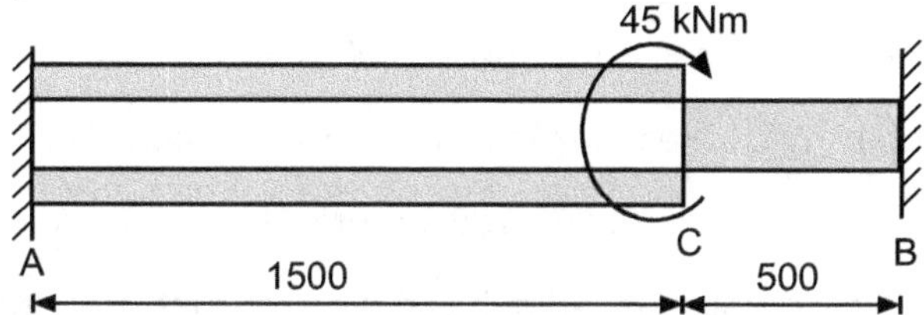


**Fig. 9.32**

| AC | CB |
|---|---|
| Brass | Steel |
| D = 50 mm | D = 25 mm |
| d = 25 mm | |
| $G_b$ = 40 GPa | $G_s$ = 80 GPa |

($T_A$ = 32.142 kN.m; $T_B$ = 12.857 kN.m; $\theta_C$ = 0.12°)

15.  A shaft section 75 mm in diameter is subjected to bending moment of 5 kN.m and torque of 10 kN.m. Find the maximum normal stresses induced on section and locate the plane on which it acts. Find also what stress acting along can produce the same maximum strain ? Take $\mu$ = 0.3.               (Max. normal stresses $\sigma_1$ = 195.33 MPa; $\sigma_2$ = – 74.61 MPa;

$\theta_1$ = 31.717°, $\theta_2$ = 121.717°, $\sigma$ = 217.713 MPa)

16.  A steel shaft is subjected to torque of 20 kN.m and bending moment 15 kN.m. Calculate the principal stresses and maximum shear stress if diameter of shaft is 115 mm.

($\sigma_1$ = 133.948 MPa; $\sigma_2$ = – 33.487 MPa; $\theta_1$ = 26.56°, $\theta_2$ = 116.56°, $\tau_{max}$ = 83.717 MPa)

17.  A hollow shaft is subjected to torque of 500 kN.m and bending moment of 250 kN.m. Internal diameter of shaft is 0.75 times the external diameter. If maximum normal stress is not to exceed 150 MPa and shear stress is not to exceed 80 MPa, design the cross-section of shaft.               (D = 373.395 mm, d = 280 mm)

18.  A solid shaft in a small hydraulic turbine is 125 mm in diameters, it supports an axial compressive load of 500 kN. Determine the maximum power that will be developed at a speed of 250 r.p.m. without exceeding maximum shear stress of 70 MPa and maximum normal stress of 90 MPa.

($\sigma$ = 40.74 MPa, $\tau$ = 66.58 MPa, T = 25.53 × 10³ N.m, Safe power = 668.455 kW)

19.  A steel bar 40 mm diameter 500 mm long when tested under an axial tensile load of 150 kN found to stretch by 0.24 mm. The same bar when subjected to a torque of 1.5 kN.m is found to twist by 2°. Determine the values of four elastic constants.

(E = 248.67 GPa; G = 85.48 GPa; $\mu$ = 0.4545; K = 910.912 GPa)

20.  A metal bar 15 mm $\phi$ subjected to a pull of 40 kN elongated by 0.5 mm over a gauge length of 500 mm in a torsion test on the same material maximum shear stress of 45 MPa was measured on a bar of 50 mm $\phi$ and angle of twist over a length of 300 mm was measured to be 0.4°. Determine Poisson's ratio for the material.               ($\mu$ = 0.463)

21. A circular shaft supported on bearings 5 m apart transmits 80 kW power at 130 r.p.m. A pulley provided at 2 m from one bearing exerts a transverse load of 50 kN on the shaft. Determine the suitable diameter of shaft if

   (i) Maximum normal stress is not to exceed 90 MPa.

   (ii) Maximum intensity of shear stress is not to exceed 40 MPa.

   ((i) D = 189.52 mm, D = 197.26 mm, Select D = 197.26 mm)

22. Fig. 9.33 shows a horizontal shaft AB subjected to torques at C and D. Determine  (i) The end fixing couples in magnitude and direction. (ii) The diameter of the shaft if the maximum shear stress is not to exceed 80 MPa. (iii) The position of section where the shaft suffers no angular twist.

   ($T_A$ = 12.25 kN.m; $T_B$ = 13.75 kN.m; D = 95.7 mm;  1.182 m)

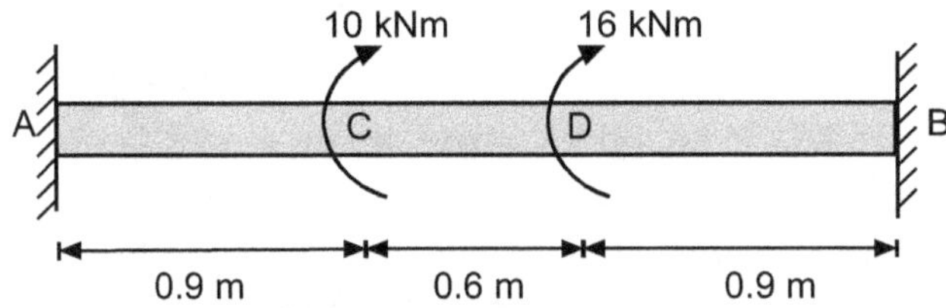


**Fig. 9.33**

23. A circular shaft supported on bearings 4 m apart transmits 75 kW power at 120 r.p.m. A pulley provided at 1.5 m from one bearing exerts a transverse load of 40 kN on the shaft. Determine the suitable diameter of shaft if (i) Maximum normal stress is not to exceed    90 MPa. (ii) Maximum shear stress is not to exceed 40 MPa.

   ((i) D = 162 mm, (ii) D = 169 mm  ∴  use D = 169 mm)

24. A solid alloy shaft 50 mm diameter is to be coupled in series with a hollow steel shaft of the same external diameter. If the angle of twist per unit length of the steel shaft is to be 70% of that of alloy shaft, find the diameter of the steel shaft. Also find the speed at which the shaft should be driven to transmit 20 kW if allowable shear stresses in alloy and steel are 56 MPa and 80 MPa respectively. Assume $G_{steel}$ = 2.25 $G_{alloy}$. (38.87 mm; 153.3 r.p.m.)

25. Two shafts are of length 'L' and outside diameter D. The first one is solid while the second one is hollow with inside diameter D/2. What is the ratio of strain energies that two steel shafts can absorb without exceeding the allowable shear stress ?  $\left(\dfrac{\mu_S}{\mu_H} = \dfrac{16}{15}\right)$.

26. A hollow circular shaft 20 mm thick transmits 294 kW at 200 r.p.m. Determine the diameters of the shaft if shear strain due to torsion is not to exceed $8 \times 10^{-4}$. Assume G = 80 GPa.                                                        (D = 110 mm; d = 70 mm)

## UNIVERSITY QUESTION PAPERS

### MAY 2014

1. Compare the weights of equal lengths of a solid and a hollow shaft to transit a given torque for the same maximum stress, if the inside diameter of the shaft is three fourth of the outside.  **[6]**

2. Following Fig. 1 shows a stepped steel shaft. It is subjected to a torque 'T' at the free end and a torque '2T' in the opposite direction at the junction of the two sizes. Determine the total angle of twist, if the maximum shear stress is limited to 80 MPa. Take G = 80 GPa. **[6]**

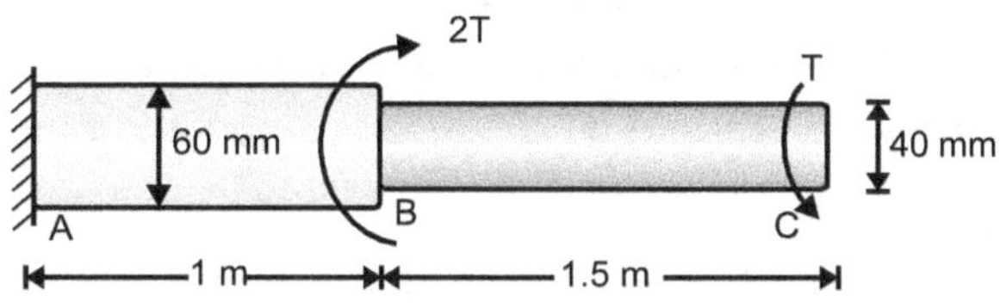


**Fig. 1**

### DECEMBER 2014

1. A hollow steel shaft 2 m long is required to transmit a torque of 15 kN-m. The total angle of twist in this length is not to exceed 3° and the allowable shearing stress is 110 MPa. Determine the inside and outside diameter of the shaft if G = 90 GPa.  **[6]**

2. A solid circular shaft is required to transmit 114 kW while turning at 24 rev/s. The allowable shearing stress is 90 MPa. Find the required shaft diameter.  **[6]**

### MAY 2015

1. A hollow steel shaft 1 m long is required to transmit a torque of 10 kN-m. The total angle of twist in this length is not to exceed 1° and the allowable shearing stress is 100 MPa. Determine the inside and outside diameter of the shaft if G = 100 GPa.  **[6]**

2. Steel bar of rectangular cross-section 33 mm × 66 mm and pinned at each end is subject to axial compression. If the proportional limit of the material is 330 MPa and E = 222 GPa, determine the minimum length for which Euler's equation may be used to determine the buckling load.  **[6]**

## November 2015

1. A hollow steel shaft 1.5 m long is required to transmit a torque of 12 kN-m. The total angle of twist in this length is not to exceed 2° and the allowable shearing stress is 100 MPa. Determine the inside and outside diameter of the shaft if G = 83 GPa.    **[6]**

2. A solid circular shaft is required to transmit 90 kW while turning at 50 rev/s. The allowable shearing stress is 120 MPa. Find the required shaft diameter.    **[6]**

## May 2016

1. A hollow, shaft, having an internal diameter 40% of its external diameter, transmits, 562.5 kW power at 100 r.p.m. Determine the external diameter of the shaft if the shear stress is not exceed 60 N/mm$^2$ and the twist in a length of 2.5 m should not exceed 1.3 degrees. Assume maximum torque = 1.25 mean torque and modulus of rigidity = $9 \times 10^4$ N/mm$^2$.

    **[6]**

2. The stepped steel shaft shown in Fig. 1 is 600 mm long and fixed at both ends subjected to a torque 120 kNm at C. Determine the fixing torque at the ends, the maximum shear in the AC and BC and angle of twist of section C.    **[6]**

    Take G = 80 GPa.

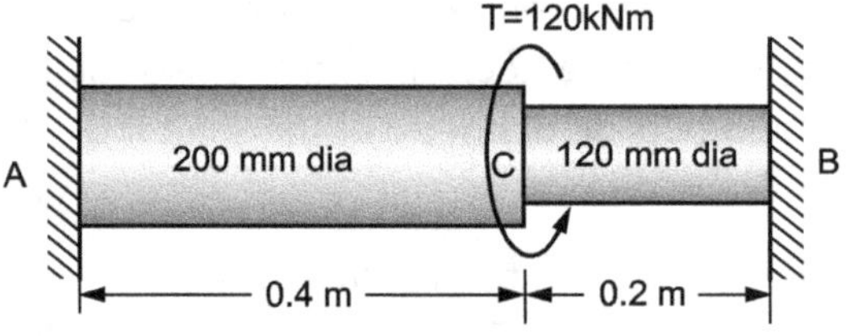

**Fig. 1**

◈ ◈ ◈

# Chapter 10

# BUCKLING OF COLUMNS

## 10.1 INTRODUCTION

*A column or a strut is a structural member subjected to axial compressive load.* However, a *vertical compression member* is called as *column* while *non-vertical compression member* is called as *strut.*

Columns are basically of two types (i) Long column, (ii) Short column. A long column fails by buckling while short column fails by crushing.

A column tends to buckle about an axis of least moment of inertia called as minor axis due to any of the following reasons :

  (i)    The section is not uniform.

  (ii)   The load is not axial.

  (iii)  The member is not initially straight.

  (iv)   The material is not homogeneous.

On account of tendency to buckle, the critical load decreases with the increase in length and finally the column fails due to the combined effect of bending, shear and compression.

The actual column will always have small imperfections of material, fabrication and eccentricities of load which causes it to buckle.

If the eccentricity is small, then for the short members, lateral deflection is less and therefore bending stress is insignificant compared to direct compressive stress. And if the member is long, eccentricity causes large deflections; and therefore bending stresses are of large magnitude compared to direct compressive stresses. Thus, the kind of stresses set up over the cross-section largely depends on length of compression member. It is difficult to draw exact line of demarcation between long column and short column.

## 10.2 CRITICAL LOAD

Once the column buckles, its section is subjected to bending moment which further adds to the deflection and the process continues. A critical load, therefore, can be defined as 'the maximum axial load to which a member can be subjected and still it remains straight'. A very small lateral load at this unstable condition will cause buckling of column. Critical load is also called as *buckling load.* For the same length of column, buckling load is different for different end conditions. Euler's theory is discussed in the next article for computation of this buckling load.

## 10.3 EULER'S THEORY OF LONG COLUMNS

Following are the assumptions made in Euler's theory :

(i)     The column is long i.e. direct stresses are insignificant compared to bending stresses.

(ii)    The column is perfectly straight, prismatic and made of homogeneous material.

(iii)   The load is axial compressive.

(iv)    The Young's modulus for the material is same for tension and compression.

(v)     Stresses are within elastic limit.

(vi)    Plane cross-sections of the column remain plane and normal to the centre line during the buckling.

(vii)   Longitudinal fibres of the column are free to expand or contract independently without any constraint of adjoining fibres.‼

## 10.3.1 Different Cases to Find Buckling Load (P)

**Case 1 : When Both Ends of the Column are Pinned or Hinged :**

Fig. 10.1 shows a column AB of length L and uniform sectional area A, hinged at both the ends A and B. Let P be the buckling load.

Consider any section at a distance x from the end B. Let y be the deflection (lateral displacement) at the section.

The bending moment at the section is given by,

$$EI \frac{d^2y}{dx^2} = -Py \qquad \ldots (10.1)$$

$$\therefore \quad EI \frac{d^2y}{dx^2} + Py = 0 \qquad \ldots (10.2)$$

$$\therefore \quad \frac{d^2y}{dx^2} + \frac{P}{EI} y = 0 \qquad \ldots (10.3)$$

The solution to the above differential equation is

$$\boxed{y = C_1 \cos\left(x\sqrt{\frac{P}{EI}}\right) + C_2 \sin\left(x\sqrt{\frac{P}{EI}}\right)} \qquad \ldots (10.4)$$

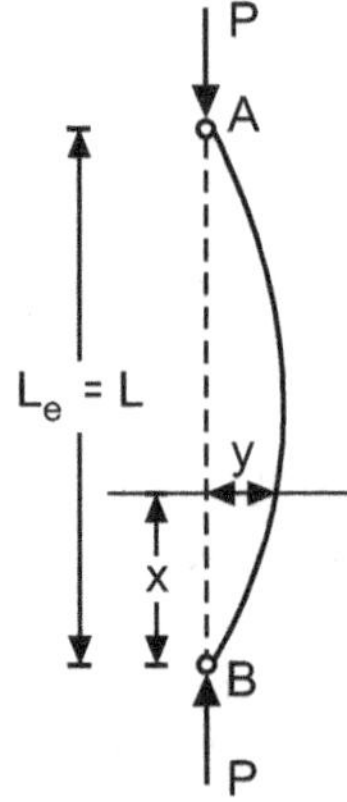

**Fig. 10.1 : Column hinged at both ends**

where $C_1$ and $C_2$ are constants of integration.

At B, the deflection is zero.

$$\therefore \quad \text{At } x = 0, \quad y = 0 \quad \text{put in equation (10.4)}$$

$$\therefore \quad C_1 = 0$$

At A also, the deflection is zero.

$$\text{i.e., at} \quad x = L, \quad y = 0 \quad \text{put in equation (10.4)}$$

$$\therefore \quad 0 = C_2 \sin\left(L\sqrt{\frac{P}{EI}}\right)$$

Since $C_1 = 0$, we conclude that $C_2$ cannot be zero.

This is because if both $C_1$ and $C_2$ are zero, the column will not buckle at all.

Hence
$$\sin\left(L\sqrt{\frac{P}{EI}}\right) = 0$$

$$\therefore \quad \left(L\sqrt{\frac{P}{EI}}\right) = 0,\ \pi,\ 2\pi,\ 3\pi,\ 4\pi$$

Considering the least practical value,

$$L\sqrt{\frac{P}{EI}} = \pi$$

$$\therefore \quad P = \frac{\pi^2\,EI}{L^2} \qquad \dots (10.5)$$

### Case 2 : When One End is Fixed and the Other is Free :

Fig. 10.2 shows a column AB of length L whose lower end B is fixed, the upper end A being free. Let P be the buckling load for column and 'a' be the deflection at the free end.

At any section, distant x from the fixed end B, the bending moment is given by

$$EI\frac{d^2y}{dx^2} = + P\,(a - y) \quad \dots (10.6)$$

where y is the deflection at x.

$$\therefore \quad EI\frac{d^2y}{dx^2} + Py = Pa \qquad \dots (10.7)$$

$$\therefore \quad \frac{d^2y}{dx^2} + \frac{P}{EI}\,y = \frac{Pa}{EI} \qquad \dots (10.8)$$

The solution to the above differential equation is

$$\boxed{\,y_1 = C_1 \cos\left(x\sqrt{\frac{P}{EI}}\right) + C_2 \sin\left(x\sqrt{\frac{P}{EI}}\right) + a\,} \qquad \dots (10.9)$$

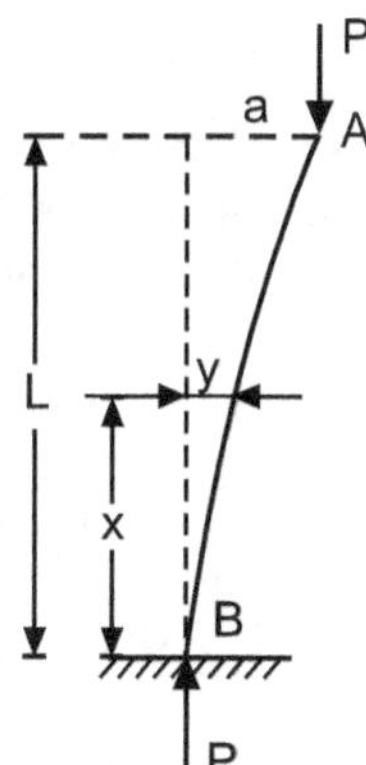


**Fig. 10.2 : Column fixed at one end free at other end**

where $C_1$ and $C_2$ are constants of integration.

At B, the deflection is zero.

$\therefore$ At $x = 0$,  $y = 0$  put in equation (10.9)

$\therefore \qquad 0 = C_1 + 0 \qquad \therefore \quad C_1 = -a$

The slope at any section is given by

$$\frac{dy}{dx} = -C_1\sqrt{\frac{P}{EI}}\sin\left(x\sqrt{\frac{P}{EI}}\right) + C_2\sqrt{\frac{P}{EI}}\cos\left(x\sqrt{\frac{P}{EI}}\right) \qquad \dots (10.10)$$

At B, the slope is zero.

$\therefore$ At $x = 0$, $\dfrac{dy}{dx} = 0$ put in equation (10.10)

$$0 = C_2 \sqrt{\frac{P}{EI}}$$

$$\therefore \quad C_2 = 0$$

At A, the deflection is a.

$$\therefore \quad \text{At } x = L; \ y = a$$

$$a = -a \cos\left(L\sqrt{\frac{P}{EI}}\right) + a$$

$$\therefore \quad \cos\left(L\sqrt{\frac{P}{EI}}\right) = 0$$

$$\therefore \quad L\sqrt{\frac{P}{EI}} = \frac{\pi}{2}, \ \frac{3\pi}{2}, \ \frac{5\pi}{2}, \ \dots$$

Considering the first practical value,

$$L\sqrt{\frac{P}{EI}} = \frac{\pi}{2}$$

$$\therefore \quad P = \frac{\pi^2 \, EI}{4 \, L^2} \qquad \dots (10.11)$$

## Case 3 : When Both Ends of the Column are Fixed :

Fig. 10.3 shows a column AB of length L whose ends A and B are both fixed. Let P be the buckling load and M be the fixed end moment.

Consider any section at x from the lower end B. The bending moment at the section is given by,

$$EI\frac{d^2y}{dx^2} = M - Py \qquad \dots (10.12)$$

$$\therefore \quad EI\frac{d^2y}{dx^2} + Py = M \qquad \dots (10.13)$$

$$\therefore \quad \frac{d^2y}{dx^2} + \frac{P}{EI}\, y = \frac{M}{EI} \qquad \dots (10.14)$$

The solution to the above differential equation is,

$$y = C_1 \cos\left(x\sqrt{\frac{P}{EI}}\right) + C_2 \sin\left(x\sqrt{\frac{P}{EI}}\right) + \frac{M}{P}$$

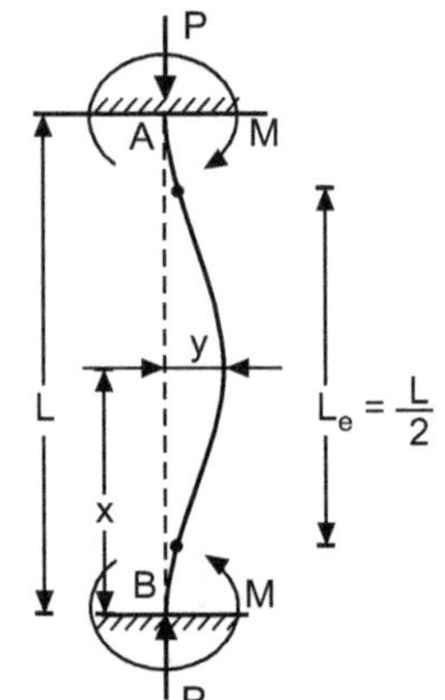


**Fig. 10.3 : Column with both fixed ends**

where $C_1$ and $C_2$ are constants of integration. The slope at any section is given by

$$\frac{dy}{dx} = -C_1\sqrt{\frac{P}{EI}}\sin\left(x\sqrt{\frac{P}{EI}}\right) + C_2\sqrt{\frac{P}{EI}}\cos\left(x\sqrt{\frac{P}{EI}}\right) \qquad \dots (10.16)$$

At B, the deflection is zero.

$$\therefore \quad \text{At } x = 0, \ y = 0 \ \text{ put in equation (10.15)}$$

$$\therefore \quad 0 = C_1 + \frac{M}{P} \quad \therefore \ C_1 = -\frac{M}{P}$$

At B, the slope is zero.

$\therefore$  At  $x = 0$, $\dfrac{dy}{dx} = 0$  put in equation (10.16)

$\therefore$
$$0 = C_2 \sqrt{\dfrac{P}{EI}} \quad \therefore \quad C_2 = 0$$

At A, the deflection is zero.

$\therefore$  At  $x = L$, $y = 0$

$\therefore$
$$0 = -\dfrac{M}{P} \cos\left(L \sqrt{\dfrac{P}{EI}}\right) + \dfrac{M}{P}$$

$\therefore$
$$\dfrac{M}{P}\left[1 - \cos\left(L \sqrt{\dfrac{P}{EI}}\right)\right] = 0$$

$\therefore$
$$\cos\left(L \sqrt{\dfrac{P}{EI}}\right) = 1$$

$\therefore$
$$L \sqrt{\dfrac{P}{EI}} = 0, 2\pi, 4\pi, 6\pi, \ldots\ldots$$

Considering the first practical value,

$$L \sqrt{\dfrac{P}{EI}} = 2\pi$$

$\therefore$
$$P = \dfrac{4\pi^2 \, EI}{L^2} \qquad \ldots (10.17)$$

### Case 4 : When One End of the Column is Fixed and the Other End is Pinned or Hinged :

Fig. 10.4 shows a column AB of length L, whose upper end A is hinged while its lower end B is fixed.

Let P be the buckling load and $M_B$ be the moment at fixed end. Also let, H be the horizontal force at A and B due to moment '$M_B$'.

Consider any section at a distance x from the lower fixed end B. The bending moment at the section is given by,

$$EI \dfrac{d^2y}{dx^2} = -Py + H(L - x) \qquad \ldots (10.18)$$

$\therefore$
$$EI \dfrac{d^2y}{dx^2} + Py = H(L - x) \qquad \ldots (10.19)$$

$\therefore$
$$\dfrac{d^2y}{dx^2} + \dfrac{P}{EI}\, y = \dfrac{H}{EI}(L - x) \qquad \ldots (10.20)$$

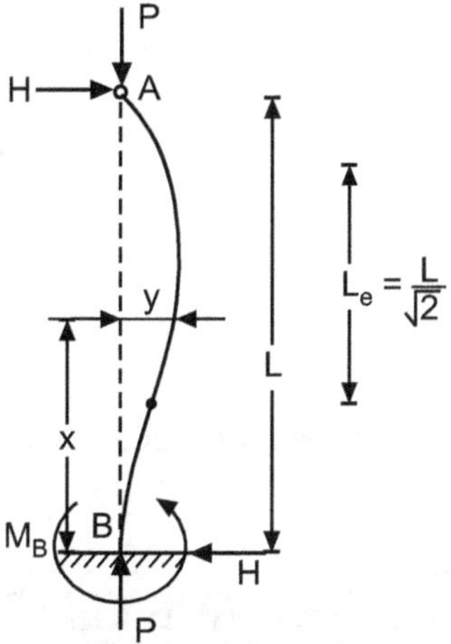


**Fig. 10.4 : Column with one end fixed and other hinged**

The solution to the above differential equation is,

$$y = C_1 \cos\left(x \sqrt{\dfrac{P}{EI}}\right) + C_2 \sin\left(x \sqrt{\dfrac{P}{EI}}\right) + \dfrac{H}{P}(L - x) \qquad \ldots (10.21)$$

where $C_1$ and $C_2$ are constants of integration. The slope at any section is given by,

$$\frac{dy}{dx} = -C_1 \sqrt{\frac{P}{EI}} \sin\left(x\sqrt{\frac{P}{EI}}\right) + C_2 \sqrt{\frac{P}{EI}} \cos\left(x\sqrt{\frac{P}{EI}}\right) - \frac{H}{P} \quad \dots(10.22)$$

At B, the deflection is zero.

$\therefore$     At $x = 0$, $y = 0$ put in equation (10.21)

$\therefore$ 
$$0 = C_1 + \frac{H}{P}L \quad \therefore \quad C_1 = -\frac{H}{P}L$$

At B, the slope is zero.

$\therefore$     At $x = 0$, $\dfrac{dy}{dx} = 0$ put in equation (10.22)

$\therefore$ 
$$0 = C_2\sqrt{\frac{P}{EI}} - \frac{H}{P} \quad \therefore \quad C_2 = \frac{H}{P}\sqrt{\frac{EI}{P}}$$

At A, the deflection is zero.

$\therefore$     At $x = L$, $y = 0$ put in equation (10.21)

$\therefore$ 
$$0 = -\frac{H}{P}L\cos\left(L\sqrt{\frac{P}{EI}}\right)$$
$$+ \left(\frac{H}{P}\sqrt{\frac{EI}{P}}\right)\sin\left(L\sqrt{\frac{P}{EI}}\right)$$

Simplifying, we get $\tan L\left(\sqrt{\frac{P}{EI}}\right) = \left(L\sqrt{\frac{P}{EI}}\right)$

The solution to this equation is

$$L\sqrt{\frac{P}{EI}} = 4.5 \text{ radians}$$

$\therefore$ 
$$\frac{L^2 P}{EI} = (4.5)^2 = 20.25$$

$\therefore$ 
$$P = \frac{20.25\,EI}{L^2}$$

Approximately $20.25 = 2\pi^2$

$\therefore$ 
$$P = \frac{2\pi^2\,EI}{L^2} \quad\quad\quad \dots(10.23)$$

## 10.4 EFFECTIVE LENGTH OF A COLUMN

It is defined as *distance between points of zero bending moment*. It depends on end conditions of column. In general, Euler's buckling load is given by

$$P_E = \frac{\pi^2\,EI}{L_e^2} \quad\quad\quad \dots(10.24)$$

For different end conditions, Euler's buckling load obtained earlier is tabulated as in Table 10.1.

**Table 10.1**

| Sr. No. | End conditions of column | $L_e$ | $P_E$ |
|---|---|---|---|
| 1. | Both ends hinged | $L$ | $\dfrac{\pi^2 EI}{L_e^2} = \dfrac{\pi^2 EI}{L^2}$ |
| 2. | One end fixed, other end free | $2L$ | $\dfrac{\pi^2 EI}{L_e^2} = \dfrac{\pi^2 EI}{4L^2}$ |
| 3. | Both ends fixed | $\dfrac{L}{2}$ | $\dfrac{\pi^2 EI}{L_e^2} = \dfrac{4\pi^2 EI}{L^2}$ |
| 4. | One end fixed, other end hinged | $\dfrac{L}{\sqrt{2}}$ | $\dfrac{\pi^2 EI}{L_e^2} = \dfrac{2\pi^2 EI}{L^2}$ |

where;
$L$ = Unsupported length of column
$L_e$ = Effective length of column
$I$ = Moment of inertia of column cross-section @ minor axis.

## 10.5 LIMITATIONS TO EULER'S FORMULA

We have,

$$P_E = \frac{\pi^2 EI}{L_e^2} = \frac{\pi^2 E (Ar^2)}{L_e^2}$$

where,

$A$ = Cross-sectional area and

$r$ = Radius of gyration

$\therefore$

$$\frac{P_E}{A} = \frac{\pi^2 Er^2}{L_e^2}$$

$$F_{CC} = \frac{\pi^2 E}{\left(\dfrac{L_e}{r}\right)^2}$$

$$\boxed{F_{CC} = \frac{\pi^2 E}{\lambda^2}}$$

where,

$F_{CC}$ = Elastic critical stress i.e. stress corresponding to Euler's buckling load and

$\lambda$ = Slenderness ratio = ratio of effective length to radius of gyration

However, *elastic critical stress can not be greater than yield or crushing stress for the column material ($F_y$). Thus, when slenderness ratio ($\lambda$) is less than a certain value, Euler's formula gives a value of buckling load even greater than crushing load. Therefore, for Euler's formula to hold good,*

$$\lambda \geq \sqrt{\frac{\pi^2 E}{F_y}} \hspace{4cm} \text{... (10.25)}$$

This is the limitation to Euler's formula.

For example, for mild steel, $F_y$ = 250 MPa and  E = 200 GPa, substituting we get,

$$\lambda \;\geq\; \sqrt{\dfrac{\pi^2 \times 200 \times 10^3}{250}}$$

$$\geq\; 88.85 \cong 90 \text{ (say) for Euler's formula to hold good.}$$

Thus, *for mild steel column, if $\lambda \geq 90$, column will fail by buckling and if $\lambda < 90$, it will fail by crushing.*

Therefore, critical $\lambda = \lambda_{cr} = 90$ for mild steel column.

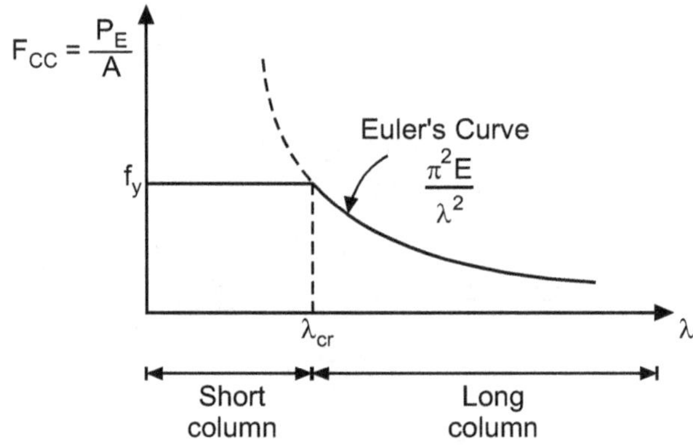


**Fig. 10.5 : Euler's curve**

Fig. 10.5 shows that allowable stress on a column decreases rapidly as slenderness ratio increases. It should be noted that Euler's formula gives critical load and not the working load, hence suitable factor of safety must be used to obtain the working load.

## 10.6  RANKINE'S FORMULA

As discussed in article 10.5 before we use Euler's formula, first it is required to determine whether column is long or short. If column is long then only Euler's formula can be used. To overcome this limitation of Euler's formula, Rankine has suggested an empirical formula which can be used for long as well as short columns.

Let,  $P_R$  =  Rankine's load

$P_C$  =  Crushing load = $F_y \cdot A$

$P_E$  =  Euler's load

Then, Rankine's load is given by,

$$\frac{1}{P_R} \;=\; \frac{1}{P_C} + \frac{1}{P_E} \hspace{4cm} \text{... (10.26)}$$

It should be observed from the above equation that for *long column, $P_E$ will be small and hence* $\dfrac{1}{P_E}$

*will be large enough so that $P_R$ will tend to $P_E$ and if column is short, $P_E$ will be large and hence* $\dfrac{1}{P_E}$

*will be small enough so that $P_R$ will tend to $P_C$. Thus, the Rankine's formula gives satisfactory results for long as well as short columns.*

We have,

$$\frac{1}{P_R} = \frac{1}{P_C} + \frac{1}{P_E}$$

$$\therefore \quad \frac{1}{P_R} = \frac{P_C + P_E}{P_C \cdot P_E}$$

$$\therefore \quad P_R = \frac{P_C \cdot P_E}{P_C + P_E}$$

$$P_R = \frac{P_C}{1 + \dfrac{P_C}{P_E}} = \frac{F_y \cdot A}{1 + \dfrac{F_y \cdot A}{\pi^2 EI/L_e^2}}$$

$$= \frac{F_y A}{1 + \dfrac{F_y \cdot A \cdot L_e^2}{\pi^2 E \, Ar^2}} \qquad (\because I = Ar^2)$$

$$= \frac{F_y \cdot A}{1 + \dfrac{F_y}{\pi^2 E}(\lambda)^2} \qquad \left(\because \lambda = \frac{L_e}{r}\right)$$

$$\mathbf{P_R = \frac{F_y\, A}{1 + a\lambda^2}} \qquad \ldots (10.27)$$

where, $\qquad a = $ Rankine's constant $= \dfrac{F_y}{\pi^2 E}$

*Thus, '$F_y$' and 'a' are constants for a given column material.*

Table 10.2 shows the values of '$F_y$' and 'a' for different column materials. Instead of calculating value of Rankine's constant from known values of $F_y$ and E, it is a practice to decide the value experimentally.

**Table 10.2**

| Sr. No. | Material | $F_y$ (MPa) | a |
|---------|----------|-------------|---|
| 1. | Mild steel | 325 | $\dfrac{1}{7500}$ |
| 2. | Cast iron | 557 | $\dfrac{1}{1600}$ |
| 3. | Wrought iron | 230 | $\dfrac{1}{9000}$ |
| 4. | Timber | 50 | $\dfrac{1}{750}$ |

In comparison with the curves for crushing load and Euler's buckling load, the curve for Rankine's crippling load is shown in Fig. 10.6.

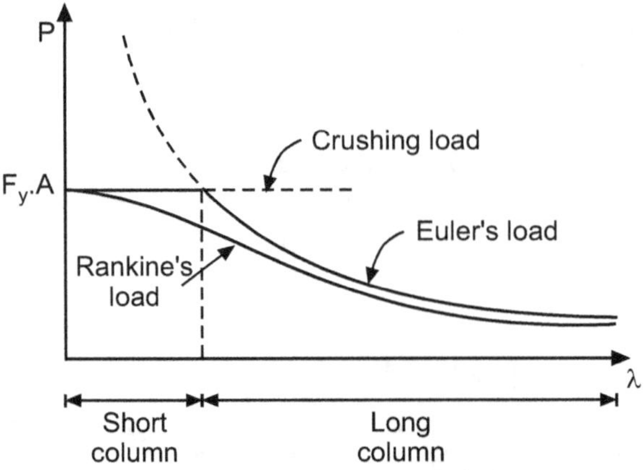



**Fig. 10.6 : Curves for Euler's and Rankine's load**

## SOLVED EXAMPLES

**Example 10.1 :** *A mild steel tube 22 mm φ, 3 mm thick is 2 m long. It is used as a strut, hinged at two ends. Calculate the crippling load by Euler's formula. Assume E = 200 GPa.*

**Data**       :   D = 22 mm; d = 16 mm; L = 2 m; both ends hinged; E = 200 GPa.

**Required**  :  Cripling load by Euler's formula.

**Concept**   :  $L_e = L$ for both ends hinged; $P_E = \dfrac{\pi^2 \, EI_{min}}{L_e^{\,2}}$.

**Solution :** (i) Geometric properties :

$$I_{min} = \frac{\pi}{64}(D^4 - d^4)$$

$$= \frac{\pi}{64}(22^4 - 16^4) = 8.282 \times 10^3 \text{ mm}^4$$

$$L_e = L = \textbf{2000 mm}$$

(ii)   Euler's load ($P_E$) :

$$P_E = \frac{\pi^2 \, EI_{min}}{L_e^{\,2}}$$

$$= \frac{\pi^2 \times 200 \times 8.282 \times 10^3}{(2000)^2}$$

$$= \textbf{4.087 kN}$$

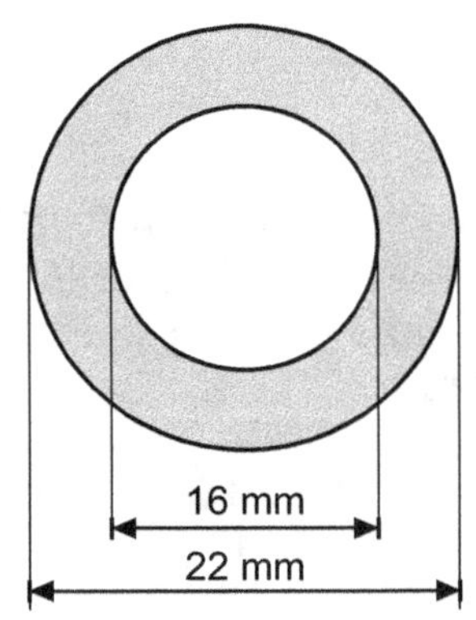



**Fig. 10.7 : C/s of tube**

**Example 10.2 :** *Find the crushing load by Rankine's formula for a hollow CI column of 200 mm external diameter and 25 mm thickness of metal. If length of column = 8 m; both ends fixed. Assume $F_y$ = 550 MPa; $a = \dfrac{1}{1600}$.*

**Data**         :   D = 200 mm; d = 150 mm; L = 8 m both ends fixed; $F_y$ = 550 MPa;

$$a = \frac{1}{1600}.$$

**Required**   :   Crushing load by Rankine's formula.

**Concept**    :   $L_e = \dfrac{L}{2}$ for both ends fixed.

**Solution**   :   (i) Geometric properties :

$$A = \frac{\pi}{4}(D^2 - d^2)$$

$$= \frac{\pi}{4}(200^2 - 150^2) = 13.74 \times 10^3 \text{ mm}^2$$

$$I_{min} = \frac{\pi}{64}(D^4 - d^4)$$

$$= \frac{\pi}{64}(200^4 - 150^4) = 53.69 \times 10^6 \text{ mm}^4$$

$$r_{min} = \sqrt{\frac{I_{min}}{A}} = \sqrt{\frac{53.69 \times 10^6}{13.74 \times 10^3}}$$

$$= 62.5 \text{ mm}$$

$$\lambda = \frac{L_e}{r_{min}} = \frac{4000}{62.5} = \mathbf{64}$$

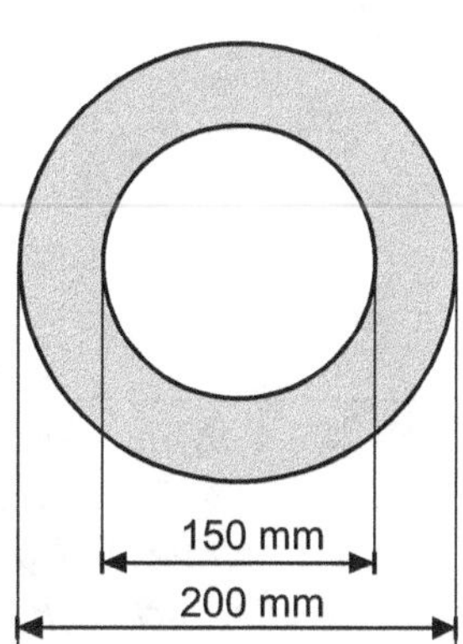

**Fig. 10.8 : C/s of column**

(ii)   Rankine's load ($P_R$) :

$$P_R = \frac{F_y A}{1 + a\lambda^2}$$

$$= \frac{550 \times 13.74 \times 10^3}{1 + \dfrac{(64)^2}{1600}}$$

$$= 2122.75 \times 10^3 \text{ N}$$

$$= \mathbf{2122.75 \text{ kN}}$$

---

**Example 10.3 :** *A square column of 100 mm × 100 mm cross-section has a concentric longitudinal hole of 50 mm diameter. The length of column is 5 m; one end fixed and other hinged. Determine the Euler's buckling load assuming E = 200 GPa.*

**Data**         :   L = 5 m;  one end fixed, other hinged; E = 200 GPa.

**Required**   :   Euler's load ($P_E$)

**Concept**    :   Application of Euler's formula.

**Solution**   :   (i) Geometric properties :

$$A = 100 \times 100 - \frac{\pi}{4}(50)^2$$

$$= 8036.5 \text{ mm}^2$$

$$I_{min} = I_{xx} = I_{yy} = \frac{100^4}{12} - \frac{\pi}{64}(50)^4$$

$$= 8.026 \times 10^6 \text{ mm}^4$$

$$L_e = \frac{L}{\sqrt{2}} = \frac{5000}{\sqrt{2}} = \textbf{3535.53 mm}$$

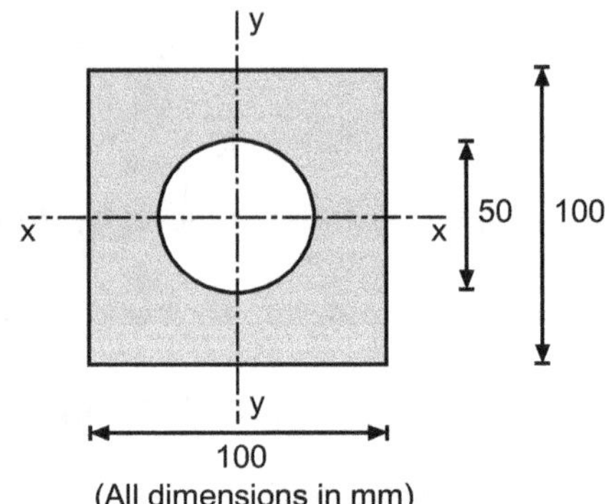



**Fig. 10.9 : C/s of column**

(ii)    Euler's load ($P_E$) :

$$P_E = \frac{\pi^2 E I_{min}}{L_e^2} = \frac{\pi^2 \times 200 \times 10^3 \times 8.026 \times 10^6}{(3535.53)^2} = 1.267 \times 10^6 \text{ N}$$

$$= 1267 \text{ kN}$$

**Example 10.4 :** *The cross-section of column is hollow rectangular section having outside dimension 200 mm × 120 mm and inside dimension 180 mm × 100 mm with uniform thickness of 10 mm. It is fixed at one end and hinged at other end. If the buckling load given by Rankine's formula is 800 kN, find actual length of column. Assume crushing stress = 300 MPa; E = 200 GPa;*
$$a = \frac{1}{7500}.$$

**Data**        :    C/s of column as shown in Fig. 10.10; $P_R$ = 800 kN; $F_y$ = 300 MPa;

$$E = 200 \text{ GPa}; \quad a = \frac{1}{7500}.$$

**Required**  :    Length of column.

**Concept**   :    Application of Rankine's formula.

**Solution**   :    (i) Geometric properties :

$$A = 200 \times 120 - 180 \times 100$$

$$= 6000 \text{ mm}^2$$

$$I_{min} = I_{xx} = \frac{200 \times 120^3}{12} - \frac{180 \times 100^3}{12}$$

$$I_{xx} = 13.8 \times 10^6 \text{ mm}^4$$

$$r_{min} = \sqrt{\frac{I_{min}}{A}} = \sqrt{\frac{13.8 \times 10^6}{6000}}$$

$$= 47.96 \text{ mm}$$

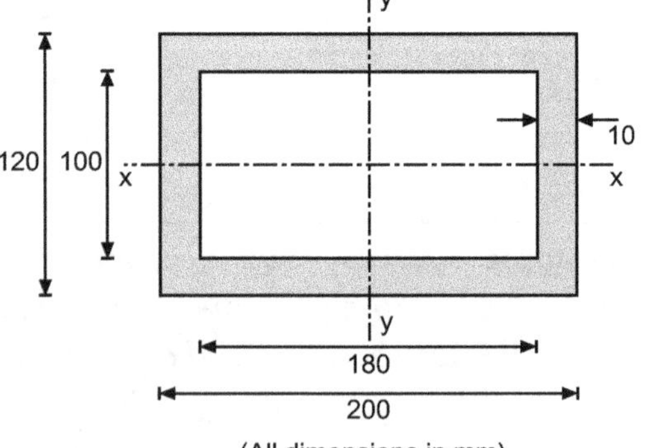



**Fig. 10.10 : C/s of column**

$$\text{Slenderness ratio} = \lambda = \frac{L_e}{r_{min}} = \frac{L_e}{47.96}$$

(ii)    Application of Rankine's formula.

$$P_R = \frac{F_y A}{1 + a\lambda^2}$$

$$800 \times 10^3 = \frac{300 \times 6000}{1 + \dfrac{(L_e/47.96)^2}{7500}}$$

$$\therefore \quad L_e = 4643.7 \text{ mm}$$

$$= \frac{L}{\sqrt{2}} \text{ for column with one end fixed and other hinged.}$$

$$\therefore \quad L = 6567.19 \text{ mm}$$

$$= \mathbf{6.56 \ m}$$

**Example 10.5 :** *A short length of tube 36 mm outside diameter and 24 mm inside diameter is tested under axial compression. In this test, tube failed at a load of 175 kN without buckling. When the tube of same section was tested as a strut with L = 1500 mm both ends hinged, the Euler's load noted was 75 kN. Determine Rankine's constant.*

**Data** : $D = 36$ mm; $d = 24$ mm; crushing failure load $P_C = F_y \cdot A = 175$ kN; Euler's load $= 75$ kN.

**Required** : Rankine's constant (a).

**Concept** : Using $\dfrac{1}{P_R} = \dfrac{1}{P_C} + \dfrac{1}{P_E}$ find $P_R$ and then find Rankine's constant (a).

**Solution** : (i) Geometric properties :

$$A = \frac{\pi}{4}(D^2 - d^2) = \frac{\pi}{4}(36^2 - 24^2)$$

$$= 565.48 \text{ mm}^2$$

$$I_{min} = \frac{\pi}{64}(D^4 - d^4) = \frac{\pi}{64}(36^4 - 24^4)$$

$$= 66.16 \times 10^3 \text{ mm}^4$$

$$r_{min} = \sqrt{\frac{I_{min}}{A}} = \sqrt{\frac{66.16 \times 10^3}{565.48}} = 10.82 \text{ mm}$$

$$L_e = L = 1500 \text{ mm}$$

$$\lambda = \frac{L_e}{r_{min}} = \frac{1500}{10.82} = \mathbf{138.63}$$

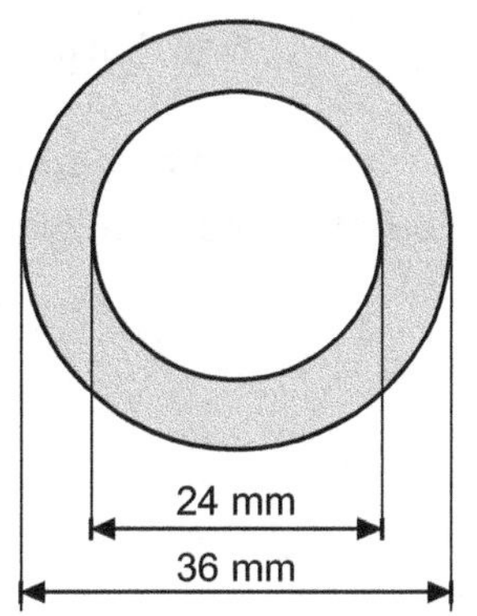



**Fig. 10.11 : C/s of column**

(ii) Rankine's constant (a) :

We have;

$$\frac{1}{P_R} = \frac{1}{P_C} + \frac{1}{P_E}$$

$$\frac{1}{P_R} = \frac{1}{175} + \frac{1}{75}$$

$$\therefore \quad P_R = 52.5 \text{ kN}$$

$$P_R = \frac{F_y \cdot A}{1 + a\lambda^2}$$

$$52.5 \times 10^3 = \frac{175 \times 10^3}{1 + a\,(138.63)^2}$$

$$\therefore \quad a = \frac{1}{8236.4}$$

**Example 10.6 :** *Find the shortest length 'L' for a pin ended steel column 60 mm × 100 mm in cross-section for which Euler's formula is applicable. Take E = 200 GPa and proportional limit = 250 MPa.*

**Data :**      b = 60 mm; D = 100 mm; E = 200 GPa; $F_y$ = 250 MPa; both ends hinged.

**Required :**    Maximum length for which Euler's formula is applicable.

**Concept :**    For Euler's formula to hold good, $\lambda \geq \sqrt{\dfrac{\pi^2 E}{F_y}}$ .

**Solution :**    (i) Geometric properties :

$$A = 60 \times 100 = 6 \times 10^3 \text{ mm}^2$$

$$I_{min} = I_{yy} = \frac{Db^3}{12}$$

$$= \frac{100 \times 60^3}{12}$$

$$= 1.8 \times 10^6 \text{ mm}^4$$

**Note :**    $I_{xx} = \dfrac{bD^3}{12} > I_y$

$$\therefore \quad r_{min} = \sqrt{\frac{I_{min}}{A}} = \sqrt{\frac{1.8 \times 10^6}{6 \times 10^3}}$$

$$= 17.32 \text{ mm}$$



**Fig. 10.12 : C/s of column**

(ii)     Length of column (L) :

For Euler's formula to hold good, $\lambda \geq \sqrt{\dfrac{\pi^2 E}{F_y}}$

$$\geq \sqrt{\frac{\pi^2 \times 200 \times 10^3}{250}}$$

$$\geq 88.86$$

$$\therefore \quad \lambda = \frac{L_e}{r_{min}} \geq 88.86$$

$$\therefore \quad L_e \geq 88.86 \times 17.32$$

$$\geq \mathbf{1539 \text{ mm}}$$

For both ends hinged column, $L_e$ = L = 1539 mm.

$\therefore$     If L ≥ 1.539 m, only then Euler's formula is applicable.

**Example 10.7 :** *A certain machine element has a cross-section b = 30 mm and D = 40 mm. The distance between end connections is 1.2 m. It behaves as a strut hinged at both ends for buckling about x-x axis and fixed at both ends for buckling about y-y axis. Find the safe load using Rankine's formula. Assume $F_y$ = 330 MPa; $a = \dfrac{1}{7500}$ and factor of safety = 2. x-x axis shall be considered parallel to 30 mm side.*

**Data** : $b = 30$ mm; $D = 40$ mm; $L = 1.2$ m ; $L_{ex} = L$ ; $L_{ey} = \dfrac{L}{2}$ ; $F_y = 330$ MPa;

$a = \dfrac{1}{7500}$ ; factor of safety = 2.

**Required** : Safe load on column by Rankine's formula.

**Concept** : Slenderness ratio $\lambda$ about x axis and y axis is different. Greater of $\lambda_x$ and $\lambda_y$ will govern the strength of column.

**Solution** : (i) Geometric properties :

$A = 30 \times 40 = 1200$ mm$^2$

$$I_{xx} = \frac{bD^3}{12} = \frac{30 \times 40^3}{12}$$

$$= 160 \times 10^3 \text{ mm}^4$$

$$I_{yy} = \frac{Db^3}{12} = \frac{40 \times 30^3}{12}$$

$$= 90 \times 10^3 \text{ mm}^4$$

$$r_{xx} = \sqrt{\frac{I_{xx}}{A}} = \sqrt{\frac{160 \times 10^3}{1200}}$$

$$= 11.55 \text{ mm}$$

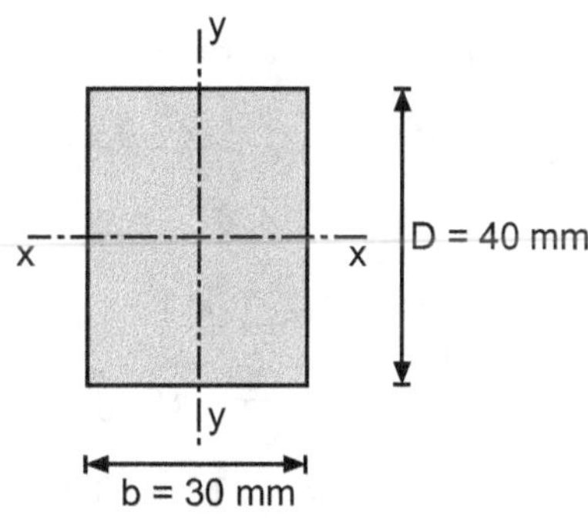


**Fig. 10.13 : C/s of column**

$$r_{yy} = \sqrt{\frac{I_{yy}}{A}} = \sqrt{\frac{90 \times 10^3}{1200}} = 8.66 \text{ mm}$$

$$L_{ex} = L = 1200 \text{ mm}$$

$$L_{ey} = \frac{L}{2} = 600 \text{ mm}$$

$$\lambda_x = \frac{L_{ex}}{r_{xx}} = \frac{1200}{11.55} = \mathbf{103.89}$$

$$\lambda_y = \frac{L_{ey}}{r_{yy}} = \frac{600}{8.66} = \mathbf{69.28}$$

Governing $\lambda = \lambda_x = 103.89$ (Greater of $\lambda_x$ and $\lambda_y$)

(ii) Safe load by Rankine's formula

$$P_R = \frac{F_y \cdot A}{1 + a\,\lambda^2} = \frac{330 \times 1200}{1 + \dfrac{(103.89)^2}{7500}} = 162.36 \times 10^3 \text{ N}$$

$\therefore$      $P_R = \mathbf{162.36 \text{ kN}}$

$$P_{safe} = \frac{P_R}{\text{factor of safety}} = \frac{162.36}{2} = \mathbf{81.18 \text{ kN}}$$

---

**Example 10.8 :** *Compare the crippling load given by Euler's and Rankine's formula for a tubular steel strut 2.3 m long having external diameter = 38 mm and internal diameter = 33 mm; strut is fixed at one end and hinged at other end. $F_y = 335$ MPa; $E = 205$ GPa; $a = \dfrac{1}{7500}$.*

---

For what length of strut does the Euler's formula cease to apply ?

**Data**    :   $D = 38$ mm; $d = 33$ mm; $L = 2.3$ m, one end fixed, other hinged; $F_y = 335$ MPa; $E = 205$ GPa; $a = \dfrac{1}{7500}$.

**Required**  :   Euler's load ($P_E$); Rankine's load ($P_R$); shortest length for which Euler's formula is applicable.

**Concept**   :   For Euler's formula to hold good, $\lambda \geq \sqrt{\dfrac{\pi^2 E}{F_y}}$.

**Solution**   :   (i) Geometric properties :

$$A = \frac{\pi}{4}(D^2 - d^2) \ = \ \frac{\pi}{4}(38^2 - 33^2)$$

$$= \ 278.82 \text{ mm}^2$$

$$I_{min} \ = \ \frac{\pi}{64}(D^4 - d^4)$$

$$= \ \frac{\pi}{64}(38^4 - 33^4)$$

$$= \ 44.14 \times 10^3 \text{ mm}^4$$

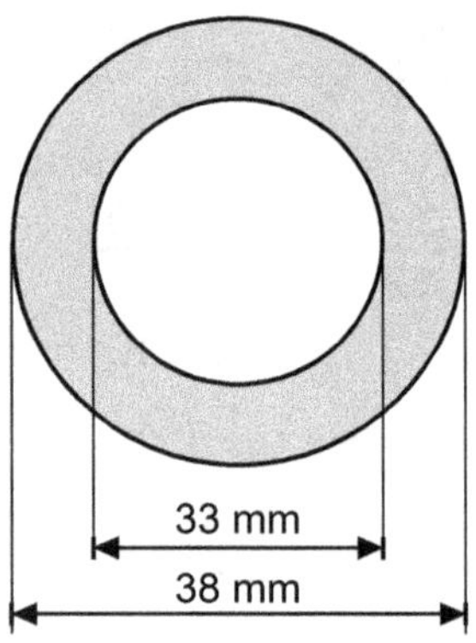


**Fig. 10.14 : C/s of strut**

$$r_{min} \ = \ \sqrt{\frac{I_{min}}{A}} = \sqrt{\frac{44.14 \times 10^3}{278.82}} = 12.58 \text{ mm}$$

$$L_e \ = \ \frac{L}{\sqrt{2}} \text{ for column with one end fixed, one end hinged.}$$

$$L_e \ = \ \frac{2300}{\sqrt{2}} = 1626.35 \text{ mm}$$

$$\lambda \ = \ \frac{L_e}{r_{min}} \ = \ \frac{1626.35}{12.58} = \mathbf{129.28}$$

(ii)     Euler's load ($P_E$).

$$P_E = \frac{\pi^2 E\, I_{min}}{L_e^2} \ = \ \frac{\pi^2 \times 205 \times 10^3 \times 44.14 \times 10^3}{(1626.35)^2}$$

$$= \ 33.76 \times 10^3 \text{ N}$$

$$= \ \mathbf{33.76 \text{ kN}}$$

(iii)    Rankine's load ($P_R$).

$$P_R = \frac{F_y \cdot A}{1 + a\,\lambda^2} \ = \ \frac{335 \times 278.82}{1 + \dfrac{(129.28)^2}{7500}}$$

$$= \ 28.93 \times 10^3 \text{ N} = \mathbf{28.93 \text{ kN}}$$

(iv)    Comparison of $P_E$ and $P_R$

$$\frac{P_E}{P_R} = \frac{33.76}{28.93} = \mathbf{1.17}$$

(v)    Shortest length for which Euler's formula is applicable.

$$\lambda \geq \sqrt{\frac{\pi^2 E}{F_y}}$$

$$\frac{L_e}{12.58} \geq \sqrt{\frac{\pi^2 \times 205 \times 10^3}{335}}$$

$$L_e \geq 977.65 \text{ mm}$$

$$\therefore \quad L \geq \sqrt{2} \times 977.65$$

$$\geq 1382.61 \text{ mm}$$

$$\therefore \quad L \geq \mathbf{1.382 \text{ m}}$$

**Example 10.9 :** *A hollow C.I. column with fixed ends supports an axial load of 1000 kN. If the column is 5 m long and has an external diameter of 250 mm, find the thickness of metal required. Use Rankine's formula. Assume $a = \dfrac{1}{1600}$ and $F_y = 80$ MPa.*

**Data**        :    $P_R = 1000$ kN; $L = 5$ m; both ends fixed; $D = 250$ mm;

$$a = \frac{1}{1600}; \ F_y = 80 \text{ MPa.}$$

**Required**   :    Thickness (t).

**Concept**   :    Geometric properties shall be found in terms of (t) and then use Rankine's formula.

**Solution**   :    (i) Geometric properties : Let d = Internal diameter of column.

$$A = \frac{\pi}{4}(D^2 - d^2) = \frac{\pi}{4}(250^2 - d^2)$$

$$I_{min} = \frac{\pi}{64}(D^4 - d^4)$$

$$= \frac{\pi}{64}(250^4 - d^4)$$

$$r_{min} = \sqrt{\frac{I_{min}}{A}} = \sqrt{\frac{(\pi/64)(250^4 - d^4)}{(\pi/4)(250^2 - d^2)}}$$

$$r_{min}^2 = 0.0625\,(250^2 + d^2)$$

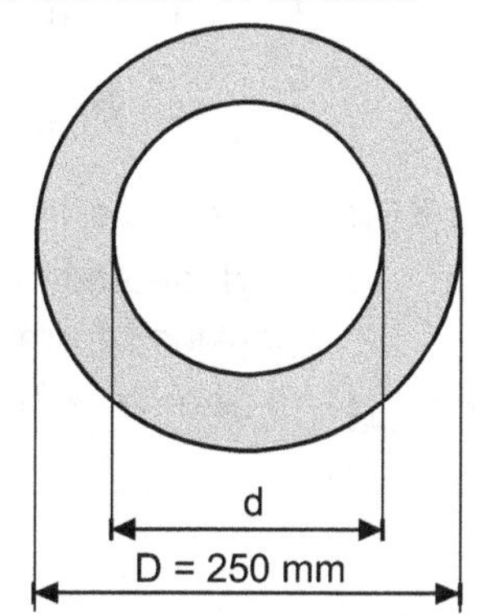


**Fig. 10.15 : C/s of column**

$$L_e = \frac{L}{2} = \frac{5000}{2} = 2500 \text{ mm}$$

$$\lambda = \frac{L_e}{r_{min}} \qquad \therefore \quad \lambda^2 = \left(\frac{L_e}{r_{min}}\right)^2$$

$$\lambda^2 = \frac{2500^2}{0.0625\,(250^2 + d^2)}$$

$$= \frac{100 \times 10^6}{(250^2 + d^2)}$$

(ii)    Application of Rankine's formula :

$$P_R = \frac{F_y \cdot A}{1 + a\,\lambda^2} = \frac{80\left(\frac{\pi}{4}\right)(250^2 - d^2)}{1 + \frac{100 \times 10^6}{1600\,(250^2 + d^2)}}$$

$\therefore$          $1000 \times 10^3 = \dfrac{62.83\,(250^4 - d^4)}{(250^2 + d^2) + 62500}$

Put          $d^2 = a$

$1000 \times 10^3 = \dfrac{62.83\,(250^4 - a^2)}{(250^2 + a) + 62500}$

$\therefore$          $(6.283 \times 10^{-5})\,a^2 + a - 120.43 \times 10^3 = 0$

Solving          $a = d^2 = 36540.2$

$\therefore$          $d = 191.15$ mm

$\therefore$          Thickness $= t = \dfrac{D - d}{2} = \dfrac{250 - 191.15}{2}$ = **29.42 mm  say 30 mm**

---

**Example 10.10 :** *A C.I. column of hollow circular cross-section is 5 m long, with both ends firmly built in. It safely carries an axial load of 800 kN. Determine the section of the column, using factor of safety 3. Assume internal diameter of column as 80% of the external diameter. Use Rankine's formula with $F_y$ = 550 MPa and $a = \dfrac{1}{6400}$.*

**Data**          :   L = 5 m; both ends fixed; $P_{safe}$ = 800 kN; factor of safety = 3; d = 0.8 D;

$F_y$ = 550 MPa; $a = \dfrac{1}{6400}$.

**Required**   :   Design of cross-section of column.

**Concept**   :   Find geometric properties in terms of unknown diameter 'D' and using Rankine's formula, evaluate D and d.

**Solution**   :   (i) Geometric properties :

$A = \dfrac{\pi}{4}\,(D^2 - d^2) = \dfrac{\pi}{4}\,(D^2 - (0.8\,D)^2)$

$I_{min} = \dfrac{\pi}{64}\,(D^4 - d^4)$

$= \dfrac{\pi}{64}\,(D^4 - (0.8\,D)^4) = \dfrac{D^4}{34.5}$

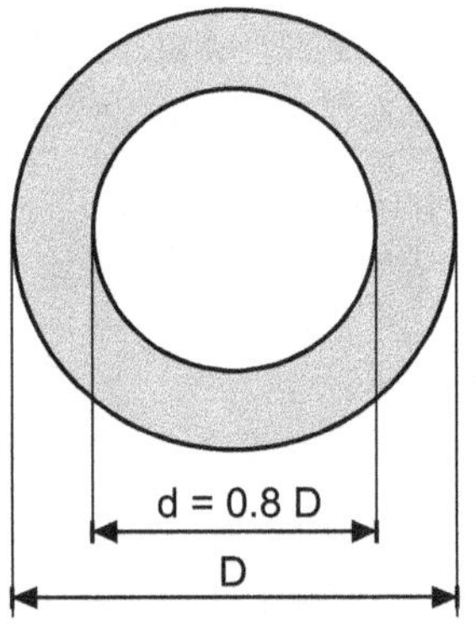


**Fig. 10.16 : C/s of column**

$$r_{min} = \sqrt{\frac{I_{min}}{A}} = \sqrt{\frac{D^4 / 34.5}{0.283\ D^2}} = 0.32\ D$$

$$L_e = \frac{L}{2} \text{ for column with both ends fixed.}$$

$$= \frac{5000}{2} = 2500 \text{ mm}$$

$$\therefore \quad \text{Slenderness ratio} = \lambda = \frac{L_e}{r_{min}} = \frac{2500}{0.32\ D} = \frac{7812.5}{D}$$

(ii)  Design of cross-section of column :

$$P_R = P_{safe} \times \text{factor of safety}$$

$$= 800 \times 3 = 2400 \text{ kN}$$

$$P_R = \frac{F_y \cdot A}{1 + a\ \lambda^2}$$

$$2400 \times 10^3 = \frac{550 \times 0.283\ D^2}{1 + \dfrac{(7812.5 / D)^2}{6400}}$$

$$15360\ D^2 + 146.48 \times 10^6 = D^4 \qquad \text{(put } a = D^2)$$

Solving;

$$D = 148.5 \text{ mm} \cong \mathbf{150\ mm}$$

$$d = 0.8 \times 150 = \mathbf{120\ mm}$$

**Example 10.11 :** *A long hollow circular column and a solid circular column of same material have same cross-sectional areas. Inside diameter of hollow column is 0.8 times external diameter. Find the ratio of their load carrying capacities if they have equal lengths.*

**Data**      :  d = 0.8 D for hollow circular column;

$D_s$ = Diameter of solid circular column;

**Required**  :  Comparison of strength for hollow and solid circular column.

**Concept**   :  Hollow circular column has better strength as compared to solid circular column having same area because of higher moment of inertia.

**Solution**  :  (i) Geometric properties :

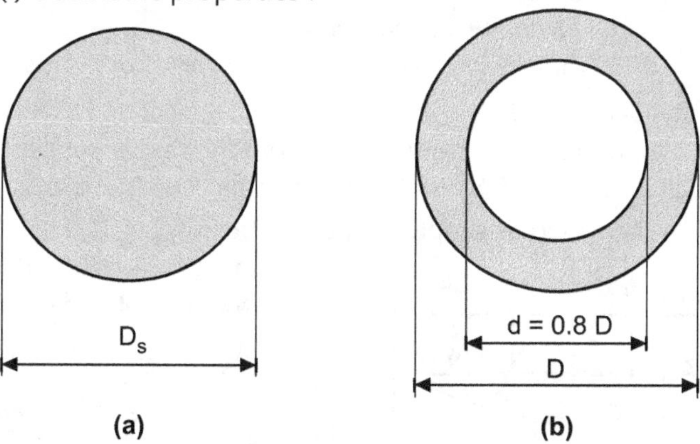


**Fig. 10.17 : Cross-sections of solid and hollow circular columns**

$$A_S = \frac{\pi}{4} (D_S)^2$$

$$A_H = \frac{\pi}{4} (D^2 - (0.8\,D)^2) = \frac{\pi}{4} (0.36\,D^2)$$

We have

$$A_S = A_H$$

$$\therefore \quad \frac{\pi}{4} (D_S)^2 = \frac{\pi}{4} (0.36\,D^2)$$

$$\therefore \quad D_S = 0.6\,D$$

$$(I_{min})_S = \frac{\pi}{64} (D_S)^4 = \frac{\pi}{64} (0.6\,D)^4 = \frac{D^4}{157.2}$$

$$(I_{min})_H = \frac{\pi}{64} (D^4 - d^4) = \frac{\pi}{64} (D^4 - (0.8\,D)^4)$$

$$= \frac{D^4}{34.5}$$

(ii)    Comparison of Euler's load for solid and hollow circular column :

For solid circular column;  $\quad (P_E)_S = \dfrac{\pi^2 E\,(I_{min})_S}{L_e^2} = \dfrac{\pi^2 E\,(D^4 / 157.2)}{L_e^2}$

For hollow circular column;  $\quad (P_E)_H = \dfrac{\pi^2 E\,(I_{min})_H}{L_e^2}$

$$= \frac{\pi E^2 \,(D^4/34.5)}{L_e^2}$$

$$\therefore \quad \frac{(P_E)_S}{(P_E)_H} = \frac{34.5}{157.2} = \mathbf{0.22}$$

$$\therefore \quad (P_E)_S = 0.22\,(P_E)_H \quad \text{OR} \quad (P_E)_H = 4.54\,(P_E)_S$$

**Example 10.12 :** *A bar of circular cross-section, 3 m long weighing 75 N initially straight is freely supported at its ends in horizontal position. The central deflection due to its own weight is found to be 1.8 mm. If this bar is used as a vertical strut, fixed at both ends and loaded axially, find the theoretical buckling load by using Euler's formula.*

**Data**       :   L = 3000 mm; W = 75 N; $Y_{centre}$ = 1.8 mm; both ends fixed for strut.

**Required**   :   Euler's load $(P_E)$.

**Concept**    :   Using equation of central deflection for simply supported beam with UDL; EI will be obtained. Using Euler's formula, $P_E$ is found out.

**Solution**   :   (i) When used as simply supported beam :

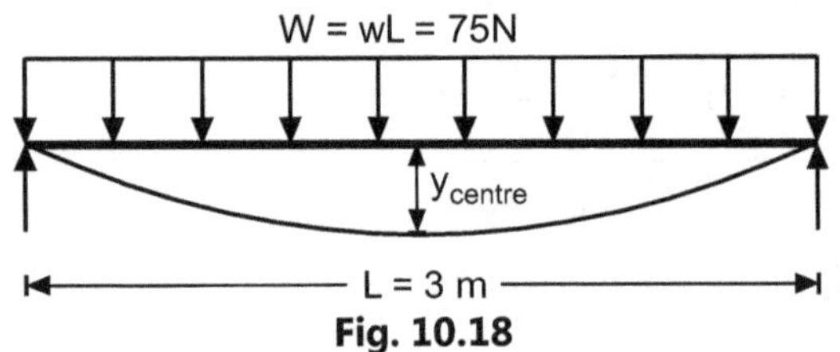


$w$ = Intensity of UDL in N/m
$W$ = Total load due to UDL.

$$Y_{centre} = \frac{5}{384} \left(\frac{wL^4}{EI}\right) = \frac{5}{384} \left(\frac{WL^3}{EI}\right)$$

$$1.8 = \frac{5}{384} \left[\frac{75 \times (3000)^3}{EI}\right]$$

$$\therefore \quad EI = \mathbf{1.465 \times 10^{10} \ N.mm^2.}$$

(ii)    When used as a strut :    $P_E = \dfrac{\pi^2 E\, I_{min}}{L_e^2} = \dfrac{\pi^2 \times 1.465 \times 10^{10}}{(3000/2)^2}$

$\therefore$                                $P_E = 64262$ N

                                                $= \mathbf{64.262}$ **kN**

**Example 10.13 :** *A pin ended wooden member AB acts in axial compression in the planer arrangement shown in Fig. 10.19. This member has rectangular cross-section of 60 mm $\times$ 100 mm. If factor of safety of 2 is to be maintained against buckling, what can be the maximum value of applied force F ? Use Euler's formula and E = 12 GPa.*

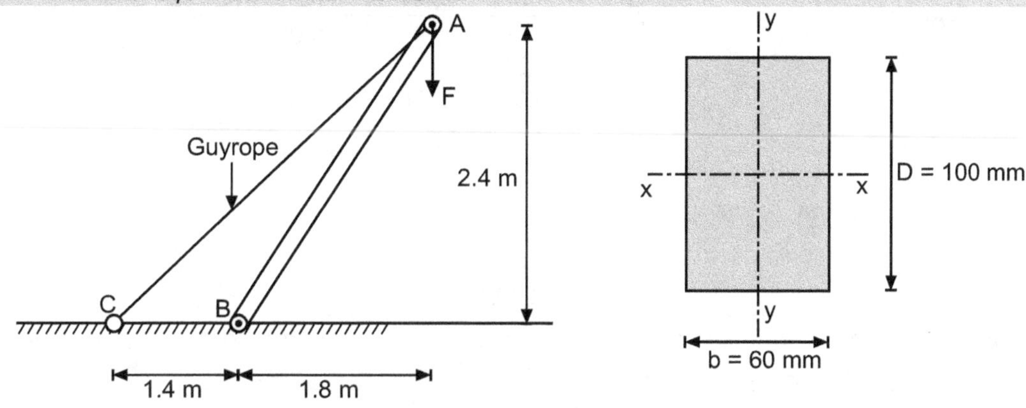



**(a) Planer arrangement**          **(b) C/s of member AB**

**Fig. 10.19**

**Data**       :   c/s of AB = 60 mm $\times$ 100 mm; factor of safety = 2; E = 12 GPa.

**Required**  :   Safe value of F.

**Concept**   :   Analyze joint 'A' and find axial force in member AB, '$F_{AB}$' in terms of 'F'. Equate $P_{safe}$ by Euler's formula and $F_{AB}$ to find F.

**Solution**  :   (i) Analysis :

FBD of joint A is shown in Fig. 10.20.

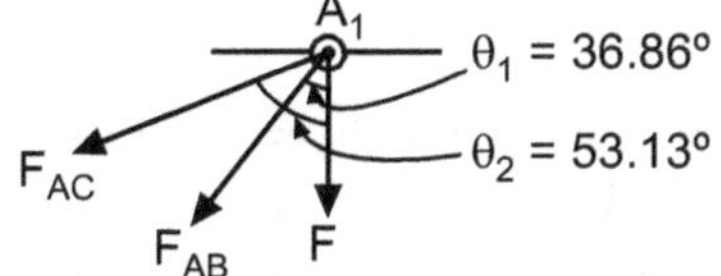



**Fig. 10.20 : FBD of joint A**

From geometry,

$\tan(\theta_1) = \dfrac{1.8}{2.4}$        $\therefore \theta_1 = 36.86°$

$\tan(\theta_2) = \dfrac{3.2}{2.4}$        $\therefore \theta_2 = 53.13°$

$\sum F_x = 0;$        $- F_{AC}\sin(53.13) - F_{AB}\sin(36.86) = 0$

$\therefore$                        $F_{AC} = -0.75\, F_{AB}$                                 ... (i)

$\sum F_y = 0;$        $- F_{AC}\cos(53.13) - F_{AB}\cos(36.86) - F = 0$

$\therefore$            $- 0.6\, F_{AC} - 0.8\, F_{AB} = F$                                 ... (ii)

Solving (i) and (ii),            $F_{AC} = 2.137\, F$

                                    $F_{AB} = -2.85\, F$                                 ... (A)

($\because$ $-$ ve sign indicates compression for AB)

(ii)  Geometric properties for AB :

$$I_{min} = \frac{Db^3}{12} = \frac{100 \times 60^3}{12} = 1.8 \times 10^6 \text{ mm}^4$$

$$L_e = \text{L for both ends hinged strut}$$

$$= \sqrt{1800^2 + 2400^2}$$

$$= 3000 \text{ mm}$$

(iii)  Safe value of 'F' :

For AB;

$$P_E = \frac{\pi^2 \, EI_{min}}{L_e^{\,2}} = \frac{\pi^2 \times 12 \times 10^3 \times 1.8 \times 10^6}{(3000)^2}$$

$$= 23.69 \times 10^3 \text{ N} = 23.69 \text{ kN}$$

$$P_{safe} = \frac{P_E}{2} = \frac{23.69}{2} = 11.845 \text{ kN} \qquad \text{... (B)}$$

Equating (A) and (B),

$$2.85 \, F = 11.845$$

$$F = \textbf{4.16 kN}$$

**Example 10.14 :** *In an experimental determination of buckling load for 12 mm $\phi$ mild steel pin ended strut of various lengths, two of the values obtained are as under.*

| (i) | Length (mm) | 500 | 200 |
|-----|-------------|-----|-----|
| (ii) | Load (kN) | 8.0 | 22.0 |

(a)  *Make necessary calculations and state whether either of the values confirms to Euler's formula for critical load.*

(b)  *Assuming that both the values are in agreement with Rankine's formula, find the values of Rankine's constant and yield stress in compression. Assume E = 200 GPa.*

**Data**  :  D = 12 mm;  (i) for L = 500 mm; P = 8.0 kN; (ii) for L = 200 mm;
P = 22 kN; E = 200 GPa.

**Required**  :  To check whether observation confirm to Euler's formula, and to find '$F_y$' and 'a'.

**Concept**  :  Euler's load will be calculated for both cases and observation made will be checked with values obtained by calculations. Using Rankine's formula, two equations will be developed for two observations and solving these equations, '$F_y$' and 'a' will be obtained.

**Solution**  :  (i) Geometric properties :

$$A = \frac{\pi}{4} (D)^2 = \frac{\pi}{4} (12)^2 = 113.09 \text{ mm}^2$$

$$I_{min} = \frac{\pi}{64} (D)^4 = \frac{\pi}{64} (12)^4 = 1017.87 \text{ mm}^4$$

$$r_{min} = \sqrt{\frac{I_{min}}{A}} = \sqrt{\frac{1017.87}{113.09}} = 3 \text{ mm}$$

For both ends hinged,        $L_e = L$

$\therefore$   Case (I) : For L = 500 mm;   $\lambda_1 = \dfrac{L_e}{r_{min}} = \dfrac{500}{3} = 166.67$

Case (II) : For L = 200 mm;   $\lambda_2 = \dfrac{L_e}{r_{min}} = \dfrac{200}{3} = 66.67$

(ii)   To check Euler's load :

Case (I) : For   $L = L_e = 500$ mm

$$P_E = \frac{\pi^2 \, EI_{min}}{L_e^{\,2}} = \frac{\pi^2 \times 200 \times 10^3 \times 1017.87}{500^2}$$

$$= 8036.7 \text{ N}$$

$$= \mathbf{8.03 \text{ kN}} \cong \mathbf{8 \text{ kN}}$$

$\therefore$   Observation for case (I) is in agreement with Euler's formula.

Case (II) : For   $L = L_e = 200$ mm

$$P_E = \frac{\pi^2 \, EI_{min}}{L_e^{\,2}} = \frac{\pi^2 \times 200 \times 10^3 \times 1017.87}{200^2}$$

$\therefore$   $$P_E = 50229.7 \text{ N}$$

$$= \mathbf{50.23 \text{ kN}} \neq \mathbf{22 \text{ kN}}$$

$\therefore$   Observation for case (II) is not in agreement with Euler's formula.

(iii) To find yield stress ($F_y$) and Rankine's constant (a) :

For case (I),   $$P_R = 8 \times 10^3 = \frac{F_y \cdot A}{1 + a\,\lambda_1^{\,2}}$$

$$8 \times 10^3 = \frac{F_y \times 113.09}{1 + a\,(166.67)^2} \qquad \dots (i)$$

For case (II),   $$P_R = 22 \times 10^3 = \frac{F_y \cdot A}{1 + a\,\lambda_2^{\,2}}$$

$\therefore$   $$22 \times 10^3 = \frac{F_y \times 113.09}{1 + a\,(66.67)^2} \qquad \dots (ii)$$

Divide equation (i) by equation (ii)

$$\frac{8}{22} = \frac{1 + a\,(66.67)^2}{1 + a\,(166.67)^2}$$

$\therefore$   $$a = \frac{1}{8888.89} \qquad \dots \text{ put in (i)}$$

$\therefore$   $$F_y = \mathbf{291.8 \text{ MPa}}$$

---

**Example 10.15 :** *The cross-section of the column is as shown in Fig. 10.21. Calculate the length of the member for which crippling load by Euler's formula and Rankine's formula will be same. Assume yield stress = $F_y$ = 330 MPa; E = 210 GPa and a = $\dfrac{1}{7500}$.*

---

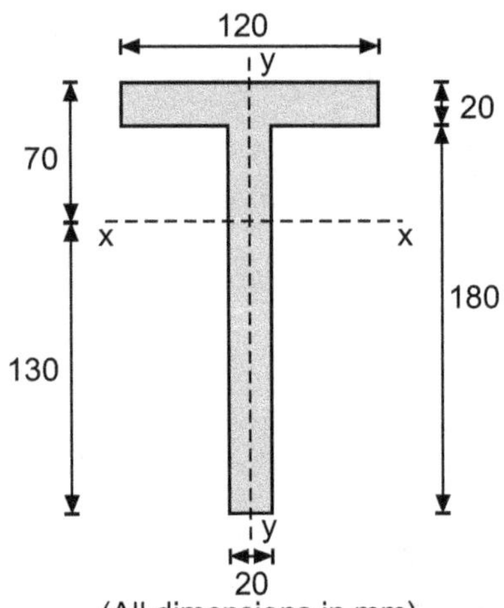



(All dimensions in mm)

**Fig. 10.21 : C/s of column**

**Data :** C/s of column as shown in Fig. 10.21.

$$F_y = 330 \text{ MPa}; \quad E = 210 \text{ GPa};$$

$$a = \frac{1}{7500}$$

**Required :** Length of column for which $P_E = P_R$

**Concept :** Euler's and Rankine's load in terms of '$L_e$' shall be equated.

**Solution** : (i) Geometric properties :

(a) To locate CG;

$\quad$ y-y is axis of symmetry.

$\quad$ Let, bottommost fibre as a reference.

$$a_1 = 120 \times 20 = 2400 \text{ mm}^2 ; \quad y_1 = 180 + \frac{20}{2} = 190 \text{ mm}$$

$$a_2 = 180 \times 20 = 3600 \text{ mm}^2 ; \quad y_2 = \frac{180}{2} = 90 \text{ mm}$$

$$\bar{y} = \frac{a_1 y_1 + a_2 y_2}{a_1 + a_2} = \frac{2400 \times 190 + 3600 \times 90}{2400 + 3600}$$

$$= 130 \text{ mm from bottom as shown in Fig. 10.21.}$$

$$A = a_1 + a_2 = 6000 \text{ mm}^2$$

(b) Moment of inertia :

$$I_{xx} = I_{xx_1} + I_{xx_2} = \frac{120 \times 20^3}{12} + (2400)(190 - 130)^2$$

$$+ \frac{20 \times 180^3}{12} + (3600)(130 - 90)^2$$

$$= 24.2 \times 10^6 \text{ mm}^4$$

$$I_{yy} = I_{yy_1} + I_{yy_2} = \frac{20 \times 120^3}{12} + \frac{180 \times 20^3}{12}$$

$$= 3 \times 10^6 \text{ mm}^4$$

$$\therefore \quad I_{min} = I_{yy} = 3 \times 10^6 \text{ mm}^4$$

(c)
$$r_{min} = \sqrt{\frac{I_{min}}{A}} = \sqrt{\frac{3 \times 10^6}{6000}} = 22.36 \text{ mm}$$

(d)
$$\lambda = \frac{L_e}{r_{min}} = \frac{L_e}{22.36}$$

(ii)   Euler's load ($P_E$) :   $P_E = \dfrac{\pi^2 \, E \, I_{min}}{L_e^2} = \dfrac{\pi^2 \times 210 \times 10^3 \times 3 \times 10^6}{L_e^2}$

$$= \dfrac{6.21 \times 10^{12}}{L_e^2} \qquad \qquad \ldots (i)$$

(iii)   Rankine's load ($P_R$) :

$$P_R = \dfrac{F_y \cdot A}{1 + a\,\lambda^2} = \dfrac{330 \times 6000}{1 + \dfrac{(L_e / 22.36)^2}{7500}}$$

$$= \dfrac{1.485 \times 10^{10}}{7500 + \left(\dfrac{L_e}{22.36}\right)^2} \qquad \qquad \ldots (ii)$$

(iv)   Length for which $P_E = P_R$ :
       Equating (i) and (ii),

$$\dfrac{6.21 \times 10^{12}}{L_e^2} = \dfrac{1.485 \times 10^{10}}{7500 + \left(\dfrac{L_e}{22.36}\right)^2}$$

$$418.18 = \dfrac{L_e^2}{7500 + \left(\dfrac{L_e}{22.36}\right)^2}$$

$\therefore$ $\qquad\qquad\qquad\qquad\qquad L_e = 4378.6$ mm

we have $\qquad\qquad\qquad\qquad L_e = \dfrac{L}{\sqrt{2}}$ for one end fixed, other end hinged.

$$L = \left(\sqrt{2}\right) L_e = \sqrt{2} \times 4.378 = \mathbf{6.19 \ m}$$

**Example 10.16** : *A built-up column consists of two channels placed back to back as shown in Fig. 10.22. The column is fixed at one end and hinged at the other end. Actual length of column is 6 m. Find the clear back to back distance between channels such that radius of gyration, for built-up section about both the principal axes is same. Also find safe axial load on column using factor of safety = 2. The properties of individual channel sections are as under.*

*$I_{xx} = 9312 \times 10^4 \ mm^4$; $I_{yy} = 394 \times 10^4 \ mm^4$; $A = 4900 \ mm^2$;*

*Distance of CG from outer face of web = $C_y = 24$ mm.*

*Use Rankine's formula. Take $F_y = 270$ MPa and $a = \dfrac{1}{7500}$.*

**Data** :   L = 6 m; one end fixed, other hinged; factor of safety = 2;

$\qquad\qquad F_y = 270$ MPa; $a = \dfrac{1}{7500}$.

**Required** :   Back to back distance between channel; safe load on column.

**Concept** :   For the optimum utility of cross-section, moment of inertia about both the principal axes should be same.

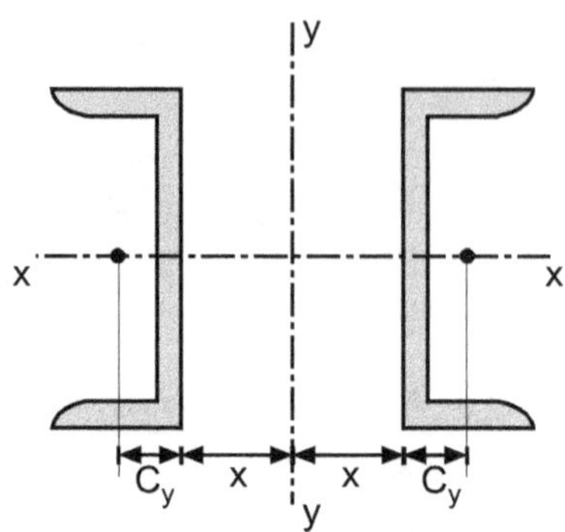


**Fig. 10.22 : C/s of column**

**Solution** : (i) Back to back distance between channels.

$$I_{xx} \text{ for built-up section} = 2 \times I_{xx} \text{ of each channel}$$
$$= 2 \times 9312 \times 10^4 \text{ mm}^4 \qquad ...\ (i)$$
$$I_{yy} \text{ for built-up section} = 2\,[I_{yy} + Ak^2] \text{ for each channel.}$$

Let, $\quad 2x$ = clear gap between channels

$$I_{yy} = 2\,[394 \times 10^4 + 4900\,(x + 24)^2] \qquad ...\ (ii)$$

[**Note :** For calculation of $I_{yy}$, parallel axis theorem is used. k = perpendicular distance from y-y axis of built-up section to C.G. of individual channel.]

Equating (i) and (ii),

$$2\,(9312 \times 10^4) = 2\,[394 \times 10^4 + 4900\,(x + 24)^2]$$
$$\therefore \qquad x = 110.9 \text{ mm}$$
$$\therefore \qquad \text{Clear gap} = 2x = 221.8 \text{ mm}$$

(ii)  Geometric properties :

$$A = 2 \times 4900 = 9800 \text{ mm}^2$$
$$I_{min} = I_{xx} = I_{yy} = 2 \times 9312 \times 10^4 = 186.24 \times 10^6 \text{ mm}^4$$
$$r_{min} = \sqrt{\frac{I_{min}}{A}} = \sqrt{\frac{186.24 \times 10^6}{9800}} = 137.85 \text{ mm}$$
$$L_e = \frac{L}{\sqrt{2}} = \frac{600}{\sqrt{2}} = 4242.64 \text{ mm}$$
$$\text{Slenderness ratio} = \lambda = \frac{L_e}{r_{min}} = \frac{4242.64}{137.85} = 30.78$$

(iii)  Safe load by Rankine's formula :

$$P_R = \frac{F_y \cdot A}{1 + a\,\lambda^2} = \frac{270 \times 9800}{1 + \dfrac{(30.78)^2}{7500}} = 2.35 \times 10^6 \text{ N}$$

$$P_{safe} = \frac{P_R}{\text{Factor of safety}} = \frac{P_R}{2} = \frac{2.35 \times 10^6}{2}$$
$$= 1.175 \times 10^6 \text{ N}$$
$$= \mathbf{1175 \text{ kN}}$$

**Example 10.17 :** *A built-up column consists of two channels with two plates connected symmetrically as shown in Fig. 10.23. The actual length of column is 7 m and it is fixed at one end and hinged at the other end. Find the safe load in axial compression using factor of safety = 2. The properties of individual channel sections are as under :*

$I_{xx} = 1819.3 \times 10^4 \ mm^4; \ I_{yy} = 140.4 \times 10^4 \ mm^4; \ A = 2821 \ mm^2;$

*Distance of CG* $= C_y = 21.7$ *mm. Use Rankine's formula,* $a = \dfrac{1}{7500}$ *and* $F_y = 300$ *MPa.*

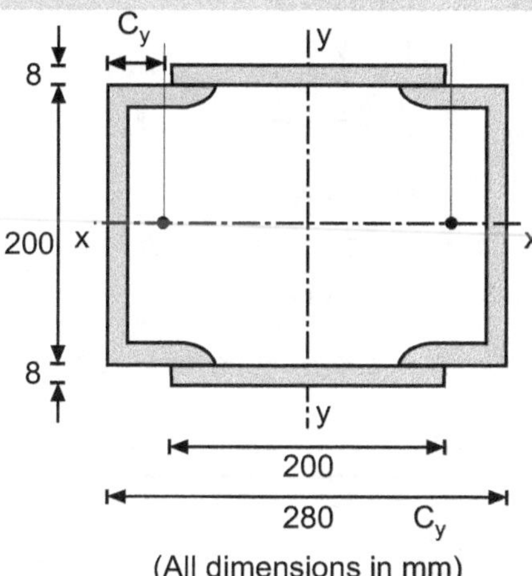


(All dimensions in mm)

**Fig. 10.23 : C/s of column**

**Data**        :   L = 7 m; one end fixed and other hinged; factor of safety = 2; $a = \dfrac{1}{7500}$;

$F_y = 300$ MPa.

**Required**   :   Safe load on column.

**Concept**    :   Application of Rankine's formula.

**Solution**   :   (i) Geometric properties :

(a)
$$A = 2\,(2821 + 200 \times 8) = 8842 \ mm^2$$

(b)
$$I_{xx} = 2\,(1819.3 \times 10^4) + 2\left(\frac{200 \times 8^3}{12} + (200 \times 8)\,(104)^2\right)$$

$$= 71.01 \times 10^6 \ mm^4$$

$$I_{yy} = 2\,(140.4 \times 10^4 + 2821\,(140 - 21.7)^2) + 2\left(\frac{8 \times 200^3}{12}\right)$$

$$= 92.43 \times 10^6 \ mm^4$$

$$\therefore \quad I_{min} = I_{xx} = 71.01 \times 10^6 \ mm^4$$

(c)
$$r_{min} = \sqrt{\frac{I_{min}}{A}} = \sqrt{\frac{71.01 \times 10^6}{8842}} = 89.62 \ mm$$

(d)
$$L_e = \frac{L}{\sqrt{2}} \quad \text{for one end fixed and other hinged.}$$

$$= \frac{7000}{\sqrt{2}} = 4949.75 \ mm$$

$\therefore$  Slenderness ratio $= \lambda = \dfrac{L_e}{r_{min}} = \dfrac{4949.75}{89.62} = 55.23$

(ii)    Safe load on column :

$$P_R = \frac{F_y \cdot A}{1 + a\lambda^2} = \frac{300 \times 8842}{1 + \dfrac{(55.23)^2}{7500}}$$

$\therefore$ 

$$P_R = 1.885 \times 10^6 \, N$$
$$= 1885 \, kN$$

$\therefore$ 

$$P_{safe} = \frac{P_R}{2} = \frac{1885}{2}$$

$$= \mathbf{942.5 \ kN}$$

**Example 10.18 :** *A steel compound column 3 m long is consisting of two 'I' sections 200 mm × 100 mm × 10 mm joined by steel plates 300 mm × 10 mm as shown in Fig. 10.24. Find the Rankine's crippling load if both ends of column are hinged. Assume $F_y$ = 550 MPa; $a = \dfrac{1}{1600}$.*

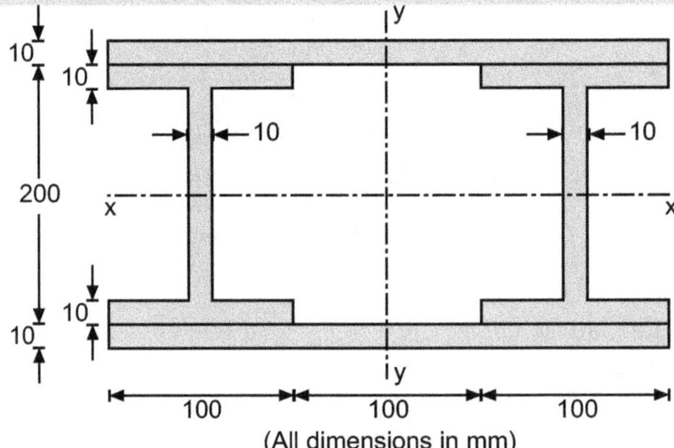


**Fig. 10.24 : C/s of column**

**Data**        :  $L$ = 3 m;  $F_y$ = 550 MPa;  $a = \dfrac{1}{1600}$.

**Required**  :  Crippling load by Rankine's formula.

**Concept**  :  Application of Rankine's formula.

**Solution**  :  (i) Geometric properties :

(a) For each I section,

$$A = 2 \times 100 \times 10 + 180 \times 10 = 3800 \ mm^2$$

$$I_{xx} = \frac{100 \times 200^3}{12} - \frac{90 \times 180^3}{12} = 22.93 \times 10^6 \ mm^4$$

$$I_{yy} = 2\left(\frac{10 \times 100^3}{12}\right) + \frac{180 \times 10^3}{12} = 1.68 \times 10^6 \ mm^4$$

(b) For each plate,

$$A = 300 \times 10 = 3000 \ mm^2$$

$$I_{xx} = \frac{300 \times 10^3}{12} = 25 \times 10^3 \text{ mm}^4$$

$$I_{yy} = \frac{10 \times 300^3}{12} = 22.5 \times 10^6 \text{ mm}^4$$

(c) For built-up section,

$$A = 2 \times 3800 + 2 \times 3000 = 13.6 \times 10^3 \text{ mm}^2$$

$$I_{xx} = 2\,(22.93 \times 10^6) + 2\,(25 \times 10^3 + 3000\,(105)^2)$$

$$= 112.06 \times 10^6 \text{ mm}^4$$

$$I_{yy} = 2\,(1.68 \times 10^6 + 3800\,(100)^2) + 2\,(22.5 \times 10^6)$$

$$= 124.36 \times 10^6 \text{ mm}^4$$

$$\therefore \quad I_{min} = I_{xx} = 112.06 \times 10^6 \text{ mm}^4$$

$$r_{min} = \sqrt{\frac{I_{min}}{A}} = \sqrt{\frac{112.06 \times 10^6}{13.6 \times 10^3}} = 90.77$$

$$L_e = L = 3000 \text{ mm}$$

$$\lambda = \frac{L_e}{r_{min}} = \frac{3000}{90.77} = 33$$

(ii)    Rankine's load $(P_R)$ :

$$P_R = \frac{F_y \cdot A}{1 + a\lambda^2} = \frac{550 \times 13.6 \times 10^3}{1 + \dfrac{(33)^2}{1600}}$$

$$= 4.450 \times 10^3 \text{ N}$$

$$= \mathbf{4450 \text{ kN}}$$

**Example 10.19 :** *A built-up column consists of 4 ISA 80 × 80 × 8 to form a box section as shown in Fig. 10.25. Length of column is 6 m; hinged at both ends. Find the strength of column using Rankine's formula. If E = 200 GPa; $F_y$ = 250 MPa.*

*Properties of each ISA (80 × 80 × 8) are as under,*

$$I_{xx} = I_{yy} = 87.4 \times 10^4 \text{ mm}^4$$

$$A = 1505 \text{ mm}^2$$

$$C_x = C_y = 23.4 \text{ mm}$$

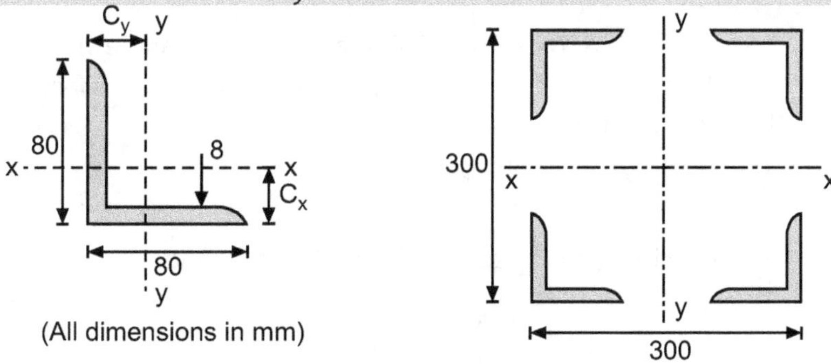


**Fig. 10.25 : C/s of column**

**Data**    :    As shown in Fig. 10.25; E = 200 GPa; $F_y$ = 250 MPa; L = 6 m.

**Required** : Strength of column by Rankine's formula.

**Concept** : It should be noted that for built-up section, $I_{xx} = I_{yy}$ due to symmetry.

Also Rankine's constant 'a' is not given; which is to be obtained as $a = \dfrac{F_y}{\pi^2 E}$.

**Solution** : (i) Geometric properties :

For built-up section,

$$A = 4 \times 1505 = 6020 \text{ mm}^2$$

$$I_{xx} = I_{yy} = I_{min} = 4[87.4 \times 10^4 + 1505(150 - 23.4)^2]$$

$$= 99.98 \times 10^6 \text{ mm}^4$$

$$r_{min} = \sqrt{\dfrac{I_{min}}{A}} = \sqrt{\dfrac{99.98 \times 10^6}{6020}} = 128.87 \text{ mm}$$

$$L_e = L = 6000 \text{ mm}$$

$$\lambda = \dfrac{L_e}{r_{min}} = \dfrac{6000}{128.87} = 46.56$$

(ii) Strength of column by Rankine's formula :

$$P_R = \dfrac{F_y \cdot A}{1 + a\lambda^2}$$

where ; $a$ = Rankine's constant

$$= \dfrac{F_y}{\pi^2 E} = \dfrac{250}{\pi^2 \times 200 \times 10^3} = \dfrac{1}{7895.68}$$

$$\therefore \quad P_R = \dfrac{250 \times 6020}{1 + \dfrac{(46.56)^2}{7895.68}}$$

$$= 1.180 \times 10^6 \text{ N}$$

$$= \mathbf{1180 \text{ kN}}$$

**Example 10.20 :** *Find by Rankine's formula the safe axial load with an angle strut ISA 70 × 70 × 8; 1.5 m long; both ends hinged will carry using factor of safety of 2. Assume $F_y = 250$ MPa and $a = \dfrac{1}{7500}$.*

**Data** : c/s of strut ISA 70 × 70 × 8 (Indian Standard Angle having each leg length = 70 mm and thickness = 8 mm); L = 1.5 m; factor of safety = 2; $F_y = 250$ MPa; a = .

**Required** : Safe load by Rankine's formula.

**Concept** : From basics; $I_{xx} = \displaystyle\int_0^A dA \cdot y^2$ ; $I_{yy} = \displaystyle\int_0^A dA \cdot x^2$ and

Product of inertia $= I_{xy} = \displaystyle\int_0^A dA \cdot x \cdot y$

Principal axes will be located using $\tan(2\theta_1) = \dfrac{I_{xy}}{I_{yy} - I_{xx}}$ and $\theta_2 = \theta_1 + 90°$.

Principal moment of inertia @ major and minor axes $I_{uu}$ and $I_{vv}$ respectively is given by,

$$I_{uu},\ I_{vv} = \frac{I_{xx} + I_{yy}}{2} \pm \sqrt{\left(\frac{I_{xx} - I_{yy}}{2}\right)^2 + I_{xy}^2}$$

**Solution**    :    (i) Geometric properties :

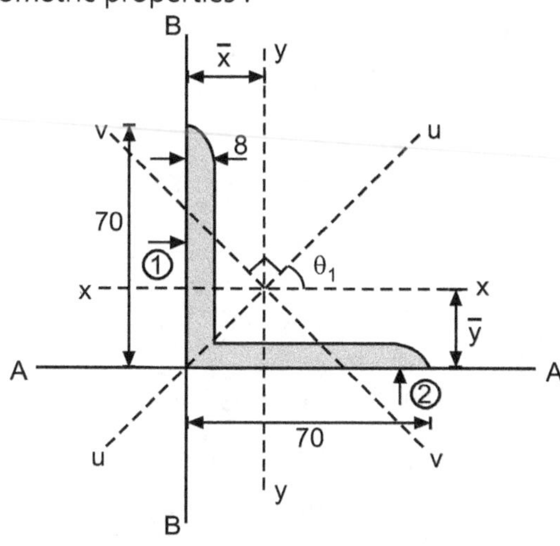


(All dimensions in mm)

**Fig. 10.26 : C/s of strut**

Consider two rectangular areas (i) and (ii) as marked in Fig. 10.26 and let, AA and BB are reference axes to locate CG of cross-section.

$$a_1 = 70 \times 8 = 560 \text{ mm}^2;\ x_1 = 4 \text{ mm};\ y_1 = \frac{70}{2} = 35 \text{ mm}$$

$$a_2 = (70 - 8)\,8 = 496 \text{ mm}^2;\ x_2 = 8 + \frac{(70 - 8)}{2} = 39 \text{ mm}; y_2 = 4 \text{ mm}$$

$\therefore$     $A = 560 + 496 = 1056 \text{ mm}^2$

$$\bar{x} = \frac{a_1 x_1 + a_2 x_2}{a_1 + a_2} = \frac{560 \times 4 + 496 \times 39}{1056} = 20.44 \text{ mm} = \bar{y}$$

$$I_{xx} = \frac{8 \times 70^3}{12} + (560)(35 - 20.44)^2 + (70 - 8)\frac{8^3}{12} + (496)(20.44 - 4)^2$$

$$= 484.08 \times 10^3 \text{ mm}^4$$

$$= I_{yy}$$

Product of inertia, $I_{xy} = 560\,(20.44 - 4)\,(35 - 20.44)$

$$+ 496\,(39 - 20.44)\,(20.44 - 4)$$

$$= 285.38 \times 10^3 \text{ mm}^4$$

Principal moment of inertia,

$$I_{uu} = I_{vv} = \frac{I_{xx} + I_{yy}}{2} \pm \sqrt{\left(\frac{I_{xx} - I_{yy}}{2}\right)^2 + I_{xy}^2}$$

$$= \frac{(484.08 + 484.08) \times 10^3}{2} \pm \sqrt{0 + (285.38 \times 10^3)^2}$$

$$= [(484.08) \pm (285.38)] \times 10^3$$

$$I_{uu} = 769.46 \times 10^3 \text{ mm}^4$$

$$I_{vv} = 198.7 \times 10^3 \text{ mm}^4$$

Location of principal planes,

$$\tan(2\theta_1) = \frac{I_{xy}}{I_{yy} - I_{xx}} \text{ , but } I_{xx} = I_{yy}$$

$\therefore \qquad \tan(2\theta_1) = \times$

$\therefore \qquad \dfrac{\sin(2\theta_1)}{\cos(2\theta_1)} = \times \qquad \therefore \cos(2\theta_1) = 0$

$\therefore \qquad 2\theta_1 = 90° \qquad \therefore \theta_1 = 45° \text{ and } \theta_2 = 135°$

Thus, $\qquad I_{min} = I_{vv} = 198.7 \times 10^3 \text{ mm}^4$

$$r_{min} = r_{vv} = \sqrt{\frac{I_{vv}}{A}} = \sqrt{\frac{198.7 \times 10^3}{1056}} = 13.71 \text{ mm}$$

Governing, $\qquad \lambda = \dfrac{L_e}{r_{min}} = \dfrac{1500}{13.71} = 109.41 \qquad\qquad (\because L_e = L)$

(ii)    Safe load by Rankine's formula :

$$P_R = \frac{F_y A}{1 + a\lambda^2}$$

$$= \frac{250 \times 1056}{1 + \dfrac{(109.41)^2}{7500}}$$

$$= 101.69 \times 10^3 \text{ N}$$

$$= 101.69 \text{ kN}$$

$\therefore \qquad P_{safe} = \dfrac{101.69}{2} = \textbf{50.84 kN}$

---

**Example 10.21 :** *A straight bar of steel 1150 mm long and 20 mm × 6 mm in cross section is loaded axially till it buckles. Assuming Euler's formula is valid, find the maximum central deflection of the bar. The ends of the bar are hinged. Yield stress for the bar is 355 MPa; E = 205 GPa.*

---

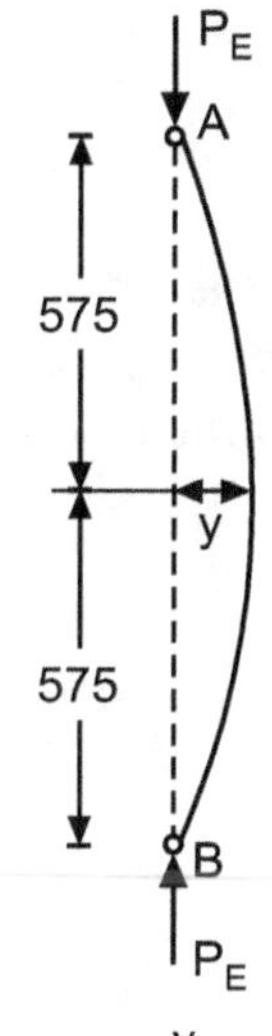

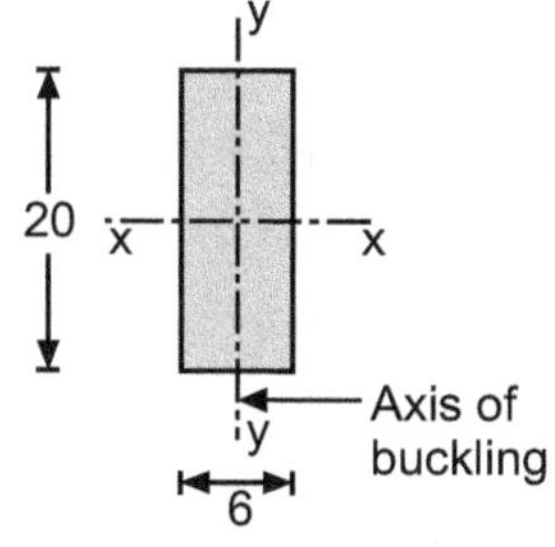



(All dimensions in mm)

**Fig. 10.27**

**Data :** L = 1150 mm; c/s = 20 mm × 6 mm

$F_y$ = 355 MPa;  E = 205 GPa.

**Required :** Central deflection (y) of the bar.

**Concept :** Cross-section at mid-span is subjected to direct and bending stresses. Maximum resultant stress shall be equated to '$F_y$' to find central deflection.

**Solution :** (i) Geometric properties :

$$A = 20 \times 6 = 120 \text{ mm}^2$$

$$I_{min} = I_{yy} = \frac{20 \times 6^3}{12} = 360 \text{ mm}^4$$

$$r_{min} = \sqrt{\frac{I_{min}}{A}} = \sqrt{\frac{360}{120}} = 1.73 \text{ mm}$$

Section modulus @ y axis =

$$Z_{yy} = \frac{I_{yy}}{y_{max}} = \frac{360}{3} = 120 \text{ mm}^3$$

$$L_e = L = 1150 \text{ mm}$$

(ii)  Euler's buckling load ($P_E$) :

$$P_E = \frac{\pi^2 \, EI_{min}}{L_e^2} = \frac{\pi^2 \times 205 \times 10^3 \times 360}{1150^2}$$

$$= 550.75 \text{ N}$$

(iii)  Direct stress ($\sigma_d$) :

$$\sigma_d = \frac{P_E}{A} = \frac{550.75}{120} = 4.59 \text{ MPa}$$

(iv)  Bending stress ($\sigma_b$) :

$$\sigma_b = \pm \frac{M}{Z_{yy}} = \pm \frac{(P_E) \, y}{Z_{yy}}$$

$$= \pm \frac{(550.75) \times y}{120}$$

$$= \pm 4.59 \, (y) \text{ MPa}$$

where;                    Y = Central deflection in 'mm'

(v)  Central deflection (y) :

Maximum resultant stress = $\sigma_{max} = \sigma_d + \sigma_b = 4.59 + 4.59 \, (y)$

Equating,                    $\sigma_{max}$  =  $F_y$  i.e. yield stress

$4.59 + 4.59\,(y)$  =  $355$

$\therefore$                    $y$  =  **76.34 mm**

**Example 10.22 :** *A column has hollow rectangular cross-section. Outside dimensions 120 mm × 60 mm. Thickness 10 mm, uniform throughout. Length of the column is 3 m. It is fixed at bottom and free at top. Calculate safe load by : (i) Euler's formula, (ii) Rankine's formula. Take E = 200 GPa, $F_y = 320$ MPa and $a = \dfrac{1}{7500}$.*                    **(May 2002)**

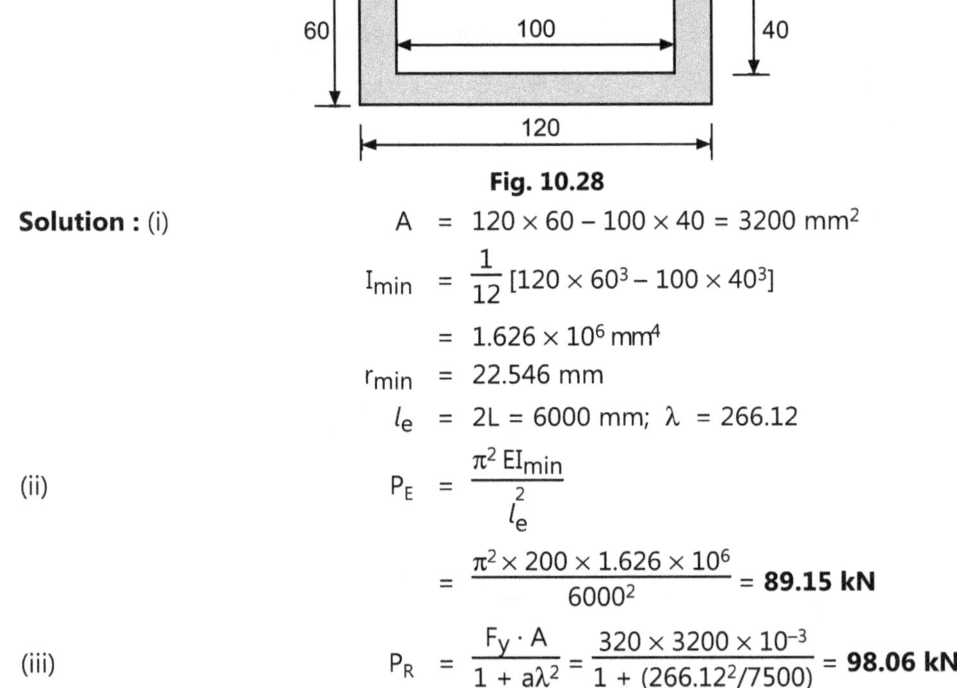


**Fig. 10.28**

**Solution :** (i)                    $A = 120 \times 60 - 100 \times 40 = 3200 \text{ mm}^2$

$I_{min} = \dfrac{1}{12}[120 \times 60^3 - 100 \times 40^3]$

$= 1.626 \times 10^6 \text{ mm}^4$

$r_{min} = 22.546 \text{ mm}$

$l_e = 2L = 6000 \text{ mm}; \quad \lambda = 266.12$

(ii)                    $P_E = \dfrac{\pi^2\, EI_{min}}{l_e^2}$

$= \dfrac{\pi^2 \times 200 \times 1.626 \times 10^6}{6000^2} = \textbf{89.15 kN}$

(iii)                    $P_R = \dfrac{F_y \cdot A}{1 + a\lambda^2} = \dfrac{320 \times 3200 \times 10^{-3}}{1 + (266.12^2/7500)} = \textbf{98.06 kN}$

**Example 10.23 :** *Explain Johnson's formula for crippling load. Make it clear that how it is modified from Rankine's formula.*                    **(May 2002)**

**Solution :** A simple expansion of the Rankine's formula will give a parabolic expression which is convenient in use.

$\dfrac{P}{A} = F_y\,[1 - a\lambda^2]$ approximately or

$\dfrac{P}{A} = F_y - b\lambda^2$

b is approximately $\dfrac{F_y^2}{4\pi^2 E}$

Above expression is called as *Johnson's* formula.

**Example 10.24 :** *Compare the crippling loads given by Euler's formula and Rankine's formula for a tubular strut with hinged ends, 2.5 m long, 40 mm outer diameter and 30 mm internal diameter. Assume E = 200 GPa, Rankine's constant, $\alpha$ = 1/7500, crushing stress = 320 MPa.*

**Solution :** (i)

$$l_e = L = 2500 \text{ mm}$$
$$I_{min} = (\pi/64)(40^4 - 30^4) = 85.9 \times 10^3 \text{ mm}^4$$
$$A = (\pi/4)(40^2 - 30^2) = 549.78 \text{ mm}^2$$
$$r_{min} = 12.49 \text{ mm} \quad \therefore \quad \lambda = 200$$

(ii)
$$P_E = \frac{\pi^2 \times 200 \times 85.9 \times 10^3}{(2500)^2} = \textbf{27.13 kN}$$

(iii)
$$P_R = \frac{F_y A}{1 + \alpha\lambda^2}$$

$$= \frac{320 \times 549.78 \times 10^{-3}}{1 + \dfrac{200^2}{7500}} = \textbf{27.78 kN} \quad \therefore \quad \frac{P_E}{P_R} = \textbf{0.976}$$

**Example 10.25 :** *A horizontal bar AB is pin supported at end A and carries a load Q at end B, as shown in Fig. 10.29. It is supported at C and D by two identical pinned end columns of length L. Each column has flexural rigidity EI. At what load Q does the system collapse by buckling of the columns ?*

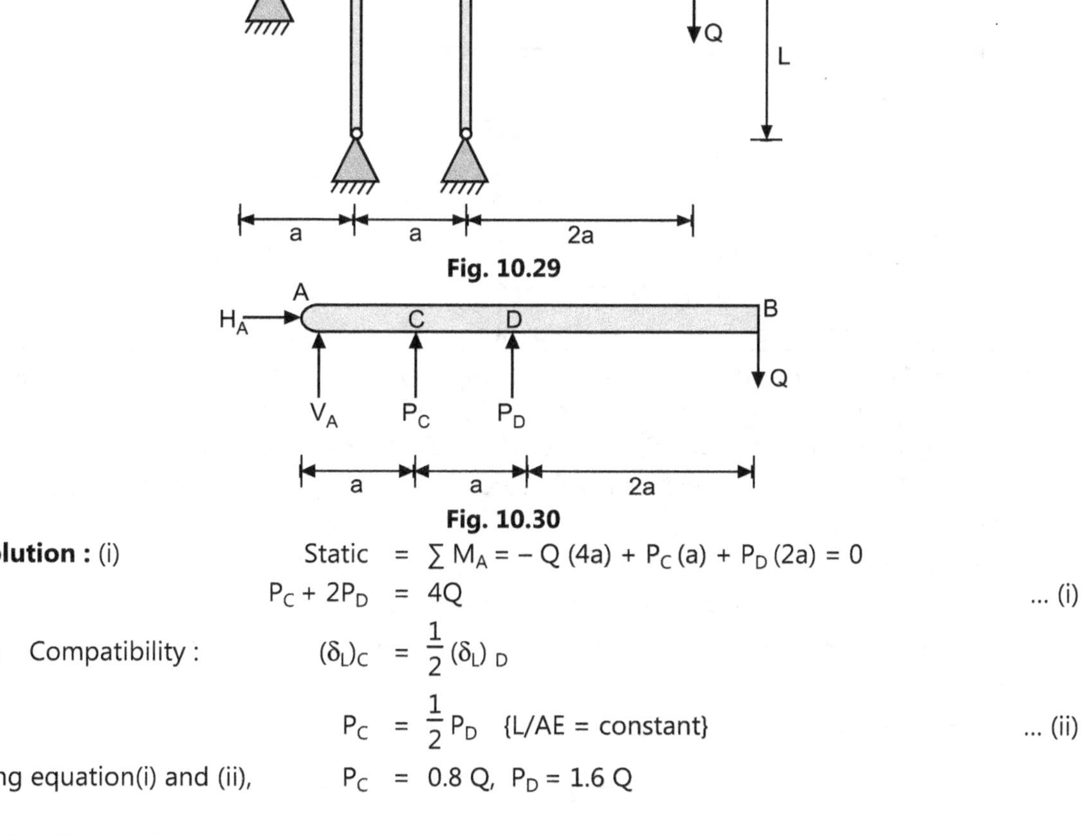


**Solution :** (i)

$$\text{Static} = \sum M_A = -Q(4a) + P_C(a) + P_D(2a) = 0$$

$$\therefore \qquad P_C + 2P_D = 4Q \qquad \qquad \text{... (i)}$$

(ii)   Compatibility :
$$(\delta_L)_C = \frac{1}{2}(\delta_L)_D$$

$$P_C = \frac{1}{2}P_D \quad \{L/AE = \text{constant}\} \qquad \qquad \text{... (ii)}$$

Solving equation(i) and (ii),   $P_C = 0.8\,Q, \; P_D = 1.6\,Q$

(iii) $\qquad P_D = 1.6\,Q = \pi^2\,EI/l_e^2$

$\therefore \qquad Q = \dfrac{\pi^2\,EI}{1.6\,L^2} \qquad (l_e = L).$

**Example 10.26 :** *A steel column is to be fabricated I section as shown in Fig. 10.31. It is 6 m in height, fixed at one end and free at the other, and is designed to carry a compressive load of 92 kN at the central axis O of the section. Determine the minimum dimensions b and d of the column and the compressive stress. Take E = 200 GPa.*

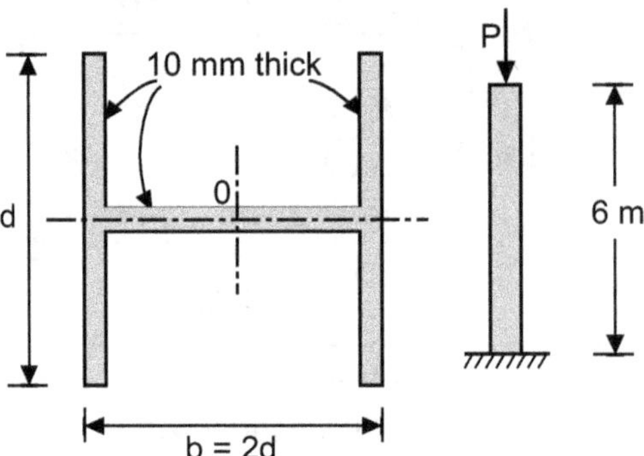


**Fig. 10.31**

**Solution :** $\qquad P_E = \dfrac{(\pi^2\,EI_{min})}{l_e^2}$

$\qquad 92 = \dfrac{(\pi^2 \times 200\,I_{min})}{(12000)^2}$

$\therefore \qquad I_{min} = 6.71 \times 10^6 \text{ mm}^4$

For the given c/s, $\qquad I_{min} = I_y = 2\,\{10d^3/12\} + (2d - 20)\,(10)^3/12$

$\qquad 1.67\,d^3 + 166.67\,d - 1666.67 = 6.71 \times 10^6$

Solving by trial and error, $\qquad d = \textbf{160 mm} \quad \therefore\ b = \textbf{320 mm}$

**Example 10.27 :** *A hollow cast from iron whose outside diameter is 200 mm and has a thickness of 20 mm is 4.5 m long and is fixed at both ends. Calculate the safe load by Rankine's formula, using a factor of safety of 2.5. Find the ratio of Euler's to Rankine's loads.*

*Take E = 1 × 10⁵ N/mm² and Rankine's constant = 1/1600 for both ends pinned case and $\sigma_c$ = 550 N/mm².*

**Data :** $D_o$ = 200 mm, t = 20 mm, $D_i$ = 160 mm, 1 = 4.5 m, F.S. = 2.5, a = 1/1600, E = 1 × 10⁵ N.mm² and $\sigma_c$ = 550 N/mm², both ends pinned.

**Required :** Safe load by Rankine's formula, ratio of Euler's to Rankine's load.

**Concept :** Standard formulae.

**Solution :** (i) Geometric properties :

$$A = \frac{\pi}{4}(200^2 - 160^2) = 11.31 \times 10^3 \text{ mm}^2$$

$$I = \frac{\pi}{64}(200^4 - 160^4) = 46.37 \times 10^6 \text{ mm}^4$$

Radius of Gyration (r) :　　$r^2 = \dfrac{I}{A} = \dfrac{46.37 \times 10^6}{11.31 \times 10^3} = 4100 \text{ mm}^2$

Both ends pinned :　　　$L_e = L = 4500 \text{ mm}$

(ii) Rankine's and Euler's Load :

$$P_R = \frac{\sigma_c \cdot A}{1 + a\left(\dfrac{L_e}{k}\right)^2}$$

$$= \frac{550 \times 11.31 \times 10^3}{1 + \dfrac{1}{1600}\left(\dfrac{4500}{4100}\right)^2} = \mathbf{1.52 \times 10^6 \text{ N}}$$

$\therefore$　　　$(P_R)_{safe} = \dfrac{1.52 \times 10^6}{2.5} = 608.82 \times 10^3 \text{ N}$

$$P_E = \frac{\pi^2 EI}{L_e^2} = \frac{\pi^2 \times 1 \times 10^5 \times 46.37 \times 10^6}{4500^2}$$

$$= \mathbf{2.26 \times 10^6 \text{ N}}$$

$\therefore$　　　$\boxed{\dfrac{(P_R)_{safe}}{P_E} = \dfrac{608.82 \times 10^3}{2.26 \times 10^6}}$

$\therefore$　　　$\dfrac{P_E}{(P_R)_{safe}} = \dfrac{2.26 \times 10^6}{608.82 \times 10^3} = \mathbf{3.71}$

**Example 10.28 :** *Compare the crippling load given by Euler's and Rankine's formula for a tabular steel strut 2.3 m long having external diameter = 38 mm and internal diameter = 33 mm, strut is fixed at one end and hinged at other end. Take $\sigma_c$ = 335 MPa, E = 205 GPa, $a = \dfrac{1}{7500}$.*

**Data :** $D_o$ = 38 mm, $D_i$ = 33 mm, $\sigma_c$ = 335 MPa, E = 205 GPa, $a = \dfrac{1}{7500}$, length of strut = 2.3 m.

**Required :** Comparison of Euler's and Rankine's load.

**Concept :** Standard formulae.

**Solution :** (i) Geometric properties :

$$A = \frac{\pi}{4}(D_o^2 - D_i^2)$$

$$= \frac{\pi}{4}(38^2 - 33^2) = 278.82 \text{ mm}^2$$

$$I = \frac{\pi}{64}(D_o^4 - D_i^4)$$

$$= \frac{\pi}{64}(38^4 - 33^4) = 44.14 \times 10^3 \text{ mm}^4$$

$$r^2 = \frac{I}{A} = \frac{44.14 \times 10^3}{278.82} = 158.31 \text{ mm}^2$$

and $\qquad$ Effective length $= Le = \dfrac{L}{\sqrt{2}} = \dfrac{2300}{\sqrt{2}} = 1626.35 \text{ mm}$

(ii) Euler's formula : $\qquad P_E = \dfrac{\pi^2 \, EI}{L_e^2}$

$$= \frac{\pi^2 \times 205 \times 10^3 \times 44.14 \times 10^3}{(1626.35)^2}$$

$$= \mathbf{337.65 \times 10^3 \ N}$$

(iii) Rankine's formula : $\qquad P_R = \dfrac{\sigma_c \, A}{Ha \times \left(\dfrac{L_e}{r}\right)^2} = \dfrac{335 \times 278.82}{1 + \dfrac{1}{7500} \times \left(\dfrac{(1626.35)^2}{158.31}\right)}$

$$= \mathbf{289.38 \times 10^3 \ N}$$

(iv) Ratio of $\dfrac{P_E}{P_R}$ : $\qquad \dfrac{P_E}{P_R} = \dfrac{337.65}{289.38} = \mathbf{1.17}$

## EXERCISE

1. A solid round bar 60 mm in diameter, 3 m long is used as a strut. One end of the strut is fixed, while its other end is hinged. Find the safe compressive load, for this strut using Euler's formula. Assume E = 200 GPa and factor of safety = 3. $\hfill$ (93 kN)

2. Calculate the safe compressive load on hollow cast iron column of 150 mm external diameter, 100 mm internal diameter and 5 m long. Use Euler's formula with factor of safety of 5 and E = 100 GPa. Assume one end of the column fixed and other end hinged.

$\hfill$ (314.9 kN)

3. A slender pin ended aluminium column 2m long and of circular cross-section is to have an outside diameter of 50 mm. Calculate the necessary internal diameter to prevent failure by buckling if critical load is 25 kN. Assume E = 70 GPa. $\hfill$ (42.63 mm)

4. A vertical steel strut, of uniform section, 40 mm in diameter and 3 m long, has pinned ends. Evaluate the maximum central deflection of the strut on buckling if yield stress of 270 MPa is reached. Neglect the direct stress due to axial thrust and assume E = 215 GPa. $\hfill$ (57.25 mm)

5. A hollow alloy tube 5 m long with diameters 40 mm and 25 mm respectively was found to extend 7 mm under a tensile load of 60 kN. Find the buckling load for the tube, when used as a strut with both ends pinned. $\hfill$ (2.35 kN)

6. Fig. 10.32 shows the cross-section of column, 7 m long, fixed at both ends. Find Euler's crippling load for the column assuming E = 200 GPa. $\hfill$ (2153.58 kN)

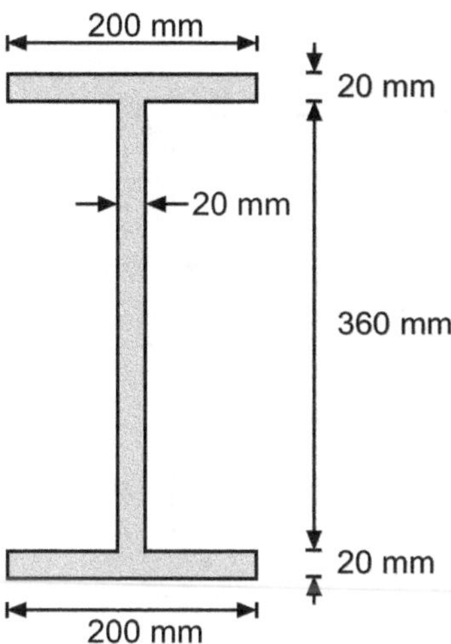


**Fig. 10.32**

7.  A 'T' section shown in Fig. 10.33 is used as a strut of 5 m length, hinged at both ends. Calculate Euler's crippling load, assuming E = 200 GPa.                    (449.26 kN)

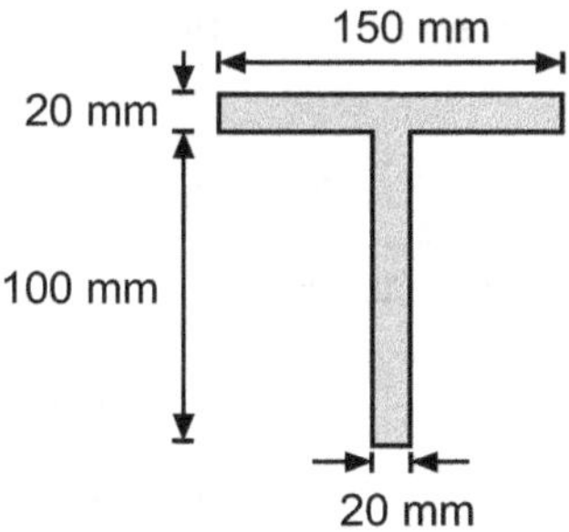


**Fig. 10.33**

8.  Determine the ratio of the strengths of a solid steel column to that of a hollow column of the same material and having the same cross-sectional area. The internal diameter of the hollow column is half of its external diameter. Both the columns are of same length and are pinned at their ends.                    (5/3)

9.  A 4 m long circular bar was found to deflect by 22 mm, when it was used as a simply supported beam subjected to load of 110 N at centre. If this bar is now used as a column, with both ends hinged, determine the crippling load it can carry.                    (4.11 kN)

10. Fig. 10.34 shows the cross-section of simply supported beam. When it is loaded with UDL of 50 kN/m it deflects by 10 mm. Find the safe load, if this beam is used as a column with both ends fixed. Assume a factor of safety of 4 and E = 200 GPa.                    (2541.47 kN)

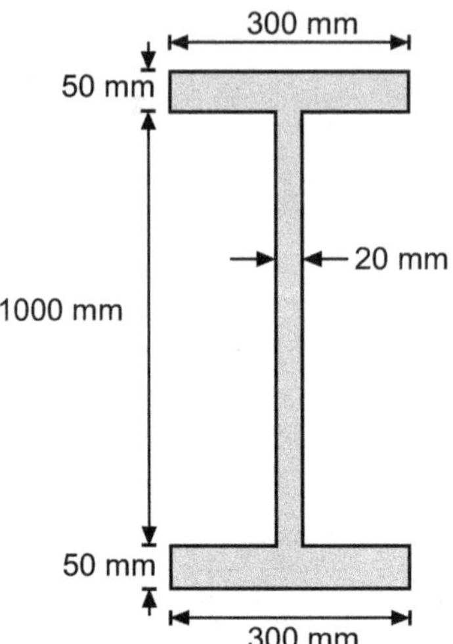

**Fig. 10.34**

11. A cast iron hollow column having 80 mm external diameter and 60 mm internal diameter is 2 m long with both ends fixed. Using Rankine's formula, find the crippling load. Assume $F_y = 600$ MPa and a $= \dfrac{1}{1600}$.                    (660 kN)

12. Compare the crippling loads given by Rankine's and Euler's formula for a tubular strut 3m long having outer and inner diameters of 37.5 mm and 32.5 mm loaded through pin joints at both ends. Assume $F_y = 315$ MPa; a $= \dfrac{1}{7500}$, and $E = 200$ GPa. If elastic limit of the material is 200 MPa, below what length of strut does the Euler's formula cease to apply ?                    ($P_E = 9.27$ kN; $P_R = 9.83$ kN; L = 1.23 m)

13. Fig. 10.35 shows the cross-section of column. Calculate the safe load, the column can carry, if it is 5m long having one end fixed and other hinged. Assume factor of safety = 3.5; $F_y = 315$ MPa; a $= \dfrac{1}{7500}$ . Properties of I section are : A = 2167 mm$^2$; $I_{xx} = 839.1 \times 10^4$ mm$^4$; $I_{yy} = 94.8 \times 10^4$ mm$^4$.                    (156.29 kN)

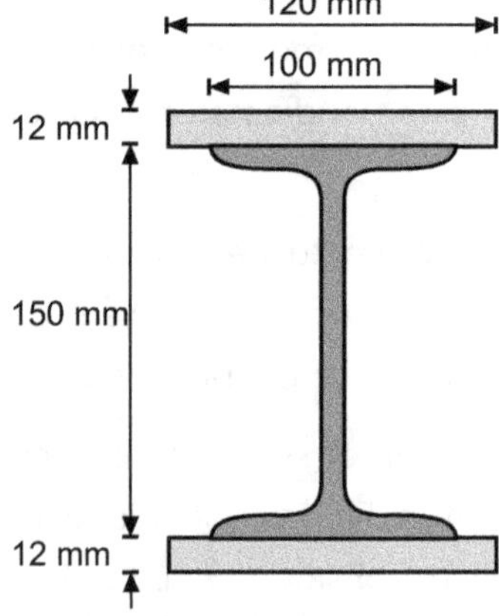

**Fig. 10.35**

14. Fig. 10.36 shows the cross-section of built-up column. Determine the safe load by Rankine's formula if length of column is 7 m, both ends fixed. Assume factor of safety = 4; $F_y$ = 320 MPa; a = 1/7500. The properties of channel section are : A = 1777 mm$^2$, $I_{xx}$ = 1161.2 × 10$^4$ mm$^4$; $I_{yy}$ = 84.2 × 10$^4$ mm$^4$ ; distance of centroid from back of the web = 19.7 mm.

(522 kN)

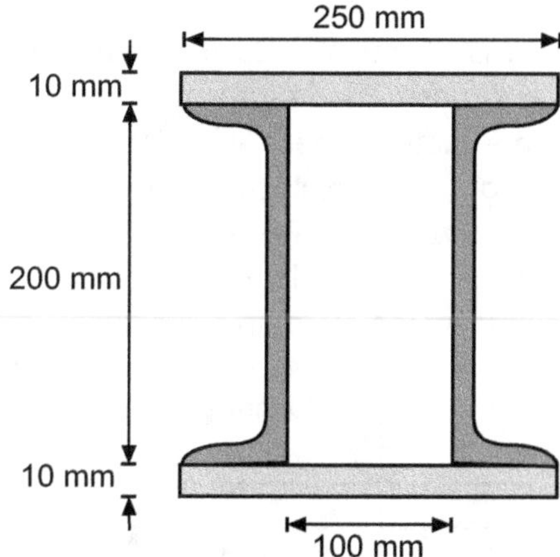


**Fig. 10.36**

15. From the following data, determine the thickness of cast iron column :

    (i)    Length of column = 6 m  (ii) External diameter = 200 mm (iii) Load = 750 kN

    (iv)   Factor of safety = 4 (v) Assume both ends fixed (vi) $F_y$ = 570 MPa

    (vii)  $a = \dfrac{1}{1600}$.                                             (22.8 mm)

16. A short length of tube 50 mm external and 30 mm internal diameter, failed in compression at a load of 250 kN. When 2 m length of same tube was tested as a strut with fixed ends, the load at the failure was 132 kN. Find Rankine's constant.        (1/5263)

17. Find the greatest length for which a mild steel strut of 'T' shaped cross-section, having area = 30 cm$^2$ and minimum moment of inertia = 240 cm$^4$, may be used with one end fixed and other end free to carry a load of 800 kN. Assume $a = \dfrac{1}{7500}$ and $F_y$ = 330 MPa.

(596 mm)

18. The following particulars refer to an engine cylinder :

    (i)    Diameter of the cylinder = 350 mm

    (ii)   Steam pressure in cylinder = 0.18 MPa

    (iii) Distance between piston and cross head = 1.25 m.

    (iv) Factor of safety = 4, $a = \dfrac{1}{7500}$ ; $F_y$ = 330 MPa.

Assuming that, the piston is firmly fixed to the piston and cross head, determine the diameter of the piston rod.

(25 mm)

19. A hollow cast iron column 5 m long is fixed at both ends and has an external diameter 300 mm. The column supports an axial load of 1200 kN. Find the internal diameter of column using factor of safety = 5; $F_y$ = 550 MPa and a = $\frac{1}{1600}$.

(266 mm)

20. A rectangular box section is 80 mm × 120 mm outside and 60 mm × 100 mm inside, having 10 mm uniform thickness. The length of the member is 3.5 m. To strengthen the member, four rods of same material, each with 20 mm diameter, 3.5 m long are welded longitudinally to the box from outside, such that there is one rod at the centre of each of the four faces. The member is used as a column fixed at the bottom and free at the top. Compute the value of Euler's buckling load. If the actual load on column is 50% of the buckling load, find the compression stress in the column. Take E = 200 GPa.

($P_E$ = 198.287 kN, $\sigma$ = 20.41 MPa)

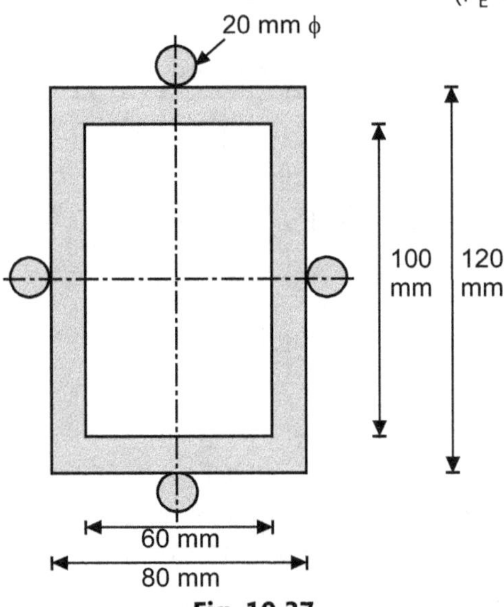


**Fig. 10.37**

21. The external diameter of hollow cylindrical column is 1.25 times its internal diameter. The length of the column is 3 m. When hinged at both ends, it has a critical buckling load of 'P' kN. If the same column is fixed at both ends, the buckling load increases by 300 kN. Taking E = 100 GPa, determine the cross- section of column. Use Euler's formula.

(D = 75 mm ; d = 60 mm)

22. A hollow cylindrical strut of external diameter 80 mm and internal diameter 70 mm is tested in direct compression and fails at 480 kN. If the same strut is tested for both ends fixed, over a length of 4 m, the axial load for the collapse is 280 kN. Find Rankine's constant.

$\left(\dfrac{1}{7930}\right)$

# UNIVERSITY QUESTION PAPERS

## MAY 2014

1. Determine the buckling load for a strut of tee section, the flange width being 100 mm, overall depth 80 mm and both flange and stem 10 mm thick. The strut is 3 m long and is hinged at both ends. Take E = 200 GN/m$^2$.  **[7]**

2. A straight cylindrical bar of 15 mm diameter and 1.2 m long is freely supported at its two ends in a horizontal position. It is loaded with a concentrated load of 100 N at the centre when the centre deflection is observed to be 5 mm. If placed in the vertical position and loaded vertically, what load would cause it to buckle? Also find the ratio of the maximum stress in the two cases.  **[7]**

## DECEMBER 2014

1. A steel bar of rectangular cross-section 60 mm × 80 mm and pinned at each end is subject to axial compression. If the proportional limit of the material is 210 MPa and E = 210 GPa, determine the minimum length for which Euler's equation may be used to determine the buckling load.  **[7]**

2. A rectangular steel bar 45 mm × 55 mm in cross-section, pinned at each end and subjected to axial compression. The bar is 2.3 m long and E = 210 GPa. Determine the buckling load using Euler's formula and corresponding stress.  **[7]**

## MAY 2015

1. Determine the ratio of the buckling strengths of a solid steel column to that of a hollow column of same material and having same cross-sectional area. The internal diameter of hollow column is half of its external diameter. Both the columns are of the same length and are pinned at both ends.  **[7]**

2. A hollow shaft of diameter ratio 3/5 is required to transmit 482 kW at 125 rpm. The shearing stress in the shaft must not to exceed 65 N/mm$^2$ and the twist in a length of 2 m not to exceed 1 degree. Calculate minimum external diameter of shaft which would satisfy these conditions.

   Take G = 8 × 10$^4$ N/mm$^2$.  **[7]**

## November 2015

1. A steel bar of rectangular cross-section 80 mm × 120 mm and pinned at each end is subject to axial compression. If the proportional limit of the material is 235 MPa and E = 207 GPa, determine the minimum length for which Euler's equation may be used to determine the buckling load.  **[7]**

2. A rectangular steel bar 65 mm × 85 mm in cross-section, pinned at each end and subjected to axial compression. The bar is 3 m long and E = 235 GPa. Determine the buckling load using Euler's formula and corresponding stress. **[7]**

## May 2016

1. A horizontal beam ABC 1.6 m long is pinned to a support at C and supported by a vertical aluminum tube 2.25 m long as shown in Fig. 1. The upper end of the tube is hinged to the beam while its lower end is firmly fixed. The beam carries a load of 250 kN at A. Find the thickness of the tube if its outer diameter is 120 mm. Allow a factor of safety 2.5 with respect to Euler critical load. Take $E = 7.2 \times 10^4$ N/mm$^2$ **[10]**

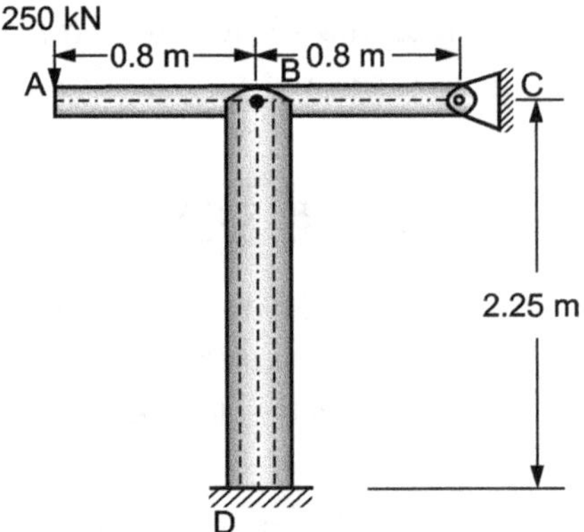


**Fig. 1**

2. A hollow cylindrical cast iron column is 4 m long, both end fixed. Design the column to carry an axial load of 250 kN. Use Rankine's formula and adopt a factor of safety of 5. The internal diameter may be taken as 0.8 times the external diameter. Take $F_c = 550$ N/mm$^2$ and $\alpha = 1/1600$. **[7]**

# Chapter 11

# PRINCIPAL STRESSES AND STRAINS

## 11.1 INTRODUCTION

The problems studied so far include direct tension, compression and shear separately, but there are many structures in which these various stresses occur in combination. Hence, it is of practical importance to find the resultant stresses which may be greater than the applied ones and also the planes on which they act when subjected to complex stress system.

In general, a three dimensional state of stress is as shown in Fig. 11.1 (a) which indicates nine stress components.

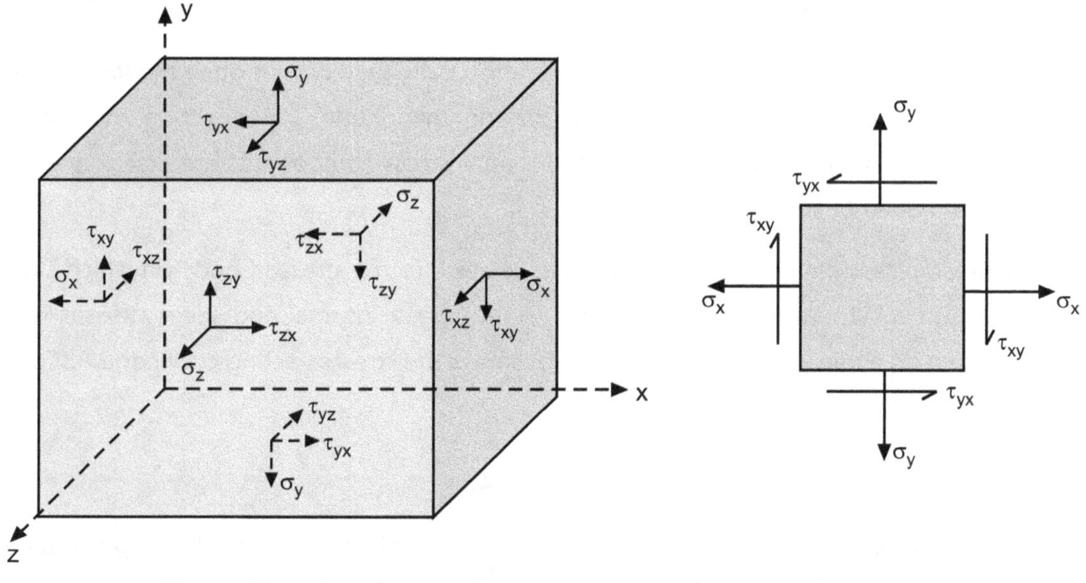

**(a) Three dimensional state of stress**　　　　**(b) State of plane stress**

**Fig. 11.1**

The notation used here defines a normal stress by means of single subscript corresponding to the face on which it acts. A face takes the name of the axis normal to it; for example, the x face is perpendicular to x-axis. A shear stress is indicated by double subscript, the first letter corresponding to the face on which it acts and second indicating its direction. Thus, the shear stress on x face acting in the y-direction is denoted by $\tau_{xy}$. It should be noted that $\tau_{xy} = \tau_{yx}$ since, the shear stresses on perpendicular planes are equal.

In this text, we consider only plane stress i.e. state of stress that can be represented by components that act parallel to a single plane i.e. stress components normal to the plane of body are zero. State of plane stress is shown in Fig. 11.1 (b).

## 11.2 TRANSFORMATION OF PLANE STRESS

The stress acting at a point is represented by the stresses acting on the faces of the element enclosing the point. These stresses will change as a function of the inclination of the planes passing through that point. Thus, the stresses on the faces of the element vary as the angular position of the element changes.

Two algebraic expressions, one for the normal stress and one for the shear stress, can be developed to give these stresses in terms of the initially known stresses and of an angle of inclination of the plane being investigated. These equations are called *equations of stress transformation*. The derivatives of these algebraic equations with respect to the angle of inclination, when equated to zero, locate the planes on which either the normal or the shear stress reaches maximum or minimum values.

Stress components are vectorial in nature but mathematically they do not obey the laws of vector addition and subtraction, since in addition to having magnitude and direction they are also associated with unit of area over which they act. Hence, stress components are first converted to forces and then added or subtracted vectorially.

Consider an elementary area of uniform thickness isolated from a stressed body on which stresses are as shown in Fig. 11.2 (a). Let, it be required to investigate normal and shear stresses on any plane AC making an angle $\theta$ as shown. Fig. 11.2 (b) shows the stresses acting on wedge ABC.

Let ,

$$A \quad = \quad \text{Area of wedge face AC}$$

$\therefore \qquad A \cos\theta, A \sin\theta \quad = \quad$ Areas of vertical face AB and horizontal face BC respectively.

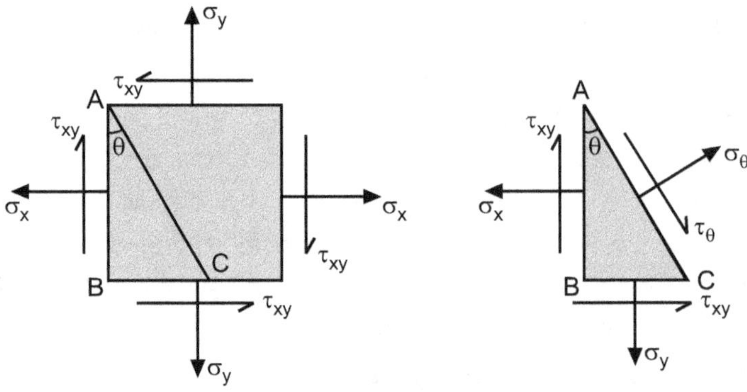


**(a) State of plane stress**              **(b) Stresses on wedge ABC**

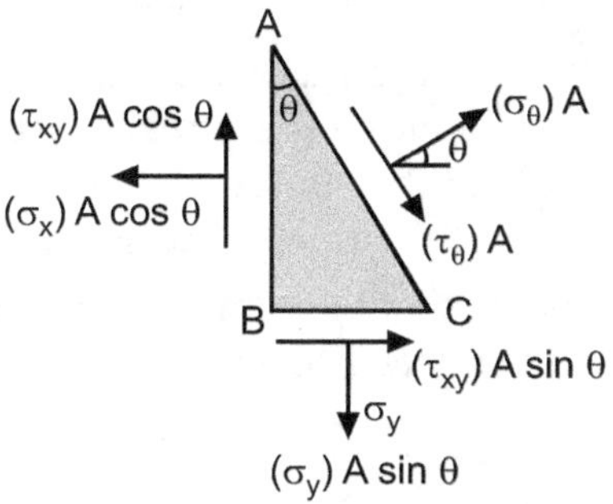


**(c) FBD of wedge ABC**

**Fig. 11.2**

Stresses acting on wedge having converted to forces, FBD of wedge ABC can be drawn as shown in Fig. 11.2 (c).

Using equations of statics ;

Algebraic sum of all the forces acting normal to the face $AC = \sum F_\theta = 0$

$\therefore \qquad (\sigma_\theta)\,A \;=\; (\sigma_x\,A \cos\theta)\cos\theta + (\sigma_y\,A\sin\theta)\sin\theta$

$$- (\tau_{xy} \cdot A\cos\theta)\sin\theta - (\tau_{xy}\,A\sin\theta)\cos\theta$$

$\therefore \qquad \sigma_\theta \;=\; \sigma_x \cdot \cos^2\theta + \sigma_y \cdot \sin^2\theta - 2\,\tau_{xy}\sin\theta\cos\theta \qquad\qquad …\,(11.1)$

Algebraic sum of all the forces acting tangential to the face $AC = \sum F_t = 0$

$\therefore \qquad (\tau_\theta)\,A \;=\; (\sigma_x\,A\cos\theta)\sin\theta - (\sigma_y\,A\sin\theta)\cos\theta$

$$+ (\tau_{xy}\,A\cos\theta)\cos\theta - (\tau_{xy}\,A\sin\theta)\sin\theta$$

$\therefore \qquad \tau_\theta \;=\; (\sigma_x - \sigma_y)\sin\theta\cos\theta + \tau_{xy}(\cos^2\theta - \sin^2\theta) \qquad\qquad …\,(11.2)$

We have, $\qquad \cos^2\theta \;=\; \dfrac{1 + \cos 2\theta}{2}$

$$\sin^2\theta \;=\; \dfrac{1 - \cos 2\theta}{2}$$

$$\sin\theta\cos\theta \;=\; \dfrac{\sin 2\theta}{2}$$

Using these relations for equations (11.1) and (11.2),

$$\sigma_\theta \;=\; \frac{\sigma_x + \sigma_y}{2} + \frac{\sigma_x - \sigma_y}{2}\cos(2\theta) - \tau_{xy}\sin(2\theta) \qquad\qquad …\,(11.3)$$

$$\tau_\theta \;=\; \frac{\sigma_x - \sigma_y}{2}\sin(2\theta) + \tau_{xy}\cos(2\theta) \qquad\qquad …\,(11.4)$$

These equations (11.3) and (11.4) are called as the *equations of stress transformation.*

The angle that the line of action of resultant stress makes with the normal to the plane is called the *obliquity* $(\phi)$.

$$\tan\phi \;=\; \frac{\tau_\theta}{\sigma_\theta} \qquad\qquad …\,(11.5)$$

## 11.3 PRINCIPAL STRESSES

The planes on which maximum or minimum normal stresses occur, there is no shear stress. These planes are called as **principal planes** and the stresses acting on these planes - the maximum and minimum normal stresses – are called as the **principal stresses.**

To locate the planes of maximum and minimum normal stresses, differentiate equation (11.3) with respect to '$\theta$' and equate it to zero i.e.

$$\frac{d}{d\theta}(\sigma_\theta) = -\frac{\sigma_x - \sigma_y}{2} 2 \cdot \sin(2\theta) - 2\,\tau_{xy} \cdot \cos(2\theta) = 0$$

$$\therefore \quad -(\sigma_x - \sigma_y)\sin(2\theta) - 2\,\tau_{xy}\cos(2\theta) = 0$$

$$\therefore \quad -(\sigma_x - \sigma_y)\tan(2\theta) = 2\,\tau_{xy}$$

$$\therefore \qquad \tan(2\theta_n) = -\frac{2\,\tau_{xy}}{\sigma_x - \sigma_y} \qquad \qquad \dots (11.6)$$

where, $\theta_n$ = Orientation of plane of maximum normal stress.

**Note :** These planes can also be located by setting $\tau_\theta$ equal to zero from equation (11.4) which indicates that there is no shear stress on the plane of maximum or minimum normal stress. Equation (11.6) gives two values of $(2\theta_n)$ that differ by 180°, hence *principal planes are 90° apart.*

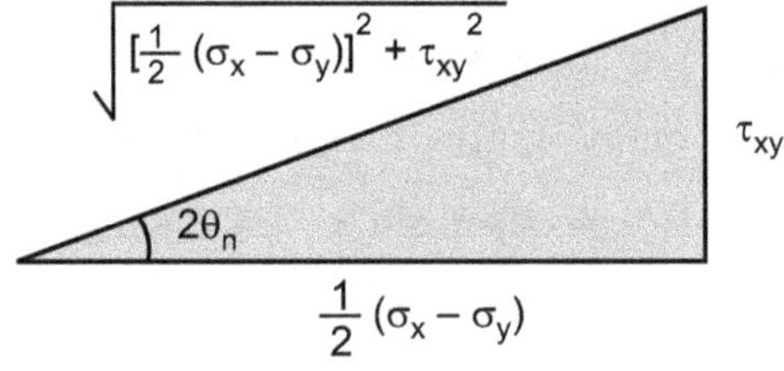

**Fig. 11.3**

From equation (11.6), we can write

$$\left.\begin{array}{l} \sin(2\theta_n) = \dfrac{\tau_{xy}}{\sqrt{\left[\dfrac{1}{2}(\sigma_x - \sigma_y)\right]^2 + \tau_{xy}^2}} \\[4ex] \cos(2\theta_n) = \dfrac{\dfrac{1}{2}(\sigma_x - \sigma_y)}{\sqrt{\left[\dfrac{1}{2}(\sigma_x - \sigma_y)\right]^2 + \tau_{xy}^2}} \end{array}\right\} \qquad \dots (11.7)$$

Substituting these values of sin $(2\theta_n)$ and cos $(2\theta_n)$ from equation (11.7) in equation (11.3), we get principal stresses as,

$$\sigma_1, \sigma_2 = \frac{\sigma_x + \sigma_y}{2} \pm \sqrt{\left(\frac{\sigma_x - \sigma_y}{2}\right)^2 + (\tau_{xy})^2} \qquad \dots (11.8)$$

where;　　　　$\sigma_1 \,;\, \sigma_2$ = Major and minor principal stresses.

**Note :** + ve sign shall be used to get major principal stress while – ve sign shall be used to get minor principal stress.

## 11.4 MAXIMUM SHEAR STRESS

To locate the plane of maximum shear stress, differentiate equation (11.4) with respect to $\theta$ and equate it to zero. i.e.

$$\frac{d}{d\theta}(\tau_\theta) = \left(\frac{\sigma_x - \sigma_y}{2}\right) 2 \cdot \cos(2\theta) - (\tau_{xy}) 2 \sin(2\theta) = 0$$

$$\therefore \quad (\sigma_x - \sigma_y)\cos(2\theta) = 2\,\tau_{xy}\sin(2\theta)$$

$$\therefore \quad \tan(2\theta_s) = \frac{\sigma_x - \sigma_y}{2\,\tau_{xy}} \qquad \qquad \text{... (11.9)}$$

where, $\theta_s$ = orientation of plane of maximum shear stress.

Equation (11.9) is negative reciprocal of equation (11.6). That means values of ($2\theta_n$) defined by equation (11.6) and that of ($2\theta_s$) defined by equation (11.9) differ by $90^\circ$. In other words, *planes of maximum shear stress are inclined at $45^\circ$ to the principal planes.*

From equation (11.8), we can write,

$$\left.\begin{array}{l} \sin(2\theta_s) = \dfrac{\frac{1}{2}(\sigma_x - \sigma_y)}{\sqrt{\left[\frac{1}{2}(\sigma_x - \sigma_y)\right]^2 + \tau_{xy}^2}} \\[2.5em] \cos(2\theta_s) = \dfrac{\tau_{xy}}{\sqrt{\left[\frac{1}{2}(\sigma_x - \sigma_y)\right]^2 + \tau_{xy}^2}} \end{array}\right\} \qquad \text{... (11.10)}$$

Substituting these values of $\sin(2\theta_s)$ and $\cos(2\theta_s)$ from equation (11.10) in equation (11.4), we get

$$\tau_{max}\,;\,\tau_{min} = \pm\sqrt{\left(\frac{\sigma_x - \sigma_y}{2}\right)^2 + (\tau_{xy})^2} \qquad \text{... (11.11)}$$

If $\sigma_x$ and $\sigma_y$ are principal stresses of $\sigma_1$ and $\sigma_2$ then $\tau_{xy}$ is zero and equation (11.11) simplifies to

$$\tau_{max} = \pm\frac{\sigma_1 - \sigma_2}{2} \qquad \text{... (11.12)}$$

Thus the maximum shear stress differs from minimum shear stress only in sign.

On the principal planes, shear stresses are zero but on the planes of maximum shear stress, normal stress is not zero. Substituting equation (11.10) in equation (11.3), the magnitude of normal stress ($\sigma'$) on the plane of maximum shear stress is obtained as ;

$$\sigma' = \frac{\sigma_x + \sigma_y}{2} \qquad \text{... (11.13)}$$

Therefore, normal stress ($\sigma'$) acts simultaneously with the maximum shear stress.

## SOLVED EXAMPLES

**Example 11.1 :** *A circular bar 40 mm diameter carries as axial tensile load of 100 kN. What is the value of shear stress on the plane on which normal stress has value of 50 MPa, tensile ?*

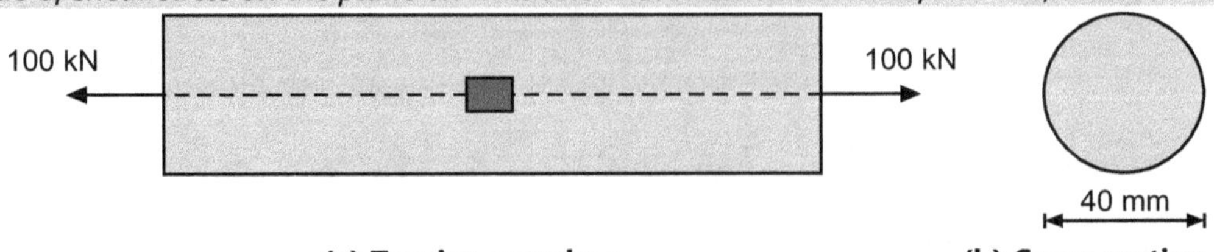


**Fig. 11.4**

**Data**       :   As shown in Fig. 11.4.

**Required**   :   Value of shear stress on the plane on which normal stress is 50 MPa, tensile.

**Concept**    :   Considering an element as shown in Fig. 11.4 find normal stress $\sigma_x$ and then use standard formulae.

**Solution**   :   (i) State of stress :

$$\text{Normal stress} = \sigma_x = \frac{P}{A} = \frac{100 \times 10^3}{\frac{\pi}{4}(40)^2}$$

$$= 79.57 \text{ MPa (Tensile)}$$

State of stress is as shown in Fig. 11.5.

**Fig. 11.5 : State of stress on element**

(ii) Plane on which normal stress is 50 MPa (tensile)

$$\sigma_\theta = \frac{\sigma_x}{2} + \frac{\sigma_x}{2}\cos(2\theta) \qquad (\because \sigma_y = \tau_{xy} = 0)$$

$$50 = \frac{79.57}{2} + \frac{79.57}{2}\cos(2\theta)$$

$$\theta = 37.56^\circ$$

(iii) Shear stress :
$$\tau_\theta = \frac{\sigma_x}{2}\sin(2\theta) \qquad \left(\because \sigma_y = \tau_{xy} = 0\right)$$

$$\tau_{37.56^\circ} = \frac{79.57}{2} \cdot \sin(2 \times 37.56)$$

$$= \mathbf{38.45 \text{ MPa}}$$

**Example 11.2 :** *If an element is subjected to state of stress as shown in Fig. 11.6, find the principal stresses. Also find the stress components on a plane at $30^\circ$ anticlockwise from x face.*

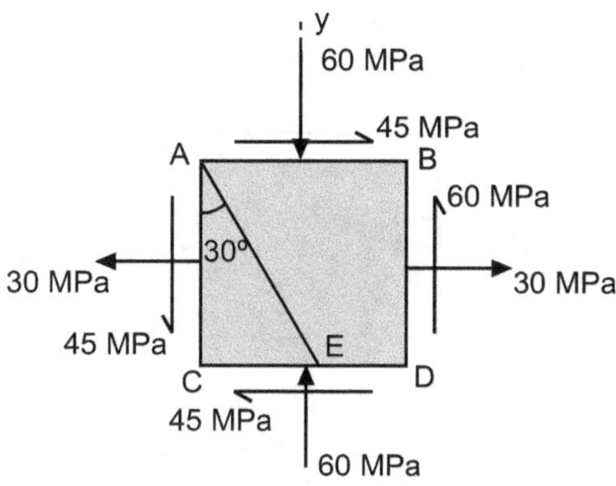


**Fig. 11.6 : Given state of stress**

**Data**        :   As shown in Fig. 11.6.

**Required**   :   Principal stresses, stress components on plane AE.

**Concept**    :   Standard formulae.

**Solution**   :   (i) Principal stresses :

$$\sigma_1, \sigma_2 = \frac{\sigma_x + \sigma_y}{2} \pm \sqrt{\left(\frac{\sigma_x - \sigma_y}{2}\right)^2 + (\tau_{xy})^2}$$

$$= \frac{30 - 60}{2} \pm \sqrt{\frac{30 - (-60)}{2} + 45^2}$$

$$= -15 \pm 63.63$$

$$\sigma_1 = -78.63 \text{ MPa} = \textbf{78.63 MPa (Compressive)}$$

$$\sigma_2 = \textbf{48.63 MPa (Tensile)}$$

(ii) Stress components on plane AE :

$$\sigma_\theta = \frac{\sigma_x + \sigma_y}{2} + \frac{\sigma_x - \sigma_y}{2} \cos(2\theta) - \tau_{xy} \sin(2\theta)$$

$$= \frac{30 - 60}{2} + \frac{30 - (-60)}{2} \cos(2 \times 30) - (-45) \sin(2 \times 30)$$

$$\sigma_{30°} = 46.47 \text{ MPa (Tensile)}$$

$$\tau_\theta = \frac{\sigma_x - \sigma_y}{2} \sin(2\theta) + \tau_{xy} \cos(2\theta)$$

$$= \frac{30 - (-60)}{2} \sin(2 \times 30) + (-45) \cos(2 \times 30)$$

$$\tau_{30°} = \textbf{16.47 MPa}$$

**Example 11.3 :** *The principal tensile stresses at a point on two perpendicular planes are 60 MPa and 30 MPa. Find normal, tangential and resultant stress and its obliquity on a plane at 20°*
*with the major principal plane as shown in Fig. 11.7. Also find the intensity of stress which acting*
*alone can produce the same maximum strain. Assume Poisson's ratio $\mu = 0.3$.*

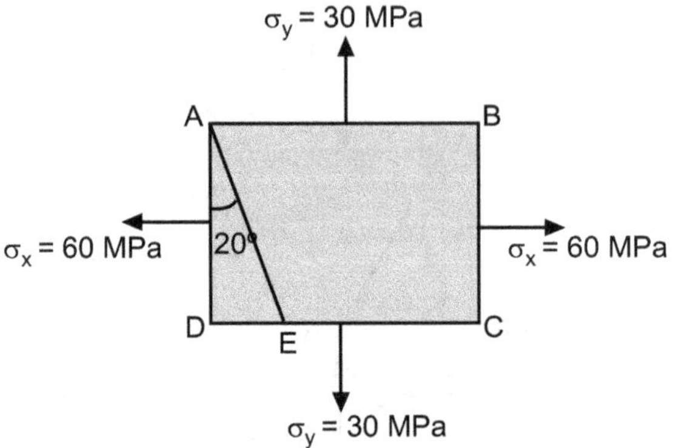


**Fig. 11.7 : Given state of stress**

**Data** : As shown in Fig. 11.7.

**Required** : Normal, tangential, resultant stress and its obliquity on a plane at 20° to major principal plane.

**Concept** : Transformation of stress.

**Solution** : (i) Normal stress on plane AE.

$$\sigma_\theta = \frac{\sigma_x + \sigma_y}{2} + \frac{\sigma_x - \sigma_y}{2}\cos(2\theta) - \tau_{xy}\sin 2\theta$$

$$= \frac{60 + 30}{2} + \frac{60 - 30}{2}\cos(2 \times 20) - 0$$

$$\sigma_{20^\circ} = \textbf{56.49 MPa (Tensile)}$$

(ii) Shear stress on plane AE :

$$\tau_\theta = \frac{\sigma_x - \sigma_y}{2}(\sin 2\theta) + \tau_{xy}\cos(2\theta)$$

$$= \frac{60 - 30}{2}\sin(2 \times 20) + 0$$

$$\tau_{20^\circ} = \textbf{9.64 MPa}$$

(iii) Resultant stress and its obliquity :

$$\text{Resultant stress} = \sqrt{\sigma_\theta^2 + \tau_\theta^2}$$

$$= \sqrt{56.49^2 + 9.64^2}$$

$$= 57.30 \text{ MPa}$$

$$\text{Obliquity} = \phi = \tan^{-1}\left(\frac{\tau_\theta}{\sigma_\theta}\right)$$

$$= \tan^{-1}\left(\frac{9.64}{56.49}\right)$$

$$= \textbf{9.68}°$$

(iv) Stress ($\sigma$) which produces the same principal strain :

$$\text{Principal strain} = \epsilon_1 = \frac{1}{E}(\sigma_1 - \mu\,\sigma_2)$$

$$= \frac{1}{E}(60 - 0.3 \times 30)$$

$$= \frac{51}{E}$$

$$\therefore \quad \frac{\sigma}{E} = \frac{51}{E}$$

$$\therefore \quad \sigma = \textbf{51 MPa}$$

**Example 11.4 :** *At a point in a strained material, the state of stress is as shown in Fig. 11.8. Determine : (i) Principal stresses, (ii) Principal planes, (iii) Maximum shear stress and plane on which it acts (iv) The tensile stress which acting alone will produce same maximum shear stress, (v) The shear stress which acting alone will produce same maximum tensile principal stress.*

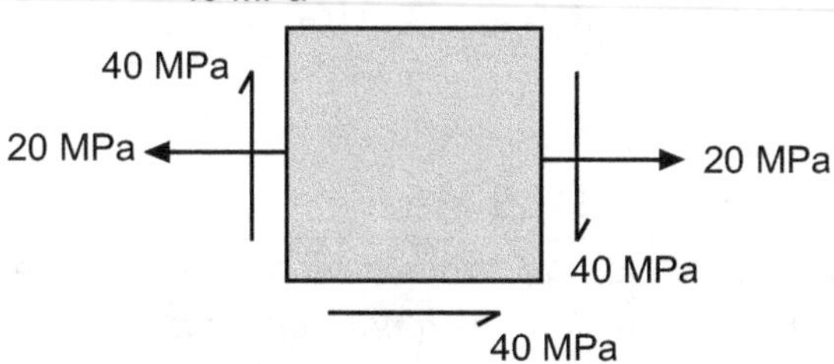


**Fig. 11.8 : Given state of stress**

**Data**         :   As shown in Fig. 11.8.
**Required**   :   As given above in the example.
**Concept**   :   Standard formulae.
**Solution**   :   (i) Principal stresses ($\sigma_1$, $\sigma_2$) :

$$(\sigma_1, \sigma_2) = \frac{\sigma_x}{2} \pm \sqrt{\left(\frac{\sigma_x}{2}\right)^2 + \tau_{xy}^2} \qquad (\because \sigma_y = 0)$$

$$(\sigma_1, \sigma_2) = \frac{20}{2} \pm \sqrt{\left(\frac{20}{2}\right)^2 + 40^2}$$

$$= 10 \pm 41.23$$

$$\sigma_1 = \textbf{51.23 MPa (Tensile)}$$

$$\sigma_2 = -31.23 \text{ MPa} = \textbf{31.23 MPa (Compressive)}$$

(ii) Principal planes :

$$\tan(2\theta) = -\frac{2\,\tau_{xy}}{\sigma_x} \qquad \left(\because \sigma_y = 0\right)$$

$$\tan(2\theta) = -\frac{2 \times 40}{20} = -4$$

$$\theta = -\textbf{37.98°} \text{ and } -\textbf{127.98°}$$

(iii) Maximum shear stress ($\tau_{max}$) :

$$\tau_{max} = \frac{\sigma_1 - \sigma_2}{2} = \frac{51.23 - (-31.23)}{2} = \textbf{41.23 MPa}$$

(iv) Planes of maximum shear :

$$\tan(2\theta) = \frac{\sigma_x}{2\,\tau_{xy}} \qquad (\because \sigma_y = 0)$$

$$= \frac{20}{2 \times 40} = 0.25$$

$$\therefore \qquad \theta = 7° \text{ and } 97°$$

(v) The tensile stress which acting alone will produce same maximum shear stress :

$$\tau_{max} = \frac{\sigma_1 - \sigma_2}{2} = \frac{\sigma_1}{2} \qquad (\because \sigma_2 = 0)$$

$$41.23 = \frac{\sigma_1}{2} \qquad \therefore \quad \sigma_1 = \textbf{82.46 MPa (Tensile)}$$

(vi) The shear stress which acting alone will produce same maximum principal tensile  stress :

$$\sigma_1 = \frac{\sigma_x + \sigma_y}{2} \pm \sqrt{\left(\frac{\sigma_x - \sigma_y}{2}\right)^2 + \tau_{xy}^2}$$

$$51.23 = 0 + \tau_{xy}$$

$$\therefore \qquad \tau_{xy} = \textbf{51.23 MPa}$$

**Example 11.5 :** *At a point in a piece of strained material, there are two planes at right angles on which the shear stress intensity is 'τ' along with normal stress intensity of 40 MPa, tensile, on one plane and 24 MPa, compressive, on the other. If the major principal stress is 56 MPa, tensile, evaluate the smaller principal stress and shear stress τ. Also evaluate maximum shear stress τ$_{max}$ and normal stress on plane of maximum shear.*

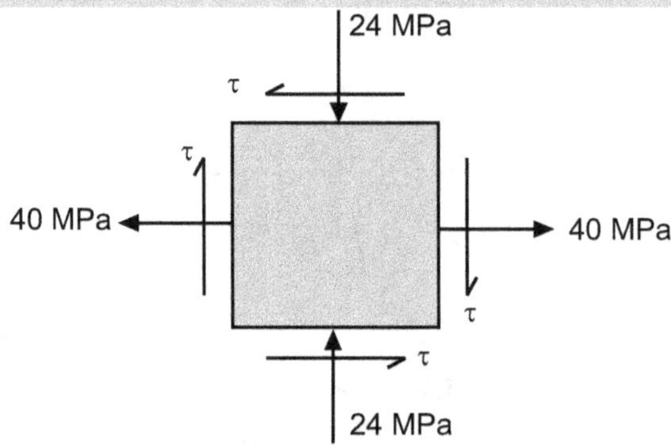


**Fig. 11.9 : Given state of stress**

| | | |
|---|---|---|
| **Data** | : | As shown in Fig. 11.9 ; $\sigma_1$ = 56 MPa, tensile |
| **Required** | : | Shear stress ($\tau$) ; minor principal stress ($\sigma_2$) ; $\tau_{max}$ and normal stress ($\sigma$) |
| | | on the plane of maximum shear. |
| **Concept** | : | Standard formulae. |
| **Solution** | : | (i) Shear stress ($\tau$) : |

$$\sigma_1 = \frac{\sigma_x + \sigma_y}{2} + \sqrt{\left(\frac{\sigma_x - \sigma_y}{2}\right)^2 + \tau_{xy}^2}$$

$$56 = \frac{40 + (-24)}{2} + \sqrt{\left(\frac{40 - (-24)}{2}\right)^2 + \tau_{xy}^2}$$

$$\therefore \qquad \tau_{xy} = \mathbf{35.78\ MPa}$$

(ii) Minor principal stress ($\sigma_2$) :

$$\sigma_2 = \frac{\sigma_x + \sigma_y}{2} - \sqrt{\left(\frac{\sigma_x - \sigma_y}{2}\right)^2 + \tau_{xy}{}^2}$$

$$= \frac{40 + (-24)}{2} - \sqrt{\left(\frac{40 - (-24)}{2}\right)^2 + 35.78^2}$$

$$= -40\ \text{MPa}$$

$$= \mathbf{40\ MPa\ (Compressive)}$$

(iii) Maximum shear stress ($\tau_{max}$) :

$$\tau_{max} = \frac{\sigma_1 - \sigma_2}{2} = \frac{56 - (-40)}{2} = \mathbf{48\ MPa}$$

(iv) Normal stress ($\sigma$) on the plane of maximum shear :

$$\sigma = \frac{\sigma_x + \sigma_y}{2} = \frac{40 - 24}{2} = \mathbf{8\ MPa\ (tensile)}$$

**Example 11.6 :** *At a point in a strained material subjected to two dimensional state of stress, one of the principal stress is 78 MPa, tensile on a plane at 60° to this principal plane, the normal stress is zero. Determine : (i) The other principal stress, (ii) The shear stress on the plane of zero normal stress, and (iii) The planes on which the normal and shear stresses are equal in magnitude.*

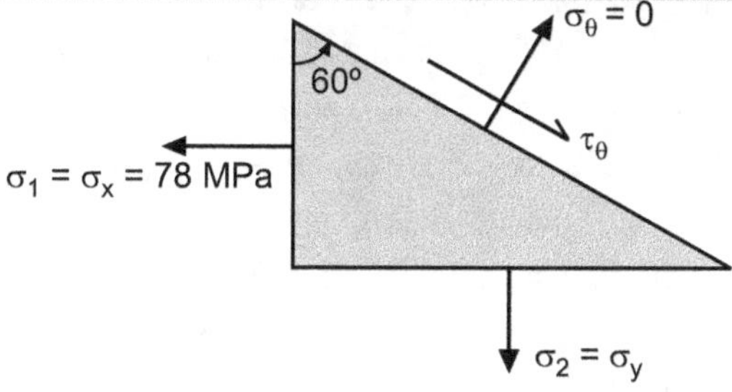


**Fig. 11.10 : Given state of stress**

**Data**   :   As shown in Fig. 11.10.

**Required**   :   (i)     Other principal stress ($\sigma_2$)

               (ii)     Shear stress ($\tau_\theta$)

               (ii)     Plane on which $\sigma_\theta = \tau_\theta$.

**Concept**   :   Standard formulae.

**Solution**   :   (i)     Principal stress $\sigma_2$ :

Let, other principal stress $\sigma_2$ be tensile in nature. See Fig. 11.10.

We have,

$$\sigma_\theta = 0 = \frac{\sigma_x + \sigma_y}{2} + \frac{\sigma_x - \sigma_y}{2}\cos(2\theta) \qquad (\because \tau_{xy} = 0)$$

$$\therefore \qquad 0 = \frac{78 + \sigma_2}{2} + \frac{78 - \sigma_2}{2}\cdot\cos(2 \times 60)$$

$$0 = 39 + 0.5\,\sigma_2 + 0.25\,\sigma_2 - 19.5$$

$\therefore$ $\qquad\qquad\qquad\sigma_2 = -26$ MPa = **26 MPa  (Compressive)**

(ii) Shear stress ($\tau_\theta$) :

$$\tau_\theta = \frac{\sigma_x - \sigma_y}{2} \cdot \sin(2\theta) = \frac{78 - (-26)}{2} \sin(2 \times 60)$$

$\therefore$ $\qquad\qquad\qquad\tau_{60} = $ **45 MPa**

(iii) The inclination of plane for which normal and shear stresses are equal in magnitude :
Equating $\sigma_\theta$ and $\tau_\theta$ from equations (11.1) and (11.2),

$$\sigma_x \cdot \cos^2\theta + \sigma_y \cdot \sin^2\theta = (\sigma_x - \sigma_y)\sin\theta\cos\theta$$

$$78 \cdot \cos^2\theta - 26\sin^2\theta = (78 - (-26)) \cdot \sin\theta \cdot \cos\theta$$

$$78\cos^2\theta - 26\sin^2\theta = 104 \cdot \sin\theta\cos\theta$$

$$\frac{78}{\tan\theta} - 26\tan\theta = 104$$

$$78 - 26\tan^2\theta = 104\tan\theta$$

$$\tan^2\theta + 4\tan\theta - 3 = 0$$

Solving ;

$$\tan\theta = 0.646 \text{ or } -4.646$$

$\therefore$ $\qquad\qquad\qquad\theta = $ **32.87° or − 77.87°**

---

**Example 11.7 :** *At a point in a stressed elastic plate, following information is known :*

*(i)    Maximum shearing strain = $\phi_{max}$ = 5 × 10⁻⁴.*

*(ii)    The sum of the normal stresses on two perpendicular planes passing through the point = 27.5 MPa.*

*(iii)    Modulus of elasticity E = 200 GPa and Poisson's ratio $\mu$ = 0.25. Compute the magnitude of principal stresses at the point.*

**Data**        :    $\phi_{max} = 5 \times 10^{-4}$ ; E = 200 GPa , $\mu$ = 0.25 ; $\sigma_1 + \sigma_2 = 27.5$ MPa.

**Required**   :    Principal stresses $\sigma_1$ and $\sigma_2$.

**Concept**    :    (i)    Knowing maximum shear strain, find $\tau_{max}$.

$\qquad\qquad$ (ii)    $\tau_{max} = \dfrac{\sigma_1 - \sigma_2}{2}$ and $\sigma_1 + \sigma_2 = 27.5$ ; Solving these two equations,

$\qquad\qquad\qquad$ principal stresses can be obtained.

**Solution**   :    (i)    Maximum shear stress ($\tau_{max}$) :

$$E = 2G(1 + \mu)$$

$$200 = 2G(1 + 0.25)$$

$\therefore$ $\qquad\qquad\qquad G = 80 \text{ GPa}$

$$\tau_{max} = \phi_{max} \cdot G = 5 \times 10^{-4} \times 80 \times 10^3 = 40 \text{ MPa}$$

(ii) Principal stresses ($\sigma_1, \sigma_2$) :

$$\sigma_1 - \sigma_2 = 2 \times 40 \qquad\qquad\qquad\qquad \text{... (i)}$$

$$\sigma_1 + \sigma_2 = 27.5 \qquad\qquad\qquad\qquad \text{... (ii)}$$

Solving equations (i) and (ii),

$$\sigma_1 = \textbf{53.75 MPa (Tensile)}$$

$$\sigma_2 = -26.25 \text{ MPa} = \textbf{26.25 MPa (Compressive)}$$

**Example 11.8 :** *At certain element; plane AB carries direct tensile stress of 30 MPa and shear stress of 20 MPa while other plane BC carries direct tensile stress of 20 MPa and a shear stress as shown in Fig. 11.11 (a). If the planes AB and BC are inclined at 30º and plane AC at right angles to plane AB which carries direct stress of unknown magnitude and nature, find (i) Shear stress on BC, (ii) Magnitude and nature of direct stress on AC, (iii) Principal stresses.*

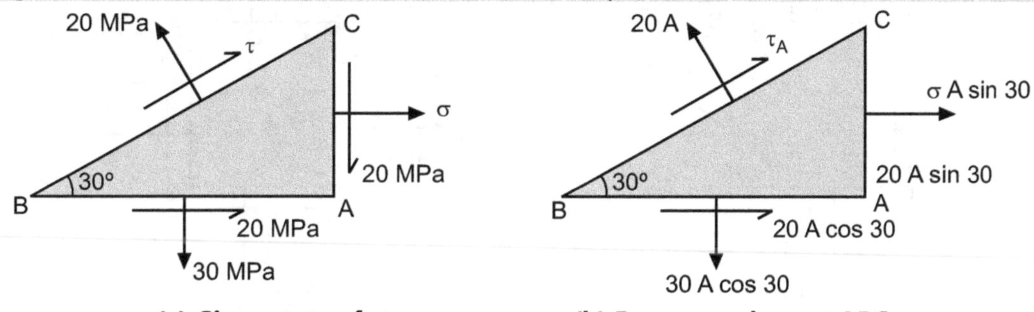

**(a) Given state of stress**          **(b) Forces on element ABC**

**Fig. 11.11**

**Data**        :   As shown in Fig. 11.11 (a).

**Required**    :   (i) Shear stress ($\tau$) on BC, (ii) Magnitude and nature of direct stress ($\sigma$) on AC, (iii) Principal stresses.

**Concept**     :   Equilibrium and standard formulae.

**Solution**    :   (i) Equilibrium : Let, A be the area along plane BC.

$\therefore$   Area of plane AC = A sin 30 and area of plane AB = A cos 30. Forces on element ABC are as shown in Fig. 11.11 (b).

$\Sigma \, F_x = 0$ ;

$$\sigma \text{ A sin } 30 + 20 \text{ A cos } 30 + \tau \text{ A cos } 30 - 20 \text{ A sin } 30 = 0$$

$$0.5 \, \sigma + 0.86 \, \tau + 7.32 = 0 \qquad \qquad \text{... (i)}$$

$\Sigma \, F_y = 0$ ;

$$- 20 \text{ A sin } 30 - 30 \text{ A cos } 30 + \tau \text{ A sin } 30 + 20 \text{ A cos } 30 = 0 \qquad \text{... (ii)}$$

$\therefore$        $\tau = 37.32$ MPa  put in equation (i)

$\sigma = -79.28$ MPa = **79.28 MPa (Compressive)**

(ii) Principal stresses ($\sigma_1$, $\sigma_2$) :

$$\sigma_1, \sigma_2 \;=\; \frac{\sigma_x + \sigma_y}{2} \pm \sqrt{\left(\frac{\sigma_x - \sigma_y}{2}\right)^2 + \tau_{xy}{}^2}$$

$$=\; \frac{-79.28 + 30}{2} \pm \sqrt{\left(\frac{-79.28 - 30}{2}\right)^2 + 20^2}$$

$$=\; -24.64 \pm 58.18$$

$$\sigma_1 \;=\; -82.82 \text{ MPa} = \textbf{82.82 MPa (Compressive)}$$

$$\sigma_2 \;=\; \textbf{33.54 MPa (Tensile)}$$

**Example 11.9 :** *At a point in a strained material, the state of stress is as shown in Fig. 11.12 (a). Locate the principal planes and evaluate the principal stresses.*

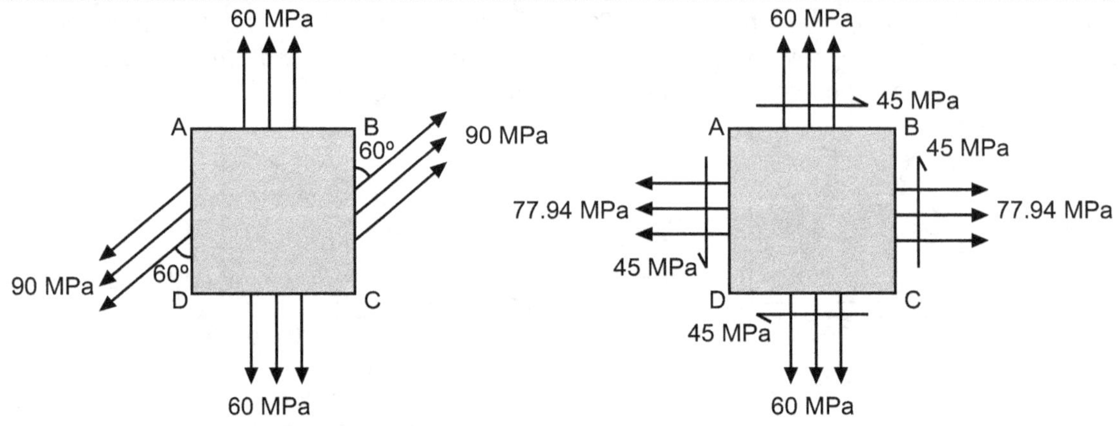


**(a) Given state of stress**          **(b) Equivalent state of stress**

**Fig. 11.12**

**Data**        :   As shown in Fig. 11.12 (a).

**Required**    :   Principal planes and principal stresses.

**Concept**     :   Standard formulae.

**Solution**    :   (i) Equivalent state of stress :

Stress normal to faces BC and AD = $90 \times \sin 60 = 77.94$ MPa

   and shear stress = $90 \cos 60 = 45$ MPa

Equivalent state of stress is as shown in Fig. 11.12 (b).

(ii) Principal stresses ($\sigma_1$, $\sigma_2$) :

$$\sigma_1, \sigma_2 = \frac{\sigma_x + \sigma_y}{2} \pm \sqrt{\left(\frac{\sigma_x - \sigma_y}{2}\right)^2 + \tau_{xy}^2}$$

$$\sigma_1, \sigma_2 = \frac{77.94 + 60}{2} \pm \sqrt{\left(\frac{77.94 - 60}{2}\right)^2 + 45^2}$$

$$= 68.97 \pm 45.88$$

$$\sigma_1 = \textbf{114.85 MPa (Tensile)}$$

$$\sigma_2 = \textbf{23.09 MPa (Tensile)}$$

(iii) Principal planes :

$$\tan (2\theta) = -\frac{2\,\tau_{xy}}{\sigma_x - \sigma_y}$$

$$= \frac{2 \times 45}{77.94 - 60} \qquad \left(\because \tau_{xy} \text{ is} - \text{ve}\right)$$

$$= 5.016$$

$$\therefore \quad \theta_1 = \textbf{39.36°}, \ \theta_2 = \theta_1 + 90° = \textbf{129.36°}$$

**Example 11.10 :** *At a point in a strained material under two-dimensional stress condition, the normal stress on a certain plane is 80 MPa compressive and the shear stress is 56 MPa. On a plane at right angles to this plane, there is no normal stress. If the maximum permissible stresses for the material are 150 MPa in compression, 130 MPa in tension and 65 MPa in shear; examine the safety of section giving reasons.*

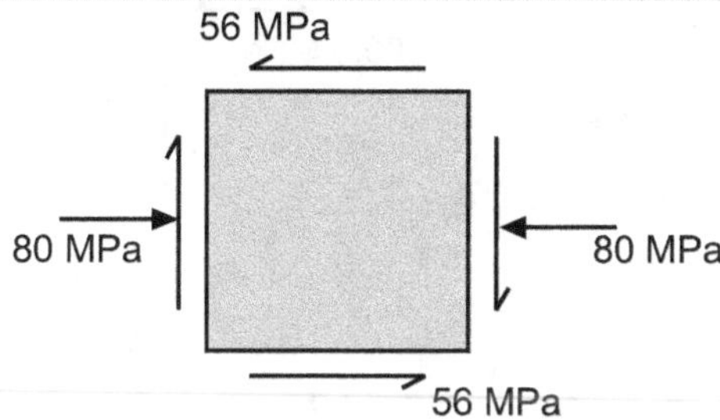


**Fig. 11.13 : Given state of stress**

**Data**       :   State of stress as shown in Fig. 11.13.

              Allowable stresses : In compression : 150 MPa, In tension : 130 MPa

              In shear : 65 MPa.

**Required**  :   To check safety of the section.

**Concept**   :   If actual stresses induced are less than respective allowable stresses, section is safe.

**Solution**  :   (i) Principal stresses ($\sigma_1$, $\sigma_2$) :

$$\sigma_1, \sigma_2 = \frac{\sigma_x}{2} \pm \sqrt{\left(\frac{\sigma_x}{2}\right)^2 + \tau_{xy}^2} \qquad (\because \sigma_y = 0)$$

$$\sigma_1, \sigma_2 = \frac{-80}{2} \pm \sqrt{\left(\frac{-80}{2}\right)^2 + 56^2}$$

$$= -40 \pm 68.82 \text{ MPa}$$

$$\sigma_1 = -108.82 \text{ MPa}$$

$$= \textbf{108.82 MPa (Compressive) < 150 MPa} \qquad \text{... (Safe)}$$

$$\sigma_2 = \textbf{28.82 MPa (Tensile) < 130 MPa} \qquad \text{... (Safe)}$$

(ii) Maximum shear stress ($\tau_{max}$) :

$$\tau_{max} = \frac{\sigma_1 - \sigma_2}{2} = \pm \textbf{68.82 MPa > 65 MPa} \qquad \text{... (Unsafe)}$$

∴   The section is unsafe in shear.

**Example 11.11 :** *At a point in a strained material, the resultant stress on vertical plane is 100 MPa, tensile, making 30° angle with normal. On horizontal plane through the point, the resultant compressive stress makes an angle of 60° with the normal as shown in Fig. 11.14 (a). Determine : (i) The principal stresses and principal planes, (ii) Maximum shear stress, (iii) On properly oriented element, show principal stresses.*

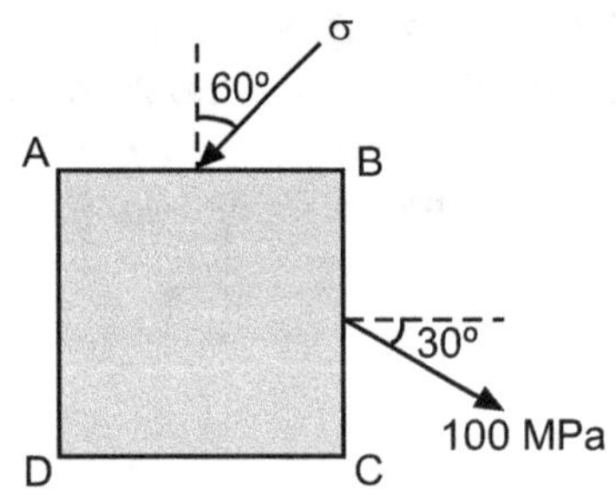


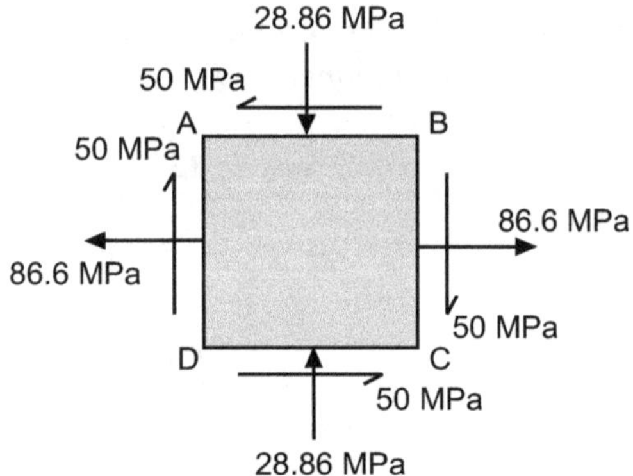


**(a) Given state of stress**                    **(b) Equivalent state of stress**

**Fig. 11.14**

**Data**        :  As shown in Fig. 11.14 (a).

**Required**    :  Principal planes and principal stresses, Maximum shear stress.

**Concept**     :  Standard formulae.

**Solution**    :  (i) Equivalent state of stress :

Normal stress on faces BC and AD = 100 cos 30 = 86.6 MPa (Tensile)

Shear stress = 100 sin 30 = 50 MPa (on all faces)

Compressive stress σ on face AB = $\dfrac{50}{\sin 60}$ = 57.73 MPa.

Normal stress on faces AB and CD = 57.73 cos 60 = 28.86 MPa (Compressive)

Equivalent state of stress is as shown in Fig. 11.14 (b).

(ii) Principal stresses ($\sigma_1$, $\sigma_2$) :

$$\sigma_1, \sigma_2 = \frac{\sigma_x + \sigma_y}{2} \pm \sqrt{\left(\frac{\sigma_x - \sigma_y}{2}\right)^2 + \tau_{xy}^2}$$

$$= \frac{86.6 - 28.86}{2} \pm \sqrt{\left(\frac{86.6 - (-28.86)}{2}\right)^2 + 50^2}$$

$$= 28.87 \pm 76.37$$

$$\sigma_1 = \textbf{105.24 MPa (Tensile)}$$

$$\sigma_2 = -47.50 \text{ MPa} = \textbf{47.5 MPa (Compressive)}$$

(iii) Principal planes :

$$\tan(2\theta) = -\frac{2\,\tau_{xy}}{\sigma_x - \sigma_y}$$

$$= -\frac{2 \times 50}{86.6 - (-28.86)}$$

$$= -0.866$$

$$\theta = \textbf{-20.44°} \text{ and } \textbf{-110.44°}$$

(iv) Maximum shear stress ($\tau_{max}$) :

$$\tau_{max} = \frac{\sigma_1 - \sigma_2}{2} = \frac{105.24 - (-47.5)}{2} = 76.37 \text{ MPa}$$

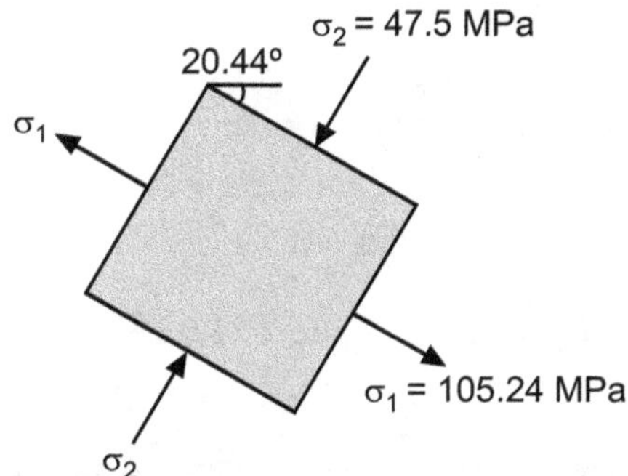


**Fig. 11.14 (c) : Principal stresses on oriented element**

**Example 11.12 :** *A circle 40 mm in diameter is marked on a steel plate before it is stressed as shown in Fig. 11.15. As a result of these stresses, the circle deforms to an ellipse. Calculate the lengths of the major and minor axes of the ellipse and their directions. Assume E = 200 GPa and μ = 0.25.*

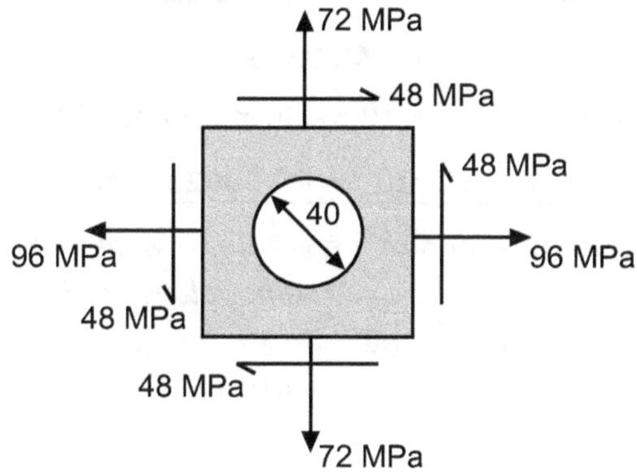


**Fig. 11.15 : State of stress on a plate**

**Data**       :   State of stress as shown in Fig. 11.15.

**Required**   :   Lengths and directions of major and minor axes of the ellipse.

**Concept**    :   Principal stresses and principal strains.

**Solution**   :   (i) Principal stresses ($\sigma_1$, $\sigma_2$) :

$$\sigma_1, \sigma_2 = \frac{\sigma_x + \sigma_y}{2} \pm \sqrt{\left(\frac{\sigma_x - \sigma_y}{2}\right)^2 + \tau_{xy}^2}$$

$$= \frac{96 + 72}{2} \pm \sqrt{\left(\frac{96 - 72}{2}\right)^2 + 48^2}$$

$$= 84 \pm 49.47$$

$$\sigma_1 = \textbf{133.47 MPa (Tensile)}$$

$$\sigma_2 = \textbf{34.53 MPa (Tensile)}$$

**(ii) Principal planes :**

$$\tan(2\theta) \;=\; \frac{2\,\tau_{xy}}{\sigma_x - \sigma_y} \qquad (\because \tau_{xy} \text{ is } - \text{ve})$$

$$= \frac{2 \times 48}{96 - 72} = 4$$

$$\theta \;=\; \mathbf{37.98^o} \text{ and } \mathbf{127.98^o}$$

**(iii) Principal strains ($\epsilon_1$, $\epsilon_2$) :**

$$\epsilon_1 = \frac{1}{E}\,(\sigma_1 - \mu\,\sigma_2) \;=\; \frac{1}{200 \times 10^3}\,(133.47 - 0.25 \times 34.53)$$

$$= \mathbf{6.24 \times 10^{-4}}$$

$$\epsilon_2 = \frac{1}{E}\,(\sigma_2 - \mu\,\sigma_1) \;=\; \frac{1}{200 \times 10^3}\,(34.53 - 0.25 \times 133.47)$$

$$= \mathbf{5.81 \times 10^{-6}}$$

Increase in diameter $= \delta d_1 = 6.24 \times 10^{-4} \times 40 = \mathbf{0.0249\ mm}$

$\therefore$  Length of major axis $= 40 + 0.0249 = \mathbf{40.0249\ mm}$

Increase in diameter $= \delta d_2 = 5.81 \times 10^{-6} \times 40 = \mathbf{2.32 \times 10^{-4}\ mm}$

Length of minor axis $= 40 + 2.32 \times 10^{-4} = \mathbf{40.000232\ mm}$

---

**Example 11.13 :** *A small block is 60 mm long, 40 mm wide and 5 mm thick. It is subjected to uniformly distributed tensile forces having the resultant values as shown in Fig. 11.16. Compute the stress components developed along the diagonal AB.*

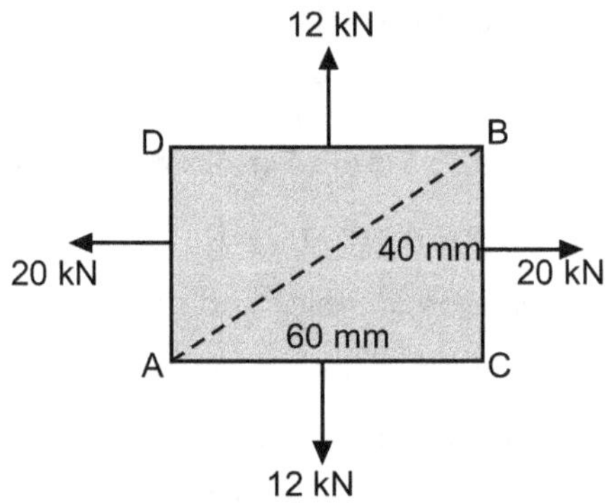


**Fig. 11.16 : State of stress on a block**

**Data**       :  As shown in Fig. 11.16.

**Required**  :  Stress components on diagonal AB.

**Concept**   :  FBD and equations of statics.

**Solution**  :  (i) FBD of wedge ABC :

Let $F_n$ and $F_t$ be the forces normal and tangential to diagonal AB for equilibrium as shown in Fig. 11.17.

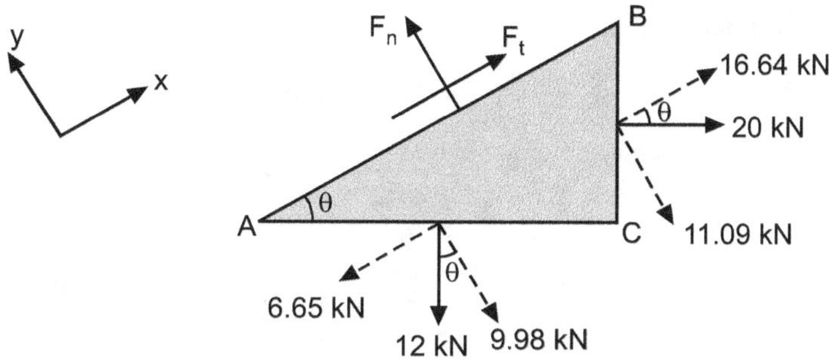



**Fig. 11.17 : Forces on wedge ABC**

$$\theta = \tan^{-1}\left(\frac{40}{60}\right) = 33.7^\circ$$

Resolving forces normal and tangential to plane AB, the components are obtained as shown in Fig. 11.17.

$\sum F_x = 0;$

$$F_t + 16.64 - 6.65 = 0$$

$\therefore$　　　　$F_t = 10 \text{ kN } (\nearrow)$

$\sum F_y = 0;$　　　$F_n - 11.09 - 9.98 = 0$

$\therefore$　　　　$F_n = 21.07 \text{ kN } (\nwarrow)$

(ii) Stress components :

$$l\,(AB) = \sqrt{60^2 + 40^2} = 72.11 \text{ mm}$$

$\therefore$　　Area of plane AB = A　$= l\,(AB) \times \text{thickness}$

$$= 72.11 \times 5$$

$$A = 360.55 \text{ mm}^2$$

$\therefore$　　Normal stress $= \sigma_n = \dfrac{F_n}{A} = \dfrac{21.07 \times 10^3}{360.55}$

$$= \mathbf{58.43 \text{ MPa (Tensile)}}$$

Shear stress $= \tau = \dfrac{F_t}{A} = \dfrac{10 \times 10^3}{360.55}$

$$= \mathbf{27.73 \text{ MPa}}$$

---

**Example 11.14 :** *The principal strains at a point in a two-dimensional stress system were observed to be 0.00035 extension and 0.00025 contraction. Determine the principal stresses. Also find the maximum shear stress.*　　　　**(Dec. 1998)**

$$E = 200 \text{ GPa}, \quad \mu = \frac{1}{m} = 0.3$$

**Data :** $\epsilon_1 = 0.00035$, $\epsilon_2 = -0.00025$, $E = 200$ GPa, $\mu = \dfrac{1}{m} = 0.3$

**Required :** $\sigma_1$, $\sigma_2$, $\tau_{max}$ and plane on which maximum shear stress acts.

**Concept :** Generalised Hooke's law.

---

**Solution :** (i) Principal stresses :

$$\epsilon_1 = \frac{1}{E}(\sigma_1 - \mu\,\sigma_2)$$

$$0.00035 = \frac{1}{200 \times 10^3}(\sigma_1 - 0.3\,\sigma_2)$$

$$\sigma_1 - 0.3\sigma_2 = 70 \qquad \qquad \dots \text{(i)}$$

$$\epsilon_2 = \frac{1}{E}(\sigma_2 - \mu\,\sigma_1)$$

$$-0.00025 = \frac{1}{200 \times 10^3}(\sigma_2 - 0.3\,\sigma_1)$$

$$\sigma_2 - 0.3\,\sigma_1 = -50 \qquad \qquad \dots\text{(ii)}$$

Solving equations (i) and (ii),

$$\sigma_1 = \textbf{60.44 MPa (Tensile)}$$

$$\sigma_2 = -31.87 \text{ MPa} = \textbf{31.87 MPa (Compressive)}$$

(ii)    Maximum shear stress :

$$\tau_{max} = \frac{\sigma_1 - \sigma_2}{2}$$

$$= \frac{60.44 - (-31.87)}{2}$$

$$\tau_{max} = \textbf{46.155 MPa (Tensile)}$$

**Example 11.15 :** *At a point in a strained material, direct stresses of 102 MPa (tensile) and 76.5 MPa (compressive) exist on two perpendicular planes. These planes also carry shear stresses. The major principal stress is 127.5 MPa. Find shear stresses on these planes. Also find the maximum shear stress.* **(Dec. 1999)**

**Data :** $\sigma_x = 102$ MPa, $\sigma_y = -76.5$ MPa, $\sigma_1 = 127.5$ MPa.

**Required :** $\tau_{xy}$, $\tau_{max}$.

**Concept :** Standard formulae.

**Solution :** (i) $\tau_{xy}$ :

$$\sigma_1 = \frac{\sigma_x + \sigma_y}{2} + \sqrt{\left(\frac{\sigma_x - \sigma_y}{2}\right)^2 + \tau_{xy}^2}$$

$$127.5 = \frac{102 - 76.5}{2} + \sqrt{\left(\frac{102 + 76.5}{2}\right)^2 + \tau_{xy}^2}$$

$$= 12.75 + \sqrt{7965.56 + \tau_{xy}^2}$$

$$13167.56 = 7965.56 + \tau_{xy}^2$$

$$\therefore \qquad \tau_{xy} = \textbf{72.12 MPa}$$

(ii)

$$\sigma_2 = \frac{\sigma_x + \sigma_y}{2} - \sqrt{\left(\frac{\sigma_x - \sigma_y}{2}\right)^2 + \tau_{xy}^2} = 12.75 - 114.74$$

$$\sigma_2 = -\textbf{101.99 MPa} = \textbf{101.99 MPa (Compressive)}$$

(iii) Maximum shear stress :

$$\tau_{max} = \frac{\sigma_1 - \sigma_2}{2} = \frac{127.5 - (-101.99)}{2}$$

$$\tau_{max} = \textbf{114.745 MPa (Tensile)}$$

**Example 11.16 :** *A piece of material is subjected to a tensile stress of 80 MPa in one direction, a compressive stress of 60 MPa in a direction at right angle to the tensile stress, and a shearing stress of 50 MPa. Find the normal, tangential and resultant component of the stress on the plane, the normal of which makes an angle of 30° with the tensile stress.*　　　　　　**(Dec. 2000)**

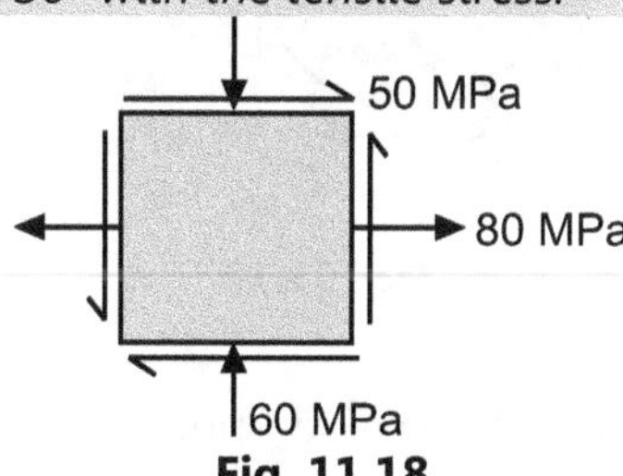


**Fig. 11.18**

**Data :** As shown in Fig. 11.18, $\theta = 60°$.

**Required :** Normal, tangential and resultant component of the stress.

**Concept :** Standard formulae.

**Solution :** (i) Normal stress :

$$\sigma_\theta = \frac{\sigma_x + \sigma_y}{2} + \frac{\sigma_x - \sigma_y}{2} \cos 2\theta - \tau_{xy} \sin 2\theta$$

$$= \frac{80 - 60}{2} + \frac{80 - (-60)}{2} \cos 120 - 50 \sin 120$$

$$= 10 - 35 - 43.30$$

$\therefore$　　　　　$\sigma_\theta = \textbf{− 68.3 MPa = 68.3 MPa (Compressive)}$

(ii)　Shear stress :

$$\tau_\theta = \frac{\sigma_x - \sigma_y}{2} \sin 2\theta + \tau_{xy} \cos 2\theta$$

$$= \frac{80 - (-60)}{2} \sin 120 + 50 \cos 120$$

$$= 60.62 - 25 = 35.62$$

$$\tau_\theta = \textbf{35.62 (Tensile)}$$

(iii) Resultant stress and its obliquity :

$$\text{Resultant stress} = \sqrt{\sigma_\theta^2 + \tau_\theta^2}$$

$$= \sqrt{(-68.3)^2 + (35.62)^2}$$

$$= \textbf{77.03 MPa}$$

$$\text{Obliquity} = \phi = \tan^{-1}\left(\frac{\tau_\theta}{\sigma_\theta}\right)$$

$$= \tan^{-1}\left(\frac{35.62}{-68.3}\right) = \textbf{− 27.54°}$$

**Example 11.17 :** *A steel bolt 30 mm diameter is subjected to direct tension of 20 kN and shearing force of 15 kN. Determine the intensities of normal and shear stresses across a plane at an angle of 70° to the axis of bolt. Also calculate the principal stresses.*                    **(May 2002)**

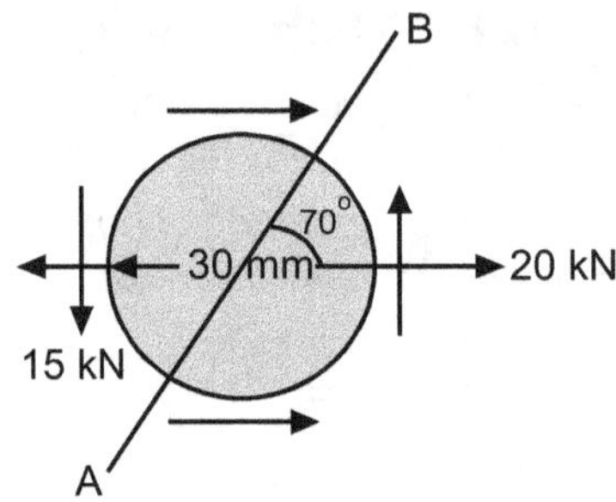


**Fig. 11.19**

**Data :** As shown in Fig. 11.19,   $\theta = 20°$.

**Required :** Stress component on plane AB and principal stresses.

**Concept :** Standard formulae.

**Solution :** (i) State of stress :

$$\text{Normal stress} \;=\; \frac{P}{A} = \frac{20 \times 10^3}{\frac{\pi}{4} \times 30^2} \;=\; 28.29 \text{ MPa}$$

$$\text{Shear stress} \;=\; \frac{S}{A} = \frac{15 \times 10^3}{\frac{\pi}{4} \times 30^2} = 21.22 \text{ MPa}$$

(ii)    Principal stresses :

$$\sigma_1, \sigma_2 \;=\; \frac{\sigma_x}{2} \pm \sqrt{\left(\frac{\sigma_x}{2}\right)^2 + \tau_{xy}^2}$$

$$=\; \frac{28.29}{2} \pm \sqrt{\left(\frac{28.29}{2}\right)^2 + 21.22^2} \;=\; 14.145 \pm 25.50$$

$$\sigma_1 \;=\; \mathbf{39.645 \text{ MPa (Tensile)}}$$

$$\sigma_2 \;=\; \mathbf{-11.355 \text{ MPa} = 11.355 \text{ (Compressive)}}$$

(iii)   Stress component on plane AE :

$$\sigma_\theta \;=\; \frac{\sigma_x}{2} + \frac{\sigma_x}{2} \cos 2\theta - \tau_{xy} \sin 2\theta$$

$$=\; \frac{28.29}{2} + \frac{28.29}{2} \cos 40 - 21.22 \sin 40$$

$$\sigma_\theta \;=\; \mathbf{11.34 \text{ MPa (Tensile)}}$$

$$\tau_\theta \;=\; \frac{\sigma_x}{2} \sin 2\theta + \tau_{xy} \cos 2\theta$$

$$=\; \frac{28.29}{2} \sin 40 + 21.22 \cos 40$$

$$\tau_\theta \;=\; \mathbf{25.35 \text{ MPa (Tensile)}}$$

**Example 11.18 :** *An element in a plane stress is subjected to stresses as shown in Fig. 11.20. Obtain the principal stresses and show them on a properly oriented element.* **(May 2003)**

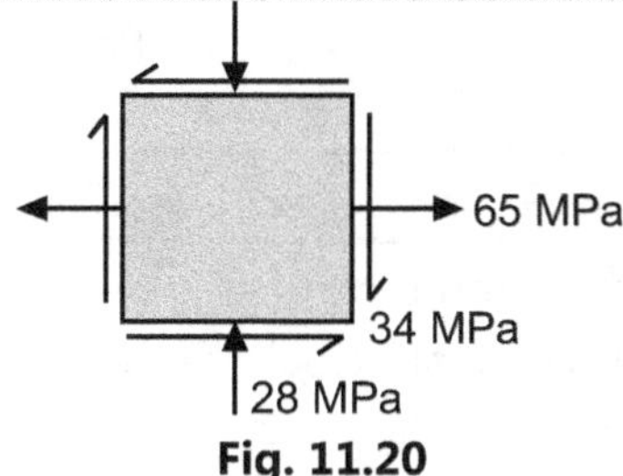

**Fig. 11.20**

**Data :** As shown in Fig. 11.20.

**Required :** $\sigma_1$, $\sigma_2$.

**Concept :** Standard formulae.

**Solution :** Principal stresses :

$$\sigma_1, \sigma_2 = \frac{\sigma_x + \sigma_y}{2} \pm \sqrt{\left(\frac{\sigma_x - \sigma_y}{2}\right)^2 + \tau_{xy}^2}$$

$$= \frac{65 - 28}{2} \pm \sqrt{\left(\frac{65 + 28}{2}\right)^2 + 34^2}$$

$$= 18.5 \pm 57.60$$

$$\sigma_1 = \textbf{76.10 MPa (Tensile)}$$

$$\sigma_2 = \textbf{– 39.10 MPa = 39.10 MPa  (Compressive)}$$

$$\tan 2\theta = -\frac{2\tau_{xy}}{\sigma_x - \sigma_y} = \frac{-2 \times 34}{(65 - (-28))} = -0.73$$

$\therefore$ $$\theta = -18.08, \ \theta = -108.09°$$

**Example 11.19 :** *At a particular point in a wooden member, the state of stress is as shown in Fig. 11.21. The direction of grain in the wood makes a 30° angle with the horizontal.*

*If the allowable shearing stress parallel to the grain is 1 MPa, verify that, this state of stress is permissible.* **(May 2003)**

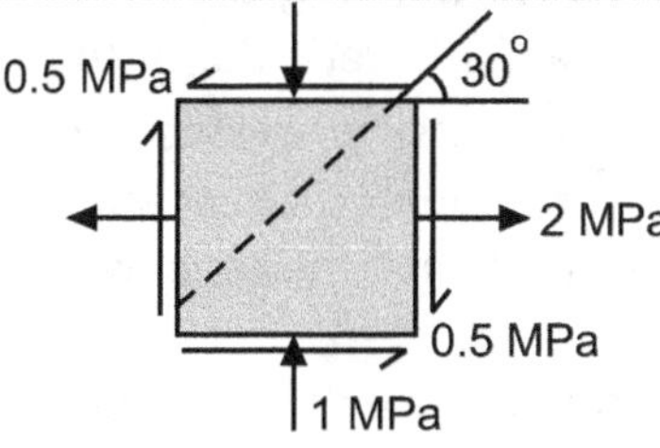

**Fig. 11.21**

**Data :** As shown in Fig. 11.21, $\tau_\theta = 1$ MPa, $\theta = 60°$.

**Required :** Check for shearing stress.

**Solution :** Standard formulae.

$$\tau_\theta = \frac{\sigma_x - \sigma_y}{2} \sin 2\theta + \tau_{xy} \cos 2\theta$$

$$= \frac{2 - (-1)}{2} \sin 120 + 0.5 \cos 120$$

$$= 1.3 + 0.25 = 1.55 \text{ MPa} > 1 \text{ MPa}$$

State of stress is not permissible.

## 11.5 MOHR'S CIRCLE

Mohr's circle is a graphical representation of a general state of stress at a point. It is a graphical method used for evaluation of principal stresses, maximum shear stress; normal and tangential stresses on any given plane.

Equations (11.3) and (11.4) are rewritten as

$$\sigma_\theta - \frac{\sigma_x + \sigma_y}{2} = \frac{\sigma_x - \sigma_y}{2} \cos (2\theta) - \tau_{xy}, \sin (2\theta)$$

$$\tau_\theta = \frac{\sigma_x - \sigma_y}{2} \sin (2\theta) + \tau_{xy} \cdot \cos (2\theta)$$

Squaring and adding these equations give,

$$\left(\sigma_\theta - \frac{\sigma_x + \sigma_y}{2}\right)^2 + \tau_\theta^2 = \left(\frac{\sigma_x - \sigma_y}{2}\right)^2 + (\tau_{xy})^2 \qquad \qquad \text{... (11.14)}$$

It should be noted that, $\sigma_x$, $\sigma_y$ and $\tau_{xy}$ are constants for a given state of stress while $\sigma_\theta$ and $\tau_\theta$ are variables. Equation (11.13) is the equation of circle of the form

$$(\sigma_\theta - a)^2 + \tau_\theta^2 = R^2 \qquad \qquad \text{... (11.15)}$$

where, $\qquad \qquad a = \dfrac{\sigma_x + \sigma_y}{2}$

and $\qquad \qquad R = \sqrt{\left(\dfrac{\sigma_x - \sigma_y}{2}\right)^2 + \tau_{xy}^2}$

The centre of Mohr's circle lies at (a, 0) i.e. $\left(\dfrac{\sigma_x + \sigma_y}{2}, 0\right)$.

Following important points must be noted for graphical analysis by Mohr's circle :

(i)   The normal stresses $\sigma_x$, $\sigma_y$ are plotted along the abscissa. The tensile stresses are considered positive and the compressive stresses are considered negative.

(ii)  The shear stress $\tau$ is plotted as ordinates. Shear stress which causes clockwise rotation of element is considered positive while the one which causes anticlockwise rotation is considered negative.

(iii) Co-ordinates of various points on Mohr's circle represent the state of stress at different planes.

(iv)  The radius of the circle to any point on its circumference represents the axis directed normal to the plane whose stress components are given by the co-ordinates of that point.

(v)   The angle between radii to points on Mohr's circle is twice the angle between the normals to the actual planes represented by these points. The rotational sense of this angle is same as that of rotational sense of the actual angle between the normals to the plane.

---

**Example 11.20 :** *At a certain point in a stressed body, the principal stresses are as shown in Fig. 11.22 (a). Determine normal and shear stress components on the planes whose normals are at $20^\circ$ and $110^\circ$ with x-axis. Show your result on properly oriented element.*

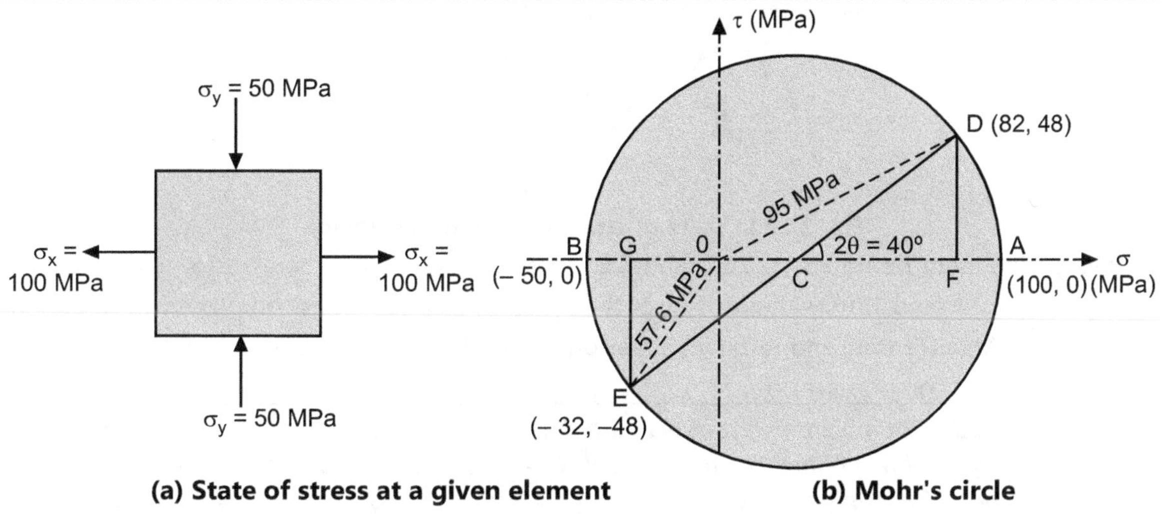


|                                        |                    |
| :------------------------------------: | :----------------: |
| **(a) State of stress at a given element** | **(b) Mohr's circle** |

**Fig. 11.22**

**Data**       :   State of stress as shown in Fig. 11.22 (a).

**Required**   :   Normal and shear stress components on the planes whose normals are at $20^\circ$ and $110^\circ$ with x axis.

**Concept**    :   Mohr's circle.

**Solution**   :

(i)   Draw a set of rectangular axes and label them as $\sigma$ and $\tau$ axes as shown in Fig. 11.22 (b).

(ii)  Along the x-axis, OA and OB are set-off equal in length to $\sigma_x$ and $\sigma_y$ respectively. Please note that $\sigma_x$ is + ve while $\sigma_y$ is − ve.

(iii) AB represents the diameter of Mohr's circle. Mark centre 'C' of AB and with 'C' as centre and AC as radius, draw Mohr's circle.

(iv)  Normal and tangential stress components are required on the planes whose normals are at $20^\circ$ and $110^\circ$ with x-axis. Hence, draw CD and CE at $40^\circ$ and $220^\circ$ anticlockwise as shown in Fig. 11.22 (b).

(v)   The co-ordinates of points D and E represent state of stress on the planes whose normals are at $20^\circ$ and $110^\circ$ with x-axis respectively.

**Ans.** : On plane, whose normal is at $20^\circ$ to x axis,

$\sigma$ = 82 MPa (Tensile) and $\tau$ = 48 MPa (clockwise)

On plane, whose normal is at $110^\circ$ to x-axis, $\sigma$ = − 32 MPa = 32 MPa (Compressive) and $\tau$ = − 48 MPa = 48 MPa (anticlockwise), as shown in Fig. 11.23.

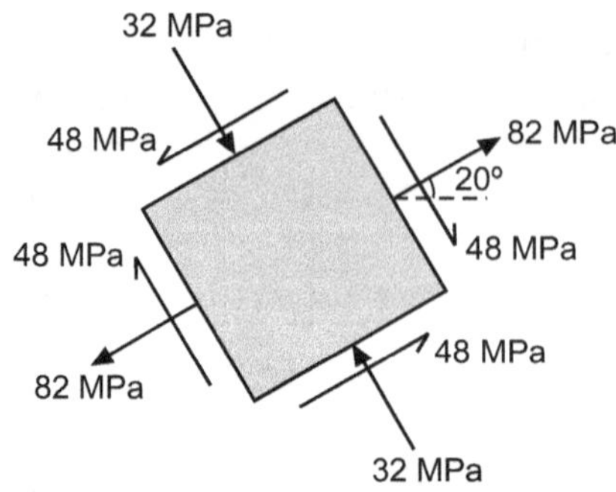


**Fig. 11.23 : State of stress on oriented element**

**Note :** It should be noted that OD and OE represent the resultant stresses on planes whose normals are at 20° and 110° with x-axis respectively. Thus, resultant stress on plane whose normal is at 20° = 95 MPa (Tensile) and resultant stress on plane whose normal is at 110° = 57.6 MPa (Compressive).

**Example 11.21 :** *At a point in a strained material, two-dimensional state of stress is as shown in Fig. 11.24 (a). Determine graphically : (i) Principal stresses, (ii) Principal planes, (iii) Maximum shear stress, (iv) Planes of maximum shear, (v) Normal and shear stress components on planes whose normals are at 35° and 125° with x-axis.*

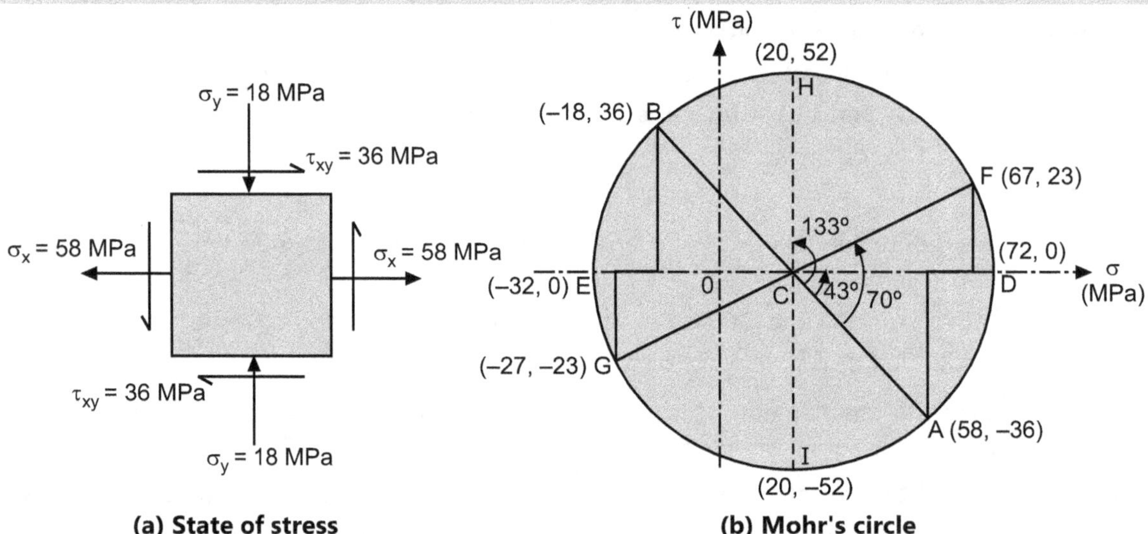


**(a) State of stress**                    **(b) Mohr's circle**

**Fig. 11.24**

**Data**          :   State of stress as shown in Fig. 11.24 (a).

**Required**   :   (i) Principal planes and principal stresses, (ii) Maximum shear stress and its plane, (iii) Normal and shear stress components on plane whose normals are at 35° and 125° with x-axis.

**Concept**   :   Mohr's circle.

**Solution**   :

(i)   Draw a set of rectangular axes and label them as σ and τ axes.

(ii)  Locate points A (58, – 36) and B (– 18, 36) representing state of stress on x and y planes respectively. It should be noted that shear on x plane is negative while that on y plane is positive.

(iii) AB is the diameter of Mohr's circle whose centre lies at C. With 'C' as centre and CA as radius draw Mohr's circle as shown in Fig. 11.24 (b); which cuts the x-axis at D and E. Measure and write the co-ordinates of points D and E which represent principal planes. Thus, $\sigma_1$ = 72 MPa (Tensile) and $\sigma_2$ = – 32 MPa = 32 MPa (Compressive)

(iv)  Measure   ACD = $2\theta_n$ = 43°

  ∴  $\theta_1$ = 21.5° and $\theta_2$ = 111.5° represent directions of principal planes. See Fig. 11.25 (a).

(v)   Locate points H (20, 52) and I (20, – 52) on vertical diameter. These are the planes of maximum shear stress.
Thus, maximum shear stress = $\tau_{max}$ = ± 52 MPa and normal stress on the plane of maximum shear is 20 MPa (Tensile).

(vi)  Measure ∠ ACH = $2\theta_s$ = 133°

  ∴  $\theta_3$ = 66.5° and $\theta_4$ = 156.5° represent the directions of planes of maximum shear. See Fig. 11.25 (b).

(vii) Normal and tangential stress components are required on planes whose normals are at 35° and 125° with x axis. Hence, draw CF and CG at 70° and 250° anticlockwise with respect to CA as shown in Fig. 11.24 (b). The co-ordinates of points F and G represent the state of stress on planes whose normals are at 35° and 125° with x-axis, respectively.

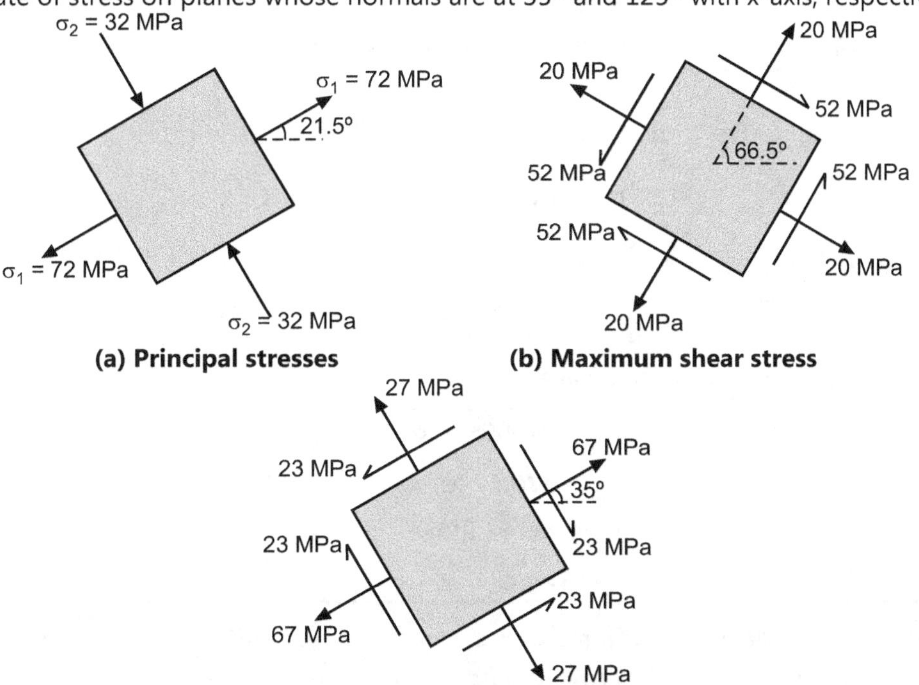



**(a) Principal stresses**          **(b) Maximum shear stress**

**(c) State of stress on element whose normals are at 35° and 125° to x-axis**

**Fig. 11.25**

Thus, on plane whose normal is at 35° with x-axis, normal stress = $\sigma$ = 67 MPa (Tensile) and shear stress = $\tau$ = 23 MPa (clockwise).

On plane whose normal is at 125° with x-axis, normal stress = $\sigma$ = $-27$ MPa = 27 MPa (Compressive) and shear stress = $\tau$ = $-23$ MPa = 23 MPa (anticlockwise). See Fig. 11.25 (c).

**Example 11.22 :** *At a point in a strained material, the normal and tangential stresses, on a plane inclined at 40° to the plane carrying major principal tensile stress, are 68 N/mm$^2$ tensile and 158 N/mm$^2$ respectively. Find the magnitude and nature of principal stresses. Also find the resultant stress on the given inclined plane.* **(Dec. 2001)**

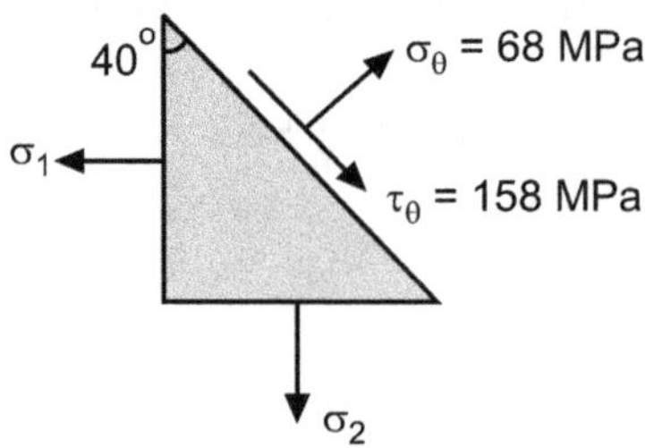


**Fig. 11.26**

**Solution :** (i)
$$\sigma_\theta = 68 = \frac{\sigma_1 + \sigma_2}{2} + \left\{\frac{\sigma_1 - \sigma_2}{2}\right\} \cos (2 \times 40)$$

$\therefore$
$$136 = 1.1736\,\sigma_1 + 0.8264\,\sigma_2 \qquad \text{... (I)}$$

$$\tau_\theta = 156 = \left\{\frac{\sigma_1 - \sigma_2}{2}\right\} \sin (2 \times 40)$$

$\therefore$
$$316.81 = \sigma_1 - \sigma_2 \qquad \text{... (II)}$$

Solving (I) and (II),

$$\sigma_1 = 198.9 \text{ MPa}, \quad \sigma_2 = 117.9 \text{ MPa}$$

(ii)   Resultant stress on inclined plane,

$$\sigma_R = \sqrt{68^2 + 156^2}$$

$$= \mathbf{170.17 \text{ MPa}}$$

$$\phi = \tan^{-1}(\tau_\theta/\sigma_\theta)$$

$$= \mathbf{66.41°}$$

**Example 11.23 :** *At a point in an strained material, stress pattern is as shown in Fig. 11.27. Determine (i) Magnitude of principal stresses and their orientation. (ii) Maximum shear stress and its orientation.*

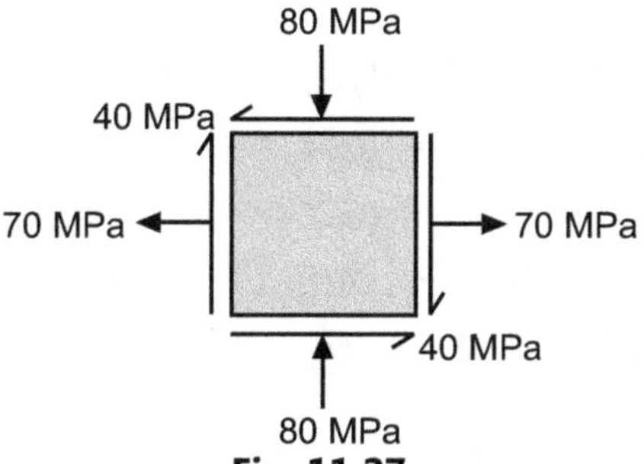



**Fig. 11.27**

**Solution :** (i) Principal stresses and its planes :

$$\sigma_1, \sigma_2 = \frac{\sigma_x + \sigma_y}{2} \pm \sqrt{\left(\frac{\sigma_x - \sigma_y}{2}\right)^2 + \tau_{xy}^2} = \frac{70 - 80}{2} \pm \sqrt{\frac{(70 + 80)^2}{2} + 40^2}$$

$$\sigma_1 = -\,90\ \textbf{MPa} \text{ and } \sigma_2 = \textbf{80 MPa}$$

$$\tan(2\theta_1) = -\frac{2\tau_{xy}}{\sigma_x - \sigma_y}$$

$$\theta_1 = \textbf{14.03°}, \ \theta_2 = \textbf{104.03°}$$

(ii)   Maximum shear stresses and its planes :

$$\tau_{max} = \pm\,(\sigma_1 - \sigma_2)/2 = \pm\,\textbf{85 MPa}$$

$$\theta_3 = -\,\textbf{30.96°} \text{ and } \theta_4 = -\,\textbf{120.96°}$$

**Example 11.24 :** $\sigma_x$, $\sigma_y$ and $\tau_{xy}$ are the stress components along the rectangular axes x and y, whereas $\sigma_{x'}$, $\sigma_{y'}$ and $\tau_{xy'}$ are the components along the rectangular axes x' and y' as shown in Fig. 11.28. Prove that $\sigma_{x'}, \sigma_{y'} - \tau_{x'y'}^2$ is independent of the orientation, as defined by $\theta$, of x' and y'. Using this invariance property, express the shear stress $\tau_{xy}$ in terms of $\sigma_x$, $\sigma_y$ and the principal stresses $\sigma_1$, $\sigma_2$.

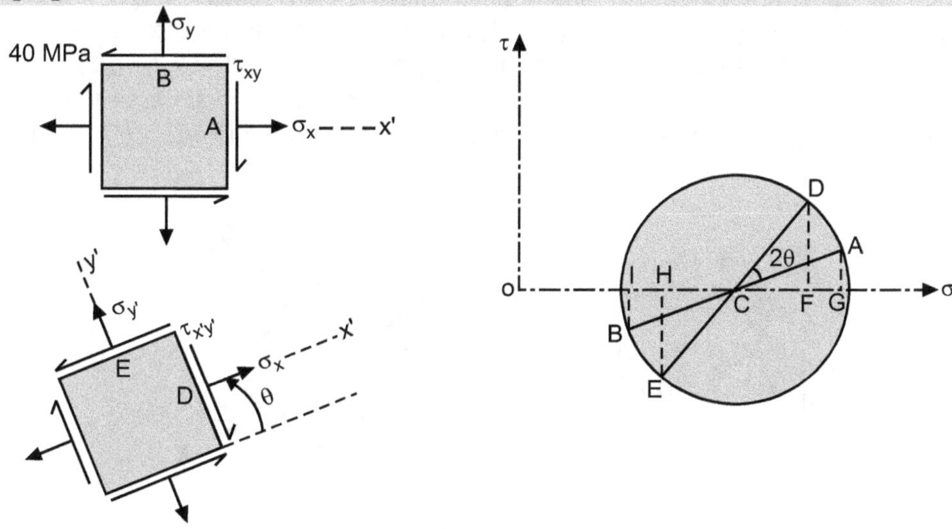



**Fig. 11.28**

**Solution : Required :** $\sigma_x \cdot \sigma_y - \sigma_{xy}^2 = \sigma_x' \cdot \sigma_y' - \tau_{x'y'}^2$ = constant.

$$(OG)(OI) - AG^2 = (OF)(OH) - DF^2$$

$$(OC + CG)(OC - CI) - AG^2 = (OC + CF)(OC - CH) - DF^2$$

$$OC^2 - CG^2 - AG^2 = OC^2 - CF^2 - DF^2$$

$$CG^2 + AG^2 = CF^2 + DF^2 = R^2 = \text{constant. Hence proved.}$$

Also

$$\sigma_x \cdot \sigma_y - \tau_{xy}^2 = \sigma_1 \cdot \sigma_2$$

$$\tau_{xy} = \sqrt{\sigma_x \cdot \sigma_y - \sigma_1 \cdot \sigma_2}$$

**Example 11.25 :** *If $\sigma_x$ = 60 MPa, $\sigma_y$ = –120 MPa, $\tau_{xy}$ = 100 MPa and $\theta$ = 30°, obtain the values of $\sigma_x'$, $\sigma_y'$ and $\tau_{xy}'$. Locate the planes of principal stresses and the planes of maximum shear stresses. Find the magnitude of these stresses.* **(Dec. 2002)**

**Solution :**

$$\sigma_x' = \sigma_\theta = \frac{\sigma_x + \sigma_y}{2} + \frac{\sigma_x - \sigma_y}{2}\cos(2\theta) - \tau_{xy}\sin(2\theta)$$

$$= -\,\textbf{71.6 MPa}$$

$$\sigma_y' = \frac{\sigma_x + \sigma_y}{2} + \frac{\sigma_x - \sigma_y}{2}\cos(2(\theta + 90)) - \tau_{xy}\sin(2(\theta + 90))$$

$$= \textbf{11.6 MPa}$$

$$\tau_{xy} = \frac{\sigma_x - \sigma_y}{2}\sin(2\theta) + \tau_{xy}\cos(2\theta) = \pm\,\textbf{127.94 MPa}$$

$$\sigma_1 = \textbf{104.5 MPa}, \; \sigma_2 = -\,\textbf{164.5 MPa}$$

$$\theta_1 = \textbf{24°}, \; \theta_2 = \textbf{114°}, \; \theta_3 = -\,\textbf{21°}, \; \theta_4 = -\,\textbf{111°}$$

$$\tau_{max} = \pm\,\textbf{134.5 MPa}$$

**Example 11.26 :** *At a point in a structure subjected to plane stress, the stresses have magnitude and directions shown acting on element A in the first part of Fig. 11.29, Element B, located at the same point, is rotated through an angle $\theta$ of such magnitude that the stresses have the values shown in the second part of Fig. 11.30. Calculate the normal stress $\sigma$ and the angle $\theta$.* **(May 2003)**

**Solution :**

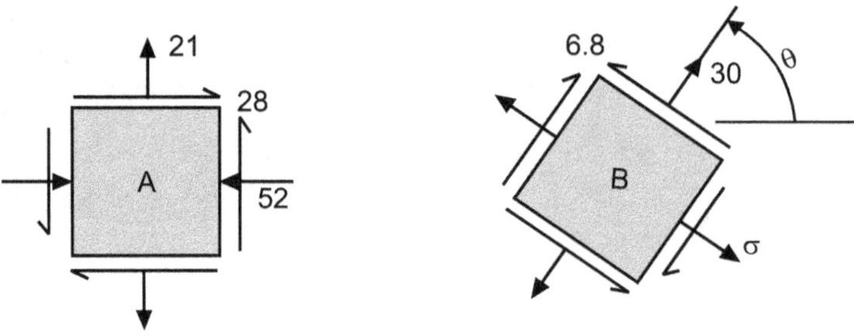


**Fig. 11.29**

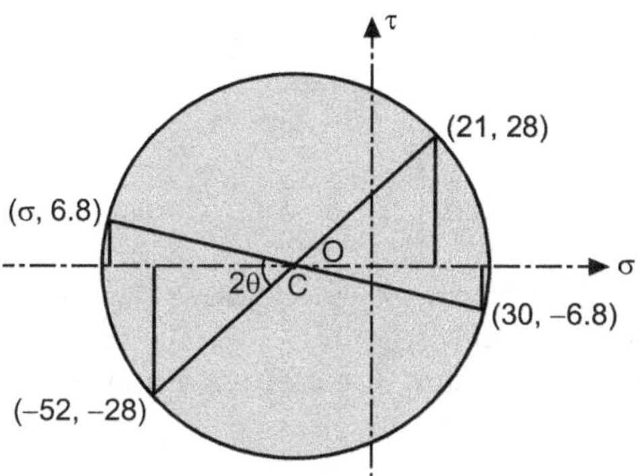

**Fig. 11.30**

From Mohr's circle,          $\sigma$ = **– 61 MPa**, $\theta$ = **24°**.

**Example 11.27 :** *The state of stress at a point is the result of the three separate actions that produce the three states of stresses as shown in Fig. 11.31. Determine the principal stresses caused by the superposition of these three stress states.*          **(May 2003)**

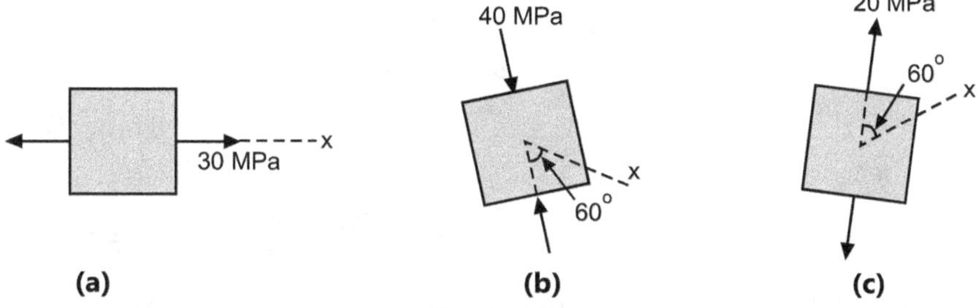


**Fig. 11.31**

**Solution :**

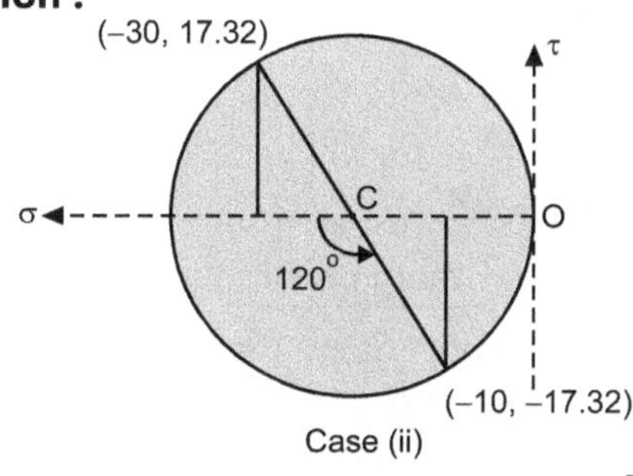


**Fig. 11.32**

Case (i) :          $\sigma_x$ = 30 MPa,          $\sigma_y$ = 0,          $\tau_{xy}$ = 0

Case (ii) :          $\sigma_x$ = – 10 MPa,          $\sigma_y$ = – 30 MPa,          $\tau_{xy}$ = – 17.32 MPa

Case (iii) :          $\sigma_x$ = 5 MPa,          $\sigma_y$ = 15 MPa,          $\tau_{xy}$ = – 8.6 MPa

∴ Resultant,          $\sigma_x$ = 25 MPa,          $\sigma_y$ = – 15 MPa,          $\tau_{xy}$ = – 25.92 MPa

$$\sigma_1, \sigma_2 = \frac{\sigma_x + \sigma_y}{2} \pm \sqrt{\left(\frac{\sigma_x - \sigma_y}{2}\right)^2 + \tau_{xy}^2}$$

$$= (25 - 15)/2 \pm \sqrt{((25 + 15)/2)^2 + (25.92)^2}$$

$$\sigma_1 = \textbf{37.73 MPa} \text{ and } \sigma_2 = \textbf{– 27.7 MPa}$$

**Example 11.28 :** *At a point in the web of a girder, bending stress is 80 MPa, tensile and shearing stress at the same point is 40 MPa calculate :*

(i)     *Principal stresses.*

(ii)    *Maximum shear stress.*

(iii)   *The tensile stress which when acting alone would produce the same maximum shear stress.*

(iv)    *The shear stress when acting along would produce the same maximum principal stress.*

**Data :** $\sigma_x = 80$ MPa, $\sigma_y = 0$, $\tau_{xy} = 40$ MPa.

**Required :** Principal stresses, maximum shear stress, equivalent alone tensile stress and shear stresses.

**Concept :** Standard formulae.

**Solution :** (i) Principal stresses :

$$\sigma_1, \sigma_2 = \frac{\sigma_x + \sigma_y}{2} \pm \sqrt{\left(\frac{\sigma_x - \sigma_y}{2}\right)^2 + \tau_{xy}^2}$$

$$\sigma_1, \sigma_2 = \frac{80}{2} \pm \sqrt{\left(\frac{80}{2}\right)^2 + 40^2}$$

$\therefore \qquad \sigma_1, \sigma_2 = 40 \pm 56.57$

$\therefore \qquad\qquad \sigma_1 = 96.57$ N/mm$^2$ (comp.)

$\qquad\qquad \sigma_2 = -16.57$ N/mm$^2$ = **16.57 N/mm$^2$ (Tension)**

(ii) Maximum shear stress :

$\therefore \qquad \tau_{max} = \dfrac{\sigma_1 - \sigma_2}{2} = \dfrac{96.57 - (-16.57)}{2} =$ **56.57 N/mm$^2$**

(iii) Tensile stress which acting alone produce same maximum shear stress :

$$\tau_{max} = \frac{\sigma_1 - \sigma_2}{2} = \frac{\sigma_1}{2}$$

$$56.57 = \frac{\sigma_1}{2}$$

$\therefore \qquad\qquad \sigma_1 =$ **113.14 N/mm$^2$**

(iv) The shear stress which acting alone produce same maximum principal stress :

$$\sigma_1 = \frac{\sigma_x + \sigma_y}{2} \pm \sqrt{\left(\frac{\sigma_x - \sigma_y}{2}\right)^2 + \tau_{xy}^2}$$

$$96.57 = \tau_{xy}$$

$\therefore \qquad\qquad \tau_{xy} =$ **96.57 N/mm$^2$**

## EXERCISE

1.  A circular bar is subjected to an axial pull of 80 kN. If the maximum intensity of shear stress on any oblique plane is not to exceed 50 MPa, determine the diameter of the bar.

    (31.91 mm)

2.  A short metallic column of 500 mm$^2$ cross-sectional area carries an axial compressive load of 80 kN. For a plane inclined at 60° with the direction of load, calculate (i) Normal stress, (ii) Shear stress, (iii) Resultant stress, (iv) Maximum shear stress, and (v) Obliquity of the resultant stress.

$$(\sigma_n = 120.08 \text{ MPa} \; ; \tau = 69.28 \text{ MPa}, \sigma = 138.63 \text{ MPa}, \tau_{max} = 80 \text{ MPa}, \phi = 30^\circ)$$

3. The principal tensile stresses at a point across two perpendicular planes are 100 MPa and 50 MPa. Find the normal and shear stresses and the resultant stress and its obliquity on a plane at $20^\circ$ with the major principal plane. Find also the intensity of stress which acting alone can produce the same strain assuming $\mu = 0.25$.

$$(\sigma_n = 94.15 \text{ MPa}, \tau = 16.08 \text{ MPa} \; ; \text{Resultant } \sigma = 95.51 \text{ MPa}, \phi = 9.68^\circ \; ; \sigma = 87.5 \text{ MPa})$$

4. The principal stresses at a point are 150 MPa (tensile) and 75 MPa (compressive). Determine the resultant stress in magnitude and direction on a plane inclined at $60^\circ$ to the axis of major principal stress. Also determine the maximum intensity of shear stress.

$$(\sigma_n = 93.75 \text{ MPa}, \; \tau = 97.425 \text{ MPa}, \text{Resultant } \sigma = 135.2 \text{ MPa} \; ;$$
$$\phi = 46.1^\circ; \tau_{max} = 112.5 \text{ MPa})$$

5. A prismatic bar carrying an axial tensile stress $\sigma_x$ is cut by an oblique section. If the normal and shear stresses on this section are 73.8 MPa and 24.6 MPa respectively, find values of $\sigma_x$ and angle $\theta$ defining the aspect of the section. $\quad\quad (\sigma_x = 83.0 \text{ MPa}; \theta = 18.43^\circ)$

6. The principal stresses acting on an element subjected to plane stresses are 12 MPa and 4.5 MPa (both tensile) respectively. Find out the position of the plane AA when the resultant stress makes the maximum angle with the normal to the plane. $\quad\quad (\phi = 27^\circ)$

7. A piece of material is subjected to two compressive stresses at right angles, their values being 60 MPa and 90 MPa. Find the position of plane across which the resultant stress is most inclined to the normal and determine the value of this resultant stress.

$$(\theta = 39.14^\circ; \text{ Resultant, } \sigma = 73.5 \text{ MPa})$$

8. At a point in a strained material, state of stress is as shown in Fig. 11.33. Find (i) The direction of principal planes, (ii) The magnitude of principal stresses, (iii) The magnitude of greatest shear stress.

$$(\sigma_1 = 116.1 \text{ MPa} \; ; \sigma_2 = 6.3 \text{ MPa} \; ; \theta_1 = 31.6^\circ \; ; \theta_2 = 121.6^\circ \; ;$$
$$\tau_{max} = 54.9 \text{ MPa} \; ; \theta_3 = 76.6^\circ , \theta_4 = 166.6^\circ)$$

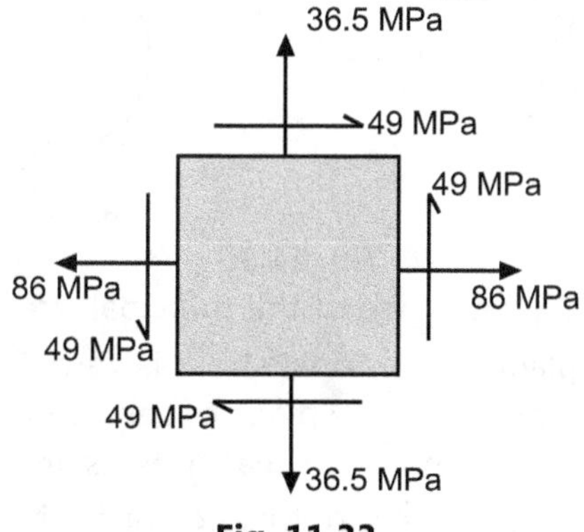

**Fig. 11.33**

9. State of stress at a point in a strained material is as shown in Fig. 11.34. Determine :
(i) The resultant stress on plane AB.

(ii)   The principal stresses and their directions.

(iii)  The maximum shear stresses and their planes.

(Normal stress on AB = 86.6 MPa; shear stress on AB = 50 MPa, $\sigma_1$ = 131.13 MPa;

$\sigma_2$ = 30.46 MPa, $\theta_1$ = 41.69°, $\theta_2$ = 131.69°, $\tau_{max}$ = 50.33 MPa, $\theta_3$ = 86.69°,

$\theta_4$ = 176.69°)

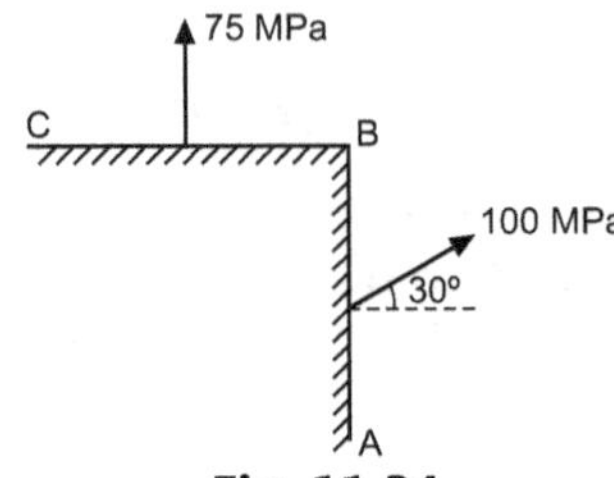

**Fig. 11.34**

10.   Draw Mohr's circles for the elements subjected to state of stress as shown in Fig. 11.35.

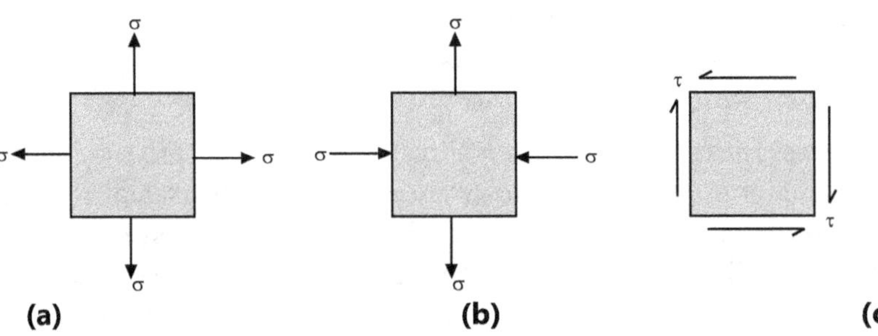

**(a)**                    **(b)**                    **(c)**

**Fig. 11.35**

(a)   No Mohr's circle

(b)                              (c)

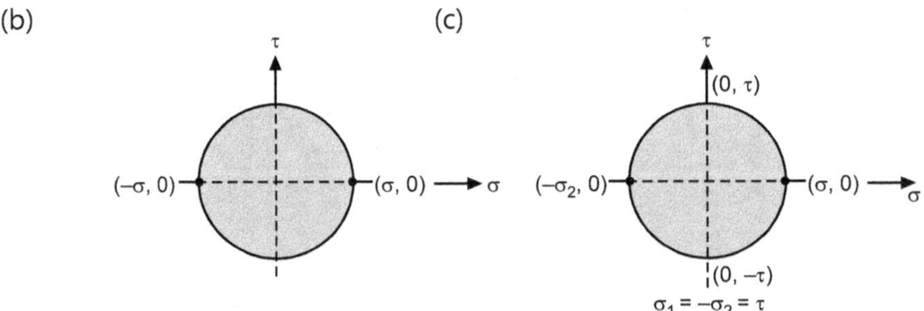

**Fig. 11.36**

11.   At a point in a strained material, one of the principal stress is 60 MPa tensile. On a plane at 60° to this principal plane, the normal stress is zero. Determine (i) the other principal stress, (ii) the shear stress on the above plane of zero normal stress, (iii) the planes on which the normal and shear stresses are equal in magnitude.

($\sigma_2$ = – 20 MPa = 20 MPa (compressive), $\tau_{60°}$ = 34.64 MPa, $\theta$ = 32.85°)

12.   An element in a two-dimensional stress system is subjected to $\sigma_x$ = 150 MPa tensile, $\sigma_y$ = 100 MPa compressive and $\tau_{xy}$ = $\tau_{yx}$ = 50 MPa. Determine the planes of zero shear and maximum shear. Also find the normal and shear stress intensities on these planes.

($\theta_1$ = 10.9°, $\theta_2$ = 100.9°, $\theta_3$ = 55.9°, $\theta_4$ = 145.9°, $\sigma_1$ = 159.63 MPa (tensile), $\sigma_2$ = 109.63 MPa (compressive), $\tau_{max}$ = 134.63 MPa)

13. At a point in a strained material, the principal stresses are 135 MPa and 54 MPa, both tensile. Locate graphically the planes for which the resultant stress is inclined at 15° to the normal. Find this resultant stress. Find also the planes for which the resultant stress is most inclined with the normal.

    ($\theta_1$ = 26°, $\theta_2$ = 79°, $\theta_3$ = 101°, $\theta_4$ = 154°, Resultant stresses = 92 MPa, 43.5 MPa, Angular position of planes of maximum obliquity = 125°)

14. Fig. 11.37 shows the normal and tangential stresses on two planes. Determine the principal stresses.

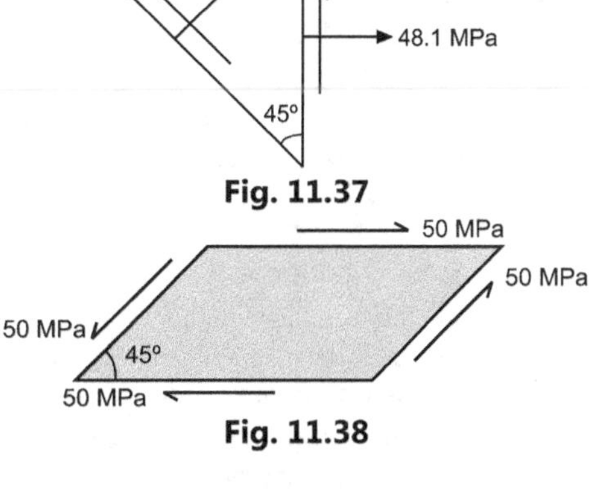

**Fig. 11.37**

15. A thin plate is under a state of stress as shown in Fig. 11.38. Find the principal stresses and their directions by using the Mohr's circle method.
    ($\sigma_1$ = 53.73 MPa, $\sigma_2$ = 22.4 MPa)
    ($\sigma_1$ = 121.42 MPa (tensile), $\sigma_2$ = 21.43 MPa (compressive))

**Fig. 11.38**

17. A triangular prism of material is subjected to two-dimensional state of stress as shown in Fig. 11.39. Determine (i) The angle 'θ' between the planes AC and BC.
    (ii) The tangential, normal and resultant stress on BC, and (iii) other principal stress.

    ((i) θ = 33.34°; (ii) On plane BC; $\sigma_n$ = 69.7 MPa (tensile), τ = 19.13 MPa (clockwise), Resultant stress = 72.29 MPa, (iii) $\sigma_2$ = 39.71 MPa (tensile)).

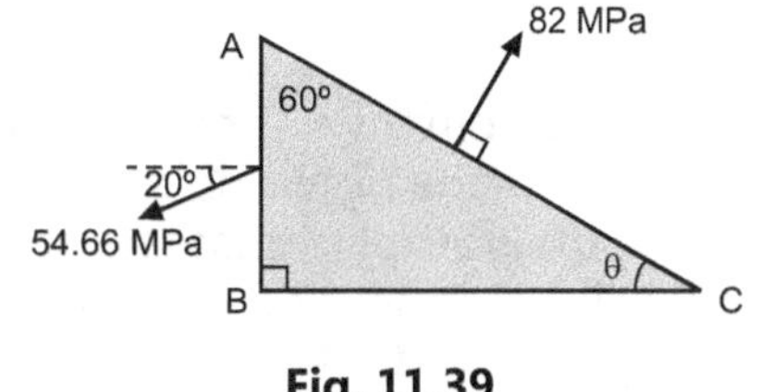

**Fig. 11.39**

## UNIVERSITY QUESTION PAPERS

### MAY 2014

1. In a 2D stress system, stresses at a point in a material are 50 MPa compression and 30 MPa shearing in one plane and 20 MPa tensile and a shearing stress in another plane at 60° to the first one. Determine the value of the shearing stress in the second plane and the principal stresses and position of their planes. Use analytical methos.**[7]**

2. The stresses on two perpendicular planes through a point in a body are        30 MPa and 15 MPa both tensile along with shear stress of 25 MPa. Find :        **[7]**
   (i)   Magnitude and direction of principal stresses
   (ii)  Maximum shear stress and their planes
   (iii) Normal and shear stresses on the planes of maximum shearing stress
   Use Mohr's circle method.

## DECEMBER 2014

1.  A material is subjected to two mutually perpendicular direct stresses of 93.5 MPa tensile (in 'y' direction) and 42.5 MPa compressive (in 'x' direction), together with a shear stress of 44 MPa. The shear couple acting on planes carrying the 93.5 MPa stress is clockwise in effect. Calculate :                                                                                        **[13]**
    (a)  Magnitude and nature of the principal stresses;
    (b)  Magnitude of the maximum shear stresses in the plane of the given stress system.
    (c)  Direction of the planes on which these stresses act.

## MAY 2015

1.  A material is subjected to two mutually perpendicular direct stresses of 92 MPa tensile and 29 MPa compressive, together with a shear stress of 22 MPa. The shear couple acting on planes carrying the 92 MPa stress is clockwise in effect. Calculate : (i) Magnitude and nature of the principal stresses; (ii) Magnitude of the maximum shear stresses in the plane of the given stress system; (iii) Direction of the planes on which these stresses act.      **[13]**

## November 2015

1.  Stressed element in a machine component is subjected to 185 MPa tensile stress in x-direction, 55 MPa compressive stress in y-direction and 75 MPa shear stress clockwise on x-face. Compute the values and orientation of the principal stresses and maximum shear stress using graphical method proposed by Mohr. Mohr's circle must be drawn on GRAPH paper using appropriate scale. (Note : Analytical solution and solution without GRAPH paper will not be evaluated.)                                                           **[13]**

## May 2016

1.  At a point in a strained material the normal stresses acting are +50 MPa and –30MPa at a plane right angle to each other, with a shear stress of 20 MPa. Determine:
    (i)    Principal stresses and their nature
    (ii)   Normal and tangential stress on a plane inclined at an angle of 25° with the plane of 50 MPa.                                                                                            **[7]**
2.  A 100 mm diameter bar with a built in bracket is fixed to the wall and loaded as shown in Fig. 1. Determine the principle stresses at the top extremity of the vertical diameter for the section market A.                                                                                          **[7]**

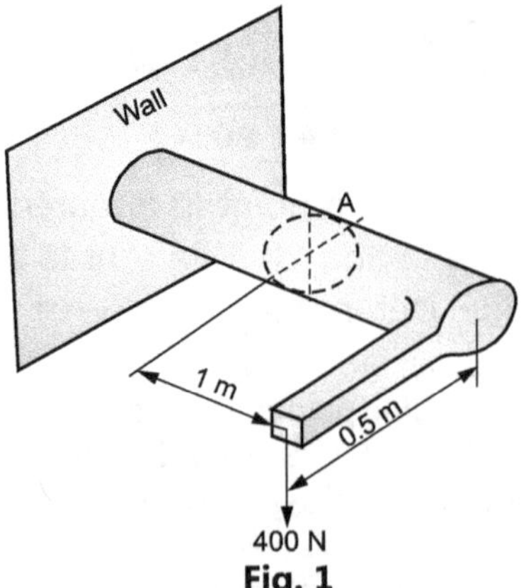


**Fig. 1**

◈ ◈ ◈

# Chapter 12

# COMBINED LOADING AND THEORIES OF ELASTIC FAILURES

## 12.1 INTRODUCTION

In chapter 9, we study the stresses and strains set up by the cross-section of circular shaft to resist the action of torsional moment. But sometimes shaft has to resist bending moment and/or axial thrust along with the torsional moment, also called as *combined actions*. In this chapter, we are going to discuss the combined action on the shaft.

## 12.2  COMBINED ACTIONS

### 12.2.1 Bending and Torsion

In practice, members are generally subjected to combined bending and torsion. In this article, we shall discuss the evaluation of principal stresses and maximum shear stress for such combined action.

Consider a solid circular shaft subjected to bending moment and torsion as shown in Fig. 12.1.

Let,                          M  =  Bending moment (sagging)

T  =  Torsional moment

D  =  Diameter of shaft

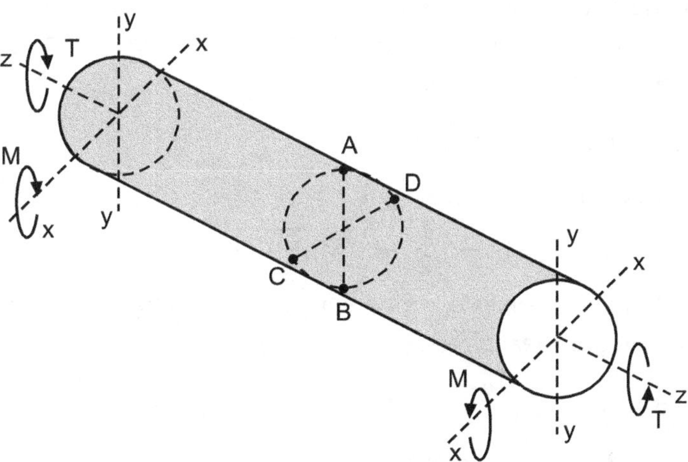


**Fig. 12.1 : Combined bending and torsion**

Consider an intermediate cross-section of shaft as shown in Fig. 12.1.

Shear stress due to torque $T = \tau = \dfrac{16\,T}{\pi D^3}$     ... (12.1)

Bending stress due to $M = \sigma = \dfrac{32M}{\pi D^3}$     ... (12.2)

It should be noted that shear stress $\tau$ is uniform at all elements A, B, C and D while bending stress $\sigma$ is compressive in nature at A, tensile in nature at B while zero at elements C and D. Hence, elements C and D are subjected to state of pure shear while principal stresses will occur at elements A and B. Principal stresses $\sigma_1$ and $\sigma_2$ at any of these two points are given by

$$\sigma_1,\ \sigma_2 \;=\; \frac{\sigma}{2} \pm \sqrt{\left(\frac{\sigma}{2}\right)^2 + \tau^2} \qquad \text{... (12.3)}$$

Substituting equations (12.1) and (12.2) in equation (12.3), we get

$$\sigma_1,\ \sigma_2 \;=\; \frac{32M}{2\pi D^3} \pm \sqrt{\left(\frac{32M}{2\pi D^3}\right)^2 + \left(\frac{16T}{\pi D^3}\right)^2}$$

$$=\; \frac{16M}{\pi D^3} \pm \sqrt{\left(\frac{16M}{\pi D^3}\right)^2 + \left(\frac{16T}{\pi D^3}\right)^2}$$

$$\sigma_1,\ \sigma_2 \;=\; \frac{16}{\pi D^3}\left[M \pm \sqrt{M^2 + T^2}\right] \qquad \text{... (12.4)}$$

Principal planes can be located by using

$$\tan(2\theta_1) \;=\; \frac{2\tau}{\sigma} = \frac{T}{M} \qquad \text{... (12.5)}$$

and $\qquad\qquad \theta_2 \;=\; \theta_1 + 90^\circ$

Maximum shear stress is given by,

$$\tau_{max} = \frac{\sigma_1 - \sigma_2}{2} \;=\; \frac{16}{\pi D^3}\sqrt{M^2 + T^2} \qquad \text{... (12.6)}$$

**Equivalent Bending and Torsional Moment :**

Let     $M_e$ = Equivalent bending moment, which acting alone, produces the same maximum normal stress.

Bending stress due to $M_e = \sigma \;=\; \dfrac{32\,M_e}{\pi D^3}$     ... (12.7)

Equating equations (12.4) and (12.7), we get

$$M_e \;=\; \frac{1}{2}\left[M + \sqrt{M^2 + T^2}\right] \qquad \text{... (12.8)}$$

Let     $T_e$ = Equivalent torsional moment, which acting alone, produces the same maximum shear stress.

Shear stress due to $T_e = \tau = \dfrac{16\,T_e}{\pi D^3}$     ... (12.9)

Equating equations (12.6) and (12.9), we get

$$T_e \;=\; \sqrt{M^2 + T^2} \qquad \text{... (12.10)}$$

## 12.2.2 Axial Force and Torsion

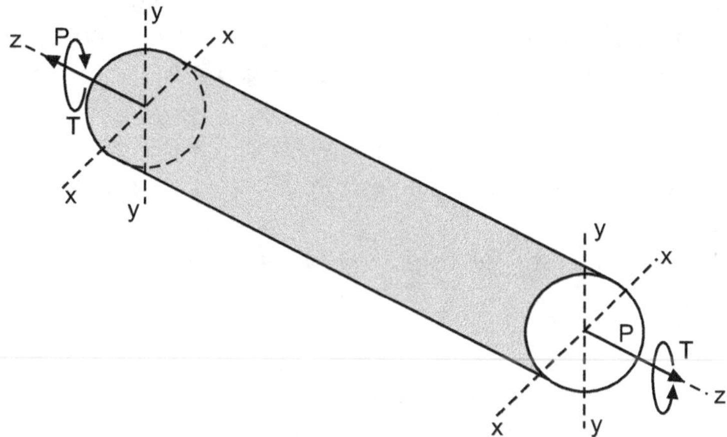

**Fig. 12.2 : Combined axial force and torsion**

Consider a solid circular shaft subjected to axial force and torsional moment as shown in Fig. 12.2.

Let      $P$ = Axial force (tensile)

        $T$ = Torsional moment

        $D$ = Diameter of shaft

Normal stress due to axial force $P = \sigma = \dfrac{4P}{\pi D^2}$        ... (12.11)

Shear stress due to torque $T$ is obtained from equation (12.1).

It should be noted that normal stress '$\sigma$' due to axial force is uniform over the entire cross-section while shear stress $\tau$ due to torque is same at any point on the surface of the shaft.

Principal stresses can be evaluated by equation (12.3) and principal planes can be located by,

$$\tan 2\theta_1 \;=\; \frac{2\tau}{\sigma} \quad \text{and} \quad \theta_2 = \theta_1 + 90^\circ$$

## 12.2.3 Axial force, Bending and Torsion

When shaft is subjected to all these three actions, for elements farthest from neutral axis of bending; normal stresses due to bending and axial force will get added algebraically and shear stress due to torque is same on all the elements at surface of the shaft. Nature of normal stresses on various elements will depend on nature of axial force and bending moment. Algebraic addition of normal stresses is possible within elastic behaviour of the material since, principle of superposition is valid till then. Principal stresses can then be obtained by using same equations discussed earlier.

# SOLVED EXAMPLES

**Example 12.1 :** *A shaft section 80 mm in diameter is subjected to bending moment of 3 kN.m and torque of 8 kN.m. Find the maximum normal stresses induced on section and locate the plane on which it acts. Find also what stress acting alone can produce the same maximum strain. Take $\mu$ = 0.3.*

**Data** : $D$ = 80 mm;  $M$ = 3 kN.m;  $T$ = 8 kN.m;  $\mu$ = 0.3

**Required** : Principal stresses and single normal stress to produce equivalent principal strain.

**Concept** : Principal stresses for combined bending and torsion using equations (12.4), (12.5).

**Solution** : (i) Principal stresses :

$$\sigma_1, \sigma_2 = \frac{16}{\pi D^3}\left(M \pm \sqrt{M^2 + T^2}\right) = \frac{16}{\pi \times 80^3}\left(3 \pm \sqrt{3^2 + 8^2}\right) \times 10^6$$

$$= 9.95\,(3 \pm 8.54)$$

$$\sigma_1 = \textbf{114.82 MPa} \text{ and}$$

$$\sigma_2 = \textbf{– 55.12 MPa}$$

(ii) Principal planes :

$$\tan(2\theta_1) = \frac{T}{M} = \frac{8}{3}$$

$\therefore$ $\theta_1$ = **34.72°**  and  $\theta_2 = \theta_1 + 90° = 34.72 + 90 = $ **124.72°**

(iii) Major principal strain :

$$\epsilon_1 = \frac{1}{E}(\sigma_1 - \mu\,\sigma_2) = \frac{1}{E}(114.82 - 0.3\,(-55.12))$$

$$= \frac{131.36}{E}$$

(iv) Single normal stress to produce major principal strain :

Let, $\sigma$ = Normal stress to produce major principal strain

$\therefore$ 
$$\frac{\sigma}{E} = \frac{131.36}{E}$$

$\therefore$ $\sigma$ = **131.36 MPa**

**Example 12.2 :** *A steel shaft is subjected to torque of 15 kN.m and bending moment of 12 kN.m. Calculate the principal stresses and maximum shear stress if diameter of shaft is 100 mm.*

**Data** : $T$ = 15 kN.m;  $M$ = 12 kN.m;   $D$ = 100 mm

**Required** : Principal stresses, maximum shear stress.

**Concept** : Same as Example (12.1).

**Solution** : (i) Principal stresses.

$$\sigma_1, \sigma_2 = \frac{16}{\pi D^3}\left(M \pm \sqrt{M^2 + T^2}\right)$$

$$= \frac{16}{\pi \times 100^3}\left(12 \pm \sqrt{12^2 + 15^2}\right) \times 10^6$$

$$= 5.09\,(12 \pm 19.2)$$

$$\sigma_1 = \textbf{158.8 MPa} \text{ and}$$

$$\sigma_2 = \textbf{– 36.65 MPa}$$

(ii)    Position of principal planes :

$$\tan (2\theta_1) = \frac{T}{M} = \frac{15}{12}$$

$\therefore \qquad \theta_1 = \textbf{25.67}^\textbf{o} \text{ and } \theta_2 = \theta_1 + 90^\text{o} = 25.67 + 90^\text{o} = \textbf{115.67}^\textbf{o}$

(iii)   Maximum shear stress :

$$\tau_{max} = \frac{16}{\pi D^3} \sqrt{M^2 + T^2}$$

$$= \frac{16}{\pi \times 100^3} \left(\sqrt{12^2 + 15^2}\right) \times 10^6$$

$$\tau_{max} = \textbf{97.83 MPa}$$

**Example 12.3 :** *A hollow shaft is subjected to torque of 400 kN.m and bending moment of 200 kN.m. Internal diameter of shaft is 0.6 times the external diameter. If maximum normal stress is not to exceed 150 MPa and shear stress is not to exceed 80 MPa, design the cross-section of shaft.*

**Data**          :    T = 400 kN.m; M = 200 kN.m; d = 0.6 D; $\sigma_{max} \leq$ 150 MPa; $\tau_{max} \leq$ 80 MPa.

**Required**   :    Design of cross section of shaft.

**Concept**    :    Design of shaft based on maximum normal stress and maximum shear stress criteria. Governing dimensions will be greater of that obtained for above two conditions.

**Solution**   :    (i) Cross-section based on maximum normal stress.

Principal stresses $\qquad (\sigma_1, \sigma_2) = \dfrac{16D}{\pi (D^4 - d^4)} \left(M \pm \sqrt{M^2 + T^2}\right)$

Major principal stress, $\qquad \sigma_1 = 150$ MPa

$$\sigma_1 = \frac{16D}{\pi [D^4 - (0.6\,D)^4]} \left(200 + \sqrt{200^2 + 400^2}\right) \times 10^6$$

$$= \frac{3.296 \times 10^9 \, D}{0.8704 \, D^4}$$

$\therefore \qquad$ D $= \textbf{293.36 mm}$ and $\textbf{d = 176.02 mm}$ $\qquad\qquad$ ... (i)

(ii)    Cross-section based on maximum shear stress.

$$\tau_{max} = \frac{16\,D}{\pi (D^4 - d^4)} \cdot \sqrt{M^2 + T^2}$$

$$80 = \frac{16\,D}{\pi [D^4 - (0.6\,D)^4]} \cdot \left(\sqrt{200^2 + 400^2}\right) \times 10^6$$

$$= \frac{2.278 \times 10^9}{0.8704 \, D^3}$$

$\therefore \qquad$ D $= \textbf{319.8 mm}$ and $\textbf{d = 191.89 mm}$ $\qquad\qquad$ ... (ii)

$\therefore \qquad$ Use $\qquad$ D $= \textbf{320 mm}$ and $\textbf{d}$ = 0.6 × 320 = $\textbf{192 mm}$

(Greater of (i) and (ii))

**Example 12.4 :** *A flywheel weighing 4 kN is mounted on a shaft 50 mm $\phi$, 600 mm long. Shaft is free to rotate at ends and flywheel is mounted on centre of shaft. If shaft is transmitting 44 kW at 300 rpm, calculate the principal stresses and maximum shear stresses in the shaft at the ends of horizontal and vertical diameter of cross-section close to that of flywheel.*

**Data**        :   Weight of flywheel = W = 4 kN; diameter of shaft = D = 50 mm;
L = 600 mm; Power = 44 kW;  N = 300 r.p.m.

**Required**   :   Principal stresses and maximum shear stresses in the shaft at the ends of horizontal and vertical diameter of cross-section close to flywheel.

**Concept**    :   (i)    Self weight of flywheel will produce bending moment and shear force for shaft and knowing power and speed of shaft, torque can be obtained.

(ii)   Stresses at the ends of horizontal diameter (AB)

   (a)   Shear stresses due to shear force.

   (b)   Shear stresses due to torque.

Normal stresses due to bending moment are zero at horizontal diameter.

(iii)  Stresses at the ends of vertical diameter (CD)

   (a)   Shear stresses due to torque.

   (b)   Normal stresses due to bending moment.

Shear stresses due to shear force are zero at the ends of vertical diameter.

**Solution**   :   (i) Analysis of forces :

Reactions at supports due to self weight of flywheel = 2 kN ($\uparrow$)

Maximum B.M. at centre $= \dfrac{WL}{4} = \dfrac{4 \times 0.6}{4} = 0.6$ kN.m.

SF and BM diagrams are drawn as shown in Fig. 12.3.

Also      $P = \dfrac{2\pi NT}{60}$   $\therefore$      $44 \times 10^3 = \dfrac{2\pi \times 300 \times T}{60}$

$\therefore$               T  = **1400.56 N.m**

(ii)   Geometric properties of shaft :

$$I_x = \frac{\pi}{64} \cdot D^4 = \frac{\pi}{64} (50)^4 = 306.796 \times 10^3 \text{ mm}^4$$

$$J = \frac{\pi}{32} \cdot D^4 = \frac{\pi}{32} (50)^4 = 613.592 \times 10^3 \text{ mm}^4$$

$$\text{Section modulus @ x axis} = Z_x = \frac{I_x}{y_{max}}$$

$$= \frac{306.796 \times 10^3}{50/2} = \textbf{12.27} \times \textbf{10}^3 \textbf{ mm}^3$$

$$\text{Polar section modulus} = \frac{J}{R} = \frac{613.592 \times 10^3}{50/2} = \textbf{24.54} \times \textbf{10}^3 \textbf{ mm}^3$$

$$A = \frac{\pi}{4} \cdot D^2 = \frac{\pi}{4} (50)^2 = \textbf{1963.49 mm}^2$$

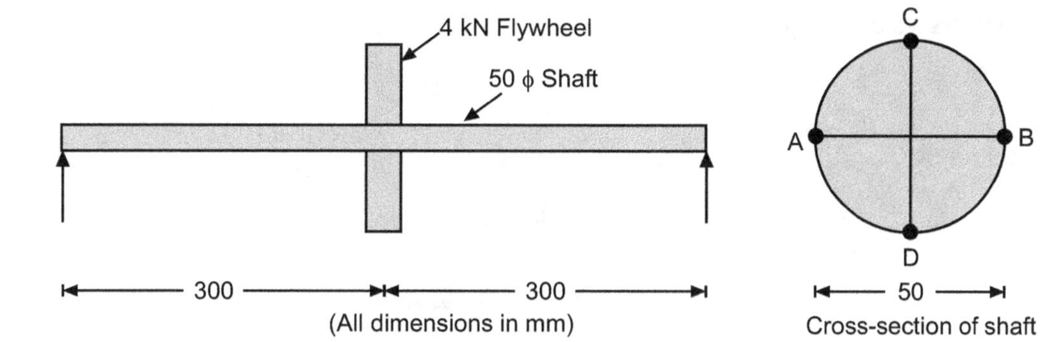

**(a) Flywheel arrangement**

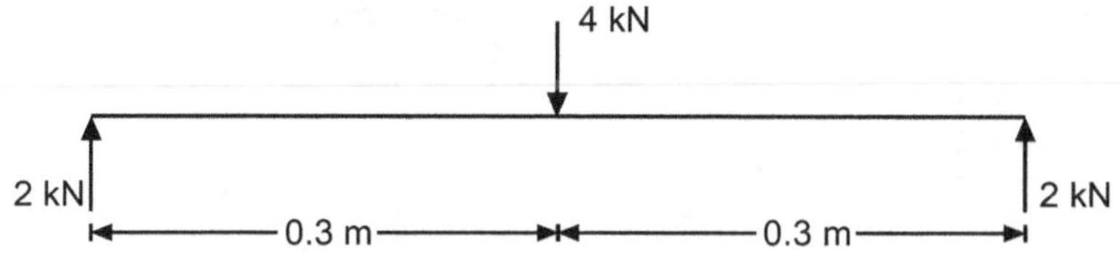

**(b) FBD of shaft**

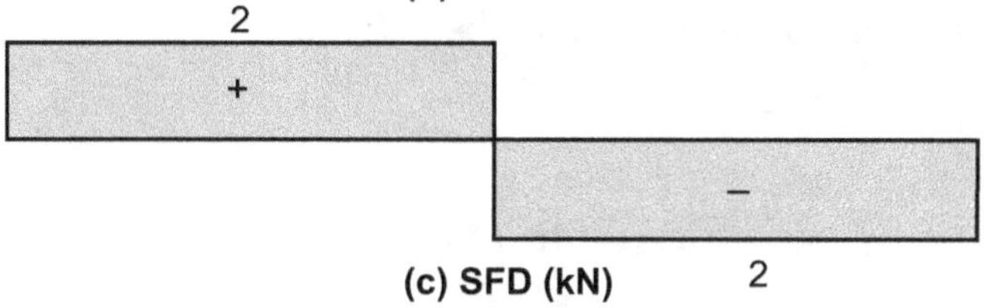

**(c) SFD (kN)**                2

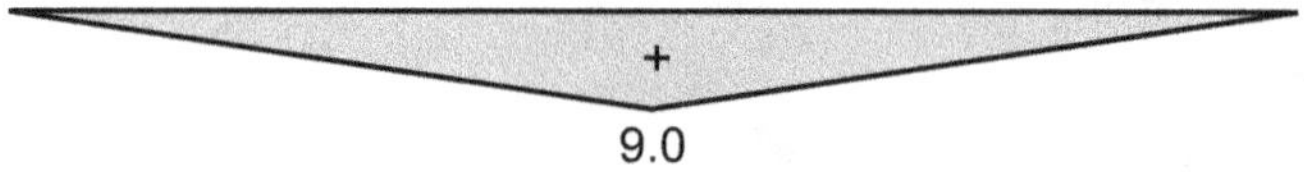

**(d) BMD (kNm)**

**Fig. 12.3**

(iii)    Evaluation of different stresses :

Shear stresses due to torque,

$$\tau_1 = \frac{T}{J/R} = \frac{1400.56 \times 10^3}{24.54 \times 10^3}$$

$$= \textbf{57.07 MPa}$$

[**Note :** $\tau_1$ = 57.07 MPa is same at all elements A, B, C and D.]

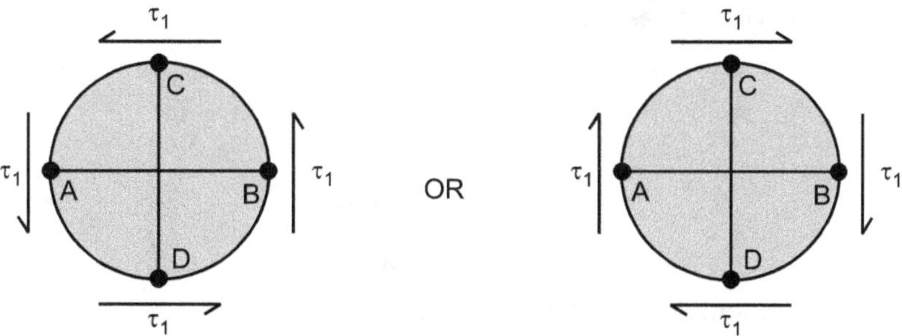



**Fig. 12.4 : Shear stresses due to torque**

Shear stresses due to shear force,

$$\tau_2 = \frac{4}{3}\tau_a$$

where;  $\tau_a$ = Average shear stress = $\dfrac{\text{Shear force}}{\text{c/s area}}$

$$= \frac{2 \times 10^3}{1963.49} = \textbf{1.02 MPa}$$

$$\therefore \qquad \tau_2 = \frac{4}{3} \times 1.02 = \textbf{1.36 MPa}$$

[**Note :** $\tau_2$ = 1.36 MPa is at A and B only]

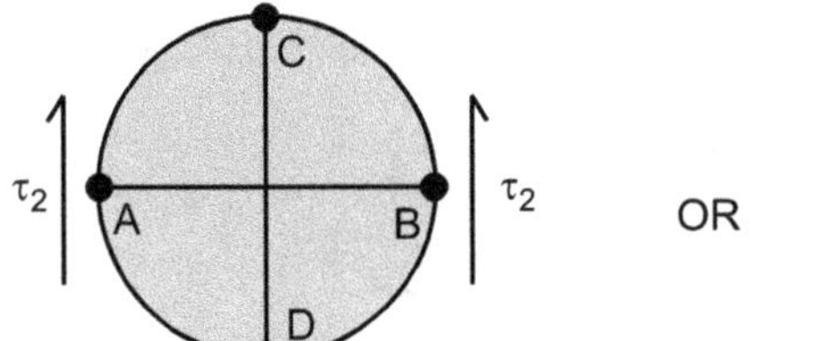

**Fig. 12.5 : Shear stresses due to shear force**

Bending stresses,  $\sigma = \dfrac{\text{B.M.}}{Z_x}$

$$= \frac{0.6 \times 10^6}{12.27 \times 10^3} = \textbf{48.9 MPa}$$

[**Note :** $\sigma$ = 48.9 MPa is at C and D only]

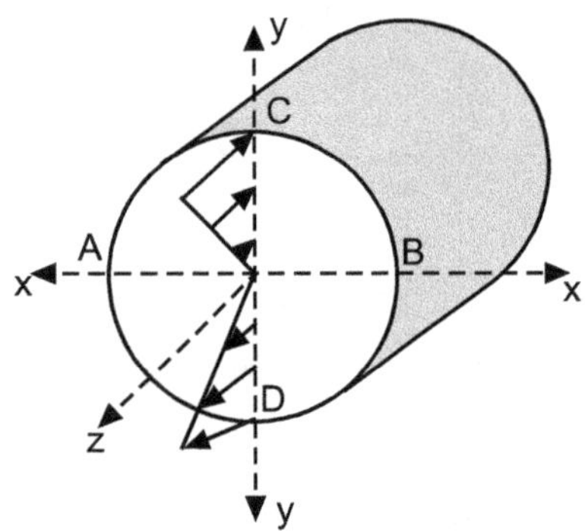

Bending compression at C.

Bending tension at D.

**Fig. 12.6 : Bending stresses**

(iv)   Analysis of stresses at elements A and B :

Out of A and B, one element will have resultant shear stress

$$= \tau_1 + \tau_2$$

$$= 57.07 + 1.36$$

$$= \textbf{58.43 MPa}$$

While other elements will have resultant shear stress

$$= \tau = -\tau_1 + \tau_2$$

$$= -57.07 + 1.36$$

$$= \mathbf{-55.71 \text{ MPa}}$$

**Note :** Because the direction of torque is not specified and position of cross-section of shaft whether on left or on right of flywheel is not defined, no comment can be made about whether the maximum shear stress is at element A or B. However, both these elements are subjected to state of pure shear.

Selecting maximum shear stress

$$\tau_{max} = \mathbf{58.43 \text{ MPa}}$$

∴  Principal stresses        $\sigma_1 = \sigma_2 = \mathbf{\pm 58.43 \text{ MPa}}$

**Note :** For element subjected to state of pure shear stress '$\tau$', principal stresses $\sigma_1 = \sigma_2 = \tau$. Out of the two, one principal stress is tensile in nature while other is compressive.

(v)    Analysis of stresses C and D.

$$\sigma_1, \sigma_2 = \frac{\sigma}{2} \pm \sqrt{\left(\frac{\sigma}{2}\right)^2 + \tau_1^2}$$

$$= \frac{48.9}{2} \pm \sqrt{\left(\frac{48.9}{2}\right)^2 + 57.07^2}$$

$$= 24.45 \pm 62.08$$

$$\sigma_1 = \mathbf{86.53 \text{ MPa}} \text{ and } \sigma_2 = \mathbf{-37.63 \text{ MPa}}$$

$$\text{Maximum shear stress} = \tau_{max} = \frac{\sigma_1 - \sigma_2}{2} = \frac{86.53 + 37.63}{2} = \mathbf{62.08 \text{ MPa}}$$

However, principal stresses at elements C and D subjected to stresses due to bending and torsion can be worked out by standard expression as ;

$$\sigma_1, \sigma_2 = \frac{16}{\pi D^3}\left(M \pm \sqrt{M^2 + T^2}\right)$$

$$= \frac{16}{\pi \times 50^3}\left(0.6 \pm \sqrt{0.6^2 + 1.4^2}\right) \times 10^6$$

$$\sigma_1 = \mathbf{86.5 \text{ MPa}} \text{ and } \sigma_2 = \mathbf{-37.6 \text{ MPa}}$$

**Note :** + ve sign of $\sigma_1$ OR $\sigma_2$ indicates that it is of the same nature as that of normal stress produced by B.M. Thus, normal stress of 86.53 MPa is compressive at 'C' and tensile at 'D' while normal stress of 37.63 MPa is tensile at 'C' and compressive at 'D' because bending moment produces compression at 'C' and tension at 'D'.

**Example 12.5 :** *A cantilever steel rod with 25 mm diameter is supporting force 'F' as shown in Fig. 12.7. Determine the maximum force 'F' that can be applied if (a) The bending stress is not to exceed 125 MPa and (b) Resultant shear stress due to bending and torsion is not to exceed 100 MPa.*

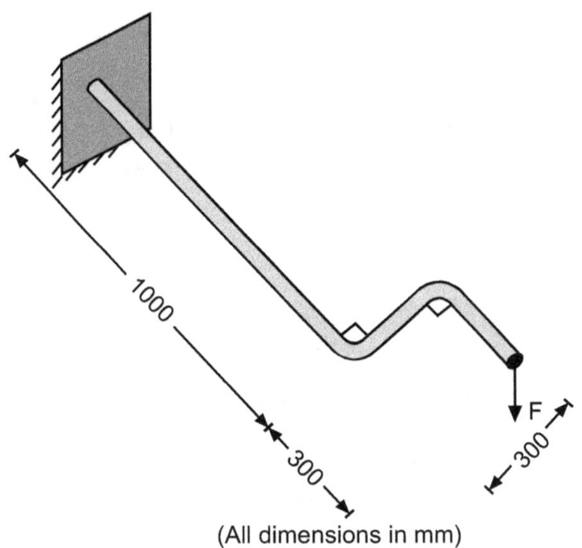



**Fig. 12.7**

**Data**      :   As shown in Fig. 12.7; bending stress ≤ 125 MPa and maximum shear stress ≤ 100 MPa.

**Required**  :   Safe value of F

**Concept**   :   Maximum bending moment is at fixed end; Bending stresses; Shear stresses due to bending and torsion.

**Solution**  :   (i) Analysis :

Let 'F' be the force in newtons.

Maximum bending moment at fixed end = **1300 F N.mm**

Maximum torque at fixed end = **300 F N.mm.**

(ii)   From bending stress criteria,

$$I_x = \frac{\pi}{64}D^4 = \frac{\pi}{64} \times 25^4 = 19.17 \times 10^3 \text{ mm}^4$$

$$y_{max} = \frac{25}{2} = 12.5 \text{ mm}$$

∴   Section modulus $= Z_x = \dfrac{I_x}{y_{max}} = \dfrac{19.17 \times 10^3}{12.5} = 1533.98 \text{ mm}^3$

$$\text{Bending stress} = \sigma = 125 = \frac{BM}{Z_x}$$

$$= \frac{1300\ F}{1533.98}$$

∴                        F  =  **147.49 N**                        ... (i)

(iii)   From resultant shear stress due to bending and torsion,

$$\tau_{max} \;=\; \frac{16}{\pi D^3}\sqrt{M^2 + T^2}$$

$$100 \;=\; \frac{16}{\pi \times 25^3}\left(\sqrt{(1300\,F)^2 + (300\,F)^2}\right)$$

$\therefore \qquad\qquad\qquad\quad F \;=\; \textbf{229.95 N} \qquad\qquad\qquad\qquad\qquad\qquad \text{... (ii)}$

$\therefore \qquad\quad$ Safe value of F $\;=\;$ Least of (i) and (ii)

$\therefore \qquad\quad$ Safe value of F $\;=\;$ **147.49 N**

---

**Example 12.6 :** *A solid circular shaft 20 mm $\phi$ is loaded as shown in Fig. 12.8.*

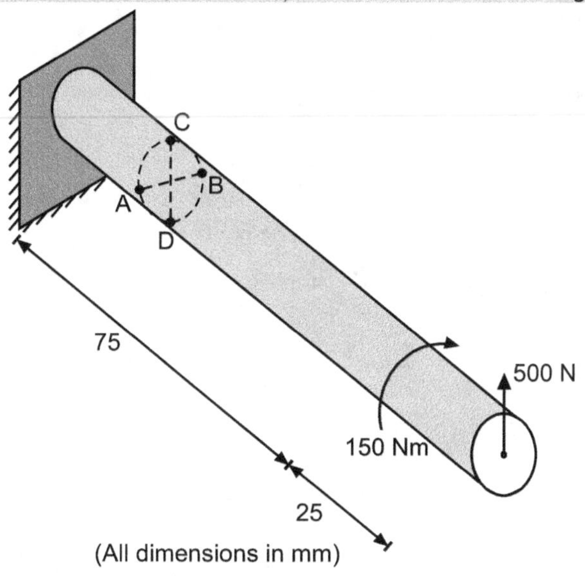


**Fig. 12.8**

Determine (i) Maximum shear stress on horizontal diameter AB and (ii) Principal stresses at element C of vertical diameter.

**Data**      :   As shown in Fig. 12.8.

**Required**    :   Maximum shear stress on AB and principal stresses at element C.

**Concept**    :   Combined stresses : Normal stresses due to bending moment and shear stresses due to torque and shear force.

**Solution**    :   (i) Geometric properties :

$$A \;=\; \frac{\pi}{4}(20)^2 = 314.16 \text{ mm}^2$$

$$I_x \;=\; \frac{\pi}{64}(20)^4 = 7853.98 \text{ mm}^4$$

$$y_{max} \;=\; \frac{20}{2} = \textbf{10 mm}$$

---

$$\therefore \qquad \text{Section modulus} = Z_X = \frac{I_X}{y_{max}}$$

$$= \frac{7853.98}{10} = \mathbf{785.39 \ mm^3}$$

$$J = \frac{\pi}{32}(20)^4 = 15.71 \times 10^3 \ mm^4$$

$$\frac{J}{R} = \frac{15.71 \times 10^3}{10} = \mathbf{1.57 \times 10^3 \ mm^3}$$

(ii)   Evaluation of different stresses :

$$\text{Shear stress due to torque} = \tau_1 = \frac{T}{J/R}$$

$$= \frac{150 \times 10^3}{1.57 \times 10^3}$$

$$= \mathbf{95.54 \ MPa}$$

$$\text{Shear stress due to shear force} = \tau_2 = \frac{4}{3}\left(\frac{SF}{A}\right)$$

$$\therefore \qquad \tau_2 = \frac{4}{3} \times \frac{500}{314.16} = 2.14 \ MPa$$

Bending stresses due to B.M. ($\sigma$)

$$\sigma = \frac{B.M.}{Z_X} \ \text{where ; } \ B.M. = 500 \times 100 \ N.mm$$

$$\therefore \qquad \sigma = \frac{500 \times 100}{785.39} = \mathbf{63.66 \ MPa}$$

Compressive at C and tensile at D.

(iii)   Maximum shear stress on horizontal diameter :

$$\tau_{max} = \tau_1 + \tau_2 = 95.54 + 2.14$$

$$= \mathbf{97.68 \ MPa}$$

(iv)   Principal stresses at C, $\sigma_1, \sigma_2 = \dfrac{\sigma}{2} \pm \sqrt{\left(\dfrac{\sigma}{2}\right)^2 + \tau_1^2}$

$$= \frac{63.66}{2} \pm \sqrt{\left(\frac{63.66}{2}\right)^2 + 95.54^2}$$

$$= 31.83 \pm 100.7$$

$$\sigma_1 = \mathbf{132.53 \ MPa \ i.e. \ compressive \ at \ C.}$$

$$\sigma_2 = \mathbf{-68.87 \ MPa \ i.e. \ tensile \ at \ C.}$$

**Note :** + ve sign of $\sigma_1$ or $\sigma_2$ indicates that principal stress is of same nature as that of $\sigma$.

Principal planes :

$$\therefore \qquad \tan(2\theta_1) \;=\; \frac{2\tau_1}{\sigma} = \frac{2 \times 95.54}{63.66}$$

$$\theta_1 \;=\; \mathbf{35.78^o}$$

and

$$\theta_2 \;=\; \theta_1 + 90^o$$

$$=\; 35.78 + 90$$

$$=\; \mathbf{125.78^o}$$

**Example 12.7 :** *A solid shaft of 100 mm diameter transmits 500 kW at 500 r.p.m. and is also subjected to an axial thrust of 200 kN. If the maximum principal stress is not to exceed 100 MPa, find what additional bending moment may safely be carried ?*

**Data**      :   D = 100 mm;  Power = 500 kW;  N = 500 r.p.m.;

                 P = 200 kN;  Maximum principal stress = 100 MPa.

**Required**   :   Additional bending moment carrying capacity.

**Concept**   :   Combined stresses : Normal stresses due to bending moment and axial force and shear stresses due to torsion.

**Solution**   :   (i) Geometric properties :

$$A \;=\; \frac{\pi}{4} D^2 = \frac{\pi}{4}(100)^2 = 7.85 \times 10^3 \, mm^2$$

$$I_x \;=\; \frac{\pi}{64}(D)^4 = \frac{\pi}{64}(100)^4 = 4.91 \times 10^6 \, mm^4$$

$$y_{max} \;=\; \frac{100}{2} = 50 \, mm$$

$$Z_x \;=\; \frac{I_x}{y_{max}} = \frac{4.91 \times 10^6}{50} = 98.17 \times 10^3 \, mm^3$$

$$J \;=\; \frac{\pi}{32}(D)^4 = \frac{\pi}{32}(100)^4 = 9.82 \times 10^6 \, mm^4$$

$$\frac{J}{R} \;=\; \frac{9.82 \times 10^6}{50} = \mathbf{196.4 \times 10^3 \, mm^3}$$

(ii)     Evaluation of different stresses :

Normal stress due to axial force

$$\sigma_a \;=\; \frac{P}{A} = \frac{200 \times 10^3}{7.85 \times 10^3} = 25.48 \, MPa$$

$$Power \;=\; \frac{2\pi \, NT}{60}$$

$$500 \times 10^3 \;=\; \frac{2\pi \times 500 \times T}{60}$$

$$\therefore \qquad T \;=\; 9.55 \times 10^3 \, N.m$$

$$= 9.55 \times 10^6 \text{ N.mm}$$

$\therefore$  Shear stresses due to torque  $= \dfrac{T}{J/R}$

$$= \dfrac{9.55 \times 10^6}{196.4 \times 10^3} = 48.62 \text{ MPa}$$

(iii)  Additional maximum bending moment :

For an element subjected to normal stress in one direction and shear stress,

$$\text{Principal stresses } \sigma_1, \sigma_2 = \dfrac{\sigma}{2} \pm \sqrt{\left(\dfrac{\sigma}{2}\right)^2 + \tau^2}$$

$\therefore$  Maximum principal stress $= \sigma_1 = \dfrac{\sigma}{2} + \sqrt{\left(\dfrac{\sigma}{2}\right)^2 + \tau^2}$

$$100 = \dfrac{\sigma}{2} + \sqrt{\left(\dfrac{\sigma}{2}\right)^2 + 48.62^2}$$

$\therefore$  $\qquad\qquad\qquad\quad \sigma = \mathbf{76.36 \text{ MPa}}$

$$= \text{Stress due to axial force} +$$
$$\text{Stress due to bending moment}$$
$$= \sigma_a + \sigma_b$$
$$= \mathbf{25.48 + \sigma_b}$$

$\therefore$  $\sigma_b = 50.88$ MPa = Maximum additional normal stress.

$\therefore$  Additional maximum B.M.  $= \sigma_b \times Z_x$

$$= 50.88 \times 98.17 \times 10^3$$
$$= 4.99 \times 10^6 \text{ N.mm}$$
$$= \mathbf{4.99 \text{ kN.m}}$$

---

**Example 12.8 :** *A solid shaft in a small hydraulic turbine is 100 mm in diameter. It supports an axial compressive load of 440 kN. Determine the maximum power that will be developed at a speed of 240 r.p.m. without exceeding maximum shear stress of 70 MPa and maximum normal stress of 90 MPa.*

**Data**  :  D = 100 mm;  Axial compressive load = P = 440 kN;  N = 240 r.p.m.;

$\tau_{max}$ = 70 MPa and Maximum normal stress = 90 MPa.

**Required**  :  Safe power P.

**Concept**  :  Combined stresses : Normal stress due to axial force and shear stress due to torsion.

**Solution**  :  (i) Geometric properties :

$$A = \dfrac{\pi}{4} D^2 = \dfrac{\pi}{4} (100)^2 = 7853.98 \text{ mm}^2$$

$$J = \dfrac{\pi}{32} (D)^4 = \dfrac{\pi}{32} (100)^4 = 9.82 \times 10^6 \text{ mm}^4$$

---

$$R = \frac{100}{2} = 50 \text{ mm}$$

$$\frac{J}{R} = \frac{9.82 \times 10^6}{50}$$

$$= \mathbf{196.35 \times 10^3 \text{ mm}^3}$$

(ii)    Normal stress due to axial force ($\sigma$)

$$\sigma = \frac{P}{A} = \frac{440 \times 10^3}{7853.98} = \mathbf{56.02 \text{ MPa}}$$

(iii)   From maximum normal stress criteria,

$$\sigma_1 = \frac{\sigma}{2} + \sqrt{\left(\frac{\sigma}{2}\right)^2 + \tau^2}$$

$$90 = \frac{56.02}{2} + \sqrt{\left(\frac{56.02}{2}\right)^2 + \tau^2}$$

$$\therefore \quad \tau = \mathbf{55.3 \text{ MPa}} \qquad\qquad \text{... (i)}$$

(iv)    From maximum shear stress criteria,

$$\tau_{max} = \sqrt{\left(\frac{\sigma}{2}\right)^2 + \tau^2}$$

$$70 = \sqrt{\left(\frac{56.02}{2}\right)^2 + \tau^2}$$

$$\tau = \mathbf{64.15 \text{ MPa}} \qquad\qquad \text{... (ii)}$$

(v)     Safe torque.

Shear stress due to torque to be allowed for safety = 55.3 MPa.

(Least of (i) and (ii))

$$\therefore \quad \tau = \frac{T}{(J/R)}$$

$$55.3 = \frac{T}{196.35 \times 10^3}$$

$$\therefore \quad T = 10.86 \times 10^6 \text{ N.mm}$$

$$= \mathbf{10.86 \times 10^3 \text{ N.m}}$$

(vi)    Safe power,

$$P = \frac{2\pi NT}{60}$$

$$= \frac{2\pi \times 240 \times 10.86 \times 10^3}{60}$$

$$= 272.94 \times 10^3 \text{ W}$$

$$= \mathbf{272.94 \text{ kW}}$$

**Example 12.9 :** *The torsional pendulum shown in Fig. 12.9 consists of a circular disc of mass 60 kg suspended by a steel wire (G = 80 GPa) of length 2 m and diameter 4 mm. Calculate the maximum angle of rotation $\theta_{max}$ that the disc can have without exceeding an allowable stress in tension of 100 MPa and allowable stress in shear of 50 MPa in the wire.*

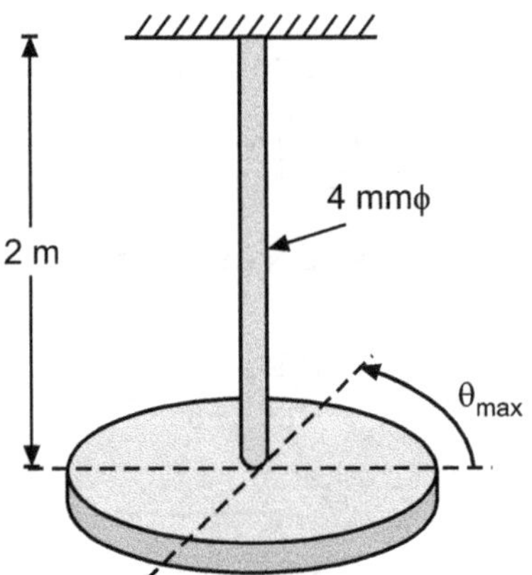


**Fig. 12.9**

**Data** : As shown in Fig. 12.9; G = 80 GPa, mass of pendulum = 60 kg. Allowable stress in tension and shear = 100 MPa and 50 MPa respectively.

**Required** : Maximum angle of rotation $\theta_{max}$.

**Concept** : Combined stresses – Normal stress due to axial force and shear stress due to torsion.

**Solution** : (i) Geometric properties of wire :

$$A = \frac{\pi}{4}(D)^2 = \frac{\pi}{4}(4)^2 = 12.57 \text{ mm}^2$$

$$J = \frac{\pi}{32}(D)^4 = \frac{\pi}{32}(4)^4 = 25.13 \text{ mm}^4$$

$$R = \frac{D}{2} = \frac{4}{2} = 2 \text{ mm}$$

$$\frac{J}{R} = \frac{25.13}{2} = \textbf{12.57 mm}^3$$

(ii)   Normal stress due to axial force ($\sigma$)

$$\sigma = \frac{P}{A} = \frac{60 \times 9.81}{12.57} = \textbf{46.83 MPa}$$

(iii)   From maximum normal stress criteria,

$$\sigma_1 = \frac{\sigma}{2} + \sqrt{\left(\frac{\sigma}{2}\right)^2 + \tau^2}$$

$$100 = \frac{46.83}{2} + \sqrt{\left(\frac{46.83}{2}\right)^2 + \tau^2}$$

$$\tau = \textbf{72.92 MPa} \qquad\qquad\qquad \text{... (i)}$$

(iv)   From maximum shear stress criteria,

$$\tau_{max} = \sqrt{\left(\frac{\sigma}{2}\right)^2 + \tau^2}$$

$$50 = \sqrt{\left(\frac{46.83}{2}\right)^2 + \tau^2}$$

$$\tau = \mathbf{44.18\ MPa} \qquad \qquad \text{... (ii)}$$

(v)  Safe torque (T) :

Shear stress due to torque to be allowed for safety = 44.18 MPa     (Least of (i) & (ii))

$$\therefore \qquad \tau = 44.18 = \frac{T}{J/R}$$

$$\therefore \qquad T = 44.18 \times 12.57 = \mathbf{555.34\ N.mm}$$

(v)  Safe angle of twist ($\theta_{max}$)

$$\frac{T}{J} = \frac{G\theta}{L}$$

$$\therefore \qquad \theta = \frac{TL}{GJ} = \frac{555.34 \times 2000}{80 \times 10^3 \times 25.13} = 0.552\ \text{rad} = \mathbf{31.63^o}$$

## 12.3 STRAIN ENERGY DUE TO TORSION

Refer to Fig. 12.10. Total strain energy of a shaft of length L, under the action of torque T is the work done in twisting i.e. for gradually applied torque,

$$U = \frac{1}{2}T\theta \qquad \qquad \text{... (12.12)}$$

Expressed in terms of maximum shear stress,

$$U = \frac{1}{2}\left(\frac{J}{R}\tau_{max}\right)\left(\frac{\tau_{max}}{R}\cdot\frac{L}{G}\right) \qquad \qquad \text{... (12.13)}$$

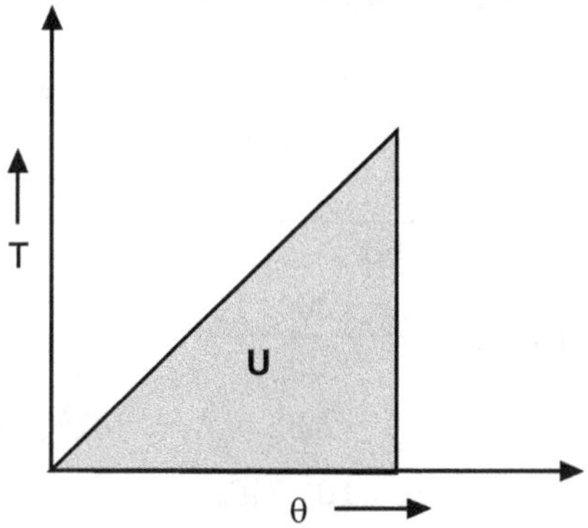

T

U

$\theta$ →

**Fig. 12.10**

(a)  For solid circular shaft,

$$U = \frac{1}{2}\left[\frac{\pi D^3}{16}\times\tau_{max}\right]\left[\frac{\tau_{max}}{D/2}\times\frac{L}{G}\right] = \frac{\tau_{max}^2}{4G}\times\frac{\pi}{4}D^2L$$

$$= \frac{\tau_{max}^2}{4G}\times(\text{Volume}) \qquad \qquad \text{... (12.14)}$$

(b)  For hollow circular shaft,

$$U = \frac{1}{2}\cdot\left[\frac{\pi}{16\ D}\cdot(D^4-d^4)\times\tau_{max}\right]\left[\frac{\tau_{max}}{D/2}\times\frac{L}{G}\right]$$

$$= \frac{\tau_{max}^2}{4G} \cdot \left[\frac{D^2 + d^2}{D^2}\right] \times (\text{Volume}) \qquad \text{... (12.15)}$$

**Example 12.10 :** *A hollow shaft subjected to a pure torque, attains maximum shear stress $\tau$. Given that strain energy per unit volume is $\tau^2/3G$.*
*(i)    Calculate the ratio of shaft diameters.*
*(ii)    Determine the actual diameters of such a shaft to transmit 4 MW at 100 r.p.m.*
*        when energy stored is 25 kN.m/m³ and G = 80 GPa.*

**Data**          :    Power = 4 MW,  N = 100 r.p.m.; U = 25 kN.m/m³,  G = 80 GPa.

**Required**   :    (i) Ratio of shaft diameters (ii) Diameter of shaft.

**Concept**    :    Strain energy due to torsion.

**Solution**    :    (i) Let, 'D' and 'd' be the external and internal diameters respectively.

From equation (12.15),

$$\frac{U}{\text{Volume}} = \frac{\tau^2}{4G}\left(\frac{D^2}{D^2 + d^2}\right) = \frac{\tau^2}{3G}$$

$$\therefore \qquad \frac{D^2 + d^2}{D^2} = \frac{4}{3}$$

$$\therefore \qquad 1 + \frac{d^2}{D^2} = \frac{4}{3}$$

$$\frac{d}{D} = \sqrt{\frac{1}{3}}$$

$$\therefore \qquad \frac{D}{d} = \mathbf{1.732}$$

(ii)    Diameters of shaft,    $P = 4 \text{ MW} = 4 \times 10^6 \text{ N.m/sec}$

$$N = 100 \text{ r.p.m.}$$

$$P = \frac{2\pi\, NT_a}{60}$$

$$4 \times 10^6 = \frac{2\pi \times 100 \times T_a}{60}$$

$$T_a = 381971.86 \text{ N.m} = 381971.86 \times 10^3 \text{ N.mm}$$

Also, it is given that,    $G = 80 \times 10^3 \text{ MPa}$

Energy stored $= 25 \text{ kN.m/m}^3 = 25 \times 10^{-3} \text{ N.mm/mm}^3$

i.e. 
$$\frac{\tau^2}{3G} = 25 \times 10^{-3}$$

$$\frac{\tau^2}{3 \times 80 \times 10^3} = 25 \times 10^{-3}$$

$$\tau = \mathbf{77.46 \text{ MPa}}$$

Using 
$$\frac{T}{J} = \frac{\tau}{R}$$

$$\frac{J}{R} = \frac{T}{\tau} = \frac{381971.86 \times 10^3}{77.46} = \mathbf{4931214.3 \text{ mm}^3}$$

$$\therefore \qquad \frac{J}{R} = \frac{\pi}{16\,D}\,(D^4 - d^4) = 4931214.3$$

$$\frac{\pi}{16 \times 1.732\,d}\,[(1.732\,d)^4 - d^4] = 4931214.3$$

$$d = \mathbf{175.85\ mm}$$

$$D = \mathbf{304.57\ mm}$$

## 12.4  THEORIES OF FAILURE

Following are the theories of failure adopted for design of structural members.

**(i)     Maximum principal stress theory :** As per this theory, maximum principal stress shall not exceed the working stress for the material. i.e. $\sigma_1 \le \sigma_{safe}$. This theory is known as Rankine's theory.

**(ii)     Maximum principal strain theory :** If $\sigma_1$ and $\sigma_2$ are the principal stresses at a point in the strained material, the major principal strain is given by

$$\epsilon_1 = \frac{1}{E}\,(\sigma_1 - \mu\,\sigma_2)$$

Let $\sigma$ be the stress which acting alone produces the same principal strain, then

$$\frac{\sigma}{E} = \frac{1}{E}\,(\sigma_1 - \mu\,\sigma_2)$$

$$\therefore \qquad \sigma = \sigma_1 - \mu\,\sigma_2$$

The criteria of design will therefore be

$$\sigma = \sigma_1 - \mu\,\sigma_2 \le \sigma_{safe}$$

This theory was given by St. Venant.

**(iii)     Maximum shear stress theory :** If $\sigma_1$ and $\sigma_2$ are the principal stresses, maximum shear stress

$$\tau_{max} = \frac{\sigma_1 - \sigma_2}{2}$$

This maximum shear stress shall not exceed the working stress in shear for the material i.e. $\tau_{max} \le \tau_{safe}$. This theory was given by Sir J. J. Guest.

**(iv)     Maximum strain energy theory :** If $\sigma_1$ and $\sigma_2$ are the principal stresses then the strain energy stored per unit volume

$$= \frac{1}{2\,E}\left(\sigma_1^2 + \sigma_2^2 - 2\,\mu\,\sigma_1\sigma_2\right)$$

Let $\sigma$ be the stress acting alone, to store the same amount of strain energy per unit volume, then

$$\frac{\sigma^2}{2E} = \frac{1}{2E}\left(\sigma_1^2 + \sigma_2^2 - 2\,\mu\,\sigma_1\sigma_2\right)$$

$$\therefore \qquad \sigma = \sqrt{\sigma_1^2 + \sigma_2^2 - 2\,\mu\,\sigma_1\sigma_2} \le \sigma_{safe}$$

This theory was given by Beltrami and Haigh.

**Example 12.11 :** *A member, solid circular in cross-section is subjected to an axial pull of 13 kN and a shear force of 5 kN. Design the cross section of member based on (i) the maximum principal stress theory, (ii) the maximum principal strain theory, (iii) the maximum shear stress theory, (iv) the maximum strain energy theory. For the material of member, elastic limit in axial tension is 250 MPa, Poisson's ratio = 0.3. Use factor of safety = 2.5.*

**Data**      :   Axial pull = 13 kN, Shear force = 5 kN, Elastic limit in axial tension
                  = 250 MPa, $\mu$ = 0.3, Factor of safety = 2.5.

**Required**  :   Design of cross-section based on various theories of failure.

**Concept**   :   Failure theories.

**Solution**  :   (i) Geometric properties and allowable stresses :

Let 'a' be the cross-sectional area of member in mm$^2$.

$$\text{Safe stress in axial tension} = \sigma_{safe} = \frac{250}{2.5} = 100 \text{ MPa}$$

$$\text{Safe stress in shear} = \tau_{safe} = \frac{100}{2} = \textbf{50 MPa.}$$

(ii)   Maximum principal stress theory,

$$\text{Direct stress on cross-section} = \sigma = \frac{P}{A} = \frac{13 \times 10^3}{a} \text{ MPa}$$

$$\text{Shear stress on cross-section} = \tau = \frac{SF}{A} = \frac{5 \times 10^3}{a} \text{ MPa}$$

Principal stresses are,

$$\sigma_1, \sigma_2 = \frac{\sigma}{2} \pm \sqrt{\left(\frac{\sigma}{2}\right)^2 + \tau^2}$$

$$= \frac{13 \times 10^3}{2a} \pm \sqrt{\left(\frac{13 \times 10^3}{2a}\right)^2 + \left(\frac{5 \times 10^3}{a}\right)^2} = \frac{6500}{a} \pm \frac{8200.6}{a}$$

$$\therefore \quad \sigma_1 = \frac{14700.6}{a} \text{ MPa}$$

$$\sigma_2 = -\frac{1700.6}{a} \text{ MPa}$$

As per this theory ;           $\sigma_1 \leq \sigma_{safe}$

$$\therefore \quad \frac{14700.6}{a} \leq 100$$

$$\therefore \quad a \geq 147 \text{ mm}^2$$

$$\therefore \quad \text{Diameter of the cross-section} = d = \sqrt{\frac{4 \times 147}{\pi}} = \textbf{13.68 mm}$$

(iii)   Maximum principal strain theory :

Let, $\sigma$ be the stress alone which produces same maximum strain.

$$\sigma = \sigma_1 - \mu \, \sigma_2 = \frac{14700.6}{a} - 0.3\left(-\frac{1700.6}{a}\right) = \frac{15210.78}{a} \text{ MPa}$$

As per this theory ;        $\sigma \leq \sigma_{safe}$ i.e. $\dfrac{15210.78}{a} \leq 100$

$$\therefore \quad a \geq 152.1 \text{ mm}^2$$

$\therefore$     Diameter of the cross-section $= d = \sqrt{\dfrac{4 \times 152.1}{\pi}} = $ **13.91 mm**

(iv)    Maximum shear stress theory,

$$\tau_{max} = \frac{\sigma_1 - \sigma_2}{2} = \frac{1}{2}\left[\frac{14700.6}{a} - \left(\frac{-1700.6}{a}\right)\right] = \frac{8200.6}{a} \text{ MPa}$$

As per this theory ; $\tau_{max} \leq \tau_{safe}$

$\therefore$          $\dfrac{8200.6}{a} \leq 50$

$\therefore$          $a \geq 164.01 \text{ mm}^2$

$\therefore$     Diameter of the cross-section $= d = \sqrt{\dfrac{4 \times 164.01}{\pi}} = $ **14.45 mm**

(v)    Maximum strain energy theory.

Strain energy stored per unit volume

$$= \frac{1}{2E}\left(\sigma_1^2 + \sigma_2^2 - 2\mu\,\sigma_1\,\sigma_2\right)$$

$$= \frac{1}{2E}\left[\left(\frac{14700.6}{a}\right)^2 + \left(-\frac{1700.6}{a}\right)^2 - 2 \times 0.3\left(\frac{14700.6}{a}\right)\left(-\frac{1700.6}{a}\right)\right]$$

$$= \frac{116.99 \times 10^6}{a^2 E}$$

As per this theory ; $\dfrac{1}{2E}\left(\sigma_1^2 + \sigma_2^2 - 2\mu\,\sigma_1\,\sigma_2\right) \leq \dfrac{\sigma_{safe}^2}{2E}$

$$\frac{116.99 \times 10^6}{a^2 E} \leq \frac{100^2}{2E}$$

$\therefore$          $a \geq 152.97 \text{ mm}^2$

$\therefore$     Diameter of the cross-section $= d = \sqrt{\dfrac{4 \times 152.97}{\pi}} = $ **13.95 mm**

**Example 12.12 :** *A square pin is required to resist a pull of 40 kN and shear force at 15 kN. Derive a suitable section according to strain energy theory. Maximum tensile stress is 350 MPa and Poisson's ratio is 0.3. Adopt a factor of safety of 2.5.*      **(May 2007)**

**Data :** Axial pull = 40 kN, shear force = 15 kN, Elastic limit in axial tension = 350 MPa, $\mu = 0.3$ and F.S. = 2.5.

**Required :** Required section.

**Concept :** Failure theory.

**Solution :** (i) Geometric properties and allowable stresses :

Let 'a' be the cross-section and x be the side of square cross-section.

Safe stress in axial tension $= \dfrac{350}{2.5} = 140$ MPa.

Let $\sigma$ be the stress,

$\therefore$       $\sigma_1, \sigma_2 = \dfrac{\sigma}{2} \pm \sqrt{\left(\dfrac{\sigma}{2}\right)^2 + \tau_{xy}^2}$

$$\sigma_1, \sigma_2 = \frac{40000}{2x^2} \pm \sqrt{\left(\frac{40000}{2x^2}\right)^2 + \left(\frac{15000}{x^2}\right)^2}$$

$$= \frac{20000}{x^2} \pm \sqrt{\left(\frac{20000}{x^2}\right)^2 + \left(\frac{15000}{x^2}\right)^2} = \frac{20000 \pm 25000}{x^2}$$

$$\therefore \qquad \sigma_1 = \frac{45000}{x^2}$$

$$\text{and} \qquad \sigma_2 = \frac{-5000}{x^2}$$

$$\therefore \qquad \sigma^2 = \sigma_1^2 - 2\,\mu\,\sigma_1\,\sigma_2 + \sigma_2^2$$

$$\therefore \qquad 140^2 = \left(\frac{45000}{x^2}\right)^2 - 2 \times 0.3 \left(\frac{45000}{x^2}\right)\left(\frac{-5000}{x^2}\right) + \left(\frac{5000}{x^2}\right)^2$$

$$140^2 = \frac{2.025 \times 10^9}{x^4} + \frac{135 \times 10^6}{x^4} + \frac{25 \times 10^6}{x^4}$$

$$\therefore \qquad x = \mathbf{18.27\ mm}$$

## EXERCISE

1.  A propeller shaft of 240 mm external diameter and 180 mm internal diameter has to transmit 1000 kW at 100 r.p.m. It is additionally subjected to bending moment of 10 kN/m and an end thrust of 200 kN. Determine : (i) principal stresses and their planes, (ii) maximum shear stress.($\sigma_1$ = 62.94 MPa (compressive),

    $\sigma_2$ = 42.05 MPa (tensile), $\theta_1$ = 39.26°, $\theta_2$ = 129.26°, $Z_{max}$ = 52.49 MPa)

2.  A propeller shaft 200 mm in diameter transmits 2250 kW at 240 rev/min. The propeller weighing 50 kN is carried by the shaft overhanging the support by 400 mm. If the propeller thrust is 150 kN, calculate the maximum direct stress induced in the cross-section of the propeller shaft.    ($\tau$ = 74 N/mm$^2$)

3.  A solid shaft 127 mm diameter transmits 600 kW at 300 r.p.m. It is also subjected to a bending moment of 9.1 kN/m and an end thrust. If the maximum principal stress is limited to 77 N/mm$^2$, find the end thrust.    (End thrust = 39 kN)

4.  In a shaft subjected to bending moment and twisting moment, the greater principal stress is numerically 5 times the lesser one. Find the ratio of M : T and the angle which the plane of greater principal stresses makes with plane of bending stress.    ($2\sqrt{5}$ , 24°5')

5.  At a certain section of a shaft of 80 mm diameter, there is a bending moment of 35 kN.m and a twisting moment of 50 kN.m. Determine the principal stresses and the plane where they act.($\sigma_1$ = 95.5 N/mm$^2$ (compression),

    $\sigma_2$ = 26.0 N/mm$^2$ (tension), $\theta_1$ = 27°30' and $\theta_2$ = 117° 30')

6.  A mild steel bar 50 mm square in section and 150 mm long is subjected to an axial compressive force of 150 kN. Half the lateral strain is prevented by application of uniform external pressure of suitable intensity. If E = 200 GPa, $\mu$ = 0.3, calculate the change in length of bar.    (0.0392 mm, decrease)

7.  A bolt is under an axial thrust of 9.6 kN together with a transverse shear force of 4.8 kN. Calculate its diameter according to (i) maximum principal stress theory; (ii) maximum shear stress theory. Assume factor of safety = 3; yield strength of material of bolt = 270 MPa and Poisson's ratio, $\mu$ = 0.3.    ((i) 12.8 mm, (ii) 13.8 mm)

## UNIVERSITY QUESTION PAPERS

### MAY 2014

1. An axial pull of 20 kN along with a shear force of 15 kN is applied to a circular bar of 20 mm diameter. The elastic limit of the bar material is 230 MPa and the Poisson's ratio, $\mu = 0.3$. **[6]**

   Determine the factor of safety against failure based on

   (a) Maximum shear stress theory.

   (b) Maximum strain energy theory.

   (c) Maximum principal strain energy theory.

   (d) Maximum shear strain energy theory.

2. A solid circular shaft is subjected to a bending moment of 40 kN-m and a torque of 10 kN-m. Design the diameter of the shaft according to **[6]**

   (i) Maximum principal stress theory

   (ii) Maximum shear stress theory

   (iii) Maximum strain energy theory

   Take $\mu = 0.25$, stress at elastic limit = 200 N/mm$^2$ and factor of safety = 2.

### DECEMBER 2014

1. A cylindrical steel shell is subjected to an internal pressure of 5.6 MPa. The mean radius of the cylinder is 325 mm and thickness is 12 mm. If the material has a yield point of 300 MPa, determine the factor of safety using : **[13]**
   (a) The maximum normal stress theory, and
   (b) The von mises theory.

### MAY 2015

1. A solid circular shaft is subjected to a bending moment of 8 kNm and a torque of 12 kNm. In a uniaxial test the shaft material gave the following results : Modulus of elasticity = 200 GN/m$^2$, Stress at yield point = 300 N/mm$^2$, Poisson's ratio = 0.3, Factor of safety = 3. Estimate the least diameter of the shaft using : (i) Maximum principal stress theory (ii) Maximum principal strain theory and (iii) Shear strain energy theory. **[13]**

### November 2015

1. A solid circular shaft made from plain carbon steel with a yield point of 250 MPa is subjected to peak bending moment of 530 N-m due to transverse loading and twisting moment of 600 N-m. For a factor of safety of 3 determine required diameter of the shaft using :

(a)  Maximum Normal Stress Theory
(b) Maximum Shear Stress Theory and
(c)  Maximum Strain Energy Theory.                                                    **[13]**

## May 2016

1.  A bolt is subjected to an axial pull of 40 kN and  a transverse shear force of 15 kN. Determine the diameter of the bolt required based on:

    (i)    Maximum principal stress theory

    (ii)   Maximum shear stress theory

    (iii)  Maximum strain energy theory.

    Take elastic limit in simple tension is equal to 350 MPa and Posisson's ratio = 0.3. Assume FOS = 2.5.                                                                **[6]**

2.  According to the theory of maximum shear stress, determine the diameter of a bolt which is subjected to an axial pull of 9 kN together with a transverse shear force of 4.5 kN. Elastic limit in tension is 225 N/mm$^2$, factor of safety = 3 and Poisson's ration = 0.3                                                                          **[6]**

◈ ◈ ◈

# SAMPLE QUESTION PAPER - I
## End Sem (Theory) Examination

**Time : 2 Hours**          **Max. Marks : 50**

(1) Answer four questions out of eight.
(2) Solve Q. 1 or Q. 2, Q. 3 or Q. 4, Q. 5 or Q. 6, Q. 7 or Q. 8.
(3) All the four questions should be solved in one answer book and attach extra supplements if required.
(4) Draw diagrams wherever necessary.
(5) Use of scientific calculator is allowed.
(6) Assume suitable data wherever necessary.

**1. (a)** Determine the reactions, at supports for the composite bar as shown in fig. 1    **[6]**

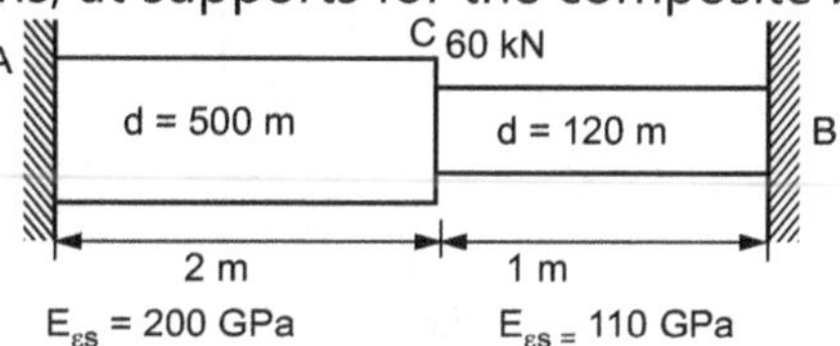


**Fig. 1**

**(b)** Draw S.F.D. and BMD for beam loaded and supported and shown in fig. 2    **[6]**

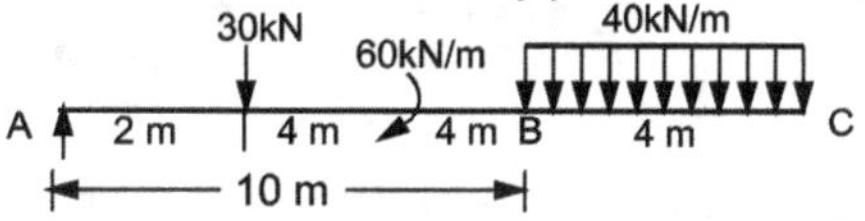


**Fig. 2**          **OR**

**2. (a)** Two vertical Rod are attached to bar as shown in fig. 3 determine position of force 5 kN from steel rod so that bar remains horizontal.    **[6]**

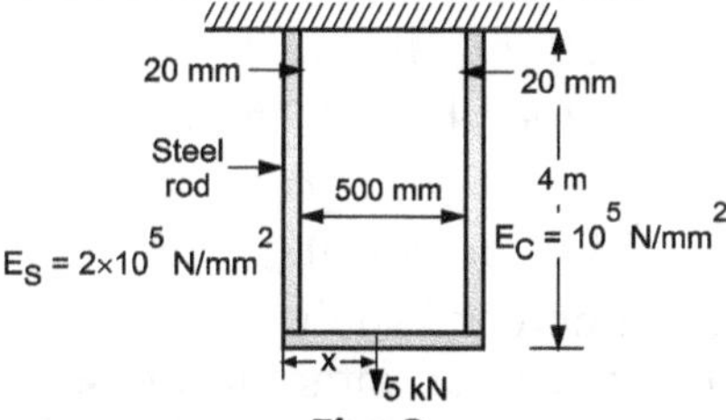


**Fig. 3**

**(b)** Draw SFD and BMD for beam loaded and supported as shown in fig. 4    **[6]**

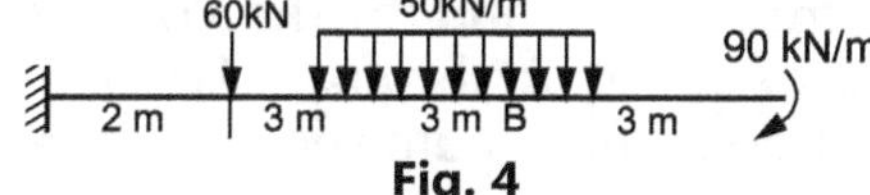


**Fig. 4**

**3. (a)** Draw bending stress distribution diagram for cross section as shown in fig. 5 take B.M. = 50 kN-m.    **[6]**

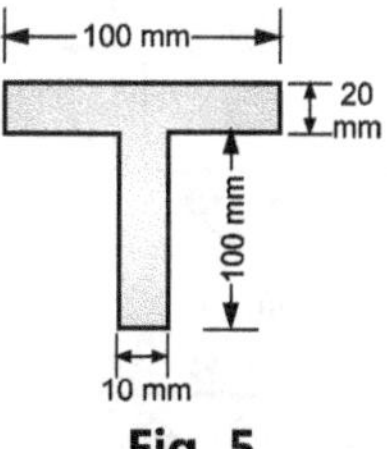


**Fig. 5**

---

**(b)** Determine deflection at free end for beam loaded and supported as shown in fig. 6 **[6]**

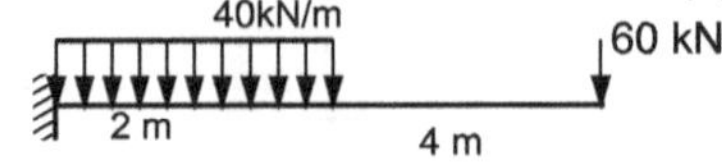


**Fig. 6**                                                                                  **OR**

**4. (a)** Maximum B.M. of a simply supported beam is 15 kNm. The cross section is shown in fig. 7 Draw bending stress distribution diagram.                                    **[6]**

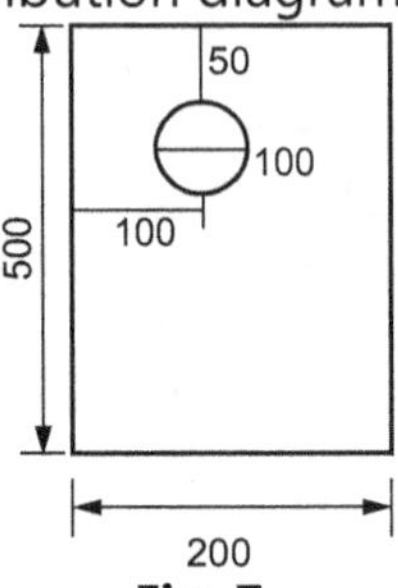


**Fig. 7**

**(b)** Determine maximum deflection for beam loaded and supported as shown in fig.8 **[6]**

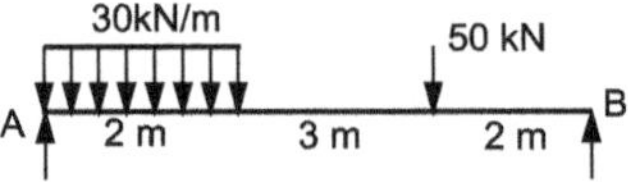


**Fig. 8**

**5. (a)** Derive the Euler's expression for column with both ends hinged.                    **[6]**

**(b)** A solid steal shaft of 80 mm diameter is to replacing by hollow steel shaft of the same material with internal diameter equal to half of the external diameter. Find the diameter of the diameter of the hollow shaft and saving in material if the maximum allowable shear sterss is same for both shafts.                                    **[7] OR**

**6. (a)** Determine the crippling load for a hollow circular cast iron column of outer diameter 100 mm and thickness 10 mm. Height of column is 7 m and both ends are fixed.   **[6]**

**(b)** A solid shaft transmits 225 kW power at 120 rpm. The allowable shearing stress is 100 MPa. Determine the diameter of shaft.                                    **[7]**

**7.**     A cylindrical sheel is subjected to an internal pressure of 8 MPa. The mean radius of cylinder is 350 mm and thickness is 19 mm. If Iy 320 MPa, determine the factor of safty using.                                                                    **[13]**
The maximum normal stress theory and (b) The Von mises theory                    **OR**

**8.**     A material is subjected to stress as shown in fig. 8 Determine the magnitude and nature of the principal stresses, maximum shear stress and angle of obliquity.    **[13]**

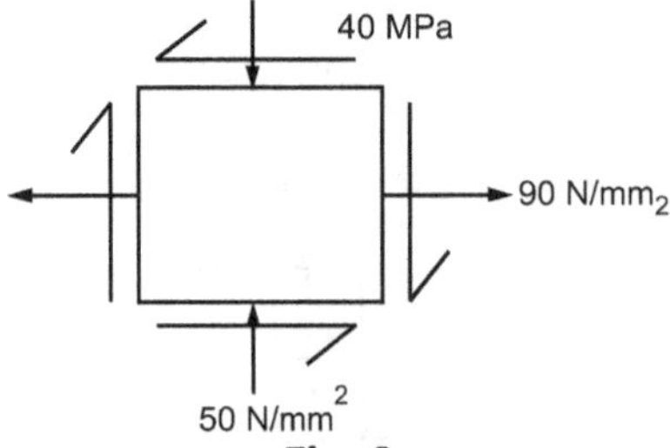


**Fig. 9**

◈ ◈ ◈

# SAMPLE QUESTION PAPER - II
### End Sem (Theory) Examination

**Time : 2 Hours**                                    **Max. Marks : 50**

**1. (a)** A bar of metal 100 mm × 50 mm in cross-section is 250 mm long. It carries a tensile load of 400 kN in the direction of its length, a compressive load of 4000 kN on its 100 mm × 250 mm faces and a tensile load of 2000 kN on its 50 mm × 250 mm faces. If $E = 2 \times 10^5$ N/mm$^2$ and Poisson's ratio is 0.25, find the change in volume of the bar.   **[6]**

**(b)** Draw SFD and BMD for the beam loaded as shown in the Fig. 1 below :   **[6]**

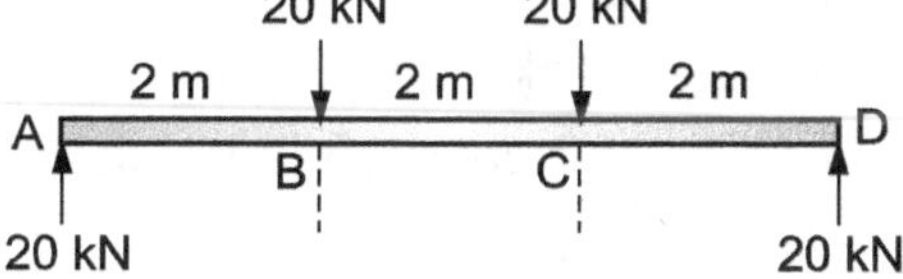


**Fig. 1**                                              **OR**

**2. (a)** An aluminum rod is rigidity attached between a steel rod and a bronze rod as shown in the Fig. 2. Axial loads are applied at the positions indicated. Find the maximum value of P that will not exceed a stress in steel of 140 MPa, in aluminum of 90 MPa, or in bronze of 100 MPa.   **[6]**

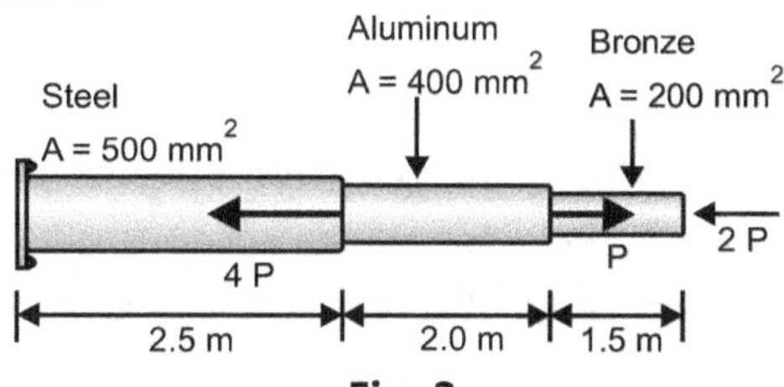


**Fig. 2**

**(b)** Draw SFD and BMD for the beam loaded as shown in Fig. 3 below.   **[6]**

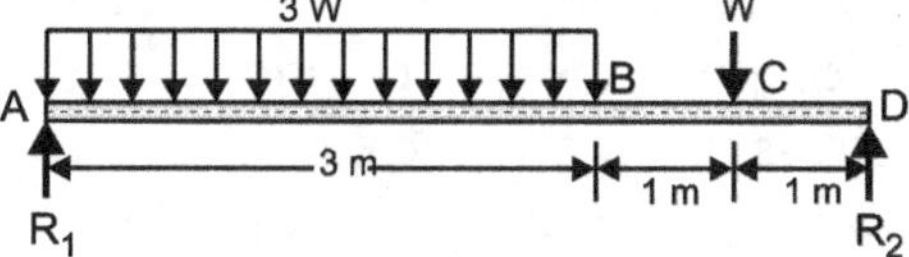


**Fig. 3**

**3. (a)** A rectangular steel bar, 15 mm wide by 30 mm high and 6 m long, is simply supported at its ends. If the density of steel is 7850 kg/m$^3$, determine the maximum bending stress caused by the self-weight of the bar.   **[6]**

**(b)** A cantilever beam, 60 mm wide by 100 mm high and 2 m long, carries UDL of 3000 N/m over entire span. find the maximum deflection and slope (in radians) of the beam. Take E = 210 GPa.   **[6] OR**

**4. (a)** A cantilever beam, 60 mm wide by 100 mm high and 2 m long, carries UDL of 3000 N/m over entire span. determine the type and magnitude of the stress in a fiber 20 mm from the top of the beam at fixed end.   **[6]**

**(b)** A horizontal cantilever of uniform section of length L carries two point loads W at the free end and 2 W at a distance of 'a' from the free end. Find the maximum deflection due to this loading. **[6]**

**5. (a)** A hollow, shaft, having an internal diameter 40% of its external diameter, transmits, 562.5 kW power at 100 r.p.m. Determine the external diameter of the shaft if the shear stress is not exceed 60 N/mm$^2$ and the twist in a length of 2.5 m should not exceed 1.3 degrees. Assume maximum torque = 1.25 mean torque and modulus of rigidity = $9 \times 10^4$ N/mm$^2$. **[6]**

**(b)** Determine the buckling load for a strut of tee section, the flange width being 100 mm, overall depth 80 mm and both flange and stem 10 mm thick. The strut is 3 m long and is hinged at both ends. Take E = 200 GN/m$^2$. **[7] OR**

**6. (a)** Following Fig. 4 shows a stepped steel shaft. It is subjected to a torque 'T' at the free end and a torque '2T' in the opposite direction at the junction of the two sizes. Determine the total angle of twist, if the maximum shear stress is limited to 80 MPa. Take G = 80 GPa. **[6]**

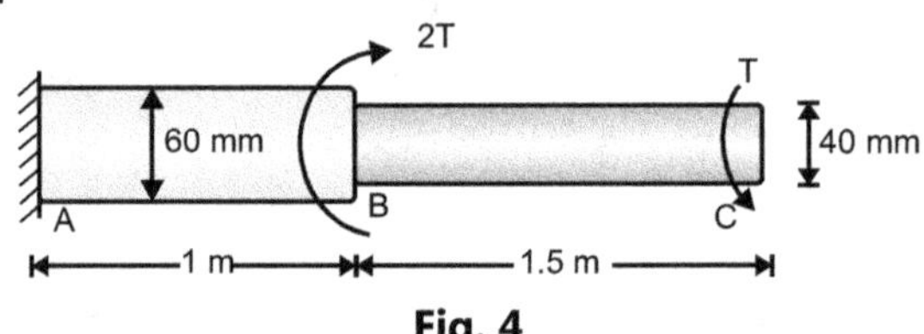


**Fig. 4**

**(b)** A hollow cylindrical cast iron column is 4 m long, both end fixed. Design the column to carry an axial load of 250 kN. Use Rankine's formula and adopt a factor of safety of 5. The internal diameter may be taken as 0.8 times the external diameter. Take $F_c$ = 550 N/mm$^2$ and $\alpha$ = 1/1600. **[7]**

**7.** Stressed element in a machine component is subjected to 175 MPa tensile stress in x-direction, 50 MPa compressive stress in y-direction and 70 MPa shear stress clockwise on x-face. Compute the values and orientation of the principal stresses and maximum shear stress using graphical method proposed by Mohr. Mohr's circle must be drawn on GRAPH paper using appropriate scale. (Note : Analytical solution and solution without GRAPH paper will not be evaluated.) **[13] OR**

**8.** A solid circular shaft made from plain carbon steel with a yield point of 250 MPa is subjected to peak bending moment of 520 N-m due to transverse loading and twisting moment of 500 N-m. For a factor of safety of 3 determine required diameter of the shaft using : **[13**

(a) Maximum Normal Stress Theory

(b) Maximum Strain Energy Theory

(c) Maximum Shear Stress Theory

## UNIVERSITY QUESTION PAPERS

### MAY 2014

**Time : 2 Hours**                                                          **Max. Marks : 50**

**Instructions :**

    (1)  Answer four questions out of 8.

           Solve Q. 1 or Q. 2, Q. 3 or Q. 4, Q. 5 or Q. 6, Q. 7 or Q. 8.

    (2)  All the four questions should be solved in one answer book and attach extra supplements if required.

    (3)  Draw diagrams wherever necessary.

    (4)  Use of scientific calculator is allowed.

    (5)  Assume suitable data wherever necessary.

---

**1.** **(a)** A bar of metal 100 mm × 50 mm in cross-section is 250 mm long. It carries a tensile load of 400 kN in the direction of its length, a compressive load of 4000 kN on its 100 mm × 250 mm faces and a tensile load of 2000 kN on its 50 mm × 250 mm faces. If E = $2 \times 10^5$ N/mm$^2$ and Poisson's ratio is 0.25, find the change in volume of the bar. **[6]**

    **(b)** A beam AB 10 meters long has supports at its ends A and B. It carries a point load of 5 kN at 3 meters from A and a point load of 5 kN at 7 meters from A and a uniformly distributed load of 1 kN per meter between the point loads. Draw SF and BM diagrams for the beam. **[6] OR**

**2.** **(a)** A steel rod of 30 mm diameter is enclosed in a brass tube of 42 mm external diameter and 32 mm internal diameter. Each is 360 mm long and the assembly is rigidly held between two stops 360 mm apart. The temperature of the assembly is then raised by 50°C. Determine:

    (i)  Stresses in the tube and the rod

    (ii)  Stresses in the tube and the rod, if the stops yields by 0.15 mm.

    $E_s$ = 205 GPa,             $E_b$ = 90 GPa

    $\alpha_s$ = $11 \times 10^{-6}$ per°C,    $\alpha_b$ = $19 \times 10^{-6}$ per°C                 **[6]**

    **(b)** Draw SF and BM diagrams for the beam ABCDE shown in following Fig. 1.     **[6]**

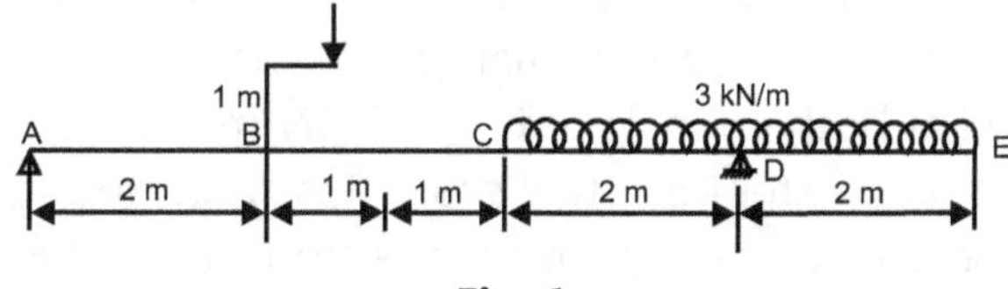


**Fig. 1**

---

P.1

**3. (a)** A cast iron pipe of internal diameter 450 mm is 15 mm thick and is supported on a span of 8 m. Find the maximum bending stress in the pipe when it is full of water. Take specific weight of cast iron = 71600 $N/m^3$ and that of water = 9810 $N/m^3$.

**(b)** Compare the strain energy stored in the two bars of the same material shown in following Fig. 2, if gradually applied load is same. **[6]**

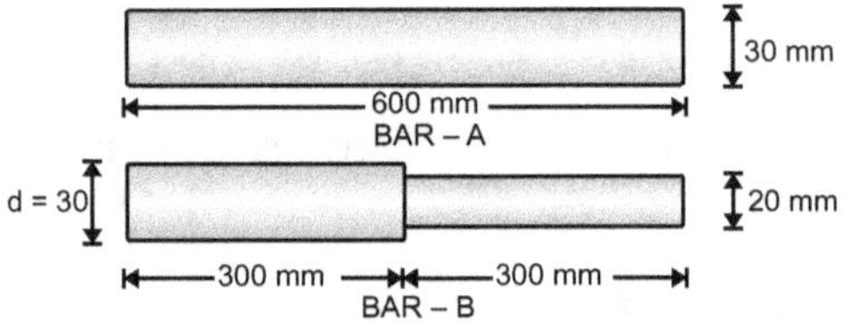


**Fig. 2**                                                                    **OR**

**4. (a)** A horizontal beam of the section shown in following Fig. 3 is 3 m long and is simply supported at the ends. Find the maximum uniformly distributed load it can carry, if the compressive and tensile stresses must not exceed 55 $N/mm^2$ and 30 $N/mm^2$ respectively. **[6]**

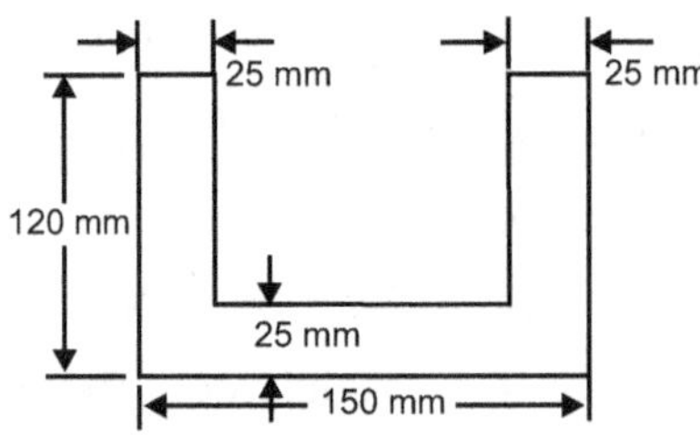


**Fig. 3**

**(b)** Following Fig. 4 shows a simply supported beam of uniform section whose moment of inertia is $4.3 \times 10^8$ $mm^4$. For the loading shown, find the position and magnitude of the maximum deflection. Take E = 200 $kN/mm^2$. **[6]**

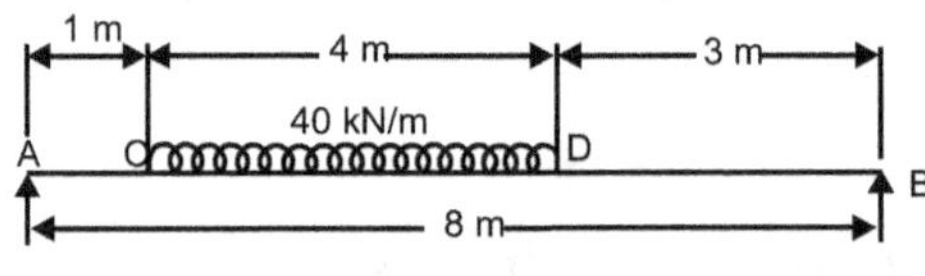


**Fig. 4**

**5. (a)** Compare the weights of equal lengths of a solid and a hollow shaft to transit a given torque for the same maximum stress, if the inside diameter of the shaft is three fourth of the outside. **[6]**

**(b)** Determine the buckling load for a strut of tee section, the flange width being 100 mm, overall depth 80 mm and both flange and stem 10 mm thick. The strut is 3 m long and is hinged at both ends. Take E = 200 $GN/m^2$. **[7] OR**

**6. (a)** Following Fig. 5 shows a stepped steel shaft. It is subjected to a torque 'T' at the free end and a torque '2T' in the opposite direction at the junction of the two sizes.

Determine the total angle of twist, if the maximum shear stress is limited to 80 MPa. Take G = 80 GPa. **[6]**

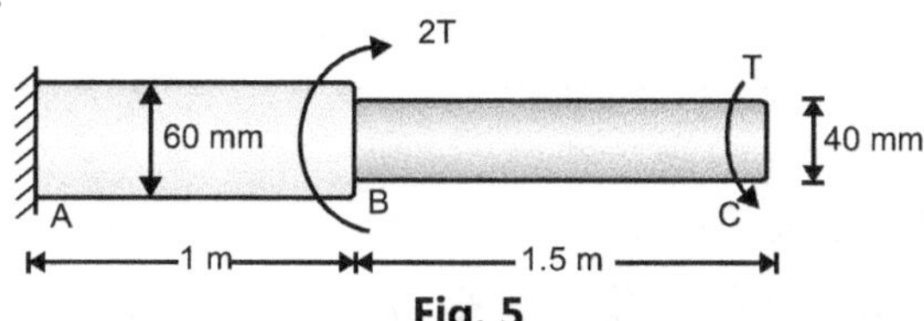


**Fig. 5**

**(b)** A straight cylindrical bar of 15 mm diameter and 1.2 m long is freely supported at its two ends in a horizontal position. It is loaded with a concentrated load of 100 N at the centre when the centre deflection is observed to be 5 mm. If placed in the vertical position and loaded vertically, what load would cause it to buckle? Also find the ratio of the maximum stress in the two cases. **[7]**

**7. (a)** An axial pull of 20 kN along with a shear force of 15 kN is applied to a circular bar of 20 mm diameter. The elastic limit of the bar material is 230 MPa and the Poisson's ratio, $\mu = 0.3$. **[6]**

Determine the factor of safety against failure based on

(a) Maximum shear stress theory.

(b) Maximum strain energy theory.

(c) Maximum principal strain energy theory.

(d) Maximum shear strain energy theory.

**(b)** In a 2D stress system, stresses at a point in a material are 50 MPa compression and 30 MPa shearing in one plane and 20 MPa tensile and a shearing stress in another plane at 60° to the first one. Determine the value of the shearing stress in the second plane and the principal stresses and position of their planes. Use analytical methos.**[7]**

**OR**

**8. (a)** A solid circular shaft is subjected to a bending moment of 40 kN-m and a torque of 10 kN-m. Design the diameter of the shaft according to **[6]**

(i)  Maximum principal stress theory

(ii) Maximum shear stress theory

(iii) Maximum strain energy theory

Take $\mu = 0.25$, stress at elastic limit = 200 N/mm$^2$ and factor of safety = 2.

**(b)** The stresses on two perpendicular planes through a point in a body are 30 MPa and 15 MPa both tensile along with shear stress of 25 MPa. Find : **[7]**

(i)  Magnitude and direction of principal stresses

(ii) Maximum shear stress and their planes

(iii) Normal and shear stresses on the planes of maximum shearing stress

Use Mohr's circle method.

## DECEMBER 2014

**Time : 2 Hours**                                                        **Max. Marks : 50**

**Instructions :**

(1) Answer four questions out of 8.

   Solve Q. 1 or Q. 2, Q. 3 or Q. 4, Q. 5 or Q. 6, Q. 7 or Q. 8.

(2) All the four questions should be solved in one answer book and attach extra supplements if required.

(3) Draw diagrams wherever necessary.

(4) Use of scientific calculator is allowed.

(5) Assume suitable data wherever necessary.

1.  **(a)** A homogeneous 800 kg bar AB is supported at either end by a cable as shown in Fig. 1. Calculate the smallest area of each cable if the stress is not to exceed 90 MPa in bronze and 120 MPa in steel.                                              **[6]**

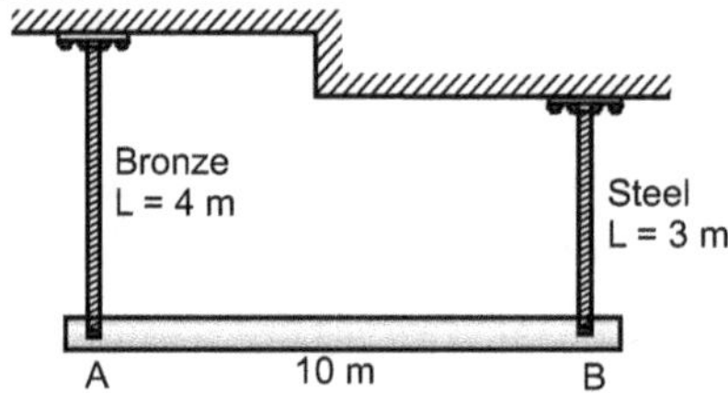


**Fig. 1**

**(b)** Draw SFD and BMD for the beam loaded as shown in the Fig. 2 below :          **[6]**

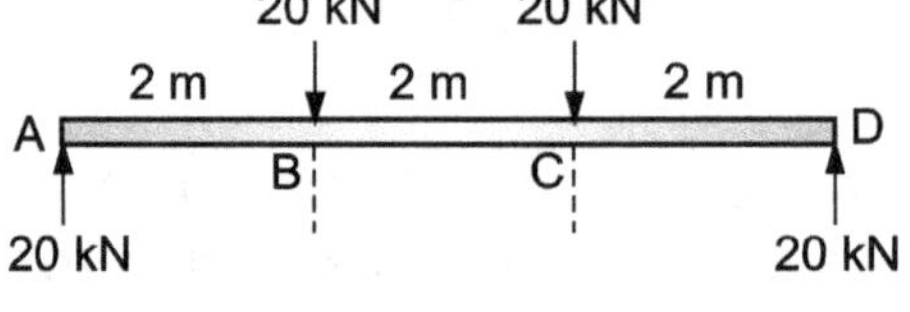


**Fig. 2**                                                                      **OR**

2.  **(a)** An aluminum rod is rigidity attached between a steel rod and a bronze rod as shown in the Fig. 3. Axial loads are applied at the positions indicated. Find the maximum value of P that will not exceed a stress in steel of 140 MPa, in aluminum of 90 MPa, or in bronze of 100 MPa.                                              **[6]**

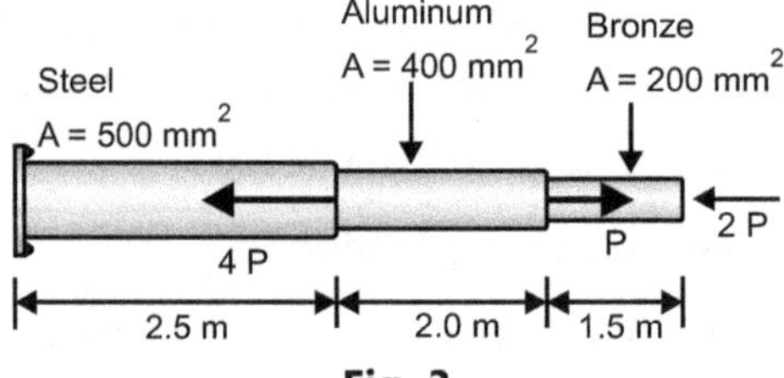


**Fig. 3**

**(b)** Draw SFD and BMD for the beam loaded as shown in the Fig. 4.                    **[6]**

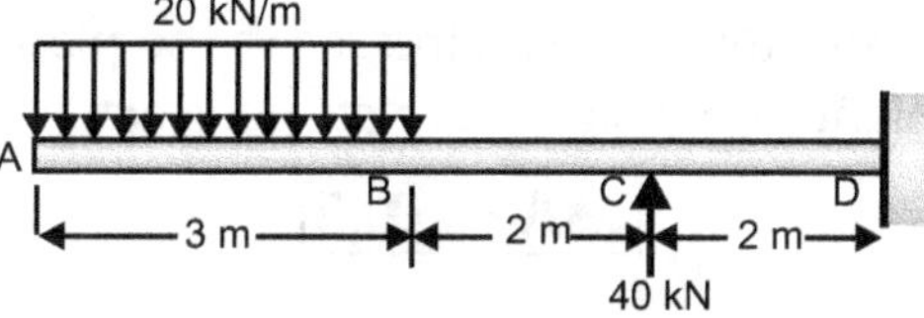


**Fig. 4**

3. **(a)** A cantilever beam, 30 mm wide by 100 mm high and 3 m long, carries a load that varies uniformly from zero at the free end to 2000 N/m at the wall. Compute the magnitude and location of the maximum flexural stress.                    **[6]**

   **(b)** The cantilever beam has rectangular cross-section of 50 mm (W) $\times$ 150 mm (H) is 3 m long and loaded by an end force of 10 kN. The material is steel with E = 210 GPa. Find the maximum deflection of the beam and maximum stress. Take E = 200 GPa.**OR**

4. **(a)** For the problem described in question 3(b) determine the type and magnitude of the stress in a fiber 20 mm from the top of the beam at a section 2 m from the free end.

                    **[6]**

   **(b)** For the problem described in question 3(b) determine the slope of free end of the cantilever beam.                    **[6]**

5. **(a)** A hollow steel shaft 2 m long is required to transmit a torque of 15 kN-m. The total angle of twist in this length is not to exceed 3° and the allowable shearing stress is 110 MPa. Determine the inside and outside diameter of the shaft if G = 90 GPa.

   **(b)** A steel bar of rectangular cross-section 60 mm $\times$ 80 mm and pinned at each end is subject to axial compression. If the proportional limit of the material is 210 MPa and E = 210 GPa, determine the minimum length for which Euler's equation may be used to determine the buckling load.                    **[7] OR**

6. **(a)** A solid circular shaft is required to transmit 114 kW while turning at 24 rev/s. The allowable shearing stress is 90 MPa. Find the required shaft diameter.                    **[6]**

   **(b)** A rectangular steel bar 45 mm $\times$ 55 mm in cross-section, pinned at each end and subjected to axial compression. The bar is 2.3 m long and E = 210 GPa. Determine the buckling load using Euler's formula and corresponding stress.                    **[7]**

7.    A cylindrical steel shell is subjected to an internal pressure of 5.6 MPa. The mean radius of the cylinder is 325 mm and thickness is 12 mm. If the material has a yield point of 300 MPa, determine the factor of safety using :                    **[13]**

   (a) The maximum normal stress theory, and

   (b) The von mises theory.                    **OR**

8.    A material is subjected to two mutually perpendicular direct stresses of 93.5 MPa tensile (in 'y' direction) and 42.5 MPa compressive (in 'x' direction), together with a shear stress of 44 MPa. The shear couple acting on planes carrying the 93.5 MPa stress is clockwise in effect. Calculate :                    **[13]**

(a) Magnitude and nature of the principal stresses;

(b) Magnitude of the maximum shear stresses in the plane of the given stress system.

(c) Direction of the planes on which these stresses act.

## MAY 2015

**Time: 2 Hours**                                                                 **Max. Marks: 50**

**Instructions :**

(1) Answer four questions out of 8.

Solve Q. 1 or Q. 2, Q. 3 or Q. 4, Q. 5 or Q. 6, Q. 7 or Q. 8.

(2) All the four questions should be solved in one answer book and attach extra supplements if required.

(3) Draw diagrams wherever necessary.

(4) Use of scientific calculator is allowed.

(5) Assume suitable data wherever necessary.

**1.** **(a)** A steel bar 25 mm diameter and length 250 mm is pulled by 0.001 mm by application of tensile load. Find the diameter of the bar if the linear strain is to be reduced by 10% without changing the load. **[6]**

**(b)** Draw SFD and BMD for the beam loaded as shown in Fig. 1 below. **[6]**

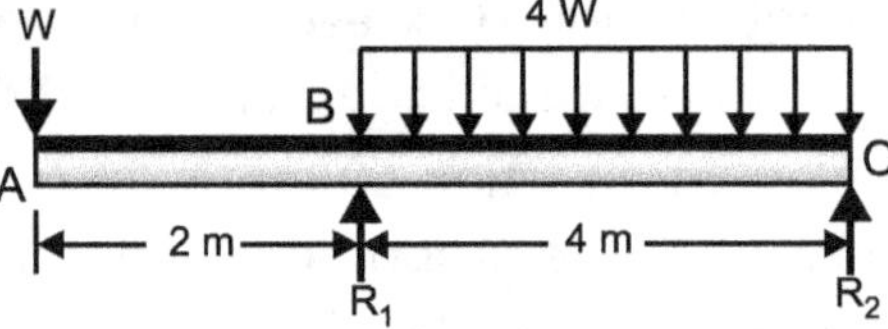


**Fig. 1**                                                                                **OR**

**2.** **(a)** A steel bar of 35 mm diameter and length 350 mm is pulled by 0.002 mm by application of tensile load. If the diameter of the bar is changed to 30 mm find the change in length for the same load. **[6]**

**(b)** Draw SFD and BMD for the beam loaded as shown in Fig. 2 below. **[6]**

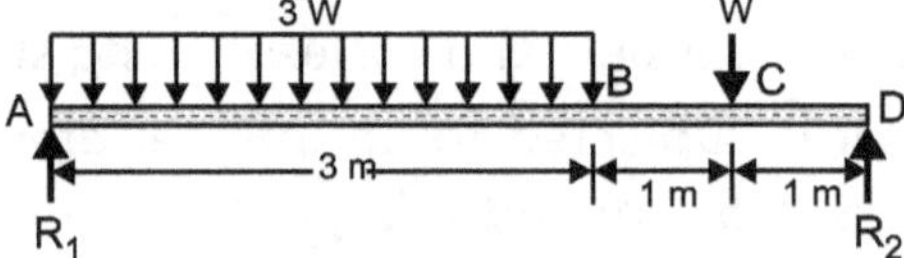


**Fig. 2**

**3.** **(a)** A rectangular steel bar, 15 mm wide by 30 mm high and 6 m long, is simply supported at its ends. If the density of steel is 7850 kg/m³, determine the maximum bending stress caused by the self-weight of the bar. **[6]**

**(b)** Determine the deflection at the free end of a cantilever of length 4 m carrying a uniformly distributed load of 12 kN/m over a length of 3 m from fixed end.
Take $EI = 2 \times 10^{13}$ N/mm². **[6] OR**

**4. (a)** Determine the minimum height h of the beam shown in Fig. 3 below if the flexural stress is not to exceed 20 MPa. **[6]**

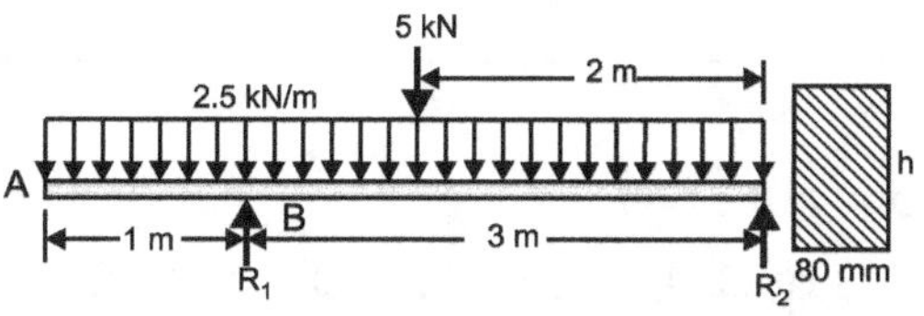


**Fig. 3**

**(b)** For the problem described in question 3(b) determine the slope at the free end of the cantilever. **[6]**

**5. (a)** A hollow steel shaft 1 m long is required to transmit a torque of 10 kN-m. The total angle of twist in this length is not to exceed 1° and the allowable shearing stress is 100 MPa. Determine the inside and outside diameter of the shaft if G = 100 GPa. **[6]**

**(b)** Determine the ratio of the buckling strengths of a solid steel column to that of a hollow column of same material and having same cross-sectional area. The internal diameter of hollow column is half of its external diameter. Both the columns are of the same length and are pinned at both ends. **[7] OR**

**6. (a)** A steel bar of rectangular cross-section 33 mm × 66 mm and pinned at each end is subject to axial compression. If the proportional limit of the material is 330 MPa and E = 222 GPa, determine the minimum length for which Euler's equation may be used to determine the buckling load. **[6]**

**(b)** A hollow shaft of diameter ratio 3/5 is required to transmit 482 kW at 125 rpm. The shearing stress in the shaft must not to exceed 65 N/mm$^2$ and the twist in a length of 2 m not to exceed 1 degree. Calculate minimum external diameter of shaft which would satisfy these conditions.

Take G = $8 \times 10^4$ N/mm$^2$. **[7]**

**7.** A solid circular shaft is subjected to a bending moment of 8 kNm and a torque of 12 kNm. In a uniaxial test the shaft material gave the following results : Modulus of elasticity = 200 GN/m$^2$, Stress at yield point = 300 N/mm$^2$, Poisson's ratio = 0.3, Factor of safety = 3. Estimate the least diameter of the shaft using : (i) Maximum principal stress theory (ii) Maximum principal strain theory and  (iii) Shear strain energy theory. **[13] OR**

**8.** A material is subjected to two mutually perpendicular direct stresses of 92 MPa tensile and 29 MPa compressive, together with a shear stress of 22 MPa. The shear couple acting on planes carrying the 92 MPa stress is clockwise in effect. Calculate : (i) Magnitude and nature of the principal stresses; (ii) Magnitude of the maximum shear stresses in the plane of the given stress system; (iii) Direction of the planes on which these stresses act. **[13]**

## November 2015

**Time : 2 Hours**                                                                    **Max. Marks : 50**

**Instructions :**

(1) Answer four questions out of 8.

Solve Q. 1 or Q. 2, Q. 3 or Q. 4, Q. 5 or Q. 6, Q. 7 or Q. 8.

(2) All the four questions should be solved in one answer book and attach extra supplements if required.

(3) Draw diagrams wherever necessary.

(4) Use of scientific calculator is allowed.

(5) Assume suitable data wherever necessary.

---

**1. (a)** A hollow steel tube with an inside diameter of 100 mm must carry a tensile load of 400 kN. Determine the outside diameter of the tube if the stress is limited to 120 MN/m². **[6]**

**(b)** Draw SFD and BMD for the beam loaded as shown in Fig. 1 below. **[6]**

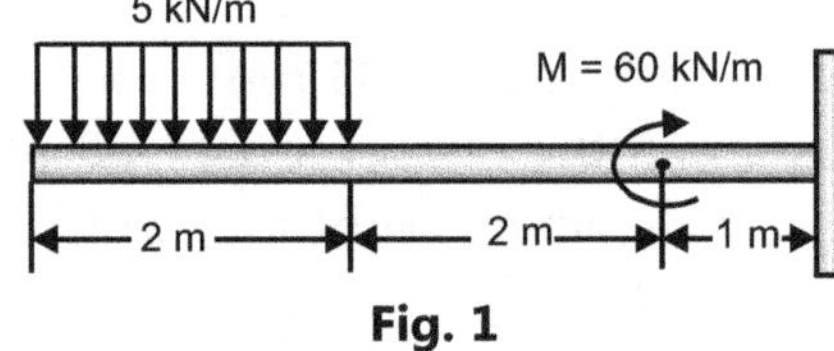


**Fig. 1**

**OR**

**2. (a)** The following data were recorded during the tensile test of a 14 mm diameter mild steel rod. The gauge length was 50 mm. **[6]**

[6]

| Load, (N) | Elongation (mm) | Load (N) | Elongation (mm) | Load (N) | Elongation, (mm) |
|---|---|---|---|---|---|
| 0 | 0 | 38090 | 0.061 | 68190 | 7.501 |
| 6500 | 0.011 | 40290 | 0.164 | 59190 | 12.501 |
| 12790 | 0.021 | 41790 | 0.434 | 67990 | 15.501 |
| 18990 | 0.031 | 46390 | 1.251 | 65190 | 20.001 |
| 25290 | 0.041 | 52590 | 2.501 | 61690 | 20.001 |
| 31490 | 0.051 | 58690 | 4.501 | | |

Plot the stress-strain diagram on GRAPH paper and determine the following mechanical properties :

(i)  Proportional limit          (ii)   Modulus of elasticity

(iii) Yield point and           (iv)   Ultimate strength.

**(b)** Draw moment and load diagrams corresponding to the shear diagram as shown in Fig. 2 below. Specify values at all change of load positions and at all points of zero shear. **[6]**

---

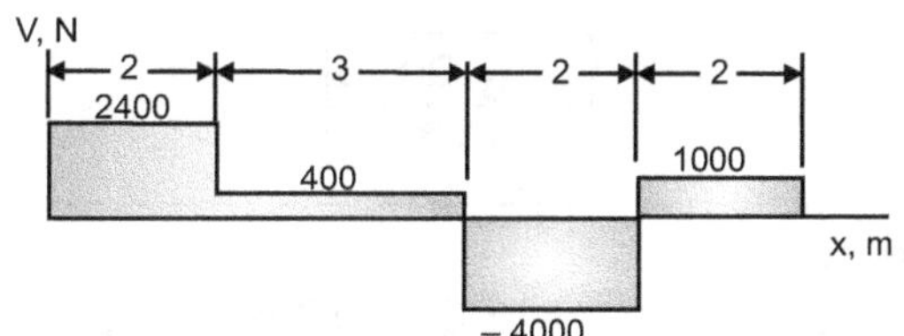

Fig. 2

3. **(a)** A cantilever beam, 60 mm wide by 100 mm high and 2 m long, carries UDL of 3000 N/m over entire span. Compute the magnitude and location of the maximum flexural stress. **[6]**

   **(b)** For the problem described in equation 3(a), find the maximum deflection and slope (in radians) of the beam. Take E = 210 GPa. **[6] OR**

4. **(a)** For the problem described in equation 3(a) determine the type and magnitude of the stress in a fiber 20 mm from the top of the beam at fixed end. **[6]**

   **(b)** A simply supported beam length 3 m is loaded centrally by a point load of 5 kN, find the location and values of maximum deflection and slope (in radians) of the beam. Take flexural rigidity of the beam section as 400 kN-m$^2$. **[6]**

5. **(a)** A hollow steel shaft 1.5 m long is required to transmit a torque of 12 kN-m. The total angle of twist in this length is not to exceed 2° and the allowable shearing stress is 100 MPa. Determine the inside and outside diameter of the shaft if G = 83 GPa. **[6]**

   **(b)** A steel bar of rectangular cross-section 80 mm × 120 mm and pinned at each end is subject to axial compression. If the proportional limit of the material is 235 MPa and E = 207 GPa, determine the minimum length for which Euler's equation may be used to determine the buckling load. **[7] OR**

6. **(a)** A solid circular shaft is required to transmit 90 kW while turning at 50 rev/s. The allowable shearing stress is 120 MPa. Find the required shaft diameter. **[6]**

   **(b)** A rectangular steel bar 65 mm × 85 mm in cross-section, pinned at each end and subjected to axial compression. The bar is 3 m long and E = 235 GPa. Determine the buckling load using Euler's formula and corresponding stress. **[7]**

7. Stressed element in a machine component is subjected to 185 MPa tensile stress in x-direction, 55 MPa compressive stress in y-direction and 75 MPa shear stress clockwise on x-face. Compute the values and orientation of the principal stresses and maximum shear stress using graphical method proposed by Mohr. Mohr's circle must be drawn on GRAPH paper using appropriate scale. (Note : Analytical solution and solution without GRAPH paper will not be evaluated.) **[13] OR**

8. A solid circular shaft made from plain carbon steel with a yield point of 250 MPa is subjected to peak bending moment of 530 N-m due to transverse loading and twisting moment of 600 N-m. For a factor of safety of 3 determine required diameter of the shaft using :

   (a) Maximum Normal Stress Theory

   (b) Maximum Shear Stress Theory and

   (c) Maximum Strain Energy Theory. **[13]**

## May 2016

**Time : 2 Hour**                                              **Max. Marks : 50**

**Instructions to the candidates :**
   (1) Attempt Q.1 or Q.2, Q.3 or Q.4, Q.5 or Q.6, Q.7 or Q.8, Q.9 or Q.10.
   (2) Neat diagrams must be drawn wherever necessary.
   (3) Figures to the right indicate full marks.
   (4) Assume suitable data, if necessary.

1. **(a)** A reinforced concrete column is 300 mm × 300 mm in section. The column is provided with 8 bars of 20 mm diameter. The column carries a load of 360 kN. Find the tresses in concrete and the steel bars. Take $E = 2.1 \times 10^5$ N/mm$^2$ and $E = 0.14 \times 10^5$ N/mm$^2$. **[6]**

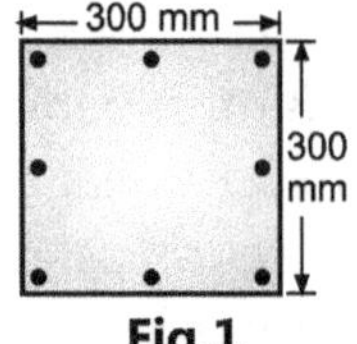


**Fig.1**

   **(b)** Draw shear force and bending moment diagrams [SFD and BMD] for a single side overhanging beam subjected to loading as shown in Fig.2 given below. Locate points of contra flexure, if any. **[6]**

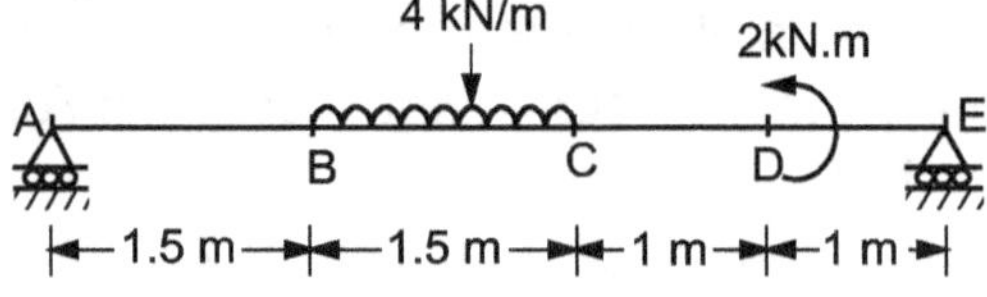


**Fig.2**                                                          **OR**

2. **(a)** A steel rod of 32 mm diameter is enclosed in a brass tube of 48 mm external diameter and 34 mm internal diameter. Each is 400 mm long and the assembly is rigidly held between two stops 400 mm apart. The temperature of the assembly is then raised by 60°C. Determine:
   (i) Stresses in the tube and the rod if the distance between the stops remains constant.
   (ii) Stresses in the tube and the rod, if the stops yields by 0.25 mm.
   $E_S = 200$ GPa; $E_b = 90$ GPa
   $\alpha_s = 12 \times 10^{-6}$ per °C; $\alpha_b = 21 \times 10^{-6}$ per °C.

   **(b)** Draw SF and BM diagrams for the beam ABCDE shown in the following Fig. 3 **[6]**

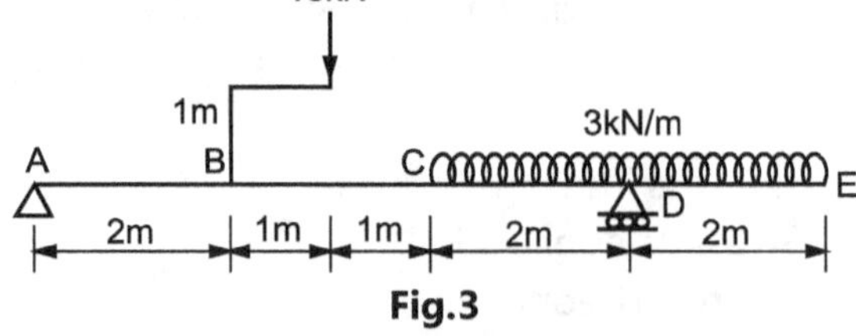


**Fig.3**

**3.** **(a)** A square beam 20 mm × 20 mm in section and 2 m long is supported at the ends. The beam fails when a point load of 400 N is applied at the centre of the beam. What uniformly distributed load per meter length will break a cantilever of the same material 40 mm wide, 60 mm. Deep and 3 m long? **[6]**

**(b)** A cantilever of length 'L' carrier a uniformly distributed load of 'w' N/m for a length of 'a' from the fixed end, find the deflection at the free end. **[6] OR**

**4.** **(a)** A simply supported beam carriers a uniformly distributed load of intensity 30 N/mm over the entire span of 1 m. The cross-section of the beam is a T-section having the dimension as shown in Fig. 4. Calculate the maximum shear for the section of the beam. **[6]**

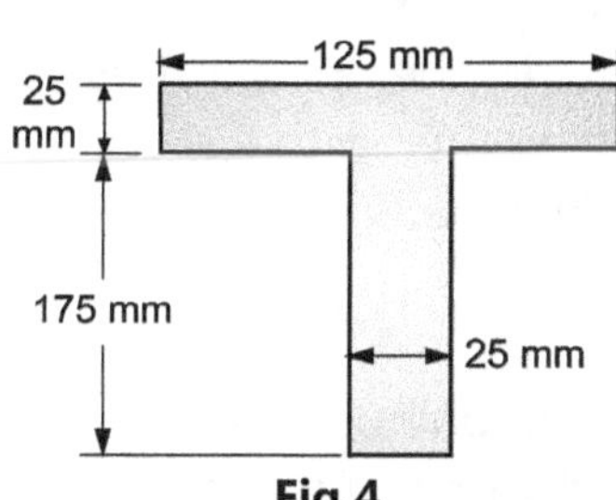


**Fig.4**

**(b)** A horizontal cantilever of uniform section of length L carries two point loads W at the free end and 2 W at a distance of 'a' from the free end. Find the maximum deflection due to this loading. **[6]**

**5.** **(a)** A hollow, shaft, having an internal diameter 40% of its external diameter, transmits, 562.5 kW power at 100 r.p.m. Determine the external diameter of the shaft if the shear stress is not exceed 60 N/mm$^2$ and the twist in a length of 2.5 m should not exceed 1.3 degrees. Assume maximum torque = 1.25 mean torque and modulus of rigidity = $9 \times 10^4$ N/mm$^2$. **[6]**

**(b)** A horizontal beam ABC 1.6 m long is pinned to a support at C and supported by a vertical aluminum tube 2.25 m long as shown in Fig.5. The upper end of the tube is hinged to the beam while its lower end is firmly fixed. The beam carries a load of 250 kN at A. Find the thickness of the tube if its outer diameter is 120 mm. Allow a factor of safety 2.5 with respect to Euler critical load.        Take E = $7.2 \times 10^4$ N/mm$^2$ **[10]**

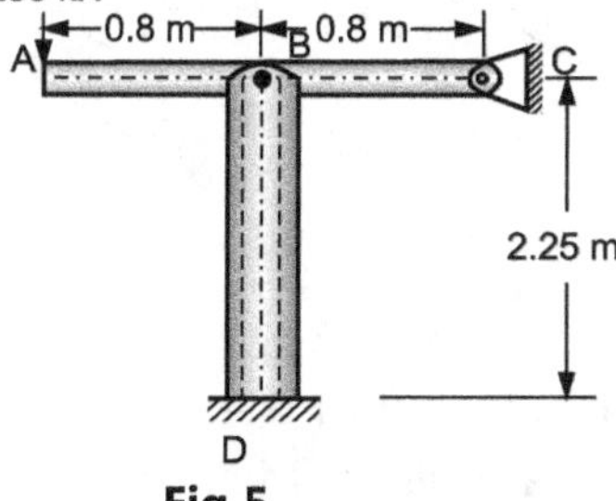


**Fig.5**                                                        **OR**

**6.** **(a)** The stepped steel shaft shown in Fig.6 is 600 mm long and fixed at both ends subjected to a torque 120 kNm at C. Determine the fixing torque at the ends, the maximum shear in the AC and BC and angle of twist of section C. **[6]**

Take G = 80 GPa.

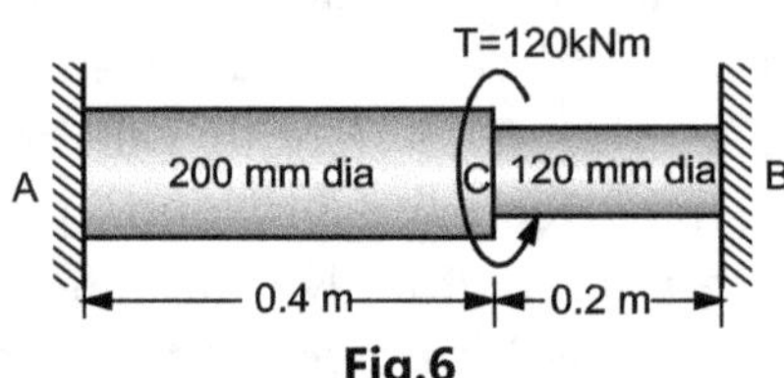


**Fig.6**

**(b)** A hollow cylindrical cast iron column is 4 m long, both end fixed. Design the column to carry an axial load of 250 kN. Use Rankine's formula and adopt a factor of safety of 5. The internal diameter may be taken as 0.8 times the external diameter. Take $F_c$ = 550 N/mm$^2$ and $\alpha$ = 1/1600. **[7]**

**7. (a)** At a point in a strained material the normal stresses acting are +50 MPa and −30MPa at a plane right angle to each other, with a shear stress of 20 MPa. Determine:
(i)   Principal stresses and their nature
(ii)   Normal and tangential stress on a plane inclined at an angle of 25° with the plane of 50 MPa. **[7]**

**(b)** A bolt is subjected to an axial pull of 40 kN and  a transverse shear force of 15 kN. Determine the diameter of the bolt required based on:
(i)   Maximum principal stress theory
(ii)   Maximum shear stress theory
(iii)  Maximum strain energy theory.
Take elastic limit in simple tension is equal to 350 MPa and Posisson's ratio = 0.3. Assume FOS = 2.5. **[6] OR**

**8. (a)** A 100 mm diameter bar with a built in bracket is fixed to the wall and loaded as shown in Fig. 7. Determine the principle stresses at the top extremity of the vertical diameter for the section market A. **[7]**

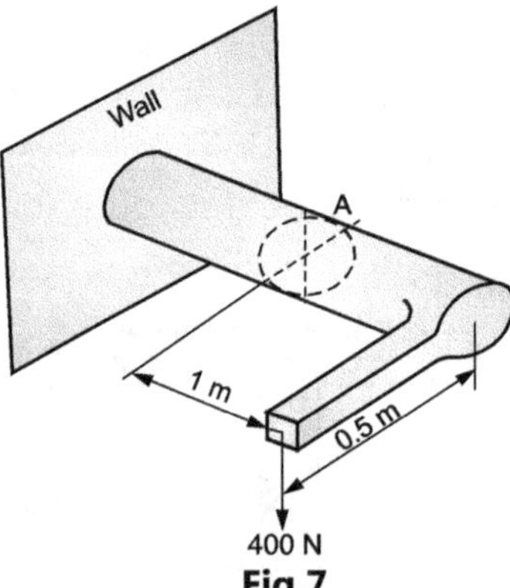


**Fig.7**

**(b)**  According to the theory of maximum shear stress, determine the diameter of a bolt which is subjected to an axial pull of 9 kN together with a transverse shear force of 4.5 kN. Elastic limit in tension is 225 N/mm$^2$, factor of safety = 3 and Poisson's ration = 0.3 **[6]**

## NOVEMBER 2016

**Time : 2 Hours**                                                    **Max. Marks : 50**

**N.B. :-** (1)  Assume suitable data, wherever necessary.

(2)  Neat diagrams must be drawn wherever necessary.

(3)  Use of electronic pocket calculator is allowed.

(4)  Figures to the right indicate full marks.

1. **(a)** Calculate the vertical displacement of point C for the structure shown in Fig. 1. Neglect the weight of the bar and beam. **[6]**

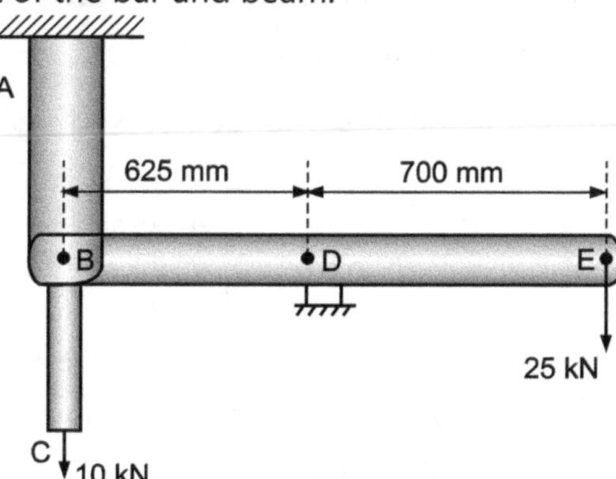


**Fig. 1**

**(b)** Draw the SFD and BMD for the beam as shown in Fig. 2. Also find the point of contra-flexure if any. **[6]**

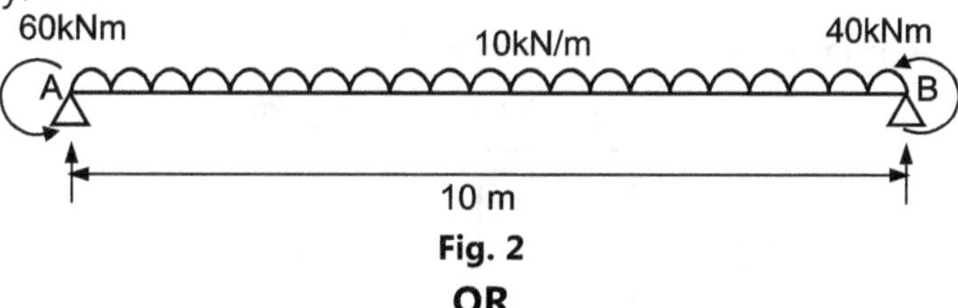


**Fig. 2**

**OR**

2. **(a)** The bulk modulus for a material is 50 GPa. A 12 mm diameter rod of the material was subjected to an axial pull of 14 kN and the change in diameter was observed to be $3.6 \times 10^{-3}$ mm. Calculate the poisson's ratio and modulud of elasticity for the material. **[6]**

**(b)** Draw the SFD and BMD for the beam as shown fig. 3. Also find the point of contra-flexure if any. **[6]**

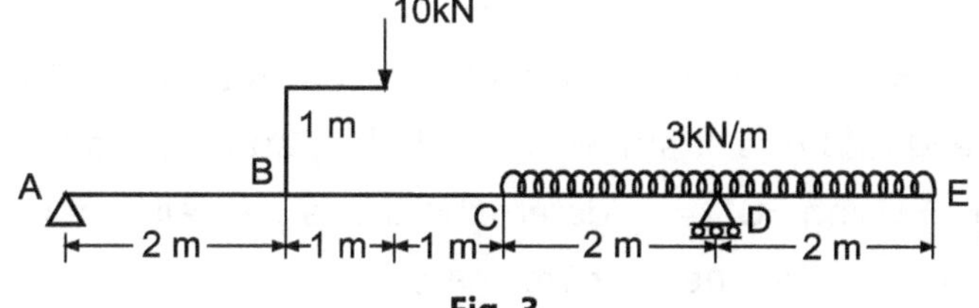


**Fig. 3**

**3. (a)** A steel channel of C section is used as a simply supported beam on a span of 4 m. The channel is to be designed for a working bending stress of 100 MPa. It has to carry a udl for the whole span. Calculate the permissible load when: **[6]**

   (i)   The channel stands upright 225 mm high.

   (ii)  The channel lies flat with the 225 mm horizontal.

   Take : A = 3053 mm$^2$, $l_{xx}$ = 2547.9 × 10$^4$mm$^4$, $l_{yy}$ = 209.5 × 10$^4$ mm$^4$, Position of N.A. for horizontal case is 24.6 mm from the web othermost fibre, overall depth of the channel 225 mm and flange width 90 mm.

**(b)** Find the deflection at C for the beam loaded as shown in Fig. 4. Take EI = 40,000 kNm$^2$. **[6]**

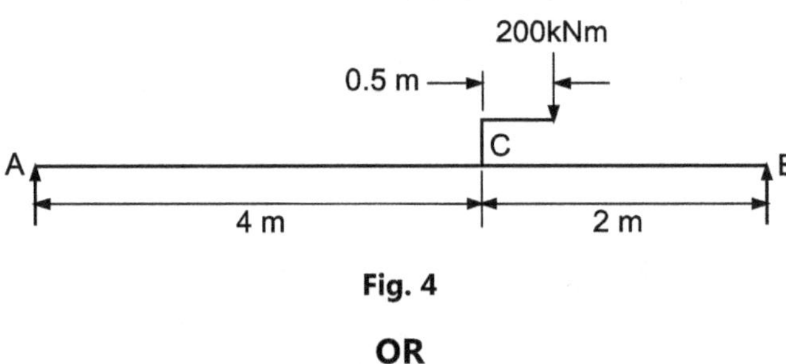



**Fig. 4**

**OR**

**4. (a)** Calculate the shear stress at the salient positions and also draw the shear stress distribution diagram for the beam section shown in Fig. 5. **[6]**

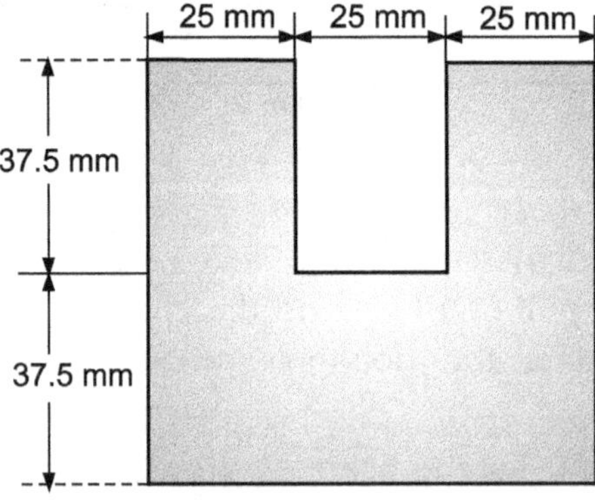



**Fig. 5**

**(b)** A uniform rod AB has $\sigma_y$ = 250 MPa and E = 200 GPa Collar D moves along the rod and has a speed of 3 m/s. It strikes a small plate attached to the end B of the rod as shown in Fig. 6. Using FOS = 4, determine the largest allowable mass of the collar if the rod is not to be permanently deformed. **[6]**

**5.** **(a)** A hollow marine propeller shaft turning at 110 rpm is required to propel a vessel at 12 m/s for the expenditure of 6337.5 kW of shaft power, the efficiency of the propeller being 68 %. The diameter ratio of the shaft is to be 2/3 and the direct stress due to the thrust is not to exceed 8 MPa.

Calculate : **[7]**

(i)  the shaft diameter,

(ii)  the maximum shearing stress due to the torque.

**(b)** Find the Euler's critical load for a hollow cylindrical cast iron column with 200 mm O.D. and 25 mm thickness, if it is 6 m long and hinged at both ends.

Take $E = 8 \times 10^4$ MPa.

Compare Euler's critical load with Rankine's critical load taking $\sigma_c = 550$ MPa and $\alpha = 1/1600$. **[6]**

**OR**

**6.** **(a)** Fig. 6 shows a horizontal shaft ABCD fixed to a rigid base at D and subjected to torques. A hole 60 mm in diameter has been drilled into the part CD of the shaft. Determine the angle of twist at the end A. Take $G = 7.7 \times 10^4$ MPa. **[6]**

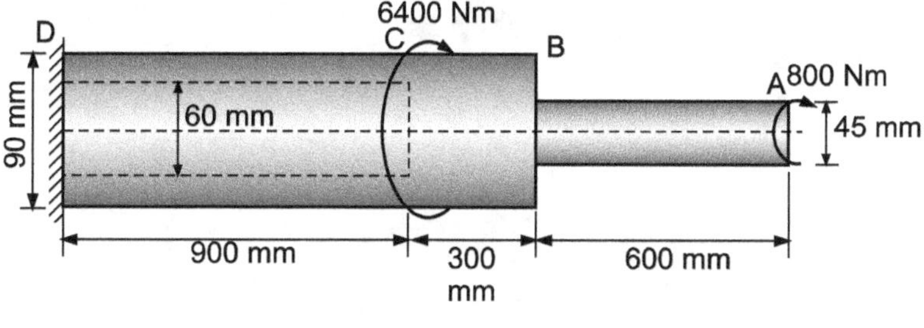


**Fig. 6**

**(b)** The following particulars refer to an engine cylinder,

Diameter of the cylinder = 400 mm.

Steam pressure in cylinder = 0.6 MPa.

Distance between the piston and cross head = 1.25 m. Find the diameter of the piston rod allowing a F.O.S. of 4. Assume that the piston rod is firmly fixed to the piston and the cross head. Take $\sigma_c = 330$ MPa and $\alpha = 1/7500$. Use Rankine's method. **[7]**

**7.** **(a)** At a certain point on an strained material the principal stresses are 100 MPa and 40 MPa, both tensile. Find the normal, tangential and resultant stresses across a plane through the point at 48 degrees to the major principal plane, using Mohr's circle. **[7]**

**(b)** The stresses induced at a critical point in a machine component made of steel are $\sigma_x$ = 100 MPa, $\sigma_y$ = 40 MPa, $T_{xy}$ = 80 MPa. Calculate the F.O.S. by maximum shear stress theory and maximum distortion energy theory. Assume $S_{yt}$ = 380 MPa. **[6]**

**OR**

**8.** **(a)** The principal tensile stresses at a point across two mutual perpendicular planes are 80 MPa and 40 MPa. Find the normal, tangential, resultant stresses and its obliquity on a plane at 20 degrees to the major principal plane. Find also the intensity of the stress which acting alone can produce the same maximum strain. Take Poisson's ratio as 0.25. Use analytical method only. **[7]**

**(b)** A solid circular shaft is subjected to a bending moment of 40 kN-m and a torque of 10 kN-m. Design the diameter of the shaft according to : **[6]**

(i) Max. principal stress theory,

(ii) Max. shear stress theory.

Take $\mu$ = 0.25, stress at elastic limit = 200 MPa, F.O.S. = 2.

✽✽✽

## MAY 2017

**Time : 2 Hours**                                                        **Max. Marks : 50**

**N.B. :-** (1)  Neat diagrams must be drawn wherever necessary.

(2)  Figures to the right indicate full marks.

(3)  Use of electronic pocket calculator is allowed.

(4)  Assume suitable data, wherever necessary.

1.  **(a)** Determine the stress in each section of the circular bar as shown in figure when subjected to an axial tensile load of 20 kN.                              **[4]**

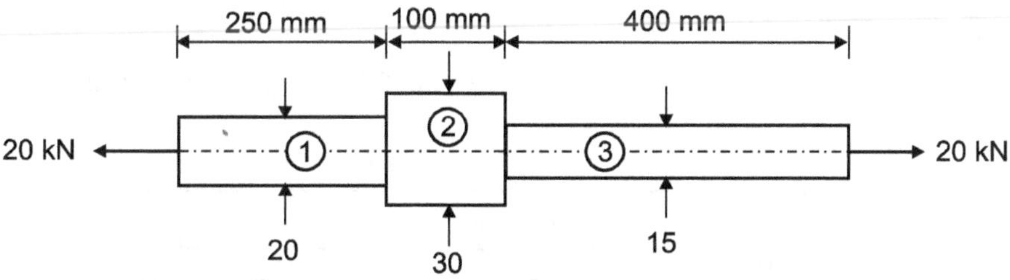


**Fig. 1**

**(b)** Draw SF and BM diagrams for the given beam.                              **[8]**



**Fig. 2**

**OR**

2.  **(a)** The composite bar as shown in figure is rigidly fixed at the ends A and B. Determine the reaction developed at ends when the temperature is raised by 18°C. Given $E_{Al}$ = 70 kN/mm$^2$, $E_a$ = 200 kN/mm$^2$, $a_{Al}$ = 11 × 10$^{-6}$/°C $\alpha_{st}$ = 12 × 10$^{-6}$/°C.                              **[6]**

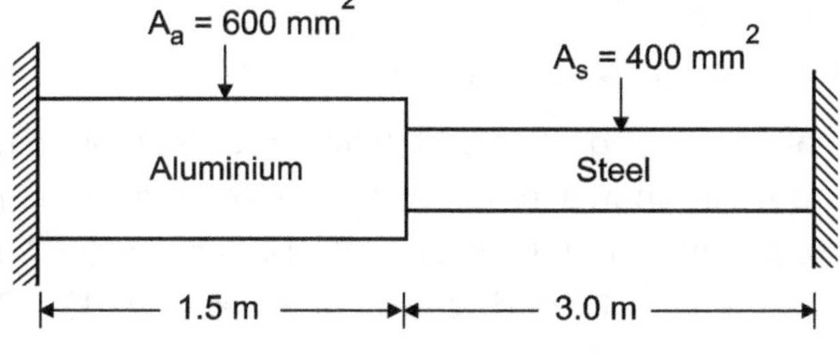


**Fig. 3**

**(b)** Derive SF and BM equations and then draw SFD and BMD of given beam.                **[6]**

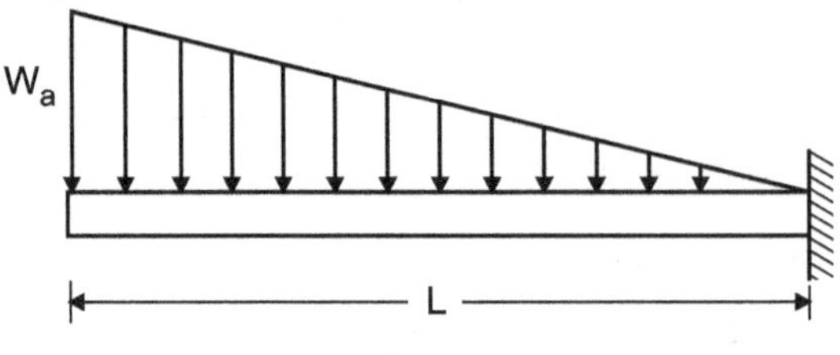


**Fig. 4**

**3. (a)** A symmetrical H section with height 120 mm, width 120 mm and thickness 20 mm is used as a simply supported beam and carries UDL of 60 kN/m over a span of 3 m. Determine shear stress at the neutral axis of H section if moment of inertia about neutral axis is $5.75 \times 10^6$ mm$^4$.                **[6]**

**(b)** Determine slope at the simple supports $R_1$ and $R_2$ of given overhang beam in terms of EI.                **[6]**

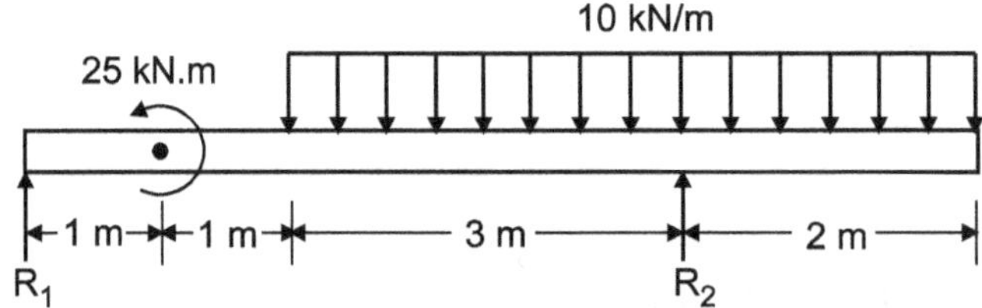


**Fig. 5**

**OR**

**4. (a)** Simply supported beam with point load W at the center and length 2 m. The cross-section of beam is T section (flange 100 m × 12 mm and web 38 mm × 12 mm). The allowable bending stress in tension and compression are 100 MPa and 150 MPa. Find safe load W.                **[6]**

**(b)** A cantilever beam of length 4 m and UDL of 60 N/m. Determine strain energy stored in the beam. Assume I = $1 \times 10^{-6}$ m$^4$ and E = 200 GPa                **[6]**

**5. (a)** A solid circular bar 25 m long and 120 mm was found to be extended 1.2 mm under tensile load of 52 kN. Now the same bar is used as a strut. Determine critical load and safe load taking FOS = 3 with the following end conditions :

(i)    Both ends fixed, and

(ii)   One end fixed and other end hinged.                **[6]**

**(b)** A compound shaft consisting of a steel segment and an aluminum segment is acted upon by two torques as shown in fig. Determine the maximum permissible value of T subject to the following conditions $\tau_{st}$ = 83 MPa $\tau_{Al}$ = 55 MPa, and the angle of rotation of the free end is limited to 6°. For steel, G = 83 GPa and for aluminium G = 28 GPa.                **[7]**

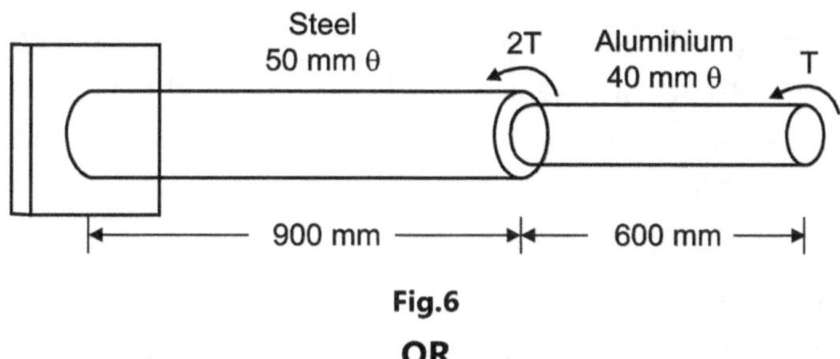


**Fig.6**

**OR**

6. **(a)** The compound shaft shown in Fig. is attached to rigid supports. For the bronze segment AB, The diameter is 75 mm, $\tau \leq 60$ MPa and G = 35 GPa. For the steel segment BC, the diameter is 50 mm. $\tau \leq 80$ MPa, and G = 83 GPa. If a = 2 m and b = 1.5 m, compute the maximum torque T that can be applied.          **[7]**

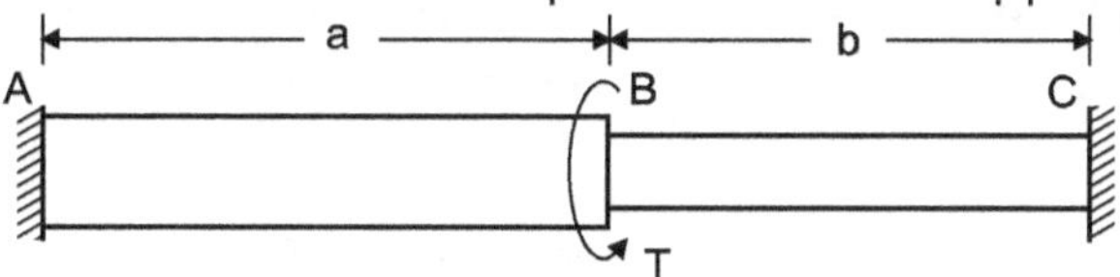


**Fig. 7**

**(b)** The rod PQ of length L and Flexural rigidity EI is hinged at both ends. For what minimum force F is it expected to buckle?          **[6]**

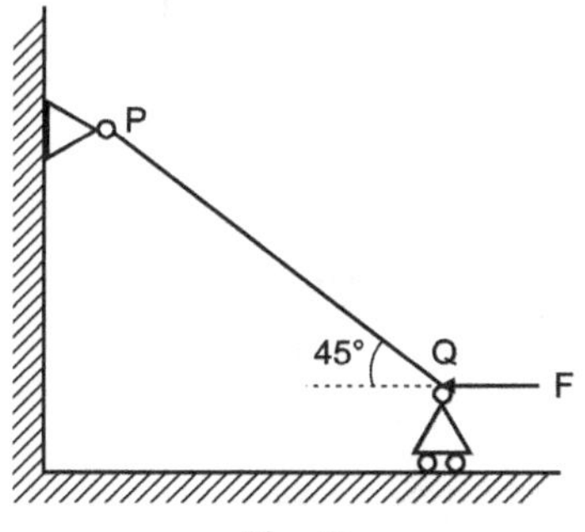


**Fig. 8**

7. **(a)** State of stress for an element of unit thickness is shown in Figure. Find the normal stress and shear stress that must act on an inclined dotted plane to keep the element in equilibrium and show the result on inclined plane with proper orientation.          **[7]**

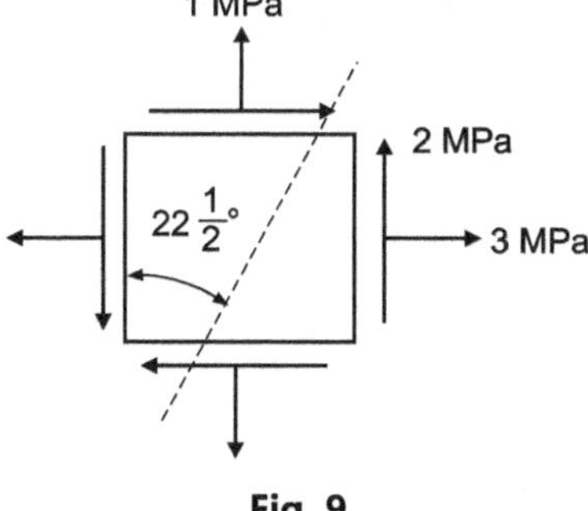


**Fig. 9**

**(b)** At a certain position of circular structure of diameter d is subjected to shear force of 10 kN together with an axial tensile load of 20 kN. If the allowable working stress is 67.5 MPa. Estimate the magnitude of 'd' required according to the maximum principal stress theory. **[6]**

**OR**

**8.** For the given state of plane stress. **[13]**

   (a)  Construct Mohr's circle with proper scale on graph paper.

   (b)  Determine principal stresses and its orientation from Mohr's ircle

   (c)  Determine shear stress and normal stress on maximum shear plane and its orientation from Mohr's circle

   (d)  Represent all the stresses and plane orientations in Mohrs' circle.

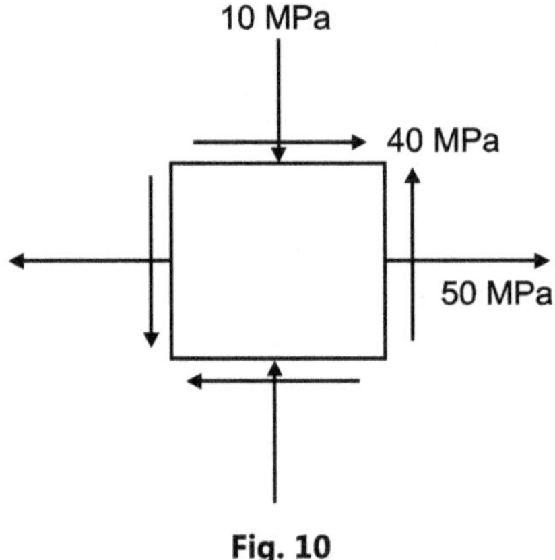


**Fig. 10**

❊ ❊ ❊